PENGUIN CLASSICS

MOBY-DICK

OR, THE WHALE

Harold Beaver is Professor of American Literature at the University of Amsterdam. He has also edited for the Penguin English Library Herman Melville's *Redburn* and *Billy Budd, Sailor and Other Stories*, as well as Edgar Allan Poe's *The Narrative of Arthur Gordon Pym* and *The Science Fiction of Edgar Allan Poe*.

HERMAN MELVILLE

Moby-Dick;

or, The Whale

EDITED WITH AN

INTRODUCTION AND COMMENTARY

BY HAROLD BEAVER

PENGUIN BOOKS

Penguin Books Ltd, Harmondsworth, Middlesex, England
Viking Penguin Inc., 40 West 23rd Street, New York, New York 10010, U.S.A.
Penguin Books Australia Ltd, Ringwood, Victoria, Australia
Penguin Books Canada Ltd, 2801 John Street, Markham, Ontario, Canada L3R 1B4
Penguin Books (N.Z.) Ltd, 182–190 Wairau Road, Auckland 10, New Zealand

—

First published as *The Whale* in 1851
Published in the Penguin English Library 1972
Reprinted 1975 (twice), 1977 (twice), 1978 (twice), 1980, 1981, 1982, 1983, 1984, 1985
Published in Penguin Classics 1985

—

—

Made and printed in Great Britain by
Hazell Watson & Viney Limited,
Member of the BPCC Group,
Aylesbury, Bucks
Set in Linotype Georgian

CONTENTS

LIST OF PLATES AND ACKNOWLEDGEMENTS

Old Dartmouth Historical Society, New Bedford, Massachusetts)

12. Forecastle Scene aboard a New Bedford Whaler. (Whaling Museum, Old Dartmouth Historical Society, New Bedford, Massachusetts)
13. 'Skeleton of the Great Northern Rorqual' from *The Naturalist's Library*. (Whaling Museum, Old Dartmouth Historical Society, New Bedford, Massachusetts)
14. Detail from a Colour Sketch by a New Bedford Whaleman. (Whaling Museum, Old Dartmouth Historical Society, New Bedford, Massachusetts)

HERMAN MELVILLE

A Biographical Note

BORN 1 August 1819 in New York City, Herman Melville grew up on Manhattan. His father, Allan Melvill, a merchant, was of New England stock; his mother, Maria Gansevoort, of a wealthy Dutch family, long established in New York State. By the time Herman was nine, however, his father was plunged into debt; and in 1830, declared bankrupt, he moved his family to Albany. There Herman attended the Albany Academy (1830–32) until his father died, worn out by financial setbacks, delirious, after several weeks' bouts of insanity. His widow, with eight children, was left largely dependent on family charity for support.

Her third oldest was only twelve at the time. After little more than elementary schooling, Herman had to leave the Academy for work as a bank clerk. But he was restless by temperament. In 1834 he went to work on an uncle's farm in Massachusetts and from 1835–7 assisted his older brother Gansevoort in the cap and fur store left by their father. Meanwhile he doubled as part-time student at the Albany Classical School and in 1837, aged eighteen, was appointed an elementary schoolteacher near Pittsfield, Massachusetts.

By spring, however, he was back with mother, in the village of Lansingburgh on the Hudson, tackling an engineering and surveying course. There was talk of a career on the Erie Canal. But hopes were soon dashed; not an opening was to be found. So, in June 1839, he signed on as merchant seaman instead for a round trip to Liverpool.

He was twenty and this was his first taste of life at sea. Yet life ashore – 'Are the green fields gone?' – still beckoned. For in 1839–40 he again took up schoolteaching; and in June

1840 set off west, along the Erie Canal, via the Great Lakes to Chicago, and on by horse or stagecoach to Galena on the upper Mississippi to join his pioneering uncle, Thomas Melville. But neither banker, nor schoolteacher, nor frontiersman, he was soon off once more, sailing down the Mississippi as far as Cairo, then up the Ohio, and so back overland to New York by a 'drizzly November', 1840.

Now nothing remained but 'to get to sea'. On 3 January 1841, he shipped aboard the whaler *Acushnet* on her maiden voyage from Fairhaven, Massachusetts, bound for Cape Horn and the Pacific. He was to be away for almost four years.

In June 1842 the *Acushnet* reached Nukahiva in the Marquesas Islands; and there, on 9 July, Melville, with a friend, deserted. They headed inland, were separated, and after a month alone among the 'cannibals' of the Taipi Valley Melville escaped on an Australian whaler, the *Lucy Ann*, which took him to Tahiti by September. Off Papeete harbour, like ten other crew members, he refused duty; the mutineers were imprisoned by the British consul; but again, with a friend, he escaped. After a month's tramp round the nearby island of Moorea, he shipped as boat-steerer on the Nantucket whaler *Charles and Henry*, to be discharged at Hawaii in April 1843. He spent almost half a year in Honolulu; and it was not till 17 August that he was enlisted into the U.S. navy as ordinary seaman aboard the frigate *United States*. The voyage home, with long delays off Peru, took over a year. On 14 October 1844 Melville was discharged at Boston and rejoined his family at Lansingburgh. He had just turned twenty-five.

There, on the Hudson, the compulsive story-teller, entertaining his mother and sisters, turned writer. Those escapades on the Marquesas and beachcombing on Moorea became *Typee* (1846) and *Omoo* (1847). Both won him instant success. Early in 1845 he had moved to New York; and in August 1847, launched as a popular author, he married Elizabeth Shaw, daughter of Lemuel Shaw, Chief Justice of Massachusetts. Their honeymoon took them across Maine into Canada; the young couple settled in New York, at 103 Fourth Avenue, sharing a household with Melville's younger brother and wife, his mother and several sisters.

He had turned professional; at last he had found his career. He was accepted by 'Young America', the literary circle gathered round Evert Duyckinck; and drawn on by Duyckinck – publisher of *The Literary World* and owner of a considerable library – his ambitions grew correspondingly literary. But *Mardi* (1849), a Spenserian romance set in the South Seas, was a flop. To recoup his fortune, he wrote both *Redburn* (1849), on his Liverpool trip, and *White-Jacket* (1850), on his return from Honolulu, within five months. Then he crossed the Atlantic to sell proof sheets of *White-Jacket* to an English publisher. Money was tight; after only a brief tour to Paris and the Rhineland, he returned home to New York (February, 1850).

Of all his sea-adventures only one topic remained: his original service aboard the whaler *Acushnet*. From that recent Atlantic crossing and memories of his longest service afloat grew a new venture: *The Whale*. But in these last five years education had at last caught up with experience. As he was to write to Nathaniel Hawthorne, in the final, intoxicated stages of composition:

> Until I was twenty-five, I had no development at all. From my twenty-fifth year I date my life. Three weeks have scarcely passed, at any time between then and now, that I have not unfolded within myself. But I feel that I am now come to the inmost leaf of the bulb, and that shortly the flower must fall to the mould.[1]

For, in the meantime, he had met the author of *The Scarlet Letter* and bought an estate of one hundred and sixty acres – with a loan from his father-in-law – near Pittsfield, in the Berkshire Hills of west Massachusetts. There as gentleman farmer, in August 1851, he completed *Moby-Dick*.

In October a second son was born. By December he had begun a seventh novel *Pierre* – in tortured memory of his father and mother's family – published in 1852. The reception

1. 1? June 1851.

of *Moby-Dick* had been disheartening; the failure of *Pierre* proved catastrophic. 'What I feel most moved to write, that is banned,' he had sworn in that same letter to Hawthorne, '– it will not pay. Yet, altogether, write the *other* way I cannot. So the product is a final hash, and all my books are botches.'

Reputation faded as fast as it had bloomed. As his imagination grew steadily more embittered and complex, the debts mounted. He was now father of two sons and two daughters. In 1853 efforts were made to find him a consular post abroad. He turned to anonymous story-writing for the magazines (selected in 1856 as *The Piazza Tales*). He serialized an historical potboiler, *Israel Potter*, published in book form in 1855. But the strain had begun to tell; on top of literary and financial worries, he was crippled – 'helpless', in his wife's phrase, with 'severe rheumatism'. *The Confidence-Man* was completed in the summer of 1856. That wily, sardonic achievement – recalling his Mississippi River trip of 1840 – wrote 'FINIS' in 1857 to Melville's one professional decade.

Fearful for his sanity, the family urged him to travel. Judge Shaw again advanced the funds; and in October 1856 he began a leisurely trip to England (where he visited Hawthorne), the Mediterranean and the Holy Land. After the age of thirty-seven an uncaring public were to hear no more, verse apart, from this wayward writer, this haunted, restless poet and supreme artificer. 'I do not wonder', wrote Hawthorne in his Liverpool journal, 'that he found it necessary to take an airing through the world, after so many years of toilsome pen-labor and domestic life, following upon so wild and adventurous youth as his was.'

On his return in May 1857, he tried the midwestern lecture circuit for a couple of years (a fiasco!) and in 1860 sailed to San Francisco, in the clipper *Meteor*, under the command of his young brother Tom. But stuck there – after planning to sail round the world – he hurried home by steamer. Then civil war broke out; he vainly tried for a commission in the navy; and in 1863 sold the last of his Pittsfield estate and moved back to New York. But not back to fiction. In the winter of 1866 Melville was at last offered public employment: a Deputy Inspectorship in the New York Custom House – outdoor work. 'Herman's position in the Custom House', wrote Elizabeth Melville in 1885, 'is in the Surveyor's Department – a *district inspector* – his work is all on the uptown piers nearly to Harlem ...' Gauguin, that other victim of the South Seas, abandoned his Danish wife and children for the dream of Tahiti: Melville abandoned the dream and for almost twenty years trod the New York pavements daily, from 104 East 26th Street, uptown to work.

Or had he abandoned it? Found glued to the inside of the desk on which he wrote *Billy Budd* was a tiny clipping: 'Keep true to the dreams of thy youth.' Like Hardy in his later years, Melville turned entirely from prose; but in 1859 or 1860 he began to write verse, printed in small, privately subsidized editions. In the quarter of a century between 1866 and 1891, three collections and one long speculative poem – almost a novel in verse – were published: *Battle-Pieces and Aspects of the War* (1866), *Clarel: A Poem and Pilgrimage in the Holy Land* (1876), *John Marr and Other Sailors* (1888), and *Timoleon* (1891). None attracted much notice. That Prometheus of American letters had declined to this seemingly sedate and gentlemanly amateur – his calm life shattered only in 1867 when his eighteen-year-old son, 'in his night clothes in bed with a pistol', shot himself.

Was it then, perhaps, that the seed of Captain Vere's dramatic dilemma took root – of an Abraham on whom his son's sacrifice is unwillingly thrust? For in December 1885, having inherited some money, Melville at last felt able to retire; and it was then at long last he turned again to prose. On 28 September 1891 – forty years after the publication of *Moby-Dick* – at the age of seventy-two almost totally forgotten, Melville died. But a draft of a final prose work, *Billy Budd, Sailor*, was left unfinished and uncollated. Packed tidily away by his widow, it was not rediscovered, or published to an attentive world, until 1924.

ON THE COMPOSITION OF *MOBY-DICK*

The Whale must have long sounded through Melville's mind. Nothing apparently was on paper before his return from London in February 1850. Yet by 1 May he could write to Richard Henry Dana, Jr.:

> About the 'whaling voyage' – I am half way in the work, & am very glad that your suggestion so jumps with mine. It will be a strange sort of a book, tho', I fear; blubber is blubber you know; tho' you may get oil out of it, the poetry runs as hard as sap from a frozen maple tree; – & to cook the thing up, one must needs throw in a little fancy, which from the nature of the thing, must be ungainly as the gambols of the whales themselves. Yet I mean to give the truth of the thing, spite of this.

His European tour was the turning-point. The years of youth and adventure were inevitably past; the resources of his art, rapidly exploited. At last with the sale of *White-Jacket* in London, he felt free to explore his one remaining asset, his one remaining mystery of life at sea: his experiences aboard the whalers *Acushnet* and *Charles and Henry*. Like Dana's *Two Years Before the Mast*, the work was to be in part documentary. Facts were what he needed. Only two days previously he had borrowed William Scoresby's *An Account of the Arctic Regions* from the New York Society Library. It was now that he must have ordered Thomas Beale's *The Natural History of the Sperm Whale* from Putnams.

Diving into Scoresby, he continued his 'voyage' with gusto. By 27 June he could tell his British publisher, Richard Bentley:

In the latter part of the coming autumn I shall have ready a new work ... a romance of adventure, founded upon certain wild legends in the Southern Sperm Whale Fisheries, and illustrated by the author's own personal experience, of two years & more, as a harpooneer ... I do not know that the subject treated of has ever been worked up by a romancer; or, indeed, by any writer, in any adequate manner.

By August 1850 a first draft was 'mostly done', yet it was to be another year before the book reached his publishers – a restless year in which his themes continued to shift and haunt him. A whole trunkful of literature, brought back from London, had cast its spell. He plunged into Shakespeare; explored Emerson;[1] borrowed Carlyle;[2] and on 18 July, with delighted amazement, discovered Hawthorne.

Literally discovered him, living in Lenox, six miles away. For he was staying in Pittsfield that summer, in the Berkshire Hills of western Massachusetts, when his aunt, Mary Melville, presented him with a copy of *Mosses from an Old Manse*. His excited marginalia can still be seen in the Harvard College Library.[3] These running comments led to an essay, 'Hawthorne and his Mosses. By a Virginian Spending July in Vermont', which Evert Duyckinck published in his journal, *The Literary World* (17 and 24 August); and Duyckinck, it seems, contrived their introduction on a literary ramble up Monument Mountain, followed by a lunch party in Stockbridge on 5 August. Melville had just turned thirty-one; Hawthorne was forty-six; and Hawthorne, willy-nilly, found himself cast as 'Hero' for 'Hero-Worship'.

1. cf. The letter to E. A. Duyckinck: 'I had heard of him as full of transcendentalisms, myths & oracular gibberish; I had only glanced at a book of his once in Putnam's store – that was all I knew of him, till I heard him lecture.' (3 March 1849) Either then or, more likely, in the summer of 1850, Melville followed up that Boston lecture.

2. Both *Sartor Resartus* and *Heroes and Hero-Worship* were borrowed from E. A. Duyckinck in late July or early August.

3. Though this was not the first of Hawthorne he had read. In 1849 Melville had borrowed *Twice-Told Tales* from Duyckinck, and in *White-Jacket* delivered a formal bow to 'my fine countryman, Hawthorne of Salem'. (ch. 68)

This meeting, this budding acquaintance more than anything, must have prompted Melville to buy 'Arrowhead', a house and farm of a hundred and sixty acres, two miles from Pittsfield. In September he moved his wife and one-year-old son from New York. By December he was again Arion afloat on his 'Whale':

'I have a sort of sea-feeling here in the country', he wrote Duyckinck

now that the ground is all covered with snow. I look out of my window in the morning when I rise as I would out of a port-hole of a ship in the Atlantic. My room seems a ship's cabin; & at nights when I wake up & hear the wind shrieking, I almost fancy there is too much sail on the house, & I had better go on the roof & rig in the chimney.

Do you want to know how I pass my time? – I rise at eight – thereabouts – & go to my barn – say good-morning to the horse, & give him his breakfast. (It goes to my heart to give him a cold one, but it can't be helped.) Then, pay a visit to my cow – cut up a pumpkin or two for her, & stand by to see her eat it – for its a pleasant sight to see a cow move her jaws – she does it so mildly & with such a sanctity. – My own breakfast over, I go to my work-room & light my fire – then spread my M.S.S. on the table – take one business squint at it, & fall to with a will. At 2½ P.M. I hear a preconcerted knock at my door, which (by request) continues till I rise & go to the door, which serves to wean me effectively from my writing, however interested I may be. My friends the horse & cow now demand their dinner – & I go & give it to them. My own dinner over, I rig my sleigh & with my mother or sisters start off for the village – & if it be a Literary World day, great is the satisfaction thereof. – My evenings I spend in a sort of mesmeric state in my room – not being able to read – only now & then skimming over some large-printed book. – Can you send me about fifty fast-writing youths, with an easy style & not averse to polishing their labors? If you can, I wish you would, because since I have been here I have planned about that number of future works & cant find enough time to think about them separately. – But I don't know but a book in a man's brain is better off than a book bound in calf – at any rate it is safer from criticism. And taking a book off the brain, is akin to the ticklish and dangerous business of taking an old painting off a panel – you have to scrape off the whole brain in order to get at it with due safety – & even then, the painting may not be worth the trouble.

Years later his wife drew a rather gloomier picture of that winter and spring, 1850–51:

Wrote White Whale or Moby Dick under unfavorable circumstances – would sit at his desk all day not eating any thing till four or five o'clock – then ride to the village after dark would be up early and out walking before breakfast – sometimes splitting wood for exercise.[4]

On their mutual visits, Hawthorne and Melville exchanged several gifts. In March 1851 Hawthorne presented Melville with *The Mariner's Chronicle*, a four-volume collection of sea disasters (Philadelphia, 1806). But Owen Chase's *Narrative of the Most Extraordinary and Distressing Shipwreck of the Whale-Ship Essex, of Nantucket* (New York, 1821) – a rare work, long out of print – was missing. Chief Justice Lemuel Shaw, however, succeeded in obtaining a copy from Nantucket and sent it to his son-in-law that April. Stirred and excited, Melville annotated the copy:

Somewhere about the latter part of A.D. 1841, in this same ship the Acushnet, we spoke the 'Charles Carroll' of Nantucket, & Owen Chace was the captain, & so it came to pass that I saw him. He was a large, powerful well made man; rather tall; to all appearances something past forty-five or so; with a handsome face for a Yankee, & expressive of great uprightness & calm unostentatious courage. His whole appearance impressed me pleasurably. He was the most prepossessing-looking whale-hunter I think I ever saw.

Being a mear foremast-hand I had no opportunity of conversing with Owen (tho' he was on board our ship for two hours at a time) nor have I ever seen him since.

But I should have before mentioned, that before seeing Chace's ship, we spoke another Nantucket craft & *gammed* with her. In the forecastle I made the acquaintance of a fine lad of sixteen or thereabouts, a son of Owen Chace. I questioned him concerning his father's adventure; and when I left his ship to

4. Elizabeth Melville, *Memoir* (Jay Leyda, *The Melville Log*, p. 412).

return again the next morning (for the two vessels were to sail in company for a few days) he went to his chest & handed me a complete copy (same edition as this one) of the *Narrative.* This was the first printed account of it I had ever seen, & the only copy of Chace's Narrative (regular & authentic) except the present one. The reading of this wondrous story upon the landless sea, & close to the very latitude of the shipwreck had a surprising effect upon me.

The *Essex*, too, had been rammed and sunk by a Pacific whale. Myth and memory had come full circle.

By June 1851 Melville wrote Hawthorne that he was off 'to New York, to bury myself in a third-story room, and work and slave on my "Whale" ... As the fishermen say, "He's in his flurry" when I left him some three weeks ago. I'm going to take him by his jaw, however, before long, and finish him up in some fashion or other.'

Then the Scoresby volumes, retained for over thirteen months, were returned to the New York Society Library. Disgusted with the heat and dust of New York, he went home 'to feel the grass – and end the book reclining on it'. Soon after he wrote, to parry a female neighbour:

> Dont you buy it – dont you read it, when it does come out, because it is by no means the sort of book for you. It is not a peice of fine feminine Spitalfields silk – but it is of the horrible texture of a fabric that should be woven of ships' cables and hausers. A Polar wind blows through it, & birds of prey hover over it. Warn all gentle fastidious people from so much as peeping into the book – on risk of a lumbago & sciatics.

It was Nantucket Ahab, apparently, who for that whole year stalled publication.[5] What was conceived in New York as romantic comedy, it seems, had been revised in New England to tragic proportions. What was begun as the quixotic pact of a cannibal don with his christian squire (chs. 1–22) had been displaced by the Faustian fate of their monomaniac captain. What was planned as an authentic-sounding cruise in quest of a legendary White Whale

5. As, years later, the emergence of Captain Vere, at a similar late stage, was to confound *Billy Budd*.

(February–August 1850) had been turned to the inverted gospel by one Ishmael of a hell-bent voyage through all space and time (August 1850–August 1851).[6] In an early version of that legend,[7] a tall negro – a proto-Queequeg, as it were – with a thrust of his harpoon won the life of the White Whale and claimed an American bride; but in Melville's final catastrophe, the stricken whale claimed ship, captain and crew.

On 18 October *The Whale* was published in London; on 14 November *Moby-Dick*, unexpurgated, in New York. Nature herself arranged the advance publicity: on 5 November rumour reached New York that the *Ann Alexander* of New Bedford had been rammed and sunk, in mid-Pacific, by a whale. From the *Panama Herald* to *Punch* this incredible news circled the globe.

6. cf. Leon Howard, *Herman Melville: A Biography*, pp. 162–79; Howard P. Vincent, *The Trying-Out of MOBY DICK*, pp. 22–49; George R. Stewart, 'The Two *Moby-Dicks*', *American Literature*, vol. 25 (January 1954), pp. 417–48.

7. 'Le Cachalot Blanc', recorded by Janez Stanonik, *Moby Dick: The Myth and the Symbol*, pp. 32–41, 189–95. See Appendix.

INTRODUCTION

In 1907, when Joseph Conrad was asked to introduce a World's Classics edition of *Moby-Dick*, he replied:

> Years ago I looked into *Typee* and *Omoo*, but as I didn't find there what I am looking for when I open a book I did go no further. Lately I had in my hand *Moby Dick*. It struck me as a rather strained rhapsody with whaling for a subject and not a single sincere line in the 3 vols of it.[1]

Even now when *Moby-Dick* is generally acclaimed a world classic – extolled among the dozen or so indubitable landmarks of nineteenth-century fiction – there may still be some rebel support for such a view. But even by 1907, that shows, *Moby-Dick* was regarded a masterpiece; and this judgement was universally confirmed a generation after Melville's death.

Not that Melville himself seemed wholly conscious of his achievement. 'Leviathan is not the biggest fish;' he wrote triumphantly to Hawthorne; ' – I have heard of Krakens.'[2] And *Pierre*, begun only five months after the completion of *Moby-Dick*, far more obviously indulged his own darkest and most confused psychological needs. *The Whale*, from the start, had slipped into a well-established wake: to be shaped into yet another 'romance' at sea with a topical slant. Only this time the primitive savagery (of *Typee*) or colonial missionaries (of *Omoo*), English slum conditions (in *Redburn*) or U.S. naval abuses (in *White-Jacket*), were to be replaced by a less passionately weighted theme: a rigorous

1. Letter to (Sir) Humphrey Milford, 15 January 1907.
2. Letter dated 17 November 1851.

account (sperm and all) of the New England whaling industry.

Yet profitable as such a survey might prove, to what length could it be drawn? *Redburn* and *White-Jacket* had both been written in a five months' spell. Was this to have been another potboiler? Another instalment of fictional autobiography to keep creditors at bay? 'I am so pulled hither and thither by circumstances', he told Hawthorne. 'The calm, the coolness, the silent grass-growing mood in which a man *ought* always to compose, – that, I fear, can seldom be mine. Dollars damn me; and the malicious Devil is forever grinning in upon me, holding the door ajar.'[3]

As usual, of course, he surveyed the technical field: Beale, Bennett, Scoresby, J. Ross Browne. Melville always worked with a small reference library close at hand. Again he used the first person; even Ishmael, his new persona, seems hardly distinguishable from his previous narrators. And again his new book was to be a quest. All his books had been quests: back to primal innocence (*Typee* and *Omoo*) or forwards home (*White-Jacket*); in search of a father (*Redburn*) or dream-maiden (*Mardi*). Such quests, confused to metaphysical jests by Herman the jester, had long proved ambiguous. The rover ('omoo'), like a prodigal son, returns to port; but the meaning of that port – like that of Ishmael's salvation, or of Ahab's witch-hunt, or of the White Whale's guile – was riddled with myths and a contradictory symbolism. Though *Mardi*, set in the 'faerie' wastes of the South Seas, had failed, in *The Whale* he again intended to confront the deepest meanings of life's dreams, anchored to a single whaleboat, launched on a three years' voyage around the world. *The Whale*, that 'mighty, misty monster', transcending the shaggy dog hoax of its Yankee origins, was to become – in a sense unconceived by George Eliot's Mr Casaubon – an unfinished 'Key to all Mythologies'.

'My development', he continued his letter to Hawthorne, 'has been all within a few years past. I am like one of those seeds taken out of the Egyptian Pyramids, which, after

3. 1 (?) June 1851.

being three thousand years a seed and nothing but a seed, being planted in English soil, it developed itself, grew to greenness, and then fell to mould. So I.' That development, that growth, is all reflected in *Moby-Dick*. Not *what* can be learnt, but theoretically *how*, impels the course; and if 'one did survive the wreck', like the ageing Faust, it is because he was capable of further energies of growth and education. Such were *Ishmaels Lehrjahre*, his university years;[4] and if *Moby-Dick* survives, it is precisely because (in a Goethean sense) it is Ishmael's own *Bildungsroman*: 'for a whale-ship was my Yale College and my Harvard'.[5]

But to grasp this education, it is essential to recall the American background from which it sprang. By mid-century the United States was dizzily entering an era of expanding wealth and power. The ever-shifting frontier expressed the untold opportunities of the vast power-house of American life. Emerson, Thoreau, Whitman – the writers of the eastern seaboard – all felt this as keenly as the pioneers. 'Go visit the Prairies in June ...' But, far more than James Fenimore Cooper or Richard Henry Dana, Melville added whole oceans to the American imagination. If the West lay open, so did the Atlantic and the Pacific; and the Yankee whaling fleet, outstripping all others, was as reckless and hardy as any waggon trails crossing the Rockies. Between land and sea spread boundless prospects for that free American spirit transcending both. 'Transcendentalism' itself was the expression of this free play of mind, rapturously caught up in an infinite, spiritual quest, as American democracy was grounded on the recognition of the infinite in every man; and Melville quite consciously was writing in a Jacksonian vein:

> But this august dignity I treat of, is not the dignity of kings and robes, but that abounding dignity which has no robed investiture. Thou shalt see it shining in the arm that wields a pick or drives a spike; that democratic dignity which, on all hands,

4. Goethe's novel, *Wilhelm Meisters Lehrjahre* (the Apprenticeship of Wilhelm Meister) had been translated in 1824 by Carlyle.

5. Ch. 24, THE ADVOCATE.

radiates without end from God; Himself! The great God absolute! The centre and circumference of all democracy! His omnipresence, our divine equality! [6]

A more immediate influence was that of the Duyckinck circle, to which Melville was introduced soon after settling in New York. 'Young America' they called themselves and their journal, *The Literary World*, promoted a fresh and restless concept of literature fit for that new, spontaneous age. Melville, in his anonymous review *Hawthorne and His Mosses*, caught their ebullient tone:

The world is as young today, as when it was created; and this Vermont morning dew is as wet to my feet, as Eden's dew to Adam's. Nor has Nature been all over ransacked by our progenitors, so that no new charms and mysteries remain for this latter generation to find. Far from it. The trillionth part has not yet been said; and all that has been said, but multiplies the avenues to what remains to be said. It is not so much paucity, as superabundance of material that seems to incapacitate modern authors.[7]

Cooper had made a start in the right direction, though too ensnared by Sir Walter Scott. Dana lacked the creative fire. Was Melville, then, to be the chosen prophet of 'Young America'? A man

... bound to carry republican progressiveness into Literature, as well as into Life? Believe me, my friends, that men not very much inferior to Shakespeare, are this day being born on the banks of the Ohio. And the day will come, when you shall say who reads a book by an Englishman that is a modern? [7]

The Whale was already well launched when Melville chanced upon Hawthorne. There – far from the open frontier, the epic sweep, the expansive vision – he stumbled into twilight, sniffed the smell of decay, sensed a hint of doom: 'Whether Hawthorne has simply availed himself of this mystical blackness', he pondered aloud

as a means to the wondrous effects he makes it to produce in his

6. Ch. 26, KNIGHTS AND SQUIRES.
7. *The Literary World*, 17 and 24 August 1850.

lights and shades; or whether there really lurks in him, perhaps unknown to himself, a touch of Puritanic gloom, – this, I cannot altogether tell. Certain it is, however, that this great power of blackness in him derives its force from its appeals to that Calvinistic sense of Innate Depravity and Original Sin, from whose visitations, in some shape or other, no deeply thinking mind is always and wholly free.[7]

It was that 'power of blackness' which so fixed and fascinated Melville; out of those epic insights and that dark, hereditary strain – a bifocal vision that is both Ishmael's and Ahab's – were born the complex splendours of *Moby-Dick*.

But there was a still wider world that Melville encountered in bookshops, in private libraries (like Duyckinck's) and the New York Public Library: the whole world of the classics and the Elizabethans – from Virgil and Homer (in Pope's translation) to Dante, Spenser and *Paradise Lost*; from Rabelais and Montaigne to Burton and Sir Thomas Browne. But, above all, Shakespeare. As Hawthorne dominated the present, so Shakespeare crowned the past. For

... it is those deep far-away things in him; those occasional flashings-forth of the intuitive Truth in him; those short, quick probings at the very axis of reality: – these are the things that make Shakespeare, Shakespeare. Through the mouths of the dark characters of Hamlet, Timon, Lear and Iago, he craftily says, or sometimes insinuates the things, which we feel to be so terrifically true, that it were all but madness for any good man, in his own proper character, to utter, or even hint of them. Tormented into desperation, Lear the frantic King tears off the mask, and speaks the sane madness of vital truth.[7]

Shakespeare became his mentor in 'the great Art of Telling the Truth'.

Page after page he exulted over his 'glorious' seven-volume Shakespeare. But this was far removed from his living experience of Music Halls, Penny Theatres, Promenade Concerts and playhouses in New York, London and Paris. His great *ensembles*, viewed as through a proscenium arch, seem mounted on a stage (with traps, flies, orchestral pit) to the full complement of bombastic solos and operatic choruses in one of Edwin Forrest's or Macready's Shakespearian extravaganzas. 'Enter Ahab: Then, all.' But the comic brogues (Yankee, Feegee, Negro, Quaker), suggest rather some variety act of farces and entr'actes, merged with the blackface minstrels of a Mississippi river town or travelling road show. For in this medley the worlds of high art and 'pop' art, east and west, all meet. Such was this American bard, this Shakespeare turned impresario to rival the great Phineas T. Barnum. Like him, he would mount 'a big picture of a whale ... stretched across the front of his Museum;'[8] like him, proclaim 'the greatest show on earth'.

For his own personal library he selected mainly classics from the romantic and pre-romantic age: Rousseau's *Confessions*, De Quincey's *Confessions*, Coleridge's *Biographia Literaria*, Goethe's *Dichtung und Wahrheit* and *Wilhelm Meister*. But the key to *Moby-Dick* was Carlyle. It was through *Sartor Resartus*, above all, that Melville conceived his romantic vision: the search for an absolute revelation in nature; the inflation of self; the fascination with dreams, with demonic possession, with self-sacrificing love. The cultural time lag across the Atlantic had always been marked. Now not only Carlyle and Ruskin, Wagner and Baudelaire became Melville's contemporaries, but Byron, Coleridge and Shelley of *Prometheus Unbound*.

Like Wagner in *The Flying Dutchman* (that proto-Ahab), he could blend theme with counter theme into a single harmony, elliptic as a hieroglyph: '*the coffin life-buoy*' redeeming a death-trance through love. *Der Ring des Nibelungen* was conceived within the precise creative span of its Yankee counterpart, the wheeling *Whale*. What Baudelaire and Rimbaud were sketching in scattered *ébauches* and *illuminations*, Melville had already orchestrated to epic dimensions by the year of the Prince Consort's Great Exhibition. That 'Grand Œuvre', of which Mallarmé was merely to

8. George Duyckinck to Joann Miller, 14 November 1849.

dream a whole generation later,[9] Melville had long ago attempted. Born in New York, he was perhaps the first, wholly self-conscious expatriate from the old European heartland – like Borges in Buenos Aires or Nabokov in St Petersburg a century later – to indulge in those scholastic parodies and acrostic games now commonplace *inside* our socially obsolete, but still intellectually fertile, high culture. Pages of mock-bibliography and glossaries package his *Whale* (or 'little treatise on Eternity'), as if none but an American might realize that traditional learning and technology could converge only by hyperboles of philological, ironic or occult fantasies. For Melville was also heir to the protestant tradition of New England, parodying with astonishing provincial vigour the old emblematic discourses of a Cotton Mather or Jonathan Edwards.

The strain was immense, pulling away from his romantic roots, on an epic quest of inner consciousness, to some unforeseen destination. His was to be the drama of an individual soul: of an Ishmael trapped in a moment of intense and anguished crisis, stripped of obsessions with class or job or nationality, crossing 'the frontiers into Eternity with nothing but a carpet-bag – that is to say, the Ego'.[10] The whole seed of the modernist movement already inheres in *Moby-Dick*: the withdrawal, or indifference of God; the collapse of reason; the disappearance of plot; the demise of naturalism. Divine Truth and divine inspiration are submerged by the magical, the mad, the absurd (THE HYENA, THE CASTAWAY). Logic and analytic reason give way to intuition and 'inner light' (in a most perverted, unQuakerly sense). Plot is dissolved in patterns of consciousness; direction in indirection (THE DOUBLOON). Naturalism is stifled by juxtaposition, or the mystical coexistence of all time. His whole aesthetic remained one of the sketch, the tentative essay or draft, however huge and swollen the CETOLOGY:

9. Letter to Paul Verlaine, 16 November 1885.

10. Letter to Hawthorne, 16 April 1851. cf. THE CARPET-BAG (Ch. 2).

For small erections may be finished by their first architects; grand ones, true ones, ever leave the copestone to posterity. God keep me from ever completing anything. This whole book is but a draught – nay, but the draught of a draught. Oh, Time, Strength, Cash, and Patience! [11]

Like Walt Whitman, his fellow New Yorker, Melville actively solicits you and me, his future readers. 'Call me Ishmael', he accosts us. That 'grand', that 'true' erection depends on successive generations of posterity to give it renewed and effective potency.[12]

For how call a work 'allegory' if it contains no maps, no complex interpretative guide, but (as in Kafka's *The Castle*) their very antithesis? If anything it seems a kind of allegory *à rebours* – a clue to the impossibility of any final map, a clue to mysterious, pervasive and malicious *dis*order – that heralds the end of all formal allegorical vision. We gaze at our own risk, till 'the palsied universe lies before us a leper'! Till blinded by 'the monumental white shroud that wraps all the prospect around' us.[13]

So allegory, of course, Ishmael rejects.[14] But philosophy, too, he resists: Locke's head and Kant's, see-sawing on either side of the *Pequod*, cancel each other out. Tumble them overboard! For his mind, as Claude Lévi-Strauss would say of a Bororo or Arawak Indian, is instinctively pre-scientific, pre-rationalistic, pre-analytic – moving in closed and circular modes to reel in the universe. Melville, the myth-maker, needs only the age-old devices of symmetry, symbolic inversions and permutations, contrasts, antitheses, dissociations and binomial groupings to order, interpret and transmit his experience of life.[15] His *Whale* is explicitly 'mystic-

11. Ch. 32, CETOLOGY.

12. See Robert Shulman, 'The Serious Functions of Melville's Phallic Jokes' (*American Literature* 33, No. 2, 1961).

13. Ch. 42, THE WHITENESS OF THE WHALE.

14. Ch. 45: 'So ignorant are most landsmen of some of the plainest and most palpable wonders of the world, that . . . they might scout at Moby Dick as a monstrous fable, or still worse and more detestable, a hideous and intolerable allegory.' (THE AFFIDAVIT.)

15. See *La Pensée sauvage*, passim.

marked';[16] for at its core, as in the earliest ritual myths, blazes the sun, a flash of gold, Promethean fire.

According to Lévi-Strauss three prime factors underlie the structure of primitive mythology: a culinary motif, a seasonal or astronomic theme, and a sociological code. All make their bow in LOOMINGS, linked to the widespread mythical theme of the limping man – Richard III, Timur Leng, or Oedipus Swellfoot – who enters later. The sequence may seem haphazard; for the meaning is effected by a continual overlayering (*im*position, not *com*position) of myths and metaphors: 'but cut into it, and you find that three distinct strata compose it: upper, middle, and lower ... This triune structure, as much as anything else, imparts power to' the tale. [17]

Mythopoeia itself, in layer upon layer of contrasting mythologies, is the driving fuse of Melville's heroics. His very theme is the mythopoeic imagination: the neurosis of man in usurping the ritual role of Gods; the trauma that converts the pretensions of an Ahab to a suicidal re-enactment of myth. Mythopoeia, in fact, far from contriving a mask, or prophylactic screen, is shown by Melville (as later by Jung) to disclose the deepest layers of psychological awareness.

Such roundness alone, in Jungian terms, betrays a search for individual wholeness. Such a *mandala* – spinning in rings or squaring of the circle – seems to project a path for the union of the conscious and the unconscious. For *The Whale* is a *wheel*: both an heroic, and a pastoral, and a metaphysical tour. The whole *wail* is a *vale* is a *veil*, – or else a *wall*, all *wile*: and 'unless you own the whale, you are but a provincial and sentimentalist in Truth'.[18]

*

'To enter into the belly of the monster', writes Mircea Eliade, 'is equivalent to a regression into the primal

16. Ch. 68, THE BLANKET.
17. Ch. 86, THE TAIL.
18. Ch. 76, THE BATTERING-RAM.

indistinctness, into the cosmic Night – and to come out of the monster is equivalent to a cosmogony: it is to pass from Chaos to Creation ... Every initiatory adventure of this type ends in the *creation* of something, in the founding of a new world or a new mode of being.'[19] In that suicidal sounding and regurgitation, in that total immersion or death-trance in the belly of *The Whale*, Ishmael – as 'most young candidates for the pains and penalties of whaling' – both confirms and confounds the gospel of Christ: 'An evil and adulterous generation seeketh after a sign; and there shall no sign be given to it, but the sign of the prophet Jonas.' (*Matthew* xii, 29)

But 'unlettered Ishmael' alone completes this *rite de passage*, this symbolic descent and resurrection. Only the 'Entered Apprentice', here too, is confirmed to the second and third degree; only Ishmael is enrolled as 'Fellow Craftsman' and finally 'Master Mason' of Blue Lodge. His captain remains for ever a masonic candidate, blindfold and led by a hangman's noose to his self-inflicted end.

'What is *The Whale*?' asks the Worshipful Master.

'A peculiar system of morality, veiled in Allegory, and illustrated by Symbols,' replies the scholar-candidate of this elaborate hoax on the rituals of masonic initiation.

'Name the grand principles on which the Order is founded.'

'Brotherly Love, Relief, and Truth.'

'Who are fit and proper persons to be made Whalemen?'

'Just, upright and free men, of mature age ...'[20]

19. *Myths, Dreams and Mysteries*, ch. 8: 'Mysteries and Spiritual Regeneration', p. 224 (Paris: Gallimard, 1957; London: Harvill Press, 1960).

20. 'In an extensive herd, so remarkable, occasionally, are these mystic gestures, that I have heard hunters who have declared them akin to Free-Mason signs and symbols; that the whale, indeed, by these methods intelligently conversed with the world'. (THE TAIL.) cf. *Typee*, chs. 24 and 30.

Freemasonry was so much part of American life that some first hand acquaintance with masonic temples was a commonplace. In February 1849, for example, Melville had visited Boston's Masonic Temple to hear Fanny Kemble Butler give a reading of *Macbeth*.

'In a Symbol there is concealment and yet revelation,' Carlyle long ago had noted; and this *Whale* too – with its cargo of religious and political and sexual improprieties – 'wears a false brow to the common world'.[21] Every revelation for Melville, as for the hermetics and mystics who taught him, conceals yet further revelations. The very act of writing, much as the parables of earlier rabbis or Zen Buddhists, itself conceals yet further probes. It is not simple precision that is its goal, but a precise response to the complex simultaneity of all things:

> True, one portrait may hit the mark much nearer than another, but none can hit it with any very considerable degree of exactness. So there is no earthly way of finding out precisely what the whale really looks like.[22]

This simultaneity of *The Whale* – as of whales – finds its most obvious expression in the pun. Literally we must learn to 'read about whales through their own spectacles'. Does not the siting of their eyes even correspond to that of human ears?

> True, both his eyes, in themselves, must simultaneously act; but is his brain so much more comprehensive, combining, and subtle than man's, that he can at the same moment of time attentively examine two distinct prospects, one on one side of him, and the other in an exactly opposite direction? If he can, then is it as marvellous a thing in him, as if a man were able simultaneously to go through the demonstrations of two distinct problems in Euclid.[23]

But this virtuoso 'solo' performance is precisely more comprehensive, combining and subtle than its contemporaries in this: that Ishmael can at the same moment of time attentively examine not merely two, but three, four, or five distinct prospects in exactly opposing directions. He scores his

21. Ch. 80, THE NUT.
22. Ch. 55, OF THE MONSTROUS PICTURES OF WHALES.
23. Ch. 74, THE SPERM WHALE'S HEAD – CONTRASTED VIEW.

prose polyphonally, as it were, via puns, through overlapping ranges of meaning, across radiating axes of reference. This shifting filigree of quotations requires marvels of hermeneutic exegesis or cryptanalysis. For every name is a cryptonym; every chapter, a cryptogram; and Ishmael, the supreme cryptographer: 'The subterranean miner that works in us all, how can one tell whither leads his shaft by the ever shifting, muffled sound of his pick?'[24]

Thus that Narcissus myth (for 'young candidates') is dissolved in that wider masonic ritual (closed to women); the masonic epic of 'Brotherly Love' is disclosed as a Brotherhood of Sodom, a descent to Gomorrha; a monomaniac's revenge is clinched, by an harpoon's thrust, in attempted buggery. The joke of THE CASSOCK, after all, is that by turning the all-pervading biblical allegory and Hebrew symbolism against the very Calvinist soil that so long had bred them, it reveals no longer *Images or Shadows of Divine Things* but of things carnal. The irony of A BOSOM FRIEND lies precisely in its immediate juxtaposition to THE SERMON.

*

For illiterate Queequeg and 'unlettered Ishmael' are matched. At that emblematic entry (or SPOUTER-INN) is set not only a large black 'oil-painting', but a little black wooden idol; not only a 'half-foundered ship', but a baby-sized 'manikin'. 'If man will strike, strike through the mask!' cries Ahab. But Queequeg's very first gesture was to swap 'a man striking a whale' for his ebony hunchback. 'How can the prisoner reach outside except by thrusting through the wall?' asks Ahab. But Queequeg simply removed the pasteboard screen from an empty fire-place.

Yet it is Yojo (O Joy!) who in the first place, indirectly, picks out the *Pequod*. All motivation, all drives at root prove erotic: the sterile emasculated solipsism of Ahab as much as the narcissism of Queequeg, groping at his crotch. Both are endowed with formidable harpoons. But while Queequeg –

24. Ch. 41, MOBY DICK.

flush in bed and whaleboat – lances his prey, neurotic Ahab is foiled of his revenge.

For Queequeg, not Ahab, is truly a High Priest's nephew and a Prince of Whales. Queequeg, not Ahab, is the ultimate *isolato*, 'cool as an icicle', 'always equal to himself', a walking 'treatise on the art of attaining truth'. Queequeg, not Ahab, proves the priest-king and lantern-bearer of *Moby-Dick*: for him, and him alone, 'to live or die was a matter of his own sovereign will and pleasure'.

Yet his role in the self-conscious moral order, as in order of appearance, lies between that mysterious Southerner, whose advent precedes him, and his mysterious captain – between Bulkington's 'deep, earnest thinking' and professorial Ahab who has 'been in colleges, as well as 'mong the cannibals'. For what is Bulkington – Ishmael's silent or 'sleeping-partner', gone before Ahab comes on deck – but a thumbnail sketch of the Emersonian hero? [25] His 'six-inch' epitaph might read:

SACRED

To the Memory

OF

PALINURUS

virtuous and self-reliant transcendentalist,
dedicated to the solitary search for truth,
who was swept overboard at night
from the helm of the ship *Pequod.*

THIS TABLET

is erected to his Memory

BY

A SHIPMATE

And what is his captain but Emerson's transcendental philosopher turned satanic, living 'wholly from within', at war

25. See S. A. Cowan, 'In praise of Self-Reliance: the role of Bulkington in *Moby-Dick*' (*American Literature* 38, pp. 547–56).

with the visible world of nature, swept overboard by day from a rocking whaleboat? Like his mentor, Ahab might cry: 'if I am the Devil's child, I will live then from the Devil.'

More of a philosopher than Stubb, less of a metaphysician than Ahab (with his 'sky-light on top'), Ishmael's is a cult of buffoonery, or *humeur noire*. He becomes not only 'an ostrich of potent digestion', gobbling down bullets and gun flints, but 'a Catskill eagle', diving down into blackest gorges and soaring out again to disappear in the sunny spaces. He swoops between the polar nihilism of Stubb and Ahab, that is, soaring between 'the sunny spaces' of the one and 'blackest gorges' of the other. For Stubb's loaded rack of pipes is mirrored by Ahab's rack of loaded muskets. Ahab's 'is a woe that is madness'; but Ishmael's 'a wisdom that is woe'. 'Ishmael saves himself from despair by laughing at what threatens his body; Ahab dooms himself by laughing at what threatens his soul.'[26] Ishmael, 'exchanging puffs' on Queequeg's wild tomahawk pipe, first senses this ultimate secret of the hyena laugh, which is 'the fine hammered steel of woe' and of *Ecclesiastes*: 'All is vanity.'

From the start Ishmael declared: 'I love to sail forbidden seas, and land on barbarous coasts. Not ignoring what is good, I am quick to perceive a horror, and could still be social with it ...' But that barbarous coast-line began in New England. Cuddling with cannibals, thrilling to blood-pacts, 'a wild, mystical, sympathetical feeling' was in him.[27] Alone he clinches his oath 'because of the dread' in his soul. Alone he can confront the 'horror' – that heart of darkness – and survive. For he alone encompasses the vision of the others (THE DOUBLOON). He alone, in the end, achieves wholeness, transcending both Ahab and Queequeg, fire and water, thanatos and eros, the brotherhood of violence and the brotherhood of lust, the destructive baptism of blood and the redemptive baptism of sperm.

Quaker Ahab, on the other hand, appears to have been

26. E. H. Rosenberry, *Melville and the Comic Spirit*, p. 123.
27. Ch. 41, MOBY DICK.

some kind of Deist, until assaulted by Moby Dick; a Deist turned Zoroastrian 'till in the sacramental act so burned' that he was scarred for life. Twice this ex-transcendentalist is shocked to a metaphysical inversion. But it was the first occasion – the loss of his leg – that consecrated this whale to an absolute focus of malice in the world. Then it was Ahab turned werewolf – were-bear, were-whale – 'with the infixed, unrelenting fangs' of his 'incurable idea'.

All Ahab utters rebounds on Ahab. This whole *Revenger's Tragedy* turns on a kind of self-castration or suicidal impulse.[28] The inscrutable wall of the whale is Ahab's own wall that masks him from the world. For to gaze too long into hell-fire is to become, 'in some enchanted way, inverted' – prow to stern – as Ishmael one fateful night at the tiller:

> A stark, bewildered feeling, as of death, came over me ... My God! what is the matter with me? thought I. Lo! in my brief sleep I had turned myself about, and was fronting the ship's stern, with my back to her prow and the compass.[29]

But what was for Ishmael a unique hallucination is now Ahab's permanent condition. This Faustus of the quarter-deck, who inverts compasses, himself aptly proves a metaphysical invert. THE NEEDLE itself aims an inverted pointer at his obsession.

Thus Ahab takes divinity upon his own humped shoulders, 'staggering beneath the piled centuries since Paradise.' Ahab Agonistes – 'noble soul! grand old heart'! [30] – is the focus and nerve-centre of the *Pequod*, condensing 'to one deep pang the sum total of those shallow pains kindly diffused through feebler men's whole lives.' [31] The 'queenly personality lives in me,' [32] he cries – like 'the British Empire,' declaring 'himself a sovereign nature (in himself) amid the

28. See ch. 106, AHAB'S LEG.
29. Ch. 96, THE TRY-WORKS.
30. Ch. 132, THE SYMPHONY.
31. Ch. 133, THE CHASE – FIRST DAY.
32. Ch. 119, THE CANDLES.

powers of heaven, hell, and earth'.[33] Grand Turk, Grand Lama, Grand Master of Grand Lodge ('at this grim sign of the Thunder Cloud'), his is 'a witchery of social czarship'.

Such intellectual pride, such deceptions and self-deceptions are all satanic. As Coleridge, long ago, had observed of Milton:

> The character of Satan is pride and sensual indulgence, finding in self the sole motive of action. It is the character so often seen *in little* on the political stage. It exhibits all the restlessness, temerity, and cunning which have marked the mighty hunters of mankind from Nimrod to Napoleon ... But around this character, he has thrown a singularity of daring, a grandeur of sufferance, and a ruined splendour, which constitute the very height of poetic sublimity.[34]

No longer cast in his Zoroastrian role, this Great Mysticetus finally appears as last of the Gnostic prophets, self-proclaimed son of Sophia, the fallen 'mother' and eternal adversary of the 'mechanical' fire of the Creator. In the midst of the typhoon, below that 'tri-pointed trinity' of corposants, he renders allegiance to none but Wisdom, who breathed the spiritual essence into man at his creation:

> To be Ahab is to be unable to resist the hypnotic attraction of the self with its impulse to envelop and control the universe. To be Ishmael is to be able at the last minute to resist the plunge from the masthead into the sea one has with rapt fascination been gazing at, to assert at the critical moment the difference between the self and the not-self.[35]

Thus Ishmael's suicidal impulse is transferred to Ahab's suicidal fate. Both are variations on the myth of Narcissus – self-infatuated, self-deceivers both. Though one imperils only himself; the other draws a whole world to destruction.

For *Moby-Dick* is not only a water eclogue, a dream idyll afloat with Noah in the ark (where shepherds turn sailors,

33. To Nathaniel Hawthorne, 16 April 1851.

34. 'A Course of Lectures' X, *The Literary Remains*, vol. I, pp. 173–4.

35. Richard Chase, 'Melville and *Moby-Dick*', p. 59 (*A Collection of Critical Essays*, 1962).

their solitary pine-tree to a towering mast), but a Fire Sermon and Argonaut quest. The whole text is coded through green and blue, in contrasting mock-pastorals of earth and sea, arched by the sun: the whale circles the equator through all the signs of the zodiac; Ahab as Phaeton, Icarus, Helios, Lucifer (Platonic Absolute and Zoroastrian magus), heroically ousts the sun. 'Talk not to me of blasphemy, man.' That solar disc, whether as gold doubloon nailed to the *Pequod*'s mast, or as the stricken whale radiating harpoons, or inverted to midnight fire in the try-works, marks the cabbalistic centre of *Moby-Dick*.

So Moby Dick, too, must reflect that wholeness of ultimate being. The Whale, too, must transcend that 'last phallic being' (of D. H. Lawrence's dreams)[36] to embody both generative principles: 'Androgyny' writes Mircea Eliade

> is an archaic and universal formula for the expression of *wholeness*, the co-existence of the contraries, or *coincidentia oppositorum*. More than a state of sexual completeness and autarchy, androgny symbolises the perfection of a primordial, non-conditioned state.[37]

Both a *vagina dentata* and buoyant with sperm, both bridal chamber and battering ram, this whale is a true amphibium, dual-sexed as Gabriel's 'Shaker God incarnated'.[38] Only thus can it evoke the solar godhead within nature and controlling nature. For

> ... *androgyny extends even to divinities who are pre-eminently masculine, or feminine*. This means that androgyny has become a general formula signifying *autonomy, strength, wholeness*; to say of a divinity that it is androgyne is as much as to say that it is the ultimate being, the ultimate reality.[37]

But what is play of superstition for sailors hardens in Ahab to neurosis. Convulsed with pain, he is shocked to a

36. 'Herman Melville's "Moby Dick"' (*Studies in Classic American Literature*, 1923).

37. *Myths, Dreams and Mysteries*, ch. 7: 'Mother Earth and the Cosmic Hierogamies', pp. 174–5.

38. Ch. 71, THE JEROBOAM'S STORY.

traumatic transference of emotion; mutilated, to a masochistic identification with his 'dismemberer', till the 'White Whale swam before him as the monomaniac incarnation of all those malicious agencies which some deep men feel eating in them ...'[39]

Thus fantasy is transformed to myth; superstition, to fanatic religion, 'chasing with curses a Job's whale round the world'. Now the whole crew, subjected to Ahab's will, drive on to their metaphysical and moral doom. Now 'to their unconscious understandings, also, in some dim, unsuspected way, he might have seemed the gliding great demon of the seas of life.' His cult, proclaimed in this myth of a demon-hunt, is further exalted by ironic glosses parodying Egyptian, Hindu, Babylonian, Hebrew, Persian, Greco-Roman, Gnostic and Christian myths of divine incarnation. Now as Tyrian Baal and Babylonian Bel Ahab is double-cast both as water dragon and sun god who hunts the water-dragon. In his monomania he re-enacts the role of dragon-slayer – Osiris to Moby Dick's Typhon, Christ to Leviathan, godlike deliverer (Prometheus, Noah, Perseus) in his most 'godlike ungodly', solitary, self-indulgent confinement.[40] Not only do 'men think in myths', as Lévi-Strauss has shown; myths, too, 'think themselves out in men'.[41]

But, demon-hunt though it seems, Ahab is hunting a real whale, with a name (Moby Dick), who snapped off his leg.

39. cf. C. G. Jung: 'The idea of the *coniunctio* of masculine and feminine, which became almost a technical concept in Hermetic philosophy, appears in Gnosticism as the *mysterium iniquitatis*, probably not uninfluenced by the Old Testament 'divine marriage' as performed, for instance, by Hosea'. ('The psychology of the child-archetype', in C. G. Jung and C. Kerényi, *Introduction to a Science of Mythology*, 1951.)

40. An explicit totemism, or cult of the whale, is ridiculed aboard the *Jeroboam*, not the *Pequod*. To *worship* a 'golden calf' is displayed not merely in terms of parody, but of farce.

41. 'Nous ne prétendons donc pas montrer comment les hommes pensent dans les mythes mais comment les mythes se pensent dans les hommes, et à leur insu.' (*Mythologiques* I. *Le cru et le cuit*, p. 20.)

It is through Ishmael's eyes that we see the awful, void, dazzling whiteness of this whale. It is through Ishmael's hypochondriac eyes that the whale turns a blank. Not only the whale; this tormented somnambulist, too, turns a blank. A blank is hunting a blank, in his madness pursuing a mirror image of his own mad self – both dumb, vacated things. Narcissus is drawn through an enchanted labyrinth of reflections. Or rather, it is a mirror image which he himself provokes: Ahab's vindictiveness confronts the whale's 'wilful, deliberate designs of destruction'. The very trail is circular; the kill, inevitably, a boomerang.

So Nietzsche: 'He who fights with monsters should be careful lest he thereby becomes a monster. And if thou gaze long into an abyss, the abyss will also gaze into thee.'[42] Such is the voyage of the *Pequod*; such Ishmael's candidacy 'for the pains and penalties of whaling', whose existential guide is THE HYENA. He must accept 'this whole universe for a vast practical joke, though the wit thereof he but dimly discerns'. He must accept the meaningless absurdity of this posturing in an unfeeling universe. His religion must be that of *no* religion, of the whiteness of the *veil*, of self-realization in total Death-in-Life, opening among the coffin warehouses of Manhattan to end in coffin resurrection. Even the antics of his intellectual pride – shoring these fragments, statistics, quotations against his ruins – is capable of no justification except the now meaningless Cartesian proof: 'Cogito, ergo sum.' Over such 'Cartesian vortices' Ishmael hovers. This Cartesian nightmare is his sole heritage: the capacity of human consciousness to reflect upon itself and to entertain its own end. 'Il n'y a qu'un problème philosophique vraiment sérieux:' wrote Albert Camus, 'c'est le suicide.' The opening of *Le Mythe de Sisyphe* is merely a variant of the opening of *Moby-Dick*.[43]

As is the conclusion: 'We must consider Sisyphus happy.' For 'philosophical suicide', in Camus' phrase, was never a

42. Apothegm 146, *Beyond Good and Evil*, ch. 4 (1886).

43. Written between 1938 and 1941. Camus by that time had read, and was indebted to, Melville.

temptation. It took Kierkegaard, a contemporary – not Ishmael – to react to the irrationalism of the universe by a 'leap into faith'. Ishmael's first existentialist lesson rather was to trust, drowning in the treachery of the infinite: 'Up from the spray of thy ocean-perishing – straight up, leaps thy apotheosis!'[44] Followed by a second, after his first lowering: that the howl of the infinite is the cruelty of the absurd; that we must accept the universe for what it *is*, with a creed whose only certainty (in Heisenberg's phrase) is an uncertainty principle – a game of Tarot where 'La Force' may be trumped by 'Le Pendu'; 'Le Pendu', at any moment, by 'La Mort':[45]

> This is it, that for ever keeps God's true princes of the Empire from the world's hustings; and leaves the highest honors that this air can give, to those men who become famous more through their infinite inferiority to the choice hidden handful of the Divine Inert . . .[46]

Ishmael's own role throughout remains essentially passive, as Queequeg's squaw.

So he wrote in THE GILDER:

> There is no steady unretracing progress in this life; we do not advance through fixed gradations, and at the last one pause: – through infancy's unconscious spell, boyhood's thoughtless faith, adolescence' doubt (the common doom), then scepticism, then disbelief, resting at last in manhood's pondering repose of If. But once gone through, we trace the round again; and are infants, boys, and men, and Ifs eternally.

Or as Melville was to write to Hawthorne:

> And perhaps after all, there is *no* secret. We incline to think that the Problem of the Universe is like the Freemason's mighty secret, so terrible to all children. It turns out, at last, to consist

44. Ch. 23, THE LEE SHORE.
45. Melville's last words to Hawthorne, on the sand-dunes of Lancashire, are a resigned echo. Referring to life after death, Hawthorne noted: 'He had pretty much made up his mind to be annihilated.'
46. Ch. 33, THE SPECKSYNDER.

in a triangle, a mallet, and an apron, – nothing more! We incline to think that God cannot explain His own secrets, and that He would like a little information upon certain points Himself.[47]

'Round and round ... like another Ixion' he revolves. For ever bound to 'that slowly wheeling circle', we too must consider Ixion happy. That 'Job's whale' remains, to the end, irreducible – an albino, a *lusus naturae*, unique.

*

> On earth's shelter, cometh oft to me,
> Eager and ready, the crying lone-flyer,
> Whets for the whale-path the heart irresistibly,
> O'er tracks of ocean ...[48]

So Melville felt, landlocked in Pittsfield, writing and rewriting *Moby-Dick*:

I look out of my window in the morning when I rise as I would out of a port-hole of a ship in the Atlantic. My room seems a ship's cabin ...[49]

After the success of *Typee* and *Omoo*, he might have continued for years spinning his yarns or making brief platform appearances in whaleman or cannibal gear. The formula for launching such adventures was simple enough: a young white (male of course, preferably alone) makes for some outpost – island, jungle, desert, prairie – as remote as possible from Victorian London or New York. R. M. Ballantyne, for example, after his success with *Hudson's Bay; or Every-Day Life in the Wilds of North America* (1848), spent the next forty odd years in penning such sequels as *The Gorilla Hunters, Fighting the Whales, The Coral Island* and a hundred more. Or Melville might have turned to the stage. He might have followed his bent for popular melodrama by joining forces with Dion Boucicault, say, in an adaptation of *Typee* on the lines of *The Corsican Brothers* or the future *Shaughraun*.

47. From Pittsfield, 16 April (?) 1851.
48. Ezra Pound, *The Seafarer* (from the Anglo-Saxon).
49. To Evert A. Duyckinck, 13 December 1850.

But Melville was neither a Ballantyne nor a Boucicault; he was a compatriot of Ralph Waldo Emerson. 'A man is the whole encyclopaedia of facts,' wrote that sage:

> The creation of a thousand forests is in one acorn; and Egypt, Greece, Rome, Gaul, Britain, America, lie folded already in the first man . . . The Sphynx must solve her own riddle.[50]

In acknowledging this – in personally testing and asserting this – Melville proved a true American child of his time. Thrust into a new world, he himself needed to renew a whole lost Atlantis of western experience. His complete inner life was to be the 'text'; the complete storehouse of the world's books, its interpretative 'commentary'. *Moby-Dick* presents his individually forged passport to a universal culture.

For as the *Pequod* circles the world, so this universal and global book must range through universal and global references in space and time, through all religious creeds and philosophical ideas (ancient and modern). The imagery thus plays its own independent role: as an intellectual subplot to the drama – an attempt to focus each gesture within the space-time of universal history, to illumine Ahab's demonic self-sacrifice, like Christ's, within the total tragedy of Man. For like another Saint Brendan, this navigator celebrates mass on the back of his *Whale*.

So spin me – not a yarn, but a whole *cyclo*paedia! Like harpooneers we flounder about, half on *The Whale* and half in the water, 'as the vast mass revolves like a tread-mill' beneath us. A whale is a whale is a whale: and within that circling word-play the mystery is left open – now turned to acrostics, by a riddling extension of that single word; now to some magical rune, with a Celtic abandon of twining, ser-

50. 'History', from *Essays* (*First Series*). Emerson continues: 'The student is to read history actively and not passively; to esteem his own life the text, and books the commentary . . . He should see that he can live all history in his own person. He must sit solidly at home, and not suffer himself to be bullied by kings or empires, but know that he is greater than all the geography and all the government of the world . . .' (1841)

pentine forms; now in an infinitive regress, to one dazzling, blinding blank.

Of all this 'the Albino whale was the symbol'. Wonder ye then at THE WHITENESS OF *THE WHALE*? wonder ye then at the fiery hunt?

HAROLD BEAVER

A NOTE ON THE TEXT

THE English were quick off the mark. On 3 July 1851 Richard Bentley wrote accepting the new book. Melville replied, accepting his terms, on 20 July – with the last sheets of *The Whale* already 'passing thro' the press' – and on 13 August the agreement was signed: Melville was to receive £150 on delivery of the manuscript, as an advance of 50 per cent share of the profits; the English edition was to appear at least a fortnight before the American.[1] A month later, on 10 September, proof sheets were shipped to Richard Bentley, London. On the 12th Allan Melville, acting for his brother, signed an agreement with Harper & Brothers, New York.

Bentley's editor must have raced through the sheets, rushing them off batch by batch to the printer. For by late September, when Allan Melville wrote requesting a change of title to *Moby-Dick* ('a particular whale who if I may so express myself is the hero of the volume'), it was already too late. On 18 October the English edition of *The Whale*, in 500 sets of three octavo volumes, was published. American publication of *Moby-Dick*, in a one-volume edition of 2,915 copies, followed on 14 November. Thus London gained a slight head start on New York and opened a Pandora's boxful of textual mischief.

For, date-line apart, the English text had little to commend it. Exceptions only seemed to prove the rule: 'worthy Captain Bildad' for 'Captain Peleg' (THE SHIP) was cer-

1. For reasons of copyright, though the gesture lacked legal sanction: 'I have been defending for a long series of years the right of American authors & publishers to protection, if their productions are published here first.' (Bentley to Evert Duyckinck, 8 July 1850.)

tainly correct; so too was the shift from 'plaintiffs' to 'defendants' in FAST-FISH AND LOOSE-FISH; the dating of a moment of composition to 'December, A.D. 1850,' not '1851' (THE FOUNTAIN) was equally compelling; while a single footnote to THE GRAND ARMADA (ch. 87), unless cancelled in proof, had apparently slipped out of the New York edition to vanish completely. All else was suspect. The English editor had freely sliced and hacked away. Wherever his prudish nose sniffed something subversive, whenever his ear caught some dubious sexual, or political, or religious overtone, his blue pencil slashed. The final bowdlerized version was a monument of decorum, a landmark of Victorian taste to match the Great Exhibition, but as a guide to Melville it seemed worthless. Even the EPILOGUE – that key in the lock – was lost.[2]

Not that the American text was beyond suspicion. But the basic norm seemed incontrovertible: 'Lacking any manuscript or printer's proof of *Moby-Dick*, we are closest to Melville's own intention in the first American edition, and save for the *obvious* misprints ... its readings must be followed. Misspellings must be allowed to stand.' (Mansfield and Vincent, pp. 833–4.[3]) Its very vagaries, that is, of archaic forms and peculiar capitalization, may lead into the maze of Melville's meanings and double-meanings.

Except, possibly, in the list of Contents. For there the English edition named the chapters as they appear, chapter-head by chapter-head, in the text itself; while on the

2. As early as 1932 William S. Ament collated the following: thirty-five cuts of a sentence or more; the loss of one footnote and the whole of chapter 25 (POSTSCRIPT) in addition to the EPILOGUE; roughly one hundred and fifty omissions or changes of less than one sentence; as well as countless changes in spelling, punctuation and style. ('Bowdler and the Whale', *American Literature*, 4, pp. 39–46.)

3. In their 'Textual Notes' Mansfield and Vincent list only nineteen emendations. But more changes were, in fact, made than listed. Twenty further silent departures from the first American edition were collated by William H. Hutchinson ('A Definitive Edition of Moby-Dick', *American Literature* 25, pp. 472–8, May 1954).

American Contents page some thirty-four chapters differ slightly from the chapter-heads found in the text – fifteen in capitalization and spelling only; nine in straightforward abbreviations; and ten with variations far in excess of normal printer's licence. But the chapter-heads, almost certainly, represent Melville's final decision. They are curter, less repetitive, less cluttered with stage directions. Why then embalm traces of Melville's frantic, last minute revision, just because Harpers left their Contents page unrevised? [4]

But what prompted Harpers to leave their list of Contents unrevised? Here Mansfield and Vincent, in their final paragraph, unwittingly stumbled on a clue: 'Possibly the author made revisions in the text which were not incorporated in the American Contents ... If the listings in the Contents were early versions and the text forms of these chapter titles were Melville's final forms, the author must have been revising and polishing his novel up to the very moment of the dispatch of the proof sheets to England in early September 1851.' (p. 838)

It was left to Harrison Hayford and Hershel Parker to draw the lesson. They were the first to recognize that it was Melville himself who had intervened in the English text; that the footnote on '*gallied*' (ch. 87), long recognized as his, far from slipping *out* of the Harper edition had been slipped *into* Bentley's, so that other additions and revisions might also be his. With the publication of their Norton Critical Edition in 1967 the English *Whale* again reared its head.

Proof lay to hand, in Melville's contract with Harpers.[5] That agreement specified for the publication of 'The Whale' from 'the plates in the possession of R. Craighead'. But who

4. Not only Mansfield and Vincent (in the Hendricks House edition) but Hayford and Parker (in the Norton edition) perpetuate the confusion. Thus three chapters, for example, are varyingly entitled THE DECK: ch. 108, in the Contents; ch. 120, again in the Contents; and ch. 127, in the text itself!

5. Melville's copy is now in the Melville Collection of the Harvard College Library. The relevant clause was not excerpted in Jay Leyda, *The Melville Log.*

was Craighead? Why should Craighead have had the plates? Was it Melville or Harpers who had authorized this minor publisher to set 'The Whale'?

The rough time-table of publication, so far known, is readily summarized:

27 June 1850 Melville writes to Richard Bentley, announcing an almost completed work 'founded upon certain wild legends in the Southern Sperm Whale Fisheries'. As a regular Harpers author, Melville clearly assumed that Harpers would print the new book: 'In case of an arrangement, I shall, of course, put you in early & certain possession of the proof sheets, as in previous cases. Being desirous of early arranging this matter in London, – so as to lose no time, when the book has passed thro' the Harpers' press here – I beg, Mr Bentley, that you at once write me as to your views concerning it.'

29 April 1851 Melville's Harper account is so deep in the red that he is refused an advance on *The Whale*.

1 May 1851 Melville borrows $2,050 from 'T.D.S.' in Pittsfield, with the intention, it seems, of having the book set at his own expense. The printer Craighead, who had stereotyped *Typee*, is now engaged.

1(?) June 1851 Melville writes to Hawthorne: 'In a week or so, I go to New York, to bury myself in a third-storey room, and work and slave on my "Whale" while it is driving through the press. *That* is the only way I can finish it now, – I am so pulled hither and thither by circumstances.'

29 June 1851 In the middle of proof-reading, Melville returns to Pittsfield. Again he writes to Hawthorne: 'The "Whale" is only half through the press; for, wearied with the long delay of the printers, and disgusted with the heat and dust of the babylonish brick-kiln of New York, I came back to the country to feel the grass – and end the book reclining on it, if I may.'

3 July 1851 Bentley offers Melville £150 on account of half profits for his new work, adding gloomily 'that, as we shall

be in the same boat, this mode of publication is the most suitable to meet all the contingencies of the case.'

20 July 1851 Melville accepts Bentley's offer, 'but not without strong hope that before long, we shall be able to treat upon a firmer basis than now, & heretofore ...' He adds: 'I am now passing thro' the press, the closing sheets of my new work; so that I shall be able to forward it to you in the course of two or three weeks – perhaps a little longer.'

29 July 1851 The letter, enclosing a signed and witnessed contract for the London publication of *The Whale*, is finally posted.

7 August 1851 Though proof-reading was now complete, or as good as complete, *The Whale* had still not been firmly placed in America. Evert Duyckinck urged Melville to let Redfield have it, though adding that the decision to give it to Harpers 'appears to have been concluded' (letter to his wife from Pittsfield).

13 August 1851 Richard Bentley signs the contract.

10 September 1851 Page proofs are mailed to England.

12 September 1851 Allan Melville, as his brother's attorney, at last signs a contract with Harper & Brothers by which they 'agreed to publish and sell and keep for sale a certain work entitled "The Whale" whereof the said Herman Melville is the author'. *The Whale* was to be printed from 'the plates in the possession of R. Craighead'.

12(?) September 1851 On the same day perhaps Melville writes to a Pittsfield neighbour; 'Concerning my own forthcoming book – it is off my hands, but must cross the sea before publication here.'

This calendar makes two things clear. First, Melville must have owned the plates; for whatever reasons he had arranged the stereotyping, he alone had controlled that long and complex text. Second, the lapse between early August and 10 September 1851 had given him five to six weeks for making final revisions on the proofs. 'Since he knew the book would be entirely reset for the English edition,

Melville was free to make whatever corrections and revisions he wanted and had time to make. He was *not* equally free to make revisions for the American edition, since the book was already plated and he would have to pay for any changes himself.' (Hayford and Parker, p. 475.) Collation of the first American edition with the first English proves, beyond doubt, that Melville did tinker with the proofs.

But so, beyond doubt, did Bentley's editor. Certain substantive changes can only be Melville's and must be adopted. But with the difficulty, verging on impossibility, of disentangling one set of scattered, last minute revisions from another of hurried, ruthless corrections, the American first edition (*A*) must still remain our closest reliable guide to Melville's intention. This Penguin edition (*P*), therefore, reproduces *A* as the copy-text, with a minimum of emendation (typographical and factual), while incorporating only a limited list of the most compelling readings from the first English edition (*E*). No attempt is made to construct, or conflate, a full *critical* text, as in the Melville Edition Project (under preparation at Northwestern University and the Newberry Library), which aims at an ideal transcending both first editions.

Such was the aim, too, of the Norton Critical Edition (*N*). But while calling themselves 'cautious', and even 'conservative', Hayford and Parker naturally fell for the heady attractions of their new-found trust in *E*. Again and again they accepted the common sense of Bentley's 'judicious literary friend'[6] at the expense of 'the unequal cross-lights', those puns and innuendoes that chart the *Pequod's* course. For 'ungodly, god-like' Ahab commands the deck; not the roundabout logic, the hollow boom, of the *Samuel Enderby*'s Boomer. This is a Yankee book, not a British.

6. On 5 May 1852, Bentley answered Melville's plea to 'let bygones be bygones' by refusing to go ahead with *Pierre* unless Melville agreed to let him 'make or have made by a judicious literary friend such alterations as are absolutely necessary to "Pierre" being properly appreciated here ...'

Even spelling changes adopted from *E* point this dangerous procedure, e.g.:

E and N	gulp	*A*	gulph
E and N	Bel	*A*	Bell
E and N	Quohog	*A*	Quohag
E and N	demogorgon	*A*	demigorgon
E and N	THE PRAIRIE	*A*	THE PRAIRE

as well as further, spontaneous changes made in *N*, e.g.

N	onions	*A*	inions
N	Sal	*A*	Sall
N	Niskayuna	*A*	Neskyeuna

All taste or sense of Melville's personal vagaries – often the clue to his phonetic overlappings and puns – is lost. What in *A* remains close to oral story-telling is in *E*, and to a larger extent in *N*, reduced to the cold orthography of print.

The following tables list:

1. English readings adopted.
2. English readings considered.
3. Other emendations adopted.
4. Other emendations considered.
5. Treatment of Accidentals.

For the reader curious enough to look at the emendations in these tables, references to this edition have been included at the beginning of each line. For convenience the page and line numbers are simply separated by a full stop.

I. ENGLISH READINGS ADOPTED

I.a. This table records all substantive emendations (words added, revised or corrected) which are certainly Melville's. Only Melville could have penned the long footnote on '*gallied*'. Only Melville could have added such striking new attributes as 'out-hanging' to 'light' or 'embryo' to the hull'. Only Melville could have spotted such subtle misreadings as 'her near appearance' for 'her mere appearance' (his second-hand source was J. Ross Browne); or 'direct swing' for 'direst swing' (which has bothered no one since); or 'correctly' for 'covertly'; or 'once leaving him' for 'laving him'. It seems likelier even that Melville spotted his own slips in the Bunyan and Pope Extracts, or the Sir Thomas Browne quotation at the head of ch. 91, than the English editor.

80.25	*E, N and P*	*Holy War.*	*A*	*Pilgrim's Progress.*
83.7	*E, N and P*	Tho' stiff	*A*	Tho' stuffed
89.23	*E, N and P*	her mere	*A*	her near
101.11–12	*E, N and P*	of out-hanging light	*A*	of light
227.13	*E, N and P*	never speak quick to him	*A*	never speak to him
244.14	*E, N and P*	direst swing	*A*	direct swing
253.27–8	*E, N and P*	coolish weather	*A*	cold weather
301.12	*E, N and P*	been covertly selected	*A*	been correctly selected
401.10	*E, N and P*	'Dough you is	*A*	'Do you is
428.38–429.1	*E, N and P*	the sort of bellows by which he blows back the breath	*A*	the sort of bitters by which he blows back the life
477.26	*E, N and P*	1850	*A*	1851
493.24–38	*E, N and P*	* To *gally* . . . the New World	*A*	(*Not present*)
511.31	*E, N and P*	denying that	*A*	denying not
559.8	*E, N and P*	untrussing the points of his hose	*A*	untagging the points of his hose
564.23	*E, N and P*	the embryo hull	*A*	the hull
626.24	*E, N and P*	were braced hard up	*A*	were hard up
656.34	*E, N and P*	once laving him	*A*	once leaving him

1.b. The rest are routine misreadings whose correction, whether by Melville or by Bentley's editor, plainly fulfils the need of the context.

75.10	*E, N and P*	(*Omitted*)	*A*	ETYMOLOGY
79.18–19	*E, N and P*	a boiling pan	*A*	boiling pan
94.19	*E, N and P*	in the needles	*A*	of the needles
108.26	*E, N and P*	any decent	*A*	my decent
140.27	*E, N and P*	become	*A*	became

170.29	*E, N and P*	worthy Captain Bildad	*A*	worthy Captain Peleg
180.32	*E, N and P*	knob	*A*	knot
181.15	*E, N and P*	all I could do	*A*	all he could do
192.38	*E, N and P*	stowage	*A*	storage
249.23	*E, N and P*	the whetstones	*A*	the whetstone
252.4	*E, N and P*	even when most	*A*	ever when most
264.10	*E, N and P*	wert not thou	*A*	wer't not thou
313.18	*E, N and P*	stands	*A*	stand
319.27	*E, N and P*	back! – Never heed	*A*	back!' (*New Paragraph*) 'Never heed
322.28	*E, N and P*	along his oar!'	*A*	along his oars!'
356.8	*E, Harper's Magazine, N and P*	boys' business	*A*	boy's business
386.33	*E, N and P*	horrible contortions	*A*	horrible contortion
418.22	*E, N and P*	lives in matter	*A*	lives on matter
418.28	*E, N and P*	stranger's	*A*	strangers'
434.7	*E, N and P*	lets	*A*	let's
461.38	*E, N and P*	diagonally	*A*	diagonically
468.27–8	*E, N and P*	one of that sort goes down	*A*	one of that sort go down
507.14	*E, N and P*	the defendants afterwards took	*A*	the plaintiffs afterwards took
525.15	*E, N and P*	such considerateness towards	*A*	such considerations towards
540.27	*E, N and P*	flow	*A*	flows
567.23	*E, N and P*	ante-chronical	*A*	antichronical
568.26	*E, N and P*	ante-chronical	*A*	antichronical
568.38	*E, N and P*	Pharaohs'	*A*	Pharaoh's
609.21–2	*E, N and P*	unearthly passionlessness	*A*	earthly passionlessness
614.23	*E, N and P*	to sailors, oaths	*A*	to sailors' oaths
631.3	*E, N and P*	intently	*A*	intenting
653.19	*E, N and P*	air	*A*	airs
660.31	*E, N and P*	prow was pointed	*A*	prows were pointed
670.38	*E, N and P*	boats'	*A*	boat's
673.11	*E, N and P*	set due eastward	*A*	sat due eastward
673.33	*E, N and P*	turn to ice,	*A*	turned to ice,
674.25	*E, N and P*	shift and swerve	*A*	swift and swerve

1.c. Spelling changes adopted are:

88.17	*E, N and P*	*Cruise*	*A*	*Cruize*
110.12	*E, N and P*	airley	*A*	early
125.27	*E, N and P*	Tongatabooans	*A*	Tongataboоarrs
153.38	*E, N and P*	Kokovoko	*A*	Rokovoko
154.5	*E, N and P*	Kokovoko	*A*	Rokovoko
158.27	*E, N and P*	Behring's	*A*	Bhering's
162.14	*E, N and P*	vertebræ	*A*	vertebra
162.30	*E, N and P*	ony	*A*	only
162.33	*E, N and P*	a-night	*A*	at night
166.28	*E, N and P*	Marchant	*A*	Merchant
172.32	*E, N and P*	net	*A*	nett
218.1	*E, N and P*	warranty	*A*	warrantry
290.2	*E, N and P*	Prairies	*A*	Praries
378.14	*E, N and P*	bridle-bits	*A*	bridle-bitts
401.22	*E, N and P*	yourselbs	*A*	yoursebls
415.9	*E, N and P*	vulturism	*A*	vultureism
498.6	*E, N and P*	vicissitudes	*A*	vicisitudes
527.9	*E, N and P*	petulance	*A*	petulence
543.10	*E, N and P*	Jimini	*A*	Jimimi
595.12	*E, N and P*	petulance	*A*	petulence

2. ENGLISH READINGS CONSIDERED

This table records a variety of English readings, some of which are attractive and most of which are incorporated by *N*. But, in each case, the emendation as readily indicates an intervening English hand as Melville's final revision. Two vexed cruces, on the 'Poor Alabama boy!' (KNIGHTS AND SQUIRES) and the strange case of 'whale-trover' (FAST-FISH AND LOOSE-FISH), are aired in the commentary: the deletion in the first instance points to Melville, but is inconclusive; the re-editing of the second points to Bentley's editor, but is equally not conclusive. Variants of special note include the opening of Father Mapple's hymn, the rightful substitution of 'Wickliff's' for 'Cranmer's', and Tashtego's last, emblematic 'death-gasp' – or should it be 'death-grasp'? – as 'the submerged savage ... kept his hammer frozen' to the mast (THE CHASE – THIRD DAY).

The most striking new reading discovered, but not adopted, by Hayford/Parker, replaces 'Is Ahab, Ahab?' – that famous sigh – with 'Is it Ahab, Ahab? Is it I, God, or who, that lifts this arm?' (THE SYMPHONY). But such questions cannot merely be grammatically resolved. Such problems, on the present bare evidence, seem beyond resolution.

83.13	*A and P*	Goldsmith, Nat. His.	*E and N*	Goldsmith's Nat. Hist.
95.20–21	*A and P*	and own brother	*E and N*	and make him the own brother
113.7–8	*A and P*	as you see the same in	*E and N*	the same as in
126.2	*A and P*	they came	*E and N*	they come
134.33	*A and P*	And lift me	*E and N*	And left me
135.1	*A and P*	the opening maw	*E and N*	the open maw
150.17	*A and P*	When	*E and N*	While yet
151.17	*A and P*	might happily gain	*E and N*	might haply gain
155.16	*A and P*	dived her brows	*E and N*	dived her bows
193.30	*A and P*	came hobbling	*E and N*	came running
210.24	*A and P*	courage was	*E and N*	courage is
217.4–5	*A and P*	he never did – oh, no! he went before. Poor Alabama boy!	*E and N*	he never did! Poor Alabama boy!
236.3	*A and P*	the Tartarian tiles	*E and N*	the Tartarean tiles
242.29	*A and P*	Now, the grand distinction	*E and N*	Now, one of the grand distinctions
255.26–7	*A and P*	we South fishers	*E and N*	we Southern fishers
257.9	*A and P*	Cranmer's	*E and N*	Wickliff's
259.22	*A and P*	men.	*E and N*	men, – a doubloon.
272.11	*A and P*	a ball	*E and N*	one ball
272.11	*A and P*	you scholars	*E and N*	your scholars
273.10	*A and P*	low veiled, high palmed Tahiti!	*E and N*	low-valed, high-palmed Tahiti!
280.34	*A and P*	and as well a thing	*E and N*	and also a thing

286.4–5	*A and P*	Had any one of	*E and N*	Had any of
291.37	*A and P*	as much like the badge	*E and N*	as much the badge
300.24	*A and P*	time or place	*E and N*	time and place
316.27	*A and P*	directed by free will	*E and N*	modified by free will
318.23–4	*A and P*	wide black trowsers	*E and N*	wide trowsers
377.7	*A and P*	Dutch savage	*E and N*	German savage
377.37–8	*A and P*	else so chance-like are such observations of the hills, that your precise	*E and N*	else – so chance-like are such observations of the hills – your precise
415.28	*A, N and P*	a powerless panic	*E*	a powerful panic
447.8–9	*A and P*	irrevocably lost	*E and N*	irrecoverably lost
506.9–13	*A and P*	Northern seas; and when indeed they (the plaintiffs) had succeeded in harpooning the fish; they were at last, through peril of their lives, obliged to forsake not only their lines, but their boat itself. Ultimately	*E and N*	northern seas, they (the plaintiffs) had succeeded in harpooning the fish; but at last, through peril of their lives, were obliged to forsake, not only their lines, but their boat itself, – Furthermore: ultimately
506.15	*A and P*	plaintiffs. And when	*E and N*	plaintiffs; – Yet again: – and when
506.19	*A and P*	and boat, which	*E and N*	and boat, all of which
506.30–31	*A and P*	possession of her. Erskine was on the other side; and he then supported it by saying, that	*E and N*	possession of her. He then proceeded to say that,
583.21	*A and P*	proud as Greek god	*E and N*	proud as a Greek god

589.24	*A and P*	milky way. He added	*E and N*	milky way – after saying this he added
609.5	*A and P*	Now, in	*E and N*	Now, sometimes, in
636.32	*A and P*	out of sight.'	*E and N*	out of my sight.'
653.6	*A, N and P*	Is Ahab, Ahab?	*E*	Is it Ahab, Ahab?
656.37	*A and P*	this serenity	*E and N*	that serenity
657.31	*A and P*	could discover	*E and N*	could perceive
685.19	*A and P*	in his death-gasp	*E and N*	in his death-grasp

3. OTHER EMENDATIONS ADOPTED

This is a listing of all substantive emendations, first introduced by other editors, chiefly Mansfield/Vincent and Hayford/Parker. All clarify obvious factual errors or typographical slips. The neatest is the Hayford/Parker reading in ch. 18 (HIS MARK), where the addition of the single word 'to' replaces the cowering figure of Peleg with that of Bildad, the immediate victim of Queequeg's practical joke.

121.10	*N and P*	having the whole	*A and E*	leaving the whole
156.8	*N and P*	bery	*A and E*	bevy
186.13	*N and P*	Peleg, to his partner	*A and E*	Peleg, his partner
187.31	*N and P*	off Japan	*A and E*	on Japan
324.7	*N and P*	the second mate	*A and E*	the third mate
332.24	*N and P*	Until Archy's	*A and E*	Until Cabaco's
346.16	*N and P*	sail westward	*A and E*	sail eastward
393.8	*N and P*	said Tashtego	*A and E*	said Daggoo
445.31	*N and P*	Sais?	*A and E*	Lais?
454.35–6	*N and P*	on the now	*A and E*	in the now
456.5	*N and P*	false brow	*A and E*	false bow
524.22	*N and P*	man loves	*A and E*	man loved
555.6	*N and P*	testing cruise	*A and E*	tasting cruise
578.14	*N and P*	Stubb longs	*A and E*	Stubb longed
606.36	*N and P*	striveth, this one jetteth	*A and E*	strivest, this one jettest
611.8	*N and P*	die in it!'	*A and E*	die it!'

4. OTHER EMENDATIONS CONSIDERED

The most convincing reading is Hayford/Parker's 'augured' for 'argued' (ch. 91); since Stubb, far from arguing, is merely concocting his 'little plan'. Their most subtle reading, not adopted in *N*, is to transfer the last, long paragraph of THE GILDER (ch. 114) from Ishmael's mouth to Ahab's.

175.21	*A, E and P*	That's he; thank ye	*N* Thank ye; thank ye
193.30	*A and P*	hobbling	*E* running *Hayford/Parker* roaring
217.4	*A, E and P*	come back	*N* came back
301.30	*A, E and P*	Yes.	*N* No.
324.34	*A, E and P*	bade far	*N* bade fair
348.2	*A, E and P*	beech canoe	*N* birch canoe
515.36	*A, E and P*	Stubb argued	*N* Stubb augured
602.10–30	*A, E, N and P*	Oh, grassy . . . learn it	*Hayford/Parker* 'Oh, grassy . . . learn it.' (*making Ahab speak the paragraph*)
603.14	*A, E and P*	her mast-head	*N* her mast-heads
666.21–2	*A, E and P*	guilt and guiltiness	*N* guilt and guiltlessness

5. TREATMENT OF ACCIDENTALS

Punctuation, as Melville well knew, was not his strong suit. The aim here is merely (a) to correct obvious errors; (b) to adjust those accidentals which were actively misleading. Following Hayford/Parker the whales display 'a still, becharmed panic' (not 'a still becharmed panic'); Ahab says, 'D'ye feel brave, men, brave?' (not 'D'ye feel brave men, brave?'). But Melville's inconsistent, idiosyncratic or archaic spellings are all maintained.

Double quotation marks have been changed to single; and

single, to double. This entailed eliminating some inconsistencies, especially in THE TOWN HO'S STORY, not listed below. The only vital departure from the American text, however, follows Harper's Magazine in giving 'Jesu! what a whale!' to the stupid Teneriffe man unable to recognize Moby Dick, instead of to Ishmael at the Golden Inn.

Comma Changes:

112.13	*E, N and P*	exclaimed,	*A*	exclaimed
195.15	*E, N and P*	saying,	*A*	saying
196.23–4	*E, N and P*	him, in his broken fashion	*A*	him in his broken fashion,
252.9–10	*N and P*	however,	*A*	however
287.26	*E, N and P*	Cæsarian	*A*	Cæsarian,
306.27	*N and P*	others,	*A*	others
324.1	*E, N and P*	Though, truly, vivacious,	*A*	Though truly vivacious,
325.1	*N and P*	eyes,	*A*	eyes
366.23	*E, N and P*	honor,	*A*	honor
399.34	*E, N and P*	time,	*A*	time
407.25	*E, N and P*	two and two, for an hour each couple,	*A*	two and two for an hour, each couple,
461.20	*N and P*	Fiercely but evenly,	*A*	Fiercely, but evenly,
462.28	*N and P*	and,	*A*	and
479.20	*N and P*	necessities,	*A*	necessities
496.38	*N and P*	still,	*A*	still
507.14	*E, N and P*	Now,	*A*	Now
614.29	*E, N and P*	Tekel,	*A*	Tekel
672.25	*E, N and P*	brave,	*A*	brave

Quotation Mark Changes:

173.25–6	*N and P*	'"*Lay* not ... moth –"'	*A*	"*Lay* not ... moth –"
174.10–11	*N and P*	'"for ... also."'	*A*	"for ... also."
230.5	*E, N and P*	he' (the leviathan) 'make	*A*	he (the leviathan) make
569.34	*N and P*	Rib' (says John Leo) 'is	*A*	Rib (says John Leo) is
624.5	*E, N and P*	if –'	*A*	if' –

Apostrophe Changes:

226.11	*N and P*	'Slid	*A* Slid
258.12	*N and P*	'Twill	*A* T'will
272.25	*N and P*	the waves' – the snow-caps'	*A and E* the waves – the snow's caps
350.21	*N and P*	sailor's talk	*A and E* sailors' talk
401.38	*E, N and P*	'em	*A* em
402.8	*N and P*	till	*A* 'till
402.12	*E, N and P*	'dention	*A* dention
402.32	*E, N and P*	'noder	*A* noder
403.28	*N and P*	'tall	*A* t'all
522.26	*N and P*	kings'	*A* king's
529.27–8	*N and P*	assistant's	*A and E* assistants'
590.8	*E, N and P*	convenience'	*A* convenience
617.28	*N and P*	'tis	*A* t'is
640.1	*N and P*	boats' crews	*A* boat's crews
652.30	*E, N and P*	' 'Tis	*A* 'Tis
674.2	*E, N and P*	Vesuvius'	*A* Vesuvius

Capitalization Changes:

93.25	*E, N and P*	Battery	*A* battery
184.28	*E, N and P*	First	*A* first
189.23	*E, N and P*	Captain	*A* captain
308.16	*E, N and P*	Commodore	*A* commodore
530.12	*E, N and P*	King Asa	*A* king Asa
568.12–13	*N and P*	anatomist	*A* Anatomist
653.26	*E, N and P*	the mate	*A* the Mate

Miscellaneous Changes:

102.14–15	*E, N and P*	wrapper (he had a redder one afterwards)	*A* wrapper – (he had a redder one afterwards)
126.32	*E, N and P*	houses,	*A* houses;
153.7	*N and P*	the 'Moss,'	*A* 'the Moss,'
169.30	*E, N and P*	*thee* and *thou*	*A* thee and thou
175.29	*E, N and P*	does *he* want?'	*A* does he want?'
252.31	*E, N and P*	pleasant –	*A* pleasant
268.12	*E, N and P*	ha-ha's	*A* ha, ha's
289.4	*E, N and P*	albatross:	*A* albatross,
293.20	*E, N and P*	seas;	*A* seas:
348.7	*E, N and P*	[*New Paragraph*] 'Thus	*A* Thus

358.8	*N and P*	run amuck	*A*	run a muck
362.20–21	*Harper's Magazine, N and P*	there she rolls! Jesu! what a whale!" It was Moby Dick.' (*Harper's omit the final quotation mark*)	*A*	there she rolls!' Jesu, what a whale! It was Moby Dick.
392.3	*E, N and P*	bowsman;	*A*	bowsman!
423.9	*E, N and P*	(It	*A*	It
423.17	*E, N and P*	dead.)	*A*	dead.
493.1	*E, N and P*	*gallied.**	*A*	gallied.
511.9–10	*N and P*	'Ye tail is ye Queen's, that ye Queen's wardrobe . . . with ye whalebone.'	*A*	*prints* Ye *and* ye *passim; E prints* ye *twice*, Ye *and* ye.
543.3	*E, N and P*	almanack;	*A*	almanack
543.9–10	*E, N and P*	the Bull; –	*A*	the Bull
578.15	*N and P*	oar:	*A*	oar;

Typographical Errors Corrected:

78.3	*N and P*	(*Omitted.*)	*A and E*	EXTRACTS (*A duplicated heading. cf. ETYMOLOGY*)
86.31	*P*	*Ocean.'*	*A*	*Ocean.*
88.21	*P*	*Mutiny,'*	*A*	*Mutiny,*
89.11	*P*	*the whale-ship*	*A*	*tke whale-ship*
110.16	*P*	bamboozling	*A*	bamboozingly
137.23	*P*	' "Who's	*A*	'Who's
138.3	*P*	'Now	*A*	Now
139.17	*P*	'And	*A*	And
167.1	*P*	innuendoes	*A*	inuendoes
181.21	*P*	island?	*A*	island.
184.11	*P*	18	*A*	CHAPTER XVII
190.2	*P*	prophecy?	*A*	prophecy.
191.2	*P*	will you?'	*A*	will you?
196.11	*P*	then,	*A*	hen
210.30	*P*	Stubb,	*A*	Stbub,
218.27	*P*	the taffrail,	*A*	the taffrail.
219.10	*P*	say.	*A*	say,
226.27	*P*	"Halloa,"	*A*	'Halloa,
239.21	*P*	i.e.	*A*	i.e
261.2	*P*	that	*A*	tha
269.11	*P*	commanded –	*A*	commanded. –
271.11	*P*	comes	*A*	come's

279.3	*P*	fearfully	*A*	fearfnlly
284.36	*P*	wonderful,	*A*	wonderful.
294.18	*P*	me'?	*A*	me?"
299.23	*P*	in crossing	*A*	incrossing
317.23	*P*	steward!'	*A*	steward!
321.11	*P*	boys!)'	*A*	boys!")
337.5–6	*P*	Tormentoso	*A*	Tormentoto
353.34	*P*	plaza	*A*	plazza
359.5	*Harper's, N and P*	But all three	*A*	But all these
362.31	*P*	up	*A*	up up
362.32	*P*	Now,	*A*	Now.
378.1	*P*	Solomon	*A*	Soloma
405.17	*P*	fastidious	*A*	fastidions
472.1	*P*	versa	*A*	versâ
472.12	*P*	Brahma	*A*	Bramha
474.31	*P*	via	*A*	viâ
478.38	*P*	fishermen	*A*	fishermon
511.9	*P*	wardrobe	*A*	warbrobe
518.20	*P*	without	*A*	withont
523.5	*P*	effulgences	*A*	effulgenees
525.38	*P*	man's	*A*	nan's
545.21	*P*	Hark!'	*A*	Hark!
567.37	*P*	Dauphine	*A*	Dauphiné
606.35	*P*	power!	*A*	power?
613.9	*P*	'Yes	*A*	Yes
615.13	*P*	to	*A*	too
619.31	*P*	the holder	*A*	theh older
633.28	*P*	innuendoes	*A*	inuendoes
634.18	*P*	it's	*A*	its
635.20	*P*	*and*	*A*	*aud*
648.6	*P*	upon	*A*	upom
670.32	*P*	being.	*A*	being
679.9	*P*	While	*A*	Whilc
682.34	*P*	fit.	*A*	fit

Harrison Hayford and Hershel Parker together pioneered the textual scholarship of *Moby-Dick*. To facilitate cross-reference to their Norton Critical Edition, these lists, in both format and content, are closely aligned to their original tabulations (pp. 486–98).

BIBLIOGRAPHY

THE armada of critics in pursuit of *The Whale* grows larger and larger. Melville himself might have been surprised at these bibliographical manoeuvres surrounding his library of 'Extracts'. But of editions, or annotated texts, the list is small. The one complete publication of Melville's fiction and poetry remains that of Constable & Co. (in sixteen volumes, London: 1922–4). A new complete edition, however, has been launched at Northwestern University and The Newberry Library under contract from the United States Office of Education; their text of *Moby-Dick* is now in active preparation. The only full commentary remains that by Luther S. Mansfield and Howard P. Vincent (New York: Hendricks House, 1952), though two slighter, more recent editions are worth noting: that by Charles Feidelson Jr (Indianapolis: Bobbs-Merrill, 1964) and the 'critical text' by Harrison Hayford and Hershel Parker (New York: W. W. Norton & Co., 1967).

Some of the earlier critical responses are still the most rewarding, especially:

D. H. LAWRENCE, in *Studies in Classic American Literature* (New York: Thomas Seltzer, 1923; London: Martin Secker, 1924. Reprinted, New York: Doubleday Anchor Books, 1953; London: Penguin, 1971.)

LEWIS MUMFORD, *Herman Melville, A Study of his Life and Vision* (New York: Harcourt, Brace & Co., 1929; London: Jonathan Cape, 1929; reissued in a revised edition, London: Secker & Warburg, 1963).

F. O. MATTHIESSEN, in *American Renaissance* (New York: Oxford University Press, 1941).

W. E. SEDGWICK, *Herman Melville: The Tragedy of Mind* (Cambridge: Harvard University Press, 1944).

But it is the decades since the Second World War that brought new readings to a floodtide. Outstanding (in order of publication) are:

CHARLES OLSON, *Call Me Ishmael* (New York: Reynal & Hitchcock, 1947. Reprinted, New York: Grove Press, 1958; London: Cape Editions, 1967).

HOWARD P. VINCENT, *The Trying-Out of MOBY-DICK* (Boston: Houghton Mifflin, 1949. Reprinted, Carbondale: Southern Illinois Press, 1965).

RICHARD CHASE, *Herman Melville: A Critical Study* (New York: Macmillan, 1949).

NEWTON ARVIN, *Herman Melville* (New York: William Sloane Associates, 1950; London: Methuen, 1950. Reprinted, New York: Viking Press, 1957).

W. H. AUDEN, *The Enchafèd Flood: or The Romantic Iconography of the Sea* (New York: Random House, 1950; London: Faber & Faber, 1951).

M. O. PERCIVAL, *A Reading of MOBY-DICK* (Chicago: University of Chicago Press, 1950).

LAWRANCE THOMPSON, *Melville's Quarrel with God* (Princeton: Princeton University Press, 1952).

CHARLES FEIDELSON, Jr, *Symbolism and American Literature* (Chicago: University of Chicago Press, 1953; reprinted, 1959).

EDWARD ROSENBERRY, *Melville and the Comic Spirit* (Cambridge: Harvard University Press, 1955).

MILTON R. STERN, *The Fine Hammered Steel of Herman Melville* (Urbana: University of Illinois Press, 1957).

HARRY LEVIN, *The Power of Blackness* (New York: Alfred A. Knopf, 1958; London: Faber & Faber, 1958. Reprinted, New York: Vintage Books, 1960).

RICHARD B. SEWALL, *The Vision of Tragedy* (New Haven: Yale University Press, 1959; reissued as a Yale Paperbound, 1962).

LESLIE FIEDLER, *Love and Death in the American Novel* (New York: Criterion Books, 1960; London: Jonathan Cape, 1967. Reprinted, New York, Meridian Books, 1962; London: Paladin, 1970).

MERLIN BOWEN, *The Long Encounter: Self and Experience in the Writings of Herman Melville* (Chicago: University of Chicago Press, 1960).

DANIEL G. HOFFMAN, *Form and Fable in American Fiction* (New York: Oxford University Press, 1961).

WARNER BERTHOFF, *The Example of Melville* (Princeton: Princeton University Press, 1962).

H. BRUCE FRANKLIN, *The Wake of the Gods: Melville's Mythology* (Stanford: Stanford University Press, 1963).

LEO MARX, *The Machine in the Garden: Technology and the Pastoral Ideal in America* (New York: Oxford University Press, 1964; reissued as a Galaxy Book, 1967).

JOHN SEELYE, *Melville: The Ironic Diagram* (Evanston: Northwestern University Press, 1970).

Among studies of more specialized concern are:

WILLIAM BRASWELL, *Melville's Religious Thought: An Essay in Interpretation* (Durham: Duke University Press, 1943. Reprinted, New York: Pageant Books, 1959).

NATHALIA WRIGHT, *Melville's Use of the Bible* (Durham: Duke University Press, 1949).

HENRY F. POMMER, *Milton and Melville* (Pittsburgh: University of Pittsburgh Press, 1950).

MERTON M. SEALTS, Jr, *Melville's Reading: A Check-List of Books Owned and Borrowed* (Cambridge: Harvard University Printing Office, 1950).

MILLICENT BELL, 'Pierre Bayle and *Moby-Dick*,' *Publications of the Modern Language Association of America*, vol. 66 (September, 1951).

GEORGE R. STEWART, 'The Two *Moby-Dicks*', *American Literature*, vol. 25 (January, 1954).

PERRY MILLER, *The Raven and the Whale: The War of Words and Wits in the Era of Poe and Melville* (New York: Harcourt, Brace & Co., 1956).

JAMES BAIRD, *Ishmael* (Baltimore: Johns Hopkins Press, 1956. Reprinted, New York: Harper & Brothers, 1960).

ROBERT SHULMAN, 'The Serious Functions of Melville's Phallic Jokes', *American Literature*, vol. 33 (May, 1961).

DOROTHÉE M. FINKELSTEIN, *Melville's Orienda* (New Haven: Yale University Press, 1961).

JANEZ STANONIK, *Moby-Dick: The Myth and the Symbol* (Ljubljana: Ljubljana University Press, 1962).

ALAN HEIMERT, '*Moby Dick* and American Political Symbolism', *American Quarterly*, vol. 15 (Winter, 1963).

PAUL BROTKORB, *Ishmael's White World: A Phenomenological Reading of MOBY-DICK* (New Haven: Yale University Press, 1965).

THOMAS VARGISH, 'Gnostic *Mythos* in *Moby-Dick*', *Publications of the Modern Language Association of America*, vol. 81 (June, 1966).

HERBERT G. ELDRIDGE, '"Careful Disorder": The Structure of *Moby-Dick*', *American Literature*, vol. 39 (May, 1967).

JAMES GUETTI, *The Limits of Metaphor* (Ithaca: Cornell University Press, 1967).

The graph of Melville's reputation, during his lifetime, has been painstakingly traced by Hugh W. Hetherington, *Melville's Reviewers: British and American, 1846–1891* (Chapel Hill: University of North Carolina Press, 1961). A variety of criticism – from contemporary reviews to the academic embrace of 1938–70 – is reprinted in Hershel Parker, *The Recognition of Herman Melville* (Ann Arbor: University of Michigan Press, 1967) and in Harrison Hayford and Hershel Parker, *Moby-Dick As Doubloon* (New York: W. W. Norton & Co., 1970). Earlier catch-alls of critical chapters and essays were gathered by:

TYRUS HILLWAY and LUTHER S. MANSFIELD, *MOBY-DICK Centennial Essays* (Dallas: Southern Methodist University Press, 1953).

MILTON R. STERN, *Discussions of MOBY-DICK* (Boston: D. C. Heath & Co., 1960).

RICHARD CHASE, *Melville: A Collection of Critical Essays* (Englewood Cliffs: Prentice-Hall, 1962).

For further reading, consult *Modern Fiction Studies,* vol. 8 (Autumn, 1962): a special Melville issue, with a bibliographical 'checklist' of Melville criticism by Maurice Beebe, Harrison Hayford and Gordon Roper.

Leon Howard has written the standard life, *Herman Melville: A Biography* (Berkeley: University of California Press, 1951; reprinted 1958), while all documents relating to it have been garnered in Jay Leyda's *The Melville Log: A Documentary Life of Herman Melville, 1819–1891* (2 vols., New York: Harcourt, Brace & Co., 1951), which remains the ultimate source-book. Since then, however, Eleanor Melville Metcalf, Melville's oldest grandchild, has excerpted her own collection from the family diaries and correspondence, *Herman Melville: Cycle and Epicycle* (Cambridge: Harvard University Press, 1953), while Merrell R. Davis and William H. Gilman have published their full and authoritative edition of *The Letters of Herman Melville* (New Haven: Yale University Press, 1960).

Melville's Pacific trails were first charted by Charles R. Anderson, *Melville in the South Seas* (New York: Columbia University Press, 1939); but perhaps the most revealing introduction to the author as man are his own two diaries of the later Atlantic crossings: *Journal of a Visit to London and the Continent, 1849–1850* (edited by Eleanor M. Metcalf, Cambridge: Harvard University Press, 1948) and *Journal of a Visit to Europe and the Levant, October 11, 1856–May 6, 1857* (edited by Howard C. Horsford, Princeton: Princeton University Press, 1955).

Facsimile title page of the first American edition.

MOBY-DICK;

OR,

THE WHALE.

BY

HERMAN MELVILLE,

AUTHOR OF

"TYPEE," "OMOO," "REDBURN," "MARDI," "WHITE-JACKET."

NEW YORK:

HARPER & BROTHERS, PUBLISHERS.

LONDON: RICHARD BENTLEY.

1851.

CONTENTS

CONTENTS

In Token

of my admiration for his genius,

this book is inscribed

to

NATHANIEL HAWTHORNE

ETYMOLOGY

(SUPPLIED BY A LATE CONSUMPTIVE USHER TO A GRAMMAR SCHOOL.)

THE pale Usher – threadbare in coat, heart, body, and brain; I see him now. He was ever dusting his old lexicons and grammars, with a queer handkerchief, mockingly embellished with all the gay flags of all the known nations of the world. He loved to dust his old grammars; it somehow mildly reminded him of his mortality.

'While you take in hand to school others, and to teach them by what name a whale-fish is to be called in our tongue, leaving out, through ignorance, the letter H, which almost alone maketh up the signification of the word, you deliver that which is not true.' *Hackluyt.*

'WHALE. * * * Sw. and Dan. *hval.* This animal is named from roundness or rolling; for in Dan. *hvalt* is arched or vaulted.' *Webster's Dictionary.*

'WHALE. * * * It is more immediately from the Dut. and Ger. *Wallen*; A.S. *Walw-ian*, to roll, to wallow.'
Richardson's Dictionary.

תן,	*Hebrew.*
χητος,	*Greek.*
CETUS,	*Latin.*
WHŒL,	*Anglo-Saxon.*
HVALT,	*Danish.*
WAL,	*Dutch.*
HWAL,	*Swedish.*

WHALE,	*Icelandic.*
WHALE,	*English.*
BALEINE,	*French.*
BALLENA,	*Spanish.*
PEKEE-NUEE-NUEE,	*Fegee.*
PEHEE-NUEE-NUEE,	*Erromangoan.*

EXTRACTS

(SUPPLIED BY A SUB-SUB-LIBRARIAN.)

It will be seen that this mere painstaking burrower and grubworm of a poor devil of a Sub-Sub appears to have gone through the long Vaticans and street-stalls of the earth, picking up whatever random allusions to whales he could anyways find in any book whatsoever, sacred or profane. Therefore you must not, in every case at least, take the higgledy-piggledy whale statements, however authentic, in these extracts, for veritable gospel cetology. Far from it. As touching the ancient authors generally, as well as the poets here appearing, these extracts are solely valuable or entertaining, as affording a glancing bird's eye view of what has been promiscuously said, thought, fancied, and sung of Leviathan, by many nations and generations, including our own.

So fare thee well, poor devil of a Sub-Sub, whose commentator I am. Thou belongest to that hopeless, sallow tribe which no wine of this world will ever warm; and for whom even Pale Sherry would be too rosy-strong; but with whom one sometimes loves to sit, and feel poor-devilish, too; and grow convivial upon tears; and say to them bluntly, with full eyes and empty glasses, and in not altogether unpleasant sadness – Give it up, Sub-Subs! For by how much the more pains ye take to please the world, by so much the more shall ye for ever go thankless! Would that I could clear out Hampton Court and the Tuileries for ye! But gulp down your tears and hie aloft to the royal-mast with your hearts; for your friends who have gone before are clearing out the seven-storied heavens, and making refugees of long-pampered Gabriel, Michael, and Raphael, against your coming.

Here ye strike but splintered hearts together – there, ye shall strike unsplinterable glasses!

'And God created great whales.'
Genesis.

'Leviathan maketh a path to shine after him;
One would think the deep to be hoary.'
Job.

'Now the Lord had prepared a great fish to swallow up Jonah.' *Jonah.*

'There go the ships; there is that Leviathan whom thou hast made to play therein.' *Psalms.*

'In that day, the Lord with his sore, and great, and strong sword, shall punish Leviathan the piercing serpent, even Leviathan that crooked serpent; and he shall slay the dragon that is in the sea.' *Isaiah.*

'And what thing soever besides cometh within the chaos of this monster's mouth, be it beast, boat, or stone, down it goes all incontinently that foul great swallow of his, and perisheth in the bottomless gulf of his paunch.'
Holland's Plutarch's Morals.

'The Indian Sea breedeth the most and the biggest fishes that are: among which the Whales and Whirlpooles called Balæne, take up as much in length as four acres or arpens of land.' *Holland's Pliny.*

'Scarcely had we proceeded two days on the sea, when about sunrise a great many Whales and other monsters of the sea, appeared. Among the former, one was of a most monstrous size. * * This came towards us, open-mouthed, raising the waves on all sides, and beating the sea before him into a foam.' *Tooke's Lucian.*
'The True History.'

'He visited this country also with a view of catching horse-whales, which had bones of very great value for their teeth, of which he brought some to the king. * * * The best whales were catched in his own country, of which some were forty-eight, some fifty yards long. He said that he was one of six who had killed sixty in two days.'

Other or Octher's verbal narrative taken down from his mouth by King Alfred. A.D. 890.

'And whereas all the other things, whether beast or vessel, that enter into the dreadful gulf of this monster's (whale's) mouth, are immediately lost and swallowed up, the sea-gudgeon retires into it in great security, and there sleeps.'

MONTAIGNE. – *Apology for Raimond Sebond.*

'Let us fly, let us fly! Old Nick take me if it is not Leviathan described by the noble prophet Moses in the life of patient Job.' *Rabelais.*

'This whale's liver was two cart-loads.' *Stowe's Annals.*

'The great Leviathan that maketh the seas to seethe like a boiling pan.' *Lord Bacon's Version of the Psalms.*

'Touching that monstrous bulk of the whale or ork we have received nothing certain. They grow exceeding fat, insomuch that an incredible quantity of oil will be extracted out of one whale.' *Ibid 'History of Life and Death.'*

'The sovereignest thing on earth is parmacetti for an inward bruise.' *King Henry.*

'Very like a whale.' *Hamlet.*

'Which to secure, no skill of leach's art
Mote him availle, but to returne againe
To his wound's worker, that with lowly dart,
Dinting his breast, had bred his restless paine,
Like as the wounded whale to shore flies thro' the maine.'

The Fairie Queen.

'Immense as whales, the motion of whose vast bodies can in a peaceful calm trouble the ocean till it boil.'

Sir William Davenant. Preface to Gondibert.

'What spermacetti is, men might justly doubt, since the learned Hosmannus in his work of thirty years, saith plainly, *Nescio quid sit.*'

Sir T. Browne. Of Sperma Ceti and the Sperma Ceti Whale. Vide his V. E.

'Like Spencer's Talus with his modern flail
He threatens ruin with his ponderous tail.

* * * * *

Their fixed jav'lins in his side he wears,
And on his back a grove of pikes appears.'

Waller's Battle of the Summer Islands.

'By art is created that great Leviathan, called a Commonwealth or State – (in Latin, Civitas) which is but an artificial man.' *Opening sentence of Hobbes's Leviathan.*

'Silly Mansoul swallowed it without chewing, as if it had been a sprat in the mouth of a whale.' *Holy War.*

'That sea beast
Leviathan, which God of all his works
Created hugest that swim the ocean stream.'

Paradise Lost.

———— 'There Leviathan,
Hugest of living creatures, in the deep
Stretched like a promontory sleeps or swims,
And seems a moving land; and at his gills
Draws in, and at his breath spouts out a sea.'

Ibid.

'The mighty whales which swim in a sea of water, and have a sea of oil swimming in them.'

Fuller's Profane and Holy State.

'So close behind some promontory lie
The huge Leviathans to attend their prey,
And give no chace, but swallow in the fry,
Which through their gaping jaws mistake the way.'

Dryden's Annus Mirabilis.

'While the whale is floating at the stern of the ship, they cut off his head, and tow it with a boat as near the shore as it will come; but it will be aground in twelve or thirteen feet water.'

Thomas Edge's Ten Voyages to Spitzbergen, in Purchass.

'In their way they saw many whales sporting in the ocean, and in wantonness fuzzing up the water through their pipes and vents, which nature has placed on their shoulders.'

Sir T. Herbert's Voyages into Asia and Africa.
Harris Coll.

'Here they saw such huge troops of whales, that they were forced to proceed with a great deal of caution for fear they should run their ship upon them.'

Schouten's Sixth Circumnavigation.

'We set sail from the Elbe, wind N. E. in the ship called The Jonas-in-the-Whale. * * *

Some say the whale can't open his mouth, but that is a fable. * * *

They frequently climb up the masts to see whether they can see a whale, for the first discoverer has a ducat for his pains. * * *

I was told of a whale taken near Shetland, that had above a barrel of herrings in his belly. * * *

One of our harpooneers told me that he caught once a whale in Spitzbergen that was white all over.'

A Voyage to Greenland, A.D. 1671.
Harris Coll.

'Several whales have come in upon this coast (Fife). Anno 1652, one eighty feet in length of the whale-bone kind came in, which, (as I was informed) besides a vast quantity of oil, did afford 500 weight of baleen. The jaws of it stand for a gate in the garden of Pitferren.'

Sibbald's Fife and Kinross.

'Myself have agreed to try whether I can master and kill this Sperma-ceti whale, for I could never hear of any of that sort that was killed by any man, such is his fierceness and swiftness.'

Richard Strafford's Letter from the Bermudas.
Phil. Trans. A.D. 1668.

'Whales in the sea
God's voice obey.'

N. E. Primer.

'We saw also abundance of large whales, there being more in those southern seas, as I may say, by a hundred to one; than we have to the northward of us.'

Captain Cowley's Voyage round the Globe. A.D. 1729.

* * * * * 'and the breath of the whale is frequently attended with such an insupportable smell, as to bring on a disorder of the brain.' *Ulloa's South America.*

'To fifty chosen sylphs of special note,
We trust the important charge, the petticoat.
Oft have we known that seven-fold fence to fail,
Tho' stiff with hoops and armed with ribs of whale.'
Rape of the Lock.

'If we compare land animals in respect to magnitude, with those that take up their abode in the deep, we shall find they will appear contemptible in the comparison. The whale is doubtless the largest animal in creation.'
Goldsmith, Nat. His.

'If you should write a fable for little fishes, you would make them speak like great whales.'
Goldsmith to Johnson.

'In the afternoon we saw what was supposed to be a rock, but it was found to be a dead whale, which some Asiatics had killed, and were then towing ashore. They seemed to endeavor to conceal themselves behind the whale, in order to avoid being seen by us.' *Cook's Voyages.*

'The larger whales, they seldom venture to attack. They stand in so great dread of some of them, that when out at sea they are afraid to mention even their names, and carry dung, lime-stone, juniper-wood, and some other articles of the same nature in their boats, in order to terrify and prevent their too near approach.'
Uno Von Troil's Letters on Banks's and Solander's Voyage to Iceland in 1772.

'The Spermacetti Whale found by the Nantuckois, is an active, fierce animal, and requires vast address and boldness in the fishermen.'

Thomas Jefferson's Whale Memorial to the French minister in 1778.

'And pray, sir, what in the world is equal to it?'

Edmund Burke's reference in Parliament to the Nantucket Whale-Fishery.

'Spain – a great whale stranded on the shores of Europe.'

Edmund Burke. (somewhere.)

'A tenth branch of the king's ordinary revenue, said to be grounded on the consideration of his guarding and protecting the seas from pirates and robbers, is the right to *royal* fish, which are whale and sturgeon. And these, when either thrown ashore or caught near the coast, are the property of the king.' *Blackstone.*

'Soon to the sport of death the crews repair:
Rodmond unerring o'er his head suspends
The barbed steel, and every turn attends.'

Falconer's Shipwreck.

'Bright shone the roofs, the domes, the spires,
And rockets blew self driven,
To hang their momentary fire
Around the vault of heaven.

'So fire with water to compare,
The ocean serves on high,
Up-spouted by a whale in air,
To express unwieldy joy.'

Cowper, on the Queen's Visit to London.

'Ten or fifteen gallons of blood are thrown out of the heart at a stroke, with immense velocity.'

John Hunter's account of the dissection of a whale. (A small sized one.)

'The aorta of a whale is larger in the bore than the main pipe of the water-works at London Bridge, and the water roaring in its passage through that pipe is inferior in impetus and velocity to the blood gushing from the whale's heart.' *Paley's Theology.*

'The whale is a mammiferous animal without hind feet.'

Baron Cuvier.

'In 40 degrees south, we saw Spermacetti Whales, but did not take any till the first of May, the sea being then covered with them.'

Colnett's Voyage for the Purpose of Extending the Spermacetti Whale Fishery.

'In the free element beneath me swam,
Floundered and dived, in play, in chace, in battle,
Fishes of every color, form, and kind:
Which language cannot paint, and mariner
Had never seen; from dread Leviathan
To insect millions peopling every wave:
Gather'd in shoals immense, like floating islands,
Led by mysterious instincts through that waste
And trackless region, though on every side
Assaulted by voracious enemies,
Whales, sharks, and monsters, arm'd in front or jaw,
With swords, saws, spiral horns, or hooked fangs.'

Montgomery's World before the Flood.

'Io! Pæan! Io! sing,
To the finny people's king.
Not a mightier whale than this
In the vast Atlantic is;
Not a fatter fish than he,
Flounders round the Polar Sea.'
Charles Lamb's Triumph of the Whale.

'In the year 1690 some persons were on a high hill observing the whales spouting and sporting with each other, when one observed; there – pointing to the sea – is a green pasture where our children's grand-children will go for bread.' *Obed Macy's History of Nantucket.*

'I built a cottage for Susan and myself and made a gateway in the form of a Gothic Arch, by setting up a whale's jaw bones.' *Hawthorne's Twice Told Tales.*

'She came to bespeak a monument for her first love, who had been killed by a whale in the Pacific ocean, no less than forty years ago.' *Ibid.*

'No, Sir, 'tis a Right Whale,' answered Tom; 'I saw his spout; he threw up a pair of as pretty rainbows as a Christian would wish to look at. He's a raal oil-butt, that fellow!'
Cooper's Pilot.

'The papers were brought in, and we saw in the Berlin Gazette that whales had been introduced on the stage there.'
Eckermann's Conversations with Goethe.

'My God! Mr Chace, what is the matter?' I answered, 'we have been stove by a whale.'
'Narrative of the Shipwreck of the Whale Ship Essex of Nantucket, which was attacked and finally destroyed by a large Sperm Whale in the Pacific Ocean.' By Owen Chace of Nantucket, first mate of the said vessel. New York. 1821.

'A mariner sat in the shrouds one night,
The wind was piping free;
Now bright, now dimmed, was the moonlight pale,
And the phospher gleamed in the wake of the whale,
As it floundered in the sea.' *Elizabeth Oakes Smith.*

'The quantity of line withdrawn from the different boats engaged in the capture of this one whale, amounted altogether to 10,440 yards or nearly six English miles.' * * *
'Sometimes the whale shakes its tremendous tail in the air, which, cracking like a whip, resounds to the distance of three or four miles.' *Scoresby.*

'Mad with the agonies he endures from these fresh attacks, the infuriated Sperm Whale rolls over and over; he rears his enormous head, and with wide expanded jaws snaps at everything around him; he rushes at the boats with his head; they are propelled before him with vast swiftness, and sometimes utterly destroyed.
* * * It is a matter of great astonishment that the consideration of the habits of so interesting, and, in a commercial point of view, of so important an animal (as the Sperm Whale) should have been so entirely neglected, or should have excited so little curiosity among the numerous, and many of them competent observers, that of late years must have possessed the most abundant and the most convenient opportunities of witnessing their habitudes.'
Thomas Beale's History of the Sperm Whale, 1839.

'The Cachalot' (Sperm Whale) 'is not only better armed than the True Whale' (Greenland or Right Whale) 'in possessing a formidable weapon at either extremity of its body, but also more frequently displays a disposition to employ these weapons offensively, and in a manner at once so artful, bold, and mischievous, as to lead to its being regarded as the most dangerous to attack of all the known species of the whale tribe.' *Frederick Debell Bennett's Whaling Voyage Round the Globe.* 1840.

October 13. 'There she blows,' was sung out from the mast-head.

'Where away?' demanded the captain.

'Three points off the lee bow, sir.'

'Raise up your wheel. Steady!'

'Steady, sir.'

'Mast-head ahoy! Do you see that whale now?'

'Ay ay, sir! A shoal of Sperm Whales! There she blows! There she breaches!'

'Sing out! sing out every time!'

'Ay ay, sir! There she blows! there – there – *thar* she blows – bowes – bo-o-o-s!'

'How far off?'

'Two miles and a half.'

'Thunder and lightning! so near! Call all hands!'

J. Ross Browne's Etchings of a Whaling Cruise. 1846.

'The Whale-ship Globe, on board of which vessel occurred the horrid transactions we are about to relate, belonged to the island of Nantucket.'

'Narrative of the Globe Mutiny,' by Lay and Hussey survivors. A.D. 1828.

'Being once pursued by a whale which he had wounded, he parried the assault for some time with a lance; but the furious monster at length rushed on the boat; himself and comrades only being preserved by leaping into the water when they saw the onset was inevitable.'

Missionary Journal of Tyerman and Bennett.

'Nantucket itself,' said Mr Webster, 'is a very striking and peculiar portion of the National interest. There is a population of eight or nine thousand persons, living here in the sea, adding largely every year to the National wealth by the boldest and most persevering industry.'

Report of Daniel Webster's Speech in the U.S. Senate, on the application for the Erection of a Breakwater at Nantucket. 1828.

'The whale fell directly over him, and probably killed him in a moment.'

'The Whale and his Captors, or The Whaleman's Adventures and the Whale's Biography, gathered on the Homeward Cruise of the Commodore Preble.' By Rev. Henry T. Cheever.

'If you make the least damn bit of noise,' replied Samuel, 'I will send you to hell.'

Life of Samuel Comstock (the mutineer), by his brother, William Comstock. Another Version of the whale-ship Globe narrative.

'The voyages of the Dutch and English to the Northern Ocean, in order, if possible, to discover a passage through it to India, though they failed of their main object, laid open the haunts of the whale.'

McCulloch's Commercial Dictionary.

'These things are reciprocal; the ball rebounds, only to bound forward again; for now in laying open the haunts of the whale, the whalemen seem to have indirectly hit upon new clews to that same mystic North-West Passage.'

From 'Something' unpublished.

'It is impossible to meet a whale-ship on the ocean without being struck by her mere appearance. The vessel under short sail, with look-outs at the mast-heads, eagerly scanning the wide expanse around them, has a totally different air from those engaged in a regular voyage.'

Currents and Whaling. U. S. Ex. Ex.

'Pedestrians in the vicinity of London and elsewhere may recollect having seen large curved bones set upright in the earth, either to form arches over gateways, or entrances to alcoves, and they may perhaps have been told that these were the ribs of whales.' *Tales of a Whale Voyager to the Arctic Ocean.*

'It was not till the boats returned from the pursuit of these whales, that the whites saw their ship in bloody possession of the savages enrolled among the crew.'

Newspaper Account of the Taking and Retaking of the Whale-ship Hobomack.

'It is generally well known that out of the crews of Whaling vessels (American) few ever return in the ships on board of which they departed.' *Cruise in a Whale Boat.*

'Suddenly a mighty mass emerged from the water, and shot up perpendicularly into the air. It was the whale.'

Miriam Coffin or the Whale Fisherman.

'The Whale is harpooned to be sure; but bethink you, how you would manage a powerful unbroken colt, with the mere appliance of a rope tied to the root of his tail.'

A Chapter on Whaling in Ribs and Trucks.

'On one occasion I saw two of these monsters (whales) probably male and female, slowly swimming, one after the other, within less than a stone's throw of the shore' (Terra Del Fuego), 'over which the beech tree extended its branches.' *Darwin's Voyage of a Naturalist.*

'"Stern all!" exclaimed the mate, as upon turning his head, he saw the distended jaws of a large Sperm Whale close to the head of the boat, threatening it with instant destruction; – "Stern all, for your lives!"'

Wharton the Whale Killer.

'So be cheery, my lads, let your hearts never fail,
While the bold harpooneer is striking the whale!'

Nantucket Song.

'Oh, the rare old Whale, mid storm and gale
 In his ocean home will be
A giant in might, where might is right,
 And King of the boundless sea.'

Whale Song.

1

LOOMINGS

CALL me Ishmael. Some years ago – never mind how long precisely – having little or no money in my purse, and nothing particular to interest me on shore, I thought I would sail about a little and see the watery part of the world. It is a way I have of driving off the spleen, and regulating the circulation. Whenever I find myself growing grim about the mouth; whenever it is a damp, drizzly November in my soul; whenever I find myself involuntarily pausing before coffin warehouses, and bringing up the rear of every funeral I meet; and especially whenever my hypos get such an upper hand of me, that it requires a strong moral principle to prevent me from deliberately stepping into the street, and methodically knocking people's hats off – then, I account it high time to get to sea as soon as I can. This is my substitute for pistol and ball. With a philosophical flourish Cato throws himself upon his sword; I quietly take to the ship. There is nothing surprising in this. If they but knew it, almost all men in their degree, some time or other, cherish very nearly the same feelings towards the ocean with me.

There now is your insular city of the Manhattoes, belted round by wharves as Indian isles by coral reefs – commerce surrounds it with her surf. Right and left, the streets take you waterward. Its extreme down-town is the Battery, where that noble mole is washed by waves, and cooled by breezes, which a few hours previous were out of sight of land. Look at the crowds of water-gazers there.

Circumambulate the city of a dreamy Sabbath afternoon. Go from Corlears Hook to Coenties Slip, and from thence, by Whitehall, northward. What do you see? – Posted like silent sentinels all around the town, stand thousands upon thousands of mortal men fixed in ocean reveries. Some leaning against the spiles; some seated upon the pier-heads; some looking over the bulwarks of ships from China; some high aloft in the rigging, as if striving to get a still better seaward peep. But these are all landsmen; of week days pent up in lath and plaster – tied to counters, nailed to benches, clinched to desks. How then is this? Are the green fields gone? What do they here?

But look! here come more crowds, pacing straight for the water, and seemingly bound for a dive. Strange! Nothing will content them but the extremest limit of the land; loitering under the shady lee of yonder warehouses will not suffice. No. They must get just as nigh the water as they possibly can without falling in. And there they stand – miles of them – leagues. Inlanders all, they come from lanes and alleys, streets and avenues – north, east, south, and west. Yet here they all unite. Tell me, does the magnetic virtue in the needles of the compasses of all those ships attract them thither?

Once more. Say, you are in the country; in some high land of lakes. Take almost any path you please, and ten to one it carries you down in a dale, and leaves you there by a pool in the stream. There is magic in it. Let the most absent-minded of men be plunged in his deepest reveries – stand that man on his legs, set his feet a-going, and he will infallibly lead you to water, if water there be in all that region. Should you ever be athirst in the great American desert, try this experiment, if your caravan happen to be supplied with a metaphysical professor. Yes, as every one knows, meditation and water are wedded for ever.

But here is an artist. He desires to paint you the dreamiest, shadiest, quietest, most enchanting bit of romantic landscape in all the valley of the Saco. What is the chief element he employs? There stand his trees, each with a hollow trunk, as if a hermit and a crucifix were within; and here sleeps his meadow, and there sleep his cattle; and up from yonder cottage goes a sleepy smoke. Deep into distant woodlands winds a mazy way, reaching to overlapping spurs of mountains bathed in their hill-side blue. But though the picture lies thus tranced, and though this pine-tree shakes down its sighs like leaves upon this shepherd's head, yet all were vain, unless the shepherd's eye were fixed upon the magic stream before him. Go visit the Prairies in June, when for scores on scores of miles you wade knee-deep among Tiger-lilies – what is the one charm wanting? – Water – there is not a drop of water there! Were Niagara but a cataract of sand, would you travel your thousand miles to see it? Why did the poor poet of Tennessee, upon suddenly receiving two handfuls of silver, deliberate whether to buy him a coat, which he sadly needed, or invest his money in a pedestrian trip to Rockaway Beach? Why is almost every robust healthy boy with a robust healthy soul in him, at some time or other crazy to go to sea? Why upon your first voyage as a passenger, did you yourself feel such a mystical vibration, when first told that you and your ship were now out of sight of land? Why did the old Persians hold the sea holy? Why did the Greeks give it a separate deity, and own brother of Jove? Surely all this is not without meaning. And still deeper the meaning of that story of Narcissus, who because he could not grasp the tormenting, mild image he saw in the fountain, plunged into it and was drowned. But that same image, we ourselves see in all rivers and oceans. It is the image of the ungraspable phantom of life; and this is the key to it all.

Now, when I say that I am in the habit of going to sea whenever I begin to grow hazy about the eyes, and begin to be over conscious of my lungs, I do not mean to have it inferred that I ever go to sea as a passenger. For to go as a passenger you must needs have a purse, and a purse is but a rag unless you have something in it. Besides, passengers get sea-sick – grow quarrelsome – don't sleep of nights – do not enjoy themselves much, as a general thing; – no, I never go as a passenger; nor, though I am something of a salt, do I ever go to sea as a Commodore, or a Captain, or a Cook. I abandon the glory and distinction of such offices to those who like them. For my part, I abominate all honorable respectable toils, trials, and tribulations of every kind whatsoever. It is quite as much as I can do to take care of myself, without taking care of ships, barques, brigs, schooners, and what not. And as for going as cook, – though I confess there is considerable glory in that, a cook being a sort of officer on ship-board – yet, somehow, I never fancied broiling fowls; – though once broiled, judiciously buttered, and judgmatically salted and peppered, there is no one who will speak more respectfully, not to say reverentially, of a broiled fowl than I will. It is out of the idolatrous dotings of the old Egyptians upon broiled ibis and roasted river horse, that you see the mummies of those creatures in their huge bakehouses the pyramids.

No, when I go to sea, I go as a simple sailor, right before the mast, plumb down into the forecastle, aloft there to the royal mast-head. True, they rather order me about some, and make me jump from spar to spar, like a grasshopper in a May meadow. And at first, this sort of thing is unpleasant enough. It touches one's sense of honor, particularly if you come of an old established family in the land, the Van Rensselaers, or Randolphs, or Hardicanutes. And more than all, if just previous to putting your hand into the tar-pot, you have been lording it as a country schoolmaster, making the tallest boys stand in awe of you. The transition is a keen one, I assure you, from a schoolmaster to a sailor, and requires a strong decoction of Seneca and the Stoics to enable you to grin and bear it. But even this wears off in time.

What of it, if some old hunks of a sea-captain orders me to get a broom and sweep down the decks? What does that indignity amount to, weighed, I mean, in the scales of the New Testament? Do you think the archangel Gabriel thinks anything the less of me, because I promptly and respectfully obey that old hunks in that particular instance? Who aint a slave? Tell me that. Well, then, however the old sea-captains may order me about – however they may thump and punch me about, I have the satisfaction of knowing that it is all right; that everybody else is one way or other served in much the same way – either in a physical or metaphysical point of view, that is; and so the universal thump is passed round, and all hands should rub each other's shoulder-blades, and be content.

Again, I always go to sea as a sailor, because they make a point of paying me for my trouble, whereas they never pay passengers a single penny that I ever heard of. On the contrary, passengers themselves must pay. And there is all the difference in the world between paying and being paid. The act of paying is perhaps the most uncomfortable infliction that the two orchard thieves entailed upon us. But *being paid*, – what will compare with it? The urbane activity with which a man receives money is really marvellous, considering that we so earnestly believe money to be the root of all earthly ills, and on no account can a monied man enter heaven. Ah! how cheerfully we consign ourselves to perdition!

Finally, I always go to sea as a sailor, because of the wholesome exercise and pure air of the forecastle deck. For as in this world, head winds are far more prevalent than winds from astern (that is, if you never violate the Pythagorean maxim), so for the most part the Commodore on the quarter-deck gets his atmosphere at second hand from the sailors on the forecastle. He thinks he breathes it first; but not so. In much the same way do the commonalty lead their leaders in many other things, at the same time that the leaders little suspect it. But wherefore it was that after having repeatedly smelt the sea as a merchant sailor, I should now take it into my head to go on a whaling voyage; this the invisible police officer of the Fates, who has the constant surveillance of me, and secretly dogs me, and influences me in some unaccountable way – he can better answer than any one else. And, doubtless, my going on this whaling voyage, formed part of the grand programme of Providence that was drawn up a long time ago. It came in as a sort of brief interlude and solo between more extensive performances. I take it that this part of the bill must have run something like this:

'Grand Contested Election for the Presidency of the United States.

'WHALING VOYAGE BY ONE ISHMAEL.

'BLOODY BATTLE IN AFFGHANISTAN.'

Though I cannot tell why it was exactly that those stage managers, the Fates, put me down for this shabby part of a whaling voyage, when others were set down for magnificent parts in high tragedies, and short and easy parts in genteel comedies, and jolly parts in farces – though I cannot tell why this was exactly; yet, now that I recall all the circumstances, I think I can see a little into the springs and motives which being cunningly presented to me under various disguises, induced me to set about performing the part I did, besides cajoling me into the delusion that it was a choice resulting from my own unbiased freewill and discriminating judgment.

Chief among these motives was the overwhelming idea of the great whale himself. Such a portentous and mysterious monster roused all my curiosity. Then the wild and distant seas where he rolled his island bulk; the undeliverable, nameless perils of the whale; these, with all the attending marvels of a thousand Patagonian sights and sounds, helped to sway me to my wish. With other men, perhaps, such things would not have been inducements; but as for me, I am tormented with an everlasting itch for things remote. I love to sail forbidden seas, and land on barbarous coasts. Not ignoring what is good, I am quick to perceive a horror, and could still be social with it – would they let me – since it is but well to be on friendly terms with all the inmates of the place one lodges in.

By reason of these things, then, the whaling voyage was welcome; the great flood-gates of the wonder-world swung open, and in the wild conceits that swayed me to my purpose, two and two there floated into my inmost soul, endless processions of the whale, and, mid most of them all, one grand hooded phantom, like a snow hill in the air.

2

THE CARPET-BAG

I STUFFED a shirt or two into my old carpet-bag, tucked it under my arm, and started for Cape Horn and the Pacific. Quitting the good city of old Manhatto, I duly arrived in New Bedford. It was on a Saturday night in December. Much was I disappointed upon learning that the little packet for Nantucket had already sailed, and that no way of reaching that place would offer, till the following Monday.

As most young candidates for the pains and penalties of whaling stop at this same New Bedford, thence to embark on their voyage, it may as well be related that I, for one, had no idea of so doing. For my mind was made up to sail in no other than a Nantucket craft, because there was a fine, boisterous something about everything connected with that famous old island, which amazingly pleased me. Besides though New Bedford has of late been gradually monopolizing the business of whaling, and though in this matter poor old Nantucket is now much behind her, yet Nantucket was her great original – the Tyre of this Carthage; – the place where the first dead American whale was stranded. Where else but from Nantucket did those aboriginal whalemen, the Red-Men, first sally out in canoes to give chase to the Leviathan? And where but from Nantucket, too, did that first adventurous little sloop put forth, partly laden with imported cobble-stones – so goes the story – to throw at the whales, in order to discover when they were nigh enough to risk a harpoon from the bowsprit?

Now having a night, a day, and still another night following before me in New Bedford, ere I could embark for my destined port, it became a matter of concernment where I was to eat and sleep meanwhile. It was a very dubious-looking, nay, a very dark and dismal night, bitingly cold and cheerless. I knew no one in the place. With anxious grapnels I had sounded my pocket, and only brought up a few pieces of silver, – So, wherever you go, Ishmael, said I to myself, as I stood in the middle of a dreary street shouldering my bag, and comparing the gloom towards the north with the darkness towards the south – wherever in your wisdom you may conclude to lodge for the night, my dear Ishmael, be sure to inquire the price, and don't be too particular.

With halting steps I paced the streets, and passed the sign of 'The Crossed Harpoons' – but it looked too expensive and jolly there. Further on, from the bright red windows of the 'Sword-Fish Inn', there came such fervent rays, that it seemed to have melted the packed snow and ice from before the house, for everywhere else the congealed frost lay ten inches thick in a hard, asphaltic pavement, – rather weary for me, when I struck my foot against the flinty projections, because from hard, remorseless service the soles of my boots were in a most miserable plight. Too expensive and jolly, again thought I, pausing one moment to watch the broad glare in the street, and hear the sounds of the tinkling glasses within. But go on, Ishmael, said I at last; don't you hear? get away from before the door; your patched boots are stopping the way. So on I went. I now by instinct followed the streets that took me waterward, for there, doubtless, were the cheapest, if not the cheeriest inns.

Such dreary streets! blocks of blackness, not houses, on either hand, and here and there a candle, like a candle moving about in a tomb. At this hour of the night, of the last day of the week, that quarter of the town proved all but deserted. But presently I came to a smoky light proceeding from a low, wide building, the door of which stood invitingly open. It had a careless look, as if it were meant for the uses of the public; so, entering, the first thing I did was to stumble over an ash-box in the porch. Ha! thought I, ha, as the flying particles almost choked me, are these ashes from that destroyed city, Gomorrah? But 'The Crossed Harpoons', and 'The Sword-Fish'? – this, then, must needs be the sign of 'The Trap'. However, I picked myself up and hearing a loud voice within, pushed on and opened a second, interior door.

It seemed the great Black Parliament sitting in Tophet. A hundred black faces turned round in their rows to peer; and beyond, a black Angel of Doom was beating a book in a pulpit. It was a negro church; and the preacher's text was about the blackness of darkness, and the weeping and wailing and teeth-gnashing there. Ha, Ishmael, muttered I, backing out, Wretched entertainment at the sign of 'The Trap!'

Moving on, I at last came to a dim sort of out-hanging light not far from the docks, and heard a forlorn creaking in the air; and looking up, saw a swinging sign over the door with a white painting upon it, faintly representing a tall straight jet of misty spray, and these words underneath – 'The Spouter-Inn: – Peter Coffin.'

Coffin? – Spouter? – Rather ominous in that particular connexion, thought I. But it is a common name in Nantucket, they say, and I suppose this Peter here is an emigrant from there. As the light looked so dim, and the place, for the time, looked quiet enough, and the dilapidated little wooden house itself looked as if it might have been carted here from the ruins of some burnt district, and as the swinging sign had a poverty-stricken sort of creak to it, I thought that here was the very spot for cheap lodgings, and the best of pea coffee.

It was a queer sort of place – a gable-ended old house, one side palsied as it were, and leaning over sadly. It stood on a sharp bleak corner, where that tempestuous wind Euroclydon kept up a worse howling than ever it did about poor Paul's tossed craft. Euroclydon, nevertheless, is a mighty pleasant zephyr to any one in-doors, with his feet on the hob quietly toasting for bed. 'In judging of that tempestuous wind called Euroclydon,' says an old writer – of whose works I possess the only copy extant – 'it maketh a marvellous difference, whether thou lookest out at it from a glass window where the frost is all on the outside, or whether thou observest it from that sashless window, where the frost is on both sides, and of which the wight Death is the only glazier.' True enough, thought I, as this passage occurred to my mind – old black-letter, thou reasonest well. Yes, these eyes are windows, and this body of mine is the house. What a pity they didn't stop up the chinks and the crannies though, and thrust in a little lint here and there. But it's too late to make any improvements now. The universe is finished; the copestone is on, and the chips were carted off a million years ago. Poor Lazarus there, chattering his teeth against the curbstone for his pillow, and shaking off his tatters with his shiverings, he might plug up both ears with rags, and put a corn-cob into his mouth, and yet that would not keep out the tempestuous Euroclydon. Euroclydon! says old Dives, in his red silken wrapper (he had a redder one afterwards) – pooh, pooh! What a fine frosty night; how Orion glitters; what northern lights! Let them talk of their oriental summer climes of everlasting conservatories; give me the privilege of making my own summer with my own coals.

But what thinks Lazarus? Can he warm his blue hands by holding them up to the grand northern lights? Would not Lazarus rather be in Sumatra than here? Would he not far rather lay him down lengthwise along the line of the equator; yea, ye gods! go down to the fiery pit itself, in order to keep out this frost?

Now, that Lazarus should lie stranded there on the curbstone before the door of Dives, this is more wonderful than that an iceberg should be moored to one of the Moluccas. Yet Dives himself, he too lives like a Czar in an ice palace made of frozen sighs, and being a president of a temperance society, he only drinks the tepid tears of orphans.

But no more of this blubbering now, we are going a-whaling, and there is plenty of that yet to come. Let us scrape the ice from our frosted feet, and see what sort of a place this 'Spouter' may be.

3

THE SPOUTER-INN

ENTERING that gable-ended Spouter-Inn, you found yourself in a wide, low, straggling entry with old-fashioned wainscots, reminding one of the bulwarks of some condemned old craft. On one side hung a very large oil-painting so thoroughly be-smoked, and every way defaced, that in the unequal cross-lights by which you viewed it, it was only by diligent study and a series of systematic visits to it, and careful inquiry of the neighbors, that you could any way arrive at an understanding of its purpose. Such unaccountable masses of shades and shadows, that at first you almost thought some ambitious young artist, in the time of the New England hags, had endeavored to delineate chaos bewitched. But by dint of much and earnest contemplation, and oft repeated ponderings, and especially by throwing open the little window towards the back of the entry, you at last come to the conclusion that such an idea, however wild, might not be altogether unwarranted.

But what most puzzled and confounded you was a long, limber, portentous, black mass of something hovering in the centre of the picture over three blue, dim, perpendicular lines floating in a nameless yeast. A boggy, soggy, squitchy picture truly, enough to drive a nervous man distracted. Yet was there a sort of indefinite, half-attained, unimaginable sublimity about it that fairly froze you to it, till you involuntarily took an oath with yourself to find out what that marvellous painting meant. Ever and anon a bright, but, alas, deceptive idea would dart you through. – It's the Black Sea in a midnight gale. – It's the unnatural combat of the four primal elements. – It's a blasted heath. – It's a Hyperborean winter scene. – It's the breaking-up of the ice-bound stream of Time. But at last all these fancies yielded to that one portentous something in the picture's midst. *That* once found out, and all the rest were plain. But stop; does it not bear a faint resemblance to a gigantic fish? even the great leviathan himself?

In fact, the artist's design seemed this: a final theory of my own, partly based upon the aggregated opinions of many aged persons with whom I conversed upon the subject. The picture represents a Cape-Horner in a great hurricane; the half-foundered ship weltering there with its three dismantled masts alone visible; and an exasperated whale, purposing to spring clean over the craft, is in the enormous act of impaling himself upon the three mast-heads.

The opposite wall of this entry was hung all over with a heathenish array of monstrous clubs and spears. Some were thickly set with glittering teeth resembling ivory saws; others were tufted with knots of human hair; and one was sickle-shaped, with a vast handle sweeping round like the segment made in the new-mown grass by a long-armed mower. You shuddered as you gazed, and wondered what monstrous cannibal and savage could ever have gone a death-harvesting with such a hacking, horrifying implement. Mixed with these were rusty old whaling lances and harpoons all broken and deformed. Some were storied weapons. With this once long lance, now wildly elbowed, fifty years ago did Nathan Swain kill fifteen whales between a sunrise and a sunset. And that harpoon – so like a corkscrew now – was flung in Javan seas, and run away with by a whale, years afterward slain off the Cape of Blanco. The original iron entered nigh the tail, and, like a restless needle sojourning in the body of a man, travelled full forty feet, and at last was found imbedded in the hump.

Crossing this dusky entry, and on through yon low-arched way – cut through what in old times must have been a great central chimney with fire-places all round – you enter the public room. A still duskier place is this, with such low ponderous beams above, and such old wrinkled planks beneath, that you would almost fancy you trod some old craft's cockpits, especially of such a howling night, when this corner-anchored old ark rocked so furiously. On one side stood a long, low, shelf-like table covered with cracked glass cases, filled with dusty rarities gathered from this wide world's remotest nooks. Projecting from the further angle of the room stands a dark-looking den –the bar – a rude attempt at a right whale's head. Be that how it may, there stands the vast arched bone of the whale's jaw, so wide, a coach might almost drive beneath it. Within are shabby shelves, ranged round with old decanters, bottles, flasks; and in those jaws of swift destruction, like another cursed Jonah (by which name indeed they called him), bustles a little withered old man, who, for their money, dearly sells the sailors deliriums and death.

Abominable are the tumblers into which he pours his poison. Though true cylinders without – within, the villanous green goggling glasses deceitfully tapered downwards to a cheating bottom. Parallel meridians rudely pecked into the glass, surround these footpads' goblets. Fill to *this* mark, and your charge is but a penny; to *this* a penny more; and so on to the full glass – the Cape Horn measure, which you may gulph down for a shilling.

Upon entering the place I found a number of young seamen gathered about a table, examining by a dim light divers specimens of *skrimshander*. I sought the landlord, and telling him I desired to be accommodated with a room, received for answer that his house was full – not a bed unoccupied. 'But avast,' he added, tapping his forehead, 'you haint no objections to sharing a harpooneer's blanket, have ye? I s'pose you are goin' a whalin', so you'd better get used to that sort of thing.'

I told him that I never liked to sleep two in a bed; that if I should ever do so, it would depend upon who the harpooneer might be, and that if he (the landlord) really had no other place for me, and the harpooneer was not decidedly objectionable, why rather than wander further about a strange town on so bitter a night, I would put up with the half of any decent man's blanket.

'I thought so. All right; take a seat. Supper? – you want supper? Supper 'll be ready directly.'

I sat down on an old wooden settle, carved all over like a bench on the Battery. At one end a ruminating tar was still further adorning it with his jack-knife, stooping over and diligently working away at the space between his legs. He was trying his hand at a ship under full sail, but he didn't make much headway, I thought.

At last some four or five of us were summoned to our meal in an adjoining room. It was cold as Iceland – no fire at all – the landlord said he couldn't afford it. Nothing but two dismal tallow candles, each in a winding sheet. We were fain to button up our monkey jackets, and hold to our lips cups of scalding tea with our half frozen fingers. But the fare was of the most substantial kind – not only meat and potatoes, but dumplings; good heavens! dumplings for supper! One young fellow in a green box coat, addressed himself to these dumplings in a most direful manner.

'My boy,' said the landlord, 'you'll have the nightmare to a dead sartainty.'

'Landlord,' I whispered, 'that aint the harpooneer, is it?'

'Oh, no,' said he, looking a sort of diabolically funny, 'the harpooner is a dark complexioned chap. He never eats dumplings, he don't – he eats nothing but steaks, and likes 'em rare.'

'The devil he does,' says I. 'Where is that harpooneer? Is he here?'

'He'll be here afore long,' was the answer.

I could not help it, but I began to feel suspicious of this 'dark complexioned' harpooneer. At any rate, I made up my mind that if it so turned out that we should sleep together, he must undress and get into bed before I did.

Supper over, the company went back to the bar-room, when, knowing not what else to do with myself, I resolved to spend the rest of the evening as a looker on.

Presently a rioting noise was heard without. Starting up, the landlord cried, 'That's the Grampus's crew. I seed her reported in the offing this morning; a three years' voyage, and a full ship. Hurrah, boys; now we'll have the latest news from the Feegees.'

A tramping of sea boots was heard in the entry; the door was flung open, and in rolled a wild set of mariners enough. Enveloped in their shaggy watch coats, and with their heads muffled in woollen comforters, all bedarned and ragged, and their beards stiff with icicles, they seemed an eruption of bears from Labrador. They had just landed from their boat, and this was the first house they entered. No wonder, then, that they made a straight wake for the whale's mouth – the bar – when the wrinkled little old Jonah, there officiating, soon poured them out brimmers all round. One complained of a bad cold in his head, upon which Jonah mixed him a pitch-like potion of gin and molasses, which he swore was a sovereign cure for all colds and catarrhs whatsoever, never mind of how long standing, or whether caught off the coast of Labrador, or on the weather side of an ice-island.

The liquor soon mounted into their heads, as it generally does even with the arrantest topers newly landed from sea, and they began capering about most obstreperously.

I observed, however, that one of them held somewhat aloof, and though he seemed desirous not to spoil the hilarity of his shipmates by his own sober face, yet upon the whole he refrained from making as much noise as the rest. This man interested me at once; and since the sea-gods had ordained that he should soon become my shipmate (though but a sleeping-partner one, so far as this narrative is concerned), I will here venture upon a little description of him. He stood full six feet in height, with noble shoulders, and a chest like a coffer-dam. I have seldom seen such brawn in a man. His face was deeply brown and burnt, making his white teeth dazzling by the contrast; while in the deep shadows of his eyes floated some reminiscences that did not seem to give him much joy. His voice at once announced that he was a Southerner, and from his fine stature, I thought he must be one of those tall mountaineers from the Alleganian Ridge in Virginia. When the revelry of his companions had mounted to its height, this man slipped away unobserved, and I saw no more of him till he became my comrade on the sea. In a few minutes, however, he was missed by his shipmates, and being, it seems, for some reason a huge favorite with them, they raised a cry of 'Bulkington! Bulkington! where's Bulkington?' and darted out of the house in pursuit of him.

It was now about nine o'clock, and the room seeming almost supernaturally quiet after these orgies, I began to congratulate myself upon a little plan that had occurred to me just previous to the entrance of the seamen.

No man prefers to sleep two in a bed. In fact, you would a good deal rather not sleep with your own brother. I don't know how it is, but people like to be private when they are sleeping. And when it comes to sleeping with an unknown stranger, in a strange inn, in a strange town, and that stranger a harpooneer, then your objections indefinitely multiply. Nor was there any earthly reason why I as a sailor should sleep two in a bed, more than anybody else; for sailors no more sleep two in a bed at sea, than bachelor Kings do ashore. To be sure they all sleep together in one apartment, but you have your own hammock, and cover yourself with your own blanket, and sleep in your own skin.

The more I pondered over this harpooneer, the more I abominated the thought of sleeping with him. It was fair to presume that being a harpooneer, his linen or woollen, as the case might be, would not be of the tidiest, certainly none of the finest. I began to twitch all over. Besides, it was getting late, and any decent harpooneer ought to be home and going bedwards. Suppose now, he should tumble in upon me at midnight – how could I tell from what vile hole he had been coming?

'Landlord! I've changed my mind about that harpooneer. – I shan't sleep with him. I'll try the bench here.'

'Just as you please; I'm sorry I cant spare ye a tablecloth for a mattress, and it's a plaguy rough board here' – feeling of the knots and notches. 'But wait a bit, Skrimshander; I've got a carpenter's plane there in the bar – wait, I say, and I'll make ye snug enough.' So saying he procured the plane; and with his old silk handkerchief first dusting the bench, vigorously set to planing away at my bed, the while grinning like an ape. The shavings flew right and left; till at last the plane-iron came bump against an indestructible knot. The landlord was near spraining his wrist, and I told him for heaven's sake to quit – the bed was soft enough to suit me, and I did not know how all the planing in the world could make eider down of a pine plank. So gathering up the shavings with another grin, and throwing them into the great stove in the middle of the room, he went about his business, and left me in a brown study.

I now took the measure of the bench, and found that it was a foot too short; but that could be mended with a chair. But it was a foot too narrow, and the other bench in the room was about four inches higher than the planed one – so there was no yoking them. I then placed the first bench lengthwise along the only clear space against the wall, leaving a little interval between, for my back to settle down in. But I soon found that there came such a draught of cold air over me from under the sill of the window, that this plan would never do at all, especially as another current from the rickety door met the one from the window, and both together formed a series of small whirlwinds in the immediate vicinity of the spot where I had thought to spend the night.

The devil fetch that harpooneer, thought I, but stop, couldn't I steal a march on him – bolt his door inside, and jump into his bed, not to be wakened by the most violent knockings? It seemed no bad idea; but upon second thoughts I dismissed it. For who could tell but what the next morning, so soon as I popped out of the room, the harpooneer might be standing in the entry, all ready to knock me down!

Still, looking around me again, and seeing no possible chance of spending a sufferable night unless in some other person's bed, I began to think that after all I might be cherishing unwarrantable prejudices against this unknown harpooneer. Thinks I, I'll wait awhile; he must be dropping in before long. I'll have a good look at him then, and perhaps we may become jolly good bedfellows after all – there's no telling.

But though the other boarders kept coming in by ones, twos, and threes, and going to bed, yet no sign of my harpooneer.

'Landlord!' said I, 'what sort of a chap is he – does he always keep such late hours?' It was now hard upon twelve o'clock.

The landlord chuckled again with his lean chuckle, and seemed to be mightily tickled at something beyond my comprehension. 'No,' he answered, 'generally he's an airley bird – airley to bed and airley to rise – yes, he's the bird what catches the worm.–But tonight he went out a peddling, you see, and I don't see what on airth keeps him so late, unless, may be, he can't sell his head.'

'Can't sell his head? – What sort of a bamboozling story is this you are telling me?' getting into a towering rage. 'Do you pretend to say, landlord, that this harpooneer is actually engaged this blessed Saturday night, or rather Sunday morning, in peddling his head around this town?'

'That's precisely it,' said the landlord, 'and I told him he couldn't sell it here, the market's overstocked.'

'With what?' shouted I.

'With heads to be sure; ain't there too many heads in the world?'

'I tell you what it is, landlord,' said I, quite calmly, 'you'd better stop spinning that yarn to me – I'm not green.'

'May be not,' taking out a stick and whittling a toothpick, 'but I rayther guess you'll be done *brown* if that ere harpooneer hears you a slanderin' his head.'

'I'll break it for him,' said I, now flying into a passion again at this unaccountable farrago of the landlord's.

'It's broke a'ready,' said he.

'Broke,' said I – '*broke*, do you mean?'

'Sartain, and that's the very reason he can't sell it, I guess.'

'Landlord,' said I, going up to him as cool as Mt. Hecla in a snow storm, – 'landlord, stop whittling. You and I must understand one another, and that too without delay. I come to your house and want a bed; you tell me you can only give me half a one; that the other half belongs to a certain harpooneer. And about this harpooneer, whom I have not yet seen, you persist in telling me the most mystifying and exasperating stories, tending to beget in me an uncomfortable feeling towards the man whom you design for my bedfellow – a sort of connexion, landlord, which is an intimate and confidential one in the highest degree. I now demand of you to speak out and tell me who and what this harpooneer is, and whether I shall be in all respects safe to spend the night with him. And in the first place, you will be so good as to unsay that story about selling his head, which if true I take to be good evidence that this harpooneer is stark mad, and I've no idea of sleeping with a madman; and you, sir, *you* I mean, landlord, *you*, sir, by trying to induce me to do so knowingly, would thereby render yourself liable to a criminal prosecution.'

'Wall,' said the landlord, fetching a long breath, 'that's a purty long sarmon for a chap that rips a little now and then. But be easy, be easy, this here harpooneer I have been tellin' you of has just arrived from the south seas, where he bought up a lot of 'balmed New Zealand heads (great curios, you know), and he's sold all on 'em but one, and that one he's trying to sell tonight, cause to-morrow's Sunday, and it would not do to be sellin' human heads about the streets when folks is goin' to churches. He wanted to, last Sunday, but I stopped him just as he was goin' out of the door with four heads strung on a string, for all the airth like a string of inions.'

This account cleared up the otherwise unaccountable mystery, and showed that the landlord, after all, had had no idea of fooling me – but at the same time what could I think of a harpooneer who stayed out of a Saturday night clean into the holy Sabbath, engaged in such a cannibal business as selling the heads of dead idolators?

'Depend upon it, landlord, that harpooneer is a dangerous man.'

'He pays reg'lar,' was the rejoinder. 'But come, it's getting dreadful late, you had better be turning flukes – it's a nice bed: Sall and me slept in that ere bed the night we were spliced. There's plenty room for two to kick about in that bed; it's an almighty big bed that. Why, afore we give it up, Sal used to put our Sam and little Johnny in the foot of it. But I got a dreaming and sprawling about one night, and somehow, Sam got pitched on the floor, and came near breaking his arm. Arter that, Sal said it wouldn't do. Come along here, I'll give ye a glim in a jiffy;' and so saying he lighted a candle and held it towards me, offering to lead the way. But I stood irresolute; when looking at a clock in the corner, he exclaimed, 'I vum it's Sunday – you won't see that harpooneer tonight; he's come to anchor somewhere – come along then; *do* come; *won't* ye come?'

I considered the matter a moment, and then up stairs we went, and I was ushered into a small room, cold as a clam, and furnished, sure enough, with a prodigious bed, almost big enough indeed for any four harpooneers to sleep abreast.

'There,' said the landlord, placing the candle on a crazy old sea chest that did double duty as a wash-stand and centre table; 'there, make yourself comfortable now, and good night to ye.' I turned round from eyeing the bed, but he had disappeared.

Folding back the counterpane, I stooped over the bed. Though none of the most elegant, it yet stood the scrutiny tolerably well. I then glanced round the room; and besides the bedstead and centre table, could see no other furniture belonging to the place, but a rude shelf, the four walls, and a papered fireboard representing a man striking a whale. Of things not properly belonging to the room, there was a hammock lashed up, and thrown upon the floor in one corner; also a large seaman's bag, containing the harpooneers' wardrobe, no doubt in lieu of a land trunk. Likewise, there was a parcel of outlandish bone fish hooks on the shelf over the fire-place, and a tall harpoon standing at the head of the bed.

But what is this on the chest? I took it up, and held it close to the light, and felt it, and smelt it, and tried every way possible to arrive at some satisfactory conclusion concerning it. I can compare it to nothing but a large door mat, ornamented at the edges with little tinkling tags something like the stained porcupine quills round an Indian moccasin. There was a hole or slit in the middle of this mat, as you see the same in South American ponchos. But could it be possible that any sober harpooneer would get into a door mat, and parade the streets of any Christian town in that sort of guise? I put it on, to try it, and it weighed me down like a hamper, being uncommonly shaggy and thick, and I thought a little damp, as though this mysterious harpooneer had been wearing it of a rainy day. I went up in it to a bit of glass stuck against the wall, and I never saw such a sight in my life. I tore myself out of it in such a hurry that I gave myself a kink in the neck.

I sat down on the side of the bed, and commenced thinking about this head-peddling harpooneer, and his door mat. After thinking some time on the bed-side, I got up and took off my monkey jacket, and then stood in the middle of the room thinking. I then took off my coat, and thought a little more in my shirt sleeves. But beginning to feel very cold now, half undressed as I was, and remembering what the landlord said about the harpooneer's not coming home at all that night, it being so very late, I made no more ado, but jumped out of my pantaloons and boots, and then blowing out the light tumbled into bed, and commended myself to the care of heaven.

Whether that mattress was stuffed with corn-cobs or broken crockery, there is no telling, but I rolled about a good deal, and could not sleep for a long time. At last I slid off into a light doze, and had pretty nearly made a good offing towards the land of Nod, when I heard a heavy footfall in the passage, and saw a glimmer of light come into the room from under the door.

Lord save me, thinks I, that must be the harpooneer, the infernal head-peddler. But I lay perfectly still, and resolved not to say a word till spoken to. Holding a light in one hand, and that identical New Zealand head in the other, the stranger entered the room, and without looking towards the bed, placed his candle a good way off from me on the floor in one corner, and then began working away at the knotted cords of the large bag I before spoke of as being in the room. I was all eagerness to see his face, but he kept it averted for some time while employed in unlacing the bag's mouth. This accomplished, however, he turned round – when, good heavens! what a sight! Such a face! It was of a dark, purplish, yellow color, here and there stuck over with large, blackish looking squares. Yes, it's just as I thought, he's a terrible bedfellow; he's been in a fight, got dreadfully cut, and here he is, just from the surgeon. But at that moment he chanced to turn his face so towards the light, that I plainly saw they could not be sticking-plasters at all, those black squares on his cheeks. They were stains of some sort or other. At first I knew not what to make of this; but soon an inkling of the truth occurred to me. I remembered a story of a white man – a whaleman too – who, falling among the cannibals, had been tattooed by them. I concluded that this harpooneer, in the course of his distant voyages, must have met with a similar adventure. And what is it, thought I, after all! It's only his outside; a man can be honest in any sort of skin. But then, what to make of his unearthly complexion, that part of it, I mean, lying round about, and completely independent of the squares of tattooing. To be sure, it might be nothing but a good coat of tropical tanning; but I never heard of a hot sun's tanning a white man into a purplish yellow one. However, I had never been in the South Seas; and perhaps the sun there produced these extraordinary effects upon the skin. Now, while all these ideas were passing through me like lightning, this harpooneer never noticed me at all. But, after some difficulty having opened his bag, he commenced fumbling in it, and presently pulled out a sort of tomahawk, and a seal-skin wallet with the hair on. Placing these on the old chest in the middle of the room, he then took the New Zealand head – a ghastly thing enough – and crammed it down into the bag. He now took off his hat – a new beaver hat, when I came nigh singing out with fresh surprise. There was no hair on his head – none to speak of at least – nothing but a small scalp-knot twisted up on his forehead. His bald purplish head now looked for all the world like a mildewed skull. Had not the stranger stood between me and the door, I would have bolted out of it quicker than ever I bolted a dinner.

Even as it was, I thought something of slipping out of the window, but it was the second floor back. I am no coward, but what to make of this head-peddling purple rascal altogether passed my comprehension. Ignorance is the parent of fear, and being completely nonplussed and confounded about the stranger, I confess I was now as much afraid of him as if it was the devil himself who had thus broken into my room at the dead of night. In fact, I was so afraid of him that I was not game enough just then to address him, and demand a satisfactory answer concerning what seemed inexplicable in him.

Meanwhile, he continued the business of undressing, and at last showed his chest and arms. As I live, these covered parts of him were checkered with the same squares as his face; his back, too, was all over the same dark squares; he seemed to have been in a Thirty Years' War, and just escaped from it with a sticking-plaster shirt. Still more, his very legs were marked, as if a parcel of dark green frogs were running up the trunks of young palms. It was now quite plain that he must be some abominable savage or other shipped aboard of a whaleman in the South Seas, and so landed in this Christian country. I quaked to think of it. A peddler of heads too – perhaps the heads of his own brothers. He might take a fancy to mine – heavens! look at that tomahawk!

But there was no time for shuddering, for now the savage went about something that completely fascinated my attention, and convinced me that he must indeed be a heathen. Going to his heavy grego, or wrapall, or dreadnaught, which he had previously hung on a chair, he fumbled in the pockets, and produced at length a curious deformed image with a hunch on its back, and exactly the colour of a three days' old Congo baby. Remembering the embalmed head, at first I almost thought that this black manikin was a real baby preserved in some similar manner. But seeing that it was not at all limber, and that it glistened a good deal like polished ebony, I concluded that it must be nothing but a wooden idol, which indeed it proved to be. For now the savage goes up to the empty fire-place, and removing the papered fire-board, sets up this little hunchbacked image, like a tenpin, between the andirons. The chimney jambs and all the bricks inside were very sooty, so that I thought this fire-place made a very appropriate little shrine or chapel for his Congo idol.

I now screwed my eyes hard towards the half hidden image, feeling but ill at ease meantime – to see what was next to follow. First he takes about a double handful of shavings out of his grego pocket, and places them carefully before the idol; then laying a bit of ship biscuit on top and applying the flame from the lamp, he kindled the shavings into a sacrificial blaze. Presently, after many hasty snatches into the fire, and still hastier withdrawals of his fingers (whereby he seemed to be scorching them badly), he at last succeeded in drawing out the biscuit; then blowing off the heat and ashes a little, he made a polite offer of it to the little negro. But the little devil did not seem to fancy such dry sort of fare at all; he never moved his lips. All these strange antics were accompanied by still stranger guttural noises from the devotee, who seemed to be praying in a sing-song or else singing some pagan psalmody or other, during which his face twitched about in the most unnatural manner. At last extinguishing the fire, he took the idol up very unceremoniously, and bagged it again in his grego pocket as carelessly as if he were a sportsman bagging a dead woodcock.

All these queer proceedings increased my uncomfortableness, and seeing him now exhibiting strong symptoms of concluding his business operations, and jumping into bed with me, I thought it was high time, now or never, before the light was put out, to break the spell in which I had so long been bound.

But the interval I spent in deliberating what to say, was a fatal one. Taking up his tomahawk from the table, he examined the head of it for an instant, and then holding it to the light, with his mouth at the handle, he puffed out great clouds of tobacco smoke. The next moment the light was extinguished, and this wild cannibal, tomahawk between his teeth, sprang into bed with me. I sang out, I could not help it now; and giving a sudden grunt of astonishment he began feeling me.

Stammering out something, I knew not what, I rolled away from him against the wall, and then conjured him, whoever or whatever he might be, to keep quiet, and let me get up and light the lamp again. But his guttural responses satisfied me at once that he but ill comprehended my meaning.

'Who-e debel you?' – he at last said – 'you no speak-e, dam-me, I kill-e.' And so saying the lighted tomahawk began flourishing about me in the dark.

'Landlord, for God's sake, Peter Coffin!' shouted I. 'Landlord! Watch! Coffin! Angels! save me!'

'Speak-e! tell-ee me whoo-ee be, or dam-me, I kill-e!' again growled the cannibal, while his horrid flourishings of the tomahawk scattered the hot tobacco ashes about me till I thought my linen would get on fire. But thank heaven, at that moment the landlord came into the room light in hand, and leaping from the bed I ran up to him.

'Don't be afraid now,' said he, grinning again. 'Queequeg here wouldn't harm a hair of your head.'

'Stop your grinning,' shouted I, 'and why didn't you tell me that that infernal harpooneer was a cannibal?'

'I thought ye know'd it; – didn't I tell ye, he was a peddlin' heads around town? – but turn flukes again and go to sleep. Queequeg, look here – you sabbee me, I sabbee you – this man sleepe you – you sabbee?' –

'Me sabbee plenty' – grunted Queequeg, puffing away at his pipe and sitting up in bed.

'You gettee in,' he added, motioning to me with his tomahawk, and throwing the clothes to one side. He really did this in not only a civil but a really kind and charitable way. I stood looking at him a moment. For all his tattooings he was on the whole a clean, comely looking cannibal. What's all this fuss I have been making about, thought I to myself – the man's a human being just as I am: he has just as much reason to fear me, as I have to be afraid of him. Better sleep with a sober cannibal than a drunken Christian.

'Landlord,' said I, 'tell him to stash his tomahawk there, or pipe, or whatever you call it; tell him to stop smoking, in short, and I will turn in with him. But I don't fancy having a man smoking in bed with me. It's dangerous. Besides, I ain't insured.'

This being told to Queequeg, he at once complied, and again politely motioned me to get into bed – rolling over to one side as much as to say – I wont touch a leg of ye.

'Good night, landlord,' said I, 'you may go.'

I turned in, and never slept better in my life.

4

THE COUNTERPANE

UPON waking next morning about daylight, I found Queequeg's arm thrown over me in the most loving and affectionate manner. You had almost thought I had been his wife. The counterpane was of patchwork, full of odd little parti-colored squares and triangles; and this arm of his tattooed all over with an interminable Cretan labyrinth of a figure, no two parts of which were of one precise shade – owing I suppose to his keeping his arm at sea unmethodically in sun and shade, his shirt sleeves irregularly rolled up at various times – this same arm of his, I say, looked for all the world like a strip of that same patchwork quilt. Indeed, partly lying on it as the arm did when I first awoke, I could hardly tell it from the quilt, they so blended their hues together; and it was only by the sense of weight and pressure that I could tell that Queequeg was hugging me.

My sensations were strange. Let me try to explain them. When I was a child, I well remember a somewhat similar circumstance that befell me; whether it was a reality or a dream, I never could entirely settle. The circumstance was this. I had been cutting up some caper or other – I think it was trying to crawl up the chimney, as I had seen a little sweep do a few days previous; and my stepmother who, somehow or other, was all the time whipping me, or sending me to bed supperless, – my mother dragged me by the legs out of the chimney and packed me off to bed, though it was only two o'clock in the afternoon of the 21st June, the longest day in the year in our hemisphere. I felt dreadfully. But there was no help for it, so up stairs I went to my little room in the third floor, undressed myself as slowly as possible so as to kill time, and with a bitter sigh got between the sheets.

I lay there dismally calculating that sixteen entire hours must elapse before I could hope for a resurrection. Sixteen hours in bed! the small of my back ached to think of it. And it was so light too; the sun shining in at the window, and a great rattling of coaches in the streets, and the sound of gay voices all over the house. I felt worse and worse – at last I got up, dressed, and softly going down in my stockinged feet, sought out my stepmother, and suddenly threw myself at her feet, beseeching her as a particular favor to give be a good slippering for my misbehavior; anything indeed but condemning me to lie abed such an unendurable length of time. But she was the best and most conscientious of stepmothers, and back I had to go to my room. For several hours I lay there broad awake, feeling a great deal worse than I have ever done since, even from the greatest subsequent misfortunes. At last I must have fallen into a troubled nightmare of a doze; and slowly waking from it – half steeped in dreams – I opened my eyes, and the before sun-lit room was now wrapped in outer darkness. Instantly I felt a shock running through all my frame; nothing was to be seen, and nothing was to be heard; but a supernatural hand seemed placed in mine. My arm hung over the counterpane, and the nameless, unimaginable, silent form or phantom, to which the hand belonged, seemed closely seated by my bedside. For what seemed ages piled on ages, I lay there, frozen with the most awful fears, not daring to drag away my hand; yet ever thinking that if I could but stir it one single inch, the horrid spell would be broken. I knew not how this consciousness at last glided away from me; but waking in the morning, I shudderingly remembered it all, and for days and weeks and months afterwards I lost myself in confounding attempts to explain the mystery. Nay, to this very hour, I often puzzle myself with it.

Now, take away the awful fear, and my sensations at feeling the supernatural hand in mine were very similar, in their strangeness, to those which I experienced on waking up and seeing Queequeg's pagan arm thrown round me. But at length all the past night's events soberly recurred, one by one, in fixed reality, and then I lay only alive to the comical predicament. For though I tried to move his arm – unlock his bridegroom clasp – yet, sleeping as he was, he still hugged me tightly, as though naught but death should part us twain. I now strove to rouse him – 'Queequeg!' – but his only answer was a snore. I then rolled over, my neck feeling as if it were in a horse-collar; and suddenly felt a slight scratch. Throwing aside the counterpane, there lay the tomahawk sleeping by the savage's side, as if it were a hatchet-faced baby. A pretty pickle, truly, thought I; abed here in a strange house in the broad day, with a cannibal and a tomahawk! 'Queequeg! – in the name of goodness, Queequeg, wake!' At length, by dint of much wriggling, and loud and incessant expostulations upon the unbecomingness of his hugging a fellow male in that matrimonial sort of style, I succeeded in extracting a grunt; and presently, he drew back his arm, shook himself all over like a Newfoundland dog just from the water, and sat up in bed, stiff as a pike-staff, looking at me, and rubbing his eyes as if he did not altogether remember how I came to be there, though a dim consciousness of knowing something about me seemed slowly dawning over him. Meanwhile, I lay quietly eyeing him, having no serious misgivings now, and bent upon narrowly observing so curious a creature. When, at last, his mind seemed made up touching the character of his bedfellow, and he became, as it were, reconciled to the fact; he jumped out upon the floor, and by certain signs and sounds gave me to understand that, if it pleased me, he would dress first and then leave me to dress afterwards, having the whole apartment to myself. Thinks I, Queequeg, under the circumstances, this is a very civilized overture; but, the truth is, these savages have an innate sense of delicacy, say what you will; it is marvellous how essentially polite they are. I pay this particular compliment to Queequeg, because he treated me with so much civility and consideration, while I was guilty of great rudeness; staring at him from the bed, and watching all his toilette motions; for the time my curiosity getting the better of my breeding. Nevertheless, a man like Queequeg you don't see every day, he and his ways were well worth unusual regarding.

He commenced dressing at top by donning his beaver hat, a very tall one, by the by, and then – still minus his trowsers – he hunted up his boots. What under the heavens he did it for, I cannot tell, but his next movement was to crush himself – boots in hand, and hat on – under the bed; when, from sundry violent gaspings and strainings, I inferred he was hard at work booting himself; though by no law of propriety that I ever heard of, is any man required to be private when putting on his boots. But Queequeg, do you see, was a creature in the transition state – neither caterpillar nor butterfly. He was just enough civilized to show off his outlandishness in the strangest possible manner. His education was not yet completed. He was an undergraduate. If he had not been a small degree civilized, he very probably would not have troubled himself with boots at all; but then, if he had not been still a savage, he never would have dreamt of getting under the bed to put them on. At last, he emerged with his hat very much dented and crushed down over his eyes, and began creaking and limping about the room, as if, not being much accustomed to boots, his pair of damp, wrinkled cowhide ones – probably not made to order either – rather pinched and tormented him at the first go off of a bitter cold morning.

Seeing, now, that there were no curtains to the window, and that the street being very narrow, the house opposite commanded a plain view into the room, and observing more and more the indecorous figure that Queequeg made, staving about with little else but his hat and boots on; I begged him as well as I could, to accelerate his toilet somewhat, and particularly to get into his pantaloons as soon as possible. He complied, and then proceeded to wash himself. At that time in the morning any Christian would have washed his face; but Queequeg, to my amazement, contented himself with restricting his ablutions to his chest, arms, and hands. He then donned his waistcoat, and taking up a piece of hard soap on the wash-stand centre-table, dipped it into water and commenced lathering his face. I was watching to see where he kept his razor, when lo and behold, he takes the harpoon from the bed corner, slips out the long wooden stock, unsheathes the head, whets it a little on his boot, and striding up to the bit of mirror against the wall, begins a vigorous scraping, or rather harpooning of his cheeks. Thinks I, Queequeg, this is using Rogers's best cutlery with a vengeance. Afterwards I wondered the less at this operation when I came to know of what fine steel the head of a harpoon is made, and how exceedingly sharp the long straight edges are always kept.

The rest of his toilet was soon achieved, and he proudly marched out of the room, wrapped up in his great pilot monkey jacket, and sporting his harpoon like a marshal's baton.

5

BREAKFAST

I QUICKLY followed suit, and descending into the bar-room accosted the grinning landlord very pleasantly. I cherished no malice towards him, though he had been skylarking with me not a little in the matter of my bedfellow.

However, a good laugh is a mighty good thing, and rather too scarce a good thing; the more's the pity. So, if any one man, in his own proper person, afford stuff for a good joke to anybody, let him not be backward, but let him cheerfully allow himself to spend and be spent in that way. And the man that has anything bountifully laughable about him, be sure there is more in that man than you perhaps think for.

The bar-room was now full of the boarders who had been dropping in the night previous, and whom I had not as yet had a good look at. They were nearly all whalemen; chief mates, and second mates, and third mates, and sea carpenters, and sea coopers, and sea blacksmiths, and harpooneers, and ship keepers; a brown and brawny company, with bosky beards; an unshorn, shaggy set, all wearing monkey jackets for morning gowns.

You could pretty plainly tell how long each one had been ashore. This young fellow's healthy cheek is like a sun-toasted pear in hue, and would seem to smell almost as musky; he cannot have been three days landed from his Indian voyage. That man next him looks a few shades lighter; you might say a touch of satin wood is in him. In the complexion of a third still lingers a tropic tawn, but slightly bleached withal; *he* doubtless has tarried whole weeks ashore. But who could show a cheek like Queequeg? which, barred with various tints, seemed like the Andes' western slope, to show forth in one array, contrasting climates, zone by zone.

'Grub, ho!' now cried the landlord, flinging open a door, and in we went to breakfast.

They say that men who have seen the world, thereby become quite at ease in manner, quite self-possessed in company. Not always, though: Ledyard, the great New Englander traveller, and Mungo Park, the Scotch one; of all men, they possessed the least assurance in the parlor. But perhaps the mere crossing of Siberia in a sledge drawn by dogs as Ledyard did, or the taking a long solitary walk on an empty stomach, in the negro heart of Africa, which was the sum of poor Mungo's performances – this kind of travel, I say, may not be the very best mode of attaining a high social polish. Still, for the most part, that sort of thing is to be had anywhere.

These reflections just here are occasioned by the circumstance that after we were all seated at the table, and I was preparing to hear some good stories about whaling; to my no small surprise, nearly every man maintained a profound silence. And not only that, but they looked embarrassed. Yes, here were a set of sea-dogs, many of whom without the slightest bashfulness had boarded great whales on the high seas – entire strangers to them – and duelled them dead without winking; and yet, here they sat at a social breakfast table – all of the same calling, all of kindred tastes – looking round as sheepishly at each other as though they had never been out of sight of some sheepfold among the Green Mountains. A curious sight; these bashful bears, these timid warrior whalemen!

But as for Queequeg – why, Queequeg sat there among them – at the head of the table, too, it so chanced; as cool as an icicle. To be sure I cannot say much for his breeding. His greatest admirer could not have cordially justified his bringing his harpoon into breakfast with him, and using it there without ceremony; reaching over the table with it, to the imminent jeopardy of many heads, and grappling the beefsteaks towards him. But *that* was certainly very coolly done by him, and every one knows that in most people's estimation, to do anything coolly is to do it genteelly.

We will not speak of all Queequeg's peculiarities here; how he eschewed coffee and hot rolls, and applied his undivided attention to beefsteaks, done rare. Enough, that when breakfast was over he withdrew like the rest into the public room, lighted his tomahawk-pipe, and was sitting there quietly digesting and smoking with his inseparable hat on, when I sallied out for a stroll.

6

THE STREET

IF I had been astonished at first catching a glimpse of so outlandish an individual as Queequeg circulating among the polite society of a civilized town, that astonishment soon departed upon taking my first daylight stroll through the streets of New Bedford.

In thoroughfares nigh the docks, any considerable seaport will frequently offer to view the queerest looking nondescripts from foreign parts. Even in Broadway and Chestnut streets, Mediterranean mariners will sometimes jostle the affrighted ladies. Regent street is not unknown to Lascars and Malays; and at Bombay, in the Apollo Green, live Yankees have often scared the natives. But New Bedford beats all Water street and Wapping. In these last-mentioned haunts you see only sailors; but in New Bedford, actual cannibals stand chatting at street corners; savages outright; many of whom yet carry on their bones unholy flesh. It makes a stranger stare.

But, besides the Feegeeans, Tongatabooans, Erromanggoans, Pannangians, and Brighggians, and, besides the wild specimens of the whaling-craft which unheeded reel about the streets, you will see other sights still more curious, certainly more comical. There weekly arrive in this town scores of green Vermonters and New Hampshire men, all athirst for gain and glory in the fishery. They are mostly young, of stalwart frames; fellows who have felled forests, and now seek to drop the axe and snatch the whale-lance. Many are as green as the Green Mountains whence they came. In some things you would think them but a few hours old. Look there! that chap strutting round the corner. He wears a beaver hat and swallow-tailed coat, girdled with a sailor-belt and sheath-knife. Here comes another with a sou'-wester and a bombazine cloak.

No town-bred dandy will compare with a country-bred one – I mean a downright bumpkin dandy – a fellow that, in the dog-days, will mow his two acres in buckskin gloves for fear of tanning his hands. Now when a country dandy like this takes it into his head to make a distinguished reputation, and joins the great whale-fishery, you should see the comical things he does upon reaching the seaport. In bespeaking his sea-outfit, he orders bell-buttons to his waistcoats; straps to his canvas trowsers. Ah, poor Hay-Seed! how bitterly will burst those straps in the first howling gale, when thou art driven, straps, buttons, and all, down the throat of the tempest.

But think not that this famous town has only harpooneers, cannibals, and bumpkins to show her visitors. Not at all. Still New Bedford is a queer place. Had it not been for us whalemen, that tract of land would this day perhaps have been in as howling condition as the coast of Labrador. As it is, parts of her back country are enough to frighten one, they look so bony. The town itself is perhaps the dearest place to live in, in all New England. It is a land of oil, true enough: but not like Canaan; a land, also, of corn and wine. The streets do not run with milk; nor in the spring-time do they pave them with fresh eggs. Yet, in spite of this, nowhere in all America will you find more patrician-like houses, parks and gardens more opulent, than in New Bedford. Whence came they? how planted upon this once scraggy scoria of a country?

Go and gaze upon the iron emblematical harpoons round yonder lofty mansion, and your question will be answered. Yes; all these brave houses and flowery gardens came from the Atlantic, Pacific, and Indian oceans. One and all, they were harpooned and dragged up hither from the bottom of the sea. Can Herr Alexander perform a feat like that?

In New Bedford, fathers, they say, give whales for dowers to their daughters, and portion off their nieces with a few porpoises a-piece. You must go to New Bedford to see a brilliant wedding; for, they say, they have reservoirs of oil in every house, and every night recklessly burn their lengths in spermaceti candles.

In summer time, the town is sweet to see; full of fine maples – long avenues of green and gold. And in August, high in air, the beautiful and bountiful horse-chestnuts, candelabra-wise, proffer the passer-by their tapering upright cones of congregated blossoms. So omnipotent is art; which in many a district of New Bedford has superinduced bright terraces of flowers upon the barren refuse rocks thrown aside at creation's final day.

And the women of New Bedford, they bloom like their own red roses. But roses only bloom in summer; whereas the fine carnation of their cheeks is perennial as sunlight in the seventh heavens. Elsewhere match that bloom of theirs, ye cannot, save in Salem, where they tell me the young girls breathe such musk, their sailor sweethearts smell them miles off shore, as though they were drawing nigh the odorous Moluccas instead of the Puritanic sands.

7

THE CHAPEL

In this same New Bedford there stands a Whaleman's Chapel, and few are the moody fishermen, shortly bound for the Indian Ocean or Pacific, who fail to make a Sunday visit to the spot. I am sure that I did not.

Returning from my first morning stroll, I again sallied out upon this special errand. The sky had changed from clear, sunny cold, to driving sleet and mist. Wrapping myself in my shaggy jacket of the cloth called bearskin, I fought my way against the stubborn storm. Entering, I found a small scattered congregation of sailors, and sailors' wives and widows. A muffled silence reigned, only broken at times by the shrieks of the storm. Each silent worshipper seemed purposely sitting apart from the other, as if each silent grief were insular and incommunicable. The chaplain had not yet arrived; and there these silent islands of men and women sat steadfastly eyeing several marble tablets, with black borders, masoned into the wall on either side the pulpit. Three of them ran something like the following, but I do not pretend to quote:

SACRED

To the Memory

OF

JOHN TALBOT,

Who, at the age of eighteen, was lost overboard,
Near the Isle of Desolation, off Patagonia,
November 1st, 1836.

THIS TABLET

Is erected to his Memory

BY HIS SISTER

SACRED

To the Memory

OF

ROBERT LONG, WILLIS ELLERY,
NATHAN COLEMAN, WALTER CANNY,
SETH MACY, AND SAMUEL GLEIG,

Forming one of the boats' crews

OF

THE SHIP ELIZA,

Who were towed out of sight by a Whale,
On the Off-shore Ground in the
PACIFIC,
December 31st, 1839.

THIS MARBLE

Is here placed by their surviving

SHIPMATES.

SACRED

To the Memory

OF

The late

CAPTAIN EZEKIEL HARDY,

Who in the bows of his boat was killed by a
Sperm Whale on the coast of Japan,
August 3d, 1833.

THIS TABLET

Is erected to his Memory

BY

HIS WIDOW.

Shaking off the sleet from my ice-glazed hat and jacket, I seated myself near the door, and turning sideways was surprised to see Queequeg near me. Affected by the solemnity of the scene, there was a wondering gaze of incredulous curiosity in his countenance. This savage was the only person present who seemed to notice my entrance; because he was the only one who could not read, and, therefore, was not reading those frigid inscriptions on the wall. Whether any of the relatives of the seamen whose names appeared there were now among the congregation, I knew not; but so many are the unrecorded accidents in the fishery, and so plainly did several women present wear the countenance if not the trappings of some unceasing grief, that I feel sure that here before me were assembled those, in whose unhealing hearts the sight of those bleak tablets sympathetically caused the old wounds to bleed afresh.

Oh! ye whose dead lie buried beneath the green grass; who standing among flowers can say – here, *here* lies my beloved, ye know not the desolation that broods in bosoms like these. What bitter blanks in those black-bordered marbles which cover no ashes! What despair in those immovable inscriptions! What deadly voids and unbidden infidelities in the lines that seem to gnaw upon all Faith, and refuse resurrections to the beings who have placelessly perished without a grave. As well might those tablets stand in the cave of Elephanta as here.

In what census of living creatures, the dead of mankind are included; why it is that a universal proverb says of them, that they tell no tales, though containing more secrets than the Goodwin Sands; how it is that to his name who yesterday departed for the other world, we prefix so significant and infidel a word, and yet do not thus entitle him, if he but embarks for the remotest Indies of this living earth; why the Life Insurance Companies pay death-forfeitures upon immortals; in what eternal, unstirring paralysis, and deadly, hopeless trance, yet lies antique Adam who died sixty round centuries ago; how it is that we still refuse to be comforted for those who we nevertheless maintain are dwelling in unspeakable bliss; why all the living so strive to hush all the dead; wherefore but the rumor of a knocking in a tomb will terrify a whole city. All these things are not without their meanings.

But Faith, like a jackal, feeds among the tombs, and even from these dead doubts she gathers her most vital hope.

It needs scarcely to be told, with what feelings, on the eve of a Nantucket voyage, I regarded those marble tablets, and by the murky light of that darkened, doleful day read the fate of the whalemen who had gone before me. Yes, Ishmael, the same fate may be thine. But somehow I grew merry again. Delightful inducements to embark, fine chance for promotion, it seems – aye, a stove boat will make me an immortal by brevet. Yes, there is death in this business of whaling – a speechlessly quick chaotic bundling of a man into Eternity. But what then? Methinks we have hugely mistaken this matter of Life and Death. Methinks that what they call my shadow here on earth is my true substance. Methinks that in looking at things spiritual, we are too much like oysters observing the sun through the water, and thinking that thick water the thinnest of air. Methinks my body is but the lees of my better being. In fact take my body who will, take it I say, it is not me. And therefore three cheers for Nantucket; and come a stove boat and stove body when they will, for stave my soul, Jove himself cannot.

8

THE PULPIT

I HAD not been seated very long ere a man of a certain venerable robustness entered; immediately as the storm-pelted door flew back upon admitting him, a quick regardful eyeing of him by all the congregation, sufficiently attested that this fine old man was the chaplain. Yes, it was the famous Father Mapple, so called by the whalemen, among whom he was a very great favorite. He had been a sailor and a harpooneer in his youth, but for many years past had dedicated his life to the ministry. At the time I now write of, Father Mapple was in the hardy winter of a healthy old age; that sort of old age which seems merging into a second flowering youth, for among all the fissures of his wrinkles, there shone certain mild gleams of a newly developing bloom – the spring verdure peeping forth even beneath February's snow. No one having previously heard his history, could for the first time behold Father Mapple without the utmost interest, because there were certain engrafted clerical peculiarities about him, imputable to that adventurous maritime life he had led. When he entered I observed that he carried no umbrella, and certainly had not come in his carriage, for his tarpaulin hat ran down with melting sleet, and his great pilot cloth jacket seemed almost to drag him to the floor with the weight of the water it had absorbed. However, hat and coat and overshoes were one by one removed, and hung up in a little space in an adjacent corner; when, arrayed in a decent suit, he quietly approached the pulpit.

Like most old fashioned pulpits, it was a very lofty one, and since a regular stairs to such a height would, by its long angle with the floor, seriously contract the already small area of the chapel, the architect, it seemed, had acted upon the hint of Father Mapple, and finished the pulpit without a stairs, substituting a perpendicular side ladder, like those used in mounting a ship from a boat at sea. The wife of a whaling captain had provided the chapel with a handsome pair of red worsted man-ropes for this ladder, which, being itself nicely headed, and stained with a mahogany color, the whole contrivance, considering what manner of chapel it was, seemed by no means in bad taste. Halting for an instant at the foot of the ladder, and with both hands grasping the ornamental knobs of the man-ropes, Father Mapple cast a look upwards, and then with a truly sailor-like but still reverential dexterity, hand over hand, mounted the steps as if ascending the main-top of his vessel.

The perpendicular parts of this side ladder, as is usually

the case with swinging ones, were of cloth-covered rope, only the rounds were of wood, so that at every step there was a joint. At my first glimpse of the pulpit, it had not escaped me that however convenient for a ship, these joints in the present instance seemed unnecessary. For I was not prepared to see Father Mapple after gaining the height, slowly turn round, and stooping over the pulpit, deliberately drag up the ladder step by step, till the whole was deposited within, leaving him impregnable in his little Quebec.

I pondered some time without fully comprehending the reason for this. Father Mapple enjoyed such a wide reputation for sincerity and sanctity, that I could not suspect him of courting notoriety by any mere tricks of the stage. No, thought I, there must be some sober reason for this thing; furthermore, it must symbolize something unseen. Can it be, then, that by that act of physical isolation, he signifies his spiritual withdrawal for the time, from all outward worldly ties and connexions? Yes, for replenished with the meat and wine of the word, to the faithful man of God, this pulpit, I see, is a self-containing strong-hold – a lofty Ehrenbreitstein, with a perennial well of water within the walls.

But the side ladder was not the only strange feature of the place, borrowed from the chaplain's former sea-farings. Between the marble cenotaphs on either hand of the pulpit, the wall which formed its back was adorned with a large painting representing a gallant ship beating against a terrible storm off a lee coast of black rocks and snowy breakers. But high above the flying scud and dark-rolling clouds, there floated a little isle of sunlight, from which beamed forth an angel's face; and this bright face shed a distinct spot of radiance upon the ship's tossed deck, something like that silver plate now inserted into the Victory's plank where Nelson fell. 'Ah, noble ship,' the angel seemed to say, 'beat on, beat on, thou noble ship, and bear a hardy helm; for lo! the sun is breaking through; the clouds are rolling off – serenest azure is at hand.'

Nor was the pulpit itself without a trace of the same sea-taste that had achieved the ladder and the picture. Its panelled front was in the likeness of a ship's bluff bows, and the Holy Bible rested on a projecting piece of scroll work, fashioned after a ship's fiddle-headed beak.

What could be more full of meaning? – for the pulpit is ever this earth's foremost part; all the rest comes in its rear; the pulpit leads the world. From thence it is the storm of God's quick wrath is first descried, and the bow must bear the earliest brunt. From thence it is the God of breezes fair or foul is first invoked for favorable winds. Yes, the world's a ship on its passage out, and not a voyage complete; and the pulpit is its prow.

9

THE SERMON

FATHER MAPPLE rose, and in a mild voice of unassuming authority ordered the scattered people to condense. 'Starboard gangway, there! side away to larboard – larboard gangway to starboard! Midships! midships!'

There was a low rumbling of heavy sea-boots among the benches, and a still slighter shuffling of women's shoes, and all was quiet again, and every eye on the preacher.

He paused a little; then kneeling in the pulpit's bows, folded his large brown hands across his chest, uplifted his closed eyes, and offered a prayer so deeply devout that he seemed kneeling and praying at the bottom of the sea.

This ended, in prolonged solemn tones, like the continual tolling of a bell in a ship that is foundering at sea in a fog – in such tones he commenced reading the following hymn; but changing his manner towards the concluding stanzas, burst forth with a pealing exultation and joy –

The ribs and terrors in the whale,
Arched over me a dismal gloom,
While all God's sun-lit waves rolled by,
And lift me deepening down to doom.

I saw the opening maw of hell,
  With endless pains and sorrows there;
Which none but they that feel can tell –
  Oh, I was plunging to despair.

In black distress, I called my God,
  When I could scarce believe him mine,
He bowed his ear to my complaints –
  No more the whale did me confine.

With speed he flew to my relief,
  As on a radiant dolphin borne;
Awful, yet bright, as lightning shone
  The face of my Deliverer God.

My song for ever shall record
  That terrible, that joyful hour;
I give the glory to my God,
  His all the mercy and the power.

Nearly all joined in singing this hymn, which swelled high above the howling of the storm. A brief pause ensued; the preacher slowly turned over the leaves of the Bible, and at last, folding his hand down upon the proper page, said: 'Beloved shipmates, clinch the last verse of the first chapter of Jonah – "And God had prepared a great fish to swallow up Jonah."

'Shipmates, this book, containing only four chapters – four yarns – is one of the smallest strands in the mighty cable of the Scriptures. Yet what depths of the soul does Jonah's deep sea-line sound! what a pregnant lesson to us is this prophet! What a noble thing is that canticle in the fish's belly! How billow-like and boisterously grand! We feel the floods surging over us; we sound with him to the kelpy bottom of the waters; sea-weed and all the slime of the sea is about us! But *what* is this lesson that the book of Jonah teaches? Shipmates, it is a two-stranded lesson; a lesson to us all as sinful men, and a lesson to me as a pilot of the living God. As sinful men, it is a lesson to us all, because it is a story of the sin, hard-heartedness, suddenly awakened fears, the swift punishment, repentance, prayers, and finally the deliverance and joy of Jonah. As with all sinners among men, the sin of this son of Amittai was in his wilful disobedience of the command of God – never mind now what that command was, or how conveyed – which he found a hard command. But all the things that God would have us do are hard for us to do – remember that – and hence, he oftener commands us than endeavors to persuade. And if we obey God, we must disobey ourselves; and it is in this disobeying ourselves, wherein the hardness of obeying God consists.

'With this sin of disobedience in him, Jonah still further flouts at God, by seeking to flee from Him. He thinks that a ship made by men, will carry him into countries where God does not reign, but only the Captains of this earth. He skulks about the wharves of Joppa, and seeks a ship that's bound for Tarshish. There lurks, perhaps, a hitherto unheeded meaning here. By all accounts Tarshish could have been no other city than the modern Cadiz. That's the opinion of learned men. And where is Cadiz, shipmates? Cadiz is in Spain; as far by water, from Joppa, as Jonah could possibly have sailed in those ancient days, when the Atlantic was an almost unknown sea. Because Joppa, the modern Jaffa, shipmates, is on the most easterly coast of the Mediterranean, the Syrian; and Tarshish or Cadiz more than two thousand miles to the westward from that, just outside the Straits of Gibraltar. See ye not then, shipmates, that Jonah sought to flee world-wide from God? Miserable man! Oh! most contemptible and worthy of all scorn; with slouched hat and guilty eye, skulking from his God; prowling among the shipping like a vile burglar hastening to cross the sea. So disordered, self-condemning is his look, that had there been policemen in those days, Jonah, on the mere suspicion of something wrong, had been arrested ere he touched a deck. How plainly he's a fugitive! no baggage, not a hat-box, valise, or carpet-bag, – no friends accompany him to the wharf with their adieux. At last, after much dodging search, he finds the Tarshish ship receiving the last items of her cargo; and as he steps on board to see its

Captain in the cabin, all the sailors for the moment desist from hoisting in the goods, to mark the stranger's evil eye. Jonah sees this; but in vain he tries to look all ease and confidence; in vain essays his wretched smile. Strong intuitions of the man assure the mariners he can be no innocent. In their gamesome but still serious way, one whispers to the other – "Jack, he's robbed a widow;" or, "Joe, do you mark him; he's a bigamist;" or, "Harry lad, I guess he's the adulterer that broke jail in old Gomorrah, or belike, one of the missing murderers from Sodom." Another runs to read the bill that's stuck against the spile upon the wharf to which the ship is moored, offering five hundred gold coins for the apprehension of a parricide, and containing a description of his person. He reads, and looks from Jonah to the bill; while all his sympathetic shipmates now crowd round Jonah, prepared to lay their hands upon him. Frighted Jonah trembles, and summoning all his boldness to his face, only looks so much the more a coward. He will not confess himself suspected; but that itself is strong suspicion. So he makes the best of it; and when the sailors find him not to be the man that is advertised, they let him pass, and he descends into the cabin.

'"Who's there?" cries the Captain at his busy desk, hurriedly making out his papers for the Customs – "Who's there?" Oh! how that harmless question mangles Jonah! For the instant he almost turns to flee again. But he rallies. "I seek a passage in this ship to Tarshish; how soon sail ye, sir?" Thus far the busy Captain had not looked up to Jonah, though the man now stands before him; but no sooner does he hear that hollow voice, than he darts a scrutinizing glance. "We sail with the next coming tide," at last he slowly answered, still intently eyeing him. "No sooner, sir?" – "Soon enough for any honest man that goes a passenger." Ha! Jonah, that's another stab. But he swiftly calls away the Captain from that scent. "I'll sail with ye," – he says, – "the passage money, how much is that? – I'll pay now." For it is particularly written, shipmates, as if it were a thing not to be overlooked in this history, "that he paid the fare thereof" ere the craft did sail. And taken with the context, this is full of meaning.

'Now Jonah's Captain, shipmates, was one whose discernment detects crime in any, but whose cupidity exposes it only in the penniless. In this world, shipmates, sin that pays its way can travel freely, and without a passport; whereas Virtue, if a pauper, is stopped at all frontiers. So Jonah's Captain prepares to test the length of Jonah's purse, ere he judge him openly. He charges him thrice the usual sum; and it's assented to. Then the Captain knows that Jonah is a fugitive; but at the same time resolves to help a flight that paves its rear with gold. Yet when Jonah fairly takes out his purse, prudent suspicions still molest the Captain. He rings every coin to find a counterfeit. Not a forger, any way, he mutters; and Jonah is put down for his passage. "Point out my state-room, Sir," says Jonah now, "I'm travel-weary; I need sleep." "Thou look'st like it," says the Captain, "there's thy room." Jonah enters, and would lock the door, but the lock contains no key. Hearing him foolishly fumbling there, the Captain laughs lowly to himself, and mutters something about the doors of convicts' cells being never allowed to be locked within. All dressed and dusty as he is, Jonah throws himself into his berth, and finds the little state-room ceiling almost resting on his forehead. The air is close, and Jonah gasps. Then, in that contracted hole, sunk, too, beneath the ship's water-line, Jonah feels the heralding presentiment of that stifling hour, when the whale shall hold him in the smallest of his bowel's wards.

'Screwed at its axis against the side, a swinging lamp slightly oscillates in Jonah's room; and the ship, heeling over towards the wharf with the weight of the last bales received, the lamp, flame and all, though in slight motion, still maintains a permanent obliquity with reference to the room; though, in truth, infallibly straight itself, it but made obvious the false, lying levels among which it hung. The lamp alarms and frightens Jonah; as lying in his berth his tormented eyes roll round the place, and this thus far successful fugitive finds no refuge for his restless glance. But that contradiction in the lamp more and more appals him. The floor, the ceiling, and the side, are all awry. "Oh! so my conscience hangs in me!" he groans, "straight upward, so it burns; but the chambers of my soul are all in crookedness!"

'Like one who after a night of drunken revelry hies to his bed, still reeling, but with conscience yet pricking him, as the plungings of the Roman race-horse but so much the more strike his steel tags into him; as one who in that miserable plight still turns and turns in giddy anguish, praying God for annihilation until the fit be passed; and at last amid the whirl of woe he feels, a deep stupor steals over him, as over the man who bleeds to death, for conscience is the wound, and there's naught to staunch it; so, after sore wrestlings in his berth, Jonah's prodigy of ponderous misery drags him drowning down to sleep.

'And now the time of tide has come; the ship casts off her cables; and from the deserted wharf the uncheered ship for Tarshish, all careening, glides to sea. That ship, my friends, was the first of recorded smugglers! the contraband was Jonah. But the sea rebels; he will not bear the wicked burden. A dreadful storm comes on, the ship is like to break. But now when the boatswain calls all hands to lighten her; when boxes, bales, and jars are clattering overboard; when the wind is shrieking, and the men are yelling, and every plank thunders with trampling feet right over Jonah's head; in all this raging tumult, Jonah sleeps his hideous sleep. He sees no black sky and raging sea, feels not the reeling timbers, and little hears he or heeds he the far rush of the mighty whale, which even now with open mouth is cleaving the seas after him. Aye, shipmates, Jonah was gone down into the sides of the ship – a berth in the cabin as I have taken it, and was fast asleep. But the frightened master comes to him, and shrieks in his dead ear, "What meanest thou, O sleeper! arise!" Startled from his lethargy by that direful cry, Jonah staggers to his feet, and stumbling to the deck, grasps a shroud, to look out upon the sea. But at that moment he is sprung upon by a panther billow leaping over the bulwarks. Wave after wave thus leaps into the ship, and finding no speedy vent runs roaring fore and aft, till the mariners come nigh to drowning while yet afloat. And ever, as the white moon shows her affrighted face from the steep gullies in the blackness overhead, aghast Jonah sees the rearing bowsprit pointing high upward, but soon beat downward again towards the tormented deep.

'Terrors upon terrors run shouting through his soul. In all his cringing attitudes, the God-fugitive is now too plainly known. The sailors mark him; more and more certain grow their suspicions of him, and at last, fully to test the truth, by referring the whole matter to high Heaven, they fall to casting lots, to see for whose cause this great tempest was upon them. The lot is Jonah's; that discovered, then how furiously they mob him with their questions. "What is thine occupation? Whence comest thou? Thy country? What people?" But mark now, my shipmates, the behavior of poor Jonah. The eager mariners but ask him who he is, and where from; whereas, they not only receive an answer to those questions, but likewise another answer to a question not put by them, but the unsolicited answer is forced from Jonah by the hard hand of God that is upon him.

'"I am a Hebrew," he cries – and then – "I fear the Lord the God of Heaven who hath made the sea and the dry land!" Fear him, O Jonah? Aye, well mightest thou fear the Lord God *then*! Straightway, he now goes on to make a full confession; whereupon the mariners become more and more appalled, but still are pitiful. For when Jonah, not yet supplicating God for mercy, since he but too well knew the darkness of his deserts, – when wretched Jonah cries out to them to take him and cast him forth into the sea, for he knew that for *his* sake this great tempest was upon them; they mercifully turn from him, and seek by other means to save the ship. But all in vain; the indignant gale howls louder; then, with one hand raised invokingly to God, with the other they not unreluctantly lay hold of Jonah.

'And now behold Jonah taken up as an anchor and dropped into the sea; when instantly an oily calmness floats out from the east, and the sea is still, as Jonah carries down the gale with him, leaving smooth water behind. He goes down in the whirling heart of such a masterless commotion that he scarce heeds the moment when he drops seething into the yawning jaws awaiting him; and the whale shoots-to all his ivory teeth, like so many white bolts, upon his prison. Then Jonah prayed unto the Lord out of the fish's belly. But observe his prayer, and learn a weighty lesson. For sinful as he is, Jonah does not weep and wail for direct deliverance. He feels that his dreadful punishment is just. He leaves all his deliverance to God, contenting himself with this, that spite of all his pains and pangs, he will still look towards His holy temple. And here, shipmates, is true and faithful repentance; not clamorous for pardon, but grateful for punishment. And how pleasing to God was this conduct in Jonah, is shown in the eventual deliverance of him from the sea and the whale. Shipmates, I do not place Jonah before you to be copied for his sin but I do place him before you as a model for repentance. Sin not; but if you do, take heed to repent of it like Jonah.'

While he was speaking these words, the howling of the shrieking, slanting storm without seemed to add new power to the preacher, who, when describing Jonah's sea-storm, seemed tossed by a storm himself. His deep chest heaved as with a ground-swell; his tossed arms seemed the warring elements at work; and the thunders that rolled away from off his swarthy brow, and the light leaping from his eye, made all his simple hearers look on him with a quick fear that was strange to them.

There now came a lull in his look, as he silently turned over the leaves of the Book once more; and, at last, standing motionless, with closed eyes, for the moment, seemed communing with God and himself.

But again he leaned over towards the people, and bowing his head lowly, with an aspect of the deepest yet manliest humility, he spake these words:

'Shipmates, God has laid but one hand upon you; both his hands press upon me. I have read ye by what murky light may be mine the lesson that Jonah teaches to all sinners; and therefore to ye, and still more to me, for I am a greater sinner than ye. And now how gladly would I come down from this mast-head and sit on the hatches there where you sit, and listen as you listen, while some one of you reads *me* that other and more awful lesson which Jonah teaches to *me*, as a pilot of the living God. How being an anointed pilot-prophet, or speaker of true things, and bidden by the Lord to sound those unwelcome truths in the ears of a wicked Nineveh, Jonah, appalled at the hostility he should raise, fled from his mission, and sought to escape his duty and his God by taking ship at Joppa. But God is everywhere; Tarshish he never reached. As we have seen, God came upon him in the whale, and swallowed him down to living gulfs of doom, and with swift slantings tore him along "into the midst of the seas," where the eddying depths sucked him ten thousand fathoms down, and "the weeds were wrapped about his head," and all the watery world of woe bowled over him. Yet even then beyond the reach of any plummet – "out of the belly of hell" – when the whale grounded upon the ocean's utmost bones, even then, God heard the engulphed, repenting prophet when he cried. Then God spake unto the fish; and from the shuddering cold and blackness of the sea, the whale came breeching up towards the warm and pleasant sun, and all the delights of air and earth; and "vomited out Jonah upon the dry land;" when the word of the Lord came a second time; and Jonah, bruised and beaten – his ears, like two sea-shells, still multitudinously murmuring of the ocean – Jonah did the Almighty's bidding. And what was that, shipmates? To preach the Truth to the face of Falsehood! That was it!

'This, shipmates, this is that other lesson; and woe to that pilot of the living God who slights it. Woe to him whom this world charms from Gospel duty! Woe to him who seeks to pour oil upon the waters when God has brewed them into a gale! Woe to him who seeks to please rather than to appal! Woe to him whose good name is more to him than goodness! Woe to him who, in this world, courts not dishonor! Woe to him who would not be true, even though to be false were salvation! Yea, woe to him who, as the great Pilot Paul has it, while preaching to others is himself a castaway!'

He drooped and fell away from himself for a moment; then lifting his face to them again, showed a deep joy in his eyes, as he cried out with a heavenly enthusiasm, – 'But oh! shipmates! on the starboard hand of every woe, there is a sure delight; and higher the top of that delight, than the bottom of the woe is deep. Is not the main-truck higher than the kelson is low? Delight is to him – a far, far upward, and inward delight – who against the proud gods and commodores of this earth, ever stands forth his own inexorable self. Delight is to him whose strong arms yet support him, when the ship of this base treacherous world has gone down beneath him. Delight is to him, who gives no quarter in the truth, and kills, burns, and destroys all sin though he pluck it out from under the robes of Senators and Judges. Delight, – top-gallant delight is to him, who acknowledges no law or lord, but the Lord his God, and is only a patriot to heaven. Delight is to him, whom all the waves of the billows of the seas of the boisterous mob can never shake from this sure Keel of the Ages. And eternal delight and deliciousness will be his, who coming to lay him down, can say with his final breath – O Father! – chiefly known to me by Thy rod – mortal or immortal, here I die. I have striven to be Thine, more than to be this world's, or mine own. Yet this is nothing; I leave eternity to Thee; for what is man that he should live out the lifetime of his God?'

He said no more, but slowly waving a benediction, covered his face with his hands, and so remained kneeling, till all the people had departed, and he was left alone in the place.

10

A BOSOM FRIEND

RETURNING to the Spouter-Inn from the Chapel, I found Queequeg there quite alone; he having left the Chapel before the benediction some time. He was sitting on a bench before the fire, with his feet on the stove hearth, and in one hand was holding close up to his face that little negro idol of his; peering hard into its face, and with a jack-knife gently whittling away at its nose, meanwhile humming to himself in his heathenish way.

But being now interrupted, he put up the image; and pretty soon, going to the table, took up a large book there, and placing it on his lap began counting the pages with deliberate regularity; at every fiftieth page – as I fancied – stopping a moment, looking vacantly around him, and giving utterance to a long-drawn gurgling whistle of astonishment. He would then begin again at the next fifty; seeming to commence at number one each time, as though he could not count more than fifty, and it was only by such a large number of fifties being found together, that his astonishment at the multitude of pages was excited.

With much interest I sat watching him. Savage though he was, and hideously marred about the face – at least to my taste – his countenance yet had a something in it which was by no means disagreeable. You cannot hide the soul. Through all his unearthly tattooings, I thought I saw the traces of a simple honest heart; and in his large, deep eyes, fiery black and bold, there seemed tokens of a spirit that would dare a thousand devils. And besides all this, there was a certain lofty bearing about the Pagan, which even his uncouthness could not altogether maim. He looked like a man who had never cringed and never had had a creditor. Whether it was, too, that his head being shaved, his forehead was drawn out in freer and brighter relief, and looked more expansive than it otherwise would, this I will not venture to decide; but certain it was his head was phrenologically an excellent one. It may seem ridiculous, but it reminded me of General Washington's head, as seen in the popular busts of him. It had the same long regularly graded retreating slope from above the brows, which were likewise very projecting, like two long promontories thickly wooded on top. Queequeg was George Washington cannibalistically developed.

Whilst I was thus closely scanning him, half-pretending meanwhile to be looking out at the storm from the casement, he never heeded my presence, never troubled himself with so much as a single glance; but appeared wholly occupied with counting the pages of the marvellous book. Considering how sociably we had been sleeping together the night previous, and especially considering the affectionate arm I had found thrown over me upon waking in the morning, I thought this indifference of his very strange. But savages are strange beings; at times you do not know exactly how to take them. At first they are overawing; their calm self-collectedness of simplicity seems a Socratic wisdom. I had noticed also that Queequeg never consorted at all, or but very little, with the other seamen in the inn. He made no advances whatever; appeared to have no desire to enlarge the circle of his acquaintances. All this struck me as mighty singular; yet, upon second thoughts, there was something almost sublime in it. Here was a man some twenty thousand miles from home, by the way of Cape Horn, that is – which was the only way he could get there – thrown among people as strange to him as though he were in the planet Jupiter; and yet he seemed entirely at his ease; preserving the utmost serenity; content with his own companionship; always equal to himself. Surely this was a touch of fine philosophy; though no doubt he had never heard there was such a thing as that. But, perhaps, to be true philosophers, we mortals should not be conscious of so living or so striving. So soon as I hear that such or such a man gives himself out for a philosopher, I conclude that, like the dyspeptic old woman, he must have 'broken his digester.'

As I sat there in that now lonely room; the fire burning low, in that mild stage when, after its first intensity has warmed the air, it then only glows to be looked at; the evening shades and phantoms gathering round the casements, and peering in upon us silent, solitary twain; the storm booming without in solemn swells; I began to be sensible of strange feelings. I felt a melting in me. No more my splintered heart and maddened hand were turned against the wolfish world. This soothing savage had redeemed it. There he sat, his very indifference speaking a nature in which there lurked no civilized hypocrisies and bland deceits. Wild he was; a very sight of sights to see; yet I began to feel myself mysteriously drawn towards him. And those same things that would have repelled most others, they were the very magnets that thus drew me. I'll try a pagan friend, thought I, since Christian kindness has proved but hollow courtesy. I drew my bench near him, and made some friendly signs and hints, doing my best to talk with him meanwhile. At first he little noticed these advances; but presently, upon my referring to his last night's hospitalities, he made out to ask me whether we were again to be bedfellows. I told him yes; whereat I thought he looked pleased, perhaps a little complimented.

We then turned over the book together, and I endeavored to explain to him the purpose of the printing, and the meaning of the few pictures that were in it. Thus I soon engaged his interest; and from that we went to jabbering the best we could about the various outer sights to be seen in this famous town. Soon I proposed a social smoke; and, producing his pouch and tomahawk, he quietly offered me a puff. And then we sat exchanging puffs from that wild pipe of his, and keeping it regularly passing between us.

If there yet lurked any ice of indifference towards me in the Pagan's breast, this pleasant, genial smoke we had, soon thawed it out, and left us cronies. He seemed to take to me quite as naturally and unbiddenly as I to him; and when our smoke was over, he pressed his forehead against mine, clasped me round the waist, and said that henceforth we were married; meaning, in his country's phrase, that we were bosom friends; he would gladly die for me, if need should be. In a countryman, this sudden flame of friendship would have seemed far too premature, a thing to be much distrusted; but in this simple savage those old rules would not apply.

After supper, and another social chat and smoke, we went to our room together. He made me a present of his embalmed head; took out his enormous tobacco wallet, and groping under the tobacco, drew out some thirty dollars in silver; then spreading them on the table, and mechanically dividing them into two equal portions, pushed one of them towards me, and said it was mine. I was going to remonstrate; but he silenced me by pouring them into my trowsers' pockets. I let them stay. He then went about his evening prayers, took out his idol, and removed the paper fireboard. By certain signs and symptoms, I thought he seemed anxious for me to join him; but well knowing what was to follow, I deliberated a moment whether, in case he invited me, I would comply or otherwise.

I was a good Christian; born and bred in the bosom of the infallible Presbyterian Church. How then could I unite with this wild idolator in worshipping his piece of wood? But what is worship? thought I. Do you suppose now, Ishmael, that the magnanimous God of heaven and earth – pagans and all included – can possibly be jealous of an insignificant bit of black wood? Impossible! But what is worship? – to do the will of God – *that* is worship. And what is the will of God? – to do to my fellow man what I would have my fellow man to do to me – *that* is the will of God. Now, Queequeg is my fellow man. And what do I wish that this Queequeg would do to me? Why, unite with me in my particular Presbyterian form of worship. Consequently, I must then unite with him in his; ergo, I must turn idolator. So I kindled the shavings; helped prop up the innocent little idol; offered him burnt biscuit with Queequeg; salamed before him twice or thrice; kissed his nose; and that done, we undressed and went to bed, at peace with our own consciences and all the world. But we did not go to sleep without some little chat.

How it is I know not; but there is no place like a bed for confidential disclosures between friends. Man and wife, they say, there open the very bottom of their souls to each other; and some old couples often lie and chat over old times till nearly morning. Thus, then, in our hearts' honeymoon, lay I and Queequeg – a cosy, loving pair.

11

NIGHTGOWN

WE had lain thus in bed, chatting and napping at short intervals, and Queequeg now and then affectionately throwing his brown tattooed legs over mine, and then drawing them back; so entirely sociable and free and easy were we; when, at last, by reason of our confabulations, what little nappishness remained in us altogether departed, and we felt like getting up again, though day-break was yet some way down the future.

Yes, we became very wakeful; so much so that our recumbent position began to grow wearisome, and by little and little we found ourselves sitting up; the clothes well tucked around us, leaning against the head-board with our four knees drawn up close together, and our two noses bending over them, as if our knee-pans were warming-pans. We felt very nice and snug, the more so since it was so chilly out of doors; indeed out of bed-clothes too, seeing that there was no fire in the room. The more so, I say, because truly to enjoy bodily warmth, some small part of you must be cold, for there is no quality in this world that is not what it is merely by contrast. Nothing exists in itself. If you flatter yourself that you are all over comfortable, and have been so a long time, then you cannot be said to be comfortable any more. But if, like Queequeg and me in the bed, the tip of your nose or the crown of your head be slightly chilled, why then, indeed, in the general consciousness you feel most delightfully and unmistakably warm. For this reason a sleeping apartment should never be furnished with a fire, which is one of the luxurious discomforts of the rich. For the height of this sort of deliciousness is to have nothing but the blanket between you and your snugness and the cold of the outer air. Then there you lie like the one warm spark in the heart of an arctic crystal.

We had been sitting in this crouching manner for some time, when all at once I thought I would open my eyes; for when between sheets, whether by day or by night, and whether asleep or awake, I have a way of always keeping my eyes shut, in order the more to concentrate the snugness of being in bed. Because no man can ever feel his own identity aright except his eyes be closed; as if darkness were indeed the proper element of our essences, though light be more congenial to our clayey part. Upon opening my eyes then, and coming out of my own pleasant and self-created darkness into the imposed and coarse outer gloom of the unilluminated twelve-o'clock-at-night, I experienced a disagreeable revulsion. Nor did I at all object to the hint from Queequeg that perhaps it were best to strike a light, seeing that we were so wide awake; and besides he felt a strong desire to have a few quiet puffs from his Tomahawk. Be it said, that though I had felt such a strong repugnance to his smoking in the bed the night before, yet see how elastic our stiff prejudices grow when love once comes to bend them. For now I liked nothing better than to have Queequeg smoking by me, even in bed, because he seemed to be full of such serene household joy then. I no more felt unduly concerned for the landlord's policy of insurance. I was only alive to the condensed confidential comfortableness of sharing a pipe and a blanket with a real friend. With our shaggy jackets drawn about our shoulders, we now passed the Tomahawk from one to the other, till slowly there grew over us a blue hanging tester of smoke, illuminated by the flame of the new-lit lamp.

Whether it was that this undulating tester rolled the savage away to far distant scenes, I know not, but he now spoke of his native island; and, eager to hear his history, I begged him to go on and tell it. He gladly complied. Though at the time I but ill comprehended not a few of his words, yet subsequent disclosures, when I had become more familiar with his broken phraseology, now enable me to present the whole story such as it may prove in the mere skeleton I give.

12

BIOGRAPHICAL

QUEEQUEG was a native of Kokovoko, an island far away to the West and South. It is not down in any map; true places never are.

When a new-hatched savage running wild about his native woodlands in a grass clout, followed by the nibbling goats, as if he were a green sapling; even then, in Queequeg's ambitious soul, lurked a strong desire to see something more of Christendom than a specimen whaler or two. His father was a High Chief, a King; his uncle a High Priest; and on the maternal side he boasted aunts who were the wives of unconquerable warriors. There was excellent blood in his veins – royal stuff; though sadly vitiated, I fear, by the cannibal propensity he nourished in his untutored youth.

A Sag Harbor ship visited his father's bay, and Queequeg sought a passage to Christian lands. But the ship, having her full complement of seamen, spurned his suit; and not all the King his father's influence could prevail. But Queequeg vowed a vow. Alone in his canoe, he paddled off to a distant strait, which he knew the ship must pass through when she quitted the island. On one side was a coral reef; on the other a low tongue of land, covered with mangrove thickets that grew out into the water. Hiding his canoe, still afloat, among these thickets, with its prow seaward, he sat down in the stern, paddle low in hand; and when the ship was gliding by, like a flash he darted out; gained her side; with one backward dash of his foot capsized and sank his canoe; climbed up the chains; and throwing himself at full length upon the deck, grappled a ring-bolt there, and swore not to let it go, though hacked in pieces.

In vain the captain threatened to throw him overboard; suspended a cutlass over his naked wrists; Queequeg was the son of a King, and Queequeg budged not. Struck by his desperate dauntlessness, and his wild desire to visit Christendom, the captain at last relented, and told him he might make himself at home. But this fine young savage – this sea Prince of Wales, never saw the captain's cabin. They put him down among the sailors, and made a whaleman of him. But like Czar Peter content to toil in the shipyards of foreign cities, Queequeg disdained no seeming ignominy, if thereby he might happily gain the power of enlightening his untutored countrymen. For at bottom – so he told me he was actuated by a profound desire to learn among the Christians, the arts whereby to make his people still happier than they were; and more than that, still better than they were. But, alas! the practices of whalemen soon convinced him that even Christians could be both miserable and wicked; infinitely more so, than all his father's heathens. Arrived at last in old Sag Harbor; and seeing what the sailors did there; and then going on to Nantucket, and seeing how they spent their wages in *that* place also, poor Queequeg gave it up for lost. Thought he, it's a wicked world in all meridians; I'll die a pagan.

And thus an old idolator at heart, he yet lived among these Christians, wore their clothes, and tried to talk their gibberish. Hence the queer ways about him, though now some time from home.

By hints, I asked him whether he did not propose going back, and having a coronation; since he might now consider his father dead and gone, he being very old and feeble at the last accounts. He answered no, not yet; and added that he was fearful Christianity, or rather Christians, had unfitted him for ascending the pure and undefiled throne of thirty pagan Kings before him. But by and by, he said, he would return, – as soon as he felt himself baptized again. For the nonce, however, he proposed to sail about, and sow his wild oats in all four oceans. They had made a harpooneer of him, and that barbed iron was in lieu of a sceptre now.

I asked him what might be his immediate purpose, touching his future movements. He answered, to go to sea again, in his own vocation. Upon this, I told him that whaling was my own design, and informed him of my intention to sail out of Nantucket, as being the most promising port for an adventurous whaleman to embark from. He at once resolved to accompany me to that island, ship aboard the same vessel, get into the same watch, the same boat, the same mess with me, in short to share my every hap; with both my hands in his, boldly dip into the Potluck of both worlds. To all this I joyously assented; for besides the affection I now felt for Queequeg, he was an experienced harpooneer, and as such, could not fail to be of great usefulness to one, who, like me, was wholly ignorant of the mysteries of whaling, though well acquainted with the sea, as known to merchant seamen.

His story being ended with his pipe's last dying puff, Queequeg embraced me, pressed his forehead against mine, and blowing out the light, we rolled over from each other, this way and that, and very soon were sleeping.

13

WHEELBARROW

NEXT morning, Monday, after disposing of the embalmed head to a barber, for a block, I settled my own and comrade's bill; using, however, my comrade's money. The grinning landlord, as well as the boarders, seemed amazingly tickled at the sudden friendship which had sprung up between me and Queequeg – especially as Peter Coffin's cock and bull stories about him had previously so much alarmed me concerning the very person whom I now companied with.

We borrowed a wheelbarrow, and embarking our things, including my own poor carpet-bag, and Queequeg's canvas sack and hammock, away we went down to the 'Moss,' the little Nantucket packet schooner moored at the wharf. As we were going along the people stared; not at Queequeg so much – for they were used to seeing cannibals like him in their streets, – but at seeing him and me upon such confidential terms. But we heeded them not, going along wheeling the barrow by turns, and Queequeg now and then stopping to adjust the sheath on his harpoon barbs. I asked him why he carried such a troublesome thing with him ashore, and whether all whaling ships did not find their own harpoons. To this, in substance, he replied, that though what I hinted was true enough, yet he had a particular affection for his own harpoon, because it was of assured stuff, well tried in many a mortal combat, and deeply intimate with the hearts of whales. In short, like many inland reapers and mowers, who go into the farmers' meadows armed with their own scythes – though in no wise obliged to furnish them – even so Queequeg, for his own private reasons, preferred his own harpoon.

Shifting the barrow from my hand to his, he told me a funny story about the first wheelbarrow he had ever seen. It was in Sag Harbor. The owners of his ship, it seems, had lent him one, in which to carry his heavy chest to his boarding house. Not to seem ignorant about the thing – though in truth he was entirely so, concerning the precise way in which to manage the barrow – Queequeg puts his chest upon it; lashes it fast; and then shoulders the barrow and marches up the wharf. 'Why,' said I, 'Queequeg, you might have known better than that, one would think. Didn't the people laugh?'

Upon this, he told me another story. The people of his island of Kokovoko, it seems, at their wedding feasts express the fragrant water of young cocoanuts into a large stained calabash like a punchbowl; and this punchbowl always forms the great central ornament on the braided mat where the feast is held. Now a certain grand merchant ship once touched at Kokovoko, and its commander – from all accounts, a very stately punctilious gentleman, at least for a sea captain – this commander was invited to the wedding feast of Queequeg's sister, a pretty young princess just turned of ten. Well; when all the wedding guests were assembled at the bride's bamboo cottage, this Captain marches in, and being assigned the post of honor, placed himself over against the punchbowl, and between the High Priest and his majesty the King, Queequeg's father. Grace being said, – for those people have their grace as well as we – though Queequeg told me that unlike us, who at such times look downwards to our platters, they, on the contrary, copying the ducks, glance upwards to the great Giver of all feasts – Grace, I say, being said, the High Priest opens the banquet by the immemorial ceremony of the island; that is, dipping his consecrated and consecrating fingers into the bowl before the blessed beverage circulates. Seeing himself placed next the Priest, and noting the ceremony, and thinking himself – being Captain of a ship – as having plain precedence over a mere island King, especially in the King's own house – the Captain coolly proceeds to wash his hands in the punch bowl; – taking it I suppose for a huge finger-glass. 'Now,' said Queequeg, 'what you tink now? – Didn't our people laugh?'

At last, passage paid, and luggage safe, we stood on board the schooner. Hoisting sail, it glided down the Acushnet river. On one side, New Bedford rose in terraces of streets, their ice-covered trees all glittering in the clear, cold air. Huge hills and mountains of casks on casks were piled upon her wharves, and side by side the world-wandering whale ships lay silent and safely moored at last; while from others came a sound of carpenters and coopers, with blended noises of fires and forges to melt the pitch, all betokening that new cruises were on the start; that one most perilous and long voyage ended, only begins a second; and a second ended, only begins a third, and so on, for ever and for aye. Such is the endlessness, yea, the intolerableness of all earthly effort.

Gaining the more open water, the bracing breeze waxed fresh; the little Moss tossed the quick foam from her bows, as a young colt his snortings. How I snuffed that Tartar air! – how I spurned that turnpike earth! – that common highway all over dented with the marks of slavish heels and hoofs; and turned me to admire the magnanimity of the sea which will permit no records.

At the same foam-fountain, Queequeg seemed to drink and reel with me. His dusky nostrils swelled apart; he showed his filed and pointed teeth. On, on we flew, and our offing gained, the Moss did homage to the blast; ducked and dived her brows as a slave before the Sultan. Sideways leaning, we sideways darted; every ropeyarn tingling like a wire; the two tall masts buckling like Indian canes in land tornadoes. So full of this reeling scene were we, as we stood by the plunging bowsprit, that for some time we did not notice the jeering glances of the passengers, a lubber-like assembly, who marvelled that two fellow beings should be so companionable; as though a white man were anything more dignified than a whitewashed negro. But there were some boobies and bumpkins there, who, by their intense greenness, must have come from the heart and centre of all verdure. Queequeg caught one of these young saplings mimicking him behind his back. I thought the bumpkin's hour of doom was come. Dropping his harpoon, the brawny savage caught him in his arms, and by an almost miraculous dexterity and strength, sent him high up bodily into the air; then slightly tapping his stern in mid-somerset, the fellow landed with bursting lungs upon his feet, while Queequeg, turning his back upon him, lighted his tomahawk pipe and passed it to me for a puff.

'Capting! Capting!' yelled the bumpkin, running towards that officer; 'Capting, Capting, here's the devil.'

'Hallo, *you* sir,' cried the Captain, a gaunt rib of the sea, stalking up to Queequeg, 'what in thunder do you mean by that? Don't you know you might have killed that chap?'

'What him say?' said Queequeg, as he mildly turned to me.

'He say,' said I, 'that you came near kill-e that man there,' pointing to the still shivering greenhorn.

'Kill-e,' cried Queequeg, twisting his tattooed face into an unearthly expression of disdain, 'ah! him bery small-e fish-e; Queequeg no kill-e so small-e fish-e; Queequeg kill-e big whale!'

'Look you,' roared the Captain, 'I'll kill-e *you*, you cannibal, if you try any more of your tricks aboard here; so mind your eye.'

But it so happened just then, that it was high time for the Captain to mind his own eye. The prodigious strain upon the main-sail had parted the weather-sheet, and the tremendous boom was now flying from side to side, completely sweeping the entire after part of the deck. The poor fellow whom Queequeg had handled so roughly, was swept overboard; all hands were in a panic; and to attempt snatching at the boom to stay it, seemed madness. It flew from right to left, and back again, almost in one ticking of a watch, and every instant seemed on the point of snapping into splinters. Nothing was done, and nothing seemed capable of being done; those on deck rushed towards the bows, and stood eyeing the boom as if it were the lower jaw of an exasperated whale. In the midst of this consternation, Queequeg dropped deftly to his knees, and crawling under the path of the boom, whipped hold of a rope, secured one end to the bulwarks, and then flinging the other like a lasso, caught it round the boom as it swept over his head, and at the next jerk, the spar was that way trapped, and all was safe. The schooner was run into the wind, and while the hands were clearing away the stern boat, Queequeg, stripped to the waist, darted from the side with a long living arc of a leap. For three minutes or more he was seen swimming like a dog, throwing his long arms straight out before him, and by turns revealing his brawny shoulders through the freezing foam. I looked at the grand and glorious fellow, but saw no one to be saved. The greenhorn had gone down. Shooting himself perpendicularly from the water, Queequeg now took an instant's glance around him, and seeming to see just how matters were, dived down and disappeared. A few minutes more, and he rose again, one arm still striking out, and with the other dragging a lifeless form. The boat soon picked them up. The poor bumpkin was restored. All hands voted Queequeg a noble trump; the captain begged his pardon. From that hour I clove to Queequeg like a barnacle; yea, till poor Queequeg took his last long dive.

Was there ever such unconsciousness? He did not seem to think that he at all deserved a medal from the Humane and Magnanimous Societies. He only asked for water – fresh water – something to wipe the brine off; that done, he put on dry clothes, lighted his pipe, and leaning against the bulwarks, and mildly eyeing those around him, seemed to be saying to himself – 'It's a mutual, joint-stock world, in all meridians. We cannibals must help these Christians.'

14

NANTUCKET

NOTHING more happened on the passage worthy the mentioning; so, after a fine run, we safely arrived in Nantucket.

Nantucket! Take out your map and look at it. See what a real corner of the world it occupies; how it stands there, away off shore, more lonely than the Eddystone lighthouse. Look at it – a mere hillock, and elbow of sand; all beach, without a background. There is more sand there than you would use in twenty years as a substitute for blotting paper. Some gamesome wights will tell you that they have to plant weeds there, they don't grow naturally; that they import Canada thistles; that they have to send beyond seas for a spile to stop a leak in an oil cask; that pieces of wood in Nantucket are carried about like bits of the true cross in

Rome; that people there plant toadstools before their houses, to get under the shade in summer time; that one blade of grass makes an oasis, three blades in a day's walk a prairie; that they wear quicksand shoes, something like Laplander snowshoes; that they are so shut up, belted about, every way inclosed, surrounded, and made an utter island of by the ocean, that to their very chairs and tables small clams will sometimes be found adhering, as to the backs of sea turtles. But these extravaganzas only show that Nantucket is no Illinois.

Look now at the wondrous traditional story of how this island was settled by the red-men. Thus goes the legend. In olden times an eagle swooped down upon the New England coast, and carried off an infant Indian in his talons. With loud lament the parents saw their child borne out of sight over the wide waters. They resolved to follow in the same direction. Setting out in their canoes, after a perilous passage they discovered the island, and there they found an empty ivory casket, – the poor little Indian's skeleton.

What wonder, then, that these Nantucketers, born on a beach, should take to the sea for a livelihood! They first caught crabs and quohogs in the sand; grown bolder, they waded out with nets for mackerel; more experienced, they pushed off in boats and captured cod; and at last, launching a navy of great ships on the sea, explored this watery world; put an incessant belt of circumnavigations round it; peeped in at Behring's Straits; and in all seasons and all oceans declared everlasting war with the mightiest animated mass that has survived the flood; most monstrous and most mountainous! That Himmalehan, salt-sea Mastodon, clothed with such portentousness of unconscious power, that his very panics are more to be dreaded than his most fearless and malicious assaults!

And thus have these naked Nantucketers, these sea hermits, issuing from their ant-hill in the sea, overrun and conquered the watery world like so many Alexanders; parcelling out among them the Atlantic, Pacific, and Indian oceans, as the three pirate powers did Poland. Let America add Mexico to Texas, and pile Cuba upon Canada; let the English overswarm all India, and hang out their blazing banner from the sun; two thirds of this terraqueous globe are the Nantucketer's. For the sea is his; he owns it, as Emperors own empires; other seamen having but a right of way through it. Merchant ships are but extension bridges; armed ones but floating forts; even pirates and privateers, though following the sea as highwaymen the road, they but plunder other ships, other fragments of the land like themselves, without seeking to draw their living from the bottomless deep itself. The Nantucketer, he alone resides and riots on the sea; he alone, in Bible language, goes down to it in ships; to and fro ploughing it as his own special plantation. *There* is his home; *there* lies his business, which a Noah's flood would not interrupt, though it overwhelmed all the millions in China. He lives on the sea, as prairie cocks in the prairie; he hides among the waves, he climbs them as chamois hunters climb the Alps. For years he knows not the land; so that when he comes to it at last, it smells like another world, more strangely than the moon would to an Earthsman. With the landless gull, that at sunset folds her wings and is rocked to sleep between billows; so at nightfall, the Nantucketer, out of sight of land, furls his sails, and lays him to his rest, while under his very pillow rush herds of walruses and whales.

15

CHOWDER

It was quite late in the evening when the little Moss came snugly to anchor, and Queequeg and I went ashore; so we could attend to no business that day, at least none but a supper and a bed. The landlord of the Spouter-Inn had recommended us to his cousin Hosea Hussey of the Try Pots, whom he asserted to be the proprietor of one of the best kept hotels in all Nantucket, and moreover he had assured us that cousin Hosea, as he called him, was famous for his chowders. In short, he plainly hinted that we could not possibly do better than try pot-luck at the Try Pots. But the directions he had given us about keeping a yellow warehouse on our starboard hand till we opened a white church to the larboard, and then keeping that on the larboard hand till we made a corner three points to the starboard, and that done, then ask the first man we met where the place was: these crooked directions of his very much puzzled us at first, especially as, at the outset, Queequeg insisted that the yellow warehouse – our first point of departure – must be left on the larboard hand, whereas I had understood Peter Coffin to say it was on the starboard. However, by dint of beating about a little in the dark, and now and then knocking up a peaceable inhabitant to inquire the way, we at last came to something which there was no mistaking.

Two enormous wooden pots painted black, and suspended by asses' ears, swung from the cross-trees of an old top-mast, planted in front of an old doorway. The horns of the cross-trees were sawed off on the other side, so that this old top-mast looked not a little like a gallows. Perhaps I was over sensitive to such impressions at the time, but I could not help staring at this gallows with a vague misgiving. A sort of crick was in my neck as I gazed up to the two remaining horns; yes, *two* of them, one for Queequeg, and one for me. It's ominous, thinks I. A Coffin my Innkeeper upon landing in my first whaling port, tombstones staring at me in the whalemen's chapel; and here a gallows! and a pair of prodigious black pots too! Are these last throwing out oblique hints touching Tophet?

I was called from these reflections by the sight of a freckled woman with yellow hair and a yellow gown, standing in the porch of the inn, under a dull red lamp swinging there, that looked much like an injured eye, and carrying on a brisk scolding with a man in a purple woollen shirt.

'Get along with ye,' said she to the man, 'or I'll be combing ye!'

'Come on, Queequeg,' said I, 'all right. There's Mrs Hussey.'

And so it turned out; Mr Hosea Hussey being from home, but leaving Mrs Hussey entirely competent to attend to all his affairs. Upon making known our desires for a supper and a bed, Mrs Hussey, postponing further scolding for the present, ushered us into a little room, and seating us at a table spread with the relics of a recently concluded repast, turned round to us and said – 'Clam or Cod?'

'What's that about Cods, ma'am?' said I, with much politeness.

'Clam or Cod?' she repeated.

'A clam for supper? a cold clam; is *that* what you mean, Mrs Hussey?' says I; 'but that's a rather cold and clammy reception in the winter time, ain't it, Mrs Hussey?'

But being in a great hurry to resume scolding the man in the purple shirt, who was waiting for it in the entry, and seming to hear nothing but the word 'clam,' Mrs Hussey hurried towards an open door leading to the kitchen, and bawling out 'clam for two,' disappeared.

'Queequeg,' said I, 'do you think that we can make out a supper for us both on one clam?'

However, a warm savory steam from the kitchen served to belie the apparently cheerless prospect before us. But when that smoking chowder came in, the mystery was delightfully explained. Oh, sweet friends! hearken to me. It was made of small juicy clams, scarcely bigger than hazel nuts, mixed with pounded ship biscuit, and salted pork cut up into little flakes; the whole enriched with butter, and plentifully seasoned with pepper and salt. Our appetites being sharpened by the frosty voyage, and in particular, Queequeg seeing his favorite fishing food before him, and the chowder being surpassingly excellent, we despatched it with great expedition: when leaning back a moment and bethinking me of Mrs Hussey's clam and cod announcement, I thought I would try a little experiment. Stepping to the kitchen door, I uttered the word 'cod' with great emphasis, and resumed my seat. In a few moments the savory steam came forth again, but with a different flavor, and in good time a fine cod-chowder was placed before us.

We resumed business; and while plying our spoons in the bowl, thinks I to myself, I wonder now if this here has any effect on the head? What's that stultifying saying about chowder-headed people? 'But look, Queequeg, ain't that a live eel in your bowl? Where's your harpoon?'

Fishiest of all fishy places was the Try Pots, which well deserved its name; for the pots there were always boiling chowders. Chowder for breakfast, and chowder for dinner, and chowder for supper, till you began to look for fish-bones coming through your clothes. The area before the house was paved with clam-shells. Mrs Hussey wore a polished necklace of codfish vertebræ; and Hosea Hussey had his account books bound in superior old shark-skin. There was a fishy flavor to the milk, too, which I could not at all account for, till one morning happening to take a stroll along the beach among some fishermen's boats, I saw Hosea's brindled cow feeding on fish remnants, and marching along the sand with each foot in a cod's decapitated head, looking very slip-shod, I assure ye.

Supper concluded, we received a lamp, and directions from Mrs Hussey concerning the nearest way to bed; but, as Queequeg was about to precede me up the stairs, the lady reached forth her arm, and demanded his harpoon; she allowed no harpoon in her chambers. 'Why not?' said I; 'every true whaleman sleeps with his harpoon – but why not?' 'Because it's dangerous,' says she. 'Ever since young Stiggs coming from that unfort'nt v'y'ge of his, when he was gone four years and a half, with ony three barrels of *ile*, was found dead in my first floor back, with his harpoon in his side; ever since then I allow no boarders to take sich dangerous weepons in their rooms a-night. So, Mr Queequeg' (for she had learned his name), 'I will just take this here iron, and keep it for you till morning. But the chowder; clam or cod tomorrow for breakfast, men?'

'Both,' says I; 'and let's have a couple of smoked herring by way of variety.'

16

THE SHIP

In bed we concocted our plans for the morrow. But to my surprise and no small concern, Queequeg now gave me to understand, that he had been diligently consulting Yojo – the name of his black little god – and Yojo had told him two or three times over, and strongly insisted upon it everyway, that instead of our going together among the whaling-fleet in harbor, and in concert selecting our craft; instead of this, I say, Yojo earnestly enjoined that the selection of the ship should rest wholly with me, inasmuch as Yojo purposed befriending us; and, in order to do so, had already pitched upon a vessel, which, if left to myself, I, Ishmael, should infallibly light upon, for all the world as though it had turned out by chance; and in that vessel I must immediately ship myself, for the present irrespective of Queequeg.

I have forgotten to mention that, in many things, Queequeg placed great confidence in the excellence of Yojo's judgment and surprising forecast of things; and cherished Yojo with considerable esteem, as a rather good sort of god, who perhaps meant well enough upon the whole, but in all cases did not succeed in his benevolent designs.

Now, this plan of Queequeg's, or rather Yojo's, touching the selection of our craft; I did not like that plan at all. I had not a little relied upon Queequeg's sagacity to point out the whaler best fitted to carry us and our fortunes securely. But as all my remonstrances produced no effect upon Queequeg, I was obliged to acquiesce; and accordingly prepared to set about this business with a determined rushing sort of energy and vigor, that should quickly settle that trifling little affair. Next morning early, leaving Queequeg shut up with Yojo in our little bedroom – for it seemed that it was some sort of Lent or Ramadan, or day of fasting, humiliation, and prayer with Queequeg and Yojo that day; *how* it was I never could find out, for, though I applied myself to it several times, I never could master his liturgies and XXXIX Articles – leaving Queequeg, then, fasting on his tomahawk pipe, and Yojo warming himself at his sacrificial fire of shavings, I sallied out among the shipping. After much prolonged sauntering and many random inquiries, I learnt that there were three ships up for three-years' voyages – The Devil-Dam, the Tit-bit, and the Pequod. *Devil-Dam*, I do not know the origin of; *Tit-bit* is obvious; *Pequod*, you will no doubt remember, was the name of a celebrated tribe of Massachusetts Indians, now extinct as the ancient Medes. I peered and pryed about the Devil-Dam; from her, hopped over to the Tit-bit; and, finally, going on board the Pequod, looked around her for a moment, and then decided that this was the very ship for us.

You may have seen many a quaint craft in your day, for aught I know; – squared-toed luggers; mountainous Japanese junks; butter-box galliots, and what not; but take my word for it, you never saw such a rare old craft as this same rare old Pequod. She was a ship of the old school, rather small if anything; with an old fashioned claw-footed look about her. Long seasoned and weather-stained in the typhoons and calms of all four oceans, her old hull's complexion was darkened like a French grenadier's, who has alike fought in Egypt and Siberia. Her venerable bows looked bearded. Her masts – cut somewhere on the coast of Japan, where her original ones were lost overboard in a gale – her masts stood stiffly up like the spines of the three old kings of Cologne. Her ancient decks were worn and wrinkled, like the pilgrim-worshipped flag-stone in Canterbury Cathedral where Beckett bled. But to all these her old antiquities, were added new and marvellous features, pertaining to the wild business that for more than half a century she had followed. Old Captain Peleg, many years her chief-mate, before he commanded another vessel of his own, and now a retired seaman, and one of the principal owners of the Pequod, – this old Peleg, during the term of his chiefmateship, had built upon her original grotesqueness, and inlaid it, all over, with a quaintness both of material and device, unmatched by anything except it be Thorkill-Hake's carved buckler or bedstead. She was apparelled like any barbaric Ethiopian emperor, his neck heavy with pendants of polished ivory. She was a thing of trophies. A cannibal of a craft, tricking herself forth in the chased bones of her enemies. All round, her unpanelled, open bulwarks were garnished like one continuous jaw, with the long sharp teeth of the sperm whale, inserted there for pins, to fasten her old hempen thews and tendons to. Those thews ran not through base blocks of land wood, but deftly travelled over sheaves of sea-ivory. Scorning a turnstile wheel at her reverend helm, she sported there a tiller; and that tiller was in one mass, curiously carved from the long narrow lower jaw of her hereditary foe. The helmsman who steered by that tiller in a tempest, felt like the Tartar, when he holds back his fiery steed by clutching its jaw. A noble craft, but somehow a most melancholy! All noble things are touched with that.

Now when I looked about the quarter-deck, for some one having authority, in order to propose myself as a candidate for the voyage, at first I saw nobody; but I could not well overlook a strange sort of tent, or rather wigwam, pitched a little behind the main-mast. It seemed only a temporary erection used in port. It was of a conical shape, some ten feet high; consisting of the long, huge slabs of limber black bone taken from the middle and highest part of the jaws of the right-whale. Planted with their broad ends on the deck, a circle of these slabs laced together, mutually sloped towards each other, and at the apex united in a tufted point, where the loose hairy fibres waved to and fro like the top-knot on some old Pottowottamie Sachem's head. A triangular opening faced towards the bows of the ship, so that the insider commanded a complete view forward.

And half concealed in this queer tenement, I at length found one who by his aspect seemed to have authority; and who, it being noon, and the ship's work suspended, was now enjoying respite from the burden of command. He was seated on an old-fashioned oaken chair, wriggling all over with curious carving; and the bottom of which was formed of a stout interlacing of the same elastic stuff of which the wigwam was constructed.

There was nothing so very particular, perhaps, about the appearance of the elderly man I saw; he was brown and brawny, like most old seamen, and heavily rolled up in blue pilot-cloth, cut in the Quaker style; only there was a fine and almost microscopic net-work of the minutest wrinkles interlacing round his eyes, which must have arisen from his continual sailings in many hard gales, and always looking to windward; – for this causes the muscles about the eyes to become pursed together. Such eye-wrinkles are very effectual in a scowl.

'Is this the Captain of the Pequod?' said I, advancing to the door of the tent.

'Supposing it be the Captain of the Pequod, what dost thou want of him?' he demanded.

'I was thinking of shipping.'

'Thou wast, wast thou? I see thou art no Nantucketer – ever been in a stove boat?'

'No, Sir, I never have.'

'Dost know nothing at all about whaling, I dare say – eh?'

'Nothing, Sir; but I have no doubt I shall soon learn. I've been several voyages in the merchant service, and I think that –'

'Marchant service be damned. Talk not that lingo to me. Dost see that leg? – I'll take that leg away from thy stern, if ever thou talkest of the marchant service to me again. Marchant service indeed! I suppose now ye feel considerable proud of having served in those marchant ships. But flukes! man, what makes thee want to go a whaling, eh? – it looks a little suspicious, don't it, eh? – Hast not been a pirate, hast thou? – Didst not rob thy last Captain, didst thou? – Dost not think of murdering the officers when thou gettest to sea?'

I protested my innocence of these things. I saw that under

the mask of these half humorous innuendoes, this old seaman, as an insulated Quakerish Nantucketer, was full of his insular prejudices, and rather distrustful of all aliens, unless they hailed from Cape Cod or the Vineyard.

'But what takes thee a-whaling? I want to know that before I think of shipping ye.'

'Well, sir, I want to see what whaling is. I want to see the world.'

'Want to see what whaling is, eh? Have ye clapped eye on Captain Ahab?'

'Who is Captain Ahab, sir?'

'Aye, aye, I thought so. Captain Ahab is the Captain of this ship.'

'I am mistaken then. I thought I was speaking to the Captain himself.'

'Thou art speaking to Captain Peleg – that's who ye are speaking to, young man. It belongs to me and Captain Bildad to see the Pequod fitted out for the voyage, and supplied with all her needs, including crew. We are part owners and agents. But as I was going to say, if thou wantest to know what whaling is, as thou tellest ye do, I can put ye in a way of finding it out before ye bind yourself to it, past backing out. Clap eye on Captain Ahab, young man, and thou wilt find that he has only one leg.'

'What do you mean, sir? Was the other one lost by a whale?'

'Lost by a whale! Young man, come nearer to me: it was devoured, chewed up, crunched by the monstrousest parmacetty that ever chipped a boat! – ah, ah!'

I was a little alarmed by his energy, perhaps also a little touched at the hearty grief in his concluding exclamation, but said as calmly as I could, 'What you say is no doubt true enough, sir; but how could I know there was any peculiar ferocity in that particular whale, though indeed I might have inferred as much from the simple fact of the accident.'

'Look ye now, young man, thy lungs are a sort of soft, d'ye see; thou dost not talk shark a bit. *Sure*, ye've been to sea before now; sure of that?'

'Sir,' said I, 'I thought I told you that I had been four voyages in the merchant –'

'Hard down out of that! Mind what I said about the marchant service – don't aggravate me – I won't have it. But let us understand each other. I have given thee a hint about what whaling is; do ye yet feel inclined for it?'

'I do, sir.'

'Very good. Now, art thou the man to pitch a harpoon down a live whale's throat, and then jump after it? Answer, quick!'

'I am, sir, if it should be positively indispensable to do so; not to be got rid of, that is; which I don't take to be the fact.'

'Good again. Now then, thou not only wantest to go a-whaling, to find out by experience what whaling is, but ye also want to go in order to see the world? Was not that what ye said? I thought so. Well then, just step forward there, and take a peep over the weather-bow, and then back to me and tell me what ye see there.'

For a moment I stood a little puzzled by this curious request, not knowing exactly how to take it, whether humorously or in earnest. But concentrating all his crow's feet into one scowl, Captain Peleg started me on the errand.

Going forward and glancing over the weather bow, I perceived that the ship swinging to her anchor with the flood-tide, was now obliquely pointing towards the open ocean. The prospect was unlimited, but exceedingly monotonous and forbidding; not the slightest variety that I could see.

'Well, what's the report?' said Peleg when I came back; 'what did ye see?'

'Not much,' I replied – 'nothing but water; considerable horizon though, and there's a squall coming up, I think.'

'Well, what dost thou think then of seeing the world? Do ye wish to go round Cape Horn to see any more of it, eh? Can't ye see the world where you stand?'

I was a little staggered, but go a-whaling I must, and I

would; and the Pequod was as good a ship as any – I thought the best – and all this I now repeated to Peleg. Seeing me so determined, he expressed his willingness to ship me.

'And thou mayest as well sign the papers right off,' he added – 'come along with ye.' And so saying, he led the way below deck into the cabin.

Seated on the transom was what seemed to me a most uncommon and surprising figure. It turned out to be Captain Bildad, who along with Captain Peleg was one of the largest owners of the vessel; the other shares, as is sometimes the case in these ports, being held by a crowd of old annuitants; widows, fatherless children, and chancery wards; each owning about the value of a timber head, or a foot of plank, or a nail or two in the ship. People in Nantucket invest their money in whaling vessels, the same way that you do yours in approved state stocks bringing in good interest.

Now, Bildad, like Peleg, and indeed many other Nantucketers, was a Quaker, the island having been originally settled by that sect; and to this day its inhabitants in general retain in an uncommon measure the peculiarities of the Quaker, only variously and anomalously modified by things altogether alien and heterogeneous. For some of these same Quakers are the most sanguinary of all sailors and whale-hunters. They are fighting Quakers; they are Quakers with a vengeance.

So that there are instances among them of men, who, named with Scripture names – a singularly common fashion on the island – and in childhood naturally imbibing the stately dramatic *thee* and *thou* of the Quaker idiom; still, from the audacious, daring, and boundless adventure of their subsequent lives, strangely blend with these unoutgrown peculiarities, a thousand bold dashes of character, not unworthy a Scandinavian sea-king, or a poetical Pagan Roman. And when these things unite in a man of greatly superior natural force, with a globular brain and a ponderous heart; who has also by the stillness and seclusion of many long night-watches in the remotest waters, and beneath constellations never seen here at the north, been led to think untraditionally and independently; receiving all nature's sweet or savage impressions fresh from her own virgin voluntary and confiding breast, and thereby chiefly, but with some help from accidental advantages, to learn a bold and nervous lofty language – that man makes one in a whole nation's census – a mighty pageant creature, formed for noble tragedies. Nor will it at all detract from him, dramatically regarded, if either by birth or other circumstances, he have what seems a half wilful over-ruling morbidness at the bottom of his nature. For all men tragically great are made so through a certain morbidness. Be sure of this, O young ambition, all mortal greatness is but disease. But, as yet we have not to do with such an one, but with quite another; and still a man, who, if indeed peculiar, it only results again from another phase of the Quaker, modified by individual circumstances.

Like Captain Peleg, Captain Bildad was a well-to-do, retired whaleman. But unlike Captain Peleg – who cared not a rush for what are called serious things, and indeed deemed those self-same serious things the veriest of all trifles – Captain Bildad had not only been originally educated according to the strictest sect of Nantucket Quakerism, but all his subsequent ocean life, and the sight of many unclad, lovely island creatures, round the Horn – all that had not moved this native born Quaker one single jot, had not so much as altered one angle of his vest. Still, for all this immutableness, was there some lack of common consistency about worthy Captain Bildad. Though refusing, from conscientious scruples, to bear arms against land invaders, yet himself had illimitably invaded the Atlantic and Pacific; and though a sworn foe to human bloodshed, yet had he in his straight-bodied coat, spilled tuns upon tuns of leviathan gore. How now in the contemplative evening of his days, the pious Bildad reconciled these things in the reminiscence, I do not know; but it did not seem to concern him much, and very probably he had long since come to the sage and sensible conclusion that a man's religion is one thing, and this practical world quite another. This world pays dividends. Rising from a little cabin-boy in short clothes of the drabbest drab, to a harpooneer in a broad shad-bellied waistcoat; from that becoming boat-header, chief-mate, and captain, and finally a ship-owner; Bildad, as I hinted before, had concluded his adventurous career by wholly retiring from active life at the goodly age of sixty, and dedicating his remaining days to the quiet receiving of his well-earned income.

Now Bildad, I am sorry to say, had the reputation of being an incorrigible old hunks, and in his sea-going days, a bitter, hard task-master. They told me in Nantucket, though it certainly seems a curious story, that when he sailed the old Categut whaleman, his crew, upon arriving home, were mostly all carried ashore to the hospital, sore exhausted and worn out. For a pious man, especially for a Quaker, he was certainly rather hard-hearted, to say the least. He never used to swear, though, at his men, they said; but somehow he got an inordinate quantity of cruel, unmitigated hard work out of them. When Bildad was a chief-mate, to have his drab-colored eye intently looking at you, made you feel completely nervous, till you could clutch something – a hammer or a marling-spike, and go to work like mad, at something or other, never mind what. Indolence and idleness perished from before him. His own person was the exact embodiment of his utilitarian character. On his long, gaunt body, he carried no spare flesh, no superfluous beard, his chin having a soft, economical nap to it, like the worn nap of his broad-brimmed hat.

Such, then, was the person that I saw seated on the transom when I followed Captain Peleg down into the cabin. The space between the decks was small; and there, bolt-upright, sat old Bildad, who always sat so, and never leaned, and this to save his coat tails. His broad-brim was placed beside him; his legs were stiffly crossed; his drab vesture was buttoned up to his chin; and spectacles on nose, he seemed absorbed in reading from a ponderous volume.

'Bildad,' cried Captain Peleg, 'at it again, Bildad, eh? Ye

have been studying those Scriptures, now, for the last thirty years, to my certain knowledge. How far ye got, Bildad?'

As if long habituated to such profane talk from his old shipmate, Bildad, without noticing his present irreverence, quietly looked up, and seeing me, glanced again inquiringly towards Peleg.

'He says he's our man, Bildad,' said Peleg, 'he wants to ship.'

'Dost thee?' said Bildad, in a hollow tone, and turning round to me.

'I *dost,*' said I unconsciously, he was so intense a Quaker.

'What do ye think of him, Bildad?' said Peleg.

'He'll do,' said Bildad, eyeing me, and then went on spelling away at his book in a mumbling tone quite audible.

I thought him the queerest old Quaker I ever saw, especially as Peleg, his friend and old shipmate, seemed such a blusterer. But I said nothing, only looking round me sharply. Peleg now threw open a chest, and drawing forth the ship's articles, placed pen and ink before him, and seated himself at a little table. I began to think it was high time to settle with myself at what terms I would be willing to engage for the voyage. I was already aware that in the whaling business they paid no wages; but all hands, including the captain, received certain shares of the profits called *lays*, and that these lays were proportioned to the degree of importance pertaining to the respective duties of the ship's company. I was also aware that being a green hand at whaling, my own lay would not be very large; but considering that I was used to the sea, could steer a ship, splice a rope, and all that, I made no doubt that from all I had heard I should be offered at least the 275th lay – that is, the 275th part of the clear net proceeds of the voyage, whatever that might eventually amount to. And though the 275th lay was what they call a rather *long lay*, yet it was better than nothing; and if we had a lucky voyage, might pretty nearly pay for the clothing I would wear out on it, not to speak of my three years' beef and board, for which I would not have to pay one stiver.

It might be thought that this was a poor way to accumulate a princely fortune – and so it was, a very poor way indeed. But I am one of those that never take on about princely fortunes, and am quite content if the world is ready to board and lodge me, while I am putting up at this grim sign of the Thunder Cloud. Upon the whole, I thought that the 275th lay would be about the fair thing, but would not have been surprised had I been offered the 200th, considering I was of a broad-shouldered make.

But one thing, nevertheless, that made me a little distrustful about receiving a generous share of the profits was this: Ashore, I had heard something of both Captain Peleg and his unaccountable old crony Bildad; how that they being the principal proprietors of the Pequod, therefore the other and more inconsiderable and scattered owners, left nearly the whole management of the ship's affairs to these two. And I did not know but what the stingy old Bildad might have a mighty deal to say about shipping hands, especially as I now found him on board the Pequod, quite at home there in the cabin, and reading his Bible as if at his own fireside. Now while Peleg was vainly trying to mend a pen with his jack-knife, old Bildad, to my no small surprise, considering that he was such an interested party in these proceedings; Bildad never heeded us, but went on mumbling to himself out of his book, '"*Lay* not up for yourselves treasures upon earth, where moth—"'

'Well, Captain Bildad,' interrupted Peleg, 'what d'ye say, what lay shall we give this young man?'

'Thou knowest best,' was the sepulchral reply, 'the seven hundred and seventy-seventh wouldn't be too much, would it? – "where moth and rust do corrupt, but *lay* –"'

Lay, indeed, thought I, and such a lay! the seven hundred and seventy-seventh! Well, old Bildad, you are determined that I, for one, shall not *lay* up many *lays* here below, where moth and rust do corrupt. It was an exceedingly *long lay* that, indeed; and though from the magnitude of the figure it might at first deceive a landsman, yet the slightest consideration will show that though seven hundred and seventy-seven is a pretty large number, yet, when you come to make a *teenth* of it, you will then see, I say, that the seven hundred and seventy-seventh part of a farthing is a good deal less than seven hundred and seventy-seven gold doubloons; and so I thought at the time.

'Why, blast your eyes, Bildad,' cried Peleg, 'thou dost not want to swindle this young man! he must have more than that.'

'Seven hundred and seventy-seventh,' again said Bildad, without lifting his eyes; and then went on mumbling – ' "for where your treasure is, there will your heart be also." '

'I am going to put him down for the three hundredth,' said Peleg, 'do ye hear that, Bildad! The three hundredth lay, I say.'

Bildad laid down his book, and turning solemnly towards him said, 'Captain Peleg, thou hast a generous heart; but thou must consider the duty thou owest to the other owners of this ship – widows and orphans, many of them – and that if we too abundantly reward the labors of this young man, we may be taking the bread from those widows and those orphans. The seven hundred and seventy-seventh lay, Captain Peleg.'

'Thou Bildad!' roared Peleg, starting up and clattering about the cabin. 'Blast ye, Captain Bildad, if I had followed thy advice in these matters, I would afore now had a conscience to lug about that would be heavy enough to founder the largest ship that ever sailed round Cape Horn.'

'Captain Peleg,' said Bildad steadily, 'thy conscience may be drawing ten inches of water, or ten fathoms, I can't tell; but as thou art still an impenitent man, Captain Peleg, I greatly fear lest thy conscience be but a leaky one; and will in the end sink thee foundering down to the fiery pit, Captain Peleg.'

'Fiery pit! fiery pit! ye insult me, man; past all natural bearing, ye insult me. It's an all-fired outrage to tell any human creature that he's bound to hell. Flukes and flames! Bildad, say that again to me, and start my soul-bolts, but I'll – I'll – yes, I'll swallow a live goat with all his hair and horns on. Out of the cabin, ye canting, drab-colored son of a wooden gun – a straight wake with ye!'

As he thundered out this he made a rush at Bildad, but with a marvellous oblique, sliding celerity, Bildad for that time eluded him.

Alarmed at this terrible outburst between the two principal and responsible owners of the ship, and feeling half a mind to give up all idea of sailing in a vessel so questionably owned and temporarily commanded, I stepped aside from the door to give egress to Bildad, who, I made no doubt, was all eagerness to vanish from before the awakened wrath of Peleg. But to my astonishment, he sat down again on the transom very quietly, and seemed to have not the slightest intention of withdrawing. He seemed quite used to impenitent Peleg and his ways. As for Peleg, after letting off his rage as he had, there seemed no more left in him, and he, too, sat down like a lamb, though he twitched a little as if still nervously agitated. 'Whew!' he whistled at last – 'the squall's gone off to leeward, I think. Bildad, thou used to be good at sharpening a lance, mend that pen, will ye. My jack-knife here needs the grindstone. That's he; thank ye, Bildad. Now then, my young man, Ishmael's thy name, didn't ye say? Well then, down ye go here, Ishmael, for the three hundredth lay.'

'Captain Peleg,' said I, 'I have a friend with me who wants to ship too – shall I bring him down tomorrow?'

'To be sure,' said Peleg. 'Fetch him along, and we'll look at him.'

'What lay does *he* want?' groaned Bildad, glancing up from the book in which he had again been burying himself.

'Oh! never thee mind about that, Bildad,' said Peleg. 'Has he ever whaled it any?' turning to me.

'Killed more whales than I can count, Captain Peleg.'

'Well, bring him along then.'

And, after signing the papers, off I went; nothing doubting but that I had done a good morning's work, and that the Pequod was the identical ship that Yojo had provided to carry Queequeg and me round the Cape.

But I had not proceeded far, when I began to bethink me that the captain with whom I was to sail yet remained unseen by me; though, indeed, in many cases, a whale-ship will be completely fitted out, and receive all her crew on board, ere the captain makes himself visible by arriving to take command; for sometimes these voyages are so prolonged, and the shore intervals at home so exceedingly brief, that if the captain have a family, or any absorbing concernment of that sort, he does not trouble himself much about his ship in port, but leaves her to the owners till all is ready for sea. However, it is always as well to have a look at him before irrevocably committing yourself into his hands. Turning back I accosted Captain Peleg, inquiring where Captain Ahab was to be found.

'And what dost thou want of Captain Ahab? It's all right enough; thou art shipped.'

'Yes, but I should like to see him.'

'But I don't think thou wilt be able to at present. I don't know exactly what's the matter with him; but he keeps close inside the house; a sort of sick, and yet he don't look so. In fact, he ain't sick; but no, he isn't well either. Any how, young man, he won't always see me, so I don't suppose he will thee. He's a queer man, Captain Ahab – so some think – but a good one. Oh, thou'lt like him well enough; no fear, no fear. He's a grand, ungodly, god-like man, Captain Ahab; doesn't speak much; but, when he does speak, then you may well listen. Mark ye, be forewarned; Ahab's above the common; Ahab's been in colleges, as well as 'mong the cannibals; been used to deeper wonders than the waves; fixed his fiery lance in mightier, stranger foes than whales. His lance! aye, the keenest and the surest that out of all our isle! Oh! he ain't Captain Bildad; no, and he ain't Captain Peleg; *he's Ahab*, boy; and Ahab of old, thou knowest, was a crowned king!'

'And a very vile one. When that wicked king was slain, the dogs, did they not lick his blood?'

'Come hither to me – hither, hither,' said Peleg, with a significance in his eye that almost startled me. 'Look ye, lad; never say that on board the Pequod. Never say it anywhere. Captain Ahab did not name himself. 'Twas a foolish, ignorant whim of his crazy, widowed mother, who died when he was only a twelvemonth old. And yet the old squaw Tistig, at Gayhead, said that the name would somehow prove prophetic. And, perhaps, other fools like her may tell thee the same. I wish to warn thee. It's a lie. I know Captain Ahab well; I've sailed with him as mate years ago; I know what he is – a good man – not a pious, good man, like Bildad, but a swearing good man – something like me – only there's a good deal more of him. Aye, aye, I know that he was never very jolly; and I know that on the passage home, he was a little out of his mind for a spell; but it was the sharp shooting pains in his bleeding stump that brought that about, as any one might see. I know, too, that ever since he lost his leg last voyage by that accursed whale, he's been a kind of moody – desperate moody, and savage sometimes; but that will all pass off. And once for all, let me tell thee and assure thee, young man, it's better to sail with a moody good captain than a laughing bad one. So good-bye to thee – and wrong not Captain Ahab, because he happens to have a wicked name. Besides, my boy, he has a wife – not three voyages wedded – a sweet, resigned girl. Think of that; by that sweet girl that old man has a child: hold ye then there can be any utter, hopeless harm in Ahab? No, no, my lad; stricken, blasted, if he be, Ahab has his humanities!'

As I walked away, I was full of thoughtfulness; what had been incidentally revealed to me of Captain Ahab, filled me with a certain wild vagueness of painfulness concerning him. And somehow, at the time, I felt a sympathy and a sorrow for him, but for I don't know what, unless it was the cruel loss of his leg. And yet I also felt a strange awe of him; but that sort of awe, which I cannot at all describe, was not exactly awe; I do not know what it was. But I felt it; and it did not disincline me towards him; though I felt impatience at what seemed like mystery in him, so imperfectly as he was known to me then. However, my thoughts were at length carried in other directions, so that for the present dark Ahab slipped my mind.

17

THE RAMADAN

As Queequeg's Ramadan, or Fasting and Humiliation, was to continue all day, I did not choose to disturb him till towards night-fall; for I cherish the greatest respect towards everybody's religious obligations, never mind how comical, and could not find it in my heart to undervalue even a congregation of ants worshipping a toad-stool; or those other creatures in certain parts of our earth, who with a degree of footmanism quite unprecedented in other planets, bow down before the torso of a deceased landed proprietor merely on account of the inordinate possessions yet owned and rented in his name.

I say, we good Presbyterian Christians should be charitable in these things, and not fancy ourselves so vastly superior to other mortals, pagans and what not, because of their half-crazy conceits on these subjects. There was Queequeg, now, certainly entertaining the most absurd notions about Yojo and his Ramadan; – but what of that? Queequeg thought he knew what he was about, I suppose; he seemed to be content; and there let him rest. All our arguing with him would not avail; let him be, I say: and Heaven have mercy on us all – Presbyterians and Pagans alike – for we are all somehow dreadfully cracked about the head, and sadly need mending.

Towards evening, when I felt assured that all his performances and rituals must be over, I went up to his room and knocked at the door; but no answer. I tried to open it, but it was fastened inside. 'Queequeg,' said I softly through the key-hole: – all silent. 'I say, Queequeg! why don't you speak? It's I – Ishmael.' But all remained still as before. I began to grow alarmed. I had allowed him such abundant time; I thought he might have had an apoplectic fit. I looked through the key-hole; but the door opening into an odd corner of the room, the key-hole prospect was but a crooked and sinister one. I could only see part of the foot-board of the bed and a line of the wall, but nothing more. I was surprised to behold resting against the wall the wooden shaft of Queequeg's harpoon, which the landlady the evening previous had taken from him, before our mounting to the chamber. That's strange, thought I; but at any rate, since the harpoon stands yonder, and he seldom or never goes abroad without it, therefore he must be inside here, and no possible mistake.

'Queequeg! – Queequeg!' – all still. Something must have happened. Apoplexy! I tried to burst open the door; but it stubbornly resisted. Running down stairs, I quickly stated my suspicions to the first person I met – the chambermaid. 'La! La!' she cried, 'I thought something must be the matter. I went to make the bed after breakfast, and the door was locked; and not a mouse to be heard; and it's been just so silent ever since. But I thought, may be, you had both gone off and locked your baggage in for safe keeping. La! La, ma'am! Mistress! murder! Mrs Hussey! apoplexy!' – and with these cries, she ran towards the kitchen, I following.

Mrs Hussey soon appeared, with a mustard-pot in one hand and a vinegar-cruet in the other, having just broken away from the occupation of attending to the castors, and scolding her little black boy meantime.

'Wood-house!' cried I, 'which way to it? Run for God's sake, and fetch something to pry open the door – the axe! – the axe! – he's had a stroke; depend upon it!' – and so saying I was unmethodically rushing up stairs again empty-handed, when Mrs Hussey interposed the mustard-pot and vinegar-cruet, and the entire castor of her countenance.

'What's the matter with you, young man?'

'Get the axe! For God's sake, run for the doctor, some one, while I pry it open!'

'Look here,' said the landlady, quickly putting down the vinegar-cruet, so as to have one hand free; 'look here; are you talking about prying open any of my doors?' – and with that she seized my arm. 'What's the matter with you? What's the matter with you, shipmate?'

In as calm, but rapid a manner as possible, I gave her to understand the whole case. Unconsciously clapping the vinegar-cruet to one side of her nose, she ruminated for an instant; then exclaimed – 'No! I haven't seen it since I put it there.' Running to a little closet under the landing of the stairs, she glanced in, and returning, told me that Queequeg's harpoon was missing. 'He's killed himself,' she cried. 'It's unfort'nate Stiggs done over again – there goes another counterpane – God pity his poor mother! – it will be the ruin of my house. Has the poor lad a sister? Where's that girl? – there, Betty, go to Snarles the Painter, and tell him to paint me a sign, with – "no suicides permitted here, and no smoking in the parlor;" – might as well kill both birds at once. Kill? The Lord be merciful to his ghost! What's that noise there? You, young man, avast there!'

And running up after me, she caught me as I was again trying to force open the door.

'I won't allow it; I won't have my premises spoiled. Go for the locksmith, there's one about a mile from here. But avast!' putting her hand in her side-pocket, 'here's a key that'll fit, I guess; let's see.' And with that, she turned it in the lock; but, alas! Queequeg's supplemental bolt remained unwithdrawn within.

'Have to burst it open,' said I, and was running down the entry a little, for a good start, when the landlady caught at me, again vowing I should not break down her premises; but I tore from her, and with a sudden bodily rush dashed myself full against the mark.

With a prodigious noise the door flew open, and the knob slamming against the wall, sent the plaster to the ceiling; and there, good heavens! there sat Queequeg, altogether cool and self-collected; right in the middle of the room; squatting on his hams, and holding Yojo on top of his head. He looked neither one way nor the other way, but sat like a carved image with scarce a sign of active life.

'Queequeg,' said I, going up to him, 'Queequeg, what's the matter with you?'

'He hain't been a sittin' so all day, has he?' said the landlady.

But all we said, not a word could we drag out of him; I almost felt like pushing him over, so as to change his position, for it was almost intolerable, it seemed so painfully and unnaturally constrained; especially, as in all probability he had been sitting so for upwards of eight or ten hours, going too without his regular meals.

'Mrs Hussey,' said I, 'he's *alive* at all events; so leave us, if you please, and I will see to this strange affair myself.'

Closing the door upon the landlady, I endeavored to prevail upon Queequeg to take a chair; but in vain. There he sat; and all I could do – for all my polite arts and blandishments – he would not move a peg, nor say a single word, nor even look at me, nor notice my presence in any the slightest way.

I wonder, thought I, if this can possibly be a part of his Ramadan; do they fast on their hams that way in his native island? It must be so; yes, it's part of his creed, I suppose; well, then, let him rest; he'll get up sooner or later, no doubt. It can't last for ever, thank God, and his Ramadan only comes once a year; and I don't believe it's very punctual then.

I went down to supper. After sitting a long time listening to the long stories of some sailors who had just come from a plum-pudding voyage, as they called it (that is, a short whaling-voyage in a schooner or brig, confined to the north of the line, in the Atlantic Ocean only); after listening to these plum-puddingers till nearly eleven o'clock, I went up stairs to go to bed, feeling quite sure by this time Queequeg must certainly have brought his Ramadan to a termination. But no; there he was just where I had left him; he had not stirred an inch. I began to grow vexed with him; it seemed so downright senseless and insane to be sitting there all day and half the night on his hams in a cold room, holding a piece of wood on his head.

'For heaven's sake, Queequeg, get up and shake yourself; get up and have some supper. You'll starve; you'll kill yourself, Queequeg.' But not a word did he reply.

Despairing of him, therefore, I determined to go to bed and to sleep; and no doubt, before a great while, he would follow me. But previous to turning in, I took my heavy bearskin jacket, and threw it over him, as it promised to be a very cold night; and he had nothing but his ordinary round jacket on. For some time, do all I would, I could not get into the faintest doze. I had blown out the candle; and the mere thought of Queequeg – not four feet off – sitting there in that uneasy position, stark alone in the cold and dark; this made me really wretched. Think of it; sleeping all night in the same room with a wide awake pagan on his hams in this dreary, unaccountable Ramadan!

But somehow I dropped off at last, and knew nothing more till break of day; when, looking over the bedside, there squatted Queequeg, as if he had been screwed down to the floor. But as soon as the first glimpse of sun entered the window, up he got, with stiff and grating joints, but with a cheerful look; limped towards me where I lay; pressed his forehead again against mine; and said his Ramadan was over.

Now, as I before hinted, I have no objection to any person's religion, be it what it may, so long as that person does not kill or insult any other person, because that other person don't believe it also. But when a man's religion becomes really frantic; when it is a positive torment to him; and, in fine, makes this earth of ours an uncomfortable inn to lodge in; then I think it high time to take that individual aside and argue the point with him.

And just so I now did with Queequeg. 'Queequeg,' said I, 'get into bed now, and lie and listen to me.' I then went on, beginning with the rise and progress of the primitive religions, and coming down to the various religions of the present time, during which time I labored to show Queequeg that all these Lents, Ramadans, and prolonged ham-squattings in cold, cheerless rooms were stark nonsense; bad for the health; useless for the soul; opposed, in short, to the obvious laws of Hygiene and common sense. I told him, too, that he being in other things such an extremely sensible and sagacious savage, it pained me, very badly pained me, to see him now so deplorably foolish about this ridiculous Ramadan of his. Besides, argued I, fasting makes the body cave in; hence the spirit caves in; and all thoughts born of a fast must necessarily be half-starved. This is the reason why most dyspeptic religionists cherish such melancholy notions about their hereafters. In one word, Queequeg, said I, rather digressively; hell is an idea first born on an undigested apple-dumpling; and since then perpetuated through the hereditary dyspepsias nurtured by Ramadans.

I then asked Queequeg whether he himself was ever troubled with dyspepsia; expressing the idea very plainly, so that he could take it in. He said no; only upon one memorable occasion. It was after a great feast given by his father the king, on the gaining of a great battle wherein fifty of the enemy had been killed by about two o'clock in the afternoon, and all cooked and eaten that very evening.

'No more, Queequeg,' said I, shuddering; 'that will do;' for I knew the inferences without his further hinting them. I had seen a sailor who had visited that very island, and he told me that it was the custom, when a great battle had been gained there, to barbecue all the slain in the yard or garden of the victor; and then, one by one, they were placed in great wooden trenchers, and garnished round like a pilau, with breadfruit and cocoanuts; and with some parsley in their mouths, were sent round with the victor's compliments to all his friends, just as though these presents were so many Christmas turkeys.

After all, I do not think that my remarks about religion made much impression upon Queequeg. Because, in the first place, he somehow seemed dull of hearing on that important subject, unless considered from his own point of view; and, in the second place, he did not more than one third understand me, couch my ideas simply as I would;

and, finally, he no doubt thought he knew a good deal more about the true religion than I did. He looked at me with a sort of condescending concern and compassion, as though he thought it a great pity that such a sensible young man should be so hopelessly lost to evangelical pagan piety.

At last we rose and dressed; and Queequeg, taking a prodigiously hearty breakfast of chowders of all sorts, so that the landlady should not make much profit by reason of his Ramadan, we sallied out to board the Pequod, sauntering along, and picking our teeth with halibut bones.

18

HIS MARK

As we were walking down the end of the wharf towards the ship, Queequeg carrying his harpoon, Captain Peleg in his gruff voice loudly hailed us from his wigwam, saying he had not suspected my friend was a cannibal, and furthermore announcing that he let no cannibals on board that craft, unless they previously produced their papers.

'What do you mean by that, Captain Peleg!' said I, now jumping on the bulwarks, and leaving my comrade standing on the wharf.

'I mean,' he replied, 'he must show his papers.'

'Yea,' said Captain Bildad in his hollow voice, sticking his head from behind Peleg's, out of the wigwam. 'He must show that he's converted. Son of darkness,' he added, turning to Queequeg, 'art thou at present in communion with any christian church?'

'Why,' said I, 'he's a member of the First Congregational Church.' Here be it said, that many tattooed savages sailing in Nantucket ships at last come to be converted into the churches.

'First Congregational Church,' cried Bildad, 'what! that worships in Deacon Deuteronomy Coleman's meeting-house?' and so saying, taking out his spectacles, he rubbed them with his great yellow bandana handkerchief, and putting them on very carefully, came out of the wigwam, and leaning stiffly over the bulwarks, took a good long look at Queequeg.

'How long hath he been a member?' he then said, turning to me; 'not very long, I rather guess, young man.'

'No,' said Peleg, 'and he hasn't been baptized right either, or it would have washed some of that devil's blue off his face.'

'Do tell, now,' cried Bildad, 'is this Philistine a regular member of Deacon Deuteronomy's meeting? I never saw him going there, and I pass it every Lord's day.'

'I don't know anything about Deacon Deuteronomy or his meeting,' said I, 'all I know is, that Queequeg here is a born member of the First Congregational Church. He is a deacon himself, Queequeg is.'

'Young man,' said Bildad sternly, 'thou art skylarking with me explain thyself, thou young Hittite. What church dost thee mean? answer me.'

Finding myself thus hard pushed, I replied. 'I mean, sir, the same ancient Catholic Church to which you and I, and Captain Peleg there, and Queequeg here, and all of us, and every mother's son and soul of us belong; the great and everlasting First Congregation of this whole worshipping world; we all belong to that; only some of us cherish some queer crotchets noways touching the grand belief; in *that* we all join hands.'

'Splice, thou mean'st *splice* hands,' cried Peleg, drawing nearer. 'Young man, you'd better ship for a missionary, instead of a fore-mast hand; I never heard a better sermon. Deacon Deuteronomy – why Father Mapple himself couldn't beat it, and he's reckoned something. Come aboard, come aboard; never mind about the papers. I say, tell Quohog there – what's that you call him? tell Quohog to step along. By the great anchor, what a harpoon he's got there! looks like good stuff that; and he handles it about right. I say, Quohog, or whatever your name is, did you ever stand in the head of a whale-boat? did you ever strike a fish?'

Without saying a word, Queequeg, in his wild sort of way, jumped upon the bulwarks, from thence into the bows of one of the whale-boats hanging to the side; and then bracing his left knee, and poising his harpoon, cried out in some such way as this:–

'Cap'ain, you see him small drop tar on water dere? You see him? well, spose him one whale eye, well, den!' and taking sharp aim at it, he darted the iron right over old Bildad's broad brim, clean across the ship's decks, and struck the glistening tar spot out of sight.

'Now,' said Queequeg, quietly hauling in the line, 'spos-ee him whale-e eye; why, dad whale dead.'

'Quick, Bildad,' said Peleg, to his partner, who, aghast at the close vicinity of the flying harpoon, had retreated towards the cabin gangway. 'Quick, I say, you Bildad, and get the ship's papers. We must have Hedgehog there, I mean Quohog, in one of our boats. Look ye, Quohog, we'll give ye the ninetieth lay, and that's more than ever was given a harpooneer yet out of Nantucket.'

So down we went into the cabin, and to my great joy Queequeg was soon enrolled among the same ship's company to which I myself belonged.

When all preliminaries were over and Peleg had got everything ready for signing, he turned to me and said, 'I guess, Quohog there don't know how to write, does he? I say, Quohog, blast ye! dost thou sign thy name or make thy mark?'

But at this question, Queequeg, who had twice or thrice before taken part in similar ceremonies, looked no ways abashed; but taking the offered pen, copied upon the paper, in the proper place, an exact counterpart of a queer round figure which was tattooed upon his arm; so that through Captain Peleg's obstinate mistake touching his appellative, it stood something like this:–

Quohog.
his ✠ mark.

Meanwhile Captain Bildad sat earnestly and steadfastly eyeing Queequeg, and at last rising solemnly and fumbling in the huge pockets of his broad-skirted drab coat, took out a bundle of tracts, and selecting one entitled 'The Latter Day Coming; or No Time to Lose,' placed it in Queequeg's hands, and then grasping them and the book with both his, looked earnestly into his eyes, and said, 'Son of darkness, I must do my duty by thee; I am part owner of this ship, and feel concerned for the souls of all its crew; if thou still clingest to thy Pagan ways, which I sadly fear, I beseech thee, remain not for aye a Belial bondsman. Spurn the idol Bell, and the hideous dragon; turn from the wrath to come; mind thine eye, I say; oh! goodness gracious! steer clear of the fiery pit!'

Something of the salt sea yet lingered in old Bildad's language, heterogeneously mixed with Scriptural and domestic phrases.

'Avast there, avast there, Bildad, avast now spoiling our harpooneer,' cried Peleg. 'Pious harpooneers never make good voyagers – it takes the shark out of 'em; no harpooneer is worth a straw who aint pretty sharkish. There was young Nat Swaine, once the bravest boat-header out of all Nantucket and the Vineyard; he joined the meeting, and never came to good. He got so frightened about his plaguy soul, that he shrinked and sheered away from whales, for fear of after-claps in case he got stove and went to Davy Jones.'

'Peleg! Peleg!' said Bildad, lifting his eyes and hands, 'thou thyself, as I myself, hast seen many a perilous time; thou knowest, Peleg, what it is to have the fear of death; how, then, can'st thou prate in this ungodly guise. Thou beliest thine own heart, Peleg. Tell me, when this same Pequod here had her three masts overboard in that typhoon off Japan, that same voyage when thou went mate with Captain Ahab, did'st thou not think of Death and the Judgment then?'

'Hear him, hear him now,' cried Peleg, marching across the cabin, and thrusting his hands far down into his pockets, – 'hear him, all of ye. Think of that! When every moment we thought the ship would sink! Death and the Judgment then? What? With all three masts making such an everlasting thundering against the side; and every sea breaking over us, fore and aft. Think of Death and the Judgment then? No! no time to think about Death then. Life was what Captain Ahab and I was thinking of; and how to save all hands – how to rig jury-masts – how to get into the nearest port; that was what I was thinking of.'

Bildad said no more, but buttoning up his coat, stalked on deck, where we followed him. There he stood, very quietly overlooking some sail-makers who were mending a top-sail in the waist. Now and then he stooped to pick up a patch, or save an end of the tarred twine, which otherwise might have been wasted.

19

THE PROPHET

'SHIPMATES, have ye shipped in that ship?'

Queequeg and I had just left the Pequod, and were sauntering away from the water, for the moment each occupied with his own thoughts, when the above words were put to us by a stranger, who, pausing before us, levelled his massive forefinger at the vessel in question. He was but shabbily apparelled in faded jacket and patched trowsers; a rag of a black handkerchief investing his neck. A confluent small-pox had in all directions flowed over his face, and left it like the complicated ribbed bed of a torrent, when the rushing waters have been dried up.

'Have ye shipped in her?' he repeated.

'You mean the ship Pequod, I suppose,' said I, trying to gain a little more time for an uninterrupted look at him.

'Aye, the Pequod – that ship there,' he said, drawing back his whole arm, and then rapidly shoving it straight out from him, with the fixed bayonet of his pointed finger darted full at the object.

'Yes,' said I, 'we have just signed the articles.'

'Anything down there about your souls?'

'About what?'

'Oh, perhaps you hav'n't got any,' he said quickly. 'No matter though, I know many chaps that hav'n't got any, – good luck to 'em; and they are all the better off for it. A soul's a sort of a fifth wheel to a wagon.'

'What are you jabbering about, shipmate?' said I.

'*He's* got enough, though, to make up for all deficiencies of that sort in other chaps,' abruptly said the stranger, placing a nervous emphasis upon the word *he*.

'Queequeg,' said I, 'let's go; this fellow has broken loose from somewhere; he's talking about something and somebody we don't know.'

'Stop!' cried the stranger. 'Ye said true – ye hav'n't seen Old Thunder yet, have ye?'

'Who's Old Thunder?' said I, again riveted with the insane earnestness of his manner.

'Captain Ahab.'

'What! the captain of our ship, the Pequod?'

'Aye, among some of us old sailor chaps, he goes by that name. Ye hav'n't seen him yet, have ye?'

'No, we hav'n't. He's sick they say, but is getting better, and will be all right again before long.'

'All right again before long!' laughed the stranger, with a solemnly derisive sort of laugh. 'Look ye; when Captain Ahab is all right, then this left arm of mine will be all right; not before.'

'What do you know about him?'

'What did they *tell* you about him? Say that!'

'They didn't tell much of anything about him; only I've heard that he's a good whale-hunter, and a good captain to his crew.'

'That's true, that's true – yes, both true enough. But you must jump when he gives an order. Step and growl; growl and go – that's the word with Captain Ahab. But nothing about that thing that happened to him off Cape Horn, long ago, when he lay like dead for three days and nights; nothing about that deadly skrimmage with the Spaniard afore the altar in Santa? – heard nothing about that, eh? Nothing about the silver calabash he spat into? And nothing about his losing his leg last voyage, according to the prophecy? Didn't ye hear a word about them matters and something more, eh? No, I don't think ye did; how could ye? Who knows it? Not all Nantucket, I guess. But hows'ever, mayhap, ye've heard tell about the leg, and how he lost it; aye, ye have heard of that, I dare say. Oh yes, *that* every one knows a'most – I mean they know he's only one leg; and that a parmacetti took the other off.'

'My friend,' said I, 'what all this gibberish of yours is about, I don't know, and I don't much care; for it seems to me that you must be a little damaged in the head. But if you are speaking of Captain Ahab, of that ship there, the Pequod, then let me tell, that I know all about the loss of his leg.'

'*All* about it, eh – sure you do? – all?'

'Pretty sure.'

With finger pointed and eye levelled at the Pequod, the beggar-like stranger stood a moment, as if in a troubled reverie; then starting a little, turned and said: –'Ye've shipped, have ye? Names down on the papers? Well, well, what's signed, is signed; and what's to be, will be; and then again, perhaps it wont be, after all. Any how, it's all fixed and arranged a'ready; and some sailors or other must go with him, I suppose; as well these as any other men, God pity 'em! Morning to ye, shipmates, morning; the ineffable heavens bless ye; I'm sorry I stopped ye.'

'Look here, friend,' said I, 'if you have anything important to tell us, out with it; but if you are only trying to bamboozle us, you are mistaken in your game; that's all I have to say.'

'And it's said very well, and I like to hear a chap talk up that way; you are just the man for him – the likes of ye. Morning to ye, shipmates, morning! Oh! when ye get there, tell 'em I've concluded not to make one of 'em.'

'Ah, my dear fellow, you can't fool us that way – you can't fool us. It is the easiest thing in the world for a man to look as if he had a great secret in him.'

'Morning to ye, shipmates, morning.'

'Morning it is,' said I. 'Come along, Queequeg, let's leave this crazy man. But stop, tell me your name, will you?'

'Elijah.'

Elijah! thought I, and we walked away, both commenting, after each other's fashion, upon this ragged old sailor; and agreed that he was nothing but a humbug, trying to be a bugbear. But we had not gone perhaps above a hundred yards, when chancing to turn a corner, and looking back as I did so, who should be seen but Elijah following us, though at a distance. Somehow, the sight of him struck me so, that I said nothing to Queequeg of his being behind, but passed on with my comrade, anxious to see whether the stranger would turn the same corner that we did. He did; and then it seemed to me that he was dogging us, but with what intent I could not for the life of me imagine. This circumstance, coupled with his ambiguous, half-hinting, half-revealing, shrouded sort of talk, now begat in me all kinds of vague wonderments and half-apprehensions, and all connected with the Pequod; and Captain Ahab; and the leg he had lost; and the Cape Horn fit; and the silver calabash; and what Captain Peleg had said of him, when I left the ship the day previous; and the prediction of the squaw Tistig; and the voyage we had bound ourselves to sail; and a hundred other shadowy things.

I was resolved to satisfy myself whether this ragged Elijah was really dogging us or not, and with that intent crossed the way with Queequeg, and on that side of it retraced our steps. But Elijah passed on, without seeming to notice us. This relieved me; and once more, and finally as it seemed to me, I pronounced him in my heart, a humbug.

20

ALL ASTIR

A DAY or two passed, and there was great activity aboard the Pequod. Not only were the old sails being mended, but new sails were coming on board, and bolts of canvas, and coils of rigging; in short, everything betokened that the ship's preparations were hurrying to a close. Captain Peleg seldom or never went ashore, but sat in his wigwam keeping a sharp look-out upon the hands; Bildad did all the purchasing and providing at the stores; and the men employed in the hold and on the rigging were working till long after night-fall.

On the day following Queequeg's signing the articles, word was given at all the inns where the ship's company were stopping, that their chests must be on board before night, for there was no telling how soon the vessel might be sailing. So Queequeg and I got down our traps, resolving, however, to sleep ashore till the last. But it seems they always give very long notice in these cases, and the ship did not sail for several days. But no wonder; there was a good deal to be done, and there is no telling how many things to be thought of, before the Pequod was fully equipped.

Every one knows what a multitude of things – beds, saucepans, knives and forks, shovels and tongs, napkins, nutcrackers, and what not, are indispensable to the business of housekeeping. Just so with whaling, which necessitates a three-years' housekeeping upon the wide ocean, far from all grocers, costermongers, doctors, bakers, and bankers. And though this also holds true of merchant vessels, yet not by any means to the same extent as with whalemen. For besides the great length of the whaling voyage, the numerous articles peculiar to the prosecution of the fishery, and the impossibility of replacing them at the remote harbors usually frequented, it must be remembered, that of all ships, whaling vessels are the most exposed to accidents of all kinds, and especially to the destruction and loss of the very things upon which the success of the voyage most depends. Hence, the spare boats, spare spars, and spare lines and harpoons, and spare everythings, almost, but a spare Captain and duplicate ship.

At the period of our arrival at the Island, the heaviest stowage of the Pequod had been almost completed; comprising her beef, bread, water, fuel, and iron hoops and staves. But, as before hinted, for some time there was a continual fetching and carrying on board of divers odds and ends of things, both large and small.

Chief among those who did this fetching and carrying was Captain Bildad's sister, a lean old lady of a most determined and indefatigable spirit, but withal very kindhearted, who seemed resolved that, if *she* could help it, nothing should be found wanting in the Pequod, after once fairly getting to sea. At one time she would come on board with a jar of pickles for the steward's pantry; another time with a bunch of quills for the chief mate's desk, where he kept his log; a third time with a roll of flannel for the small of some one's rheumatic back. Never did any woman better deserve her name, which was Charity – Aunt Charity, as everybody called her. And like a sister of charity did this charitable Aunt Charity bustle about hither and thither, ready to turn her hand and heart to anything that promised to yield safety, comfort, and consolation to all on board a ship in which her beloved brother Bildad was concerned, and in which she herself owned a score or two of well-saved dollars.

But it was startling to see this excellent hearted Quakeress coming on board, as she did the last day, with a long oil-ladle in one hand, and a still longer whaling lance in the other. Nor was Bildad himself nor Captain Peleg at all backward. As for Bildad, he carried about with him a long list of the articles needed, and at every fresh arrival, down went his mark opposite that article upon the paper. Every once and a while Peleg came hobbling out of his whalebone den, roaring at the men down the hatchways, roaring up to the riggers at the mast-head, and then concluded by roaring back into his wigwam.

During these days of preparation, Queequeg and I often visited the craft, and as often I asked about Captain Ahab, and how he was, and when he was going to come on board his ship. To these questions they would answer, that he was getting better and better, and was expected aboard every day; meantime, the two Captains, Peleg and Bildad, could attend to everything necessary to fit the vessel for the voyage. If I had been downright honest with myself, I would have seen very plainly in my heart that I did but half fancy being committed this way to so long a voyage, without once laying my eyes on the man who was to be the absolute dictator of it, so soon as the ship sailed out upon the open sea. But when a man suspects any wrong, it sometimes happens that if he be already involved in the matter, he insensibly strives to cover up his suspicions even from himself. And much this way it was with me. I said nothing, and tried to think nothing.

At last it was given out that some time next day the ship would certainly sail. So next morning, Queequeg and I took a very early start.

21

GOING ABOARD

It was nearly six o'clock, but only grey imperfect misty dawn, when we drew nigh the wharf.

'There are some sailors running ahead there, if I see right,' said I to Queequeg, 'it can't be shadows; she's off by sunrise, I guess; come on!'

'Avast!' cried a voice, whose owner at the same time coming close behind us, laid a hand upon both our shoulders, and then insinuating himself between us, stood stooping forward a little, in the uncertain twilight, strangely peering from Queequeg to me. It was Elijah.

'Going aboard?'

'Hands off, will you,' said I.

'Lookee here,' said Queequeg, shaking himself, 'go 'way!'

'Aint going aboard, then?'

'Yes, we are,' said I, 'but what business is that of yours? Do you know, Mr Elijah, that I consider you a little impertinent?'

'No, no, no; I wasn't aware of that,' said Elijah, slowly

and wonderingly looking from me to Queequeg, with the most unaccountable glances.

'Elijah,' said I, 'you will oblige my friend and me by withdrawing. We are going to the Indian and Pacific Oceans, and would prefer not to be detained.'

'Ye be, be ye? Coming back afore breakfast?'

'He's cracked, Queequeg,' said I, 'come on.'

'Holloa!' cried stationary Elijah, hailing us when we had removed a few paces.

'Never mind him,' said I, 'Queequeg, come on.'

But he stole up to us again, and suddenly clapping his hand on my shoulder, said – 'Did ye see anything looking like men going towards that ship a while ago?'

Struck by this plain matter-of-fact question, I answered, saying, 'Yes, I thought I did see four or five men; but it was too dim to be sure.'

'Very dim, very dim,' said Elijah. 'Morning to ye.'

Once more we quitted him; but once more he came softly after us; and touching my shoulder again, said, 'See if you can find 'em now, will ye?'

'Find who?'

'Morning to ye! morning to ye!' he rejoined, again moving off. 'Oh! I was going to warn ye against – but never mind, never mind – it's all one, all in the family too; – sharp frost this morning, ain't it? Good bye to ye. Shan't see ye again very soon, I guess; unless it's before the Grand Jury.' And with these cracked words he finally departed, leaving me, for the moment, in no small wonderment at his frantic impudence.

At last, stepping on board the Pequod, we found everything in profound quiet, not a soul moving. The cabin entrance was locked within; the hatches were all on, and lumbered with coils of rigging. Going forward to the forecastle, we found the slide of the scuttle open. Seeing a light, we went down, and found only an old rigger there, wrapped in a tattered pea-jacket. He was thrown at whole length upon two chests, his face downwards and inclosed in his folded arms. The profoundest slumber slept upon him.

'Those sailors we saw, Queequeg, where can they have gone to?' said I, looking dubiously at the sleeper. But it seemed that, when on the wharf, Queequeg had not at all noticed what I now alluded to; hence I would have thought myself to have been optically deceived in that matter, were it not for Elijah's otherwise inexplicable question. But I beat the thing down; and again marking the sleeper, jocularly hinted to Queequeg that perhaps we had best sit up with the body; telling him to establish himself accordingly. He put his hand upon the sleeper's rear, as though feeling if it was soft enough; and then, without more ado, sat quietly down there.

'Gracious! Queequeg, don't sit there,' said I.

'Oh! perry dood seat,' said Queequeg, 'my country way; won't hurt him face.'

'Face!' said I, 'call that his face? very benevolent countenance then; but how hard he breathes, he's heaving himself; get off, Queequeg, you are heavy, it's grinding the face of the poor. Get off, Queequeg! Look, he'll twitch you off soon. I wonder he don't wake.'

Queequeg removed himself to just beyond the head of the sleeper, and lighted his tomahawk pipe. I sat at the feet. We kept the pipe passing over the sleeper, from one to the other. Meanwhile, upon questioning him, in his broken fashion, Queequeg gave me to understand that, in his land, owing to the absence of settees and sofas of all sorts, the king, chiefs, and great people generally, were in the custom of fattening some of the lower orders for ottomans; and to furnish a house comfortably in that respect, you had only to buy up eight or ten lazy fellows, and lay them round in the piers and alcoves. Besides, it was very convenient on an excursion; much better than those garden-chairs which are convertible into walking-sticks; upon occasion, a chief calling his attendant, and desiring him to make a settee of himself under a spreading tree, perhaps in some damp marshy place.

While narrating these things, every time Queequeg received the tomahawk from me, he flourished the hatchet-side of it over the sleeper's head.

'What's that for, Queequeg?'

'Perry easy, kill-e; oh! perry easy!'

He was going on with some wild reminiscences about his tomahawk-pipe, which, it seemed, had in its two uses both brained his foes and soothed his soul, when we were directly attracted to the sleeping rigger. The strong vapor now completely filling the contracted hole, it began to tell upon him. He breathed with a sort of muffledness; then seemed troubled in the nose; then revolved over once or twice; then sat up and rubbed his eyes.

'Holloa!' he breathed at last, 'who be ye smokers?'

'Shipped men,' answered I, 'when does she sail?'

'Aye, aye, ye are going in her, be ye? She sails to-day. The Captain came aboard last night.'

'What Captain? – Ahab?'

'Who but him indeed?'

I was going to ask him some further questions concerning Ahab, when we heard a noise on deck.

'Halloa! Starbuck's astir,' said the rigger. 'He's a lively chief mate, that; good man, and a pious; but all alive now, I must turn to.' And so saying he went on deck, and we followed.

It was now clear sunrise. Soon the crew came on board in twos and threes; the riggers bestirred themselves; the mates were actively engaged; and several of the shore people were busy in bringing various last things on board. Meanwhile Captain Ahab remained invisibly enshrined within his cabin.

22

MERRY CHRISTMAS

At length, towards noon, upon the final dismissal of the ship's riggers, and after the Pequod had been hauled out from the wharf, and after the ever-thoughtful Charity had come off in a whaleboat, with her last gift – a night-cap for

Stubb, the second mate, her brother-in-law, and a spare Bible for the steward – after all this, the two captains, Peleg and Bildad, issued from the cabin, and turning to the chief mate, Peleg said:

'Now, Mr Starbuck, are you sure everything is right? Captain Ahab is all ready – just spoke to him – nothing more to be got from shore, eh? Well, call all hands, then. Muster 'em aft here – blast 'em!'

'No need of profane words, however great the hurry, Peleg,' said Bildad, 'but away with thee, friend Starbuck, and do our bidding.'

How now! Here upon the very point of starting for the voyage, Captain Peleg and Captain Bildad were going it with a high hand on the quarter-deck, just as if they were to be joint-commanders at sea, as well as to all appearances in port. And, as for Captain Ahab, no sign of him was yet to be seen; only, they said he was in the cabin. But then, the idea was, that his presence was by no means necessary in getting the ship under weigh, and steering her well out to sea. Indeed, as that was not at all his proper business, but the pilot's; and as he was not yet completely recovered – so they said – therefore, Captain Ahab stayed below. And all this seemed natural enough; especially as in the merchant service many captains never show themselves on deck for a considerable time after heaving up the anchor, but remain over the cabin table, having a farewell merry-making with their shore friends, before they quit the ship for good with the pilot.

But there was not much chance to think over the matter, for Captain Peleg was now all alive. He seemed to do most of the talking and commanding, and not Bildad.

'Aft here, ye sons of bachelors,' he cried, as the sailors lingered at the main-mast. 'Mr Starbuck, drive 'em aft.'

'Strike the tent there!' – was the next order. As I hinted before, this whalebone marquee was never pitched except in port; and on board the Pequod, for thirty years, the order to strike the tent was well known to be the next thing to heaving up the anchor.

'Man the capstan! Blood and thunder! – jump!' – was the next command, and the crew sprang for the handspikes.

Now, in getting under weigh, the station generally occupied by the pilot is the forward part of the ship. And here Bildad, who, with Peleg, be it known, in addition to his other offices, was one of the licensed pilots of the port – he being suspected to have got himself made a pilot in order to save the Nantucket pilot-fee to all the ships he was concerned in, for he never piloted any other craft – Bildad, I say, might now be seen actively engaged in looking over the bows for the approaching anchor, and at intervals singing what seemed a dismal stave of psalmody, to cheer the hands at the windlass, who roared forth some sort of a chorus about the girls in Booble Alley, with hearty good will. Nevertheless, not three days previous, Bildad had told them that no profane songs would be allowed on board the Pequod, particularly in getting under weigh; and Charity, his sister, had placed a small choice copy of Watts in each seaman's berth.

Meantime, overseeing the other part of the ship, Captain Peleg ripped and swore astern in the most frightful manner. I almost thought he would sink the ship before the anchor could be got up; involuntarily I paused on my handspike, and told Queequeg to do the same, thinking of the perils we both ran, in starting on the voyage with such a devil for a pilot. I was comforting myself, however with the thought that in pious Bildad might be found some salvation, spite of his seven hundred and seventy-seventh lay; when I felt a sudden sharp poke in my rear, and turning round, was horrified at the apparition of Captain Peleg in the act of withdrawing his leg from my immediate vicinity. That was my first kick.

'Is that the way they heave in the marchant service?' he roared. 'Spring, thou sheep-head; spring, and break thy back-bone! Why don't ye spring, I say, all of ye – spring! Quohag! spring, thou chap with the red whiskers; spring there, Scotch-cap; spring, thou green pants. Spring, I say, all of ye, and spring your eyes out!' And so saying, he moved along the windlass, here and there using his leg very freely, while imperturbable Bildad kept leading off with his psalmody. Thinks I, Captain Peleg must have been drinking something to-day.

At last the anchor was up, the sails were set, and off we glided. It was a short, cold Christmas; and as the short northern day merged into night, we found ourselves almost broad upon the wintry ocean, whose freezing spray cased us in ice, as in polished armor. The long rows of teeth on the bulwarks glistened in the moonlight; and like the white ivory tusks of some huge elephant, vast curving icicles depended from the bows.

Lank Bildad, as pilot, headed the first watch, and ever and anon, as the old craft deep dived into the green seas, and sent the shivering frost all over her, and the winds howled, and the cordage rang, his steady notes were heard, –

'Sweet fields beyond the swelling flood,
Stand dressed in living green.
So to the Jews old Canaan stood,
While Jordan rolled between.'

Never did those sweet words sound more sweetly to me than then. They were full of hope and fruition. Spite of this frigid winter night in the boisterous Atlantic, spite of my wet feet and wetter jacket, there was yet, it then seemed to me, many a pleasant haven in store; and meads and glades so eternally vernal, that the grass shot up by the spring, untrodden, unwilted, remains at midsummer.

At last we gained such an offing, that the two pilots were needed no longer. The stout sail-boat that had accompanied us began ranging alongside.

It was curious and not unpleasing, how Peleg and Bildad were affected at this juncture, especially Captain Bildad. For loath to depart, yet; very loath to leave, for good, a ship bound on so long and perilous a voyage – beyond both stormy Capes; a ship in which some thousands of his hard earned dollars were invested; a ship, in which an old shipmate sailed as captain; a man almost as old as he, once more starting to encounter all the terrors of the pitiless jaw; loath to say good-bye to a thing so every way brimful of every interest to him, – poor old Bildad lingered long; paced the deck with anxious strides; ran down into the cabin to speak another farewell word there; again came on deck, and looked to windward; looked towards the wide and endless waters, only bounded by the far-off unseen Eastern Continents; looked towards the land; looked aloft; looked right and left; looked everywhere and nowhere; and at last, mechanically coiling a rope upon its pin, convulsively grasped stout Peleg by the hand, and holding up a lantern, for a moment stood gazing heroically in his face, as much as to say, 'Nevertheless, friend Peleg, I can stand it; yes, I can.'

As for Peleg himself, he took it more like a philosopher; but for all his philosophy, there was a tear twinkling in his eye, when the lantern came too near. And he, too, did not a little run from cabin to deck – now a word below, and now a word with Starbuck, the chief mate.

But, at last, he turned to his comrade, with a final sort of look about him, – 'Captain Bildad – come, old shipmate, we must go. Back the main-yard there! Boat ahoy! Stand by to come close alongside, now! Careful, careful! – come, Bildad, boy – say your last. Luck to ye, Starbuck – luck to ye, Mr Stubb – luck to ye, Mr Flask – good bye, and good luck to ye all – and this day three years I'll have a hot supper smoking for ye in old Nantucket. Hurrah and away!'

'God bless ye, and have ye in His holy keeping, men,' murmured old Bildad, almost incoherently. 'I hope ye'll have fine weather now, so that Captain Ahab may soon be moving among ye – a pleasant sun is all he needs, and ye'll have plenty of them in the tropic voyage ye go. Be careful in the hunt, ye mates. Don't stave the boats needlessly, ye harpooneers; good white cedar plank is raised full three per cent. within the year. Don't forget your prayers, either. Mr Starbuck, mind that cooper don't waste the spare staves. Oh! the sail-needles are in the green locker! Don't whale it too much a' Lord's days, men; but don't miss a fair chance either, that's rejecting Heaven's good gifts. Have an eye to the molasses tierce, Mr Stubb; it was a little leaky, I thought. If ye touch at the islands, Mr Flask, beware of fornication. Good-bye, good-bye! Don't keep that cheese too long down in the hold, Mr Starbuck; it'll spoil. Be careful with the butter – twenty cents the pound it was, and mind ye, if –'

'Come, come, Captain Bildad; stop palavering, – away!' and with that, Peleg hurried him over the side, and both dropt into the boat.

Ship and boat diverged; the cold, damp night breeze blew between; a screaming gull flew overhead; the two hulls wildly rolled; we gave three heavy-hearted cheers, and blindly plunged like fate into the lone Atlantic.

23

THE LEE SHORE

SOME chapters back, one Bulkington was spoken of, a tall, new-landed mariner, encountered in New Bedford at the inn.

When on that shivering winter's night, the Pequod thrust her vindictive bows into the cold malicious waves, who should I see standing at her helm but Bulkington! I looked with sympathetic awe and fearfulness upon the man, who in mid-winter just landed from a four years' dangerous voyage, could so unrestingly push off again for still another tempestuous term. The land seemed scorching to his feet. Wonderfullest things are ever the unmentionable; deep memories yield no epitaphs; this six-inch chapter is the stoneless grave of Bulkington. Let me only say that it fared with him as with the storm-tossed ship, that miserably drives along the leeward land. The port would fain give succor; the port is pitiful; in the port is safety, comfort, hearthstone, supper, warm blankets, friends, all that's kind to our mortalities. But in that gale, the port, the land, is that ship's direst jeopardy; she must fly all hospitality; one touch of land, though it but graze the keel, would make her shudder through and through. With all her might she crowds all sail off shore; in so doing, fights 'gainst the very winds that fain would blow her homeward; seeks all the lashed sea's landlessness again; for refuge's sake forlornly rushing into peril; her only friend her bitterest foe!

Know ye, now, Bulkington? Glimpses do ye seem to see of that mortally intolerable truth; that all deep, earnest thinking is but the intrepid effort of the soul to keep the open independence of her sea; while the wildest winds of heaven and earth conspire to cast her on the treacherous, slavish shore?

But as in landlessness alone resides the highest truth, shoreless, indefinite as God – so, better is it to perish in that howling infinite, than be ingloriously dashed upon the lee, even if that were safety! For worm-like, then, oh! who would craven crawl to land! Terrors of the terrible! is all this agony so vain? Take heart, take heart, O Bulkington! Bear thee grimly, demigod! Up from the spray of thy ocean-perishing – straight up, leaps thy apotheosis!

24

THE ADVOCATE

As Queequeg and I are now fairly embarked in this business of whaling; and as this business of whaling has somehow come to be regarded among landsmen as a rather unpoetical and disreputable pursuit; therefore, I am all anxiety to convince ye, ye landsmen, of the injustice hereby done to us hunters of whales.

In the first place, it may be deemed almost superfluous to establish the fact, that among people at large, the business of whaling is not accounted on a level with what are called the liberal professions. If a stranger were introduced into any miscellaneous metropolitan society, it would but slightly advance the general opinion of his merits, were he presented to the company as a harpooneer, say; and if in emulation of the naval officers he should append the initials S.W.F. (Sperm Whale Fishery) to his visiting card, such a procedure would be deemed pre-eminently presuming and ridiculous.

Doubtless one leading reason why the world declines honoring us whalemen, is this: they think that, at best, our vocation amounts to a butchering sort of business; and that when actively engaged therein, we are surrounded by all manner of defilements. Butchers we are, that is true. But butchers, also, and butchers of the bloodiest badge have been all Martial Commanders whom the world invariably delights to honor. And as for the matter of the alleged uncleanliness of our business, ye shall soon be initiated into certain facts hitherto pretty generally unknown, and which, upon the whole, will triumphantly plant the sperm whale-ship at least among the cleanliest things of this tidy earth. But even granting the charge in question to be true; what disordered slippery decks of a whale-ship are comparable to the unspeakable carrion of those battle-fields from which so many soldiers return to drink in all ladies' plaudits? And if the idea of peril so much enhances the popular conceit of the soldier's profession; let me assure ye that many a veteran who has freely marched up to a battery, would quickly recoil at the apparition of the sperm whale's vast tail, fanning into eddies the air over his head. For what are the comprehensible terrors of man compared with the interlinked terrors and wonders of God!

But, though the world scouts at us whale hunters, yet does it unwittingly pay us the profoundest homage; yea an all-abounding adoration! for almost all the tapers, lamps, and candles that burn round the globe, burn, as before so many shrines, to our glory!

But look at this matter in other lights; weigh it in all sorts of scales; see what we whalemen are, and have been.

Why did the Dutch in DeWitt's time have admirals of their whaling fleets? Why did Louis XVI of France, at his own personal expense, fit out whaling ships from Dunkirk, and politely invite to that town some score or two of families from our own island of Nantucket? Why did Britain between the years 1750 and 1788 pay to her whalemen in bounties upwards of £1,000,000? And lastly, how comes it that we whalemen of America now outnumber all the rest of the banded whalemen in the world; sail a navy of upwards of seven hundred vessels; manned by eighteen thousand men; yearly consuming 4,000,000 of dollars; the ships worth, at the time of sailing, $20,000,000; and every year importing into our harbors a well reaped harvest of $7,000,000. How comes all this, if there be not something puissant in whaling?

But this is not the half; look again.

I freely assert, that the cosmopolite philosopher cannot, for his life, point out one single peaceful influence, which within the last sixty years has operated more potentially upon the whole broad world, taken in one aggregate, than the high and mighty business of whaling. One way and another, it has begotten events so remarkable in themselves, and so continuously momentous in their sequential issues, that whaling may well be regarded as that Egyptian mother, who bore offspring themselves pregnant from her womb. It would be a hopeless, endless task to catalogue all these things. Let a handful suffice. For many years past the whale-ship has been the pioneer in ferreting out the remotest and least known parts of the earth. She has explored seas and archipelagoes which had no chart, where no Cook or Vancouver had ever sailed. If American and European men-of-war now peacefully ride in once savage harbors, let them fire salutes to the honor and the glory of the whale-ship, which originally showed them the way, and first interpreted between them and the savages. They may celebrate as they will the heroes of Exploring Expeditions, your Cookes, your Krusensterns; but I say that scores of anonymous Captains have sailed out of Nantucket, that were as great, and greater than your Cooke and your Krusenstern. For in their succorless empty-handedness, they, in the heathenish sharked waters, and by the beaches of unrecorded, javelin islands, battled with virgin wonders and terrors that Cooke with all his marines and muskets would not willingly have dared. All that is made such a flourish of in the old South Sea Voyages, those things were but the life-time commonplaces of our heroic Nantucketers. Often, adventures which Vancouver dedicates three chapters to, these men accounted unworthy of being set down in the ship's common log. Ah, the world! Oh, the world!

Until the whale fishery rounded Cape Horn, no commerce but colonial, scarcely any intercourse but colonial, was carried on between Europe and the long line of the opulent Spanish provinces on the Pacific coast. It was the whalemen who first broke through the jealous policy of the Spanish crown, touching those colonies; and, if space permitted, it might be distinctly shown how from those whalemen at last eventuated the liberation of Peru, Chili, and Bolivia from the yoke of Old Spain, and the establishment of the eternal democracy in those parts.

That great America on the other side of the sphere, Australia, was given to the enlightened world by the whalemen. After its first blunder-born discovery by a Dutchman, all other ships long shunned those shores as pestiferously barbarous; but the whale-ship touched there. The whale-ship is the true mother of that now mighty colony. Moreover, in the infancy of the first Australian settlement, the emigrants were several times saved from starvation by the benevolent biscuit of the whale-ship luckily dropping an anchor in their waters. The uncounted isles of all Polynesia confess the same truth, and do commercial homage to the whale-ship, that cleared the way for the missionary and the merchant, and in many cases carried the primitive missionaries to their first destinations. If that double-bolted land, Japan, is ever to become hospitable, it is the whale-ship alone to whom the credit will be due; for already she is on the threshold.

But if, in the face of all this, you still declare that whaling has no aesthetically noble associations connected with it, then am I ready to shiver fifty lances with you there, and unhorse you with a split helmet every time.

The whale has no famous author, and whaling no famous chronicler, you will say.

The whale no famous author, and whaling no famous chronicler? Who wrote the first account of our Leviathan? Who but mighty Job! And who composed the first narrative of a whaling-voyage? Who, but no less a prince than Alfred the Great, who, with his own royal pen, took down the words from Other, the Norwegian whale-hunter of those times! And who pronounced our glowing eulogy in Parliament? Who, but Edmund Burke!

True enough, but then whalemen themselves are poor devils; they have no good blood in their veins.

No good blood in their veins? They have something better than royal blood there. The grandmother of Benjamin Franklin was Mary Morrel; afterwards, by marriage, Mary Folger, one of the old settlers of Nantucket, and the ancestress to a long line of Folgers and harpooneers – all kith and kin to noble Benjamin – this day darting the barbed iron from one side of the world to the other.

Good again; but then all confess that somehow whaling is not respectable.

Whaling not respectable? Whaling is imperial! By old English statutory law, the whale is declared 'a royal fish'.*

Oh, that's only nominal! The whale himself has never figured in any grand imposing way.

The whale never figured in any grand imposing way? In one of the mighty triumphs given to a Roman general upon his entering the world's capital, the bones of a whale, brought all the way from the Syrian coast, were the most conspicuous object in the cymballed procession.*

Grant it, since you cite it; but, say what you will, there is no real dignity in whaling.

No dignity in whaling? The dignity of our calling the very heavens attest. Cetus is a constellation in the South! No more! Drive down your hat in presence of the Czar, and

* See subsequent chapters for something more on this head.

take it off to Queequeg! No more! I know a man that, in his lifetime, has taken three hundred and fifty whales. I account that man more honorable than that great captain of antiquity who boasted of taking as many walled towns.

And, as for me, if, by any possibility, there be any as yet undiscovered prime thing in me; if I shall ever deserve any real repute in that small but high hushed world which I might not be unreasonably ambitious of; if hereafter I shall do anything that, upon the whole, a man might rather have done than to have left undone; if, at my death, my executors, or more properly my creditors, find any precious MSS. in my desk, then here I prospectively ascribe all the honor and the glory to whaling; for a whale-ship was my Yale College and my Harvard.

25

POSTSCRIPT

In behalf of the dignity of whaling, I would fain advance naught but substantiated facts. But after embattling his facts, an advocate who should wholly suppress a not unreasonable surmise, which might tell eloquently upon his cause – such an advocate, would he not be blameworthy?

It is well known that at the coronation of kings and queens, even modern ones, a certain curious process of seasoning them for their functions is gone through. There is a saltcellar of state, so called, and there may be a caster of state. How they use the salt, precisely – who knows? Certain I am, however, that a king's head is solemnly oiled at his coronation, even as a head of salad. Can it be, though, that they anoint it with a view of making its interior run well, as they anoint machinery? Much might be ruminated here, concerning the essential dignity of this regal process, because in common life we esteem but meanly and contemptibly a fellow who anoints his hair, and palpably smells of that anointing. In truth, a mature man who uses hair-oil, unless medicinally, that man has probably got a quoggy spot in him somewhere. As a general rule, he can't amount to much in his totality.

But the only thing to be considered here, is this – what kind of oil is used at coronations? Certainly it cannot be olive oil, nor macassar oil, nor castor oil, nor bear's oil, nor train oil, nor cod-liver oil. What then can it possibly be, but sperm oil in its unmanufactured, unpolluted state, the sweetest of all oils?

Think of that, ye loyal Britons! we whalemen supply your kings and queens with coronation stuff!

26

KNIGHTS AND SQUIRES

THE chief mate of the Pequod was Starbuck, a native of Nantucket, and a Quaker by descent. He was a long, earnest man, and though born on an icy coast, seemed well adapted to endure hot latitudes, his flesh being hard as twice-baked biscuit. Transported to the Indies, his live blood would not spoil like bottled ale. He must have been born in some time of general drought and famine, or upon one of those fast days for which his state is famous. Only some thirty arid summers had he seen; those summers had dried up all his physical superfluousness. But this, his thinness, so to speak, seemed no more the token of wasting anxieties and cares, than it seemed the indication of any bodily blight. It was merely the condensation of the man. He was by no means ill-looking; quite the contrary. His pure tight skin was an excellent fit; and closely wrapped up in it, and embalmed with inner health and strength, like a revivified Egyptian, this Starbuck seemed prepared to endure for long ages to come, and to endure always, as now; for be it Polar snow or torrid sun, like a patent chronometer, his interior vitality was warranted to do well in all climates. Looking into his eyes, you seemed to see there the yet lingering images of those thousand-fold perils he had calmly confronted through life. A staid, steadfast man, whose life for the most part was a telling pantomime of action, and not a tame chapter of sounds. Yet, for all his hardy sobriety and fortitude, there were certain qualities in him which at times affected, and in some cases seemed well nigh to overbalance all the rest. Uncommonly conscientious for a seaman, and endued with a deep natural reverence, the wild watery loneliness of his life did therefore strongly incline him to superstition; but to that sort of superstition, which in some organizations seems rather to spring, somehow, from intelligence than from ignorance. Outward portents and inward presentiments were his. And if at times these things bent the welded iron of his soul, much more did his far-away domestic memories of his young Cape wife and child, tend to bend him still more from the original ruggedness of his nature, and open him still further to those latent influences which, in some honest-hearted men, restrain the gush of dare-devil daring, so often evinced by others in the more perilous vicissitudes of the fishery. 'I will have no man in my boat,' said Starbuck, 'who is not afraid of a whale.' By this, he seemed to mean, not only that the most reliable and useful courage was that which arises from the fair estimation of the encountered peril, but that an utterly fearless man is a far more dangerous comrade than a coward.

'Aye, aye,' said Stubb, the second mate, 'Starbuck, there, is as careful a man as you'll find anywhere in this fishery.' But we shall ere long see what that word 'careful' precisely means when used by a man like Stubb, or almost any other whale hunter.

Starbuck was no crusader after perils; in him courage was not a sentiment; but a thing simply useful to him, and always at hand upon all mortally practical occasions. Besides, he thought, perhaps, that in this business of whaling, courage was one of the great staple outfits of the ship, like her beef and her bread, and not to be foolishly wasted. Wherefore he had no fancy for lowering for whales after sun-down; nor for persisting in fighting a fish that too much persisted in fighting him. For, thought Starbuck, I am here in this critical ocean to kill whales for my living, and not to be killed by them for theirs; and that hundreds of men had been so killed Starbuck well knew. What doom was his own father's? Where, in the bottomless deeps, could he find the torn limbs of his brother?

With memories like these in him, and, moreover, given to a certain superstitiousness, as has been said; the courage of this Starbuck which could, nevertheless, still flourish, must indeed have been extreme. But it was not in reasonable nature that a man so organized, and with such terrible experiences and remembrances as he had; it was not in nature that these things should fail in latently engendering an element in him, which, under suitable circumstances, would break out from its confinement, and burn all his courage up. And brave as he might be, it was that sort of bravery chiefly, visible in some intrepid men, which, while generally abiding firm in the conflict with seas, or winds, or whales, or any of the ordinary irrational horrors of the world, yet cannot withstand those more terrific, because more spiritual terrors, which sometimes menace you from the concentrating brow of an enraged and mighty man.

But were the coming narrative to reveal, in any instance, the complete abasement of poor Starbuck's fortitude, scarce might I have the heart to write it; for it is a thing most sorrowful, nay shocking, to expose the fall of valor in the soul. Men may seem detestable as joint stock-companies and nations; knaves, fools, and murderers there may be; men may have mean and meagre faces; but man, in the ideal, is so noble and so sparkling, such a grand and glowing creature, that over any ignominious blemish in him all his fellows should run to throw their costliest robes. That immaculate manliness we feel within ourselves, so far within us, that it remains intact though all the outer character seem gone; bleeds with keenest anguish at the undraped spectacle of a valor-ruined man. Nor can piety itself, at such a shameful sight, completely stifle her upbraidings against the permitting stars. But this august dignity I treat of, is not the dignity of kings and robes, but that abounding dignity which has no robed investiture. Thou shalt see it shining in the arm that wields a pick or drives a spike; that democratic dignity which, on all hands, radiates without end from God; Himself! The great God absolute! The centre and circumference of all democracy! His omnipresence, our divine equality!

If, then, to meanest mariners, and renegades and castaways, I shall hereafter ascribe high qualities, though dark; weave round them tragic graces; if even the most mournful, perchance the most abased, among them all, shall at times lift himself to the exalted mounts; if I shall touch that workman's arm with some ethereal light; if I shall spread a rainbow over his disastrous set of sun; then against all mortal critics bear me out in it, thou just Spirit of Equality, which hast spread one royal mantle of humanity over all my kind! Bear me out in it, thou great democratic God! who didst not refuse to the swart convict, Bunyan, the pale, poetic pearl; Thou who didst clothe with doubly hammered leaves of finest gold, the stumped and paupered arm of old Cervantes; Thou who didst pick up Andrew Jackson from the pebbles; who didst hurl him upon a war-horse; who didst thunder him higher than a throne! Thou who, in all Thy mighty, earthly marchings, ever cullest Thy selectest champions from the kingly commons; bear me out in it, O God!

27

KNIGHTS AND SQUIRES

STUBB was the second mate. He was a native of Cape Cod; and hence, according to local usage, was called a Cape-Codman. A happy-go-lucky; neither craven nor valiant; taking perils as they came with an indifferent air; and while engaged in the most imminent crisis of the chase, toiling away, calm and collected as a journeyman joiner engaged for the year. Good-humored, easy, and careless, he presided over his whale-boat as if the most deadly encounter were but a dinner, and his crew all invited guests. He was as particular about the comfortable arrangement of his part of the boat, as an old stage-driver is about the snugness of his box. When close to the whale, in the very death-lock of the fight, he handled his unpitying lance coolly and off-handedly, as a whistling tinker his hammer. He would hum over his old rigadig tunes while flank and flank with the most exasperated monster. Long usage had, for this Stubb, converted the jaws of death into an easy chair. What he thought of death itself, there is no telling. Whether he ever thought of it at all, might be a question; but, if he ever did chance to cast his mind that way after a comfortable dinner, no doubt, like a good sailor, he took it to be a sort of call of the watch to tumble aloft, and bestir themselves there, about something which he would find out when he obeyed the order, and not sooner.

What, perhaps, with other things, made Stubb such an easy-going, unfearing man, so cheerily trudging off with the burden of life in a world full of grave peddlers, all bowed to the ground with their packs; what helped to bring about that almost impious good-humor of his; that thing must have been his pipe. For, like his nose, his short, black little pipe was one of the regular features of his face. You would almost as soon have expected him to turn out of his bunk without his nose as without his pipe. He kept a whole row of pipes there ready loaded, stuck in a rack, within easy reach of his hand; and, whenever he turned in, he smoked them all out in succession, lighting one from the other to the end of the chapter; then loading them again to be in readiness anew. For, when Stubb dressed, instead of first putting his legs into his trowsers, he put his pipe into his mouth.

I say this continual smoking must have been one cause, at least, of his peculiar disposition; for every one knows that this earthly air, whether ashore or afloat, is terribly infected with the nameless miseries of the numberless mortals who have died exhaling it; and as in time of the cholera, some people go about with a camphorated handkerchief to their mouths; so, likewise, against all mortal tribulations, Stubb's tobacco smoke might have operated as a sort of disinfecting agent.

The third mate was Flask, a native of Tisbury, in Martha's Vineyard. A short, stout, ruddy young fellow, very pugnacious concerning whales, who somehow seemed to think that the great Leviathans had personally and hereditarily affronted him; and therefore it was a sort of point of honor with him, to destroy them whenever encountered. So utterly lost was he to all sense of reverence for the many marvels of their majestic bulk and mystic ways; and so dead to anything like an apprehension of any possible danger from encountering them; that in his poor opinion, the wondrous whale was but a species of magnified mouse, or at least water-rat, requiring only a little circumvention and some small application of time and trouble in order to kill and boil. This ignorant, unconscious fearlessness of his made him a little waggish in the matter of whales; he followed these fish for the fun of it; and a three years' voyage round Cape Horn was only a jolly joke that lasted that length of time. As a carpenter's nails are divided into wrought nails and cut nails; so mankind may be similarly divided. Little Flask was one of the wrought ones; made to clinch tight and last long. They called him King-Post on board of the Pequod; because, in form, he could be well likened to the short, square timber known by that name in Arctic whalers; and which by the means of many radiating side timbers inserted into it, serves to brace the ship against the icy concussions of those battering seas.

Now these three mates – Starbuck, Stubb, and Flask, were momentous men. They it was who by universal prescription commanded three of the Pequod's boats as headsmen. In that grand order of battle in which Captain Ahab would probably marshal his forces to descend on the whales, these three headsmen were as captains of companies. Or, being armed with their long keen whaling spears, they were as a picked trio of lancers; even as the harpooneers were flingers of javelins.

And since in this famous fishery, each mate or headsman, like a Gothic Knight of old, is always accompanied by his boat-steerer or harpooneer, who in certain conjunctures provides him with a fresh lance, when the former one has been badly twisted, or elbowed in the assault; and moreover, as there generally subsists between the two, a close intimacy and friendliness; it is therefore but meet, that in this place we set down who the Pequod's harpooneers were, and to what headsman each of them belonged.

First of all was Queequeg, whom Starbuck, the chief mate, had selected for his squire. But Queequeg is already known.

Next was Tashtego, an unmixed Indian from Gay Head, the most westerly promontory of Martha's Vineyard, where there still exists the last remnant of a village of red men, which has long supplied the neighboring island of Nantucket with many of her most daring harpooneers. In the fishery, they usually go by the generic name of Gay-Headers. Tashtego's long, lean, sable hair, his high cheek bones, and black rounding eyes – for an Indian, Oriental in their largeness, but Antarctic in their glittering expression – all this sufficiently proclaimed him an inheritor of the unvitiated blood of those proud warrior hunters, who, in quest of the great New England moose, had scoured, bow in hand, the aboriginal forests of the main. But no longer snuffing in the trail of the wild beasts of the woodland, Tashtego now hunted in the wake of the great whales of the sea; the unerring harpoon of the son fitly replacing the infallible arrow of the sires. To look at the tawny brawn of his lithe snaky limbs, you would almost have credited the superstitions of some of the earlier Puritans, and half believed this wild Indian to be a son of the Prince of the Powers of the Air. Tashtego was Stubb the second mate's squire.

Third among the harpooneers was Daggoo, a gigantic, coal-black negro-savage, with a lion-like tread – an Ahasuerus to behold. Suspended from his ears were two golden hoops, so large that the sailors called them ring-bolts, and would talk of securing the top-sail halyards to them. In his youth Daggoo had voluntarily shipped on board of a whaler, lying in a lonely bay on his native coast. And never having been anywhere in the world but in Africa, Nantucket, and the pagan harbors most frequented by whalemen; and having now led for many years the bold life of the fishery in the ships of owners uncommonly heedful of what manner of men they shipped; Daggoo retained all his barbaric virtues, and erect as a giraffe, moved about the decks in all the pomp of six feet five in his socks. There was a corporeal humility in looking up at him; and a white man standing before him seemed a white flag come to beg truce of a fortress. Curious to tell, this imperial negro, Ahasuerus Daggoo, was the Squire of little Flask, who looked like a chess-man beside him. As for the residue of the Pequod's company, be it said, that at the present day not one in two of the many thousand men before the mast employed in the American whale fishery, are Americans born, though pretty nearly all the officers are. Herein it is the same with the American whale fishery as with the American army and military and merchant navies, and the engineering forces employed in the construction of the American Canals and Railroads. The same, I say, because in all these cases the native American liberally provides the brains, the rest of the world as generously supplying the muscles. No small number of these whaling seamen belong to the Azores, where the outward bound Nantucket whalers frequently touch to augment their crews from the hardy peasants of those rocky shores. In like manner, the Greenland whalers sailing out of Hull or London, put in at the Shetland Islands, to receive the full complement of their crew. Upon the passage homewards, they drop them there again. How it is, there is no telling, but Islanders seem to make the best whalemen. They were nearly all Islanders in the Pequod, *Isolatoes* too, I call such, not acknowledging the common continent of men, but each *Isolato* living on a separate continent of his own. Yet now, federated along one keel, what a set these Isolatoes were! An Anacharsis Clootz deputation from all the isles of the sea, and all the ends of the earth, accompanying Old Ahab in the Pequod to lay the world's grievances before that bar from which not very many of them ever come back. Black Little Pip – he never did – oh, no! he went before. Poor Alabama boy! On the grim Pequod's forecastle, ye shall ere long see him, beating his tambourine; prelusive of the eternal time, when sent for, to the great quarter-deck on high, he was bid strike in with angels, and beat his tambourine in glory; called a coward here, hailed a hero there!

28

AHAB

For several days after leaving Nantucket, nothing above hatches was seen of Captain Ahab. The mates regularly relieved each other at the watches, and for aught that could be seen to the contrary, they seemed to be the only commanders of the ship; only they sometimes issued from the cabin with orders so sudden and peremptory, that after all it was plain they but commanded vicariously. Yes, their supreme lord and dictator was there, though hitherto unseen by any eyes not permitted to penetrate into the now sacred retreat of the cabin.

Every time I ascended to the deck from my watches below, I instantly gazed aft to mark if any strange face were visible; for my first vague disquietude touching the unknown captain, now in the seclusion of the sea, became almost a perturbation. This was strangely heightened at times by the ragged Elijah's diabolical incoherences uninvitedly recurring to me, with a subtle energy I could not have before conceived of. But poorly could I withstand them, much as in other moods I was almost ready to smile at the solemn whimsicalities of that outlandish prophet of the wharves. But whatever it was of apprehensiveness or uneasiness – to call it so – which I felt, yet whenever I came to look about me in the ship, it seemed against all warranty to cherish such emotions. For though the harpooneers, with the great body of the crew, were a far more barbaric, heathenish, and motley set than any of the tame merchant-ship companies which my previous experiences had made me acquainted with, still I ascribed this – and rightly ascribed it – to the fierce uniqueness of the very nature of that wild Scandinavian vocation in which I had so abandonedly embarked. But it was especially the aspect of the three chief officers of the ship, the mates, which was most forcibly calculated to allay these colorless misgivings, and induce confidence and cheerfulness in every presentment of the voyage. Three better, more likely sea-officers and men, each in his own different way, could not readily be found, and they were every one of them Americans; a Nantucketer, a Vineyarder, a Cape man. Now, it being Christmas when the ship shot from out her harbor, for a space we had biting Polar weather, though all the time running away from it to the southward; and by every degree and minute of latitude which we sailed, gradually leaving that merciless winter, and all its intolerable weather behind us. It was one of those less lowering, but still grey and gloomy enough mornings of the transition, when with a fair wind the ship was rushing through the water with a vindictive sort of leaping and melancholy rapidity, that as I mounted to the deck at the call of the forenoon watch, so soon as I levelled my glance towards the taffrail, foreboding shivers ran over me. Reality outran apprehension; Captain Ahab stood upon his quarter-deck.

There seemed no sign of common bodily illness about him, nor of the recovery from any. He looked like a man cut away from the stake, when the fire has overrunningly wasted all the limbs without consuming them, or taking away one particle from their compacted aged robustness. His whole high, broad form, seemed made of solid bronze, and shaped in an unalterable mould, like Cellini's cast Perseus. Threading its way out from among his grey hairs, and continuing right down one side of his tawny scorched face and neck, till it disappeared in his clothing, you saw a slender rod-like mark, lividly whitish. It resembled that perpendicular seam sometimes made in the straight, lofty trunk of a great tree, when the upper lightning tearingly darts down it, and without wrenching a single twig, peels and grooves out the bark from top to bottom, ere running off into the soil, leaving the tree still greenly alive, but branded. Whether that mark was born with him, or whether it was the scar left by some desperate wound, no one could certainly say. By some tacit consent, throughout the voyage little or no allusion was made to it, especially by the mates. But once Tashtego's senior, an old Gay-Head Indian among the crew, superstitiously asserted that not till he was full forty years old did Ahab become that way branded, and then it came upon him, not in the fury of any mortal fray, but in an elemental strife at sea. Yet, this wild hint seemed inferentially negatived, by what a grey Manxman insinuated, an old sepulchral man, who, having never before sailed out of Nantucket, had never ere this laid eye upon wild Ahab. Nevertheless, the old sea-traditions, the immemorial credulities, popularly invested this old Manxman with preternatural powers of discernment. So that no white sailor seriously contradicted him when he said that if ever Captain Ahab should be tranquilly laid out – which might hardly come to pass, so he muttered – then, whoever should do that last office for the dead, would find a birth-mark on him from crown to sole.

So powerfully did the whole grim aspect of Ahab affect me, and the livid brand which streaked it, that for the first few moments I hardly noted that not a little of this overbearing grimness was owing to the barbaric white leg upon which he partly stood. It had previously come to me that this ivory leg had at sea been fashioned from the polished bone of the sperm whale's jaw. 'Aye, he was dismasted off Japan,' said the old Gay-Head Indian once; 'but like his dismasted craft, he shipped another mast without coming home for it. He has a quiver of 'em.'

I was struck with the singular posture he maintained.

Upon each side of the Pequod's quarter deck, and pretty close to the mizen shrouds, there was an auger hole, bored about half an inch or so, into the plank. His bone leg steadied in that hole; one arm elevated, and holding by a shroud; Captain Ahab stood erect, looking straight out beyond the ship's ever-pitching prow. There was an infinity of firmest fortitude, a determinate, unsurrenderable wilfulness, in the fixed and fearless, forward dedication of that glance. Not a word he spoke; nor did his officers say aught to him; though by all their minutest gestures and expressions, they plainly showed the uneasy, if not painful, consciousness of being under a troubled master-eye. And not only that, but moody stricken Ahab stood before them with a crucifixion in his face; in all the nameless regal overbearing dignity of some mighty woe.

Ere long, from his first visit in the air, he withdrew into his cabin. But after that morning, he was every day visible to the crew; either standing in his pivot-hole, or seated upon an ivory stool he had; or heavily walking the deck. As the sky grew less gloomy; indeed, began to grow a little genial, he became still less and less a recluse; as if, when the ship had sailed from home, nothing but the dead wintry bleakness of the sea had then kept him so secluded. And, by and by, it came to pass, that he was almost continually in the air; but, as yet, for all that he said, or perceptibly did, on the at last sunny deck, he seemed as unnecessary there as another mast. But the Pequod was only making a passage now; not regularly cruising; nearly all whaling preparatives needing supervision the mates were fully competent to, so that there was little or nothing, out of himself, to employ or excite Ahab, now; and thus chase away, for that one interval, the clouds that layer upon layer were piled upon his brow, as ever all clouds choose the loftiest peaks to pile themselves upon.

Nevertheless, ere long, the warm, warbling persuasiveness of the pleasant, holiday weather we came to, seemed gradually to charm him from his mood. For, as when the red-cheeked, dancing girls, April and May, trip home to the wintry, misanthropic woods; even the barest, ruggedest, most thunder-cloven old oak will at least send forth some few green sprouts, to welcome such glad-hearted visitants; so Ahab did, in the end, a little respond to the playful allurings of that girlish air. More than once did he put forth the faint blossom of a look, which, in any other man, would have soon flowered out in a smile.

29

ENTER AHAB; TO HIM, STUBB

SOME days elapsed, and ice and icebergs all astern, the Pequod now went rolling through the bright Quito spring, which, at sea, almost perpetually reigns on the threshold of the eternal August of the Tropic. The warmly cool, clear, ringing, perfumed, overflowing, redundant days, were as crystal goblets of Persian sherbet, heaped up – flaked up, with rose-water snow. The starred and stately nights seemed haughty dames in jewelled velvets, nursing at home in lonely pride, the memory of their absent conquering Earls, the golden helmeted suns! For sleeping man, 'twas hard to choose between such winsome days and such seducing nights. But all the witcheries of that unwaning weather did not merely lend new spells and potencies to the outward world. Inward they turned upon the soul, especially when the still mild hours of eve came on; then, memory shot her crystals as the clear ice most forms of noiseless twilights. And all these subtle agencies, more and more they wrought on Ahab's texture.

Old age is always wakeful; as if, the longer linked with life, the less man has to do with aught that looks like death. Among sea-commanders, the old greybeards will oftenest leave their berths to visit the night-cloaked deck. It was so with Ahab; only that now, of late, he seemed so much to live in the open air, that truly speaking, his visits were more to the cabin, than from the cabin to the planks. 'It feels like going down into one's tomb,' – he would mutter to himself, – 'for an old captain like me to be descending this narrow scuttle, to go to my grave-dug berth.'

So, almost every twenty-four hours, when the watches of the night were set, and the band on deck sentinelled the slumbers of the band below; and when if a rope was to be hauled upon the forecastle, the sailors flung it not rudely down, as by day, but with some cautiousness dropt it to its place, for fear of disturbing their slumbering shipmates; when this sort of steady quietude would begin to prevail, habitually, the silent steersman would watch the cabin-scuttle; and ere long the old man would emerge, griping at the iron banister, to help his crippled way. Some considerating touch of humanity was in him; for at times like these, he usually abstained from patrolling the quarter-deck; because to his wearied mates, seeking repose within six inches of his ivory heel, such would have been the reverberating crack and din of that bony step, that their dreams would have been of the crunching teeth of sharks. But once, the mood was on him too deep for common regardings; and as with heavy, lumber-like pace he was measuring the ship from taffrail to mainmast, Stubb, the odd second mate, came up from below, and with a certain unassured, deprecating humorousness, hinted that if Captain Ahab was pleased to walk the planks, then, no one could say nay; but there might be some way of muffling the noise; hinting something indistinctly and hesitatingly about a globe of tow, and the insertion into it, of the ivory heel. Ah! Stubb, thou did'st not know Ahab then.

'Am I a cannon-ball, Stubb,' said Ahab, 'that thou wouldst wad me that fashion? But go thy ways; I had forgot. Below to thy nightly grave; where such as ye sleep between shrouds, to use ye to the filling one at last. – Down, dog, and kennel!'

Starting at the unforeseen concluding exclamation of the so suddenly scornful old man, Stubb was speechless a moment; then said excitedly, 'I am not used to be spoken to that way, sir; I do but less than half like it, sir.'

'Avast!' gritted Ahab between his set teeth, and violently moving away, as if to avoid some passionate temptation.

'No, sir; not yet,' said Stubb, emboldened, 'I will not tamely be called a dog, sir.'

'Then be called ten times a donkey, and a mule, and an ass, and begone, or I'll clear the world of thee!'

As he said this, Ahab advanced upon him with such overbearing terrors in his aspect, that Stubb involuntarily retreated.

'I was never served so before without giving a hard blow for it,' muttered Stubb, as he found himself descending the cabin-scuttle. 'It's very queer. Stop, Stubb; somehow, now, I don't well know whether to go back and strike him, or – what's that? – down here on my knees and pray for him? Yes, that was the thought coming up in me; but it would be the first time I ever *did* pray. It's queer; very queer; and he's queer too; aye, take him fore and aft, he's about the queerest old man Stubb ever sailed with. How he flashed at me! – his eyes like powder-pans! is he mad? Anyway there's something on his mind, as sure as there must be something on a deck when it cracks. He aint in his bed now, either, more than three hours out of the twenty-four; and he don't sleep then. Didn't that Dough-Boy, the steward, tell me that of a morning he always finds the old man's hammock clothes all rumpled and tumbled, and the sheets down at the foot, and the coverlid almost tied into knots, and the pillow a sort of frightful hot, as though a baked brick had been on it? A hot old man! I guess he's got what some folks ashore call a conscience; it's a kind of Tic-Dolly-row they say – worse nor a toothache. Well, well; I don't know what it is, but the Lord keep me from catching it. He's full of riddles; I wonder what he goes into the after hold for, every night, as Dough-Boy tells me he suspects; what's that for, I should like to know? Who's made appointments with him in the hold? Ain't that queer, now? But there's no telling, it's the old game – Here goes for a snooze. Damn me, it's worth a fellow's while to be born into the world, if only to fall right asleep. And now that I think of it, that's about the first thing babies do, and that's a sort of queer, too. Damn me, but all things are queer, come to think of 'em. But that's against my principles. Think not, is my eleventh commandment; and sleep when you can, is my twelfth – So here goes again. But how's that? didn't he call me a dog? blazes! he called me ten times a donkey, and piled a lot of jackasses on top of *that!* He might as well have kicked me, and done with it. Maybe he *did* kick me, and I didn't observe it, I was so taken all aback with his brow, somehow. It flashed like a bleached bone. What the devil's the matter with me? I don't stand right on my legs. Coming afoul of that old man has a sort of turned me wrong side out. By the Lord, I must have been dreaming, though – How? how? how? – but the only way's to stash it; so here goes to hammock again; and in the morning, I'll see how this plaguey juggling thinks over by day-light.'

30

THE PIPE

WHEN Stubb had departed, Ahab stood for a while leaning over the bulwarks; and then, as had been usual with him of late, calling a sailor of the watch, he sent him below for his ivory stool, and also his pipe. Lighting the pipe at the binnacle lamp and planting the stool on the weather side of the deck, he sat and smoked.

In old Norse times, the thrones of the sea-loving Danish kings were fabricated, saith tradition, of the tusks of the narwhale. How could one look at Ahab then, seated on that tripod of bones, without bethinking him of the royalty it symbolized? For a Khan of the plank, and a king of the sea, and a great lord of Leviathans was Ahab.

Some moments passed, during which the thick vapor came from his mouth in quick and constant puffs, which blew back again into his face. 'How now,' he soliloquized at last, withdrawing the tube, 'this smoking no longer soothes. Oh, my pipe! hard must it go with me if thy charm be gone! Here have I been unconsciously toiling, not pleasuring, – aye, and ignorantly smoking to windward all the while; to windward, and with such nervous whiffs, as if, like the dying whale, my final jets were the strongest and fullest of trouble. What business have I with this pipe? This thing that is meant for sereneness, to send up mild white vapors among mild white hairs, not among torn iron-grey locks like mine. I'll smoke no more –'

He tossed the still lighted pipe into the sea. The fire hissed in the waves; the same instant the ship shot by the bubble the sinking pipe made. With slouched hat, Ahab lurchingly paced the planks.

31

QUEEN MAB

NEXT morning Stubb accosted Flask.

'Such a queer dream, King-Post, I never had. You know the old man's ivory leg, well I dreamed he kicked me with it; and when I tried to kick back, upon my soul, my little man, I kicked my leg right off! And then, presto! Ahab seemed a pyramid, and I, like a blazing fool, kept kicking at it. But what was still more curious, Flask – you know how curious all dreams are – through all this rage that I was in, I somehow seemed to be thinking to myself, that after all, it was not much of an insult, that kick from Ahab. "Why," thinks I, "what's the row! It's not a real leg, only a false leg." And there's a mighty difference between a living thump and a dead thump. That's what makes a blow from the hand, Flask, fifty times more savage to bear than a blow from a cane. The living member – that makes the living insult, my little man. And thinks I to myself all the while, mind, while I was stubbing my silly toes against that cursed pyramid – so confoundedly contradictory was it all, all the while, I say, I was thinking to myself, "what's his leg now, but a cane – a whalebone cane. Yes," thinks I, "it was only a playful cudgelling – in fact, only a whaleboning that he gave me – not a base kick. Besides," thinks I, "look at it once; why, the end of it – the foot part – what a small sort of end it is; whereas, if a broad footed farmer kicked me, *there's* a devilish broad insult. But this insult is whittled down to a point only." But now comes the greatest joke of the dream, Flask. While I was battering away at the pyramid, a sort of badger-haired old merman, with a hump on his back, takes me by the shoulders, and slews me round. "What are you 'bout?" says he. 'Slid! man, but I was frightened. Such a phiz! But, somehow, next moment I was over the fright. "What am I about?" says I at last. "And what business is that of yours, I should like to know, Mr Humpback? Do *you* want a kick?" By the lord, Flask, I had no sooner said that, than he turned round his stern to me, bent over, and dragging up a lot of seaweed he had for a clout – what do you think, I saw? – why thunder alive, man, his stern was stuck full of marlinspikes, with the points out. Says I, on second thoughts, "I guess I won't kick you, old fellow." "Wise Stubb," said he, "wise Stubb;" and kept muttering it all the time, a sort of eating of his own gums like a chimney hag. Seeing he wasn't going to stop saying over his "wise Stubb, wise Stubb," I thought I might as well fall to kicking the pyramid again. But I had only just lifted my foot for it, when he roared out, "Stop that kicking!" "Halloa," says I, "what's the matter now, old fellow?" "Look ye here," says he; "let's argue the insult. Captain Ahab kicked ye, didn't he?" "Yes, he did," says I – "right *here* it was." "Very good," says he – "he used his ivory leg, didn't he?" "Yes, he did," says I. "Well then," says he, "wise Stubb, what have you to complain of? Didn't he kick with right good will? it wasn't a common pitch pine leg he kicked with, was it? No, you were kicked by a great man, and with a beautiful ivory leg, Stubb. It's an honor; I consider it an honor. Listen, wise Stubb. In old England the greatest lords think it great glory to be slapped by a queen, and made garter-knights of; but, be *your* boast, Stubb, that ye were kicked by old Ahab, and made a wise man of. Remember what I say; *be* kicked by him; account his kicks honors; and on no account kick back; for you can't help yourself, wise Stubb. Don't you see that pyramid?" With that, he all of a sudden seemed somehow, in some queer fashion, to swim off into the air. I snored; rolled over; and there I was in my hammock! Now, what do you think of that dream, Flask?'

'I don't know; it seems a sort of foolish to me, tho'.'

'May be; may be. But it's made a wise man of me, Flask. D'ye see Ahab standing there, sideways looking over the stern? Well, the best thing you can do, Flask, is to let that old man alone; never speak quick to him, whatever he says. Halloa! what's that he shouts? Hark!'

'Mast-head, there! Look sharp, all of ye! There are whales hereabouts! If ye see a white one, split your lungs for him!'

'What d'ye think of that now, Flask? ain't there a small drop of something queer about that, eh? A white whale – did ye mark that, man? Look ye – there's something special in the wind. Stand by for it, Flask. Ahab has that that's bloody on his mind. But, mum; he comes this way.'

32

CETOLOGY

Already we are boldly launched upon the deep; but soon we shall be lost in its unshored, harborless immensities. Ere that come to pass; ere the Pequod's weedy hull rolls side by side with the barnacled hulls of the leviathan; at the outset it is but well to attend to a matter almost indispensable to a thorough appreciative understanding of the more special leviathanic revelations and allusions of all sorts which are to follow.

It is some systematized exhibition of the whale in his broad genera, that I would now fain put before you. Yet is it no easy task. The classification of the constituents of a chaos, nothing less is here essayed. Listen to what the best and latest authorities have laid down.

'No branch of Zoology is so much involved as that which is entitled Cetology,' says Captain Scoresby, A.D. 1820.

'It is not my intention, were it in my power, to enter into the inquiry as to the true method of dividing the cetacea into groups and families. * * * Utter confusion exists among the historians of this animal' (sperm whale), says Surgeon Beale, A.D. 1839.

'Unfitness to pursue our research in the unfathomable waters.' 'Impenetrable veil covering our knowledge of the cetacea.' 'A field strewn with thorns.' 'All these incomplete indications but serve to torture us naturalists.'

Thus speak of the whale, the great Cuvier, and John Hunter, and Lesson, those lights of zoology and anatomy. Nevertheless, though of real knowledge there be little, yet of books there are a plenty; and so in some small degree, with cetology, or the science of whales. Many are the men, small and great, old and new, landsmen and seamen, who have at large or in little, written of the whale. Run over a few:– The Authors of the Bible; Aristotle; Pliny; Aldrovandi; Sir Thomas Browne; Gesner; Ray; Linnæus; Rondeletius; Willoughby; Green; Artedi; Sibbald; Brisson; Marten; Lacépède; Bonneterre; Desmarest; Baron Cuvier; Frederick Cuvier; John Hunter; Owen; Scoresby; Beale; Bennett; J. Ross Browne; the Author of Miriam Coffin; Olmstead; and the Rev. T. Cheever. But to what ultimate generalizing purpose all these have written, the above cited extracts will show.

Of the names in this list of whale authors, only those following Owen ever saw living whales; and but one of them was a real professional harpooneer and whaleman. I mean Captain Scoresby. On the separate subject of the Greenland or right-whale, he is the best existing authority. But Scoresby knew nothing and says nothing of the great sperm whale, compared with which the Greenland whale is almost unworthy mentioning. And here be it said, that the Greenland whale is an usurper upon the throne of the seas. He is not even by any means the largest of the whales. Yet, owing to the long priority of his claims, and the profound ignorance which, till some seventy years back, invested the then fabulous or utterly unknown sperm-whale, and which ignorance to this present day still reigns in all but some few scientific retreats and whale-ports; this usurpation has been every way complete. Reference to nearly all the leviathanic allusions in the great poets of past days, will satisfy you that the Greenland whale, without one rival, was to them the monarch of the seas. But the time has at last come for a new proclamation. This is Charing Cross; hear ye! good people all, – the Greenland whale is deposed, – the great sperm whale now reigneth!

There are only two books in being which at all pretend to put the living sperm whale before you, and at the same time, in the remotest degree succeed in the attempt. Those books are Beale's and Bennett's; both in their time surgeons to English South-Sea whale-ships, and both exact and reliable men. The original matter touching the sperm whale to be found in their volumes is necessarily small; but so far as it goes, it is of excellent quality, though mostly confined to scientific description. As yet, however, the sperm whale, scientific or poetic, lives not complete in any literature. Far above all other hunted whales, his is an unwritten life.

Now the various species of whales need some sort of popular comprehensive classification, if only an easy outline one for the present, hereafter to be filled in all its departments by subsequent laborers. As no better man advances to take this matter in hand, I hereupon offer my own poor endeavors. I promise nothing complete; because any human thing supposed to be complete, must for that very reason infallibly be faulty. I shall not pretend to a minute anatomical description of the various species, or – in this place at least – to much of any description. My object here is simply to project the draught of a systematization of cetology. I am the architect, not the builder.

But it is a ponderous task; no ordinary letter-sorter in the Post-office is equal to it. To grope down into the bottom of the sea after them; to have one's hands among the unspeakable foundations, ribs, and very pelvis of the world; this is a fearful thing. What am I that I should essay to hook the nose of this leviathan! The awful tauntings in Job might well appal me. 'Will he' (the leviathan) 'make a covenant with thee? Behold the hope of him is vain!' But I have swam through libraries and sailed through oceans; I have had to do with whales with these visible hands; I am in earnest; and I will try. There are some preliminaries to settle.

First: The uncertain, unsettled condition of this science of Cetology is in the very vestibule attested by the fact, that in some quarters it still remains a moot point whether a whale be a fish. In his System of Nature, A.D. 1776, Linnæus declares, 'I hereby separate the whales from the fish.' But of my own knowledge, I know that down to the year 1850, sharks and shad, alewives and herring, against Linnæus's express edict, were still found dividing the possession of the same seas with the Leviathan.

The grounds upon which Linnæus would fain have banished the whales from the waters, he states as follows: 'On account of their warm bilocular heart, their lungs, their movable eyelids, their hollow ears, penem intrantem feminam mammis lactantem,' and finally, 'ex lege naturae jure meritoque.' I submitted all this to my friends Simeon Macey and Charley Coffin, of Nantucket, both messmates of mine in a certain voyage, and they united in the opinion that the reasons set forth were altogether insufficient. Charley profanely hinted they were humbug.

Be it known that, waiving all argument, I take the good old fashioned ground that the whale is a fish, and call upon holy Jonah to back me. This fundamental thing settled, the next point is, in what internal respect does the whale differ from other fish. Above, Linnæus has given you those items. But in brief, they are these: lungs and warm blood; whereas, all other fish are lungless and cold blooded.

Next: how shall we define the whale, by his obvious externals, so as conspicuously to label him for all time to come? To be short, then, a whale is *a spouting fish with a horizontal tail.* There you have him. However contracted, that definition is the result of expanded meditation. A walrus spouts much like a whale, but the walrus is not a fish, because he is amphibious. But the last term of the definition is still more cogent, as coupled with the first. Almost any one must have noticed that all the fish familiar to landsmen have not a flat, but a vertical, or up-and-down tail. Whereas, among spouting fish the tail, though it may be similarly shaped, invariably assumes a horizontal position.

By the above definition of what a whale is, I do by no means exclude from the leviathanic brotherhood any sea creature hitherto identified with the whale by the best informed Nantucketers; nor, on the other hand, link with it any fish hitherto authoritatively regarded as alien.* Hence, all the smaller, spouting, and horizontal tailed fish must be included in this ground-plan of Cetology. Now, then, come the grand divisions of the entire whale host.

First: According to magnitude I divide the whales into three primary BOOKS (subdivisible into CHAPTERS), and these shall comprehend them all, both small and large.

I. The FOLIO WHALE; II. the OCTAVO WHALE; III. the DUODECIMO WHALE.

As the type of the FOLIO I present the *Sperm Whale*; of the OCTAVO, the *Grampus*; of the DUODECIMO, the *Porpoise.*

FOLIOS. Among these I here include the following chapters: – I. The *Sperm Whale*; II. the *Right Whale*; III. the *Fin Back Whale*; IV. the *Hump-backed Whale*; V. the *Razor Back Whale*; VI. the *Sulphur Bottom Whale.*

BOOK I. (*Folio*), CHAPTER I. (*Sperm Whale*). – This whale, among the English of old vaguely known as the

*I am aware that down to the present time, the fish styled Lamatins and Dugongs (Pig-fish and Sow-fish of the Coffins of Nantucket) are included by many naturalists among the whales. But as these pig-fish are a nosy, contemptible set, mostly lurking in the mouths of rivers, and feeding on wet hay, and especially as they do not spout, I deny their credentials as whales; and have presented them with their passports to quit the Kingdom of Cetology.

Trumpa whale, and the Physeter whale, and the Anvil Headed whale, is the present Cachalot of the French, and the Pottsfich of the Germans, and the Macrocephalus of the Long Words. He is, without doubt, the largest inhabitant of the globe; the most formidable of all whales to encounter; the most majestic in aspect; and lastly, by far the most valuable in commerce; he being the only creature from which that valuable substance, spermaceti, is obtained. All his peculiarities will, in many other places, be enlarged upon. It is chiefly with his name that I now have to do. Philologically considered, it is absurd. Some centuries ago, when the Sperm whale was almost wholly unknown in his own proper individuality, and when his oil was only accidentally obtained from the stranded fish; in those days spermaceti, it would seem, was popularly supposed to be derived from a creature identical with the one then known in England as the Greenland or Right Whale. It was the idea also, that this same spermaceti was that quickening humor of the Greenland Whale which the first syllable of the word literally expresses. In those times, also, spermaceti was exceedingly scarce, not being used for light, but only as an ointment and medicament. It was only to be had from the druggists as you nowadays buy an ounce of rhubarb. When, as I opine, in the course of time, the true nature of spermaceti became known, its original name was still retained by the dealers; no doubt to enhance its value by a notion so strangely significant of its scarcity. And so the appellation must at last have come to be bestowed upon the whale from which this spermaceti was really derived.

BOOK I. (*Folio*), CHAPTER II. (*Right Whale*). – In one respect this is the most venerable of the leviathans, being the one first regularly hunted by man. It yields the article commonly known as whalebone or baleen; and the oil specially known as 'whale oil', an inferior article in commerce. Among the fishermen, he is indiscriminately designated by all the following titles: The Whale; the Greenland Whale; the Black Whale; the Great Whale; the True Whale; the Right Whale. There is a deal of obscurity concerning the identity of the species thus multitudinously baptized. What then is the whale, which I include in the second species of my Folios? It is the Great Mysticetus of the English naturalists; the Greenland Whale of the English whalemen; the Baliene Ordinaire of the French whalemen; the Growlands Walfish of the Swedes. It is the whale which for more than two centuries past has been hunted by the Dutch and English in the Arctic seas; it is the whale which the American fishermen have long pursued in the Indian ocean, on the Brazil Banks, on the Nor' West Coast, and various other parts of the world, designated by them Right Whale Cruising Grounds.

Some pretend to see a difference between the Greenland whale of the English and the right whale of the Americans. But they precisely agree in all their grand features; nor has there yet been presented a single determinate fact upon which to ground a radical distinction. It is by endless subdivisions based upon the most inconclusive differences, that some departments of natural history become so repellingly intricate. The right whale will be elsewhere treated of at some length, with reference to elucidating the sperm whale.

BOOK I. (*Folio*), CHAPTER III. (*Fin-Back*). – Under this head I reckon a monster which, by the various names of Fin-Back, Tall-Spout, and Long-John, has been seen almost in every sea and is commonly the whale whose distant jet is so often descried by passengers crossing the Atlantic, in the New York packet-tracks. In the length he attains, and in his baleen, the Fin-back resembles the right whale, but is of a less portly girth, and a lighter color, approaching to olive. His great lips present a cable-like aspect, formed by the intertwisting, slanting folds of large wrinkles. His grand distinguishing feature, the fin, from which he derives his name, is often a conspicuous object. This fin is some three or four feet long, growing vertically from the hinder part of the back, of an angular shape, and with a very sharp pointed end. Even if not the slightest other part of the creature be visible, this isolated fin will, at times, be seen plainly projecting from the surface. When the sea is moderately calm, and slightly marked with spherical ripples, and this gnomon-like fin stands up and casts shadows upon the wrinkled surface, it may well be supposed that the watery circle surrounding it somewhat resembles a dial, with its style and wavy hour-lines graved on it. On that Ahaz-dial the shadow often goes back. The Fin-Back is not gregarious. He seems a whale-hater, as some men are man-haters. Very shy; always going solitary; unexpectedly rising to the surface in the remotest and most sullen waters; his straight and single lofty jet rising like a tall misanthropic spear upon a barren plain; gifted with such wondrous power and velocity in swimming, as to defy all present pursuit from man; this leviathan seems the banished and unconquerable Cain of his race, bearing for his mark that style upon his back. From having the baleen in his mouth, the Fin-Back is sometimes included with the right whale, among a theoretic species denominated *Whalebone whales*, that is, whales with baleen. Of these so called Whalebone whales, there would seem to be several varieties, most of which, however, are little known. Broad-nosed whales and beaked whales; pike-headed whales; bunched whales; under-jawed whales and rostrated whales, are the fishermen's names for a few sorts.

In connexion with this appellative of 'Whalebone whales,' it is of great importance to mention, that however such a nomenclature may be convenient in facilitating allusions to some kind of whales, yet it is in vain to attempt a clear classification of the Leviathan, founded upon either his baleen, or hump, or fin, or teeth; notwithstanding that those marked parts or features very obviously seem better adapted to afford the basis for a regular system of Cetology than any other detached bodily distinctions, which the whale, in his kinds, presents. How then? The baleen, hump, back-fin, and teeth; these are things whose peculiarities are indiscriminately dispersed among all sorts of whales, without any regard to what may be the nature of their structure in other and more essential particulars. Thus, the sperm whale and the humpbacked whale, each has a hump; but there the similitude ceases. Then, this same humpbacked whale and the

Greenland whale, each of these has baleen; but there again the similitude ceases. And it is just the same with the other parts above mentioned. In various sorts of whales, they form such irregular combinations; or, in the case of any one of them detached, such an irregular isolation; as utterly to defy all general methodization formed upon such a basis. On this rock every one of the whale-naturalists has split.

But it may possibly be conceived that, in the internal parts of the whale, in his anatomy – there, at least, we shall be able to hit the right classification. Nay; what thing, for example, is there in the Greenland whale's anatomy more striking than his baleen? Yet we have seen that by his baleen it is impossible correctly to classify the Greenland whale. And if you descend into the bowels of the various leviathans, why there you will not find distinctions a fiftieth part as available to the systematizer as those external ones already enumerated. What then remains? nothing but to take hold of the whales bodily, in their entire liberal volume, and boldly sort them that way. And this is the Bibliographical system here adopted; and it is the only one that can possibly succeed, for it alone is practicable. To proceed.

BOOK I. (*Folio*), CHAPTER IV. (*Hump Back*). – This whale is often seen on the northern American coast. He has been frequently captured there, and towed into harbor. He has a great pack on him like a peddler; or you might call him the Elephant and Castle whale. At any rate, the popular name for him does not sufficiently distinguish him, since the sperm whale also has a hump, though a smaller one. His oil is not very valuable. He has baleen. He is the most gamesome and light-hearted of all the whales, making more gay foam and white water generally than any other of them.

BOOK I. (*Folio*), CHAPTER V. (*Razor Back*). – Of this whale little is known but his name. I have seen him at a distance off Cape Horn. Of a retiring nature, he eludes both hunters and philosophers. Though no coward, he has never yet shown any part of him but his back, which rises in a long sharp ridge. Let him go. I know little more of him, nor does anybody else.

BOOK I. (*Folio*), CHAPTER VI. (*Sulphur Bottom*). – Another retiring gentleman, with a brimstone belly, doubtless got by scraping along the Tartarian tiles in some of his profounder divings. He is seldom seen; at least I have never seen him except in the remoter southern seas, and then always at too great a distance to study his countenance. He is never chased; he would run away with rope-walks of line. Prodigies are told of him. Adieu, Sulphur Bottom! I can say nothing more that is true of ye, nor can the oldest Nantucketer.

Thus ends BOOK I (*Folio*), and now begins BOOK II. (*Octavo*).

OCTAVOES.* These embrace the whales of middling magnitude, among which at present may be numbered: – I., the *Grampus*; II., the *Black Fish*; III., the *Narwhale*; IV., the *Thrasher*; V., the *Killer*.

BOOK II. (*Octavo*), CHAPTER I. (*Grampus*). – Though this fish, whose loud sonorous breathing, or rather blowing, has furnished a proverb to landsmen, is so well known a denizen of the deep, yet is he not popularly classed among whales. But possessing all the grand distinctive features of the leviathan, most naturalists have recognised him for one. He is of moderate octavo size, varying from fifteen to twenty-five feet in length, and of corresponding dimensions round the waist. He swims in herds; he is never regularly hunted, though his oil is considerable in quantity, and pretty good for light. By some fishermen his approach is regarded as premonitory of the advance of the great sperm whale.

BOOK II. (*Octavo*), CHAPTER II. (*Black Fish*). – I give the popular fishermen's names for all these fish, for generally they are the best. Where any name happens to be

*Why this book of whales is not denominated the Quarto is very plain. Because, while the whales of this order, though smaller than those of the former order, nevertheless retain a proportionate likeness to them in figure, yet the bookbinder's Quarto volume in its diminished form does not preserve the shape of the Folio volume, but the Octavo volume does.

vague or inexpressive, I shall say so, and suggest another. I do so now, touching the Black Fish, so called, because blackness is the rule among almost all whales. So, call him the Hyena Whale, if you please. His voracity is well known, and from the circumstance that the inner angles of his lips are curved upwards, he carries an everlasting Mephistophelean grin on his face. This whale averages some sixteen or eighteen feet in length. He is found in almost all latitudes. He has a peculiar way of showing his dorsal hooked fin in swimming, which looks something like a Roman nose. When not more profitably employed, the sperm whale hunters sometimes capture the Hyena whale, to keep up the supply of cheap oil for domestic employment – as some frugal housekeepers, in the absence of company, and quite alone by themselves, burn unsavory tallow instead of odorous wax. Though their blubber is very thin, some of these whales will yield you upwards of thirty gallons of oil.

BOOK II. (*Octavo*), CHAPTER III. (*Narwhale*), that is, *Nostril whale.* – Another instance of a curiously named whale, so named I suppose from his peculiar horn being originally mistaken for a peaked nose. The creature is some sixteen feet in length, while its horn averages five feet, though some exceed ten, and even attain to fifteen feet. Strictly speaking, this horn is but a lengthened tusk, growing out from the jaw in a line a little depressed from the horizontal. But it is only found on the sinister side, which has an ill effect, giving its owner something analogous to the aspect of a clumsy left-handed man. What precise purpose this ivory horn or lance answers, it would be hard to say. It does not seem to be used like the blade of the swordfish and bill fish; though some sailors tell me that the Narwhale employs it for a rake in turning over the bottom of the sea for food. Charley Coffin said it was used for an ice-piercer; for the Narwhale, rising to the surface of the Polar Sea, and finding it sheeted with ice, thrusts his horn up, and so breaks through. But you cannot prove either of these surmises to be correct. My own opinion is, that however this one-sided horn may really be used by the Narwhale –

however that may be – it would certainly be very convenient to him for a folder in reading pamphlets. The Narwhale I have heard called the Tusked whale, the Horned whale, and the Unicorn whale. He is certainly a curious example of the Unicornism to be found in almost every kingdom of animated nature. From certain cloistered old authors I have gathered that this same sea-unicorn's horn was in ancient days regarded as the great antidote against poison, and as such, preparations of it brought immense prices. It was also distilled to a volatile salts for fainting ladies, the same way that the horns of the male deer are manufactured into hartshorn. Originally it was in itself accounted an object of great curiosity. Black Letter tells me that Sir Martin Frobisher on his return from that voyage, when Queen Bess did gallantly wave her jewelled hand to him from a window of Greenwich Palace, as his bold ship sailed down the Thames; 'when Sir Martin returned from that voyage,' saith Black Letter, 'on bended knees he presented to her highness a prodigious long horn of the Narwhale, which for a long period after hung in the castle at Windsor.' An Irish author avers that the Earl of Leicester, on bended knees, did likewise present to her highness another horn, pertaining to a land beast of the unicorn nature.

The Narwhale has a very picturesque, leopard-like look, being of a milk-white ground color, dotted with round and oblong spots of black. His oil is very superior, clear and fine; but there is little of it, and he is seldom hunted. He is mostly found in the circumpolar seas.

BOOK II. (*Octavo*), CHAPTER IV. (*Killer*). – Of this whale little is precisely known to the Nantucketer, and nothing at all to the professed naturalist. From what I have seen of him at a distance, I should say that he was about the bigness of a grampus. He is very savage – a sort of Feegee fish. He sometimes takes the great Folio whales by the lip, and hangs there like a leech, till the mighty brute is worried to death. The Killer is never hunted. I never heard what sort of oil he has. Exception might be taken to the name bestowed upon this whale, on the ground of its indistinctness. For we are all killers, on land and on sea; Bonapartes and Sharks included.

BOOK II. (*Octavo*), CHAPTER V. (*Thrasher*). – This gentleman is famous for his tail, which he uses for a ferule in thrashing his foes. He mounts the Folio whale's back, and as he swims, he works his passage by flogging him; as some schoolmasters get along in the world by a similar process. Still less is known of the Thrasher than of the Killer. Both are outlaws, even in the lawless seas.

Thus ends BOOK II. (*Octavo*), and begins BOOK III. (*Duodecimo*).

DUODECIMOES. – These include the smaller whales. I. The Huzza Porpoise. II. The Algerine Porpoise. III. The Mealy-mouthed Porpoise.

To those who have not chanced specially to study the subject, it may possibly seem strange, that fishes not commonly exceeding four or five feet should be marshalled among WHALES – a word, which, in the popular sense, always conveys an idea of hugeness. But the creatures set down above as Duodecimoes are infallibly whales, by the terms of my definition of what a whale is – i.e. a spouting fish, with a horizontal tail.

BOOK III. (*Duodecimo*), CHAPTER I. (*Huzza Porpoise*). – This is the common porpoise found almost all over the globe. The name is of my own bestowal; for there are more than one sort of porpoises, and something must be done to distinguish them. I call him thus, because he always swims in hilarious shoals, which upon the broad sea keep tossing themselves to heaven like caps in a Fourth-of-July crowd. Their appearance is generally hailed with delight by the mariner. Full of fine spirits, they invariably come from the breezy billows to windward. They are the lads that always live before the wind. They are accounted a lucky omen. If you yourself can withstand three cheers at beholding these vivacious fish, then heaven help ye; the spirit of godly gamesomeness is not in ye. A well-fed, plump Huzza Porpoise will yield you one good gallon of good oil. But the fine and delicate fluid extracted from his jaws is exceedingly valuable. It is in request among jewellers and watchmakers. Sailors put it on their hones. Porpoise meat is good eating, you know. It may never have occurred to you that a porpoise spouts. Indeed, his spout is so small that it is not very readily discernible. But the next time you have a chance, watch him; and you will then see the great Sperm whale himself in miniature.

BOOK III. (*Duodecimo*), CHAPTER II. (*Algerine Porpoise*). – A pirate. Very savage. He is only found, I think, in the Pacific. He is somewhat larger than the Huzza Porpoise, but much of the same general make. Provoke him, and he will buckle to a shark. I have lowered for him many times, but never yet saw him captured.

BOOK III. (*Duodecimo*), CHAPTER III. (*Mealy-mouthed Porpoise*). – The largest kind of Porpoise; and only found in the Pacific, so far as it is known. The only English name, by which he has hitherto been designated, is that of the fishers – Right-Whale Porpoise, from the circumstance that he is chiefly found in the vicinity of that Folio. In shape, he differs in some degree from the Huzza Porpoise, being of a less rotund and jolly girth; indeed, he is of quite a neat and gentleman-like figure. He has no fins on his back (most other porpoises have), he has a lovely tail, and sentimental Indian eyes of a hazel hue. But his mealy-mouth spoils all. Though his entire back down to his side fins is of a deep sable, yet a boundary line, distinct as the mark in a ship's hull, called the 'bright waist,' that line streaks him from stem to stern, with two separate colors, black above and white below. The white comprises part of his head, and the whole of his mouth, which makes him look as if he had just escaped from a felonious visit to a meal-bag. A most mean and mealy aspect! His oil is much like that of the common porpoise.

* * * * * * *

Beyond the DUODECIMO, this system does not proceed, inasmuch as the Porpoise is the smallest of the whales. Above, you have all the Leviathans of note. But there are a rabble of uncertain, fugitive, half-fabulous whales, which, as an American whaleman, I know by reputation, but not personally. I shall enumerate them by their forecastle appellations; for possibly such a list may be valuable to future investigators, who may complete what I have here but begun. If any of the following whales, shall hereafter be caught and marked, then he can readily be incorporated into this System, according to his Folio, Octavo, or Duodecimo magnitude: – The Bottle-Nose Whale; the Junk Whale; the Pudding-Headed Whale; the Cape Whale; the Leading Whale; the Cannon Whale; the Scragg Whale; the Coppered Whale; the Elephant Whale; the Iceberg Whale; the Quog Whale; the Blue Whale; &c. From Icelandic, Dutch and old English authorities, there might be quoted other lists of uncertain whales, blessed with all manner of uncouth names. But I omit them as altogether obsolete; and can hardly help suspecting them for mere sounds, full of Leviathanism, but signifying nothing.

Finally: It was stated at the outset, that this system would not be here, and at once, perfected. You cannot but plainly see that I have kept my word. But I now leave my cetological System standing thus unfinished, even as the great Cathedral of Cologne was left, with the crane still standing upon the top of the uncompleted tower. For small erections may be finished by their first architects, grand ones, true ones, ever leave the copestone to posterity. God keep me from ever completing anything. This whole book is but a draught – nay, but the draught of a draught. Oh, Time, Strength, Cash, and Patience!

33

THE SPECKSYNDER

CONCERNING the officers of the whale-craft, this seems as good a place as any to set down a little domestic peculiarity on ship-board, arising from the existence of the harpooneer class of officers, a class unknown of course in any other marine than the whale-fleet.

The large importance attached to the harpooneer's vocation is evinced by the fact, that originally in the old Dutch Fishery, two centuries and more ago, the command of a whale ship was not wholly lodged in the person now called the captain, but was divided between him and an officer called the Specksynder. Literally this word means Fat-Cutter; usage, however, in time made it equivalent to Chief Harpooneer. In those days, the captain's authority was restricted to the navigation and general management of the vessel: while over the whale-hunting department and all its concerns, the Specksynder or Chief Harpooneer reigned supreme. In the British Greenland Fishery, under the corrupted title of Specksioneer, this old Dutch official is still retained, but his former dignity is sadly abridged. At present he ranks simply as senior Harpooneer; and as such, is but one of the captain's more inferior subalterns. Nevertheless, as upon the good conduct of the harpooneers the success of a whaling voyage largely depends, and since in the American Fishery he is not only an important officer in the boat, but under certain circumstances (night watches on a whaling ground) the command of the ship's deck is also his; therefore the grand political maxim of the sea demands, that he should nominally live apart from the men before the mast, and be in some way distinguished as their professional superior; though always, by them, familiarly regarded as their social equal.

Now, the grand distinction drawn between officer and man at sea, is this – the first lives aft, the last forward. Hence, in whale-ships and merchantmen alike, the mates have their quarters with the captain; and so, too, in most of the American whalers the harpooneers are lodged in the after part of the ship. That is to say, they take their meals in the captain's cabin, and sleep in a place indirectly communicating with it.

Though the long period of a Southern whaling voyage (by far the longest of all voyages now or ever made by man), the peculiar perils of it, and the community of interest prevailing among a company, all of whom, high or low, depend for their profits, not upon fixed wages, but upon their common luck, together with their common vigilance, intrepidity, and hard work; though all these things do in some cases tend to beget a less rigorous discipline than in merchantmen generally; yet, never mind how much like an old Mesopotamian family these whalemen may, in some primitive instances, live together; for all that, the punctilious externals, at least, of the quarter-deck are seldom materially relaxed, and in no instance done away. Indeed, many are the Nantucket ships in which you will see the skipper parading his quarter-deck with an elated grandeur not surpassed in any military navy; nay, extorting almost as much homage as if he wore the imperial purple, and not the shabbiest of pilot-cloth.

And though of all men the moody captain of the Pequod was the least given to that sort of shallowest assumption; and though the only homage he ever exacted, was implicit, instantaneous obedience; though he required no man to remove the shoes from his feet ere stepping upon the quarter-deck; and though there were times when, owing to peculiar circumstances connected with events hereafter to be detailed, he addressed them in unusual terms, whether of condescension or *in terrorem*, or otherwise; yet even Captain Ahab was by no means unobservant of the paramount forms and usages of the sea.

Nor, perhaps, will it fail to be eventually perceived, that behind those forms and usages, as it were, he sometimes masked himself; incidentally making use of them for other and more private ends than they were legitimately intended to subserve. That certain sultanism of his brain, which had otherwise in a good degree remained unmanifested; through those forms that same sultanism became incarnate in an irresistible dictatorship. For be a man's intellectual superiority what it will, it can never assume the practical, available supremacy over other men, without the aid of some sort of external arts and entrenchments, always, in themselves, more or less paltry and base. This it is, that for ever keeps

God's true princes of the Empire from the world's hustings; and leaves the highest honors that this air can give, to those men who become famous more through their infinite inferiority to the choice hidden handful of the Divine Inert, than through their undoubted superiority over the dead level of the mass. Such large virtue lurks in these small things when extreme political superstitions invest them, that in some royal instances even to idiot imbecility they have imparted potency. But when, as in the case of Nicholas the Czar, the ringed crown of geographical empire encircles an imperial brain; then, the plebeian herds crouch abased before the tremendous centralization. Nor, will the tragic dramatist who would depict mortal indomitableness in its fullest sweep and direst swing, ever forget a hint, incidentally so important in his art, as the one now alluded to.

But Ahab, my Captain, still moves before me in all his Nantucket grimness and shagginess; and in this episode touching Emperors and Kings, I must not conceal that I have only to do with a poor old whale-hunter like him; and, therefore, all outward majestical trappings and housings are denied me. Oh, Ahab! what shall be grand in thee, it must needs be plucked at from the skies, and dived for in the deep, and featured in the unbodied air!

34

THE CABIN-TABLE

It is noon; and Dough-Boy, the steward, thrusting his pale loaf-of-bread face from the cabin-scuttle, announces dinner to his lord and master; who, sitting in the lee quarter-boat, has just been taking an observation of the sun; and is now mutely reckoning the latitude on the smooth, medallion-shaped tablet, reserved for that daily purpose on the upper part of his ivory leg. From his complete inattention to the tidings, you would think that moody Ahab had not heard his menial. But presently, catching hold of the mizen shrouds, he swings himself to the deck, and in an even, unexhilarated voice, saying, 'Dinner, Mr Starbuck,' disappears into the cabin.

When the last echo of his sultan's step has died away, and Starbuck, the first Emir, has every reason to suppose that he is seated, then Starbuck rouses from his quietude, takes a few turns along the planks, and, after a grave peep into the binnacle, says, with some touch of pleasantness, 'Dinner, Mr Stubb,' and descends the scuttle. The second Emir lounges about the rigging awhile, and then slightly shaking the main brace, to see whether it be all right with that important rope, he likewise takes up the old burden, and with a rapid 'Dinner, Mr Flask,' follows after his predecessors.

But the third Emir, now seeing himself all alone on the quarter-deck, seems to feel relieved from some curious restraint; for, tipping all sorts of knowing winks in all sorts of directions, and kicking off his shoes, he strikes into a sharp but noiseless squall of a hornpipe right over the Grand Turk's head; and then, by a dexterous sleight, pitching his cap into the mizen-top for a shelf, he goes down rollicking, so far at least as he remains visible from the deck, reversing all other processions, by bringing up the rear with music. But ere stepping into the cabin doorway below, he pauses, ships a new face altogether, and, then, independent, hilarious little Flask enters King Ahab's presence, in the character of Abjectus, or the Slave.

It is not the least among the strange things bred by the intense artificialness of sea-usages, that while in the open air of the deck some officers will, upon provocation, bear themselves boldly and defyingly enough towards their commander; yet, ten to one, let those very officers the next moment go down to their customary dinner in that same commander's cabin, and straightway their inoffensive, not to say deprecatory and humble air towards him, as he sits at the head of the table; this is marvellous, sometimes most comical. Wherefore this difference? A problem? Perhaps not. To have been Belshazzar, King of Babylon; and to have been Belshazzar, not haughtily but courteously, therein certainly must have been some touch of mundane grandeur. But he who in the rightly regal and intelligent spirit presides over his own private dinner-table of invited guests, that man's unchallenged power and dominion of individual influence for the time; that man's royalty of state transcends Belshazzar's, for Belshazzar was not the greatest. Who has but once dined his friends, has tasted what it is to be Cæsar. It is a witchery of social czarship which there is no withstanding. Now, if to this consideration you superadd the official supremacy of a ship-master, then, by inference, you will derive the cause of that peculiarity of sea-life just mentioned.

Over his ivory-inlaid table, Ahab presided like a mute, maned sea-lion on the white coral beach, surrounded by his warlike but still deferential cubs. In his own proper turn, each officer waited to be served. They were as little children before Ahab; and yet, in Ahab, there seemed not to lurk the smallest social arrogance. With one mind, their intent eyes all fastened upon the old man's knife, as he carved the chief dish before him. I do not suppose that for the world they would have profaned that moment with the slightest observation, even upon so neutral a topic as the weather. No! And when reaching out his knife and fork, between which the slice of beef was locked, Ahab thereby motioned Starbuck's plate towards him, the mate received his meat as though receiving alms; and cut it tenderly; and a little started if, perchance, the knife grazed against the plate; and chewed it noiselessly; and swallowed it, not without circumspection. For, like the Coronation banquet at Frankfort, where the German Emperor profoundly dines with the seven Imperial Electors, so these cabin meals were somehow solemn meals, eaten in awful silence; and yet at table old Ahab forbade not conversation; only he himself was dumb. What a relief it was to choking Stubb, when a rat made a sudden racket in the hold below. And poor little Flask, he was the youngest son, and little boy of this weary family party. His were the shinbones of the saline beef; his would have been the drumsticks. For Flask to have presumed to help himself, this must have seemed to him tantamount to larceny in the first degree. Had he helped himself at that table, doubtless, never more would he have been able to hold his hand up in this honest world; nevertheless, strange to say, Ahab never forbade him. And had Flask helped himself, the chances were Ahab had never so much as noticed it. Least of all, did Flask presume to help himself to butter. Whether he thought the owners of the ship denied it to him, on account of its clotting his clear, sunny complexion; or whether he deemed that, on so long a voyage in such marketless waters, butter was at a premium, and therefore was not for him, a subaltern; however it was, Flask, alas! was a butterless man!

Another thing. Flask was the last person down at the dinner, and Flask is the first man up. Consider! For hereby Flask's dinner was badly jammed in point of time. Starbuck and Stubb both had the start of him; and yet they also have the privilege of lounging in the rear. If Stubb even, who is but a peg higher than Flask, happens to have but a small appetite, and soon shows symptoms of concluding his repast, then Flask must bestir himself, he will not get more than three mouthfuls that day; for it is against holy usage for Stubb to precede Flask to the deck. Therefore it was that Flask once admitted in private, that ever since he had arisen to the dignity of an officer, from that moment he had never known what it was to be otherwise than hungry, more or less. For what he ate did not so much relieve his hunger, as keep it immortal in him. Peace and satisfaction, thought Flask, have for ever departed from my stomach. I am an officer; but, how I wish I could fist a bit of old-fashioned beef in the forecastle, as I used to when I was before the mast. There's the fruits of promotion now; there's the vanity of glory: there's the insanity of life! Besides, if it were so that any mere sailor of the Pequod had a grudge against Flask in Flask's official capacity, all that sailor had to do, in order to obtain ample vengeance, was to go aft at dinner-time, and get a peep at Flask through the cabin sky-light, sitting silly and dumfoundered before awful Ahab.

Now, Ahab and his three mates formed what may be called the first table in the Pequod's cabin. After their departure, taking place in inverted order to their arrival, the canvas cloth was cleared, or rather was restored to some hurried order by the pallid steward. And then the three harpooneers were bidden to the feast, they being its residuary legatees. They made a sort of temporary servants' hall of the high and mighty cabin.

In strange contrast to the hardly tolerable constraint and nameless invisible domineerings of the captain's table, was the entire care-free license and ease, the almost frantic democracy of those inferior fellows the harpooneers. While their masters, the mates, seemed afraid of the sound of the hinges of their own jaws, the harpooneers chewed their food with such a relish that there was a report to it. They dined like lords; they filled their bellies like Indian ships all day loading with spices. Such portentous appetites had Queequeg and Tashtego, that to fill out the vacancies made by the previous repast, often the pale Dough-Boy was fain to bring on a great baron of salt-junk, seemingly quarried out of the solid ox. And if he were not lively about it, if he did not go with a nimble hop-skip-and-jump, then Tashtego had an ungentlemanly way of accelerating him by darting a fork at his back, harpoonwise. And once Daggoo, seized with a sudden humor, assisted Dough-Boy's memory by snatching him up bodily, and thrusting his head into a great empty wooden trencher, while Tashtego, knife in hand, began laying out the circle preliminary to scalping him. He was naturally a very nervous, shuddering sort of little fellow, this bread-faced steward; the progeny of a bankrupt baker and a hospital nurse. And what with the standing spectacle of the black terrific Ahab, and the periodical tumultuous visitations of these three savages, Dough-Boy's whole life was one continual lip-quiver. Commonly, after seeing the harpooneers furnished with all things they demanded, he would escape from their clutches into his little pantry adjoining, and fearfully peep out at them through the blinds of its door, till all was over.

It was a sight to see Queequeg seated over against Tashtego, opposing his filed teeth to the Indian's: crosswise to them, Daggoo seated on the floor, for a bench would have brought his hearse-plumed head to the low carlines; at every motion of his colossal limbs, making the low cabin framework to shake, as when an African elephant goes passenger in a ship. But for all this, the great negro was wonderfully abstemious, not to say dainty. It seemed hardly possible that by such comparatively small mouthfuls he could keep up the vitality diffused through so broad, baronial, and superb a person. But, doubtless, this noble savage fed strong and drank deep of the abounding element of air; and through his dilated nostrils snuffed in the sublime life of the worlds. Not by beef or by bread, are giants made or nourished. But Queequeg, he had a mortal, barbaric smack of the lip in eating – an ugly sound enough – so much so, that the trembling Dough-Boy almost looked to see whether any marks of teeth lurked in his own lean arms. And when he would hear Tashtego singing out for him to produce himself, that his bones might be picked, the simple-witted Steward all but shattered the crockery hanging round him in the pantry, by his sudden fits of the palsy. Nor did the whetstones which the harpooneers carried in their pockets, for their lances and other weapons; and with which whetstones, at dinner, they would ostentatiously sharpen their knives; that grating sound did not at all tend to tranquillize poor Dough-Boy. How could he forget that in his Island days, Queequeg, for one, must certainly have been guilty of some murderous, convivial indiscretions. Alas! Dough-Boy! hard fares the white waiter who waits upon cannibals. Not a napkin should he carry on his arm, but a buckler. In good time, though, to his great delight, the three salt-sea warriors would rise and depart; to his credulous, fable-mongering ears, all their martial bones jingling in them at every step, like Moorish scimetars in scabbards.

But, though these barbarians dined in the cabin, and nominally lived there; still, being anything but sedentary in their habits, they were scarcely ever in it except at mealtimes, and just before sleeping-time, when they passed through it to their own peculiar quarters.

In this one matter, Ahab seemed no exception to most American whale captains, who, as a set, rather incline to the opinion that by rights the ship's cabin belongs to them; and that it is by courtesy alone that anybody else is, at any time, permitted there. So that, in real truth, the mates and harpooneers of the Pequod might more properly be said to have lived out of the cabin than in it. For when they did enter it, it was something as a street-door enters a house; turning inwards for a moment, only to be turned out the next; and, as a permanent thing, residing in the open air. Nor did they lose much hereby; in the cabin was no companionship; socially, Ahab was inaccessible. Though nominally included in the census of Christendom, he was still an alien to it. He lived in the world, as the last of the Grisly Bears lived in settled Missouri. And as when Spring and Summer had departed, that wild Logan of the woods, burying himself in the hollow of a tree, lived out the winter there, sucking his own paws; so, in his inclement, howling old age, Ahab's soul, shut up in the caved trunk of his body, there fed upon the sullen paws of its gloom!

35

THE MAST-HEAD

It was during the more pleasant weather, that in due rotation with the other seamen my first mast-head came round.

In most American whalemen the mast-heads are manned almost simultaneously with the vessel's leaving her port; even though she may have fifteen thousand miles, and more, to sail ere reaching her proper cruising ground. And if, after a three, four, or five years' voyage she is drawing nigh home with anything empty in her – say, an empty vial even – then, her mast-heads are kept manned to the last; and not till her skysail poles sail in among the spires of the port, does she altogether relinquish the hope of capturing one whale more.

Now, as the business of standing mast-heads, ashore or afloat, is a very ancient and interesting one, let us in some measure expatiate here. I take it, that the earliest standers of mast-heads were the old Egyptians; because, in all my researches, I find none prior to them. For though their progenitors, the builders of Babel, must doubtless, by their tower, have intended to rear the loftiest mast-head in all Asia, or Africa either; yet (ere the final truck was put to it) as that great stone mast of theirs may be said to have gone by the board, in the dread gale of God's wrath; therefore, we cannot give these Babel builders priority over the Egyptians. And that the Egyptians were a nation of mast-head standers, is an assertion based upon the general belief among archæologists, that the first pyramids were founded for astronomical purposes: a theory singularly supported by the peculiar stair-like formation of all four sides of those edifices; whereby, with prodigious long upliftings of their legs, those old astronomers were wont to mount to the apex, and sing out for new stars; even as the look-outs of a modern ship sing out for a sail, or a whale just bearing in sight. In Saint Stylites, the famous Christian hermit of old times, who built him a lofty stone pillar in the desert and spent the whole latter portion of his life on its summit, hoisting his food from the ground with a tackle; in him we have a remarkable instance of a dauntless stander-of-mast-heads; who was not to be driven from his place by fogs or frosts, rain, hail, or sleet; but valiantly facing everything out to the last, literally died at his post. Of modern standers-of-mast-heads we have but a lifeless set; mere stone, iron, and bronze men; who, though well capable of facing out a stiff gale, are still entirely incompetent to the business of singing out upon discovering any strange sight. There is Napoleon; who, upon the top of the column of Vendome, stands with arms folded, some one hundred and fifty feet in the air; careless, now, who rules the decks below; whether Louis Philippe, Louis Blanc, or Louis the Devil. Great Washington, too, stands high aloft on his towering main-mast in Baltimore, and like one of Hercules' pillars, his column marks that point of human grandeur beyond which few mortals will go. Admiral Nelson, also, on a capstan of gun-metal, stands his mast-head in Trafalgar Square; and even when most obscured by that London smoke, token is yet given that a hidden hero is there; for where there is smoke, must be fire. But neither great Washington, nor Napoleon, nor Nelson, will answer a single hail from below, however madly invoked to befriend by their counsels the distracted decks upon which they gaze; however, it may be surmised, that their spirits penetrate through the thick haze of the future, and descry what shoals and what rocks must be shunned.

It may seem unwarrantable to couple in any respect the mast-head standers of the land with those of the sea; but that in truth it is not so, is plainly evinced by an item for which Obed Macy, the sole historian of Nantucket, stands accountable. The worthy Obed tells us, that in the early times of the whale fishery, ere ships were regularly launched in pursuit of the game, the people of that island erected lofty spars along the sea-coast, to which the look-outs ascended by means of nailed cleats, something as fowls go upstairs in a hen-house. A few years ago this same plan was adopted by the Bay whalemen of New Zealand, who, upon descrying the game, gave notice to the ready-manned boats nigh the beach. But this custom has now become obsolete; turn we then to the one proper mast-head, that of a whale-ship at sea.

The three mast-heads are kept manned from sun-rise to sun-set; the seamen taking their regular turns (as at the helm), and relieving each other every two hours. In the serene weather of the tropics it is exceedingly pleasant – the mast-head; nay, to a dreamy meditative man it is delightful. There you stand, a hundred feet above the silent decks, striding along the deep, as if the masts were gigantic stilts, while beneath you and between your legs, as it were, swim the hugest monsters of the sea, even as ships once sailed between the boots of the famous Colossus at old Rhodes. There you stand, lost in the infinite series of the sea, with nothing ruffled but the waves. The tranced ship indolently rolls; the drowsy trade winds blow; everything resolves you into languor. For the most part, in this tropic whaling life, a sublime uneventfulness invests you; you hear no news; read no gazettes; extras with startling accounts of commonplaces never delude you into unnecessary excitements; you hear of no domestic afflictions; bankrupt securities; fall of stocks; are never troubled with the thought of what you shall have for dinner – for all your meals for three years and more are snugly stowed in casks, and your bill of fare is immutable.

In one of those southern whalemen, on a long three or four years' voyage, as often happens, the sum of the various hours you spend at the mast-head would amount to several entire months. And it is much to be deplored that the place to which you devote so considerable a portion of the whole term of your natural life, should be so sadly destitute of anything approaching to a cosy inhabitiveness, or adapted to breed a comfortable localness of feeling, such as pertains to a bed, a hammock, a hearse, a sentry box, a pulpit, a coach, or any other of those small and snug contrivances in which men temporarily isolate themselves. Your most usual point of perch is the head of the t' gallant-mast, where you stand upon two thin parallel sticks (almost peculiar to whalemen) called the t' gallant cross-trees. Here, tossed about by the sea, the beginner feels about as cosy as he would standing on a bull's horns. To be sure, in coolish weather you may carry your house aloft with you, in the shape of a watch-coat; but properly speaking the thickest watch-coat is no more of a house than the unclad body; for as the soul is glued inside of its fleshly tabernacle, and cannot freely move about in it, nor even move out of it, without running great risk of perishing (like an ignorant pilgrim crossing the snowy Alps in winter); so a watch-coat is not so much of a house as it is a mere envelope, or additional skin encasing you. You cannot put a shelf or chest of drawers in your body, and no more can you make a convenient closet of your watch-coat.

Concerning all this, it is much to be deplored that the mast-heads of a southern whale ship are unprovided with those enviable little tents or pulpits, called *crow's-nests*, in which the lookouts of a Greenland whaler are protected from the inclement weather of the frozen seas. In the fire-side narrative of Captain Sleet, entitled 'A Voyage among the Icebergs, in quest of the Greenland Whale, and incidentally for the re-discovery of the Lost Icelandic Colonies of Old Greenland;' in this admirable volume, all standers of mast-heads are furnished with a charmingly circumstantial account of the then recently invented *crow's-nest* of the Glacier, which was the name of Captain Sleet's good craft. He called it the *Sleet's crow's-nest*, in honor of himself; he being the original inventor and patentee, and free from all ridiculous false delicacy, and holding that if we call our own children after our own names (we fathers being the original inventors and patentees), so likewise should we denominate after ourselves any other apparatus we may beget. In shape, the Sleet's crow's-nest is something like a large tierce or pipe; it is open above, however, where it is furnished with a movable side-screen to keep to windward of your head in a hard gale. Being fixed on the summit of the mast, you ascend into it through a little trap-hatch in the bottom. On the after side, or side next the stern of the ship, is a comfortable seat, with a locker underneath for umbrellas, comforters, and coats. In front is a leather rack, in which to keep your speaking trumpet, pipe, telescope, and other nautical conveniences. When Captain Sleet in person stood his mast-head in this crow's nest of his, he tells us that he always had a rifle with him (also fixed in the rack), together with a powder flask and shot, for the purpose of popping off the stray narwhales, or vagrant sea unicorns infesting those waters; for you cannot successfully shoot at them from the deck owing to the resistance of the water, but to shoot down upon them is a very different thing. Now, it was plainly a labor of love for Captain Sleet to describe, as he does, all the little detailed conveniences of his crow's-nest; but though he so enlarges upon many of these, and though he treats us to a very scientific account of his experiments in this crow's-nest, with a small compass he kept there for the purpose of counteracting the errors resulting from what is called the 'local attraction' of all binnacle magnets; an error ascribable to the horizontal vicinity of the iron in the ship's planks, and in the Glacier's case, perhaps, to there having been so many broken-down black-smiths among her crew; I say, that though the Captain is very discreet and scientific here, yet, for all his learned 'binnacle deviations,' 'azimuth compass observations,' and 'approximate errors,' he knows very well, Captain Sleet, that he was not so much immersed in those profound magnetic meditations, as to fail being attracted occasionally towards that well replenished little case-bottle, so nicely tucked in on one side of his crow's nest, within easy reach of his hand. Though, upon the whole, I greatly admire and even love the brave, the honest, and learned Captain; yet I take it very ill of him that he should so utterly ignore that case-bottle, seeing what a faithful friend and comforter it must have been, while with mittened fingers and hooded head he was studying the mathematics aloft there in that bird's nest within three or four perches of the pole.

But if we Southern whale-fishers are not so snugly housed aloft as Captain Sleet and his Greenland-men were; yet that disadvantage is greatly counterbalanced by the widely contrasting serenity of those seductive seas in which we South fishers mostly float. For one, I used to lounge up the rigging very leisurely, resting in the top to have a chat with Queequeg, or any one else off duty whom I might find there; then ascending a little way further, and throwing a lazy leg over the top-sail yard, take a preliminary view of the watery pastures, and so at last mount to my ultimate destination.

Let me make a clean breast of it here, and frankly admit that I kept but sorry guard. With the problem of the universe revolving in me, how could I – being left completely to myself at such a thought-engendering altitude, – how could I but lightly hold my obligations to observe all whale-ships' standing orders, 'Keep your weather eye open, and sing out every time.'

And let me in this place movingly admonish you, ye ship-owners of Nantucket! Beware of enlisting in your vigilant fisheries any lad with lean brow and hollow eye; given to unseasonable meditativeness; and who offers to ship with the Phædon instead of Bowditch in his head. Beware of such an one, I say: your whales must be seen before they can be killed; and this sunken-eyed young Platonist will tow you ten wakes round the world, and never make you one pint of sperm the richer. Nor are these monitions at all unneeded. For nowadays, the whale-fishery furnishes an asylum for many romantic, melancholy, and absent-minded young men, disgusted with the carking cares of earth, and seeking sentiment in tar and blubber. Childe Harold not unfrequently perches himself upon the mast-head of some luckless disappointed whale-ship, and in moody phrase ejaculates:–

> 'Roll on, thou deep and dark blue ocean, roll!
> Ten thousand blubber-hunters sweep over thee in vain.'

Very often do the captains of such ships take those absent-minded young philosophers to task, upbraiding them with not feeling sufficient 'interest' in the voyage; half-hinting that they are so hopelessly lost to all honorable ambition, as that in their secret souls they would rather not see whales than otherwise. But all in vain; those young Platonists have a notion that their vision is imperfect; they are short-sighted; what use, then, to strain the visual nerve? They have left their opera-glasses at home.

'Why, thou monkey,' said a harpooneer to one of these lads, 'we've been cruising now hard upon three years, and thou hast not raised a whale yet. Whales are scarce as hen's teeth whenever thou art up here.' Perhaps they were; or perhaps there might have been shoals of them in the far horizon; but lulled into such an opium-like listlessness of vacant, unconscious reverie is this absent-minded youth by the blending cadence of waves with thoughts, that at last he loses his identity; takes the mystic ocean at his feet for the visible image of that deep, blue, bottomless soul, pervading mankind and nature; and every strange, half-seen, gliding, beautiful thing that eludes him; every dimly-discovered, uprising fin of some undiscernible form, seems to him the embodiment of those elusive thoughts that only people the soul by continually flitting through it. In this enchanted mood, thy spirit ebbs away to whence it came; becomes diffused through time and space; like Cranmer's sprinkled Pantheistic ashes, forming at last a part of every shore the round globe over.

There is no life in thee, now, except that rocking life imparted by a gently rolling ship; by her, borrowed from the sea; by the sea, from the inscrutable tides of God. But while this sleep, this dream is on ye, move your foot or hand an inch; slip your hold at all; and your identity comes back in horror. Over Descartian vortices you hover. And perhaps, at mid-day, in the fairest weather, with one half-throttled shriek you drop through that transparent air into the summer sea, no more to rise for ever. Heed it well, ye Pantheists!

36

THE QUARTER-DECK

(*Enter Ahab: Then, all.*)

It was not a great while after the affair of the pipe, that one morning shortly after breakfast, Ahab, as was his wont, ascended the cabin-gangway to the deck. There most sea-captains usually walk at that hour, as country gentlemen, after the same meal, take a few turns in the garden.

Soon his steady, ivory stride was heard, as to and fro he paced his old rounds, upon planks so familiar to his tread, that they were all over dented, like geological stones, with the peculiar mark of his walk. Did you fixedly gaze, too, upon that ribbed and dented brow; there also, you would see still stranger foot-prints – the foot-prints of his one unsleeping, ever-pacing thought.

But on the occasion in question, those dents looked deeper, even as his nervous step that morning left a deeper mark. And, so full of his thought was Ahab, that at every uniform turn that he made, now at the main-mast and now at the binnacle, you could almost see that thought turn in him as he turned, and pace in him as he paced; so completely possessing him, indeed, that it all but seemed the inward mould of every outer movement.

'D'ye mark him, Flask?' whispered Stubb; 'the chick that's in him pecks the shell. 'Twill soon be out.'

The hours wore on; – Ahab now shut up within his cabin; anon, pacing the deck, with the same intense bigotry of purpose in his aspect.

It drew near the close of day. Suddenly he came to a halt by the bulwarks, and inserting his bone leg in the auger-hole there, and with one hand grasping a shroud, he ordered Starbuck to send everybody aft.

'Sir!' said the mate, astonished at an order seldom or never given on ship-board except in some extraordinary case.

'Send everybody aft,' repeated Ahab. 'Mast-heads, there! come down!'

When the entire ship's company were assembled, and with curious and not wholly unapprehensive faces, were eyeing him, for he looked not unlike the weather horizon when a storm is coming up, Ahab, after rapidly glancing over the bulwarks, and then darting his eyes among the crew, started from his standpoint; and as though not a soul were nigh him resumed his heavy turns upon the deck. With bent head and half-slouched hat he continued to pace, unmindful of the wondering whispering among the men; till Stubb cautiously whispered to Flask, that Ahab must have summoned them there for the purpose of witnessing a pedestrian feat. But this did not last long. Vehemently pausing, he cried: –

'What do ye do when ye see a whale, men?'

'Sing out for him!' was the impulsive rejoinder from a score of clubbed voices.

'Good!' cried Ahab, with a wild approval in his tones; observing the hearty animation into which his unexpected question had so magnetically thrown them.

'And what do ye next, men?'

'Lower away, and after him!'

'And what tune is it ye pull to, men?'

'A dead whale or a stove boat!'

More and more strangely and fiercely glad and approving, grew the countenance of the old man at every shout; while the mariners began to gaze curiously at each other, as if marvelling how it was that they themselves became so excited at such seemingly purposeless questions.

But, they were all eagerness again, as Ahab, now half-revolving in his pivot-hole, with one hand reaching high up a shroud, and tightly, almost convulsively grasping it, addressed them thus:–

'All ye mast-headers have before now heard me give orders about a white whale. Look ye! d'ye see this Spanish ounce of gold?' – holding up a broad bright coin to the sun – 'it is a sixteen dollar piece, men. D'ye see it? Mr Starbuck, hand me yon top-maul.'

While the mate was getting the hammer, Ahab, without speaking, was slowly rubbing the gold piece against the skirts of his jacket, as if to heighten its lustre, and without using any words was meanwhile lowly humming to himself, producing a sound so strangely muffled and inarticulate that it seemed the mechanical humming of the wheels of his vitality in him.

Receiving the top-maul from Starbuck, he advanced towards the main-mast with the hammer uplifted in one hand, exhibiting the gold with the other, and with a high raised voice exclaiming: 'Whosoever of ye raises me a white-headed whale with a wrinkled brow and a crooked jaw; whosoever of ye raises me that white-headed whale, with three holes punctured in his starboard fluke – look ye, whosoever of ye raises me that same white whale, he shall have this gold ounce, my boys!'

'Huzza! huzza!' cried the seamen, as with swinging tarpaulins they hailed the act of nailing the gold to the mast.

'It's a white whale, I say,' resumed Ahab, as he threw down the top-maul; 'a white whale. Skin your eyes for him, men; look sharp for white water; if ye see but a bubble, sing out.'

All this while Tashtego, Daggoo, and Queequeg had looked on with even more intense interest and surprise than the rest, and at the mention of the wrinkled brow and crooked jaw they had started as if each was separately touched by some specific recollection.

'Captain Ahab,' said Tashtego, 'that white whale must be the same that some call Moby Dick.'

'Moby Dick?' shouted Ahab. 'Do ye know the white whale then, Tash?'

'Does he fan-tail a little curious, sir, before he goes down?' said the Gay-Header deliberately.

'And has he a curious spout, too,' said Daggoo, 'very bushy, even for a parmacetty, and mighty quick, Captain Ahab?'

'And he have one, two, tree – oh! good many iron in him hide, too, Captain,' cried Queequeg disjointedly, 'all twiske-tee be-twisk, like him – him –' faltering hard for a word, and screwing his hand round and round as though uncorking a bottle – 'like him – him –'

'Corkscrew!' cried Ahab, 'aye, Queequeg, the harpoons lie all twisted and wrenched in him; aye, Daggoo, his spout is a big one, like a whole shock of wheat, and white as a pile of our Nantucket wool after the great annual sheep-shearing; aye, Tashtego, and he fan-tails like a split jib in a squall. Death and devils! men, it is Moby Dick ye have seen – Moby Dick – Moby Dick!'

'Captain Ahab,' said Starbuck, who, with Stubb and Flask, had thus far been eyeing his superior with increasing surprise, but at last seemed struck with a thought which somewhat explained all the wonder. 'Captain Ahab, I have heard of Moby Dick – but it was not Moby Dick that took off thy leg?'

'Who told thee that?' cried Ahab; then pausing, 'Aye, Starbuck; aye, my hearties all round; it was Moby Dick that dismasted me; Moby Dick that brought me to this dead stump I stand on now. Aye, aye,' he shouted with a terrific, loud, animal sob, like that of a heart-stricken moose; 'Aye, aye! it was that accursed white whale that razeed me; made a poor pegging lubber of me for ever and a day!' Then tossing both arms, with measureless imprecations he shouted out: 'Aye, aye! and I'll chase him round Good Hope, and round the Horn, and round the Norway Maelstrom, and round perdition's flames before I give him up. And this is what ye have shipped for, men! to chase that white whale on both sides of land, and over all sides of earth, till he spouts black blood and rolls fin out. What say ye, men, will ye splice hands on it, now? I think ye do look brave.'

'Aye, aye!' shouted the harpooneers and seamen, running closer to the excited old man: 'A sharp eye for the White Whale; a sharp lance for Moby Dick!'

'God bless ye,' he seemed to half sob and half shout. 'God bless ye, men. Steward! go draw the great measure of grog. But what's this long face about, Mr Starbuck; wilt thou not chase the white whale? art not game for Moby Dick?'

'I am game for his crooked jaw, and for the jaws of Death too, Captain Ahab, if it fairly comes in the way of the business we follow; but I came here to hunt whales, not my commander's vengeance. How many barrels will thy vengeance yield thee even if thou gettest it, Captain Ahab? it will not fetch thee much in our Nantucket market.'

'Nantucket market! Hoot! But come closer, Starbuck; thou requirest a little lower layer. If money's to be the measurer, man, and the accountants have computed their great counting-house the globe, by girdling it with guineas, one to every three parts of an inch; then, let me tell thee, that my vengeance will fetch a great premium *here*!'

'He smites his chest,' whispered Stubb, 'what's that for? methinks it rings most vast, but hollow.'

'Vengeance on a dumb brute!' cried Starbuck, 'that simply

smote thee from blindest instinct! Madness! To be enraged with a dumb thing, Captain Ahab, seems blasphemous.'

'Hark ye yet again, – the little lower layer. All visible objects, man, are but as pasteboard masks. But in each event – in the living act, the undoubted deed – there, some unknown but still reasoning thing puts forth the mouldings of its features from behind the unreasoning mask. If man will strike, strike through the mask! How can the prisoner reach outside except by thrusting through the wall? To me, the white whale is that wall, shoved near to me. Sometimes I think there's naught beyond. But 'tis enough. He tasks me; he heaps me; I see in him outrageous strength, with an inscrutable malice sinewing it. That inscrutable thing is chiefly what I hate; and be the white whale agent, or be the white whale principal, I will wreak that hate upon him. Talk not to me of blasphemy, man; I'd strike the sun if it insulted me. For could the sun do that, then could I do the other; since there is ever a sort of fair play herein, jealousy presiding over all creations. But not my master, man, is even that fair play. Who's over me? Truth hath no confines. Take off thine eye! more intolerable than fiends' glarings is a doltish stare! So, so; thou reddenest and palest; my heat has melted thee to anger-glow. But look ye, Starbuck, what is said in heat, that thing unsays itself. There are men from whom warm words are small indignity. I meant not to incense thee. Let it go. Look! see yonder Turkish cheeks of spotted tawn – living, breathing pictures painted by the sun. The Pagan leopards – the unrecking and unworshipping things, that live; and seek, and give no reasons for the torrid life they feel! The crew, man, the crew! Are they not one and all with Ahab, in this matter of the whale? See Stubb! he laughs! See yonder Chilian! he snorts to think of it. Stand up amid the general hurricane, thy one tost sapling cannot, Starbuck! And what is it? Reckon it. 'Tis but to help strike a fin; no wondrous feat for Starbuck. What is it more? From this one poor hunt, then, the best lance out of all Nantucket, surely he will not hang back, when every foremast-hand has clutched a whetstone? Ah!

constrainings seize thee; I see! the billow lifts thee! Speak, but speak! – Aye, aye! thy silence, then, *that* voices thee. (*Aside*) Something shot from my dilated nostrils, he has inhaled it in his lungs. Starbuck now is mine; cannot oppose me now, without rebellion.'

'God keep me! – keep us all!' murmured Starbuck, lowly.

But in his joy at the enchanted, tacit acquiescence of the mate, Ahab did not hear his foreboding invocation; nor yet the low laugh from the hold; nor yet the presaging vibrations of the winds in the cordage; nor yet the hollow flap of the sails against the masts, as for a moment their hearts sank in. For again Starbuck's downcast eyes lighted up with the stubbornness of life; the subterranean laugh died away; the winds blew on; the sails filled out; the ship heaved and rolled as before. Ah, ye admonitions and warnings! why stay ye not when ye come? But rather are ye predictions than warnings, ye shadows! Yet not so much predictions from without, as verifications of the foregoing things within. For with little external to constrain us, the innermost necessities in our being, these still drive us on.

'The measure! the measure!' cried Ahab.

Receiving the brimming pewter, and turning to the harpooneers, he ordered them to produce their weapons. Then ranging them before him near the capstan, with their harpoons in their hands, while his three mates stood at his side with their lances, and the rest of the ship's company formed a circle round the group; he stood for an instant searchingly eyeing every man of his crew. But those wild eyes met his, as the bloodshot eyes of the prairie wolves meet the eye of their leader, ere he rushes on at their head in the trail of the bison; but, alas! only to fall into the hidden snare of the Indian.

'Drink and pass!' he cried, handing the heavy charged flagon to the nearest seaman. 'The crew alone now drink. Round with it, round! Short draughts – long swallows, men; 'tis hot as Satan's hoof. So, so; it goes round excellently. It spiralizes in ye; forks out at the serpent-snapping eye. Well done; almost drained. That way it went, this way it comes.

Hand it me – here's a hollow! Men, ye seem the years; so brimming life is gulped and gone. Steward, refill!

'Attend now, my braves. I have mustered ye all round this capstan; and ye mates, flank me with your lances; and ye harpooneers, stand there with your irons; and ye, stout mariners, ring me in, that I may in some sort revive a noble custom of my fishermen fathers before me. O men, you will yet see that – Ha! boy, come back? bad pennies come not sooner. Hand it me. Why, now, this pewter had run brimming again, wert not thou St. Vitus' imp – away, thou ague!

'Advance, ye mates! Cross your lances full before me. Well done! Let me touch the axis.' So saying, with extended arm, he grasped the three level, radiating lances at their crossed centre; while so doing, suddenly and nervously twitched them; meanwhile, glancing intently from Starbuck to Stubb; from Stubb to Flask. It seemed as though, by some nameless, interior volition, he would fain have shocked into them the same fiery emotion accumulated within the Leyden jar of his own magnetic life. The three mates quailed before his strong, sustained, and mystic aspect. Stubb and Flask looked sideways from him; the honest eye of Starbuck fell downright.

'In vain!' cried Ahab; 'but, maybe, 'tis well. For did ye three but once take the full-forced shock, then mine own electric thing, *that* had perhaps expired from out me. Perchance, too, it would have dropped ye dead. Perchance ye need it not. Down lances! And now, ye mates, I do appoint ye three cup-bearers to my three pagan kinsmen there – yon three most honorable gentlemen and noblemen, my valiant harpooneers. Disdain the task? What, when the great Pope washes the feet of beggars, using his tiara for ewer? Oh, my sweet cardinals! your own condescension, *that* shall bend ye to it. I do not order ye; ye will it. Cut your seizings and draw the poles, ye harpooneers!'

Silently obeying the order, the three harpooneers now stood with the detached iron part of their harpoons, some three feet long, held, barbs up, before him.

'Stab me not with that keen steel! Cant them; cant them

over! know ye not the goblet end? Turn up the socket! So, so; now, ye cup-bearers, advance. The irons! take them; hold them while I fill!' Forthwith, slowly going from one officer to the other, he brimmed the harpoon sockets with the fiery waters from the pewter.

'Now, three to three, ye stand. Commend the murderous chalices! Bestow them, ye who are now made parties to this indissoluble league. Ha! Starbuck! but the deed is done! Yon ratifying sun now waits to sit upon it. Drink, ye harpooneers! drink and swear, ye men that man the deathful whaleboat's bow – Death to Moby Dick! God hunt us all, if we do not hunt Moby Dick to his death!' The long, barbed steel goblets were lifted; and to cries and maledictions against the white whale, the spirits were simultaneously quaffed down with a hiss. Starbuck paled, and turned, and shivered. Once more, and finally, the replenished pewter went the rounds among the frantic crew; when, waving his free hand to them, they all dispersed; and Ahab retired within his cabin.

37

SUNSET

The cabin; by the stern windows; Ahab sitting alone, and gazing out.

I LEAVE a white and turbid wake; pale waters, paler cheeks, where'er I sail. The envious billows sidelong swell to whelm my track; let them; but first I pass.

Yonder, by the ever-brimming goblet's rim, the warm waves blush like wine. The gold brow plumbs the blue. The diver sun – slow dived from noon, – goes down; my soul mounts up! she wearies with her endless hill. Is, then, the crown too heavy that I wear? this Iron Crown of Lombardy. Yet is it bright with many a gem; I, the wearer, see not its far flashings; but darkly feel that I wear that, that dazzlingly confounds. 'Tis iron – that I know – not gold. 'Tis split, too – that I feel; the jagged edge galls me so, my brain seems to beat against the solid metal; aye, steel skull, mine; the sort that needs no helmet in the most brain-battering fight!

Dry heat upon my brow? Oh! time was, when as the sunrise nobly spurred me, so the sunset soothed. No more. This lovely light, it lights not me; all loveliness is anguish to me, since I can ne'er enjoy. Gifted with the high perception, I lack the low, enjoying power; damned, most subtly and most malignantly! damned in the midst of Paradise! Good night – good night! (*waving his hand, he moves from the window.*)

'Twas not so hard a task. I thought to find one stubborn, at the least; but my one cogged circle fits into all their various wheels, and they revolve. Or, if you will, like so many ant-hills of powder, they all stand before me; and I their match. Oh, hard! that to fire others, the match itself must needs be wasting! What I've dared, I've willed; and what I've willed, I'll do! They think me mad – Starbuck does; but I'm demoniac, I am madness maddened! That wild madness that's only calm to comprehend itself! The prophecy was that I should be dismembered; and – Aye! I lost this leg. I now prophesy that I will dismember my dismemberer. Now, then, be the prophet and the fulfiller one. That's more than ye, ye great gods, ever were. I laugh and hoot at ye, ye cricket-players, ye pugilists, ye deaf Burkes and blinded Bendigoes! I will not say as schoolboys do to bullies, – Take some one of your own size; don't pommel *me*! No, ye've knocked me down, and I am up again; but *ye* have run and hidden. Come forth from behind your cotton bags! I have no long gun to reach ye. Come, Ahab's compliments to ye; come and see if ye can swerve me. Swerve me? ye cannot swerve me, else ye swerve yourselves! man has ye there. Swerve me? The path to my fixed purpose is laid with iron rails, whereon my soul is grooved to run. Over unsounded gorges, through the rifled hearts of mountains, under torrents' beds, unerringly I rush! Naught's an obstacle, naught's an angle to the iron way!

38

DUSK

By the Mainmast; Starbuck leaning against it.

My soul is more than matched; she's overmanned; and by a madman! Insufferable sting, that sanity should ground arms on such a field! But he drilled deep down, and blasted all my reason out of me! I think I see his impious end; but feel that I must help him to it. Will I, nill I, the ineffable thing has tied me to him; tows me with a cable I have no knife to cut. Horrible old man! Who's over him, he cries; – aye, he would be a democrat to all above; look, how he lords it over all below! Oh! I plainly see my miserable office, – to obey, rebelling; and worse yet, to hate with touch of pity! For in his eyes I read some lurid woe would shrivel me up, had I it. Yet is there hope. Time and tide flow wide. The hated whale has the round watery world to swim in, as the small gold-fish has its glassy globe. His heaven-insulting purpose, God may wedge aside. I would up heart, were it not like lead. But my whole clock's run down; my heart the all-controlling weight, I have no key to lift again.

A burst of revelry from the forecastle.

Oh, God! to sail with such a heathen crew that have small touch of human mothers in them! Whelped somewhere by the sharkish sea. The white whale is their demigorgon. Hark! the infernal orgies! that revelry is forward! mark the unfaltering silence aft! Methinks it pictures life. Foremost through the sparkling sea shoots on the gay, embattled, bantering bow, but only to drag dark Ahab after it, where he broods within his sternward cabin, builded over the dead water of the wake, and further on, hunted by its wolfish gurglings. The long howl thrills me through! Peace! ye revellers, and set the watch! Oh, life! 'tis in an hour like this, with soul beat down and held to knowledge, – as wild, untutored things are forced to feed – Oh, life! 'tis now that I do feel the latent horror in thee! but 'tis not me! that horror's out of me! and with the soft feeling of the human in me, yet will I try to fight ye, ye grim, phantom futures! Stand by me, hold me, bind me, O ye blessed influences!

39

FIRST NIGHT-WATCH

FORE-TOP

(*Stubb solus, and mending a brace.*)

HA! ha! ha! ha! hem! clear my throat! – I've been thinking over it ever since, and that ha-ha's the final consequence. Why so? Because a laugh's the wisest, easiest answer to all that's queer; and come what will, one comfort's always left – that unfailing comfort is, it's all predestinated. I heard not all his talk with Starbuck; but to my poor eye Starbuck then looked something as I the other evening felt. Be sure the old Mogul has fixed him, too. I twigged it, knew it; had had the gift, might readily have prophesied it – for when I clapped my eye upon his skull I saw it. Well, Stubb, *wise* Stubb – that's my title – well, Stubb, what of it, Stubb? Here's a carcase. I know not all that may be coming, but be it what it will, I'll go to it laughing. Such a waggish leering as lurks in all your horribles! I feel funny. Fa, la! lirra, skirra! What's my juicy little pear at home doing now? Crying its eyes out? – Giving a party to the last arrived harpooneers, I dare say, gay as a frigate's pennant, and so am I – fa, la! lirra, skirra! Oh –

We'll drink to-night with hearts as light,
  To love, as gay and fleeting
As bubbles that swim, on the beaker's brim,
  And break on the lips while meeting.

A brave stave that – who calls? Mr. Starbuck? Aye, aye, sir – (*Aside*) he's my superior, he has his too, if I'm not mistaken. – Aye, aye, sir, just through with this job – coming.

40

MIDNIGHT, FORECASTLE

HARPOONEERS AND SAILORS

(*Forcsail rises and discovers the watch standing, lounging, leaning, and lying in various attitudes, all singing in chorus.*)

Farewell and adieu to you, Spanish ladies!
Farewell and adieu to you, ladies of Spain!
    Our captain's commanded –

1ST NANTUCKET SAILOR

Oh, boys, don't be sentimental; it's bad for the digestion! Take a tonic, follow me!

(*Sings, and all follow.*)

Our captain stood upon the deck,
    A spy-glass in his hand,
A viewing of those gallant whales
    That blew at every strand.
Oh, your tubs in your boats, my boys,
    And by your braces stand,
And we'll have one of those fine whales,
    Hand, boys, over hand!
So, be cheery, my lads! may your hearts never fail!
While the bold harpooneer is striking the whale!

MATE'S VOICE FROM THE QUARTER-DECK

Eight bells there, forward!

2D NANTUCKET SAILOR

Avast the chorus! Eight bells there! d'ye hear, bell-boy? Strike the bell eight, thou Pip! thou blackling! and let me call the watch. I've the sort of mouth for that – the hogshead mouth. So, so, (*thrusts his head down the scuttle,*) Star–bo–l-e-e-n-s, a-h-o-y! Eight bells there below! Tumble up!

DUTCH SAILOR

Grand snoozing to-night, maty; fat night for that. I mark this in our old Mogul's wine; it's quite as deadening to some as filliping to others. We sing; they sleep – aye, lie down there, like ground-tier butts. At 'em again! There, take this copper-pump, and hail 'em through it. Tell 'em to avast dreaming of their lasses. Tell 'em it's the resurrection; they must kiss their last, and come to judgment. That's the way – *that's* it; thy throat ain't spoiled with eating Amsterdam butter.

FRENCH SAILOR

Hist, boys! let's have a jig or two before we ride to anchor in Blanket Bay. What say ye? There comes the other watch. Stand by all legs! Pip! little Pip! hurrah with your tambourine!

PIP

(*Sulky and sleepy.*)

Don't know where it is.

FRENCH SAILOR

Beat thy belly, then, and wag thy ears. Jig it, men, I say; merry's the word; hurrah! Damn me, won't you dance? Form, now, Indian-file, and gallop into the double-shuffle? Throw yourselves! Legs! legs!

ICELAND SAILOR

I don't like your floor, maty; it's too springy to my taste. I'm used to ice-floors. I'm sorry to throw cold water on the subject; but excuse me.

MALTESE SAILOR

Me too; where's your girls? Who but a fool would take his left hand by his right, and say to himself, how d'ye do? Partners! I must have partners!

SICILIAN SAILOR

Aye; girls and a green! – then I'll hop with ye; yea, turn grasshopper!

LONG-ISLAND SAILOR

Well, well, ye sulkies, there's plenty more of us. Hoe corn when you may, say I. All legs go to harvest soon. Ah! here comes the music; now for it!

AZORE SAILOR

(*Ascending, and pitching the tambourine up the scuttle.*)
Here you are, Pip; and there's the windlass-bitts; up you mount! Now, boys!
(*The half of them dance to the tambourine; some go below; some sleep or lie among the coils of rigging. Oaths a-plenty.*)

AZORE SAILOR

(*Dancing.*)

Go it, Pip! Bang it, bell-boy! Rig it, dig it, stig it, quig it, bell-boy! Make fire-flies; break the jinglers!

PIP

Jinglers, you say? – there goes another, dropped off, I pound it so.

CHINA SAILOR

Rattle thy teeth, then, and pound away; make a pagoda of thyself.

FRENCH SAILOR

Merry-mad! Hold up thy hoop, Pip, till I jump through it! Split jibs! tear yourselves!

TASHTEGO

(*Quietly smoking.*)

That's a white man; he calls that fun: humph; I save my sweat.

OLD MANX SAILOR

I wonder whether those jolly lads bethink them of what they are dancing over. I'll dance over your grave, I will – that's the bitterest threat of your night-women, that beat head-winds round corners. O Christ! to think of the green navies and the green-skulled crews! Well, well; belike, the whole world's a ball, as you scholars have it; and so 'tis right to make one ball-room of it. Dance on, lads, you're young; I was once.

3D NANTUCKET SAILOR

Spell oh! – whew! this is worse than pulling after whales in a calm – give us a whiff, Tash.

(*They cease dancing, and gather in clusters. Meantime the sky darkens – the wind rises.*)

LASCAR SAILOR

By Brahma! boys, it'll be douse sail soon. The sky-born, high-tide Ganges turned to wind! Thou showest thy black brow, Seeva!

MALTESE SAILOR

(*Reclining and shaking his cap.*)

It's the waves' – the snow-caps' turn to jig it now. They'll shake their tassels soon. Now would all the waves were women, then I'd go drown, and chassee with them evermore! There's naught so sweet on earth – heaven may not match it! – as those swift glances of warm, wild bosoms in the dance, when the over-arboring arms hide such ripe, bursting grapes.

SICILIAN SAILOR

(*Reclining.*)

Tell me not of it! Hark ye. lad – fleet interlacings of the limbs – lithe swayings – coyings – flutterings! lip! heart! hip! all graze: unceasing touch and go! not taste, observe ye, else come satiety. Eh, Pagan? (*Nudging.*)

TAHITAN SAILOR

(*Reclining on a mat.*)

Hail, holy nakedness of our dancing girls! – the Heeva-Heeva! Ah! low veiled, high palmed Tahiti! I still rest me on thy mat, but the soft soil has slid! I saw thee woven in the wood, my mat! green the first day I brought ye thence; now worn and wilted quite. Ah me! – not thou nor can I bear the change! How then, if so be transplanted to yon sky? Hear I the roaring streams from Pirohitee's peak of spears, when they leap down the crags and drown the villages? – The blast! the blast! Up, spine, and meet it! (*Leaps to his feet.*)

PORTUGUESE SAILOR

How the sea rolls swashing 'gainst the side! Stand by for reefing, hearties! the winds are just crossing swords, pell-mell they'll go lunging presently.

DANISH SAILOR

Crack, crack, old ship! so long as thou crackest, thou holdest! Well done! The mate there holds ye to it stiffly. He's no more afraid than the isle fort at Cattegat, put there to fight the Baltic with storm-lashed guns, on which the sea-salt cakes!

4TH NANTUCKET SAILOR

He has his orders, mind ye that. I heard old Ahab tell him he must always kill a squall, something as they burst a water-spout with a pistol – fire your ship right into it!

ENGLISH SAILOR

Blood! but that old man's a grand old cove! We are the lads to hunt him up his whale!

ALL

Aye! aye!

OLD MANX SAILOR

How the three pines shake! Pines are the hardest sort of tree to live when shifted to any other soil, and here there's none but the crew's cursed clay. Steady, helmsman! steady. This is the sort of weather when brave hearts snap ashore, and keeled hulls split at sea. Our captain has his birth-mark; look yonder, boys, there's another in the sky – lurid-like, ye see, all else pitch black.

DAGGOO

What of that? Who's afraid of black's afraid of me! I'm quarried out of it!

SPANISH SAILOR

(*Aside.*) He wants to bully, ah! – the old grudge makes me touchy. (*Advancing.*) Aye, harpooneer, thy race is the undeniable dark side of mankind – devilish dark at that. No offence.

DAGGOO (*grimly*)

None.

ST. JAGO'S SAILOR

That Spaniard's mad or drunk. But that can't be, or else in his one case our old Mogul's fire-waters are somewhat long in working.

5TH NANTUCKET SAILOR

What's that I saw – lightning? Yes.

SPANISH SAILOR

No; Daggoo showing his teeth.

DAGGOO (*springing*)

Swallow thine, mannikin! White skin, white liver!

SPANISH SAILOR (*meeting him*)

Knife thee heartily! big frame, small spirit!

ALL

A row! a row! a row!

TASHTEGO (*with a whiff*)

A row a'low, and a row aloft – Gods and men – both brawlers! Humph!

BELFAST SAILOR

A row! arrah a row! The Virgin be blessed, a row! Plunge in with ye!

ENGLISH SAILOR

Fair play! Snatch the Spaniard's knife! A ring, a ring!

OLD MANX SAILOR

Ready formed. There! the ringed horizon. In that ring Cain struck Abel. Sweet work, right work! No? Why then, God, mad'st thou the ring?

MATE'S VOICE FROM THE QUARTER DECK

Hands by the halyards! in top-gallant sails! Stand by to reef topsails!

ALL

The squall! the squall! jump, my jollies! (*They scatter.*)

PIP (*shrinking under the windlass*)

Jollies? Lord help such jollies! Crish, crash! there goes the jib-stay! Blang-whang! God! Duck lower, Pip, here comes the royal yard! It's worse than being in the whirled woods, the last day of the year! Who'd go climbing after chestnuts now? But there they go, all cursing, and here I don't. Fine prospects to 'em; they're on the road to heaven. Hold on hard! Jimmini, what a squall! But those chaps there are worse yet – they are your white squalls, they. White squalls? white whale, shirr! shirr! Here have I heard all their chat just now, and the white whale – shirr! shirr! – but spoken of once! and only this evening – it makes me jingle all over like my tambourine – that anaconda of an old man swore 'em in to hunt him! Oh, thou big white God aloft there somewhere in yon darkness, have mercy on this small black boy down here; preserve him from all men that have no bowels to feel fear!

* * * * * * *

41

MOBY DICK

I, ISHMAEL, was one of that crew; my shouts had gone up with the rest; my oath had been welded with theirs; and stronger I shouted, and more did I hammer and clinch my oath, because of the dread in my soul. A wild, mystical, sympathetical feeling was in me; Ahab's quenchless feud seemed mine. With greedy ears I learned the history of that murderous monster against whom I and all the others had taken our oaths of violence and revenge.

For some time past, though at intervals only, the unaccompanied, secluded White Whale had haunted those uncivilized seas mostly frequented by the Sperm Whale fishermen. But not all of them knew of his existence; only a few of them, comparatively, had knowingly seen him; while the number who as yet had actually and knowingly given battle to him, was small indeed. For, owing to the large number of whale-cruisers; the disorderly way they were sprinkled over the entire watery circumference, many of them adventurously pushing their quest along solitary latitudes, so as seldom or never for a whole twelvemonth or more on a stretch, to encounter a single news-telling sail of any sort; the inordinate length of each separate voyage; the irregularity of the times of sailing from home; all these, with other circumstances, direct and indirect, long obstructed the spread through the whole world-wide whaling-fleet of the special individualizing tidings concerning Moby Dick. It was hardly to be doubted, that several vessels reported to have encountered, at such or such a time, or on such or such a meridian, a Sperm Whale of uncommon magnitude and malignity, which whale, after doing great mischief to his assailants, had completely escaped them; to some minds it was not an unfair presumption, I say, that the whale in question must have been no other than Moby Dick. Yet as of late the Sperm Whale fishery had been marked by various and not infrequent instances of great ferocity, cunning, and malice in the monster attacked; therefore it was, that those who by accident ignorantly gave battle to Moby Dick; such hunters, perhaps, for the most part, were content to ascribe the peculiar terror he bred, more, as it were, to the perils of the Sperm Whale fishery at large, than to the individual cause. In that way, mostly, the disastrous encounter between Ahab and the whale had hitherto been popularly regarded.

And as for those who, previously hearing of the White Whale, by chance caught sight of him; in the beginning of the thing they had every one of them, almost, as boldly and fearlessly lowered for him, as for any other whale of that species. But at length, such calamities did ensue in these assaults – not restricted to sprained wrists and ancles, broken limbs, or devouring amputations – but fatal to the last degree of fatality; those repeated disastrous repulses, all accumulating and piling their terrors upon Moby Dick; those things had gone far to shake the fortitude of many brave hunters, to whom the story of the White Whale had eventually come.

Nor did wild rumors of all sorts fail to exaggerate, and still the more horrify the true histories of these deadly encounters. For not only do fabulous rumors naturally grow out of the very body of all surprising terrible events, – as the smitten tree gives birth to its fungi; but, in maritime life, far more than in that of terra firma, wild rumors abound, wherever there is any adequate reality for them to cling to. And as the sea surpasses the land in this matter, so the whale fishery surpasses every other sort of maritime life, in the wonderfulness and fearfulness of the rumors which sometimes circulate there. For not only are whalemen as a body unexempt from that ignorance and superstitiousness hereditary to all sailors; but of all sailors, they are by all odds the most directly brought into contact with whatever is appallingly astonishing in the sea; face to face they not only eye its greatest marvels, but, hand to jaw, give battle to them. Alone, in such remotest waters, that though you sailed a thousand miles, and passed a thousand shores, you would not come to any chiselled hearthstone, or aught hospitable beneath that part of the sun; in such latitudes and longitudes, pursuing too such a calling as he does, the whaleman is wrapped by influences all tending to make his fancy pregnant with many a mighty birth.

No wonder, then, that ever gathering volume from the mere transit over the widest watery spaces, the outblown rumors of the White Whale did in the end incorporate with themselves all manner of morbid hints, and half-formed fœtal suggestions of supernatural agencies, which eventually invested Moby Dick with new terrors unborrowed from anything that visibly appears. So that in many cases such a panic did he finally strike, that few who by those rumors, at least, had heard of the White Whale, few of those hunters were willing to encounter the perils of his jaw.

But there were still other and more vital practical influences at work. Not even at the present day has the original prestige of the Sperm Whale, as fearfully distinguished from all other species of the leviathan, died out of the minds of the whalemen as a body. There are those this day among them, who, though intelligent and courageous enough in offering battle to the Greenland or Right whale, would perhaps – either from professional inexperience, or incompetency, or timidity, decline a contest with the Sperm Whale; at any rate, there are plenty of whalemen, especially among those whaling nations not sailing under the American flag, who have never hostilely encountered the Sperm Whale, but whose sole knowledge of the leviathan is restricted to the ignoble monster primitively pursued in the North; seated on their hatches, these men will hearken with a childish fire-side interest and awe, to the wild, strange tales of Southern whaling. Nor is the pre-eminent tremendousness of the great Sperm Whale anywhere more feelingly comprehended, than on board of those prows which stem him.

And as if the now tested reality of his might had in former legendary times thrown its shadow before it; we find some book naturalists – Olassen and Povelson – declaring the Sperm Whale not only to be a consternation to every other creature in the sea, but also to be so incredibly ferocious as continually to be athirst for human blood. Nor even down to so late a time as Cuvier's, were these or almost similar impressions effaced. For in his Natural History, the Baron himself affirms that at sight of the Sperm Whale, all fish (sharks included) are 'struck with the most lively terrors,' and 'often in the precipitancy of their flight dash themselves against the rocks with such violence as to cause instantaneous death.' And however the general experiences in the fishery may amend such reports as these; yet in their full terribleness, even to the bloodthirsty item of Povelson, the superstitious belief in them is, in some vicissitudes of their vocation, revived in the minds of the hunters.

So that overawed by the rumors and portents concerning

him, not a few of the fishermen recalled, in reference to Moby Dick, the earlier days of the Sperm Whale fishery, when it was oftentimes hard to induce long practised Right whalemen to embark in the perils of this new and daring warfare; such men protesting that although other leviathans might be hopefully pursued, yet to chase and point lance at such an apparition as the Sperm Whale was not for mortal man. That to attempt it, would be inevitably to be torn into a quick eternity. On this head, there are some remarkable documents that may be consulted.

Nevertheless, some there were, who even in the face of these things were ready to give chase to Moby Dick; and a still greater number who, chancing only to hear of him distantly and vaguely, without the specific details of any certain calamity, and without superstitious accompaniments, were sufficiently hardy not to flee from the battle if offered.

One of the wild suggestings referred to, as at last coming to be linked with the White Whale in the minds of the superstitiously inclined, was the unearthly conceit that Moby Dick was ubiquitous; that he had actually been encountered in opposite latitudes at one and the same instant of time.

Nor, credulous as such minds must have been, was this conceit altogether without some faint show of superstitious probability. For as the secrets of the currents in the seas have never yet been divulged, even to the most erudite research; so the hidden ways of the Sperm Whale when beneath the surface remain, in great part, unaccountable to his pursuers; and from time to time have originated the most curious and contradictory speculations regarding them, especially concerning the mystic modes whereby, after sounding to a great depth, he transports himself with such vast swiftness to the most widely distant points.

It is a thing well known to both American and English whaleships, and as well a thing placed upon authoritative record years ago by Scoresby, that some whales have been captured far north in the Pacific, in whose bodies have been found the barbs of harpoons darted in the Greenland seas. Nor is it to be gainsaid, that in some of these instances it has been declared that the interval of time between the two assaults could not have exceeded very many days. Hence, by inference, it has been believed by some whalemen, that the Nor' West Passage, so long a problem to man, was never a problem to the whale. So that here, in the real living experience of living men, the prodigies related in old times of the inland Strello mountain in Portugal (near whose top there was said to be a lake in which the wrecks of ships floated up to the surface); and that still more wonderful story of the Arethusa fountain near Syracuse (whose waters were believed to have come from the Holy Land by an underground passage); these fabulous narrations are almost fully equalled by the realities of the whaleman.

Forced into familiarity, then, with such prodigies as these; and knowing that after repeated, intrepid assaults, the White Whale had escaped alive; it cannot be much matter of surprise that some whalemen should go still further in their superstitions; declaring Moby Dick not only ubiquitous, but immortal (for immortality is but ubiquity in time); that though groves of spears should be planted in his flanks, he would still swim away unharmed, or if indeed he should ever be made to spout thick blood, such a sight would be but a ghastly deception; for again in unensanguined billows hundreds of leagues away, his unsullied jet would once more be seen.

But even stripped of these supernatural surmisings, there was enough in the earthly make and incontestable character of the monster to strike the imagination with unwonted power. For, it was not so much his uncommon bulk that so much distinguished him from other sperm whales, but, as was elsewhere thrown out – a peculiar snow-white wrinkled forehead, and a high, pyramidical white hump. These were his prominent features; the tokens whereby, even in the limitless, uncharted seas, he revealed his identity, at a long distance, to those who knew him.

The rest of his body was so streaked, and spotted, and marbled with the same shrouded hue, that, in the end, he had gained his distinctive appellation of the White Whale;

a name, indeed, literally justified by his vivid aspect, when seen gliding at high noon through a dark blue sea, leaving a milky-way wake of creamy foam, all spangled with golden gleamings.

Nor was it his unwonted magnitude, nor his remarkable hue, nor yet his deformed lower jaw, that so much invested the whale with natural terror, as that unexampled, intelligent malignity which, according to specific accounts, he had over and over again evinced in his assaults. More than all, his treacherous retreats struck more of dismay than perhaps aught else. For, when swimming before his exulting pursuers, with every apparent symptom of alarm, he had several times been known to turn round suddenly, and, bearing down upon them, either stave their boats to splinters, or drive them back in consternation to their ship.

Already several fatalities had attended his chase. But though similar disasters, however little bruited ashore, were by no means unusual in the fishery; yet, in most instances, such seemed the White Whale's infernal aforethought of ferocity, that every dismembering or death that he caused, was not wholly regarded as having been inflicted by an unintelligent agent.

Judge, then, to what pitches of inflamed, distracted fury the minds of his more desperate hunters were impelled, when amid the chips of chewed boats, and the sinking limbs of torn comrades, they swam out of the white curds of the whale's direful wrath into the serene, exasperating sunlight, that smiled on, as if at a birth or a bridal.

His three boats stove around him, and oars and men both whirling in the eddies; one captain, seizing the line-knife from his broken prow, had dashed at the whale, as an Arkansas duellist at his foe, blindly seeking with a six inch blade to reach the fathom-deep life of the whale. That captain was Ahab. And then it was, that suddenly sweeping his sickle-shaped lower jaw beneath him, Moby Dick had reaped away Ahab's leg, as a mower a blade of grass in the field. No turbaned Turk, no hired Venetian or Malay, could have smote him with more seeming malice. Small reason was there to doubt, then, that ever since that almost fatal encounter, Ahab had cherished a wild vindictiveness against the whale, all the more fell for that in his frantic morbidness he at last came to identify with him, not only all his bodily woes, but all his intellectual and spiritual exasperations. The White Whale swam before him as the monomaniac incarnation of all those malicious agencies which some deep men feel eating in them, till they are left living on with half a heart and half a lung. That intangible malignity which has been from the beginning; to whose dominion even the modern Christians ascribe one-half of the worlds; which the ancient Ophites of the east reverenced in their statue devil; – Ahab did not fall down and worship it like them; but deliriously transferring its idea to the abhorred white whale, he pitted himself, all mutilated, against it. All that most maddens and torments; all that stirs up the lees of things; all truth with malice in it; all that cracks the sinews and cakes the brain; all the subtle demonisms of life and thought; all evil, to crazy Ahab, were visibly personified, and made practically assailable in Moby Dick. He piled upon the whale's white hump the sum of all the general rage and hate felt by his whole race from Adam down; and then, as if his chest had been a mortar, he burst his hot heart's shell upon it.

It is not probable that this monomania in him took its instant rise at the precise time of his bodily dismemberment. Then, in darting at the monster, knife in hand, he had but given loose to a sudden, passionate, corporal animosity; and when he received the stroke that tore him, he probably but felt the agonizing bodily laceration, but nothing more. Yet, when by this collision forced to turn towards home, and for long months of days and weeks, Ahab and anguish lay stretched together in one hammock, rounding in mid winter that dreary, howling Patagonian Cape; then it was, that his torn body and gashed soul bled into one another; and so interfusing, made him mad. That it was only then, on the homeward voyage, after the encounter, that the final monomania seized him, seems all but certain from the fact that, at intervals during the passage, he was a raving lunatic; and, though unlimbed of a leg, yet such vital strength yet lurked in his Egyptian chest, and was moreover intensified by his delirium, that his mates were forced to lace him fast, even there, as he sailed, raving in his hammock. In a strait-jacket, he swung to the mad rockings of the gales. And, when running into more sufferable latitudes, the ship, with mild stun'sails spread, floated across the tranquil tropics, and, to all appearances, the old man's delirium seemed left behind him with the Cape Horn swells, and he came forth from his dark den into the blessed light and air; even then, when he bore that firm, collected front, however pale, and issued his calm orders once again; and his mates thanked God the direful madness was now gone; even then, Ahab, in his hidden self, raved on. Human madness is oftentimes a cunning and most feline thing. When you think it fled, it may have but become transfigured into some still subtler form. Ahab's full lunacy subsided not, but deepeningly contracted; like the unabated Hudson, when that noble Northman flows narrowly, but unfathomably through the Highland gorge. But, as in his narrow-flowing monomania, not one jot of Ahab's broad madness had been left behind; so in that broad madness, not one jot of his great natural intellect had perished. That before living agent, now became the living instrument. If such a furious trope may stand, his special lunacy stormed his general sanity, and carried it, and turned all its concentred cannon upon its own mad mark; so that far from having lost his strength, Ahab, to that one end, did now possess a thousand fold more potency than ever he had sanely brought to bear upon any one reasonable object.

This is much; yet Ahab's larger, darker, deeper part remains unhinted. But vain to popularize profundities, and all truth is profound. Winding far down from within the very heart of this spiked Hotel de Cluny where we here stand – however grand and wonderful, now quit it; – and take your way, ye nobler, sadder souls, to those vast Roman halls of Thermes; where far beneath the fantastic towers of man's upper earth, his root of grandeur, his whole awful essence sits in bearded state; an antique buried beneath antiquities, and throned on torsoes! So with a broken throne, the great gods mock that captive king; so like a Caryatid, he patient sits, upholding on his frozen brow the piled entablatures of ages. Wind ye down there, ye prouder, sadder souls! question that proud, sad king! A family likeness! aye, he did beget ye, ye young exiled royalties; and from your grim sire only will the old State-secret come.

Now, in his heart, Ahab had some glimpse of this, namely: all my means are sane, my motive and my object mad. Yet without power to kill, or change, or shun the fact; he likewise knew that to mankind he did long dissemble; in some sort, did still. But that thing of his dissembling, was only subject to his perceptibility, not to his will determinate. Nevertheless, so well did he succeed in that dissembling, that when with ivory leg he stepped ashore at last, no Nantucketer thought him othewise than but naturally grieved, and that to the quick, with the terrible casualty which had overtaken him.

The report of his undeniable delirium at sea was likewise popularly ascribed to a kindred cause. And so too, all the added moodiness which always afterwards, to the very day of sailing in the Pequod on the present voyage, sat brooding on his brow. Nor is it so very unlikely, that far from distrusting his fitness for another whaling voyage, on account of such dark symptoms, the calculating people of that prudent isle were inclined to harbor the conceit, that for those very reasons he was all the better qualified and set on edge, for a pursuit so full of rage and wildness as the bloody hunt of whales. Gnawed within and scorched without, with the infixed, unrelenting fangs of some incurable idea; such an one, could he be found, would seem the very man to dart his iron and lift his lance against the most appalling of all brutes. Or, if for any reason thought to be corporeally incapacitated for that, yet such an one would seem superlatively competent to cheer and howl on his underlings to the attack. But be all this as it may, certain it is, that with the mad secret of his unabated rage bolted up and keyed in him, Ahab had purposely sailed upon the present voyage with the one only and all-engrossing object of hunting the White Whale. Had any one of his old acquaintances on shore but half dreamed of what was lurking in him then, how soon would their aghast and righteous souls have wrenched the ship from such a fiendish man! They were bent on profitable cruises, the profit to be counted down in dollars from the mint. He was intent on an audacious, immitigable, and supernatural revenge.

Here, then, was this grey-headed, ungodly old man, chasing with curses a Job's whale round the world, at the head of a crew, too, chiefly made up of mongrel renegades, and castaways, and cannibals – morally enfeebled also, by the incompetence of mere unaided virtue or right-mindedness in Starbuck, the invulnerable jollity of indifference and recklessness in Stubb, and the pervading mediocrity in Flask. Such a crew, so officered, seemed specially picked and packed by some infernal fatality to help him to his monomaniac revenge. How it was that they so aboundingly responded to the old man's ire – by what evil magic their souls were possessed, that at times his hate seemed almost theirs; the White Whale as much their insufferable foe as his; how all this came to be – what the White Whale was to them, or how to their unconscious understandings, also, in some dim, unsuspected way, he might have seemed the gliding great demon of the seas of life, – all this to explain, would be to dive deeper than Ishmael can go. The subterranean miner that works in us all, how can one tell whither leads his shaft by the ever shifting, muffled sound of his pick? Who does not feel the irresistible arm drag? What skiff in tow of a seventy-four can stand still? For one, I gave myself up to the abandonment of the time and the place; but while yet all a-rush to encounter the whale, could see naught in that brute but the deadliest ill.

42

THE WHITENESS OF THE WHALE

WHAT the white whale was to Ahab, has been hinted; what, at times, he was to me, as yet remains unsaid.

Aside from those more obvious considerations touching Moby Dick, which could not but occasionally awaken in any man's soul some alarm, there was another thought, or rather vague, nameless horror concerning him, which at times by its intensity completely overpowered all the rest; and yet so mystical and well nigh ineffable was it, that I almost despair of putting it in a comprehensible form. It was the whiteness of the whale that above all things appalled me. But how can I hope to explain myself here; and yet, in some dim, random way, explain myself I must, else all these chapters might be naught.

Though in many natural objects, whiteness refiningly enhances beauty, as if imparting some special virtue of its own, as in marbles, japonicas, and pearls; and though various nations have in some way recognised a certain royal pre-eminence in this hue; even the barbaric, grand old kings of Pegu placing the title 'Lord of the White Elephants' above all their other magniloquent ascriptions of dominion; and the modern kings of Siam unfurling the same snow-white quadruped in the royal standard; and the Hanoverian flag bearing the one figure of a snow-white charger; and the great Austrian Empire, Cæsarian heir to overlording Rome, having for the imperial color the same imperial hue; and though this pre-eminence in it applies to the human race itself, giving the white man ideal mastership over every dusky tribe; and though, besides all this, whiteness has been even made significant of gladness, for among the Romans a white stone marked a joyful day; and though in other mortal sympathies and symbolizings, this same hue is made the emblem of many touching, noble things – the innocence of brides, the benignity of age; though among the Red Men of America the giving of the white belt of wampum was the deepest pledge of honor; though in many climes, whiteness typifies the majesty of Justice in the ermine of the Judge, and contributes to the daily state of kings and queens drawn by milk-white steeds; though even in the higher mysteries of the most august religions it has been made the symbol of the divine spotlessness and power; by the Persian fire worshippers, the white forked flame being held the holiest on the altar; and in the Greek mythologies, Great Jove himself being made incarnate in a snow-white bull; and though to the noble Iroquois, the midwinter sacrifice of the sacred White Dog was by far the holiest festival of their theology, that spotless, faithful creature being held the purest envoy they could send to the Great Spirit with the annual tidings of their own fidelity; and though directly from the Latin word for white, all Christian priests derive the name of one part of their sacred vesture, the alb or tunic, worn beneath the cassock; and though among the holy pomps of the Romish faith, white is specially employed in the celebration of the Passion of our Lord; though in the Vision of St. John, white robes are given to the redeemed, and the four-and-twenty elders stand clothed in white before the great white throne, and the Holy One that sitteth there white like wool; yet for all these accumulated associations, with whatever is sweet, and honorable, and sublime, there yet lurks an elusive something in the innermost idea of this hue, which strikes more of panic to the soul than that redness which affrights in blood.

This elusive quality it is, which causes the thought of whiteness, when divorced from more kindly associations, and coupled with any object terrible in itself, to heighten that terror to the furthest bounds. Witness the white bear of the poles, and the white shark of the tropics; what but their smooth, flaky whiteness makes them the transcendent horrors they are? That ghastly whiteness it is which imparts such an abhorrent mildness, even more loathsome than terrific, to the dumb gloating of their aspect. So that not the fierce-fanged tiger in his heraldic coat can so stagger courage as the white-shrouded bear or shark.*

Bethink thee of the albatross: whence come those clouds of spiritual wonderment and pale dread, in which that white phantom sails in all imaginations? Not Coleridge first threw that spell; but God's great, unflattering laureate, Nature.†

* With reference to the Polar bear, it may possibly be urged by him who would fain go still deeper into this matter, that it is not the whiteness, separately regarded, which heightens the intolerable hideousness of that brute; for, analysed, that heightened hideousness, it might be said, only arises from the circumstances, that the irresponsible ferociousness of the creature stands invested in the fleece of celestial innocence and love; and hence, by bringing together two such opposite emotions in our minds, the Polar bear frightens us with so unnatural a contrast. But even assuming all this to be true; yet, were it not for the whiteness, you would not have that intensified terror.

As for the white shark, the white gliding ghostliness of repose in that creature, when beheld in his ordinary moods, strangely tallies with the same quality in the Polar quadruped. This peculiarity is most vividly hit by the French in the name they bestow upon that fish. The Romish mass for the dead begins with 'Requiem eternam' (eternal rest), whence *Requiem* denominating the mass itself, and any other funereal music. Now, in allusion to the white, silent stillness of death in this shark, and the mild deadliness of his habits, the French call him *Requin*.

† I remember the first albatross I ever saw. It was during a prolonged gale, in waters hard upon the Antarctic seas. From my forenoon watch below, I ascended to the overclouded deck; and there, dashed upon the main hatches, I saw a regal, feathery thing of unspotted whiteness, and with a hooked, Roman bill sublime. At intervals, it arched forth its vast archangel wings, as if to embrace some holy ark. Wondrous flutterings and throbbings shook it. Though bodily unharmed, it uttered cries, as some king's ghost in supernatural distress. Through its inexpressible, strange eyes, methought I peeped to secrets which took hold of God. As Abraham before the angels, I bowed myself; the white thing was so white, its wings so wide, and in those for ever exiled waters, I had lost the miserable warping memories of traditions and of towns. Long I gazed at that prodigy of plumage. I cannot tell, can only hint, the things that darted through me then. But at last I awoke; and turning, asked a sailor what bird was this. A goney, he replied. Goney! I never had

Most famous in our Western annals and Indian traditions is that of the White Steed of the Prairies; a magnificent milk-white charger, large-eyed, small-headed, bluff-chested, and with the dignity of a thousand monarchs in his lofty, overscorning carriage. He was the elected Xerxes of vast herds of wild horses, whose pastures in those days were only fenced by the Rocky Mountains and the Alleghanies. At their flaming head he westward trooped it like that chosen star which every evening leads on the hosts of light. The flashing cascade of his mane, the curving comet of his tail, invested him with housings more resplendent than gold and silver-beaters could have furnished him. A most imperial and archangelical apparition of that unfallen, western world, which to the eyes of the old trappers and hunters revived the glories of those primeval times when Adam walked majestic as a god, bluff-bowed and fearless as this mighty steed. Whether marching amid his aides and marshals in the van of countless cohorts that endlessly streamed it over the plains, like an Ohio; or whether with his circumambient subjects browsing all

---

heard that name before; is it conceivable that this glorious thing is utterly unknown to men ashore! never! But some time after, I learned that goney was some seaman's name for albatross. So that by no possibility could Coleridge's wild Rhyme have had aught to do with those mystical impressions which were mine, when I saw that bird upon our deck. For neither had I then read the Rhyme, nor knew the bird to be an albatross. Yet, in saying this, I do but indirectly burnish a little brighter the noble merit of the poem and the poet.

I assert, then, that in the wondrous bodily whiteness of the bird chiefly lurks the secret of the spell; a truth the more evinced in this, that by a solecism of terms there are birds called grey albatrosses; and these I have frequently seen, but never with such emotions as when I beheld the Antarctic fowl.

But how had the mystic thing been caught? Whisper it not, and I will tell; with a treacherous hook and line, as the fowl floated on the sea. At last the Captain made a postman of it; tying a lettered, leathern tally round its neck, with the ship's time and place; and then letting it escape. But I doubt not, that leathern tally, meant for man, was taken off in Heaven, when the white fowl flew to join the wing-folding, the invoking, and adoring cherubim!

around at the horizon, the White Steed gallopingly reviewed them with warm nostrils reddening through his cool milkiness; in whatever aspect he presented himself, always to the bravest Indians he was the object of trembling reverence and awe. Nor can it be questioned from what stands on legendary record of this noble horse, that it was his spiritual whiteness chiefly, which so clothed him with divineness; and that this divineness had that in it which, though commanding worship, at the same time enforced a certain nameless terror.

But there are other instances where this whiteness loses all that accessory and strange glory which invests it in the White Steed and Albatross.

What is it that in the Albino man so peculiarly repels and often shocks the eye, as that sometimes he is loathed by his own kith and kin! It is that whiteness which invests him, a thing expressed by the name he bears. The Albino is as well made as other men – has no substantive deformity – and yet this mere aspect of all-pervading whiteness makes him more strangely hideous than the ugliest abortion. Why should this be so?

Nor, in quite other aspects, does Nature in her least palpable but not the less malicious agencies, fail to enlist among her forces this crowning attribute of the terrible. From its snowy aspect, the gauntleted ghost of the Southern Seas has been denominated the White Squall. Nor, in some historic instances, has the art of human malice omitted so potent an auxiliary. How wildly it heightens the effect of that passage in Froissart, when, masked in the snowy symbol of their faction, the desperate White Hoods of Ghent murder their bailiff in the market-place!

Nor, in some things, does the common, hereditary experience of all mankind fail to bear witness to the supernaturalism of this hue. It cannot well be doubted, that the one visible quality in the aspect of the dead which most appals the gazer, is the marble pallor lingering there; as if indeed that pallor were as much like the badge of consternation in the other world, as of mortal trepidation here. And from that pallor of the dead, we borrow the expressive hue of the shroud in which we wrap them. Nor even in our superstitions do we fail to throw the same snowy mantle round our phantoms; all ghosts rising in a milk-white fog – Yea, while these terrors seize us, let us add, that even the king of terrors, when personified by the evangelist, rides on his pallid horse.

Therefore, in his other moods, symbolise whatever grand or gracious thing he will by whiteness, no man can deny that in its profoundest idealized significance it calls up a peculiar apparition to the soul.

But though without dissent this point be fixed, how is mortal man to account for it? To analyse it, would seem impossible. Can we, then, by the citation of some of those instances wherein this thing of whiteness – though for the time either wholly or in great part stripped of all direct associations calculated to impart to it aught fearful, but, nevertheless, is found to exert over us the same sorcery, however modified; – can we thus hope to light upon some chance clue to conduct us to the hidden cause we seek?

Let us try. But in a matter like this, subtlety appeals to subtlety, and without imagination no man can follow another into these halls. And though, doubtless, some at least of the imaginative impressions about to be presented may have been shared by most men, yet few perhaps were entirely conscious of them at the time, and therefore may not be able to recall them now.

Why to the man of untutored ideality, who happens to be but loosely acquainted with the peculiar character of the day, does the bare mention of Whitsuntide marshal in the fancy such long, dreary, speechless processions of slow-pacing pilgrims, down-cast and hooded with new-fallen snow? Or, to the unread, unsophisticated Protestant of the Middle American States, why does the passing mention of a White Friar or a White Nun, evoke such an eyeless statue in the soul?

Or what is there apart from the traditions of dungeoned warriors and kings (which will not wholly account for it) that makes the White Tower of London tell so much more strongly on the imagination of an untravelled American, than those other storied structures, its neighbors – the Byward Tower, or even the Bloody? And those sublimer towers, the White Mountains of New Hampshire, whence, in peculiar moods, comes that gigantic ghostliness over the soul at the bare mention of that name, while the thought of Virginia's Blue Ridge is full of a soft, dewy, distant dreaminess? Or why, irrespective of all latitudes and longitudes, does the name of the White Sea exert such a spectralness over the fancy, while that of the Yellow Sea lulls us with mortal thoughts of long lacquered mild afternoons on the waves, followed by the gaudiest and yet sleepiest of sunsets? Or, to choose a wholly unsubstantial instance, purely addressed to the fancy, why, in reading the old fairy tales of Central Europe, does 'the tall pale man' of the Hartz forests, whose changeless pallor unrustlingly glides through the green of the groves – why is this phantom more terrible than all the whooping imps of the Blocksburg?

Nor is it, altogether, the remembrance of her cathedral-toppling earthquakes; nor the stampedoes of her frantic seas; nor the tearlessness of arid skies that never rain; nor the sight of her wide field of leaning spires, wrenched cope-stones, and crosses all adroop (like canted yards of anchored fleets); and her suburban avenues of house-walls lying over upon each other, as a tossed pack of cards; – it is not these things alone which make tearless Lima, the strangest, saddest city thou can'st see. For Lima has taken the white veil; and there is a higher horror in this whiteness of her woe. Old as Pizarro, this whiteness keeps her ruins for ever new; admits not the cheerful greenness of complete decay; spreads over her broken ramparts the rigid pallor of an apoplexy that fixes its own distortions.

I know that, to the common apprehension, this phenomenon of whiteness is not confessed to be the prime agent in exaggerating the terror of objects otherwise terrible; nor to the unimaginative mind is there aught of terror in those appearances whose awfulness to another mind almost solely consists in this one phenomenon, especially when exhibited under any form at all approaching to muteness or universality. What I mean by these two statements may perhaps be respectively elucidated by the following examples.

First: The mariner, when drawing nigh the coasts of foreign lands, if by night he hear the roar of breakers, starts to vigilance, and feels just enough of trepidation to sharpen all his faculties; but under precisely similar circumstances, let him be called from his hammock to view his ship sailing through a midnight sea of milky whiteness – as if from encircling headlands shoals of combed white bears were swimming round him, then he feels a silent, superstitious dread; the shrouded phantom of the whitened waters is horrible to him as a real ghost; in vain the lead assures him he is still off soundings; heart and helm they both go down; he never rests till blue water is under him again. Yet where is the mariner who will tell thee, 'Sir, it was not so much the fear of striking hidden rocks, as the fear of that hideous whiteness that so stirred me'?

Second: To the native Indian of Peru, the continual sight of the snow-howdahed Andes conveys naught of dread, except, perhaps, in the mere fancying of the eternal frosted desolateness reigning at such vast altitudes, and the natural conceit of what a fearfulness it would be to lose oneself in such inhuman solitudes. Much the same is it with the backwoodsman of the West, who with comparative indifference views an unbounded prairie sheeted with driven snow, no shadow of tree or twig to break the fixed trance of whiteness. Not so the sailor, beholding the scenery of the Antarctic seas; where at times, by some infernal trick of legerdemain in the powers of frost and air, he, shivering and half shipwrecked, instead of rainbows speaking hope and solace to his misery, views what seems a boundless church-yard grinning upon him with its lean ice monuments and splintered crosses.

But thou sayest, methinks this white-lead chapter about whiteness is but a white flag hung out from a craven soul; thou surrenderest to a hypo, Ishmael.

Tell me, why this strong young colt, foaled in some peaceful valley of Vermont, far removed from all beasts of prey –

why is it that upon the sunniest day, if you but shake a fresh buffalo robe behind him, so that he cannot even see it, but only smells its wild animal muskiness – why will he start, snort, and with bursting eyes paw the ground in phrensies of affright? There is no remembrance in him of any gorings of wild creatures in his green northern home, so that the strange muskiness he smells cannot recall to him anything associated with the experience of former perils; for what knows he, this New England colt, of the black bisons of distant Oregon?

No: but here thou beholdest even in a dumb brute, the instinct of the knowledge of the demonism in the world. Though thousands of miles from Oregon, still when he smells that savage musk, the rending, goring bison herds are as present as to the deserted wild foal of the prairies, which this instant they may be trampling into dust.

Thus, then, the muffled rollings of a milky sea; the bleak rustlings of the festooned frosts of mountains; the desolate shiftings of the windrowed snows of prairies; all these, to Ishmael, are as the shaking of that buffalo robe to the frightened colt!

Though neither knows where lie the nameless things of which the mystic sign gives forth such hints; yet with me, as with the colt, somewhere those things must exist. Though in many of its aspects this visible world seems formed in love, the invisible spheres were formed in fright.

But not yet have we solved the incantation of this whiteness, and learned why it appeals with such power to the soul; and more strange and far more portentous – why, as we have seen, it is at once the most meaning symbol of spiritual things, nay, the very veil of the Christian's Deity; and yet should be as it is, the intensifying agent in things the most appalling to mankind.

Is it that by its indefiniteness it shadows forth the heartless voids and immensities of the universe, and thus stabs us from behind with the thought of annihilation, when beholding the white depths of the milky way? Or is it, that as in essence whiteness is not so much a color as the visible absence of color, and at the same time the concrete of all colors; is it for these reasons that there is such a dumb blankness, full of meaning, in a wide landscape of snows – a colorless, all-color of atheism from which we shrink? And when we consider that other theory of the natural philosophers, that all other earthly hues – every stately or lovely emblazoning – the sweet tinges of sunset skies and woods; yea, and the gilded velvets of butterflies, and the butterfly cheeks of young girls; all these are but subtile deceits, not actually inherent in substances, but only laid on from without; so that all deified Nature absolutely paints like the harlot, whose allurements cover nothing but the charnel-house within; and when we proceed further, and consider that the mystical cosmetic which produces every one of her hues, the great principle of light, for ever remains white or colorless in itself, and if operating without medium upon matter, would touch all objects, even tulips and roses, with its own blank tinge – pondering all this, the palsied universe lies before us a leper; and like wilful travellers in Lapland, who refuse to wear colored and coloring glasses upon their eyes, so the wretched infidel gazes himself blind at the monumental white shroud that wraps all the prospect around him. And of all these things the Albino whale was the symbol. Wonder ye then at the fiery hunt?

43

HARK!

'HIST! Did you hear that noise, Cabaco?'

It was the middle-watch: a fair moonlight; the seamen were standing in a cordon, extending from one of the fresh-water butts in the waist, to the scuttle-butt near the taffrail. In this manner, they passed the buckets to fill the scuttle-butt. Standing, for the most part, on the hallowed precincts of the quarter-deck, they were careful not to speak or rustle their feet. From hand to hand, the buckets went in the deepest silence, only broken by the occasional flap of a sail, and the steady hum of the unceasingly advancing keel.

It was in the midst of this repose, that Archy, one of the cordon, whose post was near the after-hatches, whispered to his neighbor, a Cholo, the words above.

'Hist! did you hear that noise, Cabaco?'

'Take the bucket, will ye, Archy? what noise d'ye mean?'

'There it is again – under the hatches – don't you hear it – a cough – it sounded like a cough.'

'Cough be damned! Pass along that return bucket.'

'There again – there it is! – it sounds like two or three sleepers turning over, now!'

'Caramba! have done, shipmate, will ye? It's the three soaked biscuits ye eat for supper turning over inside of ye – nothing else. Look to the bucket!'

'Say what ye will, shipmate; I've sharp ears.'

'Aye, you are the chap, ain't ye, that heard the hum of the old Quakeress's knitting-needles fifty miles at sea from Nantucket; you're the chap.'

'Grin away; we'll see what turns up. Hark ye, Cabaco, there is somebody down in the after hold that has not yet been seen on deck; and I suspect our old Mogul knows something of it too. I heard Stubb tell Flask, one morning watch, that there was something of that sort in the wind.'

'Tish! the bucket!'

44

THE CHART

HAD you followed Captain Ahab down into his cabin after the squall that took place on the night succeeding that wild ratification of his purpose with his crew, you would have seen him go to a locker in the transom, and bringing out a large wrinkled roll of yellowish sea charts, spread them before him on his screwed-down table. Then seating himself before it, you would have seen him intently study the various lines and shadings which there met his eye; and with slow but steady pencil trace additional courses over spaces that before were blank. At intervals, he would refer to piles of old log-books beside him, wherein were set down the seasons and places in which, on various former voyages of various ships, sperm whales had been captured or seen.

While thus employed, the heavy pewter lamp suspended in chains over his head, continually rocked with the motion of the ship, and for ever threw shifting gleams and shadows of lines upon his wrinkled brow, till it almost seemed that while he himself was marking out lines and courses on the wrinkled charts, some invisible pencil was also tracing lines and courses upon the deeply marked chart of his forehead.

But it was not this night in particular that, in the solitude of his cabin, Ahab thus pondered over his charts. Almost every night they were brought out; almost every night some pencil marks were effaced, and others were substituted. For with the charts of all four oceans before him, Ahab was threading a maze of currents and eddies, with a view to the more certain accomplishment of that monomaniac thought of his soul.

Now, to any one not fully acquainted with the ways of the leviathans, it might seem an absurdly hopeless task thus to seek out one solitary creature in the unhooped oceans of this planet. But not so did it seem to Ahab, who knew the sets of all tides and currents; and thereby calculating the driftings of the sperm whale's food; and, also, calling to mind the regular, ascertained seasons for hunting him in particular latitudes; could arrive at reasonable surmises, almost approaching to certainties, concerning the timeliest day to be upon this or that ground in search of his prey.

So assured, indeed, is the fact concerning the periodicalness of the sperm whale's resorting to given waters, that many hunters believe that, could he be closely observed and studied throughout the world; were the logs for one voyage of the entire whale fleet carefully collated, then the migrations of the sperm whale would be found to correspond in invariability to those of the herring-shoals or the flights of swallows. On this hint, attempts have been made to construct elaborate migratory charts of the sperm whale.*

Besides, when making a passage from one feeding-ground to another, the sperm whales, guided by some infallible instinct – say, rather, secret intelligence from the Deity – mostly swim in *veins*, as they are called; containing their way along a given ocean-line with such undeviating exactitude, that no ship ever sailed her course, by any chart, with one tithe of such marvellous precision. Though, in these cases, the direction taken by any one whale be straight as a surveyor's parallel, and though the line of advance be strictly confined to its own unavoidable, straight wake, yet the arbitrary *vein* in which at these times he is said to swim, generally embraces some few miles in width (more or less, as the vein is presumed to expand or contract); but never exceeds the visual sweep from the whale-ship's mast-heads, when circumspectly gliding along this magic zone. The sum is, that at particular seasons within that breadth and along that path, migrating whales may with great confidence be looked for.

And hence not only at substantiated times, upon well known separate feeding-grounds, could Ahab hope to encounter his prey; but in crossing the widest expanses of water between those grounds he could, by his art, so place and time himself on his way, as even then not to be wholly without prospect of a meeting.

There was a circumstance which at first sight seemed to

*Since the above was written, the statement is happily borne out by an official circular, issued by Lieutenant Maury, of the National Observatory, Washington, April 16th, 1851. By that circular, it appears that precisely such a chart is in course of completion; and portions of it are presented in the circular. 'This chart divides the ocean into districts of five degrees of latitude by five degrees of longitude; perpendicularly through each of which districts are twelve columns for the twelve months; and horizontally through each of which districts are three lines; one to show the number of days that have been spent in each month in every district, and the two others to show the number of days in which whales, sperm or right, have been seen.'

entangle his delirious but still methodical scheme. But not so in the reality, perhaps. Though the gregarious sperm whales have their regular seasons for particular grounds, yet in general you cannot conclude that the herds which haunted such and such a latitude or longitude this year, say, will turn out to be identically the same with those that were found there the preceding season; though there are peculiar and unquestionable instances where the contrary of this has proved true. In general, the same remark, only within a less wide limit, applies to the solitaries and hermits among the matured, aged sperm whales. So that though Moby Dick had in a former year been seen, for example, on what is called the Seychelle ground in the Indian ocean, or Volcano Bay on the Japanese Coast; yet it did not follow, that were the Pequod to visit either of those spots at any subsequent corresponding season, she would infallibly encounter him there. So, too, with some other feeding grounds, where he had at times revealed himself. But all these seemed only his casual stopping-places and ocean-inns, so to speak, not his places of prolonged abode. And where Ahab's chances of accomplishing his object have hitherto been spoken of, allusion has only been made to whatever wayside, antecedent, extra prospects were his, ere a particular set time or place were attained, when all possibilities would become probabilities, and, as Ahab fondly thought, every possibility the next thing to a certainty. That particular set time and place were conjoined in the one technical phrase – the Season-on-the-Line. For there and then, for several consecutive years, Moby Dick had been periodically descried, lingering in those waters for awhile, as the sun, in its annual round, loiters for a predicted interval in any one sign of the Zodiac. There it was, too, that most of the deadly encounters with the white whale had taken place; there the waves were storied with his deeds; there also was that tragic spot where the monomaniac old man had found the awful motive to his vengeance. But in the cautious comprehensiveness and unloitering vigilance with which Ahab threw his brooding soul into this unfaltering hunt, he would not permit himself to rest all his hopes upon the one crowning fact above mentioned, however flattering it might be to those hopes; nor in the sleeplessness of his vow could he so tranquillize his unquiet heart as to postpone all intervening quest.

Now, the Pequod had sailed from Nantucket at the very beginning of the Season-on-the-Line. No possible endeavor then could enable her commander to make the great passage southwards, double Cape Horn, and then running down sixty degrees of latitude arrive in the equatorial Pacific in time to cruise there. Therefore, he must wait for the next ensuing season. Yet the premature hour of the Pequod's sailing had, perhaps, been covertly selected by Ahab, with a view to this very complexion of things. Because, an interval of three hundred and sixty-five days and nights was before him; an interval which, instead of impatiently enduring ashore, he would spend in a miscellaneous hunt; if by chance the White Whale, spending his vacation in seas far remote from his periodical feeding-grounds, should turn up his wrinkled brow off the Persian Gulf, or in the Bengal Bay, or China Seas, or in any other waters haunted by his race. So that Monsoons, Pampas, Nor-Westers, Harmattans, Trades; any wind but the Levanter and Simoom, might blow Moby Dick into the devious zig-zag world-circle of the Pequod's circumnavigating wake.

But granting all this; yet, regarded discreetly and coolly, seems it not but a mad idea, this; that in the broad boundless ocean, one solitary whale, even if encountered, should be thought capable of individual recognition from his hunter, even as a white-bearded Mufti in the thronged thoroughfares of Constantinople? Yes. For the peculiar snow-white brow of Moby Dick, and his snow-white hump, could not but be unmistakable. And have I not tallied the whale, Ahab would mutter to himself, as after poring over his charts till long after midnight he would throw himself back in reveries – tallied him, and shall he escape? His broad fins are bored, and scalloped out like a lost sheep's ear! And here, his mad mind would run on in a breathless race; till a weariness and faintness of pondering came over him; and in the open air of the deck he would seek to recover his strength. Ah, God! what trances of torments does that man endure who is consumed with one unachieved revengeful desire. He sleeps with clenched hands; and wakes with his own bloody nails in his palms.

Often, when forced from his hammock by exhausting and intolerably vivid dreams of the night, which, resuming his own intense thoughts through the day, carried them on amid a clashing of phrensies, and whirled them round and round in his blazing brain, till the very throbbing of his life-spot became insufferable anguish; and when, as was sometimes the case, these spiritual throes in him heaved his being up from its base, and a chasm seemed opening in him, from which forked flames and lightnings shot up, and accursed fiends beckoned him to leap down among them; when this hell in himself yawned beneath him, a wild cry would be heard through the ship; and with glaring eyes Ahab would burst from his state room, as though escaping from a bed that was on fire. Yet these, perhaps, instead of being the unsuppressable symptoms of some latent weakness, or fright at his own resolve, were but the plainest tokens of its intensity. For, at such times, crazy Ahab, the scheming, unappeasedly steadfast hunter of the white whale; this Ahab that had gone to his hammock, was not the agent that so caused him to burst from it in horror again. The latter was the eternal, living principle or soul in him; and in sleep, being for the time dissociated from the characterizing mind, which at other times employed it for its outer vehicle or agent, it spontaneously sought escape from the scorching contiguity of the frantic thing, of which, for the time, it was no longer an integral. But as the mind does not exist unless leagued with the soul, therefore it must have been that, in Ahab's case, yielding up all his thoughts and fancies to his one supreme purpose; that purpose, by its own sheer inveteracy of will, forced itself against gods and devils into a kind of self-assumed, independent being of its own. Nay, could grimly live and burn, while the common vitality to which it was conjoined, fled horror-stricken from the unbidden and unfathered birth. Therefore, the tormented spirit that glared out of bodily eyes, when what seemed Ahab rushed from his room, was for the time but a vacated thing, a formless somnambulistic being, a ray of living light, to be sure, but without an object to color, and therefore a blankness in itself. God help thee, old man, thy thoughts have created a creature in thee; and he whose intense thinking thus makes him a Prometheus; a vulture feeds upon that heart for ever; that vulture the very creature he creates.

45

THE AFFIDAVIT

So far as what there may be of a narrative in this book; and, indeed, as indirectly touching one or two very interesting and curious particulars in the habits of sperm whales, the foregoing chapter, in its earlier part, is as important a one as will be found in this volume; but the leading matter of it requires to be still further and more familiarly enlarged upon, in order to be adequately understood, and moreover to take away any incredulity which a profound ignorance of the entire subject may induce in some minds, as to the natural verity of the main points of this affair.

I care not to perform this part of my task methodically; but shall be content to produce the desired impression by separate citations of items, practically or reliably known to me as a whaleman; and from these citations, I take it – the conclusion aimed at will naturally follow of itself.

First: I have personally known three instances where a whale, after receiving a harpoon, has effected a complete escape; and, after an interval (in one instance of three years), has been again struck by the same hand, and slain; when the two irons, both marked by the same private cypher, have been taken from the body. In the instance where three years intervened between the flinging of the two harpoons; and I think it may have been something more than that; the man who darted them happening, in the interval, to go in a trading ship on a voyage to Africa, went ashore there, joined a discovery party, and penetrated far into the interior, where he travelled for a period of nearly two years, often endangered by serpents, savages, tigers, poisonous miasmas, with all the other common perils incident to wandering in the heart of unknown regions. Meanwhile, the whale he had struck must also have been on its travels; no doubt it had thrice circumnavigated the globe, brushing with its flanks all the coasts of Africa; but to no purpose. This man and this whale again came together, and the one vanquished the other. I say I, myself, have known three instances similar to this; that is in two of them I saw the whales struck; and, upon the second attack, saw the two irons with the respective marks cut in them, afterwards taken from the dead fish. In the three-year instance, it so fell out that I was in the boat both times, first and last, and the last time distinctly recognized a peculiar sort of huge mole under the whale's eye, which I had observed there three years previous. I say three years, but I am pretty sure it was more than that. Here are three instances, then, which I personally know the truth of; but I have heard of many other instances from persons whose veracity in the matter there is no good ground to impeach.

Secondly: It is well known in the Sperm Whale Fishery, however ignorant the world ashore may be of it, that there have been several memorable historical instances where a particular whale in the ocean has been at distant times and places popularly cognisable. Why such a whale became thus marked was not altogether and originally owing to his bodily peculiarities as distinguished from other whales; for however peculiar in that respect any chance whale may be, they soon put an end to his peculiarities by killing him, and boiling him down into a peculiarly valuable oil. No: the reason was this: that from the fatal experiences of the fishery there hung a terrible prestige of perilousness about such a whale as there did about Rinaldo Rinaldini, insomuch that most fishermen were content to recognise him by merely touching their tarpaulins when he would be discovered lounging by them on the sea, without seeking to cultivate a more intimate acquaintance. Like some poor devils ashore that happen to know an irascible great man, they make distant unobtrusive salutations to him in the street, lest if they pursued the acquaintance further, they might receive a summary thump for their presumption.

But not only did each of these famous whales enjoy great individual celebrity – nay, you may call it an ocean-wide renown; not only was he famous in life and now is immortal in forecastle stories after death, but he was admitted into all the rights, privileges, and distinctions of a name; had as much a name indeed as Cambyses or Cæsar. Was it not so, O Timor Tom! thou famed leviathan, scarred like an iceberg, who so long did'st lurk in the Oriental straits of that name, whose spout was oft seen from the palmy beach of Ombay? Was it not so, O New Zealand Jack! thou terror of all cruisers that crossed their wakes in the vicinity of the Tattoo Land? Was it not so, O Morquan! King of Japan, whose lofty jet they say at times assumed the semblance of a snow-white cross against the sky? Was it not so, O Don Miguel! thou Chilian whale, marked like an old tortoise with mystic hieroglyphics upon the back! In plain prose, here are four whales as well known to the students of Cetacean History as Marius or Sylla to the classic scholar.

But this is not all. New Zealand Tom and Don Miguel, after at various times creating great havoc among the boats of different vessels, were finally gone in quest of, systematically hunted out, chased and killed by valiant whaling captains, who heaved up their anchors with that express object as much in view, as in setting out through the Narragansett Woods, Captain Butler of old had it in his mind to capture that notorious murderous savage Annawon, the headmost warrior of the Indian King Philip.

I do not know where I can find a better place than just here, to make mention of one or two other things, which to me seem important, as in printed form establishing in all respects the reasonableness of the whole story of the White Whale, more especially the catastrophe. For this is one of those disheartening instances where truth requires full as much bolstering as error. So ignorant are most landsmen of some of the plainest and most palpable wonders of the world, that without some hints touching the plain facts, historical and otherwise, of the fishery, they might scout at Moby Dick as a monstrous fable, or still worse and more detestable, a hideous and intolerable allegory.

First: Though most men have some vague flitting ideas of the general perils of the grand fishery, yet they have nothing like a fixed, vivid conception of those perils, and the frequency with which they recur. One reason perhaps is, that not one in fifty of the actual disasters and deaths by casualties in the fishery, ever finds a public record at home, however transient and immediately forgotten that record. Do you suppose that that poor fellow there, who this moment perhaps caught by the whale-line off the coast of New Guinea, is being carried down to the bottom of the sea by the sounding leviathan – do you suppose that that poor fellow's name will appear in the newspaper obituary you will read to-morrow at your breakfast? No: because the mails are very irregular between here and New Guinea. In fact, did you ever hear what might be called regular news direct or indirect from New Guinea? Yet I tell you that upon one particular voyage which I made to the Pacific, among many others, we spoke thirty different ships, every one of which had had a death by a whale, some of them more than one, and three that had each lost a boat's crew. For God's sake, be economical with your lamps and candles! not a gallon you burn, but at least one drop of man's blood was spilled for it.

Secondly: People ashore have indeed some indefinite idea that a whale is an enormous creature of enormous power; but I have ever found that when narrating to them some specific example of this two-fold enormousness, they have significantly complimented me upon my facetiousness; when, I declare upon my soul, I had no more idea of being facetious than Moses, when he wrote the history of the plagues of Egypt.

But fortunately the special point I here seek can be established upon testimony entirely independent of my own. That point is this: The Sperm Whale is in some cases sufficiently powerful, knowing, and judiciously malicious, as with direct aforethought to stave in, utterly destroy, and sink a large ship; and what is more, the Sperm Whale *has* done it.

First: in the year 1820 the ship Essex, Captain Pollard, of Nantucket, was cruising in the Pacific Ocean. One day she saw spouts, lowered her boats, and gave chase to a shoal of sperm whales. Ere long, several of the whales were wounded; when, suddenly, a very large whale escaping from the boats, issued from the shoal, and bore directly down upon the ship. Dashing his forehead against her hull, he so stove her in, that in less than 'ten minutes' she settled down and fell over. Not a surviving plank of her has been seen since. After the severest exposure, part of the crew reached the land in their boats. Being returned home at last, Captain Pollard once more sailed for the Pacific in command of another ship, but the gods shipwrecked him again upon unknown rocks and breakers; for the second time his ship was utterly lost, and forthwith forswearing the sea, he has never tempted it since. At this day Captain Pollard is a resident of Nantucket. I have seen Owen Chace, who was chief mate of the Essex at the time of the tragedy; I have read his plain and faithful narrative; I have conversed with his son; and all this within a few miles of the scene of the catastrophe.*

*The following are extracts from Chace's narrative: 'Every fact seemed to warrant me in concluding that it was anything but chance which directed his operations; he made two several attacks upon the ship, at a short interval between them, both of which, according to their direction, were calculated to do us the most injury, by being made ahead, and thereby combining the speed of the two objects for the shock; to effect which, the exact manœuvres which he made were necessary. His aspect was most horrible, and such as indicated resentment and fury. He came directly from the shoal which we had just before entered, and in which we had struck three of his companions, as if fired with revenge for their sufferings.' Again: 'At all

Secondly: The ship Union, also of Nantucket, was in the year 1807 totally lost off the Azores by a similar onset, but the authentic particulars of this catastrophe I have never chanced to encounter, though from the whale hunters I have now and then heard casual allusions to it.

Thirdly: Some eighteen or twenty years ago Commodore J—— then commanding an American sloop-of-war of the first class, happened to be dining with a party of whaling captains, on board a Nantucket ship in the harbor of Oahu, Sandwich Islands. Conversation turning upon whales, the Commodore was pleased to be sceptical touching the amazing strength ascribed to them by the professional gentlemen present. He peremptorily denied for example, that any whale could so smite his stout sloop-of-war as to cause her to leak so much as a thimbleful. Very good; but there is more coming. Some weeks after, the Commodore set sail in this impregnable craft for Valparaiso. But he was stopped on the way by a portly sperm whale, that begged a few moments' confidential business with him. That business consisted in fetching the Commodore's craft such a thwack, that with all his pumps going he made straight for the nearest port to heave down and repair. I am not superstitious, but

---

events, the whole circumstances taken together, all happening before my own eyes, and producing, at the time, impressions in my mind of decided, calculating mischief, on the part of the whale (many of which impressions I cannot now recall), induce me to be satisfied that I am correct in my opinion.'

Here are his reflections some time after quitting the ship, during a black night in an open boat, when almost despairing of reaching any hospitable shore. 'The dark ocean and swelling waters were nothing; the fears of being swallowed up by some dreadful tempest, or dashed upon hidden rocks, with all the other ordinary subjects of fearful contemplation, seemed scarcely entitled to a moment's thought; the dismal looking wreck, and *the horrid aspect and revenge of the whale*, wholly engrossed my reflections, until day again made its appearance.'

In another place – p. 45, – he speaks of *'the mysterious and mortal attack of the animal.'* * * * * * * * * *

* * * * * * * * * * * * *

I consider the Commodore's interview with that whale as providential. Was not Saul of Tarsus converted from unbelief by a similar fright? I tell you, the sperm whale will stand no nonsense.

I will now refer you to Langsdorff's Voyages for a little circumstance in point, peculiarly interesting to the writer hereof. Langsdorff, you must know by the way, was attached to the Russian Admiral Krusenstern's famous Discovery Expedition in the beginning of the present century. Captain Langsdorff thus begins his seventeenth chapter.

'By the thirteenth of May our ship was ready to sail, and the next day we were out in the open sea, on our way to Ochotsh. The weather was very clear and fine, but so intolerably cold that we were obliged to keep on our fur clothing. For some days we had very little wind; it was not till the nineteenth that a brisk gale from the northwest sprang up. An uncommon large whale, the body of which was larger than the ship itself, lay almost at the surface of the water, but was not perceived by any one on board till the moment when the ship, which was in full sail, was almost upon him, so that it was impossible to prevent its striking against him. We were thus placed in the most imminent danger, as this gigantic creature, setting up its back, raised the ship three feet at least out of the water. The masts reeled, and the sails fell altogether, while we who were below all sprang instantly upon the deck, concluding that we had struck upon some rock; instead of this we saw the monster sailing off with the utmost gravity and solemnity. Captain D'Wolf applied immediately to the pumps to examine whether or not the vessel had received any damage from the shock, but we found that very happily it had escaped entirely uninjured.'

Now, the Captain D'Wolf here alluded to as commanding the ship in question, is a New Englander, who, after a long life of unusual adventures as a sea-captain, this day resides in the village of Dorchester near Boston. I have the honor of being a nephew of his. I have particularly questioned him concerning this passage in Langsdorff. He substantiates every word. The ship, however, was by no means a large one: a Russian craft built on the Siberian coast, and purchased by my uncle after bartering away the vessel in which he sailed from home.

In that up and down manly book of old-fashioned adventure, so full, too, of honest wonders – the voyage of Lionel Wafer, one of ancient Dampier's old chums – I found a little matter set down so like that just quoted from Langsdorff, that I cannot forbear inserting it here for a corroborative example, if such be needed.

Lionel, it seems, was on his way to 'John Ferdinando,' as he calls the modern Juan Fernandes. 'In our way thither,' he says, 'about four o'clock in the morning, when we were about one hundred and fifty leagues from the Main of America, our ship felt a terrible shock, which put our men in such consternation that they could hardly tell where they were or what to think; but every one began to prepare for death. And, indeed, the shock was so sudden and violent, that we took it for granted the ship had struck against a rock; but when the amazement was a little over, we cast the lead, and sounded, but found no ground. * * * * The suddenness of the shock made the guns leap in their carriages, and several of the men were shaken out of their hammocks. Captain Davis, who lay with his head on a gun, was thrown out of his cabin!' Lionel then goes on to impute the shock to an earthquake, and seems to substantiate the imputation by stating that a great earthquake, somewhere about that time, did actually do great mischief along the Spanish land. But I should not much wonder if, in the darkness of that early hour of the morning, the shock was after all caused by an unseen whale vertically bumping the hull from beneath.

I might proceed with several more examples, one way or another known to me, of the great power and malice at times of the sperm whale. In more than one instance, he has been known, not only to chase the assailing boats back to their ships, but to pursue the ship itself, and long withstand all the lances hurled at him from its decks. The English ship Pusie Hall can tell a story on that head; and, as for his strength, let me say, that there have been examples where the lines attached to a running sperm whale have, in a calm, been transferred to the ship, and secured there; the whale towing her great hull through the water, as a horse walks off with a cart. Again, it is very often observed that, if the sperm whale, once struck, is allowed time to rally, he then acts, not so often with blind rage, as with wilful, deliberate designs of destruction to his pursuers; nor is it without conveying some eloquent indication of his character, that upon being attacked he will frequently open his mouth, and retain it in that dread expansion for several consecutive minutes. But I must be content with only one more and a concluding illustration; a remarkable and most significant one, by which you will not fail to see, that not only is the most marvellous event in this book corroborated by plain facts of the present day, but that these marvels (like all marvels) are mere repetitions of the ages; so that for the millionth time we say amen with Solomon – Verily there is nothing new under the sun.

In the sixth Christian century lived Procopius, a Christian magistrate of Constantinople, in the days when Justinian was Emperor and Belisarius general. As many know, he wrote the history of his own times, a work every way of uncommon value. By the best authorities, he has always been considered a most trustworthy and unexaggerating historian, except in some one or two particulars, not at all affecting the matter presently to be mentioned.

Now, in this history of his, Procopius mentions that, during the term of his prefecture at Constantinople, a great sea-monster was captured in the neighboring Propontis, or Sea of Marmora, after having destroyed vessels at intervals in those waters for a period of more than fifty years. A fact thus set down in substantial history cannot easily be gainsaid. Nor is there any reason it should be. Of what precise species this sea-monster was, is not mentioned. But as he destroyed ships, as well as for other reasons, he must have been a whale; and I am strongly inclined to think a sperm whale. And I will tell you why. For a long time I fancied that the sperm whale had been always unknown in the Mediterranean and the deep waters connecting with it. Even now I am certain that those seas are not, and perhaps never can be, in the present constitution of things, a place for his habitual gregarious resort. But further investigations have recently proved to me, that in modern times there have been isolated instances of the presence of the sperm whale in the Mediterranean. I am told, on good authority, that on the Barbary coast, a Commodore Davis of the British navy found the skeleton of a sperm whale. Now, as a vessel of war readily passes through the Dardanelles, hence a sperm whale could, by the same route, pass out of the Mediterranean into the Propontis.

In the Propontis, as far as I can learn, none of that peculiar substance called *brit* is to be found, the aliment of the right whale. But I have every reason to believe that the food of the sperm whale – squid or cuttle-fish – lurks at the bottom of that sea, because large creatures, but by no means the largest of that sort, have been found at its surface. If, then, you properly put these statements together, and reason upon them a bit, you will clearly perceive that, according to all human reasoning, Procopius's sea-monster, that for half a century stove the ships of a Roman Emperor, must in all probability have been a sperm whale.

46

SURMISES

THOUGH, consumed with the hot fire of his purpose, Ahab in all his thoughts and actions ever had in view the ultimate capture of Moby Dick; though he seemed ready to sacrifice all mortal interests to that one passion; nevertheless it may have been that he was by nature and long habituation far too wedded to a fiery whaleman's way, altogether to abandon the collateral prosecution of the voyage. Or at least if this were otherwise, there were not wanting other motives much more influential with him. It would be refining too much, perhaps, even considering his monomania, to hint that his vindictiveness towards the White Whale might have possibly extended itself in some degree to all sperm whales, and that the more monsters he slew by so much the more he multiplied the chances that each subsequently encountered whale would prove to be the hated one he hunted. But if such an hypothesis be indeed exceptionable, there were still additional considerations which, though not so strictly according with the wildness of his ruling passion, yet were by no means incapable of swaying him.

To accomplish his object Ahab must use tools; and of all tools used in the shadow of the moon, men are most apt to get out of order. He knew, for example, that however magnetic his ascendency in some respects was over Starbuck, yet that ascendency did not cover the complete spiritual man any more than mere corporeal superiority involves intellectual mastership; for to the purely spiritual, the intellectual but stands in a sort of corporeal relation. Starbuck's body and Starbuck's coerced will were Ahab's, so long as Ahab kept his magnet at Starbuck's brain; still he knew that for all this the chief mate, in his soul, abhorred his captain's quest, and could he, would joyfully disintegrate himself from it, or even frustrate it. It might be that a long interval would elapse ere the White Whale was seen. During that long interval Starbuck would ever be apt to fall into open relapses of rebellion against his captain's leadership, unless some ordinary, prudential, circumstantial influences were brought to bear upon him. Not only that, but the subtle insanity of Ahab respecting Moby Dick was noways more significantly manifested than in his superlative sense and shrewdness in foreseeing that, for the present, the hunt should in some way be stripped of that strange imaginative impiousness which naturally invested it; that the full terror of the voyage must be kept withdrawn into the obscure background (for few men's courage is proof against protracted meditation unrelieved by action); that when they stood their long night watches, his officers and men must have some nearer things to think of than Moby Dick. For however eagerly and impetuously the savage crew had hailed the announcement of his quest; yet all sailors of all sorts are more or less capricious and unreliable – they live in the varying outer weather, and they inhale its fickleness – and when retained for any object remote and blank in the pursuit, however promissory of life and passion in the end, it is above all things requisite that temporary interests and employments should intervene and hold them healthily suspended for the final dash.

Nor was Ahab unmindful of another thing. In times of strong emotion mankind disdain all base considerations; but such times are evanescent. The permanent constitutional condition of the manufactured man, thought Ahab, is sordidness. Granting that the White Whale fully incites the hearts of this my savage crew, and playing round their savageness even breeds a certain generous knight-errantism in them, still, while for the love of it they give chase to Moby Dick, they must also have food for their more common, daily appetites. For even the high lifted and chivalric Crusaders of old times were not content to traverse two thousand miles of land to fight for their holy sepulchre, without committing burglaries, picking pockets, and gaining other pious perquisites by the way. Had they been strictly held to their one final and romantic object – that final and romantic object, too many would have turned from in disgust. I will not strip these men, thought Ahab, of all hopes of cash – aye, cash. They may scorn cash now; but let some months go by, and no perspective promise of it to them, and then this same quiescent cash all at once mutinying in them, this same cash would soon cashier Ahab.

Nor was there wanting still another precautionary motive more related to Ahab personally. Having impulsively, it is probable, and perhaps somewhat prematurely revealed the prime but private purpose of the Pequod's voyage, Ahab was now entirely conscious that, in so doing, he had indirectly laid himself open to the unanswerable charge of usurpation; and with perfect impunity, both moral and legal, his crew if so disposed, and to that end competent, could refuse all further obedience to him, and even violently wrest from him the command. From even the barely hinted imputation of usurpation, and the possible consequences of such a suppressed impression gaining ground, Ahab must of course have been most anxious to protect himself. That protection could only consist in his own predominating brain and heart and hand, backed by a heedful, closely calculating attention to every minute atmospheric influence which it was possible for his crew to be subjected to.

For all these reasons then, and others perhaps too analytic to be verbally developed here, Ahab plainly saw that he must still in a good degree continue true to the natural, nominal purpose of the Pequod's voyage; observe all customary usages; and not only that, but force himself to evince all his well known passionate interest in the general pursuit of his profession.

Be all this as it may, his voice was now often heard hailing the three mast-heads and admonishing them to keep a bright look-out, and not omit reporting even a porpoise. This vigilance was not long without reward.

47

THE MAT-MAKER

It was a cloudy, sultry afternoon; the seamen were lazily lounging about the decks, or vacantly gazing over into the lead-colored water. Queequeg and I were mildly employed weaving what is called a sword-mat, for an additional lashing to our boat. So still and subdued and yet somehow preluding was all the scene, and such an incantation of revery lurked in the air, that each silent sailor seemed resolved into his own invisible self.

I was the attendant or page of Queequeg, while busy at the mat. As I kept passing and repassing the filling or woof of marline between the long yarns of the warp, using my own hand for the shuttle, and as Queequeg, standing sideways, ever and anon slid his heavy oaken sword between the threads, and idly looking off upon the water, carelessly and unthinkingly drove home every yarn: I say so strange a dreaminess did there then reign all over the ship and all over the sea, only broken by the intermitting dull sound of the sword, that it seemed as if this were the Loom of Time, and I myself were a shuttle mechanically weaving and weaving away at the Fates. There lay the fixed threads of the warp subject to but one single, ever returning, unchanging vibration, and that vibration merely enough to admit of the crosswise interblending of other threads with its own. This warp seemed necessity; and here, thought I, with my own hand I ply my own shuttle and weave my own destiny into these unalterable threads. Meantime, Queequeg's impulsive, indifferent sword, sometimes hitting the woof slantingly, or crookedly, or strongly, or weakly, as the case might be; and by this difference in the concluding blow producing a corresponding contrast in the final aspect of the completed fabric; this savage's sword, thought I, which thus finally shapes and fashions both warp and woof; this easy, indifferent sword must be chance – aye, chance, free will, and necessity – no wise incompatible – all interweavingly working together. The straight warp of necessity, not to be swerved from its ultimate course – its every alternating vibration, indeed, only tending to that; free will still free to ply her shuttle between given threads; and chance, though restrained in its play within the right lines of necessity, and sideways in its motions directed by free will, though thus prescribed to by both, chance by turns rules either, and has the last featuring blow at events.

* * * * * * *

Thus we were weaving and weaving away when I started at a sound so strange, long drawn, and musically wild and unearthly, that the ball of free will dropped from my hand, and I stood gazing up at the clouds whence that voice dropped like a wing. High aloft in the cross-trees was that mad Gay-Header, Tashtego. His body was reaching eagerly forward, his hand stretched out like a wand, and at brief sudden intervals he continued his cries. To be sure the same sound was that very moment perhaps being heard all over the seas, from hundreds of whalemen's look-outs perched as high in the air; but from few of those lungs could that accustomed old cry have derived such a marvellous cadence as from Tashtego the Indian's.

As he stood hovering over you half suspended in air, so wildly and eagerly peering towards the horizon, you would have thought him some prophet or seer beholding the shadows of Fate, and by those wild cries announcing their coming.

'There she blows! there! there! there! she blows! she blows!'

'Where-away?'

'On the lee-beam, about two miles off! a school of them!'

Instantly all was commotion.

The Sperm Whale blows as a clock ticks, with the same undeviating and reliable uniformity. And thereby whalemen distinguish this fish from other tribes of his genus.

'There go flukes!' was now the cry from Tashtego; and the whales disappeared.

'Quick, steward!' cried Ahab. 'Time! time!'

Dough-Boy hurried below, glanced at the watch, and reported the exact minute to Ahab.

The ship was now kept away from the wind, and she went gently rolling before it. Tashtego reporting that the whales had gone down heading to leeward, we confidently looked to see them again directly in advance of our bows. For that singular craft at times evinced by the Sperm Whale when, sounding with his head in one direction, he nevertheless, while concealed beneath the surface, mills round, and swiftly swims off in the opposite quarter – this deceitfulness of his could not now be in action; for there was no reason to suppose that the fish seen by Tashtego had been in any way alarmed, or indeed knew at all of our vicinity. One of the men selected for shipkeepers – that is, those not appointed to the boats, by this time relieved the Indian at the main-mast head. The sailors at the fore and mizzen had come down; the line tubs were fixed in their places; the cranes were thrust out; the mainyard was backed, and the three boats swung over the sea like three samphire baskets over high cliffs. Outside of the bulwarks their eager crews with one hand clung to the rail, while one foot was expectantly poised on the gunwale. So look the long line of man-of-war's men about to throw themselves on board an enemy's ship.

But at this critical instant a sudden exclamation was heard that took every eye from the whale. With a start all glared at dark Ahab, who was surrounded by five dusky phantoms that seemed fresh formed out of air.

48

THE FIRST LOWERING

THE phantoms, for so they then seemed, were flitting on the other side of the deck, and, with a noiseless celerity, were casting loose the tackles and bands of the boat which swung there. This boat had always been deemed one of the spare boats, though technically called the captain's, on account of its hanging from the starboard quarter. The figure that now stood by its bows was tall and swart, with one white tooth evilly protruding from its steel-like lips. A rumpled Chinese jacket of black cotton funereally invested him, with wide black trowsers of the same dark stuff. But strangely crowning this ebonness was a glistening white plaited turban, the living hair braided and coiled round and round upon his head. Less swart in aspect, the companions of this figure were of that vivid, tiger-yellow complexion peculiar to some of the aboriginal natives of the Manillas; – a race notorious for a certain diabolism of subtilty, and by some honest white mariners supposed to be the paid spies and secret confidential agents on the water of the devil, their lord, whose counting-room they suppose to be elsewhere.

While yet the wondering ship's company were gazing

upon these strangers, Ahab cried out to the white-turbaned old man at their head, 'All ready there, Fedallah?'

'Ready,' was the half-hissed reply.

'Lower away then; d'ye hear?' shouting across the deck. 'Lower away there, I say.'

Such was the thunder of his voice, that spite of their amazement the men sprang over the rail; the sheaves whirled round in the blocks; with a wallow, the three boats dropped into the sea; while, with a dexterous, off-handed daring, unknown in any other vocation, the sailors, goat-like, leaped down the rolling ship's side into the tossed boats below.

Hardly had they pulled out from under the ship's lee, when a fourth keel, coming from the windward side, pulled round under the stern, and showed the five strangers rowing Ahab, who, standing erect in the stern, loudly hailed Starbuck, Stubb, and Flask, to spread themselves widely, so as to cover a large expanse of water. But with all their eyes again riveted upon the swart Fedallah and his crew, the inmates of the other boats obeyed not the command.

'Captain Ahab? –' said Starbuck.

'Spread yourselves,' cried Ahab; 'give way, all four boats. Thou, Flask, pull out more to leeward!'

'Aye, aye, sir,' cheerily cried little King-Post, sweeping round his great steering oar. 'Lay back!' addressing his crew. 'There! – there! – there again! There she blows right ahead, boys! – lay back! – Never heed yonder yellow boys, Archy.'

'Oh, I don't mind 'em, sir,' said Archy; 'I knew it all before now. Didn't I hear 'em in the hold? And didn't I tell Cabaco here of it? What say ye, Cabaco? They are stowaways, Mr Flask.'

'Pull, pull, my fine hearts-alive; pull, my children; pull, my little ones,' drawlingly and soothingly sighed Stubb to his crew, some of whom still showed signs of uneasiness. 'Why don't you break your backbones, my boys? What is it you stare at? Those chaps in yonder boat? Tut! They are only five more hands come to help us – never mind from where –

the more the merrier. Pull, then, do pull; never mind the brimstone – devils are good fellows enough. So, so; there you are now; that's the stroke for a thousand pounds; that's the stroke to sweep the stakes! Hurrah for the gold cup of sperm oil, my heroes! Three cheers, men – all hearts alive! Easy, easy; don't be in a hurry – don't be in a hurry. Why don't you snap your oars, you rascals? Bite something, you dogs! So, so, so, then; – softly, softly! That's it – that's it! long and strong. Give way there, give way! The devil fetch ye, ye ragamuffin rapscallions; ye are all asleep. Stop snoring, ye sleepers, and pull. Pull, will ye? pull, can't ye? pull, won't ye? Why in the name of gudgeons and ginger-cakes don't ye pull? – pull and break something! pull, and start your eyes out! Here!' whipping out the sharp knife from his girdle; 'every mother's son of ye draw his knife, and pull with the blade between his teeth. That's it – that's it. Now ye do something; that looks like it, my steel-bits. Start her – start her, my silver-spoons! Start her, marling-spikes!'

Stubb's exordium to his crew is given here at large, because he had rather a peculiar way of talking to them in general, and especially in inculcating the religion of rowing. But you must not suppose from this specimen of his sermonizings that he ever flew into downright passions with his congregation. Not at all; and therein consisted his chief peculiarity. He would say the most terrific things to his crew, in a tone so strangely compounded of fun and fury, and the fury seemed so calculated merely as a spice to the fun, that no oarsman could hear such queer invocations without pulling for dear life, and yet pulling for the mere joke of the thing. Besides he all the time looked so easy and indolent himself, so loungingly managed his steering-oar, and so broadly gaped – open-mouthed at times – that the mere sight of such a yawning commander, by sheer force of contrast, acted like a charm upon the crew. Then again, Stubb was one of those odd sort of humorists, whose jollity is sometimes so curiously ambiguous, as to put all inferiors on their guard in the matter of obeying them.

In obedience to a sign from Ahab, Starbuck was now pulling obliquely across Stubb's bow; and when for a minute or so the two boats were pretty near to each other, Stubb hailed the mate.

'Mr Starbuck! larboard boat there, ahoy! a word with ye, sir, if ye please!'

'Halloa!' returned Starbuck, turning round not a single inch as he spoke; still earnestly but whisperingly urging his crew; his face set like a flint from Stubb's.

'What think ye of those yellow boys, sir!'

'Smuggled on board, somehow, before the ship sailed. (Strong, strong, boys!)' in a whisper to his crew, then speaking out loud again: 'A sad business, Mr Stubb! (seethe her, seethe her, my lads!) but never mind, Mr Stubb, all for the best. Let all your crew pull strong, come what will. (Spring, my men, spring!) There's hogsheads of sperm ahead, Mr Stubb, and that's what ye came for. (Pull, my boys!) Sperm, sperm's the play! This at least is duty; duty and profit hand in hand!'

'Aye, aye, I thought as much,' soliloquized Stubb, when the boats diverged, 'as soon as I clapt eye on 'em, I thought so. Aye, and that's what he went into the after hold for, so often, as Dough-Boy long suspected. They were hidden down there. The White Whale's at the bottom of it. Well, well, so be it! Can't be helped! All right! Give way, men! It ain't the White Whale to-day! Give way!'

Now the advent of these outlandish strangers at such a critical instant as the lowering of the boats from the deck, this had not unreasonably awakened a sort of superstitious amazement in some of the ship's company; but Archy's fancied discovery having some time previous got abroad among them, though indeed not credited then, this had in some small measure prepared them for the event. It took off the extreme edge of their wonder; and so what with all this and Stubb's confident way of accounting for their appearance, they were for the time freed from superstitious surmisings; though the affair still left abundant room for all manner of wild conjectures as to dark Ahab's precise agency in the matter from the beginning. For me, I silently recalled the mysterious shadows I had seen creeping on board the Pequod during the dim Nantucket dawn, as well as the enigmatical hintings of the unaccountable Elijah.

Meantime, Ahab, out of hearing of his officers, having sided the furthest to windward, was still ranging ahead of the other boats; a circumstance bespeaking how potent a crew was pulling him. Those tiger yellow creatures of his seemed all steel and whalebone; like five trip-hammers they rose and fell with regular strokes of strength, which periodically started the boat along the water like a horizontal burst boiler out of a Mississippi steamer. As for Fedallah, who was seen pulling the harpooneer oar, he had thrown aside his black jacket, and displayed his naked chest with the whole part of his body above the gunwale, clearly cut against the alternating depressions of the watery horizon; while at the other end of the boat Ahab, with one arm, like a fencer's, thrown half backward into the air, as if to counterbalance any tendency to trip; Ahab was seen steadily managing his steering oar as in a thousand boat lowerings ere the White Whale had torn him. All at once the out-stretched arm gave a peculiar motion and then remained fixed, while the boat's five oars were seen simultaneously peaked. Boat and crew sat motionless on the sea. Instantly the three spread boats in the rear paused on their way. The whales had irregularly settled bodily down into the blue, thus giving no distantly discernible token of the movement, though from his closer vicinity Ahab had observed it.

'Every man look out along his oar!' cried Starbuck. 'Thou, Queequeg, stand up!'

Nimbly springing up on the triangular raised box in the bow, the savage stood erect there, and with intensely eager eyes gazed off towards the spot where the chase had last been descried. Likewise upon the extreme stern of the boat where it was also triangularly platformed level with the gunwale, Starbuck himself was seen coolly and adroitly balancing himself to the jerking tossings of his chip of a craft, and silently eyeing the vast blue eye of the sea.

Not very far distant Flask's boat was also lying breathlessly still; its commander recklessly standing upon the top of the loggerhead, a stout sort of post rooted in the keel, and rising some two feet above the level of the stern platform. It is used for catching turns with the whale line. Its top is not more spacious than the palm of a man's hand, and standing upon such a base as that, Flask seemed perched at the mast-head of some ship which had sunk to all but her trucks. But little King-Post was small and short, and at the same time little King-Post was full of a large and tall ambition, so that this loggerhead stand-point of his did by no means satisfy King-Post.

'I can't see three seas off; tip us up an oar there, and let me on to that.'

Upon this, Daggoo, with either hand upon the gunwale to steady his way, swiftly slid aft, and then erecting himself volunteered his lofty shoulders for a pedestal.

'Good a mast-head as any, sir. Will you mount?'

'That I will, and thank ye very much, my fine fellow; only I wish you fifty feet taller.'

Whereupon planting his feet firmly against two opposite planks of the boat, the gigantic negro, stooping a little, presented his flat palm to Flask's foot, and then putting Flask's hand on his hearse-plumed head and bidding him spring as he himself should toss, with one dexterous fling landed the little man high and dry on his shoulders. And here was Flask now standing, Daggoo with one lifted arm furnishing him with a breast-band to lean against and steady himself by.

At any time it is a strange sight to the tyro to see with what wondrous habitude of unconscious skill the whaleman will maintain an erect posture in his boat, even when pitched about by the most riotously perverse and cross-running seas. Still more strange to see him giddily perched upon the loggerhead itself, under such circumstances. But the sight of little Flask mounted upon gigantic Daggoo was yet more curious; for sustaining himself with a cool, indifferent, easy, unthought of, barbaric majesty, the noble negro to every roll of the sea harmoniously rolled his fine form. On his broad back, flaxen-haired Flask seemed a snow-flake. The bearer looked nobler than the rider. Though, truly, vivacious, tumultuous, ostentatious little Flask would now and then stamp with impatience; but not one added heave did he thereby give to the negro's lordly chest. So have I seen Passion and Vanity stamping the living magnanimous earth, but the earth did not alter her tides and her seasons for that.

Meanwhile Stubb, the second mate, betrayed no such far-gazing solicitudes. The whales might have made one of their regular soundings, not a temporary dive from mere fright; and if that were the case, Stubb, as his wont in such cases, it seems, was resolved to solace the languishing interval with his pipe. He withdrew it from his hatband, where he always wore it aslant like a feather. He loaded it, and rammed home the loading with his thumb-end; but hardly had he ignited his match across the rough sand-paper of his hand, when Tashtego, his harpooneer, whose eyes had been setting to windward like two fixed stars, suddenly dropped like light from his erect attitude to his seat, crying out in a quick phrensy of hurry, 'Down, down all, and give way! – there they are!'

To a landsman, no whale, nor any sign of a herring, would have been visible at that moment; nothing but a troubled bit of greenish white water, and thin scattered puffs of vapor hovering over it, and suffusingly blowing off to leeward, like the confused scud from white rolling billows. The air around suddenly vibrated and tingled, as it were, like the air over intensely heated plates of iron. Beneath this atmospheric waving and curling, and partially beneath a thin layer of water, also, the whales were swimming. Seen in advance of all the other indications, the puffs of vapor they spouted, seemed their forerunning couriers and detached flying outriders.

All four boats were now in keen pursuit of that one spot of troubled water and air. But it bade far to outstrip them; it flew on and on, as a mass of interblending bubbles borne down a rapid stream from the hills.

'Pull, pull, my good boys,' said Starbuck, in the lowest possible but intensest concentrated whisper to his men; while the sharp fixed glance from his eyes, darted straight ahead of the bow, almost seemed as two visible needles in two unerring binnacle compasses. He did not say much to his crew, though, nor did his crew say anything to him. Only the silence of the boat was at intervals startlingly pierced by one of his peculiar whispers, now harsh with command, now soft with entreaty.

How different the loud little King-Post. 'Sing out and say something, my hearties. Roar and pull, my thunderbolts! Beach me, beach me on their black backs, boys; only do that for me, and I'll sign over to you my Martha's Vineyard plantation, boys; including wife and children, boys. Lay me on – lay me on! O Lord, Lord! but I shall go stark, staring mad: See! see that white water!' And so shouting, he pulled his hat from his head, and stamped up and down on it; then picking it up, flirted it far off upon the sea; and finally fell to rearing and plunging in the boat's stern like a crazed colt from the prairie.

'Look at that chap now,' philosophically drawled Stubb, who, with his unlighted short pipe, mechanically retained between his teeth, at a short distance, followed after – 'He's got fits, that Flask has. Fits? yes, give him fits – that's the very word – pitch fits into 'em. Merrily, merrily, hearts-alive. Pudding for supper, you know; – merry's the word. Pull, babes – pull, sucklings – pull, all. But what the devil are you hurrying about? Softly, softly, and steadily, my men. Only pull, and keep pulling; nothing more. Crack all your backbones, and bite your knives in two – that's all. Take it easy – why don't ye take it easy, I say, and burst all your livers and lungs!'

But what it was that inscrutable Ahab said to that tiger-yellow crew of his – these were words best omitted here; for you live under the blessed light of the evangelical land. Only the infidel sharks in the audacious seas may give ear to such words, when, with tornado brow, and eyes of red murder, and foam-glued lips, Ahab leaped after his prey.

Meanwhile, all the boats tore on. The repeated specific allusions of Flask to 'that whale,' as he called the fictitious monster which he declared to be incessantly tantalizing his boat's bow with its tail – these allusions of his were at times so vivid and life-like, that they would cause some one or two of his men to snatch a fearful look over the shoulder. But this was against all rule; for the oarsmen must put out their eyes, and ram a skewer through their necks; usage pronouncing that they must have no organs but ears, and no limbs but arms, in these critical moments.

It was a sight full of quick wonder and awe! The vast swells of the omnipotent sea; the surging, hollow roar they made, as they rolled along the eight gunwales, like gigantic bowls in a boundless bowling-green; the brief suspended agony of the boat, as it would tip for an instant on the knife-like edge of the sharper waves, that almost seemed threatening to cut it in two; the sudden profound dip into the watery glens and hollows; the keen spurrings and goadings to gain the top of the opposite hill; the headlong, sled-like slide down its other side; – all these, with the cries of the headsmen and harpooneers, and the shuddering gasps of the oarsmen, with the wondrous sight of the ivory Pequod bearing down upon her boats with outstretched sails, like a wild hen after her screaming brood; – all this was thrilling. Not the raw recruit, marching from the bosom of his wife into the fever heat of his first battle; not the dead man's ghost encountering the first unknown phantom in the other world; – neither of these can feel stranger and stronger emotions than that man does, who for the first time finds himself pulling into the charmed, churned circle of the hunted sperm whale.

The dancing white water made by the chase was now becoming more and more visible, owing to the increasing darkness of the dun cloud-shadows flung upon the sea. The jets of vapor no longer blended, but tilted everywhere to right and left; the whales seemed separating their wakes. The boats were pulled more apart; Starbuck giving chase to three whales running dead to leeward. Our sail was now set, and, with the still rising wind, we rushed along; the boat going with such madness through the water, that the lee oars could scarcely be worked rapidly enough to escape being torn from the row-locks.

Soon we were running through a suffusing wide veil of mist; neither ship nor boat to be seen.

'Give way, men,' whispered Starbuck, drawing still further aft the sheet of his sail; 'there is time to kill a fish yet before the squall comes. There's white water again! – close to! Spring!'

Soon after, two cries in quick succession on each side of us denoted that the other boats had got fast; but hardly were they overheard, when with a lightning-like hurtling whisper Starbuck said: 'Stand up!' and Queequeg, harpoon in hand, sprang to his feet.

Though not one of the oarsmen was then facing the life and death peril so close to them ahead, yet with their eyes on the intense countenance of the mate in the stern of the boat, they knew that the imminent instant had come; they heard, too, an enormous wallowing sound as of fifty elephants stirring in their litter. Meanwhile the boat was still booming through the mist, the waves curling and hissing around us like the erected crests of enraged serpents.

'That's his hump. *There, there*, give it to him!' whispered Starbuck.

A short rushing sound leaped out of the boat; it was the darted iron of Queequeg. Then all in one welded commotion came an invisible push from astern, while forward the boat seemed striking on a ledge; the sail collapsed and exploded; a gush of scalding vapor shot up near by; something rolled and tumbled like an earthquake beneath us. The whole crew were half suffocated as they were tossed helter-skelter into the white curdling cream of the squall. Squall, whale, and harpoon had all blended together; and the whale, merely grazed by the iron, escaped.

Though completely swamped, the boat was nearly unharmed. Swimming round it we picked up the floating oars, and lashing them across the gunwale, tumbled back to our places. There we sat up to our knees in the sea, the water covering every rib and plank, so that to our downward gazing eyes the suspended craft seemed a coral boat grown up to us from the bottom of the ocean.

The wind increased to a howl; the waves dashed their bucklers together; the whole squall roared, forked, and crackled around us like a white fire upon the prairie, in which, unconsumed, we were burning; immortal in these jaws of death! In vain we hailed the other boats; as well roar to the live coals down the chimney of a flaming furnace as hail those boats in that storm. Meanwhile the driving scud, rack, and mist, grew darker with the shadows of night; no sign of the ship could be seen. The rising sea forbade all attempts to bale out the boat. The oars were useless as propellers, performing now the office of life-preservers. So, cutting the lashing of the waterproof match keg, after many failures Starbuck contrived to ignite the lamp in the lantern; then stretching it on a waif pole, handed it to Queequeg as the standard-bearer of this forlorn hope. There, then, he sat, holding up that imbecile candle in the heart of that almighty forlornness. There, then, he sat, the sign and symbol of a man without faith, hopelessly holding up hope in the midst of despair.

Wet, drenched through, and shivering cold, despairing of ship or boat, we lifted up our eyes as the dawn came on. The mist still spread over the sea, the empty lantern lay crushed in the bottom of the boat. Suddenly Queequeg started to his feet, hollowing his hand to his ear. We all heard a faint creaking, as of ropes and yards hitherto muffled by the storm. The sound came nearer and nearer; the thick mists were dimly parted by a huge, vague form. Affrighted, we all sprang into the sea as the ship at last loomed into view, bearing right down upon us within a distance of not much more than its length.

Floating on the waves we saw the abandoned boat, as for one instant it tossed and gaped beneath the ship's bows like a chip at the base of a cataract; and then the vast hull rolled over it, and it was seen no more till it came up weltering astern. Again we swam for it, were dashed against it by the seas, and were at last taken up and safely landed on board.

Ere the squall came close to, the other boats had cut loose from their fish and returned to the ship in good time. The ship had given us up, but was still cruising, if haply it might light upon some token of our perishing, – an oar or a lance pole.

49

THE HYENA

THERE are certain queer times and occasions in this strange mixed affair we call life when a man takes this whole universe for a vast practical joke, though the wit thereof he but dimly discerns, and more than suspects that the joke is at nobody's expense but his own. However, nothing dispirits, and nothing seems worth while disputing. He bolts down all events, all creeds, and beliefs, and persuasions, all hard things visible and invisible, never mind how knobby; as an ostrich of potent digestion gobbles down bullets and gun flints. And as for small difficulties and worryings, prospects of sudden disaster, peril of life and limb; all these, and death itself, seem to him only sly, good-natured hits, and jolly punches in the side bestowed by the unseen and unaccountable old joker. That odd sort of wayward mood I am speaking of, comes over a man only in some time of extreme tribulation; it comes in the very midst of his earnestness, so that what just before might have seemed to him a thing most momentous, now seems but a part of the general joke. There is nothing like the perils of whaling to breed this free and easy sort of genial, desperado philosophy; and with it I now regarded this whole voyage of the Pequod, and the great White Whale its object.

'Queequeg,' said I, when they had dragged me, the last man, to the deck, and I was still shaking myself in my jacket to fling off the water; 'Queequeg, my fine friend, does this sort of thing often happen?' Without much emotion, though soaked through just like me, he gave me to understand that such things did often happen.

'Mr Stubb,' said I, turning to that worthy, who, buttoned up in his oil-jacket, was now calmly smoking his pipe in the rain; 'Mr Stubb, I think I have heard you say that of all whalemen you ever met, our chief mate, Mr Starbuck, is by far the most careful and prudent. I suppose then, that going plump on a flying whale with your sail set in a foggy squall is the height of a whaleman's discretion?'

'Certain. I've lowered for whales from a leaking ship in a gale off Cape Horn.'

'Mr Flask,' said I, turning to little King-Post, who was standing close by; 'you are experienced in these things, and I am not. Will you tell me whether it is an unalterable law in this fishery, Mr Flask, for an oarsman to break his own back pulling himself back-foremost into death's jaws?'

'Can't you twist that smaller?' said Flask. 'Yes, that's the law. I should like to see a boat's crew backing water up to a whale face foremost. Ha, ha! the whale would give them squint for squint, mind that!'

Here then, from three impartial witnesses, I had a deliberate statement of the entire case. Considering, therefore, that squalls and capsizings in the water and consequent bivouacks on the deep, were matters of common occurrence in this kind of life; considering that at the superlatively critical instant of going on to the whale I must resign my life into the hands of him who steered the boat – oftentimes a fellow who at that very moment is in his impetuousness upon the point of scuttling the craft with his own frantic stampings; considering that the particular disaster to our own particular boat was chiefly to be imputed to Starbuck's driving on to his whale almost in the teeth of a squall, and considering that Starbuck, notwithstanding, was famous for his great heedfulness in the fishery; considering that I belonged to this uncommonly prudent Starbuck's boat; and finally considering in what a devil's chase I was implicated, touching the White Whale: taking all things together, I say, I thought I might as well go below and make a rough draft of my will. 'Queequeg,' said I, 'come along, you shall be my lawyer, executor, and legatee.'

It may seem strange that of all men sailors should be tinkering at their last wills and testaments, but there are no people in the world more fond of that diversion. This was the fourth time in my nautical life that I had done the same thing. After the ceremony was concluded upon the present occasion, I felt all the easier; a stone was rolled away from my heart. Besides, all the days I should now live would be as good as the days that Lazarus lived after his resurrection; a supplementary clean gain of so many months or weeks as the case might be. I survived myself; my death and burial were locked up in my chest. I looked round me tranquilly and contentedly, like a quiet ghost with a clean conscience sitting inside the bars of a snug family vault.

Now then, thought I, unconsciously rolling up the sleeves of my frock, here goes for a cool, collected dive at death and destruction, and the devil fetch the hindmost.

50

AHAB'S BOAT AND CREW. FEDALLAH

'WHO would have thought it, Flask!' cried Stubb; 'if I had but one leg you would not catch me in a boat, unless maybe to stop the plug-hole with my timber toe. Oh! he's a wonderful old man!'

'I don't think it so strange, after all, on that account,' said Flask. 'If his leg were off at the hip, now, it would be a different thing. That would disable him; but he has one knee, and good part of the other left, you know.'

'I don't know that, my little man; I never yet saw him kneel.'

* * * * * * *

Among whale-wise people it has often been argued whether, considering the paramount importance of his life to the success of the voyage, it is right for a whaling captain to jeopardize that life in the active perils of the chase. So

Tamerlane's soldiers often argued with tears in their eyes, whether that invaluable life of his ought to be carried into the thickest of the fight.

But with Ahab the question assumed a modified aspect. Considering that with two legs man is but a hobbling wight in all times of danger; considering that the pursuit of whales is always under great and extraordinary difficulties; that every individual moment, indeed, then comprises a peril; under these circumstances is it wise for any maimed man to enter a whale-boat in the hunt? As a general thing, the joint-owners of the Pequod must have plainly thought not.

Ahab well knew that although his friends at home would think little of his entering a boat in certain comparatively harmless vicissitudes of the chase, for the sake of being near the scene of action and giving his orders in person, yet for Captain Ahab to have a boat actually apportioned to him as a regular headsman in the hunt – above all for Captain Ahab to be supplied with five extra men, as that same boat's crew, he well knew that such generous conceits never entered the heads of the owners of the Pequod. Therefore he had not solicited a boat's crew from them, nor had he in any way hinted his desires on that head. Nevertheless he had taken private measures of his own touching all that matter. Until Archy's published discovery, the sailors had little foreseen it, though to be sure when, after being a little while out of port, all hands had concluded the customary business of fitting the whaleboats for service; when some time after this Ahab was now and then found bestirring himself in the matter of making thole-pins with his own hands for what was thought to be one of the spare boats, and even solicitously cutting the small wooden skewers, which when the line is running out are pinned over the groove in the bow: when all this was observed in him, and particularly his solicitude in having an extra coat of sheathing in the bottom of the boat, as if to make it better withstand the pointed pressure of his ivory limb; and also the anxiety he evinced in exactly shaping the thigh board, or clumsy cleat, as it is sometimes called, the horizontal piece in the boat's bow for bracing the knee against in darting or stabbing at the whale; when it was observed how often he stood up in that boat with his solitary knee fixed in the semi-circular depression in the cleat, and with the carpenter's chisel gouged out a little here and straightened it a little there; all these things, I say, had awakened much interest and curiosity at the time. But almost everybody supposed that this particular preparative heedfulness in Ahab must only be with a view to the ultimate chase of Moby Dick; for he had already revealed his intention to hunt that mortal monster in person. But such a supposition did by no means involve the remotest suspicion as to any boat's crew being assigned to that boat.

Now, with the subordinate phantoms, what wonder remained soon waned away; for in a whaler wonders soon wane. Besides, now and then such unaccountable odds and ends of strange nations come up from the unknown nooks and ash-holes of the earth to man these floating outlaws of whalers; and the ships themselves often pick up such queer castaway creatures found tossing about the open sea on planks, bits of wreck, oars, whaleboats, canoes, blown-off Japanese junks, and what not; that Beelzebub himself might climb up the side and step down into the cabin to chat with the captain, and it would not create any unsubduable excitement in the forecastle.

But be all this as it may, certain it is that while the subordinate phantoms soon found their place among the crew, though still as it were somehow distinct from then, yet that hair-turbaned Fedallah remained a muffled mystery to the last. Whence he came in a mannerly world like this, by what sort of unaccountable tie he soon evinced himself to be linked with Ahab's peculiar fortunes; nay, so far as to have some sort of a half-hinted influence; Heaven knows, but it might have been even authority over him; all this none knew. But one cannot sustain an indifferent air concerning Fedallah. He was such a creature as civilized, domestic people in the temperate zone only see in their dreams, and that but dimly; but the like of whom now and then glide among the unchanging Asiatic communities, especially the Oriental isles to the east of the continent – those insulated, immemorial, unalterable countries, which even in these modern days still preserve much of the ghostly aboriginalness of earth's primal generations, when the memory of the first man was a distinct recollection, and all men his descendants, unknowing whence he came, eyed each other as real phantoms, and asked of the sun and the moon why they were created and to what end; when though, according to Genesis, the angels indeed consorted with the daughters of men, the devils also, add the uncanonical Rabbins, indulged in mundane amours.

51

THE SPIRIT-SPOUT

DAYS, weeks passed, and under easy sail, the ivory Pequod had slowly swept across four several cruising-grounds; that off the Azores; off the Cape de Verdes; on the Plate (so called), being off the mouth of the Rio de la Plata; and the Carrol Ground, an unstaked, watery locality, southerly from St Helena.

It was while gliding through these latter waters that one serene and moonlight night, when all the waves rolled by like scrolls of silver; and, by their soft, suffusing seethings, made what seemed a silvery silence, not a solitude: on such a silent night a silvery jet was seen far in advance of the white bubbles at the bow. Lit up by the moon, it looked celestial; seemed some plumed and glittering god uprising from the sea. Fedallah first descried this jet. For of these moonlight nights, it was his wont to mount to the mainmast head, and stand a look-out there, with the same precision as if it had been day. And yet, though herds of whales were seen by night, not one whaleman in a hundred would venture a lowering for them. You may think with what emotions, then, the seamen beheld this old Oriental perched aloft at such unusual hours; his turban and the moon, companions in one sky. But when, after spending his uniform interval there for several successive nights without uttering a single sound; when, after all this silence, his unearthly voice was heard announcing that silvery, moon-lit jet, every reclining mariner started to his feet as if some winged spirit had lighted in the rigging, and hailed the mortal crew. 'There she blows!' Had the trump of judgment blown, they could not have quivered more; yet still they felt no terror; rather pleasure. For though it was a most unwonted hour, yet so impressive was the cry, and so deliriously exciting, that almost every soul on board instinctively desired a lowering.

Walking the deck with quick, side-lunging strides, Ahab commanded the t'gallant sails and royals to be set, and every stunsail spread. The best man in the ship must take the helm. Then, with every mast-head manned, the piled-up craft rolled down before the wind. The strange, upheaving, lifting tendency of the taffrail breeze filling the hollows of so many sails, made the buoyant, hovering deck to feel like air beneath the feet; while still she rushed along, as if two antagonistic influences were struggling in her – one to mount direct to heaven, the other to drive yawingly to some horizontal goal. And had you watched Ahab's face that night, you would have thought that in him also two different things were warring. While his one live leg made lively echoes along the deck, every stroke of his dead limb sounded like a coffin-tap. On life and death this old man walked. But though the ship so swiftly sped, and though from every eye, like arrows, the eager glances shot, yet the silvery jet was no more seen that night. Every sailor swore he saw it once, but not a second time.

This midnight-spout had almost grown a forgotten thing, when, some days after, lo! at the same silent hour, it was again announced: again it was descried by all; but upon making sail to overtake it, once more it disappeared as if it had never been. And so it served us night after night, till no one heeded it but to wonder at it. Mysteriously jetted into the clear moonlight, or starlight, as the case might be; disappearing again for one whole day, or two days, or three;

and somehow seeming at every distinct repetition to be advancing still further and further in our van, this solitary jet seemed for ever alluring us on.

Nor with the immemorial superstition of their race, and in accordance with the preternaturalness, as it seemed, which in many things invested the Pequod, were there wanting some of the seamen who swore that whenever and wherever descried; at however remote times, or in however far apart latitudes and longitudes, that unnearable spout was cast by one self-same whale; and that whale, Moby Dick. For a time, there reigned, too, a sense of peculiar dread at this flitting apparition, as if it were treacherously beckoning us on and on, in order that the monster might turn round upon us, and rend us at last in the remotest and most savage seas.

These temporary apprehensions, so vague but so awful, derived a wondrous potency from the contrasting serenity of the weather, in which, beneath all its blue blandness, some thought there lurked a devilish charm, as for days and days we voyaged along, through seas so wearily, lonesomely mild, that all space, in repugnance to our vengeful errand, seemed vacating itself of life before our urn-like prow.

But, at last, when turning to the eastward, the Cape winds began howling around us, and we rose and fell upon the long, troubled seas that are there; when the ivory-tusked Pequod sharply bowed to the blast, and gored the dark waves in her madness, till, like showers of silver chips, the foam-flakes flew over her bulwarks; then all this desolate vacuity of life went away, but gave place to sights more dismal than before.

Close to our bows, strange forms in the water darted hither and thither before us; while thick in our rear flew the inscrutable sea-ravens. And every morning, perched on our stays, rows of these birds were seen; and spite of our hootings, for a long time obstinately clung to the hemp, as though they deemed our ship some drifting, uninhabited craft; a thing appointed to desolation, and therefore fit roosting-place for their homeless selves. And heaved and heaved, still unrestingly heaved the black sea, as if its vast tides were a conscience; and the great mundane soul were in anguish and remorse for the long sin and suffering it had bred.

Cape of Good Hope, do they call ye? Rather Cape Tormentoso, as called of yore; for long allured by the perfidious silences that before had attended us, we found ourselves launched into this tormented sea, where guilty beings transformed into those fowls and these fish, seemed condemned to swim on everlastingly without any haven in store, or beat that black air without any horizon. But calm, snow-white, and unvarying; still directing its fountain of feathers to the sky; still beckoning us on from before, the solitary jet would at times be descried.

During all this blackness of the elements, Ahab, though assuming for the time the almost continual command of the drenched and dangerous deck, manifested the gloomiest reserve; and more seldom than ever addressed his mates. In tempestuous times like these, after everything above and aloft has been secured, nothing more can be done but passively to wait the issue of the gale. Then Captain and crew become practical fatalists. So, with his ivory leg inserted into its accustomed hole, and with one hand firmly grasping a shroud, Ahab for hours and hours would stand gazing dead to windward, while an occasional squall of sleet or snow would all but congeal his very eyelashes together. Meantime, the crew driven from the forward part of the ship by the perilous seas that burstingly broke over its bows, stood in a line along the bulwarks in the waist; and the better to guard against the leaping waves, each man had slipped himself into a sort of bowline secured to the rail, in which he swung as in a loosened belt. Few or no words were spoken; and the silent ship, as if manned by painted sailors in wax, day after day tore on through all the swift madness and gladness of the demoniac waves. By night the same muteness of humanity before the shrieks of the ocean prevailed; still in silence the men swung in the bowlines; still wordless Ahab stood up to the blast. Even when wearied nature seemed demanding repose he would not seek that repose in his hammock. Never could Starbuck forget the old man's aspect, when one night going down into the cabin to mark how the barometer stood, he saw him with closed eyes sitting straight in his floor-screwed chair; the rain and half-melted sleet of the storm from which he had some time before emerged, still slowly dripping from the unremoved hat and coat. On the table beside him lay unrolled one of those charts of tides and currents which have previously been spoken of. His lantern swung from his tightly clenched hand. Though the body was erect, the head was thrown back so that the closed eyes were pointed towards the needle of the tell-tale that swung from a beam in the ceiling.*

Terrible old man! thought Starbuck with a shudder, sleeping in this gale, still thou steadfastly eyest thy purpose.

52

THE ALBATROSS

SOUTH-EASTWARD from the Cape, off the distant Crozetts, a good cruising ground for Right Whalemen, a sail loomed ahead, the Goney (Albatross) by name. As she slowly drew nigh, from my lofty perch at the fore-mast-head, I had a good view of that sight so remarkable to a tyro in the far ocean fisheries – a whaler at sea, and long absent from home.

As if the waves had been fullers, this craft was bleached like the skeleton of a stranded walrus. All down her sides, this spectral appearance was traced with long channels of reddened rust, while all her spars and her rigging were like the thick branches of trees furred over with hoar-frost. Only her lower sails were set. A wild sight it was to see her long-bearded look-outs at those three mast-heads. They seemed clad in the skin of beasts, so torn and bepatched the raiment

*The cabin-compass is called the tell-tale, because without going to the compass at the helm, the Captain, while below, can inform himself of the course of the ship.

that had survived nearly four years of cruising. Standing in iron hoops nailed to the mast, they swayed and swung over a fathomless sea; and though, when the ship slowly glided close under our stern, we six men in the air came so nigh to each other that we might almost have leaped from the mast-heads of one ship to those of the other; yet, those forlorn-looking fishermen, mildly eyeing us as they passed, said not one word to our own look-outs, while the quarter-deck hail was being heard from below.

'Ship ahoy! Have ye seen the White Whale?'

But as the strange captain, leaning over the pallid bulwarks, was in the act of putting his trumpet to his mouth, it somehow fell from his hand into the sea; and the wind now rising amain, he in vain strove to make himself heard without it. Meantime his ship was still increasing the distance between. While in various silent ways the seamen of the Pequod were evincing their observance of this ominous incident at the first mere mention of the White Whale's name to another ship, Ahab for a moment paused; it almost seemed as though he would have lowered a boat to board the stranger, had not the threatening wind forbade. But taking advantage of his windward position, he again seized his trumpet, and knowing by her aspect that the stranger vessel was a Nantucketer and shortly bound home, he loudly hailed – 'Ahoy there! This is the Pequod, bound round the world! Tell them to address all future letters to the Pacific ocean! and this time three years, if I am not at home, tell them to address them to –'

At that moment the two wakes were fairly crossed, and instantly, then, in accordance with their singular ways, shoals of small harmless fish, that for some days before had been placidly swimming by our side, darted away with what seemed shuddering fins, and ranged themselves fore and aft with the stranger's flanks. Though in the course of his continual voyagings Ahab must often before have noticed a similar sight, yet, to any monomaniac man, the veriest trifles capriciously carry meanings.

'Swim away from me, do ye?' murmured Ahab, gazing

over into the water. There seemed but little in the words, but the tone conveyed more of deep helpless sadness than the insane old man had ever before evinced. But turning to the steersman, who thus far had been holding the ship in the wind to diminish her headway, he cried out in his old lion voice, – 'Up helm! Keep her off round the world!'

Round the world! There is much in that sound to inspire proud feelings; but whereto does all that circumnavigation conduct? Only through numberless perils to the very point whence we started, where those that we left behind secure, were all the time before us.

Were this world an endless plain, and by sailing eastward we could for ever reach new distances, and discover sights more sweet and strange than any Cyclades or Islands of King Solomon, then there were promise in the voyage. But in pursuit of those far mysteries we dream of, or in tormented chase of that demon phantom that, some time or other, swims before all human hearts; while chasing such over this round globe, they either lead us on in barren mazes or midway leave us whelmed.

53

THE GAM

THE ostensible reason why Ahab did not go on aboard of the whaler we had spoken was this: the wind and sea betokened storms. But even had this not been the case, he would not after all, perhaps, have boarded her – judging by his subsequent conduct on similar occasions – if so it had been that, by the process of hailing, he had obtained a negative answer to the question he put. For, as it eventually turned out, he cared not to consort, even for five minutes, with any stranger captain, except he could contribute some of that information he so absorbingly sought. But all this might remain inadequately estimated, were not something said here of the peculiar usages of whaling-vessels when meeting each other in foreign seas, and especially on a common cruising-ground.

If two strangers crossing the Pine Barrens in New York State, or the equally desolate Salisbury Plain in England; if casually encountering each other in such inhospitable wilds, these twain, for the life of them, cannot well avoid a mutual salutation; and stopping for a moment to interchange the news; and, perhaps, sitting down for a while and resting in concert: then, how much more natural that upon the illimitable Pine Barrens and Salisbury Plains of the sea, two whaling vessels descrying each other at the ends of the earth – off lone Fanning's Island, or the far away King's Mills; how much more natural, I say, that under such circumstances these ships should not only interchange hails, but come into still closer, more friendly and sociable contact. And especially would this seem to be a matter of course, in the case of vessels owned in one seaport, and whose captains, officers, and not a few of the men are personally known to each other: and consequently, have all sorts of dear domestic things to talk about.

For the long absent ship, the outward-bounder, perhaps, has letters on board; at any rate, she will be sure to let her have some papers of a date a year or two later than the last one on her blurred and thumb-worn files. And in return for that courtesy, the outward bound ship would receive the latest whaling intelligence from the cruising-ground to which she may be destined, a thing of the utmost importance to her. And in degree, all this will hold true concerning whaling vessels crossing each other's track on the cruising-ground itself, even though they are equally long absent from home. For one of them may have received a transfer of letters from some third, and now far remote vessel; and some of those letters may be for the people of the ship she now meets. Besides, they would exchange the whaling news, and have an agreeable chat. For not only would they meet with all the sympathies of sailors, but likewise with all the peculiar congenialities arising from a common pursuit and mutually shared privations and perils.

Nor would difference of country make any very essential difference; that is, so long as both parties speak one language, as is the case with Americans and English. Though, to be sure, from the small number of English whalers, such meetings do not very often occur, and when they do occur there is too apt to be a sort of shyness between them; for your Englishman is rather reserved, and your Yankee, he does not fancy that sort of thing in anybody but himself. Besides, the English whalers sometimes affect a kind of metropolitan superiority over the American whalers; regarding the long, lean Nantucketer, with his nondescript provincialisms, as a sort of sea-peasant. But where this superiority in the English whalemen does really consist, it would be hard to say, seeing that the Yankees in one day, collectively, kill more whales than all the English, collectively, in ten years. But this is a harmless little foible in the English whale-hunters, which the Nantucketer does not take much to heart; probably, because he knows that he has a few foibles himself.

So, then, we see that of all ships separately sailing the sea, the whalers have most reason to be sociable – and they are so. Whereas, some merchant ships crossing each other's wake in the mid-Atlantic, will oftentimes pass on without so much as a single word of recognition, mutually cutting each other on the high seas, like a brace of dandies in Broadway; and all the time indulging, perhaps, in finical criticism upon each other's rig. As for Men-of-War, when they chance to meet at sea, they first go through such a string of silly bowings and scrapings, such a ducking of ensigns, that there does not seem to be much right-down hearty good-will and brotherly love about it at all. As touching Slave-ships meeting, why, they are in such a prodigious hurry, they run away from each other as soon as possible. And as for Pirates, when they chance to cross each other's cross-bones, the first hail is – 'How many skulls?' – the same way that whalers hail – 'How many barrels?' And that question once answered, pirates straightway steer apart, for they are infernal villains on both sides, and don't like to see overmuch of each other's villainous likenesses.

But look at the godly, honest, unostentatious, hospitable, sociable, free-and-easy whaler! What does the whaler do when she meets another whaler in any sort of decent weather? She has a '*Gam*,' a thing so utterly unknown to all other ships that they never heard of the name even; and if by chance they should hear of it, they only grin at it, and repeat gamesome stuff about 'spouters' and 'blubber-boilers,' and such like pretty exclamations. Why it is that all Merchant-seamen, and also all Pirates and Man-of-War's men, and Slave-ship sailors, cherish such a scornful feeling towards Whale-ships; this is a question it would be hard to answer. Because, in the case of pirates, say, I should like to know whether that profession of theirs has any peculiar glory about it. It sometimes ends in uncommon elevation, indeed; but only at the gallows. And besides, when a man is elevated in that odd fashion, he has no proper foundation for his superior altitude. Hence, I conclude, that in boasting himself to be high lifted above a whaleman, in that assertion the pirate has no solid basis to stand on.

But what is a *Gam*? You might wear out your index-finger running up and down the columns of dictionaries, and never find the word. Dr Johnson never attained to that erudition; Noah Webster's ark does not hold it. Nevertheless, this same expressive word has now for many years been in constant use among some fifteen thousand true born Yankees. Certainly, it needs a definition, and should be incorporated into the Lexicon. With that view, let me learnedly define it.

GAM. Noun – *A social meeting of two (or more) Whale-ships, generally on a cruising-ground; when, after exchanging hails, they exchange visits by boats' crews: the two captains remaining, for the time, on board of one ship, and the two chief mates on the other.*

There is another little item about Gamming which must not be forgotten here. All professions have their own little peculiarities of detail; so has the whale fishery. In a pirate, man-of-war, or slave ship, when the captain is rowed anywhere in his boat, he always sits in the stern sheets on a comfortable, sometimes cushioned seat there, and often steers himself with a pretty little milliner's tiller decorated with gay cords and ribbons. But the whale-boat has no seat astern, no sofa of that sort whatever, and no tiller at all. High times indeed, if whaling captains were wheeled about the water on castors like gouty old aldermen in patent chairs. And as for a tiller, the whale-boat never admits of any such effeminacy; and therefore as in gamming a complete boat's crew must leave the ship, and hence as the boat steerer or harpooneer is of the number, that subordinate is the steersman upon the occasion, and the captain, having no place to sit in, is pulled off to his visit all standing like a pine tree. And often you will notice that being conscious of the eyes of the whole visible world resting on him from the sides of the two ships, this standing captain is all alive to the importance of sustaining his dignity by maintaining his legs. Nor is this any very easy matter; for in his rear is the immense projecting steering oar hitting him now and then in the small of his back, the after-oar reciprocating by rapping his knees in front. He is thus completely wedged before and behind, and can only expand himself sideways by settling down on his stretched legs; but a sudden, violent pitch of the boat will often go far to topple him, because length of foundation is nothing without corresponding breadth. Merely make a spread angle of two poles, and you cannot stand them up. Then, again, it would never do in plain sight of the world's riveted eyes, it would never do, I say, for this straddling captain to be seen steadying himself the slightest particle by catching hold of anything with his hands; indeed, as token of his entire, buoyant self-command, he generally carries his hands in his trowsers' pockets; but perhaps being generally very large, heavy hands, he carries them there for ballast. Nevertheless there have occurred instances, well authenticated ones too, where the captain has been known for an uncommonly critical moment or two, in a sudden squall say – to seize hold of the nearest oarsman's hair, and hold on there like grim death.

54

THE TOWN-HO'S STORY

(As told at the Golden Inn.)

THE Cape of Good Hope, and all the watery region round about there, is much like some noted four corners of a great highway, where you meet more travellers than in any other part.

It was not very long after speaking the Goney that another homeward-bound whaleman, the Town-Ho,* was encountered. She was manned almost wholly by Polynesians. In the short gam that ensued she gave us strong news of Moby Dick. To some the general interest in the White Whale was now wildly heightened by a circumstance of the Town-Ho's story, which seemed obscurely to involve with the whale a certain wondrous, inverted visitation of one of those so called judgments of God which at times are said to overtake some men. This latter circumstance, with its own particular accompaniments, forming what may be called the secret part of the tragedy about to be narrated, never reached the ears of Captain Ahab or his mates. For that secret part of the story was unknown to the captain of the Town-Ho himself. It was the private property of three confederate white seamen of that ship, one of whom, it seems, communicated it to Tashtego with Romish injunctions of secresy, but the following night Tashtego rambled in his sleep, and revealed so much of it in that way, that when he was awakened he could not well withhold the rest. Nevertheless, so potent an influence did this thing have on those seamen in the Pequod who came to the full knowledge of it, and by such a strange delicacy, to call it so, were they governed in this matter, that they

*The ancient whale-cry upon first sighting a whale from the masthead, still used by whalemen in hunting the famous Gallipagos terrapin.

kept the secret among themselves so that it never transpired abaft the Pequod's main-mast. Interweaving in its proper place this darker thread with the story as publicly narrated on the ship, the whole of this strange affair I now proceed to put on lasting record.

For my humor's sake, I shall preserve the style in which I once narrated it at Lima, to a lounging circle of my Spanish friends, one saint's eve, smoking upon the thick-gilt tiled piazza of the Golden Inn. Of those fine cavaliers, the young Dons, Pedro and Sebastian, were on the closer terms with me; and hence the interluding questions they occasionally put, and which are duly answered at the time.

'Some two years prior to my first learning the events which I am about rehearsing to you, gentlemen, the Town-Ho, Sperm Whaler of Nantucket, was cruising in your Pacific here, not very many days' sail westward from the eaves of this good Golden Inn. She was somewhere to the northward of the Line. One morning upon handling the pumps, according to daily usage, it was observed that she made more water in her hold than common. They supposed a sword-fish had stabbed her, gentlemen. But the captain, having some unusual reason for believing that rare good luck awaited him in those latitudes; and therefore being very averse to quit them, and the leak not being then considered at all dangerous, though, indeed, they could not find it after searching the hold as low down as was possible in rather heavy weather, the ship still continued her cruisings, the mariners working at the pumps at wide and easy intervals; but no good luck came; more days went by, and not only was the leak yet undiscovered, but it sensibly increased. So much so, that now taking some alarm, the captain, making all sail, stood away for the nearest harbor among the islands, there to have his hull hove out and repaired.

'Though no small passage was before her, yet, if the commonest chance favored, he did not at all fear that his ship would founder by the way, because his pumps were of the best, and being periodically relieved at them, those six-and-thirty men of his could easily keep the ship free; never mind if the leak should double on her. In truth, well nigh the whole of this passage being attended by very prosperous breezes, the Town-Ho had all but certainly arrived in perfect safety at her port without the occurrence of the least fatality, had it not been for the brutal overbearing of Radney, the mate, a Vineyarder, and the bitterly provoked vengeance of Steelkilt, a Lakeman and desperado from Buffalo.'

'Lakeman! – Buffalo! Pray, what is a Lakeman, and where is Buffalo?' said Don Sebastian, rising in his swinging mat of grass.

'On the eastern shore of our Lake Erie, Don; but – I crave your courtesy – may be, you shall soon hear further of all that. Now, gentlemen, in square-sail brigs and three-masted ship, well nigh as large and stout as any that ever sailed out of your old Callao to far Manilla; this Lakeman, in the land-locked heart of our America, had yet been nurtured by all those agrarian freebooting impressions popularly connected with the open ocean. For in their interflowing aggregate, those grand fresh-water seas of ours, – Erie, and Ontario, and Huron, and Superior, and Michigan, – possess an ocean-like expansiveness, with many of the ocean's noblest traits; with many of its rimmed varieties of races and of climes. They contain round archipelagoes of romantic isles, even as the Polynesian waters do; in large part, are shored by two great contrasting nations, as the Atlantic is; they furnish long maritime approaches to our numerous territorial colonies from the East, dotted all round their banks; here and there are frowned upon by batteries, and by the goat-like craggy guns of lofty Mackinaw; they have heard the fleet thunderings of naval victories; at intervals, they yield their beaches to wild barbarians, whose red painted faces flash from out their peltry wigwams; for leagues and leagues are flanked by ancient and unentered forests, where the gaunt pines stand like serried lines of kings in Gothic genealogies; those same woods harboring wild Afric beasts of prey, and silken creatures whose exported furs give robes to Tartar Emperors; they mirror the paved capitals of Buffalo and Cleveland, as well as Winnebago villages; they float alike the full-rigged merchant ship, the armed cruiser of the State, the steamer, and the beech canoe; they are swept by Borean and dismasting blasts as direful as any that lash the salted wave; they know what shipwrecks are, for out of sight of land, however inland, they have drowned full many a midnight ship with all its shrieking crew.

'Thus, gentlemen, though an inlander, Steelkilt was wild-ocean born, and wild-ocean nurtured; as much of an audacious mariner as any. And for Radney, though in his infancy he may have laid him down on the lone Nantucket beach, to nurse at his maternal sea; though in after life he had long followed our austere Atlantic and your contemplative Pacific; yet was he quite as vengeful and full of social quarrel as the backwoods seamen, fresh from the latitudes of buck-horn handled Bowie-knives. Yet was this Nantucketer a man with some good-hearted traits; and this Lakeman, a mariner, who though a sort of devil indeed, might yet by inflexible firmness, only tempered by that common decency of human recognition which is the meanest slave's right; thus treated, this Steelkilt had long been retained harmless and docile. At all events, he had proved so thus far; but Radney was doomed and made mad, and Steelkilt – but, gentlemen, you shall hear.

'It was not more than a day or two at the furthest after pointing her prow for her island haven, that the Town-Ho's leak seemed again increasing, but only so as to require an hour or more at the pumps every day. You must know that in a settled and civilized ocean like our Atlantic, for example, some skippers think little of pumping their whole way across it; though of a still, sleepy night, should the officer of the deck happen to forget his duty in that respect, the probability would be that he and his shipmates would never again remember it, on account of all hands gently subsiding to the bottom. Nor in the solitary and savage seas far from you to the westward, gentlemen, is it altogether unusual for ships to keep clanging at their pump-handles in full chorus even for a voyage of considerable length; that is, if it lie along a tolerably accessible coast, or if any other reasonable retreat is afforded them. It is only when a leaky vessel is in some very out of the way part of those waters, some really landless latitude, that her captain begins to feel a little anxious.

'Much this way had it been with the Town-Ho; so when her leak was found gaining once more, there was in truth some small concern manifested by several of her company; especially by Radney the mate. He commanded the upper sails to be well hoisted, sheeted home anew, and every way expanded to the breeze. Now this Radney, I suppose, was as little of a coward, and as little inclined to any sort of nervous apprehensiveness touching his own person as any fearless, unthinking creature on land or on sea that you can conveniently imagine, gentlemen. Therefore when he betrayed this solicitude about the safety of the ship, some of the seamen declared that it was only on account of his being a part owner in her. So when they were working that evening at the pumps, there was on this head no small gamesomeness slily going on among them, as they stood with their feet continually overflowed by the rippling clear water; clear as any mountain spring, gentlemen – that bubbling from the pumps ran across the deck, and poured itself out in steady spouts at the lee scupper-holes.

'Now, as you well know, it is not seldom the case in this conventional world of ours – watery or otherwise; that when a person placed in command over his fellow-men finds one of them to be very significantly his superior in general pride of manhood, straightway against that man he conceives an unconquerable dislike and bitterness; and if he have a chance he will pull down and pulverise that subaltern's tower, and make a little heap of dust of it. Be this conceit of mine as it may, gentlemen, at all events Steelkilt was a tall and noble animal with a head like a Roman, and a flowing golden beard like the tasseled housings of your last viceroy's snorting charger; and a brain, and a heart, and a soul in him, gentlemen, which had made Steelkilt Charlemagne, had he been born son to Charlemagne's father. But Radney, the mate, was ugly as a mule; yet as hardy, as stubborn, as malicious. He did not love Steelkilt, and Steelkilt knew it.

'Espying the mate drawing near as he was toiling at the pump with the rest, the Lakeman affected not to notice him, but unawed, went on with his gay banterings.

'"Aye, aye, my merry lads, it's a lively leak this; hold a cannikin, one of ye, and let's have a taste. By the Lord, it's worth bottling! I tell ye what, men, old Rad's investment must go for it! he had best cut away his part of the hull and tow it home. The fact is, boys, that sword-fish only began the job; he's come back again with a gang of ship-carpenters, saw-fish, and file-fish, and what not; and the whole posse of 'em are now hard at work cutting and slashing at the bottom; making improvements, I suppose. If old Rad were here now, I'd tell him to jump overboard and scatter 'em. They're playing the devil with his estate, I can tell him. But he's a simple old soul, – Rad, and a beauty too. Boys, they say the rest of his property is invested in looking-glasses. I wonder if he'd give a poor devil like me the model of his nose."

'"Damn your eyes! what's that pump stopping for?" roared Radney, pretending not to have heard the sailor's talk. "Thunder away at it!"

'"Aye, aye, sir," said Steelkilt, merry as a cricket. "Lively, boys, lively, now!" And with that the pump clanged like fifty fire-engines; the men tossed their hats off to it, and ere long that peculiar gasping of the lungs was heard which denotes the fullest tension of life's utmost energies.

'Quitting the pump at last, with the rest of his band, the Lakeman went forward all panting, and sat himself down on the windlass; his face fiery red, his eyes bloodshot, and wiping the profuse sweat from his brow. Now what cozening fiend it was, gentlemen, that possessed Radney to meddle with such a man in that corporeally exasperated state, I know not; but so it happened. Intolerably striding along the deck, the mate commanded him to get a broom and sweep down the planks, and also a shovel, and remove some offensive matters consequent upon allowing a pig to run at large.

'Now, gentlemen, sweeping a ship's deck at sea is a piece of household work which in all times but raging gales is regularly attended to every evening; it has been known to be done in the case of ships actually foundering at the time. Such, gentlemen, is the inflexibility of sea-usages and the instinctive love of neatness in seamen; some of whom would not willingly drown without first washing their faces. But in all vessels this broom business is the prescriptive province of the boys, if boys there be aboard. Besides, it was the stronger men in the Town-Ho that had been divided into gangs, taking turns at the pumps; and being the most athletic seaman of them all, Steelkilt had been regularly assigned captain of one of the gangs; consequently he should have been freed from any trivial business not connected with truly nautical duties, such being the case with his comrades. I mention all these particulars so that you may understand exactly how this affair stood between the two men.

'But there was more than this: the order about the shovel was almost as plainly meant to sting and insult Steelkilt, as though Radney had spat in his face. Any man who has gone sailor in a whale-ship will understand this; and all this and doubtless much more, the Lakeman fully comprehended when the mate uttered his command. But as he sat still for a moment, and as he steadfastly looked into the mate's malignant eye and perceived the stacks of powder-casks heaped up in him and the slow-match silently burning along towards them; as he instinctively saw all this, that strange forbearance and unwillingness to stir up the deeper passionateness in any already ireful being – a repugnance most felt, when felt at all, by really valiant men even when aggrieved – this nameless phantom feeling, gentlemen, stole over Steelkilt.

'Therefore, in his ordinary tone, only a little broken by the bodily exhaustion he was temporarily in, he answered him saying that sweeping the deck was not his business, and he would not do it. And then, without at all alluding to the shovel, he pointed to three lads as the customary sweepers; who, not being billeted at the pumps, had done little or nothing all day. To this, Radney replied with an oath, in a most domineering and outrageous manner unconditionally reiterating his command; meanwhile advancing upon the still seated Lakeman, with an uplifted cooper's club hammer which he had snatched from a cask near by.

'Heated and irritated as he was by his spasmodic toil at the pumps, for all his first nameless feeling of forbearance the sweating Steelkilt could but ill brook this bearing in the mate; but somehow still smothering the conflagration within him, without speaking he remained doggedly rooted to his seat, till at last the incensed Radney shook the hammer within a few inches of his face, furiously commanding him to do his bidding.

'Steelkilt rose, and slowly retreating round the windlass, steadily followed by the mate with his menacing hammer, deliberately repeated his intention not to obey. Seeing, however, that his forbearance had not the slightest effect, by an awful and unspeakable intimation with his twisted hand he warned off the foolish and infatuated man; but it was to no purpose. And in this way the two went once slowly round the windlass; when, resolved at last no longer to retreat, bethinking him that he had now forborne as much as comported with his humor, the Lakeman paused on the hatches and thus spoke to the officer:

'"Mr Radney, I will not obey you. Take that hammer away, or look to yourself." But the predestinated mate coming still closer to him, where the Lakeman stood fixed, now shook the heavy hammer within an inch of his teeth; meanwhile repeating a string of insufferable maledictions. Retreating not the thousandth part of an inch; stabbing him in the eye with the unflinching poniard of his glance, Steelkilt, clenching his right hand behind him and creepingly drawing it back, told his persecutor that if the hammer but grazed his cheek he (Steelkilt) would murder him. But, gentlemen, the fool had been branded for the slaughter by the gods. Immediately the hammer touched the cheek; the next instant the lower jaw of the mate was stove in his head; he fell on the hatch spouting blood like a whale.

'Ere the cry could go aft Steelkilt was shaking one of the

backstays leading far aloft to where two of his comrades were standing their mast-heads. They were both Canallers.'

'Canallers!' cried Don Pedro. 'We have seen many whale-ships in our harbors, but never heard of your Canallers. Pardon: who and what are they?'

'Canallers, Don, are the boatmen belonging to our grand Erie Canal. You must have heard of it.'

'Nay, Senor; hereabouts in this dull, warm, most lazy, and hereditary land, we know but little of your vigorous North.'

'Aye? Well then, Don, refill my cup. Your chicha's very fine; and ere proceeding further I will tell ye what our Canallers are; for such information may throw side-light upon my story.

'For three hundred and sixty miles, gentlemen, through the entire breadth of the state of New York; through numerous populous cities and most thriving villages; through long, dismal, uninhabited swamps, and affluent, cultivated fields, unrivalled for fertility; by billiard-room and bar-room; through the holy-of-holies of great forests; on Roman arches over Indian rivers; through sun and shade; by happy hearts or broken; through all the wide contrasting scenery of those noble Mohawk counties; and especially, by rows of snow-white chapels, whose spires stand almost like mile-stones, flows one continual stream of Venetianly corrupt and often lawless life. There's your true Ashantee, gentlemen; there howl your pagans; where you ever find them, next door to you; under the long-flung shadow, and the snug patronizing lee of churches. For by some curious fatality, as it is often noted of your metropolitan freebooters that they ever encamp around the halls of justice, so sinners, gentlemen, most abound in holiest vicinities.'

'Is that a friar passing?' said Don Pedro, looking downwards into the crowded plaza, with humorous concern.

'Well for our northern friend, Dame Isabella's Inquisition wanes in Lima,' laughed Don Sebastian. 'Proceed, Senor.'

'A moment! Pardon!' cried another of the company.

'In the name of all us Limeese, I but desire to express to you, sir sailor, that we have by no means overlooked your delicacy in not substituting present Lima for distant Venice in your corrupt comparison. Oh! do not bow and look surprised; you know the proverb all along this coast – "Corrupt as Lima." It but bears out your saying, too; churches more plentiful than billiard-tables, and for ever open – and "Corrupt as Lima." So, too, Venice; I have been there; the holy city of the blessed evangelist, St Mark! – St Dominic, purge it! Your cup! Thanks: here I refill; now, you pour out again.'

'Freely depicted in his own vocation, gentlemen, the Canaller would make a fine dramatic hero, so abundantly and picturesquely wicked is he. Like Mark Antony, for days and days along his green-turfed, flowery Nile, he indolently floats, openly toying with his red-cheeked Cleopatra, ripening his apricot thigh upon the sunny deck. But ashore, all this effeminacy is dashed. The brigandish guise which the Canaller so proudly sports; his slouched and gaily-ribboned hat betoken his grand features. A terror to the smiling innocence of the villages through which he floats; his swart visage and bold swagger are not unshunned in cities. Once a vagabond on his own canal, I have received good turns from one of these Canallers; I thank him heartily; would fain be not ungrateful; but it is often one of the prime redeeming qualities of your man of violence, that at times he has as stiff an arm to back a poor stranger in a strait, as to plunder a wealthy one. In sum, gentlemen, what the wildness of this canal life is, is emphatically evinced by this; that our wild whale-fishery contains so many of its most finished graduates, and that scarce any race of mankind, except Sydney men, are so much distrusted by our whaling captains. Nor does it at all diminish the curiousness of this matter, that to many thousands of our rural boys and young men born along its line, the probationary life of the Grand Canal furnishes the sole transition between quietly reaping in a Christian corn-field, and recklessly ploughing the waters of the most barbaric seas.'

'I see! I see!' impetuously exlaimed Don Pedro, spilling his chicha upon his silvery ruffles. 'No need to travel! The world's one Lima. I had thought, now, that at your temperate North the generations were cold and holy as the hills. – But the story.'

'I left off, gentlemen, where the Lakeman shook the backstay. Hardly had he done so, when he was surrounded by the three junior mates and the four harpooneers, who all crowded him to the deck. But sliding down the ropes like baleful comets, the two Canallers rushed into the uproar, and sought to drag their man out of it towards the forecastle. Others of the sailors joined with them in this attempt, and a twisted turmoil ensued; while standing out of harm's way, the valiant captain danced up and down with a whale-pike, calling upon his officers to manhandle that atrocious scoundrel, and smoke him along to the quarter-deck. At intervals, he ran close up to the revolving border of the confusion, and prying into the heart of it with his pike, sought to prick out the object of his resentment. But Steelkilt and his desperadoes were too much for them all; they succeeded in gaining the forecastle deck, where, hastily slewing about three or four large casks in a line with the windlass, these sea-Parisians entrenched themselves behind the barricade.'

'"Come out of that, ye pirates!" roared the captain, now menacing them with a pistol in each hand, just brought to him by the steward. "Come out of that, ye cut-throats!"

'Steelkilt leaped on the barricade, and striding up and down there, defied the worst the pistols could do; but gave the captain to understand distinctly, that his (Steelkilt's) death would be the signal for a murderous mutiny on the part of all hands. Fearing in his heart lest this might prove but too true, the captain a little desisted, but still commanded the insurgents instantly to return to their duty.

'"Will you promise not to touch us, if we do?" demanded their ringleader.

'"Turn to! turn to! – I make no promise; – to your duty! Do you want to sink the ship, by knocking off at a time like this? Turn to!" and he once more raised a pistol.

'"Sink the ship?" cried Steelkilt. "Aye, let her sink. Not a man of us turns to, unless you swear not to raise a rope-yarn against us. What say ye, men?" turning to his comrades. A fierce cheer was their response.

'The Lakeman now patrolled the barricade, all the while keeping his eye on the Captain, and jerking out such sentences as these: – "It's not our fault; we didn't want it; I told him to take his hammer away; it was boys' business; he might have known me before this; I told him not to prick the buffalo; I believe I have broken a finger here against his cursed jaw; ain't those mincing knives down in the forecastle there, men? look to those handspikes, my hearties. Captain, by God, look to yourself; say the word; don't be a fool; forget it all; we are ready to turn to; treat us decently, and we're your men; but we won't be flogged."

'"Turn to! I make no promises, turn to, I say!"

'"Look ye, now," cried the Lakeman, flinging out his arm towards him, "there are a few of us here (and I am one of them) who have shipped for the cruise, d'ye see; now as you well know, sir, we can claim our discharge as soon as the anchor is down; so we don't want a row; it's not our interest; we want to be peaceable; we are ready to work, but we won't be flogged."

'"Turn to!" roared the Captain.

'Steelkilt glanced round him a moment, and then said: – "I tell you what it is now, Captain, rather than kill ye, and be hung for such a shabby rascal, we won't lift a hand against ye unless ye attack us; but till you say the word about not flogging us, we don't do a hand's turn."

'"Down into the forecastle then, down with ye, I'll keep ye there till ye're sick of it. Down ye go."

'"Shall we?" cried the ringleader to his men. Most of them were against it; but at length, in obedience to Steelkilt, they preceded him down into their dark den, growlingly disappearing, like bears into a cave.

'As the Lakeman's bare head was just level with the planks, the Captain and his posse leaped the barricade, and rapidly drawing over the slide of the scuttle, planted their group of hands upon it, and loudly called for the steward to bring the heavy brass padlock belonging to the companion-way. Then opening the slide a little, the Captain whispered something down the crack, closed it, and turned the key upon them – ten in number – leaving on deck some twenty or more, who thus far had remained neutral.

'All night a wide-awake watch was kept by all the officers, forward and aft, especially about the forecastle scuttle and fore hatchway; at which last place it was feared the insurgents might emerge, after breaking through the bulkhead below. But the hours of darkness passed in peace; the men who still remained at their duty toiling hard at the pumps, whose clinking and clanking at intervals through the dreary night dismally resounded through the ship.

'At sunrise the Captain went forward, and knocking on the deck, summoned the prisoners to work; but with a yell they refused. Water was then lowered down to them, and a couple of handfuls of biscuit were tossed after it; when again turning the key upon them and pocketing it, the Captain returned to the quarter-deck. Twice every day for three days this was repeated; but on the fourth morning a confused wrangling, and then a scuffling was heard, as the customary summons was delivered; and suddenly four men burst up from the forecastle, saying they were ready to turn to. The fetid closeness of the air, and a famishing diet, united perhaps to some fears of ultimate retribution, had constrained them to surrender at discretion. Emboldened by this, the Captain reiterated his demand to the rest, but Steelkilt shouted up to him a terrific hint to stop his babbling and betake himself where he belonged. On the fifth morning three others of the mutineers bolted up into the air from the desperate arms below that sought to restrain them. Only three were left.

'"Better turn to, now?" said the Captain with a heartless jeer.

'"Shut us up again, will ye!" cried Steelkilt.

'"Oh! certainly," said the Captain, and the key clicked.

'It was at this point, gentlemen, that enraged by the defection of seven of his former associates, and stung by the mocking voice that had last hailed him, and maddened by his long entombment in a place as black as the bowels of despair; it was then that Steelkilt proposed to the two Canallers, thus far apparently of one mind with him, to burst out of their hole at the next summoning of the garrison; and armed with their keen mincing knives (long, crescentic, heavy implements with a handle at each end) run amuck from the bowsprit to the taffrail; and if by any devilishness of desperation possible, seize the ship. For himself, he would do this, he said, whether they joined him or not. That was the last night he should spend in that den. But the scheme met with no opposition on the part of the other two; they swore they were ready for that, or for any other mad thing, for anything in short but a surrender. And what was more, they each insisted upon being the first man on deck, when the time to make the rush should come. But to this their leader as fiercely objected, reserving that priority for himself; particularly as his two comrades would not yield, the one to the other, in the matter; and both of them could not be first, for the ladder would but admit one man at a time. And here, gentlemen, the foul play of these miscreants must come out.

'Upon hearing the frantic project of their leader, each in his own separate soul had suddenly lighted, it would seem, upon the same piece of treachery, namely: to be foremost in breaking out, in order to be the first of the three, though the last of the ten, to surrender; and thereby secure whatever small chance of pardon such conduct might merit. But when Steelkilt made known his determination still to lead them to the last, they in some way, by some subtle chemistry of villany, mixed their before secret treacheries together; and when their leader fell into a doze, verbally opened their souls to each other in three sentences; and bound the sleeper with cords, and gagged him with cords; and shrieked out for the Captain at midnight.

'Thinking murder at hand, and smelling in the dark for the blood, he and all his armed mates and harpooneers rushed for the forecastle. In a few minutes the scuttle was opened, and, bound hand and foot, the still struggling ringleader was shoved up into the air by his perfidious allies, who at once claimed the honor of securing a man who had been fully ripe for murder. But all three were collared, and dragged along the deck like dead cattle; and, side by side, were seized up into the mizen rigging, like three quarters of meat, and there they hung till morning. "Damn ye," cried the Captain, pacing to and fro before them, "the vultures would not touch ye, ye villains!"

'At sunrise he summoned all hands; and separating those who had rebelled from those who had taken no part in the mutiny, he told the former that he had a good mind to flog them all round – thought, upon the whole, he would do so – he ought to – justice demanded it; but for the present, considering their timely surrender, he would let them go with a reprimand, which he accordingly administered in the vernacular.

'"But as for you, ye carrion rogues," turning to the three men in the rigging – "for you, I mean to mince ye up for the try-pots;" and, seizing a rope, he applied it with all his might to the backs of the two traitors, till they yelled no more, but lifelessly hung their heads sideways, as the two crucified thieves are drawn.

'"My wrist is sprained with ye!" he cried, at last; "but there is still rope enough left for you, my fine bantam, that wouldn't give up. Take that gag from his mouth, and let us hear what he can say for himself."

'For a moment the exhausted mutineer made a tremulous motion of his cramped jaws, and then painfully twisting round his head, said in a sort of hiss, "What I say is this – and mind it well – if you flog me, I murder you!"

'"Say ye so? then see how ye frighten me" – and the Captain drew off with the rope to strike.

'"Best not," hissed the Lakeman.

'"But I must," – and the rope was once more drawn back for the stroke.

'Steelkilt here hissed out something, inaudible to all but

the Captain; who, to the amazement of all hands, started back, paced the deck rapidly two or three times, and then suddenly throwing down his rope, said, "I won't do it – let him go – cut him down: d'ye hear?"

'But as the junior mates were hurrying to execute the order, a pale man, with a bandaged head, arrested them – Radney the chief mate. Ever since the blow, he had lain in his berth; but that morning, hearing the tumult on the deck, he had crept out, and thus far had watched the whole scene. Such was the state of his mouth, that he could hardly speak; but mumbling something about *his* being willing and able to do what the captain dared not attempt, he snatched the rope and advanced to his pinioned foe.

'"You are a coward!" hissed the Lakeman.

'"So I am, but take that." The mate was in the very act of striking, when another hiss stayed his uplifted arm. He paused: and then pausing no more, made good his word, spite of Steelkilt's threat, whatever that might have been. The three men were then cut down, all hands were turned to, and, sullenly worked by the moody seamen, the iron pumps clanged as before.

'Just after dark that day, when one watch had retired below, a clamor was heard in the forecastle; and the two trembling traitors running up, besieged the cabin door, saying they durst not consort with the crew. Entreaties, cuffs, and kicks could not drive them back, so at their own instance they were put down in the ship's run for salvation. Still, no sign of mutiny reappeared among the rest. On the contrary, it seemed, that mainly at Steelkilt's instigation, they had resolved to maintain the strictest peacefulness, obey all orders to the last, and, when the ship reached port, desert her in a body. But in order to insure the speediest end to the voyage, they all agreed to another thing – namely, not to sing out for whales, in case any should be discovered. For, spite of her leak, and spite of all her other perils, the Town-Ho still maintained her mast-heads, and her captain was just as willing to lower for a fish that moment, as on the day his craft first struck the cruising ground; and Radney the mate was quite as ready to change his berth for a boat, and with his bandaged mouth seek to gag in death the vital jaw of the whale.

'But though the Lakeman had induced the seamen to adopt this sort of passiveness in their conduct, he kept his own counsel (at least till all was over) concerning his own proper and private revenge upon the man who had stung him in the ventricles of his heart. He was in Radney the chief mate's watch; and as if the infatuated man sought to run more than half way to meet his doom, after the scene at the rigging, he insisted, against the express counsel of the captain, upon resuming the head of his watch at night. Upon this, and one or two other circumstances, Steelkilt systematically built the plan of his revenge.

'During the night, Radney had an unseamanlike way of sitting on the bulwarks of the quarter-deck, and leaning his arm upon the gunwale of the boat which was hoisted up there, a little above the ship's side. In this attitude, it was well known, he sometimes dozed. There was a considerable vacancy between the boat and the ship, and down between this was the sea. Steelkilt calculated his time, and found that his next trick at the helm would come round at two o'clock, in the morning of the third day from that in which he had been betrayed. At his leisure, he employed the interval in braiding something very carefully in his watches below.

'"What are you making there?" said a shipmate.

'"What do you think? what does it look like?"

'"Like a lanyard for your bag; but it's an odd one, seems to me."

'"Yes, rather oddish," said the Lakeman, holding it at arm's length before him; "but I think it will answer. Shipmate, I haven't enough twine, – have you any?"

'But there was none in the forecastle.

'"Then I must get some from old Rad;" and he rose to go aft.

'"You don't mean to go a begging to *him*!" said a sailor.

'"Why not? Do you think he won't do me a turn, when it's to help himself in the end, shipmate?" and going to the mate, he looked at him quietly, and asked him for some twine to mend his hammock. It was given him – neither twine nor lanyard were seen again; but the next night an iron ball, closely netted, partly rolled from the pocket of the Lakeman's monkey jacket, as he was tucking the coat into his hammock for a pillow. Twenty-four hours after, his trick at the silent helm – nigh to the man who was apt to doze over the grave always ready dug to the seaman's hand – that fatal hour was then to come; and in the fore-ordaining soul of Steelkilt, the mate was already stark and stretched as a corpse, with his forehead crushed in.

'But, gentlemen, a fool saved the would-be murderer from the bloody deed he had planned. Yet complete revenge he had, and without being the avenger. For by a mysterious fatality, Heaven itself seemed to step in to take out of his hands into its own the damning thing he would have done.

'It was just between daybreak and sunrise of the morning of the second day, when they were washing down the decks, that a stupid Teneriffe man, drawing water in the main-chains, all at once shouted out, "There she rolls! there she rolls! Jesu! what a whale!" It was Moby Dick.'

'Moby Dick!' cried Don Sebastian; 'St Dominic! Sir sailor, but do whales have christenings? Whom call you Moby Dick?'

'A very white, and famous, and most deadly immortal monster, Don; – but that would be too long a story.'

'How how?' cried all the young Spaniards, crowding.

'Nay, Dons, Dons – nay, nay! I cannot rehearse that now. Let me get more into the air, Sirs.'

'The chicha; the chicha;' cried Don Pedro; 'our vigorous friend looks faint; – fill up his empty glass!'

'No need, gentlemen; one moment, and I proceed. – Now, gentlemen, so suddenly perceiving the snowy whale within fifty yards of the ship – forgetful of the compact among the crew – in the excitement of the moment, the Teneriffe man had instinctively and involuntarily lifted his voice for the monster, though for some little time past it had been plainly beheld from the three sullen mast-heads. All was now a phrensy. "The White Whale – the White Whale!" was the cry from captain, mates, and harpooneers, who, undeterred by fearful rumors, were all anxious to capture so famous and precious a fish; while the dogged crew eyed askance, and with curses, the appalling beauty of the vast milky mass, that lit up by a horizontal spangling sun, shifted and glistened like a living opal in the blue morning sea. Gentlemen, a strange fatality pervades the whole career of these events, as if verily mapped out before the world itself was charted. The mutineer was the bowsman of the mate, and when fast to a fish, it was his duty to sit next him, while Radney stood up with his lance in the prow, and haul in or slacken the line, at the word of command. Moreover, when the four boats were lowered, the mate's got the start; and none howled more fiercely with delight than did Steelkilt, as he strained at his oar. After a stiff pull, their harpooneer got fast, and, spear in hand, Radney sprang to the bow. He was always a furious man, it seems, in a boat. And now his bandaged cry was, to beach him on the whale's topmost back. Nothing loath, his bowsman hauled him up and up, through a blinding foam that blent two whitenesses together; till of a sudden the boat struck as against a sunken ledge, and keeling over, spilled out the standing mate. That instant, as he fell on the whale's slippery back, the boat righted, and was dashed aside by the swell, while Radney was tossed over into the sea, on the other flank of the whale. He struck out through the spray, and, for an instant, was dimly seen through that veil, wildly seeking to remove himself from the eye of Moby Dick. But the whale rushed round in a sudden maelstrom; seized the swimmer between his jaws; and rearing high up with him, plunged headlong again, and went down.

'Meantime, at the first tap of the boat's bottom, the Lakeman had slackened the line, so as to drop astern from the whirlpool; calmly looking on, he thought his own thoughts. But a sudden, terrific, downward jerking of the boat, quickly brought his knife to the line. He cut it; and the whale was free. But, at some distance, Moby Dick rose again, with some tatters of Radney's red woollen shirt, caught in the teeth that had destroyed him. All four boats gave chase again; but the whale eluded them, and finally wholly disappeared.

'In good time, the Town-Ho reached her port – a savage, solitary place – where no civilized creature resided. There, headed by the Lakeman, all but five or six of the foremastmen deliberately deserted among the palms; eventually, as it turned out, seizing a large double war-canoe of the savages, and setting sail for some other harbor.

'The ship's company being reduced to but a handful, the captain called upon the Islanders to assist him in the laborious business of heaving down the ship to stop the leak. But to such unresting vigilance over their dangerous allies was this small band of whites necessitated, both by night and by day, and so extreme was the hard work they underwent, that upon the vessel being ready again for sea, they were in such a weakened condition that the captain durst not put off with them in so heavy a vessel. After taking counsel with his officers, he anchored the ship as far off shore as possible; loaded and ran out his two cannon from the bows; stacked his muskets on the poop; and warning the Islanders not to approach the ship at their peril, took one man with him, and setting the sail of his best whaleboat, steered straight before the wind for Tahiti, five hundred miles distant, to procure a reinforcement to his crew.

'On the fourth day of the sail, a large canoe was descried, which seemed to have touched at a low isle of corals. He steered away from it; but the savage craft bore down on him; and soon the voice of Steelkilt hailed him to heave to, or he would run him under water. The captain presented a pistol. With one foot on each prow of the yoked war-canoes, the Lakeman laughed him to scorn; assuring him that if the pistol so much as clicked in the lock, he would bury him in bubbles and foam.

'"What do you want of me?" cried the captain.

'"Where are you bound? and for what are you bound?" demanded Steelkilt; "no lies."

'"I am bound to Tahiti for more men."

'"Very good. Let me board you a moment – I come in peace." With that he leaped from the canoe, swam to the boat; and climbing the gunwale, stood face to face with the captain.

'"Cross your arms, sir; throw back your head. Now, repeat after me. As soon as Steelkilt leaves me, I swear to beach this boat on yonder island, and remain there six days. If I do not, may lightning strike me!"

'"A pretty scholar," laughed the Lakeman. "Adios, Senor!" and leaping into the sea, he swam back to his comrades.

'Watching the boat till it was fairly beached, and drawn up to the roots of the cocoa-nut trees, Steelkilt made sail again, and in due time arrived at Tahiti, his own place of destination. There, luck befriended him; two ships were about to sail for France, and were providentially in want of precisely that number of men which the sailor headed. They embarked; and so for ever got the start of their former captain, had he been at all minded to work them legal retribution.

'Some ten days after the French ships sailed, the whale-boat arrived, and the captain was forced to enlist some of the more civilized Tahitians, who had been somewhat used to the sea. Chartering a small native schooner, he returned with them to his vessel; and finding all right there, again resumed his cruisings.

'Where Steelkilt now is, gentlemen, none know; but upon the island of Nantucket, the widow of Radney still turns to the sea which refuses to give up its dead; still in dreams sees the awful white whale that destroyed him.' * * *

'Are you through?' said Don Sebastian, quietly.

'I am, Don.'

'Then I entreat you, tell me if to the best of your own convictions, this your story is in substance really true? It is so passing wonderful! Did you get it from an unquestionable source? Bear with me if I seem to press.'

'Also bear with all of us, sir sailor; for we all join

in Don Sebastian's suit,' cried the company, with exceeding interest.

'Is there a copy of the Holy Evangelists in the Golden Inn, gentlemen?'

'Nay,' said Don Sebastian; 'but I know a worthy priest near by, who will quickly procure one for me. I go for it; but are you well advised? this may grow too serious.'

'Will you be so good as to bring the priest also, Don?'

'Though there are no Auto-da-Fés in Lima now,' said one of the company to another; 'I fear our sailor friend runs risk of the archiepiscopacy. Let us withdraw more out of the moonlight. I see no need of this.'

'Excuse me for running after you, Don Sebastian; but may I also beg that you will be particular in procuring the largest sized Evangelist you can.'

* * * * * * *

'This is the priest, he brings you the Evangelists,' said Don Sebastian, gravely, returning with a tall and solemn figure.

'Let me remove my hat. Now, venerable priest, further into the light, and hold the Holy Book before me that I may touch it.'

'So help me Heaven, and on my honor, the story I have told ye, gentlemen, is in substance and its great items, true. I know it to be true; it happened on this ball; I trod the ship; I knew the crew; I have seen and talked with Steelkilt since the death of Radney.'

55

OF THE MONSTROUS PICTURES OF WHALES

I SHALL ere long paint to you as well as one can without canvas, something like the true form of the whale as he actually appears to the eye of the whaleman when in his own absolute body the whale is moored alongside the whale-ship so that he can be fairly stepped upon there. It may be worth while, therefore, previously to advert to those curious imaginary portraits of him which even down to the present day confidently challenge the faith of the landsman. It is time to set the world right in this matter, by proving such pictures of the whale all wrong.

It may be that the primal source of all those pictorial delusions will be found among the oldest Hindoo, Egyptian, and Grecian sculptures. For ever since those inventive but unscrupulous times when on the marble panellings of temples, the pedestals of statues, and on shields, medallions, cups, and coins, the dolphin was drawn in scales of chain-armor like Saladin's, and a helmeted head like St George's; ever since then has some thing of the same sort of license prevailed, not only in most popular pictures of the whale, but in many scientific presentations of him.

Now, by all odds, the most ancient extant portrait any-ways purporting to be the whale's, is to be found in the famous cavern-pagoda of Elephanta, in India. The Brahmins maintain that in the almost endless sculptures of that immemorial pagoda, all the trades and pursuits, every conceivable avocation of man, were prefigured ages before any of them actually came into being. No wonder then, that in some sort our noble profession of whaling should have been there shadowed forth. The Hindoo whale referred to, occurs in a separate department of the wall, depicting the incarnation of Vishnu in the form of leviathan, learnedly known as the Matse Avatar. But though this sculpture is half man and half whale, so as only to give the tail of the latter, yet that small section of him is all wrong. It looks more like the tapering tail of an anaconda, than the broad palms of the true whale's majestic flukes.

But go to the old Galleries, and look now at a great Christian painter's portrait of this fish; for he succeeds no better than the antediluvian Hindoo. It is Guido's picture of Perseus rescuing Andromeda from the sea-monster or whale. Where did Guido get the model of such a strange creature as that? Nor does Hogarth, in painting the same scene in his own 'Perseus Descending,' make out one whit better. The huge corpulence of that Hogarthian monster undulates on the surface, scarcely drawing one inch of water. It has a sort of howdah on its back, and its distended tusked mouth into which the billows are rolling, might be taken for the Traitors' Gate leading from the Thames by water into the Tower. Then, there are the Prodromus whales of old Scotch Sibbald, and Jonah's whale, as depicted in the prints of old Bibles and the cuts of old primers. What shall be said of these? As for the book-binder's whale winding like a vine-stalk round the stock of a descending anchor – as stamped and gilded on the backs and title-pages of many books both old and new – that is a very picturesque but purely fabulous creature, imitated, I take it, from the like figures on antique vases. Though universally denominated a dolphin, I nevertheless call this book-binder's fish an attempt at a whale; because it was so intended when the device was first introduced. It was introduced by an old Italian publisher somewhere about the 15th century, during the Revival of Learning; and in those days, and even down to a comparatively late period, dolphins were popularly supposed to be a species of the Leviathan.

In the vignettes and other embellishments of some ancient books you will at times meet with very curious touches at the whale, where all manner of spouts, jets d'eau, hot springs and cold, Saratoga and Baden-Baden, come bubbling up from his unexhausted brain. In the title-page of the original edition of the 'Advancement of Learning' you will find some curious whales.

But quitting all these unprofessional attempts, let us glance at those pictures of leviathan purporting to be sober, scientific delineations, by those who know. In old Harris's collection of voyages there are some plates of whales extracted from a Dutch book of voyages, A.D. 1671, entitled 'A Whaling Voyage to Spitzbergen in the ship Jonas in the Whale, Peter Peterson of Friesland, master.' In one of those plates the whales, like great rafts of logs, are represented lying among ice-isles, with white bears running over their living backs. In another plate, the prodigious blunder is made of representing the whale with perpendicular flukes.

Then again, there is an imposing quarto, written by one Captain Colnett, a Post Captain in the English navy, entitled 'A Voyage round Cape Horn into the South Seas, for the purpose of extending the Spermaceti Whale Fisheries.' In this book is an outline purporting to be a 'Picture of a Physeter or Spermaceti whale, drawn by scale from one killed on the coast of Mexico, August, 1793, and hoisted on deck.' I doubt not the captain had this veracious picture taken for the benefit of his marines. To mention but one thing about it, let me say that it has an eye which applied, according to the accompanying scale, to a full grown sperm whale, would make the eye of that whale a bow-window some five feet long. Ah, my gallant captain, why did ye not give us Jonah looking out of that eye!

Nor are the most conscientious compilations of Natural History for the benefit of the young and tender, free from the same heinousness of mistake. Look at that popular work 'Goldsmith's Animated Nature.' In the abridged London edition of 1807, there are plates of an alleged 'whale' and a 'narwhale.' I do not wish to seem inelegant, but this unsightly whale looks much like an amputated sow; and, as for the narwhale, one glimpse at it is enough to amaze one, that in this nineteenth century such a hippogriff could be palmed for genuine upon any intelligent public of schoolboys.

Then, again, in 1825, Bernard Germain, Count de Lacépède, a great naturalist, published a scientific systemized whale book, wherein are several pictures of the different species of the Leviathan. All these are not only incorrect, but the picture of the Mysticetus or Greenland whale (that is to say, the Right whale), even Scoresby, a long experienced man as touching that species, declares not to have its counterpart in nature.

But the placing of the cap-sheaf to all this blundering business was reserved for the scientific Frederick Cuvier, brother to the famous Baron. In 1836 he published a

Natural History of Whales, in which he gives what he calls a picture of the Sperm Whale. Before showing that picture to any Nantucketer, you had best provide for your summary retreat from Nantucket. In a word, Frederick Cuvier's Sperm Whale is not a Sperm Whale, but a squash. Of course, he never had the benefit of a whaling voyage (such men seldom have), but whence he derived that picture, who can tell? Perhaps he got it as his scientific predecessor in the same field, Desmarest, got one of his authentic abortions; that is, from a Chinese drawing. And what sort of lively lads with the pencil those Chinese are, many queer cups and saucers inform us.

As for the sign-painters' whales seen in the streets hanging over the shops of oil-dealers, what shall be said of them? They are generally Richard III whales, with dromedary humps, and very savage; breakfasting on three or four sailor tarts, that is whaleboats full of mariners: their deformities floundering in seas of blood and blue paint.

But these manifold mistakes in depicting the whale are not so very surprising after all. Consider! Most of the scientific drawings have been taken from the stranded fish; and these are about as correct as a drawing of a wrecked ship, with broken back, would correctly represent the noble animal itself in all its undashed pride of hull and spars. Though elephants have stood for their full-lengths, the living Leviathan has never yet fairly floated himself for his portrait. The living whale, in his full majesty and significance, is only to be seen at sea in unfathomable waters; and afloat the vast bulk of him is out of sight, like a launched line-of-battle ship; and out of that element it is a thing eternally impossible for mortal man to hoist him bodily into the air, so as to preserve all his mighty swells and undulations. And, not to speak of the highly presumable difference of contour between a young sucking whale and a full-grown Platonian Leviathan; yet, even in the case of one of those young sucking whales hoisted to a ship's deck, such is then the outlandish, eel-like, limbered, varying shape of him, that his precise expression the devil himself could not catch.

But it may be fancied, that from the naked skeleton of the stranded whale, accurate hints may be derived touching his true form. Not at all. For it is one of the more curious things about this Leviathan, that his skeleton gives very little idea of his general shape. Though Jeremy Bentham's skeleton, which hangs for candelabra in the library of one of his executors, correctly conveys the idea of a burly-browed utilitarian old gentleman, with all Jeremy's other leading personal characteristics; yet nothing of this kind could be inferred from any leviathan's articulated bones. In fact, as the great Hunter says, the mere skeleton of the whale bears the same relation to the fully invested and padded animal as the insect does to the chrysalis that so roundingly envelopes it. This peculiarity is strikingly evinced in the head, as in some part of this book will be incidentally shown. It is also very curiously displayed in the side fin, the bones of which almost exactly answer to the bones of the human hand, minus only the thumb. This fin has four regular bone-fingers, the index, middle, ring, and little finger. But all these are permanently lodged in their fleshy covering, as the human fingers in an artificial covering. 'However recklessly the whale may sometimes serve us,' said humorous Stubb one day, 'he can never be truly said to handle us without mittens.'

For all these reasons, then, any way you may look at it, you must needs conclude that the great Leviathan is that one creature in the world which must remain unpainted to the last. True, one portrait may hit the mark much nearer than another, but none can hit it with any very considerable degree of exactness. So there is no earthly way of finding out precisely what the whale really looks like. And the only mode in which you can derive even a tolerable idea of his living contour, is by going a whaling yourself; but by so doing, you run no small risk of being eternally stove and sunk by him. Wherefore, it seems to me you had best not be too fastidious in your curiosity touching this Leviathan.

56

OF THE LESS ERRONEOUS PICTURES OF WHALES, AND THE TRUE PICTURES OF WHALING SCENES

In connexion with the monstrous pictures of whales, I am strongly tempted here to enter upon those still more monstrous stories of them which are to be found in certain books, both ancient and modern, especially in Pliny, Purchas, Hackluyt, Harris, Cuvier, &c. But I pass that matter by.

I know of only four published outlines of the great Sperm Whale; Colnett's, Huggins's, Frederick Cuvier's, and Beale's. In the previous chapter Colnett and Cuvier have been referred to. Huggins's is far better than theirs; but, by great odds, Beale's is the best. All Beale's drawings of this whale are good, excepting the middle figure in the picture of three whales in various attitudes, capping his second chapter. His frontispiece, boats attacking Sperm Whales, though no doubt calculated to excite the civil scepticism of some parlor men, is admirably correct and life-like in its general effect. Some of the Sperm Whale drawings in J. Ross Browne are pretty correct in contour; but they are wretchedly engraved. That is not his fault though.

Of the Right Whale, the best outline pictures are in Scoresby; but they are drawn on too small a scale to convey a desirable impression. He has but one picture of whaling scenes, and this is a sad deficiency, because it is by such pictures only, when at all well done, that you can derive anything like a truthful idea of the living whale as seen by his living hunters.

But, taken for all in all, by far the finest, though in some details not the most correct, presentations of whales and whaling scenes to be anywhere found, are two large French engravings, well executed, and taken from paintings by one Garnery. Respectively, they represent attacks on the Sperm and Right Whale. In the first engraving a noble Sperm

Whale is depicted in full majesty of might, just risen beneath the boat from the profundities of the ocean, and bearing high in the air upon his back the terrific wreck of the stoven planks. The prow of the boat is partially unbroken, and is drawn just balancing upon the monster's spine; and standing in that prow, for that one single incomputable flash of time, you behold an oarsman, half shrouded by the incensed boiling spout of the whale, and in the act of leaping, as if from a precipice. The action of the whole thing is wonderfully good and true. The half-emptied line-tub floats on the whitened sea; the wooden poles of the spilled harpoons obliquely bob in it; the heads of the swimming crew are scattered about the whale in contrasting expressions of affright; while in the black stormy distance the ship is bearing down upon the scene. Serious fault might be found with the anatomical details of this whale, but let that pass; since, for the life of me, I could not draw so good a one.

In the second engraving, the boat is in the act of drawing alongside the barnacled flank of a large running Right Whale, that rolls his black weedy bulk in the sea like some mossy rock-slide from the Patagonian cliffs. His jets are erect, full, and black like soot; so that from so abounding a smoke in the chimney, you would think there must be a brave supper cooking in the great bowels below. Sea fowls are pecking at the small crabs, shell-fish, and other sea candies and maccaroni, which the Right Whale sometimes carries on his pestilent back. And all the while the thick-lipped leviathan is rushing through the deep, leaving tons of tumultuous white curds in his wake, and causing the slight boat to rock in the swells like a skiff caught nigh the paddle-wheels of an ocean steamer. Thus, the foreground is all raging commotion; but behind, in admirable artistic contrast, is the glassy level of a sea becalmed, the drooping unstarched sails of the powerless ship, and the inert mass of a dead whale, a conquered fortress, with the flag of capture lazily hanging from the whale-pole inserted into his spout-hole.

Who Garnery the painter is, or was, I know not. But my life for it he was either practically conversant with his subject, or else marvellously tutored by some experienced whaleman. The French are the lads for painting action. Go and gaze upon all the paintings of Europe, and where will you find such a gallery of living and breathing commotion on canvas, as in that triumphal hall at Versailles; where the beholder fights his way, pell-mell, through the consecutive great battles of France; where every sword seems a flash of the Northern Lights, and the successive armed kings and Emperors dash by, like a charge of crowned centaurs? Not wholly unworthy of a place in that gallery, are these sea battle-pieces of Garnery.

The natural aptitude of the French for seizing the picturesqueness of things seems to be peculiarly evinced in what paintings and engravings they have of their whaling scenes. With not one tenth of England's experience in the fishery, and not the thousandth part of that of the Americans, they have nevertheless furnished both nations with the only finished sketches at all capable of conveying the real spirit of the whale hunt. For the most part, the English and American whale draughtsmen seem entirely content with presenting the mechanical outline of things, such as the vacant profile of the whale; which, so far as picturesqueness of effect is concerned, is about tantamount to sketching the profile of a pyramid. Even Scoresby, the justly renowned Right whaleman, after giving us a stiff full length of the Greenland whale, and three or four delicate miniatures of narwhales and porpoises, treats us to a series of classical engravings of boat hooks, chopping knives, and grapnels; and with the microscopic diligence of a Leuwenhoeck submits to the inspection of a shivering world ninety-six facsimiles of magnified Arctic snow crystals. I mean no disparagement to the excellent voyager (I honor him for a veteran), but in so important a matter it was certainly an oversight not to have procured for every crystal a sworn affidavit taken before a Greenland Justice of the Peace.

In addition to those fine engravings from Garnery, there

are two other French engravings worthy of note, by some one who subscribes himself 'H. Durand.' One of them, though not precisely adapted to our present purpose, nevertheless deserves mention on other accounts. It is a quiet noon-scene among the isles of the Pacific; a French whaler anchored, inshore, in a calm, and lazily taking water on board; the loosened sails of the ship, and the long leaves of the palms in the background, both drooping together in the breezeless air. The effect is very fine, when considered with reference to its presenting the hardy fishermen under one of their few aspects of oriental repose. The other engraving is quite a different affair: the ship hove-to upon the open sea, and in the very heart of the Leviathanic life, with a Right Whale alongside; the vessel (in the act of cutting-in) hove over to the monster as if to a quay; and a boat, hurriedly pushing off from this scene of activity, is about giving chase to whales in the distance. The harpoons and lances lie levelled for use; three oarsmen are just setting the mast in its hole; while from a sudden roll of the sea, the little craft stands half-erect out of the water, like a rearing horse. From the ship, the smoke of the torments of the boiling whale is going up like the smoke over a village of smithies; and to windward, a black cloud, rising up with earnest of squalls and rains, seems to quicken the activity of the excited seamen.

57

OF WHALES IN PAINT; IN TEETH; IN WOOD; IN SHEET-IRON; IN STONE; IN MOUNTAINS; IN STARS

On Tower-hill, as you go down to the London docks, you may have seen a crippled beggar (or *kedger*, as the sailors say) holding a painted board before him, representing the tragic scene in which he lost his leg. There are three whales and three boats; and one of the boats (presumed to contain the missing leg in all its original integrity) is being crunched by the jaws of the foremost whale. Any time these ten years, they tell me, has that man held up that picture, and exhibited that stump to an incredulous world. But the time of his justification has now come. His three whales are as good whales as were ever published in Wapping, at any rate; and his stump as unquestionable a stump as any you will find in the western clearings. But, though for ever mounted on that stump, never a stump-speech does the poor whaleman make; but, with downcast eyes, stands ruefully contemplating his own amputation.

Throughout the Pacific, and also in Nantucket, and New Bedford, and Sag Harbor, you will come across lively sketches of whales and whaling-scenes, graven by the fishermen themselves on Sperm Whale-teeth, or ladies' busks wrought out of the Right Whale-bone, and other like skrimshander articles, as the whalemen call the numerous little ingenious contrivances they elaborately carve out of the rough material, in their hours of ocean leisure. Some of them have little boxes of dentistical-looking implements, specially intended for the skrimshandering business. But, in general, they toil with their jack-knives alone; and, with that almost omnipotent tool of the sailor, they will turn you out anything you please, in the way of a mariner's fancy.

Long exile from Christendom and civilization inevitably restores a man to that condition in which God placed him, *i.e.* what is called savagery. Your true whale-hunter is as much a savage as an Iroquois. I myself am a savage, owning no allegiance but to the King of the Cannibals; and ready at any moment to rebel against him.

Now, one of the peculiar characteristics of the savage in his domestic hours, is his wonderful patience of industry. An ancient Hawaiian war-club or spear-paddle, in its full multiplicity and elaboration of carving, is as great a trophy of human perseverance as a Latin lexicon. For, with but a bit of broken sea-shell or a shark's tooth, that miraculous intricacy of wooden net-work has been achieved; and it has cost steady years of steady application.

As with the Hawaiian savage, so with the white sailor-savage. With the same marvellous patience, and with the same single shark's tooth, of his one poor jack-knife, he will carve you a bit of bone sculpture, not quite as workmanlike, but as close packed in its maziness of design, as the Greek savage, Achilles's shield; and full of barbaric spirit and suggestiveness, as the prints of that fine old Dutch savage, Albert Durer.

Wooden whales, or whales cut in profile out of the small dark slabs of the noble South Sea war-wood, are frequently met with in the forecastles of American whalers. Some of them are done with much accuracy.

At some gable-roofed country houses you will see brass whales hung by the tail for knockers to the road-side door. When the porter is sleepy, the anvil-headed whale would be best. But these knocking whales are seldom remarkable as faithful essays. On the spires of some old-fashioned churches you will see sheet-iron whales placed there for weather-cocks; but they are so elevated, and besides that are to all intents and purposes so labelled with *'Hands off!'* you cannot examine them closely enough to decide upon their merit.

In bony, ribby regions of the earth, where at the base of high broken cliffs masses of rock lie strewn in fantastic groupings upon the plain, you will often discover images of the petrified forms of the Leviathan partly merged in grass, which of a windy day breaks against them in a surf of green surges.

Then, again, in mountainous countries where the traveller is continually girdled by amphitheatrical heights; here and there from some lucky point of view you will catch passing glimpses of the profiles of whales defined along the undulating ridges. But you must be a thorough whaleman, to see these sights; and not only that, but if you wish to return to such a sight again, you must be sure and take the exact intersecting latitude and longitude of your first stand-point, else so chance-like are such observations of the hills, that your precise, previous stand-point would require a laborious re-discovery; like the Solomon islands, which still remain incognita, though once high-ruffed Mendanna trod them and old Figuera chronicled them.

Nor when expandingly lifted by your subject, can you fail to trace out great whales in the starry heavens, and boats in pursuit of them; as when long filled with thoughts of war the Eastern nations saw armies locked in battle among the clouds. Thus at the North have I chased Leviathan round and round the Pole with the revolutions of the bright points that first defined him to me. And beneath the effulgent Antarctic skies I have boarded the Argo-Navis, and joined the chase against the starry Cetus far beyond the utmost stretch of Hydrus and the Flying Fish.

With a frigate's anchors for my bridle-bits and fasces of harpoons for spurs, would I could mount that whale and leap the topmost skies, to see whether the fabled heavens with all their countless tents really lie encamped beyond my mortal sight!

58

BRIT

STEERING north-eastward from the Crozetts, we fell in with vast meadows of brit, the minute, yellow substance, upon which the Right Whale largely feeds. For leagues and leagues it undulated round us, so that we seemed to be sailing through boundless fields of ripe and golden wheat.

On the second day, numbers of Right Whales were seen, who, secure from the attack of a Sperm Whaler like the Pequod, with open jaws sluggishly swam through the brit, which, adhering to the fringing fibres of that wondrous Venetian blind in their mouths, was in that manner separated from the water that escaped at the lip.

As morning mowers, who side by side slowly and seethingly advance their scythes through the long wet grass of marshy meads; even so these monsters swam, making a strange, grassy, cutting sound; and leaving behind them endless swaths of blue upon the yellow sea.*

But it was only the sound they made as they parted the brit which at all reminded one of mowers. Seen from the mast-heads, especially when they paused and were stationary for a while, their vast black forms looked more like lifeless masses of rock than anything else. And as in the great hunting countries of India, the stranger at a distance will sometimes pass on the plains recumbent elephants without knowing them to be such, taking them for bare, blackened elevations of the soil; even so, often, with him, who for the first time beholds this species of the leviathans of the sea. And even when recognized at last, their immense magnitude renders it very hard really to believe that such bulky masses of overgrowth can possibly be instinct, in all parts, with the same sort of life that lives in a dog or a horse.

Indeed, in other respects, you can hardly regard any creatures of the deep with the same feelings that you do those of the shore. For though some old naturalists have maintained that all creatures of the land are of their kind in the sea; and though taking a broad general view of the thing, this may very well be; yet coming to specialities, where, for example, does the ocean furnish any fish that in disposition answers to the sagacious kindness of the dog? The accursed shark alone can in any generic respect be said to bear comparative analogy to him.

But though, to landsmen in general, the native inhabitants of the seas have ever been regarded with emotions unspeakably unsocial and repelling; though we know the sea to be an everlasting terra incognita, so that Columbus sailed over numberless unknown worlds to discover his one superficial western one; though, by vast odds, the most

*That part of the sea known among whalemen as the 'Brazil Banks' does not bear that name as the Banks of Newfoundland do, because of there being shallows and soundings there, but because of this remarkable meadow-like appearance, caused by the vast drifts of brit continually floating in those latitudes, where the Right Whale is often chased.

terrific of all mortal disasters have immemorially and indiscriminately befallen tens and hundreds of thousands of those who have gone upon the waters; though but a moment's consideration will teach, that however baby man may brag of his science and skill, and however much, in a flattering future, that science and skill may augment; yet for ever and for ever, to the crack of doom, the sea will insult and murder him, and pulverize the stateliest, stiffest frigate he can make; nevertheless, by the continual repetition of these very impressions, man has lost that sense of the full awfulness of the sea which aboriginally belongs to it.

The first boat we read of, floated on an ocean, that with Portuguese vengeance had whelmed a whole world without leaving so much as a widow. That same ocean rolls now; that same ocean destroyed the wrecked ships of last year. Yea, foolish mortals, Noah's flood is not yet subsided; two thirds of the fair world it yet covers.

Wherein differ the sea and the land, that a miracle upon one is not a miracle upon the other? Preternatural terrors rested upon the Hebrews, when under the feet of Korah and his company the live ground opened and swallowed them up for ever; yet not a modern sun ever sets, but in precisely the same manner the live sea swallows up ships and crews.

But not only is the sea such a foe to man who is an alien to it, but it is also a fiend to its own offspring; worse than the Persian host who murdered his own guests; sparing not the creatures which itself hath spawned. Like a savage tigress that tossing in the jungle overlays her own cubs, so the sea dashes even the mightiest whales against the rocks, and leaves them there side by side with the split wrecks of ships. No mercy, no power but its own controls it. Panting and snorting like a mad battle steed that has lost its rider, the masterless ocean overruns the globe.

Consider the subtleness of the sea; how its most dreaded creatures glide under water, unapparent for the most part, and treacherously hidden beneath the loveliest tints of azure. Consider also the devilish brilliance and beauty of many of its most remorseless tribes, as the dainty embellished shape of many species of sharks. Consider, once more, the universal cannibalism of the sea; all whose creatures prey upon each other, carrying on eternal war since the world began.

Consider all this; and then turn to this green, gentle, and most docile earth; consider them both, the sea and the land; and do you not find a strange analogy to something in yourself? For as this appalling ocean surrounds the verdant land, so in the soul of man there lies one insular Tahiti, full of peace and joy, but encompassed by all the horrors of the half known life. God keep thee! Push not off from that isle, thou canst never return!

59

SQUID

SLOWLY wading through the meadows of brit, the Pequod still held on her way north-eastward towards the island of Java; a gentle air impelling her keel, so that in the surrounding serenity her three tall tapering masts mildly waved to that languid breeze, as three mild palms on a plain. And still, at wide intervals in the silvery night, the lonely, alluring jet would be seen.

But one transparent blue morning, when a stillness almost preternatural spread over the sea, however unattended with any stagnant calm; when the long burnished sun-glade on the waters seemed a golden finger laid across them, enjoining some secrecy; when the slippered waves whispered together as they softly ran on; in this profound hush of the visible sphere a strange spectre was seen by Daggoo from the main-mast-head.

In the distance, a great white mass lazily rose, and rising higher and higher, and disentangling itself from the azure, at last gleamed before our prow like a snow-slide, new slid from the hills. Thus glistening for a moment, as slowly it subsided, and sank. Then once more arose, and silently gleamed. It seemed not a whale; and yet is this Moby Dick? thought Daggoo. Again the phantom went down, but on re-appearing once more, with a stiletto-like cry that startled every man from his nod, the negro yelled out – 'There! there again! there she breaches! right ahead! The White Whale, the White Whale!'

Upon this, the seamen rushed to the yard-arms, as in swarming-time the bees rush to the boughs. Bare-headed in the sultry sun, Ahab stood on the bowsprit, and with one hand pushed far behind in readiness to wave his orders to the helmsman, cast his eager glance in the direction indicated aloft by the outstretched motionless arm of Daggoo.

Whether the flitting attendance of the one still and solitary jet had gradually worked upon Ahab, so that he was now prepared to connect the ideas of mildness and repose with the first sight of the particular whale he pursued; however this was, or whether his eagerness betrayed him; whichever way it might have been, no sooner did he distinctly perceive the white mass, than with a quick intensity he instantly gave orders for lowering.

The four boats were soon on the water; Ahab's in advance, and all swiftly pulling towards their prey. Soon it went down, and while, with oars suspended, we were awaiting its re-appearance, lo! in the same spot where it sank, once more it slowly rose. Almost forgetting for the moment all thoughts of Moby Dick, we now gazed at the most wondrous phenomenon which the secret seas have hitherto revealed to mankind. A vast pulpy mass, furlongs in length and breadth, of a glancing cream-color, lay floating on the water, innumerable long arms radiating from its centre, and curling and twisting like a nest of anacondas, as if blindly to clutch at any hapless object within reach. No perceptible face or front did it have; no conceivable token of either sensation or instinct; but undulated there on the billows, an unearthly, formless, chance-like apparition of life.

As with a low sucking sound it slowly disappeared again,

Starbuck still gazing at the agitated waters where it had sunk, with a wild voice exclaimed – 'Almost rather had I seen Moby Dick and fought him, than to have seen thee, thou white ghost!'

'What was it, Sir?' said Flask.

'The great live squid, which, they say, few whale-ships ever beheld, and returned to their ports to tell of it.'

But Ahab said nothing; turning his boat, he sailed back to the vessel; the rest as silently following.

Whatever superstitions the sperm whalemen in general have connected with the sight of this object, certain it is, that a glimpse of it being so very unusual, that circumstance has gone far to invest it with portentousness. So rarely is it beheld, that though one and all of them declare it to be the largest animated thing in the ocean, yet very few of them have any but the most vague ideas concerning its true nature and form; notwithstanding, they believe it to furnish to the sperm whale his only food. For though other species of whales find their food above water, and may be seen by man in the act of feeding, the spermaceti whale obtains his whole food in unknown zones below the surface; and only by inference is it that any one can tell of what, precisely, that food consists. At times, when closely pursued, he will disgorge what are supposed to be the detached arms of the squid; some of them thus exhibited exceeding twenty and thirty feet in length. They fancy that the monster to which these arms belonged ordinarily clings by them to the bed of the ocean; and that the sperm whale, unlike other species, is supplied with teeth in order to attack and tear it.

There seems some ground to imagine that the great Kraken of Bishop Pontoppodan may ultimately resolve itself into Squid. The manner in which the Bishop describes it, as alternately rising and sinking, with some other particulars he narrates, in all this the two correspond. But much abatement is necessary with respect to the incredible bulk he assigns it.

By some naturalists who have vaguely heard rumors of the mysterious creature, here spoken of, it is included among the class of cuttle-fish, to which, indeed, in certain external respects it would seem to belong, but only as the Anak of the tribe.

60

THE LINE

WITH reference to the whaling scene shortly to be described, as well as for the better understanding of all similar scenes elsewhere presented, I have here to speak of the magical, sometimes horrible whale-line.

The line originally used in the fishery was of the best hemp, slightly vapored with tar, not impregnated with it, as in the case of ordinary ropes; for while tar, as ordinarily used, makes the hemp more pliable to the rope-maker, and also renders the rope itself more convenient to the sailor for common ship use; yet, not only would the ordinary quantity too much stiffen the whale-line for the close coiling to which it must be subjected; but as most seamen are beginning to learn, tar in general by no means adds to the rope's durability or strength, however much it may give it compactness and gloss.

Of late years the Manilla rope has in the American fishery almost entirely superseded hemp as a material for whale-lines; for, though not so durable as hemp, it is stronger, and far more soft and elastic; and I will add (since there is an aesthetics in all things), is much more handsome and becoming to the boat, than hemp. Hemp is a dusky, dark fellow, a sort of Indian; but Manilla is as a golden-haired Circassian to behold.

The whale line is only two thirds of an inch in thickness. At first sight, you would not think it so strong as it really is. By experiment its one and fifty yarns will each suspend a weight of one hundred and twenty pounds; so that the whole rope will bear a strain nearly equal to three tons. In length, the common sperm whale-line measures something over two hundred fathoms. Towards the stern of the boat it is spirally coiled away in the tub, not like the worm-pipe of a still though, but so as to form one round, cheese-shaped mass of densely bedded 'sheaves', or layers of concentric spiralizations, without any hollow but the 'heart', or minute vertical tube formed at the axis of the cheese. As the least tangle or kink in the coiling would, in running out, infallibly take somebody's arm, leg, or entire body off, the utmost precaution is used in stowing the line in its tub. Some harpooneers will consume almost an entire morning in this business, carrying the line high aloft and then reeving it downwards through a block towards the tub, so as in the act of coiling to free it from all possible wrinkles and twists.

In the English boats two tubs are used instead of one; the same line being continuously coiled in both tubs. There is some advantage in this; because these twin-tubs being so small they fit more readily into the boat, and do not strain it so much; whereas, the American tub, nearly three feet in diameter and of proportionate depth, makes a rather bulky freight for a craft whose planks are but one half-inch in thickness; for the bottom of the whale-boat is like critical ice, which will bear up a considerable distributed weight, but not very much of a concentrated one. When the painted canvas cover is clapped on the American line-tub, the boat looks as if it were pulling off with a prodigious great wedding-cake to present to the whales.

Both ends of the line are exposed; the lower end terminating in an eye-splice or loop coming up from the bottom against the side of the tub, and hanging over its edge completely disengaged from everything. This arrangement of the lower end is necessary on two accounts. First: In order to facilitate the fastening to it of an additional line from a neighboring boat, in case the stricken whale should sound so deep as to threaten to carry off the entire line originally attached to the harpoon. In these instances, the whale of course is shifted like a mug of ale, as it were, from the one boat to the other; though the first boat always hovers at hand to assist its consort. Second: This arrangement is indispensable for common safety's sake; for were the lower end of the line in any way attached to the boat, and were the whale then to run the line out to the end almost in a single, smoking minute as he sometimes does, he would not stop there, for the doomed boat would infallibly be dragged down after him into the profundity of the sea; and in that case no town-crier would ever find her again.

Before lowering the boat for the chase, the upper end of the line is taken aft from the tub, and passing round the loggerhead there, is again carried forward the entire length of the boat, resting crosswise upon the loom or handle of every man's oar, so that it jogs against his wrist in rowing; and also passing between the men, as they alternately sit at the opposite gunwales, to the leaded chocks or grooves in the extreme pointed prow of the boat, where a wooden pin or skewer the size of a common quill, prevents it from slipping out. From the chocks it hangs in a slight festoon over the bows, and is then passed inside the boat again; and some ten or twenty fathoms (called box-line) being coiled upon the box in the bows, it continues its way to the gunwale still a little further aft, and is then attached to the short-warp – rope which is immediately connected with the harpoon; but previous to that connexion, the short-warp goes through sundry mystifications too tedious to detail.

Thus the whale-line folds the whole boat in its complicated coils, twisting and writhing around it in almost every direction. All the oarsmen are involved in its perilous contortions; so that to the timid eye of the landsman, they seem as Indian jugglers, with the deadliest snakes sportively festooning their limbs. Nor can any son of mortal woman, for the first time, seat himself amid those hempen intricacies, and while straining his utmost at the oar, bethink him that at any unknown instant the harpoon may be darted, and all these horrible contortions be put in play like ringed lightnings; he cannot be thus circumstanced without a shudder that makes the very marrow in his bones to quiver in him like a shaken jelly. Yet habit – strange thing! what cannot habit accomplish? – Gayer sallies, more merry mirth, better jokes, and brighter repartees, you never heard over your mahogany, than you will hear over the half-inch white cedar of the whale-boat, when thus hung in hangman's nooses; and, like the six burghers of Calais before King Edward, the six men composing the crew pull into the jaws of death, with a halter around every neck, as you may say.

Perhaps a very little thought will now enable you to account for those repeated whaling disasters – some few of which are casually chronicled – of this man or that man being taken out of the boat by the line, and lost. For, when the line is darting out, to be seated then in the boat, is like being seated in the midst of the manifold whizzings of a steam-engine in full play, when every flying beam, and shaft, and wheel, is grazing you. It is worse; for you cannot sit motionless in the heart of these perils, because the boat is rocking like a cradle, and you are pitched one way and the other, without the slightest warning; and only by a certain self-adjusting buoyancy and simultaneousness of volition and action, can you escape being made a Mazeppa of, and run away with where the all-seeing sun himself could never pierce you out.

Again: as the profound calm which only apparently precedes and prophesies of the storm, is perhaps more awful than the storm itself; for, indeed, the calm is but the wrapper and envelope of the storm; and contains it in itself, as the seemingly harmless rifle holds the fatal powder, and the ball, and the explosion; so the graceful repose of the line, as it silently serpentines about the oarsmen before being brought into actual play – this is a thing which carries more of true terror than any other aspect of this dangerous affair. But why say more? All men live enveloped in whale-lines. All are born with halters round their necks; but it is only when caught in the swift, sudden turn of death, that mortals realize the silent, subtle, ever-present perils of life. And if you be a philosopher, though seated in the whale-boat, you would not at heart feel one whit more of terror, than though seated before your evening fire with a poker, and not a harpoon, by your side.

61

STUBB KILLS A WHALE

If to Starbuck the apparition of the Squid was a thing of portents, to Queequeg it was quite a different object.

'When you see him 'quid,' said the savage, honing his harpoon in the bow of his hoisted boat, 'then you quick see him 'parm whale.'

The next day was exceedingly still and sultry, and with nothing special to engage them, the Pequod's crew could hardly resist the spell of sleep induced by such a vacant sea. For this part of the Indian Ocean through which we then were voyaging is not what whalemen call a lively ground; that is, it affords fewer glimpses of porpoises, dolphins, flying-fish, and other vivacious denizens of more stirring waters, than those off the Rio de la Plata, or the in-shore ground off Peru.

It was my turn to stand at the foremast-head; and with my shoulders leaning against the slackened royal shrouds, to and fro I idly swayed in what seemed an enchanted air. No resolution could withstand it; in that dreamy mood losing all consciousness, at last my soul went out of my body; though my body still continued to sway as a pendulum will, long after the power which first moved it is withdrawn.

Ere forgetfulness altogether came over me, I had noticed that the seamen at the main and mizen mast-heads were already drowsy. So that at last all three of us lifelessly swung from the spars, and for every swing that we made there was a nod from below from the slumbering helmsman. The waves, too, nodded their indolent crests; and across the wide trance of the sea, east nodded to west, and the sun over all.

Suddenly bubbles seemed bursting beneath my closed eyes; like vices my hands grasped the shrouds; some invisible, gracious agency preserved me; with a shock I came back to life. And lo! close under our lee, not forty fathoms off, a gigantic Sperm Whale lay rolling in the water like the capsized hull of a frigate, his broad, glossy back, of an Ethiopian hue, glistening in the sun's rays like a mirror. But lazily undulating in the trough of the sea, and ever and anon tranquilly spouting his vapory jet, the whale looked like a portly burgher smoking his pipe of a warm afternoon. But that pipe, poor whale, was thy last. As if struck by some enchanter's wand, the sleepy ship and every sleeper in it all at once started into wakefulness; and more than a score of voices from all parts of the vessel, simultaneously with the three notes from aloft, shouted forth the accustomed cry, as the great fish slowly and regularly spouted the sparkling brine into the air.

'Clear away the boats! Luff!' cried Ahab. And obeying his own order, he dashed the helm down before the helmsman could handle the spokes.

The sudden exclamations of the crew must have alarmed the whale; and ere the boats were down, majestically turning, he swam away to the leeward, but with such a steady tranquillity, and making so few ripples as he swam, that thinking after all he might not as yet be alarmed, Ahab gave orders that not an oar should be used, and no man must speak but in whispers. So seated like Ontario Indians on the gunwales of the boats, we swiftly but silently paddled along; the calm not admitting of the noiseless sails being set. Presently, as we thus glided in chase, the monster perpendicularly flitted his tail forty feet into the air, and then sank out of sight like a tower swallowed up.

'There go flukes!' was the cry, an announcement immediately followed by Stubb's producing his match and igniting his pipe, for now a respite was granted. After the full interval of his sounding had elapsed, the whale rose again, and being now in advance of the smoker's boat, and much nearer to it than to any of the others, Stubb counted upon the honor of the capture. It was obvious, now, that the whale had at length become aware of his pursuers. All silence of cautiousness was therefore no longer of use. Paddles were dropped, and oars came loudly into play. And still puffing at his pipe, Stubb cheered on his crew to the assault.

Yes, a mighty change had come over the fish. All alive to his jeopardy, he was going 'head out'; that part obliquely projecting from the mad yeast which he brewed.*

'Start her, start her, my men! Don't hurry yourselves; take plenty of time – but start her; start her like thunder-claps, that's all,' cried Stubb, spluttering out the smoke as he spoke. 'Start her, now; give 'em the long and strong stroke, Tashtego. Start her, Tash, my boy – start her, all; but keep cool, keep cool – cucumbers is the word – easy, easy – only start her like grim death and grinning devils, and raise the buried dead perpendicular out of their graves, boys – that's all. Start her!'

'Woo-hoo! Wa-hee!' screamed the Gay-Header in reply, raising some old war-whoop to the skies; as every oarsman in the strained boat involuntarily bounced forward with the one tremendous leading stroke which the eager Indian gave.

But his wild screams were answered by others quite as wild. 'Kee-hee! Kee-hee!' yelled Daggoo, straining forwards and backwards on his seat, like a pacing tiger in his cage.

'Ka-la! Koo-loo!' howled Queequeg, as if smacking his lips over a mouthful of Grenadier's steak. And thus with oars and yells the keels cut the sea. Meanwhile, Stubb retaining his place in the van, still encouraged his men to the onset, all the while puffing the smoke from his mouth. Like desperadoes they tugged and they strained, till the welcome cry was heard – 'Stand up, Tashtego! – give it to him!' The harpoon was hurled. 'Stern all!' The oarsmen backed water;

*It will be seen in some other place of what a very light substance the entire interior of the sperm whale's enormous head consists. Though apparently the most massive, it is by far the most buoyant part about him. So that with ease he elevates it in the air, and invariably does so when going at his utmost speed. Besides, such is the breadth of the upper part of the front of his head, and such the tapering cut-water formation of the lower part, that by obliquely elevating his head, he thereby may be said to transform himself from a bluff-bowed sluggish galliot into a sharp-pointed New York pilot-boat.

the same moment something went hot and hissing along every one of their wrists. It was the magical line. An instant before, Stubb had swiftly caught two additional turns with it round the loggerhead, whence, by reason of its increased rapid circlings, a hempen blue smoke now jetted up and mingled with the steady fumes from his pipe. As the line passed round and round the loggerhead; so also, just before reaching that point, it blisteringly passed through and through both of Stubb's hands, from which the hand-cloths, or squares of quilted canvas sometimes worn at these times, had accidentally dropped. It was like holding an enemy's sharp two-edged sword by the blade, and that enemy all the time striving to wrest it out of your clutch.

'Wet the line! wet the line!' cried Stubb to the tub oarsman (him seated by the tub) who, snatching off his hat, dashed the sea-water into it.* More turns were taken, so that the line began holding its place. The boat now flew through the boiling water like a shark all fins. Stubb and Tashtego here changed places – stem for stern – a staggering business truly in that rocking commotion.

From the vibrating line extending the entire length of the upper part of the boat, and from its now being more tight than a harpstring, you would have thought the craft had two keels – one cleaving the water, the other the air – as the boat churned on through both opposing elements at once. A continual cascade played at the bows; a ceaseless whirling eddy in her wake; and, at the slightest motion from within, even but of a little finger, the vibrating, cracking craft canted over her spasmodic gunwale into the sea. Thus they rushed; each man with might and main clinging to his seat, to prevent being tossed to the foam; and the tall form of Tashtego at the steering oar crouching almost double, in order to bring down his centre of gravity. Whole Atlantics

*Partly to show the indispensableness of this act, it may here be stated, that, in the old Dutch fishery, a mop was used to dash the running line with water; in many other ships, a wooden piggin, or bailer, is set apart for that purpose. Your hat, however, is the most convenient.

and Pacifics seemed passed as they shot on their way, till at length the whale somewhat slackened his flight.

'Haul in – haul in!' cried Stubb to the bowsman; and, facing round towards the whale, all hands began pulling the boat up to him, while yet the boat was being towed on. Soon ranging up by his flank, Stubb, firmly planting his knee in the clumsy cleat, darted dart after dart into the flying fish; at the word of command, the boat alternately sterning out of the way of the whale's horrible wallow, and then ranging up for another fling.

The red tide now poured from all sides of the monster like brooks down a hill. His tormented body rolled not in brine but in blood, which bubbled and seethed for furlongs behind in their wake. The slanting sun playing upon this crimson pond in the sea, sent back its reflection into every face, so that they all glowed to each other like red men. And all the while, jet after jet of white smoke was agonizingly shot from the spiracle of the whale, and vehement puff after puff from the mouth of the excited headsman; as at every dart, hauling in upon his crooked lance (by the line attached to it), Stubb straightened it again and again, by a few rapid blows against the gunwale, then again and again sent it into the whale.

'Pull up – pull up!' he now cried to the bowsman, as the waning whale relaxed in his wrath. 'Pull up – close to!' and the boat ranged along the fish's flank. When reaching far over the bow, Stubb slowly churned his long sharp lance into the fish, and kept it there, carefully churning and churning, as if cautiously seeking to feel after some gold watch that the whale might have swallowed, and which he was fearful of breaking ere he could hook it out. But that gold watch he sought was the innermost life of the fish. And now it is struck; for, starting from his trance into that unspeakable thing called his 'flurry,' the monster horribly wallowed in his blood, overwrapped himself in impenetrable, mad, boiling spray, so that the imperilled craft, instantly dropping astern, had much ado blindly to struggle out from that phrensied twilight into the clear air of the day.

And now abating in his flurry, the whale once more rolled out into view; surging from side to side; spasmodically dilating and contracting his spout-hole, with sharp, cracking, agonized respirations. At last, gush after gush of clotted red gore, as if it had been the purple lees of red wine, shot into the frighted air; and falling back again, ran dripping down his motionless flanks into the sea. His heart had burst!

'He's dead, Mr Stubb,' said Tashtego.

'Yes; both pipes smoked out!' and withdrawing his own from his mouth, Stubb scattered the dead ashes over the water; and, for a moment, stood thoughtfully eyeing the vast corpse he had made.

62

THE DART

A WORD concerning an incident in the last chapter.

According to the invariable usage of the fishery, the whale-boat pushes off from the ship, with the headsman or whale-killer as temporary steersman, and the harpooneer or whale-fastener pulling the foremost oar, the one known as the harpooneer-oar. Now it needs a strong, nervous arm to strike the first iron into the fish; for often, in what is called a long dart, the heavy implement has to be flung to the distance of twenty or thirty feet. But however prolonged and exhausting the chase, the harpooneer is expected to pull his oar meanwhile to the uttermost; indeed, he is expected to set an example of superhuman activity to the rest, not only by incredible rowing, but by repeated loud and intrepid exclamations; and what it is to keep shouting at the top of one's compass, while all the other muscles are strained and half started – what that is none know but those who have tried it. For one, I cannot bawl very heartily and work very recklessly at one and the same time. In this straining, bawling state, then, with his back to the fish, all at once the exhausted harpooneer hears the exciting cry – 'Stand up, and give it to him!' He now has to drop and secure his oar, turn round on his centre half way, seize his harpoon from the crotch, and with what little strength may remain, he essays to pitch it somehow into the whale. No wonder, taking the whole fleet of whalemen in a body, that out of fifty fair chances for a dart, not five are successful; no wonder that so many hapless harpooneers are madly cursed and disrated; no wonder that some of them actually burst their blood-vessels in the boat; no wonder that some sperm whalemen are absent four years with four barrels; no wonder that to many ship owners, whaling is but a losing concern; for it is the harpooneer that makes the voyage, and if you take the breath out of his body how can you expect to find it there when most wanted!

Again, if the dart be successful, then at the second critical instant, that is, when the whale starts to run, the boat-header and harpooneer likewise start to running fore and aft, to the imminent jeopardy of themselves and every one else. It is then they change places; and the headsman, the chief officer of the little craft, takes his proper station in the bows of the boat.

Now, I care not who maintains the contrary, but all this is both foolish and unnecessary. The headsman should stay in the bows from first to last; he should both dart the harpoon and the lance, and no rowing whatever should be expected of him, except under circumstances obvious to any fisherman. I know that this would sometimes involve a slight loss of speed in the chase; but long experience in various whalemen of more than one nation has convinced me that in the vast majority of failures in the fishery, it has not by any means been so much the speed of the whale as the before described exhaustion of the harpooneer that has caused them.

To insure the greatest efficiency in the dart, the harpooneers of this world must start to their feet from out of idleness, and not from out of toil.

63

THE CROTCH

OUT of the trunk, the branches grow; out of them, the twigs. So, in productive subjects, grow the chapters.

The crotch alluded to on a previous page deserves independent mention. It is a notched stick of a peculiar form, some two feet in length, which is perpendicularly inserted into the starboard gunwale near the bow, for the purpose of furnishing a rest for the wooden extremity of the harpoon, whose other naked, barbed end slopingly projects from the prow. Thereby the weapon is instantly at hand to its hurler, who snatches it up as readily from its rest as a backwoodsman swings his rifle from the wall. It is customary to have two harpoons reposing in the crotch, respectively called the first and second irons.

But these two harpoons, each by its own cord, are both connected with the line; the object being this: to dart them both, if possible, one instantly after the other into the same whale; so that if, in the coming drag, one should draw out, the other may still retain a hold. It is a doubling of the chances. But it very often happens that owing to the instantaneous, violent, convulsive running of the whale upon receiving the first iron, it becomes impossible for the harpooneer, however lightning-like in his movements, to pitch the second iron into him. Nevertheless, as the second iron is already connected with the line, and the line is running, hence that weapon must, at all events, be anticipatingly tossed out of the boat, somehow and somewhere; else the most terrible jeopardy would involve all hands. Tumbled into the water, it accordingly is in such cases; the spare coils of box line (mentioned in a preceding chapter) making this feat, in most instances, prudently practicable. But this critical act is not always unattended with the saddest and most fatal casualties.

Furthermore: you must know that when the second iron is thrown overboard, it thenceforth becomes a dangling, sharp-edged terror, skittishly curvetting about both boat and whale, entangling the lines, or cutting them, and making a prodigious sensation in all directions. Nor, in general, is it possible to secure it again until the whale is fairly captured and a corpse.

Consider, now, how it must be in the case of four boats all engaging one unusually strong, active, and knowing whale; when owing to these qualities in him, as well as to the thousand concurring accidents of such an audacious enterprise, eight or ten loose second irons may be simultaneously dangling about him. For, of course, each boat is supplied with several harpoons to bend on to the line should the first one be ineffectually darted without recovery. All these particulars are faithfully narrated here, as they will not fail to elucidate several most important, however intricate passages, in scenes hereafter to be painted.

64

STUBB'S SUPPER

STUBB's whale had been killed some distance from the ship. It was a calm; so, forming a tandem of three boats, we commenced the slow business of towing the trophy to the Pequod. And now, as we eighteen men with our thirty-six arms, and one hundred and eighty thumbs and fingers, slowly toiled hour after hour upon that inert, sluggish corpse in the sea; and it seemed hardly to budge at all, except at long intervals; good evidence was hereby furnished of the enormousness of the mass we moved. For, upon the great canal of Hang-Ho, or whatever they call it, in China, four or five laborers on the foot-path will draw a bulky freighted junk at the rate of a mile an hour; but this grand argosy we towed heavily forged along, as if laden with pig-lead in bulk.

Darkness came on; but three lights up and down in the

Pequod's main-rigging dimly guided our way; till drawing nearer we saw Ahab dropping one of several more lanterns over the bulwarks. Vacantly eyeing the heaving whale for a moment, he issued the usual orders for securing it for the night, and then handing his lantern to a seaman, went his way into the cabin, and did not come forward again until morning.

Though, in overseeing the pursuit of this whale, Captain Ahab had evinced his customary activity, to call it so; yet now that the creature was dead, some vague dissatisfaction, or impatience, or despair, seemed working in him; as if the sight of that dead body reminded him that Moby Dick was yet to be slain; and though a thousand other whales were brought to his ship, all that would not one jot advance his grand, monomaniac object. Very soon you would have thought from the sound on the Pequod's decks, that all hands were preparing to cast anchor in the deep; for heavy chains are being dragged along the deck, and thrust rattling out of the port-holes. But by those clanking links, the vast corpse itself, not the ship, is to be moored. Tied by the head to the stern, and by the tail to the bows, the whale now lies with its black hull close to the vessel's, and seen through the darkness of the night, which obscured the spars and rigging aloft, the two – ship and whale, seemed yoked together like colossal bullocks, whereof one reclines while the other remains standing.*

*A little item may as well be related here. The strongest and most reliable hold which the ship has upon the whale when moored alongside, is by the flukes or tail; and as from its greater density that part is relatively heavier than any other (excepting the side-fins), its flexibility even in death, causes it to sink low beneath the surface; so that with the hand you cannot get at it from the boat, in order to put the chain round it. But this difficulty is ingeniously overcome: a small, strong line is prepared with a wooden float at its outer end, and a weight in its middle, while the other end is secured to the ship. By adroit management the wooden float is made to rise on the other side of the mass, so that now having girdled the whale, the chain is readily made to follow suit; and being slipped along the body, is at last locked fast round the smallest part of the tail, at the point of junction with its broad flukes or lobes.

If moody Ahab was now all quiescence, at least so far as could be known on deck, Stubb, his second mate, flushed with conquest, betrayed an unusual but still good-natured excitement. Such an unwonted bustle was he in that the staid Starbuck, his official superior, quietly resigned to him for the time the sole management of affairs. One small, helping cause of all this liveliness in Stubb, was soon made strangely manifest. Stubb was a high liver; he was somewhat intemperately fond of the whale as a flavorish thing to his palate.

'A steak, a steak, ere I sleep! You, Daggoo! overboard you go, and cut me one from his small!'

Here be it known, that though these wild fishermen do not, as a general thing, and according to the great military maxim, make the enemy defray the current expenses of the war (at least before realizing the proceeds of the voyage), yet now and then you find some of these Nantucketers who have a genuine relish for that particular part of the Sperm Whale designated by Stubb; comprising the tapering extremity of the body.

About midnight that steak was cut and cooked; and lighted by two lanterns of sperm oil, Stubb stoutly stood up to his spermaceti supper at the capstan-head, as if that capstan were a sideboard. Nor was Stubb the only banqueter on whale's flesh that night. Mingling their mumblings with his own mastication, thousands on thousands of sharks, swarming round the dead leviathan, smackingly feasted on its fatness. The few sleepers below in their bunks were often startled by the sharp slapping of their tails against the hull, within a few inches of the sleepers' hearts. Peering over the side you could just see them (as before you heard them) wallowing in the sullen, black waters, and turning over on their backs as they scooped out huge globular pieces of the whale of the bigness of a human head. This particular feat of the shark seems all but miraculous. How, at such an apparently unassailable surface, they contrive to gouge out such symmetrical mouthfuls, remains a part of the universal problem of all things. The mark they thus leave on the whale, may best be likened to the hollow made by a carpenter in countersinking for a screw.

Though amid all the smoking horror and diabolism of a sea-fight, sharks will be seen longingly gazing up to the ship's decks, like hungry dogs round a table where red meat is being carved, ready to bolt down every killed man that is tossed to them; and though, while the valiant butchers over the deck-table are thus cannibally carving each other's live meat with carving-knives all gilded and tasselled, the sharks, also, with their jewel-hilted mouths, are quarrelsomely carving away under the table at the dead meat; and though, were you to turn the whole affair upside down, it would still be pretty much the same thing, that is to say, a shocking sharkish business enough for all parties; and though sharks also are the invariable outriders of all slave ships crossing the Atlantic, systematically trotting alongside, to be handy in case a parcel is to be carried anywhere, or a dead slave to be decently buried; and though one or two other like instances might be set down, touching the set terms, places, and occasions, when sharks do most socially congregate, and most hilariously feast; yet is there no conceivable time or occasion when you will find them in such countless numbers, and in gayer or more jovial spirits, than around a dead sperm whale, moored by night to a whale-ship at sea. If you have never seen that sight, then suspend your decision about the propriety of devil-worship, and the expediency of conciliating the devil.

But, as yet, Stubb heeded not the mumblings of the banquet that was going on so nigh him, no more than the sharks heeded the smacking of his own epicurean lips.

'Cook, cook! – where's that old Fleece?' he cried at length, widening his legs still further, as if to form a more secure base for his supper; and, at the same time, darting his fork into the dish, as if stabbing with his lance; 'cook, you cook! – sail this way, cook!'

The old black, not in any very high glee at having been previously roused from his warm hammock at a most unseasonable hour, came shambling along from his galley, for, like many old blacks, there was something the matter with his knee-pans, which he did not keep well scoured like his other pans; this old Fleece, as they called him, came shuffling and limping along, assisting his step with his tongs, which, after a clumsy fashion, were made of straightened iron hoops; this old Ebony floundered along, and in obedience to the word of command, came to a dead stop on the opposite side of Stubb's sideboard; when, with both hands folded before him, and resting on his two-legged cane, he bowed his arched back still further over, at the same time sideways inclining his head, so as to bring his best ear into play.

'Cook,' said Stubb, rapidly lifting a rather reddish morsel to his mouth, 'don't you think this steak is rather overdone? You've been beating this steak too much, cook; it's too tender. Don't I always say that to be good, a whale-steak must be tough? There are those sharks now over the side, don't you see they prefer it tough and rare? What a shindy they are kicking up! Cook, go and talk to 'em; tell 'em they are welcome to help themselves civilly, and in moderation, but they must keep quiet. Blast me, if I can hear my own voice. Away, cook, and deliver my message. Here, take this lantern,' snatching one from his sideboard; 'now then, go and preach to 'em!'

Sullenly taking the offered lantern, old Fleece limped across the deck to the bulwarks; and then, with one hand dropping his light low over the sea, so as to get a good view of his congregation, with the other hand he solemnly flourished his tongs, and leaning far over the side in a mumbling voice began addressing the sharks, while Stubb, softly crawling behind, overheard all that was said.

'Fellow-critters: I'se ordered here to say dat you must stop dat dam noise dare. You hear? Stop dat dam smackin' ob de lip! Massa Stubb say dat you can fill your dam bellies up to de hatchings, but by Gor! you must stop dat dam racket!'

'Cook,' here interposed Stubb, accompanying the word

with a sudden slap on the shoulder, – 'Cook! why, damn your eyes, you mustn't swear that way when you're preaching. That's no way to convert sinners, Cook!'

'Who dat? Den preach to him yourself,' sullenly turning to go.

'No, Cook; go on, go on.'

'Well, den, Belubed fellow-critters:' –

'Right!' exclaimed Stubb, approvingly, 'coax 'em to it; try that,' and Fleece continued.

'Dough you is all sharks, and by natur wery woracious, yet I zay to you, fellow-critters, dat dat woraciousness – 'top dat dam slappin' ob de tail! How you tink to hear, 'spose you keep up such a dam slappin' and bitin' dare?'

'Cook,' cried Stubb, collaring him, 'I wont have that swearing. Talk to 'em gentlemanly.'

Once more the sermon proceeded.

'Your woraciousness, fellow-critters, I don't blame ye so much for; dat is natur, and can't be helped; but to gobern dat wicked natur, dat is de pint. You is sharks, sartin; but if you gobern de shark in you, why den you be angel; for all angel is not'ing more dan de shark well goberned. Now, look here, bred'ren, just try wonst to be cibil, a helping yourselbs from dat whale. Don't be tearin' de blubber out your neighbour's mout, I say. Is not one shark dood right as toder to dat whale? And, by Gor, none on you has de right to dat whale; dat whale belong to some one else. I know some o' you has berry brig mout, brigger dan oders; but den de brig mouts sometimes has de small bellies; so dat de brigness ob de mout is not to swallar wid, but to bite off de blubber for de small fry ob sharks, dat can't get into de scrouge to help demselves.'

'Well done, old Fleece!' cried Stubb, 'that's Christianity; go on.'

'No use goin' on; de dam willains will keep a scrougin' and slappin' each oder, Massa Stubb; dey don't hear one word; no use a-preachin' to such dam g'uttons as you call 'em, till dare bellies is full, and dare bellies is bottomless; and when dey do get 'em full, dey wont hear you den; for den dey sink in de sea, go fast to sleep on de coral, and can't hear not'ing at all, no more, for eber and eber.'

'Upon my soul, I am about of the same opinion; so give the benediction, Fleece, and I'll away to my supper.'

Upon this, Fleece, holding both hands over the fishy mob, raised his shrill voice, and cried –

'Cussed fellow-critters! Kick up de damndest row as ever you can; fill your dam' bellies till dey bust – and den die.'

'Now, cook,' said Stubb, resuming his supper at the capstan; 'Stand just where you stood before, there, over against me, and pay particular attention.'

'All 'dention,' said Fleece, again stooping over upon his tongs in the desired position.

'Well,' said Stubb, helping himself freely meanwhile; 'I shall now go back to the subject of this steak. In the first place, how old are you, cook?'

'What dat do wid de 'teak,' said the old black, testily.

'Silence! How old are you, cook?'

''Bout ninety, dey say,' he gloomily muttered.

'And have you lived in this world hard upon one hundred years, cook, and don't know yet how to cook a whale-steak?' rapidly bolting another mouthful at the last word, so that that morsel seemed a continuation of the question. 'Where were you born, cook?'

''Hind de hatchway, in ferry-boat, goin' ober de Roanoke.'

'Born in a ferry-boat! That's queer, too. But I want to know what country you were born in, cook?'

'Didn't I say de Roanoke country?' he cried, sharply.

'No, you didn't, cook; but I'll tell you what I'm coming to, cook. You must go home and be born over again; you don't know how to cook a whale-steak yet.'

'Bress my soul, if I cook 'noder one,' he growled, angrily, turning round to depart.

'Come back, cook; – here, hand me those tongs; – now take that bit of steak there, and tell me if you think that steak cooked as it should be? Take it, I say' – holding the tongs towards him – 'take it, and taste it.'

Faintly smacking his withered lips over it for a moment,

the old negro muttered, 'Best cooked 'teak I eber taste; joosy, berry joosy.'

'Cook,' said Stubb, squaring himself once more; 'do you belong to the church?'

'Passed one once in Cape-Down,' said the old man sullenly.

'And you have once in your life passed a holy church in Cape-Town, where you doubtless overheard a holy parson addressing his hearers as his beloved fellow-creatures, have you, cook! And yet you come here, and tell me such a dreadful lie as you did just now, eh?' said Stubb. 'Where do you expect to go to, cook?'

'Go to bed berry soon,' he mumbled, half-turning as he spoke.

'Avast! heave to! I mean when you die, cook. It's an awful question. Now what's your answer?'

'When dis old brack man dies,' said the negro slowly, changing his whole air and demeanor, 'he hisself won't go nowhere; but some bressed angel will come and fetch him.'

'Fetch him? How? In a coach and four, as they fetched Elijah? And fetch him where?'

'Up dere,' said Fleece, holding his tongs straight over his head, and keeping it there very solemnly.

'So, then, you expect to go up into our main-top, do you, cook, when you are dead? But don't you know the higher you climb, the colder it gets? Main-top, eh?'

'Didn't say dat 'tall,' said Fleece, again in the sulks.

'You said up there, didn't you? and now look yourself, and see where your tongs are pointing. But, perhaps you expect to get into heaven by crawling through the lubber's hole, cook; but, no, no, cook, you don't get there, except you go the regular way, round by the rigging. It's a ticklish business, but must be done, or else it's no go. But none of us are in heaven yet. Drop your tongs, cook, and hear my orders. Do ye hear? Hold your hat in one hand, and clap t'other a'top of your heart, when I'm giving my orders, cook. What! that your heart, there? – that's your gizzard! Aloft! aloft!

– that's it – now you have it. Hold it there now, and pay attention.'

'All 'dention,' said the old black, with both hands placed as desired, vainly wriggling his grizzled head, as if to get both ears in front at one and the same time.

'Well then, cook, you see this whale-steak of yours was so very bad, that I have put it out of sight as soon as possible; you see that, don't you? Well, for the future, when you cook another whale-steak for my private table here, the capstan, I'll tell you what to do so as not to spoil it by overdoing. Hold the steak in one hand, and show a live coal to it with the other; that done, dish it; d'ye hear? And now to-morrow, cook, when we are cutting in the fish, be sure you stand by to get the tips of his fins; have them put in pickle. As for the ends of the flukes, have them soused, cook. There, now ye may go.'

But Fleece had hardly got three paces off, when he was recalled.

'Cook, give me cutlets for supper to-morrow night in the mid-watch. D'ye hear? away you sail, then. – Halloa! stop! make a bow before you go. – Avast heaving again! Whale-balls for breakfast – don't forget.'

'Wish, by gor! whale eat him, 'stead of him eat whale. I'm bressed if he ain't more of shark dan Massa Shark hisself,' muttered the old man, limping away; with which sage ejaculation he went to his hammock.

65

THE WHALE AS A DISH

THAT mortal man should feed upon the creature that feeds his lamp, and, like Stubb, eat him by his own light, as you may say; this seems so outlandish a thing that one must needs go a little into the history and philosophy of it.

It is upon record, that three centuries ago the tongue of the Right Whale was esteemed a great delicacy in France, and commanded large prices there. Also, that in Henry VIIIth's time, a certain cook of the court obtained a handsome reward for inventing an admirable sauce to be eaten with barbacued porpoises, which, you remember, are a species of whale. Porpoises, indeed, are to this day considered fine eating. The meat is made into balls about the size of billiard balls, and being well seasoned and spiced might be taken for turtle-balls or veal balls. The old monks of Dunfermline were very fond of them. They had a great porpoise grant from the crown.

The fact is, that among his hunters at least, the whale would by all hands be considered a noble dish, were there not so much of him; but when you come to sit down before a meat-pie nearly one hundred feet long, it takes away your appetite. Only the most unprejudiced of men like Stubb, nowadays partake of cooked whales; but the Esquimaux are not so fastidious. We all know how they live upon whales, and have rare old vintages of prime old train oil. Zogranda, one of their most famous doctors, recommends strips of blubber for infants, as being exceedingly juicy and nourishing. And this reminds me that certain Englishmen, who long ago were accidentally left in Greenland by a whaling vessel – that these men actually lived for several months on the mouldy scraps of whales which had been left ashore after trying out the blubber. Among the Dutch whalemen these scraps are called 'fritters'; which, indeed, they greatly resemble, being brown and crisp, and smelling something like old Amsterdam housewives' dough-nuts or oly-cooks, when fresh. They have such an eatable look that the most self-denying stranger can hardly keep his hands off.

But what further depreciates the whale as a civilized dish, is his exceeding richness. He is the great prize ox of the sea, too fat to be delicately good. Look at his hump, which would be as fine eating as the buffalo's (which is esteemed a rare dish), were it not such a solid pyramid of fat. But the spermaceti itself, how bland and creamy that is; like the transparent, half-jellied, white meat of a cocoanut in the third month of its growth, yet far too rich to supply a substitute for butter. Nevertheless, many whalemen have a method of absorbing it into some other substance, and then partaking of it. In the long try watches of the night it is a common thing for the seamen to dip their ship-biscuit into the huge oil-pots and let them fry there awhile. Many a good supper have I thus made.

In the case of a small Sperm Whale the brains are accounted a fine dish. The casket of the skull is broken into with an axe, and the two plump, whitish lobes being withdrawn (precisely resembling two large puddings), they are then mixed with flour, and cooked into a most delectable mess, in flavor somewhat resembling calves' heads, which is quite a dish among some epicures; and every one knows that some young bucks among the epicures, by continually dining upon calves' brains, by and by get to have a little brains of their own, so as to be able to tell a calf's head from their own heads; which, indeed, requires uncommon discrimination. And that is the reason why a young buck with an intelligent looking calf's head before him, is somehow one of the saddest sights you can see. The head looks a sort of reproachfully at him, with an 'Et tu Brute!' expression.

It is not, perhaps, entirely because the whale is so excessively unctuous that landsmen seem to regard the eating of him with abhorrence; that appears to result, in some way, from the consideration before mentioned: i.e. that a man should eat a newly murdered thing of the sea, and eat it too by its own light. But no doubt the first man that ever murdered an ox was regarded as a murderer; perhaps he was hung; and if he had been put on his trial by oxen, he certainly would have been; and he certainly deserved it if any murderer does. Go to the meat-market of a Saturday night and see the crowds of live bipeds staring up at the long rows of dead quadrupeds. Does not that sight take a tooth out of the cannibal's jaw? Cannibals? who is not a cannibal? I tell you it will be more tolerable for the Fejee that salted down a lean missionary in his cellar against a coming famine; it will be more tolerable for that provident Fejee, I say, in the day of judgment, than for thee, civilized and enlightened gourmand, who nailest geese to the ground and feastest on their bloated livers in thy paté-de-foie-gras.

But Stubb, he eats the whale by its own light, does he? and that is adding insult to injury, is it? Look at your knife-handle, there, my civilized and enlightened gourmand dining off that roast beef, what is that handle made of? – what but the bones of the brother of the very ox you are eating? And what do you pick your teeth with, after devouring that fat goose? With a feather of the same fowl. And with what quill did the Secretary of the Society for the Suppression of Cruelty to Ganders formally indite his circulars? It is only within the last month or two that that society passed a resolution to patronize nothing but steel pens.

66

THE SHARK MASSACRE

WHEN in the Southern Fishery, a captured Sperm Whale, after long and weary toil, is brought alongside late at night, it is not, as a general thing at least, customary to proceed at once to the business of cutting him in. For that business is an exceedingly laborious one; is not very soon completed; and requires all hands to set about it. Therefore, the common usage is to take in all sail; lash the helm a'lee; and then send every one below to his hammock till daylight, with the reservation that, until that time, anchor-watches shall be kept; that is, two and two, for an hour each couple, the crew in rotation shall mount the deck to see that all goes well.

But sometimes, especially upon the Line in the Pacific, this plan will not answer at all; because such incalculable hosts of sharks gather round the moored carcase, that were he left so for six hours, say, on a stretch, little more than the skeleton would be visible by morning. In most other parts of the ocean, however, where these fish do not so largely abound, their wondrous voracity can be at times considerably diminished, by vigorously stirring them up with sharp whaling-spades, a procedure notwithstanding, which, in some instances, only seems to tickle them into still greater activity. But it was not thus in the present case with the Pequod's sharks; though, to be sure, any man unaccustomed to such sights, to have looked over her side that night, would have almost thought the whole round sea was one huge cheese, and those sharks the maggots in it.

Nevertheless, upon Stubb setting the anchor-watch after his supper was concluded; and when, accordingly, Queequeg and a forecastle seaman came on deck, no small excitement was created among the sharks; for immediately suspending the cutting stages over the side, and lowering three lanterns, so that they cast long gleams of light over the turbid sea, these two mariners, darting their long whaling-spades, kept up an incessant murdering of the sharks,* by striking the keen steel deep into their skulls, seemingly their only vital part. But in the foamy confusion of their mixed and struggling hosts, the marksmen could not always hit their marks; and this brought about new revelations of the incredible ferocity of the foe. They viciously snapped, not only at each other's disembowelments, but like flexible bows, bent round, and bit their own; till those entrails seemed swallowed over and over again by the same mouth, to be oppositely voided by the gaping wound. Nor was this all. It was unsafe to meddle with the corpses and ghosts of these creatures. A sort of generic or Pantheistic vitality seemed to lurk in their very joints and bones, after what might be called the individual life had departed. Killed and hoisted on deck for the sake of his skin, one of these

*The whaling-spade used for cutting-in is made of the very best steel; is about the bigness of a man's spread hand; and in general shape, corresponds to the garden implement after which it is named; only its sides are perfectly flat, and its upper end considerably narrower than the lower. This weapon is always kept as sharp as possible; and when being used is occasionally honed, just like a razor. In its socket, a stiff pole, from twenty to thirty feet long, is inserted for a handle.

sharks almost took poor Queequeg's hand off, when he tried to shut down the dead lid of his murderous jaw.

'Queequeg no care what god made him shark,' said the savage, agonizingly lifting his hand up and down; 'wedder Fejee god or Nantucket god; but de god wat made shark must be one dam Ingin.'

67

CUTTING IN

IT was a Saturday night, and such a Sabbath as followed! Ex officio professors of Sabbath breaking are all whalemen. The ivory Pequod was turned into what seemed a shamble; every sailor a butcher. You would have thought we were offering up ten thousand red oxen to the sea gods.

In the first place, the enormous cutting tackles, among other ponderous things comprising a cluster of blocks generally painted green, and which no single man can possibly lift – this vast bunch of grapes was swayed up to the maintop and firmly lashed to the lower mast-head, the strongest point anywhere above a ship's deck. The end of the hawser-like rope winding through these intricacies, was then conducted to the windlass, and the huge lower block of the tackles was swung over the whale; to this block the great blubber hook, weighing some one hundred pounds, was attached. And now suspended in stages over the side, Starbuck and Stubb, the mates, armed with their long spades, began cutting a hole in the body for the insertion of the hook just above the nearest of the two side-fins. This done, a broad, semicircular line is cut round the hole, the hook is inserted, and the main body of the crew striking up a wild chorus, now commence heaving in one dense crowd at the windlass. When instantly, the entire ship careens over on her side; every bolt in her starts like the nail-heads of an old house in frosty weather; she trembles, quivers, and nods her frighted mast-heads to the sky. More and more she leans over to the whale, while every gasping heave of the windlass is answered by a helping heave from the billows; till at last, a swift, startling snap is heard; with a great swash the ship rolls upwards and backwards from the whale, and the triumphant tackle rises into sight dragging after it the disengaged semicircular end of the first strip of blubber. Now as the blubber envelopes the whale precisely as the rind does an orange, so is it stripped off from the body precisely as an orange is sometimes stripped by spiralizing it. For the strain constantly kept up by the windlass continually keeps the whale rolling over and over in the water, and as the blubber in one strip uniformly peels off along the line called the 'scarf', simultaneously cut by the spades of Starbuck and Stubb, the mates; and just as fast as it is thus peeled off, and indeed by that very act itself, it is all the time being hoisted higher and higher aloft till its upper end grazes the main-top; the men at the windlass then cease heaving, and for a moment or two the prodigious blood-dripping mass sways to and fro as if let down from the sky, and every one present must take good heed to dodge it when it swings, else it may box his ears and pitch him headlong overboard.

One of the attending harpooneers now advances with a long, keen weapon called a boarding-sword, and watching his chance he dexterously slices out a considerable hole in the lower part of the swaying mass. Into this hole, the end of the second alternating great tackle is then hooked so as to retain a hold upon the blubber, in order to prepare for what follows. Whereupon, this accomplished swordsman, warning all hands to stand off, once more makes a scientific dash at the mass, and with a few sidelong, desperate, lunging slicings, severs it completely in twain; so that while the short lower part is still fast, the long upper strip, called a blanket-piece, swings clear, and is all ready for lowering. The heavers forward now resume their song, and while the one tackle is peeling and hoisting a second strip from the whale, the other is slowly slackened away, and down goes the first strip through the main hatchway right beneath, into an unfurnished parlor called the blubber-room. Into this twilight apartment sundry nimble hands keep coiling away the long blanket-piece as if it were a great live mass of plaited serpents. And thus the work proceeds; the two tackles hoisting and lowering simultaneously; both whale and windlass heaving, the heavers singing, the blubber-room gentlemen coiling, the mates scarfing, the ship straining, and all hands swearing occasionally, by way of assuaging the general friction.

68

THE BLANKET

I HAVE given no small attention to that not unvexed subject, the skin of the whale. I have had controversies about it with experienced whalemen afloat, and learned naturalists ashore. My original opinion remains unchanged; but it is only an opinion.

The question is, what and where is the skin of the whale? Already you know what his blubber is. That blubber is something of the consistence of firm, close-grained beef, but tougher, more elastic and compact, and ranges from eight or ten to twelve and fifteen inches in thickness.

Now, however preposterous it may at first seem to talk of any creature's skin as being of that sort of consistence and thickness, yet in point of fact these are no arguments against such a presumption; because you cannot raise any other dense enveloping layer from the whale's body but that same blubber; and the outermost enveloping layer of any animal, if reasonably dense, what can that be but the skin? True, from the unmarred dead body of the whale, you may scrape off with your hand an infinitely thin, transparent substance, somewhat resembling the thinnest shreds of isinglass, only it is almost as flexible and soft as satin; that is, previous to being dried, when it not only contracts and thickens, but becomes rather hard and brittle. I have several such dried bits, which I use for marks in my whale-books. It is transparent, as I said before; and being laid upon the printed page, I have sometimes pleased myself with fancying it exerted a magnifying influence. At any rate, it is pleasant to read about whales through their own spectacles, as you may say. But what I am driving at here is this. That same infinitely thin, isinglass substance, which, I admit, invests the entire body of the whale, is not so much to be regarded as the skin of the creature, as the skin of the skin, so to speak; for it were simply ridiculous to say, that the proper skin of the tremendous whale is thinner and more tender than the skin of a new-born child. But no more of this.

Assuming the blubber to be the skin of the whale; then, when this skin, as in the case of a very large Sperm Whale, will yield the bulk of one hundred barrels of oil; and, when it is considered that, in quantity, or rather weight, that oil, in its expressed state, is only three fourths, and not the entire substance of the coat; some idea may hence be had of the enormousness of that animated mass, a mere part of whose mere integument yields such a lake of liquid as that. Reckoning ten barrels to the ton, you have ten tons for the net weight of only three quarters of the stuff of the whale's skin.

In life, the visible surface of the Sperm Whale is not the least among the many marvels he presents. Almost invariably it is all over obliquely crossed and re-crossed with numberless straight marks in thick array, something like those in the finest Italian line engravings. But these marks do not seem to be impressed upon the isinglass substance above mentioned, but seem to be seen through it, as if they were engraved upon the body itself. Nor is this all. In some instances, to the quick, observant eye, those linear marks, as in a veritable engraving, but afford the ground for far other delineations. These are hieroglyphical; that is, if you call those mysterious cyphers on the walls of pyramids hieroglyphics, then that is the proper word to use in the present connexion. By my retentive memory of the hieroglyphics upon one Sperm Whale in particular, I was much struck with a plate representing the old Indian characters chiselled on the famous hieroglyphic palisades on the banks of the Upper Mississippi. Like those mystic rocks, too, the mystic-marked whale remains undecipherable. This allusion to the Indian rocks reminds me of another thing. Besides all the other phenomena which the exterior of the Sperm Whale presents, he not seldom displays the back, and more especially his flanks, effaced in great part of the regular linear appearance, by reason of numerous rude scratches, altogether of an irregular, random aspect. I should say that those New England rocks on the sea-coast, which Agassiz imagines to bear the marks of violent scraping contact with vast floating icebergs – I should say, that those rocks must not a little resemble the Sperm Whale in this particular. It also seems to me that such scratches in the whale are probably made by hostile contact with other whales; for I have most remarked them in the large, full-grown bulls of the species.

A word or two more concerning this matter of the skin or blubber of the whale. It has already been said, that it is stript from him in long pieces, called blanket-pieces. Like most sea-terms, this one is very happy and significant. For the whale is indeed wrapt up in his blubber as in a real blanket or counterpane; or, still better, an Indian poncho slipt over his head, and skirting his extremity. It is by reason of this cosy blanketing of his body, that the whale is enabled to keep himself comfortable in all weathers, in all seas, times, and tides. What would become of a Greenland whale, say, in those shuddering, icy seas of the North, if unsupplied with his cosy surtout? True, other fish are found exceedingly brisk in those Hyperborean waters; but these, be it observed, are your cold-blooded, lungless fish, whose very bellies are refrigerators; creatures, that warm themselves under the lee of an iceberg, as a traveller in winter would bask before an inn fire, whereas, like man, the whale has lungs and warm blood. Freeze his blood, and he dies. How wonderful is it then – except after explanation – that this great monster, to whom corporeal warmth is as indispensable as it is to man; how wonderful that he should be found at home, immersed to his lips for life in those Arctic waters! where, when seamen fall overboard, they are sometimes found, months afterwards, perpendicularly frozen into the hearts of fields of ice, as a fly is found glued in amber. But more surprising is it to know, as has been proved by experiment, that the blood of a Polar whale is warmer than that of a Borneo negro in summer.

It does seem to me, that herein we see the rare virtue of a strong individual vitality, and the rare virtue of thick walls, and the rare virtue of interior spaciousness. Oh, man! admire and model thyself after the whale! Do thou, too, remain warm among ice. Do thou, too, live in this world without being of it. Be cool at the equator; keep thy blood fluid at the Pole. Like the great dome of St Peter's, and like the great whale, retain, O man! in all seasons a temperature of thine own.

But how easy and how hopeless to teach these fine things! Of erections, how few are domed like St Peter's! of creatures, how few vast as the whale!

69

THE FUNERAL

'HAUL in the chains! Let the carcase go astern!'

The vast tackles have now done their duty. The peeled white body of the beheaded whale flashes like a marble sepulchre; though changed in hue, it has not perceptibly lost anything in bulk. It is still colossal. Slowly it floats more and more away, the water round it torn and splashed by the insatiate sharks, and the air above vexed with rapacious flights of screaming fowls, whose beaks are like so many insulting poniards in the whale. The vast white headless phantom floats further and further from the ship, and every rod that it so floats, what seem square roods of sharks and cubic roods of fowls, augment the murderous din. For hours and hours from the almost stationary ship that hideous sight is seen. Beneath the unclouded and mild azure sky, upon the fair face of the pleasant sea, wafted by the joyous breezes, that great mass of death floats on and on, till lost in infinite perspectives.

There's a most doleful and most mocking funeral! The sea-vultures all in pious mourning, the air-sharks all punctiliously in black or speckled. In life but few of them would have helped the whale, I ween, if peradventure he had needed it; but upon the banquet of his funeral they most piously do pounce. Oh, horrible vulturism of earth! from which not the mightiest whale is free.

Nor is this the end. Desecrated as the body is, a vengeful ghost survives and hovers over it to scare. Espied by some timid man-of-war or blundering discovery-vessel from afar, when the distance obscuring the swarming fowls, nevertheless still shows the white mass floating in the sun, and the white spray heaving high against it; straightway the whale's unharming corpse, with trembling fingers is set down in the log – *shoals, rocks, and breakers hereabouts: beware!* And for years afterwards, perhaps, ships shun the place; leaping over it as silly sheep leap over a vacuum, because their leader originally leaped there when a stick was held. There's your law of precedents; there's your utility of traditions; there's the story of your obstinate survival of old beliefs never bottomed on the earth, and now not even hovering in the air! There's orthodoxy!

Thus, while in life the great whale's body may have been a real terror to his foes, in his death his ghost becomes a powerless panic to a world.

Are you a believer in ghosts, my friend? There are other ghosts than the Cock-Lane one, and far deeper men than Doctor Johnson who believe in them.

70

THE SPHYNX

It should not have been omitted that previous to completely stripping the body of the leviathan, he was beheaded. Now, the beheading of the Sperm Whale is a scientific anatomical feat, upon which experienced whale surgeons very much pride themselves: and not without reason.

Consider that the whale has nothing that can properly be called a neck; on the contrary, where his head and body seem to join, there, in that very place, is the thickest part of him. Remember, also, that the surgeon must operate from above, some eight or ten feet intervening between him and his subject, and that subject almost hidden in a discolored, rolling, and oftentimes tumultuous and bursting sea. Bear in mind, too, that under these untoward circumstances he has to cut many feet deep in the flesh; and in that subterraneous manner, without so much as getting one single peep into the ever-contracting gash thus made, he must skilfully steer clear of all adjacent, interdicted parts, and exactly divide the spine at a critical point hard by its insertion into the skull. Do you not marvel, then, at Stubb's boast, that he demanded but ten minutes to behead a sperm whale?

When first severed, the head is dropped astern and held there by a cable till the body is stripped. That done, if it belong to a small whale it is hoisted on deck to be deliberately disposed of. But, with a full grown leviathan this is impossible; for the sperm whale's head embraces nearly one third of his entire bulk, and completely to suspend such a burden as that, even by the immense tackles of a whaler, this were as vain a thing as to attempt weighing a Dutch barn in jewellers' scales.

The Pequod's whale being decapitated and the body

stripped, the head was hoisted against the ship's side – about half way out of the sea, so that it might yet in great part be buoyed up by its native element. And there with the strained craft steeply leaning over to it, by reason of the enormous downward drag from the lower mast-head, and every yard-arm on that side projecting like a crane over the waves; there, that blood-dripping head hung to the Pequod's waist like the giant Holofernes's from the girdle of Judith.

When this last task was accomplished it was noon, and the seamen went below to their dinner. Silence reigned over the before tumultuous but now deserted deck. An intense copper calm, like a universal yellow lotus, was more and more unfolding its noiseless measureless leaves upon the sea.

A short space elapsed, and up into this noiselessness came Ahab alone from his cabin. Taking a few turns on the quarter-deck, he paused to gaze over the side, then slowly getting into the main-chains he took Stubb's long spade – still remaining there after the whale's decapitation – and striking it into the lower part of the half-suspended mass, placed its other end crutch-wise under one arm, and so stood leaning over with eyes attentively fixed on this head.

It was a black and hooded head; and hanging there in the midst of so intense a calm, it seemed the Sphynx's in the desert. 'Speak, thou vast and venerable head,' muttered Ahab, 'which, though ungarnished with a beard, yet here and there lookest hoary with mosses; speak, mighty head, and tell us the secret thing that is in thee. Of all divers, thou hast dived the deepest. That head upon which the upper sun now gleams, has moved amid this world's foundations. Where unrecorded names and navies rust, and untold hopes and anchors rot; where in her murderous hold this frigate earth is ballasted with bones of millions of the drowned; there, in that awful water-land, there was thy most familiar home. Thou hast been where bell or diver never went; hast slept by many a sailor's side, where sleepless mothers would give their lives to lay them down. Thou saw'st the locked lovers when leaping from their flaming ship; heart to heart they sank beneath the exulting wave; true to each other, when heaven seemed false to them. Thou saw'st the murdered mate when tossed by pirates from the midnight deck; for hours he fell into the deeper midnight of the insatiate maw; and his murderers still sailed on unharmed – while swift lightnings shivered the neighboring ship that would have borne a righteous husband to outstretched, longing arms. O head! thou hast seen enough to split the planets and make an infidel of Abraham, and not one syllable is thine!'

'Sail ho!' cried a triumphant voice from the main-mast-head.

'Aye? Well, now, that's cheering,' cried Ahab, suddenly erecting himself, while whole thunder-clouds swept aside from his brow. 'That lively cry upon this deadly calm might almost convert a better man. – Where away?'

'Three points on the starboard bow, sir, and bringing down her breeze to us!'

'Better and better, man. Would now St Paul would come along that way, and to my breezelessness bring his breeze! O Nature, and O soul of man! how far beyond all utterance are your linked analogies! not the smallest atom stirs or lives in matter, but has its cunning duplicate in mind.'

71

THE JEROBOAM'S STORY

HAND in hand, ship and breeze blew on; but the breeze came faster than the ship, and soon the Pequod began to rock.

By and by, through the glass the stranger's boats and manned mast-heads proved her a whale-ship. But as she was so far to windward, and shooting by, apparently making a passage to some other ground, the Pequod could not hope to reach her. So the signal was set to see what response would be made.

Here be it said, that like the vessels of military marines,

the ships of the American Whale Fleet have each a private signal; all which signals being collected in a book with the names of the respective vessels attached, every captain is provided with it. Thereby, the whale commanders are enabled to recognise each other upon the ocean, even at considerable distances, and with no small facility.

The Pequod's signal was at last responded to by the stranger's setting her own; which proved the ship to be the Jeroboam of Nantucket. Squaring her yards, she bore down, ranged abeam under the Pequod's lee, and lowered a boat; it soon drew nigh; but, as the side-ladder was being rigged by Starbuck's order to accommodate the visiting captain, the stranger in question waved his hand from his boat's stern in token of that proceeding being entirely unnecessary. It turned out that the Jeroboam had a malignant epidemic on board, and that Mayhew, her captain, was fearful of infecting the Pequod's company. For, though himself and boat's crew remained untainted, and though his ship was half a rifle-shot off, and an incorruptible sea and air rolling and flowing between; yet conscientiously adhering to the timid quarantine of the land, he peremptorily refused to come into direct contact with the Pequod.

But this did by no means prevent all communication. Preserving an interval of some few yards between itself and the ship, the Jeroboam's boat by the occasional use of its oars contrived to keep parallel to the Pequod, as she heavily forged through the sea (for by this time it blew very fresh), with her main-topsail aback; though, indeed, at times by the sudden onset of a large rolling wave, the boat would be pushed some way ahead; but would be soon skilfully brought to her proper bearings again. Subject to this, and other the like interruptions now and then, a conversation was sustained between the two parties; but at intervals not without still another interruption of a very different sort.

Pulling an oar in the Jeroboam's boat, was a man of a singular appearance, even in that wild whaling life where individual notabilities make up all totalities. He was a small, short, youngish man, sprinkled all over his face with freckles, and wearing redundant yellow hair. A long-skirted, cabalistically-cut coat of a faded walnut tinge enveloped him; the overlapping sleeves of which were rolled up on his wrists. A deep, settled, fanatic delirium was in his eyes.

So soon as this figure had been first descried, Stubb had exclaimed – 'That's he! that's he! – the long-togged scaramouch the Town-Ho's company told us of!' Stubb here alluded to a strange story told of the Jeroboam, and a certain man among her crew, some time previous when the Pequod spoke the Town-Ho. According to this account and what was subsequently learned, it seemed that the scaramouch in question had gained a wonderful ascendency over almost everybody in the Jeroboam. His story was this:

He had been originally nurtured among the crazy society of Neskyeuna Shakers, where he had been a great prophet; in their cracked, secret meetings having several times descended from heaven by the way of a trap-door, announcing the speedy opening of the seventh vial, which he carried in his vest-pocket; but, which, instead of containing gunpowder, was supposed to be charged with laudanum. A strange, apostolic whim having seized him, he had left Neskyeuna for Nantucket, where, with that cunning peculiar to craziness, he assumed a steady, common sense exterior, and offered himself as a green-hand candidate for the Jeroboam's whaling voyage. They engaged him; but straightway upon the ship's getting out of sight of land, his insanity broke out in a freshet. He announced himself as the archangel Gabriel, and commanded the captain to jump overboard. He published his manifesto, whereby he set himself forth as the deliverer of the isles of the sea and vicar-general of all Oceanica. The unflinching earnestness with which he declared these things; – the dark, daring play of his sleepless, excited imagination, and all the preternatural terrors of real delirium, united to invest this Gabriel in the minds of the majority of the ignorant crew, with an atmosphere of sacredness. Moreover, they were afraid of him. As such a man, however, was not of much practical use in the ship, especially as he refused to work except when he pleased, the incredulous captain would fain have been rid of him; but apprised that that individual's intention was to land him in the first convenient port, the archangel forthwith opened all his seals and vials – devoting the ship and all hands to unconditional perdition, in case this intention was carried out. So strongly did he work upon his disciples among the crew, that at last in a body they went to the captain and told him if Gabriel was sent from the ship, not a man of them would remain. He was therefore forced to relinquish his plan. Nor would they permit Gabriel to be any way maltreated, say or do what he would; so that it came to pass that Gabriel had the complete freedom of the ship. The consequence of all this was, that the archangel cared little or nothing for the captain and mates; and since the epidemic had broken out, he carried a higher hand than ever; declaring that the plague, as he called it, was at his sole command; nor should it be stayed but according to his good pleasure. The sailors, mostly poor devils, cringed, and some of them fawned before him; in obedience to his instructions, sometimes rendering him personal homage, as to a god. Such things may seem incredible; but, however wondrous, they are true. Nor is the history of fanatics half so striking in respect to the measureless self-deception of the fanatic himself, as his measureless power of deceiving and bedevilling so many others. But it is time to return to the Pequod.

'I fear not thy epidemic, man,' said Ahab from the bulwarks, to Captain Mayhew, who stood in the boat's stern; 'come on board.'

But now Gabriel started to his feet.

'Think, think of the fevers, yellow and bilious! Beware of the horrible plague!'

'Gabriel, Gabriel!' cried Captain Mayhew; 'thou must either –' But that instant a headlong wave shot the boat far ahead, and its seethings drowned all speech.

'Hast thou seen the White Whale?' demanded Ahab, when the boat drifted back.

'Think, think of thy whale-boat, stoven and sunk! Beware of the horrible tail!'

'I tell thee again, Gabriel, that –' But again the boat tore ahead as if dragged by fiends. Nothing was said for some moments, while a succession of riotous waves rolled by, which by one of those occasional caprices of the seas were tumbling, not heaving it. Meantime, the hoisted sperm whale's head jogged about very violently, and Gabriel was seen eyeing it with rather more apprehensiveness than his archangel nature seemed to warrant.

When this interlude was over, Captain Mayhew began a dark story concerning Moby Dick; not, however, without frequent interruptions from Gabriel, whenever his name was mentioned, and the crazy sea that seemed leagued with him.

It seemed that the Jeroboam had not long left home, when upon speaking a whale-ship, her people were reliably apprised of the existence of Moby Dick, and the havoc he had made. Greedily sucking in this intelligence, Gabriel solemnly warned the captain against attacking the White Whale, in case the monster should be seen; in his gibbering insanity, pronouncing the White Whale to be no less a being than the Shaker God incarnated; the Shakers receiving the Bible. But when, some year or two afterwards, Moby Dick was fairly sighted from the mast-heads, Macey, the chief mate, burned with ardor to encounter him; and the captain himself being not unwilling to let him have the opportunity, despite all the archangel's denunciations and forewarnings, Macey succeeded in persuading five men to man his boat. With them he pushed off; and, after much weary pulling, and many perilous, unsuccessful onsets, he at last succeeded in getting one iron fast. Meantime, Gabriel, ascending to the main-royal mast-head, was tossing one arm in frantic gestures, and hurling forth prophecies of speedy doom to the sacrilegious assailants of his divinity. Now, while Macey, the mate, was standing up in his boat's bow, and with all the reckless energy of his tribe was venting his wild exclamations upon the whale, and essaying to get a fair chance for his poised lance, lo! a broad white shadow rose from the sea; by its quick, fanning motion, temporarily taking the breath out of the bodies of the oarsmen. Next instant, the luckless mate, so full of furious life, was smitten bodily into the air, and making a long arc in his descent, fell into the sea at the distance of about fifty yards. Not a chip of the boat was harmed, nor a hair of any oarsman's head; but the mate for ever sank.

(It is well to parenthesize here, that of the fatal accidents in the Sperm-Whale Fishery, this kind is perhaps almost as frequent as any. Sometimes, nothing is injured but the man who is thus annihilated; oftener the boat's bow is knocked off, or the thighboard, in which the headsman stands, is torn from its place and accompanies the body. But strangest of all is the circumstance, that in more instances than one, when the body has been recovered, not a single mark of violence is discernible; the man being stark dead.)

The whole calamity, with the falling form of Macey, was plainly descried from the ship. Raising a piercing shriek – 'The vial; the vial!' Gabriel called off the terror-stricken crew from the further hunting of the whale. This terrible event clothed the archangel with added influence; because his credulous disciples believed that he had specifically foreannounced it, instead of only making a general prophecy, which any one might have done, and so have chanced to hit one of many marks in the wide margin allowed. He became a nameless terror to the ship.

Mayhew having concluded his narration, Ahab put such questions to him, that the stranger captain could not forbear inquiring whether he intended to hunt the White Whale, if opportunity should offer. To which Ahab answered – 'Aye.' Straightway, then, Gabriel once more started to his feet, glaring upon the old man, and vehemently exclaimed, with downward pointed finger – 'Think, think of the blasphemer – dead, and down there! – beware of the blasphemer's end!'

Ahab stolidly turned aside; then said to Mayhew, 'Captain, I have just bethought me of my letter-bag; there is a letter for one of thy officers, if I mistake not. Starbuck, look over the bag.'

Every whale-ship takes out a goodly number of letters for various ships, whose delivery to the persons to whom they may be addressed, depends upon the mere chance of encountering them in the four oceans. Thus, most letters never reach their mark; and many are only received after attaining an age of two or three years or more.

Soon Starbuck returned with a letter in his hand. It was sorely tumbled, damp, and covered with a dull, spotted, green mould, in consequence of being kept in a dark locker of the cabin. Of such a letter, Death himself might well have been the post-boy.

'Can'st not read it?' cried Ahab. 'Give it me, man. Aye, aye, it's but a dim scrawl; – what's this?' As he was studying it out, Starbuck took a long cutting-spade pole, and with his knife slightly split the end, to insert the letter there, and in that way, hand it to the boat, without its coming any closer to the ship.

Meantime, Ahab holding the letter, muttered, 'Mr Har – yes, Mr Harry – (a woman's pinny hand, – the man's wife, I'll wager) – Aye – Mr Harry Macey, Ship Jeroboam; – why it's Macey, and he's dead!'

'Poor fellow! poor fellow! and from his wife,' sighed Mayhew; 'but let me have it.'

'Nay, keep it thyself,' cried Gabriel to Ahab; 'thou art soon going that way.'

'Curses throttle thee!' yelled Ahab. 'Captain Mayhew, stand by now to receive it;' and taking the fatal missive from Starbuck's hands, he caught it in the slit of the pole, and reached it over towards the boat. But as he did so, the oarsmen expectantly desisted from rowing; the boat drifted a little towards the ship's stern; so that, as if by magic, the letter suddenly ranged along with Gabriel's eager hand. He clutched it in an instant, seized the boat-knife, and impaling the letter on it, sent it thus loaded back into the ship. It fell at Ahab's feet. Then Gabriel shrieked out to his comrades to give way with their oars, and in that manner the mutinous boat rapidly shot away from the Pequod.

As, after this interlude, the seamen resumed their work upon the jacket of the whale, many strange things were hinted in reference to this wild affair.

72

THE MONKEY-ROPE

In the tumultuous business of cutting-in and attending to a whale, there is much running backwards and forwards among the crew. Now hands are wanted here, and then again hands are wanted there. There is no staying in any one place; for at one and the same time everything has to be done everywhere. It is much the same with him who endeavors the description of the scene. We must now retrace our way a little. It was mentioned that upon first breaking ground in the whale's back, the blubber-hook was inserted into the original hole there cut by the spades of the mates. But how did so clumsy and weighty a mass as that same hook get fixed in that hole? It was inserted there by my particular friend Queequeg, whose duty it was, as harpooneer, to descend upon the monster's back for the special purpose referred to. But in very many cases, circumstances require that the harpooneer shall remain on the whale till the whole flensing or stripping operation is concluded. The whale, be it observed, lies almost entirely submerged, excepting the immediate parts operated upon. So down there, some ten feet below the level of the deck, the poor harpooneer flounders about, half on the whale and half in the water, as the vast mass revolves like a tread-mill beneath him. On the occasion in question, Queequeg figured in the Highland costume – a shirt and socks – in which to my eyes, at least, he appeared to uncommon advantage; and no one had a better chance to observe him, as will presently be seen.

Being the savage's bowsman, that is, the person who

pulled the bow-oar in his boat (the second one from forward), it was my cheerful duty to attend upon him while taking that hard-scrabble scramble upon the dead whale's back. You have seen Italian organ-boys holding a dancing-ape by a long cord. Just so, from the ship's steep side, did I hold Queequeg down there in the sea, by what is technically called in the fishery a monkey-rope, attached to a strong strip of canvas belted round his waist.

It was a humorously perilous business for both of us. For, before we proceed further, it must be said that the monkey-rope was fast at both ends; fast to Queequeg's broad canvas belt, and fast to my narrow leather one. So that for better or for worse, we two, for the time, were wedded; and should poor Queequeg sink to rise no more, then both usage and honor demanded, that instead of cutting the cord, it should drag me down in his wake. So, then, an elongated Siamese ligature united us. Queequeg was my own inseparable twin brother; nor could I any way get rid of the dangerous liabilities which the hempen bond entailed.

So strongly and metaphysically did I conceive of my situation then, that while earnestly watching his motions, I seemed distinctly to perceive that my own individuality was now merged in a joint stock company of two: that my free will had received a mortal wound; and that another's mistake or misfortune might plunge innocent me into unmerited disaster and death. Therefore, I saw that here was a sort of interregnum in Providence; for its even-handed equity never could have sanctioned so gross an injustice. And yet still further pondering – while I jerked him now and then from between the whale and the ship, which would threaten to jam him – still further pondering, I say, I saw that this situation of mine was the precise situation of every mortal that breathes; only, in most cases, he, one way or other, has this Siamese connexion with a plurality of other mortals. If your banker breaks, you snap; if your apothecary by mistake sends you poison in your pills, you die. True, you may say that, by exceeding caution, you may possibly escape these and the multitudinous other evil chances of life. But handle Queequeg's monkey-rope heedfully as I would, sometimes he jerked it so, that I came very near sliding overboard. Nor could I posibly forget that, do what I would, I only had the management of one end of it.*

I have hinted that I would often jerk poor Queequeg from between the whale and the ship – where he would occasionally fall, from the incessant rolling and swaying of both. But this was not the only jamming jeopardy he was exposed to. Unappalled by the massacre made upon them during the night, the sharks now freshly and more keenly allured by the before pent blood which began to flow from the carcase – the rabid creatures swarmed round it like bees in a beehive.

And right in among those sharks was Queequeg; who often pushed them aside with his floundering feet. A thing altogether incredible were it not that attracted by such prey as a dead whale, the otherwise miscellaneously carnivorous shark will seldom touch a man.

Nevertheless, it may well be believed that since they have such a ravenous finger in the pie, it is deemed but wise to look sharp to them. Accordingly, besides the monkey-rope, with which I now and then jerked the poor fellow from too close a vicinity to the maw of what seemed a peculiarly ferocious shark – he was provided with still another protection. Suspended over the side in one of the stages, Tashtego and Daggoo continually flourished over his head a couple of keen whale-spades, wherewith they slaughtered as many sharks as they could reach. This procedure of theirs, to be sure, was very disinterested and benevolent of them. They meant Queequeg's best happiness, I admit; but in their hasty zeal to befriend him, and from the circumstance that both he and the sharks were at times half hidden by the blood-

*The monkey-rope is found in all whalers; but it was only in the Pequod that the monkey and his holder were ever tied together. This improvement upon the original usage was introduced by no less a man than Stubb, in order to afford to the imperilled harpooneer the strongest possible guarantee for the faithfulness and vigilance of his monkey-rope holder.

mudded water, those indiscreet spades of theirs would come nearer amputating a leg than a tail. But poor Queequeg, I suppose, straining and gasping there with that great iron hook – poor Queequeg, I suppose, only prayed to his Yojo, and gave up his life into the hands of his gods.

Well, well, my dear comrade and twin-brother, thought I, as I drew in and then slacked off the rope to every swell of the sea – what matters it, after all? Are you not the precious image of each and all of us men in this whaling world? That unsounded ocean you gasp in, is Life; those sharks, your foes; those spades, your friends; and what between sharks and spades you are in a sad pickle and peril, poor lad.

But courage! there is good cheer in store for you, Queequeg. For now, as with blue lips and bloodshot eyes the exhausted savage at last climbs up the chains and stands all dripping and involuntarily trembling over the side; the steward advances, and with a benevolent, consolatory glance hands him – what? Some hot Cogniac? No! hands him, ye gods! hands him a cup of tepid ginger and water!

'Ginger? Do I smell ginger?' suspiciously asked Stubb, coming near. 'Yes, this must be ginger,' peering into the as yet untasted cup. Then standing as if incredulous for a while, he calmly walked towards the astonished steward slowly saying, 'Ginger? ginger? and will you have the goodness to tell me, Mr Dough-Boy, where lies the virtue of ginger? Ginger! is ginger the sort of fuel you use, Dough-Boy, to kindle a fire in this shivering cannibal? Ginger! – what the devil is ginger? – sea-coal? – fire-wood? – lucifer matches? – tinder? – gun-powder? – what the devil is ginger, I say, that you offer this cup to our poor Queequeg here?'

'There is some sneaking Temperance Society movement about this business,' he suddenly added, now approaching Starbuck, who had just come from forward. 'Will you look at that kannakin, sir: smell of it, if you please.' Then watching the mate's countenance, he added: 'The steward, Mr Starbuck, had the face to offer that calomel and jalap to Queequeg, there, this instant off the whale. Is the steward an apothecary, sir? and may I ask whether this is the sort of bellows by which he blows back the breath into a half-drowned man?'

'I trust not,' said Starbuck, 'it is poor stuff enough.'

'Aye, aye, steward,' cried Stubb, 'we'll teach you to drug a harpooneer; none of your apothecary's medicine here; you want to poison us, do ye? You have got out insurances on our lives and want to murder us all, and pocket the proceeds, do ye?'

'It was not me,' cried Dough-Boy, 'it was Aunt Charity that brought the ginger on board; and bade me never give the harpooneers any spirits, but only this ginger-jub – so she called it.'

'Ginger-jub! you gingerly rascal! take that! and run along with ye to the lockers, and get something better. I hope I do no wrong, Mr Starbuck. It is the captain's orders – grog for the harpooneer on a whale.'

'Enough,' replied Starbuck, 'only don't hit him again, but –'

'Oh, I never hurt when I hit, except when I hit a whale or something of that sort; and this fellow's a weazel. What were you about saying, sir?'

'Only this: go down with him, and get what thou wantest thyself.'

When Stubb reappeared, he came with a dark flask in one hand, and a sort of tea-caddy in the other. The first contained strong spirits, and was handed to Queequeg; the second was Aunt Charity's gift, and that was freely given to the waves.

73

STUBB AND FLASK KILL A RIGHT WHALE; AND THEN HAVE A TALK OVER HIM

It must be borne in mind that all this time we have a Sperm Whale's prodigious head hanging to the Pequod's side. But we must let it continue hanging there a while till we can get a chance to attend to it. For the present other matters press, and the best we can do now for the head, is to pray heaven the tackles may hold.

Now, during the past night and forenoon, the Pequod had gradually drifted into a sea, which, by its occasional patches of yellow brit, gave unusual tokens of the vicinity of Right Whales, a species of the Leviathan that but few supposed to be at this particular time lurking anywhere near. And though all hands commonly disdained the capture of those inferior creatures; and though the Pequod was not commissioned to cruise for them at all, and though she had passed numbers of them near the Crozetts without lowering a boat; yet now that a Sperm Whale had been brought alongside and beheaded, to the surprise of all, the announcement was made that a Right Whale should be captured that day, if opportunity offered.

Nor was this long wanting. Tall spouts were seen to leeward; and two boats, Stubb's and Flask's, were detached in pursuit. Pulling further and further away, they at last became almost invisible to the men at the mast-head. But suddenly in the distance, they saw a great heap of tumultuous white water, and soon after news came from aloft that one or both the boats must be fast. An interval passed and the boats were in plain sight, in the act of being dragged right towards the ship by the towing whale. So close did the monster come to the hull, that at first it seemed as if he meant it malice; but suddenly going down in a maelstrom, within three rods of the planks, he wholly disappeared from view, as if diving under the keel. 'Cut, cut!' was the cry from the ship to the boats, which, for one instant, seemed on the point of being brought with a deadly dash against the vessel's hide. But having plenty of line yet in the tubs, and the whale not sounding very rapidly, they paid out abundance of rope, and at the same time pulled with all their might so as to get ahead of the ship. For a few minutes the struggle was intensely critical; for while they still slacked out the tightened line in one direction, and still plied their oars in another, the contending strain threatened to take them under. But it was only a few feet advance they sought to gain. And they stuck to it till they did gain it; when instantly, a swift tremor was felt running like lightning along the keel, as the strained line, scraping beneath the ship, suddenly rose to view under her bows, snapping and quivering; and so flinging off its drippings, that the drops fell like bits of broken glass on the water, while the whale beyond also rose to sight, and once more the boats were free to fly. But the fagged whale abated his speed, and blindly altering his course, went round the stern of the ship towing the two boats after him, so that they performed a complete circuit.

Meantime, they hauled more and more upon their lines, till close flanking him on both sides, Stubb answered Flask with lance for lance; and thus round and round the Pequod the battle went, while the multitudes of sharks that had before swum round the Sperm Whale's body, rushed to the fresh blood that was spilled, thirstily drinking at every new gash, as the eager Israelites did at the new bursting fountains that poured from the smitten rock.

At last his spout grew thick, and with a frightful roll and vomit, he turned upon his back a corpse.

While the two headsmen were engaged in making fast cords to his flukes, and in other ways getting the mass in readiness for towing, some conversation ensued between them.

"I wonder what the old man wants with this lump of foul lard,' said Stubb, not without some disgust at the thought of having to do with so ignoble a leviathan.

'Wants with it?' said Flask, coiling some spare line in the boat's bow, 'did you never hear that the ship which but once has a Sperm Whale's head hoisted on her starboard side, and at the same time a Right Whale's on the larboard; did you never hear, Stubb, that that ship can never afterwards capsize?'

'Why not?'

'I don't know, but I heard that gamboge ghost of a Fedallah saying so, and he seems to know all about ships' charms. But I sometimes think he'll charm the ship to no good at last. I don't half like that chap, Stubb. Did you ever notice how that tusk of his is a sort of carved into a snake's head, Stubb?'

'Sink him! I never look at him at all; but if ever I get a chance of a dark night, and he standing hard by the bulwarks, and no one by; look down there, Flask' – pointing into the sea with a peculiar motion of both hands – 'Aye, will I! Flask, I take that Fedallah to be the devil in disguise. Do you believe that cock and bull story about his having been stowed away on board ship? He's the devil, I say. The reason why you don't see his tail, is because he tucks it up out of sight; he carries it coiled away in his pocket, I guess. Blast him! now that I think of it, he's always wanting oakum to stuff into the toes of his boots.'

'He sleeps in his boots, don't he? He hasn't got any hammock; but I've seen him lay of nights in a coil of rigging.'

'No doubt, and it's because of his cursed tail; he coils it down, do ye see, in the eye of the rigging.'

'What's the old man have so much to do with him for?'

'Striking up a swap or a bargain, I suppose.'

'Bargain? – about what?'

'Why, do ye see, the old man is hard bent after that White Whale, and the devil there is trying to come round him, and get him to swap away his silver watch, or his soul, or something of that sort, and then he'll surrender Moby Dick.'

'Pooh! Stubb, you are skylarking; how can Fedallah do that?'

'I don't know, Flask, but the devil is a curious chap, and a wicked one, I tell ye. Why, they say as how he went a sauntering into the old flag-ship once, switching his tail about devilish easy and gentlemanlike, and inquiring if the old governor was at home. Well, he was at home, and asked the devil what he wanted. The devil, switching his hoofs, up and says, "I want John." "What for?" says the old governor. "What business is that of yours," says the devil, getting mad, – "I want to use him." "Take him," says the governor – and by the Lord, Flask, if the devil didn't give John the Asiatic cholera before he got through with him, I'll eat this whale in one mouthful. But look sharp – aint you all ready there? Well, then, pull ahead, and let's get the whale alongside.'

'I think I remember some such story as you were telling,' said Flask, when at last the two boats were slowly advancing with their burden towards the ship, 'but I can't remember where.'

'Three Spaniards? Adventures of those three bloody-minded soldadoes? Did ye read it there, Flask? I guess ye did?'

'No: never saw such a book; heard of it, though. But now, tell me, Stubb, do you suppose that that devil you was speaking of just now, was the same you say is now on board the Pequod?'

'Am I the same man that helped kill this whale? Doesn't the devil live for ever; who ever heard that the devil was dead? Did you ever see any parson a wearing mourning for the devil? And if the devil has a latch-key to get into the admiral's cabin, don't you suppose he can crawl into a port-hole? Tell me that, Mr Flask?'

'How old do you suppose Fedallah is, Stubb?'

'Do you see that mainmast there?' pointing to the ship; 'well, that's the figure one; now take all the hoops in the Pequod's hold, and string 'em along in a row with that mast, for oughts, do you see; well, that wouldn't begin to be Fedallah's age. Nor all the coopers in creation couldn't show hoops enough to make oughts enough.'

'But see here, Stubb, I thought you a little boasted just now, that you meant to give Fedallah a sea-toss, if you got a good chance. Now, if he's so old as all those hoops of yours come to, and if he is going to live for ever, what good will it do to pitch him overboard – tell me that?'

'Give him a good ducking, anyhow.'

'But he'd crawl back.'

'Duck him again; and keep ducking him.'

'Suppose he should take it into his head to duck you, though – yes, and drown you – what then?'

'I should like to see him try it; I'd give him such a pair of black eyes that he wouldn't dare to show his face in the admiral's cabin again for a long while, let alone down in the orlop there, where he lives, and hereabouts on the upper decks where he sneaks so much. Damn the devil, Flask; do you suppose I'm afraid of the devil? Who's afraid of him, except the old governor who daresn't catch him and put him in double-darbies, as he deserves, but lets him go about kidnapping people; aye, and signed a bond with him, that all the people the devil kidnapped, he'd roast for him? There's a governor!'

'Do you suppose Fedallah wants to kidnap Captain Ahab?'

'Do I suppose it? You'll know it before long, Flask. But I am going now to keep a sharp look-out on him; and if I see anything very suspicious going on, I'll just take him by the nape of his neck, and say – Look here, Beelzebub, you don't do it! and if he makes any fuss, by the Lord I'll make a grab into his pocket for his tail, take it to the capstan, and give him such a wrenching and heaving, that his tail will come short off at the stump – do you see; and then, I rather guess when he finds himself docked in that queer fashion, he'll sneak off without the poor satisfaction of feeling his tail between his legs.'

'And what will you do with the tail, Stubb?'

'Do with it? Sell it for an ox whip when we get home; – what else?'

'Now, do you mean what you say, and have been saying all along, Stubb?'

'Mean or not mean, here we are at the ship.'

The boats were here hailed, to tow the whale on the larboard side, where fluke chains and other necessaries were already prepared for securing him.

'Didn't I tell you so?' said Flask; 'yes, you'll soon see this right whale's head hoisted up opposite that parmacetti's.'

In good time, Flask's saying proved true. As before, the Pequod steeply leaned over towards the sperm whale's head, now, by the counterpoise of both heads, she regained her even keel; though sorely strained, you may well believe. So, when on one side you hoist in Locke's head, you go over that way; but now, on the other side, hoist in Kant's and you come back again; but in very poor plight. Thus, some minds for ever keep trimming boat. Oh, ye foolish! throw all these thunder-heads overboard, and then you will float light and right.

In disposing of the body of a right whale, when brought alongside the ship, the same preliminary proceedings commonly take place as in the case of a sperm whale; only, in the latter instance, the head is cut off whole, but in the former the lips and tongue are separately removed and hoisted on deck, with all the well known black bone attached to what is called the crown-piece. But nothing like this, in the present case, had been done. The carcases of both whales had dropped astern; and the head-laden ship not a little resembled a mule carrying a pair of overburdening panniers.

Meantime, Fedallah was calmly eyeing the right whale's head, and ever and anon glancing from the deep wrinkles there to the lines in his own hand. And Ahab chanced so to stand, that the Parsee occupied his shadow; while, if the Parsee's shadow was there at all it seemed only to blend with, and lengthen Ahab's. As the crew toiled on, Laplandish speculations were bandied among them, concerning all these passing things.

74

THE SPERM WHALE'S HEAD – CONTRASTED VIEW

HERE, now, are two great whales, laying their heads together; let us join them, and lay together our own.

Of the grand order of folio leviathans, the Sperm Whale and the Right Whale are by far the most noteworthy. They are the only whales regularly hunted by man. To the Nantucketer, they present the two extremes of all the known varieties of the whale. As the external difference between them is mainly observable in their heads; and as a head of each is this moment hanging from the Pequod's side; and as we may freely go from one to the other, by merely stepping across the deck: – where, I should like to know, will you obtain a better chance to study practical cetology than here?

In the first place, you are struck by the general contrast between these heads. Both are massive enough in all conscience; but there is a certain mathematical symmetry in the Sperm Whale's which the Right Whale's sadly lacks. There is more character in the Sperm Whale's head. As you behold it, you involuntarily yield the immense superiority to him, in point of pervading dignity. In the present instance, too, this dignity is heightened by the pepper and salt color of his head at the summit, giving token of advanced age and large experience. In short, he is what the fishermen technically call a 'grey-headed whale.'

Let us now note what is least dissimilar in these heads – namely, the two most important organs, the eye and the ear. Far back on the side of the head, and low down, near the angle of either whale's jaw, if you narrowly search, you will at last see a lashless eye, which you would fancy to be a young colt's eye; so out of all proportion is it to the magnitude of the head.

Now, from this peculiar sideway position of the whale's eyes, it is plain that he can never see an object which is exactly ahead, no more than he can one exactly astern. In a word, the position of the whale's eyes corresponds to that of a man's ears; and you may fancy, for yourself, how it would fare with you, did you sideways survey objects through your ears. You would find that you could only command some thirty degrees of vision in advance of the straight side-line of sight; and about thirty more behind it. If your bitterest foe were walking straight towards you, with dagger uplifted in broad day, you would not be able to see him, any more than if he were stealing upon you from behind. In a word, you would have two backs, so to speak; but, at the same time, also, two fronts (side fronts): for what is it that makes the front of a man – what, indeed, but his eyes?

Moreover, while in most other animals that I can now think of, the eyes are so planted as imperceptibly to blend their visual power, so as to produce one picture and not two to the brain; the peculiar position of the whale's eyes, effectually divided as they are by many cubic feet of solid head, which towers between them like a great mountain separating two lakes in valleys; this, of course, must wholly separate the impressions which each independent organ imparts. The whale, therefore, must see one distinct picture on this side, and another distinct picture on that side; while all between must be profound darkness and nothingness to him. Man may, in effect, be said to look out on the world from a sentry-box with two joined sashes for his window. But with the whale, these two sashes are separately inserted, making two distinct windows, but sadly impairing the view. This peculiarity of the whale's eyes is a thing always to be borne in mind in the fishery; and to be remembered by the reader in some subsequent scenes.

A curious and most puzzling question might be started concerning this visual matter as touching the Leviathan. But I must be content with a hint. So long as a man's eyes are open in the light, the act of seeing is involuntary; that is, he cannot then help mechanically seeing whatever objects are before him. Nevertheless, any one's experience will teach him, that though he can take in an undiscriminating sweep of things at one glance, it is quite impossible for him, attentively, and completely, to examine any two things – however large or however small – at one and the same instant of time; never mind if they lie side by side and touch each other. But if you now come to separate these two objects, and surround each by a circle of profound darkness; then, in order to see one of them, in such a manner as to bring your mind to bear on it, the other will be utterly excluded from your contemporary consciousness. How is it, then, with the whale? True, both his eyes, in themselves, must simultaneously act; but is his brain so much more comprehensive, combining, and subtle than man's, that he can at the same moment of time attentively examine two distinct prospects, one on one side of him, and the other in an exactly opposite direction? If he can, then is it as marvellous a thing in him, as if a man were able simultaneously to go through the demonstrations of two distinct problems in Euclid. Nor, strictly investigated, is there any incongruity in this comparison.

It may be but an idle whim, but it has always seemed to me, that the extraordinary vacillations of movement displayed by some whales when beset by three or four boats; the timidity and liability to queer frights, so common to such whales; I think that all this indirectly proceeds from the helpless perplexity of volition, in which their divided and diametrically opposite powers of vision must involve them.

But the ear of the whale is full as curious as the eye. If you are an entire stranger to their race, you might hunt over these two heads for hours, and never discover that organ. The ear has no external leaf whatever; and into the hole itself you can hardly insert a quill, so wondrously minute is it. It is lodged a little behind the eye. With respect to their ears, this important difference is to be observed between the sperm whale and the right. While the ear of the former has an external opening, that of the latter is entirely and evenly covered over with a membrane, so as to be quite imperceptible from without.

Is it not curious, that so vast a being as the whale should see the world through so small an eye, and hear the thunder through an ear which is smaller than a hare's? But if his eyes were broad as the lens of Herschel's great telescope; and his ears capacious as the porches of cathedrals; would that make him any longer of sight, or sharper of hearing? Not at all. – Why then do you try to 'enlarge' your mind? Subtilize it.

Let us now with whatever levers and steam-engines we have at hand, cant over the sperm whale's head, so that it may lie bottom up; then, ascending by a ladder to the summit, have a peep down the mouth; and were it not that the body is now completely separated from it, with a lantern we might descend into the great Kentucky Mammoth Cave of his stomach. But let us hold on here by this tooth, and look about us where we are. What a really beautiful and chaste-looking mouth! from floor to ceiling, lined, or rather papered with a glistening white membrane, glossy as bridal satins.

But come out now, and look at this portentous lower jaw, which seems like the long narrow lid of an immense snuff-box, with the hinge at one end, instead of one side. If you pry it up, so as to get it overhead, and expose its rows of teeth, it seems a terrific portcullis; and such, alas! it proves to many a poor wight in the fishery, upon whom these spikes fall with impaling force. But far more terrible is it to behold, when fathoms down in the sea, you see some sulky whale, floating there suspended, with his prodigious jaw, some fifteen feet long, hanging straight down at right-angles with his body, for all the world like a ship's jib-boom. This whale is not dead; he is only dispirited; out of sorts, perhaps; hypochondriac; and so supine, that the hinges of his jaw have relaxed, leaving him there in that ungainly sort of plight, a reproach to all his tribe, who must, no doubt, imprecate lock-jaws upon him.

In most cases this lower jaw – being easily unhinged by a practised artist – is disengaged and hoisted on deck for the purpose of extracting the ivory teeth, and furnishing a supply of that hard white whalebone with which the fishermen fashion all sorts of curious articles, including canes, umbrella-stocks, and handles to riding-whips.

With a long, weary hoist the jaw is dragged on board, as if it were an anchor; and when the proper time comes – some few days after the other work – Queequeg, Daggoo, and Tashtego, being all accomplished dentists, are set to drawing teeth. With a keen cutting-spade, Queequeg lances the gums; then the jaw is lashed down to ringbolts, and a tackle being rigged from aloft, they drag out these teeth, as Michigan oxen drag stumps of old oaks out of wild wood-lands. There are generally forty-two teeth in all; in old whales, much worn down, but undecayed; nor filled after our artificial fashion. The jaw is afterwards sawn into slabs, and piled away like joists for building houses.

75

THE RIGHT WHALE'S HEAD – CONTRASTED VIEW

CROSSING the deck, let us now have a good long look at the Right Whale's head.

As in general shape the noble Sperm Whale's head may be compared to a Roman war-chariot (especially in front, where it is so broadly rounded); so, at a broad view, the Right Whale's head bears a rather inelegant resemblance to a gigantic galliot-toed shoe. Two hundred years ago an old Dutch voyager likened its shape to that of a shoemaker's last. And in this same last or shoe, that old woman of the nursery tale, with the swarming brood, might very comfortably be lodged, she and all her progeny.

But as you come nearer to this great head it begins to assume different aspects, according to your point of view. If you stand on its summit and look at these two *f*-shaped spout-holes, you would take the whole head for an enormous bass-viol, and these spiracles, the apertures in its sounding-board. Then, again, if you fix your eye upon this strange, crested, comb-like incrustation on the top of the mass – this green, barnacled thing, which the Greenlanders call the 'crown,' and the Southern fishers the 'bonnet' of the Right Whale; fixing your eyes solely on this, you would take the head for the trunk of some huge oak, with a bird's nest in its crotch. At any rate, when you watch those live crabs that nestle here on this bonnet, such an idea will be almost sure to occur to you; unless, indeed, your fancy has been fixed by the technical term 'crown' also bestowed upon it; in which case you will take great interest in thinking how this mighty monster is actually a diademed king of the sea, whose green crown has been put together for him in this marvellous manner. But if this whale be a king, he is a very sulky looking fellow to grace a diadem. Look at that hanging lower lip! what a huge sulk and pout is there! a sulk and pout, by carpenter's measurement, about twenty feet long and five feet deep; a sulk and pout that will yield you some 500 gallons of oil and more.

A great pity, now, that this unfortunate whale should be harelipped. The fissure is about a foot across. Probably the mother during an important interval was sailing down the Peruvian coast, when earthquakes caused the beach to gape. Over this lip, as over a slippery threshold, we now slide into the mouth. Upon my word were I at Mackinaw, I should take this to be the inside of an Indian wigwam. Good Lord! is this the road that Jonah went? The roof is about twelve feet high, and runs to a pretty sharp angle, as if there were a regular ridge-pole there; while these ribbed, arched, hairy sides, present us with those wondrous, half vertical, scimetar-shaped slats of whalebone, say three hundred on a side, which depending from the upper part of the head or crown bone, form those Venetian blinds which have elsewhere been cursorily mentioned. The edges of these bones are fringed with hairy fibres, through which the Right Whale strains the water, and in whose intricacies he retains the small fish, when open mouthed he goes through the seas of brit in feeding time. In the central blinds of bone, as they stand in their natural order, there are certain curious marks, curves, hollows, and ridges, whereby some whalemen calculate the creature's age, as the age of an oak by its circular rings. Though the certainty of this criterion is far from demonstrable, yet it has the savor of analogical probability. At any rate, if we yield to it, we must grant a far greater age to the Right Whale than at first glance will seem reasonable.

In old times, there seem to have prevailed the most curious fancies concerning these blinds. One voyager in Purchas calls them the wondrous 'whiskers' inside of the whale's mouth;* another, 'hogs' bristles;' a third old gentleman in

*This reminds us that the Right Whale really has a sort of whisker, or rather a moustache, consisting of a few scattered white hairs on the upper part of the outer end of the lower jaw. Sometimes these tufts impart a rather brigandish expression to his otherwise solemn countenance.

Hackluyt uses the following elegant language: 'There are about two hundred and fifty fins growing on each side of his upper *chop*, which arch over his tongue on each side of his mouth.'

As every one knows, these same 'hogs' bristles', 'fins', 'whiskers', 'blinds', or whatever you please, furnish to the ladies their busks and other stiffening contrivances. But in this particular, the demand has long been on the decline. It was in Queen Anne's time that the bone was in its glory, the farthingale being then all the fashion. And as those ancient dames moved about gaily, though in the jaws of the whale, as you may say; even so, in a shower, with the like thoughtlessness, do we nowadays fly under the same jaws for protection; the umbrella being a tent spread over the same bone.

But now forget all about blinds and whiskers for a moment, and, standing in the Right Whale's mouth, look around you afresh. Seeing all these colonnades of bone so methodically ranged about, would you not think you were inside of the great Haarlem organ, and gazing upon its thousand pipes? For a carpet to the organ we have a rug of the softest Turkey – the tongue, which is glued, as it were, to the floor of the mouth. It is very fat and tender, and apt to tear in pieces in hoisting it on deck. This particular tongue now before us; at a passing glance I should say it was a six-barreler; that is, it will yield you about that amount of oil.

Ere this, you must have plainly seen the truth of what I started with – that the Sperm Whale and the Right Whale have almost entirely different heads. To sum up, then: in the Right Whale's there is no great well of sperm; no ivory teeth at all; no long, slender mandible of a lower jaw, like the Sperm Whale's. Nor in the Sperm Whale are there any of those blinds of bone; no huge lower lip; and scarcely anything of a tongue. Again, the Right Whale has two external spout-holes, the Sperm Whale only one.

Look your last, now, on these venerable hooded heads, while they yet lie together; for one will soon sink, unrecorded, in the sea; the other will not be very long in following.

Can you catch the expression of the Sperm Whale's there? It is the same he died with, only some of the longer wrinkles in the forehead seem now faded away. I think his broad brow to be full of a prairie-like placidity, born of a speculative indifference as to death. But mark the other head's expression. See that amazing lower lip, pressed by accident against the vessel's side, so as firmly to embrace the jaw. Does not this whole head seem to speak of an enormous practical resolution in facing death? This Right Whale I take to have been a Stoic; the Sperm Whale, a Platonian, who might have taken up Spinoza in his latter years.

76

THE BATTERING-RAM

ERE quitting, for the nonce, the Sperm Whale's head, I would have you, as a sensible physiologist, simply – particularly remark its front aspect, in all its compacted collectedness. I would have you investigate it now with the sole view of forming to yourself some unexaggerated, intelligent estimate of whatever battering-ram power may be lodged there. Here is a vital point; for you must either satisfactorily settle this matter with yourself, or for ever remain an infidel as to one of the most appalling, but not the less true events, perhaps anywhere to be found in all recorded history.

You observe that in the ordinary swimming position of the Sperm Whale, the front of his head presents an almost wholly vertical plane to the water; you observe that the lower part of that front slopes considerably backwards, so as to furnish more of a retreat for the long socket which receives the boom-like lower jaw; you observe that the mouth is entirely under the head, much in the same way, indeed, as though your own mouth were entirely under your chin. Moreover you observe that the whale has no external nose;

and that what nose he has – his spout hole – is on the top of his head; you observe that his eyes and ears are at the sides of his head, nearly one third of his entire length from the front. Wherefore, you must now have perceived that the Sperm Whale's head is a dead, blind wall, without a single organ or tender prominence of any sort whatsoever. Furthermore, you are now to consider that only in the extreme, lower, backward sloping part of the front of the head, is there the slightest vestige of bone; and not till you get near twenty feet from the forehead do you come to the full cranial development. So that this whole enormous boneless mass is as one wad. Finally, though, as will soon be revealed, its contents partly comprise the most delicate oil; yet, you are now to be apprised of the nature of the substance which so impregnably invests all that apparent effeminacy. In some previous place I have described to you how the blubber wraps the body of the whale, as the rind wraps an orange. Just so with the head; but with this difference : about the head this envelope, though not so thick, is of a boneless toughness, inestimable by any man who has not handled it. The severest pointed harpoon, the sharpest lance darted by the strongest human arm, impotently rebounds from it. It is as though the forehead of the Sperm Whale were paved with horses' hoofs. I do not think that any sensation lurks in it.

Bethink yourself also of another thing. When two large, loaded Indiamen chance to crowd and crush towards each other in the docks, what do the sailors do? They do not suspend between them, at the point of coming contact, any merely hard substance, like iron or wood. No, they hold there a large, round wad of tow and cork, enveloped in the thickest and toughest of ox-hide. That bravely and uninjured takes the jam which would have snapped all their oaken handspikes and iron crowbars. By itself this sufficiently illustrates the obvious fact I drive at. But supplementary to this, it has hypothetically occurred to me, that as ordinary fish possess what is called a swimming bladder in them, capable, at will, of distension or contraction; and as the Sperm Whale, as far as I know, has no such provision in him; considering, too, the otherwise inexplicable manner in which he now depresses his head altogether beneath the surface, and anon swims with it high elevated out of the water; considering the unobstructed elasticity of its envelop; considering the unique interior of his head; it has hypothetically occurred to me, I say, that those mystical lung-celled honeycombs there may possibly have some hitherto unknown and unsuspected connexion with the outer air, so as to be susceptible to atmospheric distension and contraction. If this be so, fancy the irresistibleness of that might, to which the most impalpable and destructive of all elements contributes.

Now, mark. Unerringly impelling this dead, impregnable, uninjurable wall, and this most buoyant thing within; there swims behind it all a mass of tremendous life, only to be adequately estimated as piled wood is – by the cord; and all obedient to one volition, as the smallest insect. So that when I shall hereafter detail to you all the specialties and concentrations of potency everywhere lurking in this expansive monster; when I shall show you some of his more inconsiderable braining feats; I trust you will have renounced all ignorant incredulity, and be ready to abide by this; that though the Sperm Whale stove a passage through the Isthmus of Darien, and mixed the Atlantic with the Pacific, you would not elevate one hair of your eye-brow. For unless you own the whale, you are but a provincial and sentimentalist in Truth. But clear Truth is a thing for salamander giants only to encounter; how small the chances for the provincials then? What befel the weakling youth lifting the dread goddess's veil at Sais?

77

THE GREAT HEIDELBURGH TUN

Now comes the Baling of the Case. But to comprehend it aright, you must know something of the curious internal structure of the thing operated upon.

Regarding the Sperm Whale's head as a solid oblong, you may, on an inclined plane, sideways divide it into two quoins,* whereof the lower is the bony structure, forming the cranium and jaws, and the upper an unctuous mass wholly free from bones; its broad forward end forming the expanded vertical apparent forehead of the whale. At the middle of the forehead horizontally subdivide this upper quoin, and then you have two almost equal parts, which before were naturally divided by an internal wall of a thick tendinous substance.

The lower subdivided part, called the junk, is one immense honeycomb of oil, formed by the crossing and recrossing, into ten thousand infiltrated cells, of tough elastic white fibres throughout its whole extent. The upper part, known as the Case, may be regarded as the great Heidelburgh Tun of the Sperm Whale. And as that famous great tierce is mystically carved in front, so the whale's vast plaited forehead forms innumerable strange devices for the emblematical adornment of his wondrous tun. Moreover, as that of Heidelburgh was always replenished with the most excellent of the wines of the Rhenish valleys, so the tun of the whale contains by far the most precious of all his oily vintages; namely, the highly-prized spermaceti, in its absolutely pure, limpid, and odoriferous state. Nor is this pre-

*Quoin is not a Euclidean term. It belongs to the pure nautical mathematics. I know not that it has been defined before. A quoin is a solid which differs from a wedge in having its sharp end formed by the steep inclination of one side, instead of the mutual tapering of both sides.

cious substance found unalloyed in any other part of the creature. Though in life it remains perfectly fluid, yet, upon exposure to the air, after death, it soon begins to concrete; sending forth beautiful crystalline shoots, as when the first thin delicate ice is just forming in water. A large whale's case generally yields about five hundred gallons of sperm, though from unavoidable circumstances, considerable of it is spilled, leaks, and dribbles away, or is otherwise irrevocably lost in the ticklish business of securing what you can.

I know not with what fine and costly material the Heidelburgh Tun was coated within, but in superlative richness that coating could not possibly have compared with the silken pearl-colored membrane, like the lining of a fine pelisse, forming the inner surface of the Sperm Whale's case.

It will have been seen that the Heidelburgh Tun of the Sperm Whale embraces the entire length of the entire top of the head; and since – as has been elsewhere set forth – the head embraces one third of the whole length of the creature, then setting that length down at eighty feet for a good sized whale, you have more than twenty-six feet for the depth of the tun, when it is length-wise hoisted up and down against a ship's side.

As in decapitating the whale, the operator's instrument is brought close to the spot where an entrance is subsequently forced into the spermaceti magazine; he has, therefore, to be uncommonly heedful, lest a careless, untimely stroke should invade the sanctuary and wastingly let out its invaluable contents. It is this decapitated end of the head, also, which is at last elevated out of the water, and retained in that position by the enormous cutting tackles, whose hempen combinations, on one side, make quite a wilderness of ropes in that quarter.

Thus much being said, attend now, I pray you, to that marvellous and – in this particular instance – almost fatal operation whereby the Sperm Whale's great Heidelburgh Tun is tapped.

78

CISTERN AND BUCKETS

NIMBLE as a cat, Tashtego mounts aloft; and without altering his erect posture, runs straight out upon the overhanging main-yard-arm, to the part where it exactly projects over the hoisted Tun. He has carried with him a light tackle called a whip, consisting of only two parts, travelling through a single-sheaved block. Securing this block, so that it hangs down from the yard-arm, he swings one end of the rope, till it is caught and firmly held by a hand on deck. Then, hand-over-hand, down the other part, the Indian drops through the air, till dexterously he lands on the summit of the head. There – still high elevated above the rest of the company, to whom he vivaciously cries – he seems some Turkish Muezzin calling the good people to prayers from the top of a tower. A short-handled sharp spade being sent up to him, he diligently searches for the proper place to begin breaking into the Tun. In this business he proceeds very heedfully, like a treasure-hunter in some old house, sounding the walls to find where the gold is masoned in. By the time this cautious search is over, a stout iron-bound bucket, precisely like a well-bucket, has been attached to one end of the whip; while the other end, being stretched across the deck, is there held by two or three alert hands. These last now hoist the bucket within grasp of the Indian, to whom another person has reached up a very long pole. Inserting this pole into the bucket, Tashtego downward guides the bucket into the Tun, till it entirely disappears; then giving the word to the seamen at the whip, up comes the bucket again, all bubbling like a dairy-maid's pail of new milk. Carefully lowered from its height, the full-freighted vessel is caught by an appointed hand, and quickly emptied into a large tub. Then re-mounting aloft, it again goes through the same round until the deep cistern will yield no more. Towards the end, Tashtego has to ram his long pole harder and harder, and deeper and deeper into the Tun, until some twenty feet of the pole have gone down.

Now, the people of the Pequod had been baling some time in this way; several tubs had been filled with the fragrant sperm; when all at once a queer accident happened. Whether it was that Tashtego, that wild Indian, was so heedless and reckless as to let go for a moment his one-handed hold on the great cabled tackles suspending the head; or whether the place where he stood was so treacherous and oozy; or whether the Evil One himself would have it to fall out so, without stating his particular reasons; how it was exactly, there is no telling now; but, on a sudden, as the eightieth or ninetieth bucket came suckingly up – my God! poor Tashtego – like the twin reciprocating bucket in a veritable well, dropped head-foremost down into this great Tun of Heidelburgh, and with a horrible oily gurgling, went clean out of sight!

'Man overboard!' cried Daggoo, who amid the general consternation first came to his senses. 'Swing the bucket this way!' and putting one foot into it, so as the better to secure his slippery hand-hold on the whip itself, the hoisters ran him high up to the top of the head, almost before Tashtego could have reached its interior bottom. Meantime, there was a terrible tumult. Looking over the side, they saw the before lifeless head throbbing and heaving just below the surface of the sea, as if that moment seized with some momentous idea; whereas it was only the poor Indian unconsciously revealing by those struggles the perilous depth to which he had sunk.

At this instant, while Daggoo, on the summit of the head, was clearing the whip – which had somehow got foul of the great cutting tackles – a sharp cracking noise was heard; and to the unspeakable horror of all, one of the two enormous hooks suspending the head tore out, and with a vast vibration the enormous mass sideways swung, till the drunk ship reeled and shook as if smitten by an iceberg. The one remaining hook, upon which the entire strain now depended, seemed every instant to be on the point of giving way; an event still more likely from the violent motions of the head.

'Come down, come down!' yelled the seamen to Daggoo, but with one hand holding on to the heavy tackles, so that if the head should drop, he would still remain suspended; the negro having cleared the foul line, rammed down the bucket into the now collapsed well, meaning that the buried harpooneer should grasp it, and so be hoisted out.

'In heaven's name, man,' cried Stubb, 'are you ramming home a cartridge there? – Avast! How will that help him; jamming that iron-bound bucket on top of his head? Avast, will ye!'

'Stand clear of the tackle!' cried a voice like the bursting of a rocket.

Almost in the same instant, with a thunder-boom, the enormous mass dropped into the sea, like Niagara's Table-Rock into the whirlpool; the suddenly relieved hull rolled away from it, to far down her glittering copper; and all caught their breath, as half swinging – now over the sailors' heads, and now over the water – Daggoo, through a thick mist of spray, was dimly beheld clinging to the pendulous tackles, while poor, buried-alive Tashtego was sinking utterly down to the bottom of the sea! But hardly had the blinding vapor cleared away, when a naked figure with a boarding-sword in its hand, was for one swift moment seen hovering over the bulwarks. The next, a loud splash announced that my brave Queequeg had dived to the rescue. One packed rush was made to the side, and every eye counted every ripple, as moment followed moment, and no sign of either the sinker or the diver could be seen. Some hands now jumped into a boat alongside, and pushed a little off from the ship.

'Ha! ha!' cried Daggoo, all at once, from his now quiet, swinging perch overhead; and looking further off from the side, we saw an arm thrust upright from the blue waves; a sight strange to see, as an arm thrust forth from the grass over a grave.

'Both! both! – it is both!' – cried Daggoo again with a joyful shout; and soon after, Queequeg was seen boldly striking out with one hand, and with the other clutching the long hair of the Indian. Drawn into the waiting boat, they were quickly brought to the deck; but Tashtego was long in coming to, and Queequeg did not look very brisk.

Now, how had this noble rescue been accomplished? Why, diving after the slowly descending head, Queequeg with his keen sword had made side lunges near its bottom, so as to scuttle a large hole there; then dropping his sword, had thrust his long arm far inwards and upwards, and so hauled out our poor Tash by the head. He averred, that upon first thrusting in for him, a leg was presented; but well knowing that that was not as it ought to be, and might occasion great trouble; – he had thrust back the leg, and by a dexterous heave and toss, had wrought a somerset upon the Indian; so that with the next trial, he came forth in the good old way – head foremost. As for the great head itself, that was doing as well as could be expected.

And thus, through the courage and great skill in obstetrics of Queequeg, the deliverance, or rather, delivery of Tashtego, was successfully accomplished, in the teeth, too, of the most untoward and apparently hopeless impediments; which is a lesson by no means to be forgotten. Midwifery should be taught in the same course with fencing and boxing, riding and rowing.

I know that this queer adventure of the Gay-Header's will be sure to seem incredible to some landsmen, though they themselves may have either seen or heard of some one's falling into a cistern ashore; an accident which not seldom happens, and with much less reason too than the Indian's, considering the exceeding slipperiness of the curb of the Sperm Whale's well.

But, peradventure, it may be sagaciously urged, how is this? We thought the tissued, infiltrated head of the Sperm Whale, was the lightest and most corky part about him; and yet thou makest it sink in an element of a far greater specific gravity than itself. We have thee there. Not at all, but I have ye; for at the time poor Tash fell in, the case had been nearly emptied of its lighter contents, leaving little but the dense tendinous wall of the well – a double welded, hammered substance, as I have before said, much heavier than the sea water, and a lump of which sinks in it like lead almost. But the tendency to rapid sinking in this substance was in the present instance materially counteracted by the other parts of the head remaining undetached from it, so that it sank very slowly and deliberately indeed, affording Queequeg a fair chance for performing his agile obstetrics on the run, as you may say. Yes, it was a running delivery, so it was.

Now, had Tashtego perished in that head, it had been a very precious perishing; smothered in the very whitest and daintiest of fragrant spermaceti; coffined, hearsed, and tombed in the secret inner chamber and sanctum sanctorum of the whale. Only one sweeter end can readily be recalled – the delicious death of an Ohio honey-hunter, who seeking honey in the crotch of a hollow tree, found such exceeding store of it, that leaning too far over, it sucked him in, so that he died embalmed. How many, think ye, have likewise fallen into Plato's honey head, and sweetly perished there?

79

THE PRAIRE

To scan the lines of his face, or feel the bumps on the head of this Leviathan; this is a thing which no Physiognomist or Phrenologist has as yet undertaken. Such an enterprise would seem almost as hopeful as for Lavater to have scrutinized the wrinkles on the Rock of Gibraltar, or for Gall to have mounted a ladder and manipulated the Dome of the Pantheon. Still, in that famous work of his, Lavater not only treats of the various faces of men, but also attentively studies the faces of horses, birds, serpents, and fish; and dwells in detail upon the modifications of expression discernible therein. Nor have Gall and his disciple Spurzheim failed to throw out some hints touching the phrenological characteristics of other beings than man. Therefore, though I am but ill qualified for a pioneer, in the application of these two semi-sciences to the whale, I will do my endeavor. I try all things; I achieve what I can.

Physiognomically regarded, the Sperm Whale is an anomalous creature. He has no proper nose. And since the nose is the central and most conspicuous of the features; and since it perhaps most modifies and finally controls their combined expression; hence it would seem that its entire absence, as an external appendage, must very largely affect the countenance of the whale. For as in landscape gardening, a spire, cupola, monument, or tower of some sort, is deemed almost indispensable to the completion of the scene; so no face can be physiognomically in keeping without the elevated open-work belfry of the nose. Dash the nose from Phidias's marble Jove, and what a sorry remainder! Nevertheless, Leviathan is of so mighty a magnitude, all his proportions are so stately, that the same deficiency which in the sculptured Jove were hideous, in him is no blemish at all. Nay, it is an added grandeur. A nose to the whale would have been impertinent. As on your physiognomical voyage you sail round his vast head in your jolly-boat, your noble conceptions of him are never insulted by the reflection that he has a nose to be pulled. A pestilent conceit, which so often will insist upon obtruding even when beholding the mightiest royal beadle on his throne.

In some particulars, perhaps the most imposing physiognomical view to be had of the Sperm Whale, is that of the full front of his head. This aspect is sublime.

In thought, a fine human brow is like the East when troubled with the morning. In the repose of the pasture, the curled brow of the bull has a touch of the grand in it. Pushing heavy cannon up mountain defiles, the elephant's brow is majestic. Human or animal, the mystical brow is as that great golden seal affixed by the German emperors to their decrees. It signifies – 'God: done this day by my hand.' But in most creatures, nay in man himself, very often the brow is but a mere strip of alpine land lying along the snow line. Few are the foreheads which like Shakspeare's or Melancthon's rise so high, and descend so low, that the eyes themselves seem clear, eternal, tideless mountain lakes; and all above them in the forehead's wrinkles, you seem to track the antlered thoughts descending there to drink, as the Highland hunters track the snow prints of the deer. But in the great Sperm Whale, this high and mighty god-like dignity inherent in the brow is so immensely amplified, that gazing on it, in that full front view, you feel the Deity and the dread powers more forcibly than in beholding any other object in living nature. For you see no one point precisely; not one distinct feature is revealed; no nose, eyes, ears, or mouth; no face; he has none, proper; nothing but that one broad firmament of a forehead, pleated with riddles; dumbly lowering with the doom of boats, and ships, and men. Nor, in profile, does this wondrous brow diminish; though that way viewed, its grandeur does not domineer upon you so. In profile, you plainly perceive that horizontal, semi-crescentic depression in the forehead's middle, which, in man, is Lavater's mark of genius.

But how? Genius in the Sperm Whale? Has the Sperm Whale ever written a book, spoken a speech? No, his great genius is declared in his doing nothing particular to prove it. It is moreover declared in his pyramidical silence. And this reminds me that had the great Sperm Whale been known to the young Orient World, he would have been deified by their child-magian thoughts. They deified the crocodile of the Nile, because the crocodile is tongueless; and the Sperm Whale has no tongue, or at least it is so exceedingly small, as to be incapable of protrusion. If hereafter any highly cultured, poetical nation shall lure back to their birth-right, the merry May-day gods of old; and livingly enthrone them again in the now egotistical sky; on the now unhaunted hill; then be sure, exalted to Jove's high seat, the great Sperm Whale shall lord it.

Champollion deciphered the wrinkled granite hieroglyphics. But there is no Champollion to decipher the Egypt of every man's and every being's face. Physiognomy, like every other human science, is but a passing fable. If then, Sir William Jones, who read in thirty languages, could not read the simplest peasant's face in its profounder and more subtle meanings, how may unlettered Ishmael hope to read the awful Chaldee of the Sperm Whale's brow? I but put that brow before you. Read it if you can.

80

THE NUT

If the Sperm Whale be physiognomically a Sphinx, to the phrenologist his brain seems that geometrical circle which it is impossible to square.

In the full-grown creature the skull will measure at least twenty feet in length. Unhinge the lower jaw, and the side view of this skull is as the side view of a moderately inclined plane resting throughout on a level base. But in life – as we have elsewhere seen – this inclined plane is angularly filled up, and almost squared by the enormous superincumbent mass of the junk and sperm. At the high end the skull forms a crater to bed that part of the mass; while under the long floor of this crater – in another cavity seldom exceeding ten inches in length and as many in depth – reposes the mere handful of this monster's brain. The brain is at least twenty feet from his apparent forehead in life; it is hidden away behind its vast outworks, like the innermost citadel within the amplified fortifications of Quebec. So like a choice casket is it secreted in him, that I have known some whalemen who peremptorily deny that the Sperm Whale has any other brain than that palpable semblance of one formed by the cubic-yards of his sperm magazine. Lying in strange folds, courses, and convolutions, to their apprehensions, it seems more in keeping with the idea of his general might to regard that mystic part of him as the seat of his intelligence.

It is plain, then, that phrenologically the head of this Leviathan, in the creature's living intact state, is an entire delusion. As for his true brain, you can then see no indications of it, nor feel any. The whale, like all things that are mighty, wears a false brow to the common world.

If you unload his skull of its spermy heaps and then take a rèar view of its rear end, which is the high end, you will be struck by its resemblance to the human skull, beheld in the same situation, and from the same point of view. Indeed, place this reversed skull (scaled down to the human magnitude) among a plate of men's skulls, and you would involuntarily confound it with them; and remarking the depressions on one part of its summit, in phrenological phrase you would say – This man had no self-esteem, and no veneration. And by those negations, considered along with the affirmative fact of his prodigious bulk and power, you can best form to yourself the truest, though not the most exhilarating conception of what the most exalted potency is.

But if from the comparative dimensions of the whale's proper brain, you deem it incapable of being adequately charted, then I have another idea for you. If you attentively regard almost any quadruped's spine, you will be struck with the resemblance of its vertebræ to a strung necklace of dwarfed skulls, all bearing rudimental resemblance to the skull proper. It is a German conceit, that the vertebræ are absolutely undeveloped skulls. But the curious external resemblance, I take it the Germans were not the first men to perceive. A foreign friend once pointed it out to me, in the skeleton of a foe he had slain, and with the vertebræ of which he was inlaying, in a sort of basso-relievo, the beaked prow of his canoe. Now, I consider that the phrenologists have omitted an important thing in not pushing their investigations from the cerebellum through the spinal canal. For I believe that much of a man's character will be found betokened in his backbone. I would rather feel your spine than your skull, whoever you are. A thin joist of a spine never yet upheld a full and noble soul. I rejoice in my spine, as in the firm audacious staff of that flag which I fling half out to the world.

Apply this spinal branch of phrenology to the Sperm Whale. His cranial cavity is continuous with the first neck-vertebra; and in that vertebra the bottom of the spinal canal will measure ten inches across, being eight in height, and of a triangular figure with the base downwards. As it passes through the remaining vertebræ the canal tapers in size, but for a considerable distance remains of large capacity. Now, of course, this canal is filled with much the same strangely fibrous substance – the spinal cord – as the brain; and directly communicates with the brain. And what is still more, for many feet after emerging from the brain's cavity, the spinal cord remains of an undecreasing girth, almost equal to that of the brain. Under all these circumstances, would it be unreasonable to survey and map out the whale's spine phrenologically? For, viewed in this light, the wonderful comparative smallness of his brain proper is more than compensated by the wonderful comparative magnitude of his spinal cord.

But leaving this hint to operate as it may with the phrenologists, I would merely assume the spinal theory for a moment, in reference to the Sperm Whale's hump. This august hump, if I mistake not, rises over one of the larger vertebræ, and is, therefore, in some sort, the outer convex mould of it. From its relative situation then, I should call this high hump the organ of firmness or indomitableness in the Sperm Whale. And that the great monster is indomitable, you will yet have reason to know.

81

THE PEQUOD MEETS THE VIRGIN

THE predestinated day arrived, and we duly met the ship Jungfrau, Derick De Deer, master, of Bremen.

At one time the greatest whaling people in the world, the Dutch and Germans are now among the least; but here and there at very wide intervals of latitude and longitude, you still occasionally meet with their flag in the Pacific.

For some reason, the Jungfrau seemed quite eager to pay her respects. While yet some distance from the Pequod, she rounded to, and dropping a boat, her captain was impelled towards us, impatiently standing in the bows instead of the stern.

'What has he in his hand there?' cried Starbuck, pointing to something wavingly held by the German. 'Impossible! – a lamp-feeder!'

'Not that,' said Stubb, 'no, no, it's a coffee-pot, Mr Starbuck; he's coming off to make us our coffee, is the Yarman; don't you see that big tin can there alongside of him? – that's his boiling water. Oh! he's all right, is the Yarman.'

'Go along with you,' cried Flask, 'it's a lamp-feeder and an oil-can. He's out of oil, and has come a-begging.'

However curious it may seem for an oil-ship to be borrowing oil on the whale-ground, and however much it may inversely contradict the old proverb about carrying coals to Newcastle, yet sometimes such a thing really happens; and in the present case Captain Derick De Deer did indubitably conduct a lamp-feeder as Flask did declare.

As he mounted the deck, Ahab abruptly accosted him, without at all heeding what he had in his hand; but in his broken lingo, the German soon evinced his complete ignorance of the White Whale; immediately turning the conversation to his lamp-feeder and oil-can, with some remarks touching his having to turn into his hammock at night in profound darkness – his last drop of Bremen oil being gone, and not a single flying-fish yet captured to supply the deficiency; concluding by hinting that his ship was indeed what in the Fishery is technically called a *clean* one (that is, an empty one), well deserving the name of Jungfrau or the Virgin.

His necessities supplied, Derick departed; but he had not gained his ship's side, when whales were almost simultaneously raised from the mast-heads of both vessels; and so eager for the chase was Derick, that without pausing to put his oil-can and lamp-feeder aboard, he slewed round his boat and made after the leviathan lamp-feeders.

Now, the game having risen to leeward, he and the other three German boats that soon followed him, had considerably the start of the Pequod's keels. There were eight whales, an average pod. Aware of their danger, they were going all abreast with great speed straight before the wind, rubbing their flanks as closely as so many spans of horses in harness. They left a great, wide wake, as though continually unrolling a great wide parchment upon the sea.

Full in this rapid wake, and many fathoms in the rear, swam a huge, humped old bull, which by his comparatively slow progress, as well as by the unusual yellowish incrustations overgrowing him, seemed afflicted with the jaundice, or some other infirmity. Whether this whale belonged to the pod in advance, seemed questionable; for it is not customary for such venerable leviathans to be at all social. Nevertheless, he stuck to their wake, though indeed their back water must have retarded him, because the white-bone or swell at his broad muzzle was a dashed one, like the swell formed when two hostile currents meet. His spout was short, slow, and laborious; coming forth with a choking sort of gush, and spending itself in torn shreds, followed by strange subterranean commotions in him, which seemed to have egress at his other buried extremity, causing the waters behind him to upbubble.

'Who's got some paregoric?' said Stubb, 'he has the stomach-ache, I'm afraid. Lord, think of having half an acre of stomach-ache! Adverse winds are holding mad Christmas in him, boys. It's the first foul wind I ever knew to blow from astern; but look, did ever whale yaw so before? it must be, he's lost his tiller.'

As an overladen Indiaman bearing down the Hindostan coast with a deck load of frightened horses, careens, buries, rolls, and wallows on her way; so did this old whale heave his aged bulk, and now and then partly turning over on his cumbrous rib-ends, expose the cause of his devious wake in the unnatural stump of his starboard fin. Whether he had lost that fin in battle, or had been born without it, it were hard to say.

'Only wait a bit, old chap, and I'll give ye a sling for that wounded arm,' cried cruel Flask, pointing to the whale-line near him.

'Mind he don't sling thee with it,' cried Starbuck. 'Give way, or the German will have him.'

With one intent all the combined rival boats were pointed for this one fish, because not only was he the largest, and therefore the most valuable whale, but he was nearest to them, and the other whales were going with such great velocity, moreover, as almost to defy pursuit for the time. At this juncture, the Pequod's keels had shot by the three German boats last lowered; but from the great start he had had, Derick's boat still led the chase, though every moment neared by his foreign rivals. The only thing they feared, was, that from being already so nigh to his mark, he would be enabled to dart his iron before they could completely overtake and pass him. As for Derick, he seemed quite confident that this would be the case, and occasionally with a deriding gesture shook his lamp-feeder at the other boats.

'The ungracious and ungrateful dog!' cried Starbuck; 'he mocks and dares me with the very poor-box I filled for him not five minutes ago!' – then in his old intense whisper – 'give way, greyhounds! Dog to it!'

'I tell ye what it is, men' – cried Stubb to his crew – 'It's against my religion to get mad; but I'd like to eat that villanous Yarman – Pull – wont ye? Are you going to let that rascal beat ye? Do ye love brandy? A hogshead of brandy, then, to the best man. Come, why don't some of ye burst a blood-vessel? Who's that been dropping an anchor overboard – we don't budge an inch – we're becalmed. Halloo, here's grass growing in the boat's bottom – and by the Lord, the mast there's budding. This won't do, boys. Look at that Yarman! The short and long of it is, men, will ye spit fire or not?'

'Oh! see the suds he makes!' cried Flask, dancing up and down – 'What a hump – Oh, *do* pile on the beef – lays like a log! Oh! my lads, *do* spring – slap-jacks and quohogs for supper, you know, my lads – baked clams and muffins – oh, *do, do,* spring – he's a hundred barreler – don't lose him now – don't, oh, *don't!* – see that Yarman – Oh! won't ye pull for your duff, my lads – such a sog! such a sogger! Don't ye love sperm? There goes three thousand dollars, men! – a bank! – a whole bank! The bank of England! – Oh, *do, do, do!* – What's that Yarman about now?'

At this moment Derick was in the act of pitching his lamp-feeder at the advancing boats, and also his oil-can; perhaps with the double view of retarding his rivals' way, and at the same time economically accelerating his own by the momentary impetus of the backward toss.

'The unmannerly Dutch dogger!' cried Stubb. 'Pull now, men, like fifty thousand line-of-battle-ship loads of red-haired devils. What d'ye say, Tashtego; are you the man to snap your spine in two-and-twenty pieces for the honor of old Gay-head? What d'ye say?'

'I say, pull like god-dam,' – cried the Indian.

Fiercely but evenly, incited by the taunts of the German, the Pequod's three boats now began ranging almost abreast; and, so disposed, momentarily neared him. In that fine, loose, chivalrous attitude of the headsman when drawing near to his prey, the three mates stood up proudly, occasionally backing the after oarsman with an exhilarating cry of, 'There she slides, now! Hurrah for the white-ash breeze! Down with the Yarman! Sail over him!'

But so decided an original start had Derick had, that spite of all their gallantry, he would have proved the victor in this race, had not a righteous judgment descended upon him in a crab which caught the blade of his midship oarsman. While this clumsy lubber was striving to free his white-ash, and while, in consequence, Derick's boat was nigh to capsizing, and he thundering away at his men in a mighty rage; – that was a good time for Starbuck, Stubb, and Flask. With a shout, they took a mortal start forwards, and slantingly ranged up on the German's quarter. An instant more, and all four boats were diagonally in the whale's immediate wake, while stretching from them, on both sides, was the foaming swell that he made.

It was a terrific, most pitiable, and maddening sight. The whale was now going head out, and sending his spout before him in a continual tormented jet; while his one poor fin beat his side in an agony of fright. Now to this hand, now to that, he yawed in his faltering flight, and still at every billow that he broke, he spasmodically sank in the sea, or sideways rolled towards the sky his one beating fin. So have I seen a bird with clipped wing, making affrighted broken circles in the air, vainly striving to escape the piratical hawks. But the bird has a voice, and with plaintive cries will make known her fear; but the fear of this vast dumb brute of the sea, was chained up and enchanted in him; he had no voice, save that choking respiration through his spiracle, and this made the sight of him unspeakably pitiable; while still, in his amazing bulk, portcullis jaw, and omnipotent tail, there was enough to appal the stoutest man who so pitied.

Seeing now that but a very few moments more would give the Pequod's boats the advantage, and rather than be thus foiled of his game, Derick chose to hazard what to him must have seemed a most unusually long dart, ere the last chance would for ever escape.

But no sooner did his harpooneer stand up for the stroke, than all three tigers – Queequeg, Tashtego, Daggoo – instinctively sprang to their feet, and standing in a diagonal row, simultaneously pointed their barbs; and, darted over the head of the German harpooneer, their three Nantucket irons entered the whale. Blinding vapors of foam and white-fire! The three boats, in the first fury of the whale's headlong rush, bumped the German's aside with such force, that both Derick and his baffled harpooneer were spilled out, and sailed over by the three flying keels.

'Don't be afraid, my butter-boxes,' cried Stubb, casting a passing glance upon them as he shot by; 'ye'll be picked up presently – all right – I saw some sharks astern – St Bernard's dogs, you know – relieve distressed travellers. Hurrah! this is the way to sail now. Every keel a sun-beam! Hurrah! – Here we go like three tin kettles at the tail of a mad cougar! This puts me in mind of fastening to an elephant in a tilbury on a plain – makes the wheel-spokes fly, boys, when you fasten to him that way; and there's danger of being pitched out too, when you strike a hill. Hurrah! this is the way a fellow feels when he's going to Davy Jones – all a rush down an endless inclined plane! Hurrah! this whale carries the everlasting mail!'

But the monster's run was a brief one. Giving a sudden gasp, he tumultuously sounded. With a grating rush, the three lines flew round the loggerheads with such a force as to gouge deep grooves in them; while so fearful were the harpooneers that this rapid sounding would soon exhaust the lines, that using all their dexterous might, they caught repeated smoking turns with the rope to hold on; till at last – owing to the perpendicular strain from the lead-lined chocks of the boats, whence the three ropes went straight down into the blue – the gunwales of the bows were almost even with the water, while the three sterns tilted high in the air. And the whale soon ceasing to sound, for some time they remained in that attitude, fearful of expending more line, though the position was a little ticklish. But though boats have been taken down and lost in this way, yet it is this 'holding on', as it is called; this hooking up by the sharp barbs of his live flesh from the back; this it is that often torments the Leviathan into soon rising again to meet the sharp lance of his foes. Yet not to speak of the peril of the thing, it is to be doubted whether this course is always the best; for it is but reasonable to presume, that the longer the stricken whale stays under water, the more he is exhausted. Because, owing to the enormous surface of him – in a full grown sperm whale something less than 2000 square feet – the pressure of the water is immense. We all know what an astonishing atmospheric weight we ourselves stand up under; even here, above-ground, in the air; how vast, then, the burden of a whale, bearing on his back a column of two hundred fathoms of ocean! It must at least equal the weight of fifty atmospheres. One whaleman has estimated it at the weight of twenty line-of-battle ships, with all their guns, and stores, and men on board.

As the three boats lay there on that gently rolling sea, gazing down into its eternal blue noon; and as not a single groan or cry of any sort, nay, not so much as a ripple or a bubble came up from its depths; what landsman would have thought, that beneath all that silence and placidity, the utmost monster of the seas was writhing and wrenching in agony! Not eight inches of perpendicular rope were visible at the bows. Seems it credible that by three such thin threads the great Leviathan was suspended like the big weight to an eight day clock. Suspended? and to what? To three bits of board. Is this the creature of whom it was once so triumphantly said – 'Canst thou fill his skin with barbed irons? or his head with fish-spears? The sword of him that layeth at him cannot hold, the spear, the dart, nor the habergeon: he esteemeth iron as straw; the arrow cannot make him flee; darts are counted as stubble; he laugheth at the shaking of a spear!' This the creature? this he? Oh! that unfulfilments should follow the prophets. For with the strength of a thousand thighs in his tail, Leviathan had run his head under the mountains of the sea, to hide him from the Pequod's fish-spears!

In that sloping afternoon sunlight, the shadows that the three boats sent down beneath the surface, must have been long enough and broad enough to shade half Xerxes' army. Who can tell how appalling to the wounded whale must have been such huge phantoms flitting over his head!

'Stand by, men; he stirs,' cried Starbuck, as the three lines suddenly vibrated in the water, distinctly conducting upwards to them, as by magnetic wires, the life and death throbs of the whale, so that every oarsman felt them in his seat. The next moment, relieved in great part from the downward strain at the bows, the boats gave a sudden bounce upwards, as a small ice-field will, when a dense herd of white bears are scared from it into the sea.

'Haul in! Haul in!' cried Starbuck again; 'he's rising.'

The lines, of which, hardly an instant before, not one hand's breadth could have been gained, were now in long quick coils flung back all dripping into the boats, and soon the whale broke water within two ship's lengths of the hunters.

His motions plainly denoted his extreme exhaustion. In most land animals there are certain valves or flood-gates in many of their veins, whereby when wounded, the blood is in some degree at least instantly shut off in certain directions. Not so with the whale; one of whose peculiarities it is, to have an entire non-valvular structure of the blood-vessels, so that when pierced even by so small a point as a harpoon, a deadly drain is at once begun upon his whole arterial system; and when this is heightened by the extraordinary pressure of water at a great distance below the surface, his life may be said to pour from him in incessant streams. Yet so vast is the quantity of blood in him, and so distant and numerous its interior fountains, that he will keep thus bleeding and bleeding for a considerable period; even as in a drought a river will flow, whose source is in the well-springs of far-off and undiscernible hills. Even now, when the boats pulled upon this whale, and perilously drew over his swaying flukes, and the lances were darted into him, they were followed by steady jets from the new made wound, which kept continually playing, while the natural spout-hole in his head was only at intervals, however rapid, sending its affrighted moisture into the air. From this last vent no blood yet came, because no vital part of him had thus far been struck. His life, as they significantly call it, was untouched.

As the boats now more closely surrounded him, the whole upper part of his form, with much of it that is ordinarily submerged, was plainly revealed. His eyes, or rather the places where his eyes had been, were beheld. As strange misgrown masses gather in the knot-holes of the noblest oaks when prostrate, so from the points which the whale's eyes had once occupied, now protruded blind bulbs, horribly pitiable to see. But pity there was none. For all his old age, and his one arm, and his blind eyes, he must die the death and be murdered, in order to light the gay bridals and other merry-makings of men, and also to illuminate the solemn churches that preach unconditional inoffensiveness by all to all. Still rolling in his blood, at last he partially disclosed a strangely discolored bunch or protuberance, the size of a bushel, low down on the flank.

'A nice spot,' cried Flask; 'just let me prick him there once.'

'Avast!' cried Starbuck, 'there's no need of that!'

But humane Starbuck was too late. At the instant of the dart an ulcerous jet shot from this cruel wound, and goaded by it into more than sufferable anguish, the whale now spouting thick blood, with swift fury blindly darted at the craft, bespattering them and their glorying crews all over with showers of gore, capsizing Flask's boat and marring the bows. It was his death stroke. For, by this time, so spent was he by loss of blood, that he helplessly rolled away from the wreck he had made; lay panting on his side, impotently flapped with his stumped fin, then over and over slowly revolved like a waning world; turned up the white secrets of his belly; lay like a log, and died. It was most piteous, that last expiring spout. As when by unseen hands the water is gradually drawn off from some mighty fountain, and with half-stifled melancholy gurglings the spray-column lowers and lowers to the ground – so the last long dying spout of the whale.

Soon, while the crews were awaiting the arrival of the ship, the body showed symptoms of sinking with all its treasures unrifled. Immediately, by Starbuck's orders, lines were secured to it at different points, so that ere long every boat was a buoy; the sunken whale being suspended a few inches beneath them by the cords. By very heedful management, when the ship drew nigh, the whale was transferred to her side, and was strongly secured there by the stiffest fluke-chains, for it was plain that unless artificially upheld, the body would at once sink to the bottom.

It so chanced that almost upon first cutting into him with

the spade, the entire length of a corroded harpoon was found imbedded in his flesh, on the lower part of the bunch before described. But as the stumps of harpoons are frequently found in the dead bodies of captured whales, with the flesh perfectly healed around them, and no prominence of any kind to denote their place; therefore, there must needs have been some other unknown reason in the present case fully to account for the ulceration alluded to. But still more curious was the fact of a lance-head of stone being found in him, not far from the buried iron, the flesh perfectly firm about them. Who had darted that stone lance? And when? It might have been darted by some Nor' West Indian long before America was discovered.

What other marvels might have been rummaged out of this monstrous cabinet there is no telling. But a sudden stop was put to further discoveries, by the ship's being unprecedently dragged over sideways to the sea, owing to the body's immensely increasing tendency to sink. However, Starbuck, who had the ordering of affairs, hung on to it to the last; hung on to it so resolutely, indeed, that when at length the ship would have been capsized, if still persisting in locking arms with the body, then, when the command was given to break clear from it, such was the immovable strain upon the timber-heads to which the fluke-chains and cables were fastened, that it was impossible to cast them off. Meantime everything in the Pequod was aslant. To cross to the other side of the deck was like walking up the steep gabled roof of a house. The ship groaned and gasped. Many of the ivory inlayings of her bulwarks and cabins were started from their places, by the unnatural dislocation. In vain handspikes and crows were brought to bear upon the immovable fluke-chains, to pry them adrift from the timber-heads; and so low had the whale now settled that the submerged ends could not be at all approached, while every moment whole tons of ponderosity seemed added to the sinking bulk, and the ship seemed on the point of going over.

'Hold on, hold on, won't ye?' cried Stubb to the body,

'don't be in such a devil of a hurry to sink! By thunder, men, we must do something or go for it. No use prying there; avast, I say with your handspikes, and run one of ye for a prayer book and a pen-knife, and cut the big chains.'

'Knife? Aye, aye,' cried Queequeg, and seizing the carpenter's heavy hatchet, he leaned out of a porthole, and steel to iron, began slashing at the largest fluke-chains. But a few strokes, full of sparks, were given, when the exceeding strain effected the rest. With a terrific snap, every fastening went adrift; the ship righted, the carcase sank.

Now, this occasional inevitable sinking of the recently killed Sperm Whale is a very curious thing; nor has any fisherman yet adequately accounted for it. Usually the dead Sperm Whale floats with great buoyancy, with its side or belly considerably elevated above the surface. If the only whales that thus sank were old, meagre, and broken-hearted creatures, their pads of lard diminished and all their bones heavy and rheumatic; then you might with some reason assert that this sinking is caused by an uncommon specific gravity in the fish so sinking, consequent upon this absence of buoyant matter in him. But it is not so. For young whales, in the highest health, and swelling with noble aspirations, prematurely cut off in the warm flush and May of life, with all their panting lard about them; even these brawny, buoyant heroes do sometimes sink.

Be it said, however, that the Sperm Whale is far less liable to this accident than any other species. Where one of that sort goes down, twenty Right Whales do. This difference in the species is no doubt imputable in no small degree to the greater quantity of bone in the Right Whale; his Venetian blinds alone sometimes weighing more than a ton; from this incumbrance the Sperm Whale is wholly free. But there are instances where, after the lapse of many hours or several days, the sunken whale again rises, more buoyant than in life. But the reason of this is obvious. Gases are generated in him; he swells to a prodigious magnitude; becomes a sort of animal balloon. A line-of-battle ship could hardly keep him under then. In the Shore Whaling, on soundings, among the Bays of New Zealand, when a Right Whale gives token of sinking, they fasten buoys to him, with plenty of rope; so that when the body has gone down, they know where to look for it when it shall have ascended again.

It was not long after the sinking of the body that a cry was heard from the Pequod's mast-heads, announcing that the Jungfrau was again lowering her boats; though the only spout in sight was that of a Fin-Back, belonging to the species of uncapturable whales, because of its incredible power of swimming. Nevertheless, the Fin-Back's spout is so similar to the Sperm Whale's, that by unskilful fishermen it is often mistaken for it. And consequently Derick and all his host were now in valiant chase of this unnearable brute. The Virgin crowding all sail, made after her four young keels, and thus they all disappeared far to leeward, still in bold, hopeful chase.

Oh! many are the Fin-Backs, and many are the Dericks, my friend.

82

THE HONOR AND GLORY OF WHALING

There are some enterprises in which a careful disorderliness is the true method.

The more I dive into this matter of whaling, and push my researches up to the very spring-head of it, so much the more am I impressed with its great honorableness and antiquity; and especially when I find so many great demi-gods and heroes, prophets of all sorts, who one way or other have shed distinction upon it, I am transported with the reflection that I myself belong, though but subordinately, to so emblazoned a fraternity.

The gallant Perseus, a son of Jupiter, was the first whaleman; and to the eternal honor of our calling be it said, that the first whale attacked by our brotherhood was not killed with any sordid intent. Those were the knightly days of our profession, when we only bore arms to succor the distressed, and not to fill men's lamp-feeders. Every one knows the fine story of Perseus and Andromeda; how the lovely Andromeda, the daughter of a king, was tied to a rock on the sea-coast, and as Leviathan was in the very act of carrying her off, Perseus, the prince of whalemen, intrepidly advancing, harpooned the monster, and delivered and married the maid. It was an admirable artistic exploit, rarely achieved by the best harpooneers of the present day; inasmuch as this Leviathan was slain at the very first dart. And let no man doubt this Arkite story; for in the ancient Joppa, now Jaffa, on the Syrian coast, in one of the Pagan temples, there stood for many ages the vast skeleton of a whale, which the city's legends and all the inhabitants asserted to be the identical bones of the monster that Perseus slew. When the Romans took Joppa, the same skeleton was carried to Italy in triumph. What seems most singular and suggestively important in this story, is this: it was from Joppa that Jonah set sail.

Akin to the adventure of Perseus and Andromeda – indeed, by some supposed to be indirectly derived from it – is that famous story of St George and the Dragon; which dragon I maintain to have been a whale; for in many old chronicles whales and dragons are strangely jumbled together, and often stand for each other. 'Thou art as a lion of the waters, and as a dragon of the sea,' saith Ezekiel; hereby, plainly meaning a whale; in truth, some versions of the Bible use that word itself. Besides, it would much subtract from the glory of the exploit had St George but encountered a crawling reptile of the land, instead of doing battle with the great monster of the deep. Any man may kill a snake, but only a Perseus, a St George, a Coffin, have the heart in them to march boldly up to a whale.

Let not the modern paintings of this scene mislead us; for though the creature encountered by that valiant whaleman of old is vaguely represented of a griffin-like shape, and though the battle is depicted on land and the saint on horseback, yet considering the great ignorance of those times, when the true form of the whale was unknown to artists; and considering that as in Perseus' case, St George's whale might have crawled up out of the sea on the beach; and considering that the animal ridden by St George might have been only a large seal, or sea-horse; bearing all this in mind, it will not appear altogether incompatible with the sacred legend and the ancientest draughts of the scene, to hold this so-called dragon no other than the great Leviathan himself. In fact, placed before the strict and piercing truth, this whole story will fare like that fish, flesh, and fowl idol of the Philistines, Dagon by name; who being planted before the ark of Israel, his horse's head and both the palms of his hands fell off from him, and only the stump or fishy part of him remained. Thus, then, one of our own noble stamp, even a whaleman, is the tutelary guardian of England; and by good rights, we harpooneers of Nantucket should be enrolled in the most noble order of St George. And therefore, let not the knights of that honorable company (none of whom, I venture to say, have ever had to do with a whale like their great patron), let them never eye a Nantucketer with disdain, since even in our woollen frocks and tarred trowsers we are much better entitled to St George's decoration than they.

Whether to admit Hercules among us or not, concerning this I long remained dubious: for though according to the Greek mythologies, that antique Crockett and Kit Carson – that brawny doer of rejoicing good deeds, was swallowed down and thrown up by a whale; still, whether that strictly makes a whaleman of him, that might be mooted. It nowhere appears that he ever actually harpooned his fish, unless, indeed, from the inside. Nevertheless, he may be deemed a sort of involuntary whaleman; at any rate the whale caught him, if he did not the whale. I claim him for one of our clan.

But, by the best contradictory authorities, this Grecian story of Hercules and the whale is considered to be derived from the still more ancient Hebrew story of Jonah and the whale; and vice versa; certainly they are very similar. If I claim the demigod then, why not the prophet?

Nor do heroes, saints, demigods, and prophets alone comprise the whole roll of our order. Our grand master is still to be named; for like royal kings of old times, we find the head-waters of our fraternity in nothing short of the great gods themselves. That wondrous oriental story is now to be rehearsed from the Shaster, which gives us the dread Vishnoo, one of the three persons in the godhead of the Hindoos; gives us this divine Vishnoo himself for our Lord; – Vishnoo, who, by the first of his ten earthly incarnations, has for ever set apart and sanctified the whale. When Brahma, or the God of Gods, saith the Shaster, resolved to recreate the world after one of its periodical dissolutions, he gave birth to Vishnoo, to preside over the work; but the Vedas, or mystical books, whose perusal would seem to have been indispensable to Vishnoo before beginning the creation, and which therefore must have contained something in the shape of practical hints to young architects, these Vedas were lying at the bottom of the waters; so Vishnoo became incarnate in a whale, and sounding down in him to the uttermost depths, rescued the sacred volumes. Was not this Vishnoo a whaleman, then? even as a man who rides a horse is called a horseman?

Perseus, St George, Hercules, Jonah, and Vishnoo! there's a member-roll for you! What club but the whaleman's can head off like that?

83

JONAH HISTORICALLY REGARDED

REFERENCE was made to the historical story of Jonah and the whale in the preceding chapter. Now some Nantucketers rather distrust this historical story of Jonah and the whale. But then there were some sceptical Greeks and Romans, who, standing out from the orthodox pagans of their times, equally doubted the story of Hercules and the whale, and Arion and the dolphin; and yet their doubting those traditions did not make those traditions one whit the less facts, for all that.

One old Sag-Harbor whaleman's chief reason for questioning the Hebrew story was this: – He had one of those quaint old-fashioned Bibles, embellished with curious, unscientific plates; one of which represented Jonah's whale with two spouts in his head – a peculiarity only true with respect to a species of the Leviathan (the Right Whale, and the varieties of that order), concerning which the fishermen have this saying, 'A penny roll would choke him;' his swallow is so very small. But, to this, Bishop Jebb's anticipative answer is ready. It is not necessary, hints the Bishop, that we consider Jonah as tombed in the whale's belly, but as temporarily lodged in some part of his mouth. And this seems reasonable enough in the good Bishop. For truly, the Right Whale's mouth would accommodate a couple of whist-tables, and comfortably seat all the players. Possibly, too, Jonah might have ensconced himself in a hollow tooth; but, on second thoughts, the Right Whale is toothless.

Another reason which Sag-Harbor (he went by that name) urged for his want of faith in this matter of the prophet, was something obscurely in reference to his incarcerated body and the whale's gastric juices. But this objection likewise falls to the ground, because a German exegetist supposes that Jonah must have taken refuge in the floating body of a *dead* whale – even as the French soldiers in the Russian campaign turned their dead horses into tents, and crawled into them. Besides, it has been divined by other continental commentators, that when Jonah was thrown overboard from the Joppa ship, he straightway effected his escape to another vessel near by, some vessel with a whale for a figure-head; and, I would add, possibly called 'The Whale,' as some craft are nowadays christened the 'Shark,' the 'Gull,' the 'Eagle.' Nor have there been wanting learned exegetists who have opined that the whale mentioned in the book of Jonah merely meant a life-preserver –

an inflated bag of wind – which the endangered prophet swam to, and so was saved from a watery doom. Poor Sag-Harbor, therefore, seems worsted all round. But he had still another reason for his want of faith. It was this, if I remember right: Jonah was swallowed by the whale in the Mediterranean Sea, and after three days he was vomited up somewhere within three days' journey of Nineveh, a city on the Tigris, very much more than three days' journey across from the nearest point of the Mediterranean coast. How is that?

But was there no other way for the whale to land the prophet within that short distance of Nineveh? Yes. He might have carried him round by the way of the Cape of Good Hope. But not to speak of the passage through the whole length of the Mediterranean, and another passage up the Persian Gulf and Red Sea, such a supposition would involve the complete circumnavigation of all Africa in three days, not to speak of the Tigris waters, near the site of Nineveh, being too shallow for any whale to swim in. Besides, this idea of Jonah's weathering the Cape of Good Hope at so early a day would wrest the honor of the discovery of that great headland from Bartholomew Diaz, its reputed discoverer, and so make modern history a liar.

But all these foolish arguments of old Sag-Harbor only evinced his foolish pride of reason – a thing still more reprehensible in him, seeing that he had but little learning except what he had picked up from the sun and the sea. I say it only shows his foolish, impious pride, and abominable, devilish rebellion against the reverend clergy. For by a Portuguese Catholic priest, this very idea of Jonah's going to Nineveh via the Cape of Good Hope was advanced as a signal magnification of the general miracle. And so it was. Besides, to this day, the highly enlightened Turks devoutly believe in the historical story of Jonah. And some three centuries ago, an English traveller in old Harris's Voyages, speaks of a Turkish Mosque built in honor of Jonah, in which mosque was a miraculous lamp that burnt without any oil.

84

PITCHPOLING

To make them run easily and swiftly, the axles of carriages are anointed; and for much the same purpose, some whalers perform an analogous operation upon their boat; they grease the bottom. Nor is it to be doubted that as such a procedure can do no harm, it may possibly be of no contemptible advantage; considering that oil and water are hostile, that oil is a sliding thing, and that the object in view is to make the boat slide bravely. Queequeg believed strongly in anointing his boat, and one morning not long after the German ship Jungfrau disappeared, took more than customary pains in that occupation; crawling under its bottom, where it hung over the side, and rubbing in the unctuousness as though diligently seeking to insure a crop of hair from the craft's bald keel. He seemed to be working in obedience to some particular presentiment. Nor did it remain unwarranted by the event.

Towards noon whales were raised; but so soon as the ship sailed down to them, they turned and fled with swift precipitancy; a disordered flight, as of Cleopatra's barges from Actium.

Nevertheless, the boats pursued, and Stubb's was foremost. By great exertion, Tashtego at last succeeded in planting one iron; but the stricken whale, without at all sounding, still continued his horizontal flight, with added fleetness. Such unintermitted strainings upon the planted iron must sooner or later inevitably extract it. It became imperative to lance the flying whale, or be content to lose him. But to haul the boat up to his flank was impossible, he swam so fast and furious. What then remained?

Of all the wondrous devices and dexterities, the sleights of hand and countless subtleties, to which the veteran whaleman is so often forced, none exceed that fine manœuvre with the lance called pitchpoling. Small sword, or broad sword, in all its exercises boasts nothing like it. It is only indispensable with an inveterate running whale; its grand fact and feature is the wonderful distance to which the long lance is accurately darted from a violently rocking, jerking boat, under extreme headway. Steel and wood included, the entire spear is some ten or twelve feet in length; the staff is much slighter than that of the harpoon, and also of a lighter material – pine. It is furnished with a small rope called a warp, of considerable length, by which it can be hauled back to the hand after darting.

But before going further, it is important to mention here, that though the harpoon may be pitchpoled in the same way with the lance, yet it is seldom done; and when done, is still less frequently successful, on account of the greater weight and inferior length of the harpoon as compared with the lance, which in effect become serious drawbacks. As a general thing, therefore, you must first get fast to a whale, before any pitchpoling comes into play.

Look now at Stubb, a man who from his humorous, deliberate coolness and equanimity in the direst emergencies, was specially qualified to excel in pitchpoling. Look at him; he stands upright in the tossed bow of the flying boat; wrapt in fleecy foam, the towing whale is forty feet ahead. Handling the long lance lightly, glancing twice or thrice along its length to see if it be exactly straight, Stubb whistlingly gathers up the coil of the warp in one hand, so as to secure its free end in his grasp, leaving the rest unobstructed. Then holding the lance full before his waistband's middle, he levels it at the whale; when, covering him with it, he steadily depresses the butt-end in his hand, thereby elevating the point till the weapon stands fairly balanced upon his palm, fifteen feet in the air. He minds you somewhat of a juggler, balancing a long staff on his chin. Next moment with a rapid, nameless impulse, in a superb lofty arch the bright steel spans the foaming distance, and quivers in the life spot of the whale. Instead of sparkling water, he now spouts red blood.

'That drove the spigot out of him!' cries Stubb. ''Tis July's immortal Fourth; all fountains must run wine to-day! Would now, it were old Orleans whiskey, or old Ohio, or unspeakable old Monongahela! Then, Tashtego, lad, I'd have ye hold a canakin to the jet, and we'd drink round it! Yea, verily, hearts alive, we'd brew choice punch in the spread of his spout-hole there, and from that live punch-bowl quaff the living stuff!'

Again and again to such gamesome talk, the dexterous dart is repeated, the spear returning to its master like a greyhound held in skilful leash. The agonized whale goes into his flurry; the tow-line is slackened, and the pitchpoler dropping astern, folds his hands, and mutely watches the monster die.

85

THE FOUNTAIN

THAT for six thousand years – and no one knows how many millions of ages before – the great whales should have been spouting all over the sea, and sprinkling and mistifying the gardens of the deep, as with so many sprinkling or mistifying pots; and that for some centuries back, thousands of hunters should have been close by the fountain of the whale, watching these sprinklings and spoutings – that all this should be, and yet, that down to this blessed minute (fifteen and a quarter minutes past one o'clock P.M. of this sixteenth day of December, A.D. 1850), it should still remain a problem, whether these spoutings are, after all, really water, or nothing but vapor – this is surely a noteworthy thing.

Let us, then, look at this matter, along with some interesting items contingent. Every one knows that by the peculiar cunning of their gills, the finny tribes in general breathe the air which at all times is combined with the element in which they swim hence, a herring or a cod might live a century, and never once raises its head above the surface. But owing to his marked internal structure which gives him regular lungs, like a human being's, the whale can only live by inhaling the disengaged air in the open atmosphere. Wherefore the necessity for his periodical visits to the upper world. But he cannot in any degree breathe through his mouth, for, in his ordinary attitude, the Sperm Whale's mouth is buried at least eight feet beneath the surface; and what is still more, his windpipe has no connexion with his mouth. No, he breathes through his spiracle alone; and this is on the top of his head.

If I say, that in any creature breathing is only a function indispensable to vitality, inasmuch as it withdraws from the air a certain element, which being subsequently brought into contact with the blood imparts to the blood its vivifying principle, I do not think I shall err; though I may possibly use some superfluous scientific words. Assume it, and it follows that if all the blood in a man could be aerated with one breath, he might then seal up his nostrils and not fetch another for a considerable time. That is to say, he would then live without breathing. Anomalous as it may seem, this is precisely the case with the whale, who systematically lives, by intervals, his full hour and more (when at the bottom) without drawing a single breath, or so much as in any way inhaling a particle of air; for, remember, he has no gills. How is this? Between his ribs and on each side of his spine he is supplied with a remarkable involved Cretan labyrinth of vermicelli-like vessels, which vessels, when he quits the surface, are completely distended with oxygenated blood. So that for an hour or more, a thousand fathoms in the sea, he carries a surplus stock of vitality in him, just as the camel crossing the waterless desert carries a surplus supply of drink for future use in its four supplementary stomachs. The anatomical fact of this labyrinth is indisputable; and that the supposition founded upon it is reasonable and true, seems the more cogent to me, when I consider the otherwise inexplicable obstinacy of that leviathan in *having his spoutings out*, as the fishermen phrase it. This is what I mean. If unmolested, upon rising to the surface, the Sperm Whale will continue there for a period of time exactly uniform with all his other unmolested risings. Say he stays eleven minutes, and jets seventy times, that is, respires seventy breaths; then whenever he rises again, he will be sure to have his seventy breaths over again, to a minute. Now, if after he fetches a few breaths you alarm him, so that he sounds, he will be always dodging up again to make good his regular allowance of air. And not till those seventy breaths are told, will he finally go down to stay out his full term below. Remark, however, that in different individuals these rates are different; but in any one they are alike. Now, why should the whale thus insist upon having his spoutings out, unless it be to replenish his reservoir of air, ere descending for good? How obvious is it, too, that this necessity for the whale's rising exposes him to all the fatal hazards of the chase. For not by hook or by net could this vast leviathan be caught, when sailing a thousand fathoms beneath the sunlight. Not so much thy skill, then, O hunter, as the great necessities, that strike the victory to thee!

In man, breathing is incessantly going on – one breath only serving for two or three pulsations; so that whatever other business he has to attend to, waking or sleeping, breathe he must, or die he will. But the Sperm Whale only breathes about one seventh or Sunday of his time.

It has been said that the whale only breathes through his spout-hole; if it could truthfully be added that his spouts are mixed with water, then I opine we should be furnished with the reason why his sense of smell seems obliterated in him; for the only thing about him that at all answers to his nose is that identical spout-hole; and being so clogged with two elements, it could not be expected to have the power of smelling. But owing to the mystery of the spout – whether it be water or whether it be vapor – no absolute certainty can as yet be arrived at on this head. Sure it is, nevertheless, that the Sperm Whale has no proper olfactories. But what does he want of them? No roses, no violets, no Cologne-water in the sea.

Furthermore, as his windpipe solely opens into the tube of his spouting canal, and as that long canal – like the grand Erie Canal – is furnished with a sort of locks (that open and shut) for the downward retention of air or the upward exclusion of water, therefore the whale has no voice, unless you insult him by saying, that when he so strangely rumbles, he talks through his nose. But then again, what has the whale to say? Seldom have I known any profound being that had anything to say to this world, unless forced to stammer out something by way of getting a living. Oh! happy that the world is such an excellent listener!

Now, the spouting canal of the Sperm Whale, chiefly intended as it is for the conveyance of air, and for several feet laid along, horizontally, just beneath the upper surface of his head, and a little to one side; this curious canal is very much like a gas-pipe laid down in a city on one side of a street. But the question returns whether this gas-pipe is also a water-pipe; in other words, whether the spout of the Sperm Whale is the mere vapor of the exhaled breath, or whether that exhaled breath is mixed with water taken in at the mouth, and discharged through the spiracle. It is certain that the mouth indirectly communicates with the spouting canal; but it cannot be proved that this is for the purpose of discharging water through the spiracle. Because the greatest necessity for so doing would seem to be, when in feeding he accidentally takes in water. But the Sperm Whale's food is far beneath the surface, and there he cannot spout even if he would. Besides, if you regard him very closely, and time him with your watch, you will find that when unmolested, there is an undeviating rhyme between the periods of his jets and the ordinary periods of respiration.

But why pester one with all this reasoning on the subject? Speak out! You have seen him spout; then declare what the spout is; can you not tell water from air? My dear sir, in this world it is not so easy to settle these plain things. I have ever found your plain things the knottiest of all. And as for this whale spout, you might almost stand in it, and yet be undecided as to what it is precisely.

The central body of it is hidden in the snowy sparkling mist enveloping it; and how can you certainly tell whether any water falls from it, when, always, when you are close enough to a whale to get a close view of his spout, he is in a prodigious commotion, the water cascading all around him. And if at such times you should think that you really perceived drops of moisture in the spout, how do you know that they are not merely condensed from its vapor; or how do you know that they are not those identical drops superficially lodged in the spout-hole fissure, which is countersunk into the summit of the whale's head? For even when tranquilly swimming through the mid-day sea in a calm, with his elevated hump sun-dried as a dromedary's in the desert; even then, the whale always carries a small basin of water on his head, as under a blazing sun you will sometimes see a cavity in a rock filled up with rain.

Nor is it at all prudent for the hunter to be over curious touching the precise nature of the whale spout. It will not do for him to be peering into it, and putting his face in it. You cannot go with your pitcher to this fountain and fill it, and bring it away. For even when coming into slight contact with the outer, vapory shreds of the jet, which will often happen, your skin will feverishly smart, from the acridness of the thing so touching it. And I know one, who coming into still closer contact with the spout, whether with some scientific object in view, or otherwise, I cannot say, the skin peeled off from his cheek and arm. Wherefore, among whalemen, the spout is deemed poisonous; they try to evade it. Another thing; I have heard it said, and I do not much doubt it, that if the jet is fairly spouted into your eyes, it will blind you. The wisest thing the investigator can do then, it seems to me, is to let this deadly spout alone.

Still, we can hypothesize, even if we cannot prove and establish. My hypothesis is this: that the spout is nothing but mist. And besides other reasons, to this conclusion I am impelled, by considerations touching the great inherent dignity and sublimity of the Sperm Whale; I account him no common, shallow being, inasmuch as it is an undisputed fact that he is never found on soundings, or near shores; all other whales sometimes are. He is both ponderous and profound. And I am convinced that from the heads of all ponderous profound beings, such as Plato, Pyrrho, the Devil, Jupiter, Dante, and so on, there always goes up a certain semi-visible steam, while in the act of thinking deep thoughts. While composing a little treatise on Eternity, I had the curiosity to place a mirror before me; and ere long saw reflected there, a curious involved worming and undulation in the atmosphere over my head. The invariable moisture of my hair, while plunged in deep thought, after six cups of hot tea in my thin shingled attic, of an August noon; this seems an additional argument for the above supposition.

And how nobly it raises our conceit of the mighty, misty monster, to behold him solemnly sailing through a calm tropical sea; his vast, mild head overhung by a canopy of vapor, engendered by his incommunicable contemplations, and that vapor – as you will sometimes see it – glorified by a rainbow, as if Heaven itself had put its seal upon his thoughts. For, d'ye see, rainbows do not visit the clear air; they only irradiate vapor. And so, through all the thick mists of the dim doubts in my mind, divine intuitions now and then shoot, enkindling my fog with a heavenly ray. And for this I thank God; for all have doubts; many deny; but doubts or denials, few along with them, have intuitions. Doubts of all things earthly, and intuitions of some things heavenly; this combination makes neither believer nor infidel, but makes a man who regards them both with equal eye.

86

THE TAIL

OTHER poets have warbled the praises of the soft eye of the antelope, and the lovely plumage of the bird that never alights; less celestial, I celebrate a tail.

Reckoning the largest sized Sperm Whale's tail to begin at that point of the trunk where it tapers to about the girth of a man, it comprises upon its upper surface alone, an area of at least fifty square feet. The compact round body of its root expands into two broad, firm, flat palms or flukes, gradually shoaling away to less than an inch in thickness. At the crotch or junction, these flukes slightly overlap, then sideways recede from each other like wings, leaving a wide vacancy between. In no living thing are the lines of beauty more exquisitely defined than in the crescentic borders of these flukes. At its utmost expansion in the full grown whale, the tail will considerably exceed twenty feet across.

The entire member seems a dense webbed bed of welded sinews; but cut into it, and you find that three distinct strata compose it: – upper, middle, and lower. The fibres in the upper and lower layers, are long and horizontal; those of the middle one, very short, and running crosswise between the outside layers. This triune structure, as much as anything else, imparts power to the tail. To the student of old Roman walls, the middle layer will furnish a curious parallel to the thin course of tiles always alternating with the stone in those wonderful relics of the antique, and which undoubtedly contribute so much to the great strength of the masonry.

But as if this vast local power in the tendinous tail were not enough, the whole bulk of the leviathan is knit over with a warp and woof of muscular fibres and filaments, which passing on either side the loins and running down into the flukes, insensibly blend with them, and largely contribute to their might; so that in the tail the confluent measureless force of the whole whale seems concentrated to a point. Could annihilation occur to matter, this were the thing to do it.

Nor does this – its amazing strength, at all tend to cripple the graceful flexion of its motions; where infantileness of ease undulates through a Titanism of power. On the contrary, those motions derive their most appalling beauty from it. Real strength never impairs beauty or harmony, but it often bestows it; and in everything imposingly beautiful, strength has much to do with the magic. Take away the tied tendons that all over seem bursting from the marble in the carved Hercules, and its charm would be gone. As devout Eckerman lifted the linen sheet from the naked corpse of Goethe, he was overwhelmed with the massive chest of the man, that seemed as a Roman triumphal arch. When Angelo paints even God the Father in human form, mark what robustness is there. And whatever they may reveal of the divine love in the Son, the soft, curled, hermaphroditical Italian pictures, in which his idea has been most successfully embodied; these pictures, so destitute as they are of all brawniness, hint nothing of any power, but the mere negative, feminine one of submission and endurance, which on all hands it is conceded, form the peculiar practical virtues of his teachings.

Such is the subtle elasticity of the organ I treat of, that whether wielded in sport, or in earnest, or in anger, whatever be the mood it be in, its flexions are invariably marked by exceeding grace. Therein no fairy's arm can transcend it.

Five great motions are peculiar to it. First, when used as a fin for progression; Second, when used as a mace in battle; Third, in sweeping; Fourth, in lobtailing; Fifth, in peaking flukes.

First: Being horizontal in its position, the Leviathan's tail acts in a different manner from the tails of all other sea creatures. It never wriggles. In man or fish, wriggling is a sign of inferiority. To the whale, his tail is the sole means of propulsion. Scroll-wise coiled forwards beneath the body, and then rapidly sprung backwards, it is this which gives that singular darting, leaping motion to the monster when furiously swimming. His side-fins only serve to steer by.

Second: It is a little significant, that while one sperm whale only fights another sperm whale with his head and jaw, nevertheless, in his conflicts with man, he chiefly and contemptuously uses his tail. In striking at a boat, he swiftly curves away his flukes from it, and the blow is only inflicted by the recoil. If it be made in the unobstructed air, especially if it descend to its mark, the stroke is then simply irresistible. No ribs of man or boat can withstand it. Your only salvation lies in eluding it; but if it comes sideways through the opposing water, then partly owing to the light buoyancy of the whale-boat, and the elasticity of its materials, a cracked rib or a dashed plank or two, a sort of stitch in the side, is generally the most serious result. These submerged side blows are so often received in the fishery, that they are accounted mere child's play. Some one strips off a frock, and the hole is stopped.

Third: I cannot demonstrate it, but it seems to me, that in the whale the sense of touch is concentrated in the tail; for in this respect there is a delicacy in it only equalled by the daintiness of the elephant's trunk. This delicacy is chiefly evinced in the action of sweeping, when in maidenly gentleness the whale with a certain soft slowness moves his immense flukes from side to side upon the surface of the sea; and if he feel but a sailor's whisker, woe to that sailor, whiskers and all. What tenderness there is in that preliminary touch! Had this tail any prehensile power, I should straightway bethink me of Darmonodes' elephant that so frequented the flower-market, and with low salutations presented nosegays to damsels, and then caressed their zones. On more accounts than one, a pity it is that the whale does not possess this prehensile virtue in his tail; for I have heard of yet another elephant, that when wounded in the fight, curved round his trunk and extracted the dart.

Fourth: Stealing unawares upon the whale in the fancied security of the middle of solitary seas, you find him unbent from the vast corpulence of his dignity, and kitten-like, he plays on the ocean as if it were a hearth. But still you see his power in his play. The broad palms of his tail are flirted high into the air; then smiting the surface, the thunderous concussion resounds for miles. You would almost think a great gun had been discharged; and if you noticed the light wreath of vapor from the spiracle at his other extremity, you would think that that was the smoke from the touch-hole.

Fifth: As in the ordinary floating posture of the leviathan the flukes lie considerably below the level of his back, they are then completely out of sight beneath the surface; but when he is about to plunge into the deeps, his entire flukes with at least thirty feet of his body are tossed erect in the air, and so remain vibrating a moment, till they downwards shoot out of view. Excepting the sublime *breach* – somewhere else to be described – this peaking of the whale's flukes is perhaps the grandest sight to be seen in all animated nature. Out of the bottomless profundities the gigantic tail seems spasmodically snatching at the highest heaven. So in dreams, have I seen majestic Satan thrusting forth his tormented colossal claw from the flame Baltic of Hell. But in gazing at such scenes, it is all in all what mood you are in; if in the Dantean, the devils will occur to you; if in that of Isaiah, the archangels. Standing at the mast-head of my ship during a sunrise that crimsoned sky and sea, I once saw a large herd of whales in the east, all heading towards the sun, and for a moment vibrating in concert with peaked flukes. As it seemed to me at the time, such a grand embodiment of adoration of the gods was never beheld, even in Persia, the home of the fire worshippers. As Ptolemy Philopater testified of the African elephant, I then testified of the whale, pronouncing him the most devout of all beings. For according to King Juba, the military elephants of antiquity often hailed the morning with their trunks uplifted in the profoundest silence.

The chance comparison in this chapter, between the whale and the elephant, so far as some aspects of the tail of the one and the trunk of the other are concerned, should not tend to place those two opposite organs on an equality, much less the creatures to which they respectively belong. For as the mightiest elephant is but a terrier to Leviathan, so, compared with Leviathan's tail, his trunk is but the stalk of a lily. The most direful blow from the elephant's trunk were as the playful tap of a fan, compared with the measureless crush and crash of the sperm whale's ponderous flukes, which in repeated instances have one after the other hurled entire boats with all their oars and crews into the air, very much as an Indian juggler tosses his balls.*

The more I consider this mighty tail, the more do I deplore my inability to express it. At times there are gestures in it, which, though they would well grace the hand of man, remain wholly inexplicable. In an extensive herd, so remarkable, occasionally, are these mystic gestures, that I have heard hunters who have declared them akin to Free-Mason signs and symbols; that the whale, indeed, by these methods intelligently conversed with the world. Nor are there wanting other motions of the whale in his general body, full of strangeness, and unaccountable to his most experienced assailant. Dissect him how I may, then, I but go skin deep; I know him not, and never will. But if I know not even the tail of this whale, how understand his head? much more, how comprehend his face, when face he has none? Thou shalt see my back parts, my tail, he seems to say, but my face shall not be seen. But I cannot completely make out his back parts; and hint what he will about his face, I say again he has no face.

87

THE GRAND ARMADA

THE long and narrow peninsula of Malacca, extending south-eastward from the territories of Birmah, forms the most southerly point of all Asia. In a continuous line from that peninsula stretch the long islands of Sumatra, Java, Bally, and Timor; which, with many others, form a vast mole, or rampart, lengthwise connecting Asia with Australia,

*Though all comparison in the way of general bulk between the whale and the elephant is preposterous, inasmuch as in that particular the elephant stands in much the same respect to the whale that the dog does to the elephant; nevertheless, there are not wanting some points of curious similitude; among these is the spout. It is well known that the elephant will often draw up water or dust in his trunk, and then elevating it, jet it forth in a stream.

and dividing the long unbroken Indian ocean from the thickly studded oriental archipelagoes. This rampart is pierced by several sally-ports for the convenience of ships and whales; conspicuous among which are the straits of Sunda and Malacca. By the straits of Sunda, chiefly, vessels bound to China from the west, emerge into the China seas.

Those narrow straits of Sunda divide Sumatra from Java; and standing midway in that vast rampart of islands, buttressed by that bold green promontory, known to seamen as Java Head; they not a little correspond to the central gateway opening into some vast walled empire: and considering the inexhaustible wealth of spices, and silks, and jewels, and gold, and ivory, with which the thousand islands of that oriental sea are enriched, it seems a significant provision of nature, that such treasures, by the very formation of the land, should at least bear the appearance, however ineffectual, of being guarded from the all-grasping western world. The shores of the Straits of Sunda are unsupplied with those domineering fortresses which guard the entrances to the Mediterranean, the Baltic, and the Propontis. Unlike the Danes, these Orientals do not demand the obsequious homage of lowered top-sails from the endless procession of ships before the wind, which for centuries past, by night and by day, have passed between the islands of Sumatra and Java, freighted with the costliest cargoes of the east. But while they freely waive a ceremonial like this, they do by no means renounce their claim to more solid tribute.

Time out of mind the piratical proas of the Malays, lurking among the low shaded coves and islets of Sumatra, have sallied out upon the vessels sailing through the straits, fiercely demanding tribute at the point of their spears. Though by the repeated bloody chastisements, they have received at the hands of European cruisers, the audacity of these corsairs has of late been somewhat repressed; yet, even at the present day, we occasionally hear of English and American vessels, which, in those waters, have been remorselessly boarded and pillaged.

With a fair, fresh wind, the Pequod was now drawing nigh

to these straits; Ahab purposing to pass through them into the Javan sea, and thence, cruising northwards, over waters known to be frequented here and there by the Sperm Whale, sweep inshore by the Philippine Islands, and gain the far coast of Japan, in time for the great whaling season there. By these means, the circumnavigating Pequod would sweep almost all the known Sperm Whale cruising grounds of the world, previous to descending upon the Line in the Pacific; where Ahab, though everywhere else foiled in his pursuit, firmly counted upon giving battle to Moby Dick, in the sea he was most known to frequent; and at a season when he might most reasonably be presumed to be haunting it.

But how now? in this zoned quest, does Ahab touch no land? does his crew drink air? Surely, he will stop for water. Nay. For a long time, now, the circus-running sun has raced within his fiery ring, and needs no sustenance but what's in himself. So Ahab. Mark this, too, in the whaler. While other hulls are loaded down with alien stuff, to be transferred to foreign wharves; the world-wandering whale-ship carries no cargo but herself and crew, their weapons and their wants. She has a whole lake's contents bottled in her ample hold. She is ballasted with utilities; not altogether with unusable pig-lead and kentledge. She carries years' water in her. Clear old prime Nantucket water; which, when three years afloat, the Nantucketer, in the Pacific, prefers to drink before the brackish fluid, but yesterday rafted off in casks, from the Peruvian or Indian streams. Hence it is, that, while other ships may have gone to China from New York, and back again, touching at a score of ports, the whale-ship, in all that interval, may not have sighted one grain of soil; her crew having seen no man but floating seamen like themselves. So that did you carry them the news that another flood had come; they would only answer – 'Well, boys, here's the ark!'

Now, as many Sperm Whales had been captured off the western coast of Java, in the near vicinity of the Straits of Sunda; indeed, as most of the ground, roundabout, was generally recognized by the fishermen as an excellent spot for cruising; therefore, as the Pequod gained more and more upon Java Head, the look-outs were repeatedly hailed, and admonished to keep wide awake. But though the green palmy cliffs of the land soon loomed on the starboard bow, and with delighted nostrils the fresh cinnamon was snuffed in the air, yet not a single jet was descried. Almost renouncing all thought of falling in with any game hereabouts, the ship had well nigh entered the straits, when the customary cheering cry was heard from aloft, and ere long a spectacle of singular magnificence saluted us.

But here be it premised, that owing to the unwearied activity with which of late they have been hunted over all four oceans, the Sperm Whales, instead of almost invariably sailing in small detached companies, as in former times, are now frequently met with in extensive herds, sometimes embracing so great a multitude, that it would almost seem as if numerous nations of them had sworn solemn league and covenant for mutual assistance and protection. To this aggregation of the Sperm Whale into such immense caravans, may be imputed the circumstance that even in the best cruising grounds, you may now sometimes sail for weeks and months together, without being greeted by a single spout; and then be suddenly saluted by what sometimes seems thousands on thousands.

Broad on both bows, at the distance of some two or three miles, and forming a great semicircle, embracing one half of the level horizon, a continuous chain of whale-jets were up-playing and sparkling in the noon-day air. Unlike the straight perpendicular twin-jets of the Right Whale, which, dividing at top, fall over in two branches, like the cleft drooping boughs of a willow, the single forward-slanting spout of the Sperm Whale presents a thick curled bush of white mist, continually rising and falling away to leeward.

Seen from the Pequod's deck, then, as she would rise on a high hill of the sea, this host of vapory spouts, individually curling up into the air, and beheld through a blending atmosphere of bluish haze, showed like the thousand cheerful chimneys of some dense metropolis, descried of a balmy autumnal morning, by some horseman on a height.

As marching armies approaching an unfriendly defile in the mountains, accelerate their march, all eagerness to place that perilous passage in their rear, and once more expand in comparative security upon the plain; even so did this vast fleet of whales now seem hurrying forward through the straits; gradually contracting the wings of their semicircle, and swimming on, in one solid, but still crescentic centre.

Crowding all sail the Pequod pressed after them; the harpooneers handling their weapons, and loudly cheering from the heads of their yet suspended boats. If the wind only held, little doubt had they, that chased through these Straits of Sunda, the vast host would only deploy into the Oriental seas to witness the capture of not a few of their number. And who could tell whether, in that congregated caravan, Moby Dick himself might not temporarily be swimming, like the worshipped white-elephant in the coronation procession of the Siamese! So with stun-sail piled on stun-sail, we sailed along, driving these leviathans before us; when, of a sudden, the voice of Tashtego was heard, loudly directing attention to something in our wake.

Corresponding to the crescent in our van, we beheld another in our rear. It seemed formed of detached white vapors, rising and falling something like the spouts of the whales; only they did not so completely come and go; for they constantly hovered, without finally disappearing. Levelling his glass at this sight, Ahab quickly revolved in his pivot-hole, crying, 'Aloft there, and rig whips and buckets to wet the sails; – Malays, sir, and after us!'

As if too long lurking behind the headlands, till the Pequod should fairly have entered the straits, these rascally Asiatics were now in hot pursuit, to make up for their over-cautious delay. But when the swift Pequod, with a fresh leading wind, was herself in hot chase; how very kind of these tawny philanthropists to assist in speeding her on to her own chosen pursuit, – mere riding-whips and rowels to her, that they were. As with glass under arm, Ahab to-and-fro paced the deck; in his forward turn beholding the monsters he chased, and in the after one the bloodthirsty pirates chasing *him*; some such fancy as the above seemed his. And when he glanced upon the green walls of the watery defile in which the ship was then sailing, and bethought him that through that gate lay the route to his vengeance, and beheld, how that through that same gate he was now both chasing and being chased to his deadly end; and not only that, but a herd of remorseless wild pirates and inhuman atheistical devils were infernally cheering him on with their curses; – when all these conceits had passed through his brain, Ahab's brow was left gaunt and ribbed, like the black sand beach after some stormy tide has been gnawing it, without being able to drag the firm thing from its place.

But thoughts like these troubled very few of the reckless crew; and when, after steadily dropping and dropping the pirates astern, the Pequod at last shot by the vivid green Cockatoo Point on the Sumatra side, emerging at last upon the broad waters beyond; then, the harpooneers seemed more to grieve that the swift whales had been gaining upon the ship, than to rejoice that the ship had so victoriously gained upon the Malays. But still driving on in the wake of the whales, at length they seemed abating their speed; gradually the ship neared them; and the wind now dying away, word was passed to spring to the boats. But no sooner did the herd, by some presumed wonderful instinct of the Sperm Whale, become notified of the three keels that were after them, – though as yet a mile in their rear, – than they rallied again, and forming in close ranks and battalions, so that their spouts all looked like flashing lines of stacked bayonets, moved on with redoubled velocity.

Stripped to our shirts and drawers, we sprang to the white-ash, and after several hours' pulling were almost disposed to renounce the chase, when a general pausing commotion among the whales gave animating token that they were now at last under the influence of that strange perplexity of inert irresolution, which, when the fishermen perceive it in the whale, they say he is *gallied.** The compact martial columns in which they had been hitherto rapidly and steadily swimming, were now broken up in one measureless rout; and like King Porus' elephants in the Indian battle with Alexander, they seemed going mad with consternation. In all directions expanding in vast irregular circles, and aimlessly swimming hither and thither, by their short thick spoutings, they plainly betrayed their distraction of panic. This was still more strangely evinced by those of their number, who, completely paralysed as it were, helplessly floated like water-logged dismantled ships on the sea. Had these leviathans been but a flock of simple sheep, pursued over the pasture by three fierce wolves, they could not possibly have evinced such excessive dismay. But this occasional timidity is characteristic of almost all herding creatures. Though banding together in tens of thousands, the lion-maned buffaloes of the West have fled before a solitary horseman. Witness, too, all human beings, how when herded together in the sheepfold of a theatre's pit, they will, at the slightest alarm of fire, rush helter-skelter for the outlets, crowding, trampling, jamming, and remorselessly dashing each other to death. Best, therefore, withhold any amazement at the strangely gallied whales before us, for there is

*To *gally*, or *gallow*, is to frighten excessively, – to confound with fright. It is an old Saxon word. It occurs once in Shakspere:—

> 'The wrathful skies
> *Gallow* the very wanderers of the dark,
> And make them keep their caves.'
>
> *Lear*, Act III. sc. ii.

To common land usages, the word is now completely obsolete. When the polite landsman first hears it from the gaunt Nantucketer, he is apt to set it down as one of the whaleman's self-derived savageries. Much the same is it with many other sinewy Saxonisms of this sort, which emigrated to the New-England rocks with the noble brawn of the old English emigrants in the time of the Commonwealth. Thus, some of the best and furthest-descended English words – the etymological Howards and Percys – are now democratised, nay, plebeianised – so to speak – in the New World.

no folly of the beasts of the earth which is not infinitely outdone by the madness of men.

Though many of the whales, as has been said, were in violent motion, yet it is to be observed that as a whole the herd neither advanced nor retreated, but collectively remained in one place. As is customary in those cases, the boats at once separated, each making for some one lone whale on the outskirts of the shoal. In about three minutes' time, Queequeg's harpoon was flung; the stricken fish darted blinding spray in our faces, and then running away with us like light, steered straight for the heart of the herd. Though such a movement on the part of the whale struck under such circumstances, is in no wise unprecedented; and indeed is almost always more or less anticipated; yet does it present one of the more perilous vicissitudes of the fishery. For as the swift monster drags you deeper and deeper into the frantic shoal, you bid adieu to circumspect life and only exist in a delirious throb.

As, blind and deaf, the whale plunged forward, as if by sheer power of speed to rid himself of the iron leech that had fastened to him; as we thus tore a white gash in the sea, on all sides menaced as we flew, by the crazed creatures to and fro rushing about us; our beset boat was like a ship mobbed by ice-isles in a tempest, and striving to steer through their complicated channels and straits, knowing not at what moment it may be locked in and crushed.

But not a bit daunted, Queequeg steered us manfully; now sheering off from this monster directly across our route in advance; now edging away from that, whose colossal flukes were suspended overhead, while all the time, Starbuck stood up in the bows, lance in hand, pricking out of our way whatever whales he could reach by short darts, for there was no time to make long ones. Nor were the oarsmen quite idle, though their wonted duty was now altogether dispensed with. They chiefly attended to the shouting part of the business. 'Out of the way, Commodore!' cried one, to a great dromedary that of a sudden rose bodily to the surface, and for an instant threatened to swamp us. 'Hard down with your tail, there!' cried a second to another, which, close to our gunwale, seemed calmly cooling himself with his own fan-like extremity.

All whaleboats carry certain curious contrivances, originally invented by the Nantucket Indians, called druggs. Two thick squares of wood of equal size are stoutly clenched together, so that they cross each other's grain at right angles; a line of considerable length is then attached to the middle of this block, and the other end of the line being looped, it can in a moment be fastened to a harpoon. It is chiefly among gallied whales that this drugg is used. For then, more whales are close round you than you can possibly chase at one time. But sperm whales are not every day encountered; while you may, then, you must kill all you can. And if you cannot kill them all at once, you must wing them, so that they can be afterwards killed at your leisure. Hence it is, that at times like these the drugg comes into requisition. Our boat was furnished with three of them. The first and second were successfully darted, and we saw the whales staggeringly running off, fettered by the enormous sidelong resistance of the towing drugg. They were cramped like malefactors with the chain and ball. But upon flinging the third, in the act of tossing overboard the clumsy wooden block, it caught under one of the seats of the boat, and in an instant tore it out and carried it away, dropping the oarsman in the boat's bottom as the seat slid from under him. On both sides the sea came in at the wounded planks, but we stuffed two or three drawers and shirts in, and so stopped the leaks for the time.

It had been next to impossible to dart these drugged-harpoons, were it not that as we advanced into the herd, our whale's way greatly diminished; moreover, that as we went still further and further from the circumference of commotion, the direful disorders seemed waning. So that when at last the jerking harpoon drew out, and the towing whale sideways vanished; then, with the tapering force of his parting momentum, we glided between two whales into the innermost heart of the shoal, as if from some mountain torrent we had slid into a serene valley lake. Here the storms in the roaring glens between the outermost whales, were heard but not felt. In this central expanse the sea presented that smooth satin-like surface, called a sleek, produced by the subtle moisture thrown off by the whale in his more quiet moods. Yes, we were now in that enchanted calm which they say lurks at the heart of every commotion. And still in the distracted distance we beheld the tumults of the outer concentric circles, and saw successive pods of whales, eight or ten in each, swiftly going round and round, like multiplied spans of horses in a ring; and so closely shoulder to shoulder, that a Titanic circus-rider might easily have over-arched the middle ones, and so have gone round on their backs. Owing to the density of the crowd of reposing whales, more immediately surrounding the embayed axis of the herd, no possible chance of escape was at present afforded us. We must watch for a breach in the living wall that hemmed us in; the wall that had only admitted us in order to shut us up. Keeping at the centre of the lake, we were occasionally visited by small tame cows and calves; the women and children of this routed host.

Now, inclusive of the occasional wide intervals between the revolving outer circles, and inclusive of the spaces between the various pods in any one of those circles, the entire area at this juncture, embraced by the whole multitude, must have contained at least two or three square miles. At any rate – though indeed such a test at such a time might be deceptive – spoutings might be discovered from our low boat that seemed playing up almost from the rim of the horizon. I mention this circumstance, because, as if the cows and calves had been purposely locked up in this innermost fold; and as if the wide extent of the herd had hitherto prevented them from learning the precise cause of its stopping; or, possibly, being so young, unsophisticated, and every way innocent and inexperienced; however it may have been, these smaller whales – now and then visiting our becalmed boat from the margin of the lake – evinced a wondrous fearlessness and confidence, or else a still, becharmed panic which it was impossible not to marvel at. Like household dogs they came snuffling round us, right up to our gunwales, and touching them; till it almost seemed that some spell had suddenly domesticated them. Queequeg patted their foreheads; Starbuck scratched their backs with his lance; but fearful of the consequences, for the time refrained from darting it.

But far beneath this wondrous world upon the surface, another and still stranger world met our eyes as we gazed over the side. For, suspended in those watery vaults, floated the forms of the nursing mothers of the whales, and those that by their enormous girth seemed shortly to become mothers. The lake, as I have hinted, was to a considerable depth exceedingly transparent; and as human infants while suckling will calmly and fixedly gaze away from the breast, as if leading two different lives at the time; and while yet drawing mortal nourishment, be still spiritually feasting upon some unearthly reminiscence; – even so did the young of these whales seem looking up towards us, but not at us, as if we were but a bit of Gulf-weed in their new-born sight. Floating on their sides, the mothers also seemed quietly eyeing us. One of these little infants, that from certain queer tokens seemed hardly a day old, might have measured some fourteen feet in length, and some six feet in girth. He was a little frisky; though as yet his body seemed scarce yet recovered from that irksome position it had so lately occupied in the maternal reticule; where, tail to head, and all ready for the final spring, the unborn whale lies bent like a Tartar's bow. The delicate side-fins, and the palms of his flukes, still freshly retained the plaited crumpled appearance of a baby's ears newly arrived from foreign parts.

'Line! line!' cried Queequeg, looking over the gunwale; 'him fast! him fast! – Who line him! Who struck? – Two whale; one big, one little!'

'What ails ye, man?' cried Starbuck.

'Look-e here,' said Queequeg pointing down.

As when the stricken whale, that from the tub has reeled

out hundreds of fathoms of rope; as, after deep sounding, he floats up again, and shows the slackened curling line buoyantly rising and spiralling towards the air; so now, Starbuck saw long coils of the umbilical cord of Madame Leviathan, by which the young cub seemed still tethered to its dam. Not seldom in the rapid vicissitudes of the chase, this natural line, with the maternal end loose, becomes entangled with the hempen one, so that the cub is thereby trapped. Some of the subtlest secrets of the seas seemed divulged to us in this enchanted pond. We saw young Leviathan amours in the deep.*

And thus, though surrounded by circle upon circle of consternations and affrights, did these inscrutable creatures at the centre freely and fearlessly indulge in all peaceful concernments; yea, serenely revelled in dalliance and delight. But even so, amid the tornadoed Atlantic of my being, do I myself still for ever centrally disport in mute calm; and while ponderous planets of unwaning woe revolve round me, deep down and deep inland there I still bathe me in eternal mildness of joy.

Meanwhile, as we thus lay entranced, the occasional sudden frantic spectacles in the distance evinced the activity of the other boats, still engaged in drugging the whales on the frontier of the host; or possibly carrying on the war within the first circle, where abundance of room and some convenient retreats were afforded them. But the sight of the enraged drugged whales now and then blindly darting to

*The sperm whale, as with all other species of the Leviathan, but unlike most other fish, breeds indifferently at all seasons; after a gestation which may probably be set down at nine months, producing but one at a time; though in some few known instances giving birth to an Esau and Jacob:– a contingency provided for in suckling by two teats, curiously situated, one on each side of the anus; but the breasts themselves extend upwards from that. When by chance these precious parts in a nursing whale are cut by the hunter's lance, the mother's pouring milk and blood rivallingly discolor the sea for rods. The milk is very sweet and rich; it has been tasted by man; it might do well with strawberries. When overflowing with mutual esteem, the whales salute *more hominum.*

and fro across the circles, was nothing to what at last met our eyes. It is sometimes the custom when fast to a whale more than commonly powerful and alert, to seek to hamstring him, as it were, by sundering or maiming his gigantic tail-tendon. It is done by darting a short-handled cutting-spade, to which is attached a rope for hauling it back again. A whale wounded (as we afterwards learned) in this part, but not effectually, as it seemed, had broken away from the boat, carrying along with him half of the harpoon line; and in the extraordinary agony of the wound, he was now dashing among the revolving circles like the lone mounted desperado Arnold, at the battle of Saratoga, carrying dismay wherever he went.

But agonizing as was the wound of this whale, and an appalling spectacle enough, any way; yet the peculiar horror with which he seemed to inspire the rest of the herd, was owing to a cause which at first the intervening distance obscured from us. But at length we perceived that by one of the unimaginable accidents of the fishery, this whale had become entangled in the harpoon-line that he towed; he had also run away with the cutting-spade in him; and while the free end of the rope attached to that weapon, had permanently caught in the coils of the harpoon-line round his tail, the cutting-spade itself had worked loose from his flesh. So that tormented to madness, he was now churning through the water, violently flailing with his flexible tail, and tossing the keen spade about him, wounding and murdering his own comrades.

This terrific object seemed to recall the whole herd from their stationary fright. First, the whales forming the margin of our lake began to crowd a little, and tumble against each other, as if lifted by half spent billows from afar; then the lake itself began faintly to heave and swell; the submarine bridal-chambers and nurseries vanished; in more and more contracting orbits the whales in the more central circles began to swim in thickening clusters. Yes, the long calm was departing. A low advancing hum was soon heard; and then like to the tumultuous masses of block-ice when the great river Hudson breaks up in Spring, the entire host of whales came tumbling upon their inner centre, as if to pile themselves up in one common mountain. Instantly Starbuck and Queequeg changed places; Starbuck taking the stern.

'Oars! Oars!' he intensely whispered, seizing the helm – 'gripe your oars, and clutch your souls, now! My God, men, stand by! Shove him off, you Queequeg – the whale there! – prick him! – hit him! Stand up – stand up, and stay so! Spring, men – pull, men; never mind their backs – scrape them! – scrape away!'

The boat was now all but jammed between two vast black bulks, leaving a narrow Dardanelles between their long lengths. But by desperate endeavor we at last shot into a temporary opening; then giving way rapidly, and at the same time earnestly watching for another outlet. After many similar hair-breadth escapes, we at last swiftly glided into what had just been one of the outer circles, but now crossed by random whales, all violently making for one centre. This lucky salvation was cheaply purchased by the loss of Queequeg's hat, who, while standing in the bows to prick the fugitive whales, had his hat taken clean from his head by the air-eddy made by the sudden tossing of a pair of broad flukes close by.

Riotous and disordered as the universal commotion now was, it soon resolved itself into what seemed a systematic movement; for having clumped together at last in one dense body, they then renewed their onward flight with augmented fleetness. Further pursuit was useless; but the boats still lingered in their wake to pick up what drugged whales might be dropped astern, and likewise to secure one which Flask had killed and waifed. The waif is a pennoned pole, two or three of which are carried by every boat; and which, when additional game is at hand, are inserted upright into the floating body of a dead whale, both to mark its place on the sea, and also as token of prior possession, should the boats of any other ship draw near.

The result of this lowering was somewhat illustrative of that sagacious saying in the Fishery, – the more whales the less fish. Of all the drugged whales only one was captured. The rest contrived to escape for the time, but only to be taken, as will hereafter be seen, by some other craft than the Pequod.

88

SCHOOLS AND SCHOOLMASTERS

THE previous chapter gave account of an immense body or herd of Sperm Whales, and there was also then given the probable cause inducing those vast aggregations.

Now, though such great bodies are at times encountered, yet, as must have been seen, even at the present day, small detached bands are occasionally observed, embracing from twenty to fifty individuals each. Such bands are known as schools. They generally are of two sorts; those composed almost entirely of females, and those mustering none but young vigorous males, or bulls, as they are familiarly designated.

In cavalier attendance upon the school of females, you invariably see a male of full grown magnitude, but not old; who, upon any alarm, evinces his gallantry by falling in the rear and covering the flight of his ladies. In truth, this gentleman is a luxurious Ottoman, swimming about over the watery world, surroundingly accompanied by all the solaces and endearments of the harem. The contrast between this Ottoman and his concubines is striking; because, while he is always of the largest leviathanic proportions, the ladies, even at full growth, are not more than one third of the bulk of an average-sized male. They are comparatively delicate, indeed; I dare say, not to exceed half a dozen yards round the waist. Nevertheless, it cannot be denied, that upon the whole they are hereditarily entitled to *en bon point.*

It is very curious to watch this harem and its lord in their indolent ramblings. Like fashionables, they are for ever on the move in leisurely search of variety. You meet them on the Line in time for the full flower of the Equatorial feeding season, having just returned, perhaps, from spending the summer in the Northern seas, and so cheating summer of all unpleasant weariness and warmth. By the time they have lounged up and down the promenade of the Equator awhile, they start for the Oriental waters in anticipation of the cool season there, and so evade the other excessive temperature of the year.

When serenely advancing on one of these journeys, if any strange suspicious sights are seen, my lord whale keeps a wary eye on his interesting family. Should any unwarrantably pert young Leviathan coming that way, presume to draw confidentially close to one of the ladies, with what prodigious fury the Bashaw assails him, and chases him away! High times, indeed, if unprincipled young rakes like him are to be permitted to invade the sanctity of domestic bliss; though do what the Bashaw will, he cannot keep the most notorious Lothario out of his bed; for, alas! all fish bed in common. As ashore, the ladies often cause the most terrible duels among their rival admirers; just so with the whales, who sometimes come to deadly battle, and all for love. They fence with their long lower jaws, sometimes locking them together, and so striving for the supremacy like elks that warringly interweave their antlers. Not a few are captured having the deep scars of these encounters, – furrowed heads, broken teeth, scolloped fins; and in some instances, wrenched and dislocated mouths.

But supposing the invader of domestic bliss to betake himself away at the first rush of the harem's lord, then is it very diverting to watch that lord. Gently he insinuates his vast bulk among them again and revels there awhile, still in tantalizing vicinity to young Lothario, like pious Solomon devoutly worshipping among his thousand concubines. Granting other whales to be in sight, the fishermen will seldom give chase to one of these Grand Turks; for these Grand Turks are too lavish of their strength, and hence their unctuousness is small. As for the sons and the daughters they beget, why, those sons and daughters must take care of themselves; at least, with only the maternal help. For like certain other omnivorous roving lovers that might be named, my Lord Whale has no taste for the nursery, however much for the bower; and so, being a great traveller, he leaves his anonymous babies all over the world; every baby an exotic. In good time, nevertheless, as the ardor of youth declines; as years and dumps increase; as reflection lends her solemn pauses; in short, as a general lassitude overtakes the sated Turk; then a love of ease and virtue supplants the love for maidens; our Ottoman enters upon the impotent, repentant, admonitory stage of life, forswears, disbands the harem, and grown to an exemplary, sulky old soul, goes about all alone among the meridians and parallels saying his prayers, and warning each young Leviathan from his amorous errors.

Now, as the harem of whales is called by the fishermen a school, so is the lord and master of that school technically known as the schoolmaster. It is therefore not in strict character, however admirably satirical, that after going to school himself, he should then go abroad inculcating not what he learned there, but the folly of it. His title, schoolmaster, would very naturally seem derived from the name bestowed upon the harem itself, but some have surmised that the man who first thus entitled this sort of Ottoman whale, must have read the memoirs of Vidocq, and informed himself what sort of a country-schoolmaster that famous Frenchman was in his younger days, and what was the nature of those occult lessons he inculcated into some of his pupils.

The same secludedness and isolation to which the schoolmaster whale betakes himself in his advancing years, is true of all aged Sperm Whales. Almost universally, a lone whale – as a solitary Leviathan is called – proves an ancient one. Like venerable moss-bearded Daniel Boone, he will have no one near him but Nature herself; and her he takes to wife in the wilderness of waters, and the best of wives she is, though she keeps so many moody secrets.

The schools composing none but young and vigorous males, previously mentioned, offer a strong contrast to the harem schools. For while those female whales are characteristically timid, the young males, or forty-barrel-bulls, as they call them, are by far the most pugnacious of all Leviathans, and proverbially the most dangerous to encounter; excepting those wondrous grey-headed, grizzled whales, sometimes met, and these will fight you like grim fiends exasperated by a penal gout.

The Forty-barrel-bull schools are larger than the harem schools. Like a mob of young collegians, they are full of fight, fun, and wickedness, tumbling round the world at such a reckless, rollicking rate, that no prudent underwriter would insure them any more than he would a riotous lad at Yale or Harvard. They soon relinquish this turbulence though, and when about three fourths grown, break up, and separately go about in quest of settlements, that is, harems.

Another point of difference between the male and female schools is still more characteristic of the sexes. Say you strike a Forty-barrel-bull – poor devil! all his comrades quit him. But strike a member of the harem school, and her companions swim around her with every token of concern, sometimes lingering so near her and so long, as themselves to fall a prey.

89

FAST-FISH AND LOOSE-FISH

THE allusion to the waifs and waif-poles in the last chapter but one, necessitates some account of the laws and regulations of the whale fishery, of which the waif may be deemed the grand symbol and badge.

It frequently happens that when several ships are cruising in company, a whale may be struck by one vessel, then escape, and be finally killed and captured by another vessel;

and herein are indirectly comprised many minor contingencies, all partaking of this one grand feature. For example, – after a weary and perilous chase and capture of a whale, the body may get loose from the ship by reason of a violent storm; and drifting far away to leeward, be retaken by a second whaler, who, in a calm, snugly tows it alongside, without risk of life or line. Thus the most vexatious and violent disputes would often arise between the fishermen, were there not some written or unwritten, universal, undisputed law applicable to all cases.

Perhaps the only formal whaling code authorized by legislative enactment, was that of Holland. It was decreed by the States-General in A.D. 1695. But though no other nation has ever had any written whaling law, yet the American fishermen have been their own legislators and lawyers in this matter. They have provided a system which for terse comprehensiveness surpasses Justinian's Pandects and the By-laws of the Chinese Society for the Suppression of Meddling with other People's Business. Yes; these laws might be engraven on a Queen Anne's farthing, or the barb of a harpoon, and worn round the neck, so small are they.

I. A Fast Fish belongs to the party fast to it.

II. A Loose-Fish is fair game for anybody who can soonest catch it.

But what plays the mischief with this masterly code is the admirable brevity of it, which necessitates a vast volume of commentaries to expound it.

First: What is a Fast-Fish? Alive or dead a fish is technically fast, when it is connected with an occupied ship or boat, by any medium at all controllable by the occupant or occupants, – a mast, an oar, a nine-inch cable, a telegraph wire, or a strand of cobweb, it is all the same. Likewise a fish is technically fast when it bears a waif, or any other recognised symbol of possession; so long as the party waifing it plainly evince their ability at any time to take it alongside, as well as their intention so to do.

These are scientific commentaries; but the commentaries of the whalemen themselves sometimes consist in hard words and harder knocks – the Coke-upon-Littleton of the fist. True, among the more upright and honorable whalemen allowances are always made for peculiar cases, where it would be an outrageous moral injustice for one party to claim possession of a whale previously chased or killed by another party. But others are by no means so scrupulous.

Some fifty years ago there was a curious case of whale-trover litigated in England, wherein the plaintiffs set forth that after a hard chase of a whale in the Northern seas; and when indeed they (the plaintiffs) had succeeded in harpooning the fish; they were at last, through peril of their lives, obliged to forsake not only their lines, but their boat itself. Ultimately the defendants (the crew of another ship) came up with the whale, struck, killed, seized, and finally appropriated it before the very eyes of the plaintiffs. And when those defendants were remonstrated with, their captain snapped his fingers in the plaintiffs' teeth, and assured them that by way of doxology to the deed he had done, he would now retain their line, harpoons, and boat, which had remained attached to the whale at the time of the seizure. Wherefore the plaintiffs now sued for the recovery of the value of their whale, line, harpoons, and boat.

Mr Erskine was counsel for the defendants; Lord Ellenborough was the judge. In the course of the defence, the witty Erskine went on to illustrate his position, by alluding to a recent crim. con. case, wherein a gentleman, after in vain trying to bridle his wife's viciousness, had at last abandoned her upon the seas of life; but in the course of years, repenting of that step, he instituted an action to recover possession of her. Erskine was on the other side; and he then supported it by saying, that though the gentleman had originally harpooned the lady, and had once had her fast, and only by reason of the great stress of her plunging viciousness, had at last abandoned her; yet abandon her he did, so that she became a loose-fish; and therefore when a subsequent gentleman re-harpooned her, the lady then became that subsequent gentleman's property, along with whatever harpoon might have been found sticking in her.

Now in the present case Erskine contended that the examples of the whale and the lady were reciprocally illustrative of each other.

These pleadings, and the counter pleadings, being duly heard, the very learned judge in set terms decided, to wit, – That as for the boat, he awarded it to the plaintiffs, because they had merely abandoned it to save their lives; but that with regard to the controverted whale, harpoons, and line, they belonged to the defendants; the whale, because it was a Loose-Fish at the time of the final capture; and the harpoons and line because when the fish made off with them, it (the fish) acquired a property in those articles; and hence anybody who afterwards took the fish had a right to them. Now, the defendants afterwards took the fish; ergo, the aforesaid articles were theirs.

A common man looking at this decision of the very learned Judge, might possibly object to it. But ploughed up to the primary rock of the matter, the two great principles laid down in the twin whaling laws previously quoted, and applied and elucidated by Lord Ellenborough in the above cited case; these two laws touching Fast-Fish and Loose-Fish, I say, will, on reflection, be found the fundamentals of all human jurisprudence; for notwithstanding its complicated tracery of sculpture, the Temple of the Law, like the Temple of the Philistines, has but two props to stand on.

Is it not a saying in every one's mouth, Possession is half of the law: that is, regardless of how the thing came into possession? But often possession is the whole of the law. What are the sinews and souls of Russian serfs and Republican slaves but Fast-Fish, whereof possession is the whole of the law? What to the rapacious landlord is the widow's last mite but a Fast-Fish? What is yonder undetected villain's marble mansion with a door-plate for a waif; what is that but a Fast-Fish? What is the ruinous discount which Mordecai, the broker, gets from poor Woebegone, the bankrupt, on a loan to keep Woebegone's family from starvation; what is that ruinous discount but a Fast-Fish? What is the Archbishop of Savesoul's income of £100,000 seized from the scant bread and cheese of hundreds of thousands of broken-backed laborers (all sure of heaven without any of Savesoul's help) what is that globular 100,000 but a Fast-Fish? What are the Duke of Dunder's hereditary towns and hamlets but Fast-Fish? What to that redoubted harpooneer, John Bull, is poor Ireland, but a Fast-Fish? What to that apostolic lancer, Brother Jonathan, is Texas but a Fast-Fish? And concerning all these, is not Possession the whole of the law?

But if the doctrine of Fast-Fish be pretty generally applicable, the kindred doctrine of Loose-Fish is still more widely so. That is internationally and universally applicable.

What was America in 1492 but a Loose-Fish, in which Columbus struck the Spanish standard by way of waifing it for his royal master and mistress? What was Poland to the Czar? What Greece to the Turk? What India to England? What at last will Mexico be to the United States? All Loose-Fish.

What are the Rights of Man and the Liberties of the World but Loose-Fish? What all men's minds and opinions but Loose-Fish? What is the principle of religious belief in them but a Loose-Fish? What to the ostentatious smuggling verbalists are the thoughts of thinkers but Loose-Fish? What is the great globe itself but a Loose-Fish? And what are you, reader, but a Loose-Fish and a Fast-Fish, too?

90

HEADS OR TAILS

'De balena vero sufficit, si rex habeat caput, et regina caudam.'

Bracton, l. 3, c. 3.

LATIN from the books of the Laws of England, which taken along with the context, means, that of all whales captured by anybody on the coast of that land, the King, as Honorary Grand Harpooneer, must have the head, and the Queen be respectfully presented with the tail. A division which, in the whale, is much like halving an apple; there is no intermediate remainder. Now as this law, under a modified form, is to this day in force in England; and as it offers in various respects a strange anomaly touching the general law of Fast and Loose-Fish, it is here treated of in a separate chapter, on the same courteous principle that prompts the English railways to be at the expense of a separate car, specially reserved for the accommodation of royalty. In the first place, in curious proof of the fact that the above-mentioned law is still in force, I proceed to lay before you a circumstance that happened within the last two years.

It seems that some honest mariners of Dover, or Sandwich, or some one of the Cinque Ports, had after a hard chase succeeded in killing and beaching a fine whale which they had originally descried afar off from the shore. Now the Cinque Ports are partially or somehow under the jurisdiction of a sort of policeman or beadle, called a Lord Warden. Holding the office directly from the crown, I believe, all the royal emoluments incident to the Cinque Port territories become by assignment his. By some writers this office is called a sinecure. But not so. Because the Lord Warden is busily employed at times in fobbing his perquisites; which are his chiefly by virtue of that same fobbing of them.

Now when these poor sun-burnt mariners, bare-footed, and with their trowsers rolled high up on their eely legs, had wearily hauled their fat fish high and dry, promising themselves a good £150 from the precious oil and bone; and in fantasy sipping rare tea with their wives, and good ale with their cronies, upon the strength of their respective shares; up steps a very learned and most Christian and charitable gentleman, with a copy of Blackstone under his arm; and laying it upon the whale's head, he says – 'Hands off! this fish, my masters, is a Fast-Fish. I seize it as the Lord Warden's.' Upon this the poor mariners in their respectful consternation – so truly English – knowing not what to say, fall to vigorously scratching their heads all round; meanwhile ruefully glancing from the whale to the stranger. But that did in nowise mend the matter, or at all soften the hard heart of the learned gentleman with the copy of Blackstone. At length one of them, after long scratching about for his ideas, made bold to speak.

'Please, sir, who is the Lord Warden?'

'The Duke.'

'But the duke had nothing to do with taking this fish?'

'It is his.'

'We have been at great trouble, and peril, and some expense, and is all that to go to the Duke's benefit; we getting nothing at all for our pains but our blisters?'

'It is his.'

'Is the Duke so very poor as to be forced to this desperate mode of getting a livelihood?'

'It is his.'

'I thought to relieve my old bed-ridden mother by part of my share of this whale.'

'It is his.'

'Won't the Duke be content with a quarter or a half?'

'It is his.'

In a word, the whale was seized and sold, and his Grace the Duke of Wellington received the money. Thinking that viewed in some particular lights, the case might by a bare possibility in some small degree be deemed, under the circumstances, a rather hard one, an honest clergyman of the town respectfully addressed a note to his Grace, begging him to take the case of those unfortunate mariners into full consideration. To which my Lord Duke in substance replied (both letters were published) that he had already done so, and received the money, and would be obliged to the reverend gentleman if for the future he (the reverend gentleman) would decline meddling with other people's business. Is this the still militant old man, standing at the corners of the three kingdoms, on all hands coercing alms of beggars?

It will readily be seen that in this case the alleged right of the Duke to the whale was a delegated one from the Sovereign. We must needs inquire then on what principle the Sovereign is originally invested with that right. The law itself has already been set forth. But Plowdon gives us the reason for it. Says Plowdon, the whale so caught belongs to the King and Queen, 'because of its superior excellence.' And by the soundest commentators this has ever been held a cogent argument in such matters.

But why should the King have the head, and the Queen the tail? A reason for that, ye lawyers!

In his treatise on 'Queen-Gold,' or Queen-pinmoney, an old King's Bench author, one William Prynne, thus discourseth: 'Ye tail is ye Queen's, that ye Queen's wardrobe may be supplied with ye whalebone.' Now this was written at a time when the black limber bone of the Greenland or Right whale was largely used in ladies' bodices. But this same bone is not in the tail; it is in the head, which is a sad mistake for a sagacious lawyer like Prynne. But is the Queen a mermaid, to be presented with a tail? An allegorical meaning may lurk here.

There are two royal fish so styled by the English law writers – the whale and the sturgeon; both royal property under certain limitations, and nominally supplying the tenth branch of the crown's ordinary revenue. I know not that any other author has hinted of the matter; but by inference it seems to me that the sturgeon must be divided in the same way as the whale, the King receiving the highly dense and elastic head peculiar to that fish, which, symbolically regarded, may possibly be humorously grounded upon some presumed congeniality. And thus there seems a reason in all things, even in law.

91

THE PEQUOD MEETS THE ROSE-BUD

'In vain it was to rake for Ambergriese in the paunch of this Leviathan, insufferable fetor denying that inquiry.'

Sir T. Browne, V. E.

It was a week or two after the last whaling scene recounted, and when we were slowly sailing over a sleepy, vapory, mid-day sea, that the many noses on the Pequod's deck proved more vigilant discoverers than the three pairs of eyes aloft. A peculiar and not very pleasant smell was smelt in the sea.

'I will bet something now,' said Stubb, 'that somewhere hereabouts are some of those drugged whales we tickled the other day. I thought they would keel up before long.'

Presently, the vapors in advance slid aside; and there in the distance lay a ship, whose furled sails betokened that some sort of whale must be alongside. As we glided nearer, the stranger showed French colors from his peak; and by the eddying cloud of vulture sea-fowl that circled, and hovered, and swooped around him, it was plain that the whale alongside must be what the fishermen call a blasted whale, that is, a whale that has died unmolested on the sea, and so floated an unappropriated corpse. It may well be conceived, what an unsavory odor such a mass must exhale; worse than an Assyrian city in the plague, when the living are incompetent to bury the departed. So intolerable indeed is it regarded by some, that no cupidity could persuade them to moor alongside of it. Yet are there those who will still do it; notwithstanding the fact that the oil obtained from such subjects is of a very inferior quality, and by no means of the nature of attar-of-rose.

Coming still nearer with the expiring breeze, we saw that the Frenchmen had a second whale alongside; and this second whale seemed even more of a nosegay than the first. In truth, it turned out to be one of those problematical whales that seem to dry up and die with a sort of prodigious dyspepsia, or indigestion; leaving their defunct bodies almost entirely bankrupt of anything like oil. Nevertheless, in the proper place we shall see that no knowing fisherman will ever turn up his nose at such a whale as this, however much he may shun blasted whales in general.

The Pequod had now swept so nigh to the stranger, that Stubb vowed he recognized his cutting spade-pole entangled in the lines that were knotted round the tail of one of these whales.

'There's a pretty fellow, now,' he banteringly laughed,

1. New Bedford Docks: 'Huge hills and mountains of casks on casks were piled upon her wharves, and side by side the world-wandering whale ships lay silent and safely moored at last. . .' (WHEELBARROW)

2. Tattooed Mummified Maori Head: 'Holding a light in one hand, and that identical New Zealand head in the other, the stranger entered the room. . .' (THE SPOUTER-INN)

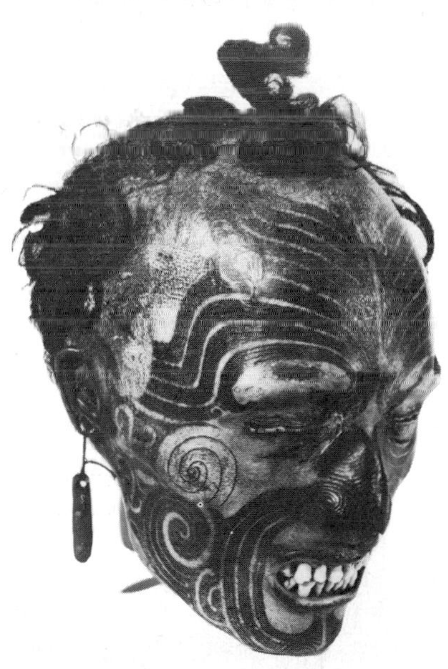

This Tablet was erected by
the Capt. Officers & Crew, of
the Ship Huntress
of New Bedford.
In memory of
WILLIAM C. J. KIRKWOOD,
of Boston Mass. aged 25 y'rs,
who fell from aloft, off
Cape Horn, Feb. 10, 1850,
and was drowned.

3. The Seamen's Bethel and Mariners' Home, New Bedford (1830): 'In this same New Bedford there stands a Whaleman's Chapel. . .' (THE CHAPEL)

4. Cenotaph at the Seamen's Bethel: '. . . and there these silent islands of men and women sat steadfastly eyeing several marble tablets, with black borders, masoned into the wall on either side the pulpit.' (THE CHAPEL)

5. The Whaleship *A. R. Tucker* of New Bedford: 'She was a ship of the old school, rather small if anything; with an old fashioned claw-footed look about her.' (THE SHIP)

6. A Quito Doubloon, dated 1839: 'look ye, whosoever of ye raises me that same white whale, he shall have this gold ounce, my boys!' (THE QUARTER-DECK)

7. *Pêche du Cachalot*, from an aquatint after Garneray: 'a noble Sperm Whale is depicted in full majesty of might, just risen beneath the boat from the profundities of the ocean, and bearing high in the air upon his back the terrific wreck of the stoven planks.' (OF THE LESS ERRONEOUS PICTURES OF WHALES)

8. Frontispiece to Thomas Beale, *The Natural History of the Sperm Whale* (London, 1839): 'His frontispiece, boats attacking Sperm Whales though no doubt calculated to excite the civil scepticism of some parlor men, is admirably correct and life-like in its general effect.' (OF THE LESS ERRONEOUS PICTURES OF WHALES)

9. J. M. W. Turner, detail from 'Whalers. *Vide Beale's Voyage p. 165*', exhibited at the Royal Academy, 1845, now usually known as *The Whale Ship*. On reading Beale, Melville noted: 'Turner's pictures of whales were suggested by this book.' (*Marginalia*)

10. 'Cutting In & Trying Out', frontispiece to J. Ross Browne, *Etchings of a Whaling Cruise* (New York, 1846): 'Now as the blubber envelopes the whale precisely as the rind does an orange, so is it stripped off from the body precisely as an orange is sometimes stripped by spiralizing it.' (CUTTING IN)

11. Detail from a Whaleman's Journal: 'When reaching far over the bow, Stubb slowly churned his long sharp lance into the fish, and kept it there, carefully churning and churning. . .'
(STUBB KILLS A WHALE)

12. Forecastle scene aboard a New Bedford Whaler: 'But the whaleman, as he seeks the food of light, so he lives in light. He makes his berth an Aladdin's lamp. . .' (THE LAMP)

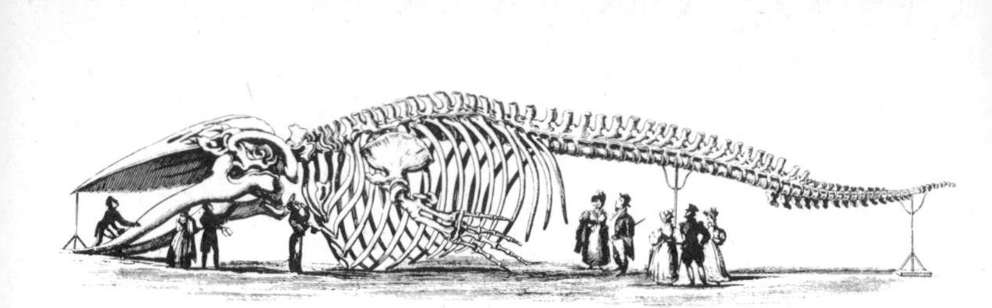

13. 'Skeleton of the Great Northern Rorqual' (from *The Naturalist's Library*, Edinburgh, 1837): 'To me this vast ivory-ribbed chest, with the long, unrelieved spine, extending far away from it in a straight line, not a little resembled the embryo hull of a great ship new-laid upon the stocks. . .' (MEASUREMENT OF THE WHALE'S SKELETON)

14. Detail from a Colour Sketch by a New Bedford Whaleman (c. 1840): 'the frail gunwales bent in, collapsed, and snapped, as both jaws, like an enormous shears, sliding further aft, bit the craft completely in twain. . .' (THE CHASE – FIRST DAY)

standing in the ship's bows, 'there's a jackal for ye! I well know that these Crappoes of Frenchmen are but poor devils in the fishery; sometimes lowering their boats for breakers, mistaking them for Sperm Whale spouts; yes, and sometimes sailing from their port with their hold full of boxes of tallow candles, and cases of snuffers, foreseeing that all the oil they will get won't be enough to dip the Captain's wick into; aye, we all know these things; but look ye, here's a Crappo that is content with our leavings, the drugged whale there, I mean; aye, and is content too with scraping the dry bones of that other precious fish he has there. Poor devil! I say, pass round a hat, some one, and let's make him a present of a little oil for dear charity's sake. For what oil he'll get from that drugged whale there, wouldn't be fit to burn in a jail; no, not in a condemned cell. And as for the other whale, why, I'll agree to get more oil by chopping up and trying out these three masts of ours, than he'll get from that bundle of bones; though, now that I think of it, it may contain something worth a good deal more than oil; yes, ambergris. I wonder now if our old man has thought of that. It's worth trying. Yes, I'm in for it;' and so saying he started for the quarter-deck.

By this time the faint air had become a complete calm; so that whether or no, the Pequod was now fairly entrapped in the smell, with no hope of escaping except by its breezing up again. Issuing from the cabin, Stubb now called his boat's crew, and pulled off for the stranger. Drawing across her bow, he perceived that in accordance with the fanciful French taste, the upper part of her stem-piece was carved in the likeness of a huge drooping stalk, was painted green, and for thorns had copper spikes projecting from it here and there; the whole terminating in a symmetrical folded bulb of a bright red color. Upon her head boards, in large gilt letters, he read 'Bouton de Rose,' – Rose-button, or Rose-bud; and this was the romantic name of this aromatic ship.

Though Stubb did not understand the *Bouton* part of the inscription, yet the word *rose*, and the bulbous figure-head put together, sufficiently explained the whole to him.

'A wooden rose-bud, eh?' he cried with his hand to his nose, 'that will do very well; but how like all creation it smells!'

Now in order to hold direct communication with the people on deck, he had to pull round the bows to the starboard side, and thus come close to the blasted whale; and so talk over it.

Arrived then at this spot, with one hand still to his nose, he bawled – 'Bouton-de-Rose, ahoy! are there any of you Bouton-de-Roses that speak English?'

'Yes,' rejoined a Guernsey-man from the bulwarks, who turned out to be the chief-mate.

'Well, then, my Bouton-de-Rose-bud, have you seen the White Whale?'

'*What* whale?'

'The *White* Whale – a Sperm Whale – Moby Dick, have ye seen him?'

'Never heard of such a whale. Cachalot Blanche? White Whale – no.'

'Very good, then; good bye now, and I'll call again in a minute.'

Then rapidly pulling back towards the Pequod, and seeing Ahab leaning over the quarter-deck rail awaiting his report, he moulded his two hands into a trumpet and shouted – 'No, Sir! No!' Upon which Ahab retired, and Stubb returned to the Frenchman.

He now perceived that the Guernsey-man, who had just got into the chains, and was using a cutting-spade, had slung his nose in a sort of bag.

'What's the matter with your nose, there?' said Stubb. 'Broke it?'

'I wish it was broken, or that I didn't have any nose at all!' answered the Guernsey-man, who did not seem to relish the job he was at very much. 'But what are you holding *yours* for?'

'Oh, nothing! It's a wax nose; I have to hold it on. Fine day, aint it? Air rather gardenny, I should say; throw us a bunch of posics, will ye, Bouton-de-Rose?'

'What in the devil's name do you want here?' roared the Guernsey-man, flying into a sudden passion.

'Oh! keep cool – cool? yes, that's the word; why don't you pack those whales in ice while you're working at 'em? But joking aside, though; do you know, Rose-bud, that it's all nonsense trying to get any oil out of such whales? As for that dried up one, there, he hasn't a gill in his whole carcase.'

'I know that well enough; but, d'ye see, the Captain here won't believe it; this is his first voyage; he was a Cologne manufacturer before. But come aboard, and mayhap he'll believe you, if he won't me; and so I'll get out of this dirty scrape.'

'Anything to oblige ye, my sweet and pleasant fellow,' rejoined Stubb, and with that he soon mounted to the deck. There a queer scene presented itself. The sailors, in tasselled caps of red worsted, were getting the heavy tackles in readiness for the whales. But they worked rather slow and talked very fast, and seemed in anything but a good humor. All their noses upwardly projected from their faces like so many jib-booms. Now and then pairs of them would drop their work, and run up to the mast-head to get some fresh air. Some thinking they would catch the plague, dipped oakum in coal-tar, and at intervals held it to their nostrils. Others having broken the stems of their pipes almost short off at the bowl, were vigorously puffing tobacco-smoke, so that it constantly filled their olfactories.

Stubb was struck by a shower of outcries and anathemas proceeding from the Captain's round-house abaft; and looking in that direction saw a fiery face thrust from behind the door, which was held ajar from within. This was the tormented surgeon, who, after in vain remonstrating against the proceedings of the day, had betaken himself to the Captain's round-house (*cabinet* he called it) to avoid the pest; but still, could not help yelling out his entreaties and indignations at times.

Marking all this, Stubb argued well for his scheme, and turning to the Guernsey-man had a little chat with him, during which the stranger mate expressed his detestation of his Captain as a conceited ignoramus, who had brought them all into so unsavory and unprofitable a pickle. Sounding him carefully, Stubb further perceived that the Guernsey-man had not the slightest suspicion concerning the ambergris. He therefore held his peace on that head, but otherwise was quite frank and confidential with him, so that the two quickly concocted a little plan for both circumventing and satirizing the Captain, without his at all dreaming of distrusting their sincerity. According to this little plan of theirs, the Guernsey-man, under cover of an interpreter's office, was to tell the Captain what he pleased, but as coming from Stubb; and as for Stubb, he was to utter any nonsense that should come uppermost in him during the interview.

By this time their destined victim appeared from his cabin. He was a small and dark, but rather delicate looking man for a sea-captain, with large whiskers and moustache, however; and wore a red cotton velvet vest with watch-seals at his side. To this gentleman, Stubb was now politely introduced by the Guernsey-man, who at once ostentatiously put on the aspect of interpreting between them.

'What shall I say to him first?' said he.

'Why,' said Stubb, eyeing the velvet vest and the watch and seals, 'you may as well begin by telling him that he looks a sort of babyish to me, though I don't pretend to be a judge.'

'He says, Monsieur,' said the Guernsey-man, in French, turning to his captain, 'that only yesterday his ship spoke a vessel, whose captain and chief-mate, with six sailors, had all died of a fever caught from a blasted whale they had brought alongside.'

Upon this the captain started, and eagerly desired to know more.

'What now?' said the Guernsey-man to Stubb.

'Why, since he takes it so easy, tell him that now I have eyed him carefully, I'm quite certain that he's no more fit to command a whale-ship than a St Jago monkey. In fact, tell him from me he's a baboon.'

'He vows and declares, Monsieur, that the other whale,

the dried one, is far more deadly than the blasted one; in fine, Monsieur, he conjures us, as we value our lives, to cut loose from these fish.'

Instantly the captain ran forward, and in a loud voice commanded his crew to desist from hoisting the cutting-tackles, and at once cast loose the cables and chains confining the whales to the ship.

'What now?' said the Guernsey-man, when the captain had returned to them.

'Why, let me see; yes, you may as well tell him now that – that – in fact, tell him I've diddled him, and (aside to himself) perhaps somebody else.'

'He says, Monsieur, that he's very happy to have been of any service to us.'

Hearing this, the captain vowed that they were the grateful parties (meaning himself and mate) and concluded by inviting Stubb down into his cabin to drink a bottle of Bordeaux.

'He wants you to take a glass of wine with him,' said the interpreter.

'Thank him heartily; but tell him it's against my principles to drink with the man I've diddled. In fact, tell him I must go.'

'He says, Monsieur, that his principles won't admit of his drinking; but that if Monsieur wants to live another day to drink, then Monsieur had best drop all four boats, and pull the ship away from these whales, for it's so calm they won't drift.'

By this time Stubb was over the side, and getting into his boat, hailed the Guernsey-man to this effect, – that having a long tow-line in his boat, he would do what he could to help them, by pulling out the lighter whale of the two from the ship's side. While the Frenchman's boats, then, were engaged in towing the ship one way, Stubb benevolently towed away at his whale the other way, ostentatiously slacking out a most unusually long tow-line.

Presently a breeze sprang up; Stubb feigned to cast off from the whale; hoisting his boats, the Frenchman soon increased his distance, while the Pequod slid in between him and Stubb's whale. Whereupon Stubb quickly pulled to the floating body, and hailing the Pequod to give notice of his intentions, at once proceeded to reap the fruit of his unrighteous cunning. Seizing his sharp boat-spade, he commenced an excavation in the body, a little behind the side fin. You would almost have thought he was digging a cellar there in the sea; and when at length his spade struck against the gaunt ribs, it was like turning up old Roman tiles and pottery buried in fat English loam. His boat's crew were all in high excitement, eagerly helping their chief, and looking as anxious as gold-hunters.

And all the time numberless fowls were diving, and ducking, and screaming, and yelling, and fighting around them. Stubb was beginning to look disappointed, especially as the horrible nosegay increased, when suddenly from out of the very heart of this plague, there stole a faint stream of perfume, which flowed through the tide of bad smells without being absorbed by it, as one river will flow into and then along with another, without at all blending with it for a time.

'I have it, I have it,' cried Stubb, with delight, striking something in the subterranean regions, 'a purse! a purse!'

Dropping his spade, he thrust both hands in, and drew out handfuls of something that looked like ripe Windsor soap, or rich mottled old cheese; very unctuous and savory withal. You might easily dent it with your thumb; it is of a hue between yellow and ash color. And this, good friends, is ambergris, worth a gold guinea an ounce to any druggist. Some six handfuls were obtained; but more was unavoidably lost in the sea, and still more, perhaps, might have been secured were it not for impatient Ahab's loud command to Stubb to desist, and come on board, else the ship would bid them good bye.

92

AMBERGRIS

Now this ambergris is a very curious substance, and so important as an article of commerce, that in 1791 a certain Nantucket-born Captain Coffin was examined at the bar of the English house of Commons on that subject. For at that time, and indeed until a comparatively late day, the precise origin of ambergris remained, like amber itself, a problem to the learned. Though the word ambergris is but the French compound for grey amber, yet the two substances are quite distinct. For amber, though at times found on the sea-coast, is also dug up in some far inland soils, whereas ambergris is never found except upon the sea. Besides, amber is a hard, transparent, brittle, odorless substance, used for mouth-pieces to pipes, for beads and ornaments; but ambergris is soft, waxy, and so highly fragrant and spicy, that it is largely used in perfumery, in pastiles, precious candles, hair-powders, and pomatum. The Turks use it in cooking, and also carry it to Mecca, for the same purpose that frankincense is carried to St Peter's in Rome. Some wine merchants drop a few grains into claret, to flavor it.

Who would think, then, that such fine ladies and gentlemen should regale themselves with an essence found in the inglorious bowels of a sick whale! Yet so it is. By some, ambergris is supposed to be the cause, and by others the effect, of the dyspepsia in the whale. How to cure such a dyspepsia it were hard to say, unless by administering three or four boat loads of Brandreth's pills, and then running out of harm's way, as laborers do in blasting rocks.

I have forgotten to say that there were found in this ambergris, certain hard, round, bony plates, which at first Stubb thought might be sailors' trousers buttons; but it afterwards turned out that they were nothing more than pieces of small squid bones embalmed in that manner.

Now that the incorruption of this most fragrant ambergris should be found in the heart of such decay; is this nothing? Bethink thee of that saying of St Paul in Corinthians, about corruption and incorruption; how that we are sown in dishonor, but raised in glory. And likewise call to mind that saying of Paracelsus about what it is that maketh the best musk. Also forget not the strange fact that of all things of ill-savor, Cologne-water, in its rudimental manufacturing stages, is the worst.

I should like to conclude the chapter with the above appeal, but cannot, owing to my anxiety to repel a charge often made against whalemen, and which, in the estimation of some already biased minds, might be considered as indirectly substantiated by what has been said of the Frenchman's two whales. Elsewhere in this volume the slanderous aspersion has been disproved, that the vocation of whaling is throughout a slatternly, untidy business. But there is another thing to rebut. They hint that all whales always smell bad. Now how did this odious stigma originate?

I opine, that it is plainly traceable to the first arrival of the Greenland whaling ships in London, more than two centuries ago. Because those whalemen did not then, and do not now, try out their oil at sea as the Southern ships have always done; but cutting up the fresh blubber in small bits, thrust it through the bung holes of large casks, and carry it home in that manner; the shortness of the season in those Icy Seas, and the sudden and violent storms to which they are exposed, forbidding any other course. The consequence is, that upon breaking into the hold, and unloading one of these whale cemeteries, in the Greenland dock, a savor is given forth somewhat similar to that arising from excavating an old city grave-yard, for the foundations of a Lying-in Hospital.

I partly surmise also, that this wicked charge against whalers may be likewise imputed to the existence on the coast of Greenland, in former times, of a Dutch village called Schmerenburgh or Smeerenberg, which latter name is the one used by the learned Fogo Von Slack, in his great work on Smells, a textbook on that subject. As its name imports (smeer, fat; berg, to put up), this village was founded in order to afford a place for the blubber of the Dutch whale fleet to be tried out, without being taken home to Holland for that purpose. It was a collection of furnaces, fat-kettles, and oil sheds; and when the works were in full operation certainly gave forth no very pleasant savor. But all this is quite different with a South Sea Sperm Whaler; which in a voyage of four years perhaps, after completely filling her hold with oil, does not, perhaps, consume fifty days in the business of boiling out; and in the state that it is casked, the oil is nearly scentless. The truth is, that living or dead, if but decently treated, whales as a species are by no means creatures of ill odor; nor can whalemen be recognised, as the people of the middle ages affected to detect a Jew in the company, by the nose. Nor indeed can the whale possibly be otherwise than fragrant, when, as a general thing, he enjoys such high health; taking abundance of exercise; always out of doors; though, it is true, seldom in the open air. I say, that the motion of a Sperm Whale's flukes above water dispenses a perfume, as when a musk-scented lady rustles her dress in a warm parlor. What then shall I liken the Sperm Whale to for fragrance, considering his magnitude? Must it not be to that famous elephant, with jewelled tusks, and redolent with myrrh, which was led out of an Indian town to do honor to Alexander the Great?

93

THE CASTAWAY

It was but some few days after encountering the Frenchman, that a most significant event befell the most insignificant of the Pequod's crew; an event most lamentable; and which ended in providing the sometimes madly merry and predestinated craft with a living and ever accompanying prophecy of whatever shattered sequel might prove her own.

Now, in the whale ship, it is not every one that goes in the boats. Some few hands are reserved called ship-keepers, whose province it is to work the vessel while the boats are pursuing the whale. As a general thing, these ship-keepers are as hardy fellows as the men comprising the boats' crews. But if there happen to be an unduly slender, clumsy, or timorous wight in the ship, that wight is certain to be made a ship-keeper. It was so in the Pequod with the little negro Pippin by nick-name, Pip by abbreviation. Poor Pip! ye have heard of him before; ye must remember his tambourine on that dramatic midnight, so gloomy-jolly.

In outer aspect, Pip and Dough-Boy made a match, like a black pony and a white one, of equal developments, though of dissimilar color, driven in one eccentric span. But while hapless Dough-Boy was by nature dull and torpid in his intellects, Pip, though over tender-hearted, was at bottom very bright, with that pleasant, genial, jolly brightness peculiar to his tribe; a tribe, which ever enjoy all holidays and festivities with finer, freer relish than any other race. For blacks, the year's calendar should show naught but three hundred and sixty-five Fourth of Julys and New Year's Days. Nor smile so, while I write that this little black was brilliant, for even blackness has its brilliancy; behold yon lustrous ebony, panelled in kings' cabinets. But Pip loved life, and all life's peaceable securities; so that the panic-striking business in which he had somehow unaccountably become entrapped, had most sadly blurred his brightness; though, as ere long will be seen, what was thus temporarily subdued in him, in the end was destined to be luridly illumined by strange wild fires, that fictitiously showed him off to ten times the natural lustre with which in his native Tolland County in Connecticut, he had once enlivened many a fiddler's frolic on the green; and at melodious even-tide, with his gay ha-ha! had turned the round horizon into one star-belled tambourine. So, though in the clear air of day, suspended against a blue-veined neck, the pure-watered diamond drop will healthful glow; yet, when the cunning jeweller would show you the diamond in its most impressive lustre, he lays it against a gloomy ground, and then lights it up, not by the sun, but by some unnatural gases. Then come out those fiery effulgences, infernally superb; then the evil-blazing diamond, once the divinest symbol of the crystal skies, looks like some crown-jewel stolen from the King of Hell. But let us to the story.

It came to pass, that in the ambergris affair Stubb's after-oarsman chanced so to sprain his hand, as for a time to become quite maimed; and, temporarily, Pip was put into his place.

The first time Stubb lowered with him, Pip evinced much nervousness; but happily, for that time, escaped close contact with the whale; and therefore came off not altogether discreditably; though Stubb observing him, took care, afterwards, to exhort him to cherish his courageousness to the utmost, for he might often find it needful.

Now upon the second lowering, the boat paddled upon the whale; and as the fish received the darted iron, it gave its customary rap, which happened, in this instance, to be right under poor Pip's seat. The involuntary consternation of the moment caused him to leap, paddle in hand, out of the boat; and in such a way, that part of the slack whale line coming against his chest, he breasted it overboard with him, so as to become entangled in it, when at last plumping into the water. That instant the stricken whale started on a fierce run, the line swiftly straightened; and presto! poor Pip came all foaming up to the chocks of the boat, remorselessly dragged there by the line, which had taken several turns around his chest and neck.

Tashtego stood in the bows. He was full of the fire of the hunt. He hated Pip for a poltroon. Snatching the boat-knife from its sheath, he suspended its sharp edge over the line, and turning towards Stubb, exclaimed interrogatively, 'Cut?' Meantime Pip's blue, choked face plainly looked, Do, for God's sake! All passed in a flash. In less than half a minute, this entire thing happened.

'Damn him, cut!' roared Stubb; and so the whale was lost and Pip was saved.

So soon as he recovered himself, the poor little negro was assailed by yells and execrations from the crew. Tranquilly permitting these irregular cursings to evaporate, Stubb then in a plain, business-like, but still half humorous manner, cursed Pip officially; and that done, unofficially gave him much wholesome advice. The substance was, Never jump from a boat, Pip, except – but all the rest was indefinite, as the soundest advice ever is. Now, in general, *Stick to the boat*, is your true motto in whaling; but cases will sometimes happen when *Leap from the boat*, is still better. Moreover, as if perceiving at last that if he should give undiluted conscientious advice to Pip, he would be leaving him too wide a margin to jump in for the future; Stubb suddenly dropped all advice, and concluded with a peremptory command, 'Stick to the boat, Pip, or by the Lord, I wont pick you up if you jump; mind that. We can't afford to lose whales by the likes of you; a whale would sell for thirty times what you would, Pip, in Alabama. Bear that in mind, and don't jump any more.' Hereby perhaps Stubb indirectly hinted, that though man loves his fellow, yet man is a money-making animal, which propensity too often interferes with his benevolence.

But we are all in the hands of the Gods; and Pip jumped again. It was under very similar circumstances to the first performance; but this time he did not breast out the line; and hence, when the whale started to run, Pip was left behind on the sea, like a hurried traveller's trunk. Alas! Stubb was but too true to his word. It was a beautiful, bounteous, blue day; the spangled sea calm and cool, and flatly stretching away, all round, to the horizon, like gold-beater's skin hammered out to the extremest. Bobbing up and down in that sea, Pip's ebon head showed like a head of cloves. No boat-knife was lifted when he fell so rapidly astern. Stubb's inexorable back was turned upon him; and the whale was winged. In three minutes, a whole mile of shoreless ocean was between Pip and Stubb. Out from the centre of the sea, poor Pip turned his crisp, curling, black head to the sun, another lonely castaway, though the loftiest and the brightest.

Now, in calm weather, to swim in the open ocean is as easy to the practised swimmer as to ride in a spring-carriage ashore. But the awful lonesomeness is intolerable. The intense concentration of self in the middle of such a heartless immensity, my God! who can tell it? Mark, how when sailors in a dead calm bathe in the open sea – mark how closely they hug their ship and only coast along her sides.

But had Stubb really abandoned the poor little negro to his fate? No; he did not mean to, at least. Because there were two boats in his wake, and he supposed, no doubt, that they would of course come up to Pip very quickly, and pick him up; though, indeed, such considerateness towards oarsmen jeopardized through their own timidity, is not always manifested by the hunters in all similar instances; and such instances not unfrequently occur; almost invariably in the fishery, a coward, so called, is marked with the same ruthless detestation peculiar to military navies and armies.

But it so happened, that those boats, without seeing Pip, suddenly spying whales close to them on one side, turned, and gave chase; and Stubb's boat was now so far away, and he and all his crew so intent upon his fish, that Pip's ringed horizon began to expand around him miserably. By the merest chance the ship itself at last rescued him; but from that hour the little negro went about the deck an idiot; such, at least, they said he was. The sea had jeeringly kept his finite body up, but drowned the infinite of his soul. Not drowned entirely, though. Rather carried down alive to wondrous depths, where strange shapes of the unwarped primal world glided to and fro before his passive eyes; and the miser-merman, Wisdom, revealed his hoarded heaps; and among the joyous, heartless, ever-juvenile eternities, Pip saw the multitudinous, God-omnipresent, coral insects, that out of the firmament of waters heaved the colossal orbs. He saw God's foot upon the treadle of the loom, and spoke it; and therefore his shipmates called him mad. So man's insanity is heaven's sense; and wandering from all mortal reason, man comes at last to that celestial thought, which, to reason, is absurd and frantic; and weal or woe, feels then uncompromised, indifferent as his God.

For the rest, blame not Stubb too hardly. The thing is common in that fishery; and in the sequel of the narrative, it will then be seen what like abandonment befell myself.

94

A SQUEEZE OF THE HAND

THAT whale of Stubb's so dearly purchased, was duly brought to the Pequod's side, where all those cutting and hoisting operations previously detailed, were regularly gone through, even to the baling of the Heidelburgh Tun, or Case.

While some were occupied with this latter duty, others were employed in dragging away the larger tubs, so soon as filled with the sperm; and when the proper time arrived, this same sperm was carefully manipulated ere going to the try-works, of which anon.

It had cooled and crystallized to such a degree, that when, with several others, I sat down before a large Constantine's bath of it, I found it strangely concreted into lumps, here and there rolling about in the liquid part. It was our business to squeeze these lumps back into fluid. A sweet and unctuous duty! No wonder that in old times this sperm was such a favorite cosmetic. Such a clearer! such a sweetener! such a softener! such a delicious mollifier! After having my hands in it for only a few minutes, my fingers felt like eels, and began, as it were, to serpentine and spiralize.

As I sat there at my ease, cross-legged on the deck; after the bitter exertion at the windlass; under a blue tranquil sky; the ship under indolent sail, and gliding so serenely along; as I bathed my hands among those soft, gentle globules of infiltrated tissues, woven almost within the hour; as they richly broke to my fingers, and discharged all their opulence, like fully ripe grapes their wine; as I snuffed up that uncontaminated aroma, – literally and truly, like the smell of spring violets; I declare to you, that for the time I lived as in a musky meadow; I forgot all about our horrible oath; in that inexpressible sperm, I washed my hands and my heart of it; I almost began to credit the old Paracelsan superstition that sperm is of rare virtue in allaying the heat of anger: while bathing in that bath, I felt divinely free from all ill-will, or petulance, or malice, of any sort whatsoever.

Squeeze! squeeze! squeeze! all the morning long; I squeezed that sperm till I myself almost melted into it; I squeezed that sperm till a strange sort of insanity came over me; and I found myself unwittingly squeezing my co-laborers' hands in it, mistaking their hands for the gentle globules. Such an abounding, affectionate, friendly, loving feeling did this avocation beget; that at last I was continually squeezing their hands, and looking up into their eyes sentimentally; as much as to say, – Oh! my dear fellow beings, why should we longer cherish any social acerbities, or know the slightest ill-humor or envy! Come; let us squeeze hands all round; nay, let us all squeeze ourselves into each other; let us squeeze ourselves universally into the very milk and sperm of kindness.

Would that I could keep squeezing that sperm for ever! For now, since by many prolonged, repeated experiences, I have perceived that in all cases man must eventually lower, or at least shift, his conceit of attainable felicity; not placing it anywhere in the intellect or the fancy; but in the wife, the heart, the bed, the table, the saddle, the fire-side, the country; now that I have perceived all this, I am ready to squeeze case eternally. In thoughts of the visions of the night, I saw long rows of angels in paradise, each with his hands in a jar of spermaceti.

* * * * * * *

Now, while discoursing of sperm, it behooves to speak of other things akin to it, in the business of preparing the sperm whale for the try-works.

First comes white-horse, so called, which is obtained from the tapering part of the fish, and also from the thicker portions of his flukes. It is tough with congealed tendons – a wad of muscle – but still contains some oil. After being severed from the whale, the white-horse is first cut into portable oblongs ere going to the mincer. They look much like blocks of Berkshire marble.

Plum-pudding is the term bestowed upon certain fragmentary parts of the whale's flesh, here and there adhering to the blanket of blubber, and often participating to a considerable degree in its unctuousness. It is a most refreshing, convivial, beautiful object to behold. As its name imports, it is of an exceedingly rich, mottled tint, with a bestreaked snowy and golden ground, dotted with spots of the deepest crimson and purple. It is plums of rubies, in pictures of citron. Spite of reason, it is hard to keep yourself from eating it. I confess, that once I stole behind the foremast to try it. It tasted something as I should conceive a royal cutlet from the thigh of Louis le Gros might have tasted, supposing him to have been killed the first day after the venison season, and that particular venison season contemporary with an unusually fine vintage of the vineyards of Champagne.

There is another substance, and a very singular one, which turns up in the course of this business, but which I feel it to be very puzzling adequately to describe. It is called slobgollion; an appellation original with the whalemen, and even so is the nature of the substance. It is an ineffably oozy, stringy affair, most frequently found in the tubs of sperm, after a prolonged squeezing, and subsequent decanting. I hold it to be the wondrously thin, ruptured membranes of the case, coalescing.

Gurry, so called, is a term properly belonging to right whalemen, but sometimes incidentally used by the sperm fishermen. It designates the dark, glutinous substance which is scraped off the back of the Greenland or right whale, and much of which covers the decks of those inferior souls who hunt that ignoble Leviathan.

Nippers. Strictly this word is not indigenous to the whale's vocabulary. But as applied by whalemen, it becomes so. A whaleman's nipper is a short firm strip of tendinous stuff cut from the tapering part of Leviathan's tail: it averages an inch in thickness, and for the rest, is about the size of the iron part of a hoe. Edgewise moved along the oily deck, it operates like a leathern squilgee; and by nameless blandishments, as of magic, allures along with it all impurities.

But to learn all about these recondite matters, your best way is at once to descend into the blubber-room, and have a long talk with its inmates. This place has previously been mentioned as the receptacle for the blanket-pieces, when stript and hoisted from the whale. When the proper time arrives for cutting up its contents, this apartment is a scene of terror to all tyros, especially by night. On one side, lit by a dull lantern, a space has been left clear for the workmen. They generally go in pairs, – a pike-and-gaff-man and a spade-man. The whaling-pike is similar to a frigate's boarding-weapon of the same name. The gaff is something like a boat-hook. With his gaff, the gaffman hooks on to a sheet of blubber, and strives to hold it from slipping, as the ship pitches and lurches about. Meanwhile, the spade-man stands on the sheet itself, perpendicularly chopping it into the portable horse-pieces. This spade is sharp as hone can make it; the spademan's feet are shoeless; the thing he stands on will sometimes irresistibly slide away from him, like a sledge. If he cuts off one of his own toes, or one of his assistant's, would you be very much astonished? Toes are scarce among veteran blubber-room men.

95

THE CASSOCK

Had you stepped on board the Pequod at a certain juncture of this post-mortemizing of the whale; and had you strolled forward nigh the windlass, pretty sure am I that you would have scanned with no small curiosity a very strange, enigmatical object, which you would have seen there, lying along lengthwise in the lee scuppers. Not the wondrous cistern in the whale's huge head; not the prodigy of his unhinged lower jaw; not the miracle of his symmetrical tail; none of these would so surprise you, as half a glimpse of that unaccountable cone, – longer than a Kentuckian is tall, nigh a foot in diameter at the base, and jet-black as Yojo, the ebony idol of Queequeg. And an idol, indeed, it is; or, rather, in old times, its likeness was. Such an idol as that found in the secret groves of Queen Maachah in Judea; and for worshipping which, King Asa, her son, did depose her, and destroyed the idol, and burnt it for an abomination at the brook Kedron, as darkly set forth in the 15th chapter of the first book of Kings.

Look at the sailor, called the mincer, who now comes along, and assisted by two allies, heavily backs the grandissimus, as the mariners call it, and with bowed shoulders, staggers off with it as if he were a grenadier carrying a dead comrade from the field. Extending it upon the forecastle deck, he now proceeds cylindrically to remove its dark pelt, as an African hunter the pelt of a boa. This done he turns the pelt inside out, like a pantaloon leg; gives it a good stretching, so as almost to double its diameter; and at last hangs it, well spread, in the rigging, to dry. Ere long, it is taken down; when removing some three feet of it, towards the pointed extremity, and then cutting two slits for armholes at the other end, he lengthwise slips himself bodily into it. The mincer now stands before you invested in the full canonicals of his calling. Immemorial to all his order, this investiture alone will adequately protect him, while employed in the peculiar functions of his office.

That office consists in mincing the horse-pieces of blubber for the pots; an operation which is conducted at a curious wooden horse, planted endwise against the bulwarks, and with a capacious tub beneath it, into which the minced pieces drop, fast as the sheets from a rapt orator's desk. Arrayed in decent black; occupying a conspicuous pulpit; intent on bible leaves; what a candidate for an archbishoprick, what a lad for a Pope were this mincer! *

96

THE TRY-WORKS

BESIDES her hoisted boats, an American whaler is outwardly distinguished by her try-works. She presents the curious anomaly of the most solid masonry joining with oak and hemp in constituting the completed ship. It is as if from the open field a brick-kiln were transported to her planks.

The try-works are planted between the foremast and main-mast, the most roomy part of the deck. The timbers beneath are of a peculiar strength, fitted to sustain the weight of an almost solid mass of brick and mortar, some ten feet by eight square, and five in height. The foundation does not penetrate the deck, but the masonry is firmly secured to the surface by ponderous knees of iron bracing it on all sides, and screwing it down to the timbers. On the flanks it is cased with wood, and at top completely covered by a large, sloping, battened hatchway. Removing this hatch we expose the great try-pots, two in number, and each of several barrels' capacity. When not in use, they are kept remarkably clean. Sometimes they are polished with soapstone and sand, till they shine within like silver punch-bowls. During the night-watches some cynical old sailors will crawl into them and coil themselves away there for a nap. While employed in polishing them – one man in each pot, side by side – many confidential communications are carried on, over the iron lips. It is a place also for profound mathematical meditation. It was in the left hand try-pot of the

*Bible leaves! Bible leaves! This is the invariable cry from the mates to the mincer. It enjoins him to be careful, and cut his work into as thin slices as possible, inasmuch as by so doing the business of boiling out the oil is much accelerated, and its quantity considerably increased, besides perhaps improving it in quality.

Pequod, with the soapstone diligently circling round me, that I was first indirectly struck by the remarkable fact, that in geometry all bodies gliding along the cycloid, my soapstone for example, will descend from any point in precisely the same time.

Removing the fire-board from the front of the try-works, the bare masonry of that side is exposed, penetrated by the two iron mouths of the furnaces, directly underneath the pots. These mouths are fitted with heavy doors of iron. The intense heat of the fire is prevented from communicating itself to the deck, by means of a shallow reservoir extending under the entire inclosed surface of the works. By a tunnel inserted at the rear, this reservoir is kept replenished with water as fast as it evaporates. There are no external chimneys; they open direct from the rear wall. And here let us go back for a moment.

It was about nine o'clock at night that the Pequod's try-works were first started on this present voyage. It belonged to Stubb to oversee the business.

'All ready there? Off hatch, then, and start her. You cook, fire the works.' This was an easy thing, for the carpenter had been thrusting his shavings into the furnace throughout the passage. Here be it said that in a whaling voyage the first fire in the try-works has to be fed for a time with wood. After that no wood is used, except as a means of quick ignition to the staple fuel. In a word, after being tried out, the crisp, shrivelled blubber, now called scraps or fritters, still contains considerable of its unctuous properties. These fritters feed the flames. Like a plethoric burning martyr, or a self-consuming misanthrope, once ignited, the whale supplies his own fuel and burns by his own body. Would that he consumed his own smoke! for his smoke is horrible to inhale, and inhale it you must, and not only that, but you must live in it for the time. It has an unspeakable, wild, Hindoo odor about it, such as may lurk in the vicinity of funereal pyres. It smells like the left wing of the day of judgment; it is an argument for the pit.

By midnight the works were in full operation. We were

clear from the carcase; sail had been made; the wind was freshening; the wild ocean darkness was intense. But that darkness was licked up by the fierce flames, which at intervals forked forth from the sooty flues, and illuminated every lofty rope in the rigging, as with the famed Greek fire. The burning ship drove on, as if remorselessly commissioned to some vengeful deed. So the pitch and sulphur-freighted brigs of the bold Hydriote, Canaris, issuing from their midnight harbors, with broad sheets of flame for sails, bore down upon the Turkish frigates, and folded them in conflagrations.

The hatch, removed from the top of the works, now afforded a wide hearth in front of them. Standing on this were the Tartarean shapes of the pagan harpooneers, always the whale-ship's stokers. With huge pronged poles they pitched hissing masses of blubber into the scalding pots, or stirred up the fires beneath, till the snaky flames darted, curling, out of the doors to catch them by the feet. The smoke rolled away in sullen heaps. To every pitch of the ship there was a pitch of the boiling oil, which seemed all eagerness to leap into their faces. Opposite the mouth of the works, on the further side of the wide wooden hearth, was the windlass. This served for a sea-sofa. Here lounged the watch, when not otherwise employed, looking into the red heat of the fire, till their eyes felt scorched in their heads. Their tawny features, now all begrimed with smoke and sweat, their matted beards, and the contrasting barbaric brilliancy of their teeth, all these were strangely revealed in the capricious emblazonings of the works. As they narrated to each other their unholy adventures, their tales of terror told in words of mirth; as their uncivilized laughter forked upwards out of them, like the flames from the furnace; as to and fro, in their front, the harpooneers wildly gesticulated with their huge pronged forks and dippers; as the wind howled on, and the sea leaped, and the ship groaned and dived, and yet steadfastly shot her red hell further and further into the blackness of the sea and the night, and scornfully champed the white bone in her mouth, and viciously spat round her on all sides; then the rushing Pequod, freighted with savages, and laden with fire, and burning a corpse, and plunging into that blackness of darkness, seemed the material counterpart of her monomaniac commander's soul.

So seemed it to me, as I stood at her helm, and for long hours silently guided the way of this fire-ship on the sea. Wrapped, for that interval, in darkness myself, I but the better saw the redness, the madness, the ghastliness of others. The continual sight of the fiend shapes before me, capering half in smoke and half in fire, these at last begat kindred visions in my soul, so soon as I began to yield to that unaccountable drowsiness which ever would come over me at a midnight helm.

But that night, in particular, a strange (and ever since inexplicable) thing occurred to me. Starting from a brief standing sleep, I was horribly conscious of something fatally wrong. The jaw-bone tiller smote my side, which leaned against it; in my ears was the low hum of sails, just beginning to shake in the wind; I thought my eyes were open; I was half conscious of putting my fingers to the lids and mechanically stretching them still further apart. But, spite of all this, I could see no compass before me to steer by; though it seemed but a minute since I had been watching the card, by the steady binnacle lamp illuminating it. Nothing seemed before me but a jet gloom, now and then made ghastly by flashes of redness. Uppermost was the impression, that whatever swift, rushing thing I stood on was not so much bound to any haven ahead as rushing from all havens astern. A stark, bewildered feeling, as of death, came over me. Convulsively my hands grasped the tiller, but with the crazy conceit that the tiller was, somehow, in some enchanted way, inverted. My God! what is the matter with me? thought I. Lo! in my brief sleep I had turned myself about, and was fronting the ship's stern, with my back to her prow and the compass. In an instant I faced back, just in time to prevent the vessel from flying up into the wind, and very probably capsizing her. How glad and how grateful the relief from this unnatural hallucination of the night, and the fatal contingency of being brought by the lee!

Look not too long in the face of the fire, O man! Never dream with thy hand on the helm! Turn not thy back to the compass; accept the first hint of the hitching tiller; believe not the artificial fire, when its redness makes all things look ghastly. To-morrow, in the natural sun, the skies will be bright; those who glared like devils in the forking flames, the morn will show in far other, at least gentler, relief; the glorious, golden, glad sun, the only true lamp – all others but liars!

Nevertheless the sun hides not Virginia's Dismal Swamp, nor Rome's accursed Campagna, nor wide Sahara, nor all the millions of miles of deserts and of griefs beneath the moon. The sun hides not the ocean, which is the dark side of this earth, and which is two thirds of this earth. So, therefore, that mortal man who hath more of joy than sorrow in him, that mortal man cannot be true – not true, or undeveloped. With books the same. The truest of all men was the Man of Sorrows, and the truest of all books is Solomon's, and Ecclesiastes is the fine hammered steel of woe. 'All is vanity.' ALL. This wilful world hath not got hold of unchristian Solomon's wisdom yet. But he who dodges hospitals and jails, and walks fast crossing grave yards, and would rather talk of operas than hell; calls Cowper, Young, Pascal, Rousseau, poor devils all of sick men; and throughout a care-free lifetime swears by Rabelais as passing wise, and therefore jolly; – not that man is fitted to sit down on tomb-stones, and break the green damp mould with unfathomably wondrous Solomon.

But even Solomon, he says, 'the man that wandereth out of the way of understanding shall remain' (*i. e.* even while living) 'in the congregation of the dead.' Give not thyself up, then, to fire, lest it invert thee, deaden thee; as for the time it did me. There is a wisdom that is woe; but there is a woe that is madness. And there is a Catskill eagle in some souls that can alike dive down into the blackest gorges, and soar out of them again and become invisible in the sunny spaces.

And even if he for ever flies within the gorge, that gorge is in the mountains; so that even in his lowest swoop the mountain eagle is still higher than other birds upon the plain, even though they soar.

97

THE LAMP

HAD you descended from the Pequod's try-works to the Pequod's forecastle, where the off duty watch were sleeping, for one single moment you would have almost thought you were standing in some illuminated shrine of canonized kings and counsellors. There they lay in their triangular oaken vaults, each mariner a chiselled muteness; a score of lamps flashing upon his hooded eyes.

In merchantmen, oil for the sailor is more scarce than the milk of queens. To dress in the dark, and eat in the dark, and stumble in darkness to his pallet, this is his usual lot. But the whaleman, as he seeks the food of light, so he lives in light. He makes his berth an Aladdin's lamp, and lays him down in it; so that in the pitchiest night the ship's black hull still houses an illumination.

See with what entire freedom the whaleman takes his handful of lamps – often but old bottles and vials, though – to the copper cooler at the try-works, and replenishes them there, as mugs of ale at a vat. He burns, too, the purest of oil, in its unmanufactured, and, therefore, unvitiated state; a fluid unknown to solar, lunar, or astral contrivances ashore. It is sweet as early grass butter in April. He goes and hunts for his oil, so as to be sure of its freshness and genuineness, even as the traveller on the prairie hunts up his own supper of game.

98

STOWING DOWN AND CLEARING UP

ALREADY has it been related how the great leviathan is afar off descried from the mast-head; how he is chased over the watery moors, and slaughtered in the valleys of the deep; how he is then towed alongside and beheaded; and how (on the principle which entitled the headsman of old to the garments in which the beheaded was killed) his great padded surtout becomes the property of his executioner; how, in due time, he is condemned to the pots, and, like Shadrach, Meshach, and Abednego, his spermaceti, oil, and bone pass unscathed through the fire; – but now it remains to conclude the last chapter of this part of the description by rehearsing – singing, if I may – the romantic proceeding of decanting off his oil into the casks and striking them down into the hold, where once again leviathan returns to his native profundities, sliding along beneath the surface as before; but, alas! never more to rise and blow.

While still warm, the oil, like hot punch, is received into the six-barrel casks; and while, perhaps, the ship is pitching and rolling this way and that in the midnight sea, the enormous casks are slewed round and headed over, end for end, and sometimes perilously scoot across the slippery deck, like so many land slides, till at last man-handled and stayed in their course; and all round the hoops, rap, rap, go as many hammers as can play upon them, for now, *ex officio*, every sailor is a cooper.

At length, when the last pint is casked, and all is cool, then the great hatchways are unsealed, the bowels of the ship are thrown open, and down go the casks to their final rest in the sea. This done, the hatches are replaced, and hermetically closed, like a closet walled up.

In the sperm fishery, this is perhaps one of the most remarkable incidents in all the business of whaling. One day the planks stream with freshets of blood and oil; on the sacred quarter-deck enormous masses of the whale's head are profanely piled; great rusty casks lie about, as in a brewery yard; the smoke from the try-works has besooted all the bulwarks; the mariners go about suffused with unctuousness; the entire ship seems great leviathan himself; while on all hands the din is deafening.

But a day or two after, you look about you, and prick your ears in this self-same ship; and were it not for the tell-tale boats and try-works, you would all but swear you trod some silent merchant vessel, with a most scrupulously neat commander. The unmanufactured sperm oil possesses a singularly cleansing virtue. This is the reason why the decks never look so white as just after what they call an affair of oil. Besides, from the ashes of the burned scraps of the whale, a potent ley is readily made; and whenever any adhesiveness from the back of the whale remains clinging to the side, that ley quickly exterminates it. Hands go diligently along the bulwarks, and with buckets of water and rags restore them to their full tidiness. The soot is brushed from the lower rigging. All the numerous implements which have been in use are likewise faithfully cleansed and put away. The great hatch is scrubbed and placed upon the try-works, completely hiding the pots; every cask is out of sight; all tackles are coiled in unseen nooks; and when by the combined and simultaneous industry of almost the entire ship's company, the whole of this conscientious duty is at last concluded, then the crew themselves proceed to their own ablutions; shift themselves from top to toe; and finally issue to the immaculate deck, fresh and all aglow, as bridegrooms new-leaped from out the daintiest Holland.

Now, with elated step, they pace the planks in twos and threes, and humorously discourse of parlors, sofas, carpets, and fine cambrics; propose to mat the deck; think of having hangings to the top; object not to taking tea by moonlight on the piazza of the forecastle. To hint to such musked mariners of oil, and bone, and blubber, were little short of audacity. They know not the thing you distantly allude to. Away, and bring us napkins!

But mark: aloft there, at the three mast heads, stand three men intent on spying out more whales, which, if caught, infallibly will again soil the old oaken furniture, and drop at least one small grease-spot somewhere. Yes; and many is the time, when, after the severest uninterrupted labors, which know no night; continuing straight through for ninety-six hours; when from the boat, where they have swelled their wrists with all day rowing on the Line, – they only step to the deck to carry vast chains, and heave the heavy windlass, and cut and slash, yea, and in their very sweatings to be smoked and burned anew by the combined fires of the equatorial sun and the equatorial try-works; when, on the heel of all this, they have finally bestirred themselves to cleanse the ship, and make a spotless dairy room of it; many is the time the poor fellows, just buttoning the necks of their clean frocks, are startled by the cry of 'There she blows!' and away they fly to fight another whale, and go through the whole weary thing again. Oh! my friends, but this is man-killing! Yet this is life. For hardly have we mortals by long toilings extracted from this world's vast bulk its small but valuable sperm; and then, with weary patience, cleansed ourselves from its defilements, and learned to live here in clean tabernacles of the soul; hardly is this done, when – *There she blows!* – the ghost is spouted up, and away we sail to fight some other world, and go through young life's old routine again.

Oh! the metempsychosis! Oh! Pythagoras, that in bright Greece, two thousand years ago, did die, so good, so wise, so mild; I sailed with thee along the Peruvian coast last voyage – and, foolish as I am, taught thee, a green simple boy, how to splice a rope!

99

THE DOUBLOON

ERE now it has been related how Ahab was wont to pace his quarter-deck, taking regular turns at either limit, the binnacle and mainmast; but in the multiplicity of other things requiring narration it has not been added how that sometimes in these walks, when most plunged in his mood, he was wont to pause in turn at each spot, and stand there strangely eyeing the particular object before him. When he halted before the binnacle, with his glance fastened on the pointed needle in the compass, that glance shot like a javelin with the pointed intensity of his purpose; and when resuming his walk he again paused before the mainmast, then, as the same riveted glance fastened upon the riveted gold coin there, he still wore the same aspect of nailed firmness, only dashed with a certain wild longing, if not hopefulness.

But one morning, turning to pass the doubloon, he seemed to be newly attracted by the strange figures and inscriptions stamped on it, as though now for the first time beginning to interpret for himself in some monomaniac way whatever significance might lurk in them. And some certain significance lurks in all things, else all things are little worth, and the round world itself but an empty cipher, except to sell by the cartload, as they do hills about Boston, to fill up some morass in the Milky Way.

Now this doubloon was of purest, virgin gold, raked somewhere out of the heart of gorgeous hills, whence, east and west, over golden sands, the head-waters of many a Pactolus flow. And though now nailed amidst all the rustiness of iron bolts and the verdigris of copper spikes, yet, untouchable and immaculate to any foulness, it still preserved its Quito glow. Nor, though placed amongst a ruthless crew and every hour passed by ruthless hands, and through the livelong nights shrouded with thick darkness which might cover any pilfering approach, nevertheless every sunrise found the doubloon where the sunset left it last. For it was set apart and sanctified to one awe-striking end; and however wanton in their sailor ways, one and all, the mariners revered it as the white whale's talisman. Sometimes they talked it over in the weary watch by night, wondering whose it was to be at last, and whether he would ever live to spend it.

Now these noble golden coins of South America are as medals of the sun and tropic token-pieces. Here palms, alpacas, and volcanoes; sun's disks and stars; ecliptics, horns-of-plenty, and rich banners waving, are in luxuriant profusion stamped; so that the precious gold seems almost to derive an added preciousness and enhancing glories, by passing through those fancy mints, so Spanishly poetic.

It so chanced that the doubloon of the Pequod was a most wealthy example of these things. On its round border it bore the letters, REPUBLICA DEL ECUADOR: QUITO. So this bright coin came from a country planted in the middle of the world, and beneath the great equator, and named after it; and it had been cast midway up the Andes, in the unwaning clime that knows no autumn. Zoned by those letters you saw the likeness of three Andes' summits; from one a flame; a tower on another; on the third a crowing cock; while arching over all was a segment of the partitioned zodiac, the signs all marked with their usual cabalistics, and the keystone sun entering the equinoctial point at Libra.

Before this equatorial coin, Ahab, not unobserved by others, was now pausing.

'There's something ever egotistical in mountain-tops and towers, and all other grand and lofty things; look here, – three peaks as proud as Lucifer. The firm tower, that is Ahab; the volcano, that is Ahab; the courageous, the undaunted, and victorious fowl, that, too, is Ahab; all are Ahab; and this round gold is but the image of the rounder globe, which, like a magician's glass, to each and every man in turn but mirrors back his own mysterious self. Great pains, small gains for those who ask the world to solve them; it cannot solve itself. Methinks now this coined sun wears a ruddy face; but see! aye, he enters the sign of storms, the equinox! and but six months before he wheeled out of a former equinox at Aries! From storm to storm! So be it, then. Born in throes, 'tis fit that man should live in pains and die in pangs! So be it, then! Here's stout stuff for woe to work on. So be it, then.'

'No fairy fingers can have pressed the gold, but devil's claws must have left their mouldings there since yesterday,' murmured Starbuck to himself, leaning against the bulwarks. 'The old man seems to read Belshazzar's awful writing. I have never marked the coin inspectingly. He goes below; let me read. A dark valley between three mighty, heaven-abiding peaks, that almost seem the Trinity, in some faint earthly symbol. So in this vale of Death, God girds us round; and over all our gloom, the sun of Righteousness still shines a beacon and a hope. If we bend down our eyes, the dark vale shows her mouldy soil; but if we lift them, the bright sun meets our glance half way, to cheer. Yet, oh, the great sun is no fixture; and if, at midnight, we would fain snatch some sweet solace from him, we gaze for him in vain! This coin speaks wisely, mildly, truly, but still sadly to me. I will quit it, lest Truth shake me falsely.'

'There now's the old Mogul,' soliloquized Stubb by the try-works, 'he's been twigging it; and there goes Starbuck from the same, and both with faces which I should say might be somewhere within nine fathoms long. And all from looking at a piece of gold, which did I have it now on Negro Hill or in Corlaer's Hook, I'd not look at it very long ere spending it. Humph! in my poor, insignificant opinion, I regard this as queer. I have seen doubloons before now in my voyagings; your doubloons of old Spain, your doubloons of Peru, your doubloons of Chili, your doubloons of Bolivia, your doubloons of Popayan; with plenty of gold moidores and pistoles, and joes, and half joes, and quarter joes. What then should there be in this doubloon of the Equator that is so killing wonderful? By Golconda! lct mc rcad it once.

Halloa! here's signs and wonders truly! That, now, is what old Bowditch in his Epitome calls the zodiac, and what my almanack below calls ditto. I'll get the almanack; and as I have heard devils can be raised with Daboll's arithmetic, I'll try my hand at raising a meaning out of these queer curvicues here with the Massachusetts calendar. Here's the book. Let's see now. Signs and wonders; and the sun, he's always among 'em. Hem, hem, hem; here they are – here they go – all alive: – Aries, or the Ram; Taurus, or the Bull; – and Jimini! here's Gemini himself, or the Twins. Well; the sun he wheels among 'em. Aye, here on the coin he's just crossing the threshold between two of twelve sitting rooms all in a ring. Book! you lie there; the fact is, you books must know your places. You'll do to give us the bare words and facts, but we come in to supply the thoughts. That's my small experience, so far as the Massachusetts calendar, and Bowditch's navigator, and Daboll's arithmetic go. Signs and wonders, eh? Pity if there is nothing wonderful in signs, and significant in wonders! There's a clue somewhere; wait a bit; hist – hark! By Jove, I have it! Look you, Doubloon, your zodiac here is the life of man in one round chapter; and now I'll read it off, straight out of the book. Come, Almanack! To begin: there's Aries, or the Ram – lecherous dog, he begets us; then, Taurus, or the Bull – he bumps us the first thing; then Gemini, or the Twins – that is, Virtue and Vice; we try to reach Virtue, when lo! comes Cancer the Crab, and drags us back; and here, going from Virtue, Leo, a roaring Lion, lies in the path – he gives a few fierce bites and surly dabs with his paw; we escape, and hail Virgo, the Virgin! that's our first love; we marry and think to be happy for aye, when pop comes Libra, or the Scales – happiness weighed and found wanting; and while we are very sad about that, Lord! how we suddenly jump, as Scorpio, or the Scorpion, stings us in rear; we are curing the wound, when whang come the arrows all round; Sagittarius, or the Archer, is amusing himself. As we pluck out the shafts, stand aside! here's the battering-ram, Capricornus, or the Goat; full tilt, he comes rushing, and head-long we are tossed; when Aquarius, or the Water-bearer, pours out his whole deluge and drowns us; and to wind up with Pisces, or the Fishes, we sleep. There's a sermon now, writ in high heaven, and the sun goes through it every year, and yet comes out of it all alive and hearty. Jollily he, aloft there, wheels through toil and trouble; and so, alow here, does jolly Stubb. Oh, jolly's the word for aye! Adieu, Doubloon! But stop; here comes little King-Post; dodge round the try-works, now, and let's hear what he'll have to say. There; he's before it; he'll out with something presently. So, so; he's beginning.'

'I see nothing here, but a round thing made of gold, and whoever raises a certain whale, this round thing belongs to him. So, what's all this staring been about? It is worth sixteen dollars, that's true; and at two cents the cigar, that's nine hundred and sixty cigars. I wont smoke dirty pipes like Stubb, but I like cigars, and here's nine hundred and sixty of them; so here goes Flask aloft to spy 'em out.'

'Shall I call that wise or foolish, now; if it be really wise it has a foolish look to it; yet, if it be really foolish, then has it a sort of wiseish look to it. But, avast; here comes our old Manxman – the old hearse-driver, he must have been, that is, before he took to the sea. He luffs up before the doubloon; halloa, and goes round on the other side of the mast; why, there's a horse-shoe nailed on that side; and now he's back again; what does that mean? Hark! he's muttering – voice like an old worn-out coffee-mill. Prick ears, and listen!'

'If the White Whale be raised, it must be in a month and a day, when the sun stands in some one of these signs. I've studied signs, and know their marks; they were taught me two score years ago, by the old witch in Copenhagen. Now, in what sign will the sun then be? The horse-shoe sign; for there it is, right opposite the gold. And what's the horse-shoe sign? The lion is the horse-shoe sign – the roaring and devouring lion. Ship, old ship! my old head shakes to think of thee.'

'There's another rendering now; but still one text. All sorts of men in one kind of world, you see. Dodge again! here comes Queequeg – all tattooing – looks like the signs of the Zodiac himself. What says the Cannibal? As I live he's comparing notes; looking at his thigh bone; thinks the sun is in the thigh, or in the calf, or in the bowels, I suppose, as the old women talk Surgeon's Astronomy in the back country. And by Jove, he's found something there in the vicinity of his thigh – I guess it's Sagittarius, or the Archer. No: he don't know what to make of the doubloon; he takes it for an old button off some king's trowsers. But, aside again! here comes that ghost-devil, Fedallah; tail coiled out of sight as usual, oakum in the toes of his pumps as usual. What does he say, with that look of his? Ah, only makes a sign to the sign and bows himself; there is a sun on the coin – fire worshipper, depend upon it. Ho! more and more. This way comes Pip – poor boy! would he had died, or I; he's half horrible to me. He too has been watching all of these interpreters – myself included – and look now, he comes to read, with that unearthly idiot face. Stand away again and hear him. Hark!'

'I look, you look, he looks; we look, ye look, they look.'

'Upon my soul, he's been studying Murray's Grammar! Improving his mind, poor fellow! But what's that he says now – hist!'

'I look, you look, he looks; we look, ye look, they look.'

'Why, he's getting it by heart – hist! again.'

'I look, you look, he looks; we look, ye look, they look.'

'Well, that's funny.'

'And I, you, and he; and we, ye, and they, are all bats; and I'm a crow, especially when I stand a'top of this pine tree here. Caw! caw! caw! caw! caw! caw! Ain't I a crow? And where's the scare-crow? There he stands; two bones stuck into a pair of old trowsers, and two more poked into the sleeves of an old jacket.'

'Wonder if he means me? – complimentary! – poor lad! – I could go hang myself. Any way, for the present, I'll quit Pip's vicinity. I can stand the rest, for they have plain wits;

but he's too crazy-witty for my sanity. So, so, I leave him muttering.'

'Here's the ship's navel, this doubloon here, and they are all on fire to unscrew it. But, unscrew your navel, and what's the consequence? Then again, if it stays here, that is ugly, too, for when aught's nailed to the mast it's a sign that things grow desperate. Ha, ha! old Ahab! the White Whale; he'll nail ye! This is a pine tree. My father, in old Tolland county, cut down a pine tree once, and found a silver ring grown over in it; some old darkey's wedding ring. How did it get there? And so they'll say in the resurrection, when they come to fish up this old mast, and find a doubloon lodged in it, with bedded oysters for the shaggy bark. Oh, the gold! the precious, precious gold! – the green miser 'll hoard ye soon! Hish! hish! God goes 'mong the worlds blackberrying. Cook! ho, cook! and cook us! Jenny! hey, hey, hey, hey, hey, Jenny, Jenny! and get your hoe-cake done!'

100

LEG AND ARM

THE PEQUOD, OF NANTUCKET, MEETS THE SAMUEL ENDERBY, OF LONDON

'SHIP, ahoy! Hast seen the White Whale?'

So cried Ahab, once more hailing a ship showing English colors, bearing down under the stern. Trumpet to mouth, the old man was standing in his hoisted quarter-boat, his ivory leg plainly revealed to the stranger captain, who was carelessly reclining in his own boat's bow. He was a darkly-tanned, burly, good-natured, fine-looking man, of sixty or thereabouts, dressed in a spacious roundabout, that hung round him in festoons of blue pilot-cloth; and one empty arm of this jacket streamed behind him like the broidered arm of a huzzar's surcoat.

'Hast seen the White Whale?'

'See you this?' and withdrawing it from the folds that had hidden it, he held up a white arm of sperm whale bone, terminating in a wooden head like a mallet.

'Man my boat!' cried Ahab, impetuously, and tossing about the oars near him – 'Stand by to lower!'

In less than a minute, without quitting his little craft, he and his crew were dropped to the water, and were soon alongside of the stranger. But here a curious difficulty presented itself. In the excitement of the moment, Ahab had forgotten that since the loss of his leg he had never once stepped on board of any vessel at sea but his own, and then it was always by an ingenious and very handy mechanical contrivance peculiar to the Pequod, and a thing not to be rigged and shipped in any other vessel at a moment's warning. Now, it is no very easy matter for anybody – except those who are almost hourly used to it, like whalemen – to clamber up a ship's side from a boat on the open sea; for the great swells now lift the boat high up towards the bulwarks, and then instantaneously drop it half way down to the kelson. So, deprived of one leg, and the strange ship of course being altogether unsupplied with the kindly invention, Ahab now found himself abjectly reduced to a clumsy landsman again; hopelessly eyeing the uncertain changeful height he could hardly hope to attain.

It has before been hinted, perhaps, that every little untoward circumstance that befel him, and which indirectly sprang from his luckless mishap, almost invariably irritated or exasperated Ahab. And in the present instance, all this was heightened by the sight of the two officers of the strange ship, leaning over the side, by the perpendicular ladder of nailed cleets there, and swinging towards him a pair of tastefully-ornamented man-ropes; for at first they did not seem to bethink them that a one-legged man must be too much of a cripple to use their sea bannisters. But this awkwardness only lasted a minute, because the strange captain, observing at a glance how affairs stood, cried out, 'I see, I see! – avast heaving there! Jump, boys, and swing over the cutting-tackle.'

As good luck would have it, they had had a whale alongside a day or two previous, and the great tackles were still aloft, and the massive curved blubber-hook, now clean and dry, was still attached to the end. This was quickly lowered to Ahab, who at once comprehending it all, slid his solitary thigh into the curve of the hook (it was like sitting in the fluke of an anchor, or the crotch of an apple tree), and then giving the word, held himself fast, and at the same time also helped to hoist his own weight, by pulling hand-over-hand upon one of the running parts of the tackle. Soon he was carefully swung inside the high bulwarks, and gently landed upon the capstan head. With his ivory arm frankly thrust forth in welcome, the other captain advanced, and Ahab, putting out his ivory leg, and crossing the ivory arm (like two sword-fish blades) cried out in his walrus way, 'Aye, aye, hearty! let us shake bones together! – an arm and a leg! – an arm that never can shrink, d'ye see; and a leg that never can run. Where did'st thou see the White Whale? – how long ago?'

'The White Whale,' said the Englishman, pointing his ivory arm towards the East, and taking a rueful sight along it, as if it had been a telescope; 'There I saw him, on the Line, last season.'

'And he took that arm off, did he?' asked Ahab, now sliding down from the capstan, and resting on the Englishman's shoulder, as he did so.

'Aye, he was the cause of it, at least; and that leg, too?'

'Spin me the yarn,' said Ahab; 'how was it?'

'It was the first time in my life that I ever cruised on the Line,' began the Englishman. 'I was ignorant of the White Whale at that time. Well, one day we lowered for a pod of four or five whales, and my boat fastened to one of them; a regular circus horse he was, too, that went milling and milling round so, that my boat's crew could only trim dish, by sitting all their sterns on the outer gunwale. Presently up breaches from the bottom of the sea a bouncing great whale, with a milky-white head and hump, all crows' feet and wrinkles.'

'It was he, it was he!' cried Ahab, suddenly letting out his suspended breath.

'And harpoons sticking in near his starboard fin.'

'Aye, aye – they were mine – *my* irons,' cried Ahab, exultingly – 'but on!'

'Give me a chance, then,' said the Englishman, good-humoredly. 'Well, this old great-grandfather, with the white head and hump, runs all afoam into the pod, and goes to snapping furiously at my fast-line.'

'Aye, I see! – wanted to part it; free the fast-fish – an old trick – I know him.'

'How it was exactly,' continued the one-armed commander, 'I do not know; but in biting the line, it got foul of his teeth, caught there somehow; but we didn't know it then; so that when we afterwards pulled on the line, bounce we came plump on to his hump! instead of the other whale's that went off to windward, all fluking. Seeing how matters stood, and what a noble great whale it was – the noblest and biggest I ever saw, sir, in my life – I resolved to capture him, spite of the boiling rage he seemed to be in. And thinking the hap-hazard line would get loose, or the tooth it was tangled to might draw (for I have a devil of a boat's crew for a pull on a whale-line); seeing all this, I say, I jumped into my first mate's boat – Mr Mounttop's here (by the way, Captain – Mounttop; Mounttop – the captain); – as I was saying, I jumped into Mounttop's boat, which, d'ye see, was gunwale and gunwale with mine, then; and snatching the first harpoon, let this old great-grandfather have it. But, Lord, look you, sir – hearts and souls alive, man – the next instant, in a jiff, I was blind as a bat – both eyes out – all befogged and bedeadened with black foam – the whale's tail looming straight up out of it, perpendicular in the air, like a marble steeple. No use sterning all, then; but as I was groping at midday, with a blinding sun, all crown-jewels; as I was groping, I say, after the second iron, to toss it overboard – down comes the tail like a Lima tower, cutting my boat in two, leaving each half in splinters; and, flukes first, the white hump backed through the wreck, as though it was all chips. We all struck out. To escape his terrible flailings, I seized hold of my harpoon-pole sticking in him, and for a moment clung to that like a sucking fish. But a combing sea dashed me off, and at the same instant, the fish, taking one good dart forwards, went down like a flash; and the barb of that cursed second iron towing along near me caught me here' (clapping his hand just below his shoulder); 'yes, caught me just here, I say, and bore me down to Hell's flames, I was thinking; when, when, all of a sudden, thank the good God, the barb ript its way along the flesh – clear along the whole length of my arm – came out nigh my wrist, and up I floated; – and that gentleman there will tell you the rest (by the way, captain – Dr Bunger, ship's surgeon: Bunger, my lad, – the captain). Now, Bunger boy, spin your part of the yarn.'

The professional gentleman thus familiarly pointed out, had been all the time standing near them, with nothing specific visible, to denote his gentlemanly rank on board. His face was an exceedingly round but sober one; he was dressed in a faded blue woollen frock or shirt, and patched trowsers; and had thus far been dividing his attention between a marlingspike he held in one hand, and a pill-box held in the other, occasionally casting a critical glance at the ivory limbs of the two crippled captains. But, at his superior's introduction of him to Ahab, he politely bowed, and straightway went on to do his captain's bidding.

'It was a shocking bad wound,' began the whale-surgeon; 'and, taking my advice, Captain Boomer here, stood our old Sammy –'

'Samuel Enderby is the name of my ship,' interrupted the one-armed captain, addressing Ahab; 'go on, boy.'

'Stood our old Sammy off to the northward, to get out of the blazing hot weather there on the Line. But it was no use – I did all I could; sat up with him nights; was very severe with him in the matter of diet –'

'Oh, very severe!' chimed in the patient himself; then suddenly altering his voice, 'Drinking hot rum toddies with me every night, till he couldn't see to put on the bandages;

and sending me to bed, half seas over, about three o'clock in the morning. Oh, ye stars! he sat up with me indeed, and was very severe in my diet. Oh! a great watcher, and very dietetically severe, is Dr Bunger. (Bunger, you dog, laugh out! why don't ye? You know you're a precious jolly rascal.) But, heave ahead, boy, I'd rather be killed by you than kept alive by any other man.'

'My captain, you must have ere this perceived, respected sir' – said the imperturbable godly-looking Bunger, slightly bowing to Ahab – 'is apt to be facetious at times; he spins us many clever things of that sort. But I may as well say – en passant, as the French remark – that I myself – that is to say, Jack Bunger, late of the reverend clergy – am a strict total abstinence man; I never drink –'

'Water!' cried the captain; 'he never drinks it; it's a sort of fits to him; fresh water throws him into the hydrophobia; but go on – go on with the arm story.'

'Yes, I may as well,' said the surgeon, coolly. 'I was about observing, sir, before Captain Boomer's facetious interruption, that spite of my best and severest endeavors, the wound kept getting worse and worse; the truth was, sir, it was as ugly gaping wound as surgeon ever saw; more than two feet and several inches long. I measured it with the lead line. In short, it grew black; I knew what was threatened, and off it came. But I had no hand in shipping that ivory arm there; that thing is against all rule' – pointing at it with the marlingspike – 'that is the captain's work, not mine; he ordered the carpenter to make it; he had that club-hammer there put to the end, to knock some one's brains out with, I suppose, as he tried mine once. He flies into diabolical passions sometimes. Do ye see this dent, sir' – removing his hat, and brushing aside his hair, and exposing a bowl-like cavity in his skull, but which bore not the slightest scarry trace, or any token of ever having been a wound – 'Well, the captain there will tell you how that came here; he knows.'

'No, I don't,' said the captain, 'but his mother did; he was born with it. Oh, you solemn rogue, you – you Bunger! was there ever such another Bunger in the watery world? Bunger, when you die, you ought to die in pickle, you dog; you should be preserved to future ages, you rascal.'

'What became of the White Whale?' now cried Ahab, who thus far had been impatiently listening to this bye-play between the two Englishmen.

'Oh!' cried the one-armed captain, 'Oh, yes! Well; after he sounded, we didn't see him again for some time; in fact, as I before hinted, I didn't then know what whale it was that had served me such a trick, till some time afterwards, when coming back to the Line, we heard about Moby Dick – as some call him – and then I knew it was he.'

'Did'st thou cross his wake again?'

'Twice.'

'But could not fasten?'

'Didn't want to try to: ain't one limb enough? What should I do without this other arm? And I'm thinking Moby Dick doesn't bite so much as he swallows.'

'Well, then,' interrupted Bunger, 'give him your left arm for bait to get the right. Do you know, gentlemen' – very gravely and mathematically bowing to each Captain in succession – 'Do you know, gentlemen, that the digestive organs of the whale are so inscrutably constructed by Divine Providence, that it is quite impossible for him to completely digest even a man's arm? And he knows it too. So that what you take for the White Whale's malice is only his awkwardness. For he never means to swallow a single limb; he only thinks to terrify by feints. But sometimes he is like the old juggling fellow, formerly a patient of mine in Ceylon, that making believe swallow jack-knives, once upon a time let one drop into him in good earnest, and there it stayed for a twelvemonth or more; when I gave him an emetic, and he heaved it up in small tacks, d'ye see. No possible way for him to digest that jack-knife, and fully incorporate it into his general bodily system. Yes, Captain Boomer, if you are quick enough about it, and have a mind to pawn one arm for the sake of the privilege of giving decent burial to the other, why in that case the arm is yours; only let the whale have another chance at you shortly, that's all.'

'No, thank ye, Bunger,' said the English Captain, 'he's welcome to the arm he has, since I can't help it, and didn't know him then; but not to another one. No more White Whales for me; I've lowered for him once, and that has satisfied me. There would be great glory in killing him, I know that; and there is a ship-load of precious sperm in him, but, hark ye, he's best let alone; don't you think so, Captain?' – glancing at the ivory leg.

'He is. But he will still be hunted, for all that. What is best let alone, that accursed thing is not always what least allures. He's all a magnet! How long since thou saw'st him last? Which way heading?'

'Bless my soul, and curse the foul fiend's,' cried Bunger, stoopingly walking round Ahab, and like a dog, strangely snuffing; 'this man's blood – bring the thermometer; – it's at the boiling point! – his pulse makes these planks beat! – sir!' – taking a lancet from his pocket, and drawing near to Ahab's arm.

'Avast!' roared Ahab, dashing him against the bulwarks 'Man the boat! Which way heading?'

'Good God!' cried the English Captain, to whom the question was put. 'What's the matter? He was heading east, I think. – Is your Captain crazy?' whispering Fedallah.

But Fedallah, putting a finger on his lip, slid over the bulwarks to take the boat's steering oar, and Ahab, swinging the cutting-tackle towards him, commanded the ship's sailors to stand by to lower.

In a moment he was standing in the boat's stern, and the Manilla men were springing to their oars. In vain the English Captain hailed him. With back to the stranger ship, and face set like a flint to his own, Ahab stood upright till alongside of the Pequod.

101

THE DECANTER

ERE the English ship fades from sight, be it set down here, that she hailed from London, and was named after the late Samuel Enderby, merchant of that city, the original of the famous whaling house of Enderby & Sons; a house which in my poor whaleman's opinion, comes not far behind the united royal houses of the Tudors and Bourbons, in point of real historical interest. How long, prior to the year of our Lord 1775, this great whaling house was in existence, my numerous fish-documents do not make plain; but in that year (1775) it fitted out the first English ships that ever regularly hunted the Sperm Whale; though for some score of years previous (ever since 1726) our valiant Coffins and Maceys of Nantucket and the Vineyard had in large fleets pursued that Leviathan, but only in the North and South Atlantic: not elsewhere. Be it distinctly recorded here, that the Nantucketers were the first among mankind to harpoon with civilized steel the great Sperm Whale; and that for half a century they were the only people of the whole globe who so harpooned him.

In 1778, a fine ship, the Amelia, fitted out for the express purpose, and at the sole charge of the vigorous Enderbys, boldly rounded Cape Horn, and was the first among the nations to lower a whale-boat of any sort in the great South Sea. The voyage was a skilful and lucky one; and returning to her berth with her hold full of the precious sperm, the Amelia's example was soon followed by other ships, English and American, and thus the vast Sperm Whale grounds of the Pacific were thrown open. But not content with this good deed, the indefatigable house again bestirred itself: Samuel and all his Sons – how many, their mother only knows – and under their immediate auspices, and partly, I think, at their expense, the British government was induced to send the sloop-of-war Rattler on a whaling voyage of discovery into the South Sea. Commanded by a naval Post-Captain, the Rattler made a rattling voyage of it, and did some service; how much does not appear. But this is not all. In 1819, the same house fitted out a discovery whale ship of their own, to go on a testing cruise to the remote waters of Japan. That ship – well called the 'Syren' – made a noble experimental cruise; and it was thus that the great Japanese Whaling Ground first became generally known. The Syren in this famous voyage was commanded by a Captain Coffin, a Nantucketer.

All honor to the Enderbies, therefore, whose house, I think, exists to the present day; though doubtless the original Samuel must long ago have slipped his cable for the great South Sea of the other world.

The ship named after him was worthy of the honor, being a very fast sailer and a noble craft every way. I boarded her once at midnight somewhere off the Patagonian coast, and drank good flip down in the forecastle. It was a fine gam we had, and they were all trumps – every soul on board. A short life to them, and a jolly death. And that fine gam I had long, very long after old Ahab touched her planks with his ivory heel – it minds me of the noble, solid, Saxon hospitality of that ship; and may my parson forget me, and the devil remember me, if I ever lose sight of it. Flip? Did I say we had flip? Yes, and we flipped it at the rate of ten gallons the hour; and when the squall came (for it's squally off there by Patagonia), and all hands – visitors and all – were called to reef topsails, we were so top-heavy that we had to swing each other aloft in bowlines; and we ignorantly furled the skirts of our jackets into the sails, so that we hung there, reefed fast in the howling gale, a warning example to all drunken tars. However, the masts did not go overboard; and by and bye we scrambled down, so sober, that we had to pass the flip again, though the savage salt spray bursting down the forecastle scuttle, rather too much diluted and pickled it to my taste.

The beef was fine – tough, but with body in it. They said

it was bull-beef; others, that it was dromedary beef; but I do not know, for certain, how that was. They had dumplings too; small, but substantial, symmetrically globular, and indestructible dumplings. I fancied that you could feel them, and roll them about in you after they were swallowed. If you stooped over too far forward, you risked their pitching out of you like billiard-balls. The bread – but that couldn't be helped; besides, it was an anti-scorbutic; in short, the bread contained the only fresh fare they had. But the forecastle was not very light, and it was very easy to step over into a dark corner when you ate it. But all in all, taking her from truck to helm, considering the dimensions of the cook's boilers, including his own live parchment boilers; fore and aft, I say, the Samuel Enderby was a jolly ship; of good fare and plenty; fine flip and strong; crack fellows all, and capital from boot heels to hat-band.

But why was it, think ye, that the Samuel Enderby, and some other English whalers I know of – not all though – were such famous, hospitable ships; that passed round the beef, and the bread, and the can, and the joke; and were not soon weary of eating, and drinking, and laughing? I will tell you. The abounding good cheer of these English whalers is matter for historical research. Nor have I been at all sparing of historical whale research, when it has seemed needed.

The English were preceded in the whale fishery by the Hollanders, Zealanders, and Danes; from whom they derived many terms still extant in the fishery; and what is yet more, their fat old fashions, touching plenty to eat and drink. For, as a general thing, the English merchant-ship scrimps her crew; but not so the English whaler. Hence, in the English, this thing of whaling good cheer is not normal and natural, but incidental and particular; and, therefore, must have some special origin, which is here pointed out, and will be still further elucidated.

During my researches in the Leviathanic histories, I stumbled upon an ancient Dutch volume, which, by the musty whaling smell of it, I knew must be about whalers.

The title was, 'Dan Coopman,' wherefore I concluded that this must be the invaluable memoirs of some Amsterdam cooper in the fishery, as every whale ship must carry its cooper. I was reinforced in this opinion by seeing that it was the production of one 'Fitz Swackhammer.' But my friend Dr Snodhead, a very learned man, professor of Low Dutch and High German in the college of Santa Claus and St Pott's, to whom I handed the work for translation, giving him a box of sperm candles for his trouble – this same Dr Snodhead, so soon as he spied the book, assured me that 'Dan Coopman' did not mean 'The Cooper,' but 'The Merchant.' In short, this ancient and learned Low Dutch book treated of the commerce of Holland; and, among other subjects, contained a very interesting account of its whale fishery. And in this chapter it was, headed 'Smeer,' or 'Fat,' that I found a long detailed list of the outfits for the larders and cellars of 180 sail of Dutch whalemen; from which list, as translated by Dr Snodhead, I transcribe the following:

400,000 lbs. of beef.
60,000 lbs. Friesland pork.
150,000 lbs. of stock fish.
550,000 lbs. of biscuit.
72,000 lbs. of soft bread.
2,800 firkins of butter.
20,000 lbs. Texel & Leyden cheese.
144,000 lbs. cheese (probably an inferior article).
550 ankers of Geneva.
10,800 barrels of beer.

Most statistical tables are parchingly dry in the reading; not so in the present case, however, where the reader is flooded with whole pipes, barrels, quarts, and gills of good gin and good cheer.

At the time, I devoted three days to the studious digesting of all this beer, beef, and bread, during which many profound thoughts were incidentally suggested to me, capable of a transcendental and Platonic application; and, furthermore, I compiled supplementary tables of my own, touching the probable quantity of stock-fish, &c., consumed by every Low Dutch harpooneer in that ancient Greenland and Spitzbergen whale fishery. In the first place, the amount of butter, and Texel and Leyden cheese consumed, seems amazing. I impute it, though, to their naturally unctuous natures, being rendered still more unctuous by the nature of their vocation, and especially by their pursuing their game in those frigid Polar Seas, on the very coasts of that Esquimaux country where the convivial natives pledge each other in bumpers of train oil.

The quantity of beer, too, is very large, 10,800 barrels. Now, as those polar fisheries could only be prosecuted in the short summer of that climate, so that the whole cruise of one of these Dutch whalemen, including the short voyage to and from the Spitzbergen sea, did not much exceed three months, say, and reckoning 30 men to each of their fleet of 180 sail, we have 5,400 Low Dutch seamen in all; therefore, I say, we have precisely two barrels of beer per man, for a twelve weeks' allowance, exclusive of his fair proportion of that 550 ankers of gin. Now, whether these gin and beer harpooneers, so fuddled as one might fancy them to have been, were the right sort of men to stand up in a boat's head, and take good aim at flying whales; this would seem somewhat improbable. Yet they did aim at them, and hit them too. But this was very far North, be it remembered, where beer agrees well with the constitution; upon the Equator, in our southern fishery, beer would be apt to make the harpooneer sleepy at the mast-head and boozy in his boat; and grievous loss might ensue to Nantucket and New Bedford.

But no more; enough has been said to show that the old Dutch whalers of two or three centuries ago were high livers; and that the English whalers have not neglected so excellent an example. For, say they, when cruising in an empty ship, if you can get nothing better out of the world, get a good dinner out of it, at least. And this empties the decanter.

102

A BOWER IN THE ARSACIDES

HITHERTO, in descriptively treating of the Sperm Whale, I have chiefly dwelt upon the marvels of his outer aspect; or separately and in detail upon some few interior structural features. But to a large and thorough sweeping comprehension of him, it behoves me now to unbutton him still further, and untrussing the points of his hose, unbuckling his garters, and casting loose the hooks and the eyes of the joints of his innermost bones, set him before you in his ultimatum; that is to say, in his unconditional skeleton.

But how now, Ishmael? How is it, that you, a mere oarsman in the fishery, pretend to know aught about the subterranean parts of the whale? Did erudite Stubb, mounted upon your capstan, deliver lectures on the anatomy of the Cetacea; and by help of the windlass, hold up a specimen rib for exhibition? Explain thyself, Ishmael. Can you land a full-grown whale on your deck for examination, as a cook dishes a roast-pig? Surely not. A veritable witness have you hitherto been, Ishmael; but have a care how you seize the privilege of Jonah alone; the privilege of discoursing upon the joists and beams; the rafters, ridge-pole, sleepers, and under-pinnings, making up the frame-work of leviathan; and belike of the tallow-vats, dairy-rooms, butteries, and cheeseries in his bowels.

I confess, that since Jonah, few whalemen have penetrated very far beneath the skin of the adult whale; nevertheless, I have been blessed with an opportunity to dissect him in miniature. In a ship I belonged to, a small cub Sperm Whale was once bodily hoisted to the deck for his poke or bag, to make sheaths for the barbs of the harpoons, and for the heads of the lances. Think you I let that chance go, without using my boat-hatchet and jack-knife, and breaking the seal and reading all the contents of that young cub?

And as for my exact knowledge of the bones of the leviathan in their gigantic, full grown development, for that rare knowledge I am indebted to my late royal friend Tranquo, king of Tranque, one of the Arsacides. For being at Tranque, years ago, when attached to the trading-ship Dey of Algiers, I was invited to spend part of the Arsacidean holidays with the Lord of Tranque, at his retired palm villa at Pupella; a sea-side glen not very far distant from what our sailors called Bamboo-Town, his capital.

Among many other fine qualities, my royal friend Tranquo, being gifted with a devout love for all matters of barbaric vertù, had brought together in Pupella whatever rare things the more ingenious of his people could invent; chiefly carved woods of wonderful devices, chiselled shells, inlaid spears, costly paddles, aromatic canoes; and all these distributed among whatever natural wonders, the wonder-freighted, tribute-rendering waves had cast upon his shores.

Chief among these latter was a great Sperm Whale, which, after an unusually long raging gale, had been found dead and stranded, with his head against a cocoa-nut tree, whose plumage-like, tufted droopings seemed his verdant jet. When the vast body had at last been stripped of its fathom-deep enfoldings, and the bones become dust dry in the sun, then the skeleton was carefully transported up the Pupella glen, where a grand temple of lordly palms now sheltered it.

The ribs were hung with trophies; the vertebræ were carved with Arsacidean annals, in strange hieroglyphics; in the skull, the priests kept up an unextinguished aromatic flame, so that the mystic head again sent forth its vapory spout; while, suspended from a bough, the terrific lower jaw vibrated over all the devotees, like the hair-hung sword that so affrighted Damocles.

It was a wondrous sight. The wood was green as mosses of the Icy Glen; the trees stood high and haughty, feeling their living sap; the industrious earth beneath was as a weaver's loom, with a gorgeous carpet on it, whereof the ground-vine tendrils formed the warp and woof, and the living flowers the figures. All the trees, with all their laden branches; all the shrubs, and ferns, and grasses; the message-carrying air; all these unceasingly were active. Through the lacings of the leaves, the great sun seemed a flying shuttle weaving the unwearied verdure. Oh, busy weaver! unseen weaver! – pause! – one word! – whither flows the fabric? what palace may it deck? wherefore all these ceaseless toilings? Speak, weaver! – stay thy hand! – but one single word with thee! Nay – the shuttle flies – the figures float from forth the loom; the freshet-rushing carpet for ever slides away. The weaver-god, he weaves; and by that weaving is he deafened, that he hears no mortal voice; and by that humming, we, too, who look on the loom are deafened; and only when we escape it shall we hear the thousand voices that speak through it. For even so it is in all material factories. The spoken words that are inaudible among the flying spindles; those same words are plainly heard without the walls, bursting from the opened casements. Thereby have villanies been detected. Ah, mortal! then, be heedful; for so, in all this din of the great world's loom, thy subtlest thinkings may be overheard afar.

Now, amid the green, life-restless loom of that Arsacidean wood, the great, white, worshipped skeleton lay lounging – a gigantic idler! Yet, as the ever-woven verdant warp and woof intermixed and hummed around him, the mighty idler seemed the cunning weaver; himself all woven over with the vines; every month assuming greener, fresher verdure; but himself a skeleton. Life folded Death; Death trellised Life; the grim god wived with youthful Life, and begat him curly-headed glories.

Now, when with royal Tranquo I visited this wondrous whale, and saw the skull an altar, and the artificial smoke ascending from where the real jet had issued, I marvelled that the king should regard a chapel as an object of vertù. He laughed. But more I marvelled that the priests should swear that smoky jet of his was genuine. To and fro I paced before this skeleton – brushed the vines aside – broke through the ribs – and with a ball of Arsacidean twine, wandered, eddied long amid its many winding, shaded collonades and arbors. But soon my line was out; and following it back, I emerged from the opening where I entered. I saw no living thing within; naught was there but bones.

Cutting me a green measuring-rod, I once more dived within the skeleton. From their arrow-slit in the skull, the priests perceived me taking the altitude of the final rib. 'How now!' they shouted; 'Dar'st thou measure this our god! That's for us.' 'Aye, priests – well, how long do ye make him, then?' But hereupon a fierce contest rose among them, concerning feet and inches; they cracked each other's sconces with their yard-sticks – the great skull echoed – and seizing that lucky chance, I quickly concluded my own admeasurements.

These admeasurements I now propose to set before you. But first, be it recorded, that, in this matter, I am not free to utter any fancied measurement I please. Because there are skeleton authorities you can refer to, to test my accuracy. There is a Leviathanic Museum, they tell me, in Hull, England, one of the whaling ports of that country, where they have some fine specimens of fin-backs and other whales. Likewise, I have heard that in the museum of Manchester, in New Hampshire, they have what the proprietors call 'the only perfect specimen of a Greenland or River Whale in the United States.' Moreover, at a place in Yorkshire, England, Burton Constable by name, a certain Sir Clifford Constable has in his possession the skeleton of a Sperm Whale, but of moderate size, by no means of the full-grown magnitude of my friend King Tranquo's.

In both cases, the stranded whales to which these two skeletons belonged, were originally claimed by their proprietors upon similar grounds. King Tranquo seizing his because he wanted it; and Sir Clifford, because he was lord of the seignories of those parts. Sir Clifford's whale has been articulated throughout; so that, like a great chest of drawers, you can open and shut him, in all his bony cavities – spread out his ribs like a gigantic fan – and swing all day upon his lower jaw. Locks are to be put upon some of his trap-doors and shutters; and a footman will show round future visitors with a bunch of keys at his side. Sir Clifford thinks of charging twopence for a peep at the whispering gallery in the spinal column; threepence to hear the echo in the hollow of his cerebellum; and sixpence for the unrivalled view from his forehead.

The skeleton dimensions I shall now proceed to set down are copied verbatim from my right arm, where I had them tattooed; as in my wild wanderings at that period, there was no other secure way of preserving such valuable statistics. But as I was crowded for space, and wished the other parts of my body to remain a blank page for a poem I was then composing – at least, what untattooed parts might remain – I did not trouble myself with the odd inches; nor, indeed, should inches at all enter into a congenial admeasurement of the whale.

103

MEASUREMENT OF THE WHALE'S SKELETON

In the first place, I wish to lay before you a particular, plain statement, touching the living bulk of this leviathan, whose skeleton we are briefly to exhibit. Such a statement may prove useful here.

According to a careful calculation I have made, and which I partly base upon Captain Scoresby's estimate, of seventy tons for the largest sized Greenland whale of sixty feet in length; according to my careful calculation, I say, a Sperm Whale of the largest magnitude, between eighty-five and ninety feet in length, and something less than forty feet in its fullest circumference, such a whale will weigh at least ninety tons; so that, reckoning thirteen men to a ton, he would considerably outweigh the combined population of a whole village of one thousand one hundred inhabitants.

Think you not then that brains, like yoked cattle, should be put to this leviathan, to make him at all budge to any landsman's imagination?

Having already in various ways put before you his skull, spout-hole, jaw, teeth, tail, forehead, fins, and divers other parts, I shall now simply point out what is most interesting in the general bulk of his unobstructed bones. But as the colossal skull embraces so very large a proportion of the entire extent of the skeleton; as it is by far the most complicated part; and as nothing is to be repeated concerning it in this chapter, you must not fail to carry it in your mind, or under your arm, as we proceed, otherwise you will not gain a complete notion of the general structure we are about to view.

In length, the Sperm Whale's skeleton at Tranque measured seventy-two feet; so that when fully invested and extended in life, he must have been ninety feet long; for in the whale, the skeleton loses about one fifth in length compared with the living body. Of this seventy-two feet, his skull and jaw comprised some twenty feet, leaving some fifty feet of plain back-bone. Attached to this back-bone, for something less than a third of its length, was the mighty circular basket of ribs which once enclosed his vitals.

To me this vast ivory-ribbed chest, with the long, unrelieved spine, extending far away from it in a straight line, not a little resembled the embryo hull of a great ship new-laid upon the stocks, when only some twenty of her naked bow-ribs are inserted, and the keel is otherwise, for the time, but a long, disconnected timber.

The ribs were ten on a side. The first, to begin from the neck, was nearly six feet long; the second, third, and fourth were each successively longer, till you came to the climax of the fifth, or one of the middle ribs, which measured eight feet and some inches. From that part, the remaining ribs diminished, till the tenth and last only spanned five feet and some inches. In general thickness, they all bore a seemly correspondence to their length. The middle ribs were the most arched. In some of the Arsacides they are used for beams whereon to lay foot-path bridges over small streams.

In considering these ribs, I could not but be struck anew with the circumstance, so variously repeated in this book, that the skeleton of the whale is by no means the mould of his invested form. The largest of the Tranque ribs, one of the middle ones, occupied that part of the fish which, in life, is greatest in depth. Now, the greatest depth of the invested body of this particular whale must have been at least sixteen feet; whereas, the corresponding rib measured but little more than eight feet. So that this rib only conveyed half of the true notion of the living magnitude of that part. Besides, for some way, where I now saw but a naked spine, all that had been once wrapped round with tons of added bulk in flesh, muscle, blood, and bowels. Still more, for the ample fins, I here saw but a few disordered joints; and in place of the weighty and majestic, but boneless flukes, an utter blank!

How vain and foolish, then, thought I, for timid untravelled man to try to comprehend aright this wondrous whale, by merely poring over his dead attenuated skeleton, stretched in this peaceful wood. No. Only in the heart of quickest perils; only when within the eddyings of his angry flukes; only on the profound unbounded sea, can the fully invested whale be truly and livingly found out.

But the spine. For that, the best way we can consider it is, with a crane, to pile its bones high up on end. No speedy enterprise. But now it's done, it looks much like Pompey's Pillar.

There are forty and odd vertebræ in all, which in the skeleton are not locked together. They mostly lie like the great knobbed blocks on a Gothic spire, forming solid courses of heavy masonry. The largest, a middle one, is in width something less than three feet, and in depth more than four. The smallest, where the spine tapers away into the tail, is only two inches in width, and looks something like a white billiard-ball. I was told that there were still smaller ones, but they had been lost by some little cannibal urchins, the priest's children, who had stolen them to play marbles with. Thus we see how that the spine of even the hugest of living things tapers off at last into simple child's play.

104

THE FOSSIL WHALE

FROM his mighty bulk the whale affords a most congenial theme whereon to enlarge, amplify, and generally expatiate. Would you, you could not compress him. By good rights he should only be treated of in imperial folio. Not to tell over again his furlongs from spiracle to tail, and the yards he measures about the waist; only think of the gigantic involutions of his intestines, where they lie in him like great cables and hausers coiled away in the subterranean orlop-deck of a line-of-battle-ship.

Since I have undertaken to manhandle this Leviathan, it behoves me to approve myself omnisciently exhaustive in the enterprise; not overlooking the minutest seminal germs of his blood, and spinning him out to the uttermost coil of his bowels. Having already described him in most of his present habitatory and anatomical peculiarities, it now remains to magnify him in an archæological, fossiliferous, and antediluvian point of view. Applied to any other creature than the Leviathan – to an ant or a flea – such portly terms might justly be deemed unwarrantably grandiloquent. But when Leviathan is the text, the case is altered. Fain am I to stagger to this emprise under the weightiest words of the dictionary. And here be it said, that whenever it has been convenient to consult one in the course of these dissertations, I have invariably used a huge quarto edition of Johnson, expressly purchased for that purpose; because that famous lexicographer's uncommon personal bulk more fitted him to compile a lexicon to be used by a whale author like me.

One often hears of writers that rise and swell with their subject, though it may seem but an ordinary one. How, them, with me, writing of this Leviathan? Unconsciously my chirography expands into placard capitals. Give me a condor's quill! Give me Vesuvius' crater for an inkstand! Friends, hold my arms! For in the mere act of penning my thoughts of this Leviathan, they weary me, and make me faint with their outreaching comprehensiveness of sweep, as if to include the whole circle of the sciences, and all the generations of whales, and men, and mastodons, past, present, and to come, with all the revolving panoramas of empire on earth, and throughout the whole universe, not excluding its suburbs. Such, and so magnifying, is the virtue of a large and liberal theme! We expand to its bulk. To produce a mighty book, you must choose a mighty theme. No great and enduring volume can ever be written on the flea, though many there be who have tried it.

Ere entering upon the subject of Fossil Whales, I present my credentials as a geologist, by stating that in my miscellaneous time I have been a stone-mason, and also a great digger of ditches, canals and wells, wine-vaults, cellars, and cisterns of all sorts. Likewise, by way of preliminary, I desire to remind the reader, that while in the earlier geological strata there are found the fossils of monsters now almost completely extinct; the subsequent relics discovered in what are called the Tertiary formations seem the connecting, or at any rate intercepted links, between the ante-chronical creatures, and those whose remote posterity are said to have entered the Ark; all the Fossil Whales hitherto discovered belong to the Tertiary period, which is the last preceding the superficial formations. And though none of them precisely answer to any known species of the present time, they are yet sufficiently akin to them in general respects, to justify their taking rank as Cetacean fossils.

Detached broken fossils of pre-adamite whales, fragments of their bones and skeletons, have within thirty years past, at various intervals, been found at the base of the Alps, in Lombardy, in France, in England, in Scotland, and in the States of Louisiana, Mississippi, and Alabama. Among the more curious of such remains is part of a skull, which in the year 1779 was disinterred in the Rue Dauphine in Paris, a short street opening almost directly upon the palace of the

Tuileries; and bones disinterred in excavating the great docks of Antwerp, in Napoleon's time. Cuvier pronounced these fragments to have belonged to some utterly unknown Leviathanic species.

But by far the most wonderful of all cetacean relics was the almost complete vast skeleton of an extinct monster, found in the year 1842, on the plantation of Judge Creagh, in Alabama. The awe-stricken credulous slaves in the vicinity took it for the bones of one of the fallen angels. The Alabama doctors declared it a huge reptile, and bestowed upon it the name of Basilosaurus. But some specimen bones of it being taken across the sea to Owen, the English anatomist, it turned out that this alleged reptile was a whale, though of a departed species. A significant illustration of the fact, again and again repeated in this book, that the skeleton of the whale furnishes but little clue to the shape of his fully invested body. So Owen re-christened the monster Zeuglodon; and in his paper read before the London Geological Society, pronounced it, in substance, one of the most extraordinary creatures which the mutations of the globe have blotted out of existence.

When I stand among these mighty Leviathan skeletons, skulls, tusks, jaws, ribs, and vertebræ, all characterized by partial resemblances to the existing breeds of sea-monsters; but at the same time bearing on the other hand similar affinities to the annihilated ante-chronical Leviathans, their incalculable seniors; I am, by a flood, borne back to that wondrous period, ere time itself can be said to have begun; for time began with man. Here Saturn's grey chaos rolls over me, and I obtain dim, shuddering glimpses into those Polar eternities; when wedged bastions of ice pressed hard upon what are now the Tropics; and in all the 25,000 miles of this world's circumference, not an inhabitable hand's breadth of land was visible. Then the whole world was the whale's; and, king of creation, he left his wake along the present lines of the Andes and the Himmalehs. Who can show a pedigree like Leviathan? Ahab's harpoon had shed older blood than the Pharaohs'. Methuselah seems a schoolboy. I look round to shake hands with Shem. I am horror-struck at this antemosaic, unsourced existence of the unspeakable terrors of the whale, which, having been before all time, must needs exist after all humane ages are over.

But not alone has this Leviathan left his pre-adamite traces in the stereotype plates of nature, and in limestone and marl bequeathed his ancient bust; but upon Egyptian tablets, whose antiquity seems to claim for them an almost fossiliferous character, we find the unmistakable print of his fin. In an apartment of the great temple of Denderah, some fifty years ago, there was discovered upon the granite ceiling a sculptured and painted planisphere, abounding in centaurs, griffins, and dolphins, similar to the grotesque figures on the celestial globe of the moderns. Gliding among them, old Leviathan swam as of yore; was there swimming in that planisphere, centuries before Solomon was cradled.

Nor must there be omitted another strange attestation of the antiquity of the whale, in his own osseous post-diluvian reality, as set down by the venerable John Leo, the old Barbary traveller.

'Not far from the Sea-side, they have a Temple, the Rafters and Beams of which are made of Whale-Bones; for Whales of a monstrous size are oftentimes cast up dead upon that shore. The Common People imagine, that by a secret Power bestowed by God upon the Temple, no Whale can pass it without immediate death. But the truth of the Matter is, that on either side of the Temple, there are Rocks that shoot two Miles into the Sea, and wound the Whales when they light upon 'em. They keep a Whale's Rib of an incredible length for a Miracle, which lying upon the Ground with its convex part uppermost, makes an Arch, the Head of which cannot be reached by a Man upon a Camel's Back. This Rib' (says John Leo) 'is said to have layn there a hundred Years before I saw it. Their Historians affirm, that a Prophet who prophesy'd of Mahomet, came from this Temple, and some do not stand to assert, that the Prophet Jonas was cast forth by the Whale at the Base of the Temple.'

In this Afric Temple of the Whale I leave you, reader, and if you be a Nantucketer, and a whaleman, you will silently worship there.

105

DOES THE WHALE'S MAGNITUDE DIMINISH? – WILL HE PERISH?

INASMUCH, then, as this Leviathan comes floundering down upon us from the head-waters of the Eternities, it may be fitly inquired, whether, in the long course of his generations, he has not degenerated from the original bulk of his sires.

But upon investigation we find, that not only are the whales of the present day superior in magnitude to those whose fossil remains are found in the Tertiary system (embracing a distinct geological period prior to man), but of the whales found in that Tertiary system, those belonging to its latter formations exceed in size those of its earlier ones.

Of all the pre-adamite whales yet exhumed, by far the largest is the Alabama one mentioned in the last chapter, and that was less than seventy feet in length in the skeleton. Whereas, we have already seen, that the tape-measure gives seventy-two feet for the skeleton of a large sized modern whale. And I have heard, on whalemen's authority, that Sperm Whales have been captured near a hundred feet long at the time of capture.

But may it not be, that while the whales of the present hour are an advance in magnitude upon those of all previous geological periods; may it not be, that since Adam's time they have degenerated?

Assuredly, we must conclude so, if we are to credit the accounts of such gentlemen as Pliny, and the ancient naturalists generally. For Pliny tells us of whales that embraced acres of living bulk, and Aldrovandus of others which measured eight hundred feet in length – Rope Walks and Thames Tunnels of Whales! And even in the days of Banks and Solander, Cooke's naturalists, we find a Danish member of the Academy of Sciences setting down certain Iceland Whales (reydan-siskur, or Wrinkled Bellies) at one hundred and twenty yards; that is, three hundred and sixty feet. And Lacépède, the French naturalist, in his elaborate history of whales, in the very beginning of his work (page 3), sets down the Right Whale at one hundred metres, three hundred and twenty-eight feet. And this work was published so late as A.D. 1825.

But will any whaleman believe these stories? No. The whale of to-day is as big as his ancestors in Pliny's time. And if ever I go where Pliny is, I, a whaleman (more than he was), will make bold to tell him so. Because I cannot understand how it is, that while the Egyptian mummies that were buried thousands of years before even Pliny was born, do not measure so much in their coffins as a modern Kentuckian in his socks; and while the cattle and other animals sculptured on the oldest Egyptian and Nineveh tablets, by the relative proportions in which they are drawn, just as plainly prove that the high-bred, stall-fed, prize cattle of Smithfield, not only equal, but far exceed in magnitude the fattest of Pharaoh's fat kine; in the face of all this, I will not admit that of all animals the whale alone should have degenerated.

But still another inquiry remains; one often agitated by the more recondite Nantucketers. Whether owing to the almost omniscient look-outs at the mast-heads of the whaleships, now penetrating even through Behring's straits, and into the remotest secret drawers and lockers of the world; and the thousand harpoons and lances darted along all continental coasts; the moot point is, whether Leviathan can long endure so wide a chase, and so remorseless a havoc; whether he must not at last be exterminated from the waters, and the last whale, like the last man, smoke his last pipe, and then himself evaporate in the final puff.

Comparing the humped herds of whales with the humped herds of buffalo, which, not forty years ago, overspread by tens of thousands the prairies of Illinois and Missouri, and shook their iron manes and scowled with their thunder-clotted brows upon the sites of populous river-capitals, where now the polite broker sells you land at a dollar an inch; in such a comparison an irresistible argument would seem furnished, to show that the hunted whale cannot now escape speedy extinction.

But you must look at this matter in every light. Though so short a period ago – not a good life-time – the census of the buffalo in Illinois exceeded the census of men now in London, and though at the present day not one horn or hoof of them remains in all that region; and though the cause of this wondrous extermination was the spear of man; yet the far different nature of the whale-hunt peremptorily forbids so inglorious an end to the Leviathan. Forty men in one ship hunting the Sperm Whale for forty-eight months think they have done extremely well, and thank God, if at last they carry home the oil of forty fish. Whereas, in the days of the old Canadian and Indian hunters and trappers of the West, when the far west (in whose sunset suns still rise) was a wilderness and a virgin, the same number of moccasined men, for the same number of months, mounted on horse instead of sailing in ships, would have slain not forty, but forty thousand and more buffaloes; a fact that, if need were, could be statistically stated.

Nor, considered aright, does it seem any argument in favor of the gradual extinction of the Sperm Whale, for example, that in former years (the latter part of the last century, say) these Leviathans, in small pods, were encountered much oftener than at present, and, in consequence, the voyages were not so prolonged, and were also much more remunerative. Because, as has been elsewhere noticed, those whales, influenced by some views to safety, now swim the seas in immense caravans, so that to a large degree the scattered solitaries, yokes, and pods, and schools of other days are now aggregated into vast but widely separated, unfrequent armies. That is all. And equally fallacious seems the conceit, that because the so-called whalebone whales no longer haunt many grounds in former years abounding with them, hencc that species also is declining.

For they are only being driven from promontory to cape; and if one coast is no longer enlivened with their jets, then, be sure, some other and remoter strand has been very recently startled by the unfamiliar spectacle.

Furthermore: concerning these last mentioned Leviathans, they have two firm fortresses, which, in all human probability, will for ever remain impregnable. And as upon the invasion of their valleys, the frosty Swiss have retreated to their mountains; so, hunted from the savannas and glades of the middle seas, the whale-bone whales can at last resort to their Polar citadels, and diving under the ultimate glassy barriers and walls there, come up among icy fields and floes; and in a charmed circle of everlasting December, bid defiance to all pursuit from man.

But as perhaps fifty of these whale-bone whales are harpooned for one cachalot, some philosophers of the forecastle have concluded that this positive havoc has already very seriously diminished their battalions. But though for some time past a number of these whales, not less than 13,000, have been annually slain on the nor' west coast by the Americans alone; yet there are considerations which render even this circumstance of little or no account as an opposing argument in this matter.

Natural as it is to be somewhat incredulous concerning the populousness of the more enormous creatures of the globe, yet what shall we say to Harto, the historian of Goa, when he tells us that at one hunting the King of Siam took 4000 elephants; that in those regions elephants are numerous as droves of cattle in the temperate climes. And there seems no reason to doubt that if these elephants, which have now been hunted for thousands of years, by Semiramis, by Porus, by Hannibal, and by all the successive monarchs of the East – if they still survive there in great numbers, much more may the great whale outlast all hunting, since he has a pasture to expatiate in, which is precisely twice as large as all Asia, both Americas, Europe and Africa, New Holland, and all the Isles of the sea combined.

Moreover: we are to consider, that from the presumed

great longevity of whales, their probably attaining the age of a century and more, therefore at any one period of time, several distinct adult generations must be contemporary. And what that is, we may soon gain some idea of, by imagining all the grave-yards, cemeteries, and family vaults of creation yielding up the live bodies of all the men, women, and children who were alive seventy-five years ago; and adding this countless host to the present human population of the globe.

Wherefore, for all these things, we account the whale immortal in his species, however perishable in his individuality. He swam the seas before the continents broke water; he once swam over the site of the Tuileries, and Windsor Castle, and the Kremlin. In Noah's flood he despised Noah's Ark; and if ever the world is to be again flooded, like the Netherlands, to kill off its rats, then the eternal whale will still survive, and rearing upon the topmost crest of the equatorial flood, spout his frothed defiance to the skies.

106

AHAB'S LEG

THE precipitating manner in which Captain Ahab had quitted the Samuel Enderby of London, had not been unattended with some small violence to his own person. He had lighted with such energy upon a thwart of his boat that his ivory leg had received a half-splintering shock. And when after gaining his own deck, and his own pivot-hole there, he so vehemently wheeled round with an urgent command to the steersman (it was, as ever, something about his not steering inflexibly enough); then, the already shaken ivory received such an additional twist and wrench, that though it still remained entire, and to all appearances lusty, yet Ahab did not deem it entirely trustworthy.

And, indeed, it seemed small matter for wonder, that for all his pervading, mad recklessness, Ahab did at times give careful heed to the condition of that dead bone upon which he partly stood. For it had not been very long prior to the Pequod's sailing from Nantucket, that he had been found one night lying prone upon the ground, and insensible; by some unknown, and seemingly inexplicable, unimaginable casualty, his ivory limb having been so violently displaced, that it had stake-wise smitten, and all but pierced his groin; nor was it without extreme difficulty that the agonizing wound was entirely cured.

Nor, at the time, had it failed to enter his monomaniac mind, that all the anguish of that then present suffering was but the direct issue of a former woe; and he too plainly seemed to see, that as the most poisonous reptile of the marsh perpetuates his kind as inevitably as the sweetest songster of the grove; so, equally with every felicity, all miserable events do naturally beget their like. Yea, more than equally, thought Ahab; since both the ancestry and posterity of Grief go further than the ancestry and posterity of Joy. For, not to hint of this: that it is an inference from certain canonic teachings, that while some natural enjoyments here shall have no children born to them for the other world, but, on the contrary, shall be followed by the joy-childlessness of all hell's despair; whereas, some guilty mortal miseries shall still fertilely beget to themselves an eternally progressive progeny of griefs beyond the grave; not at all to hint of this, there still seems an inequality in the deeper analysis of the thing. For, thought Ahab, while even the highest earthly felicities ever have a certain unsignifying pettiness lurking in them, but, at bottom, all heart-woes, a mystic significance, and, in some men, an archangelic grandeur; so do their diligent tracings-out not belie the obvious deduction. To trail the genealogies of these high mortal miseries, carries us at last among the sourceless primogenitures of the gods; so that, in the face of all the glad, hay-making suns, and soft-cymballing, round harvest-moons, we must needs give in to this: that the gods themselves are not for ever glad. The ineffaceable, sad birth-mark in the brow of man, is but the stamp of sorrow in the signers.

Unwittingly here a secret has been divulged, which perhaps might more properly, in set way, have been disclosed before. With many other particulars concerning Ahab, always had it remained a mystery to some, why it was, that for a certain period, both before and after the sailing of the Pequod, he had hidden himself away with such Grand-Lama-like exclusiveness; and, for that one interval, sought speechless refuge, as it were, among the marble senate of the dead. Captain Peleg's bruited reason for this thing appeared by no means adequate; though, indeed, as touching all Ahab's deeper part, every revelation partook more of significant darkness than of explanatory light. But, in the end, it all came out; this one matter did, at least. That direful mishap was at the bottom of his temporary recluseness. And not only this, but to that ever-contracting, dropping circle ashore, who, for any reason, possessed the privilege of a less banned approach to him; to that timid circle the above hinted casualty – remaining, as it did, moodily unaccounted for by Ahab – invested itself with terrors, not entirely underived from the land of spirits and of wails. So that, through their zeal for him, they had all conspired, so far as in them lay, to muffle up the knowledge of this thing from others; and hence it was, that not till a considerable interval had elapsed, did it transpire upon the Pequod's decks.

But be all this as it may; let the unseen, ambiguous synod in the air, or the vindictive princes and potentates of fire, have to do or not with earthly Ahab, yet, in this present matter of his leg, he took plain practical procedures; – he called the carpenter.

And when that functionary appeared before him, he bade him without delay set about making a new leg, and directed the mates to see him supplied with all the studs and joists of jaw-ivory (Sperm Whale) which had thus far been accumulated on the voyage, in order that a careful selection of the stoutest, clearest-grained stuff might be secured. This done, the carpenter received orders to have the leg completed that night; and to provide all the fittings for it, independent of those pertaining to the distrusted one in use. Moreover, the ship's forge was ordered to be hoisted out of its temporary idleness in the hold; and, to accelerate the affair, the blacksmith was commanded to proceed at once to the forging of whatever iron contrivances might be needed.

107

THE CARPENTER

SEAT thyself sultanically among the moons of Saturn, and take high abstracted man alone; and he seems a wonder, a grandeur, and a woe. But from the same point, take mankind in mass, and for the most part, they seem a mob of unnecessary duplicates, both contemporary and hereditary. But most humble though he was, and far from furnishing an example of the high, humane abstraction; the Pequod's carpenter was no duplicate; hence, he now comes in person on this stage.

Like all sea-going ship carpenters, and more especially those belonging to whaling vessels, he was, to a certain offhanded, practical extent, alike experienced in numerous trades and callings collateral to his own; the carpenter's pursuit being the ancient and outbranching trunk of all those numerous handicrafts which more or less have to do with wood as an auxiliary material. But, besides the application to him of the generic remark above, this carpenter of the Pequod was singularly efficient in those thousand nameless mechanical emergencies continually recurring in a large ship, upon a three or four years' voyage, in uncivilized and far-distant seas. For not to speak of his readiness in ordinary duties: – repairing stove boats, sprung spars, reforming the shape of clumsy-bladed oars, inserting bull's eyes in the deck, or new tree-nails in the side planks, and other miscellaneous matters more directly pertaining to his special business; he was moreover unhesitatingly expert in all manner of conflicting aptitudes, both useful and capricious.

The one grand stage where he enacted all his various parts so manifold, was his vice-bench; a long rude ponderous table furnished with several vices, of different sizes, and both of iron and of wood. At all times except when whales were alongside, this bench was securely lashed athwartships against the rear of the Try-works.

A belaying pin is found too large to be easily inserted into its hole: the carpenter claps it into one of his ever-ready vices, and straightway files it smaller. A lost land-bird of strange plumage strays on board, and is made a captive: out of clean shaved rods of right-whale bone, and cross-beams of sperm whale ivory, the carpenter makes a pagoda-looking cage for it. An oarsman sprains his wrist: the carpenter concocts a soothing lotion. Stubb longs for vermillion stars to be painted upon the blade of his every oar: screwing each oar in his big vice of wood, the carpenter symmetrically supplies the constellation. A sailor takes a fancy to wear shark-bone ear-rings: the carpenter drills his ears. Another has the toothache: the carpenter out pincers, and clapping one hand upon his bench bids him be seated there; but the poor fellow unmanageably winces under the unconcluded operation; whirling round the handle of his wooden vice, the carpenter signs him to clap his jaw in that, if he would have him draw the tooth.

Thus, this carpenter was prepared at all points, and alike indifferent and without respect in all. Teeth he accounted bits of ivory; heads he deemed but top-blocks; men themselves he lightly held for capstans. But while now upon so wide a field thus variously accomplished, and with such liveliness of expertness in him, too; all this would seem to argue some uncommon vivacity of intelligence. But not precisely so. For nothing was this man more remarkable, than for a certain impersonal stolidity as it were; impersonal, I say; for it so shaded off into the surrounding infinite of things, that it seemed one with the general stolidity discernible in the whole visible world; which while pauselessly active in uncounted modes, still eternally holds its peace, and ignores you, though you dig foundations for cathedrals. Yet was this half-horrible stolidity in him, involving, too, as it appeared, an all-ramifying heartlessness; – yet was it oddly dashed at times, with an old, crutch-like, antediluvian, wheezing humorousness, not unstreaked now and then with a certain grizzled wittiness; such as might have served to pass the time during the midnight watch on the bearded forecastle of Noah's ark. Was it that this old carpenter had been a life-long wanderer, whose much rolling, to and fro, not only had gathered no moss; but what is more, had rubbed off whatever small outward clingings might have originally pertained to him? He was a stript abstract; an unfractioned integral; uncompromised as a new-born babe; living without premeditated reference to this world or the next. You might almost say, that this strange uncompromisedness of him involved a sort of unintelligence; for in his numerous trades, he did not seem to work so much by reason or by instinct, or simply because he had been tutored to it, or by any intermixture of all these, even or uneven; but merely by a kind of deaf and dumb, spontaneous literal process. He was a pure manipulator; his brain, if he had ever had one, must have early oozed along into the muscles of his fingers. He was like one of those unreasoning but still highly useful, *multum in parvo*, Sheffield contrivances, assuming the exterior – though a little swelled – of a common pocket knife; but containing, not only blades of various sizes, but also screw-drivers, cork-screws, tweezers, awls, pens, rulers, nail-filers, countersinkers. So, if his superiors wanted to use the carpenter for a screw-driver, all they had to do was to open that part of him, and the screw was fast: or if for tweezers, take him up by the legs, and there they were.

Yet, as previously hinted, this omnitooled, open-and-shut carpenter, was, after all, no mere machine of an automaton. If he did not have a common soul in him, he had a subtle something that somehow anomalously did its duty. What that was, whether essence of quicksilver, or a few drops of hartshorn, there is no telling. But there it was; and there it had abided for now some sixty years or more. And this it was, this same unaccountable, cunning life-principle in him; this it was, that kept him a great part of the time soliloquizing; but only like an unreasoning wheel, which also hummingly soliloquizes; or rather, his body was a sentry-box and this soliloquizer on guard there, and talking all the time to keep himself awake.

108

AHAB AND THE CARPENTER

THE DECK – FIRST NIGHT WATCH

(*Carpenter standing before his vice-bench, and by the light of two lanterns busily filing the ivory joist for the leg, which joist is firmly fixed in the vice. Slabs of ivory, leather straps, pads, screws, and various tools of all sorts lying about the bench. Forward, the red flame of the forge is seen, where the blacksmith is at work.*)

DRAT the file, and drat the bone! That is hard which should be soft, and that is soft which should be hard. So we go, who file old jaws and shinbones. Let's try another. Aye, now, this works better (*sneezes*). Halloa, this bone dust is (*sneezes*) – why it's (*sneezes*) – yes it's (*sneezes*) – bless my soul, it won't let me speak! This is what an old fellow gets now for working in dead lumber. Saw a live tree, and you don't get this dust; amputate a live bone, and you don't get it (*sneezes*). Come, come, you old Smut, there, bear a hand, and let's have that ferule and buckle-screw; I'll be ready for them presently. Lucky now (*sneezes*) there's no knee-joint to make; that might puzzle a little; but a mere shin-bone – why it's easy as making hop-poles; only I should like to put a good finish on. Time, time; if I but only had the time, I could turn him out as neat a leg now as ever (*sneezes*) scraped to a lady in a parlor. Those buckskin legs and calves of legs I've seen in shop windows wouldn't compare at all. They soak water, they do; and of course get rheumatic, and have to be doctored (*sneezes*) with washes and lotions, just like live legs. There; before I saw it off, now, I must call his old Mogulship, and see whether the length will be all right; too short, if anything, I guess. Ha! that's the heel; we are in luck; here he comes, or it's somebody else, that's certain.

AHAB (*advancing*).

(*During the ensuing scene, the carpenter continues sneezing at times.*)

Well, manmaker!

Just in time, sir. If the captain pleases, I will now mark the length. Let me measure, sir.

Measured for a leg! good. Well, it's not the first time. About it! There; keep thy finger on it. This is a cogent vice thou hast here, carpenter; let me feel its grip once. So, so; it does pinch some.

Oh, sir, it will break bones – beware, beware!

No fear; I like a good grip; I like to feel something in this slippery world that can hold, man. What's Prometheus about there? – the blacksmith, I mean – what's he about?

He must be forging the buckle-screw, sir, now.

Right. It's a partnership; he supplies the muscle part. He makes a fierce red flame there!

Aye, sir; he must have the white heat for this kind of fine work.

Um-m. So he must. I do deem it now a most meaning thing, that that old Greek, Prometheus, who made men, they say, should have been a blacksmith, and animated them with fire; for what's made in fire must properly belong to fire, and so hell's probable. How the soot flies! This must be the remainder the Greek made the Africans of. Carpenter, when he's through with that buckle, tell him to forge a pair of steel shoulder-blades; there's a pedlar aboard with a crushing pack.

Sir?

Hold; while Prometheus is about it, I'll order a complete man after a desirable pattern. Imprimis, fifty feet high in his socks; then, chest modelled after the Thames Tunnel; then, legs with roots to 'em, to stay in one place; then, arms three feet through the wrist; no heart at all, brass forehead, and about a quarter of an acre of fine brains; and let me see – shall I order eyes to see outwards? No, but put a sky-light on top of his head to illuminate inwards. There, take the order, and away.

Now, what's he speaking about, and who's he speaking to, I should like to know? Shall I keep standing here? (*aside.*)

'Tis but indifferent architecture to make a blind dome; here's one. No, no, no; I must have a lantern.

Ho, ho! That's it, hey? Here are two, sir; one will serve my turn.

What art thou thrusting that thief-catcher into my face for, man? Thrusted light is worse than presented pistols.

I thought, sir, that you spoke to carpenter.

Carpenter? why that's – but no; – a very tidy, and, I may say, an extremely gentlemanlike sort of business thou art in here, carpenter; – or would'st thou rather work in clay?

Sir? – Clay? clay, sir? That's mud; we leave clay to ditchers, sir.

The fellow's impious! What art thou sneezing about?

Bone is rather dusty, sir.

Take the hint, then; and when thou art dead, never bury thyself under living people's noses.

Sir? – oh! ah! – I guess so; – yes – oh, dear!

Look ye, carpenter, I dare say thou callest thyself a right good workmanlike workman, eh? Well, then, will it speak thoroughly well for thy work, if, when I come to mount this leg thou makest, I shall nevertheless feel another leg in the same identical place with it; that is, carpenter, my old lost leg; the flesh and blood one, I mean. Canst thou not drive that old Adam away?

Truly, sir. I begin to understand somewhat now. Yes, I have heard something curious on that score, sir; how that a dismasted man never entirely loses the feeling of his old spar, but it will be still pricking him at times. May I humbly ask if it be really so, sir?

It is, man. Look, put thy live leg here in the place where mine once was; so, now, here is only one distinct leg to the eye, yet two to the soul. Where thou feelest tingling life; there, exactly there, there to a hair, do I. Is't a riddle?

I should humbly call it a poser, sir.

Hist, then. How dost thou know that some entire, living, thinking thing may not be invisibly and uninterpenetratingly standing precisely where thou now standest; aye, and standing there in thy spite? In thy most solitary hours, then, dost thou not fear eavesdroppers? Hold, don't speak! And if I still feel the smart of my crushed leg, though it be now so long dissolved; then, why mayst not thou, carpenter, feel the fiery pains of hell for ever, and without a body? Hah!

Good Lord! Truly, sir, if it comes to that, I must calculate over again; I think I didn't carry a small figure, sir.

Look ye, pudding-heads should never grant premises. – How long before the leg is done?

Perhaps an hour, sir.

Bungle away at it then, and bring it to me (*turns to go*). Oh, Life! Here I am, proud as Greek god, and yet standing debtor to this blockhead for a bone to stand on! Cursed be that mortal inter-indebtedness which will not do away with ledgers. I would be free as air; and I'm down in the whole world's books. I am so rich, I could have given bid for bid with the wealthiest Prætorians at the auction of the Roman empire (which was the world's); and yet I owe for the flesh in the tongue I brag with. By heavens! I'll get a crucible, and into it, and dissolve myself down to one small, compendious vertebra. So.

CARPENTER (*resuming his work*).

Well, well, well! Stubb knows him best of all, and Stubb always says he's queer; says nothing but that one sufficient little word queer; he's queer, says Stubb; he's queer – queer, queer; and keeps dinning it into Mr Starbuck all the time – queer, sir – queer, queer, very queer. And here's his leg! Yes, now that I think of it, here's his bedfellow! has a stick of whale's jaw-bone for a wife! And this is his leg; he'll stand on this. What was that now about one leg standing in three places, and all three places standing in one hell – how was that? Oh! I don't wonder he looked so scornful at me! I'm a sort of strange-thoughted sometimes, they say; but that's only haphazard-like. Then, a short, little old body like me, should never undertake to wade out into deep waters with tall, heron-built captains; the water chucks you under the chin pretty quick, and there's a great cry for life-boats. And here's the heron's leg! long and slim, sure enough! Now, for most folks one pair of legs lasts a lifetime, and that must be because they use them mercifully, as a tender-hearted old lady uses her roly-poly old coach-horses. But Ahab; oh he's a hard driver. Look, driven one leg to death, and spavined the other for life, and now wears out bone legs by the cord. Halloa, there, you Smut! bear a hand there with those screws, and let's finish it before the resurrection fellow comes a-calling with his horn for all legs, true or false, as brewery-men go round collecting old beer barrels, to fill 'em up again. What a leg this is! It looks like a real live leg, filed down to nothing but the core; he'll be standing on this to-morrow; he'll be taking altitudes on it. Halloa! I almost forgot the little oval slate, smoothed ivory, where he figures up the latitude. So, so; chisel, file, and sandpaper, now!

109

AHAB AND STARBUCK IN THE CABIN

ACCORDING to usage they were pumping the ship next morning; and lo! no inconsiderable oil came up with the water; the casks below must have sprung a bad leak. Much concern was shown; and Starbuck went down into the cabin to report this unfavorable affair.*

*In Sperm-whalemen with any considerable quantity of oil on board, it is a regular semi-weekly duty to conduct a hose into the hold, and drench the casks with sea-water; which afterwards, at varying intervals, is removed by the ship's pumps. Hereby the casks

Now, from the South and West the Pequod was drawing nigh to Formosa and the Bashee Isles between which lies one of the tropical outlets from the China waters into the Pacific. And so Starbuck found Ahab with a general chart of the oriental archipelagoes spread before him; and another separate one representing the long eastern coasts of the Japanese islands – Niphon, Matsmai, and Sikoke. With his snow-white new ivory leg braced against the screwed leg of his table, and with a long pruning-hook of a jack-knife in his hand, the wondrous old man, with his back to the gangway door, was wrinkling his brow, and tracing his old courses again.

'Who's there!' hearing the footstep at the door, but not turning round to it. 'On deck! Begone!'

'Captain Ahab mistakes; it is I. The oil in the hold is leaking, sir. We must up Burtons and break out.'

'Up Burtons and break out? Now that we are nearing Japan; heave-to here for a week to tinker a parcel of old hoops?'

'Either do that, sir, or waste in one day more oil than we may make good in a year. What we come twenty thousand miles to get is worth saving, sir.'

'So it is, so it is; if we get it.'

'I was speaking of the oil in the hold, sir.'

'And I was not speaking or thinking of that at all. Begone! Let it leak! I'm all aleak myself. Aye! leaks in leaks! not only full of leaky casks, but those leaky casks are in a leaky ship; and that's a far worse plight than the Pequod's, man. Yet I don't stop to plug my leak; for who can find it in the deep-loaded hull; or how hope to plug it, even if found, in this life's howling gale? Starbuck! I'll not have the Burtons hoisted.'

'What will the owners say, sir?'

'Let the owners stand on Nantucket beach and outyell the Typhoons. What cares Ahab? Owners, owners? Thou art

---

are sought to be kept damply tight; while by the changed character of the withdrawn water, the mariners readily detect any serious leakage in the precious cargo.

always prating to me, Starbuck, about those miserly owners, as if the owners were my conscience. But look ye, the only real owner of anything is its commander; and hark ye, my conscience is in this ship's keel. – On deck!'

'Captain Ahab,' said the reddening mate, moving further into the cabin, with a daring so strangely respectful and cautious that it almost seemed not only every way seeking to avoid the slightest outward manifestation of itself, but within also seemed more than half distrustful of itself; 'A better man than I might well pass over in thee what he would quickly enough resent in a younger man; aye, and in a happier, Captain Ahab.'

'Devils! Dost thou then so much as dare to critically think of me? – On deck!'

'Nay, sir, not yet; I do entreat. And I do dare, sir – to be forbearing! Shall we not understand each other better than hitherto, Captain Ahab?'

Ahab seized a loaded musket from the rack (forming part of most South-Sea-men's cabin furniture), and pointing it towards Starbuck, exclaimed: 'There is one God that is Lord over the earth, and one Captain that is lord over the Pequod. – On deck!'

For an instant in the flashing eyes of the mate, and his fiery cheeks, you would have almost thought that he had really received the blaze of the levelled tube. But, mastering his emotion, he half calmly rose, and as he quitted the cabin, paused for an instant and said: 'Thou hast outraged, not insulted me, sir; but for that I ask thee not to beware of Starbuck; thou wouldst but laugh; but let Ahab beware of Ahab; beware of thyself, old man.'

'He waxes brave, but nevertheless obeys; most careful bravery that!' murmured Ahab, as Starbuck disappeared. 'What's that he said – Ahab beware of Ahab – there's something there!' Then unconsciously using the musket for a staff, with an iron brow he paced to and fro in the little cabin; but presently the thick plaits of his forehead relaxed, and returning the gun to the rack, he went to the deck.

'Thou art but too good a fellow, Starbuck,' he said lowly

to the mate; then raising his voice to the crew: 'Furl the t'gallant-sails and close-reef the top-sails, fore and aft; back the main-yard; up Burtons, and break out in the main-hold.'

It were perhaps vain to surmise exactly why it was, that as respecting Starbuck, Ahab thus acted. It may have been a flash of honesty in him; or mere prudential policy which, under the circumstance, imperiously forbade the slightest symptom of open disaffection, however transient, in the important chief officer of his ship. However it was, his orders were executed; and the Burtons were hoisted.

110

QUEEQUEG IN HIS COFFIN

UPON searching, it was found that the casks last struck into the hold were perfectly sound, and that the leak must be further off. So, it being calm weather, they broke out deeper and deeper, disturbing the slumbers of the huge ground-tier butts; and from that black midnight sending those gigantic moles into the daylight above. So deep did they go; and so ancient, and corroded, and weedy the aspect of the lowermost puncheons, that you almost looked next for some mouldy corner-stone cask containing coins of Captain Noah, with copies of the posted placards, vainly warning the infatuated old world from the flood. Tierce after tierce, too, of water, and bread, and beef, and shooks of staves, and iron bundles of hoops, were hoisted out, till at last the piled decks were hard to get about; and the hollow hull echoed under foot, as if you were treading over empty catacombs, and reeled and rolled in the sea like an air-freighted demijohn. Top-heavy was the ship as a dinnerless student with all Aristotle in his head. Well was it that the Typhoons did not visit them then.

Now, at this time it was that my poor pagan companion, and fast bosom-friend, Queequeg, was seized with a fever, which brought him nigh to his endless end.

Be it said, that in this vocation of whaling, sinecures are

unknown; dignity and danger go hand in hand; till you get to be Captain, the higher you rise the harder you toil. So with poor Queequeg, who, as harpooneer, must not only face all the rage of the living whale, but – as we have elsewhere seen – mount his dead back in a rolling sea; and finally descend into the gloom of the hold, and bitterly sweating all day in that subterraneous confinement, resolutely manhandle the clumsiest casks and see to their stowage. To be short, among whalemen, the harpooneers are the holders, so called.

Poor Queequeg! when the ship was about half disembowelled, you should have stooped over the hatchway, and peered down upon him there; where, stripped to his woollen drawers, the tattooed savage was crawling about amid that dampness and slime, like a green spotted lizard at the bottom of a well. And a well, or an ice-house, it somehow proved to him, poor pagan; where, strange to say, for all the heat of his sweatings, he caught a terrible chill which lapsed into a fever; and at last, after some days' suffering, laid him in his hammock, close to the very sill of the door of death. How he wasted and wasted away in those few long-lingering days, till there seemed but little left of him but his frame and tattooing. But as all else in him thinned, and his cheek-bones grew sharper, his eyes, nevertheless, seemed growing fuller and fuller; they became of a strange softness of lustre; and mildly but deeply looked out at you there from his sickness, a wondrous testimony to that immortal health in him which could not die, or be weakened. And like circles on the water, which, as they grow fainter, expand; so his eyes seemed rounding and rounding, like the rings of Eternity. An awe that cannot be named would steal over you as you sat by the side of this waning savage, and saw as strange things in his face, as any beheld who were bystanders when Zoroaster died. For whatever is truly wondrous and fearful in man, never yet was put into words or books. And the drawing near of Death, which alike levels all, alike impresses all with a last revelation, which only an author from the dead could adequately tell. So that – let us say it again – no dying Chaldee or Greek had higher and holier thoughts than those, whose mysterious shades you saw creeping over the face of poor Queequeg, as he quietly lay in his swaying hammock, and the rolling sea seemed gently rocking him to his final rest, and the ocean's invisible flood-tide lifted him higher and higher towards his destined heaven.

Not a man of the crew but gave him up; and, as for Queequeg himself, what he thought of his case was forcibly shown by a curious favor he asked. He called one to him in the grey morning watch, when the day was just breaking, and taking his hand, said that while in Nantucket he had chanced to see certain little canoes of dark wood, like the rich war-wood of his native isle; and upon inquiry, he had learned that all whalemen who died in Nantucket, were laid in those same dark canoes, and that the fancy of being so laid had much pleased him; for it was not unlike the custom of his own race, who, after embalming a dead warrior, stretched him out in his canoe, and so left him to be floated away to the starry archipelagoes; for not only do they believe that the stars are isles, but that far beyond all visible horizons, their own mild, uncontinented seas, interflow with the blue heavens; and so form the white breakers of the milky way. He added, that he shuddered at the thought of being buried in his hammock, according to the usual sea-custom, tossed like something vile to the death-devouring sharks. No: he desired a canoe like those of Nantucket, all the more congenial to him, being a whaleman, that like a whale-boat these coffin-canoes were without a keel; though that involved but uncertain steering, and much lee-way adown the dim ages.

Now, when this strange circumstance was made known aft, the carpenter was at once commanded to do Queequeg's bidding, whatever it might include. There was some heathenish, coffin-colored old lumber aboard, which, upon a long previous voyage, had been cut from the aboriginal groves of the Lackaday islands, and from these dark planks the coffin was recommended to be made. No sooner was the carpenter apprised of the order, than taking his rule, he forthwith with all the indifferent promptitude of his character, proceeded into the forecastle and took Queequeg's measure with great accuracy, regularly chalking Queequeg's person as he shifted the rule.

'Ah! poor fellow! he'll have to die now,' ejaculated the Long Island sailor.

Going to his vice-bench, the carpenter for convenience' sake and general reference, now transferringly measured on it the exact length the coffin was to be, and then made the transfer permanent by cutting two notches at its extremities. This done, he marshalled the planks and his tools, and to work.

When the last nail was driven, and the lid duly planed and fitted, he lightly shouldered the coffin and went forward with it, inquiring whether they were ready for it yet in that direction.

Overhearing the indignant but half-humorous cries with which the people on deck began to drive the coffin away, Queequeg, to every one's consternation, commanded that the thing should be instantly brought to him, nor was there any denying him; seeing that, of all mortals, some dying men are the most tyrannical; and certainly, since they will shortly trouble us so little for evermore, the poor fellows ought to be indulged.

Leaning over in his hammock, Queequeg long regarded the coffin with an attentive eye. He then called for his harpoon, had the wooden stock drawn from it, and then had the iron part placed in the coffin along with one of the paddles of his boat. All by his own request, also, biscuits were then ranged round the sides within: a flask of fresh water was placed at the head, and a small bag of woody earth scraped up in the hold at the foot; and a piece of sailcloth being rolled up for a pillow, Queequeg now entreated to be lifted into his final bed, that he might make trial of its comforts, if any it had. He lay without moving a few minutes, then told one to go to his bag and bring out his little god, Yojo. Then crossing his arms on his breast with

Yojo between, he called for the coffin lid (hatch he called it) to be placed over him. The head part turned over with a leather hinge, and there lay Queequeg in his coffin with little but his composed countenance in view. 'Rarmai' (it will do; it is easy), he murmured at last, and signed to be replaced in his hammock.

But ere this was done, Pip, who had been slily hovering near by all this while, drew nigh to him where he lay, and with soft sobbings, took him by the hand; in the other, holding his tambourine.

'Poor rover! will ye never have done with all this weary roving? where go ye now? But if the currents carry ye to those sweet Antilles where the beaches are only beat with water-lilies, will ye do one little errand for me? Seek out one Pip, who's now been missing long: I think he's in those far Antilles. If ye find him, then comfort him; for he must be very sad; for look! he's left his tambourine behind; – I found it. Rig-a-dig, dig, dig! Now, Queequeg, die; and I'll beat ye your dying march.'

'I have heard,' murmured Starbuck, gazing down the scuttle, 'that in violent fevers, men, all ignorance, have talked in ancient tongues; and that when the mystery is probed, it turns out always that in their wholly forgotten childhood those ancient tongues had been really spoken in their hearing by some lofty scholars. So, to my fond faith, poor Pip, in this strange sweetness of his lunacy, brings heavenly vouchers of all our heavenly homes. Where learned he that, but there? – Hark! he speaks again: but more wildly now.'

'Form two and two! Let's make a General of him! Ho, where's his harpoon? Lay it across here. – Rig-a-dig, dig, dig! huzza! Oh for a game cock now to sit upon his head and crow! Queequeg dies game! – mind ye that; Queequeg dies game! – take ye good heed of that; Queequeg dies game! I say; game, game, game! but base little Pip, he died a coward; died all a'shiver; – out upon Pip! Hark ye; if ye find Pip, tell all the Antilles he's a runaway; a coward, a coward, a coward! Tell them he jumped from a whale-boat!

I'd never beat my tambourine over base Pip, and hail him General, if he were once more dying here. No, no! shame upon all cowards – shame upon them! Let 'em go drown like Pip, that jumped from a whale-boat. Shame! shame!'

During all this, Queequeg lay with closed eyes, as if in a dream. Pip was led away, and the sick man was replaced in his hammock.

But now that he had apparently made every preparation for death; now that his coffin was proved a good fit, Queequeg suddenly rallied; soon there seemed no need of the carpenter's box; and thereupon, when some expressed their delighted surprise, he, in substance, said, that the cause of his sudden convalescence was this; – at a critical moment, he had just recalled a little duty ashore, which he was leaving undone; and therefore had changed his mind about dying: he could not die yet, he averred. They asked him, then, whether to live or die was a matter of his own sovereign will and pleasure. He answered, certainly. In a word, it was Queequeg's conceit, that if a man made up his mind to live, mere sickness could not kill him: nothing but a whale, or a gale, or some violent, ungovernable, unintelligent destroyer of that sort.

Now, there is this noteworthy difference between savage and civilized! that while a sick, civilized man may be six months convalescing, generally speaking, a sick savage is almost half-well again in a day. So, in good time my Queequeg gained strength; and at length after sitting on the windlass for a few indolent days (but eating with a vigorous appetite) he suddenly leaped to his feet, threw out arms and legs, gave himself a good stretching, yawned a little bit, and then springing into the head of his hoisted boat, and poising a harpoon, pronounced himself fit for a fight.

With a wild whimsiness, he now used his coffin for a sea-chest; and emptying into it his canvas bag of clothes, set them in order there. Many spare hours he spent, in carving the lid with all manner of grotesque figures and drawings; and it seemed that hereby he was striving, in his rude way, to copy parts of the twisted tattooing on his body. And this tattooing, had been the work of a departed prophet and seer of his island, who, by those hieroglyphic marks, had written out on his body a complete theory of the heavens and the earth, and a mystical treatise on the art of attaining truth; so that Queequeg in his own proper person was a riddle to unfold; a wondrous work in one volume; but whose mysteries not even himself could read, though his own live heart beat against them; and these mysteries were therefore destined in the end to moulder away with the living parchment whereon they were inscribed, and so be unsolved to the last. And this thought it must have been which suggested to Ahab that wild exclamation of his, when one morning turning away from surveying poor Queequeg – 'Oh, devilish tantalization of the gods!'

111

THE PACIFIC

When gliding by the Bashee isles we emerged at last upon the great South Sea; were it not for other things, I could have greeted my dear Pacific with uncounted thanks, for now the long supplication of my youth was answered; that serene ocean rolled eastwards from me a thousand leagues of blue.

There is, one knows not what sweet mystery about this sea, whose gently awful stirrings seem to speak of some hidden soul beneath; like those fabled undulations of the Ephesian sod over the buried Evangelist St John. And meet it is, that over these sea-pastures, wide-rolling watery prairies and Potters' Fields of all four continents, the waves should rise and fall, and ebb and flow unceasingly; for here, millions of mixed shades and shadows, drowned dreams, somnambulisms, reveries; all that we call lives and souls, lie dreaming, dreaming, still; tossing like slumberers in their beds; the ever-rolling waves but made so by their restlessness.

To any meditative Magian rover, this serene Pacific, once beheld, must ever after be the sea of his adoption. It rolls the midmost waters of the world, the Indian ocean and Atlantic being but its arms. The same waves wash the moles of the new-built Californian towns, but yesterday planted by the recentest race of men, and lave the faded but still gorgeous skirts of Asiatic lands, older than Abraham; while all between float milky-ways of coral isles, and low-lying, endless, unknown Archipelagoes, and impenetrable Japans. Thus this mysterious, divine Pacific zones the world's whole bulk about; makes all coasts one bay to it; seems the tide-beating heart of earth. Lifted by those eternal swells, you needs must own the seductive god, bowing your head to Pan.

But few thoughts of Pan stirred Ahab's brain, as standing like an iron statue at his accustomed place beside the mizen rigging, with one nostril he unthinkingly snuffed the sugary musk from the Bashee isles (in whose sweet woods mild lovers must be walking), and with the other consciously inhaled the salt breath of the new found sea; that sea in which the hated White Whale must even then be swimming. Launched at length upon these almost final waters, and gliding towards the Japanese cruising-ground, the old man's purpose intensified itself. His firm lips met like the lips of a vice; the Delta of his forehead's veins swelled like overladen brooks; in his very sleep, his ringing cry ran through the vaulted hull, 'Stern all! the White Whale spouts thick blood!'

112

THE BLACKSMITH

AVAILING himself of the mild, summer-cool weather that now reigned in these latitudes, and in preparation for the peculiarly active pursuits shortly to be anticipated, Perth, the begrimed, blistered old blacksmith, had not removed his portable forge to the hold again, after concluding his contributory work for Ahab's leg, but still retained it on deck, fast lashed to ringbolts by the foremast; being now almost incessantly invoked by the headsmen, and harpooneers, and bowsmen to do some little job for them; altering, or repairing, or new shaping their various weapons and boat furniture. Often he would be surrounded by an eager circle, all waiting to be served; holding boat-spades, pike-heads, harpoons, and lances, and jealously watching his every sooty movement, as he toiled. Nevertheless, this old man's was a patient hammer wielded by a patient arm. No murmur, no impatience, no petulance did come from him. Silent, slow, and solemn; bowing over still further his chronically broken back, he toiled away, as if toil were life itself, and the heavy beating of his hammer the heavy beating of his heart. And so it was. – Most miserable!

A peculiar walk in this old man, a certain slight but painful appearing yawing in his gait, had at an early period of the voyage excited the curiosity of the mariners. And to the importunity of their persisted questionings he had finally given in; and so it came to pass that every one now knew the shameful story of his wretched fate.

Belated, and not innocently, one bitter winter's midnight, on the road running between two country towns, the blacksmith half-stupidly felt the deadly numbness stealing over him, and sought refuge in a leaning, dilapidated barn. The issue was, the loss of the extremities of both feet. Out of this revelation, part by part, at last came out the four acts of the gladness, and the one long, and as yet uncatastrophied fifth act of the grief of his life's drama.

He was an old man, who at the age of nearly sixty, had postponedly encountered that thing in sorrow's technicals called ruin. He had been an artisan of famed excellence, and with plenty to do; owned a house and garden; embraced a youthful, daughter-like, loving wife, and three blithe, ruddy children; every Sunday went to a cheerful-looking church, planted in a grove. But one night, under cover of darkness, and further concealed in a most cunning disguisement, a desperate burglar slid into his happy home, and robbed them all of everything. And darker yet to tell, the blacksmith himself did ignorantly conduct this burglar into his family's heart. It was the Bottle Conjuror! Upon the opening of that fatal cork, forth flew the fiend, and shrivelled up his home. Now, for prudent, most wise, and economic reasons the blacksmith's shop was in the basement of his dwelling, but with a separate entrance to it; so that always had the young and loving healthy wife listened with no unhappy nervousness, but with vigorous pleasure, to the stout ringing of her young-armed old husband's hammer; whose reverberations, muffled by passing through the floors and walls, came up to her, not unsweetly, in her nursery; and so, to stout Labor's iron lullaby the blacksmith's infants were rocked to slumber.

Oh, woe on woe! Oh, Death, why canst thou not sometimes be timely? Hadst thou taken this old blacksmith to thyself ere his full ruin came upon him, then had the young widow had a delicious grief, and her orphans a truly venerable, legendary sire to dream of in their after years; and all of them a care-killing competency. But Death plucked down some virtuous elder brother, on whose whistling daily toil solely hung the responsibilities of some other family, and left the worse than useless old man standing, till the hideous rot of life should make him easier to harvest.

Why tell the whole? The blows of the basement hammer every day grew more and more between; and each blow every day grew fainter than the last; the wife sat frozen at the window, with tearless eyes, glitteringly gazing into the weeping faces of her children; the bellows fell; the forge choked up with cinders; the house was sold; the mother dived down into the long church-yard grass; her children twice followed her thither; and the houseless, familyless old man staggered off a vagabond in crape; his every woe unreverenced; his grey head a scorn to flaxen curls!

Death seems the only desirable sequel for a career like this; but Death is only a launching into the region of the strange Untried; it is but the first salutation to the possibilities of the immense Remote, the Wild, the Watery, the Unshored; therefore, to the death-longing eyes of such men, who still have left in them some interior compunctions against suicide, does the all-contributed and all-receptive ocean alluringly spread forth his whole plain of unimaginable, taking terrors, and wonderful, new-life adventures; and from the hearts of infinite Pacifics, the thousand mermaids sing to them – 'Come hither, broken-hearted; here is another life without the guilt of intermediate death; here are wonders supernatural, without dying for them. Come hither! bury thyself in a life which, to your now equally abhorred and abhorring, landed world, is more oblivious than death. Come hither! put up *thy* grave-stone, too, within the churchyard, and come hither, till we marry thee!'

Hearkening to these voices, East and West, by early sunrise, and by fall of eve, the blacksmith's soul responded, Aye, I come! And so Perth went a-whaling.

113

THE FORGE

WITH matted beard, and swathed in a bristling shark-skin apron, about mid-day, Perth was standing between his forge and anvil, the latter placed upon an iron-wood log, with one hand holding a pike-head in the coals, and with the other at his forge's lungs, when Captain Ahab came along, carrying in his hand a small rusty-looking leathern bag. While yet a little distance from the forge, moody Ahab paused; till at last, Perth, withdrawing his iron from the fire, began hammering it upon the anvil – the red mass sending off the sparks in thick hovering flights, some of which flew close to Ahab.

'Are these thy Mother Carey's chickens, Perth? they are always flying in thy wake; birds of good omen, too, but not to all; – look here, they burn; but thou – thou liv'st among them without a scorch.'

'Because I am scorched all over, Captain Ahab,' answered Perth, resting for a moment on his hammer; 'I am past scorching; not easily can'st thou scorch a scar.'

'Well, well; no more. Thy shrunk voice sounds too calmly, sanely woful to me. In no Paradise myself, I am impatient of all misery in others that is not mad. Thou should'st go mad, blacksmith; say, why dost thou not go mad? How can'st thou endure without being mad? Do the heavens yet hate thee, that thou can'st not go mad? – What wert thou making there?'

'Welding an old pike-head, sir; there were seams and dents in it.'

'And can'st thou make it all smooth again, blacksmith, after such hard usage as it had?'

'I think so, sir.'

'And I suppose thou can'st smoothe almost any seams and dents; never mind how hard the metal, blacksmith?'

'Aye, sir, I think I can; all seams and dents but one.'

'Look ye here, then,' cried Ahab, passionately advancing, and leaning with both hands on Perth's shoulders; 'look ye here – *here* – can you smoothe out a seam like this, blacksmith,' sweeping one hand across his ribbed brow; 'if thou could'st, blacksmith, glad enough would I lay my head upon thy anvil, and feel thy heaviest hammer between my eyes. Answer! Can'st thou smoothe this seam?'

'Oh! that is the one, sir! Said I not all seams and dents but one?'

'Aye, blacksmith, it is the one; aye, man, it is unsmoothable; for though thou only see'st it here in my flesh, it has worked down into the bone of my skull – *that* is all wrinkles! But, away with child's play; no more gaffs and pikes to-day. Look ye here!' jingling the leathern bag, as if it were full of gold coins. 'I, too, want a harpoon made; one that a thousand yoke of fiends could not part, Perth; something that will stick in a whale like his own fin-bone. There's the stuff,' flinging the pouch upon the anvil. 'Look ye, blacksmith, these are the gathered nail-stubbs of the steel shoes of racing horses.'

'Horse-shoe stubbs, sir? Why, Captain Ahab, thou hast here, then, the best and stubbornest stuff we blacksmiths ever work.'

'I know it, old man; these stubbs will weld together like glue from the melted bones of murderers. Quick! forge me the harpoon. And forge me first, twelve rods for its shank; then wind, and twist, and hammer these twelve together like the yarns and strands of a tow-line. Quick! I'll blow the fire.'

When at last the twelve rods were made, Ahab tried them, one by one, by spiralling them, with his own hand, round a long, heavy iron bolt. 'A flaw!' rejecting the last one. 'Work that over again, Perth.'

This done, Perth was about to begin welding the twelve into one, when Ahab stayed his hand, and said he would weld his own iron. As, then, with regular, gasping hems, he hammered on the anvil, Perth passing to him the glowing rods, one after the other, and the hard pressed forge shooting up its intense straight flame, the Parsee passed silently, and bowing over his head towards the fire, seemed invoking some curse or some blessing on the toil. But, as Ahab looked up, he slid aside.

'What's that bunch of lucifers dodging about there for?' muttered Stubb, looking on from the forecastle. 'That Parsee smells fire like a fusee; and smells of it himself, like a hot musket's powder-pan.'

At last the shank, in one complete rod, received its final heat; and as Perth, to temper it, plunged it all hissing into the cask of water near by, the scalding steam shot up into Ahab's bent face.

'Would'st thou brand me, Perth?' wincing for a moment with the pain; 'have I been but forging my own branding-iron, then?'

'Pray God, not that; yet I fear something, Captain Ahab. Is not this harpoon for the White Whale?'

'For the white fiend! But now for the barbs; thou must make them thyself, man. Here are my razors – the best of steel; here, and make the barbs sharp as the needle-sleet of the Icy Sea.'

For a moment, the old blacksmith eyed the razors as though he would fain not use them.

'Take them, man, I have no need for them; for I now neither shave, sup, nor pray till—but here – to work!'

Fashioned at last into an arrowy shape, and welded by Perth to the shank, the steel soon pointed the end of the iron; and as the blacksmith was about giving the barbs their final heat, prior to tempering them, he cried to Ahab to place the water-cask near.

'No, no – no water for that; I want it of the true death-temper. Ahoy, there! Tashtego, Queequeg, Daggoo! What say ye, pagans! Will ye give me as much blood as will cover this barb?' holding it high up. A cluster of dark nods replied, Yes. Three punctures were made in the heathen flesh, and the White Whale's barbs were then tempered.

'Ego non baptizo te in nomine patris, sed in nomine diaboli!' deliriously howled Ahab, as the malignant iron scorchingly devoured the baptismal blood.

Now, mustering the spare poles from below, and selecting one of hickory, with the bark still investing it, Ahab fitted the end to the socket of the iron. A coil of new tow-line was then unwound, and some fathoms of it taken to the windlass, and stretched to a great tension. Pressing his foot upon it, till the rope hummed like a harp-string, then eagerly bending over it, and seeing no strandings, Ahab exclaimed, 'Good! and now for the seizings.'

At one extremity the rope was unstranded, and the separate spread yarns were all braided and woven round the socket of the harpoon; the pole was then driven hard up into the socket; from the lower end the rope was traced half way along the pole's length, and firmly secured so, with intertwistings of twine. This done, pole, iron, and rope – like the Three Fates – remained inseparable, and Ahab moodily stalked away with the weapon; the sound of his ivory leg, and the sound of the hickory pole, both hollowly ringing along every plank. But ere he entered his cabin, a light, unnatural, half-bantering, yet most piteous sound was heard.

Oh, Pip! thy wretched laugh, thy idle but unresting eye; all thy strange mummeries not unmeaningly blended with the black tragedy of the melancholy ship, and mocked it!

114

THE GILDER

PENETRATING further and further into the heart of the Japanese cruising ground, the Pequod was soon all astir in the fishery. Often, in mild, pleasant weather, for twelve, fifteen, eighteen, and twenty hours on the stretch, they were engaged in the boats, steadily pulling, or sailing, or paddling after the whales, or for an interlude of sixty or seventy minutes calmly awaiting their uprising; though with but small success for their pains.

At such times, under an abated sun; afloat all day upon smooth, slow heaving swells; seated in his boat, light as a birch canoe; and so sociably mixing with the soft waves themselves, that like hearth-stone cats they purr against the gunwale; these are the times of dreamy quietude, when beholding the tranquil beauty and brilliancy of the ocean's skin, one forgets the tiger heart that pants beneath it; and would not willingly remember, that this velvet paw but conceals a remorseless fang.

These are the times, when in his whale-boat the rover softly feels a certain filial, confident, land-like feeling towards the sea; that he regards it as so much flowery earth; and the distant ship revealing only the tops of her masts, seems struggling forward, not through high rolling waves, but through the tall grass of a rolling prairie: as when the western emigrants' horses only show their erected ears, while their hidden bodies widely wade through the amazing verdure.

The long-drawn virgin vales; the mild blue hill-sides; as over these there steals the hush, the hum; you almost swear that play-wearied children lie sleeping in these solitudes, in some glad May-time, when the flowers of the woods are plucked. And all this mixes with your most mystic mood; so that fact and fancy, half-way meeting, interpenetrate, and form one seamless whole.

Nor did such soothing scenes, however temporary, fail of at least as temporary an effect on Ahab. But if these secret golden keys did seem to open in him his own secret golden treasuries, yet did his breath upon them prove but tarnishing.

Oh, grassy glades! oh, ever vernal endless landscapes in the soul; in ye, – though long parched by the dead drought of the earthy life, – in ye, men yet may roll, like young horses in new morning clover; and for some few fleeting moments, feel the cool dew of the life immortal on them. Would to God these blessed calms would last. But the mingled, mingling threads of life are woven by warp and woof: calms crossed by storms, a storm for every calm. There is no steady unretracing progress in this life; we do not advance through fixed gradations, and at the last one pause: – through infancy's unconscious spell, boyhood's thoughtless faith, adolescence' doubt (the common doom), then scepticism, then disbelief, resting at last in manhood's pondering repose of If. But once gone through, we trace the round again; and are infants, boys, and men, and Ifs eternally. Where lies the final harbor, whence we unmoor no more? In what rapt ether sails the world, of which the weariest will never weary? Where is the foundling's father hidden? Our souls are like those orphans whose unwedded mothers die in bearing them: the secret of our paternity lies in their grave, and we must there to learn it.

And that same day, too, gazing far down from his boat's side into that same golden sea, Starbuck lowly murmured: –

'Loveliness unfathomable, as ever lover saw in his young bride's eye! – Tell me not of thy teeth-tiered sharks, and thy kidnapping cannibal ways. Let faith oust fact; let fancy oust memory; I look deep down and do believe.'

And Stubb, fish-like, with sparkling scales, leaped up in that same golden light: –

'I am Stubb, and Stubb has his history; but here Stubb takes oaths that he has always been jolly!'

115

THE PEQUOD MEETS THE BACHELOR

AND jolly enough were the sights and the sounds that came bearing down before the wind, some few weeks after Ahab's harpoon had been welded.

It was a Nantucket ship, the Bachelor, which had just wedged in her last cask of oil, and bolted down her bursting hatches; and now, in glad holiday apparel, was joyously, though somewhat vain-gloriously, sailing round among the widely-separated ships on the ground, previous to pointing her prow for home.

The three men at her mast-head wore long streamers of narrow red bunting at their hats; from the stern, a whale-boat was suspended, bottom down; and hanging captive from the bowsprit was seen the long lower jaw of the last whale they had slain. Signals, ensigns, and jacks of all colors were flying from her rigging, on every side. Sideways lashed in each of her three basketed tops were two barrels of sperm; above which, in her top-mast cross-trees, you saw slender breakers of the same precious fluid; and nailed to her main truck was a brazen lamp.

As was afterwards learned, the Bachelor had met with the most surprising success; all the more wonderful, for that while cruising in the same seas numerous other vessels had gone entire months without securing a single fish. Not only had barrels of beef and bread been given away to make room for the far more valuable sperm, but additional supplemental casks had been bartered for, from the ships she had met; and these were stowed along the deck, and in the captain's and officer's state-rooms. Even the cabin table itself had been knocked into kindling-wood; and the cabin mess dined off the broad head of an oil-butt, lashed down to the floor for a centrepiece. In the forecastle, the sailors had actually caulked and pitched their chests, and filled them; it was humorously added, that the cook had clapped a head on his largest boiler, and filled it; that the steward had plugged his spare coffee-pot and filled it; that the harpooneers had headed the sockets of their irons and filled them; that indeed everything was filled with sperm, except the captain's pantaloons pockets, and those he reserved to thrust his hands into, in self-complacent testimony of his entire satisfaction.

As this glad ship of good luck bore down upon the moody Pequod, the barbarian sound of enormous drums came from her forecastle; and drawing still nearer, a crowd of her men were seen standing round her huge try-pots, which, covered with the parchment-like *poke* or stomach skin of the black fish, gave forth a loud roar to every stroke of the clenched hands of the crew. On the quarter-deck, the mates and harpooneers were dancing with the olive-hued girls who had eloped with them from the Polynesian Isles; while suspended in an ornamented boat, firmly secured aloft between the foremast and mainmast, three Long Island negroes, with glittering fiddle-bows of whale ivory, were presiding over the hilarious jig. Meanwhile, others of the ship's company were tumultuously busy at the masonry of the try-works, from which the huge pots had been removed. You would have almost thought they were pulling down the cursed Bastile, such wild cries they raised, as the now useless brick and mortar were being hurled into the sea.

Lord and master over all this scene, the captain stood erect on the ship's elevated quarter-deck, so that the whole rejoicing drama was full before him, and seemed merely contrived for his own individual diversion.

And Ahab, he too was standing on his quarter-deck, shaggy and black, with a stubborn gloom; and as the two ships crossed each other's wakes – one all jubilations for things passed, the other all forebodings as to things to come – their two captains in themselves impersonated the whole striking contrast of the scene.

'Come aboard, come aboard!' cried the gay Bachelor's commander, lifting a glass and a bottle in the air.

'Hast seen the White Whale?' gritted Ahab in reply.

'No; only heard of him; but don't believe in him at all,' said the other good-humoredly. 'Come aboard!'

'Thou art too damned jolly. Sail on. Hast lost any men?'

'Not enough to speak of – two islanders, that's all; – but come aboard, old hearty, come along. I'll soon take that black from your brow. Come along, will ye (merry's the play); a full ship and homeward-bound.'

'How wondrous familiar is a fool!' muttered Ahab; then aloud, 'Thou art a full ship and homeward bound, thou sayst; well, then, call me an empty ship, and outward-bound. So go thy ways, and I will mine. Forward there! Set all sail, and keep her to the wind!'

And thus, while the one ship went cheerily before the breeze, the other stubbornly fought against it; and so the two vessels parted; the crew of the Pequod looking with grave, lingering glances towards the receding Bachelor; but the Bachelor's men never heeding their gaze for the lively revelry they were in. And as Ahab, leaning over the taffrail, eyed the homeward-bound craft, he took from his pocket a small vial of sand, and then looking from the ship to the vial, seemed thereby bringing two remote associations together, for that vial was filled with Nantucket soundings.

116

THE DYING WHALE

Not seldom in this life, when, on the right side, fortune's favorites sail close by us, we, though all adroop before, catch somewhat of the rushing breeze, and joyfully feel our bagging sails fill out. So seemed it with the Pequod. For next day after encountering the gay Bachelor, whales were seen and four were slain; and one of them by Ahab.

It was far down the afternoon; and when all the spearings

of the crimson fight were done: and floating in the lovely sunset sea and sky, sun and whale both stilly died together; then, such a sweetness and such plaintiveness, such inwreathing orisons curled up in that rosy air, that it almost seemed as if far over from the deep green convent valleys of the Manilla isles, the Spanish land-breeze, wantonly turned sailor, had gone to sea, freighted with these vesper hymns.

Soothed again, but only soothed to deeper gloom, Ahab, who had sterned off from the whale, sat intently watching his final wanings from the now tranquil boat. For that strange spectacle observable in all sperm whales dying – the turning sunwards of the head, and so expiring – that strange spectacle, beheld of such a placid evening, somehow to Ahab conveyed a wondrousness unknown before.

'He turns and turns him to it, – how slowly, but how steadfastly, his homage-rendering and invoking brow, with his last dying motions. He too worships fire; most faithful, broad, baronial vassal of the sun! – Oh that these too-favoring eyes should see these too-favoring sights. Look! here, far water-locked; beyond all hum of human weal or woe; in these most candid and impartial seas; where to traditions no rocks furnish tablets; where for long Chinese ages, the billows have still rolled on speechless and unspoken to, as stars that shine upon the Niger's unknown source; here, too, life dies sunwards full of faith; but see! no sooner dead, than death whirls round the corpse, and it heads some other way. –

'Oh, thou dark Hindoo half of nature, who of drowned bones hast builded thy separate throne somewhere in the heart of these unverdured seas; thou art an infidel, thou queen, and too truly speakest to me in the wide-slaughtering Typhoon, and the hushed burial of its after calm. Nor has this thy whale sunwards turned his dying head, and then gone round again, without a lesson to me.

'Oh, trebly hooped and welded hip of power! Oh, high aspiring, rainbowed jet! – that one striveth, this one jetteth all in vain! In vain, oh whale, dost thou seek intercedings with yon all-quickening sun, that only calls forth life, but gives it not again. Yet dost thou, darker half, rock me with a prouder, if a darker faith. All thy unnamable imminglings float beneath me here; I am buoyed by breaths of once living things, exhaled as air, but water now.

'Then hail, for ever hail, O sea, in whose eternal tossings the wild fowl finds his only rest. Born of earth, yet suckled by the sea; though hill and valley mothered me, ye billows are my foster-brothers!'

117

THE WHALE WATCH

THE four whales slain that evening had died wide apart; one, far to windward; one, less distant, to leeward; one ahead; one astern. These last three were brought alongside ere nightfall; but the windward one could not be reached till morning; and the boat that had killed it lay by its side all night; and that boat was Ahab's.

The waif-pole was thrust upright into the dead whale's spout-hole; and the lantern hanging from its top, cast a troubled flickering glare upon the black, glossy back, and far out upon the midnight waves, which gently chafed the whale's broad flank, like soft surf upon a beach.

Ahab and all his boat's crew seemed asleep but the Parsee; who crouching in the bow, sat watching the sharks, that spectrally played round the whale, and tapped the light cedar planks with their tails. A sound like the moaning in squadrons over Asphaltites of unforgiven ghosts of Gomorrah, ran shuddering through the air.

Started from his slumbers, Ahab, face to face, saw the Parsee; and hooped round by the gloom of the night they seemed the last men in a flooded world. 'I have dreamed it again,' said he.

'Of the hearses? Have I not said, old man, that neither hearse nor coffin can be thine?'

'And who are hearsed that die on the sea?'

'But I said, old man, that ere thou couldst die on this voyage, two hearses must verily be seen by thee on the sea; the first not made by mortal hands; and the visible wood of the last one must be grown in America.'

'Aye, aye! a strange sight that, Parsee: – a hearse and its plumes floating over the ocean with the waves for the pall-bearers. Ha! Such a sight we shall not soon see.'

'Believe it or not, thou canst not die till it be seen, old man.'

'And what was that saying about thyself?'

'Though it come to the last, I shall still go before thee thy pilot.'

'And when thou are so gone before – if that ever befall – then ere I can follow, thou must still appear to me, to pilot me still? – Was it not so? Well, then, did I believe all ye say, oh my pilot! I have here two pledges that I shall yet slay Moby Dick and survive it.'

'Take another pledge, old man,' said the Parsee, as his eyes lighted up like fire-flies in the gloom – 'Hemp only can kill thee.'

'The gallows, ye mean. – I am immortal then, on land and on sea,' cried Ahab with a laugh of derision; – 'Immortal on land and on sea!'

Both were silent again, as one man. The grey dawn came on, and the slumbering crew arose from the boat's bottom, and ere noon the dead whale was brought to the ship.

118

THE QUADRANT

THE season for the Line at length drew near; and every day when Ahab, coming from his cabin, cast his eyes aloft, the vigilant helmsman would ostentatiously handle his spokes, and the eager mariners quickly run to the braces, and would stand there with all their eyes centrally fixed on the nailed doubloon; impatient for the order to point the ship's prow for the equator. In good time the order came. It was hard upon high noon; and Ahab, seated in the bows of his high-hoisted boat, was about taking his wonted daily observation of the sun to determine his latitude.

Now, in that Japanese sea, the days in summer are as freshets of effulgences. That unblinkingly vivid Japanese sun seems the blazing focus of the glassy ocean's immeasurable burning-glass. The sky looks lacquered; clouds there are none; the horizon floats; and this nakedness of unrelieved radiance is as the insufferable splendors of God's throne. Well that Ahab's quadrant was furnished with colored glasses, through which to take sight of that solar fire. So, swinging his seated form to the roll of the ship, and with his astrological-looking instrument placed to his eye, he remained in that posture for some moments to catch the precise instant when the sun should gain its precise meridian. Meantime while his whole attention was absorbed, the Parsee was kneeling beneath him on the ship's deck, and with face thrown up like Ahab's, was eyeing the same sun with him; only the lids of his eyes half hooded their orbs, and his wild face was subdued to an unearthly passionlessness. At length the desired observation was taken; and with his pencil upon his ivory leg, Ahab soon calculated what his latitude must be at that precise instant. Then falling into a moment's revery, he again looked up towards the sun and murmured to himself: 'Thou sea-mark! thou high and mighty Pilot! thou tellest me truly where I *am* – but canst thou cast the least hint where I *shall* be? Or canst thou tell where some other thing besides me is this moment living? Where is Moby Dick? This instant thou must be eyeing him. These eyes of mine look into the very eye that is even now beholding him; aye, and into the eye that is even now equally beholding the objects on the unknown, thither side of thee, thou sun!'

Then gazing at his quadrant, and handling, one after the other, its numerous cabalistical contrivances, he pondered again, and muttered: 'Foolish toy! babies' plaything of haughty Admirals, and Commodores, and Captains; the world brags of thee, of thy cunning and might; but what after all canst thou do, but tell the poor, pitiful point, where thou thyself happenest to be on this wide planet, and the hand that holds thee: no! not one jot more! Thou canst not tell where one drop of water or one grain of sand will be to-morrow noon; and yet with thy impotence thou insultest the sun! Science! Curse thee, thou vain toy; and cursed be all the things that cast man's eyes aloft to that heaven, whose live vividness but scorches him, as these old eyes are even now scorched with thy light, O sun! Level by nature to this earth's horizon are the glances of man's eyes; not shot from the crown of his head, as if God had meant him to gaze on his firmament. Curse thee, thou quadrant!' dashing it to the deck, 'no longer will I guide my earthly way by thee; the level ship's compass, and the level dead-reckoning, by log and by line; *these* shall conduct me, and show me my place on the sea. Aye,' lighting from the boat to the deck, 'thus I trample on thee, thou paltry thing that feebly pointest on high; thus I split and destroy thee!'

As the frantic old man thus spoke and thus trampled with his live and dead feet, a sneering triumph that seemed meant for Ahab, and a fatalistic despair that seemed meant for himself – these passed over the mute, motionless Parsee's face. Unobserved he rose and glided away; while, awestruck by the aspect of their commander, the seamen clustered together on the forecastle, till Ahab, troubledly pacing the deck, shouted out – 'To the braces! Up helm! – square in!'

In an instant the yards swung round; and as the ship half-wheeled upon her heel, her three firm-seated graceful masts erectly poised upon her long, ribbed hull, seemed as the three Horatii pirouetting on one sufficient steed.

Standing between the knight-heads, Starbuck watched the Pequod's tumultuous way, and Ahab's also, as he went lurching along the deck.

'I have sat before the dense coal fire and watched it all aglow, full of its tormented flaming life; and I have seen it wane at last, down, down, to dumbest dust. Old man of oceans! of all this fiery life of thine, what will at length remain but one little heap of ashes!'

'Aye,' cried Stubb, 'but sea-coal ashes – mind ye that, Mr Starbuck – sea-coal, not your common charcoal. Well, well; I heard Ahab mutter, "Here some one thrusts these cards into these old hands of mine; swears that I must play them, and no others." And damn me, Ahab, but thou actest right; live in the game, and die in it!'

119

THE CANDLES

WARMEST climes but nurse the cruellest fangs: the tiger of Bengal crouches in spiced groves of ceaseless verdure. Skies the most effulgent but basket the deadliest thunders: gorgeous Cuba knows tornadoes that never swept tame northern lands. So, too, it is, that in these resplendent Japanese seas the mariner encounters the direst of all storms, the Typhoon. It will sometimes burst from out that cloudless sky, like an exploding bomb upon a dazed and sleepy town.

Towards evening of that day, the Pequod was torn of her canvas, and bare poled was left to fight a Typhoon which had struck her directly ahead. When darkness came on, sky and sea roared and split with the thunder, and blazed with the lightning, that showed the disabled masts fluttering here and there with the rags which the first fury of the tempest had left for its after sport.

Holding by a shroud, Starbuck was standing on the quarter-deck; at every flash of the lightning glancing aloft, to see what additional disaster might have befallen the intricate hamper there; while Stubb and Flask were directing the men in the higher hoisting and firmer lashing of the boats. But all their pains seemed naught. Though lifted to the very top of the cranes, the windward quarter boat (Ahab's) did not escape. A great rolling sea, dashing high up against the reeling ship's high tetering side, stove in the boat's bottom at the stern, and left it again, all dripping through like a sieve.

'Bad work, bad work! Mr Starbuck,' said Stubb, regarding the wreck, 'but the sea will have its way. Stubb, for one, can't fight it. You see, Mr Starbuck, a wave has such a great long start before it leaps, all round the world it runs, and then comes the spring! But as for me, all the start I have to meet it, is just across the deck here. But never mind; it's all in fun: so the old song says;' — (*sings.*)

Oh! jolly is the gale,
And a joker is the whale,
A' flourishin' his tail, –
Such a funny, sporty, gamy, jesty, joky, hoky-poky lad,
is the Ocean, oh!

The scud all a flyin',
That's his flip only foamin';
When he stirs in the spicin', –
Such a funny, sporty, gamy, jesty, joky, hoky-poky lad,
is the Ocean, oh!

Thunder splits the ships,
But he only smacks his lips,
A tastin' of this flip, –
Such a funny, sporty, gamy, jesty, joky, hoky-poky lad,
is the Ocean, oh!

'Avast Stubb,' cried Starbuck, 'let the Typhoon sing, and strike his harp here in our rigging; but if thou are a brave man thou wilt hold thy peace.'

'But I am not a brave man; never said I was a brave man; I am a coward; and I sing to keep up my spirits. And I tell you what it is, Mr Starbuck, there's no way to stop my singing in this world but to cut my throat. And when that's done, ten to one I sing ye the doxology for a wind-up.'

'Madman! look through my eyes if thou hast none of thine own.'

'What! how can you see better of a dark night than anybody else, never mind how foolish?'

'Here!' cried Starbuck, seizing Stubb by the shoulder, and

pointing his hand towards the weather bow, 'markest thou not that the gale comes from the eastward, the very course Ahab is to run for Moby Dick? the very course he swung to this day noon? now mark his boat there; where is that stove? In the stern-sheets, man; where he is wont to stand – his stand-point is stove, man! Now jump overboard, and sing away, if thou must!'

'I don't half understand ye: what's in the wind!'

'Yes, yes, round the Cape of Good Hope is the shortest way to Nantucket,' soliloquized Starbuck suddenly, heedless of Stubb's question. 'The gale that now hammers at us to stave us, we can turn it into a fair wind that will drive us towards home. Yonder, to windward, all is blackness of doom; but to leeward, homeward – I see it lightens up there; but not with the lightning.'

At that moment in one of the intervals of profound darkness, following the flashes, a voice was heard at his side; and almost at the same instant a volley of thunder peals rolled overhead.

'Who's there?'

'Old Thunder!' said Ahab, groping his way along the bulwarks to his pivot-hole; but suddenly finding his path made plain to him by elbowed lances of fire.

Now, as the lightning rod to a spire on shore is intended to carry off the perilous fluid into the soil; so the kindred rod which at sea some ships carry to each mast, is intended to conduct it into the water. But as this conductor must descend to considerable depth, that its end may avoid all contact with the hull; and as moreover, if kept constantly towing there, it would be liable to many mishaps, besides interfering not a little with some of the rigging, and more or less impeding the vessel's way in the water; because of all this, the lower parts of a ship's lightning-rods are not always overboard; but are generally made in long slender links, so as to be the more readily hauled up into the chains outside, or thrown down into the sea, as occasion may require.

'The rods! the rods!' cried Starbuck to the crew, suddenly admonished to vigilance by the vivid lightning that had just been darting flambeaux, to light Ahab to his post. 'Are they overboard? drop them over, fore and aft. Quick!'

'Avast!' cried Ahab; 'let's have fair play here, though we be the weaker side. Yet I'll contribute to raise rods on the Himmalehs and Andes, that all the world may be secured; but out on privileges! Let them be, sir.'

'Look aloft!' cried Starbuck. 'The corpusants! the corpusants!'

All the yard-arms were tipped with a pallid fire; and touched at each tri-pointed lightning-rod-end with three tapering white flames, each of the three tall masts was silently burning in that sulphurous air, like three gigantic wax tapers before an altar.

'Blast the boat! let it go!' cried Stubb at this instant, as a swashing sea heaved up under his own little craft, so that its gunwale violently jammed his hand, as he was passing a lashing. 'Blast it!' – but slipping backward on the deck, his uplifted eyes caught the flames; and immediately shifting his tone, he cried – 'The corpusants have mercy on us all!'

To sailors, oaths are household words; they will swear in the trance of the calm, and in the teeth of the tempest; they will imprecate curses from the topsail-yard-arms, when most they teter over to a seething sea; but in all my voyagings, seldom have I heard a common oath when God's burning finger has been laid on the ship; when His 'Mene, Mene, Tekel, Upharsin' has been woven into the shrouds and the cordage.

While this pallidness was burning aloft, few words were heard from the enchanted crew; who in one thick cluster stood on the forecastle, all their eyes gleaming in that pale phosphorescence, like a far away constellation of stars. Relieved against the ghostly light, the gigantic jet negro, Daggoo, loomed up to thrice his real stature, and seemed the black cloud from which the thunder had come. The parted mouth of Tashtego revealed his shark-white teeth, which strangely gleamed as if they too had been tipped by corpusants; while lit up by the preternatural light, Queequeg's tattooing burned like Satanic blue flames on his body.

The tableau all waned at last with the pallidness aloft; and once more the Pequod and every soul on her decks were wrapped in a pall. A moment or two passed, when Starbuck, going forward, pushed against some one. It was Stubb. 'What thinkest thou now, man; I heard thy cry; it was not the same in the song.'

'No, no, it wasn't; I said the corpusants have mercy on us all; and I hope they will, still. But do they only have mercy on long faces? – have they no bowels for a laugh? And look ye, Mr Starbuck – but it's too dark to look. Hear me, then: I take that mast-head flame we saw for a sign of good luck; for those masts are rooted in a hold that is going to be chock a' block with sperm-oil, d'ye see; and so, all that sperm will work up into the masts, like sap in a tree. Yes, our three masts will yet be as three spermaceti candles – that's the good promise we saw.'

At that moment Starbuck caught sight of Stubb's face slowly beginning to glimmer into sight. Glancing upwards, he cried: 'See! see!' and once more the high tapering flames were beheld with what seemed redoubled supernaturalness in their pallor.

'The corpusants have mercy on us all,' cried Stubb, again.

At the base of the mainmast, full beneath the doubloon and the flame, the Parsee was kneeling in Ahab's front, but with his head bowed away from him; while near by, from the arched and overhanging rigging, where they had just been engaged securing a spar, a number of the seamen, arrested by the glare, now cohered together, and hung pendulous, like a knot of numbed wasps from a drooping, orchard twig. In various enchanted attitudes, like the standing, or stepping, or running skeletons in Herculaneum, others remained rooted to the deck; but all their eyes upcast.

'Aye, aye, men!' cried Ahab. 'Look up at it; mark it well; the white flame but lights the way to the White Whale!

Hand me those main-mast links there; I would fain feel this pulse, and let mine beat against it; blood against fire! So.'

Then turning – the last link held fast in his left hand, he put his foot upon the Parsee; and with fixed upward eye, and high-flung right arm, he stood erect before the lofty tri-pointed trinity of flames.

'Oh! thou clear spirit of clear fire, whom on these seas I as Persian once did worship, till in the sacramental act so burned by thee, that to this hour I bear the scar; I now know thee, thou clear spirit, and I now know that thy right worship is defiance. To neither love nor reverence wilt thou be kind; and e'en for hate thou canst but kill; and all are killed. No fearless fool now fronts thee. I own thy speechless, placeless power; but to the last gasp of my earthquake life will dispute its unconditional, unintegral mastery in me. In the midst of the personified impersonal, a personality stands here. Though but a point at best; whencesoe'er I came; wheresoe'er I go; yet while I earthly live, the queenly personality lives in me, and feels her royal rights. But war is pain, and hate is woe. Come in thy lowest form of love, and I will kneel and kiss thee; but at thy highest, come as mere supernal power; and though thou launchest navies of full-freighted worlds, there's that in here that still remains indifferent. Oh, thou clear spirit, of thy fire thou madest me, and like a true child of fire, I breathe it back to thee.'

[*Sudden, repeated flashes of lightning; the nine flames leap lengthwise to thrice their previous height; Ahab, with the rest, closes his eyes, his right hand pressed hard upon them.*]

'I own thy speechless, placeless power; said I not so? Nor was it wrung from me; nor do I now drop these links. Thou canst blind; but I can then grope. Thou canst consume; but I can then be ashes. Take the homage of these poor eyes, and shutter-hands. I would not take it. The lightning flashes through my skull; mine eye-balls ache and ache; my whole beaten brain seems as beheaded, and rolling on some stunning ground. Oh, oh! Yet blindfold, yet will I talk to thee. Light though thou be, thou leapest out of darkness;

but I am darkness leaping out of light, leaping out of thee! The javelins cease; open eyes; see, or not? There burn the flames! Oh, thou magnanimous! now I do glory in my genealogy. But thou are but my fiery father; my sweet mother, I know not, Oh, cruel! what hast thou done with her? There lies my puzzle; but thine is greater. Thou knowest not how came ye; hence callest thyself unbegotten; certainly knowest not thy beginning, hence callest thyself unbegun. I know that of me, which thou knowest not of thyself, oh, thou omnipotent. There is some unsuffusing thing beyond thee, thou clear spirit, to whom all thy eternity is but time, all thy creativeness mechanical. Through thee, thy flaming self, my scorched eyes do dimly see it. Oh, thou foundling fire, thou hermit immemorial, thou too hast thy incommunicable riddle, thy unparticipated grief. Here again with haughty agony, I read my sire. Leap! leap up, and lick the sky! I leap with thee; I burn with thee; would fain be welded with thee, defyingly I worship thee!'

'The boat! the boat!' cried Starbuck, 'look at thy boat, old man!'

Ahab's harpoon, the one forged at Perth's fire, remained firmly lashed in its conspicuous crotch, so that it projected beyond his whale-boat's bow; but the sea that had stove its bottom had caused the loose leather sheath to drop off; and from the keen steel barb there now came a levelled flame of pale, forked fire. As the silent harpoon burned there like a serpent's tongue, Starbuck grasped Ahab by the arm – 'God, God is against thee, old man; forbear! 'tis an ill voyage! ill begun, ill continued; let me square the yards, while we may, old man, and make a fair wind of it homewards, to go on a better voyage than this.'

Overhearing Starbuck, the panic-stricken crew instantly ran to the braces – though not a sail was left aloft. For the moment all the aghast mate's thoughts seemed theirs; they raised a half mutinous cry. But dashing the rattling lightning links to the deck, and snatching the burning harpoon, Ahab waved it like a torch among them; swearing to transfix with it the first sailor that but cast loose a rope's end.

Petrified by his aspect, and still more shrinking from the fiery dart that he held, the men fell back in dismay, and Ahab spoke again: –

'All your oaths to hunt the White Whale are as binding as mine; and heart, soul, and body, lungs and life, old Ahab is bound. And that ye may know to what tune this heart beats; look ye here; thus I blow out the last fear!' And with one blast of his breath he extinguished the flame.

As in the hurricane that sweeps the plain, men fly the neighborhood of some lone, gigantic elm, whose very height and strength but render it so much the more unsafe, because so much the more a mark for thunderbolts; so at those last words of Ahab's many of the mariners did run from him in a terror of dismay.

120

THE DECK TOWARDS THE END OF THE FIRST NIGHT WATCH

Ahab standing by the helm. Starbuck approaching him.

'WE must send down the main-top-sail yard, sir. The band is working loose, and the lee lift is half-stranded. Shall I strike it, sir?'

'Strike nothing; lash it. If I had sky-sail poles, I'd sway them up now.'

'Sir? – in God's name! – sir?'

'Well.'

'The anchors are working, sir. Shall I get them inboard?'

'Strike nothing, and stir nothing, but lash everything. The wind rises, but it has not got up to my table-lands yet. Quick, and see to it. – By masts and keels! he takes me for the hunch-backed skipper of some coasting smack. Send down my main-top-sail yard! Ho, gluepots! Loftiest trucks were made for wildest winds, and this brain-truck of mine now sails amid the cloud-scud. Shall I strike that? Oh, none but cowards send down their brain-trucks in tempest time.

What a hooroosh aloft there! I would e'en take it for sublime, did I not know that the colic is a noisy malady. Oh, take medicine, take medicine!'

121

MIDNIGHT – THE FORECASTLE BULWARKS

Stubb and Flask mounted on them, and passing additional lashings over the anchors there hanging.

'No, Stubb; you may pound that knot there as much as you please, but you will never pound into me what you were just now saying. And how long ago is it since you said the very contrary? Didn't you once say that whatever ship Ahab sails in, that ship should pay something extra on its insurance policy, just as though it were loaded with powder barrels aft and boxes of lucifers forward? Stop, now; didn't you say so?'

'Well, suppose I did? What then? I've part changed my flesh since that time, why not my mind? Besides, supposing we *are* loaded with powder barrels aft and lucifers forward; how the devil could the lucifers get afire in this drenching spray here? Why, my little man, you have pretty red hair, but you couldn't get afire now. Shake yourself; you're Aquarius, or the water-bearer, Flask; might fill pitchers at your coat collar. Don't you see, then, that for these extra risks the Marine Insurance companies have extra guarantees? Here are hydrants, Flask. But hark, again, and I'll answer ye the other thing. First take your leg off from the crown of the anchor here, though, so I can pass the rope; now listen. What's the mighty difference between holding a mast's lightning-rod in the storm, and standing close by a mast that hasn't got any lightning-rod at all in a storm? Don't you see, you timber-head, that no harm can come to the holder of the rod, unless the mast is first struck? What are you talking about, then? Not one ship in a hundred carries rods, and Ahab, – aye, man, and all of us, – were in no more danger then, in my poor opinion, than all the crews in ten thousand ships now sailing the seas. Why, you King-Post, you, I suppose you would have every man in the world go about with a small lightning-rod running up the corner of his hat, like a militia officer's skewered feather, and trailing behind like his sash. Why don't ye be sensible, Flask? it's easy to be sensible; why don't ye, then? any man with half an eye can be sensible.'

'I don't know that, Stubb. You sometimes find it rather hard.'

'Yes, when a fellow's soaked through, it's hard to be sensible, that's a fact. And I am about drenched with this spray. Never mind; catch the turn there, and pass it. Seems to me we are lashing down these anchors now as if they were never going to be used again. Tying these two anchors here, Flask, seems like tying a man's hands behind him. And what big generous hands they are, to be sure. These are your iron fists, hey? What a hold they have, too! I wonder, Flask, whether the world is anchored anywhere; if she is, she swings with an uncommon long cable, though. There, hammer that knot down, and we've done. So; next to touching land, lighting on deck is the most satisfactory. I say, just wring out my jacket skirts, will ye? Thank ye. They laugh at long-togs so, Flask; but seems to me, a long tailed coat ought always to be worn in all storms afloat. The tails tapering down that way, serve to carry off the water, d'ye see. Same with cocked hats; the cocks form gable-end eave-troughs, Flask. No more monkey-jackets and tarpaulins for me; I must mount a swallow-tail, and drive down a beaver; so. Halloa! whew! there goes my tarpaulin overboard; Lord, Lord, that the winds that come from heaven should be so unmannerly! This is a nasty night, lad.'

122

MIDNIGHT ALOFT – THUNDER AND LIGHTNING

The Main-top-sail yard. – Tashtego passing new lashings around it.

'UM, um, um. Stop that thunder! Plenty too much thunder up here. What's the use of thunder? Um, um, um. We don't want thunder; we want rum; give us a glass of rum. Um, um, um!'

123

THE MUSKET

DURING the most violent shocks of the Typhoon, the man at the Pequod's jaw-bone tiller had several times been reelingly hurled to the deck by its spasmodic motions, even though preventer tackles had been attached to it – for they were slack – because some play to the tiller was indispensable.

In a severe gale like this, while the ship is but a tossed shuttlecock to the blast, it is by no means uncommon to see the needles in the compasses, at intervals, go round and round. It was thus with the Pequod's; at almost every shock the helmsman had not failed to notice the whirling velocity with which they revolved upon the cards; it is a sight that hardly any one can behold without some sort of unwonted emotion.

Some hours after midnight, the Typhoon abated so much, that through the strenuous exertions of Starbuck and Stubb – one engaged forward and the other aft – the shivered remnants of the jib and fore and main-top-sails were cut adrift from the spars, and went eddying away to leeward, like the feathers of an albatross, which sometimes are cast to the winds when that storm-tossed bird is on the wing.

The three corresponding new sails were now bent and reefed, and a storm-trysail was set further aft; so that the ship soon went through the water with some precision again; and the course – for the present, East-south-east – which he was to steer, if practicable, was once more given to the helmsman. For during the violence of the gale, he had only steered according to its vicissitudes. But as he was now bringing the ship as near her course as possible, watching the compass meanwhile, lo! a good sign! the wind seemed coming round astern; aye, the foul breeze became fair!

Instantly the yards were squared, to the lively song of '*Ho! the fair wind! oh-he-yo, cheerly, men!*' the crew singing for joy, that so promising an event should so soon have falsified the evil portents preceding it.

In compliance with the standing order of his commander – to report immediately, and at any one of the twenty-four hours any decided change in the affairs of the deck, – Starbuck had no sooner trimmed the yards to the breeze – however reluctantly and gloomily, – than he mechanically went below to apprise Captain Ahab of the circumstance.

Ere knocking at his state-room, he involuntarily paused before it a moment. The cabin lamp – taking long swings this way and that – was burning fitfully, and casting fitful shadows upon the old man's bolted door, – a thin one, with fixed blinds inserted, in place of upper panels. The isolated subterraneousness of the cabin made a certain humming silence to reign there, though it was hooped round by all the roar of the elements. The loaded muskets in the rack were shiningly revealed, as they stood upright against the forward bulkhead. Starbuck was an honest, upright man; but out of Starbuck's heart, at that instant when he saw the muskets, there strangely evolved an evil thought; but so blent with its neutral or good accompaniments that for the instant he hardly knew it for itself.

'He would have shot me once,' he murmured, 'yes, there's the very musket that he pointed at me; – that one with the studded stock; let me touch it – lift it. Strange, that I, who have handled so many deadly lances, strange, that I should shake so now. Loaded? I must see. Aye, aye; and powder in the pan; – that's not good. Best spill it? – wait. I'll cure myself of this. I'll hold the musket boldly while I think. – I come to report a fair wind to him. But how fair? Fair for death and doom, – *that*'s fair for Moby Dick. It's a fair wind that's only fair for that accursed fish. – The very tube he pointed at me! – the very one; *this* one – I hold it here; he would have killed me with the very thing I handle now. – Aye and he would fain kill all his crew. Does he not say he will not strike his spars to any gale? Has he not dashed his heavenly quadrant? and in these same perilous seas, gropes he not his way by mere dead reckoning of the error-abounding log? and in this very Typhoon, did he not swear that he would have no lightning-rods? But shall this crazed old man be tamely suffered to drag a whole ship's company down to doom with him? – Yes, it would make him the wilful murderer of thirty men and more, if this ship come to any deadly harm; and come to deadly harm, my soul swears this ship will, if Ahab have his way. If, then, he were this instant – put aside, that crime would not be his. Ha! is he muttering in his sleep? Yes, just there, – in there, he's sleeping. Sleeping? aye, but still alive, and soon awake again. I can't withstand thee, then, old man. Not reasoning; not remonstrance; not entreaty wilt thou hearken to; all this thou scornest. Flat obedience to thy own flat commands, this is all thou breathest. Aye, and say'st the men have vow'd thy vow; say'st all of us are Ahabs. Great God forbid! – But is there no other way? no lawful way? – Make him a prisoner to be taken home? What! hope to wrest this old man's living power from his own living hands? Only a fool would try it. Say he were pinioned even; knotted all over with ropes and hawsers; chained down to ring-bolts on this cabin floor; he would be more hideous than a caged tiger, then. I could not endure the sight; could not possibly fly his howlings; all comfort, sleep itself, inestimable reason would leave me on the long intolerable voyage. What, then, remains? The land is hundreds of leagues away, and locked Japan the nearest. I stand alone here upon an open sea, with two oceans and a whole continent between me and law. – Aye, aye, 'tis so. – Is heaven a murderer when its lightning strikes a would-be murderer in his bed, tindering sheets and skin together? – And would I be a murderer, then, if —' and slowly, stealthily, and half sideways looking, he placed the loaded musket's end against the door.

'On this level, Ahab's hammock swings within; his head this way. A touch, and Starbuck may survive to hug his wife and child again. – Oh Mary! Mary! – boy! boy! boy! – But if I wake thee not to death, old man, who can tell to what unsounded deeps Starbuck's body this day week may sink, with all the crew! Great God, where art thou? Shall I? shall I? — The wind has gone down and shifted, sir; the fore and main topsails are reefed and set; she heads her course.'

'Stern all! Oh Moby Dick, I clutch thy heart at last!'

Such were the sounds that now came hurtling from out the old man's tormented sleep, as if Starbuck's voice had caused the long dumb dream to speak.

The yet levelled musket shook like a drunkard's arm against the panel; Starbuck seemed wrestling with an angel; but turning from the door, he placed the death-tube in its rack, and left the place.

'He's too sound asleep, Mr Stubb; go thou down, and wake him, and tell him. I must see to the deck here. Thou know'st what to say.'

124

THE NEEDLE

NEXT morning the not-yet-subsided sea rolled in long slow billows of mighty bulk, and striving in the Pequod's gurgling track, pushed her on like giants' palms outspread. The strong, unstaggering breeze abounded so, that sky and air seemed vast outbellying sails; the whole world boomed before the wind. Muffled in the full morning light, the invisible sun was only known by the spread intensity of his place; where his bayonet rays moved on in stacks. Emblazonings, as of crowned Babylonian kings and queens, reigned over everything. The sea was as a crucible of molten gold, that bubblingly leaps with light and heat.

Long maintaining an enchanted silence, Ahab stood apart; and every time the tetering ship loweringly pitched down her bowsprit, he turned to eye the bright sun's rays produced ahead; and when she profoundly settled by the stern, he turned behind, and saw the sun's rearward place, and how the same yellow rays were blending with his undeviating wake.

'Ha, ha, my ship! thou mightest well be taken now for the sea-chariot of the sun. Ho, ho! all ye nations before my prow, I bring the sun to ye! Yoke on the further billows; hallo! a tandem, I drive the sea!'

But suddenly reined back by some counter thought, he hurried towards the helm, huskily demanding how the ship was heading.

'East-sou-east, sir,' said the frightened steersman.

'Thou liest!' smiting him with his clenched fist. 'Heading East at this hour in the morning, and the sun astern?'

Upon this every soul was confounded; for the phenomenon just then observed by Ahab had unaccountably escaped every one else; but its very blinding palpableness must have been the cause.

Thrusting his head half way into the binnacle, Ahab caught one glimpse of the compasses; his uplifted arm slowly fell; for a moment he almost seemed to stagger. Standing behind him Starbuck looked, and lo! the two compasses pointed East, and the Pequod was as infallibly going West.

But ere the first wild alarm could get out abroad among the crew, the old man with a rigid laugh exclaimed, 'I have it! It has happened before. Mr Starbuck, last night's thunder turned our compasses – that's all. Thou hast before now heard of such a thing, I take it.'

'Aye; but never before has it happened to me, sir,' said the pale mate, gloomily.

Here, it must needs be said, that accidents like this have in more than one case occurred to ships in violent storms. The magnetic energy, as developed in the mariner's needle, is, as all know, essentially one with the electricity beheld in heaven; hence it is not to be much marvelled at, that such things should be. In instances where the lightning has actually struck the vessel, so as to smite down some of the spars and rigging, the effect upon the needle has at times been still more fatal; all its loadstone virtue being annihilated, so that the before magnetic steel was of no more use than an old wife's knitting needle. But in either case, the needle never again, of itself, recovers the original virtue thus marred or lost; and if the binnacle compasses be affected, the same fate reaches all the others that may be in the ship; even were the lowermost one inserted into the kelson.

Deliberately standing before the binnacle, and eyeing the transpointed compasses, the old man, with the sharp of his extended hand, now took the precise bearing of the sun, and satisfied that the needles were exactly inverted, shouted out his orders for the ship's course to be changed accordingly. The yards were braced hard up; and once more the Pequod thrust her undaunted bows into the opposing wind, for the supposed fair one had only been juggling her.

Meanwhile, whatever were his own secret thoughts, Starbuck said nothing, but quietly he issued all requisite orders; while Stubb and Flask – who in some small degree seemed then to be sharing his feelings – likewise unmurmuringly acquiesced. As for the men, though some of them lowly rumbled, their fear of Ahab was greater than their fear of Fate. But as ever before, the pagan harpooneers remained almost wholly unimpressed; or if impressed, it was only with a certain magnetism shot into their congenial hearts from inflexible Ahab's.

For a space the old man walked the deck in rolling reveries. But chancing to slip with his ivory heel, he saw the crushed copper sight-tubes of the quadrant he had the day before dashed to the deck.

'Thou poor, proud heaven-gazer and sun's pilot! yesterday I wrecked thee, and to-day the compasses would feign have wrecked me. So, so. But Ahab is lord over the level loadstone yet. Mr Starbuck – a lance without the pole; a top-maul, and the smallest of the sail-maker's needles. Quick!'

Accessory, perhaps, to the impulse dictating the thing he was now about to do, were certain prudential motives, whose object might have been to revive the spirits of his crew by a stroke of his subtle skill, in a matter so wondrous as that of the inverted compasses. Besides, the old man well knew that to steer by transpointed needles, though clumsily practicable, was not a thing to be passed over by superstitious sailors, without some shudderings and evil portents.

'Men,' said he, steadily turning upon the crew, as the mate handed him the things he had demanded, 'my men, the thunder turned old Ahab's needles; but out of this bit of steel Ahab can make one of his own, that will point as true as any.'

Abashed glances of servile wonder were exchanged by the sailors, as this was said; and with fascinated eyes they awaited whatever magic might follow. But Starbuck looked away.

With a blow from the top-maul Ahab knocked off the steel head of the lance, and then handing to the mate the long iron rod remaining, bade him hold it upright, without its touching the deck. Then, with the maul, after repeatedly smiting the upper end of this iron rod, he placed the blunted needle endwise on the top of it, and less strongly hammered that, several times, the mate still holding the rod as before. Then going through some small strange motions with it – whether indispensable to the magnetizing of the steel, or merely intended to augment the awe of the crew, is uncertain – he called for linen thread; and moving to the binnacle, slipped out the two reversed needles there, and horizontally suspended the sail-needle by its middle, over one of the compass-cards. At first, the steel went round and round, quivering and vibrating at either end; but at last it settled to its place, when Ahab, who had been intently watching for this result, stepped frankly back from the binnacle, and pointing his stretched arm towards it, exclaimed, – 'Look ye, for yourselves, if Ahab be not lord of the level loadstone! The sun is East, and that compass swears it!'

One after another they peered in, for nothing but their own eyes could persuade such ignorance as theirs, and one after another they slunk away.

In his fiery eyes of scorn and triumph, you then saw Ahab in all his fatal pride.

125

THE LOG AND LINE

WHILE now the fated Pequod had been so long afloat this voyage, the log and line had but very seldom been in use. Owing to a confident reliance upon other means of determining the vessel's place, some merchantmen, and many whalemen, especially when cruising, wholly neglect to heave the log; though at the same time, and frequently more for form's sake than anything else, regularly putting down upon the customary slate the course steered by the ship, as well as the presumed average rate of progression every hour. It had been thus with the Pequod. The wooden reel and angular log attached hung, long untouched, just beneath the railing of the after bulwarks. Rains and spray had damped it; sun and wind had warped it; all the elements had combined to rot a thing that hung so idly. But heedless of all this, his mood seized Ahab, as he happened to glance upon the reel, not many hours after the magnet scene, and he remembered how his quadrant was no more, and recalled his frantic oath about the level log and line. The ship was sailing plungingly; astern the billows rolled in riots.

'Forward, there! Heave the log!'

Two seamen came. The golden-hued Tahitian and the grizzly Manxman. 'Take the reel, one of ye, I'll heave.'

They went towards the extreme stern, on the ship's lee side, where the deck, with the oblique energy of the wind, was now almost dipping into the creamy, sidelong-rushing sea.

The Manxman took the reel, and holding it high up, by the projecting handle-ends of the spindle, round which the spool of line revolved, so stood with the angular log hanging downwards, till Ahab advanced to him.

Ahab stood before him, and was lightly unwinding some thirty or forty turns to form a preliminary hand-coil to toss overboard, when the old Manxman, who was intently eyeing both him and the line, made bold to speak.

'Sir, I mistrust it; this line looks far gone, long heat and wet have spoiled it.'

''Twill hold, old gentleman. Long heat and wet, have they spoiled thee? Thou seem'st to hold. Or, truer perhaps, life holds thee; not thou it.'

'I hold the spool, sir. But just as my captain says. With these grey hairs of mine 'tis not worth while disputing, 'specially with a superior, who'll ne'er confess.'

'What's that? There now's a patched professor in Queen Nature's granite-founded College; but methinks he's too subservient. Where wert thou born?'

'In the little rocky Isle of Man, sir.'

'Excellent! Thou'st hit the world by that.'

'I know not, sir, but I was born there.'

'In the Isle of Man, hey? Well, the other way, it's good. Here's a man from Man; a man born in once independent Man, and now unmanned of Man; which is sucked in – by what? Up with the reel! The dead, blind wall butts all inquiring heads at last. Up with it! So.'

The log was heaved. The loose coils rapidly straightened out in a long dragging line astern, and then, instantly, the reel began to whirl. In turn, jerkingly raised and lowered by the rolling billows, the towing resistance of the log caused the old reelman to stagger strangely.

'Hold hard!'

Snap! the overstrained line sagged down in one long festoon; the tugging log was gone.

'I crush the quadrant, the thunder turns the needles, and now the mad sea parts the log-line. But Ahab can mend all. Haul in here, Tahitian; reel up, Manxman. And look ye, let the carpenter make another log, and mend thou the line. See to it.'

'There he goes now; to him nothing's happened; but to me, the skewer seems loosening out of the middle of the world. Haul in, haul in, Tahitian! These lines run whole, and whirling out: come in broken, and dragging slow. Ha, Pip? come to help; eh, Pip?'

'Pip? whom call ye Pip? Pip jumped from the whale-boat. Pip's missing. Let's see now if ye haven't fished him up here, fisherman. It drags hard; I guess he's holding on. Jerk him, Tahiti! Jerk him off; we haul in no cowards here. Ho! there's his arm just breaking water. A hatchet! a hatchet! cut it off – we haul in no cowards here. Captain Ahab! sir, sir! here's Pip, trying to get on board again.'

'Peace, thou crazy loon,' cried the Manxman, seizing him by the arm. 'Away from the quarter-deck!'

'The greater idiot ever scolds the lesser,' muttered Ahab, advancing. 'Hands off from that holiness! Where sayest thou Pip was, boy?'

'Astern there, sir, astern! Lo, lo!'

'And who art thou, boy? I see not my reflection in the vacant pupils of thy eyes. Oh God! that man should be a thing for immortal souls to sieve through! Who art thou, boy?'

'Bell-boy, sir; ship's-crier, ding, dong, ding! Pip! Pip! Pip! One hundred pounds of clay reward for Pip; five feet high – looks cowardly – quickest known by that! Ding, dong, ding! Who's seen Pip the coward?'

'There can be no hearts above the snow-line. Oh, ye frozen heavens! look down here. Ye did beget this luckless child, and have abandoned him, ye creative libertines. Here, boy; Ahab's cabin shall be Pip's home henceforth, while Ahab lives. Thou touchest my inmost centre, boy; thou art tied to me by cords woven of my heart-strings. Come, let's down.'

'What's this? here's velvet shark-skin,' intently gazing at Ahab's hand, and feeling it. 'Ah, now, had poor Pip but felt so kind a thing as this, perhaps he had ne'er been lost! This seems to me, sir, as a man-rope; something that weak souls may hold by. Oh, sir, let old Perth now come and rivet these two hands together; the black one with the white, for I will not let this go.'

'Oh, boy, nor will I thee, unless I should thereby drag thee to worse horrors than are here. Come, then, to my cabin. Lo! ye believers in gods all goodness, and in man all ill, lo you! see the omniscient gods oblivious of suffering man; and man, though idiotic, and knowing not what he does, yet full of the sweet things of love and gratitude. Come! I feel prouder leading thee by thy black hand, than though I grasped an Emperor's!'

'There go two daft ones now,' muttered the old Manxman. 'One daft with strength, the other daft with weakness. But here's the end of the rotten line – all dripping, too. Mend it, eh? I think we had best have a new line altogether. I'll see Mr Stubb about it.'

126

THE LIFE-BUOY

STEERING now south-eastward by Ahab's levelled steel, and her progress solely determined by Ahab's level log and line; the Pequod held on her path towards the Equator. Making so long a passage through such unfrequented waters, descrying no ships, and ere long, sideways impelled by unvarying trade winds, over waves monotonously mild; all these seemed the strange calm things preluding some riotous and desperate scene.

At last, when the ship drew near to the outskirts, as it were, of the Equatorial fishing-ground, and in the deep darkness that goes before the dawn, was sailing by a cluster of rocky islets; the watch – then headed by Flask – was startled by a cry so plaintively wild and unearthly – like half-articulated wailings of the ghosts of all Herod's murdered Innocents – that one and all, they started from their reveries, and for the space of some moments stood, or sat, or leaned all transfixedly listening, like the carved Roman slave, while that wild cry remained within hearing. The Christian or civilized part of the crew said it was mermaids, and shuddered; but the pagan harpooneers remained unappalled. Yet the grey Manxman – the oldest mariner of all – declared that the wild thrilling sounds that were heard, were the voices of newly drowned men in the sea.

Below in his hammock, Ahab did not hear of this till grey dawn, when he came to the deck; it was then recounted to him by Flask, not unaccompanied with hinted dark meanings. He hollowly laughed, and thus explained the wonder.

Those rocky islands the ship had passed were the resort of great numbers of seals, and some young seals that had lost their dams, or some dams that had lost their cubs, must have risen nigh the ship and kept company with her, crying and sobbing with their human sort of wail. But this only the more affected some of them, because most mariners cherish a very superstitious feeling about seals, arising not only from their peculiar tones when in distress, but also from the human look of their round heads and semi-intelligent faces, seen peeringly uprising from the water alongside. In the sea, under certain circumstances, seals have more than once been mistaken for men.

But the bodings of the crew were destined to receive a most plausible confirmation in the fate of one of their number that morning. At sun-rise this man went from his hammock to his mast-head at the fore; and whether it was that he was not yet half waked from his sleep (for sailors sometimes go aloft in a transition state), whether it was thus with the man, there is now no telling; but, be that as it may, he had not been long at his perch, when a cry was heard – a cry and a rushing – and looking up, they saw a falling phantom in the air; and looking down, a little tossed heap of white bubbles in the blue of the sea.

The life-buoy – a long slender cask – was dropped from the stern, where it always hung obedient to a cunning spring; but no hand rose to seize it, and the sun having long beat upon this cask it had shrunken, so that it slowly filled, and the parched wood also filled at its every pore; and the studded iron-bound cask followed the sailor to the bottom, as if to yield him his pillow, though in sooth but a hard one.

And thus the first man of the Pequod that mounted the mast to look out for the White Whale, on the White Whale's own peculiar ground; that man was swallowed up in the deep. But few, perhaps, thought of that at the time. Indeed, in some sort, they were not grieved at this event, at least as a portent; for they regarded it, not as a foreshadowing of evil in the future, but as the fulfilment of an evil already presaged. They declared that now they knew the reason of those wild shrieks they had heard the night before. But again the old Manxman said nay.

The lost life-buoy was now to be replaced; Starbuck was directed to see to it; but as no cask of sufficient lightness could be found, and as in the feverish eagerness of what seemed the approaching crisis of the voyage, all hands were impatient of any toil but what was directly connected with its final end, whatever that might prove to be; therefore, they were going to leave the ship's stern unprovided with a buoy, when by certain strange signs and innuendoes Queequeg hinted a hint concerning his coffin.

'A life-buoy of a coffin!' cried Starbuck, starting.

'Rather queer, that, I should say,' said Stubb.

'It will make a good enough one,' said Flask, 'the carpenter here can arrange it easily.'

'Bring it up; there's nothing else for it,' said Starbuck, after a melancholy pause. 'Rig it, carpenter; do not look at me so – the coffin, I mean. Dost thou hear me? Rig it.'

'And shall I nail down the lid, sir?' moving his hand as with a hammer.

'Aye.'

'And shall I caulk the seams, sir?' moving his hand as with a caulking-iron.

'Aye.'

'And shall I then pay over the same with pitch, sir?' moving his hand as with a pitch-pot.

'Away! what possesses thee to this? Make a life-buoy of the coffin, and no more. – Mr Stubb, Mr Flask, come forward with me.'

'He goes off in a huff. The whole he can endure; at the parts he baulks. Now I don't like this. I make a leg for Captain Ahab, and he wears it like a gentleman; but I make a bandbox for Queequeg, and he wont put his head into it. Are all my pains to go for nothing with that coffin? And now I'm ordered to make a life-buoy of it. It's like turning an old coat; going to bring the flesh on the other side now. I don't like this cobbling sort of business – I don't like it at all; it's undignified; it's not my place. Let tinkers' brats do tinkerings; we are their betters. I like to take in hand none but clean, virgin, fair-and-square mathematical jobs, something that regularly begins at the beginning, and is at the middle when midway, and comes to an end at the conclusion; not a cobbler's job, that's at an end in the middle, and at the beginning at the end. It's the old woman's tricks to be giving cobbling jobs. Lord! what an affection all old women have for tinkers. I know an old woman of sixty-five who ran away with a bald-headed young tinker once. And that's the reason I never would work for lonely widow old women ashore, when I kept my job-shop in the Vineyard; they might have taken it into their lonely old heads to run off with me. But heigh-ho! there are no caps at sea but snow-caps. Let me see. Nail down the lid; caulk the seams; pay over the same with pitch; batten them down tight, and hang it with the snap-spring over the ship's stern. Were ever such things done before with a coffin? Some superstitious old carpenters, now, would be tied up in the rigging, ere they would do the job. But I'm made of knotty Aroostook hemlock; I don't budge. Cruppered with a coffin! Sailing about with a grave-yard tray! But never mind. We workers in woods make bridal-bedsteads and card-tables, as well as coffins and hearses. We work by the month, or by the job, or by the profit; not for us to ask the why and wherefore of our work, unless it be too confounded cobbling, and then we stash it if we can. Hem! I'll do the job, now, tenderly. I'll have me – let's see – how many in the ship's company, all told? But I've forgotten. Any way, I'll have me thirty separate, Turk's-headed life-lines, each three feet long hanging all round to the coffin. Then, if the hull go down, there'll be thirty lively fellows all fighting for one coffin, a sight not seen very often beneath the sun! Come hammer, calking-iron, pitch-pot, and marling-spike! Let's to it.'

127

THE DECK

The coffin laid upon two line-tubs, between the vice-bench and the open hatchway; the Carpenter calking its seams; the string of twisted oakum slowly unwinding from a large roll of it placed in the bosom of his frock. – Ahab comes slowly from the cabin-gangway, and hears Pip following him.

'BACK, lad; I will be with ye again presently. He goes! Not this hand complies with my humor more genially than that boy. – Middle aisle of a church! What's here?'

'Life-buoy, sir. Mr Starbuck's orders. Oh, look, sir! Beware the hatchway!'

'Thank ye, man. Thy coffin lies handy to the vault.'

'Sir? The hatchway? oh! So it does, sir, so it does.'

'Art not thou the leg-maker? Look, did not this stump come from thy shop?'

'I believe it did, sir; does the ferrule stand, sir?'

'Well enough. But art thou not also the undertaker?'

'Aye, sir; I patched up this thing here as a coffin for

Queequeg; but they've set me now to turning it into something else.'

'Then tell me; art thou not an arrant, all-grasping, intermeddling, monopolizing, heathenish old scamp, to be one day making legs, and the next day coffins to clap them in, and yet again life-buoys out of those same coffins? Thou art as unprincipled as the gods, and as much of a jack-of-all-trades.'

'But I do not mean anything, sir. I do as I do.'

'The gods again. Hark ye, dost thou not ever sing working about a coffin? The Titans, they say, hummed snatches when chipping out the craters for volcanoes; and the grave-digger in the play sings, spade in hand. Dost thou never?'

'Sing, sir? Do I sing? Oh, I'm indifferent enough, sir, for that; but the reason why the grave-digger made music must have been because there was none in his spade, sir. But the calking mallet is full of it. Hark to it.'

'Aye, and that's because the lid there's a sounding-board; and what in all things makes the sounding-board is this – there's naught beneath. And yet, a coffin with a body in it rings pretty much the same, Carpenter. Hast thou ever helped carry a bier, and heard the coffin knock against the churchyard gate, going in?'

'Faith, sir, I've—'

'Faith? What's that?'

'Why, faith, sir, it's only a sort of exclamation-like – that's all, sir.'

'Um, um; go on.'

'I was about to say, sir, that—'

'Art thou a silk-worm? Dost thou spin thy own shroud out of thyself? Look at thy bosom! Despatch! and get these traps out of sight.'

'He goes aft. That was sudden, now; but squalls come sudden in hot latitudes. I've heard that the Isle of Albemarle, one of the Gallipagos, is cut by the Equator right in the middle. Seems to me some sort of Equator cuts yon old man, too, right in his middle. He's always under the Line – fiery hot, I tell ye! He's looking this way – come, oakum;

quick. Here we go again. This wooden mallet is the cork, and I'm the professor of musical glasses – tap, tap!'

(*Ahab to himself.*)

'There's a sight! There's a sound! The greyheaded woodpecker tapping the hollow tree! Blind and dumb might well be envied now. See! that thing rests on two line-tubs, full of tow-lines. A most malicious wag, that fellow. Rat-tat! So man's seconds tick! Oh! how immaterial are all materials! What things real are there, but imponderable thoughts? Here now's the very dreaded symbol of grim death, by a mere hap, made the expressive sign of the help and hope of most endangered life. A life-buoy of a coffin! Does it go further? Can it be that in some spiritual sense the coffin is, after all, but an immortality-preserver! I'll think of that. But no. So far gone am I in the dark side of earth, that its other side, the theoretic bright one, seems but uncertain twilight to me. Will ye never have done, Carpenter, with that accursed sound? I go below; let me not see that thing here when I return again. Now, then, Pip, we'll talk this over; I do suck most wondrous philosophies from thee! Some unknown conduits from the unknown worlds must empty into thee!'

128

THE PEQUOD MEETS THE RACHEL

NEXT day, a large ship, the Rachel, was descried, bearing directly down upon the Pequod, all her spars thickly clustering with men. At the time the Pequod was making good speed through the water; but as the broad-winged windward stranger shot nigh to her, the boastful sails all fell together as blank bladders that are burst, and all life fled from the smitten hull.

'Bad news; she brings bad news,' muttered the old Manxman. But ere her commander, who, with trumpet to mouth, stood up in his boat; ere he could hopefully hail, Ahab's voice was heard.

'Hast seen the White Whale?'

'Aye, yesterday. Have ye seen a whale-boat adrift?'

Throttling his joy, Ahab negatively answered this unexpected question; and would then have fain boarded the stranger, when the stranger captain himself, having stopped his vessel's way, was seen descending her side. A few keen pulls, and his boat-hook soon clinched the Pequod's main-chains, and he sprang to the deck. Immediately he was recognized by Ahab for a Nantucketer he knew. But no formal salutation was exchanged.

'Where was he? – not killed! – not killed!' cried Ahab, closely advancing. 'How was it?'

It seemed that somewhat late on the afternoon of the day previous, while three of the stranger's boats were engaged with a shoal of whales, which had led them some four or five miles from the ship; and while they were yet in swift chase to windward, the white hump and head of Moby Dick had suddenly loomed up out of the blue water, not very far to leeward; whereupon, the fourth rigged boat – a reserved one – had been instantly lowered in chase. After a keen sail before the wind, this fourth boat – the swiftest keeled of all – seemed to have succeeded in fastening – at least, as well as the man at the mast-head could tell anything about it. In the distance he saw the diminished dotted boat; and then a swift gleam of bubbling white water; and after that nothing more; whence it was concluded that the stricken whale must have indefinitely run away with his pursuers, as often happens. There was some apprehension, but no positive alarm, as yet. The recall signals were placed in the rigging; darkness came on; and forced to pick up her three far to windward boats – ere going in quest of the fourth one in the precisely opposite direction – the ship had not only been necessitated to leave that boat to its fate till near midnight, but, for the time, to increase her distance from it. But the rest of her crew being at last safe aboard, she crowded all sail – stunsail on stunsail – after the missing boat; kindling a fire in her try-pots for a beacon; and every other man aloft on the look-out. But though when she had thus sailed a sufficient distance to gain the presumed place of the absent ones when last seen; though she then paused to lower her spare boats to pull all around her; and not finding anything, had again dashed on; again paused, and lowered her boats; and though she had thus continued doing till day light; yet not the least glimpse of the missing keel had been seen.

The story told, the stranger Captain immediately went on to reveal his object in boarding the Pequod. He desired that ship to unite with his own in the search; by sailing over the sea some four or five miles apart, on parallel lines, and so sweeping a double horizon, as it were.

'I will wager something now,' whispered Stubb to Flask, 'that some one in that missing boat wore off that Captain's best coat; mayhap, his watch – he's so cursed anxious to get it back. Who ever heard of two pious whale-ships cruising after one missing whale-boat in the height of the whaling season? See, Flask, only see how pale he looks – pale in the very buttons of his eyes – look – it wasn't the coat – it must have been the –'

'My boy, my own boy is among them. For God's sake – I beg, I conjure' – here exclaimed the stranger Captain to Ahab, who thus far had but icily received his petition. 'For eight-and-forty hours let me charter your ship – I will gladly pay for it, and roundly pay for it – if there be no other way – for eight-and-forty hours only – only that – you must, oh, you must, and you *shall* do this thing.'

'His son!' cried Stubb, 'oh, it's his son he's lost! I take back the coat and watch – what says Ahab? We must save that boy.'

'He's drowned with the rest on 'em, last night,' said the old Manx sailor standing behind them; 'I heard; all of ye heard their spirits.'

Now, as it shortly turned out, what made this incident of the Rachel's the more melancholy, was the circumstance, that not only was one of the Captain's sons among the number of the missing boat's crew; but among the number of the other boats' crews, at the same time, but on the other hand, separated from the ship during the dark vicissitudes of the chase, there had been still another son; as that for a time, the wretched father was plunged to the bottom of the cruellest perplexity; which was only solved for him by his chief mate's instinctively adopting the ordinary procedure of a whale-ship in such emergencies, that is, when placed between jeopardized but divided boats, always to pick up the majority first. But the captain, for some unknown constitutional reason, had refrained from mentioning all this, and not till forced to it by Ahab's iciness did he allude to his one yet missing boy; a little lad, but twelve years old, whose father with the earnest but unmisgiving hardihood of a Nantucketer's paternal love, had thus early sought to initiate him in the perils and wonders of a vocation almost immemorially the destiny of all his race. Nor does it unfrequently occur, that Nantucket captains will send a son of such tender age away from them, for a protracted three or four years' voyage in some other ship than their own; so that their first knowledge of a whaleman's career shall be unenervated by any chance display of a father's natural but untimely partiality, or undue apprehensiveness and concern.

Meantime, now the stranger was still beseeching his poor boon of Ahab; and Ahab still stood like an anvil, receiving every shock, but without the least quivering of his own.

'I will not go,' said the stranger, 'till you say *aye* to me. Do to me as you would have me do to you in the like case. For *you* too have a boy, Captain Ahab – though but a child, and nestling safely at home now – a child of your old age too – Yes, yes, you relent; I see it – run, run, men, now, and stand by to square in the yards.'

'Avast,' cried Ahab – 'touch not a rope-yarn;' then in a voice that prolongingly moulded every word – 'Captain Gardiner, I will not do it. Even now I lose time. Good bye, good bye. God bless ye, man, and may I forgive myself, but I must go. Mr Starbuck, look at the binnacle watch, and in three minutes from this present instant warn off all strangers: then brace forward again, and let the ship sail as before.'

Hurriedly turning, with averted face, he descended into his cabin, leaving the strange captain transfixed at this unconditional and utter rejection of his so earnest suit. But starting from his enchantment, Gardiner silently hurried to the side; more fell than stepped into his boat, and returned to his ship.

Soon the two ships diverged their wakes; and long as the strange vessel was in view, she was seen to yaw hither and thither at every dark spot, however small, on the sea. This way and that her yards were swung round; starboard and larboard, she continued to tack; now she beat against a head sea; and again it pushed her before it; while all the while, her masts and yards were thickly clustered with men, as three tall cherry trees, when the boys are cherrying among the boughs.

But by her still halting course and winding, woful way, you plainly saw that this ship that so wept with spray, still remained without comfort. She was Rachel, weeping for her children, because they were not.

129

THE CABIN

(Ahab moving to go on deck; Pip catches him by the hand to follow.)

'LAD, lad, I tell thee thou must not follow Ahab now. The hour is coming when Ahab would not scare thee from him, yet would not have thee by him. There is that in thee, poor lad, which I feel too curing to my malady. Like cures like; and for this hunt, my malady becomes my most desired health. Do thou abide below here, where they shall serve thee, as if thou wert the captain. Aye, lad, thou shalt sit here in my own screwed chair; another screw to it, thou must be.'

'No, no, no! ye have not a whole body, sir; do ye but use

poor me for your one lost leg; only tread upon me, sir; I ask no more, so I remain a part of ye.'

'Oh! spite of million villains, this makes me a bigot in the fadeless fidelity of man! – and a black! and crazy! – but methinks like-cures-like applies to him too; he grows so sane again.'

'They tell me, sir, that Stubb did once desert poor little Pip, whose drowned bones now show white, for all the blackness of his living skin. But I will never desert ye, sir, as Stubb did him. Sir, I must go with ye.'

'If thou speakest thus to me much more, Ahab's purpose keels up in him. I tell thee no; it cannot be.'

'Oh good master, master, master!'

'Weep so, and I will murder thee! have a care, for Ahab too is mad. Listen, and thou wilt often hear my ivory foot upon the deck, and still know that I am there. And now I quit thee. Thy hand! – Met! True art thou, lad, as the circumference to its centre. So: God for ever bless thee; and if it come to that, – God for ever save thee, let what will befall.'

(*Ahab goes; Pip steps one step forward.*)

'Here he this instant stood; I stand in his air, – but I'm alone. Now were even poor Pip here I could endure it, but he's missing. Pip! Pip! Ding, dong, ding! Who's seen Pip? He must be up here; let's try the door. What? neither lock, nor bolt, nor bar; and yet there's no opening it. It must be the spell; he told me to stay here: Aye, and told me this screwed chair was mine. Here, then, I'll seat me, against the transom, in the ship's full middle, all her keel and her three masts before me. Here, our old sailors say, in their black seventy-fours great admirals sometimes sit at table, and lord it over rows of captains and lieutenants. Ha! what's this? epaulets! epaulets! the epaulets all come crowding! Pass round the decanters; glad to see ye; fill up, monsieurs! What an odd feeling, now, when a black boy's host to white men with gold lace upon their coats! – Monsieurs, have ye seen one Pip? – a little negro lad, five feet high, hang-dog look, and cowardly! Jumped from a whale-boat once; – seen him? No! Well then, fill up again, captains, and let's drink shame upon all cowards! I name no names. Shame upon them! Put one foot upon the table. Shame upon all cowards. – Hist! above there, I hear ivory – Oh, master! master! I am indeed downhearted when you walk over me. But here I'll stay, though this stern strikes rocks; and they bulge through; and oysters come to join me.'

130

THE HAT

AND now that at the proper time and place, after so long and wide a preliminary cruise, Ahab, – all other whaling waters swept – seemed to have chased his foe into an ocean-fold, to slay him the more securely there; now, that he found himself hard by the very latitude and longitude where his tormenting wound had been inflicted; now that a vessel had been spoken which on the very day preceding had actually encountered Moby Dick; – and now that all his successive meetings with various ships contrastingly concurred to show the demoniac indifference with which the white whale tore his hunters, whether sinning or sinned against; now it was that there lurked a something in the old man's eyes, which it was hardly sufferable for feeble souls to see. As the unsetting polar star, which through the livelong, arctic, six months' night sustains its piercing, steady, central gaze; so Ahab's purpose now fixedly gleamed down upon the constant midnight of the gloomy crew. It domineered above them so, that all their bodings, doubts, misgivings, fears, were fain to hide beneath their souls, and not sprout forth a single spear or leaf.

In this foreshadowing interval too, all humor, forced or natural, vanished. Stubb no more strove to raise a smile; Starbuck no more strove to check one. Alike, joy and sorrow, hope and fear, seemed ground to finest dust, and powdered, for the time, in the clamped mortar of Ahab's iron soul. Like machines, they dumbly moved about the deck, ever conscious that the old man's despot eye was on them.

But did you deeply scan him in his more secret confidential hours; when he thought no glance but one was on him; then you would have seen that even as Ahab's eyes so awed the crew's, the inscrutable Parsee's glance awed his; or somehow, at least, in some wild way, at times affected it. Such an added, gliding strangeness began to invest the thin Fedallah now; such ceaseless shudderings shook him; that the men looked dubious at him; half uncertain, as it seemed, whether indeed he were a mortal substance, or else a tremulous shadow cast upon the deck by some unseen being's body. And that shadow was always hovering there. For not by night, even, had Fedallah ever certainly been known to slumber, or go below. He would stand still for hours: but never sat or leaned; his wan but wondrous eyes did plainly say – We two watchmen never rest.

Nor, at any time, by night or day could the mariners now step up the deck, unless Ahab was before them; either standing in his pivot-hole, or exactly pacing the planks between two undeviating limits, – the main-mast and the mizen; or else they saw him standing in the cabin-scuttle, – his living foot advanced upon the deck, as if to step; his hat slouched heavily over his eyes; so that however motionless he stood, however the days and nights were added on, that he had not swung in his hammock; yet hidden beneath that slouching hat, they could never tell unerringly whether, for all this, his eyes were really closed at times: or whether he was still intently scanning them; no matter, though he stood so in the scuttle for a whole long hour on the stretch, and the unheeded night-damp gathered in beads of dew upon that stone-carved coat and hat. The clothes that the night had wet, the next day's sunshine dried upon him; and so, day after day, and night after night; he went no more beneath the planks; whatever he wanted from the cabin that thing he sent for.

He ate in the same open air; that is, his two only meals, – breakfast and dinner: supper he never touched; nor reaped his beard; which darkly grew all gnarled, as unearthed roots of trees blown over, which still grow idly on at naked base, though perished in the upper verdure. But though his whole life was now become one watch on deck; and though the Parsee's mystic watch was without intermission as his own; yet these two never seemed to speak – one man to the other – unless at long intervals some passing unmomentous matter made it necessary. Though such a potent spell seemed secretly to join the twain; openly, and to the awe-struck crew, they seemed pole-like asunder. If by day they chanced to speak one word; by night, dumb men were both, so far as concerned the slightest verbal interchange. At times, for longest hours, without a single hail, they stood far parted in the starlight; Ahab in his scuttle, the Parsee by the mainmast; but still fixedly gazing upon each other, as if in the Parsee Ahab saw his forethrown shadow, in Ahab the Parsee his abandoned substance.

And yet, somehow, did Ahab – in his own proper self, as daily, hourly, and every instant, commandingly revealed to his subordinates, – Ahab seemed an independent lord; the Parsee but his slave. Still again both seemed yoked together, and an unseen tyrant driving them; the lean shade siding the solid rib. For be this Parsee what he may, all rib and keel was solid Ahab.

At the first faintest glimmering of the dawn, his iron voice was heard from aft – 'Man the mast-heads!' – and all through the day, till after sunset and after twilight, the same voice every hour, at the striking of the helmsman's bell, was heard – 'What d'ye see? – sharp! sharp!'

But when three or four days had slided by, after meeting the children-seeking Rachel; and no spout had yet been seen; the monomaniac old man seemed distrustful of his crew's fidelity; at least, of nearly all except the Pagan harpooneers; he seemed to doubt, even, whether Stubb and Flask might not willingly overlook the sight he sought. But if these suspicions were really his, he sagaciously refrained from verbally expressing them, however his actions might seem to hint them.

'I will have the first sight of the whale myself,' – he said. 'Aye! Ahab must have the doubloon!' and with his own hands he rigged a nest of basketed bowlines; and sending a hand aloft, with a single sheaved block, to secure to the main-mast head, he received the two ends of the downward-reeved rope; and attaching one to his basket prepared a pin for the other end, in order to fasten it at the rail. This done, with that end yet in his hand and standing beside the pin, he looked round upon his crew, sweeping from one to the other; pausing his glance long upon Daggoo, Queequeg, Tashtego; but shunning Fedallah; and then settling his firm relying eye upon the chief mate, said, – 'Take the rope, sir – I give it into thy hands, Starbuck.' Then arranging his person in the basket, he gave the word for them to hoist him to his perch, Starbuck being the one who secured the rope at last; and afterwards stood near it. And thus, with one hand clinging round the royal mast, Ahab gazed abroad upon the sea for miles and miles, – ahead, astern, this side, and that, – within the wide expanded circle commanded at so great a height.

When in working with his hands at some lofty almost isolated place in the rigging, which chances to afford no foothold, the sailor at sea is hoisted up to that spot, and sustained there by the rope; under these circumstances, its fastened end on deck is always given in strict charge to some one man who has the special watch of it. Because in such a wilderness of running rigging, whose various different relations aloft cannot always be infallibly discerned by what is seen of them at the deck; and when the deck-ends of these ropes are being every few minutes cast down from the fastenings, it would be but a natural fatality, if, unprovided with a constant watchman, the hoisted sailor should by some carelessness of the crew be cast adrift and fall all swooping to the sea. So Ahab's proceedings in this matter were not unusual; the only strange thing about them seemed to be, that Starbuck, almost the one only man who had ever ventured to oppose him with anything in the slightest degree approaching to decision – one of those too, whose faithfulness on the look-out he had seemed to doubt somewhat; – it was strange, that this was the very man he should select for his watchman; freely giving his whole life into such an otherwise distrusted person's hands.

Now, the first time Ahab was perched aloft; ere he had been there ten minutes; one of those red-billed savage sea-hawks which so often fly incommodiously close round the manned mast-heads of whalemen in these latitudes; one of these birds came wheeling and screaming round his head in a maze of untrackably swift circlings. Then it darted a thousand feet straight up into the air; then spiralized downwards, and went eddying again round his head.

But with his gaze fixed upon the dim and distant horizon, Ahab seemed not to mark this wild bird; nor, indeed, would any one else have marked it much, it being no uncommon circumstance; only now almost the least heedful eye seemed to see some sort of cunning meaning in almost every sight.

'Your hat, your hat, sir!' suddenly cried the Sicilian seaman, who being posted at the mizen-mast-head, stood directly behind Ahab, though somewhat lower than his level, and with a deep gulf of air dividing them.

But already the sable wing was before the old man's eyes; the long hooked bill at his head: with a scream, the black hawk darted away with his prize.

An eagle flew thrice round Tarquin's head, removing his cap to replace it, and thereupon Tanaquil, his wife, declared that Tarquin would be king of Rome. But only by the replacing of the cap was that omen accounted good. Ahab's hat was never restored; the wild hawk flew on and on with it; far in advance of the prow: and at last disappeared; while from the point of that disappearance, a minute black spot was dimly discerned, falling from that vast height into the sea.

131

THE PEQUOD MEETS THE DELIGHT

THE intense Pequod sailed on; the rolling waves and days went by; the life-buoy-coffin still lightly swung; and another ship, most miserably misnamed the Delight, was descried. As she drew nigh, all eyes were fixed upon her broad beams, called shears, which, in some whaling-ships, cross the quarter-deck at the height of eight or nine feet; serving to carry the spare, unrigged, or disabled boats.

Upon the stranger's shears were beheld the shattered, white ribs, and some few splintered planks, of what had once been a whale-boat; but you now saw through this wreck, as plainly as you see through the peeled, half-unhinged, and bleaching skeleton of a horse.

'Hast seen the White Whale?'

'Look!' replied the hollow-cheeked captain from his taff-rail; and with his trumpet he pointed to the wreck.

'Hast killed him?'

'The harpoon is not yet forged that will ever do that,' answered the other, sadly glancing upon a rounded hammock on the deck, whose gathered sides some noiseless sailors were busy in sewing together.

'Not forged!' and snatching Perth's levelled iron from the crotch, Ahab held it out, exclaiming – 'Look ye, Nantucketer; here in this hand I hold his death! Tempered in blood, and tempered by lightning are these barbs; and I swear to temper them triply in that hot place behind the fin, where the White Whale most feels his accursed life!'

'Then God keep thee, old man – see'st thou that' – pointing to the hammock – 'I bury but one of five stout men, who were alive only yesterday; but were dead ere night. Only *that* one I bury; the rest were buried before they died; you sail upon their tomb.' Then turning to his crew – 'Are ye ready there? place the plank then on the rail, and lift the body; so, then – Oh! God' – advancing towards the hammock with uplifted hands – 'may the resurrection and the life—'

'Brace forward! Up helm!' cried Ahab like lightning to his men.

But the suddenly started Pequod was not quick enough to escape the sound of the splash that the corpse soon made as it struck the sea; not so quick, indeed, but that some of the flying bubbles might have sprinkled her hull with their ghostly baptism.

As Ahab now glided from the dejected Delight, the strange life-buoy hanging at the Pequod's stern came into conspicuous relief.

'Ha! yonder! look yonder, men!' cried a foreboding voice in her wake. 'In vain, oh, ye strangers, ye fly our sad burial; ye but turn us your taffrail to show us your coffin!'

132

THE SYMPHONY

It was a clear steel-blue day. The firmaments of air and sea were hardly separable in that all-pervading azure; only, the pensive air was transparently pure and soft, with a woman's look, and the robust and man-like sea heaved with long, strong, lingering swells, as Samson's chest in his sleep.

Hither, and thither, on high, glided the snow-white wings of small, unspeckled birds; these were the gentle thoughts of the feminine air; but to and fro in the deeps, far down in the bottomless blue, rushed mighty leviathans, sword-fish, and sharks; and these were the strong, troubled, murderous thinkings of the masculine sea.

But though thus contrasting within, the contrast was only in shades and shadows without; those two seemed one; it was only the sex, as it were, that distinguished them.

Aloft, like a royal czar and king, the sun seemed giving this gentle air to this bold and rolling sea; even as bride to groom. And at the girdling line of the horizon, a soft and tremulous motion – most seen here at the equator – denoted the fond, throbbing trust, the loving alarms, with which the poor bride gave her bosom away.

Tied up and twisted; gnarled and knotted with wrinkles; haggardly firm and unyielding; his eyes glowing like coals, that still glow in the ashes of ruin; untottering Ahab stood forth in the clearness of the morn; lifting his splintered helmet of a brow to the fair girl's forehead of heaven.

Oh, immortal infancy, and innocency of the azure! Invisible winged creatures that frolic all round us! Sweet childhood of air and sky! how oblivious were ye of old Ahab's close-coiled woe! But so have I seen little Miriam and Martha, laughing-eyed elves, heedlessly gambol around their old sire; sporting with the circle of singed locks which grew on the marge of that burnt-out crater of his brain.

Slowly crossing the deck from the scuttle, Ahab leaned over the side, and watched how his shadow in the water sank and sank to his gaze, the more and the more that he strove to pierce the profundity. But the lovely aromas in that enchanted air did at last seem to dispel, for a moment, the cankerous thing in his soul. That glad, happy air, that winsome sky, did at last stroke and caress him; the step-mother world, so long cruel – forbidding – now threw affectionate arms round his stubborn neck, and did seem to joyously sob over him, as if over one, that however wilful and erring, she could yet find it in her heart to save and to bless. From beneath his slouched hat Ahab dropped a tear into the sea; nor did all the Pacific contain such wealth as that one wee drop.

Starbuck saw the old man; saw him, how he heavily leaned over the side; and he seemed to hear in his own true heart the measureless sobbing that stole out of the centre of the serenity around. Careful not to touch him, or be noticed by him, he yet drew near to him, and stood there.

Ahab turned.

'Starbuck!'

'Sir.'

'Oh, Starbuck! it is a mild, mild wind, and a mild looking sky. On such a day – very much such a sweetness as this – I struck my first whale – a boy-harpooneer of eighteen! Forty – forty – forty years ago! – ago! Forty years of continual whaling! forty years of privation, and peril, and storm-time! forty years on the pitiless sea! for forty years has Ahab forsaken the peaceful land, for forty years to make war on the horrors of the deep! Aye and yes, Starbuck, out of those forty years I have not spent three ashore. When I think of this life I have led; the desolation of solitude it has been; the masoned, walled-town of a Captain's exclusiveness, which admits but small entrance to any sympathy from the green country without – oh, weariness! heaviness! Guinea-coast slavery of solitary command! – when I think of all this; only half-suspected, not so keenly known to me before – and how for forty years I have fed upon dry salted fare – fit emblem of the dry nourishment of my soul! – when the poorest landsman has had fresh fruit to his daily hand, and broken the world's fresh bread to my mouldy crusts – away, whole oceans away, from that young girl-wife I wedded past fifty, and sailed for Cape Horn the next day, leaving but one dent in my marriage pillow – wife? wife? – rather a widow with her husband alive! Aye, I widowed that poor girl when I married her, Starbuck; and then, the madness, the frenzy, the boiling blood and the smoking brow, with which, for a thousand lowerings old Ahab has furiously, foamingly chased his prey – more a demon than a man! – aye, aye! what a forty years' fool – fool – old fool, has old Ahab been! Why this strife of the chase? why weary, and palsy the arm at the oar, and the iron, and the lance? how the richer or better is Ahab now? Behold, Oh, Starbuck! is it not hard, that with this weary load I bear, one poor leg should have been snatched from under me? Here, brush this old hair aside; it blinds me, that I seem to weep. Locks so grey did never grow but from out some ashes! But do I look very old, so very, very old, Starbuck? I feel deadly faint, bowed, and humped, as though I were Adam, staggering beneath the piled centuries since Paradise. God! God! God! – crack my heart! – stave my brain! – mockery! mockery! bitter, biting mockery of grey hairs, have I lived enough joy to wear ye; and seem and feel thus intolerably old? Close! stand close to me, Starbuck; let me look into a human eye; it is better than to gaze into sea or sky; better than to gaze upon God. By the green land; by the bright hearth-stone! this is the magic glass, man; I see my wife and my child in thine eye. No, no; stay on board, on board! – lower not when I do; when branded Ahab gives chase to Moby Dick. That hazard shall not be thine. No, no! not with the far away home I see in that eye!'

'Oh, my Captain! my Captain! noble soul! grand old heart, after all! why should any one give chase to that hated fish! Away with me! let us fly these deadly waters! let us home! Wife and child, too, are Starbuck's – wife and child of his brotherly, sisterly, play-fellow youth; even as thine, sir, are the wife and child of thy loving, longing, paternal old age! Away! let us away! – this instant let me alter the course! How cheerily, how hilariously, O my Captain, would we bowl on our way to see old Nantucket again! I think, sir, they have some such mild blue days, even as this, in Nantucket.'

'They have, they have. I have seen them – some summer days in the morning. About this time – yes, it is his noon nap now – the boy vivaciously wakes; sits up in bed; and his mother tells him of me, of cannibal old me; how I am abroad upon the deep, but will yet come back to dance him again.'

''Tis my Mary, my Mary herself! She promised that my boy, every morning, should be carried to the hill to catch the first glimpse of his father's sail! Yes, yes! no more! it is done! we head for Nantucket! Come, my Captain, study out the course, and let us away! See, see! the boy's face from the window! the boy's hand on the hill!'

But Ahab's glance was averted; like a blighted fruit tree he shook, and cast his last, cindered apple to the soil.

'What is it, what nameless, inscrutable, unearthly thing

is it; what cozzening, hidden lord and master, and cruel, remorseless emperor commands me; that against all natural lovings and longings, I so keep pushing, and crowding, and jamming myself on all the time; recklessly making me ready to do what in my own proper, natural heart, I durst not so much as dare? Is Ahab, Ahab? Is it I, God, or who, that lifts this arm? But if the great sun move not of himself; but is as an errand-boy in heaven; nor one single star can revolve, but by some invisible power; how then can this one small heart beat; this one small brain think thoughts; unless God does that beating, does that thinking, does that living, and not I. By heaven, man, we are turned round and round in this world, like yonder windlass, and Fate is the handspike. And all the time, lo! that smiling sky, and this unsounded sea! Look! see yon Albicore! who put it into him to chase and fang that flying-fish? Where do murderers go, man! Who's to doom, when the judge himself is dragged to the bar? But it is a mild, mild wind, and a mild looking sky; and the air smells now, as if it blew from a far-away meadow; they have been making hay somewhere under the slopes of the Andes, Starbuck, and the mowers are sleeping among the new-mown hay. Sleeping? Aye, toil we how we may, we all sleep at last on the field. Sleep? Aye, and rust amid greenness; as last year's scythes flung down, and left in the half-cut swaths – Starbuck!'

But blanched to a corpse's hue with despair, the mate had stolen away.

Ahab crossed the deck to gaze over on the other side; but started at two reflected, fixed eyes in the water there. Fedallah was motionlessly leaning over the same rail.

133

THE CHASE – FIRST DAY

THAT night, in the mid-watch, when the old man – as his wont at intervals – stepped forth from the scuttle in which he leaned, and went to his pivot-hole, he suddenly thrust out his face fiercely, snuffing up the sea air as a sagacious ship's dog will, in drawing nigh to some barbarous isle. He declared that a whale must be near. Soon that peculiar odor, sometimes to a great distance given forth by the living sperm whale, was palpable to all the watch; nor was any mariner surprised when, after inspecting the compass, and then the dog-vane, and then ascertaining the precise bearing of the odor as nearly as possible, Ahab rapidly ordered the ship's course to be slightly altered, and the sail to be shortened.

The acute policy dictating these movements was sufficiently vindicated at daybreak, by the sight of a long sleek on the sea directly and lengthwise ahead, smooth as oil, and resembling in the pleated watery wrinkles bordering it, the polished metallic-like marks of some swift tide-rip, at the mouth of a deep, rapid stream.

'Man the mast-heads! Call all hands!'

Thundering with the butts of three clubbed handspikes on the forecastle deck, Daggoo roused the sleepers with such judgment claps that they seemed to exhale from the scuttle, so instantaneously did they appear with their clothes in their hands.

'What d'ye see?' cried Ahab, flattening his face to the sky.

'Nothing, nothing, sir!' was the sound hailing down in reply.

'T'gallant sails! – stunsails! alow and aloft, and on both sides!'

All sail being set, he now cast loose the life-line, reserved for swaying him to the main royal-mast head; and in a few moments they were hoisting him thither, when, while but two thirds of the way aloft, and while peering ahead through the horizontal vacancy between the main-top-sail and top-gallant-sail, he raised a gull-like cry in the air, 'There she blows! – there she blows! A hump like a snow-hill! It is Moby Dick!'

Fired by the cry which seemed simultaneously taken up by the three look-outs, the men on deck rushed to the rigging to behold the famous whale they had so long been pursuing. Ahab had now gained his final perch, some feet above the other look-outs, Tashtego standing just beneath him on the cap of the top-gallant-mast, so that the Indian's head was almost on a level with Ahab's heel. From this height the whale was now seen some mile or so ahead, at every roll of the sea revealing his high sparkling hump, and regularly jetting his silent spout into the air. To the credulous mariners it seemed the same silent spout they had so long ago beheld in the moonlit Atlantic and Indian Oceans.

'And did none of ye see it before?' cried Ahab, hailing the perched men all around him.

'I saw him almost that same instant, sir, that Captain Ahab did, and I cried out,' said Tashtego.

'Not the same instant; not the same – no, the doubloon is mine, Fate reserved the doubloon for me. *I* only; none of ye could have raised the White Whale first. There she blows! there she blows! – there she blows! There again! – there again!' he cried, in long-drawn, lingering, methodic tones, attuned to the gradual prolongings of the whale's visible jets. 'He's going to sound! In stunsails! Down top-gallant-sails! Stand by three boats. Mr Starbuck, remember, stay on board, and keep the ship. Helm there! Luff, luff a point! So; steady, man, steady! There go flukes! No, no; only black water! All ready the boats there? Stand by, stand by! Lower me, Mr Starbuck; lower, lower, – quick, quicker!' and he slid through the air to the deck.

'He is heading straight to leeward, sir,' cried Stubb, 'right away from us; cannot have seen the ship yet.'

'Be dumb, man! Stand by the braces! Hard down the helm! – brace up! Shiver her! – shiver her! So; well that! Boats, boats!'

Soon all the boats but Starbuck's were dropped; all the boat-sails set – all the paddles plying; with rippling swiftness, shooting to leeward; and Ahab heading the onset. A pale, death-glimmer lit up Fedallah's sunken eyes; a hideous motion gnawed his mouth.

Like noiseless nautilus shells, their light prows sped through the sea; but only slowly they neared the foe. As they neared him, the ocean grew still more smooth; seemed drawing a carpet over its waves; seemed a noon-meadow, so serenely it spread. At length the breathless hunter came so nigh his seemingly unsuspecting prey, that his entire dazzling hump was distinctly visible, sliding along the sea as if an isolated thing, and continually set in a revolving ring of finest, fleecy, greenish foam. He saw the vast, involved wrinkles of the slightly projecting head beyond. Before it, far out on the soft Turkish-rugged waters, went the glistening white shadow from his broad, milky forehead, a musical rippling playfully accompanying the shade; and behind, the blue waters interchangeably flowed over into the moving valley of his steady wake; and on either hand bright bubbles arose and danced by his side. But these were broken again by the light toes of hundreds of gay fowl softly feathering the sea, alternate with their fitful flight; and like to some flag-staff rising from the painted hull of an argosy, the tall but shattered pole of a recent lance projected from the white whale's back; and at intervals one of the cloud of soft-toed fowls hovering, and to and fro skimming like a canopy over the fish, silently perched and rocked on this pole, the long tail feathers streaming like pennons.

A gentle joyousness – a mighty mildness of repose in swiftness, invested the gliding whale. Not the white bull Jupiter swimming away with ravished Europa clinging to his graceful horns; his lovely, leering eyes sideways intent upon the maid; with smooth bewitching fleetness, rippling straight for the nuptial bower in Crete; not Jove, not that great majesty Supreme! did surpass the glorified White Whale as he so divinely swam.

On each soft side – coincident with the parted swell, that but once laving him, then flowed so wide away – on each bright side, the whale shed off enticings. No wonder there had been some among the hunters who namelessly transported and allured by all this serenity, had ventured to assail it; but had fatally found that quietude but the vesture of tornadoes. Yet calm, enticing calm, oh, whale! thou glidest on, to all who for the first time eye thee, no matter how many in that same way thou may'st have bejuggled and destroyed before.

And thus, through the serene tranquilities of the tropical sea, among waves whose hand-clappings were suspended by exceeding rapture, Moby Dick moved on, still withholding from sight the full terrors of his submerged trunk, entirely hiding the wrenched hideousness of his jaw. But soon the fore part of him slowly rose from the water; for an instant his whole marbleized body formed a high arch, like Virginia's Natural Bridge, and warningly waving his bannered flukes in the air, the grand god revealed himself, sounded, and went out of sight. Hoveringly halting, and dipping on the wing, the white sea-fowls longingly lingered over the agitated pool that he left.

With oars apeak, and paddles down, the sheets of their sails adrift, the three boats now stilly floated, awaiting Moby Dick's reappearance.

'An hour,' said Ahab, standing rooted in his boat's stern; and he gazed beyond the whale's place, towards the dim blue spaces and wide wooing vacancies to leeward. It was only an instant; for again his eyes seemed whirling round in his head as he swept the watery circle. The breeze now freshened; the sea began to swell.

'The birds! – the birds!' cried Tashtego.

In long Indian file, as when herons take wing, the white birds were now all flying towards Ahab's boat; and when within a few yards began fluttering over the water there, wheeling round and round, with joyous, expectant cries. Their vision was keener than man's; Ahab could discover no sign in the sea. But suddenly as he peered down and down into its depths, he profoundly saw a white living spot no bigger than a white weasel, with wonderful celerity uprising, and magnifying as it rose, till it turned, and then there were plainly revealed two long crooked rows of white, glistening teeth, floating up from the undiscoverable bottom. It was Moby Dick's open mouth and scrolled jaw; his vast, shadowed bulk still half blending with the blue of the sea. The glittering mouth yawned beneath the boat like an open-doored marble tomb; and giving one sidelong sweep with his steering oar, Ahab whirled the craft aside from this tremendous apparition. Then, calling upon Fedallah to change places with him, went forward to the bows, and seizing Perth's harpoon, commanded his crew to grasp their oars and stand by to stern.

Now, by reason of this timely spinning round the boat upon its axis, its bow, by anticipation, was made to face the whale's head while yet under water. But as if perceiving this strategem, Moby Dick, with that malicious intelligence ascribed to him, sidelingly transplanted himself, as it were, in an instant, shooting his pleated head lengthwise beneath the boat.

Through and through; through every plank and each rib, it thrilled for an instant, the whale obliquely lying on his back, in the manner of a biting shark, slowly and feelingly taking its bows full within his mouth, so that the long, narrow, scrolled lower jaw curled high up into the open air, and one of the teeth caught in a row-lock. The bluish pearl-white of the inside of the jaw was within six inches of Ahab's head, and reached higher than that. In this attitude the White Whale now shook the slight cedar as a mildly cruel cat her mouse. With unastonished eyes Fedallah gazed, and crossed his arms; but the tiger-yellow crew were tumbling over each other's heads to gain the uttermost stern.

And now, while both elastic gunwales were springing in and out, as the whale dallied with the doomed craft in this devilish way; and from his body being submerged beneath the boat, he could not be darted at from the bows, for the bows were almost inside of him, as it were; and while the other boats involuntarily paused, as before a quick crisis impossible to withstand, then it was that monomaniac Ahab, furious with this tantalizing vicinity of his foe, which placed him all alive and helpless in the very jaws he hated; frenzied with all this, he seized the long bone with his naked hands, and wildly strove to wrench it from its gripe. As now he thus vainly strove, the jaw slipped from him; the frail gunwales bent in, collapsed, and snapped, as both jaws, like an enormous shears, sliding further aft, bit the craft completely in twain, and locked themselves fast again in the sea, midway between the two floating wrecks. These floated aside, the broken ends drooping, the crew at the stern-wreck clinging to the gunwales, and striving to hold fast to the oars to lash them across.

At that preluding moment, ere the boat was yet snapped, Ahab, the first to perceive the whale's intent, by the crafty upraising of his head, a movement that loosed his hold for the time; at that moment his hand had made one final effort to push the boat out of the bite. But only slipping further into the whale's mouth, and tilting over sideways as it slipped, the boat had shaken off his hold on the jaw; spilled him out of it, as he leaned to the push; and so he fell flat-faced upon the sea.

Ripplingly withdrawing from his prey, Moby Dick now lay at a little distance, vertically thrusting his oblong white head up and down in the billows; and at the same time slowly revolving his whole spindled body; so that when his vast wrinkled forehead rose – some twenty or more feet out of the water – the now rising swells, with all their confluent waves, dazzlingly broke against it; vindictively tossing their shivered spray still higher into the air.* So, in a gale, the but half baffled Channel billows only recoil from the base of the Eddystone, triumphantly to overleap its summit with their scud.

But soon resuming his horizontal attitude, Moby Dick swam swiftly round and round the wrecked crew; sideways churning the water in his vengeful wake, as if lashing him

*This motion is peculiar to the sperm whale. It receives its designation (pitchpoling) from its being likened to that preliminary up-and-down poise of the whale-lance, in the exercise called pitchpoling, previously described. By this motion the whale must best and most comprehensively view whatever objects may be encircling him.

self up to still another and more deadly assault. The sight of the splintered boat seemed to madden him, as the blood of grapes and mulberries cast before Antiochus's elephants in the book of Maccabees. Meanwhile Ahab half smothered in the foam of the whale's insolent tail, and too much of a cripple to swim, – though he could still keep afloat, even in the heart of such a whirlpool as that; helpless Ahab's head was seen, like a tossed bubble which the least chance shock might burst. From the boat's fragmentary stern, Fedallah incuriously and mildly eyed him; the clinging crew, at the other drifting end, could not succor him; more than enough was it for them to look to themselves. For so revolvingly appalling was the White Whale's aspect, and so planetarily swift the ever-contracting circles he made, that he seemed horizontally swooping upon them. And though the other boats, unharmed, still hovered hard by; still they dared not pull into the eddy to strike, lest that should be the signal for the instant destruction of the jeopardized castaways, Ahab and all; nor in that case could they themselves hope to escape. With straining eyes, then, they remained on the outer edge of the direful zone, whose centre had now become the old man's head.

Meantime, from the beginning all this had been descried from the ship's mast heads; and squaring her yards, she had borne down upon the scene; and was now so nigh, that Ahab in the water hailed her; – 'Sail on the' – but that moment a breaking sea dashed on him from Moby Dick, and whelmed him for the time. But struggling out of it again, and chancing to rise on a towering crest, he shouted, – 'Sail on the whale! – Drive him off!'

The Pequod's prow was pointed; and breaking up the charmed circle, she effectually parted the white whale from his victim. As he sullenly swam off, the boats flew to the rescue.

Dragged into Stubb's boat with blood-shot, blinded eyes, the white brine caking in his wrinkles; the long tension of Ahab's bodily strength did crack, and helplessly he yielded to his body's doom: for a time, lying all crushed in the bottom of Stubb's boat, like one trodden under foot of herds of elephants. Far inland, nameless wails came from him, as desolate sounds from out ravines.

But this intensity of his physical prostration did but so much the more abbreviate it. In an instant's compass, great hearts sometimes condense to one deep pang, the sum total of those shallow pains kindly diffused through feebler men's whole lives. And so, such hearts, though summary in each one suffering; still, if the gods decree it, in their life-time aggregate a whole age of woe, wholly made up of instantaneous intensities; for even in their pointless centres, those noble natures contain the entire circumferences of inferior souls.

'The harpoon,' said Ahab, half way rising, and draggingly leaning on one bended arm – 'is it safe?'

'Aye, sir, for it was not darted; this is it,' said Stubb, showing it.

'Lay it before me; – any missing men?'

'One, two, three, four, five; – there were five oars, sir, and here are five men.'

'That's good. – Help me, man; I wish to stand. So, so, I see him! there! there! going to leeward still; what a leaping spout! – Hands off from me! The eternal sap runs up in Ahab's bones again! Set the sail; out oars; the helm!'

It is often the case that when a boat is stove, its crew, being picked up by another boat, help to work that second boat; and the chase is thus continued with what is called double-banked oars. It was thus now. But the added power of the boat did not equal the added power of the whale, for he seemed to have treble-banked his every fin; swimming with a velocity which plainly showed, that if now, under these circumstances, pushed on, the chase would prove an indefinitely prolonged, if not a hopeless one; nor could any crew endure for so long a period, such an unintermitted, intense straining at the oar; a thing barely tolerable only in some one brief vicissitude. The ship itself, then, as it sometimes happens, offered the most promising intermediate means of overtaking the chase. Accordingly, the boats now made for her, and were soon swayed up to their cranes – the two parts of the wrecked boat having been previously secured by her – and then hoisting everything to her side, and stacking her canvas high up, and sideways outstretching it with stun-sails, like the double-jointed wings of an albatross; the Pequod bore down in the leeward wake of Moby Dick. At the well known, methodic intervals, the whale's glittering spout was regularly announced from the manned mast-heads; and when he would be reported as just gone down, Ahab would take the time, and then pacing the deck, binnacle-watch in hand, so soon as the last second of the allotted hour expired, his voice was heard. – 'Whose is the doubloon now? D'ye see him?' and if the reply was, No, sir! straightway he commanded them to lift him to his perch. In this way the day wore on; Ahab, now aloft and motionless; anon, unrestingly pacing the planks.

As he was thus walking, uttering no sound, except to hail the men aloft, or to bid them hoist a sail still higher, or to spread one to a still greater breadth – thus to and fro pacing, beneath his slouched hat, at every turn he passed his own wrecked boat, which had been dropped upon the quarter-deck, and lay there reversed; broken bow to shattered stern. At last he paused before it; and as in an already over-clouded sky fresh troops of clouds will sometimes sail across, so over the old man's face there now stole some such added gloom as this.

Stubb saw him pause; and perhaps intending, not vainly, though, to evince his own unabated fortitude, and thus keep up a valiant place in his Captain's mind, he advanced, and eyeing the wreck exclaimed – 'The thistle the ass refused; it pricked his mouth too keenly, sir; ha! ha!'

'What soulless thing is this that laughs before a wreck? Man, man! did I not know thee brave as fearless fire (and as mechanical) I could swear thou wert a poltroon. Groan nor laugh should be heard before a wreck.'

'Aye, sir,' said Starbuck drawing near, ''tis a solemn sight; an omen, and an ill one.'

'Omen? omen? – the dictionary! If the gods think to

speak outright to man, they will honorably speak outright; not shake their heads, and give an old wives' darkling hint. – Begone! Ye two are the opposite poles of one thing; Starbuck is Stubb reversed, and Stubb is Starbuck; and ye two are all mankind; and Ahab stands alone among the millions of the peopled earth, nor gods nor men his neighbors! Cold, cold – I shiver! – How now? Aloft there? D'ye see him? Sing out for every spout, though he spout ten times a second!'

The day was nearly done; only the hem of his golden robe was rustling. Soon, it was almost dark, but the look-out men still remained unset.

'Can't see the spout now, sir; – too dark' – cried a voice from the air.

'How heading when last seen?'

'As before, sir, – straight to leeward.'

'Good! he will travel slower now 'tis night. Down royals and top-gallant stun-sails, Mr Starbuck. We must not run over him before morning; he's making a passage now, and may heave-to a while. Helm there! keep her full before the wind! – Aloft! come down! – Mr Stubb, send a fresh hand to the fore-mast head, and see it manned till morning.' – Then advancing towards the doubloon in the main-mast – 'Men, this gold is mine, for I earned it; but I shall let it abide here till the White Whale is dead; and then, whosoever of ye first raises him, upon the day he shall be killed, this gold is that man's; and if on that day I shall again raise him, then ten times its sum shall be divided among all of ye! Away now! – the deck is thine, sir.'

And so saying, he placed himself half way within the scuttle, and slouching his hat, stood there till dawn, except when at intervals rousing himself to see how the night wore on.

134

THE CHASE – SECOND DAY

At day-break, the three mast-heads were punctually manned afresh.

'D'ye see him?' cried Ahab, after allowing a little space for the light to spread.

'See nothing, sir.'

'Turn up all hands and make sail! he travels faster than I thought for; – the top-gallant sails! – aye, they should have been kept on her all night. But no matter – 'tis but resting for the rush.'

Here be it said, that this pertinacious pursuit of one particular whale, continued through day into night, and through night into day, is a thing by no means unprecedented in the South sea fishery. For such is the wonderful skill, prescience of experience, and invincible confidence acquired by some great natural geniuses among the Nantucket commanders; that from the simple observation of a whale when last descried, they will, under certain given circumstances, pretty accurately foretell both the direction in which he will continue to swim for a time, while out of sight, as well as his probable rate of progression during that period. And, in these cases, somewhat as a pilot, when about losing sight of a coast, whose general trending he well knows, and which he desires shortly to return to again, but at some further point; like as this pilot stands by his compass, and takes the precise bearing of the cape at present visible, in order the more certainly to hit aright the remote, unseen headland, eventually to be visited: so does the fisherman, at his compass, with the whale; for after being chased, and diligently marked, through several hours of daylight, then, when night obscures the fish, the creature's future wake through the darkness is almost as established to the sagacious mind of the hunter, as the pilot's coast is to him. So that to this hunter's wondrous skill, the proverbial evanescence of a thing writ in water, a wake, is to all desired purposes well nigh as reliable as the steadfast land. And as the mighty iron Leviathan of the modern railway is so familiarly known in its every pace, that, with watches in their hands, men time his rate as doctors that of a baby's pulse; and lightly say of it, the up train or the down train will reach such or such a spot, at such or such an hour; even so, almost, there are occasions when these Nantucketers time that other Leviathan of the deep, according to the observed humor of his speed; and say to themselves, so many hours hence this whale will have gone two hundred miles, will have about reached this or that degree of latitude or longitude. But to render this acuteness at all successful in the end, the wind and the sea must be the whaleman's allies; for of what present avail to the becalmed or windbound mariner is the skill that assures him he is exactly ninety-three leagues and a quarter from his port? Inferable from these statements, are many collateral subtile matters touching the chase of whales.

The ship tore on; leaving such a furrow in the sea as when a cannon-ball, missent, becomes a plough-share and turns up the level field.

'By salt and hemp!' cried Stubb, 'but this swift motion of the deck creeps up one's legs and tingles at the heart. This ship and I are two brave fellows! – Ha! ha! Some one take me up, and launch me, spine-wise, on the sea, – for by live-oaks! my spine's a keel. Ha, ha! we go the gait that leaves no dust behind!'

'There she blows – she blows! – she blows! – right ahead!' was now the mast-head cry.

'Aye, aye!' cried Stubb, 'I knew it – ye can't escape – blow on and split your spout, O whale! the mad fiend himself is after ye! blow your trump – blister your lungs! – Ahab will dam off your blood, as a miller shuts his water-gate upon the stream!'

And Stubb did but speak out for well nigh all that crew. The frenzies of the chase had by this time worked them bubblingly up, like old wine worked anew. Whatever pale fears and forebodings some of them might have felt before; these were not only now kept out of sight through the growing awe of Ahab, but they were broken up, and on all sides routed, as timid prairie hares that scatter before the bounding bison. The hand of Fate had snatched all their souls; and by the stirring perils of the previous day; the rack of the past night's suspense; the fixed, unfearing, blind, reckless way in which their wild craft went plunging towards its flying mark; by all these things, their hearts were bowled along. The wind that made great bellies of their sails, and rushed the vessel on by arms invisible as irresistible; this seemed the symbol of that unseen agency which so enslaved them to the race.

They were one man, not thirty. For as the one ship that held them all; though it was put together of all contrasting things – oak, and maple, and pine wood; iron, and pitch, and hemp - yet all these ran into each other in the one concrete hull, which shot on its way, both balanced and directed by the long central keel; even so, all the individualities of the crew, this man's valor, that man's fear; guilt and guiltiness, all varieties were welded into oneness, and were all directed to that fatal goal which Ahab their one lord and keel did point to.

The rigging lived. The mast-heads, like the tops of tall palms, were outspreadingly tufted with arms and legs. Clinging to a spar with one hand, some reached forth the other with impatient wavings; others, shading their eyes from the vivid sunlight, sat far out on the rocking yards; all the spars in full bearing of mortals, ready and ripe for their fate. Ah! how they still strove through that infinite blueness to seek out the thing that might destroy them!

'Why sing ye not out for him, if ye see him?' cried Ahab, when, after the lapse of some minutes since the first cry, no more had been heard. 'Sway me up, men; ye have been deceived; not Moby Dick casts one odd jet that way, and then disappears.'

It was even so; in their headlong eagerness, the men had mistaken some other thing for the whale-spout, as the event itself soon proved; for hardly had Ahab reached his perch; hardly was the rope belayed to its pin on deck, when he struck the key-note to an orchestra, that made the air vibrate as with the combined discharges of rifles. The triumphant halloo of thirty buckskin lungs was heard, as – much nearer to the ship than the place of the imaginary jet, less than a mile ahead – Moby Dick bodily burst into view! For not by any calm and indolent spoutings; not by the peaceable gush of that mystic fountain in his head, did the White Whale now reveal his vicinity; but by the far more wondrous phenomenon of breaching. Rising with his utmost velocity from the furthest depths, the Sperm Whale thus booms his entire bulk into the pure element of air, and piling up a mountain of dazzling foam, shows his place to the distance of seven miles and more. In those moments, the torn, enraged waves he shakes off, seem his mane; in some cases, this breaching is his act of defiance.

'There she breaches! there she breaches!' was the cry, as in his immeasurable bravadoes the White Whale tossed himself salmon-like to Heaven. So suddenly seen in the blue plain of the sea, and relieved against the still bluer margin of the sky, the spray that he raised, for the moment, intolerably glittered and glared like a glacier; and stood there gradually fading and fading away from its first sparkling intensity, to the dim mistiness of an advancing shower in a vale.

'Aye, breach your last to the sun, Moby Dick!' cried Ahab, 'thy hour and thy harpoon are at hand! – Down! down all of ye, but one man at the fore. The boats! – stand by!'

Unmindful of the tedious rope-ladders of the shrouds, the men, like shooting stars, slid to the deck, by the isolated backstays and halyards; while Ahab, less dartingly, but still rapidly was dropped from his perch.

'Lower away,' he cried, so soon as he had reached his boat – a spare one, rigged the afternoon previous. 'Mr Starbuck, the ship is thine – keep away from the boats, but keep near them. Lower, all!'

As if to strike a quick terror into them, by this time being the first assailant himself, Moby Dick had turned, and was now coming for the three crews. Ahab's boat was central; and cheering his men, he told them he would take the whale head-and-head, – that is, pull straight up to his forehead, – a not uncommon thing; for when within a certain limit, such a course excludes the coming onset from the whale's sidelong vision. But ere that close limit was gained, and while yet all three boats were plain as the ship's three masts to his eye; the White Whale churning himself into furious speed, almost in an instant as it were, rushing among the boats with open jaws, and a lashing tail, offered appalling battle on every side; and heedless of the irons darted at him from every boat, seemed only intent on annihilating each separate plank of which those boats were made. But skilfully manœuvred, incessantly wheeling like trained chargers in the field; the boats for a while eluded him; though, at times, but by a plank's breadth; while all the time, Ahab's unearthly slogan tore every other cry but his to shreds.

But at last in his untraceable evolutions, the White Whale so crossed and recrossed, and in a thousand ways entangled the slack of the three lines now fast to him, that they foreshortened, and, of themselves, warped the devoted boats towards the planted irons in him; though now for a moment the whale drew aside a little, as if to rally for a more tremendous charge. Seizing that opportunity, Ahab first paid out more line: and then was rapidly hauling and jerking in upon it again – hoping that way to disencumber it of some snarls – when lo! – a sight more savage than the embattled teeth of sharks!

Caught and twisted – corkscrewed in the mazes of the line, loose harpoons and lances, with all their bristling barbs and points, came flashing and dripping up to the chocks in the bows of Ahab's boat. Only one thing could be done. Seizing the boat-knife, he critically reached within – through – and then, without – the rays of steel; dragged in the line beyond, passed it, inboard, to the bowsman, and then, twice sundering the rope near the chocks – dropped the intercepted fagot of steel into the sea; and was all fast again. That instant, the White Whale made a sudden rush among the remaining tangles of the other lines; by so doing, irresistibly dragged the more involved boats of Stubb and Flask towards his flukes; dashed them together like two rolling husks on a surf-beaten beach, and then, diving down into the sea, disappeared in a boiling maelstrom, in which, for a space, the odorous cedar chips of the wrecks danced round and round, like the grated nutmeg in a swiftly stirred bowl of punch.

While the two crews were yet circling in the waters, reaching out after the revolving line-tubs, oars, and other floating furniture, while aslope little Flask bobbed up and down like an empty vial, twitching his legs upwards to escape the dreaded jaws of sharks, and Stubb was lustily singing out for some one to ladle him up; and while the old man's line – now parting – admitted of his pulling into the creamy pool to rescue whom he could; – in that wild simultaneousness of a thousand concreted perils, – Ahab's yet unstricken boat seemed drawn up towards Heaven by invisible wires, – as, arrow-like, shooting perpendicularly from the sea, the White Whale dashed his broad forehead against its bottom, and sent it, turning over and over, into the air; till it fell again – gunwale downwards – and Ahab and his men struggled out from under it, like seals from a sea-side cave.

The first uprising momentum of the whale – modifying its direction as he struck the surface – involuntarily launched him along it, to a little distance from the centre of the destruction he had made; and with his back to it, he now lay for a moment slowly feeling with his flukes from side to side; and whenever a stray oar, bit of plank, the least chip or crumb of the boats touched his skin, his tail swiftly drew back, and came sideways smiting the sea. But soon, as if satisfied that his work for that time was done, he pushed his pleated forehead through the ocean, and trailing after him the intertangled lines, continued his leeward way at a traveller's methodic pace.

As before, the attentive ship having descried the whole fight, again came bearing down to the rescue, and dropping a boat, picked up the floating mariners, tubs, oars, and whatever else could be caught at, and safely landed them on her decks. Some sprained shoulders, wrists, and ankles; livid contusions; wrenched harpoons and lances; inextricable intricacies of rope; shattered oars and planks; all these were there; but no fatal or even serious ill seemed to have befallen any one. As with Fedallah the day before, so Ahab was now found grimly clinging to his boat's broken half, which afforded a comparatively easy float; nor did it so exhaust him as the previous day's mishap.

But when he was helped to the deck, all eyes were fastened upon him; as instead of standing by himself he still half-hung upon the shoulder of Starbuck, who had thus far been the foremost to assist him. His ivory leg had been snapped off, leaving but one short sharp splinter.

'Aye aye, Starbuck, 'tis sweet to lean sometimes, be the leaner who he will; and would old Ahab had leaned oftener than he has.'

'The ferrule has not stood, sir,' said the carpenter, now coming up; 'I put good work into that leg.'

'But no bones broken, sir, I hope,' said Stubb with true concern.

'Aye! and all splintered to pieces, Stubb! – d'ye see it. – But even with a broken bone, old Ahab is untouched; and I account no living bone of mine one jot more me, than this dead one that's lost. Nor white whale, nor man, nor fiend, can so much as graze old Ahab in his own proper and inaccessible being. Can any lead touch yonder floor, any mast scrape yonder roof? – Aloft there! which way?'

'Dead to leeward, sir.'

'Up helm, then; pile on the sail again, ship keepers! down the rest of the spare boats and rig them – Mr Starbuck away, and muster the boats' crews.'

'Let me first help thee towards the bulwarks, sir.'

'Oh, oh, oh! how this splinter gores me now! Accursed fate! that the unconquerable captain in the soul should have such a craven mate!'

'Sir?'

'My body, man, not thee. Give me something for a cane – there, that shivered lance will do. Muster the men. Surely I have not seen him yet. By heaven it cannot be! – missing? – quick! call them all.'

The old man's hinted thought was true. Upon mustering the company, the Parsee was not there.

'The Parsee!' cried Stubb – 'he must have been caught in —'

'The black vomit wrench thee! – run all of ye above, alow, cabin, forecastle – find him – not gone – not gone!'

But quickly they returned to him with the tidings that the Parsee was nowhere to be found.

'Aye, sir,' said Stubb – 'caught among the tangles of your line – I thought I saw him dragging under.'

'*My* line! *my* line? Gone? – gone? What means that little word? – What death-knell rings in it, that old Ahab shakes as if he were the belfry. The harpoon, too! – toss over the litter there, – d'ye see it? – the forged iron, men, the white whale's – no, no, no, – blistered fool! this hand did dart it! – 'tis in the fish! – Aloft there! Keep him nailed – Quick! – all hands to the rigging of the boats – collect the oars – harpooneers! the irons, the irons! – hoist the royals higher – a pull on all the sheets! – helm there! steady, steady for your life! I'll ten times girdle the unmeasured globe; yea and dive straight through it, but I'll slay him yet!'

'Great God! but for one single instant show thyself,' cried Starbuck; 'never, never wilt thou capture him, old man – In Jesus' name no more of this, that's worse than devil's madness. Two days chased; twice stove to splinters; thy very leg once more snatched from under thee; thy evil shadow gone – all good angels mobbing thee with warnings: – what more wouldst thou have? – Shall we keep chasing this murderous fish till he swamps the last man? Shall we be dragged by him to the bottom of the sea? Shall we be towed by him to the infernal world? Oh, oh, – Impiety and blasphemy to hunt him more!'

'Starbuck, of late I've felt strangely moved to thee; ever since that hour we both saw – thou know'st what, in one another's eyes. But in this matter of the whale, be the front of thy face to me as the palm of this hand – a lipless, unfeatured blank. Ahab is for ever Ahab, man. This whole act's immutably decreed. 'Twas rehearsed by thee and me a billion years before this ocean rolled. Fool! I am the Fates' lieutenant; I act under orders. Look thou, underling! that thou obeyest mine. – Stand round me, men. Ye see an old man cut down to the stump; leaning on a shivered lance; propped up on a lonely foot. 'Tis Ahab – his body's part; but Ahab's soul's a centipede, that moves upon a hundred legs. I feel strained, half stranded, as ropes that tow dismasted frigates in a gale; and I may look so. But ere I break, ye'll hear me crack; and till ye hear *that*, know that Ahab's hawser tows his purpose yet. Believe ye, men, in the things called omens? Then laugh aloud, and cry encore! For ere they drown, drowning things will twice rise to the surface; then rise again, to sink for evermore. So with Moby Dick – two days he's floated – to-morrow will be the third. Aye, men, he'll rise once more, – but only to spout his last! D'ye feel brave, men, brave?'

'As fearless fire,' cried Stubb.

'And as mechanical,' muttered Ahab. Then as the men went forward, he muttered on: – 'The things called omens! And yesterday I talked the same to Starbuck there, concerning my broken boat. Oh! how valiantly I seek to drive out of others' hearts what's clinched so fast in mine! – The Parsee – the Parsee! – gone, gone? and he was to go before: – but still was to be seen again ere I could perish – How's that? – There's a riddle now might baffle all the lawyers backed by the ghosts of the whole line of judges: – like a hawk's beak it pecks my brain. *I'll, I'll* solve it, though!'

When dusk descended, the whale was still in sight to leeward.

So once more the sail was shortened, and everything passed nearly as on the previous night; only, the sound of hammers, and the hum of the grindstone was heard till nearly daylight, as the men toiled by lanterns in the complete and careful rigging of the spare boats and sharpening their fresh weapons for the morrow. Meantime, of the broken keel of Ahab's wrecked craft the carpenter made him another leg; while still as on the night before, slouched Ahab stood fixed within his scuttle; his hid, heliotrope glance anticipatingly gone backward on its dial; set due eastward for the earliest sun.

135

THE CHASE – THIRD DAY

THE morning of the third day dawned fair and fresh, and once more the solitary night-man at the fore-mast-head was relieved by crowds of the daylight look-outs, who dotted every mast and almost every spar.

'D'ye see him?' cried Ahab; but the whale was not yet in sight.

'In his infallible wake, though; but follow that wake, that's all. Helm there; steady, as thou goest, and hast been going. What a lovely day again! were it a new-made world, and made for a summer-house to the angels, and this morning the first of its throwing open to them, a fairer day could not dawn upon that world. Here's food for thought, had Ahab time to think; but Ahab never thinks; he only feels, feels, feels; *that's* tingling enough for mortal man! to think's audacity. God only has that right and privilege. Thinking is, or ought to be, a coolness and a calmness; and our poor hearts throb, and our poor brains beat too much for that. And yet, I've sometimes thought my brain was very calm – frozen calm, this old skull cracks so, like a glass in which the contents turn to ice, and shiver it. And still this hair is growing now; this moment growing, and heat must breed it; but no, it's like that sort of common grass that will grow anywhere, between the earthy clefts of Greenland ice or in Vesuvius' lava. How the wild winds blow it; they whip it about me as the torn shreds of split sails lash the tossed ship they cling to. A vile wind that has no doubt blown ere this through prison corridors and cells, and wards of hospitals, and ventilated them, and now comes blowing hither as innocent as fleeces. Out upon it! – it's tainted. Were I the wind, I'd blow no more on such a wicked, miserable world. I'd crawl somewhere to a cave, and slink there. And yet, 'tis a noble and heroic thing, the wind! who ever conquered it? In every fight it has the last and bitterest blow. Run tilting at it, and you but run through it. Ha! a coward wind that strikes stark naked men, but will not stand to receive a single blow. Even Ahab is a braver thing – a nobler thing than *that*. Would now the wind but had a body; but all the things that most exasperate and outrage mortal man, all these things are bodiless, but only bodiless as objects, not as agents. There's a most special, a most cunning, oh, a most malicious difference! And yet, I say again, and swear it now, that there's something all glorious and gracious in the wind. These warm Trade Winds, at least, that in the clear heavens blow straight on, in strong and steadfast, vigorous mildness; and veer not from their mark, however the baser currents of the sea may turn and tack, and mightiest Mississippies of the land shift and swerve about, uncertain where to go at last. And by the eternal Poles! these same Trades that so directly blow my good ship on; these Trades, or something like them – something so unchangeable, and full as strong, blow my keeled soul along! To it! Aloft there! What d'ye see?'

'Nothing, sir.'

'Nothing! and noon at hand! The doubloon goes a-begging! See the sun! Aye, aye, it must be so. I've oversailed him. How, got the start? Aye, he's chasing *me* now; not I, *him* – that's bad; I might have known it, too. Fool! the lines – the harpoons he's towing. Aye, aye, I have run him by last night. About! about! Come down, all of ye, but the regular look outs! Man the braces!'

Steering as she had done, the wind had been somewhat on the Pequod's quarter, so that now being pointed in the reverse direction, the braced ship sailed hard upon the breeze as she rechurned the cream in her own white wake.

'Against the wind he now steers for the open jaw,' murmured Starbuck to himself, as he coiled the new-hauled main-brace upon the rail. 'God keep us, but already my bones feel damp within me, and from the inside wet my flesh. I misdoubt me that I disobey my God in obeying him!'

'Stand by to sway me up!' cried Ahab, advancing to the hempen basket. 'We should meet him soon.'

'Aye, aye, sir,' and straightway Starbuck did Ahab's bidding, and once more Ahab swung on high.

A whole hour now passed; gold-beaten out to ages. Time itself now held long breaths with keen suspense. But at last, some three points off the weather bow, Ahab descried the spout again, and instantly from the three mast-heads three shrieks went up as if the tongues of fire had voiced it.

'Forehead to forehead I meet thee, this third time, Moby Dick! On deck there! – brace sharper up; crowd her into the wind's eye. He's too far off to lower yet, Mr Starbuck. The sails shake! Stand over that helmsman with a top-maul! So, so; he travels fast, and I must down. But let me have one more good round look aloft here at the sea; there's time for that. An old, old sight, and yet somehow so young; aye, and not changed a wink since I first saw it, a boy, from the sand-hills of Nantucket! The same! – the same! – the same to Noah as to me. There's a soft shower to leeward. Such lovely leewardings! They must lead somewhere – to something else than common land, more palmy than the palms. Leeward! the white whale goes that way; to look to windward, then; the better if the bitterer quarter. But good bye, good bye, old mast-head! What's this? – green? aye, tiny mosses in these warped cracks. No such green weather stains on Ahab's head! There's the difference now between man's old age and matter's. But aye, old mast, we both grow old together; sound in our hulls, though, are we not, my ship? Aye, minus a leg, that's all. By heaven this dead wood has the better of my live flesh every way. I can't compare with it; and I've known some ships made of dead trees outlast the lives of men made of the most vital stuff of vital fathers. What's that he said? he should still go before me, my pilot; and yet to be seen again? But where? Will I have eyes at the bottom of the sea, supposing I descend those endless stairs? and all night I've been sailing from him, wherever he did sink to. Aye, aye, like many more thou told'st direful truth as touching thyself, O Parsee; but, Ahab, there thy shot fell short. Good by, mast-head – keep a good eye upon the whale, the while I'm gone. We'll talk to-morrow, nay, to-night, when the white whale lies down there, tied by head and tail.'

He gave the word; and still gazing round him, was steadily lowered through the cloven blue air to the deck.

In due time the boats were lowered; but as standing in his shallop's stern, Ahab just hovered upon the point of the descent, he waved to the mate, – who held one of the tackle-ropes on deck – and bade him pause.

'Starbuck!'

'Sir?'

'For the third time my soul's ship starts upon this voyage, Starbuck.'

'Aye, sir, thou wilt have it so.'

'Some ships sail from their ports, and ever afterwards are missing, Starbuck!'

'Truth, sir: saddest truth.'

'Some men die at ebb tide; some at low water; some at the full of the flood; – and I feel now like a billow that's all one crested comb, Starbuck. I am old; – shake hands with me, man.'

Their hands met; their eyes fastened; Starbuck's tears the glue.

'Oh, my captain, my captain! – noble heart – go not – go not! – see, it's a brave man that weeps; how great the agony of the persuasion then!'

'Lower away!' – cried Ahab, tossing the mate's arm from him. 'Stand by the crew!'

In an instant the boat was pulling round close under the stern.

'The sharks! the sharks!' cried a voice from the low cabin-window there; 'O master, my master, come back!'

But Ahab heard nothing; for his own voice was high-lifted then; and the boat leaped on.

Yet the voice spake true; for scarce had he pushed from the ship, when numbers of sharks, seemingly rising from out the dark waters beneath the hull, maliciously snapped at the blades of the oars, every time they dipped in the water; and in this way accompanied the boat with their bites. It is a thing not uncommonly happening to the whale-boats in those swarming seas; the sharks at times apparently following them in the same prescient way that vultures hover over the banners of marching regiments in the east. But these were the first sharks that had been observed by the Pequod since the White Whale had been first descried; and whether it was that Ahab's crew were all such tiger-yellow barbarians, and therefore their flesh more musky to the senses of the sharks – a matter sometimes well known to affect them, – however it was, they seemed to follow that one boat without molesting the others.

'Heart of wrought steel!' murmured Starbuck gazing over the side, and following with his eyes the receding boat – 'canst thou yet ring boldly to that sight? – lowering thy keel among ravening sharks, and followed by them, open-mouthed to the chase; and this the critical third day? – For when three days flow together in one continuous intense pursuit; be sure the first is the morning, the second the noon, and the third the evening and the end of that thing – be that end what it may. Oh! my God! what is this that shoots through me, and leaves me so deadly calm, yet expectant, – fixed at the top of a shudder! Future things swim before me, as in empty outlines and skeletons; all the past is somehow grown dim. Mary, girl! thou fadest in pale glories behind me; boy! I seem to see but thy eyes grown wondrous blue. Strangest problems of life seem clearing; but clouds sweep between – Is my journey's end coming? My legs feel faint; like his who has footed it all day. Feel thy heart, – beats it yet? – Stir thyself, Starbuck! – stave it off – move, move! speak aloud! – Mast-head there! See ye my boy's hand on the hill? – Crazed; – aloft there! – keep thy keenest eye upon the boats: – mark well the whale! – Ho! again! – drive off that hawk! see! he pecks – he tears the vane' – pointing to the red flag flying at the main-truck – 'Ha! he soars away with it! – Where's the old man now? see'st thou that sight, oh Ahab! – shudder, shudder!'

The boats had not gone very far, when by a signal from the mast-heads – a downward pointed arm, Ahab knew that the whale had sounded; but intending to be near him at the next rising, he held on his way a little sideways from the vessel; the becharmed crew maintaining the profoundest silence, as the head-beat waves hammered and hammered against the opposing bow.

'Drive, drive in your nails, oh ye waves! to their uttermost heads drive them in! ye but strike a thing without a lid; and no coffin and no hearse can be mine: – and hemp only can kill me! Ha! ha!'

Suddenly the waters around them slowly swelled in broad circles; then quickly upheaved, as if sideways sliding from a submerged berg of ice, swiftly rising to the surface. A low rumbling sound was heard; a subterraneous hum; and then all held their breaths; as bedraggled with trailing ropes, and harpoons, and lances, a vast form shot lengthwise, but obliquely from the sea. Shrouded in a thin drooping veil of mist, it hovered for a moment in the rainbowed air; and then fell swamping back into the deep. Crushed thirty feet upwards, the waters flashed for an instant like heaps of fountains, then brokenly sank in a shower of flakes, leaving the circling surface creamed like new milk round the marble trunk of the whale.

'Give way!' cried Ahab to the oarsmen, and the boats darted forward to the attack; but maddened by yesterday's fresh irons that corroded in him, Moby Dick seemed combinedly possessed by all the angels that fell from heaven. The wide tiers of welded tendons overspreading his broad white forehead, beneath the transparent skin, looked knitted together; as head on, he came churning his tail among the boats; and once more flailed them apart; spilling out the irons and lances from the two mates' boats, and dashing in one side of the upper part of their bows, but leaving Ahab's almost without a scar.

While Daggoo and Queequeg were stopping the strained planks; and as the whale swimming out from them, turned, and showed one entire flank as he shot by them again; at that moment a quick cry went up. Lashed round and round to the fish's back; pinioned in the turns upon turns in which, during the past night, the whale had reeled the involutions of the lines around him, the half torn body of the Parsee was seen; his sable raiment frayed to shreds; his distended eyes turned full upon old Ahab.

The harpoon dropped from his hand.

'Befooled, befooled!' – drawing in a long lean breath – 'Aye, Parsee! I see thee again. – Aye, and thou goest before; and this, *this* then is the hearse that thou didst promise. But I hold thee to the last letter of thy word. Where is the second hearse? Away, mates, to the ship! those boats are useless now; repair them if ye can in time, and return to me; if not, Ahab is enough to die – Down, men! the first thing that but offers to jump from this boat I stand in, that thing I harpoon. Ye are not other men, but my arms and my legs; and so obey me. – Where's the whale? gone down again?'

But he looked too nigh the boat; for as if bent upon escaping with the corpse he bore, and as if the particular place of the last encounter had been but a stage in his leeward voyage, Moby Dick was now again steadily swimming forward; and had almost passed the ship, – which thus far had been sailing in the contrary direction to him, though for the present her headway had been stopped. He seemed swimming with his utmost velocity, and now only intent upon pursuing his own straight path in the sea.

'Oh! Ahab,' cried Starbuck, 'not too late is it, even now, the third day, to desist. See! Moby Dick seeks thee not. It is thou, thou, that madly seekest him!'

Setting sail to the rising wind, the lonely boat was swiftly impelled to leeward, by both oars and canvas. And at last when Ahab was sliding by the vessel, so near as plainly to distinguish Starbuck's face as he leaned over the rail, he hailed him to turn the vessel about, and follow him, not too swiftly, at a judicious interval. Glancing upwards, he saw Tashtego, Queequeg, and Daggoo, eagerly mounting to the three mast-heads; while the oarsmen were rocking in the two staved boats which had but just been hoisted to the side, and were busily at work in repairing them. One after the other, through the port-holes, as he sped, he also caught flying glimpses of Stubb and Flask, busying themselves on deck among bundles of new irons and lances. As he saw all this; as he heard the hammers in the broken boats; far other hammers seemed driving a nail into his heart. But he rallied. And now marking that the vane or flag was gone from the main-mast-head, he shouted to Tashtego, who had just gained that perch, to descend again for another flag, and a hammer and nails, and so nail it to the mast.

Whether fagged by the three days' running chase, and the resistance to his swimming in the knotted hamper he bore; or whether it was some latent deceitfulness and malice in him: whichever was true, the White Whale's way now began to abate, as it seemed, from the boat so rapidly nearing him once more; though indeed the whale's last start had not been so long a one as before. And still as Ahab glided over the waves the unpitying sharks accompanied him; and so pertinaciously stuck to the boat; and so continually bit at the plying oars, that the blades became jagged and crunched, and left small splinters in the sea, at almost every dip.

'Heed them not! those teeth but give new rowlocks to your oars. Pull on! 'tis the better rest, the shark's jaw than the yielding water.'

'But at every bite, sir, the thin blades grow smaller and smaller!'

'They will last long enough! pull on! – But who can tell' – he muttered – 'whether these sharks swim to feast on the whale or on Ahab? – But pull on! Aye, all alive, now – we near him. The helm! take the helm; let me pass,' – and so saying, two of the oarsmen helped him forward to the bows of the still flying boat.

At length as the craft was cast to one side, and ran ranging along with the White Whale's flank, he seemed strangely oblivious of its advance – as the whale sometimes will – and Ahab was fairly within the smoky mountain mist, which, thrown off from the whale's spout, curled round his great, Monadnock hump; he was even thus close to him; when, with body arched back, and both arms lengthwise high-lifted to the poise, he darted his fierce iron, and his far fiercer curse into the hated whale. As both steel and curse sank to the socket, as if sucked into a morass, Moby Dick sideways writhed; spasmodically rolled his nigh flank against the bow, and, without staving a hole in it, so suddenly canted the boat over, that had it not been for the elevated part of the gunwale to which he then clung, Ahab would once more have been tossed into the sea. As it was, three of the oarsmen – who foreknew not the precise instant of the dart, and were therefore unprepared for its effects – these were flung out; but so fell, that, in an instant two of them clutched the gunwale again, and rising to its level on a combing wave, hurled themselves bodily inboard again; the third man helplessly dropping astern, but still afloat and swimming.

Almost simultaneously, with a mighty volition of ungraduated, instantaneous swiftness, the White Whale darted through the weltering sea. But when Ahab cried out to the steersman to take new turns with the line, and hold it so; and commanded the crew to turn round on their seats, and tow the boat up to the mark; the moment the treacherous line felt that double strain and tug, it snapped in the empty air!

'What breaks in me? Some sinew cracks! – 'tis whole again; oars! oars! Burst in upon him!'

Hearing the tremendous rush of the sea-crashing boat, the whale wheeled round to present his blank forehead at bay; but in that evolution, catching sight of the nearing black hull of the ship; seemingly seeing in it the source of all his persecutions; bethinking it – it may be – a larger and nobler foe; of a sudden, he bore down upon its advancing prow, smiting his jaws amid fiery showers of foam.

Ahab staggered; his hand smote his forehead. 'I grow blind; hands! stretch out before me that I may yet grope my way. Is't night?'

'The whale! The ship!' cried the cringing oarsmen.

'Oars! oars! Slope downwards to thy depths, O sea, that ere it be for ever too late, Ahab may slide this last, last time upon his mark! I see: the ship! the ship! Dash on, my men! Will ye not save my ship?'

But as the oarsmen violently forced their boat through the sledge-hammering seas, the before whale-smitten bow-ends of two planks burst through, and in an instant almost, the temporarily disabled boat lay nearly level with the waves; its half-wading, splashing crew, trying hard to stop the gap and bale out the pouring water.

Meantime, for that one beholding instant, Tashtego's mast-head hammer remained suspended in his hand; and the red flag, half-wrapping him as with a plaid, then streamed itself straight out from him, as his own forward-flowing heart; while Starbuck and Stubb, standing upon the bowsprit beneath, caught sight of the down-coming monster just as soon as he.

'The whale, the whale! Up helm, up helm! Oh, all ye sweet powers of air, now hug me close! Let not Starbuck die, if die he must, in a woman's fainting fit. Up helm, I say – ye fools, the jaw! the jaw! Is this the end of all my bursting prayers? all my life-long fidelities? Oh, Ahab, Ahab, lo, thy work. Steady! helmsman, steady. Nay, nay! Up helm again! He turns to meet us! Oh, his unappeasable brow drives on towards one, whose duty tells him he cannot depart. My God, stand by me now!'

'Stand not by me, but stand under me, whoever you are that will now help Stubb; for Stubb, too, sticks here. I grin at thee, thou grinning whale! Who ever helped Stubb, or kept Stubb awake, but Stubb's own unwinking eye? And now poor Stubb goes to bed upon a mattrass that is all too soft; would it were stuffed with brushwood! I grin at thee, thou grinning whale! Look ye, sun, moon, and stars! I call ye assassins of as good a fellow as ever spouted up his ghost. For all that, I would yet ring glasses with ye, would ye but hand the cup! Oh, oh! oh, oh! thou grinning whale, but there'll be plenty of gulping soon! Why fly ye not, O Ahab! For me, off shoes and jacket to it; let Stubb die in his drawers! A most mouldy and over salted death, though; – cherries! cherries! cherries! Oh, Flask, for one red cherry ere we die!'

'Cherries? I only wish that we were where they grow. Oh, Stubb, I hope my poor mother's drawn my part-pay ere this; if not, few coppers will now come to her, for the voyage is up.'

From the ship's bows, nearly all the seamen now hung inactive; hammers, bits of plank, lances, and harpoons, mechanically retained in their hands, just as they had darted from their various employments; all their enchanted eyes intent upon the whale, which from side to side strangely vibrating his predestinating head, sent a broad band of overspreading semicircular foam before him as he rushed. Retribution, swift vengeance, eternal malice were in his whole aspect, and spite of all that mortal man could do, the solid white buttress of his forehead smote the ship's starboard bow, till men and timbers reeled. Some fell flat upon their faces. Like dislodged trucks, the heads of the harpooneers aloft shook on their bull-like necks. Through the breach, they heard the waters pour, as mountain torrents down a flume.

'The ship! The hearse! – the second hearse!' cried Ahab from the boat; 'its wood could only be American!'

Diving beneath the settling ship, the whale ran quivering along its keel; but turning under water, swiftly shot to the surface again, far off the other bow, but within a few yards of Ahab's boat, where, for a time, he lay quiescent.

'I turn my body from the sun. What ho, Tashtego! let me hear thy hammer. Oh! ye three unsurrendered spires of mine; thou uncracked keel; and only god-bullied hull; thou firm deck, and haughty helm, and Pole-pointed prow, – death-glorious ship! must ye then perish, and without me? Am I cut off from the last fond pride of meanest shipwrecked captains? Oh, lonely death on lonely life! Oh, now I feel my topmost greatness lies in my topmost grief. Ho, ho! from all your furthest bounds, pour ye now in, ye bold billows of my whole foregone life, and top this one piled comber of my death! Towards thee I roll, thou all-destroying but unconquering whale; to the last I grapple with thee; from hell's heart I stab at thee; for hate's sake I spit my last breath at thee. Sink all coffins and all hearses to one common pool! and since neither can be mine, let me then tow to pieces, while still chasing thee, though tied to thee, thou damned whale! *Thus*, I give up the spear!'

The harpoon was darted; the stricken whale flew forward; with igniting velocity the line ran through the groove; – ran foul. Ahab stooped to clear it; he did clear it; but the flying turn caught him round the neck, and voicelessly as Turkish mutes bowstring their victim, he was shot out of the boat, ere the crew knew he was gone. Next instant, the heavy eye-splice in the rope's final end flew out of the stark-empty tub, knocked down an oarsman, and smiting the sea, disappeared in its depths.

For an instant, the tranced boat's crew stood still; then turned. 'The ship? Great God, where is the ship?' Soon they through dim, bewildering mediums saw her sidelong fading phantom, as in the gaseous Fata Morgana; only the uppermost masts out of water; while fixed by infatuation, or fidelity, or fate, to their once lofty perches, the pagan harpooneers still maintained their sinking lookouts on the sea. And now, concentric circles seized the lone boat itself, and all its crew, and each floating oar, and every lance-pole, and spinning, animate and inanimate, all round and round in one vortex, carried the smallest chip of the Pequod out of sight.

But as the last whelmings intermixingly poured themselves over the sunken head of the Indian at the mainmast, leaving a few inches of the erect spar yet visible, together with long streaming yards of the flag, which calmly undulated, with ironical coincidings, over the destroying billows they almost touched; – at that instant, a red arm and a hammer hovered backwardly uplifted in the open air, in the act of nailing the flag faster and yet faster to the subsiding spar. A sky-hawk that tauntingly had followed the main-truck downwards from its natural home among the stars, pecking at the flag, and incommoding Tashtego there; this bird now chanced to intercept its broad fluttering wing between the hammer and the wood; and simultaneously feeling that etherial thrill, the submerged savage beneath, in his death-gasp, kept his hammer frozen there; and so the bird of heaven, with archangelic shrieks, and his imperial beak thrust upwards, and his whole captive form folded in the flag of Ahab, went down with his ship, which, like Satan, would not sink to hell till she had dragged a living part of heaven along with her, and helmeted herself with it.

Now small fowls flew screaming over the yet yawning gulf; a sullen white surf beat against its steep sides; then all collapsed, and the great shroud of the sea rolled on as it rolled five thousand years ago.

EPILOGUE

'AND I ONLY AM ESCAPED ALONE TO TELL THEE.'

Job.

The drama's done. Why then here does any one step forth? – Because one did survive the wreck.

It so chanced, that after the Parsee's disappearance, I was he whom the Fates ordained to take the place of Ahab's bowsman, when that bowsman assumed the vacant post; the same, who, when on the last day the three men were tossed from out the rocking boat, was dropped astern. So, floating on the margin of the ensuing scene, and in full sight of it, when the half-spent suction of the sunk ship reached me, I was then, but slowly, drawn towards the closing vortex. When I reached it, it had subsided to a creamy pool. Round and round, then, and ever contracting towards the button-like black bubble at the axis of that slowly wheeling circle, like another Ixion I did revolve. Till, gaining that vital centre, the black bubble upward burst; and now, liberated by reason of its cunning spring, and, owing to its great buoyancy, rising with great force, the coffin life-buoy shot lengthwise from the sea, fell over, and floated by my side. Buoyed up by that coffin, for almost one whole day and night, I floated on a soft and dirge-like main. The unharming sharks, they glided by as if with padlocks on their mouths; the savage sea-hawks sailed with sheathed beaks. On the second day, a sail drew near, nearer, and picked me up at last. It was the devious-cruising Rachel, that in her retracing search after her missing children, only found another orphan.

FINIS.

COMMENTARY

'Why then do you try to "enlarge" your mind? Subtilize it.'
(THE SPERM WHALE'S HEAD)
'My dear sir, in this world it is not so easy to settle these plain things. I have ever found your plain things the knottiest of all.'
(THE FOUNTAIN)

ANY new edition must stand on the backs of previous editors and in numerous cases – particularly those involving Melville's sourcebooks on whaling and whaling lore – I am indebted for a head start not only to work by Mansfield and Vincent, but their predecessor Willard Thorp and successor Charles Feidelson, Jr. My intention is in no way to replace their editions. The aim, rather, was to displace something of their minute concern with Melville's primary sources. What was needed, I felt, for all but the most specialized readers, was not so much a key to Melville's library, as an interpretative key to *Moby-Dick* itself.

Most readers will want help somewhere on this voyage, but not to distract the eye by overcrowding the page with notes (other than Melville's own) or confuse the text with a blur of numerals, all comments are given here with page references under their respective chapter-heads. Chapters are usually short so that passages should be easily located. Or the notes can be read separately as guide to the maze-like accretion of imagery at the heart of Melville's meaning and method. For the maze itself is the pattern, only to be traced from within: despite its bibliographical tap-roots and far-reaching aura of allusions, *Moby-Dick* is symbolically self-contained and forms its own best and sufficient commentary.

On the surface, however, all is dazzle and bluff – like the White Whale himself, to evade comprehension. Which has made it easy to overlook the sheer bravado of Melville's performance – the breath-taking, astonishingly sustained prestidigitation of this rogue masterpiece: 'Rope Walks and Thames Tunnels of Whales!' The first function of a new commentary, then, was to decode the text, unravel the threads, reveal the pattern (turned inside out) and trace the jumbled loops to their several links and knots. 'Infinite sad mischief,' Melville was to say, 'has resulted from the profane bursting open of secret recesses' (*I and My Chimney*, 1856). But in literature, as he well knew, there can be no recesses; all secrets are disclosed in the end; and even Hermes Trismegistus must expect to be exposed at last.

TITLE PAGE

The first English edition added:

There Leviathan,
Hugest of living creatures, in the deep
Stretch'd like a promontory sleeps or swims,
And seems a moving land; and at his gills
Draws in, and at his breath spouts out a sea.
Paradise Lost

But it is doubtful whether Melville would so clumsily have anticipated his Sub-Sub-Librarian's list (Extract 24), or identified Moby Dick so specifically with the Miltonic Leviathan. The reset title-page of the 1853 English issue omits the quotation.

DEDICATION

TO NATHANIEL HAWTHORNE Even before meeting Hawthorne, Melville had raised him to heroic stature. Only Shakespeare's name could adequately evoke 'those occasional flashings-forth of the intuitive Truth in him; those short, quick probings at the very axis of reality'. In two anonymous articles he hailed him as oracle and guide: 'You may be witched by his sunlight, – transported by the bright gildings in the skies he builds over you; but there is the blackness of darkness beyond; and even his bright gildings but fringe and play upon the edges of thunder-clouds (*Literary World*, 17 and 24 August 1850).

The Hawthornes, of course, were captivated. Who was this 'Virginian Spending July in Vermont'? 'The writer has a truly generous heart ...' Nathaniel wrote to the editor, Evert Duyckinck. 'But he is no common man; and next to deserving his praise, it is good to have beguiled or bewitched such a man into praising and more than I deserve' (29 August 1850). His wife, Sophia, added rapturously: 'There is such a generous, noble enthusiasm as I have not before found in any critic of any writer. While bringing out the glory of his subject ... he surrounds himself with a glory. The freshness of primeval nature is in that man, & the true Promethean fire is in him. Who can he be, so fearless, so rich in heart, of such fine intuition? Is his name altogether hidden?'

Amusingly enough it was Duyckinck, a few weeks earlier, who had introduced his two contributors (and correspondents) to each other. Melville was spending the summer in Pittsfield; Hawthorne living near by in Lenox; and to-and-fro visiting began, continued the following year after Melville had moved his family to Arrowhead, the farmhouse he had acquired in the Berkshires, two miles from Pittsfield. But this exchange of visits was never frequent – no more than a dozen either way. The younger Melville, it seems, was all puppyish devotion and zest; while Hawthorne, fifteen years his senior, was as usual diffident, shy, reserved. In any case, both were soon immersed in work: at Lenox, *The House of the Seven Gables* was in progress; at Arrowhead, *Moby-Dick*. And after publication in November 1851, coinciding with the Hawthornes' return to Concord, the contact between the two novelists slowly dwindled and cooled.

Melville had early grasped his hero's limitations: 'Still there is something lacking' he wrote to Duyckinck, '– a good deal lacking – to the plump sphericity of the man. What is that? – He does'nt patronise the butcher – he needs roast-beef, done rare' (12 February 1851). Nevertheless from their exchange of letters during those critical months, of which only Melville's side survives, it is clear that he felt free to soar in Hawthorne's company with a fine and careless rapture. Not that he utterly bared himself. Smokescreens abound. But he welcomed the fellow-writer as fellow-spirit, one of 'God's true princes of the Empire', one of 'the choice hidden handful of the Divine Inert' (THE SPECKSYNDER).

'The divine magnet is on you, and my magnet responds' (November 1851). In token of this bond – the same mystical bond as tied Ishmael to Ahab – *Moby-Dick* was dedicated.

ETYMOLOGY

75. *A LATE CONSUMPTIVE USHER* A mocking self-portrait to usher in not merely these extracts but the whole of *Moby-Dick* – with more than a hint of the queer talk to permeate this gay world. Notice is served: what we are to expect is a global range of reference, through space and time; what we ourselves must do is dust our 'old lexicons and grammars'. For not 'WHALE' (*hval, whœl, wal*) alone, but the entire *Whale*, may prove an etymological exercise.

The spirit of Dr Johnson, another 'usher' (in Boswell's phrase) turned lexicographer, is invoked at the outset.

75. *ETYMOLOGY* The quotations are from Noah Webster's *An American Dictionary of the English Language* (Springfield, 1848) and Charles Richardson's *A New Dictionary of the English Language* (Philadelphia, 1848). In Richardson, too, Melville found the passage from Richard Hakluyt, *The Principal Navigations* (1598), as quoted.

There are at least four errors in the glossary: the Hebrew for 'whale' (transliterated) is *tannin* (*Genesis* i, 21; *Job* vii, 12), not *tan*, a hypothetical singular derived from *tannim* (*Ezekiel* xxix, 3 and xxxii, 2) and possibly levia/*than* (*Job* xli, 1; *Psalm* civ, 26; *Isaiah* xxvii, 1); κῆτος is the correct Greek spelling, not χητος; *hwael* is the Anglo-Saxon form found in Alfred's account of Octhere, not *whœl* (or *wheel*, or *whirl*); *hvalt* is the adjectival form of *hval*, correctly given by Webster. Conceivably Melville consulted a Hebraist to find the most inclusive term for this 'whale', since all the biblical passages cited are utilized in either the text or the Extracts.

75. *the letter H* cf. 'HWAL', at the lexical centre, with the Hebrew Tetragrammaton 'YHWH'. Does not the aspirate 'almost alone' make up 'the signification of the word'? Its breath spells life.

76. *PEHEE-NUEE-NUEE* With 'Fish-Plenty-Plenty' from Fiji and Erromanga (in the New Hebrides) to cap errors and jokes. Cf. *Typee*, chs. 13 and 20. Cf. Captain Barnacle (*alias* Charles M. Newell), *Leaves from an Old Log, Péhe Nú-e, The Tiger Whale of the Pacific* (1877).

EXTRACTS

77. *Hampton Court and the Tuileries* The royal palace on the Thames (already a museum) Melville visited on 11 November 1849; the palace on the Seine was then the presidential residence of Louis Napoleon.

78. *Here ye strike but splintered hearts* cf. 'If ever, my dear Hawthorne, in the eternal times that are to come, you and I shall sit down in Paradise, in some little shady corner by ourselves; and if we shall by any means be able to smuggle a basket of champagne there (I won't believe in a Temperance Heaven), and if we shall then cross our celestial legs in the celestial grass that is forever tropical, and strike our glasses and our heads together, till both musically ring in concert, – then, O my dear fellow-mortal, how shall we pleasantly discourse of all the things manifold which now so distress us ...' (June 1851)

78. *EXTRACTS* As a whale is huge, the hugest beast in creation, huger even than the long extinct dinosaur, so a book about whales is bound to be huge; and its bibliography, inevitably a whale of a bibliography. The conception itself almost certainly derived from Robert Southey, *The Doctor* (1834–47). Many of the quotations Melville found in his sourcebooks or in Richardson's dictionary. Clearly there was no check with works of reference to hand. *King Henry* remains simply *King Henry*, where *King Henry IV, Part I* is meant; the first edition of Cowley's *New Voyage round the World* was 1697, not 1729; the Icelandic expedition of 1772 was led by Sir Joseph Banks (not Bank); John Stow's name is misspelt; the title of Thomas Fuller's book is reversed. Personal jottings are left unexpanded: Sir Thomas Browne's 'V.E.' stands for *Vulgar Errors*, the common title of his *Pseudodoxia Epidemica* (1646); 'N. E. Primer', for *New England Primer*; 'Harris Coll', for John Harris, *Navigantium atque Itinerantium Bibliotheca: or, a Compleat Collection of Voyages and Travels* (2 vols., London, 1705); Goldsmith's 'Nat. His.' refers to the abridgement of *Animated Nature* (London, 1774); Edmund Burke's reference in Parliament is from his *Speech on Conciliation with the American Colonies* (22 March 1775); by 'Scoresby' is meant Captain William Scoresby, *An Account of the Arctic Regions, with a History and Description of the Northern Whale-Fishery* (2 vols., Edinburgh, 1820).

But the list is artful. If *Jonah* i, 17 becomes the text for Father Mapple's sermon, and if a white whale is first sighted off Spitzbergen in 1671, the end of the *Pequod* is prefigured in the extract from Owen Chase and the very title *Miriam Coffin* – a name echoed in the 'coffin warehouses' of the opening, repeated in that of the landlord of the Spouter-Inn, confirmed in Ishmael's friend and messmate Charley Coffin, to be resurrected at last in the 'coffin life-buoy' of the *Epilogue*.

Of the eighteen or so whaling books consulted by Melville, the five principal sources are all listed here: Captain Scoresby, *An Account of the Arctic Regions* (1820); Thomas Beale, *The Natural History of the Sperm Whale* (London, 1839); Frederick Bennett, *Narrative of a Whaling Voyage Round the Globe, from the Year 1833 to 1836* (2 vols., London, 1840); J. Ross Browne, *Etchings of a Whaling Cruise, with Notes of a Sojourn on the Island of Zanzibar; and a Brief History of the Whale Fishery, in its Past and Present Condition* (New York, 1846); and Rev. Henry T. Cheever, *The Whale and his Captors; or, The Whaleman's Adventures and the Whale's Biography* (New York, 1850). (The list of general reading is further glossed and expanded in THE ADVOCATE, CETOLOGY, MOBY DICK, and OF THE MONSTROUS and OF THE LESS ERRONEOUS PICTURES OF WHALES.) But decisive was Owen Chase, *Narrative of the Most Extraordinary and Distressing Shipwreck of the Whale-Ship Essex, of Nantucket* (New York, 1821) which, ten years earlier on board the *Acushnet*, first sparked the conception of *Moby-Dick* (see pp. 276, 307 notes). Mocha Dick himself, however, is avoided. No encounter with that legendary white whale is quoted, though J. N. Reynold's sketch, *Mocha Dick: or, the White Whale of the Pacific* (the *Knickerbocker Magazine*, May 1839), for one, was obviously familiar to Melville.

Here follows the list of Extracts, numbered from one to eighty, with their exact and detailed references:

1. *Genesis* i, 21.
2. *Job* xli, 32 ('Leviathan' substituted for 'He').
3. *Jonah* i, 17.
4. *Psalms* civ, 26.
5. *Isaiah* xxvii, 1.
6. Plutarch's *Morals*, 'Which are the Most Crafty, Water-Animals or Those Creatures which Breed upon the Land?' sec. 31 (Philemon Holland's translation, 1603).

7. Pliny's *Natural History*, IX, ii, 4, quoted by Charles Richardson, under 'Whale' (Philemon Holland's translation, 1604).
8. Lucian's *The True History*, Bk 1, with unindicated omission (William Tooke's translation, 1820).
9. King Alfred's gloss in his translation of Orosius, *Historia adversus Paganos*, Pt 1, ch. 1 (inaccurately quoted from either Hakluyt, Cheever, or most likely J. Ross Browne, p. 512).
10. Montaigne, *Apology for Raimond Sebond* (*Essays*, Bk 2, ch. 12): possibly from William Hazlitt's translation.
11. Rabelais, *Gargantua and Pantagruel*, 'How Pantagruel discovered a monstrous physeter, or whirlpool, near the wild island' Bk 4, ch. 33 (from the Urquhart-Motteux translation).
12. *The Annales, or General Chronicle of England, begun first by maister John Stow* (London, 1615), p. 677, entry for 9 July 1574.
13. Bacon, *Translation of Certain Psalms in English Verse* (London, 1625), *Psalm* civ, 26.
14. Bacon, *Historia Vitae et Mortis* (1650), Topic 3, item 48.
15. Shakespeare, *King Henry IV, Part* 1, I, iii, 57–8.
16. Shakespeare, *Hamlet*, III, ii, 372.
17. Spenser, *The Faerie Queene* (1596), Bk VI, canto x, stanza 31.
18. *The Works of Sr. William Davenant Kt.* (London, 1673): 'Preface to *Gondibert*', p. 16.
19. Sir Thomas Browne, *Pseudodoxia Epidemica*, Bk III, ch. 26. (Melville owned the 1686 folio, misreading 'Hosmannus' for 'Hofmannus'.)
20. Edmund Waller, *The Battle of the Summer Islands*, canto iii, lines 11–12, 53–4 (the pronouns of the second couplet changed to the masculine).
21. Thomas Hobbes, *Leviathan* (1651): the fifth sentence of the 'Introduction'.
22. John Bunyan, *The Holy War* (1682), ch. 3 (quoted by Cheever, p. 70). The first American edition read: *'Pilgrim's Progress'*. This attribution was almost certainly corrected, for the first English edition, by Melville.

23. Milton, *Paradise Lost* I, 200–202.

24. Milton, *Paradise Lost* VII, 412–16.

25. Thomas Fuller, *The Holy State and the Profane State* (1642), Bk 2, ch. 20, 'The Good Sea-Captain'.

26. Dryden, *Annus Mirabilis* (1667), stanza 203.

27. Thomas Edge in *Hakluytus Posthumus, or Purchas His Pilgrims* (1625), Pt 2, Bk 3, ch. 2, sec. 3 (the phrasing much altered).

28. Sir Thomas Herbert, *Some Yeares Travels in Divers Parts of Asia and Afrique* (1638), Bk 1, p. 13. (Not in John Harris's *Collection*.)

29. Willem Cornelis Schouten, the sixth 'circumnavigation' in John Harris, *Navigantium atque Itinerantium Bibliotheca* (1705), vol. 1, Bk 1, ch. 1.

30. Friedrich Martens, *The Voyage to Spitzbergen and Greenland*, 1671. The plates are in Harris, vol. I, Bk 4, chs. 39–42 (provoking contemptuous comment, pp. 368–9); the full text in Tancred Robinson, *An Account of Several Late Voyages and Discoveries to the South and North* (London, 1694).

31. Sir Robert Sibbald, *The History, Ancient and Modern, of the Sheriffdoms of Fife and Kinross* (Edinburgh, 1710), Pt 4, ch. 1, 'Concerning the Coast'.

32. Richard Strafford's *Letter from the Bermudas* (1668), printed in the *Philosophical Transactions* of the Royal Society, vol. 3 (quoted by Beale, p. 137).

33. *The New England Primer For the More Easy Attaining the True Reading of English* (1727). Quoted by Cheever, p. 111.

34. Captain William Ambrose Cowley, *New Voyage round the World* (1697), from *A Collection of Voyages* (London, 1729), vol. IV, ch. 2.

35. Antonio de Ulloa, *A Voyage to South America* (1758; 5th edn, 1807), vol. 2, Bk 9, ch. 3.

36. Pope, *The Rape of the Lock*, canto ii, lines 117–20. Melville himself seems to have corrected 'stuffed', of the American edition, to 'stiff', for the English edition.

37. *Goldsmith's Natural History*, an abridgement of Oliver Goldsmith's *History of the Earth and Animated Nature* (London, 1774), for the use of schools by Mrs Pilkington (Philadelphia, 1829): 'whale', ch. 2, sec. 3.

38. Boswell, *Life of Samuel Johnson* (1791), entry for 1773.

39. Captain James Cook, *A Voyage to the Pacific ... for Making Discoveries in the Northern Hemisphere* (London, 1784), entry for 3 September 1778.

40. Uno von Troil, *Letters on Iceland* (London, 1780), Letter 12, p. 130.

41. Thomas Jefferson's note to the French foreign minister, protesting against the ban on the import of foreign whale oil (October 1788).

42. Edmund Burke, *Speech on Conciliation with the American Colonies* (22 March 1775).

43. Edmund Burke, Speech in the House of Commons, *c.* 1780 (not in complete *Works*).

44. Sir William Blackstone, *Commentaries on the Laws of England* (1765 69), Bk 1, ch. 8.

45. William Falconer, *The Shipwreck* (1762), canto ii, linking lines 71 to 75–6.

46. William Cowper, *On the Queen's Visit to London* (1789), lines 13–20.

47. John Hunter's account, quoted by Paley (see 48).

48. William Paley, *Natural Theology* (1802), ch. 10, 'Of the Vessels of Animal Bodies'.

49. Baron Georges Cuvier, *Le règne animal* (1827–35), *The Class Pisces*, vol. 10.

50. Captain James Colnett, *A Voyage to the South Atlantic and Round Cape Horn ... for the Purpose of Extending the Spermaceti Whale Fisheries* (London, 1798), ch. 4, entry for 1 May 1793.

51. James Montgomery, *The Pelican Island* (1827), canto ii, linking lines 22–4, 26–8, 37–42 (derived, errors and all, from Cheever, p. 128).

52. Charles Lamb, *The Triumph of the Whale* (1812), lines 1–6: a satire on the Prince Regent.

53. Obed Macy, *History of Nantucket* (Boston, 1835).

54. Hawthorne, 'The Village Uncle' in *Twice-Told Tales* (2nd edn, 1842).

55. Hawthorne, 'Chippings with a Chisel' in *Twice-Told Tales.*

56. James Fenimore Cooper, *The Pilot* (1823), ch. 17.

57. Johann Eckermann, *Conversations with Goethe* (1836–48, English translation, 1850), entry for 31 January 1830.

58. Owen Chase, *Narrative of the Most Extraordinary and Distressing Shipwreck of the Whale-Ship Essex, of Nantucket* (New York, 1821), ch. 2.

59. Elizabeth Oakes Smith, *The Drowned Mariner* (1845), lines 1–5.

60. Captain William Scoresby, *An Account of the Arctic Regions* (1820), vol. 2, ch. 4, sec. 9 and vol. 1, ch. 6, sec. 1.

61. Thomas Beale, *The Natural History of the Sperm Whale* (1839), p. 165 and p. 33.

62. Frederick Bennett, *Narrative of a Whaling Voyage Round the Globe* (1840), vol. 2, ch. 6, p. 213.

63. J. Ross Browne, *Etchings of a Whaling Cruise* (1846), p. 115.

64. William Lay and Cyrus M. Hussey, *A Narrative of the Mutiny, on Board the Ship Globe* (1828), ch. 1, p. 15.

65. Daniel Tyerman and George Bennett, *Journal of Voyages and Travels* (Boston, 1832), vol. 1, ch. 1, p. 3.

66. Daniel Webster, On the breakwater at Nantucket, in the U.S. Senate, 2 May 1828.

67. Henry T. Cheever, *The Whale and his Captors* (1850), p. 151.

68. *Life of Samuel Comstock,* a local pamphlet perhaps.

69. John Ramsay McCulloch, *A Dictionary, practical, theoretical, and historical, of Commerce and Commercial Navigation* (London, 1832–39). Quoted by J. Ross Browne, p. 514.

70. From *'Something'*, possibly an early draft of *Moby-Dick,* ch. 41.

71. Charles Wilkes, *Narrative of the U.S. Exploring Expedition* (1845), vol. 5, ch. 12, 'Currents and Whaling'. Quoted by J. Ross Browne.

72. Robert Pearse Gillies, *Tales of a Voyager to the Arctic Ocean*, First Series (London, 1826), vol. 2, p. 316.

73. The *Hobomack* of Falmouth is apparently confused with the *Sharon* of Fairhaven: 'ten days out from the Island of Ascension, 9 November 1842, the *Sharon* was left in charge of three savages recently recruited from the Kingsmill islands, when two boats were lowered for whales; the savages killed Captain Norris, and only through the timely giving of the alarm by a Portuguese boy ... and the daring of the third mate in swimming aboard, entering by the cabin windows, and single-handedly fighting the mutineers with a whaling-spade, was the *Sharon* recaptured' (Mansfield and Vincent, p. 586).

74. James A. Rhodes, *Cruise in a Whale Boat* (New York, 1848).

75. Joseph C. Hart, *Miriam Coffin, or, the Whale-Fishermen* (New York, 1834), vol. 2, ch. 10.

76. W. A. G., *Ribs and Trucks, from Davy's Locker; being Magazine Matter Broke Loose, and Fragments of Sundry Things In-Edited* (Boston, 1842), 'A Chapter on Whaling', p. 13.

77. Charles Darwin, *Journal of Researches into the Geology and Natural History of the Various Countries visited by H.M.S. Beagle under the command of Captain Fitzroy, R.N. from 1832 to 1836* (London, 1839), entry for 28 January 1833.

78. Harry Halyard, *Wharton the Whale-Killer or, The Pride of the Pacific. A Tale of the Ocean* (Boston, 1848).

79. *Nantucket Song*, quoted by J. Ross Browne, p. 17.

80. *Whale Song*, on Cheever's title-page.

'But I have swam through libraries and sailed through oceans': for the whole point of these Extracts, supplied by a sallow grub of a Sub-Sub, is that Melville – through this screen of tomfoolery – takes learning profoundly seriously. He works with all whaling myth, legend and literature in his bones. From the very start he displays the breadth of his reading.

In his entrance-hall, or 'vestibule', that is, he sets up a library stack, its shelves lined with the Bible, the Greek and Roman classics, Bacon, Spenser, Shakespeare, Milton, Pope, the early voyagers of the South Seas, contemporaries, fellow whalers. The reader must run the gauntlet of this dictionary of quotations before he too can hie aloft, like the poor devil of a Sub-Sub, to the royal-mast with his heart. Not for nothing had Melville been schoolmaster before turning sailor.

Dry as dust as this burrowing may seem, it emphasizes at least one thing: the importance, the universality, of his subject. But in hinting at depths, it also raises the question of Melville's ultimate aim: that such a vast chronological vista – a range of Extracts extending from *Genesis* to the present – should be gulped by this *Whale* in a few preliminary pagefuls as a snack, a kind of *hors d'œuvre*, suggests that Melville intends us to read his own work as their culmination, a *summa* of all pre-Melvillean whaling literature. The gesture, like all his gestures, is at once hyperbolic and deliberate.

Just as whales, moreover, from *Job* to *Hamlet* to *Paradise Lost*, have continually surfaced through the greatest works of world literature, so perhaps this *Whale* will prove in the end not only a *summa* of whaling literature, but reveal the art of whaling itself as a *summa* of human existence, by welding all 'higgledy-piggledy whale statements' to their 'veritable gospel cetology' at last.

'To produce a mighty book, you must choose a mighty theme. No great and enduring volume can ever be written on the flea ...' (THE FOSSIL WHALE)

I LOOMINGS

LOOMINGS 'Let us try. But in a matter like this, subtlety appeals to subtlety, and without imagination no man can follow another into these halls.' (THE WHITENESS OF THE WHALE)

This is the overture – the prelude to sound all the main themes, and keys, and shifts of key, on which the rest of *Moby-Dick* will play its prolonged and fugal variations. With a triple flourish Melville first casts his spell:

'Call me Ishmael ...'

'There now is your insular city of the Manhattoes ...'

'Circumambulate the city of a dreamy Sabbath afternoon ...' Each new start strikes a new and separate chord: the first (with its coffin warehouses and suicide) of death, to be echoed in the myth of Narcissus drowned, Egyptian mummies and pyramids; the second (with its wharves and moles) of commerce, since to go whaling is a commercial business centring on blubber, try-works and casks of spermaceti; the third ('fixed in ocean reveries') of a universal, implacable, metaphysical urge. 'Yes, as every one knows, meditation and water are wedded for ever.'

'Surely all this is not without meaning': nothing will prove without meaning – neither myth, memories, nor metaphors. 'And still deeper the meaning of that story of Narcissus, who because he could not grasp the tormenting, mild image he saw in the fountain, plunged into it and was drowned.' Still deeper the complex of modern illusions linked with the fate of that Greek shepherd. 'But that same image, we ourselves see in all rivers and oceans. It is the image of the ungraspable phantom of life; and this is the key to it all.' The pastoral of self-contemplation, that is, of fascinated self-exploration of intellect by intellect, imagination by imagination (the myth of Narcissus beloved by the nymph Echo), is 'the key to it all': all the sterile, inturned processes of modern man, all the sterile, inturned processes of modern art. For *Moby Dick* will prove as inturned and self-tormented as the myth on which it is based.

Ishmael, for one, is apt to succumb entirely to pastoral myth: 'As I sat there at my case, cross-legged on the deck ... as I snuffed up that uncontaminated aroma, – literally and truly, like the smell of spring violets; I declare to you, that for the time I lived as in a musky meadow ...' (A SQUEEZE OF THE HAND) But this version of pastoral glances back to an earlier, as well as on to the coming, *fin de siècle*; its hero metamorphosed not to a jonquil (of the aesthetic movement), but to a self-destructive Satan (of Gothic horror and romance).

The quest for Moby Dick, then, is to be read as a pastoral turned demoniac, an extension of the Narcissus myth in which the whole ocean becomes the mirror image of man. In its pastoral opening the valley of the Saco lies 'thus tranced' – a pine-tree shaking sighs like leaves upon some shepherd's head; in its demoniac close, when Ahab Narcissus-like is plunged into the sea, the picture yet again lies 'tranced'. Amid nightmares, day-dreams, enchantments, the book moves from trance to trance. In the end is the beginning.

Only after this withdrawal to shipboard, this slow relinquishing of *terra firma*–of 'landsmen', 'inlanders all', and their last toehold on Manhattan – is Melville ready, at last, to introduce 'the great whale himself'. For death, commerce, metaphysics apart, this will prove, above all, a tale of adventure 'with an everlasting itch for things remote'. Not of adventure only, but of mystery, centring on 'a portentous and mysterious monster'. Nor of mystery only, but of imagination, as 'quick to perceive a horror' as any tale of Edgar Allan Poe's. Opening in Whitehall, the chapter ends with a vision of the White Whale, 'one grand hooded phantom, like a snow hill in the air': and all the themes are announced; the stage is set; the spell is bound.

Bound equally by its rhythm and its intonation, a tone which is not that of pastoral only, or of Gothic romance, but of heroic extravaganza: 'thousands upon thousands of mortal men ... and there they stand – miles of them – leagues. Inlanders all, they come from lanes and alleys, streets and avenues – north, east, south, and west ...' Which is the voice of the frontier, of the hunter back from the hunt, of the fisherman back on shore telling that tallest of all tall tales: of the whale that got away. Through the pastoral vision (of shepherds tranced by their magic streams and 'a grasshopper in a May meadow') blurring uneasily to something demoniac – a metaphysical horror – rises this slow, yarning, deadpan, garrulous voice of a sailor gazing out to sea or, turned Yankee farmer now, jawing round his stove: 'yet, somehow, I never fancied broiling fowls; – though once broiled, judiciously buttered, and judgmatically salted and peppered, there is no one who will speak more respectfully, not to say reverentially, of a broiled fowl than I will.'

It seems a leisurely, lollopping, long-winded gait, with the ambling narrative pace of other home-bred, loquacious Yankees – like Robert Frost, say, or Mark Twain from further West – where Adam and Eve are quaintly turned to 'the two orchard thieves' amid hoary Pythagorean allusions to flatulence and beans.

Yet 'not without azure loomings': 'on the utmost verge of our actual horizon' is there 'not a looming as of Land; a promise of new Fortunate Islands, perhaps whole undiscovered Americas, for such as have canvas to sail thither? – As exordium to the whole, stand here the following ...: – "Who am I; what is this ME?"' (Carlyle, *Sartor Resartus*, I, viii, 'The World out of Clothes')

93. *Call me Ishmael* In Hebrew 'God hears', son of Abraham

and his wife Sarah's Egyptian handmaid, Hagar: 'And he will be a wild man; his hand will be against every man, and every man's hand against him; and he shall dwell in the presence of all his brethren.' (*Genesis* xvi, 12)

From his boyhood reading Melville no doubt recalled the surly pioneer whom James Fenimore Cooper had given the same symbolic name: Ishmael Bush of *The Prairie* (1827).

93. *my hypos* viz. Hypochondria, or 'the spleen' – linking thoughts of suicide with the sea. For 'Death is only a launching into the region of the strange Untried; it is but the first salutation to the possibilities of the immense Remote, the Wild, the Watery, the Unshored; therefore, to the death-longing eyes of such men, who still have left in them some interior compunctions against suicide, does the all-contributed and all-receptive ocean alluringly spread forth his whole plain of unimaginable, taking terrors, and wonderful, new-life adventures; and from the hearts of infinite Pacifics, the thousand mermaids sing to them . . .' (THE BLACKSMITH)

93. *With a philosophical flourish Cato throws himself* Since Cato the Younger, according to Plutarch, spent several hours reading Plato's *Phaedo* before committing suicide. But what of Ishmael? Had he not also displayed Stoic self-control? 'Beware of enlisting in your vigilant fisheries any lad with lean brow and hollow eye; given to unseasonable meditativeness; and who offers to ship with the Phædon instead of Bowditch in his head.' (THE MAST-HEAD, p. 256, note)

93. *your insular city of the Manhattoes* Linking bourgeois commerce, from the start, with the Red Indian; men's 'hats off' with 'Manhattoes'; 'your insular city' with a whale's 'island bulk'.

The phrase echoes Washington Irving's *Knickerbocker History of New York*; cf. 'the ancient city of Manhattoes' (in 'The Legend of Sleepy Hollow').

93. *Its extreme down-town is the Battery* A park of some twenty acres at the southern tip of Manhattan. The original British fort (built in 1693) was succeeded by a U.S. fort (built in 1807). Called Castle Garden at this time, it was used mainly for civic receptions.

93. *from Corlears Hook to Coenties Slip, and from thence, by*

Whitehall From the East River, that is, near the present Williamsburg Bridge, to quays between the tip of Manhattan and Wall Street; and so from the lower East Side north-west to Broadway, and north to the docks along the Hudson. The whole area was familiar to Melville from his earliest childhood on Pearl Street to his shipping as 'boy' for Liverpool in 1839 (see *Redburn*, ch. 1).

'Corlear' preserves the Iroquois name for the Dutch, and later British, authorities of New York and Albany.

94. *the valley of the Saco ... into distant woodlands* Rising at the base of Mt Washington, the river meets the Atlantic in southern Maine. The 'bit of romantic landscape' looks like the work of the Hudson River School – something by Thomas Doughty or Asher Durand perhaps – with its horizon of 'overlapping spurs of mountains bathed in their hill-side blue'. But Melville knew the valley from his own tour through the White Mountains, on his honeymoon, in 1847.

95. *the shepherd's eye ... fixed upon the magic stream* The 'I' mingling with the object in the act of perception: 'at times transparent, at others a mirror, water bemuses us with the possibility of penetrating the surface of nature, yet it flatters and disturbs us by casting back our own image. What do we actually see – the object or ourselves? ... What makes water the telltale element in landscape is that it so clearly elicits the narcissistic response.' (Leo Marx, *The Machine in the Garden*, pp. 291–2)

95. *Go visit the Prairies in June* As he himself had visited Illinois in the summer of 1840, to stay with his uncle Thomas Melville in Galena on the upper Mississippi.

95. *the poor poet of Tennessee ... in a pedestrian trip to Rockaway Beach* On the south-west corner of Long Island, in Queens borough, New York City. There seems to be a private joke here at the expense of Bayard Taylor, the pedestrian poet from Pennsylvania. Melville owned his *Views-A-Foot* (1846) and knew him well. Both contributed to the *Literary World*; and Taylor's cousin and companion, Dr Franklin Taylor, also accompanied Melville on part of his European trip in 1849.

95. *the old Persians hold the sea holy* cf. 'The Parsees and Ghebers never willingly throw filth either into fire or water ... This reverence for the elements prevents them from being sailors, as in a long voyage they might be forced to defile the sea.' (James

B. Fraser, *Historical and Descriptive Account of Persia*, New York, 1841, p. 120)

95. *the image of the ungraspable phantom* cf. Ovid, *Metamorphoses*, Bk 3, 432–6. Ovid's Narcissus, far from plunging, however, wilted on *terra firma* and died.

96. *broiled ibis ... in their huge bake-houses the pyramids* Transforming 'pyramids' to 'pyres'. So Milton's Satan, indulging a pun:

Springs upward like a Pyramid of fire ...
(*Paradise Lost* II, 1013)

'The vaults of Saccara had just been opened and more than five hundred mummies of the ibis had been found in a sepulchral cave.' (Vivant Denon, *Travels in Upper and Lower Egypt, during the campaigns of General Bonaparte in That Country*, vol. I, ch. 9, 296: New York, 1803)

96. *of an old established family in the land* Melville's mother was of the old established Gansevoort family of Albany, New York; his grandfather, General Peter Gansevoort, had won renown in the Revolutionary War as 'the hero of Fort Stanwix' (1777). His paternal grandfather, Thomas Melvill, celebrated in Oliver Wendell Holmes' *The Last Leaf*, had been a leader of the Boston Tea Party and served as major in the Revolution: 'a personification of the spirit of 1776, one of the earliest to venture in the cause of liberty' (Daniel Webster, 1832)

The Melville House in Pittsfield was 'a rare place – an old family mansion, wainscoted and stately, with large halls & chimneys – quite a piece of mouldering rural grandeur' (Evert Duyckinck, 4 August 1850)

To Sophia Hawthorne, however, Melville emphasized his 'Scotch descent – of noble lineage – of the Lords of Melville & Leven', no doubt echoing his father's pride: 'The name you bear should also inspirit you to services of the highest estimation in private society, & to deeds of noble daring in public life; descended through a long line of respectable Ancestors, from a scottish Hero, who emblazoned by his achievements an hereditary title, which came down to him from remote antiquity, & who fell on Floden Field in defence of his Country's freedom ...' (Letter to Midshipman Thomas Melville, 1826)

96. *the Van Rensselaers* Wealthy landed family, founded by

the Dutch diamond and pearl merchant, Kiliaen Van Rensselaer (c. 1585–1644). A charter member of the Dutch West India Company, he was one of the first to develop a patroonship in New Netherland. Called Rensselaerswyck, it comprised most of the present Albany, Rensselaer and Columbia counties. On Stephen Van Rensselaer's death (1839), the family estates still included the major part of Albany and Rensselaer counties.

96. *or Randolphs* Among the most notable of this prominent Virginia family are: Peyton Randolph of Williamsburg, a close friend of George Washington; his nephew Edmund Randolph, Washington's aide-de-camp, later first his Attorney-General, then Secretary of State; and John Randolph of Roanoke.

96. *or Hardicanutes* Less hardy than they sound, though. For the death of Hardi- (or, Hartha-) canute ended the male line of the royal Danish house in England. For the deeper implications, see 'a Scandinavian sea-king'. (p. 169, note)

96. *as a country schoolmaster* The late consumptive usher recalls his own short career as assistant schoolmaster in the Sykes District of Richmond, near Pittsfield (1837–8) and at Greenbush, New York.

97. *the root of all earthly ills ... a monied man 1 Timothy* vi, 10; *Matthew* xix, 24.

97. *the Pythagorean maxim* 'To abstain from beans because they are flatulent and partake most of the breath of life.' (Diogenes Laertius, *Lives of Eminent Philosophers*, Bk 8)

Pythagoras claims a niche here as a mock patron of *Moby-Dick*. For the ascetic ideals of his brotherhood, translating all things to number, increasingly came to subvert accepted religious doctrine. While his adoption of the Orphic belief in metempsychosis first imbued the western mind with oriental ideas: 'like a universal yellow lotus ... more and more unfolding its noiseless measureless leaves'. (THE SPHYNX)

98. *'Grand Contested Election for the Presidency ... BLOODY BATTLE IN AFFGHANISTAN'* The 1840 presidential campaign was the first 'rip-roaring' campaign in U.S. history. William Henry Harrison, who had helped open Ohio and Indiana to white settlement, twice defeating the Indian forces of Tecumseh (at Tippecanoe river and again, during the *War of 1812*, at the battle of the Thames), had picked John Tyler as running mate. With slogans like 'Log Cabin and Hard

Cider' and 'Tippecanoe and Tyler Too', Harrison's Whig ticket defeated the Democratic candidate, Martin Van Buren. But the strain of the campaign was too much for Harrison who died, after only a month as ninth President of the United States, on 4 April 1841.

On 3 January, three months earlier, the whaleship *Acushnet*, with Melville aboard, had sailed out of Fairhaven down the Acushnet river on her maiden voyage. On 6 January 1842, in the first of the Afghan Wars, the British army was massacred at Kabul.

These newspaper headlines pinpoint the tale as precisely as a single minute of composition will be recorded eighty-five chapters later. (p. 477) Ishmael's lot is to be cast literally as an 'interlude' or, in Miguel de Unamuno's phrase, 'intra-history'.

98. *those stage managers ... this shabby part* Though he will change his mind: conceding his own role as 'tragic dramatist'; 'to meanest mariners, and renegades and castaways' ascribing 'high qualities, though dark'; weaving 'round them tragic graces'. (ch. 26, KNIGHTS AND SQUIRES)

98. *rolled his island bulk* From 'the Dut. and Ger. *Wallen*; A.S. *Walw-ian*, to roll, to wallow' (ETYMOLOGY): the first verb used of the whale, as it is to be the last, twice-repeated verb of the final chapter.

98. *the great flood-gates ... two and two there floated* Like Noah, to confront the wonder-land of whales in an ark.

2 THE CARPET-BAG

THE CARPET-BAG cf. 'There is the grand truth about Nathaniel Hawthorne. He says NO! in thunder; but the Devil himself cannot make him say *yes*. For all men who say *yes*, lie; and all men who say *no*, – why, they are in the happy condition of judicious, unincumbered travellers in Europe; they cross the frontiers into Eternity with nothing but a carpet-bag, – that is to say, the Ego.' (Melville to Hawthorne, reviewing *The House of the Seven Gables*, April 1851)

99. *duly arrived in New Bedford* A 'drizzly November' in Manhattan turns to a dark December in New Bedford, at the mouth of the Acushnet, Buzzards Bay, southern Massachusetts.

99. *As most young candidates ... of whaling* Here beginneth a whole underworld of masonic allusions, opening – as befits a new recruit – at a local 'lodge': 'wherever in your wisdom you may conclude to lodge for the night, my dear Ishmael', 'it is but well to be on friendly terms with all the inmates of the place one lodges in'.

See 'the whole roll of our order. Our grand master is still to be named'. (p. 472, note)

99. *poor old Nantucket ... the Tyre of this Carthage* Lying forty miles to the south-east, beyond Martha's Vineyard. It was a Nantucket Quaker, in the late eighteenth century, who founded Fairhaven on the east, and New Bedford on the west, bank of the Acushnet, securing for both the privilege of importing whale oil duty free, on which their joint prosperity rested; by the early 1820's a bridge connecting the twin ports had been constructed.

By 1841, when Melville sailed downstream from Fairhaven, New Bedford alone, with a population fast rising to 12,000, employed some 170 whale-ships, requiring some 4,000 hands. More than 75,000 barrels of sperm oil and 85,000 barrels of common whale oil (over a third of the total U.S. product) were imported annually up the Acushnet, making it the chief whaling entrepôt of the world.

100. *blocks of blackness ... like a candle moving about in a tomb* cf. 'For thou wilt light my candle: the Lord my God will enlighten my darkness.' (*Psalm* xviii, 28) Sounding the first variation on the psalmist's doom:

> The sorrows of death compassed me, and the floods of ungodly men made me afraid.
> The sorrows of hell compassed me about: the snares of death prevented me ...

100. *the door ... stood invitingly open* cf. 'For there are certain men crept in unawares, who were before of old ordained to this condemnation, ungodly men, turning the grace of our God into lasciviousness, and denying the only Lord God, and our Lord Jesus Christ.' (*Jude*, 4)

100. *But 'The Crossed Harpoons', and 'The Sword-Fish'?* Signs of Sodom? On the shores of Milton's '*Asphaltick* Pool' (*Paradise Lost*, I, 411), or the Dead Sea? Thus the 'asphaltic pavement' so hard on miserable 'soles'. Thus the 'bright red windows',

smoke and 'glare': 'And he looked toward Sodom and Gomorrah ... and, lo, the smoke of the country went up as the smoke of a furnace.' (*Genesis* xix, 28)

101. *the great Black Parliament sitting in Tophet* The 'valley of slaughter' (*Jeremiah* vii, 31–2), south of Jerusalem – named for hell-fire from the human sacrifice to Moloch once held there, and later the smoke of its refuse dumps. Of the fourteen churches of New Bedford in Melville's time at least one was Negro.

101. *the preacher's text was about the blackness of darkness* The whole context is Jude's: 'And the angels which kept not their first estate, but left their own habitation, he hath reserved in everlasting chains under darkness unto the judgement of the great day. Even as Sodom and Gomorrha, and the cities about them in like manner, giving themselves over to fornication, and going after strange flesh, are set forth for an example, suffering the vengeance of eternal fire. Likewise also these filthy dreamers defile the flesh, despise dominion, and speak evil of dignities ... Woe unto them! for they have gone in the way of Cain ... to whom is reserved the blackness of darkness for ever.' (*Jude* 6–13)

A sardonic loan (by 'patched boots') from Carlyle's *Sartor Resartus*: 'The Universe was a mighty Sphynx-riddle, which I knew so little of, yet must rede, or be devoured. In red streaks of unspeakable grandeur, yet also in the blackness of darkness, was Life, to my too-unfurnished Thought, unfolding itself.' (II, iv, 'Getting Under Way') For Ishmael, of course, is the interloper. It is Ishmael who imposes his own sexual obsessions. It is Ishmael who rejects not the 'ash-box', it appears, but St Jude.

In 'Hawthorne and his Mosses' Melville had merely inverted the text (DEDICATION, note); here he parodies the whole *General Epistle*, transforming 'a negro church' to visions of Gomorrah and Tophet.

101. *the weeping and wailing ... at the sign of 'The Trap!'* cf.

> Yea, the light of the wicked shall be put out, and the spark of his fire shall not shine.
> The light shall be dark in his tabernacle, and his candle shall be put out with him ...
> The snare is laid for him in the ground, and a trap for him in the way.
>
> (*Job* xviii, 5–10)

101. *Coffin? – Spouter? –* To find a 'room . . . in the inn' (*Luke* ii, 7)? 'Rather ominous' in the connection. This novice, having bypassed *The Cross* (ed Harpoons) and *The Sword* (-Fish), now settles deliberately for a Spouter's *Coffin.*

101. *the best of pea coffee* Kentucky coffee, ground from the brown seeds of the Kentucky coffee tree, or 'pea locust'. Its pods resemble those of the Virginian locust tree.

101. *Euroclydon* The tempestuous east wind that shipwrecked Paul off the coast of Malta (*Acts* xxvii, 14); a 'zephyr', of course, is a west wind.

101. *an old writer . . . the only copy extant* The 'wight Death' ironically prompting this fictitious 'old black-letter', or Gothic text.

102. *Poor Lazarus* Luke xvi, 19–31. The rich man's epithet in the Vulgate is '*dives*'.

102. *an iceberg . . . moored to one of the Moluccas* Or Spice Islands, between Celebes and New Guinea: in 'those Polar eternities; when wedged bastions of ice pressed hard upon what are now the Tropics'. (THE FOSSIL WHALE)

102. *a Czar in an ice palace* Built annually in St Petersburg for the winter carnival.

102. *being a president of a temperance society* The first temperance society was formed in Saratoga, N.Y., in 1808. But it was in the 1840s that the national temperance movement began its crusade culminating in the Prohibition Amendment of 1919.

102. *the tepid tears of orphans* Resolved in a pun: 'no more of this blubbering'. Yet Ishmael himself, like another Lazarus, will rise 'from the dead'. (*Luke* xvi, 31) He too (his final words) will become 'another orphan'.

For a further onslaught on the mid-Victorian gulf between rich and poor, cf. FAST-FISH AND LOOSE-FISH. (pp. 507–8)

3 THE SPOUTER INN

103. *the unnatural combat of the four primal elements* 'Ignei, aerii, aquatici, terreni spiritus' of medieval demonology (hailed by Marlowe's Faustus, I. iii. 17).

104. *The picture represents a Cape-Horner* And an 'overwhelming idea of the great whale' in the 'act of impaling him-

self upon the three mast-heads'. Turner's *The Whale Ship* (cradled by the diving whale, as this is arched) may possibly have been in Melville's mind. Exhibited as 'Whalers. *Vide Beale's Voyage p. 165*' at the Royal Academy in 1845, it is a fine example of that 'sort of indefinite, half-attained, unimaginable sublimity' of Turner's mature style (Plate 9). As this, of Melville's.

The language is so thoroughly teased with 'unequal cross-lights' and cross-references that it is 'only by diligent study and a series of systematic visits' that you can 'any way arrive at an understanding of its purpose'. 'Portentous' remains the *leitmotif* of this *Whale*. But a 'black mass' offers the first clue to its metamorphosis; a boggy, soggy 'morass', to its final aim and destination – 'enough to drive a nervous man distracted'. While 'a blasted heath' launches a whole landslide of allusions to *King Lear* (III, ii) and *Macbeth*.

Turner painted four whaling pictures in 1845–6, derived from Beale's *Natural History of the Sperm Whale*. *The Whale Ship* has hung in the Metropolitan Museum of Art, New York, since 1896. The rest, part of the Turner Bequest of 1851, are now in the Tate Gallery, London. (See p. 372, note)

104. *Nathan Swain* cf. 'There was young Nat Swaine, once the bravest boat-header out of all Nantucket and the Vineyard ...' (HIS MARK) The name – evoking a countryman, particularly a shepherd or, in pastoral terms, lover – is set as a prototype, or figurehead, at the entry to this inn. On the one side a whale, on the other 'a long-armed mower'; on the one wall pastoral, on the other the sea. The two are complementary. Hebrew prophet confronts 'New England hags'. Between these twin emblems leads the path to Moby Dick.

104. *the Cape of Blanco* There are several such capes; probably Cabo Blanco on the Peruvian coast is meant (*Acushnet* Log, 27 December 1841; *Omoo*, ch. 52). But its presence here is merely one of those 'mystic gestures' surrounding the whiteness of the whale.

105. *gulph down for a shilling* Archaism disguising a pun, not revealed until '"out of the belly of hell" – when the whale grounded upon the ocean's utmost bones, even then, God heard the engulphed, repenting prophet when he cried.' (THE SERMON)

105. *skrimshander* Or 'scrimshaw', as 'the whalemen call the numerous little ingenious contrivances they elaborately carve out of' whale-bone. (OF WHALES IN PAINT; IN TEETH etc.)

106. *a ruminating tar* Or Jack Tar with jack-knife: further symptom of 'th' *Asphaltick* Pool'.

106. *each in a winding sheet* Of solidified drippings.

106. *our monkey jackets* Short, close-fitting jackets, worn by sailors.

106. *in a green box coat* A loose overcoat for driving, fitted only at the shoulders. Throughout his visit to London Melville had been self-conscious about his coat: 'for I find my green coat plays the devil with my respectability here'. (*Journal*, 14 December 1849)

106. *the Grampus's crew ... from the Feejees* The *Grampus* ('whose loud sonorous breathing ... has furnished a proverb to landsmen') is a fitting enough name for this boisterous ship: 'By some fishermen ... regarded as premonitory of the advance of the great sperm whale.' (CETOLOGY)

cf. Extract 75: 'Suddenly a mighty mass emerged from the water, and shot up perpendicularly, with inconceivable velocity, into the air. It was the whale; – and the last effort was his last expiring throe! – He fell dead; – but in his descent, he pitched headlong across the bows of the *Grampus*, and, in one fell swoop, carried away the entire fore-part of the vessel!

'The crew escaped, by throwing themselves into boats alongside, and rowing quickly off. The gallant ship instantly filled with water, and settled away from their sight.' (Joseph C. Hart, *Miriam Coffin, or, The Whale-Fishermen*, pp. 292–3)

A Quaker Peleg, too, was owner of that ill-fated *Grampus*; another Starbuck, her mate.

107. *one of them held somewhat aloof* Like Emerson's 'great man ... who in the midst of the crowd keeps with perfect sweetness the independence of solitude'. (*Self-Reliance*)

107. *though but a sleeping-partner* In a single pun uniting two idols of Ishmael's dreams: Queequeg (his bedfellow) and Bulkington (the Bull/king), himself soon to rise a 'demigod'. (THE LEE SHORE)

107. *from the Alleganian Ridge in Virginia* To salute Edgar Allan Poe, a fellow Virginian? Since it was on another *Grampus*

that Pym, a young stowaway, set sail for the South Seas? cf. *The Narrative of Arthur Gordon Pym, of Nantucket* (New York, 1838). cf. THE WHITENESS OF THE WHALE (p. 296, note)

The Allegheny Mountains, a western ridge of the Appalachians, extend from northern Pennsylvania through Maryland to Virginia. Their eastern section, known as the Allegheny Front, is particularly rugged.

108. *with his old silk handkerchief* A second usher 'with a queer handkerchief, mockingly embellished ...'

110. *jolly good bedfellows after all* An adjective firmly linked with 'The Crossed Harpoons' and 'The Sword-Fish'. But may not 'The Spouter-Inn', too, belong to the Cities of the Plain – 'a queer sort of place', like 'some condemned old craft', 'as if it might have been carted here from the ruins of some burnt district'?

110. *cool as Mt Hecla* Mt Hekla, the volcano in south-west Iceland, had erupted six years earlier.

111. *a purty long sarmon for a chap that rips a little* viz. 'lets rip', 'flies into a passion'. cf. 'What's the reason, Mr Hawthorne, that in the last stages of metaphysics a fellow always falls to *swearing* so? I could rip an hour.' (April 1851)

111. *a lot of 'balmed New Zealand heads ... last Sunday* The trade in tattooed heads between New Zealand and Sydney was prohibited in 1831. cf. Charles Wilkes' account of the steward of a missionary brig: 'He then proceeded to inform them that he had two preserved heads of New Zealand chiefs, which he would sell for ten pounds ... The penalty for selling them was fifty guineas, and he conjured them to the most perfect secrecy.' (*Narrative of the U.S. Exploring Expedition ... 1838–1842*, II, 399–400) See Plate 2.

112. *be turning flukes* With the triangular tail of the whale: i.e. dive under.

112. *Sall and me slept in that ere bed* Nothing in *Moby-Dick* is fortuitous. Why 'Sall' – or 'Sal'? If 'Ishmael', by a pun, suggests 'is male', 'is male', by a partial anagram, reveals 'I'm Sal'. The name, that is, by picking out alternate letters, is turned to 'Sal', just as its owner will be turned to a wife in the Coffins' wedding bed.

The landlord's Christian name by her side evokes not an

'Angel', but Apostle, 'of Doom' – 'Sall and me' turning literally to *salpetre*, or 'saltpetre', the chief constituent of gunpowder. The offspring of Peter and Sal are Samuel and John – each 'a prophet of the Lord', uniting the Old and the New Testaments. (It is Sam, of course, who is kicked out of bed during father's nightmare.)

Ishmael turns out, in every way, to be 'Sal', not only as Queequeg's 'wife', but his salvage – the *Pequod*'s sole survivor ('salmon' or 'salamander'): 'AND I ONLY AM ESCAPED ALONE TO TELL THEE'. (EPILOGUE)

112. *I vum it's Sunday* I vow

113. *weighed me down like a hamper ... a kink in the neck* Second sign of 'The Trap!'. cf. the gallows outside the Try Pots: 'A sort of crick was in my neck as I gazed up to the two remaining horns ...' (CHOWDER, p. 160, note)

115. *in a Thirty Years' War* Heralding a whole range of allusions to the Holy Roman Empire.

115. *as if a parcel of dark green frogs* 'And I saw three unclean spirits like frogs ... For they are the spirits of devils, working miracles ...' (*Revelation* xvi, 13–14)

115. *his heavy grego* Literally 'greek' – a coarse jacket with a hood, worn in the Levant. This 'devil' too, in his grego, is 'one grand hooded phantom'.

116. *as if he were a sportsman bagging a dead woodcock.* This pun – and this pun alone – suggests that Queequeg's 'black manikin' may be a phallic idol. The hint is revived by its later identification with 'that unaccountable cone', 'the grandissimus' of THE CASSOCK; and confirmed by Queequeg's reaction to the doubloon. What the cannibal worships is the image of his own masculinity, his own potency 'stiff as a pike-staff'.

The very vocabulary is already compromising: his face twitching 'in the most unnatural manner' during 'these queer proceedings'. So too Ishmael, with his 'everlasting itch', after that 'squitchy picture', had begun 'to twitch all over'. So too the diabolical landlord of this 'queer sort of place' – this 'old ark' where whalers are paired in bed, these 'cockpits' where sailors orgiastically caper – specializes in ambiguities:

' "yea, he's the bird what catches the worm."

' "I s'pose you are goin' a whalin', so you'd better get used to that sort of thing." Though there was no "earthly reason", muses Ishmael, "why I as a sailor should sleep two in a bed, more than anybody else." '

117. *scattered the hot tobacco ashes* 'Ha! thought I, ha, as the flying particles almost choked me, are these ashes from that destroyed city, Gomorrah?' 'The devil fetch that harpooneer, thought I.'

117. *Queequeg here* cf. the Marquesan Marbonna, 'large and muscular, well made as a statue, and with an arm like a degenerate Tahitian's thigh' (*Omoo*, ch. 81). Melville met this tattooed Polynesian on Eimeo: 'In my frequent conversations with him ... I found this islander a philosopher of nature – a wild heathen, moralising upon the vices and follies' of Christendom. Like Queequeg, Marbonna too had embarked 'at his native island, as a sailor, on board' a whaler.

4 THE COUNTERPANE

118. *The counterpane was of patchwork* And the 'exact counterpart' of the symbols 'tattooed upon his arm'. (HIS MARK, p. 186, note) With a further touch of *Sartor Resartus*: for was it not Professor Teufelsdröckh who concluded that all symbols – all human institutions, in fact – are clothes?

118. *an interminable Cretan labyrinth* A further cabbalistic sign at the entrance to this labyrinthine *Whale*. cf. *Paradise Lost* IX, 182–8.

119. *cutting up some caper or other* 'Caper', for Ishmael, always carries a hint of the caprine, and so of sex. cf. The *Grampus*'s crew, after their 'pitch-like potion', 'capering about'; and the room 'almost supernaturally quiet after these orgies'. cf. Young Ishmael's attempt 'to crawl up' his stepmother's 'chimney'; and the dead grasp of that 'supernatural hand'.

119. *in the afternoon of the 21st June* At the midsummer solstice.

120. *his bridegroom clasp* In a matrimonial bed, in New Bedford, male hugs fellow male ('till death us do part'), their baby between neither Sam nor little Johnny, but a Tom/ahawk.

120. *like a Newfoundland dog* A favourite image (cf. *Benito Cereno*, 1855). Melville himself owned 'a large Newfoundland' (Julian Hawthorne, *Hawthorne and his Circle*).

122. *Rogers's best cutlery* For 'roger' has long meant a 'penis'; 'to roger', by antonomasia, 'to copulate'.

Rogers (a Connecticut firm) is still a major manufacturer of household silver. For years their most famous line of silver-plate table settings was known and advertised as 'Rogers "1847"'.

5 BREAKFAST

124. *drawn by dogs as Ledyard* John Ledyard (1751–89), born in Groton, Connecticut, was a member of Captain Cook's last expedition. Failing to finance a Northwest Passage expedition of his own, he walked across Europe, arriving at St Petersburg in 1787; permitted to continue across the Urals, he eventually reached Yakutsk by horse-drawn troika, before being arrested and sent back.

124. *poor Mungo's performances* Mungo Park (1771–1806), whose first expedition to the Niger is described in his *Travels in the Interior Districts of Africa* (1799), was drowned in the river on his return.

124. *some sheepfold among the Green Mountains* Of northern Vermont.

125. *sallied out for a stroll* With a final pun: 'You had almost thought I had been his wife.' (THE COUNTERPANE)

6 THE STREET

125. *Broadway and Chestnut streets ... Regent Street* New York, Philadelphia and London thoroughfares at some distance from the docks. But their choice is not entirely haphazard. England, as usual, is linked to royalty; the 'City of Brotherly Love', to those congregated 'cones' at the close; these queer-looking nondescripts in Broadway, to *Matthew* vii, 13: 'for wide is the gate, and broad is the way, that leadeth to destruction, and many there be which go in thereat'.

For 'New Bedford is a queer place' – Canaanite, if not exactly 'like Canaan'.

125. *in the Apollo Green* By the Apollo Bunder, or harbour of old Bombay. A long ground-swell of Indian allusions is launched, next to emerge in 'the cave of Elephanta'. (THE CHAPEL)

125. *all Water Street and Wapping* In Liverpool, and the London dock area.

125. *Feegeeans ... Brighggians* Natives of Fiji, Tongatabu (largest of the Tonga Islands), Erromanga (in the New Hebrides), trailing off to brigandish 'brigs'.

126. *this once scraggy scoria* Literally 'dung': the slag or dross left after smelting, as well as a clinker-like mass of cooled lava.

127. *Herr Alexander* A German magician confounding New York audiences at Palmo's Opera House, Niblo's Theatre, the Alhambra and the Chinese Museum in the late 1840s.

127. *horse-chestnuts, candelabra-wise ... their tapering upright cones* As the houses recklessly burn their spermaceti candles, so the horse-chestnuts bountifully proffer their sea-born candelabra to the passer-by.

But even this image is doomed. Next it will be 'Jeremy Bentham's skeleton, which hangs for candelabra', linking Utilitarianism and tapers in death. (OF THE MONSTROUS PICTURES OF WHALES)

7 THE CHAPEL

127. *a Whaleman's Chapel* The Seamen's Bethel, built by the Port Society in 1830, still stands (Plate 3).

129. *JOHN TALBOT ... Off Patagonia* While Ishmael dreams of all the 'marvels of a thousand Patagonian sights and sounds', this young sea-dog found nothing but an 'Isle of Desolation'. His 'tablet' merely anagrammatizes John 'Talbot', to signify a young candidate 'masoned into the wall'. (cf. Plate 4.)

130. *the cave of Elephanta* An island in Bombay harbour with six rock-hewn caves, dedicated to Siva the Destroyer. (See OF THE MONSTROUS PICTURES OF WHALES, p. 367, note.)

130. *more secrets than the Goodwin Sands* That both the evil and the good 'win sands' is the ultimate secret of those treacherous shoals near the mouth of the Thames.

130. *why the Life Insurance Companies pay death-forfeitures* But Ishmael is detached from all established orthodoxies: 'Besides, I aint insured.'

130. *in what eternal, unstirring paralysis ... yet lies antique*

Adam Aimed at Paul: 'For as in Adam all die, even so in Christ shall all be made alive.' (*1 Corinthians* xv, 22) For a further twist, see AMBERGRIS (p. 520, note).

130. *who died sixty round centuries ago* According to biblical time, though precisely whose chronology Ishmael follows is not quite clear. By Archbishop Ussher's reckoning (1650–54), the date of the Creation fell in 4004 B.C. Nineteenth-century argument, however, favoured a return to the Septuagint chronology, fixing the date at 5411 B.C. Since the life-span of Adam (it is agreed) was 930 years, his death, according to the Septuagint school, occurred 6,332 years before the publication of *Moby-Dick*; according to the Irish Archbishop, only 4,952 years.

cf. 'for six thousand years' (p. 477, note), where Ishmael apparently follows the Archbishop rather than the Septuagint. cf. Also 'as it rolled five thousand years ago' (p. 685, note), where again he appears to prefer the Septuagint.

Before history, however, stretch 'antemosaic' vistas of geological time, measured in millions of years. (p. 102) Melville eagerly studied contemporary scientific debate, with its rival views of iceberg versus glacier, to account for 'those Polar eternities'. (THE FOSSIL WHALE)

131. *an immortal by brevet* As in the army, by conferring a nominal rank without extra pay.

131. *my shadow here on earth ... my true substance* Further confounding the Platonic paradox: for 'there are few who, going to the images, behold in them the realities, and these only with difficulty ...' For we are 'enshrined in that living tomb which we carry about, now that we are imprisoned in the body, like an oyster in his shell'. (*Phaedrus*, 250)

131. *take my body who will ... it is not me* But the immediate source of the paradox, yet again, is Carlyle's *Sartor Resartus* (itself derived from Swift's *Tale of a Tub*), concluding that the material world is a mere clothing of the spiritual: 'but properly speaking the thickest watch-coat is no more of a house than the unclad body; for as the soul is glued inside of its fleshly tabernacle ... so a watch-coat is not so much of a house as it is a mere envelope, or additional skin encasing you.' (THE MAST-HEAD)

8 THE PULPIT

131. *the famous Father Mapple* As those 'congregated' cones were transformed to a 'congregation of sailors', so the 'fine maples' are converted to 'this fine old man ... Father Mapple' – to chime with *chapel*, though concealing that fruit of 'the two orchard thieves', an *apple*.

Father Mapple, it seems, is a composite portrait of the Reverend Enoch Mudge, the sixty-five year old pastor of the New Bedford Bethel at the time of Melville's first visit, and the more famous Edward Taylor of the Boston Bethel, whose nautical sermons became something of a tourist attraction in the 1830s and 1840s. Emerson, Harriet Martineau, Dickens (*American Notes for General Circulation*, 1842) all came to hear Taylor preach. Father Taylor, unlike Mudge, moreover, 'had been a sailor ... in his youth'.

133. *deliberately drag up the ladder* cf. Emerson's 'Shakespeare': 'the Genius draws up the ladder after him, when the creative age goes up to heaven ...' (*Representative Men*, 1850)

133. *replenished with the meat and wine of the word* Or Holy Communion with 'the Word ... made flesh' (*John* i, 14).

133. *a lofty Ehrenbreitstein* In his *Journal*, for 10 December 1849, Melville described the panoramic view from this 'famous Quebec fortress' looking across the Rhine to Coblenz.

133. *a large painting representing a gallant ship ... off a lee coast* Which will also serve as Bulkington's epitaph. (THE LEE SHORE)

cf. John Ross Dix's description of Father Taylor's Boston Bethel: 'the only ornament being a large painting at the back of the pulpit representing a ship in a stiff breeze off a lee shore, we believe; for we are not seaman enough to be certain on the point. High over the mast-head are dark storm-clouds, from one of which a remarkably small angel is seen, with outstretched arms, – the celestial individual having just flung down a golden anchor bigger than itself.' (Quoted in Gilbert Haven and Thomas Russell, *Father Taylor, the Sailor Preacher*, Boston, 1872, pp. 357–8)

9 THE SERMON

134. *the following hymn* A free adaptation of a rhymed version of Psalm xviii ('Deliverance from despair') used in the Dutch Reformed Church, in which Melville was brought up:

> Death, and the terrors of the grave,
> Spread over me their dismal shade;
> While floods of high temptations rose,
> And made my sinking soul afraid.
>
> I saw the opening gates of hell,
> With endless pains and sorrows there,
> Which none but they that feel, can tell;
> While I was hurried to despair.
>
> In my distress I call'd my God,
> When I could scarce believe him mine;
> He bow'd his ear to my complaints;
> Then did his grace appear divine.
>
> With speed he flew to my relief,
> As on a cherub's wings he rode:
> Awful and bright as lightning shone
> The face of my deliv'rer, God.
>
> My song for ever shall record
> That terrible, that joyful hour;
> And give the glory to the Lord,
> Due to his mercy and his pow'r.
>
> (*The Psalms and Hymns ... of the Reformed Protestant Dutch Church in North America*, Philadelphia 1854, pp. 34–5)

For a full text – including verses one, six and seven, not utilized by Melville – see *American Literature* XXVII (1955), pp. 393–6.

134. *Arched over me* For 'in Dan. *hvalt* is arched or vaulted'. (ETYMOLOGY)

134. *And lift me deepening* The oxymoron reflecting the original see-saw of 'high temptations ... sinking soul'. The English editor substituted a dull, commonsensical 'left'.

135. *the last verse of the first chapter of Jonah* The text of the Authorized Version is correctly given in Extract 3. Father

Mapple's sermon paraphrases, and quotes extensively from, *Jonah* i to iii, 3, stopping short at the repentance of Nineveh.

135. *to the kelpy bottom* 'The waters compassed me about, even to the soul: the depth closed me round about, the weeds were wrapped about my head.' (*Jonah* ii, 5)

137. *broke jail in old Gomorrah, or belike ... from Sodom* Again raising a suspicion of the pander-like role of that 'wrinkled little old Jonah' on those 'old wrinkled planks' in the Spouter-Inn.

141. *Jonah carries down the gale ... leaving smooth water behind* The whole universe centres on Jonah's plight: the ship 'heeling' as his conscience reels; the deep 'tormented' as his rolling eyes; his conscience crooked as the 'slanting storm' outside the Bethel, or the 'swift slantings' of the Mediterranean sea.

142. *Woe to him who seeks to please rather than to appal!* With that final pun on his own name Father M/*appal* (shrouded 'beneath February's snow') anticipates THE WHITENESS OF THE WHALE (p. 295, note).

143. *as the great Pilot Paul has it* 'But I keep under my body, and bring it into subjection: lest that by any means, when I have preached to others, I myself should be a castaway.' (*1 Corinthians* ix, 27)

143. *ever stands forth his own inexorable self* Thus Ishmael's two peculiar heroes: the 'aloof' Bulkington, and Queequeg 'cool as an icicle'. Thus Ishmael with his carpet-bag. Thus all Islanders, '*Isolatoes*', 'sitting apart from the other, as if each silent grief were insular and incommunicable'. Thus 'the great whale' himself: 'Be cool at the equator; keep thy blood fluid at the Pole ... retain, O man! in all seasons a temperature of thine own.' (THE BLANKET)

But who had 'ordered the scattered people to condense'? What else is 'a pilot of the living God' but one of the proud 'commodores of this earth'?

143. *Delight is to him whose strong arms yet support him* Foreshadowing Ishmael's final 'hope for a resurrection'. If Ahab is to be an unrepentant Jonah-sinner, and Pip a resurrected Jonah-prophet, Ishmael alone will survive 'vomited out ... upon the dry land' (*Jonah* ii, 10).

143. *from under the robes of Senators and Judges* Possibly

aimed at Massachusetts' Senior Senator (Daniel Webster) and Chief Justice (Lemuel Shaw, Melville's own father-in-law) for their connivance in the 'Compromise of 1850' and appeasement of the South. See Charles H. Foster, 'Something in Emblems: a reinterpretation of *Moby-Dick*' (*New England Quarterly* XXXIV, March 1961).

10 A BOSOM FRIEND

144. *with a jack-knife gently whittling away* Another Jack Tar 'diligently working away' – an ironical pointer to the landlord's whittled toothpick.

144. *He looked like a man who had never cringed* cf. Jonah: 'In all his cringing attitudes, the God-fugitive is now too plainly known.'

145. *as though he were in the planet Jupiter* Another bull-king, 'swimming away with ravished Europa ...' (THE CHASE – FIRST DAY)

146. *No more my splintered heart* A tinkling tag from the Spouter-Inn, with its 'cracked glass cases': 'Here ye strike but splintered hearts together ...' (p. 78, note).

147. *clasped me round the waist* A second 'bridegroom clasp'. cf. The Polynesian *tayos*: 'extravagant friendships, unsurpassed by the story of Damon and Pythias: in truth, much more wonderful; for, notwithstanding the devotion – even of life in some cases – to which they led, they were frequently entertained at first sight for some stranger from another island'. (*Omoo*, ch. 39) cf. The 'comely' Kooloo and 'handsome' Poky with his 'little pocket-idol, black as jet' (*Omoo*, chs. 39, 40).

cf. 'Every Kanaka has one particular friend, whom he considers himself bound to do everything for, and with whom he has a sort of contract, – an alliance offensive and defensive, – and for whom he will often make the greatest sacrifices. This friend they call *aikane*; and for such did Hope adopt me. I do not believe I could have wanted anything he had, that he would not have given me.' (Richard Henry Dana, Jr, *Two Years Before the Mast*, 1840)

147. *drew out some thirty dollars in silver* To confirm a Judas-like betrayal of Christ (*Matthew* xxvi, 15–16): for 'Christian kindness' had 'proved but hollow courtesy'. Literally 'this sooth-

ing savage' *redeems* (viz. pays cash to reclaim) Ishmael's 'splintered heart'.

147. *a good Christian ... the infallible Presbyterian Church* In lieu of the bosom of the Presbyterian Church, Ishmael embraces his own chosen 'elder', or 'bosom friend'.

Allan Melvill, Herman's father, was a Unitarian; his mother, Maria, like all the Gansevoorts, a member of the Dutch Reformed Church. His wife's family, too, were Unitarians, though he and Elizabeth at this time attended the Episcopal Church in Pittsfield.

147. *But what is worship? – to do the will of God?* 'But if any man love God, the same is known of him. As concerning therefore the eating of those things that are offered in sacrifice unto idols, we know that an idol is nothing in the world, and that there is none other God but one.' (*1 Corinthians* viii, 3–4)

147. *the innocent little idol* What had opened in 'a negro church' is transformed to this worship of a 'little negro'. The wedding is confirmed by this innocent 'woodcock'.

147. *salamed before him twice or thrice* With a final syncope of 'Sal and me' – joining 'man and wife', bosom friends, Platonic and 'Socratic wisdom' in 'our hearts' honeymoon'. Inevitably that 'solitary twain' become 'a cosy, loving pair'.

The whole chapter invites comparison with *Robinson Crusoe* – almost as if Ishmael's account of his relationship with a South Sea cannibal implied a critique of that famous account of the English mariner with a Carib cannibal. For Yankee and Yorkshireman have much in common. Like Crusoe, Ishmael claims to be a non-conformist, 'born and bred in the bosom of the infallible Presbyterian Church'; like young Crusoe, again, he abominates 'all honorable respectable toils', fleeing 'the middle station' of life – Manhattan counters, benches, desks – for the open sea. Like Melville, Defoe too invokes the simile of 'Jonah in the ship of Tarshish'.

But their resolution of the parable is very different. Robinson Crusoe's bond with his 'man Friday', after more than twenty-five years' solitary exile, marks the end of his voyage of regeneration; Ishmael's, in New England, before he has even left the mainland, affirms the *pre-condition* of his voyage. Crusoe contrives the bond on his own terms: he christens the young cannibal, clothes him, teaches him, converts him to his own peculiar brand of Protestantism; and only then – having recreated him, as it were, in his own image – can say 'I began really to love the creature'. But Ishmael, from the start, acknowledges his tattooed 'savage' on terms of *mutual fellowship* – joint-members of 'the great and everlasting First Congregation of this whole worshipping world'.

Later, when Ishmael does try instructing Queequeg (THE RAMADAN), the effect is almost that of deliberate parody of *Robinson Crusoe*. For Queequeg proves the true ascetic; Ishmael, merely a hollow champion of 'Hygiene and common sense'. And the pagan remains politely unimpressed 'that such a sensible young man should be so hopelessly lost to evangelical pagan piety'.

It is those anomalies, the 'fighting Quakers', who specifically prove Crusoe's heirs. For, though quick enough to utilize Queequeg, they cannot accept him. They can accept only his *function*, that is, not his *person*. Which means they must aspire to convert him, being unable to love him – thus reducing him for ever, in their eyes, to a thick-shelled clam.

11 NIGHTGOWN

149. *how elastic our stiff prejudices ... love once comes to bend them* In this homosexual idyll, the white man plays 'wife' to the 'savage' male: 'there is no quality in this world that is not what it is merely by contrast. Nothing exists in itself' – heat and cold, white legs and brown, Christian and pagan.

149. *serene household joy ... a blue hanging tester* Together recalling that 'serenest azure' of the Christian idyll at the back of the Whaleman's Chapel. For here, yet again, Ishmael resigns 'his own identity' to 'condensed' communion.

12 BIOGRAPHICAL

150. *Sag Harbor* On Gardiners Bay, near the east end of Long Island. The Whalers' Church survives.

150. *On one side ... a coral reef* Linking Manhattan to Kokovoko, Ishmael's 'everlasting itch' to Queequeg's 'strong desire'.

151. *this sea Prince of Wales ... made a whaleman* cf. Melville

at Windsor: 'On the way down from the tower, met the Queen ... God bless her, say I, & long live the "prince of whales" ...' (*Journal*, 22 November 1849)

151. *like Czar Peter* Peter the Great who, as 'Peter Mikailhov', studied gunnery at Königsberg, anatomy at Leyden, engraving at Amsterdam, and for several months worked as a common ship's carpenter in the royal navy dockyard at Deptford.

152. *the mysteries of whaling ... we rolled over from each other* With the roll of the whale – which is also 'the whole roll of our order'. (p. 472, note)

13 WHEELBARROW

152. *for a block* On which to hang wigs.

153. *Peter Coffin's cock and bull stories* From 'some old craft's cockpits' to a boarder's 'woodcock' and his native island of *Cock*/ovoko, this story of the Spouter-Inn is literally all 'cock and bull': of Queequeg and *Bul*/kington.

153. *because it was of assured stuff* That 'sheath', those 'Crossed Harpoons' affording 'stuff for a good joke', foster the same innuendo.

153. *like many inland reapers and mowers* From a homosexual idyll to the wide trance of the ocean, from a City of Brotherly Love to the Masonic Brotherhood of whaling, from the Freemasonry of Sodom to 'many a mortal combat', the path leads always by way of pastoral. On the one side a whale, on the other 'a long-armed mower'; on the one wall green meadows, on the other the sea.

So even these rolling stones, paradoxically, catch 'the "Moss"'.

154. *the Captain coolly proceeds to wash his hands* And 'every one knows that in most people's estimation, to do anything coolly, is to do it genteelly'. (BREAKFAST)

154. *the punch bowl ... for a huge finger-glass* cf. Charles Wilkes' account of a similar reception: 'After the meal was over, a small earthen finger-bowl was brought to the king to wash his hands, and as the attendant did not seem to be prepared to extend the like courtesy to our gentlemen, a desire for a similar utensil was expressed and complied with, although apparently with some reluctance. In like manner, when the jar of water was

brought to the king, one of the party seized upon it and drank, and the rest followed suit, to the evident distress of the attendant. It was afterwards understood that his anxiety arose from the vessel being tabooed, as every thing belonging or appropriated to the use of the king is.' (*Narrative of the U.S. Exploring Expedition ... 1838–1842*, III, 114–15)

155. *Gaining the more open water* All is intoxicating self-contradiction – above 'that *Tar/tar* air', below 'the magnanimity of the sea'; on the one side 'the slavish heels and hoofs', on the other a little schooner snorting like a colt and ducking like a slave.

157. *Was there ever such unconsciousness?* 'But, perhaps, to be true philosophers, we mortals should not be conscious of so living or so striving.' (A BOSOM FRIEND)

157. *mildly eyeing those around him* '... as he mildly turned to me'. For in Queequeg, as in Father Mapple, such 'mild gleams' are habitual.

157. *It's a mutual, joint-stock world* So Queequeg's self-reliance counters – and transcends – Emerson's: 'Society everywhere is in conspiracy against the manhood of every one of its members. Society is a joint-stock company, in which the members agree, for the better securing of his bread to each shareholder, to surrender the liberty and culture of the eater. The virtue in most request is conformity. Self-reliance is its aversion.' (*Self-Reliance*)

14 NANTUCKET

157. *the Eddystone lighthouse* On the Eddystone Rock, fourteen miles off the coast of Cornwall, south-west of Plymouth.

157. *Canada thistles ... true cross in Rome* For Nantucket, too, is all self-contradiction: part Holy See, part poisonous toadstools; part northern tundra, part desert oasis; no Prairie State, yet breeding 'cocks in the prairie'; utterly 'belted about', yet itself belting the globe with incessant 'circumnavigations'.

158. *like Laplander snow-shoes* From the fabled home of witches with power over winds.

158. *an eagle ... carried off an infant Indian* See *Collections of the Massachusetts Historical Society*, 2nd Series, III (1815), 34.

158. *quohogs* Or *quahog*, a thick-shelled clam.

158. *like so many Alexanders* Both conquerors and magicians (see p. 127, note).

158. *as the three pirate powers did Poland* The 'partitions of Poland' (1772, 1793 and 1795) were the spoils of Russia, Austria and Prussia.

159. *Let America add Mexico to Texas ... let the English overswarm all India* American settlers in Texas declared their independence from Mexico in March 1836. The annexation of Texas (as its twenty-eighth and largest state) by the United States in December 1845, led directly to a war with Mexico (1846–8) and the invasion by U.S. forces of New Mexico and California, with deep forays across the Rio Grande. In March 1847, U.S. forces landed at Veracruz and in September, after savage fighting, entered Mexico City. By the treaty of *Guadalupe Hidalgo* (February 1848) Mexico recognized Texas as a U.S. possession, ceding Upper California, Nevada, Utah, parts of Colorado and Wyoming, with most of New Mexico and Arizona – two-fifths of all her territory for an indemnity of 15 million dollars.

Cuba, too, was jealously eyed: Narciso López (a Venezuelan revolutionary who had fled to the United States) planned a series of expeditions, with American aid; but both the invasions of 1848 and 1850 ended in fiasco; the landing of 1851, in his capture and execution. (The South was eager to add Cuba to the slave-holding states, but attempts to purchase the island three years later from Spain were foiled.)

Though the Aroostook War had been averted and the Maine/New Brunswick border settled by the Webster–Ashburton Treaty (1842), more recent concessions on the Pacific coast still rankled. A slogan of the 1844 election had been 'Fifty-four forty or fight'; and even after the Oregon Treaty had fixed the Canadian border at the 49th latitude (1846), there was wild talk of pushing north.

The British, meanwhile, annexed Sind (now part of West Pakistan) in 1843, occupied Lahore in February 1846 (when Kashmir was also ceded), and in 1849, after victory in the Second Sikh War, annexed the whole of West Punjab.

159. *he alone ... goes down to it in ships* cf.

They that go down to the sea in ships, that do business in great waters;

These see the works of the Lord, and his wonders in the deep.
(*Psalm* cvii, 23–4)

159. There *is his home; there lies his business* cf. 'The sea, to mariners generally, is but a highway over which they travel to foreign markets; but to the whaler it is his field of labor, it is the home of his business. The Nantucket whaleman, when with his family, is but a visitor there. He touches at foreign ports merely to procure recruits to enable him to prosecute his voyage; he touches at home merely to lay enough to prepare for a new voyage. He is in the bosom of his family weeks, on the bosom of the ocean years.' (Obed Macy, *History of Nantucket*, p. 219)

15 CHOWDER

159. *his cousin Hosea Hussey ... proprietor of one of the best kept hotels* But a dubious enough name for a landlord:

'And the Lord said to Hosea, Go, take unto thee a wife of whoredoms and children of whoredoms: for the land hath committed great whoredom, departing from the Lord.' (*Hosea* i, 2)

'Then said the Lord unto me, Go yet, love a woman beloved of her friend, yet an adultress, according to the love of the Lord toward the children of Israel, who look to other gods, and love flagons of wine.' (*Hosea* iii, 1)

160. *try pot-luck at the Try Pots* and 'boldly dip into the Pot-luck of both worlds'. (BIOGRAPHICAL)

160. *till we made a corner three points* Till we reached a corner, on our right, at an angle of roughly 33°.

160. *suspended by asses' ears* Ear-shaped lugs, or handles.

160. *The horns of the cross-trees ... a little like a gallows* Third sign of 'The Trap!' – for these 'young candidates' with a hangman's noose around their necks (see p. 472, note).

160. *prodigious black pots ... hints touching Tophet* Because of the oil bubbling and boiling out of the blubber: 'and the preacher's text was about ... the weeping and wailing'. (cf. THE TRY-WORKS)

160. *yellow hair ... a dull red lamp ... a purple woollen shirt* Like the 'red windows of the "Sword-Fish Inn"', to throw out 'oblique hints'? For if yellow and purple combine to create 'a

wife of whoredoms', what of Ishmael's lover with his 'purplish, yellow' face? 'Fishiest of all fishy places was the Try Pots...'

162. *What's that stultifying saying* 'Chowder-head' means 'thick-head'.

162. *a polished necklace of codfish vertebræ* cf. 'It is a German conceit, that the vertebræ are absolutely undeveloped skulls.' (THE NUT) Thus this hussy (whore or harlot) wears a necklace of skulls – first avatar of Kali, black goddess of death (see p. 272, note)

162. *young Stiggs ... with his harpoon in his side* Meaning 'stigma'? Is not Queequeg literally stigmatized – tattooed or pricked all over?

16 THE SHIP

163. *as Yojo purposed befriending us* But the little hunch-back proves a sinister advocate. Mansfield and Vincent suggest that Yojo may be a variant of Yâjooj and Majooj, the Koranic equivalents of Gog and Magog. But this woodcock's name is merely a palindrome (mirror-writing for Narcissus by his fountain) of 'O Joy!'.

163. *some sort of Lent or Ramadan* The ninth month of the lunar year during which all Moslems must fast from dawn to sunset. Followers of Mohammed were known as Ishmaelites or Hagarenes.

164. *XXXIX Articles* The official creed of the Church of England, fixed by Convocation in 1563.

164. *I sallied out among the shipping* For a third solo turn: first into the streets of New Bedford; then to the Whaleman's Chapel.

'The town of Nantucket, in the state of Massachusetts, contains about eight thousand inhabitants; nearly a third part of the population are quakers, and they are, taken together, a very industrious and enterprising people. On this island are owned about one hundred vessels, of all descriptions, engaged in the whale trade, giving constant employment and support to upwards of sixteen hundred hardy seamen...' (Owen Chase, *Narrative of the Most Extraordinary and Distressing Shipwreck of the Whale-ship Essex, of Nantucket*, ch. 1)

Melville himself, at the time of writing, had never visited the island.

164. *Pequod ... the name of a celebrated tribe of Massachusetts Indians* Or rather Connecticut Indians, whose restless warrior spirit, under Sassacus, had led to the most serious of the New England Indian wars. In a surprise attack, on the night of 26 May 1637, their fort near Mystic, Connecticut, was attacked by militia from Hartford. Between 500 and 800 Pequot braves were massacred before dawn.

John Mason, the English commander, wrote his own *Brief History of the Pequot War*. But Melville had probably read Thomas Shepard's paean to 'the goodness of God, as to myself, so to all the country, in delivering us from the Pekoat furies...' (*The Autobiography of Thomas Shepard*, 1832) That Calvinist pastor, in distant Cambridge, breathed prophetic doom (on Job and rebellious Korah): 'At last, by the direction of one Captain Mason, their wigwams were set on fire; which being dry, and contiguous one to another, was most dreadful to the Indians; some burning, some bleeding to death by the sword, some resisting till they were cut off; some flying were beat down by the men without; until the Lord had utterly consumed the whole company, except four or five girls they took prisoners... And 'tis verily thought, scarce one man escaped, unless one or two to carry forth tidings of the lamentable end of their fellows.' So Sassacus and all his braves 'perished from among the congregation'.

The *Acushnet*, too, had borne the name of an extinct tribe of 'Massachusetts Indians'.

164. *butter-box galliots* Dutch cargo-boats or fishing-vessels. Luggers, junks, galliots – all have four-sided sails bent upon a yard which hangs obliquely to the mast.

164. *like a French grenadier's ... on the coast of Japan* For the *Pequod*, too, is all self-contradiction: both warrior Indian and Napoleonic warrior; both barbaric Viking and Ethiopian; both Middle and Far Eastern; Cannibal and Tartar; pagan and Christian. The references, like the Nantucketers, girdle 'this watery world'.

'So that did you carry them the news that another flood had come; they would only answer – "Well, boys, here's the ark."' (p. 489)

164. *the three old kings of Cologne* The bones of the three Kings, or Magi, were taken from Constantinople to Cologne in the twelfth century; placed in a silver reliquary, they are honoured by a shrine in the cathedral choir. See Melville's *Journal*: 'We went to the Cathedral, during service – saw the tomb of the *Three Kings of Cologne* – their skulls.' (9 December 1849)

164. *Her ancient decks were worn and wrinkled* Like the 'old wrinkled planks' of that other 'corner-anchored old ark'. But whale-like, too, with her long sharp teeth 'garnished like one continuous jaw'.

164. *the pilgrim-worshipped flag-stone ... where Beckett bled* 'Ugly place where they killed him ...' (*Journal*, 5 November 1849)

164. *Old Captain Peleg* Peleg (in Hebrew 'division') is named among the generations of the sons of Shem, the son of Noah: 'for in his days was the earth divided'. (*Genesis* x, 25) The divided ownership of the *Pequod* and the excessive number of 'lays' into which the profits of the voyage are to be divided both centre on Captain Peleg.

165. *Thorkill-Hake's carved buckler or bedstead* Thorkell Hákr (Thorkel Foulmouth), the eleventh-century invader of England, foster father of Knut. His great deeds were 'carved over his shut bed, and on the stool before his highseat'. (*The Story of Burnt Njal*, tr. Sir George Dasent, 1861) Melville must have been drawn to the name (suggesting 'Thunder/kill/hack') in some secondary source since, Icelandic apart, the *Njalssaga* was only available at that time in Latin.

165. *to propose myself as a candidate for the voyage* The masonic password heralds another image of Brotherly Love: another black cone, this time 'some ten feet high'. For what is the 'temporary erection', with 'a tufted point', 'pitched a little behind the main-mast', but a phallic totem? That was why perhaps Queequeg's little god 'had already pitched upon' the *Pequod*. That was why perhaps Ishmael in a moment 'decided that this was the very ship for us'.

But the full compound of sacrilege – of a Quaker 'in this queer tenement', Thomas à Becket knifed by the try-works – is not revealed until ch. 95, THE CASSOCK, in 'that unaccountable cone ... jet-black as Yojo, the ebony idol of Queequeg'. (p. 530, note)

165. *part of the jaws of the right-whale* And 'in those jaws of swift destruction' sits another wrinkled Jonah, selling 'the sailors deliriums and death'.

165. *like the top-knot on some old Pottowottamie Sachem's head* Or Queequeg's apex, with 'nothing but a small scalp-knot twisted up on his forehead'. The Potawatamies or Potawatomies, an Algonquian tribe from western New York, were gathered into a reservation in Kansas by the 1840s. The 'sachem' is a tribal chief.

166. *rolled up in blue pilot-cloth* cf. Queequeg's shirt sleeves 'irregularly rolled up'. 'Drabbest' brown, not blue, was the usual Quaker colour.

167. *from Cape Cod or the Vineyard* From Cape Cod, Massachusetts, or Martha's Vineyard, an island fifteen miles west of Nantucket.

167. *Captain Ahab* In Hebrew 'father's brother' – for Ishmael, a father by proxy. The biblical Ahab deserted Jehovah, on marrying the Phoenician Jezebel, for Canaanite Baal: 'And he reared up an altar for Baal in the house of Baal, which he had built in Samaria. And Ahab made a grove; and Ahab did more to provoke the Lord God of Israel to anger than all the kings of Israel that were before him.' (*1 Kings* xvi, 31–3)

Captain Ahab, like his namesake, is married with a son; inhabits an 'ivory house' (*1 Kings* xxii, 39); and, in the end, falls in battle.

167. *Captain Bildad* In Hebrew 'old friendship or old love' – named after the second, and least consoling, of Job's comforters: 'Doth God pervert judgment? or doth the Almighty pervert justice? ... If thou wert pure and upright; surely now he would awake for thee, and make the habitation of thy righteousness prosperous.' (*Job* viii, 3–6)

167. *Clap eye on Captain Ahab* 'Aye, aye, I thought so': another pun echoed to the end. It is a Captain Peleg (or 'Pillick') who first introduces this 'pegging lubber', or peg-leg.

167. *the monstrousest parmacetty* Popular corruption of 'spermaceti'.

168. *I had been four voyages in the merchant* Melville had only been on one voyage in the merchant service (his first to Liverpool), followed by three aboard as many whalers: on the

Acushnet, which he jumped at Nukahiva, in the Marquesas Islands (9 July 1842); on the *Lucy Ann*, of Sydney, which dropped him at Papeete, Tahiti (25 September 1842); on the *Charles and Henry*, of Nantucket, from which he was discharged at Lahaina, in the Hawaiian Islands (27 April 1843).

His fifth and last voyage, as ordinary seaman, was home to Boston from Honolulu, aboard the U.S. frigate, *United States*.

168. *all his crow's feet into one scowl* A nautical pun, to suggest not only that network of 'pursed' wrinkles, but of cords rove through a long block, or 'dead-eye'.

169. *Seated on the transom* A cross-beam bolted to the stern-post.

169. *They are fighting Quakers* Or cannibal Quakers: for this insulated, insular sect, too, is all self-contradiction – part Scandinavian, part Pagan Roman – 'anomalously modified by things altogether alien and heterogeneous'.

169. *a Scandinavian sea-king, or a poetical Pagan Roman* It is Melville who is both sea-king (of the carved bedstead) and poetical Roman (reeling with 'the plungings of the Roman race-horse). For somewhere at the mythological roots of *Moby-Dick* there lurk memories of pagan Scandinavia with its rock-carvings, or drawings, of ships and sun discs; runic knots and interlacing patterns; dancing men and men in procession with great erected phalluses; ocean quest and boat-burial. Its religion revealed mysteries as transcendent as Odin hanging nine nights on the gallows as a sacrifice to himself, and objects of veneration as intimate as the embalmed penis of a horse. Its shamans delighted in hidden truth – providing Melville with a host of creative symbols: the Great Goddess, the serpent, the ship, sky-god and bull.

As Celtic mythology and the rites of British Druids (it has been argued) control *Billy Budd*, so *Moby-Dick*, conceived almost half a century earlier, may be read – in part, at least – as Viking Saga. (cf. Carlyle, 'The Hero as Divinity. Odin. Paganism: Scandinavian Mythology', *On Heroes, Hero-Worship, and the Heroic in History*, Lecture I, 1840)

170. *all men tragically great ... a certain morbidness* Echoing Coleridge on *Hamlet*: 'one of Shakspeare's modes of creating characters is, to conceive any one intellectual or moral faculty in morbid excess, and then to place himself, Shakspeare, thus mutilated or diseased, under given circumstances'; foreshadow-

ing Ahab 'in his frantic morbidness' pitting himself 'all mutilated' against the whale. (MOBY DICK)

See Leon Howard, 'Melville's Struggle with the Angel' (*Modern Language Quarterly*, vol. I, 1940, pp. 201–5).

171. *broad shad-bellied waistcoat* Sloping away at the abdomen. 'Shad-belly' was a contemporary nickname for Quakers.

171. *an incorrigible old hunks* With a touch of old 'Hunker' – or conservative Democrat – below that Tammany Hall of a Wigwam?

171. *the old Categut* Phonetically named, it seems, after the Kattegat Strait between Denmark and Sweden.

171. *the exact embodiment of his utilitarian character* Which, in Ishmael's 'lingo', spells death. Even Bildad's voice has a 'hollow', 'sepulchral' tone as he glances up 'from the book in which he had again been burying himself'.

172. *'I dost,' said I unconsciously* 'Dost' unto 'dost': 'For dust thou art, and unto dust shalt thou return.' (*Genesis* iii, 19)

'We therefore commit his body to the ground; earth to earth, ashes to ashes, dust to dust; in sure and certain hope of the Resurrection to eternal life.' (*The Book of Common Prayer, Burial of the Dead*)

172. *certain shares of the profits called* lays Paying by 'lays' is said to have originated in the Dutch Greenland fisheries in the seventeenth century. A captain, in Melville's time, might expect a lay of between 1/8 and 1/17: the first mate, 1/20; the second mate, 1/45; the third mate, 1/60; the helmsman, from 1/80 to 1/120; the common sailor, from 1/120 to 1/150; a cabin-boy, 1/250. The normal rate for a greenhand, the 'long lay', was anything between 1/160 and 1/200. Melville himself, according to his friend, Richard Tobias Greene, received an advance of $84 when he shipped on the *Acushnet* ('Toby's Own Story', July 1846).

172. *one stiver* A small coin of the Low Countries.

173. *of a broad-shouldered make* The *Acushnet*'s crew list records Melville's age, '21', and height, '5 feet, 9½ inches'.

173. *his unaccountable old crony* As Queequeg 'with a jack-knife' was 'gently whittling away', so Peleg now is 'vainly trying to mend a pen with his jack-knife'; as Queequeg 'appeared wholly occupied with counting the pages' of his large book, so

Bildad now seems 'absorbed in reading from a ponderous volume'; as Queequeg hums, Bildad mumbles. For here is yet another pair of bosom friends, turned 'cronies'.

173. '"Lay *not up for yourselves treasures upon earth* ..."' (*Matthew* vi, 19–21)

'The light of the body is the eye... If therefore the light that is in thee be darkness, how great is that darkness! ... Ye cannot serve God and mammon': an apt enough text for this 'incorrigible old hunks', with 'his drab-colored eye', who 'had long since come to the sage and sensible conclusion that a man's religion is one thing, and this practical world quite another'.

173. *the seven hundred and seventy-seventh* 'Lay indeed' – with a further sepulchral pun: 'And all the days of Lamech were seven hundred seventy and seven years; and he died.' (*Genesis* v, 31)

175. *That's he; thank ye* Emended by Hayford and Parker to: 'Thank ye; thank ye'.

176. *a sort of sick ... In fact, he ain't sick* Yet again all is self-contradiction. Now Ahab is 'queer', as the Spouter-Inn, New Bedford, the dockside 'nondescripts', Queequeg, Peleg's wigwam, Bildad, had all been queer. This is altogether a queer book.

176. *a grand, ungodly, god-like man* Peleg's Captain Ahab is the Carlylean Hero, both as Prophet and Conqueror: 'Ever, to the true instinct of men, there is something god-like in him ... I should say, *sincerity*, a deep, great, genuine sincerity, is the first characteristic of all men in any way heroic ... Such a man is what we call an *original* man; he comes to us at first-hand.' (*On Heroes*, Lecture II)

176. *the dogs, did they not lick his blood? 1 Kings* xxi, 19.

177. *the old squaw Tistig* Meaning ''Tis a stig' (p. 162, note)? Is not Ahab literally stigmatized with 'a slender rod-like mark' from crown to sole? He 'sleeps with clenched hands; and wakes with his own bloody nails in his palms'. (THE CHART)

cf. Judith Quary, the half-breed squaw of Nantucket, dooming Thomas Starbuck to death in a whale's jaw before he sails for the Pacific (Joseph C. Hart, *Miriam Coffin, or, The Whale-Fishermen*).

177. *at Gayhead* 'The most westerly promontory of Martha's Vineyard', Tashtego's birthplace.

178. *dark Ahab* Dark as his ship: 'A noble craft, but somehow a most melancholy! All noble things are touched with that.'

17 THE RAMADAN

178. *knocked at the door ... 'It's I – Ishmael'* 'Be of good cheer; it is I; be not afraid.' (*Matthew* xiv, 27)

180. *Unconsciously clapping the vinegar-cruet to ... her nose* 'Whoredom and wine and new wine take away the heart ... Their drink is sour: they have committed whoredom continually'. (*Hosea* iv, 11, 18) 'Was there ever such unconsciousness?'

180. *Snarles the Painter* In the sense of a 'noose', or 'snare' – to paint the sign of 'The Trap!' (p. 160, note)

181. *very punctual then* By the calendar, he means, since Ramadan is reckoned by the lunar, not solar, year.

182. *screwed down to the floor ... with stiff and grating joints* cf. Bildad sitting 'bolt-upright' with his legs 'stiffly crossed'. cf. The *Pequod*'s masts standing 'stiffly up like the spines of the three old kings of Cologne'. All religious experience, Melville seems to suggest, has something in common.

183. *hell is an idea ... an undigested apple-dumpling* To return to 'the two orchard thieves': but 'so soon as I hear' *Ishmael* give 'himself out for a philosopher, I conclude that, like the dyspeptic old woman, he must have "broken his digester".' (A BOSOM FRIEND)

183. *to barbecue all the slain ... so many Christmas turkeys* cf. Montaigne: 'This done, they roast him and eat him in common and send some pieces to their absent friends.' (*Of Cannibals*) Even those 'Christmas turkeys' – or Turkish Christians in this *pilau*? – point to Montaigne's Christendom: 'I think there is more barbarity in eating a man alive than in eating him dead, in tearing by tortures and the rack a body still full of feeling, in roasting him bit by bit, having him bitten and mangled by dogs and swine (and what is worse, on the pretext of piety and religion) than in roasting and eating him after he is dead.'

183. *pilau* 'Pilaff' represents modern Turkish pronunciation.

184. *we sallied out to board* After three solo turns man and wife, bosom friends together, at last.

184. *picking our teeth with halibut bones* Or 'holy butts', so called from being commonly eaten on holy days.

18 HIS MARK

184. *a member of the First Congregational Church* 'How long hath he been a member?' A joke at Bildad's expense (lurking in that wigwam), but also the reader's, via that 'congregation of sailors', via those 'tapering upright cones of congregated blossoms'. (THE STREET)

184. *Deacon Deuteronomy Coleman's meeting-house* Or house of God: 'These words the Lord spake unto all your assembly in the mount out of the midst of the fire, of the cloud, and of the thick darkness, with a great voice... And he wrote them in two tables of stone ...' (*Deuteronomy* v, 22) cf. 'one Nathan Coleman'. (*Omoo*, ch. 56)

185. *his great yellow bandana ... over the bulwarks* In 'his broad-skirted drab coat', another 'Hussey' ('with yellow hair and a yellow gown'), leaning 'stiffly' to gaze at this 'Philistine' – from the land of Canaan.

185. *thou young Hittite* A hill-tribe of Canaan, defeated by the Israelites. (*Joshua* xi)

185. *some of us cherish some queer crotchets* Fancying ourselves 'vastly superior to other mortals, pagans and what not' – though all alike rooted at THE CROTCH (ch. 63).

185. *tell Quohog there* The implication being that Queequeg, as far as Peleg is concerned, looks as thick-skulled as the clams he has just been consuming at the Try Pots. But this 'Quohog' will soon turn 'Hedgehog' with prickly quills.

185. *what a harpoon ... and he handles it about right* 'Because it was of assured stuff', as he at once demonstrates on a small tar spot, or 'Asphaltick Pool' (p. 100, note).

186. *why, dad whale dead* And Bil/dad dead: 'We therefore commit his body to the ground ...' (p. 172, note).

186. *said Peleg, to his partner* This is Hayford and Parker's reading. For it is not Peleg, but Bildad, who is plainly retreating.

186. *Queequeg was soon enrolled* Into the masonic 'roll of our order' (p. 472, note).

186. *a queer round figure ... tattooed upon his arm* The Maltese Cross of the first edition is neither 'round' nor 'queer'. Rockwell Kent, in his illustrated edition (N.Y., Random House, 1930), substitutes ∞, the sign for infinity. Which is certainly more in line with the rest of Queequeg's 'twisted tattooing' – representing, as it does, 'a complete theory of the heavens and the earth, and a mystical treatise on the art of attaining truth'. (QUEEQUEG IN HIS COFFIN, p. 593, note)

187. *Son of darkness ... steer clear of the fiery pit!* '... and the preacher's text was about the blackness of darkness, and the weeping and wailing and teeth-gnashing there.' (THE CARPET-BAG)

187. *a Belial bondsman. Spurn the idol Bell* 'Be ye not unequally yoked together with unbelievers: for what fellowship hath righteousness with unrighteousness? and what communion hath light with darkness? and what concord hath Christ with Belial? ... And what agreement hath the temple of God with idols?' (*2 Corinthians* vi, 14–16)

In the apocryphal book, *Bel and the Dragon*, Daniel tells how he revealed to King Astyages that a Babylonian idol, or Baal, was a mere image of brass – a fraud imposed upon the people by the priests – and exploded their holy dragon by feeding it pitch, fat and hair.

Baal, or Baalim, were the local deities of Canaan, worshipped in orgiastic cults connected with fertility. 'Belial' here seems to be treated as a derivative of 'Bel': 'Now the sons of Eli were sons of Belial; they knew not the Lord.' (*1 Samuel* ii, 12) After the glare outside 'The Crossed Harpoons' and 'The Sword-Fish', and that compromising bed at 'The Spouter-Inn', Melville again seems to be evoking Milton:

And When Night
Darkens the Streets, then wander forth the Sons
Of *Belial*, flown with insolence and wine.
Witness the Streets of *Sodom*, and that night
In *Gibeah*, when hospitable Dores
Yielded thir Matrons to prevent worse rape.
(*Paradise Lost* I, 500–505)

But the pun rebounds on *Bel*/Dad: 'remain not for aye a Belial bondsman ... mind thine eye, I say'. For Bildad is all 'eye' – rubbing his spectacles to take 'a good long look at Queequeg', 'earnestly and steadfastly eyeing him', grasping his hands and looking 'earnestly into his eyes'. To the end a *voyeur*, he is caught, 'quietly overlooking some sail-makers ... in the waist'.

'Wretched entertainment at the sign of "The Trap!"'

187. *Davy Jones* The spirit of the sea, the sailors' devil.

188. *how to rig jury-masts* Temporary masts, in ironic flight from Death and Judgment; as 'jury-leg' denotes a wooden leg.

188. *stooped to pick up ... an end of the tarred twine* Another 'small drop tar' (from 'th' Asphaltick Pool') – linking Queequeg to the Quaker, dead Bildad to the 'Dead Sea', and both to Sodom.

19 THE PROPHET

THE PROPHET cf. Meyerbeer's grand opera, *Le Prophète,* first produced in Paris in 1849, the year of Melville's visit.

188. *but shabbily apparelled in ... patched trowsers* 'Though I cannot tell why it was exactly that those stage managers, the Fates, put me down for this shabby part of a whaling voyage ...' (LOOMINGS) For this is 'Sartor Resartus' himself – Ahab's doppelgänger and the whale's, with his 'ribbed', tormented face. His blazon is 'black'; his bearing a 'levelled mass'.

188. *'Anything down there about your souls?'* With the first hint of complicity in some kind of Faustian pact.

189. *this fellow has broken loose* But it is the *Pequod* which proves a lunatic's asylum.

189. *then this left arm of mine will be all right* Another pun to echo the length of the book.

189. *off Cape Horn ... like dead for three days and nights* 'And Saul arose from the earth, and when his eyes were opened, he saw no man: but they led him by the hand, and brought him into Damascus. And he was three days without sight, and neither did eat nor drink.' (*Acts* ix, 8–9)

189. *that deadly skrimmage ... afore the altar* In Santa (to compound the sacrilege), Peru: the first Pacific port touched by the *Acushnet* after rounding the Horn (23 June 1841).

189. *Nothing about the silver calabash he spat into?* Or chalice for Holy Communion.

190. *the ineffable heavens* To make a Latin joke at the expense of the Greek root of his own calling, as a spokesman (*πρό/φητης*) of God. For this Hebrew prophet literally *wears* 'ineffables' – that is to say 'patched trowsers'.

191. *Elijah* Who denounced King Ahab and foretold his doom: 'In the place where dogs licked the blood of Naboth shall dogs lick thy blood, even thine' (*1 Kings* xxi, 19). Ishmael had earlier played on the allusion (p. 176).

Like Ahab's mother, this Elijah is called 'crazy': 'yet the old squaw ... at Gayhead, said that the name would somehow prove prophetic.'

191. *that he was dogging us* As 'the invisible police officer of the Fates ... secretly dogs me'. (LOOMINGS)

20 ALL ASTIR

192. *traps* From *draps* (French), clothes – but with a token of 'traps' within a 'Trap'.

193. *did this charitable Aunt Charity bustle* Another withered old Jonah, investing in 'deliriums and death'. All Charity's gifts, ironically, are mementoes of Queequeg: the 'jar of pickles' hinting at 'a pretty pickle'; the 'bunch of quills', at 'porcupine quills'; the 'roll of flannel', at a roll in bed.

193. *down went his mark* Which is: 'Bildad. his mark.'

193. *hobbling out of his whalebone den* Came pegging Peleg – like 'a roaring lion ... seeking whom he may devour' (*Daniel* vi, 10ff.; *1 Peter* v, 8).

Or did Peleg come 'roaring out of his whalebone den' and then conclude 'by roaring back into his wigwam'? Hayford and Parker argue, on palæographic grounds, that the word was twice misread: first by his copyist or American compositor as 'hobbling'; and, when corrected in proof, again by his English compositor as 'running'.

21 GOING ABOARD

194. *some sailors ... it can't be shadows* See THE FIRST LOWERING, pp. 321–2.

195. *The cabin entrance was locked* Recalling 'something about the doors of convicts' cells being never allowed to be locked within'. (THE SERMON)

195. *old rigger ... in a tattered pea-jacket* 'pie' or 'pee-jacket': a stout short overcoat of coarse woollen cloth, commonly worn by sailors.

196. *the sleeper's rear ... he'll twitch you off soon* 'in the most unnatural manner'. (THE SPOUTER-INN, p. 116, note) But like Ishmael, this rigger, it appears, 'never slept better' in his life.

196. *fattening some of the lower orders for ottomans* With a further digression on Queequeg's 'queer ways': 'In truth this gentleman is a luxurious Ottoman, swimming about over the watery world, surroundingly accompanied by all the solaces and endearments of the harem.' (SCHOOLS AND SCHOOLMASTERS p. 501)

22 MERRY CHRISTMAS

199. *Blood and thunder! – jump!* At this lodge of Thor, 'at this grim sign of the Thunder Cloud'.

199. *at intervals ... a dismal stave of psalmody* Now the sailors roar, like 'the devil ... seeking whom he may devour'. (*1 Peter* v, 8)

Booble Alley was among 'the lowest and most abandoned neighbourhoods frequented by sailors in Liverpool'. 'The pestilent lanes and alleys which, in their vocabulary, go by the names of Rotten-row, Gibraltar-place, and Booble-alley, are putrid with vice and crime; to which, perhaps, the round world does not furnish a parallel.' (*Redburn*, ch. 39)

199. *a small choice copy of Watts* Isaac Watts' *Psalms of David Imitated in the Language of the New Testament* (1719), possibly bound together with his collected *Hymns and Spiritual Songs* (1707–09), from which brother Bildad sings the hymn beginning: 'There is a land of pure delight ...' (Bk II, No. 66, stanza 3).

200. *like the white ivory tusks ... vast curving icicles* For the *Pequod*, though very like a whale, is also strangely elephantine – forestalling that hybrid 'the Elephant Whale'.

200. *sweet fields ... in living green* sings Bildad 'as the old craft deep dived into the green seas'. For Christian pastoral is

the greenest of all pastorals. Consider the title of Watts' hymn: 'A prospect of heaven makes death easy'. Then consider Bildad's 'drab-colored eye intently looking at you ...' (THE SHIP) Then consider this whole panorama of green seas, green pants, green Canaan, viewed through the 'green goggling glasses' of the whole roll of this order.

200. *many a pleasant haven* Where the grass shoots up by the spring. 'Spring, thou sheep-head; spring ... Why don't ye spring, I say, all of ye – spring!' Which is Ishmael's evergreen paradox: for here is no *Merry Christ*, nor *Christ Mass* – only a poke in the rear, or kick in the *ass*.

201. *gazing heroically in his face* To the end a voyeur (looking, looking, looking) to gaze at last, hand in hand, at 'stout Peleg' – like Queequeg 'holding close' to his face that little idol of his, 'peering hard into its face ...' (A BOSOM FRIEND)

23 THE LEE SHORE

203. *in landlessness alone resides the highest truth* Which is Nantucketers' truth: 'He alone resides and riots on the sea ... He lives on the sea, as prairie cocks in the prairie ...' But, as for Ishmael, he 'must eventually lower, or at least shift, his conceit of attainable felicity' – returning to the hearthstone, the supper and the bed. (See A SQUEEZE OF THE HAND, p. 527.)

203. *Take heart, take heart, O Bulkington!* With a last glancing pun on that idol of radical Democrats, the 'Palinurus of Democracy', Thomas *Hart* Benton? Like Bulkington, with powerful chest and dazzling teeth, he was large physically; like Bulkington, he was from the mountains (of North Carolina); like Bulkington, he preferred the political wilderness to being cast 'on the treacherous, slavish shore' of his pro-slavery Missouri electorate. Benton was dropped from the helm of the Democratic Party for his opposition to the 'Compromise of 1850'. (See Alan Heimert, '*Moby-Dick* and American Political Symbolism', *American Quarterly* vol. XV, No. 4.)

203. *straight up, leaps thy apotheosis!* Like some Greek or Nordic hero, both bull-king and sky-god. The death of Poe, that other Virginian, was prologue to Melville's own Atlantic crossing of October, 1849.

24 THE ADVOCATE

THE ADVOCATE Compulsively marching the initiate up to an American battery of statistics. See Beale ch. 11, 'Rise and Progress of the Sperm Whale Fishery', passim; Scoresby, vol. II, pp. 117, 119; and J. Ross Browne, p. 539.

204. *the Dutch in De Witt's time* Jan de Witt (1625–72), Grand Pensionary of Holland and leading republican opponent to the House of Orange, did much to encourage industry and commerce. His brother Cornelius was a naval officer. 'At one time the greatest whaling people in the world, the Dutch and Germans are now among the least . . .'

205. *we whalemen of America now outnumber all* J. Ross Browne quotes Congressman Joseph Grinnell of New Bedford: 'I have prepared with great care a table from authentic sources, to show the consumption of domestic and foreign articles by our whaling fleet, now consisting of 650 ships, barques, brigs, and schooners, tonnaging 200,000 tons; cost at the time of sailing, $20,000,000; manned by 17,500 officers and seamen, one half of whom are green hands when the vessels sail. By this table, it will be seen that the annual consumption by this fleet is $3,845,500; only $400,000 is foreign articles ... The value of the annual import of oil and whalebone in a crude state is $7,000,000 . . .' (1844).

By 1846, the peak year, some 40,000 men were employed in U.S. whaling ports and at sea; of 900 whalers throughout the world, 735 were American; up to $120,000,000 were invested in the industry; and whale exports ranked third, after meat and lumber, in U.S. trade.

205. *that Egyptian mother* Nut, the mother of Isis (born pregnant from the womb), and of Osiris (twin foetus who impregnated her), and of Set, or Typhon (his implacable foe). cf. Plutarch: Isis and Osiris 'were in love with one another before they were born, and enjoyed each other in the dark before they came into the world.' ('Of Isis and Osiris', *Moralia* 356A)

This is Melville's one explicit allusion to the Osiris myth. See H. Bruce Franklin, *The Wake of the Gods*, ch. 3, 'Moby-Dick: An Egyptian Myth Incarnate'. (cf. p. 284, note.)

205. *Cook* Captain James Cook, who explored the Pacific in a series of expeditions throughout the 1770s.

205. *Vancouver* George Vancouver, who accompanied Captain Cook on his second and third voyage into the Pacific and charted the north-west coast of America (1792–4).

205. *your Krusensterns* Adam Johann von Krusenstern, the first Russian to circumnavigate the globe. Melville had read his *Voyage round the World, in the Years 1803–1806* (London, 1813).

206. *first blunder-born discovery by a Dutchman* Australia was probably first sighted by the Portuguese in 1601, and again by Spaniards a few years later. But the first callers, in 1606, were the Dutch who named it New Holland.

206. *that double-bolted land, Japan* Under the Tokugawa shogunate only Nagasaki, where the Dutch operated a limited trading concession, was open to foreigners. In 1853 Commodore Perry deliberately provoked the régime by anchoring four ships off Uraga in Yedo Bay. In March 1854, three years after the publication of *Moby-Dick*, a treaty was signed opening Japan to American trade.

207. *Who but might Job!* xli, 1–34 (Extract 2).

207. *Alfred the Great ... Other, the Norwegian* In his Anglo-Saxon paraphrase of Orosius, *Historia adversus Paganos* (c. 890), into which King Alfred inserted a verbatim account of the voyages of Octhere and Wulfstan: 'he sailed along the Norway coast, so far north as commonly the whale-hunters used to travel.' (See Extract 9.)

207. *Who, but Edmund Burke!* Early in his *Speech on Conciliation with the American Colonies* (1775), Burke called attention to the exploits of New England whale fishermen and 'the progress of their victorious industry'. 'Whilst we follow them among the tumbling mountains of ice, and behold them penetrating into the deepest frozen recesses of Hudson's Bay and Davis's Straits, whilst we are looking for them beneath the arctic circle, we hear that they have pierced into the opposite region of polar cold, that they are at the antipodes, and engaged under the frozen serpent of the south ... We know that whilst some of them draw the line and strike the harpoon on the coast of Africa, others run the longitude and pursue their gigantic game along the coast of Brazil. No sea but what is vexed by their fisheries. No climate that is not witness to their toils.' (See Extract 42.)

207. *a long line of Folgers* Mary Folger, with husband and

family, settled in Nantucket in 1663. It was the famed Peleg ('Pillick') Folger who made his first whaling voyage, as a twenty-one-year-old on the *Grampus*, in 1751. (See p. 106, note.) It was Capt. Timothy Folger, in 1769, who supplied Franklin with data about the Gulf Stream, giving Americans a temporary lead over the British on the Atlantic run. It was Capt. Mayhew Folger, whale-hunting on the *Topaz*, who found the mutineers from the *Bounty* on Pitcairn Island in February 1808.

207. *declared 'a royal fish'* By an Act of Edward II of 1315, and again of 1324. (See ch. 90, HEADS OR TAILS.)

207. *one of the mighty triumphs given to a Roman general* No such triumph is recorded, although Marcus Aemilius Scaurus (Aedile, 58 B.C.) brought the Joppa whale-skeleton (referred to again in ch. 82) to Rome. Dr H. P. Vincent discovered that Melville's source of information about this skeleton, believed by the inhabitants of Joppa to have been that of Perseus' monster, was the article on 'Whale' in John Kitto's *Cyclopaedia of Biblical Literature* (New York, 1846). It is Kitto's comment that the bones remained in Joppa 'till the conquering Romans carried them in triumph to the great city', which Melville is here elaborating.

208. *whales . . . as many walled towns* Another pun to resound to the end. That 'great captain of antiquity' is possibly Demetrius I of Macedonia (336–283 B.C.), *Poliorcetes*, 'Besieger of Cities'. (Plutarch, *Demetrius*, 42)

208. *for a whale-ship was my Yale College and my Harvard* cf. R. H. Dana, Jr's constant harping on his time at Harvard and plans of returning there. (*Two Years Before the Mast*) cf. Nathaniel Ames: 'I continue to regard as the happiest part of my existence, the three years passed at Harvard University, and the three and a half spent on board a man of war, two seminaries at which I had the honour to receive my polite education . . .' (*A Mariner's Sketches*, 1830)

25 POSTSCRIPT

209. *with coronation stuff!* For a final snub at loyal Britons, linking 'sperm oil' and 'stuff'. (p. 153, note)

26 KNIGHTS AND SQUIRES

209. *Starbuck* A common enough name among the Quakers of Nantucket. It was a Mary Starbuck who had been decisive in establishing the Society in the early eighteenth century; Mary too is the name of Starbuck's 'young Cape wife' (p. 624). But proper nouns in Melville always sound overtones: if 'Star' (of the Nativity) suits his 'deep natural reverence', 'buck' (or dollar) fits this professional killer of whales. Hieroglyphically '*$', then, represents the starry-eyed capitalist on the *Pequod*'s deck, while 'Starbuck' pinpoints her doom in the Pacific – near one of the Line Islands, south of Christmas, that straddle the whale cruising grounds.

210. *for all his hardy sobriety* Like Father Mapple 'in the hardy winter of a healthy old age'. cf. Thomas Fuller's 'The Good Soldier': 'He will not in bravery expose himself to needlesse perill ... He keepeth a clear and quiet conscience in his breast, which otherwise will gnaw out the roots of all valour ... None fitter to go to warre, than those who have made their peace with God in Christ; for such a man's soul is an impregnable fort: it cannot be scaled with ladders, for it reaches up to heaven ...' (*The Holy State and the Profane State*, Bk 2, ch. 19) Melville had been reading Fuller (see Extract 25) in April, 1849.

211. *shocking, to expose the fall of valor* For '*Valour* is still *value*. The first duty for a man is still that of subduing *Fear*.' (Carlyle, *On Heroes, Hero-Worship, and the Heroic in History*, Lecture 1)

As Melville noted in his Shakespeare: 'The infernal nature has a valor often denied to innocence.' (*King Lear* V, iii, 97–101)

211. *detestable as joint stock-companies* Speaking with the voice of Emerson's *Self-Reliance* (p. 157, note).

212. *that democratic dignity which ... radiates without end from God* 'Howsoever, I am sure there is a common Spirit that playes within us, yet makes no part of us; and that is the Spirit of God, and scintillation of that noble and mighty Essence, which is the life and radicall heat of spirits ... Whosoever feels not the warme gale and gentle ventilation of this Spirit, (though I feele his pulse,) I dare not say he lives ...' (Sir Thomas Browne, *Religio Medici*, Part I, sec. 32)

Which Emerson transposed to his own peculiar gospel: 'There

is one mind common to all individual men. Every man is an inlet to the same and to all of the same ...' (HISTORY) 'We live in succession, in division, in parts, in particles. Meantime within man is the soul of the whole ... to which every part and particle is equally related, the eternal ONE ...' (THE OVER-SOUL, passim)

212. *The great God absolute! The centre and circumference* 'Great Architect of the Universe', masonic 'Grand Geometrician' (p. 472, note): 'Trismegistus sayd God was a circle, whose centre, that is, his presentiall and immutable essence, from whence all things have their beinge, is every where, but his circumference, that is, his incomprehensible infinity, is noe where.' (Sir Thomas Browne, *Pseudodoxia Epidemica*, Bk 7, ch. 3)

212. *castaways ... perchance the most abased* Foreshadowing poor Pip.

212. *weave round them tragic graces* For Ahab's role is not uniquely tragic. Though Ahab Agonistes ('mighty pageant creature') proves the focus and magnetic centre of the *Pequod*, tragedy – as much as the pursuit of happiness – remains a function of 'democratic dignity', 'our divine equality'.

212. *thou just Spirit of Equality* cf. Laurence Sterne's invocation: 'Gentle Spirit of sweetest humour, who erst did sit upon the easy pen of my beloved Cervantes; Thou who glided'st daily through his lattice, and turned'st the twilight of his prison into noon-day brightness by thy presence – tinged'st his little urn of water with heaven sent nectar, and all the time he wrote of Sancho and his master, didst cast mystic mantle o'er his withered stump, and wide extended it to all the evils of his life ...' (*Tristram Shandy*, Bk 9, ch. 25) Sterne's imagery pervades these final paragraphs; while KNIGHTS AND SQUIRES, the very title, is of course quixotic.

212. *the swart convict, Bunyan* John Bunyan was arrested, by agents of the Restoration, for unlicensed preaching and kept in prison from 1660 till the Declaration of Indulgence (1672). On his return to Bedford he was again briefly reimprisoned (1675). 'Swart' presumably refers to his tinker's trade and supposed Gipsy origins.

212. *the stumped and paupered arm of old Cervantes* Miguel de Cervantes lost the use of his left arm as the result of a wound received at the battle of Lepanto, 1571 (*Don Quixote*, Pt 2, Bk 3,

'The Author's Preface'). Like Sterne, Melville assumed the hand to be amputated.

212. *Andrew Jackson from the pebbles* The seventh President of the United States, born in the Carolina backwoods, was left orphaned and destitute by the age of fourteen. His military career was crowned at New Orleans, in the *War of 1812*.

Like Walt Whitman (in Brooklyn) and 'Young America' (the Duyckincks' New York circle), Ishmael (from Manhattan) exalts Jacksonian democracy not only as the mark of an expanding frontier but of an expanding consciousness – of the infinite play of possibility inherent in every man.

212. *Thy selectest champions from the kingly commons* 'So neither are a troope of these ignorant Doradoes, of that true esteeme and value, as many a forlorne person, whose condition doth place them below their feet. Let us speake like Politicians, there is Nobility without Heraldry ...' (Sir Thomas Browne, *Religio Medici*, Pt II, sec. 1)

27 KNIGHTS AND SQUIRES

212. *Stubb* 'Stubbs' was common in New Bedford and Nantucket – but not blunt 'Stubb'.

213. *in a world full of grave peddlers* Or peddlers of graves: again alluding to Bunyan, that 'whistling tinker' – or rather, Christian fleeing the City of Destruction, bowed with a pack, on his *Pilgrim's Progress from this World to that which is to come*.

214. *as captains of companies ... flingers of javelins* For the whales *are* 'walled towns' in 'those battering seas'.

215. *Tashtego* Or 'Tash'. The last Nantucket Indian chief, according to Joseph Hart, was called Tashima.

215. *a son of the Prince of the Powers of the Air* (*Ephesians*, ii, 2) 'In the late 1830s there were still some 235 Indians living near Devil's Den and Devil's Bridge, Gayhead, in the town of Chilmark on Martha's Vineyard ... Also this area was reputedly the first spot in New England to be visited by Norsemen in 1006.' (Mansfield and Vincent, quoting John Warner Barber's *Historical Collections*, Worcester, 1829) The place was named Gay Head from its cliffs of variegated clays – red, blue, orange, tan and black – streaked with brilliant white sandy soil.

215. *Daggoo* Perhaps suggested by

> Dagon, his name, Sea Monster, upward Man
> And downward Fish . . .
>
> (*Paradise Lost* I, 462–3)

(See p. 471, note.)

215. *an Ahasuerus to behold* The Hebrew name for the Persian king Khshayarsha, 'which reigned from India even unto Ethiopia' (*Esther* i, 1); identified in Melville's time not with Xerxes, son of Darius I, but Cambyses, son of Cyrus the Great. (Nathalia Wright, *Melville's Use of the Bible*, p. 22)

216. *nearly all Islanders . . .* Isolatoes '. . . these naked Nantucketers, these sea hermits . . .' Perhaps with a glance at John Donne: 'No man is an island, entire of itself; every man is a piece of the continent, a part of the main . . .' (*Devotion* XVII)

216. *Yet now, federated along one keel* 'E Pluribus Unum': this federation of thirty '*Isolatoes*', in the very year of the 'Compromise' crisis, inevitably evokes the thirty squabbling, radically disunited states of the U.S. Republic. Longfellow, too, that year exhorted the 'Ship of State':

> For only what is sound and strong
> To this vessel shall belong.
> Cedar of Maine and Georgia pine
> Here together shall combine.
> A goodly frame, and a goodly fame,
> And the UNION be her name. . .
>
> (*The Building of the Ship*, 1850)

The *Pequod* too, though evoking a whole world (Viking, Ethiopian, Cannibal, Tartar), is all-American: her 'visible' wood 'put together of all contrasting things – oak and maple, and pine' from the three contrasting sections of the United States, whose contrasting economies were built on the Indian (the West), the Polynesian (New England), and the Negro (the South). (THE WHALE WATCH, THE CHASE – SECOND DAY)

But where Longfellow ends with a facile cheer:

Thou, too, sail on, O Ship of State!
Sail on, O UNION, strong and great!
Humanity with all its fears,
With all the hopes of future years,
Is hanging breathless on thy fate!

this new *Leviathan* ends with a close-up: of a 'Poor Alabama boy' – at the centre of the whole uproar – 'Black Little Pip'! (See Alan Heimert, '*Moby-Dick* and American Political Symbolism', *American Quarterly* vol. XV, No. 4.)

216. *An Anacharsis Clootz deputation from all the isles of the sea* 'Wherefore glorify ye the Lord in the fires, even the name of the Lord God of Israel in the isles of the sea.' (*Isaiah* xxiv, 15)

The figure of Anacharsis (*né* Baron Jean Baptiste de) Clootz – the Prussian nobleman who in 1790 presented a 'congress' of foreigners 'before the bar of the first French Assembly as Representatives of the Human Race' (*The Confidence-Man*, ch. 2; *Billy Budd, Sailor*, ch. 1) – made an indelible impression on Melville:

'... the sun's slant rays lighted a spectacle such as our foolish little Planet has not often had to show: Anacharsis Clootz entering the august Salle de Manège, with the Human Species at his heels, Swedes, Spaniards, Polacks; Turks, Chaldeans, Greeks, dwellers in Mesopotamia; behold them all; they have come to claim place in the grand Federation, having an undoubted interest in it. "Our Ambassador titles," said the fervid Clootz, "are not written on parchment, but on the living hearts of all men." These whiskered Polacks, long-flowing turbaned Ishmaelites, astrological Chaldeans, who stand so mute here, let them plead with you, august Senators, more eloquently than eloquence could.' (Carlyle, *The French Revolution* Bk 8, ch. 10)

'Anacharsis' was the self-styled name of a Scythian hero (in a contemporary romance), whose enthusiasm for ancient Greece equalled that of the Prussian for France.

217. *oh, no! he went before* These words, omitted in the first English edition, may represent an early draft in the composition of *Moby-Dick*. This was Leon Howard's argument, developed by George R. Stewart in 'The Two *Moby-Dicks*', *American Literature*, vol. 25 (January 1954), pp. 417–48. Hayford and Parker, accepting the English reading, infer that Melville, at the last minute realizing his own confusion, cancelled the clause. But they make sufficient sense as they stand. They even widen

the ironic implications. For they must refer to THE CASTAWAY, to Pip the sea-changeling, who 'saw God's foot upon the treadle of the loom, and spoke it' – 'called a coward here, hailed a hero there!'

28 AHAB

218. *with a vindictive sort of leaping* As 'the *Pequod* thrust her vindictive bows into the cold malicious waves'. (THE LEE SHORE) But 'To me belongeth vengeance, and recompense; their foot shall slide in due time ...' saith Deacon *Deuteronomy* (xxxii, 35).

218. *like Cellini's cast Perseus* Cellini's bronze, *Perseus with the head of Medusa,* stands in the Loggia dei Lanzi, Florence. The Gorgon's head, as much as the heroic Perseus, was doubtless in Melville's mind. (See 'their demigorgon' p. 267.)

219. *rod-like mark, lividly whitish* Which is 'Ahab. his mark':

> Dark'n'd so, yet shon
> Above them all th' Arch Angel: but his face
> Deep scars of Thunder had intrencht, and care
> Sat on his faded cheek, but under Browes
> Of dauntless courage, and considerate Pride
> Waiting Revenge ...
>
> (*Paradise Lost* I, 599–604)

219. *still greenly alive, but branded* For Ahab, too, is still 'green', though bearing the mark of Cain – and mark of the beast (*Revelation* xiii, 3).

A great elm in the park at Pittsfield, struck by lightning in 1841, suggested the touch. It bore a scar one hundred feet long.

219. *a grey Manxman ... an old sepulchral man* This awesome old salt – and mouthpiece of doom – reappears in various guises throughout Melville's work. His studying with an 'old witch in Copenhagen' (THE DOUBLOON) links him with the old Dansker (in *Billy Budd*); his 'preternatural powers of discernment', with Van, the old Finn, 'supposed to possess the gift of second sight' (*Omoo*, ch. 12); his 'grizzly' looks, with Melville's final *alter ego*, Daniel Orme, 'an image of the Great Grizzly of the California Sierras ... grim in his last den awaiting the last hour'.

220. *holding by a shroud; Captain Ahab stood erect* Another

Jonah, pitched by the mizzen-mast, 'looking straight out beyond the ship's ever-pitching prow'.

220. *in all the nameless regal overbearing dignity* From 'crown to sole' this 'Ecce Homo' is of an 'overbearing grimness'. 'Bear thee grimly, demi-god' resounds the echo. 'Up from the spray of thy ocean-perishing ...'

29 ENTER AHAB; TO HIM, STUBB

ENTER AHAB; TO HIM, STUBB The prologue is done; stage directions begin – with Ishmael, as chorus, to rehearse the tragedy of 'wild Ahab'.

221. *the bright Quito spring* In the capital of Ecuador, 'ciudad de primavera perpetua', seasonal temperatures usually vary by less than one degree.

222. *descending this narrow scuttle ... to my grave-dug* birth (third rite of masonic initiation, p. 472, note). 'Because strait is the gate, and narrow is the way, which leadeth unto life, and few there be that find it.' (*Matthew* vii, 14)

222. *Down, dog, and kennel!* Ahab's very first command evoking Elijah's prophecy – and *King Lear*. In the fool's words: 'Truth's a dog must to kennel.' (I, iv, 114)

223. *Tic-Dolly-row Tic douloureux,* or facial neuralgia – with a hint of the slattern.

224. *Think not, is my eleventh commandment* cf. The young Papal Guardsman to Goethe: ' "*Che pensa? non deve mai pensar l'uomo, pensando s'invecchia*"; which being interpreted is as much as to say, "What are you thinking about? a man ought never to think; thinking makes one old".' (Marked in Melville's copy of *Goethe's Autobiography and Travels*, vol. II)

30 THE PIPE

224. *at the binnacle lamp* Near the helm to illumine the compass box.

224. *on that tripod of bones* Now Ahab is Norse sea-king, *and* Tartar Khan, *and* Pythian priestess at the oracular altar of the golden helmeted sun.

224. *no longer soothes* As a 'pleasant, genial smoke' with that

'soothing savage' (A BOSOM FRIEND); as Queequeg's tomahawk pipe 'soothed his soul'.

225. *mild white vapors ... mild white hairs* For this 'great lord of Leviathans' is 'very like a whale': 'And how nobly it raises our conceit of the mighty, misty monster, to behold him solemnly sailing through a calm tropical sea; his vast mild head overhung by a canopy of vapor, engendered by his incommunicable contemplations ...' (THE FOUNTAIN)

225. *I'll smoke no more* – cf. Marlowe's Faustus, shutting the Vulgate: 'Divinity adieu!' (I, i, 47) So, with a toss of the hand, Ahab has snuffed his last 'mild gleams' and glimpse of serenity.

225. *With slouched hat ... lurchingly paced* 'See ye not then, shipmates, that Jonah sought to flee world-wide from God? Miserable man! Oh! most contemptible and worthy of all scorn; with slouched hat and guilty eye, skulking from his God; prowling among the shipping like a vile burglar hastening to cross the seas.' (THE SERMON)

31 QUEEN MAB

QUEEN MAB 'the fairies' midwife' who brings to birth hopes in the form of dreams, by driving:

> Athwart men's noses as they lie asleep ...
> And in this state she gallops night by night
> Through lovers' brains, and then they dream of love.
> (*Romeo and Juliet* I, iv, 53ff.)

cf. *White-Jacket*: 'There's Shelley, he was quite a sailor ... but they ought to have let him sleep in his sailor's grave ... and not burn his body, as they did, as if he had been a bloody Turk. But many people thought him so, White-Jacket, because he didn't go to mass, and because he wrote *Queen Mab*.' (ch. 65)

225. *he kicked me with it ... I kicked my leg right off!* cf. Peleg accosting Ishmael: 'Dost see that leg? – I'll take that leg away from thy stern ...' (p. 166) Or again: 'a sudden sharp poke in my rear ... That was my first kick.' (p. 199)

225. *Ahab seemed a pyramid* Or *pyr*/amid: 'and I, like a blazing fool, kept kicking at it.' Compare Starbuck, 'a revivified Egyptian', with this heaven-aspiring 'tomb', shrine, or 'sacred retreat' for an embalmed mummy.

'I shudder at idea of ancient Egyptians. It was in these pyramids that was conceived the idea of Jehovah. Terrible mixture of the cunning and awful. Moses learned in all the lore of the Egyptians. The idea of Jehovah born here.' (Melville's *Journal*, 3 January 1857)

cf. also the Great Seal of the United States (engraved on a one-dollar bill): a Masonic pyramid truncated, with the Eye of God at its apex.

225. *not much of an insult* 'in-saltus', literally leap or assault.

225. *The living member* Like Queequeg, a 'born member of the First Congregational Church'? (p. 184, note).

225. *stubbing my silly toes* After a pun's assault, a 'battering' – soon to extend its range, in THE BATTERING-RAM. cf. *Acts*: 'And the Lord said ... it is hard for thee to kick against the pricks.' (ix, 5)

226. *a sort of badger-haired old merman, with a hump on his back* A sort of Davy Jones with Ahab's 'iron-grey locks'. Again, cf. that 'curious little deformed image' with a hunchback and whittled nose – linking this 'queer dream' with Queequeg's 'queer proceedings'.

226. *'Slid! man, but I was frightened* Syncope of 'God's lid':

> ... and then anon
> Drums in his ear, at which he starts and wakes,
> And, being thus frighted, swears a prayer or two
> And sleeps again.
>
> (*Romeo and Juliet* I, iv, 85–8)

226. *seaweed ... for a clout* Cloth or patch, *and* (as in archery) his mark.

226. *a sort of eating of his own gums like a chimney hag* The

> ... hag, when maids lie on their backs,
> That presses them and learns them first to bear,
> Making them women of good carriage.
>
> (*Romeo and Juliet* I, iv, 92–4)

For a cross-commentary on all this humping and thumping, see THE TAIL (p. 484, note). For an earlier 'chimney' hag and 'troubled mightmare' (confounding Herman and merman) see THE COUNTERPANE.

226. *slapped by a queen . . . kicked by old Ahab* cf. The mason's investiture with his apron 'more honourable than the Garter or any other Order in existence, being the badge of innocence and the bond of friendship' (p. 472, note).

227. *and on no account kick back* cf. Shelley's notes to *Queen Mab*: 'But the doctrine of Necessity teaches us that in no case could any event have happened otherwise than it did happen, and that, if God is the author of good, he is also the author of evil; that, if he is entitled to our gratitude for the one, he is entitled to our hatred for the other. . . God made man such as he is, and then damned him for being so.' (1813) This 'fairy' became the eighteen-year-old Shelley's spokesman on the evils of marriage, commerce, and Christianity – revealing a future, regenerate world where 'all things are recreated, and the flames of consentaneous love inspires all life'.

32 CETOLOGY

CETOLOGY The facts derive mainly from Beale. It was Surgeon Beale who stressed the ignorance of writers like 'Green, Aldrovandus, Willoughby, Rondelet, Artedi, Ray, Sibbald, Linnaeus, Brisson, Marten'. Even the opening quotation from Scoresby and that cento of scraps from John Hunter, Lesson and Cuvier all appear on the fly-leaf of *The Natural History of the Sperm Whale.*

Baron Georges Cuvier (1769–1832) and René Primivère Lesson (1794–1849) were French zoologists; Dr John Hunter (1728–93) was author of an early study of whale anatomy (*Transactions of the Royal Society*)

228. *Captain Scoresby* From 1803 to 1822 William Scoresby (junior) sailed annually to Greenland – first, as a fourteen-year-old, on his father's whaler, later as captain of various British ships. He mapped and charted the coasts of Greenland, taking deep sea temperature soundings and making a special study of terrestrial magnetism. In 1825 he entered the Anglican ministry, but in 1856, a year before his death, made a final voyage to study terrestrial magnetism in Australia.

228. *Thus speak of the whale* This roll-call of names partly duplicates authorities already quoted. (See EXTRACTS.) Among historic names here newly inserted are: Ulisse Aldrovandi, the sixteenth-century Bologna naturalist and his con-

temporary, the Zurich biologist and naturalist, Konrad von Gesner; John Ray (or Wray), the seventeenth-century English naturalist and his pupil Francis Willughby, who together planned a systematic classification of both vegetable and animal kingdoms; Sir Robert Sibbald, the Scottish geographer and physician to Charles II; Linnaeus (Karl von Linné), the great Swedish botanist, and the Comte de Lacépède, a protégé of Buffon's. The list, like other such pieces of *apparatus criticus*, is meant, of course, to stun the reader rather than introduce a true note of scientific inquiry. Melville's learning – part experience, part enthusiastic research (in Bennett and Beale), part pure high spirits – tends constantly to this scholarship of the imagination: the only kind, after all, at home in a work of fiction.

228. *Olmstead* Francis Allyn Olmsted, *Incidents of a Whaling Voyage* (New York, 1840).

229. *This is Charing Cross* Geometric centre of the circumference of old London, from which mile-stones were reckoned. Here new monarchs were customarily proclaimed – and public hangings held.

229. *it is a ponderous task* For 'a ponderous heart' – to conclude, like the Scriptures no doubt, in 'a ponderous volume'.

230. *ribs, and very pelvis of the world* Like Jonah in the whale 'grounded upon the ocean's utmost bones'. (THE SERMON) 'Cetology', transposed, turns to 'theology'.

230. *The awful tauntings in Job*

Canst thou draw out leviathan with an hook? or his tongue with a cord which thou lettest down?
Canst thou put a hook into his nose? or bore his jaw through with a thorn?
Will he make many supplications unto thee? will he speak soft words unto thee?
Will he make a covenant with thee? wilt thou take him for a servant for ever? ...
Behold the hope of him is in vain: shall not one be cast down even at the sight of him?

(*Job* xli, 1–4, 9)

Though certain intermediate taunts – omitted here, to be picked up in ch. 81, p. 464 – had lost much of their sting by Melville's day.

230. *penem intrantem feminam* On account of 'the penis penetrating the female who suckles by means of teats', and 'rightly and deservedly by the law of nature'.

Naturally Linnaeus, not 'holy Jonah', is correct: the whale is an aquatic mammal, not 'a great fish', nor even 'a spouting fish'. Melville is having fun matching prophet (backed by Simeon Macey and Charley Coffin of Nantucket) versus naturalist, and classifying his whales 'in their entire liberal volume' by 'the Bibliographical system'. But once again he is wrong: it has not proved 'vain to attempt a clear classification of the Leviathan, founded upon either his baleen, or hump, or fin, or teeth', nor are these peculiarities 'indiscriminately dispersed among all sorts of whales, without any regard to what may be the nature of their structure in other and more essential particulars'.

Today whales are classified into two major groups: the whalebone or baleen whales, and toothed whales. The whalebone or baleen whales include the right whale, the grey whale, the finbacks, the rorquals, and the hump-backs: in these hundreds of fringed plates of horny whalebone suspended from the upper jaw, serve as strainers for the plankton on which they feed. The blue rorqual or sulphur-bottom whale (whom Melville admits never having seen 'except in the remoter Southern seas, and then always at too great a distance to study his countenance'), not the Sperm whale, is 'without doubt, the largest inhabitant of the globe' living or extinct, sometimes reaching about a hundred feet in length.

Among the toothed whales are the sperm whale or cachalot, the pygmy sperm whale, the beaked whale, the dolphin and the porpoise.

231. *I divide the whales into three ... BOOKS* For the whale is also *The Whale*, and a 'veil' – an 'impenetrable veil covering our knowledge of the cetacea'.

'Cetaceans are naturally divided into three distinct tribes, or families.' (Bennett, vol. 2, p. 152)

232. *the Trumpa whale* From his *trompe* (Old French), trump or spout.

232. *the Pottsfich of the Germans Pottfisch*, or 'pot fish'.

233. *the Great Mysticetus* The Arctic Right whale. (Aristotle, *Natural History* III, xii)

233. *the Baliene Ordinaire of the French Baleine ordinaire*, or common whale.

233. *the Growlands Walfish of the Swedes* Grönlands *Valfisk,* or Greenland whale.

234. *with its style* Stylus, or pointed spike, and triangular plate forming the gnomon of a sun-dial.

234. *On that Ahaz-dial the shadow often goes back* The Lord's sign that Hezekiah, the son of Ahaz, king of Judah, should recover from sickness: 'Behold, I will bring again the shadow of the degrees, which is gone down in the sun dial of Ahaz, ten degrees backward. So the sun returned ten degrees, by which degrees it was gone down.' (*Isaiah* xxxviii, 8)

234. *unconquerable Cain ... bearing for his mark* A gnomon, or masonic set-square – on that '*Ahab*-dial' at the grim lodge of the Thunder Cloud. For is not the 'great lord of Leviathans' himself a Long John, a Tall-Spout, a whale-hater, 'always going solitary', 'rising like a tall misanthropic spear upon a barren plain'?

234. *rostrated whales* i.e. terminating in a rostrum, or beaky snout.

235. *the Elephant and Castle whale* Inn-sign apart, there is to be play later with the whale as 'citadel' at one end (THE NUT), and 'elephant's trunk' at the other (THE TAIL), as if to test the amalgam.

236. *Another retiring gentleman, with a brimstone belly* Like old Bildad, old Jonah; for those 'brimmers all round', that 'broad-brimmed hat', too were the marks of Sodom: 'Then the Lord rained upon Sodom and upon Gomorrah brimstone and fire from the Lord out of heaven; and he overthrew those cities, and all the plain ...' (*Genesis* xix, 24–5)

236. *Adieu, Sulphur Bottom!* Like Jonah 'out of the belly of hell', '... and thou heardest my voice'. (Jonah ii, 2)

236. *a proverb to landsmen* To puff and blow like a grampus.

237. (Narwhale), *that is,* Nostril Whale The Narwhale, in fact, relates obscurely to Old Norse *nahvalr*, or 'corpse', 'being of a milk-white ground color, dotted with round and oblong spots of black'.

237. *peculiar horn ... mistaken for a peaked nose* For this peculiar horn ('for fainting ladies'), this sinister ivory horn or sea-unicorn's horn – ivory 'rake' or leg – is charged with over-

tones. 'Charley Coffin' masks the first of William Scoresby's many curious interventions.

238. *Black Letter* The source (not fictitious this time) is the account of Frobisher's search for a Northwest Passage recorded in Hakluyt's *Principal Navigations, Voiages, and Discoveries of the English Nation* (1598–1600). The facts, however, are slightly confused: it was on leaving for the first voyage that the crew 'shotte off our ordinance and made the best shew we could' while sailing past Greenwich, where Elizabeth 'bade us fare-well, with shaking her hand at us out of the window'; the horn was found on the second voyage, 'wreathed and straite, like in fashion to a taper made of waxe ... This horne is to be seene and reserved as a Jewell by the Queens Majesties Commandement, in her Wardrope of Robes.'

238. *An Irish author* Fictitious this time – with his horny joke at the reader's expense (and the virgin queen's!).

239. *always swims in hilarious shoals* If Ahab shares a touch with the Great Mysticetus, the solitary Fin-Back, Hump-Back, and Unicorn whales; if his mates and harpooneers are at one with the Killer; then what are the crew but Huzza Porpoises? For 'cetology' here proves disguised 'eschatology'. This bestiary is also a dumb show, or masque.

240. *called the 'bright waist'* A white band encircling the hull about halfway between the waterline and the rail. Black squares looking like gunports were painted on it, to ward off pirates.

241. *full of Leviathanism* Parodying Macbeth's soliloquy (V, v, 27–8). See p. 637 and note.

241. *the great Cathedral of Cologne ... with the crane* 'The structure itself is one of the most singular in the world. One transept is nearly complete – in new stone, and strangely contrasts with the ruinous condition of the vast unfinished tower on one side.' (*Journal*, 9 December 1849)

241. *small erections ... ever leave the copestone to posterity. God keep me* An ironic enough invocation in view of his earlier claim: 'The universe is finished; the copestone is on, and the chips were carted off a million years ago.' (THE CARPET-BAG) But with a scurrilous glance too at that queer wigwam, another 'temporary erection used in port'. (THE SHIP)

Ishmael's dislike of closed aesthetic systems is intimately 'related to his rejection of the respectable social order, including its economic, political and religious systems. Primal sexual energy is intrinsically subversive of conventional order and of respectable systems ... His enormous phallic imagery also embodies Melville's belief that the sources of artistic and sexual creation are closely related.' (Robert Shulman, 'The Serious Functions of Melville's Phallic Jokes', *American Literature* 33, No. 2, 1961)

CETOLOGY then, rightly, underlies the whole eschatology of *The Whale*.

33 THE SPECKSYNDER

THE SPECKSYNDER Dutch, *Specksnijder*. The facts derive wholly from Scoresby (vol. II, p. 39).

243. *he sometimes masked himself* Another 'insulated Quakerish Nantucketer', like Peleg, utilizing, not innuendo this time, but a strict formalism for his private ends. 'And the king of Israel disguised himself, and went into the battle.' (*1 Kings* xxii, 30)

244. *the dead level of the mass* Opening a series of enigma variations on the triad first sounded by the prophet: 'who, pausing before us, levelled his massive forefinger at the vessel in question'.

244. *Nicholas the Czar* Nicholas I, the 'Iron Czar'. He died during the Crimean War, four years after the publication of *Moby-Dick*.

244. *encircles an imperial brain ... the tremendous centralization* Himself! The great Czar absolute! The centre and circumference of all Empire! Till on the *Pequod*, too, the plebeian herds crouch abased. (p. 643)

244. *what shall be grand in thee ... plucked at from the skies* 'Grand old cove', 'grand old heart', 'Grand Turk' in Grand Lodge.

34 THE CABIN-TABLE

245. *Belshazzar* Last king of Babylon, as Ahab will be the last captain of the *Pequod*. The gold vessels from the Temple of Jerusalem at his feast, to honour the idols, foreshadow the impious pledge with which Ahab is about to consecrate his

voyage. In both banquet-hall and whaler, the handwriting is prophetic; for both are doomed. (cf. *Belshazzar's awful writing*, p. 542, and *when God's burning finger had been laid* p. 614, notes.)

246. *the Coronation banquet at Frankfort* Frankfurt-am-Main, appointed by the Golden Bull of Charles IV (1356) to be the seat of imperial elections. After 1562, when Emperors ceased to be crowned by Popes, the coronation itself took place there – the Emperor-elect, crowned 'King of the Romans' by the Archbishop-Elector of Mainz, proceeding to a banquet in the Kaisersaal (or *Römer*).

248. *baron of salt-junk* Or salted sirloin for this 'baronial' trio.

248. *knife in hand ... laying out the circle* For this pale simpleton of a steward is the merest shadow, and caricature, of his black master: a ringed scalp, not crown, encircling his servile brain; with a 'quiver' on the lip, not of ivory legs; nervously retreating behind the 'blinds' of his pantry door (cf. p. 622); till convulsed 'by his sudden fits of the palsy'.

249. *the low carlines* Or carlings, beams lying fore and aft, connecting one transverse deck-beam to another.

250. *that wild Logan* A Mingo chief on the Ohio and Scioto rivers (c. 1725–80), he was named after James Logan, William Penn's secretary, whose hospitality and trade with the Indians confirmed their peace with the colony. Long friendly with the whites, Logan only turned on the settlers after his own family was massacred in 1774. His speech refusing to collaborate in a treaty to end Lord Dunmore's War – at least Jefferson's version of it in *Notes on the State of Virginia* – was familiar to every American school boy as a set recitation piece.

35 THE MAST-HEAD

THE MAST-HEAD cf. *White-Jacket*: 'I am of a meditative humor, and at sea used often to mount aloft at night, and, seating myself on one of the upper yards, tuck my jacket about me and give loose to reflection... And it is a very fine feeling, and one that fuses us into the universe of things, and makes us a part of the All, to think that, wherever we ocean-wanderers rove, we have still the same glorious old stars to keep us company...' (ch. 19, THE JACKET ALOFT) cf. Also J. Ross Browne: 'The mast-head was a little world of peace and seclusion, where I could think over past times without interruption. There was much around me to inspire vague and visionary fancies: the ocean, a trackless waste of waters; the arched sky spread over it like a variegated curtain; the sea-birds wheeling in the air; and the myriads of albacore cleaving their way through the clear, blue waves ...' (pp. 193–4)

251. *the general belief among archæologists* Giovanni Battista Belzoni discusses the 'astronomical purposes' of the pyramids, though rejecting the theory (*Narrative of the Operations and Discoveries in Egypt and Nubia*, London, 1821).

251. *Saint Stylites ... a dauntless stander-of-mast-heads* Saint Simeon, the fifth-century Syrian, lived more than thirty-five years on his pillar.

251. *There is Napoleon ... with arms folded* On his Trajan's column in the Place Vendôme. But the original toga-clad figure had been pulled down in 1814. This Emperor in a tricorne was commissioned by Louis Philippe.

251. *whether Louis Philippe, Louis Blanc* i.e. Whether the 'Citizen King', whose inauguration after the July revolution of 1830 marked the triumph of the *haute bourgeoisie*; or the Socialist leader, whose *Organisation du Travail* (1840) first propounded the slogan: 'From each according to his abilities, to each according to his needs'. Louis Blanc's attacks on the monarchy and agitation among the workers led to the February revolution of 1848 and Louis Philippe's abdication as King of the French.

251. *or Louis the Devil* Diplomatically glossed to 'Louis Napoleon' in the English edition – then President of the Second Republic. Already at the time of Melville's visit in 1849, his rule had taken an openly dictatorial turn, leading, shortly after the publication of *Moby-Dick*, to the *coup d'état* of 2 December 1851.

251. *on his towering main-mast in Baltimore* Completed in 1829, Washington's column tops both Nelson's and Napoleon's.

252. *marks that point of human grandeur* 'First in war, first in peace, and first in the hearts of his countrymen': yet the eulogy is double-edged. For what of Queequeg, that towering Hercules, 'George Washington cannibalistically developed'?

252. *Admiral Nelson ... in Trafalgar Square* Eighteen feet tall, poised 145 feet up on the 'cap' of his top-gallant mast. The four battle scenes at the base were cast in bronze from captured French cannon. The column was completed in 1849, just prior to Melville's arrival in England.

252. *The worthy Obed tells us History of Nantucket* (Boston, 1835) p. 31.

252. *the famous Colossus at old Rhodes* Bronze statue of the sun god, Helios, over a hundred feet high. Its legs, according to legend, rested on two moles forming the entrance of the harbour.

253. *glued inside of its fleshly tabernacle* 'What? know ye not that your body is the temple of the Holy Ghost which is in you, which ye have of God, and ye are not your own?' (*1 Corinthians* vi, 19)

254. *Captain Sleet* Ishmael's nickname for William Scoresby (senior) – commemorated by his more famous son in *Memorials of the Sea. My Father: Being records of the adventurous life of the late William Scoresby, Esq., of Whitby* (London, 1851). In all he made thirty whaling voyages to the Arctic without losing a ship and was the first, after Hudson, to trace the east coast of Greenland. This whole account of *Sleet's crow's-nest* parodies Scoresby Jr: 'The one most approved by the inventor is about 4½ feet in length, and 2½ in diameter. The form is cylindrical; open above and close below. It is composed of laths of wood placed in a perpendicular position round the exterior edge of a strong wooden hoop, forming the top, and round a plane of mahogany, or other wood, which forms the bottom and the whole circumference of the cylinder is covered with canvas or leather. The entrance is by a trap-hatch at the bottom. It is fixed on the very summit of the main-top-gallant-mast, from whence the prospect on every side is unimpeded. On the after side is a seat, with a place beneath for a flag. In other parts are receptacles for a speaking trumpet, telescope, and occasionally for a *rifle piece*, with utensils for loading. For the more effectual shelter of the observer, when in an erect posture, a moveable screen is applied to the top of the windward side, which increases the height so much as effectually to shield his head.' (vol. II, pp. 203–5)

255. *so many broken-down blacksmiths* Foreshadowing THE BLACKSMITH.

255. *little case-bottle* A square bottle, to fit with others into a case.

256. *with the Phædon* Plato's *Φαιδων* records the discussion on death and immortality between Socrates and his friends in prison during the last hours of his life – an apt enough text for the *Pequod,* launched to a hymn by Watts. cf. 'I bought a set of Bayle's Dictionary the other day, & on my return to New York intend to lay the great old folios side by side & go to sleep on them thro' the summer, with the Phaedon in one hand & Tom Brown [Sir Thomas Browne] in the other.' (To Evert Duyckinck, 5 April 1849)

256. *Bowditch* Nathaniel Bowditch (1773–1838), navigator and mathematician of Salem, Massachusetts, first issued *The New American Practical Navigator* in 1802. Still the standard work, after more than sixty editions, it is referred to simply as *Bowditch's Navigator.*

256. *this sunken-eyed young Platonist* 'Those young Platonists' may never raise a whale, yet 'in their secret souls' still penetrate to the essence of Leviathan without binoculars. For the Sperm Whale, like Ishmael, will emerge 'a Platonian' (see pp. 370, 443).

256. *Roll on, thou deep and dark blue ocean, roll!* 'Ten thousand fleets sweep over thee in vain!' (Byron, *Childe Harold's Pilgrimage,* Canto VII, stanza 179)

The whole stanza anticipates the final catastrophe – and closing sentence:

> Man marks the earth with ruin – his control
> Stops with the shore; upon the watery plain
> The wrecks are all thy deed, nor doth remain
> A shadow of man's ravage, save his own,
> When, for a moment, like a drop of rain,
> He sinks into thy depths with bubbling groan,
> Without a grave, unknell'd, uncoffin'd, and unknown.

256. *their opera glasses at home* With a nod at the familiar melodramas of the contemporary stage and a jest at these displaced habitués who cannot sing out for whales.

257. *at last he loses his identity* What was merely 'absent-minded' on land becoming a vacancy, an opium-trance, a loss

of identity at sea, till drowned in 'that deep, blue, bottomless soul' or 'Over-Soul' – 'Himself! The great God absolute!': 'I am nothing; I see all; the currents of the Universal Being circulate through me; I am part or parcel of God.' (Emerson, *Works*, I, 16)

'Because no man can ever feel his own identity aright except his eyes be closed; as if darkness were indeed the proper element of our essences...' (NIGHTGOWN)

257. *like Cranmer's sprinkled Pantheistic ashes* Convicted of heresy on the return of the Roman church under Queen Mary, Thomas Cranmer, first Protestant Archbishop of Canterbury, was burnt at the stake in 1556. The ashes of heretics were often scattered so that no holy relics might be preserved. The English editor, however, changed the text, thinking that Melville must have confused Cranmer's martyrdom (of whose ashes nothing further is known) with the posthumous fate of Wycliffe, whose body was disinterred in 1428, burnt, and its ashes cast into the Swift: 'Thus this Brook hath convey'd his ashes into Avon; Avon into Severn; Severn into the narrow Seas; they, into the main Ocean. And thus the Ashes of Wickliff are the Emblem of his Doctrine, which now is dispersed all the World over.' (Thomas Fuller, *The Church-History of Britain*, Bk IV, sec. 53: London 1655; new edn Oxford, 1845)

257. *Over Descartian vortices you hover* 'With the problem of the universe revolving' in you. Descartes argued that rotation of cosmic matter round an axis accounted for the origin of the terrestrial system. The whole Cartesian universe was conceived as matter in motion within a series of whirlpools, or vortices. So creation was reduced to a theory of dynamics (later discredited by Newton); the mysteries of *Genesis* to mathematical equations; a 'Universal Being' to spontaneous, Godless, mechanical laws.

257. *perhaps, at mid-day, in the fairest weather ... you drop* Like Phaeton; or Milton's Mulciber ('Sheer o're the Chrystal Battlements', *Paradise Lost* I, 740), or Icarus 'into the summer sea' – to link a whole substratum of Minoan references, first heralded by 'an interminable Cretan labyrinth'.

But 'still deeper the meaning of that story of Narcissus, who because he could not grasp the tormenting, mild image he saw in the fountain, plunged into it and was drowned.' (LOOMINGS)

257. *Heed it well, ye Pantheists!* 'In reading some of Goethe's sayings, so worshipped by his votaries, I came across this, *"Live in the all."* That is to say, your separate identity is but a wretched one, – good; but get out of yourself, spread and expand yourself, and bring to yourself the tinglings of life that are felt in the flowers and the woods, that are felt in the planets Saturn and Venus, and the Fixed Stars. What nonsense! Here is a fellow with a raging toothache. "My dear boy," Goethe says to him, "you are sorely afflicted with that tooth; but you must *live in the all*, and then you will be happy!" As with all great genius, there is an immense deal of flummery in Goethe, and in proportion to my own contact with him, a monstrous deal of it in me.' (To Hawthorne, June 1851)

36 THE QUARTER-DECK

THE QUARTER-DECK 'The captain's word is law ... When he stands on his quarter-deck at sea, he absolutely commands as far as eye can reach. Only the moon and stars are beyond his jurisdiction. He is lord and master of the sun.' (*White-Jacket*, ch. 6)

257. *as to and fro he paced his old rounds* 'And the Lord said unto Satan, Whence comest thou? Then Satan answered the Lord, and said, From going to and fro in the earth, and from walking up and down in it.' (*Job* i, 7)

260. *Death and devils! men, it is Moby Dick* Even to name the White Whale incurs death – just as the first glimpse of Milton's Satan, 'rowling' in the flood, raises a whale:

> or that Sea-beast
> *Leviathan*, which God of all his works
> Created hugest that swim th' Ocean stream.
> (*Paradise Lost* I, 200–202; Extract 23)

For both derive ultimately from Isaiah's prophecy that 'the Lord with his sore and great and strong sword shall punish leviathan the piercing serpent, even leviathan that crooked serpent; and he shall slay the dragon that is in the sea'. (*Isaiah* xxvii, 1; Extract 5) In Ahab's mind the two are inextricably mixed. But elsewhere in *Isaiah* (li, 9), the serpent is named. His name (meaning 'proud') is R/*ahab*.

For 'Moby Dick', see note on Chap. 41.

261. *it was Moby Dick that dismasted me ... to this dead stump* 'And there's a mighty difference between a living thump and a dead thump ... The living member – that makes the living insult, my little man.' (QUEEN MAB)

Which is Ahab's agony: in lieu of a live stump he tosses both arms at his braves and bids them 'splice hands'; in the privacy of his thoughts 'dismasted' will soon turn to 'dismembered'. Are these the obsessions of impotence? Or merely the scars of Ahab's trauma – the castration complex of a pegging lover?

261. *that razeed me* Like a ship, reduced in height, with its upper deck or decks removed.

261. *Nantucket market! Hoot!* Cry of the owl, Macbeth's familiar – and signal of witchery.

261. *He smites his chest* 'for it is written, Vengeance is mine; I will repay, saith the Lord.' (*Romans* xii, 19)

262. *All visible objects ... are but as pasteboard masks* Again parodying Carlyle: 'All visible things are emblems; what thou seest is not there on its own account; strictly taken, is not there at all; Matter exists only spiritually, and to represent some Idea, and *body* it forth.' 'Rightly viewed no meanest object is insignificant; all objects are as windows, through which the philosophic eye looks into Infinitude itself.' 'So that this so solid-seeming World, after all, were ... what the Earth-Spirit in Faust names it, the living visible Garment of God.' (*Sartor Resartus* Bk 1, chs 11, 8)

But again every word rebounds, like 'the thick vapor ... from his mouth in quick and constant puffs'. (THE PIPE) For it is Ahab who plays Don Quixote, Knight of the Rueful Countenance in his Pasteboard Vizor; *he* is the prisoner in the walled city; *he* is the hypocrite schemer behind the mask; to whom the White Whale's brow piled 'layer upon layer', far from a punster's 'wall', is rather a glass shoved near: 'you could almost see that thought turn in him as he turned ... that it all but seemed the inward mould of every outer movement.'

262. *and be the white whale agent, or be the white whale principal* Melville seems constantly to shift his ground from 'agent', meaning one who acts (the efficient cause as opposed to 'instrument', that which is acted upon), to 'agent', meaning one who does the actual work (as opposed to the employer who directs it), just as he plays variations on 'principal' (the actual perpetrator,

or authority for whom another acts) and 'principle' (the origin or fundamental source of action, the ultimate basis of existence).

The sense, however, is clear: be the whale executor of another's directive or himself initiating that directive, be he a secondary or a primary cause: I shall have my revenge – a question of teleology leading inevitably to 'Talk not to me of blasphemy', i.e. the place and existence of God in Ahab's universe.

For a veiled allusion to a Gnostic heresy – be the white whale the 'Supreme Being' or merely 'a far inferior agent, the Demiurgus, or the Creator', see pp. 267, 283, 616–17, notes.

262. *I'd strike the sun if it insulted me* Like his namesake in defiant worship of his Babylonian sun-god, or Baal (*1 Kings* xvi, 31–2). But 'The Lord is thy keeper: the Lord is thy shade upon thy right hand. The sun shall not smite thee by day, nor the moon by night.' (*Psalm* cxxi, 5–6)

262. *But not my master, man, is even that fair play* Which is the voice of mock-Jacobean drama peculiar to Ahab's *Revenger's Tragedy* – 'a bold and nervous lofty language', full of inversion, antonomasia, and every form of conceit swinging into blank verse:

> But look ye, Starbuck, what is said in heat,
> That thing unsays itself. There are men
> From whom warm words are small indignity.
> I meant not to incense thee. Let it go.
> Look! see yonder Turkish cheeks of spotted tawn ...

263. *formed a circle round the group* cf. The Kokovoko High Priest 'dipping his consecrated and consecrating fingers into the bowl before the blessed beverage circulates', and this self-styled priest-king with his rite of indissoluble communion.

263. *the bloodshot eyes of the prairie wolves* Eye meeting bloodshot eye in a final 'aye, aye' of the pact.

263. *Round with it, round!* 'Aye, my hearties all round', 'round and round', to and fro pacing 'his old rounds' – 'round Good Hope, and round the Horn, and round the Norway maelstrom, and round perdition's flames ...'

264. *a noble custom of my fishermen fathers* The scene itself derives from Robert Pearse Gillies: 'The harpooners were invited into the cabin, bearing the harpoons they had selected for their boats, and each was compelled to drink a bumper of rum,

from the socket of his weapon, to the success of the fishery. The compulsion found necessary to oblige these officers to quaff a quarter of a pint of real Jamaica, was by no means so great as that occasionally requisite to force a culprit to receive the fatal noose round his neck.' (*Tales of a Voyager to the Arctic Ocean*, vol. 1, pp. 251–2: First Series, 1826)

264. *wert not thou St Vitus' imp* An omen, 'O men'! With a *tic* Ahab jerks and spills a drop. *Chorea Sancti Viti*, or St Vitus' Dance, is a convulsive disorder marked by depression, irritability, and general emotional instability. Those 'sharp shooting pains in his bleeding stump' have impaired his whole nervous system: 'such nervous whiffs', nervous language, 'nervous step'!

264. *grasped the three ... lances at their crossed centre* cf.

HORATIO Propose the oath, my lord.
HAMLET Never to speak of this that you have seen,
Swear by my sword.
GHOST (*Beneath*) Swear (*Hamlet* I, v, 152–5)

The actual pose, however, is more reminiscent of the *Oath of the Horatii*, the celebrated painting by Jacques Louis David (now in the Toledo Museum of Art). Which possibly accounts for an odd image later linking the *Pequod's* three masts to 'the three Horatii pirouetting on one sufficient steed'. (THE QUADRANT, p. 610 note)

264. *within the Leyden jar of his own magnetic life* One of the earliest forms of electrical condenser. The attraction of captain and crew, captain and his mates, is presented throughout in terms of an electro-magnetic charge – Hawthorne's metaphor for the blood-camaraderie of secret vice: 'the electric thrill' of recognition, the 'electric chain' of the adulterous Dimmesdale, Hester and Pearl on their midnight scaffold. (*The Scarlet Letter*)

264. *Cut your seizings* Of tarred rope.

265. *Now, three to three, ye stand* Before your triple-crowned captain.

265. *the rounds among the frantic crew* 'But when a man's religion becomes really frantic; when it is a positive torment to him; and, in fine, makes this earth of ours an uncomfortable inn to lodge in; then I think it high time to take that individual aside and argue the point with him.' (THE RAMADAN)

37 SUNSET

265. *this Iron Crown of Lombardy* Constantine's crown – containing, according to tradition, one of the nails used at the Crucifixion – now kept in the Cathedral of Monza. Both Charlemagne and Charles V, among other Holy Roman Emperors, were crowned with it as kings of Lombardy; and it was this crown that Napoleon assumed when he crowned himself king of Italy in 1805. But the most recent of its wearers (1838) was Ferdinand I, Emperor of Austria – another monarch, like Ahab, subject to spells of insanity.

266. *all loveliness is anguish to me* cf.

the more I see
Pleasures about me, so much more I feel
Torment within me, as from the hateful siege
Of contraries; all good to me becomes
Bane . . .

(*Paradise Lost* IX, 119–23)

266. *damned in the midst of Paradise!* As Satan 'in prospect of Eden':

And like a devillish Engine back recoiles
Upon himself; horror and doubt distract
His troubl'd thoughts, and from the bottom stirr
The Hell within him, for within him Hell
He brings, and round about him, nor from Hell
One step no more then from himself can fly
By change of place . . .

(*Paradise Lost* IV, 17–23)

266. *What I've dared, I've willed*

. . . the unconquerable Will,
And study of revenge, immortal hate,
And courage never to submit or yield.

(*Paradise Lost* I, 106–8)

266. *They think me mad . . . but I'm demoniac* Though the terms are hardly exclusive. cf. Uriel watching Satan:

his gestures fierce
He markd and mad demeanour, then alone,
As he suppos'd all unobserv'd, unseen.

(*Paradise Lost* IV, 128–30)

266. *I am madness maddened!* 'Witchcraft, and all manner of Spectre-work, and Demonology, we have now named Madness and Diseases of the Nerves. Seldom reflecting that still the new question comes upon us: What is Madness, what are Nerves? Ever, as before, does Madness remain a mysterious-terrific, altogether *infernal* boiling-up of the Nether Chaotic Deep, through this fair-painted Vision of Creation, which swims thereon, which we name the Real.' (Carlyle, *Sartor Resartus* III, viii, 'Natural Supernaturalism')

266. *The prophecy ... be dismembered* Of 'the old squaw Tistig, at Gayhead'. (p. 177, note)

266. *ye deaf Burkes and blinded Bendigoes!* Great gods! Hoot! Deaf and blinded! Hoot! Not even demanding 'fair play' now – merely a 'ring' and the chance of a bout. Jem ('Deaf') Burke and 'Bendigo' (William Thompson) were English boxing champions in 1833, and 1839–45, respectively.

266. *The path to my fixed purpose is laid with iron rails* Ahab is not satanic only, but titanic; his wheel-like mechanic hum – all cogs and rails – is deliberately linked to the fallen Titan who brought fire to mankind. cf. 'Benthamee Utility, virtue by Profit and Loss; reducing this God's-world to a dead brute Steam-engine'. (Carlyle, *On Heroes and Hero-Worship*, Lecture 2)

38 DUSK

267. *My soul is more than matched* Conceding Ahab's pun: 'and I their match. Oh, hard! that ... the match itself must needs be wasting!' (p. 266)

267. *she's overmanned; and by a madman!* By an *Übermensch*, even (to leap a generation). For what is Ahab but the very type of the Nietzschean madman searching for God? The very type of Nietzschean anguished self-transcendence: 'Caesar – with the heart of Christ!', acknowledging no light, other than lightning.

267. *The white whale is their demigorgon* Again, a conflation: of Demogorgon, primeval god of ancient mythology, and Demiurgos, the Platonic Creator. Both are ambivalent: Demogorgon was originally a nether deity invoked in magic – among medieval necromancers as part of the infernal Trinity (*Doctor Faustus*, I, iii, 19); and Demiurgos, among Gnostics at least, an

author of evil conceived as subject to the Supreme Being. A pun suggests both 'demon' and 'half Gorgon': something of all these implications seems to have been intended.

If the chief mate, like the captain, however, was linking the white whale with Gnosticism, his most likely source was Andrews Norton, *The Evidences of the Genuineness of the Gospels* (3 vols: Cambridge, Mass., 1844). Volumes II and III, 'The Evidence ... Afforded by the Early Heretics', treat – among others – of the Marcionites who taught that 'the material world, the visible universe, was not the work of the Supreme Being, but of a far inferior agent, the Demiurgus, or the Creator, who was also the God of the Jews; that the spiritual world ... over which the true Divinity presided, and the material world, the realm of the Creator, were widely separated from each other; that evil was inherent in matter; that the material world, both as being material, and as being the work of an inferior being, was full of imperfection and evil ...' (II, 21–3)

But 'demigorgon' here also suggests confused memories of Shelley's *Prometheus Unbound* (1820), where Demogorgon as a primal and eternal power surpassing even Olympian Zeus, drives the God of false theology from his throne. This atheist paean, glorying in man ('sceptreless, free, uncircumscribed'), certainly influenced *Moby-Dick*. But whereas for Shelley the Titan, instinct with love, is an unyielding champion of mankind, for Melville the fallen Titan, instinct with pride, tends rather to be the ambiguous champion of an Age of Iron.

39 FIRST NIGHT-WATCH

268. *my juicy little pear* Aunt Charity's sister. Stubb, oddly enough, is Bildad's brother-in-law. (MERRY CHRISTMAS)

268. *We'll drink to-night* Third chorus of Charles Fenno Hoffman's 'Sparkling and Bright' (first published in 1830, reprinted in *The Vigil of Faith*, 1842).

40 MIDNIGHT, FORECASTLE

MIDNIGHT ''Tis now the very witching time of night ...': hour of the hoot owl. 'Hark! the infernal orgies!' – mark this *Walpurgisnacht* of Ishmael's *Faust*.

269. *Take a tonic, follow me!* 'And he saith unto them, Follow me, and I will make you fishers of men' (*Matthew* iv, 19).

269. *Our captain stood upon the deck* First verse and chorus of 'Captain Bunker', incorporating lines from 'The Mermaid' and 'The Bonny Ship the Diamond'.

270. *Star-bo-l-e-e-n-s, a-h-o-y!* 'Starbowlines ahoy!', viz. all men of the starboard watch on deck. The *Acushnet* crew list contained four Portuguese sailors, one Irishman, one Englishman, and three American Negroes (including Backus, a 'little black').

271. *Rig it, dig it, stig it, quig it* To a 'rigadig' tune: a verbal jingle to spur on the jingling bell-boy on the windlass-bitt – in lieu of the lasses, 'girls and a green!' Not Pip (with his bells) nor the Azore Sailor (with his spell), but Melville himself ('Tis a stig, young Stiggs! Stig it!) is the ultimate jingler.

For this azure (or Azore), too, will prove a tint of deception – and self-reflection. To 'rig' means not only to romp and to banter, but to cheat and trick; and (in naval parlance) to fit out; and so clothe; and so play the wanton – act the woman or girl. If 'mounting a windlass' implied fornication, to 'rig it' here suggests something transvestite; to 'bang it', 'dig it', more than a hint of sodomy. The bell-boy is thus revealed as a *belle*-boy in ballroom drag; the pippin as a 'Fruit of that Forbidden Tree', turned apple of Sodom: 'Hold up thy hoop, Pip, till I jump through it! Split jibs! tear yourselves!'

Thus Melville, the jingler, rigging his text (manipulating it, that is, in an underhand, fraudulent manner) is also rigging his readers (in the sense of fooling, or playing 'jigs' on us) 'among the coils of rigging'. The frolic is his.

271. *make a pagoda of thyself* cf. Bildad: 'if thou still clingest to thy Pagan ways, which I sadly fear . . . Spurn the idol Bell'.

272. *your night-women, that beat head-winds* To Pip's Mr Tambo playing Mr Bones. cf. The three witches: 'I'll give thee a wind.' 'Th'art kind.' 'And I another.' (*Macbeth* I, i, 11–13)

272. *O Christ! to think of the green navies* Green because greenhorns – green from the pasture as though they had never been out of sight of some Christian 'sheep-fold among the Green Mountains' – now mildewed and sedgy on the sea bottom. 'Are the green fields gone?' The old Manxman picks up the echoes

from LOOMINGS; he plays the chorus and points the change of mood.

272. *By Brahma! ... Thou showest thy black brow, Seeva!* Siva, god of destruction (and of the regeneration that follows), with Vishnu, the preserver, and Brahma, creator of the universe, form the great trinity on which Hinduism centres. Represented with three eyes, a necklace of skulls and a serpent wound about him, he is commonly worshipped in the form of a lingam, or phallus ('the happy one who creates the elements', *Śvetāśvatara-Upanisad* V, 14). His wife Kali, black goddess of death, with her necklace of human heads and protruding blood-stained tongue, is commonly worshipped in the form of snakes, believed to be her incarnation.

273. *the Heeva-Heeva!* The heiva, ceremonial dance of peace. See A DANCE IN THE VALLEY. (*Omoo*, ch. 63)

273. *Pirohitee's peak of spears* Tahiti's quadruple-crested Olympus is dominated by Mt Orohena (7,618 ft). 'From the great central peaks of the larger peninsula – Orohena, Aorai, and Pirohitee – the land radiates on all sides to the sea in sloping green ridges.' (*Omoo*, ch. 18)

273. *the isle fort at Cattegat* On the strait between Sweden and Jutland. (See 'the old *Categut*' p. 171, note.)

274 *Our captain has his birth-mark ... there's another* As the adulterous Dimmesdale, on the midnight scaffold, 'looking upward to the zenith, beheld there the appearance of an immense letter, – the letter A, – marked out in lines of dull red light'. (*The Scarlet Letter*)

274. *The old grudge* It could be a Negro uprising, as on Santo Domingo maybe, or a slave-boat rebellion, such as Melville was to recount four years later in *Benito Cereno*.

274. *ST JAGO'S SAILOR* viz. a Portuguese-speaking sailor from San Tiago, or São Tiago, or São Thiago – largest and most populous of the Cape Verde Islands, between Maio and Fogo.

275. *Gods and men – both brawlers!* The pederastic pastoral around the 'blackling' Corydon is – point counter point – shattered by a storm and a rumble. Thus Melville's inevitable rhythm from trance to horror, from fiddler's green to Cain and Abel, is resolved in a pun: for these merry-mad jiggers, turned brawlers with knives, are not merely noisily quarrelsome but

dancing the 'bransle' or 'braule'. (It was the Frenchman, of course, who first formed the Indian-file, shouted 'Jig it' and 'Legs!', and merry-mad led with a jump.)

Thus male love frolic gives birth only to male blood frolic – eight *belles* jangled pell-mell – just as the sole fruit of Ishmael's and Queequeg's stigging it, quigging it, had been 'a hatchet-faced baby'.

'Jollies? Lord help such jollies!'

275. *Fair play! ... A ring, a ring!* The naive English voice unwittingly parrotting dark Ahab: 'since there is ever a sort of fair play herein'; 'ring me in', 'ye pugilists!'

276. *God! Duck lower* 'Pip, here comes the royal yard' (virile member, or penis)! 'Who'd go climbing after chestnuts now' (proffering 'their tapering upright cones')?

276. *Oh, thou big white God ... have mercy* 'White skin, white liver!' cried Daggoo. But to Pip, white means power; power, a plea for protection:

I have called upon thee, for thou wilt hear me, O God: incline thine ear unto me, and hear my speech.

Shew thy marvellous loving kindness, O thou that savest by thy right hand them which put their trust in thee from those that rise up against them.

Keep me as the apple of the eye, hide me under the shadow of thy wings ...

(*Psalm* xvii, 6–9)

276. *on this small black boy* cf. Blake's 'The Little Black Boy':

My mother bore me in the southern wild,
And I am black, but O! my soul is white ...

Yet whiteness itself will prove a horror. *Songs of Innocence*, at last, must turn to *Songs of Experience*. (THE CAST-AWAY) In God's service Pip too – merry mad – will drown.

41 MOBY DICK

MOBY DICK Stories of ferocious whales who had smashed into whaling ships were commonplace among sailors, but the seeds of *Moby-Dick* were planted ten years earlier, it seems, in the Pacific. In 1841 the *Acushnet* sailed for several days alongside a Nantucket whaler; on board was the sixteen-year-old son of Owen Chase, Chief Mate of the *Essex*, sunk by a whale in those same latitudes just south of the equator in 1820. The youth lent Melville his father's *Narrative of the Most Extraordinary and Distressing Shipwreck of the Whale-Ship Essex, of Nantucket* (New York, 1821), from which Melville quotes an Extract (58) and again in THE AFFIDAVIT, concluding: 'At this day Captain Pollard is a resident of Nantucket. I have seen Owen Chace, who was chief mate of the *Essex* at the time of the tragedy; I have read his plain and faithful narrative; I have conversed with his son; and all this within a few miles of the scene of the catastrophe.' A copy of Chase's *Narrative*, inscribed 'Herman Melville from Judge Shaw, April, 1851', survives with eighteen pages of commentary bound into the text. (See A BIOGRAPHICAL NOTE.) There he wrote: 'The reading of this wondrous story upon the landless sea, & close to the very latitude of the shipwreck had a surprising effect upon me.' (*What I know of Owen Chace, &*)

The name he derived from the celebrated White Whale 'Mocha Dick', sighted in 1810 off the Chilean island (between Valdivia and Conception), and given its epithet on the analogy of 'Timor Jack' or 'New Zealand Tom'. (See THE AFFIDAVIT.) The exploits of this whale were legendary: he was said to have been harpooned nineteen times, caused the death of more than thirty men, breached three whaling ships and fourteen boats, and sunk an Australian trader and a French merchantman. An early sketch by Jeremiah N. Reynolds, published in the *Knickerbocker Magazine* (May 1839), was certainly known to Melville. He transposed its title, 'Mocha Dick: or, the White Whale of the Pacific', transformed the *Penguin* to the *Pequod*, and transferred 'a lurking deviltry' to an 'intangible malignity'. That account, however, ended with the capture of Mocha Dick, tried-out to one hundred barrels of oil.

But, according to 'The Career of Mocha Dick' (*Detroit Free Press*, 3 April 1892), Mocha Dick lived on. Operating near his home base, Mocha Dick destroyed two boats belonging to the English whaler *Desmond* (5 July 1840); struck again, 300 miles south, to shatter a boat of the Russian barque *Sarepta* (30 August 1840), lingering so long that the crew were forced to desert a whale they had just killed; turned up in the Atlantic, near the Falkland Islands, to wreck two boats and kill two men of the Bristol ship *John Day* (May 1841); and in October 1842 made a climactic appearance off the Japanese coast, first ramming a light lumber ship, then engaging in simultaneous battle with the crews of the *Crieff* (Scots), the *Dudley* (English) and the *Yankee* (American), sinking two whale boats and carrying away the jib boom and bowsprit of the *Crieff*.

By July 1846 even the *Knickerbocker Magazine* had forgotten its earlier version, reminding its readers of 'the sketch of *"Mocha Dick, of the Pacific"*, published in the *Knickerbocker* many years ago; a huge mountain-whale, that rises like an island every now and then from the bosom of the Pacific, trailing from his sides hundreds of green slimy ropes, that stream like "horrid hair" upon the waters'. That account may well have led Melville to look up the earlier issue, in the very month he rediscovered his lost buddy of the *Acushnet* and fellow deserter on the Marquesas, Richard Tobias Greene, and began 'The Story of Toby'. May not 'Toby Dick' then have elided with 'Mocha Dick' to form that one euphonious compound, 'Moby Dick'?

On 16 August 1851, while *The Whale* was in the press, his own ship, the *Acushnet*, was wrecked on St Lawrence Island. On 5 November, only nine days before publication, even more awesome news reached New York: that on 20 August, in mid-Pacific, the *Ann Alexander* of New Bedford had actually been rammed and sunk by a whale. Evert Duyckinck at once informed Melville. 'Crash! comes Moby Dick himself ...' he replied excitedly, '& reminds me of what I have been about for part of the last year or two. It is really & truly a surprising coincidence – to say the least. I make no doubt it IS Moby Dick himself, for there is no account of his capture after the sad fate of the *Pequod* about fourteen years ago. – Ye Gods! What a Commentator is this Ann Alexander whale. What he has to say is short & pithy & very much to the point. I wonder if my evil art has raised this monster.' (7 November 1851)

278. *that ignorance and superstitiousness hereditary to all sailors* cf. David Hume: 'In proportion as any man's course of life is governed by accident, we always find, that he encreases in superstition; as may particularly be observed of gamesters and sailors, who, though, of all mankind, the least capable of serious reflection, abound most in frivolous and superstitious apprehensions.' (*The Natural History of Religion*)

278. *the outblown rumors of the White Whale* cf. Jules Lecomte: 'In 1828 a fine American three-master, the *Oceania,*

returned to Nantucket with a large cargo of whalebone and oil. The crew, as usual, told the strangest stories about the latest misdeeds of the indomitable white sperm whale ...' ('Le Cachalot Blanc', *Musée des familles*, January 1837) For the full text of this early French version of a Nantucket myth, see Appendix.

279. *some book naturalists – Olassen and Povelson* Olafsen and Povelsen, in *Travels in Iceland* (London, 1805), declare there is a species of whale so voracious 'that it takes whole boats with their crews into its mouth, destroys the vessels, and swallows the men alive'. Once having tasted human flesh, it 'will wait there a whole year in the hope of devouring' more.

279. *so late a time as Cuvier's* Baron Georges Cuvier (1769–1832), author of *Leçons sur l'anatomie comparée* (1800–05) and *Le règne animal* (1817). It is Beale who alludes to 'Olassen and Povelsen' and quotes the Baron (*The Natural History of the Sperm Whale*, pp. 4–5).

280. *the mystic modes whereby ... he transports himself* These mysteries *in profundis* parallel Ahab's 'mystic aspect' on high, for which Ishmael had just evinced such 'a wild, mystical, sympathetical feeling'.

281. *the Nor' West Passage* cf. Scoresby, vol. 1, pp. 8–12.

281. *the inland Strello mountain in Portugal* Serra da Estrella, source of the Mondego river. The Baronne d'Aulnoy, whose memoirs are quite as fictitious as her fairy tales, writes of 'the lake of the mountain of Strella where there are often found the wrecks of ships, broken masts, anchors, and sails, and yet the sea is above twelve leagues off, and this is upon the top of a very high hill too'. (*Relation du Voyage d'Espagne*, 1691)

281. *Arethusa* Nymph loved by the river-god Alpheus and transformed by Artemis into a fountain. Pursued out of Arcadia, she flowed beneath the sea to emerge on Ortygia, the island in the harbour of Syracuse.

281. *wrinkled forehead ... pyramidical white hump* cf. QUEEN MAB. The White Whale's and the Quaker's 'peculiarities' are linked – to a confused transposition of their joint (bodily, intellectual, spiritual) identities.

282. *as an Arkansas duellist ... blindly seeking* Or 'dualist', blindly professing the 'arcane saw' that there are two coexistent

principles: one good, one evil – 'to whose dominion even the modern Christians ascribe one-half of the worlds'? South-western duellists were literally yoked in mortal combat, their left hands linked with a knotted handkerchief.

cf. Also that *'unhuntable bar'* of the south-west, 'The Big Bear of Arkansas'. (T. B. Thorpe, in *The Spirit of the Times*, 1841)

282. *his sickle-shaped lower jaw ... reaped away Ahab's leg* In one pastoral sweep 'like a whole shock of wheat'. For that jaw mirrors the harpooneer's own tool, 'sickle-shaped, with a vast handle sweeping round' (THE SPOUTER-INN); this mower, those 'many inland reapers and mowers ... armed with their own scythes'. (p. 153, note)

283. *the ancient Ophites of the east* A Gnostic sect of the second century A.D., meaning 'Believers in the Serpent'. They followed Marcion in teaching that the Creator in the Old Testament and the Father of the New were irrevocably opposed; but went further than him in worshipping the serpent as an agent of the true God, since it was the only creature in Eden to offer Adam and Eve the knowledge that Jehovah had withheld: 'Maintaining the common opinion that the Creator was *not spiritual*, and regarding him as being opposed to the manifestation and development of the spiritual principle in man, they honoured the Serpent for having thwarted his narrow purposes, withdrawn our first parents from their allegiance to him, induced them to eat the fruit of the tree of knowledge, and thus brought them the knowledge of "that Power which is over All".' (Andrews Norton, *The Evidences of the Genuineness of the Gospels*, II, 220)

The Creator being evil, it followed that his foes of the Old Testament are really its heroes, and Ophites specially revered Cain, the Sodomites and the Egyptians. 'Hist boys!' a subtle snake-dance is weaving: from the harpooneers' gulped 'hiss' to 'that anaconda of an old man' ('damned ... most malignantly! damned in the midst of Paradise!'); from Hindu Siva to the phallic cult of the Ophites.

See Lawrence Thompson, *Melville's Quarrel with God*, pp. 430–32; and Thomas Vargish, 'Gnostic *Mythos* in *Moby-Dick*'. (*P.M.L.A.* 81, 1966, pp. 272–7)

283. *reverenced in their statue devil* Andrews Norton

continues: 'But the Creator, who was himself desirous of being regarded as the highest God, being in consequence angry with the Serpent, expelled him from heaven, where he had before dwelt, and cast him down to earth. After this fall he is made to correspond to the serpent of the Apocalypse, the Devil; and is represented as ... full of malice equally toward men and their Maker.' (*The Evidences of the Genuineness of the Gospels*, II, 221)

283. *all evil, to crazy Ahab* Doomed and denounced by a 'crazy' prophet; 'knife in hand', like a suicidal Othello:

Set you down this:
And say besides that in Aleppo once,
Where a malignant and a turban'd Turk
Beat a Venetian and traduc'd the state,
I took by th' throat the circumcised dog,
And smote him – thus.

(*Othello* V, ii, 354–9)

283. *that dreary, howling Patagonian Cape* Itself incorporating the *agoni* of Ahab's 'agonizing bodily laceration'. cf. 'I wasted away ... I would see that bar in every thing I did; *he hunted me.*' ('The Big Bear of Arkansas')

284. *such vital strength ... in his Egyptian chest* Like another Osiris, Ahab is dismembered 'in mid winter' by a leviathan/fish. Like Osiris, he revives as the sun revives. Dead 'for three days and nights', Ahab becomes literally an Osiris, intent on 'supernatural revenge'.

H. Bruce Franklin first showed how the Osiris myth underpins and shapes the structure of *Moby-Dick*. Herodotus (Bk II), Diodorus Siculus (*The Historical Library*, Bk I), Plutarch ('Of Isis and Osiris', in Philemon Holland's translation of *The Philosophie Commonly Called the Morals*, 1603), and Thomas Maurice (*Indian Antiquities*, 1794–1800; *The History of Hindostan*, 1819) were Melville's major sources:

'This version may be found in Plutarch and Maurice: Osiris is a priest-king-god who sails the world in a ship which later becomes the constellation Argo. He hunts Typhon, who is usually represented by some kind of aquatic monster and who symbolizes the ocean and all in nature that is malignant to man. Once a year, Typhon dismembers Osiris. When this happens – the date is variously given as the autumnal equinox, the winter solstice, and the period in between – Osiris disappears for a certain length of time, which is also variously given. During this absence from earth, he rules the infernal regions and a ship sails the world bearing his coffin. During this time, also, his phallus is missing and the land lies infertile. In a vernal phallic ritual, Osiris is healed and the fertility of the land is restored. His dismemberment in the fall or winter symbolizes the seasonal disaster in nature. The seasonal resurrection of the sun causes, symbolizes, or is symbolized by his resurrection.

'Ahab is also a priest-king-god who sails the world in a ship which is equated with the constellation Argo. He also hunts an aquatic monster who symbolizes the ocean and all in nature that is malignant to man. Once a year, for three successive years, he is dismembered by the aquatic monster which he hunts. The first two times, he also disappears for a length of time and then is healed with the advance of the sun. Ahab is also described as ruler of the infernal regions. Phallic rituals, fire worship, and infernal orgies are conducted on his ship, which also sails the world bearing a coffin . . .

'Like Osiris' periodic dismemberments, Ahab's periodic dismemberments are related to natural fertility and astronomical events and are inflicted by his eternal foe, the demon of life. Like Osiris' descents, Ahab's are periodic, are related to natural fertility and astronomical events, and are infernal. Unlike Osiris, however, Ahab is mortal; from one dismemberment he does not recover, from one descent he does not arise. These differences and similarities between Ahab's role and Osiris' role in part define the nature and tragedy of Ahab's cosmic struggle.'

But why Osiris? Why this insistence on 'Egyptian'? Because 'the gods are fabulously reported to be born in Egypt'. (Diodorus Siculus I, 18) 'And Moses was learned in all the wisdom of the Egyptians.' (*Acts* vii, 22) 'Melville saw Egyptian mythology as the direct source of the Hebrew mythology and therefore of the myth of the Christ. Confronted with the solecisms of the Old Testament's prophecies of the Saviour and the New Testament's biography of the Saviour, he turned to what he considered their Egyptian source. There he found a picture of the saviour which seemed to describe more accurately what he could see. He drew from this source his own version of the saviour myth – *Moby-Dick*, which he submits to us as a kind of truth not found in Christian, Hebrew, or Egyptian mythology.' (H. Bruce Franklin,

The Wake of the Gods, ch. 3, 'Moby-Dick: An Egyptian Myth Incarnate', pp. 73–4, 83, 97)

For a further account, see especially pp. 205, 225, 575, 611, notes.

284. *the unabated Hudson ... through the Highland gorge* Of the Catskill Mountains, New York.

284. *his special lunacy stormed his general sanity* For the triumph of 'sudden, passionate, corporal animosity' *is* 'Paradise Lost'. But reason not only survives in Hell; it grows. Independent of God's rule, it grows self-conscious, arrogant, wilful. Thus the proud cry of assertive reason ringing out:

> The mind is its own place, and in it self
> Can make a Heav'n of Hell, a Hell of Heav'n.
>
> (*Paradise Lost* I, 254–5)

284. *this spiked Hotel de Cluny* At whose 'very heart' there lurks a 'luny'. But 'Hark ye yet again, – the little lower layer': 'The primeval world – the Fore-World, as the Germans say – I can dive to it in myself as well as grope for it with researching fingers in catacombs, libraries, and the broken reliefs and torsos of ruined villas.' (Emerson, 'History')

On his visit to Paris Melville had been fascinated by this fifteenth-century Gothic structure, built on the site of the Roman baths of the Emperor Julian: 'Thence to the Hôtel de Cluny. A most unique collection. The house is just the house I should like to live in. Glorious old cabinets – ebony, ivory carvings. – Beautiful chapel. Tapestry, old keys. Leda & the Swan. Descended into the vaults of the old Roman palace of Thermes. Baths, &c.' (*Journal*, 5 December 1849)

The 'darker, deeper part' now hinted is that while the spiked upper stories (the work of Pierre de Chaslus, abbot of Cluny) are Christian, the baths in the basement (or *Palais de Julien*, where Constantine's nephew, the Apostate, was thought to have been crowned) are not merely pagan, but infidel. There, like Dante's Satan, sits 'that proud, sad king', 'upholding on his frozen brow the piled entablatures' of the Frigidarium:

> 'Lo imperador del doloroso regno'
>
> (*Inferno*, canto xxxiv, 28)

What royal Ahab had deliriously 'piled' on that snow-white hump, piled back now – concentred on his own frozen brow.

284. *those vast Roman halls of Thermes* or *Palais des Thermes*, meaning 'heat', 'hot springs' (or 'fiery pit'). But a non-existent spirit called 'Thermes', phonetically at least, suggests the 'Hermes', as true guardian-guide of the *Pequod*. It is surely an apt little joke that Ahab's 'whole awful essence', as bearded Caryatid, sits so hermaphroditically buried, so hermetically sealed and concealed in these halls.

285. *from you grin sire* Conflating 'grandsire' and the archaic 'grimsire' (someone morose and overbearing).

285. *all my means are sane, my motive and my object mad* Thus Ahab, the man of masks – who sees 'all visible objects ... but as pasteboard masks' – is brought to converge on his paradigm, Milton's Satan ('artificer of fraud', 'sly hypocrite'). Both are their own worst victims, self-beguiled by their own deceitful logic; both, 'intent on an audacious, immitigable, and supernatural revenge'.

286. *a Job's whale* cf. 'The awful tauntings in Job'. (p. 230, note)

286. *the gliding great demon* But it is Ahab who is 'demoniac'. It is Ahab, whose every word rebounds. The hump-backed, pyramidical White Whale is Ahab's ultimate reflection; Narcissus-like he pursues his 'monomaniac incarnation'.

286. *muffled sound of his pick*

> Yet without power to kill ...
> in some sort, did still ...
> not to his will ...
> Nevertheless so well ...
> hunting the White Whale ...

The ear alone, Ishmael warns, is a guide to those 'larger, darker, deeper' profundities: that ever 'shifting' 'shaft', the sound of that 'pick' picking up 'such a crew ... specially picked and packed'.

286. *Who does not feel the irresistible arm drag?* And in that 'arm', that 'drag', are echoes of his own indelible, childhood trauma: 'a supernatural hand seemed placed in mine. My arm hung over the counterpane, and the nameless, unimaginable, silent form or phantom ... seemed closely seated by my bedside. For what seemed ages piled on ages, I lay there, frozen with the

most awful fears, not daring to drag away my hand ...' (THE COUNTERPANE)

Thus the phantom whale and Ahab's magic phantom, too, are linked – and both, by that 'ever shifting, muffled sound' to the darker, deeper layers of Ishmael's own 'unconscious'.

42 THE WHITENESS OF THE WHALE

287. *grand old kings of Pegu* In the sixteenth century Pegu, fifty miles north-east of Rangoon, was capital of a united Burmese kingdom.

287. *even made significant of gladness* cf. Rabelais (*Gargantua and Pantagruel,* Bk 1, ch. 10, 'Of that which is Signified by the Colours White and Blue') cf. Sir Thomas Browne, 'A digression of Blacknesse'. (*Pseudodoxia Epidemica,* Bk 6, ch. 12)

287. *among the Romans a white stone* cf. *Revelation*: 'To him that overcometh will I give to eat of the hidden manna, and will give him a white stone, and in the stone a new name written ...' (ii, 17)

288. *to the noble Iroquois ... the sacred White Dog* 'In mid-winter, usually about the first of February, this religious celebration was held... They selected a dog free from physical blemish, and of pure white, if such a one could be found. The white deer, white squirrel, and other chance animals of the albino kind, were regarded as consecrated to the Great Spirit. White was the Iroquois emblem of purity and faith. In strangling the dog, they were careful neither to shed his blood nor break his bones... Around his neck was hung a string of white wampum, the pledge of their sincerity... The dog had not the slightest connexion with the sins of the people. On the contrary, the simple idea of sacrifice was, to send up the spirit of the dog as a messenger to the Great Spirit, to announce their continued fidelity to his service, and also to convey to him their united thanks for the blessings of the year.' (Lewis H. Morgan, *League of the Ho-dé-no-sau-nee or Iroquois,* 1851).

An advance excerpt, Bk 2, ch. 2, had been published in the *Literary World,* 28 December 1850, vol 7, pp. 521–3, under the heading 'New Year's Festivities of the Iroquois'.

288. *the alb or tunic* Or 'alba tunica', worn under THE CASSOCK, or pallium.

288. *white ... in the celebration of the Passion of our Lord* Only on Maundy Thursday, commemorating the first Eucharist.

288. *the four-and-twenty elders ... clothed in white* 'And round about the throne were four and twenty seats: and upon the seats I saw four and twenty elders sitting, clothed in white raiment; and they had on their heads crowns of gold.' (*Revelation* iv, 4)

288. *and the Holy One ... white like wool* 'His head and his hairs were white like wool, as white as snow; and his eyes were as a flame of fire.' (*Revelation* i, 14)

cf. Moby Dick's 'peculiar snow-white wrinkled forehead'. cf. Mocha Dick: 'From the effect of age, or more probably from a freak of nature, as exhibited in the case of the Ethiopian Albino, a singular consequence had resulted – *he was white as wool!*' (*Knickerbocker Magazine*, May 1839)

289. *the Romish mass for the dead* As a New Year gift, 1851, a complete set of Cuvier was presented to Melville by his brother Allan. In (*The Class Pisces*) of *The Animal Kingdom* (London, 1834), vol. 10, p. 632, Melville marked a note on sharks: 'The French name this terrible animal *Requin*, from requiem, the rest or stillness of death, in allusion to the deadly character of its habits ...' (Jay Leyda, *The Melville Log*, p. 402)

This, like the item on the White Dog, must have been another last minute insertion – added, possibly, after the composition of THE FUNERAL.

289. *Coleridge* 'The Rime of the Ancient Mariner' (*Lyrical Ballads*, 1798).

289. *As Abraham before the angels* *Genesis* xviii, 2.

289. *A goney, he replied* Itself a mystic sign hinting at 'flutterings and throbbings', the very name expressing 'supernatural distress'.

290. *the White Steed of the Prairies* This wild stallion – the 'pacing mustang' of frontier legend – was usually black. But see James Hall, *The Wilderness and the War Path* (New York, 1846): 'A tradition has been current for several years past, among the Indians and traders, in relation to a very remarkable horse, supposed to be the leader of a herd of these animals, roaming on the Western plains. Many profess to have seen the 'White Steed', and describe him as a horse of splendid figure and action, and

of such surpassing fleetness, sagacity, and courage, that he baffles every attempt to capture him ...' Note II, Appendix, pp. 169–70)

291. *the desperate White Hoods of Ghent* For the fracas in Ghent, see Jean Froissart, *Chronicles of England, France and Spain* (Pt I, ch. 350 in Lord Berners' translation). The White Hoods were the popular party in Ghent who in 1381 led a rebellion against the count of Flanders and his court at Bruges (the subject of Sir Henry Taylor's blank verse drama, *Philip van Artevelde*, 1834).

291. *the aspect of the dead which most appals* Shifting by a series of verbal sleights from 'pallor', via 'pall', to 'the shroud in which we wrap them'.

292. *the king of terrors ... rides on his pallid horse* The fourth horseman of the Apocalypse: 'And I looked, and behold a pale horse: and the name that sat on him was Death, and Hell followed with him.' (*Revelation* vi, 8)

292. *Whitsuntide* Whitsunday, or White Sunday. The English name for Pentecost derives from the white baptismal robes worn by the newly baptised at this feast of the Holy Ghost.

292. *a White Friar or a White Nun* Carmelites, that is, the mendicant order founded on Mount Carmel in the twelfth century; their habit is brown, distinguished by a white cloak and scapular. The great Spanish mystics, St Theresa of Avila and St John of the Cross, had reorientated the order back toward the contemplative life. Whatever the susceptibilities of midwestern Protestants, incidentally, a convent of Carmelite nuns had been established near Port Tobacco, Maryland, as early as 1790.

292. *the White Tower of London* The central keep of the Tower of London, built shortly after the Conquest, was first whitened in Henry III's reign. Like the Bloody Tower (on the inner curtain) it served as a state prison until the Restoration. Through the Byward Tower (on the outer curtain) leads the only entrance from the land side.

293. *'the tall pale man' of the Hartz forests* See De Quincey, *Suspira de Profundis*, 'The Apparition of the Brocken'.

293. *all the whooping imps of the Blocksburg* The Blocksberg,

or Brocken, highest peak of the Hartz Mountains – legendary meeting-place on Walpurgis Nacht, or eve of May, of 'the Witches' Sabbat'. (Goethe's *Faust*, Pt I, scene xxi)

293. *Lima ... Old as Pizarro* Founded in 1535 by Francisco Pizarro: 'you know the proverb all along this coast – "Corrupt as Lima".' (THE TOWN-HO'S STORY) Melville had visited the Peruvian capital on a forty-eight hours' leave in early 1844, while seaman on the frigate *United States*. But what precisely had occurred on this leave? A crew-mate, writing fifteen years later, to announce the birth of a son named after him, added: 'You probably have not forgotten all of the crew of the old frigate *United States* and more especially our visit to the city of Lima.' (4 February 1859)

The old capital of the viceroys, largely destroyed by earthquake in 1746, was again severely shaken, after Independence in 1828. But to Melville's day a 'wide field' of more than fifty 'leaning spires', including the cathedral, survived. Nor was Lima more noticably pallid, or white-washed, than any other Andean town. Possibly by 'the white veil', Melville had the local *saya y manto* in mind, a kind of double petticoat, one hung on the hips, the other drawn up over the head. Masquerade unfailingly intrigued him. Such 'rigid pallor', however, suggests not *lime* so much as the last stage of syphilitic paresis.

295. *nay, the very veil of the Christian's Deity* The Host, or consecrated bread, of the Eucharist. For what appeals, appals. And 'Woe to him', in Father Mapple's phrase, 'who seeks to please rather than to appal!'

But in that 'appalling' lurks a 'pall', till a 'palsied universe lies before us'; in that 'veil', the very whale that Ahab would pierce.

296. *white or colorless ... if operating without medium upon matter*. Operating, that is, without luminiferous ether – the hypothetical element (between the molecules of the gases that make up air) for transmitting light and heat.

It was Thomas Young, in England, and Augustin Jean Fresnel, in France, who first advanced proof for the wave theory in the early nineteenth century – at the same time as Goethe, in Germany, was pouring scorn on Newton's colour lore. (*Zur Farbenlehre*, 1810.) Throughout *Moby-Dick*, what seems traditional imagery is really an extension of scientific theory and experimental proof. Pastoral, for once, is based on Positivism.

296. *like wilful travellers in Lapland* Thus '*pal*/sied', inverted to '*lep*/er', is transformed to '*Lap*/land', or 'land of pall'. The very word-play conjures up a world of sorcerers and of witchcraft – Nantucketers in their 'quicksand shoes, something like Laplander snow-shoes'.

cf. The final vision of Arthur Gordon Pym, of Nantucket: 'The darkness had materially increased, relieved only by the glare of the water thrown back from the white curtain before us. Many gigantic and pallidly white birds flew continuously now from beyond the veil ... And now we rushed into the embraces of the cataract, where a chasm threw itself open to receive us. But there arose in our pathway a shrouded human figure, very far larger in its proportions than any dweller among men. And the hue of the skin of the figure was of the perfect whiteness of the snow.' (Edgar Allan Poe, *The Narrative of Arthur Gordon Pym*, ch. 25)

cf. Also the fate of Hawthorne's infidel, blinded by 'The Great Carbuncle'. (*Twice-Told Tales*, 1842)

For Ahab's defiant rejection of 'colored glasses', see THE QUADRANT.

296. *the Albino whale was the symbol* Or the Albino *Whale*? For the whale is a *Whale* is a veil – till a 'monumental white shroud ... wraps all the prospect around' the dazzled reader. (See p. 454, note.)

43 HARK!

297. *his neighbor, a Cholo* Half-breed of Spanish and Peruvian-Indian parentage.

297. *Caramba!* Spanish exclamation of surprise and faint disgust.

297. *the hum of the old Quakeress's knitting-needles* The Cholo, paradoxically, is deaf to the sound of Clotho (his all but anagram) spinning the web of life: which is Queequeg's heathenish hum, Stubb's rigadig hum, Ahab's mechanical hum, 'the steady hum of the unceasingly advancing keel' away from Nantucket Charity.

44 THE CHART

THE CHART For a large part, Melville's facts derive from Commodore Charles Wilkes' *Narrative of the United States Exploring Expedition ... 1832–1842* (Philadelphia, 1845), vol. 5, ch. 12, 'Currents and Whaling'. Wilkes opens: 'It may at first sight appear singular that subjects apparently so dissimilar as currents and whaling should be united to form the subject of one chapter'. But Ahab's 'large wrinkled roll' at once unites both the currents, the captain, and the whale.

297. *a locker in the transom* The cross-beams in the stern, sometimes made into a seat.

298. *the periodicalness of the sperm whale's resorting to given waters* Ishmael will develop this hint – of the περίοδος of the whales' cyclic migrations and transmigrations – in THE FOUNTAIN. (p. 478, note)

299. *an official circular, issued by Lieutenant Maury* Matthew Fontaine Maury's *Explanations and Sailing Directors to Accompany Lieut. Maury's Investigation of the Wind and Current Charts*, second, enlarged edition (16 April 1851).

300. *the Seychelle ground* Along the Seychelles Ridge, northeast of Madagascar.

300. *Volcano Bay on the Japanese Coast* Possibly Suruga Bay, below Mount Fuji.

300. *that tragic spot* 'Aye, he was dismasted off Japan', the old Gay-Head Indian had commented (AHAB), like the *Pequod* herself, it seemed, with her new trio of Japanese masts. (THE SHIP) But now the dismasting is to be viewed rather as a prologue to the final catastrophe – both plotted along the Equator. It was off the Japanese coast, however, that Mocha Dick performed one of his most notorious feats, simultaneously engaging in battle with the crews of the *Crieff*, the *Dudley* and the *Yankee* (October 1842). This heroic combat may well have confused Melville's ulterior purpose. (See MOBY DICK, ch. 41, note.)

301. *Monsoons, Pampas, Nor-Westers, Harmattans, Trades* i.e. In the Indian Ocean, off the estuary of the River Plate, in the North Atlantic, off the Guinea Coast – anywhere except the Mediterranean (Levanter), or Arabian desert (Simoom).

301. *the* Pequod'*s circumnavigating wake* The devious *Pequod* seeking the wheeling whale, round and round, through the zigzag word-circle of *Moby-Dick.*

301. *Mufti in the thronged thoroughfares of Constantinople? Yes* Now the title of any Muslim priest or legal adviser, but in Ottoman Turkey reserved for the official state head of Islam and his deputies. Hayford and Parker read, 'No', which the oratorical question logically requires.

301. *scalloped out like a lost sheep's ear!* Whose owner's tag has torn loose.

302. *Ah, God! what trances of torments* To wake with the bleeding stigmata of the damned.

302. *his own intense thoughts ... amid a clashing of phrensies* Whirling his mind (φρήν) in a frenzied Descartian vortex, round and round, like the wheeling *Pequod* or circumnavigating whale.

302. *with glaring eyes ... burst from his state room* Another Ixion escaping his bed; or King Lear, rather, snatched off that 'wheel of fire'. (IV, vii, 47)

303. *a ray of living light ... without an object to color* Another fugal variation on the theme of agent and principle, colour and light, linking (through Ishmael's eyes) the blank horror of the White Whale and the blank, tormented somnambulist.

303. *he whose intense thinking thus makes him a Prometheus* Like Satan, another Titan, and bringer of fire – to link Ishmael himself now, 'pondering' THE WHITENESS OF THE WHALE, with Ahab thus pondering over his charts, 'till a weariness and faintness of pondering came over him'.

45 THE AFFIDAVIT

303. *I care not to perform ... my task methodically* To echo Montaigne and Sterne: 'a careful disorderliness is the true method'. (THE HONOR AND GLORY OF WHALING, p. 469, note)

303. *marked by the same private cypher* cf. One of the Rev. Cheever's stories of 'old Captain Bunker, of New Bedford': '"Hallo!" said Captain Bunker, jesting, "here is my missing old iron." What he said in joke proved to be very truth, for the

blubber-kept harpoon was the identical one he had lost five years before, having on it the ship's name and his own private mark.' (*The Whale and his Captors*, pp. 157–8)

304. *Rinaldo Rinaldini* Renaud of the *chansons de geste*, rebel knight against Charlemagne; Rinaldo in the renaissance epics of Ariosto, Boiardo and Tasso; robber prince in a romance by Goethe's brother-in-law, Christian August Vulpius (1797).

305. *as Cambyses or Caesar* Son and successor of Cyrus the Great, Cambyses died, possibly by suicide, while crushing an insurrection. Julius Caesar ('supreme lord and dictator'), of course, was assassinated.

305. *O Timor Tom! ... O Don Miguel!* 'The Oriental straits of that name', or Timor Sea, lie between the Lesser Sundas of eastern Indonesia and north-west Australia; Ombai strait, due north of Timor. Timor Jack and New Zealand Tom were two notorious whales (see Beale, pp. 183 ff.); 'Morquan', 'Don Miguel' are Melville's own inventions.

New Zealand Tom, Bennett adds, was 'conspicuously distinguished by a white hump' (vol. 2, p. 220). Perhaps he was that 'Old Tom' of whom Emerson heard from a seaman in a stage coach: 'a white whale ... who rushed upon the boats which attacked him & crushed the boats to small chips in his jaws ...' (*Journal*, 19 February 1834)

At the last minute Melville – or his English editor, more likely – altered 'New Zealand Tom' to 'New Zealand Jack'; which made for consistency, while compounding the muddle. For, on reading Beale, Melville had firmly underlined 'Timor Jack'.

305. *as Marius or Sylla* Caius Marius (Caesar's uncle) and Lucius Cornelius Sulla were competing generals, whose rivalry (88–82 B.C.) involved Rome in bloody Civil War.

305. *through the Narragansett Woods ... the Indian King Philip* 'King Philip' (so called by English settlers) was Metacomet, Sachem of the Wampanoag Indians, whose uprising in 1675 led to the most bloody of all New England's Indian Wars. Allied to the populous Narragansett tribe of Rhode Island, they raided border settlements, burning and massacring women and children. Unable to draw the Indians into pitched battle, the settlers resorted to similar maquis warfare.

But the pursuit of Annawon seems to be confused here with Lt-Col. William Butler's expedition to capture Joseph Brant, the

Mohawk leader, a century later. Annawon, in fact, was captured by a Captain Benjamin Church, under commission from the Plymouth colony, in September, 1676; Butler's expedition of 1778 proved abortive.

306. *a hideous and intolerable allegory* Confronted by Sophia Hawthorne's prying formulas, Melville sent back this evasive smokescreen: 'your allusion for example to the "Spirit Spout" first showed to me that there was a subtile significance in that thing – but I did not, in that case, *mean* it. I had some vague idea while writing it, that the whole book was susceptible of an allegoric construction, & also that *parts* of it were – but the speciality of many of the particular subordinate allegories, were first revealed to me, after reading Mr Hawthorne's letter, which, without citing any particular examples, yet intimated the part-&-parcel allegoricalness of the whole.' (8 January 1852)

In fact, 'an allegorical meaning may lurk here' and there (HEADS OR TAILS); 'hints', in that 'grand fishery'; but *The Whale* as a whole – that hall of mirrors, that wheeling enigma – is *no* mere allegorical transposition. What is more Ishmael is enough of a Yankee, and nineteenth-century novelist, to insist on the veracity of his facts. Positivism, he asserts, underlies not only the colour lore, but every technical, historical, financial, geographical, biological, anatomical, statistical facet of this 'leviathanic brotherhood', this new *Leviathan.*

307. *In the year 1820 the ship Essex* 'When I was on board the ship *Acushnet* of Fairhaven, on the passage to the Pacific cruising-grounds, among other matters of forecastle conversations at times was the story of the *Essex*. It was then that I first became acquainted with her history and her truly astounding fate ...' (Melville's manuscript notes inserted in his copy of Owen Chase, *Narrative of the Most Extraordinary and Distressing Shipwreck of the Whale-Ship Essex, of Nantucket*)

On 20 November 1820, the *Essex* was cruising in latitude 0° 40′ S and longitude 119° 0′ W. Whales were sighted, boats lowered. The mate, back on deck for repairs, suddenly 'observed a very large spermaceti whale, as well as I could judge, about eighty-five feet in length; he broke water about twenty rods off our weather-bow, and was lying quietly, with his head in a direction for the ship. He spouted two or three times, and then disappeared. In less than two or three seconds he came up again, about the length of the ship off, and made directly for us, at the rate of about three knots. The ship was then going with about the same velocity...' For a full transcription of the relevant pages of the *Narrative* (ch. 2 and the beginning of ch. 3), see Appendix.

Detail for detail, that account will be echoed in THE CHASE – THIRD DAY (pp. 682–5, passim). The *Pequod*, too, is struck on the 'starboard bow'; Moby Dick, too, dives under the ship, 'grazing her keel as he went along'; orders of 'Up helm!' to steersmen are identical; in each case the whale attacks twice; 'retribution, swift vengeance, eternal malice were in his whole aspect...' Only, at the climax, the *Pequod* will sink much faster than the *Essex*.

307. *After the severest exposure, part of the crew* Such understatement attains its own grandiloquence. Only a few years previous Captain Bligh had made his famous voyage from near Tofua to Timor – a distance of almost 4,000 miles in forty-eight days. But the men of the *Essex*, covering half that distance, were at sea twice as long. The Marquesas, they knew, lay nearest. Then, the Society Islands. But, scared of being 'devoured by cannibals', the three surviving boats made for the coast of South America – only to succumb themselves, *en route*, to cannibalism.

Owen Chase is explicit: 'On the first of February, having consumed the last morsel, the captain and the three other men that remained with him, were reduced to the necessity of casting lots. It fell upon Owen Coffin to die, who with great fortitude and resignation submitted to his fate. They drew lots to see who should shoot him: he placed himself firmly to receive his death, and was immediately shot by Charles Ramsdale, whose hard fortune it was to become his executioner. On the 11th Brazilla Ray died; and on these two bodies the captain and Charles Ramsdale, the only two that were then left, subsisted until the morning of the twenty-third when they fell in with the ship *Dauphin*, as before stated, and were snatched from impending destruction.'

Melville noted: 'All the sufferings of these miserable men of the *Essex* might, in all human probability, have been avoided, had they, immediately after leaving the wreck, steered straight for Tahiti, from which they were not very distant at the time, & to which, there was a fair Trade wind. But they dreaded cannibals, & strange to tell knew not that for more than 20 years, the English missionaries had been resident in Tahiti; & that in the same year of the shipwreck – 1820 – it was entirely safe for the mariner to touch at Tahiti.

'– But they chose to stem a head wind, & make a passage of several thousand miles (an unavoidably roundabout one, too) in order to gain a civilized harbor on the coast of South America.' (*Sequel*)

This epic, two-thousand-mile long journey had been the ultimate source for Edgar Allan Poe's *The Narrative of Arthur Gordon Pym* (chs 11 and 12).

307. *shipwrecked him again upon unknown rocks* Five months out of Nantucket, the *Two Brothers* struck a reef at Raiatea, west of the Sandwich Islands. The ship was a total loss. 'Pollard, it seems, now took the hint, & after reaching home from this second shipwreck, vowed to abide ashore. He has ever since lived in Nantucket. Hall told me that he became a butcher there. I believe he is still living.' (*Sequel*)

Later Melville added in pencil and underlined three times: 'A night-watchman'. At the same time, perhaps, he annotated an earlier passage: 'Since writing the foregoing I – sometime about 1850–53 – saw Capt. Pollard on the island of Nantucket, and exchanged some words with him. To the islanders he was a nobody – to me, the most impressive man, tho' wholly unassuming, even humble – that I ever encountered.'

308. *The ship Union* The authentic particulars are recounted in Obed Macy's *The History of Nantucket* (Boston, 1835), which Melville certainly knew, as Extract 53 shows. Possibly he did not have the book to hand; his own surviving copy was not acquired until July, 1852.

308. *Commodore J—* Charles Anderson suggests this may have been Commodore Thomas ap Catesby Jones, who commanded the frigate *United States* on which Melville returned to Boston from Honolulu in 1844. He had commanded the *Peacock* on a voyage to the Sandwich Islands in 1825 (*Melville in the South Seas*, New York, 1939). Honolulu, close to Pearl Harbor, is the principal port of Oahu, third largest of the Hawaiian Islands.

309. *Ochotsh* Okhotsk, Siberian seaport on the Sea of Okhotsk, north of Sakhalin Island.

309. *Captain D'Wolf ... a New Englander* Captain John De Wolf II, husband of Allan Melvill's oldest sister Mary. He is

frequently mentioned in Georg Heinrich von Langsdorff's *Voyages and Travels in Various Parts of the World* (London, 1813), with whom he served from 1805–7, and in 1861 published his own *Voyage to the North Pacific and a Journey through Siberia More than Half a Century Ago.* De Wolf had retired in 1827; the following summer the nine-year-old Herman spent several months with him in his home at Bristol, Rhode Island (once the chief residence of Massasoit and his son, 'King Philip').

309. *Lionel Wafer, one of ancient Dampier's old chums* William Dampier (1651?–1715), buccaneer on the west coast of Spanish America and the Philippines, who later commanded a naval expedition to Australia and New Guinea, was on both privateering expeditions in which Alexander Selkirk was marooned on Juan Fernandez and rescued. Lionel Wafer (1660?–1705?), the surgeon, accompanied Dampier to the West Indies, Africa and into the Pacific. In 1699 he published *A New Voyage and Description of the Isthmus of America,* recounting a solitary stay of several months 'among the Darien Indians' (here quoted).

310. *The English ship Pusie Hall* 'In the year 1835, the ship *Pusie Hall* encountered a fighting whale, which after injuring and driving off her four boats, pursued them to the ship, and withstood for some time the lances hurled at it, by the crew, from the bows of the vessel, before it could be induced to retire: in this affair a youth in one of the boats was destroyed by a blow from the whale, and one of the officers was severely lacerated by coming in contact with the animal's jaw.' (Bennett, *Narrative of a Whaling Voyage*, vol. II, p. 218)

311. *amen with Solomon* *Ecclesiastes* i, 9.

311. *Procopius ... in the days when Justinian was Emperor and Belisarius general* In the *History of His Own Time* the Byzantine historian of the age of Justinian I – who accompanied Belisarius against the Vandals of North Africa, the Ostrogoths in Italy and the Persians – recounts: 'It was at that time also that the whale, which the Byzantines called Porphyrius, was caught. This whale had been annoying Byzantium and the towns about it for fifty years, not continually, however, but disappearing sometimes for a rather long interval. And it sank many boats and terrified the passengers of many others, driving them from their course and carrying them off to great distances.' *Porphyrius,* meaning 'purple' suggests 'imperial fish'. Again Melville's

source, almost certainly, was the article on 'Whale' in John Kitto's *Cyclopedia of Biblical Literature*, concluding: 'On the island of Zerbi, close to the African coast, the late Commander Davies, R.N., found the bones of a cachalot on the beach ...'

312. *brit* The spawn of herring and sprat: viz 'the minute, yellow substance, upon which the Right Whale largely feeds'. (BRIT)

47 THE MAT-MAKER

THE MAT-MAKER The setting derives from Olmsted, *Incidents of a Whaling Voyage*, pp. 87–8.

315. *a sword-mat, for an additional lashing* i.e. Matting for a further protection of the rigging. Queequeg handles the wooden sword with which the fabric is beaten close in the weaving.

316. *so strange a dreaminess ... mechanically weaving and weaving*

> In Being's floods, in Action's storm,
> I walk and work, above, beneath,
> Work and weave in endless motion!
> Birth and Death,
> An infinite ocean;
> A seizing and giving
> The fire of Living:
> 'Tis thus at the roaring Loom of Time I ply,
> And weave for God the Garment thou seest Him by.

(Carlyle's translation of the Earth-Spirit's claim to Goethe's Faust, *Sartor Resartus*, I, viii, 'The World out of Clothes')

From the very start Ishmael had been dogged, so he felt, by the 'invisible police officer of the Fates', cunningly urged to perform his role, cajoled into the delusion that it was a choice resulting from his own 'unbiased freewill and discriminating judgment'. (*LOOM*/INGS) Now he adjusts the hypothesis (in good Calvinist fashion) to both woof and warp, free will and necessity. cf. Jonathan Edwards' insistence on Christian freedom within the Law, free will *and* predestination (*Freedom of Will*, 1754).

316. *High aloft in the cross-trees ... Tashtego* stands suspended – madman, magician, prophet, seer – on a gallows.

317. *The Sperm Whale blows as a clock ticks* See THE FOUNTAIN, p. 478.

318. *like three samphire baskets* cf.

Half-way down
Hangs one that gathers samphire – dreadful trade!
(*King Lear* IV, vi, 14–15)

The aromatic leaves of the *herbe de Saint Pierre*, growing on cliffs by the sea, were used for pickling.

318. *their eager crews ... poised on the gunwale* Like marines from a gunship, about to throw themselves aboard a gun/whale.

48 THE FIRST LOWERING

318. *the living hair braided and coiled* A Medusa's head – for this Ahab/Perseus.

318. *secret confidential agents ... of the devil* 'And the Lord said, Who shall persuade Ahab, that he may go up and fall at Ramoth-gilead? ... And there came forth a spirit, and stood before the Lord, and said, I will persuade him. And the Lord said unto him, Wherewith? And he said, I will go forth, and I will be a lying spirit in the mouth of all his prophets. And he said, Thou shalt persuade him, and prevail also: go forth, and do so.' (*1 Kings* xxii, 20–22)

322. *like a horizontal burst boiler out of a Mississippi steamer* In the summer of 1840, aged twenty, Melville had stayed with his uncle Thomas Melville in the riverside town of Galena, Illinois. A complete novel, *The Confidence-Man: His Masquerade* (1857), was yet to be constructed of the experience.

327. *hissing ... like the erected crests of enraged serpents* For sailors and sea now shadow each other: that 'half-hissed reply', this 'hissing'; that 'erect posture', these erections; that 'living hair', these enraged serpents; their blades reflected in the 'knife-like' waves; their wolfish howl heard in the wind's howl.

327. *in one welded commotion* The booming gun boat strikes the gun/whale: 'the sail collapsed and exploded; a gush of scalding vapor shot up near by'.

328. *unconsumed, we were burning* A crew of Babylonian Jews in 'the midst of a burning fiery furnace'. (*Daniel* iii)

328. *on a waif pole* 'A pennoned pole . . . inserted upright into the floating body of a dead whale, both to mark its place on the sea, and also as token of prior possession . . .' (THE GRAND ARMADA); but here indicating only these waifs, strayed into 'that almighty forlorness'.

328. *that imbecile candle* cf.

The sorrows of hell compassed me about: the snares of death prevented me.
In my distress I called upon the Lord, and cried unto my God . . .

(*Psalm* xviii, 5ff.)

329. *The ship . . . was still cruising* Like the *Rachel*, at the close, 'in her retracing search after her missing children'. (EPILOGUE)

49 THE HYENA

THE HYENA Do not slink to safety which, in any case, will destroy you; trust, drown in the treachery of the howling infinite. That was the first existentialist lesson – of THE LEE SHORE. But this 'hyena' is, of course, a laughing hyena. Now that Ishmael too has hunted 'the Hyena Whale', he must confront the *whole* existentialist predicament in all its teasing horror: the random backlash of the Absurd.

cf. 'Deformity they signifie by a Bear; and an unstable Man by an Hyaena, because that animal yearly exchangeth its sex.' (Sir Thomas Browne, 'Of the Hieroglyphical Pictures of the Egyptians', *Pseudodoxia Epidemica* Bk. V, ch. 20)

329. *jolly punches in the side* 'Jollies? Lord help such jollies!' – shadow-boxing with such an unaccountable old Punch. cf. Ahab's mocking challenge to the gods: 'Come forth from behind your cotton bags'. (SUNSET) So modern mathematicians, following Heisenberg, talk of an Uncertainty Principle with the same assurance as Tarot players once speculated on The Joker.

329. *sort of genial, desperado philosophy* cf.

He would joke with hyaenas, returning their stare
With an impudent wag of the head:
And he once went a walk, paw-in-paw, with a bear,
'Just to keep up its spirits,' he said.

(Lewis Carroll, *The Hunting of the Snark*:
Fit the First, *The Landing*, 1876)

Having set out, it seems, as a disciple of Plato, or rather Sartor Resartus (in his 'patched boots'), Ishmael turns at last – under the impact of whaling – to this free and easy sort of philosophy, or *humeur noire*. He confronts THE HYENA, that is, not with Ahab's grim bravado, nor Stubb's bantering airs, but porpoise-like, in a 'spirit of godly gamesomeness', as a suicidal farce.

330. *what a devil's chase . . . a rough draft of my will* 'Short draughts – long swallows, men; 'tis hot as Satan's hoof'. (THE QUARTER-DECK)

331. *a stone was rolled away from my heart* This is the turning-point – the true peripeteia – of Ishmael's self-education, though his final test is yet to come. For this vaulted *Whale* is also a cunningly ghosted *Bildungsroman*: 'And, behold, there was a great earthquake: for the angel of the Lord descended from heaven, and came and rolled back the stone from the door . . .' (*Matthew* xxviii, 2)

After this ceremony of self-transcendence, that is, Ishmael too can join the ranks of the cool, collected – 'God's true princes of the Empire' who are wholly self-contained, relying on their own innermost resources. Now Ishmael's 'will' is locked up in his 'chest'. Now Ishmael, too, is beyond heaven and hell, beyond good and evil in Nietzsche's phrase. For Life – that is the joke, ha, ha! – is nothing but 'assimilation, injury, violation of the foreign and the weaker . . . not because it is moral or immoral in any sense, but because it is *alive* . . .' (*Jenseits von Gut und Böse*, 1886)

Thus it is that Ishmael has earned his right to final resurrection – to become 'poor Lazarus' himself (of THE CARPET-BAG), who alone will survive the final wreck. 'There is only one liberty,' wrote Camus in his *Notebooks*, 'to come to terms with death. After which, everything is possible.'

331. *unconsciously rolling up the sleeves* To the end Ishmael remains a simple seaman – one of the crew – though paradoxically capable of formulating his own conscious brand of philosophy. 'But, perhaps, to be true philosophers, we mortals should not be conscious of so living or so striving.' This roll of the sleeves, confirming the stone's roll, also re-echoes the roll of the charts, the roll of the whale, and a roll in bed with a bosom friend, whose shirt sleeves too were 'irregularly rolled up'. (THE COUNTERPANE)

50 AHAB'S BOAT AND CREW. FEDALLAH

FEDALLAH Arabic, 'feda' (*fedā*') + 'Allah' / 'the Sacrifice (or Ransom) of God'. Dorothée Melitsky Finkelstein interprets the name as a pun on 'fedai' (*fedā'i*), meaning 'the devoted one' or 'he who offers up his life'. (*Melville's Orienda,* pp. 223–39) The term was applied to the assassins – avenging ministers, or 'destroying angels', of the 'Old Man of the Mountain'. A sect of the Ismailiya movement, this secret brotherhood waged commando strikes against the princes of Islam in the name of 'the hidden prophet', the seventh and last Imam, Ishmael (Arabic, *Ismā'īl*).

And Ahab, 'old man of oceans'? Is not 'the last of the Grisly Bears' too an 'Old Man of the Mountain'? Does not Ahab too, in the end, despatch his own assassin? (p. 608, note) And Fedallah? Is he not a messenger of destruction? A *'fedā'ī'*, held to ransom, sacrificed at last in his secret cause?

332. *So Tamerlane's soldiers often argued* Timur Leng (Timur the Lame), the ruthless Mongol conqueror who slaughtered thousands and built pyramids of their skulls – another *alter ego* for this 'Khan of the plank' and hob-legged captain on his voyage of doom.

cf. 'The princes and Emirs of the court cast themselves at his feet and told him it was not reasonable so great a monarch should fight a duel; but he had no regard to their speeches, and continued his way.' (Petis de la Croix, *History of Timur-Bec, known by the Name of Tamerlain the Great,* I, 195)

332. *Until Archy's published discovery* cf. *HARK!* Both the American and English first editions read: 'Until Cabaco's published discovery . . .'

332. *an extra coat of sheathing* Like a harpoon's leather sheath, to withstand the pricking of that limb 'whittled down to a point'.

333. *such queer castaway creatures* Mansfield and Vincent associate 'Fedallah' with a more common Arabic name, 'Fadlallah'/'the Grace of God' (pp. 729–34). Melville may have come across it in *The Spectator* No. 578 (9 August 1714), which consists largely of a paraphrase of a tale from Ambrose Phillips' *The Thousand and One Days* (London, 1714–15).

Fadlallah, 'a Prince of great Virtues' married to the lovely Zemroude, went hunting one day with a visiting dervish. This dervish revealed a terrible secret: *'the Power of reanimating a dead Body, by flinging my own Soul into it'*. He performed the trick on a dead doe. Then Fadlallah had a turn. But no sooner had Fadlallah reanimated the doe, than the dervish shot his soul into Fadlallah's body and tried to kill the doe, which bounded off. The evil dervish then occupied the throne and claimed the unsuspecting Zemroude. Fadlallah's soul, meanwhile, migrating from the doe to a dead nightingale to the queen's dead lapdog, awaited its revenge.

The Spectator used the tale to illumine a current metaphysical conundrum. What is a 'person'? What assures us of our 'personal identity'? Locke, in equating identity with self-awareness, was anchored firmly to Descartes: 'the word *person* properly signifies a thinking intelligent being that has reason and reflection, and can consider itself as itself . . .' Viz. *Cogito ergo sum*: not identity of substance, but continuity of consciousness alone, can be the criterion.

And Fedallah? Is he not too a kind of dervish spirit? A 'lying spirit' (*1 Kings* xxii, 22)? A 'winged spirit' to raise 'the Spirit-Spout'? 'Ready' is his one 'half-hissed reply'. And Ahab? 'Is Ahab, Ahab?' Is he really a 'person', a 'being', in Locke's sense, that 'can consider itself as itself'? 'Is it I, God, or who, that lifts this arm?' (THE SYMPHONY)

333. *that Beelzebub himself might climb up the side* As Tashtego 'half suspended' seemed 'a son of the Prince of the Powers of the Air'; as Queequeg, in the 'living arc of a leap', the spirit of water; as Daggoo, shouldering Flask, 'the living magnanimous earth'; so the last of the four pagan harpooneers controls the last element. *'Ignei, aerii, aquatici spiritus salvete . . .'* The invocation is complete: *'Orientis princeps Belsibub, inferni ardentis monarcha & demigorgon, propitiamus vos, ut appareat et surgat Mephostophilis.'* (*Doctor Faustus* I, iii, 17–20)

333. *among the unchanging Asiatic communities* Sun and moon, light and dark, the spirits of good and evil in apposition, close the chapter in joint salute to Zoroastrian, and Manichaean, dualism. For Fedallah, as the crew soon learns, is a Parsee, descendant of Medes who migrated to India in the seventh and eighth centuries to escape Muslim persecution. To this day, they remain faithful to the teaching of Zarathustra and of the Magi, showing particular veneration for the god of fire. Parsees do not, in fact, worship fire; but, in Melville's eyes, magic Fedallah was

the fitting guardian angel for the 'Arkansas duellist'; a firebrand for the fire-worshipper; an insulated islander for the 'insulated Quakerish Nantucketer'. His 'half-hinted influence' represses the mere hint of Ahab's real desires; a gliding phantom, he haunts his dreams.

cf. 'Southern Asia, in general, is the seat of awful images and associations. As the cradle of the human race, it would alone have a dim and reverential feeling connected with it . . . The mere antiquity of Asiatic things, of their institutions, histories, modes of faith, &c., is so impressive, that to me the vast age of the race and name overpowers the sense of youth in the individual.' (De Quincey, 'The Pleasures of Opium', *Confessions of an English Opium Eater*, 1822)

334. *the angels indeed consorted with the daughters of men* 'And it came to pass, when men began to multiply on the face of the earth, and daughters were born unto them, that the sons of God saw the daughters of men that they were fair; and they took them wives of all which they chose . . .' (*Genesis* vi, 1–2).

334. *the devils also, add the uncanonical Rabbins* Such as the *Book of Enoch* or *Book of Jubilees* (the 'Little Genesis'), for example, which have survived outside the biblical and apocryphal canon in mainly Ethiopic versions. These pseudepigraphical texts of the second and first centuries B.C. – in their *midrashim* on *Genesis* – interpreted 'the sons of God' to have been fallen angels or devils moved by lust; their giant offspring, as violent and destructive.

'Rabbinus', the medieval latin form of 'rabbi', was used chiefly to designate Talmudic authorities. 'Uncanonical' here, however, suggests not only Jewish but *Christian* authorities outside the Scriptures and Canon Law. In particular, it evokes that indignant chorus of late medieval doctors opposed to the *canon Episcopi*, enshrined in the Canon Law.

The *canon Episcopi*, or *capitulum Episcopi*, simply asserted that night-flying and the metamorphosis of witches were hallucinations and that anyone who believed in them was 'beyond doubt an infidel and a pagan'. This remained the official doctrine of the church. But as 'Witches' Sabbats' spread relentlessly to every corner of Western Europe, a battery of sophistical, and increasingly hysterical, expositions (culminating in that encyclopedia of demonology, the *Malleus Maleficarum*, or 'Hammer of Witches', 1486) were produced to demolish the text. For by the late fifteenth century it was common knowledge that there were thousands such 'Sabbats' – some national, some international as on the Blocksberg – where witches flew to meet their demon lovers. First they circled in a dance round Satan, then kissed him, then threw themselves into promiscuous orgies with those 'whooping imps'. In one year alone, according to the *Malleus*, the Inquisitor of Como burnt forty-one witches, all of whom confessed to sexual intercourse with *incubi*.

The sexual capacity of such demons – especially the Devil's own potency – furnished matter for intense speculation: 'Some important theologians conjectured that the Devil equipped himself by squeezing the organs of the dead . . . Other experts advanced other theories, more profound than decent. But on the whole, Holy Mother Church followed the magisterial ruling of the Angelic Doctor, St Thomas Aquinas . . . According to him, the Devil could only discharge as *incubus* what he had previously absorbed as *succubus*. He therefore nimbly alternated between these postures . . .' (H. R. Trevor-Roper, *The Witch Craze in the Sixteenth and Seventeenth Centuries*, 1967)

51 THE SPIRIT-SPOUT

334. *across four several cruising-grounds* The Cape Verde islands lie due south of the Azores, off the western promontory of Africa. Unlike the *Acushnet*, the *Pequod* is bound for the Pacific by a 'devious zig-zag world-circle', doubling back from the River Plate, via the Carrol Ground, to the Cape of Good Hope: because 'an interval of three hundred and sixty-five days and nights' was before them. (THE CHART)

334. *on such a silent night a silvery jet*

> The moon shines bright. In such a night as this . . .
> (*Merchant of Venice* V, i, 1ff.)

Amid a magic murmur of half-rhymes and allusions, the *Pequod* glides, with Fedallah's gliding gait, after Fedallah's snow-white phantom jet.

334. *some plumed and glittering god* Suggesting Quetzalcoatl, the plumed serpent of the Aztecs, or Mayan Kulkulcán – an apt familiar for 'that anaconda of an old man' and his 'hair-turbaned' headsman. The feathered, solitary jet lures the *Pequod* to

those skull-piled pyramids of Teotihuacán and Cholula, greedy for human sacrifice. (See W. H. Prescott, *History of the Conquest of Mexico*, 3 vols., 1843.)

335. *as if some winged spirit had lighted in the rigging* cf. Fedallah on 'the mainmast head' with Milton's Satan in Eden:

> Thence up he flew, and on the Tree of Life,
> The middle Tree and highest there that grew,
> Sat like a Cormorant; yet not true Life
> Thereby regaind, but sat devising Death
> To them who liv'd ... (*Paradise Lost* IV, 194–8)

335. *as if two antagonistic influences* Unleashed by that 'half-hinted influence' to a permanent Manichaean dualism of light and dark, life and death, of which cleft Ahab is both the agonized focus and emblem.

336. *all its blue blandness ... lonesomely mild* Once again 'serenest azure' and 'mild gleams' are uneasy signs:

> The fair breeze blew, the white foam flew,
> The furrow followed free ...
> (Coleridge, *The Rime of the Ancient Mariner* Pt II, 103–6)

336. *Close to our bows, strange forms* 'The very deep did rot: O Christ! ...' The Ancient Mariner, natural herald of THE ALBATROSS, haunts this whole passage round the Cape:

> Beyond the shadow of the ship,
> I watched the water-snakes:
> They moved in tracks of shining white,
> And when they reared, the elfish light
> Fell off in hoary flakes. (Op. cit., Pt IV, 272–6)

336. *the inscrutable sea-ravens ... spite of our hootings* Owls, and the winds' howl, answer those birds of ill omen 'o'er the infected house'. (*Othello* IV, i, 20)

337. *Rather Cape Tormentoso Cabo Tormentoso* (the Cape of Storms) was the name originally given to the south-western horn of Africa by Bartholomew Díaz (1487). But King John II of Portugal 'hoping thence to discover the Indies, named it at his returne the "Cape of Good Hope" ...' (*Hakluytus Posthumus, or Purchas His Pilgrimes*, 1625)

Both first editions read 'Tormentoto'. Whether Melville misread a black-letter Hakluyt, or his printer erred, the pun leads unerringly from 'Hope' to 'this tormented sea'.

337. *as if manned by painted sailors in wax* Paradoxically inverting Coleridge's image:

> Day after day, day after day,
> We stuck, nor breath nor motion;
> As idle as a painted ship
> Upon a painted ocean.
> (*The Rime of the Ancient Mariner* Pt II, 115–18)

For the 'silvery silence' of the opening is now transformed to a 'muteness of humanity'; the whalers' cry, to these 'shrieks of the ocean'; the *Pequod*'s madness, to 'the swift madness and gladness' of the waves.

52 THE ALBATROSS

338. *off the distant Crozetts* The Crozet Islands, about two thousand miles south-east of the Cape of Good Hope.

338. *this craft was bleached* White as her name: 'Bethink thee of the *alba*/tross, whence come those clouds of spiritual wonderment and pale dread, in which that white phantom sails in all imaginations?' (p. 289)

338. *like the skeleton of a stranded walrus* By paronomasia suggesting *wall/rust*: 'All down her sides ... traced with long channels of reddened rust'.

> Her beams bemocked the sultry main,
> Like April hoar-frost spread;
> But where the ship's huge shadow lay,
> The charméd water burnt alway
> A still and awful red.
> (*The Rime of the Ancient Mariner* Pt IV, 267–71)

Those 'long-bearded look-outs' evoke the Mariner himself, 'whose eye is bright, whose beard with age is hoar'; 'this spectral appearance', his 'spectre-bark': 'And its ribs are seen as bars on the face of the setting Sun ...' (Pt III)

338. *so torn and bepatched the raiment* Sign of 'Sartor Resartus', whose every symbol is turned to 'patchwork'. A *Goney*: the very name seems resonant with distress. The key to this

mild and pallid skeleton – this gliding phantom – is made explicit only in the final encounter with the *Delight* (ch. 131).

> At length did cross an Albatross,
> Thorough the fog it came;
> As if it had been a Christian soul...
> (*The Rime of the Ancient Mariner* Pt I, 63–5)

340. *sights more sweet and strange than any Cyclades or Islands of King Solomon* 'Cyclades' was applied originally to the Aegean Islands forming a rough circle around Delos, Apollo's birthplace. Or was Melville perhaps thinking of the Venus de Milo, discovered on Melos in 1820? Or the quarries of white Parian marble from which she was cut?

The Solomons were discovered in the quest for biblical Ophir. (*1 Kings* x, 11) Sighted in 1568 by the Spaniard Alvaro de Mendaña, sailing from Peru in search of western islands – a fabled Inca El Dorado – they were named for King Solomon, though no gold was found. (See 'high-ruffed Mendanna', p. 378; and A BOWER IN THE ARSACIDES.)

The final dilemma poises Ishmael versus Ahab: the one still circling in amazement; the other midway whelmed.

53 THE GAM

341. *the Pine Barrens in New York State* Or rather the coastal plain – part sandy woodland, part swampland – of southern New Jersey.

341. *lone Fanning's Island* An 'uninhabited spot, but exceedingly prolific in fruit of all kinds' (*Omoo*, ch. 51): about 1,500 miles south of Hawaii, one of the Line Islands.

341. *the far away King's Mills* Grinding slow, but sure: among the Gilbert Islands, where the *Pequod* will meet her doom.

343. *Noah Webster's ark An American Dictionary of the English Language* (2 vols., 1828).

343. *GAM. NOUN* Rewriting Henry T. Cheever's definition: '*Gam* is the word by which they designate the meeting, exchanging visits, and keeping company of two or more whale ships, or a sociable family of whales.' (*The Whale and his Captors*, pp. 205–6)

54 THE TOWN-HO'S STORY

THE TOWN-HO'S STORY Itself conceivably an interpolation, this 'gam' alone became an extract, or trailer to herald the American edition: in *Harper's New Monthly Magazine* (October 1851) and the *Baltimore Weekly Sun* (8 November 1851).

345. *that secret part of the tragedy* That Moby Dick performed the inverted judgment of God – taking revenge out of Steelkilt's hands – 'never reached the ears of Captain Ahab or his mates'. The affair of the iron ball, that is, remained 'closely netted'.

347. *your old Callao* Headquarters of the U.S. Pacific squadron. Melville spent several weeks aboard the *United States* here between December 1843 and July 1844.

347. *craggy guns of lofty Mackinaw* Fort Michilimackinac, on the south shore of the straits of Mackinac (or Mackinaw), the great military post of the old Northwest throughout the fur-trading years of the eighteenth and early nineteenth centuries. In 1780–81 the fort and town were transformed from Old Mackinaw to the island.

Melville had passed through these straits, separating Lake Huron from Lake Michigan, on his way out to Galena, Illinois, in 1840 (p. 322, note). It was then he had made his own first-hand acquaintance with Steelkilt's country. The initial leg of the trip, from Albany, had taken him along the Erie Canal. At Buffalo he had embarked on the lake boat for the second and longest leg of his journey west.

347. *the fleet thunderings of naval victories* One of the first actions of the *War of 1812* was the capture of Mackinac: on 27 July, the American garrison, ignorant that war had been declared, was surprised by the British. Their attempt to recapture the fort, in August 1814, was unsuccessful and only with the Treaty of Ghent did the island pass permanently back into American hands.

347. *their peltry wigwams ... the gaunt pines* After those 'fleet thunderings', the puns crowd thick and fast. The wigwams are not only made of pelts, but paltry compared to 'lofty Mackinaw'.

347. *exported furs . . . to Tartar Emperors* Possibly of mink, or Hudson Bay sable (i.e. American marten).

347. *Winnebago villages* Of Indians of Sioux stock, centred on Lake Winnebago in east Wisconsin. For 'beech canoe', possibly read 'birch canoe'.

348. *with some good-hearted traits* The 'brutal overbearing' of 'this Nantucketer', part owner of the *Town-Ho*, is at least a partial reflection of Ahab's 'overbearing grimness': both are stubborn, hardy, 'doomed and made mad', fools 'branded for the slaughter'. The Radney/Steelkilt confrontation, then, offers at least a partial commentary on the Ahab/Starbuck impasse. For, however various the circumstances, Steelkilt – unlike Starbuck – withstands 'those more terrific, because more spiritual terrors, which sometimes menace you from the concentrating brow of an enraged and mighty man'. (KNIGHTS AND SQUIRES)

349. *his superior in general pride of manhood* The full implication of such 'unconquerable dislike' Melville was to explore again in *Billy Budd*, his swan-song, thirty-five years later. There a British warship replaces the American whaler; a dark-eyed master-at-arms, the ugly mate; an adolescent foretopman, the Lakeman desperado. There the antagonism, no longer mutual, but of crazed antipathy and naive incomprehension, involves both in disaster.

Then it will be a time of revolution; but Budd, though accused of mutiny, will prove no Parisian, entrenched behind barricades. Then a sock on the forehead (not the lower jaw) will prove fatal. Then no longer inert on the mizzen between 'the two crucified thieves' (his betrayers), but, Christ-like from the mainyard, Billy Budd will ascend to take 'the full rose of the dawn'.

Even an erotic innuendo, so typical of *Billy Budd*, is hinted. For what else is Radney but, by metathesis, 'randy'? What else that 'tower' but Steelkilt's 'pride of manhood'? A suppressed homosexual note – of swinging fist versus heavy hammer, 'fine bantam' versus sterile mule, Beauty versus the Beast – is the hallmark of Melville's devious style in confronting the mysteries of life at sea.

Here it is Radney, 'the predestined mate' alone, who is pulverized, literally crunched in the White Whale's jaw. The tragedy of *Billy Budd* will be that *all* (master-at-arms, subaltern, captain) are pulled down, *all* pulverized together.

349. *a flowing golden beard* As if to link the Lakeman with the hero of *White-Jacket* (Jack Chase of the 'abounding nut-brown beard') to whom *Billy Budd, Sailor* was one day to be dedicated.

353. *our grand Erie Canal* Connecting the Hudson at Albany to Lake Erie at Buffalo; completed in 1825. Young Melville had himself taken up surveying in the hopes of finding employment on the canal.

353. *Your chicha's very fine* A Peruvian liquor, from Inca times, made of maize and berries which are masticated and then allowed to ferment.

353. *on Roman arches over Indian rivers* 'The aqueducts, by means of which this canal is conducted over ravines and rivers, are eighteen in number. A representation is given of one which crosses the Mohawk, presenting the singular spectacle of a navigable stream, and a vessel gliding along its course, at the rate of four miles an hour, many feet above the broken and turbulent current of a river'. (*American Magazine of Useful and Entertaining Knowledge*, July 1836)

353. *those noble Mohawk counties* In central New York state.

353. *Venetianly corrupt and often lawless life* So too an urban metaphor, which is the *Town-Ho*'s mark, will pervade the *Bellipotent* – 'Cain's city', tarred and painted black. (*Billy Budd, Sailor*)

353. *There's your true Ashantee* The Ashanti, now part of Ghana, a warrior tribe long a threat to British power.

353. *Dame Isabella's Inquisition wanes in Lima* Established by Ferdinand and Isabella in 1478 to spy out converted Moors and Jews, the Spanish Inquisition survived well into the nineteenth century. Undermined by royal decrees of 1768 and 1773, the Inquisition was not abolished until 1820; the Holy Office not definitely suppressed until 1834. Only then were Spanish liberals assured unrestricted freedom to publish and think as they pleased: '... there are no Auto-da-Fé's in Lima now'.

Queen Isabella alone is singled out perhaps as the patron of Columbus and an ardent Catholic whose confessors, the Dominican Tomás de Torquemada and the Franciscan Cardinal Ximénez, both became Inquisitors General.

354. *St Dominic, purge it!* Patron of the cathedral of Lima. It was St Dominic whom Pope Innocent III sent to preach to the Albigensians – Dominicans, too, were later commissioned to root out that Manichaean heresy. Torquemada, the first Inquisitor General, was a Dominican, as were Krämer and Sprenger, the German witch hunters. As official theologians of the Inquisition, and its demonologists, Dominican friars were busy everywhere with testimonies and denunciations, racks and confessions. (cf. the imagery of the Spanish ship *San Dominick*, in *Benito Cereno*, 1855)

354. *Like Mark Antony* The triumvir, in slouched hat, floating on Roman arches over Indian rivers.

354. *except Sydney men* Ex-convicts, that is, from the first penal settlement of Australia.

355. *these sea-Parisians ... behind the barricade* On 22 February 1848, street fighting broke out in Paris. Two days later Louis Philippe abdicated and radicals, led by Louis Blanc, set up a Commune in the city hall. But feeling betrayed by their revolution, the workers rose against a decree bidding them disperse to their provinces and for four days in June there was bloody fighting in the barricaded streets of Paris. (See 'whether Louis Philippe, Louis Blanc', p. 251, note.)

359. *hissed ... inaudible to all but the Captain* 'Captain, by God, look to yourself' Steelkilt had warned; 'treat us decently, and we're your men; but we won't be flogged.' On this Golgotha, however, the final impiety is suppressed: 'Father, behold thy Son!'

360. *in the ship's run* The extreme after part of the bilge, i.e. at the furthest extremity from the forecastle.

361. *in the morning of the third day from that in which he had been betrayed* A deliberate echo of Christ-like resurrection after the tableau of the three-fold crucifixion in the mizzen rigging. 'The two trembling traitors', or 'crucified thieves' in this allegory, remain in the lowest inferno below the captain's quarters.

362. *a stupid Teneriffe man* Presumably it was being a *Canary* Islander that made him 'instinctively and involuntarily' sing out.

362. *"Jesu! what a whale!"* In a single ellipse, presenting the 'inverted visitation of one of those so called judgments of God'.

As Steelkilt stabbed Radney 'in the eye with the unflinching poniard of his glance', so Radney will be 'seen through that veil, wildly seeking to remove himself from the eye of Moby Dick'.

This text follows *Harper's New Monthly Magazine* in giving both exclamations to the Teneriffe man, the terse explanation to Ishmael at the Golden Inn. The first American edition read: '"... there she rolls!" Jesu, what a whale! It was Moby Dick.'

363. *in a sudden maelstrom ... plunged headlong* Which was Edgar Allan Poe's *A Descent into the Maelström* (1841); which will be Ahab's 'Norway maelstrom, and ... perdition's flames'. (THE QUARTER-DECK)

364. *headed by the Lakeman, all but five or six ... deliberately deserted* Are these clues to the schism within the Democratic Party, between conservatives and radicals, Hunkers and Barnburners, southern planters and northern abolitionists, slave-owners and Free Soil rebels, after the Baltimore Convention of 1844? 'The abortive mutiny of ten crewmen out of thirty, the early defection of seven of Steelkilt's associates, the ultimate capitulation of the others and the successful commandeering of another ship, follow closely the sequence of historical events from 1844, through the state-by-state bolts from the Party, to the Utica Convention of 1848 and the formation of the Free-Soil Party at Buffalo. Moreover, the geographical center of the new party was the very canal and lake region from which Steelkilt and his supporters came. The radical Free-Soil sentiment of New York and upper Ohio seems echoed in the "agrarian freebooting impressions" ascribed to the *Town-Ho*'s mutinous mate.' (Alan Heimert, '*Moby Dick* and American Political Symbolism', *American Quarterly* vol. XV, No. 4)

55 OF THE MONSTROUS PICTURES OF WHALES

OF THE MONSTROUS PICTURES OF WHALES cf. Sir Thomas Browne: 'OF MANY THINGS QUESTIONABLE AS THEY ARE COMMONLY DESCRIBED IN PICTURES'. (*Pseudodoxia Epidemica*, Bk 5)

367. *the incarnation of Vishnu ... learnedly known as the Matse Avatar* Second god in the triad Brahma-Vishnu-Siva, the Preserver. Among his nine incarnations are those of Krishna, god of fire and lightning, and of Matsya, the fish which saved Manu (the progenitor of man) from the deluge by means of an ark.

But here there is no such sculpture. Melville was misled, possibly by a too hasty glance at Thomas Maurice's *Indian Antiquities* (1798), whose account of the Matse Avatar immediately follows his tour of Elephanta; possibly by 'Varuna on a crocodile, one of the background figures for the Ardhanariśvara-Siva statue' (Mansfield and Vincent, p. 613). For the caves are devoted to Siva and his emblematic form – half *male* and half *female* – would fittingly deck this *Whale.*

367. *Guido's picture of Perseus rescuing Andromeda* In the National Gallery, London, when Melville saw it (December 1849), but on loan to the National Gallery of Ireland since 1862. Guido Reni, or Reni's studio rather, painted a series of versions on the Andromeda theme. Ahab too, of course, was modelled on a like *objet d'art*, 'Cellini's cast Perseus'.

367. *Hogarth ... in his own 'Perseus Descending'* The second of two engravings by Hogarth for *Perseus and Andromeda* (London, 1730), a play by the Shakespearean annotator, Lewis Theobald.

368. *the Prodromus whales of old Scotch Sibbald* Sir Robert Sibbald's *Scotia Illustrata, sive Prodromus historiae naturalis* (Edinburgh, 1683) contains some mention of whales, but no pictures. Melville probably had in mind not the *Prodromus* (or Introduction) but Sibbald's *Phalainologia nova, sive observationes de rarioribus quibusdam Balaenis in Scotiae littus nuper ejectis* (Edinburgh, 1692), which includes detailed information on a variety of whales, with illustrations.

368. *the book-binder's whale . . . introduced by an old Italian publisher* The dolphin and anchor – renowned colophon of the Aldine Press, founded in Venice in the 1490s by Aldus Manutius.

368. *hot springs and cold, Saratoga and Baden-Baden* Saratoga Springs, a popular spa since the 1820s, lies in eastern New York State; Baden-Baden, famous for its mineral baths since Roman times, in the Black Forest.

368. *the original edition of the 'Advancement of Learning'* (London, 1605), by Francis Bacon.

368. *in old Harris's collection of voyages* John Harris, *Navigantium atque Itinerantium Bibliotheca: or, a Compleat Collection of Voyages and Travels* (2 vols.: London, 1705). See Extract 30, note.

English whalers, too, were initiated at Spitzbergen. In 1610 the Muscovy Company sent their first ship to Spitzbergen with six Basque harpooners aboard to teach the art of catching right whales. When numbers began to fall off, the whalers pushed on to Jan Mayen, Greenland, and Davis Strait in search of quarry.

369. *one Captain Colnett* Capt. James Colnett, *A Voyage to the South Atlantic and round Cape Horn into the Pacific Ocean, for the Purpose of Extending the Spermaceti Whale Fisheries* (London, 1798) – a source for *Sketch Sixth* of *The Encantadas*, written three years later. The offending outline was by the captain himself.

369. *'Goldsmith's Animated Nature'* Like much of Goldsmith's *opus*, hackwork; his *History of the Earth and Animated Nature* (1774) was published in eight volumes, earning him a hundred guineas each.

369. *in 1825, Bernard Germain, Count de Lacépède ... a scientific systemized whale book Histoire Naturelle des Cétacés*, first published in 1804, became volume II of *Œuvres de M. le comte de Lacépède*, 1826. Melville is merely echoing Capt. Scoresby's comments in his *Account of the Arctic Regions*.

369. *the scientific Frederick Cuvier . . . Desmarest* Lacépède's *Histoire Naturelle* was further annotated by Anselme Gaëtan Desmarest (1784–1838). These glosses on both Cuvier's *De l'Histoire Naturelle des Cétacés* (Paris, 1836) and Desmarest's 'Chinese drawing' derive from Thomas Beale (pp. 13–14); but that ultimate, crushing 'squash' is Melville's.

370. *a full-grown Platonian Leviathan* Attaining the Platonic Form, or Idea, of a whale. 'Plutonian', however, would seem an apter term for this Leviathan 'only to be seen at sea in unfathomable waters'. Literally the whale is an infernal god, and the sinister echo chimes with Ahab's fatal obsession. Yet twenty chapters on the Sperm Whale proves after all 'a metaphysical professor' – 'a Platonian, who might have taken up Spinoza in his latter years'.

371. *Jeremy Bentham's skeleton, which hangs for candelabra* The father of Utilitarianism spent his last hours on a work entitled *Auto-Icon, or Farther Uses of the Dead for the Living*. His body he duly left for dissection; his skeleton (or 'auto-ikon'), fully clothed with a wax head imposed, he presented to University College, London, whose founder he is.

371. *as the great Hunter says* John Hunter, anatomist and surgeon (1728–93). The reference is to his 'Observations on the Structure and Oeconomy of Whales' (in *Philosophical Transactions of the Royal Society of London*, 1787, vol. 77). Melville's source is again Thomas Beale.

56 OF THE LESS ERRONEOUS PICTURES OF WHALES, AND THE TRUE PICTURES OF WHALING SCENES

372. *Huggins's is far better* William John Huggins (1781–1845), the marine painter. Beale refers to 'Mr Huggins' admirable print', and his composite outline is labelled 'Colnett, Huggins, and Beale'. (p. 14) Melville may also have seen aquatints after Huggins, for instance that of the *Samuel Enderby* leaving Cowes roads (1835). (See p. 555, note.)

372. *Beale's is the best* (*The Natural History of the Sperm Whale*, p. 14). The offending 'middle figure', at the head of chapter 2, is of a whale rearing so high as to seem poised on its tail. Beale's frontispiece of seven whales snapping, spouting and diving among five whale-boats is reproduced as Plate 8 of this edition. In his marginalia Melville wrote: 'Turner's pictures of whales were suggested by this book.' (See p. 104, note.)

372. *Sperm Whale drawings in J. Ross Browne* J. Ross Browne's *Etchings of a Whaling Cruise* (New York, 1846) contains eight steel engravings by J. Halpin from sketches furnished by Browne, or A. A. von Schmidt, as well as a dozen wood-cuts of poor quality referred to here. (See Plate 10.)

372. *the best outline pictures are in Scoresby* Of the twelve plates appended to volume 2 of Capt. W. Scoresby's *An Account of the Arctic Regions*, two are of the *Balaena Mysticetus*, or Right Whale.

372. *from paintings by one Garnery* Louis Garneray (1783–1857) began his marine paintings during an eight year stint as British prisoner of war. His pictures, as well as his accounts of adventures in the South Seas, were very popular in France. The two aquatints here described were published in about 1850. The first, 'Pêche du Cachalot', is reproduced as Plate 7.

374. *in that triumphal hall at Versailles* Louis Philippe transformed the royal palace into a national monument, creating the

Galerie des Batailles in its south wing. Melville had visited Versailles in December 1849.

374. *microscopic diligence of a Leuwenhoeck* Anton van Leeuwenhoek (1632–1723), the Dutch naturalist who collected over 247 microscopes and was the first to give a complete description of red blood cells.

375. *who subscribes himself 'H. Durand'* A common pseudonym among French engravers and woodcarvers.

57 OF WHALES IN PAINT; IN TEETH; IN WOOD; IN SHEET-IRON; IN STONE; IN MOUNTAINS; IN STARS

375. *On Tower-hill . . . a crippled beggar* Jay Leyda discovered this peg-legged beggar carrying a board in *Uncle Philip's Conversations with Young People about the Whale Fishery, and Polar Regions* (London, 1837).

376. *ladies' busks* Byproducts of the whale were omnipresent in sophisticated society: not only 'spermaceti candles' for brilliant weddings, whalebone stays for ladies' corsets, whalebone ribs for umbrellas, 'canes, umbrella-stocks, and handles to riding-whips', but ambergris 'soft, waxy, and so highly fragrant and spicy, that it is largely used in perfumery, in pastiles, precious candles, hair-powders, and pomatum'. (AMBERGRIS)

376. *owning no allegiance but to the King of the Cannibals* For the 'pale Usher' is now converted to a 'white sailor-savage', whose scrimshaw trophy is this sculptured *Whale*: intricate in its elaboration 'as a Latin lexicon'; as close packed in 'maziness of design' as Achilles's shield.

377. *that fine old Dutch savage, Albert Durer* Albrecht Dürer was German, of course. Melville is using 'Dutch' (or *duytsch, deutsch*) in a deliberately folksy manner, after the style of 'Pennsylvania Dutch'.

378. *once high-ruffed Mendanna trod* Though Alvaro de Mendaña in 1568 spent several months charting the Solomon islands, the idea of colonizing them had to be abandoned. (p. 340, note) His second expedition, nearly thirty years later, discovered some of the Marquesas and the Santa Cruz group, but not the Solomons. For three centuries they remained elusive.

But Dutch, English, French navigators had coasted or sighted the islands. The identification was largely achieved through the researches of French scholars, Philippe Buâche (1781) and the Count de Fleurieu (1790). By 1824 the whole archipelago had, in effect, been rediscovered. By 1848, a French mission had been founded, and again abandoned soon after the murder of the first vicar–apostolic. But the charting of the Solomons was by then almost completed.

378. *and old Figuera chronicled* The 'learned Doctor' Cristóbal Suarez de Figueroa's '*History of Mendanna's Voyage*' (Madrid, 1613), quoted in *Typee*, ch. 25.

378. *I have boarded the Argo-Navis* Argo, Hydrus, Piscis Volans, Cetus (the Whale) are all southern constellations. The hybrid Latin, linking Jason's *Argo* and Ahab's *Pequod*, transforms the Greek warriors' quest for a Golden Fleece to a chivalric cloth of gold in medieval 'heavens'. 'DENIQUE COELUM', the crusaders' cry, was Melville's family motto.

But Plutarch, oddly, supplied an Egyptian ancestry ('Of Isis and Osiris'). And Plutarch was Thomas Maurice's source in tracing the outlines of Typhon's 'everlasting wars with the beneficent Osiris' from 'the celestial Draco' of the north down through the equatorial Hydrus and Cetus to the antarctic Argo. If the 'great Polar dragon' (or Leviathan) was 'no other than the Evil Principle in nature personified', then antarctic 'Argo was the sacred ship of Osiris, and no other than the ark.' (*The History of Hindostan*, 2nd edn, Vol. I, pp. 312, 320)

When a 'grand argosy' appears at last, however, far from chasing or leaping, it is towed – heavily forging 'along, as if laden with pig-lead in bulk'. Such weightless quest is the condition of dream.

58 BRIT

378. *For leagues and leagues it undulated round . . . boundless fields of ripe and golden wheat* cf. 'Go visit the Prairies in June . . .' Not a hint in the prologue is not picked up later: 'the one charm wanting' in the Prairies is now supplied by this water pastoral of 'reapers and mowers, who go into the farmers' meadows armed with their own scythes' (pp. 153, 282). As knee-deep Tigers lurked there, so here the whole ocean will turn 'a savage tigress overlaying her own cubs'.

378. *that wondrous Venetian blind* The metaphor (and pun) flashes its coded clue of turbulent depths beyond the sluggish, inert calm of this 'meadow-like appearance'. Dream-city of masques and gondoliers – eternal water pastoral – 'Venice' here signals corruption and unmasking of pastoral illusion: 'by rows of snow-white chapels . . . flows one continual stream of Venetainly corrupt and often lawless life'. (THE TOWN-HO'S STORY)

379. *all creatures of the land are of their kind in the sea* One such 'old naturalist' was Thomas Fuller. Extract 25 continues: 'Who made the mighty whales, who swim in a sea of water, and have a sea of oyl swimming in them? who first taught the water to imitate the creatures on land? so that the sea is the stable of horse-fishes, the stall of kine-fishes, the stye of hog-fishes, the kennell of dog-fishes, and in all things the sea the ape of the land.' ('The Good Sea-Captain', *The Holy State and the Profane State*, 1642: Bk II, ch. 20)

380. *with Portuguese vengeance had whelmed a whole world* Conceivably Melville had read Southey's *History of Brazil* (1810–19). But probably he is referring to the Portuguese slave trade from the Congo and Angola that, despite the British embargo, continued booming throughout the 1840's. One Portuguese monopoly on the Dahomey coast was said to be worth £300,000 in annual imposts. As many as 50,000 slaves were reaching Brazilian ports like Pernambuco in a single year.

380 *Preternatural terrors under the feet of Korah* 'And the earth opened her mouth, and swallowed them up, and their houses, and all the men that appertained unto Korah, and all their goods. They, and all that appertained to them, went down alive into the pit, and the earth closed upon them: and they perished from among the congregation.' (*Numbers* xvi, 32–3)

As Korah stirred open rebellion against Moses, so Ahab is a self-declared rebel against God; and as Korah's fate was a pit that 'closed', so Ahab's is to be a 'yawning gulf', whose sides collapse over him. Well might the crew of the *Pequod*, like the men of Korah's company, exclaim: 'O God, the God of the spirits of all flesh, shall one man sin, and wilt thou be wroth with all the congregation?' (*Numbers* xvi, 22)

380. *worse than the Persian host* Herodotus tells the story of Oroetes, Persian satrap of Sardes, who lured Polycrates, tyrant of

Samos, across to the mainland and crucified him. (Herodotus III, 120–25)

380. *Consider the subtleness of the sea* How 'every strange, half-seen, gliding, beautiful thing that eludes him; every dimly-discovered, uprising fin . . .' has turned a delusive spectre in that Byronic blue, and emblematic, 'soul' – or *Over-Soul.* (THE MAST-HEAD, p. 257; p. 212, note)

381. *one insular Tahiti, full of peace and joy* But this, too, is western illusion. Here too, as in Conrad's *Heart of Darkness,* horrors abound: 'the roaring streams from Pirohitee's peak of spears, when they leap down the crags and drown the villages'.

59 SQUID

381. *one transparent blue morning* It is the seeming transparency of blue which is the key to its horror. And the consequences ('with one half-throttled shriek') are always the same. Now 'the long burnished sun-glade' extends the pastoral illusion; a preternatural stillness draws on 'preternatural terrors'.

382. *innumerable long arms . . . like a nest of anacondas* The water-boa, largest of anacondas, reaches a length of thirty feet.

383. *the great Kraken of Bishop Pontoppodan* In thanking Hawthorne for his 'joy-giving and exultation-breeding' letter, Melville again invoked the Kraken: 'Lord, when shall we be done growing? As long as we have anything more to do, we have done nothing. So, now, let us add Moby Dick to our blessing, and step from that. Leviathan is not the biggest fish; – I have heard of Krakens.' (7 November 1851)

This largest of all sea monsters was first mentioned by Erik Pontoppidan, Bishop of Bergen, in his *Natural History of Norway* (1752): '. . . whose back, or upper part, which seems an English mile and a half in circumference (some have affirmed more), looks at first like a number of small islands, surrounded with something that floats like sea-weeds. At last several bright points or horns appear, which grow thicker the higher they emerge, and sometimes stand up as high and large as the masts of middle-sized vessels. In a short time it slowly sinks, which is thought as dangerous as its rising, as it causes such a swell and whirlpool as draws everything down with it, like that of Maelstrom.' (John Knox, *A New Collection of Voyages*, 1767)

384. *only as the Anak of the tribe* 'And there we saw giants, the sons of Anak, which came of the giants . . .' (*Numbers* xiii, 33)

60 THE LINE

384. *the Manilla rope . . . far more soft and elastic* Of 'that vivid tiger-yellow complexion peculiar to some of the aboriginal natives of the Manillas; – a race notorious for a certain diabolism of subtilty . . .' (THE FIRST LOWERING)

384. *a golden-haired Circassian* The Cherkess region, between the Black Sea and the Caucasus, was ceded to Russia by the Ottoman Empire in 1829. It was, at this time, the scene of desperate resistance to Russian penetration by its Muslim tribes.

384. *In length . . . something over two hundred fathoms* cf. 'The quantity of line withdrawn from the different boats . . . amounted altogether to 10,440 yards or nearly six English miles'. (Extract 60)

385. *the worm-pipe of a still* The coiled tube, connected with the head of a still, in which vapour is condensed.

385. *layers of concentric spiralizations* 'Over Descartian vortices you hover' – of both rope and sea.

385. *a prodigious great wedding-cake* Because painted white presumably, and secreting 'an elongated Siamese ligature' (p. 426) to wed whaler to whale: 'Gayer sallies, more merry mirth, better jokes, and brighter repartees, you never heard . . .' The bridal is fêted with ale-mug, 'harp-string', and hung 'festoon'.

386. *as Indian jugglers, with the deadliest snakes* Or Hindu acolytes of Vishnu and Siva. Sailors and sea again shadow each other: what was the squid's 'pulpy mass', becomes the novice whaleman's 'shaken jelly'.

387. *like the six burghers of Calais before King Edward* In 1347, after an eleven month siege, Calais fell to Edward III. The story, like that of the White Hoods of Ghent, is told by Froissart: Edward had promised to spare the town if six prominent citizens offered their lives. The mayor, Eustache de Saint-Pierre, and five others, appeared before the king – barefoot, in shirts, with halters round their necks. Edward's queen, Philippa, interceded and saved their lives.

387. *being made a Mazeppa of* The Polish nobleman, hero of Byron's poem (1819); the source is Voltaire's *Charles XII*. Caught in an intrigue, the youthful Mazeppa was tied naked by the injured husband to the back of a wild horse. Lashed to madness, the horse galloped off, through forests and rivers, on and on till it reached its native steppes, where it collapsed and died. Himself on the point of death, Mazeppa was rescued by Ukrainian peasants.

387. *the seemingly harmless rifle* Conceived, yet again, by dissecting the pun implicit in 'gunwale'.

This conjunction of contraries – of whizzing steam-engine and rocking cradle, death and birth, calm and storm, rifle and ball – lies at the very roots of *Moby-Dick*. For 'all are born with halters round their necks'; all born at the sign of 'the Trap!'; initiates all 'at this grim sign of the Thunder Cloud'.

That 'swift, sudden turn' prepares for 'the flying turn' to catch first Pip, then Ahab, round the neck; this cradle, for the serene playfulness of the nursing whales. But also for the final glimpse of '*the rocking boat*', when death is literally restored to life, and the full implication of 'a certain self-adjusting buoyancy' is compressed, with almost Chinese concision, into a '*coffin life-buoy*' – the oxymoron closing on a pun.

61 STUBB KILLS A WHALE

388. *my soul went out of my body . . . sway as a pendulum will* Thus the captain's crazed somnambulism is linked to the passive drowsiness of his crew, satanic delusion to pastoral illusion – just as this swaying pendulum on the foremast-head recalls Starbuck's glimpse of Ahab in his cabin: 'the closed eyes . . . pointed towards the needle of the tell-tale that swung from a beam in the ceiling'. (THE SPIRIT-SPOUT)

All Melville's imagery is 'tell-tale': this 'spell of sleep', this 'enchanted air', this 'dreamy mood' drenched in blue, word for word deliberately recalls 'the dreamiest, shadiest, quietest, most enchanting bit of romantic landscape in all the valley of the Saco . . .' The mood of pastoral idyll is always a daze of reverie, merging into sleep, where the breeze is languid, the Right Whales sluggishly scythe, the white squid lazily disentangles itself from the azure, and the Sperm Whale lazily undulates in the trough of the sea.

'Trance' is the key-word: of the tranced valley, the tranced ship indolently rolling, 'the wide trance of the sea'. And its complement is always this 'shock' of self-possession, this re-awakening, when 'identity comes back' *in horror*.

Here begins Ishmael's second test; and 'the shrouds' he grasps, like his captain rounding the Cape, are a constant *memento mori*.

389. *like a portly burgher smoking his pipe* In a Flemish genre painting by David Teniers, the younger, say, or Adriaen Brouwer's *The Smoker*. Yet the image, so benign at first glance, has its sinister undertone. For this whale, like the burgher too, 'is supplied with teeth in order to attack and tear': the Sperm Whale is 'at once so artful, bold, and mischievous, as to lead to its being regarded as the most dangerous to attack of all the known species of the whale tribe'. (Extract 62)

Ironies within ironies lurk inside this nest of Chinese boxes. Earlier the whalemen, turned snake-charmers, had mirrored the sea-squid; now the Sperm Whale, glistening like a mirror, with a puff returns the reflection. Posing as Mayor de Saint-Pierre and his Calais burghers, the hunters confront not a king, they find, but a fellow-bourgeois.

As the whale smokes his afternoon pipe, so Stubb inevitably lights his. Puffer pursues spouter: and as the whale perpendicularly flits 'his tail forty feet into the air' to sink out of sight, so *vice versa* rings out Stubb's cry to 'raise the buried dead perpendicular out of their graves, boys'. Death answers life; life, death. On all sides man echoes ocean; the ocean, man. Till in the final slaughter – as 'jet after jet of white smoke was agonizingly shot from the spiracle of the whale, and vehement puff after puff from the mouth of the excited headsman' – whaler and whale become one.

Every image is reflected within this folding mirror: as the ocean had tossed 'like a savage tigress', so Daggoo now strains on his seat 'like a pacing tiger in his cage'; Ahab, ablaze, launches into 'boiling water'; over shark-infested depths, the boat itself becomes 'a shark all fins ... in that rocking commotion'.

'Form now, Indian-file ...': for the Ontario Indians, too, play their role, and the Indian war-whoop. Tash is a Gay-Header; his crew-mates, all warrior Pequots. And in the final blood-bath – when a slanting sun plays upon the 'crimson pond in the sea' – the six burghers are literally transformed at last to 'red men'.

The very point counterpoint of the imagery, turned over and

upside down, till reality becomes reflection, and reflection reality, is condensed to an emblem: the pivotal track of the whaleboat. Once the line is drawn taut, 'you would have thought the craft had two keels – one cleaving the water, the other the air – as the boat churned on through both opposing elements at once'.

389. *the helmsman could handle the spokes* This *wheel* seems to contradict an earlier account of the helmsman's *tiller*. (THE SHIP) But sometimes a wheel was fixed to and rode upon a tiller. The helm of the *Charles W. Morgan*, now at Mystic, Connecticut, is so designed.

390. *from the mad yeast which he brewed* Frothed, paronomastically, by a 'whale' to 'ale'.

390. *Grenadier's steak Macrurus fabricii* or *rupestris*, a deep-sea fish.

391. *something went hot and hissing ... a hempen blue smoke* This hiss of the serpent line, that heat 'like ringed lightnings', all point at Ahab. Steam-engine, fire-arms, 'devil's blue' – the symbols converge; and justice, Melville ensures, will be poetic.

392. *carefully churning and churning* The churning boat contracting shark-like to a single point, the lance; the living trance of the crew transfigured to the death trance of the whale (*Walwian*, to roll, to wallow); the spasmodic crack of the gun/wale, to these spasmodically cracking gasps; till jet after jet 'shot' into the frighted air.

392. *some gold watch that the whale might have swallowed* To become a clock the crocodile swallowed in pursuit of Captain Hook: 'it goes tick, tick, tick, tick inside him; and so before he can reach me I hear the tick and bolt. Once I heard it strike six...' (*Peter Pan*, Act II, 1904) See David Park Williams, 'Hook and Ahab: Barrie's Strange Satire on Melville'. (*P.M.L.A.* LXXX, December 1965)

393. *gush after gush of clotted red gore ... purple lees of red wine* cf. '... and he shall slay the dragon that is in the sea. In that day sing unto her, a vineyard of red wine.' (*Isaiah* xxvii, 1–2)

For 'ten or fifteen gallons of blood are thrown out of the heart at a stroke, with immense velocity.' (John Hunter, Extract 47)

393. *'Yes; both pipes smoked out!'* The 'prodigious great wedding-cake' and these smoked out pipes curiously evoke another ceremony – that of Queequeg and Ishmael 'exchanging

puffs' in the Spouter-Inn: 'as though naught but death should part us twain'.

62 THE DART

394. *long experience in various whalemen of more than one nation* Melville's own experience, of little more than two years, was aboard an American whaler, the *Acushnet* (January 1841–July 1842), the Australian *Lucy Ann,* on which he escaped from the Marquesas, and the *Charles and Henry* of Nantucket, that took him from Tahiti, via the Galapagos, to Hawaii. (p. 168, note)

63 THE CROTCH

395. *Out of the trunk ... grow the chapters* To assert, with Ishmael, that his inspiration was organic, is not to deny the structural core of his sixfold scheme, charting the *Pequod*'s course from New England, through the Atlantic and Indian oceans, via the China Sea to the Pacific and her fated rendezvous on the equator. 'Behind the chapter-clusters that define the novel's leafy configuration are solid trunk and branches'. (Herbert G. Eldridge, '"Careful Disorder": The Structure of *Moby-Dick*', *American Literature* 39, 1967)

64 STUBB'S SUPPER

396. *the great canal of Hang-Ho, or whatever they call it* From the 360-mile-long 'grand Erie Canal', Ishmael turns to the authentic 850-mile-long Grand Canal (opened in the fifth century B.C., completed by Kublai Khan in 1289 A.D.), connecting the Yangtze with the Pei River and the city of Hangchow with Tientsin. *Yün-ho,* its Chinese name, means 'transit river'; *Chah-ho,* 'river of flood gates'; part of its earliest section, however, followed the old bed of the *Hwang-ho,* or Yellow River. Thus Ishmael's own mocking ideogram for these coolies on the tow-path: *Hang-Ho,* viz. 'born with halters round their necks'.

399. *were you to turn the whole affair upside down ... a shocking sharkish business* These gilded knives and jewel-hilted mouths explicitly extend the mirror imagery. The invariable partnership of shark and man forms the ironic base not only for

Fleece's sermon ('Belubed fellow-critters') but for Queequeg's SHARK MASSACRE, its sequel. So too the sharks' social hilarity – their gay and jovial spirits around the dead Sperm Whale – echo the gay sallies of the whale-boat crew, whose harpooneer was himself a Gay-Header. All are cannibals, all laughing hyenas.

400. *something the matter with his knee-pans* Another limper, like his captain: 'I never yet saw him kneel.' (p. 331)

401. *Is not one shark dood right* 'Has not one shark as good a right ... ?'

401. *'Well done, old Fleece! ... that's Christianity'* viz. 'when the word of Stubb came a second time, Fleece did the mate's bidding. And what was that, shipmates? To preach Charity to the face of Indifference! That was it!'

Slap echoes slap. This 'sermon' from a mount parodies THE SERMON, as this grizzled nonagenarian caricatures Bildad (mumbling to a mumbling congregation) – or rather St Francis preaching to the birds, or the Good Shepherd himself 'invested in the fleece of celestial innocence and love'. For this sheep is a black sheep, 'of an Ethiopian hue' like the whale – another victim of Stubb's humour.

402. *ober de Roanoke* Flowing from the Appalachians into Albemarle Sound, North Carolina.

403. *as they fetched Elijah 2 Kings* ii, 11.

403. *the lubber's hole* A hole in the platform of the maintop, which saves climbing over the shrouds.

65 THE WHALE AS A DISH

405. *a great porpoise grant from the crown* A privilege granted the monks at 'Dunfermling' by Malcolm IV: *'Capita piscium qui dicuntur Crespeis praeter linguam, qui in meo Dominio ex illa parte Scottwatir applicuerint, in qua parte illorum Ecclesia sita est* ... The last shows, that the Meer-swine and Porpesses, and lesser sort of whales (which I guess were meant by Crespeis) were matter of Trade and the oyl was imployed, as a Charter hath it, *ad luminaria Ecclesiae*'. (Sir Robert Sibbald, *The History, Ancient and Modern, of the Sheriffdoms of Fife and Kinross*, Pt 4, ch. 1) See Extract 31.

Melville may have become immersed in this sourcebook in

tracing his family name back to Scotland. Most famous of the clan, Andrew Melville, became rector of St Andrews in 1590.

405. *Zogranda* An anagram, Willard Thorp suggested, of Sangrado, the Valladolid doctor to whom Gil Blas attached himself. The information, as usual, is Scoresby's: 'They also eat the skin of the whale raw, both adults and children; for it is not uncommon, when the females visit the whale-ships, for them to help themselves to pieces of skin, preferring those with which a little blubber is connected, and to give it as food to their infants, who suck it with apparent delight.'

405. *like old Amsterdam housewives' dough-nuts or oly-cooks* 'Olykoek' (Dutch *oliekoek*), a fried cake or cruller.

405. *a solid pyramid of fat ... white meat of a cocoanut* This culinary catalogue signals a whole range of now established imagery, reduced to telegraphic code: the 'prize ox' recalling whaler and whale 'yoked together, like colossal bullocks'; the buffalo evoking 'Ontario Indians', or backwoodsmen swinging their rifles from the wall; the creamy spermaceti, the squid's 'vast pulpy mass ... of a glancing cream-color'; the 'pyramid of fat', like the pyramid profile of the whale, a recurrent maze of Egyptian imagery initiated by 'the idolatrous dotings of the old Egyptians upon . . . their huge bake-houses the pyramids'. (LOOMINGS)

But the whale not only reflects the warrior-frenzy, horror and idolatry of the *Pequod*: the white cocoanut drops like an echo to her 'three tall tapering masts' mildly waving to a languid breeze 'as three mild palms on a plain'. Both pyramid and cocoanut, hieroglyphically speaking that is, are present in the whale; both idolatry and pastoral in those 'mysterious cyphers'; and both are illusory.

406. *In the long try watches* i.e. Night watches in the try-works.

406. *with an 'Et tu Brute!' expression* Behind the shaggy dog latin, lurks an earlier allusion to the whale as Caesar. (p. 305) For the schoolboy bathos of that pun crowns Ishmael's symbolic display: a kind of occult, or metaphysical, proof of the identity of man and beast. 'Verily I say unto you, It shall be more tolerable for the land of Sodom and Gomorrha in the day of judgment, than' for thee, civilized and enlightened gourmand. (*Matthew* x, 15)

406. *Cannibals? who is not a cannibal?* 'For we are all killers, on land and on sea; Bonapartes and Sharks included.' (CETOLOGY) 'Nay further, we are what we all abhorre, *Anthropophagi* and Cannibals, devourers not onely of men, but of our selves; and that not in an allegory, but a positive truth; for all this masse of flesh that wee behold, came in at our mouths; this frame wee looke upon, hath beene upon our trenchers; In briefe, we have devoured our selves, and yet doe live and remayne our selves.' (Sir Thomas Browne, *Religio Medici*, Pt I, sect. 37)

It was Montaigne, in his germinal essay *Of Cannibals* (familiar to both Browne and Melville), who first fostered the paradox that cannibals, far from being an ultimate aberration of mankind, should rather serve as exemplars of 'the laws of nature', and of a lost Golden Age.

66 THE SHARK MASSACRE

408. *the whole round sea was one huge cheese* It was the whale line which had first been 'one round, cheese-shaped mass' – associated not with maggots, but 'the worm-pipe of a still'.

409. *one dam Ingin* The oath, like the snap of the shark's jaw, rebounds on the cannibal, and all fellow Pequots. But the agony of that boomerang lid is itself metaphysical: if a god made the shark, he also made Queequeg who murdered the shark – and Stubb too 'more of a shark dan Massa Shark hisself'. A vision of God, whether pagan or Christian, is our own treacherous self-reflection; and the jovial blood-letting Sabbath that follows turns the whole ship to 'a shamble; every sailor a butcher'.

67 CUTTING IN

409. *this vast bunch of grapes* Where whales gush out such wine, some deeper sacrilege of Holy Communion is hinted.

410. *as an orange is ... stripped by spiralizing it* 'The coils of rigging' and whale line 'spirally coiled' have left their stigma. The blubber, flayed in 'concentric spiralizations', and coiled away, is itself now a vortex over which the tackles hover.

410. *the prodigious blood-dripping mass ... let down from the*

sky As if the corporal presence of the Eucharist itself – to 'pitch' the non-observer headlong overboard.

68 THE BLANKET

412. *the famous hieroglyphic palisades on the banks of the Upper Mississippi* The Indian symbolism, soon metamorphosed to a poncho, here rebounds literally on the whale's back. But 'palisades' conceals its own clue: to the 'Piasa' Rocks, north of Alton, Illinois.

According to the early western traveller, Edmund Flagg, 'the name is of aboriginal derivation, and, in the idiom of the Illini, denotes "the bird that devours men"' (1836–7). During the 1840s, apparently, traces of an enormous bird with spread wings were still visible. (See John W. Nichol, 'Melville and the Midwest', *P.M.L.A.*, Sept. 1951.) Melville may have heard – or even seen a reproduction – of these 'mystic rocks' on his visit to Galena in 1840.

413. *Agassiz* Louis Agassiz (1807–73), Swiss zoologist and geologist. His *Études sur les glaciers* (1840), written in Neuchâtel, presented the first exposition of glacial movement and deposit. In 1846 he visited the United States to deliver the Lowell lectures, and two years later accepted a professorship at Harvard. These icebergs on the New England coast play, as it were, prelude to a theme: the polar parable that concludes this chapter.

413. *counterpane: or, still better, an Indian poncho ... skirting his extremity* cf. Ishmael in New Bedford trying on Queequeg's poncho, or wrapt in a counterpane. cf. Professor Teufelsdröckh's conclusion that all symbols are clothes; all clothes symbols. (*Sartor Resartus*) cf. Ahab in his skirted jacket, Ishmael in his frock, Queequeg in his 'Highland costume', and the prophet Gabriel cabalistically enveloped in long skirts.

414. *the rare virtue of a strong individual vitality, and ... of thick walls* cf. Starbuck wrapt in 'his pure tight skin', with flesh 'hard as twice-baked biscuit'. But Ahab sees *only* the thick wall, the veil, the whale shoved near: 'Sometimes I think there's naught beyond.' (p. 262)

414. *remain warm among ice ... Be cool at the equator* Thus runs the gospel according to Melville – or Ishmael, the outcast. Thus his 'selectest champions from the kingly commons': Queequeg 'cool as an icicle' and the 'aloof' Bulkington.

Freighted with emblems – idolatrous pyramids, Indian treachery, entangled serpent horror – whale and whalemen are 'yoked together' for good and ill. The whale's 'rare virtue' too but reflects Nantucket virtues: '*Isolatoes* ... I call such, not acknowledging the common continent of men, but each *Isolato* living on a separate continent of his own.' (KNIGHTS AND SQUIRES)

414. *Of erections, how few are domed like St Peter's!* 'This is a world in itself; a refuge from both heat and cold; it hath a season of its own, perennial spring, which the atmosphere without can never affect.' (Mme. de Stael, *Corinne; or, Italy*, Bk 4, ch. 3)

The Sabbath shamble is sacrilegiously crowned by St Peter, just as Stubb had been mockingly posed as Eustache de Saint-Pierre, the crew as rock samphire, Queequeg as Czar Peter, and the sign on the Spouter-Inn was inscribed 'Peter Coffin'. Not 'upon this rock' (of Peter), but New England rocks, *Moby-Dick* is to be built.

'For small erections may be finished by their first architects; grand ones, true ones, ever leave the copestone to posterity.' (CETOLOGY) Those puns, in the end, erect a vast pulsing phallus, vitally transcendent of the architecture at its base.

69 THE FUNERAL

414. *The vast white headless phantom*

Prone on the Flood, extended long and large
Lay floating many a rood ...

(*Paradise Lost* I, 195–6)

Peeled, the whale becomes a squid-like horror: beneath the azure, a 'white ghost'. And 'every rod' that it floats, turned to 'square roods of sharks', marks the cross upon which Christ died; every *requin*, or shark, a *Requiem Eternam*. (p. 289, note)

415. *that great mass of death* White as the squid's 'white mass', inevitably dissolving – amid such pious mourners, at its own funeral banquet – into a parody of solemn, high, pontifical Mass.

415. *as silly sheep leap over a vacuum* In 'some sheepfold among the Green Mountains'. (p. 124) 'Silly sheep', by metathesis, prompts 'seely ship' (Old English *saelig*), recalling the original meaning 'spiritually blessed', 'holy', 'innocent'. So

'simple' (the sheep's epithet on their next appearance) evokes a whole sliding range of reference from innocence to stupidity.

cf, Erasmus: 'And such as are destin'd to eternal life are called sheep, than which creature there is not anything more foolish... And yet Christ professes to be the Shepherd of his Flock, and is himself delighted with the name of a Lamb.' (*Encomium Moriae*) Or Kierkegaard: 'Just try to imagine quite clearly to yourself that the model is called a "Lamb", that alone is a scandal to natural man; no one has any desire to be a lamb.' (*Journal*, 1849)

415. *There are other ghosts than the Cock-Lane one* 'Again, could anything be more miraculous than an actual authentic Ghost? The English Johnson longed, all his life, to see one; but could not, though he went to Cock Lane, and thence to the church-vaults, and tapped on coffins.' (Carlyle, *Sartor Resartus*, Bk 3, ch. 8)

Mysterious noises heard at No. 33 Cock Lane, Smithfield, attributed to a ghost exposing a murder, were themselves exposed in 1762 as a hoax by one William Parsons, his wife and daughter. Dr Johnson, who took part in the investigation, was not taken in. 'But the rumor of a knocking ... will terrify a whole city.' (THE CHAPEL)

Melville was either muddled (despite Boswell's account), or elaborating an artful cross reference (which seems more likely). For this Cock Lane ghost, deceiving the Anglican Johnson, suggests none other than Christ. That this cock and bull story was perpetrated by a family of 'Parsons' must have chiefly delighted Melville, strolling 'down Holborn Hill through Cock Lane (Dr Johnson's Ghost) to Smithfield (West)' (*Journal*, 10 November 1849)

70 THE SPHYNX

417. *the giant Holofernes's from the girdle of Judith* For the story of the Assyrian general and the Jewish widow, see the apocryphal book of *Judith*.

417. *the Sphynx's in the desert* Near the great pyramid at Giza. Ahab outmatches Oedipus (club-foot) in challenging the Sphynx; for this riddling head, too, can swallow men alive. (p. 449)

417. *this frigate earth ... ballasted with bones* What is the *Pequod* herself, under Ahab's command, but an emblematic device of this metaphor? A frigate with 'murderous hold', manned by 'an Anacharsis Clootz deputation from all the isles of the sea', tricked out 'in the chased bones of her enemies', symbolic of all mankind: Indian, Viking, Christian, African, Cannibal, Tartar.

418. *tossed by pirates from the midnight deck* An echo, possibly, of Hamlet's letter to Horatio (IV, vi), as this whole *memento mori* recalls his graveyard apostrophe to a jester's skull.

418. *not the smallest atom stirs ... cunning duplicate in mind* cf. Demogorgon in Shelley's *Prometheus Unbound*:

Ye elemental Genii, who have homes
From man's high mind even to the central stone
Of sullen lead; from heaven's star-fretted domes
To the dull weed some sea-worm battens on ...
(Act IV, 539–42)

cf. Coleridge on 'the everlasting broodings and superfluous activities of Hamlet's mind': 'his senses are in a state of trance, and he looks upon external things as hieroglyphics. His soliloquy – ... springs from that craving after the indefinite – for that which is not – which most easily besets men of genius.' (*Notes on Hamlet*)

The riddle of the Sphynx – or Demogorgon – is that of the whole universe.

71 THE JEROBOAM'S STORY

419. *the Jeroboam of Nantucket* Recalling Elijah's curse of King Ahab: 'Behold I will bring evil upon thee ... and will make thine house like the house of Jeroboam the son of Nebat.' (*1 Kings* xxi, 21–2)

The *Jeroboam* is named after the first ruler of the ten tribes of Israel who, on King Solomon's death, seceded from the house of David. (*1 Kings* xi, 26–xiv, 20) As Gabriel pronounces the White Whale to be none other 'than the Shaker God incarnated', so Jeroboam 'made two calves of gold, and said unto them, It is too much for you to go up to Jerusalem: behold thy gods, O Israel, which brought thee up out of the land of Egypt'. (*1 Kings* xii, 28) As Captain Mayhew lost Macey, his chief mate, by ignoring Gabriel's 'denunciations and forewarnings', so Jeroboam, by ignoring the prophet Ahijah, lost Abijah, his son, with these 'prophecies of speedy doom'.

'Therefore, behold, I will bring evil upon the house of Jeroboam, and will cut off from Jeroboam him that pisseth against the wall, and him that is shut up and left in Israel, and will take away the remnant of the house of Jeroboam, as a man taketh away dung, till it be all gone.' (*1 Kings* xiv, 10)

Ahab, seventh king of Israel, succeeded to the throne of Jeroboam half a century later.

420. *with freckles, and wearing redundant yellow hair* 'Doth not even nature itself teach you, that, if a man have long hair, it is a shame unto him? But if a woman have long hair, it is a glory to her...' (*1 Corinthians* xi, 14–15) This Adam (hailed as androgynous in Shaker hymns) reflects more than a touch of Milton's Eve; this freckled youth, of another Hussey 'with yellow hair'. (p. 160)

420. *A long-skirted, cabalistically-cut coat* Meaning 'of Jewish cut' from *Cabbala*, the rabbinic tradition of Mishnah and Talmud. But the spelling (from *cabal*) suggests that this prophet is merely one of a clique of sinister intriguers. (His sleeves, like Ishmael's, like Queequeg's, are 'irregularly rolled up'.)

The husk of the butternut, or white walnut, yields a dye commonly used to colour the homespun of pioneers.

420. *the long-togged scaramouch* The casting of this cabalistically clothed archangel as *Scaramuccia*, the lazy coward becudgelled by Harlequin, is revealing of both Melville's purpose and Gabriel's role. He is a mere stock character of the religious farce, who refuses 'to work except when he pleased' and flinches apprehensively from the Sperm Whale's head.

420. *the crazy society of Neskyeuna Shakers* Properly entitled 'The United Society of Believers in Christ's Second Appearing' (also called 'The Millenial Church'), the movement originated in England among mid-eighteenth-century Quakers. First known as 'Shaking Quakers', they found a leader in Ann Lee (a mill-girl from Manchester, whose four children had all died in infancy), who declared in a vision that Christ's Second Coming, in the maternal spirit, was fulfilled in her. Following further visions, she and eight disciples emigrated in 1774 to New York, and settled at Niskayuna, on the Hudson River, near Schenectady.

The society, though peculiar in believing in the dual sexuality of God (revealed in a male and female Christ: Jesus and 'Mother Ann'), was no more 'crazy' or 'cracked' than any latterday Tolstoyan community. But just as the Quakers had been lampooned for their excessive worldly cares (making nonsense of their spiritual concerns), their offspring, the Shakers, are here shown as fanatic quacks (living off prophecies of doom).

The odd spelling 'Neskyeuna' (suggesting *nescio*) by a Latin pun relates the Shaker sect to the agitation against supposed Irish and German Catholic political domination stirred up in 1850. The 'Know-Nothings', so called for their extreme secrecy, were a subterranean offshoot of the Native American Party, opposed to all immigrant groups, especially Roman Catholics.

Melville paid at least three visits to Shaker settlements at Hancock and Lebanon, Massachusetts, in the summer of 1850, returning with Hawthorne and Evert Duyckinck a year later: 'A glass eyed preacher was holding forth, looking like an escaped maniac. His sermon was a clumsy, impudent, disgusting affair, sufficiently so at times to have driven the ladies from the house ...' (*Duyckinck to his wife*, 11 August 1851)

It was on his first visit to Hancock that Melville acquired *A Summary View of the Millenial Church, or United Society of Believers, Commonly Called Shakers* (Albany, 1848), which he thoroughly marked and annotated.

420. *The speedy opening of the seventh vial* This apocalyptic vial, like an anarchist's time-bomb in a vest-pocket, is of course facetious. But hidden depths stir in the allusion:

> And he gathered them together into a place called in the Hebrew tongue Armageddon.
> And the seventh angel poured out his vial into the air; and there came a great voice out of the temple of heaven, from the throne, saying, It is done ...
>
> (*Revelation* xvi, 16–17)

For John the Divine, too, is resonant with allusions. As the great voice from the throne, 'It is done', is a deliberate echo of the great cry from the cross (*John* xix, 30), so 'the temple of heaven' and the 'great earthquake' specifically echo *Matthew* xxvii, 51. Melville's use of the text is thus duplicit, surreptitiously linking this 'small, short, youngish' archangel from Neskyeuna with another 'deep, settled fanatic' from Nazareth – another miracle worker who could stay plagues, who cut his cloth according to the

Torah, and 'gained a wonderful ascendency over almost everybody'.

Armageddon itself (where good will confront evil) proves a link with that set collision of contraries which marks the course of the *Pequod*. The whole of *Revelation,* it becomes clear, underscores Melville's design. Is not *Moby-Dick,* too, a book of 'leviathanic revelations'? A new testament? The apocalypse (by one Ishmael, infidel) of Death, and Hell, and Armageddon? 'And I stood upon the sand of the sea, and saw a beast rise up out of the sea . . . and upon his heads the name of blasphemy.' (*Revelation* xiii, 1)

420. *that cunning peculiar to craziness* A tell-tale phrase linking Gabriel to Ahab – 'archangel' to 'Arch Angel ruind'. (*Paradise Lost* I, 593)

420. *the deliverer of the isles of the sea* 'Wherefore glorify ye the Lord in the fires . . .' (*Isaiah* xxiv, 15). For Shaker rites of purging sexual desire, by flogging and burning, read the witness of an ex-Shaker, Thomas Brown, *An Account of the People Called Shakers: Their Faith, Doctrine, and Practice* (Troy, 1812).

420. *preternatural terrors of real delirium* Evoking the phrase used of Korah and the Hebrews (p. 380) – to link Gabriel not only to Jeroboam and Ahijah, but to the brothers Aaron and Moses. As Gabriel declared 'that the plague . . . was at his sole command; nor should it be stayed but according to his good pleasure', so 'Aaron took as Moses commanded, and ran into the midst of the congregation; and, behold, the plague was begun among the people: and he put on incense, and made an atonement for the people. And he stood between the dead and the living; and the plague was stayed.' (*Numbers* xvi, 47–8)

Like Aaron, Jeroboam was a maker of golden calves (*Exodus* xxxii, 4; *1 Kings* xii, 28). Link by link the pieces are fitted; the reputable and disreputable confounded. Moses, Aaron, Ahijah, Jesus, Mother Ann, Gabriel – all, Melville implies, are in the same cabal; one with Jeroboam's Israelite priests at Bethel and Dan, the Hindu priests of the Matse Avatar at Elephanta, the fraudulent Babylonian priests of Bel and the Dragon – shirkers all. Likewise Gabriel and Ahab are linked not only by the Old Testament myth or a common 'delirium', but their 'measureless power of deceiving and bedevilling so many others'. (What turns the *Jeroboam*'s crew simply to 'poor devils', turns the *Pequod* wholly to 'diabolism'.)

From Moses to Jesus to Gabriel, Melville has forged this all-embracing chain; the dismissive scorn – the nihilism – is implacable. All religion is either fraudulent, or mad, or both: 'an opium-like listlessness' of unconscious reverie (THE MAST-HEAD); or 'laudanum' (to anticipate Marx) for 'the terror-stricken'. In 'gazing at such scenes, it is all in what mood you are in; if in the Dantean, the devils will occur to you; if in that of Isaiah, the archangels.' (THE TAIL)

421. *forthwith opened all his seals and vials*

And I heard a great voice out of the temple saying to the seven angels, Go your ways, and pour out the vials of the wrath of God upon the earth . . .

And I saw three unclean spirits like frogs come out of the mouth of the dragon, and out of the mouth of the beast, and out of the mouth of the false prophet.

The whole of *Revelation* xvi, in fact, is relevant not only for THE JEROBOAM'S STORY, but *The Whale*. The *Pequod*'s crew, too, bear 'the mark of the beast'; their blood-bath had stained the sea crimson; and 'every living soul' aboard, except one, will die 'in the sea'. The rivers and pastoral fountains of LOOMINGS were tainted; delusions are linked; and scorched Ahab will plunge, Narcissus-like, into the sea. Sun and fire are his tokens; and his crew, held in the electric charge of his will, blaspheme the name of God 'that the way of the kings of the east might be prepared'.

422. *the Shakers receiving the Bible* Grammar, if nothing else, seems wanting, though Melville may be alluding to Shaker belief that the Bible, in itself, is not definitive. A man of God, like Gabriel, speaking in prophecy, utters the Word of God; the 'Woman of the Apocalypse', Mother Ann, was also known as 'Ann the Word'.

72 THE MONKEY-ROPE

THE MONKEY-ROPE Suggested by Francis Allyn Olmsted, *Incidents of a Whaling Voyage* (New York, 1841), p. 63.

426. *for better or for worse, we two . . . were wedded* 'as though naught but death should part us twain'. (THE COUNTERPANE) That 'bridegroom clasp' in the matrimonial bed (of New Bedford) and hug by a bosom friend is legitimatized at last.

426. *an elongated Siamese ligature . . . my own inseparable twin brother* Chang and Eng, the original 'Siamese Twins' (1811–74), were being exhibited throughout the United States by Phineas T. Barnum at this time.

426. *my free will had received a mortal wound* It was Queequeg, long ago on the *Moss*, who had embodied the ultimate lesson: 'It's a mutual, joint-stock world, in all meridians.' (WHEELBARROW, p. 157, note)

428. *that kannakin* More usually 'canikin', or 'canakin'. (p. 477) 'Kanaka' (Hawaiian, *man*) was a common appellative for a South Sea Islander.

428. *calomel and jalap* Two purgatives – Mediterranean and Mexican.

73 STUBB AND FLASK KILL A RIGHT WHALE; AND THEN HAVE A TALK OVER HIM

429. *a Sperm Whale's . . . head hanging to the Pequod's side* 'Perhaps I was over sensitive to such impressions at the time, but I could not help staring at this gallows with a vague misgiving.' (CHOWDER, p. 160)

431. *a complete circuit . . . round and round* Whose radial centre is the *Pequod*; whose blind circumference, the whale; whose satellites, two flying headsmen. (See p. 212, note.)

431. *the eager Israelites . . . at the new bursting fountains* 'Behold, I will stand before thee there upon the rock in Horeb; and thou shalt smite the rock, and there shall come water out of it, that the people may drink. And Moses did so in the sight of the elders of Israel'. (*Exodus* xvii, 6) As Stubb and Flask did, in the sight of the *Pequod*.

Not only Moses, but Yahweh himself, is now openly linked with evil; and the fountains (as in *Revelation* xvi, 4) are tainted with 'fresh blood'.

431. *that gamboge ghost* The bright yellow pigment is derived from a Cambodian gum-resin.

432. *to swap away his silver watch, or his soul* cf. p. 392, note. Stubb's 'skylarking' here is typically hell-raising – a kind of Faustian parody, like some farcical interlude from Marlowe's

Tragical History of Doctor Faustus, with the devil himself ducked and docked and given 'a pair of black eyes'.

432. *give John the Asiatic cholera* That 'Beelzebub himself might climb up the side and step down into the cabin to chat with the captain . . . would not create any unsubduable excitement in the forecastle'. (p. 333) But who is this 'old governor' on 'the old flag-ship'? Could God be in league with this sauntering devil, as the Lord was with Satan 'going to and fro in the earth, and . . . walking up and down in it'? (*Job* i, 7) Such a 'bond' strikes deeper than any Faustian pact.

cf. *White-Jacket*: 'Our Lord High Admiral will yet interpose . . . though long ages should elapse, and leave our wrongs unredressed . . .' (The End)

433. *Three Spaniards? . . . three bloody-minded soldadoes?* Flask is more likely to have heard of Cervantes, say, or *The Three Musketeers,* than of George Walker's gothic extravaganza, *The Three Spaniards* (London, 1800), at that time still unpublished in America!

433. *now take all the hoops in the Pequod's hold . . . for oughts* A *jeu d'esprit* to demonstrate 'the Pythagorean maxim' that numbers are not merely symbols but the essence of all things, that all relationships in the universe can be expressed mathematically.

Thus the crews of three whale boats had been reduced to statistics; a whale's respiration will be timed to the second; exact dimensions for parts of the whale, as for parts of the whaler, are established; and within a 6,000-year span of recorded history, the precise stroke of an instant of composition will be clocked and dated. 'I have often admired the mysticall way of *Pythagoras,* and the secret Magicke of numbers.' (Sir Thomas Browne, *Religio Medici,* Pt I, sec. 12)

Yet these 'oughts', within noughts, imply a fission to shatter such nihilism, just as Stubb's little puzzle of infinite number and finite hoops seems already to herald Kant's dialectic, soon to be hoisted on board.

434. *down in the orlop* The lowest deck covering the hold.

434. *in double darbies* Meaning 'fetters' or 'handcuffs'.

434. *hoist in Locke's head . . . hoist in Kant's* As the *Pequod* was converted ('with a philosophical flourish') to ciphers, here a conflict of metaphysical ciphers is itself converted to an image –

'so strongly and metaphysically' does Ishmael conceive each situation.

The 'counterpoise', that so strains the *Pequod*, balances Locke's head (at birth, a *tabula rasa*, a blank slate for experience to inscribe) against Kant's (from birth, by its own inner structure, determining what knowledge it acquired). In Locke's head, that is, all knowledge was *a posteriori*; in Kant's, essentially *a priori* – the 'thing-in-itself', or absolute truth, for ever evading its grasp.

The debate is airily dismissed by Ishmael. Yet this antinomy too (to use Kant's own term), like all such antitheses throughout *Moby-Dick*, may reflect an essential precondition of life. These philosophers hoisted on board are still 'thunderheads', after all, not 'dunderheads'. Indeed the whole of *Moby-Dick*, at times, seems like one vast emblem of the Kantian dialectic, proceeding by a series of antithetical images, puns, allusions, paradoxes, to demonstrate not merely – as here – the mutually conflicting character of metaphysical principles, but the antinomies inherent even in the phenomenal world itself, finding everywhere contradictions incapable of resolution.

435. *the head laden ship not a little resembled a mule* A hint of sterility now burdens the *Pequod* (and her peg-legged captain), as it burdened Radney of the *Town-Ho*, 'ugly as a mule'.

74 THE SPERM WHALE'S HEAD – CONTRASTED VIEW

THE SPERM WHALE'S HEAD 'I will not conceal his parts, nor his power, nor his comely proportion . . . Who can open the doors of his face? his teeth are terrible round about.' (*Job* xli. 12, 14)

438. *to go through the demonstrations of two distinct problems in Euclid* Has not *The Whale* too 'a certain mathematical symmetry'? Does not *The Whale* too demonstrate a kind of composite Euclidian geometry? The capacity of the whale (according to Ishmael) simultaneously to examine two wholly separate images is, of course, precisely what *Moby-Dick* demands of its readers: 'their divided and diametrically opposite powers of vision must involve them.'

In Blake's phrase: 'May God keep us from single vision and Newton's sleep.' It is not only 'pleasant', but necessary it seems, 'to read about whales through their own spectacles'. (THE BLANKET)

438. *Herschel's great telescope* Erected in 1789, with a 48-inch mirror and a focal length of 40 ft.

438. *the Great Kentucky Mammoth Cave* Long an Indian hide-out, the cave was discovered by Kentucky pioneers in 1799. Its full extent, as that of the whale's stomach, remains unexplored – a labyrinth of extraordinary limestone formations, huge chambers connected by narrow winding passages, lakes and underground streams. Known passages extend over 150 miles, the corridors occurring in five separate levels, through the lowest of which flows Echo river, draining into the Green river.

What else is this Mammoth Cave but an artfully cunning emblem, and clue, to *Moby-Dick* itself – that elaborate, vast labyrinth with its extraordinary symbolic formations, huge set scenes connected by involved and winding narrative, unexplored (even today) in all its variety of separate levels, through the lowest of which flows Echo river into the pervasive green of pastoral illusion?

439. *white membrane, glossy as bridal satins* This hint of female chastity is at once transformed to the male thrust of an impaling spike.

75 THE RIGHT WHALE'S HEAD – CONTRASTED VIEW

440. *a gigantic galliot-toed shoe* The 'old Dutch voyager' is possibly Willem Cornelis Schouten (1567?–1625), who opened a new route around Cape Horn into the Pacific. (Extract 29)

441. *the inside of an Indian wigwam* As the whale's blubber had seemed 'an Indian poncho', its mouth is now revealed to be a wigwam with ridge-pole and 'peltry' sides. Once past portcullis or Venetian blind, in fact, the Pequot hunter will find himself thoroughly at home.

442. *in Queen Anne's time . . . in the jaws of the whale* That these adjuncts of bourgeois culture – the umbrella and stay – are encompassed by the jaws of the whale, suggests that bourgeois culture itself shares all their ferocity and horror. A Quaker had lurked concealed in 'the jaws of the right-whale'. The bar of the Spouter-Inn, too, had stood in 'the vast arched bone'.

Even the whales, as if anticipating the corsets and candles, perfume and parasols, look the part: now 'like a portly burgher smoking his pipe of a warm afternoon', now like 'a musk-scented lady' rustling 'her dress in a warm parlor' – exponents all of 'the sanctity of domestic bliss'. Their Grand Armada sails into view 'like the thousand cheerful chimneys of some dense metropolis'.

442. *the great Haarlem organ . . . a rug of the softest Turkey* The eighteenth-century organ in the church of St Bavo, or Groote Kerk, with its 5,000 pipes. The tulip craze had reached Holland from Turkey in the seventeenth century.

443. *This Right Whale . . . a Stoic; the Sperm Whale, a Platonian, who might have taken up Spinoza* The seam of Dutch allusions again surfaces – now in Amsterdam where the great Jewish philosopher Spinoza (another lens grinder, like Leeuwenhoek) was born.

The immediate point of the comparison is to contrast the practical morality of the Stoics with the speculative idealism of the Platonians (for whom virtue is knowledge). But even for Plato Ideas were different from things; Spinoza saw only 'one infinite substance, of which finite existences are modes or limitations'. This whole universe, he taught, is but a manifestation of God – *is*, in a sense, God.

'Heed it well, ye Pantheists!' Ishmael might cry. For had he not himself, in like vein, invoked 'Himself! The great God absolute! The centre and circumference of all democracy! His omnipresence, our divine equality!'? Much else links Spinoza to Ishmael: the denial of free will; the denial of a transcendent distinction between good and evil; the denial, by implication, of personal immortality. Yet whereas Ishmael's 'whole universe' is beyond man's wit, Spinoza's 'intellectual love of God' implies an understanding and acceptance of God's infinite plan; whereas Ishmael suspects only 'a vast practical joke' aimed at himself, Spinoza teaches the wise man 'to view all things "*sub specie aeternitatis*".'

'O head!' Ahab had muttered, 'thou hast seen enough to split the planets and make an infidel of Abraham . . .' Expelled for his beliefs from the Jewish community, Spinoza was genuinely an infidel-Abraham, a lapsed Jew, an 'ex officio professor of Sabbath breaking'.

76 THE BATTERING-RAM

THE BATTERING-RAM Whatever the implicit pun, that hyphen implies siege warfare: 'to appoint battering rams against the gates, to cast a mount, and to build a fort.' (*Ezekiel* xxi, 22)

444. *the front of the Sperm Whale's head is a dead, blind wall* To Ahab's blind boast ('Sometimes I think there's naught beyond'), 'a sensible physiologist' now replies: 'not till you get near twenty feet from the forehead do you come to the full cranial development.'

444. *which so impregnably invests all that apparent effeminacy* This 'most delicate oil' in a wad of such 'boneless toughness' again suggests the curious bisexuality, or hermaphroditism, of the whale. A suspicion that what is impregnable might also impregnate 'all that apparent effeminacy' is raised by the impotence of 'the severest pointed harpoon' or 'sharpest lance', compared to the 'concentrations of potency everywhere lurking in this expansive monster'. The collusion of imagery makes literally a beast with 'two backs, so to speak'. (p. 436)

For, of course, that effeminacy, so apparent in 'pearl-colored' silk, masks an immense male reservoir of 'about five hundred gallons of sperm' stored 'in its crotch'. And if the head proves ambivalent, a pun in the chapter-head may better convey 'the most exalted potency' of this battering ram.

Here where all contraries meet – of life and death, good and evil – the polarities of sex, male and female, also converge: and the 'great well of sperm' will be drawn up in buckets 'all bubbling like a dairy-maid's pail of new milk'.

444. *paved with horses' hoofs* 'Indeed, I can compare it to nothing else but the inside of a horse's hoof . . .' As the butting 'ram' was Cheever's (pp. 155–6), these hoofs and harpoons are drawn from Owen Chase. (*Narrative . . . of the Whale-Ship Essex*, p. 38)

445. *clear Truth is a thing for salamander giants* Meaning Titans who can endure fire, a Promethean race. Thus Ahab. But what of Ishmael? Is he not too a youth – though 'of a broad-shouldered make'? And *sal*/amander – alone to survive the encounter with that 'veil', that Holy of Holies, the White Whale?

445. *the weakling youth lifting the dread goddess's veil at Sais*

An ancient city of the Nile Delta once famous for two shrines: to Neith (sky-goddess of joy) and Osiris (fertility god of the Underworld). For here, too, all contraries meet.

The reference is to Schiller's *Das Verschleirete Bild zu Sais* (in Bulwer-Lytton's translation), where a youth seeking Truth in the temple, lifts the forbidden veil, to find only sorrow – and an early death.

77 THE GREAT HEIDELBURGH TUN

THE GREAT HEIDELBURGH TUN A gigantic cask in the castle cellar of Heidelberg, with a capacity of about 49,000 gallons:

'This so much celebrated Tun is thirty one Foot long and twenty one high, unto which you ascend by a Pair of Stairs of fifty Steps, to a kind of Platform or Balcony of twenty Foot long, inclosed with Rails: the Elector's Arms are placed on the Front of the Tun, and *Bacchus* on the Top, attended by Satyrs, Drunkards, and such-like... Abundance of Jests and Apothegms, relating to the same Subject, are to be seen, in *High Dutch* on divers Parts of this enormous Tun.' ('The Travels of Mr Maximilian Mission', John Harris, Coll.)

447. *invade the sanctuary* Or 'magazine' of this gun/whale. As the blocks, painted green, dangled down like a 'vast bunch of grapes', the Case itself now appears as a vast vintage tun – filled with the wine and precious oils of the sacrament, awaiting desecration.

78 CISTERN AND BUCKETS

448. *he seems some Turkish Muezzin* Turkish allusions, from the Turkey carpet of the Right Whale's tongue, to his 'scimetar-shaped slats of whalebone', invoke the Muslim, the infidel, the persecutor of Christians. Thus the irony of this call to prayers – for the defilement of Christian sacraments 'till the drunk ship reeled'.

449. *Towards the end, Tashtego has to ram his long pole harder and harder, and deeper and deeper* For now the whale is 'the deep cistern'; Tashego, the battering ram. But in such abundance of 'fragrant sperm', 'apparent effeminacy' prevails. Towards the end *double entendres* sound everywhere in this

'ticklish business' of the sperm spilling and leaking and dribbling, the 'queer accident' and queerer midwifery by the naked Queequeg delivering the Gay-Header head first with such 'agile obstetrics'.

In this curious homosexual farrago where male rams male, and brave delivers long-haired brave from a bridal chamber of sperm oil, the erotic roles are as confused among men as the sexual symbolism among whales. *Cistern and Buckets*, is it, or bucks and sissies?

450. *like Niagara's Table-Rock into the whirlpool* A piece of Table-Rock collapsed on 25 June 1850. The gorge immediately below Niagara Falls is known as Whirlpool Rapids.

450. *my brave Queequeg* 'For better or for worse' Ishmael is now wholly Queequeg's – 'a bosom friend' turned squaw who may legitimately admire her 'brave'.

452. *in the secret inner chamber and sanctum sanctorum* The innermost sanctuary of the Temple at Jerusalem.

452. *an Ohio honey-hunter ... leaning too far over* Like Paul Hover, bee-hunter, in Cooper's *The Prairie*. cf. The fate of Narcissus (in LOOMINGS) with that of the 'sunken-eyed young Platonist' (of THE MAST-HEAD) or any reader of *The Whale*. How many, think ye, have likewise fallen into Melville's honey head, and sweetly perished there?

'But what plays the mischief with this masterly code is the admirable brevity of it, which necessitates a vast volume of commentaries to expound it.' (FAST-FISH AND LOOSE-FISH)

79 THE PRAIRE

THE PRAIRE This 'praire', with a bull, is also a prayer to Jove: both lower with doom; both are linked as emblems of pastoral delusion.

452. *for Lavater ... or for Gall* The Physiognomist is Lavater; Gall, the Phrenologist. Johann Kaspar Lavater (1741–1801), a Swiss theologian, fascinated the nineteenth century by his attempt to classify the correlations between men's characters and their facial characteristics: *Physiognomical Fragments for the Promotion of a Knowledge of Man and of Love of Man* (1775–8).

The German Franz Joseph Gall (1758–1828), and his disciple Johan Caspar Spurzheim (1776–1832), who died in Boston, collaborated as physicians in Vienna. On the supposition that separate attributes of the mind must be localized in separate organs of the brain, they correlated twenty-six faculties with bumps on different parts of the skull.

452. *manipulated the dome of the Pantheon.* 'Of erections, how few are domed like St Peter's!' – bar the Pantheon. For in Rome, too, all contraries meet.

453. *Phidias's marble Jove* His colossal, chryselephantine statue of Zeus in the temple of Olympia was counted one of the seven wonders of the world.

453. *the curled brow of the bull ... that great golden seal* As Jove in such pastures suggests Europa's white bull, so that great golden seal with 'mystical brow' is the Golden Bull – in one Holy Roman Empire of allusion.

454. *Few are the foreheads ... like Shakspeare's or Melancthon's* Shakespeare's, of course, is the very type of genius, and the most memorable feature of Droeshout's engraving in the First Folio is doubtless its 'mystical brow'. But why should Melanchthon, intimate friend of Luther, be thought comparable to Shakespeare?

A long article on 'Phrenology', in William and Robert Chambers' *A Popular Encyclopedia,* vol I, juxtaposed illustrations of 'the head of Melanchthon, the most virtuous and talented of the reformers' and the head of 'the atrocious criminal Hare, who murdered by wholesale'. The criminal, it was explained, had nearly as much brain as the theologian, but Melanchthon's superiority of intellect was 'obvious by one glance at the high and full forehead, compared with "the forehead villainous low", as Shakspeare would have called it' of the criminal. (*Information for the People*, Philadelphia, 1847)

454. *Lavater's mark of genius* And mark of the Turk – the whale's 'semi-crescentic depression' matching the whaleboat's 'semi-circular depression in the cleat'.

454. *his great genius is declared in his doing nothing particular to prove it* As the whale's 'rare virtue' was Nantucket virtue (Islanders both – and *Isolatoes*), so his genius proves that of 'God's true princes ... the choice hidden handful of the Divine Inert'. In the very act of writing, 'unlettered Ishmael' recognizes,

salutes, invokes, exalts his peculiar reflection in the genius of the Sperm Whale.

So Melville at the age of thirty-seven, was to lapse into inertia; or at least withdraw, as far as his public was concerned, into impenetrable silence. For almost twenty years a Custom House officer on the New York piers, 'his great genius' too was 'declared in his doing nothing particular to prove it'.

454. *moreover declared in his pyramidical silence* One oxymoron echoes another. For what is true of semantics was as true of optics; the metaphors had long been mixed: 'is it for these reasons that there is such a dumb blankness, full of meaning, in a wide landscape of snows?' (THE WHITENESS OF THE WHALE)

As the 'colorless all-color' of light ultimately shrouds Moby Dick, so the meaningless multi-meaning of language ultimately wraps *The Whale*. Its very vocabulary is self-reflexive, only mirroring, or defining itself; its etymologies and cross-references are all circular. The genius of *Moby-Dick*, too, is declared in declaring nothing: 'Dissect him how I may ... I but go skin deep; I know him not, and never will.' (THE TAIL, p. 487, note) 'Like those mystic rocks, too, the mystic-marked whale remains undecipherable.' (THE BLANKET)

cf. James Guetti, *The Languages of* 'Moby-Dick' (in *The Limits of Metaphor*, Cornell University Press, 1967) for a reading of the strategy behind Ishmael's various narrative 'masks'.

454. *They deified the crocodile of the Nile* cf. 'Neither is the crocodile set so much by among them, without some probable cause: For they say that in some respect he is the very image representing god: as being the onely creature in the world which hath no tongue: for as much as divine speech needeth neither voice nor tongue.' (Plutarch, 'Of Isis and Osiris', Holland's translation, p. 1316)

454. *Champollion* Using the Rosetta Stone, found by Napoleon's troops near the mouth of the Nile, Jean François Champollion (1790–1832) established the key for deciphering Egyptian hieroglyphics.

455. *the Egypt of every man's and every being's face* 'I hold moreover that there is a Phytognomy, or Physiognomy, not onely of men, but of Plants, and Vegetables; and in every one of them some outward figures which hang as signes and bushes of

their inward formes. The finger of God hath set an inscription upon all his workes, not graphicall or composed of Letters, but of their severall formes, constitutions, parts, and operations, which aptly joyned together make one word that doth expresse their natures ...' (Sir Thomas Browne, *Religio Medici*, Pt II, sec. 2)

455. *Sir William Jones* (1746–94) famous as jurist and Oriental linguist. Judge of the high court of Calcutta from 1783 till his death, he published two works on Muslim law and a Persian Grammar, began *The Institute of Hindu Law, or Ordinances of Manu*, translated the Greek orator Isaeus, the *Sakuntala* of Kalidasa and the *Hitopadesa* (both in Sanscrit), the poems of Hafiz (Persian), and the *Moallakat* (Arabic).

80 THE NUT

THE NUT Turning the great 'TUN' upside down: deciphering that 'firmament' of hieroglyphics to Egyptian 'NUT'; unriddling 'NUT' (the Sky) to 'that Egyptian mother, who bore offspring themselves pregnant from her womb' (Isis, Set, Osiris). See THE ADVOCATE (p. 205, note).

455. *that geometrical circle ... impossible to square* Suggesting some masonic conundrum – of the Grand Geometrician with his set-square (p. 472, note); for only quantity, not a *concept*, can by definition be multiplied by itself.

455. *the innermost citadel ... of Quebec* cf. Father Mapple 'impregnable in his little Quebec' (THE PULPIT)

456. *a strung necklace of dwarfed skulls* Both Siva and Kali, his consort, were represented wearing a necklace of skulls; and Siva commonly worshipped – amid such 'spermy heaps' – in the form of a lingam or phallus.

456. *It is a German conceit,* advanced by Lorenz Oken (1779–1851), that the skull-bones are analogous to those of the vertebral column.

456. *A foreign friend* Presumably a Typee cannibal from the Marquesan valley which first brought Melville fame.

456. *the spinal canal* From a 'freighted junk' on the 'great canal of Hang-Ho' Ishmael turns to this 'mass of the junk and sperm'; from 'our grand Erie Canal' to our 'spinal canal'.

456. *A thin joist of a spine never yet upheld a full and noble*

soul cf. The Tahitan Sailor: 'Up, spine, and meet it!' cf. The masts of the *Pequod* standing 'stiffly up like the spines of the three old kings of Cologne'.

81 THE PEQUOD MEETS THE VIRGIN

457. *the ship Jungfrau, Derick De Deer, master, of Bremen* His utter ignorance and innocence reveal a treble irony: his name recalling Low German *die Deern,* or 'girl'; his ship, not only Jesus's parable of the Wise and Foolish Virgins, but that allegorical fable of the Virgin and the Unicorn. Thus antlered De Deer – without a drop of sperm – is literally cuckolded in the end.

But the gift of a *Theo/doric, Dietrich* or *Derrick* (hangman at Tyburn) is 'the gallows'.

459. *eight whales, an average pod* In U.S. usage, a small school of seals or whales.

459. *Who's got some paregoric?* An anodyne, literally παρα/ἀγορος 'for speaking': 'but the fear of this vast dumb brute of the sea, was chained up and enchanted in him ...'

461. *slap-jacks* Griddle-cakes.

461. *such a sog! such a sogger!* From 'hog', 'log', 'quohog', 'dog', to 'dogger', 'sog' to 'sogger': such 'a large whale' (*Dictionary of American English*), such a 'lump'! (Wright, *English Dialect Dictionary*)

461. *'The unmannerly Dutch dogger!'* A two-masted fishing boat with bluff bows, used in the North Seas. (cf. Dogger Bank)

461. *to snap your spine in two-and-twenty pieces* An adult, in fact, has twenty-six vertebrae, of which seven are in the neck, twelve in the chest.

463. *a mad cougar* Also called 'catamount', 'red tiger', 'American lion'.

463. *in a tilbury* A light open two-wheeled carriage.

463. *to Davy Jones ... this whale carries the everlasting mail!* To the sailors' devil, spirit of the sea – like a mail-coach to the Dead Letter Office of Eternity. (p. 424)

464. *the weight of fifty atmospheres* viz. fifty times the pressure of 14.7 lb. on the square inch, which is that of the atmosphere on the ocean's surface.

464. *'Canst thou fill his skin with barbed irons?'* *Job* xli, 7 and 26–29, omitting the second half of verses 27 and 28. See CETOLOGY (p. 230, note).

464. *Oh! that unfulfilments should follow the prophets* But not THE PROPHET! Nor a 'Job's whale':

> The sword of him that layeth at him cannot hold . . . he laugheth at the shaking of a spear!
> He maketh the deep to boil like a pot . . . one would think the deep to be hoary.
> Upon the earth there is not his like, who is made without fear.
> He beholdeth all high things: he is a king over all the children of pride.
>
> (*Job* xli, 26–34)

465. *His eyes . . . strange misgrown masses* cf. 'A whale, perfectly blind, was taken by Captain W. Swain, now of the *Sarah and Elizabeth* whaler, of London, both eyes of which were completely disorganized, the orbits being occupied by fungous masses, protruding considerably, rendering it certain that the whale must have been deprived of vision for a long space of time. . .' (Beale, ch. 2, '*Habits of the Sperm Whale*')

467. *darted by some Nor' West Indian long before America was discovered* Evidence from old harpoons and, since 1953, international whale marking (by numbered darts, rather like ringed birds) shows that whales live at least thirty to forty years. Anatomical evidence from larger whales suggests a life of up to seventy or eighty years. But a longer span, stretching to centuries, is sailors' myth.

82 THE HONOR AND GLORY OF WHALING

469. *a careful disorderliness is the true method* cf. 'I care not to perform this part of my task methodically . . .' (THE AFFIDAVIT) But from Manhattan to Nantucket, to the Cape of Good Hope, to the straits of Sunda, past 'the Bashee isles' into the Pacific and on to the equator, the *Pequod*'s own 'zig-zag world-circle' is most methodically plotted. For monomaniac Ahab plots that course. (THE CHART) Which is also the plot – or devious word-circle – of *Moby-Dick*.

See THE CROTCH, p. 395, note.

470. *this Arkite story* Old as Noah's ark? Or linking that 'Syrian coast' to Canaanite Arca? (*Genesis* x, 17)

470. *the ancient Joppa, now Jaffa* cf. 'one of the mighty triumphs given to a Roman general...' (p. 207, note)

470. *'Thou art as a lion of the waters, and as a dragon of the sea,' saith Ezekiel ... in truth some versions of the Bible* In the King James version: 'Son of man, take up a lamentation for Pharaoh king of Egypt, and say unto him, Thou art like a young lion of the nations, and thou art as a whale in the seas: and thou camest forth with thy rivers, and troubledst the waters with thy feet, and fouledst their rivers.' (*Ezekiel* xxxii, 2)

470. *a Coffin* Such as Miriam Coffin (of *The Whale-Fishermen*). 'Coffin' is a Nantucket Quaker name. The third whaler on which Melville served, the *Charles & Henry*, was built and registered by Charles G. and Henry Coffin.

471. *a large seal, or sea-horse* Old English *horschwael*, metathesized to 'walrus'.

471. *that fish, flesh and fowl idol of the Philistines, Dagon.* 'And when they arose early on the morrow morning, behold, Dagon was fallen upon his face to the ground before the ark of the Lord; and the head of Dagon and both the palms of his hands were cut off upon the threshold; only the stump of Dagon was left to him.' (*1 Samuel* v, 4) Kitto, in his *Cyclopaedia of Biblical Literature*, derived his name from *dag*, the Hebrew for the fish that swallowed Jonah. He was possibly a fish-god of a Canaan fertility rite; but the 'horse's head' is wholly Melville's accessory.

471. *Whether to admit Hercules* 'Hercules Phoenicius', in Sir Thomas Browne's phrase: both Bayle and Kitto associated him with Jonah.

471. *that antique Crockett and Kit Carson* i.e. That frontiersman, hero of tall tales – like Colonel Davy Crockett (1786–1836), who died in the war for Texan Independence at the Alamo, or Kit Carson (1809–1868), guide on the Santa Fé trail, prominent in the capture of California during the Mexican War.

472. *the whole roll of our order. Our grand master is still to be named* The language – of 'fraternity', 'our brotherhood', 'great honorableness and antiquity' – is consciously modelled on that of Freemasonry: in whose secret fraternal order every mason calls another 'brother'; whose God is the 'Great Architect of the Uni-

verse' or 'Grand Geometrician'; whose highest office is that of 'Grand Master'; whose calendar, too, counts 'sixty round centuries'; whose apprentices, stripped of all metal, enter masonry 'poor and penniless' (as Ishmael 'having little or no money in my purse'); whose 'young candidates' take their oath blindfold, kneeling with a hangman's noose around their necks, on the black and white chequered temple floor; whose initiates to the 'second degree' step in a circle, as if ascending a spiral staircase; and to the 'third degree', are ritually 'murdered', laid in a 'grave' or 'coffin', and 'raised from the dead'; in whose ceremonies skulls and crossbones abound; whose rituals and legends supposedly stretch back to the building of King Solomon's temple; over whose higher 'degrees' preside prophets, priests and kings – from the 'mark masons', with secret code, to their offspring the Royal Ark Mariners meeting under the presidency of the 'Worshipful Master Noah'.

'*When were you made a Mason?*' asks the Worshipful Master.

'*When the Sun was at its Meridian,*' replies the candidate for initiation.

'*What is Freemasonry?*' asks the Worshipful Master.

'*A peculiar system of morality, veiled in Allegory, and illustrated by Symbols,*' replies the candidate.

'*Name the grand principles on which the Order is founded.*'

'*Brotherly Love, Relief, and Truth.*'

An initiate's bonds are in such secrets shared by the few. And the same might be said of Melville's *The Whale*: 'so remarkable, occasionally, are these mystic gestures, that I have heard hunters who have declared them akin to Free-Mason signs and symbols; that the whale, indeed, by these methods intelligently conversed with the world'.

Presenting the initiate with his apron, the Senior Warden pronounces:

'*I invest you with the distinguishing badge of a Mason. It is more ancient than the Golden Fleece or the Roman Eagle, more honourable than the Garter or any other Order in existence, being the badge of innocence and the bond of friendship.*'

By good rights, then, the harpooneers of 'this grand argosy' or Argo-Navis, too, 'should be enrolled in the most noble order of St George'. ('Listen, wise Stubb. In old England the greatest lords think it great glory to be slapped by a queen, and made garter-knights of . . .')

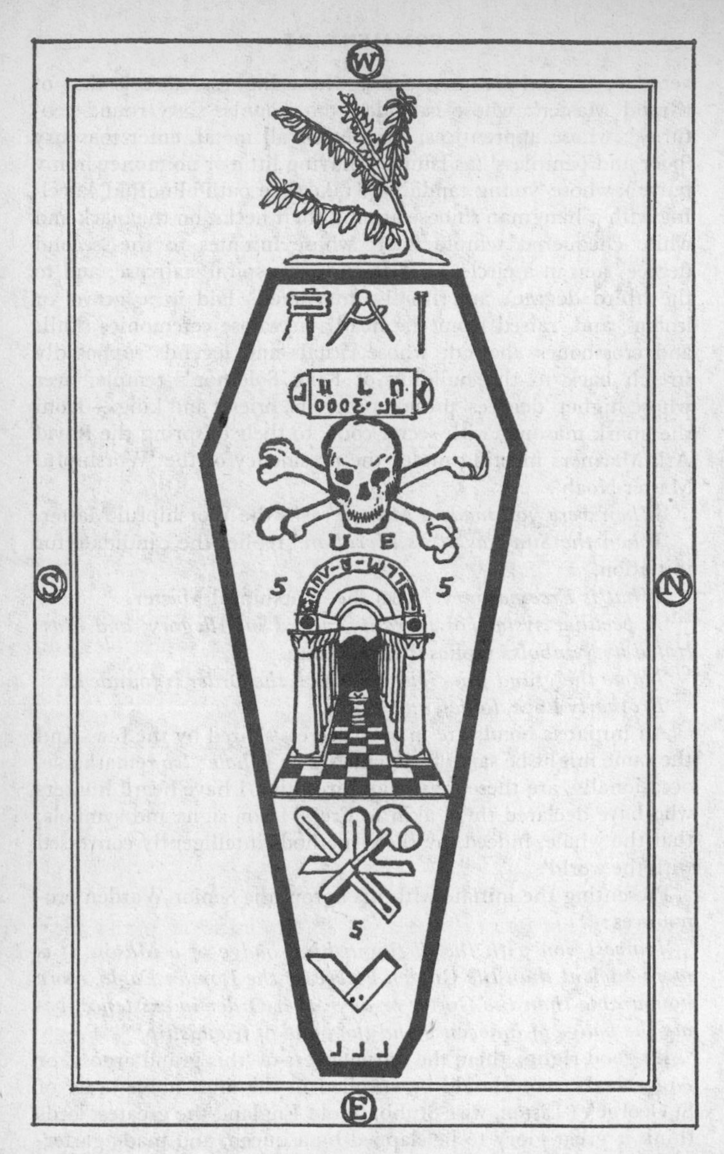

Masonic Coffin

But whatever the marks of Freemasonry here, they are not those of 'the young Orient world'. Rather they are those of the Grand Orient lodges of nineteenth-century France, Italy and Spain – anticlerical in intent, with the motto 'liberty, equality, fraternity'. To fraternity (in A SQUEEZE OF THE HAND) Ishmael will return; to the clergy also, 'to illuminate the solemn churches that preach unconditional inoffensiveness by all to all'. (p. 466)

For a brief period in Melville's youth Freemasonry was much in the news. From the late 1820s to the early 1830s an Anti-Masonic party was active in New York state, in 1831 holding the first national nominating convention and issuing the first written party platform in U.S. history.

472. *from the Shaster* Or 'Shastra', any one of the sacred books of the Hindus.

472. *the dread Vishnoo ... by the first of his ten earthly incarnations* The 'Matse Avatar' in the cavern-pagoda of Elephanta. (OF THE MONSTROUS PICTURES OF WHALES)

472. *practical hints to young architects* For 'perhaps, after all, there is *no* secret. We incline to think that the Problem of the Universe is like the Freemason's mighty secret, so terrible to all children. It turns out, at last, to consist in a triangle, a mallet, and an apron, – nothing more! We incline to think that God cannot explain His own secrets, and that He would like a little information upon certain points Himself.' (To Nathaniel Hawthorne, April 1851)

83 JONAH HISTORICALLY REGARDED

472. *this historical story of Jonah* Melville drew most of his comical illustrations of theological controversy from John Kitto's *Cyclopaedia of Biblical Literature*. In the article on 'Jonah' there are references to the theory that the tale is an allegory based on the myth of Hercules and the sea-monster; to Bishop Jebb's theory 'that the asylum of Jonah was not in the stomach of a whale, but in a cavity of its throat'; to the hypothesis of Anton, 'who fancied that the prophet took refuge in the interior of a dead whale'; to the theory of Less that Jonah 'was taken up by a ship having a large fish for a figure-head'; and to the suggestion of Charles Taylor that the Hebrew word for the creature that swallowed Jonah means, in fact, 'life-preserver'.

The circuit 'by the way of the Cape of Good Hope' derives from Pierre Bayle ('Jonas': *Dictionnaire historique et critique*, III, 579)

473. *his incarcerated body and the whale's gastric juices* cf. Bayle's paraphrase of St Augustine's forty-ninth letter: 'Is it easier to raise a dead man from the grave than to preserve a man alive in the body of a great fish? Will it be said that the digestive faculty of the stomach cannot be suspended?' (III, 578)

473. *the 'Gull'* viz. such commentators gull the public, just as such exegetists, far from being life-preservers, are themselves inflated wind-bags.

474. *an English traveller in old Harris's Voyages* 'The Travels of Mr Joannes Baptiste Tavernier Bernier thro' Turkey into Persia', in John Harris's *Navigantium atque Itinerantium Bibliotheca*. Bernier writes of Nineveh: 'Half a League from Tigris stands a little Hill, encompassed with Houses, on the top whereof is built a Mosque, in the Place where, they say, Jonas is buried. The Turks have a mighty Veneration for it, and cover it with a Persian Carpet of Silk and Silver, and at the Four Corners are great Copper Candlesticks with Wax Tapers, and several Lamps.'

Pierre Bayle adds: 'Mr Simon *affirms, that . . . there is a miraculous lamp, that burns continually without any oil or other liquor, if he will give credit to their reveries*.' ('Jonas', III, 579)

And, of course, the irony of the whole chapter is clinched by this 'highly enlightened' Muslim support for a Portuguese Catholic position, and the metamorphosis of a Hebrew miracle to an Aladdin's lamp.

84 PITCHPOLING

477. *'Tis July's immortal Fourth; all fountains must run wine to-day!* Independence Day – from immortal God – turning the *Pequod*'s crew (Nantucketers, Vineyarders, all) to diabolical blood-quaffers.

477. *unspeakable old Monongahela!* River region of southern Pennsylvania, west of the Alleghenies, settled mainly by Scottish–Irish, and famous for its whisky. But the implicit reference is to the Whisky Rebellion of 1794 against Alexander Hamilton's excise – a tax resented by these frontiersmen as discriminatory and a blow to their liberty.

85 THE FOUNTAIN

477. *for six thousand years* Or 'sixty round centuries', according to Archbishop Ussher's Old Testament chronology. (p. 130, note)

477. *as with so many sprinkling or mistifying pots* Turning 'the spread of his spout-hole' from a punch-bowl for blood-quaffers to a ciborium for the Holy Eucharist itself: 'And he took the cup, and gave thanks, and gave it to them, saying, Drink ye all of it; for this is my blood of the new testament, which is shed for many ...' (*Matthew* xxvi, 26–8)

477. *this sixteenth day of December, A.D. 1850* Like Southey's *The Doctor* (vol 7, p. 552), recording the exact point of a moment of composition.

478. *for his periodical visits to the upper world ... buried at least eight feet beneath the surface* Suggesting the cycle of death and resurrection of fertility gods – like Attis, Osiris, Adonis, Tammuz, and Jesus himself – whom Sir James Frazer was to make the subject of his study more than half a century later.

'If hereafter any highly cultured, poetical nation shall lure back to their birth right, the merry May-day gods of old;' then be sure 'the great Sperm Whale shall lord it.' (p. 454)

479. *But the Sperm Whale only breathes about one seventh or Sunday of his time* The ambivalent whale, whose Sunday breathing 'imparts to the blood its vivifying principle', is revealed as emblem of an equally ambivalent Christianity: both bourgeois and church-going – part umbrella-handle, part corsets, part gas-pipe, part Holy Eucharist.

479. *No roses, no violets, no Cologne-water in the sea* Nothing virginal, nothing modest, nothing magical in the sea. It is a world without grace (of the Blessed Virgin Mary), without heart's ease (of the *Viola tricolor*), without holy mystery (of 'the three old kings of Cologne' in their silver reliquary).

480. *furnished with a sort of locks (that open and shut)* 'And the key of the house of David will I lay upon his shoulder; so he shall open, and none shall shut; and he shall shut, and none shall open.' (*Isaiah* xxii, 22) cf. *Revelation* iii, 7.

480. *therefore the whale has no voice; unless ... when he so strangely rumbles, he talks through his nose* Despite the 'pyra-

midical silence' of 'this vast dumb brute', Ishmael admits to having heard an occasional rumble.

Until recently it was believed that whales were completely dumb. Yet Arctic whalers have long known that the Beluga, or White Whale, sometimes makes sounds audible to men on deck. When White Whales are near or underneath a ship, a whistling, musical trill is heard so often they are nicknamed 'sea canaries'.

The theory used to be that such sounds were produced by the whale releasing a fine stream of bubbles from the blowhole; they were not a true 'voice'. But the widespread use of hydrophones for undersea listening, and of echo-sounding devices, during World War II, revealed that schools of whales, far from being strong and silent, kept up a continuous hubbub.

Post-war experiments by L. V. Worthington and W. E. Schevill of the Woods Hole Oceanographic Institution, Massachusetts, have established that whales produce a wide range of noises and can hear ultrasonic vibrations up to eighty kilocycles a second; our upper limit is about twenty. The 'sonar' system of whales is analogous to radar, consisting of a sound pulse repeated from ten to over four hundred times a second. The whale, weaving his head from side to side as he approaches an object, orientates himself by the echo-signals, each ear counter-balancing the other.

481. *Wherefore, among whalemen, the spout is deemed poisonous* So these sprinkling pots and spoutings turn out, in the end, to be acrid – poisonous as the tumblers in which Peter Coffin dearly sold the sailors 'deliriums and death'. What was 'mistifying', or rather 'mystifying', in the end is literally blinding.

482. *He is both ponderous and profound* Very like *The Whale*, Ishmael's own 'ponderous task', or Bildad's Scriptures – yet another 'ponderous volume'. *All* truth, it was long ago acknowledged, 'is profound'. (MOBY DICK) 'And still deeper the meaning of that story of Narcissus, who because he could not grasp the tormenting, mild image he saw in THE FOUNTAIN, plunged into it and was drowned.' (LOOMINGS)

482. *all ponderous profound beings, such as Plato, Pyrrho, the Devil, Jupiter, Dante, and so on* The Sperm Whale itself is, of course, a 'Platonian'; recently 'exalted to Jove's high seat'; soon to evoke the Dantean torments of 'majestic Satan'. But, above all, he is a Pyrrhonian – an ambivalent mass of contradictions: polar solitary and bourgeois, *sanctum sanctorum* and killer.

Pyrrho (c. 360–270 B.C.), who accompanied Alexander the Great to India, where he may have studied Hindu and Persian philosophy, taught that nothing can be known because the contrary of every proposition can be maintained with equal plausibility. Kant's antimonies, earlier hoisted on board – in demonstrating the logical self-contradictions involved in all questions of space and time, free-will and the existence of God – elaborated, in part, the most sustained proof of Pyrrho's insight. For nothing, even direct sense-perception according to Pyrrho, is soluble by reason.

482. *a certain semi-visible steam* This rhapsody on the sublimity of the Sperm Whale as mystagogue is capped by Ishmael's own 'little treatise on Eternity' – itself to be capped by the perspiration following six cups of hot tea. The bathos is cutting; it dismisses not only Plato's or Dante's profundities, but Ishmael's own convoluted complexities. For the 'remarkable involved Cretan labyrinth of vermicelli-like vessels' of *The Whale* prove no more than a mirror reflection of the 'curious involved worming and undulation' of Ishmael's thoughts. Subjective idealism, Melville appears to say, can go no further.

Pyrrho, then – not Plato, Jupiter or Dante – is Ishmael's ultimate master. Despite the satanic psychology and pervasive myth of Narcissus, it is a Pyrrhonian sense of logical loggerheads, a simultaneous yoking of opposites, which is implicit not only in the whole dialectic, but in the *discordia consors* of individual parts – of sentences, even phrases – of *Moby-Dick*. His fourth will made, Ishmael too is imperturbable. He suspends his judgment, viewing 'this strange mixed affair we call life' with total scepticism.

482. *that vapor . . . glorified by a rainbow* In a final apotheosis, the Great Mysticetus is glimpsed like some nineteenth-century bishop, 'his vast, mild head overhung by a canopy', in the 'incommunicable contemplations' of his prayers – his ecclesiastical vapours irradiated by 'the everlasting convenant between God and every living creature of all flesh that is upon the earth'. (*Genesis* ix, 16)

So 'mistifying pots' have been turned to 'a canopy', as *ciborium*, itself once 'a canopy raised over the high altar', now means solely 'a receptacle for the reservation of the Eucharist'.

482. *Doubts of all things earthly, and intuitions of some things heavenly* As teasing coda to this hermetic, yet 'semi-visible'

symbolism, Ishmael adds a personal benediction: all, to some extent, are sceptics; many are atheists; but only few can attain (in Kant's phrase) to *Religion innerhalb der Grenzen der blossen Vernunft* (Religion within the boundaries of mere reason). 'This combination makes neither believer nor infidel', but – to forestall T. H. Huxley by some eighteen years – an 'agnostic'.

86 THE TAIL

483. *At the crotch or junction, these flukes slightly overlap* Like whalemen and whaleboat, the whale too has a 'crotch', suggesting both an idyll of angels with sideways receding wings and 'the crescentic borders' of the infidel Turk: here, too, all contraries meet.

483. *where infantileness of ease undulates through a Titanism of power* This phrase, like the rest of THE TALE, is a conscious Pyrrho-technic display of juxtaposed contraries, to lead, via those hermaphroditical Italian pictures, to a coupling – a literal copulation – of sexual imagery. The conjunction of male and female characteristics, present in both whaler and whale, now reaches a climax of robust beauty in the ascent from a muscle-bound Hercules, to that spiritual athlete Goethe, to its apogee and source in the divine champion, God the Father himself.

483. *Real strength never impairs beauty or harmony* 'It was strength and beauty,' Melville was to repeat almost forty years later. The 'charm' of the Handsome Sailor, too, would lie in 'comeliness and power, always attractive in masculine conjunction'; and Billy Budd, too, was to be compared to that 'heroic strong man, Hercules'.

The *Farnese Hercules* was clearly in Ishmael's mind. Nor did closer acquaintance with that muscle-bound prodigy in any way dampen Melville's enthusiasm. When, six years later, he actually saw the statue in Naples, he remarked in his journal on its 'gravely benevolent face' (21 February 1857); and that same year, lecturing on 'Statuary in Rome', he observed that the *Farnese Hercules* 'in its simplicity and good nature reminds us of cheerful and humane things'.

484. *As devout Eckerman lifted the linen sheet* 'The body lay naked, only wrapped in a white sheet . . . Frederick drew aside the

sheet, and I was astonished at the divine magnificence of the limbs. The breast was powerful, broad, and arched. . . A perfect man lay in great beauty before me.' (J. P. Eckermann, *Conversations with Goethe*, 23 March 1832, the final entry)

The English translation, by John Oxenford, had appeared a year earlier, in 1850. (See Extract 57.)

484. *When Angelo paints even God the Father in human form* In the 'Creation of Adam' on the ceiling of the Sistine Chapel – where the Christ presiding over the Last Judgment, however, is far from being either soft or curled.

cf. 'Of the picture of our Saviour with long haire' and 'Of the picture of God the Father ' (Sir Thomas Browne, *Pseudodoxia Epidemica* Bk 5, chs. 7 and 22)

484. *the soft, curled, hermaphroditical Italian pictures* Though an hermaphrodite, endowed with both male and female organs, might be thought to imply an ideal fusion of the sexes, it suggests here, as usual, a passive male, a 'soft, curled' Ganymede, or catamite. This hermaphrodite Jesus ('wearing redundant yellow hair') is not a synthesis Ishmael admires; he is too destitute of masculine brawniness and power, too entirely negative, feminine, submissive. His beauty, lacking 'real strength', is unimposing.

cf. Queequeg, that 'grand and glorious fellow', that 'noble trump', 'throwing his long arms straight out before him, and by turns revealing his brawny shoulders. . .' (WHEELBARROW)

484. *Therein no fairy's arm can transcend it* Was this already a code word, then, to signal the ambiguous nature of this subtly elastic 'organ', this 'member' in its webbed bed of sinews ('passing on either side the loins'), this compact, round 'root' at the crotch?

QUEEN MAB certainly suggests so. 'The fairies' midwife' brought Stubb 'such a queer dream': of an old queen, in fact, 'his stern . . . stuck full of marlinspikes, with the points out' – an old fairy of a hump-backed merman who as good as called Ahab himself 'a queen'. Those buttocks, that Hieronymus Bosch vision, suggests that a whole gamut of sailors' bawdy has remained unchanged over the centuries. 'The living member – that makes the living insult, my little man.'

So the clues begin to unravel. This TAIL and that fairy dream, this 'webbed bed' and that 'hammock', form mutual commentaries. As the whalebone cane has 'a small sort of end

... whittled down to a point', so 'in the tail the confluent measureless force of the whole whale seems concentrated to a point'. Ahab's 'dead thump' and the whale's 'living thump' are matched.

485. *Darmonodes' elephant that so frequented the flower-market* The story (also told by Montaigne) derives from Plutarch's *Moralia*: 'They feel love for many creatures, sometimes fierce and wild passions, sometimes rather charming and courtly. For instance, the elephant in Alexandria, who was a rival of Aristophanes the grammarian; they loved the same flower-girl, and the devotion of the elephant was no less manifest than that of the grammarian. For he used to bring her fruit as he passed through the fruit market; and passing his trunk like a hand inside her tunic he would gently caress the beauty around her breast'.

Extract 6 is from Plutarch's *Moralia*; Extract 7 from Pliny the Elder's *Natural History*, which also mentions the story; but the name 'Darmonodes' (itself suspiciously un-Greek) occurs in neither.

485. *yet another elephant, that when wounded ... extracted the dart* That of King Porus 'in the Indian battle with Alexander'. (THE GRAND ARMADA) Melville may have derived this touch straight from Montaigne, rather than Montaigne's source, Plutarch's *Life of Alexander*.

485. *Stealing unawares upon ... the vast corpulence of his dignity* You find no longer 'a portly burgher smoking his pipe', but a kitten upon a hearth: 'There go the ships: there is that leviathan, whom thou hast made to play therein.' (*Psalm* civ, 26: Extract 4.)

485. *You would almost think a great gun* For this idyll of 'broad palms', too, 'is but the wrapper and envelope of the storm'. Thunder resounds 'to the distance of three or four miles' (Extract 60) – by a rebus, at last, projecting the pun long implicit in 'gunwale'.

486. *majestic Satan thrusting forth his ... claw from the flame Baltic of Hell* Converting the kitten's playful claws into a satanic cat-like claw, with a touch of the Kattegat (or 'Categut'), one of 'those domineering fortresses which guard the entrances to ... the Baltic'. cf. 'Those who have noticed, in old editions of Dante, the representation of one of Satan's claws, projecting from a

lake of brimstone, will best conceive the effect this vision of a whale's tail produces.' (Robert Pearse Gillies, *Tales of a Voyager to the Arctic Ocean*, vol. 2, p. 299)

486. *even in Persia, the home of the fire worshippers* Linking the whale not only to Ahab, but his *alter ego*, Fedallah. cf. Pierre Bayle: 'the followers of the ancient religion of the Persians ... maintain that they do not adore the sun, but only turn toward it when they pray to God.' (*An Historical and Critical Dictionary*, 5, p. 637)

486. *As Ptolemy Philopater testified* Again an allusion to Plutarch's *Moralia*: 'Juba says ... also that elephants pray to the gods without being trained to the habit, purifying themselves in the sea, and they worship the risen sun, holding the trunk aloft like a hand. For this reason the beast is greatly loved by the gods, as Ptolemy Philopater testified.'

486. *The chance comparison ... between the whale and the elephant* Elephants 'stirring in their litter', 'pushing heavy cannon' up mountains, or yoked to 'a tilbury on a plain' have, in rapid succession, been multiplied by the appearance of Darmonodes's, King Porus's, and Ptolemy Philopater's elephants – soon to be joined by 'Moby Dick himself ... like the worshipped white-elephant in the coronation procession of the Siamese!'

This elephantine vista at last makes explicit the long heralded pun of 'the famous cavern-pagoda of Elephanta, in India'. But more illuminating is the elephant's role. For his trunk, like 'the stalk of a lily', inevitably points to the delicate, dainty, maidenly gentle and tender side of the whale – playful as the 'tap of a fan'. The elephant, that is, evokes damsels and zones: the Sperm Whale, 'measureless crush and crash'. Muscular force is centred in the tail: the more 'exquisitely' feminine preoccupations of knitting and stitching, in the trunk. Once paired, however, they couple. Whale and *elefant* – male and female: their all but anagrams – literally fuse when the 'tail flirted high into the air' is 'discharged'; and the maidenly gentle flukes 'are tossed erect in the air, and so remain vibrating ... till they downwards shoot out of view', 'very much as an Indian juggler tosses his balls'.

The whale is not so much philo/pater, it seems, as philoprogenitive.

487. *mystic gestures ... akin to Free-Mason signs and symbols* As the whaler in 'the whole roll' of his order sounded very like

a whale, so the whale in the brotherhood of his herd looks very like a Freemason with his 'mystic gestures' and 'signs'.

cf. Ishmael and Queequeg at the Spouter-Inn, conversing by 'friendly signs and hints', certain 'symptoms' and 'signs'. (A BOSOM FRIEND)

487. *Dissect him how I may . . . I know him not, and never will* 'So there is no earthly way of finding out precisely what *The Whale* really looks like.' (OF THE MONSTROUS PICTURES OF WHALES) All language, for 'unlettered Ishmael', is circuitous, labyrinthine, self-defeating. Yet it remains his sole access to reality: that is the paradox. This commentary, indeed, must prove his ultimate *raison d'être*; since ultimate reality itself escapes him.

But it is precisely ultimate reality (unknown, 'inscrutable', yet seeming-malicious) that his captain so tenaciously pursues.

487. *Thou shalt see my back parts* 'And the Lord said, Behold, there is a place by me, and thou shalt stand upon a rock: And it shall come to pass, while my glory passeth by, that I will put thee in a clift of the rock, and will cover thee with my hand while I pass by: And I will take away mine hand, and thou shalt see my back parts: but my face shall not be seen.' (*Exodus* xxxiii, 21–3)

cf. 'I know that he is wise in all, wonderful in that we conceive, but far more in what we comprehend not; for we behold him but asquint, upon reflex or shadow; our understanding is dimmer than *Moses* Eye; we are ignorant of the back-parts of God and the lower side of his Divinity; therefore to pry into the maze of his Counsels is not onely folly in Man, but presumption even in Angels. There is no threed or line to guide us in that labyrinth. . .' (Sir Thomas Browne, *Religio Medici*, Pt I, sec. 13)

87 THE GRAND ARMADA

487. *the most southerly point of all Asia* Birmah, of course, is Burma; Bally, Bali.

488. *domineering fortresses* Gibraltar on the Mediterranean, Kattegat on the Baltic, Istanbul on the Propontis.

488. *piratical proas* Or *prahu*, a large Malayan outrigger canoe with sails.

489. *kentledge* From *quintal*, a hundredweight: pig-iron used as permanent ballast.

491. *Corresponding to the crescent in our van ... another in our rear* As the whale's brow bore a 'horizontal, semi-crescentic depression' and his palms (or winged flukes) were 'exquisitely defined ... in the crescentic borders', his armada now sails, past palms, in one solid winged crescent – mirrored by another, in the rear, of 'rascally Asiatics'.

Between these two crescent moons Captain Ahab, like 'the circus-running sun', is trapped (by a paradox) in the straits of Sunda. But is not Tashtego too, with his cry, still a 'Turkish Muezzin'? And Ahab, a Sultan, or old Mogul? The three mates his three Emirs? Had not Moby Dick too appeared 'as a white bearded Mufti'? And will not the bull whale, attending his harem, soon reappear as 'a luxurious Ottoman', a 'Bashaw', a 'sated Turk'?

Muslims? Who is not a muslim?

492. *a herd of remorseless wild pirates* One lot of 'bloodthirsty' and 'inhuman atheistical devils' cheers on another, in a symmetrical progression, which is also a vicious circle. For as the Malays are to the *Pequod*, so the *Pequod* is to the whales; and the whales, in their turn, mirror 'these rascally Asiatics'.

493. *like King Porus' elephants* In a battle-stampede, which enabled Alexander to defeat King Porus at the Hydaspes, 326 B.C. (Q. Curtius Rufus, *History of Alexander the Great*)

495. *curious contrivances ... called druggs* Usually spelt 'drogues', from the 'dragged' wooden blocks. But Ishmael is aiming at a pun. For that 'iron leech' will turn a 'drugged-harpoon' to enrage 'drugged whales'.

496. *the embayed axis of the herd* Within 'the tumults of the outer concentric circles' lies the heart of this Descartian vortex. The whales in a whirlpool, that is, by turning are themselves turned from a school to a whole universe of Cartesian professors.

496. *a breach in the living wall* For there are walls within walls within walls, as well as wheels within wheels. And 'how can the prisoner reach outside except by thrusting through the wall?' (THE QUARTER-DECK)

497. *Like household dogs ... right up to our gunwales* This mutual trust suggests some Golden Age pastoral; Queequeg, another Adam among the gunwales.

497. *suspended in those watery vaults ... exceedingly transparent* But the whales, too, are 'vaulted' (ETYMOLOGY) – vaults within vaults.

497. *floated the forms of the nursing mothers* cf. Bennett: 'Intelligent whalers, who have occasionally seen the female Cachalot in the act of suckling her young, agree very closely in their descriptions of this process. They state, that the mother reposes upon her side, with the pectoral fin raised above the surface of the sea, while the calf, which is thus enabled to retain its spiracle in the air, receives the protruded nipple within the angle of the mouth – a part where it is reasonable to suppose that the tongue would also be found of some assistance.' (*Narrative of a Whaling Voyage*, vol. 2, pp. 178–9)

The gestation period, for most baleen whales, is about ten to twelve months. Usually one calf is born to each mother every two or three years. 'It goes under the protection of its mother, for probably a year or more...' (Scoresby, vol. I p. 470)

497. *some fourteen feet in length ... bent like a Tartar's bow* Again Bennett supplied the details, after 'an anatomical examination of a foetal Cachalot, which was removed from the abdomen of its mother, and taken on board the ship ... It was fourteen feet long and six in circumference; of a deep black colour, prettily mottled with a few white-spots; and in form, as perfect as the adult whale, with the single exception that the tail-fin was crumpled on its free border, and had the corner of each fluke folded inwards. Its position in the womb was that of a bent bow – the head and tail being approximated, and the back arched.' (vol. II, pp. 167–8)

The *discordia consors*, or violent yoking of contraries (cradle and gunwale, calm and commotion), finds its embryo reflection in the unborn whale. For the suckling – 'still spiritually feasting', it seems, upon some unearthly Wordsworthian *Intimations* – springs from the womb, switched back and poised for death. 'How I snuffed that Tartar air!' (p. 155)

Birth is launched deathward, but death itself may prove a rebirth: so the two teats are 'curiously situated, one on each side of the anus'; so the umbilical line 'becomes entangled with the hempen one'; so 'milk and blood rivallingly discolor the sea'.

498. *long coils ... of Madame Leviathan* As the whale-line 'spirally coiled' had spiralized the whale, so the embryo whale

now lies spiralized within 'the gigantic involutions' of his dam. (THE FOSSIL WHALE)

cf. Scoresby: 'In the latter end of April 1811, a sucker was taken by a Hull whaler, to which the *fumis umbilicalis* was still attached.' (vol. 1, p. 470)

498. *birth to an Esau and Jacob* About one per cent of the pregnancies among baleen whales, it has been calculated, are twins.

498. *it might do well with strawberries* 'The milk is probably very rich, for in that caught near Berkley, with its young one, the milk, which was tasted by Messrs Jenner and Ludlow, surgeons at Sudbury, was rich like cow's milk to which cream had been added.' (Beale, p. 126)

In the first three days of life a baby whale makes a *net* increase of 500 lb. a day on his mother's milk.

498. *the whales salute* more hominum '... penem intrantem feminam mammis lactantem.' (CETOLOGY) cf. Bennett: 'Like other cetaceans, they couple *more hominum*: in one instance, which came under my notice, the position of the parties was vertical; their heads being raised above the surface of the sea.' (vol. 2, p. 178)

498. *deep down and deep inland there I still bathe me in eternal mildness of joy* 'So in the soul of man there lies one insular Tahiti, full of peace and joy ...' (BRIT)

499. *the lone mounted desperado Arnold* On 17 October 1777, after a decisive American victory – in what was perhaps the decisive campaign of the Revolutionary War – General Burgoyne, outnumbered and outmanoeuvred, surrendered at Saratoga. The Springs were earlier linked to the whales' spout; now the battlefield recalls Benedict Arnold, maverick hero of the campaign, who later turned traitor to the American cause, leading devastating raids against Virginia and his native Connecticut. But Melville, no doubt, had also his grandfather in mind; for Colonel Gansevoort played a key role by gallantly holding Fort Stanwix under siege, until the advance of Arnold's forces scared the British into retreat.

500. *killed and waifed* Technical term apart, the pun is insistent. Dead, the whale is for ever outcast from the nurseries.

88 SCHOOLS AND SCHOOLMASTERS

501. en bon point In old French – now usually *embonpoint*, meaning 'in plump condition'.

501. *like fashionables* Lounging, in their turn, up and down the promenades of Saratoga or Baden-Baden (celebrated for 'jets d'eau, hot springs and cold') with their whalebone corsets and canes, 'umbrella-stocks, and handles to riding-whips'.

502. *the Bashaw* An earlier form of *pasha*, used here perhaps for its etymological derivation from *bāsh* (Turkish, 'head'), soon to be literally bashed – wrenched, scarred and broken.

502. *Solomon ... among his thousand concubines* To be precise, 'seven hundred wives, princesses, and three hundred concubines'. (*1 Kings* xi, 3)

503. *the memoirs of Vidocq* Eugène François Vidocq (1775–1857), after a career of crime, joined the Paris *Sûreté* in 1809 as a police spy, eventually rising to the head of the detective branch. In 1832 he was discharged on the grounds of instigating a crime in order to uncover it. His *Mémoires* in four volumes (1828–9) – largely spurious – tell how disguised as a friar, he taught in a school for peasant girls.

503. *venerable moss-bearded Daniel Boone* who blazed the Wilderness Road into Kentucky, lived to the age of eighty-six, moving from Boonesborough to what is now West Virginia, and in his mid-sixties to a tract granted him by the Spanish in Missouri.

504. *a riotous lad at Yale or Harvard* There is nothing like 'whaling to breed this free and easy sort of genial, desperado philosophy'. The masonic brotherhood extends to 'the leviathanic'.

cf. Beale: 'The young males ... make an immediate and rapid retreat upon one of their number being struck, who is left to take the best care he can of himself.' (pp. 52–4)

89 FAST-FISH AND LOOSE-FISH

505. *Justinian's Pandects* A compendium, or digest, of extracts from noted classical jurists – one of the four parts of the *Corpus*

Juris Civilis compiled by order of Justinian I, and issued in fifty books between 529 and 535 A.D.

505. *on a Queen Anne's farthing* A byword for rarity. Commemorative farthings – though not Queen Anne's especially – were often diminutive.

506. *the Coke-upon-Littleton of the fist* The first four volumes of Sir Edward Coke's *Institutes* (1628–44) consist of a commentary on the *Tenures* of Sir Thomas Littleton (1422–81), long the principal authority on English real property law.

506. *a curious case of whale-trover* See 'An Account of a Trial Respecting the Right of the Ship *Experiment*, to a Whale Struck by One of the Crew of the *Neptune*' (Scoresby, Appendix to vol. II, pp. 518–21)

The whole passage is re-edited in *E*, with results even more stilted than the original. Hayford and Parker accept the corrections as Melville's; but there is nothing peculiarly Melvillean about the revised draft. Surely the English editor, noting the muddle between 'plaintiffs' and 'defendants' that closed these paragraphs, took pencil in hand to sort out the rest. This very English piece of legal chicanery might be expected to appeal to an English editorial mind.

506. *Mr Erskine was counsel for the defendants; Lord Ellenborough was the judge* Thomas Erskine (1750–1823), the great forensic barrister, defended Thomas Paine's *The Rights of Man* against a charge of sedition. Lord Ellenborough (1750–1818), a repressive Lord Chief Justice of the French Revolutionary period, successfully defended Warren Hastings at his impeachment. Thus Lord Ellenborough is the reactionary; Mr Erskine, the progressive. While Lord Ellenborough, on one side, upholds the hereditary rights of archbishops and dukes, Mr Erskine, on the other, represents the 'souls of Russian serfs and Republican slaves', 'the Rights of Man and the Liberties of the World'.

The Yankee irony, at the expense of Old World sinecures, is crowned by the king himself – his head, like a sturgeon's symbolically regarded, at once 'highly dense and elastic'.

560. *a recent crim. con. case* A *criminal conversation* case – meaning 'intercourse' or 'adultery'.

506. *the gentleman had originally harpooned the lady* The phallic innuendo sounds *passim*. cf. Queequeg 'sporting his harpoon like a marshal's baton', or 'stopping to adjust the sheath'.

507. *like the Temple of the Philistines* At Gaza with its 'two middle pillars upon which the house stood'. (*Judges* xvi, 29)

507. *Republican slaves* Melville's attitude to the slave issue in this critical decade before the outbreak of Civil War was to be fully explored through the ironic mask of Captain Amasa Delano (of Duxbury, Massachusetts) in *Benito Cereno*, 1855.

507. *Mordecai, the broker* Esther's uncle and guardian, viz. a Jew.

508. *What to ... Brother Jonathan, is Texas* 'I am distressed for thee, my brother Jonathan' (2 *Samuel* i, 26): a second reference to American imperial ambitions. (pp. 158–9, note) James K. Paulding's *The Diverting History of John Bull and Brother Jonathan* (1812) had revived the old nickname, first used in England of the Roundheads.

508. *What was Poland to the Czar?* Alexander I, made king of dismembered Poland by the Congress of Vienna (1815).

508. *What at last will Mexico be to the United States?* A 'neighbour Naboth', to change the metaphor (after David Lee Child's tract, *The Taking of Naboth's Vineyard, or History of the Texas Conspiracy*, 1845). For President Polk's appeals to 'prosperity and glory' were invariably criticized as a 'coveting of Naboth's Vineyard'; and the Ahab in this allegory was inevitably John C. Calhoun. (See Alan Heimert, '*Moby-Dick* and American Political Symbolism', *American Quarterly* vol. XV, No. 4.)

90 HEADS OR TAILS

508. *Bracton, l.3, c. 3* Henry de Bracton (d. 1268), author of the *De Legibus et Consuetudinibus Angliae*, was the first to attempt a systematic treatise on the laws and customs of England. Melville's extract is from the Tractus Secundus, *De Corona*.

509. *some honest mariners of Dover* A current piece of gossip from the *Literary World*: 'Some poor fishermen captured a whale in Margate Bay, and as it was of value, Dr Wallingford addressed a letter to the Duke, endeavouring to persuade him to give up the animal to the captors, because really it was not a fish; in which assertion the doctor is fully sustained by all sound zoologists. The Duke wrote back word, that he did not see what any fellow of the College of Surgery had to do with the Warden

of the Cinque Ports; that the fishermen had been paid £28 for salvage, and the balance of the proceeds of the whale aforesaid, he intended to dispose of just as he pleased, without consulting Dr Wallingford at all!' (29 June 1850)

509. *the Cinque Ports* The five (later seven) sea-ports of south-eastern England which, until 1835, received certain privileges in return for providing a majority of the recruits for the British navy.

509. *fobbing his perquisites* viz. pocketing – into his fob pocket.

509. *promising themselves a good £150 from the precious oil and bone* A Blue Whale, it is estimated, would bring in roughly £3,000 today: in oil alone £2,000, plus the meat extract, meat meal, liver oil, liver extract, frozen meat etc. The Blue Whale, however, like the Hump-Backed Whale, is now completely protected.

509. *a copy of Blackstone* Sir William Blackstone's *Commentaries on the Laws of England* (1765–9). See Extract 44: 'A tenth branch of the king's ordinary revenue ... is the right to *royal* fish, which are whale and sturgeon. And these, when either thrown ashore or caught near the coast, are the property of the king.' (Bk I, ch. 8)

509. *their respectful consternation – so truly English* Like 'those other creatures in certain parts of our earth, who with a degree of footmanism quite unprecedented in other planets, bow down before the torso of a deceased landed proprietor merely on account of the inordinate possessions yet owned and rented in his name'. (THE RAMADAN, p. 178)

510. *meddling with other people's business* 'The Iron Duke' died a year after the publication of *Moby-Dick*, at the age of eighty-three. His reactionary politics had made him so loathed that once he was actually assaulted by a mob.

510. *Plowdon* Edmund Plowden (1518–85), English jurist. The king's right to whales is set out in section 315 of his *Commentaries ou les reportes* (1571).

511. *one William Prynne* (1600–1669), a relentless Puritan pamphleteer – who in 1660, however, affirmed Charles II's right of restoration. In *Aurum Reginae: or a compendious Tractate and ... Collection of Records ... concerning Queen-Gold* (Lon-

don, 1668), he wrote: 'The King himself shall have the Head and Body to his benefit, to make Oyle and other things; but the QUEEN the Tayle, to make whalebones for her Royal Vestments, Dresses, and other use in her Wardrobe.'

511. *An allegorical meaning may lurk here* 'But is the Queen a mere maid...?' That 'black limber bone', that tail, expose the pun.

91 THE PEQUOD MEETS THE ROSE-BUD

511. Sir T. Browne, V. E. *Vulgar Errors*, or *Pseudodoxia Epidemica* (1646), Bk III, ch. 26, 'Of Sperma-Ceti, and the Sperma-Ceti Whale' (cf. Extract 19). This is the reading of the first English edition. The American reading, 'denying not inquiry', made nonsense of the 'insufferable fetor'.

513. *these Crappoes of Frenchmen* From *crapaud*, 'toad'.

513. *'Bouton de Rose' ... the romantic name of this aromatic ship* With an anagrammatic twist Ishmael suggests that such seeming romance is essentially a-romantic, this consummately French *Roman de la Rose*, merely a confusion of contraries: a nosegay surrounded by vultures; a corpse-like odour, with a suggestion of 'crap'.

A good thing, then, 'that the Sperm Whale has no proper olfactories'. Yet the whale itself contains the base for all perfume: its ambergris, the fixative for 'attar-of-rose', for violet water, for *Eau de Cologne*; its sperm, 'literally and truly, like the smell of spring violets'. 'No roses, no violets, no Cologne-water in the sea.' (p. 479) Yet a 'Rose-bud', 'a bunch of posies', 'a Cologne manufacturer', are all to be found.

514. *Never heard of such a whale* The *Jungfrau*, too, evinced 'complete ignorance of the White Whale'. But the *Bouton de Rose* is not ignorant merely; she is disaffected. Her once revolutionary crew is back under bourgeois command. And if the captain is 'diddled' by his chief-mate, so is the chief-mate by Stubb. Both are led by the nose.

For that 'unsavory odor' conceals a political stench; within that tale of Yankee cunning lurks a Yankee jest. The ultimate jibe is at the July Revolution of 1830: drooping, yet spiked 'with impaling force'.

514. *Cachalot Blanche!* Had Melville, though, heard of 'Le

Cachalot Blanc', an article that regaled its French readers at length with one version of the 'Nantuckett' myth (*Musée des familles,* January 1837)? See Appendix.

515. *so I'll get out of this dirty scrape* A quick-witted pun for a Guernsey-man, while 'scraping the dry bones' of his noxious whale; as is his next scoff too, at the ex-Cologne manufacturer's unprofitable 'pickle'.

515. *the Captain's round-house* A Crappo aptly withdraws to a '*cabinet*', or privy – to oust one 'dirty scrape' with another. Anality aboard reflects that 'prodigious dyspepsia' (of crap) in the whale.

515. *Stubb argued well* 'Stubb augured well' is Hayford/Parker's convincing emendation.

516. *a red cotton velvet vest* The French ship is liberally daubed in red – with her bright red figure-head and red-capped crew and fiery-faced surgeon. But her captain, too, wears red. Half cotton, half velvet, half republican, half monarchist – what else in this ex-industrialist but a 'citizen king'? Who else is this whiskered 'ignoramus' but Louis Philippe? What else are his sailors but 'worsted'?

518. *'a purse! a purse!'* Though the whale may be almost 'bankrupt' of oil, the crew look on 'anxious as gold-hunters' while Stubb feels ... for another 'gold watch that the whale might have swallowed'?

518. *something that looked like ripe Windsor soap, or rich mottled old cheese* A royal fish (royally proclaimed) aptly proves to contain Windsor soap: 'This is Charing Cross; hear ye! good people all ... the great sperm whale now reigneth!' (p. 229)

So 'that drugged whale' finds its fit resting-place with a 'druggist'. So the 'old cheese' of its innards returns a whiff of the whale-line. So its 'ash color' mirrors 'the white ash' of the oars. So 'pale golden ambergris' is 'worth a gold guinea an ounce'.

92 AMBERGRIS

AMBERGRIS 'Ambergris appears to be nothing but the hardened faeces of the spermaceti whale'. (Beale) But its genesis is still uncertain. Lighter than water, it melts at about 65°C. and dissolves readily in absolute alcohol, ether, fat or volatile oils.

519. *Captain Coffin ... at the bar of the English House of Commons* Declared 'that he had lately brought home 362 ounces, troy, of this costly substance, which he had found in the anus of a *female* sperm whale that he had captured off the coast of Guinea, and which he stated was very bony and sickly...' (Beale, ch. 10, 'Ambergris', pp. 130–35)

519. *The Turks ... to St Peter's in Rome* cf. It 'is also constantly bought by the pilgrims who travel to Mecca, probably to offer it there, and make use of it in fumigations, in the same manner as frankincense is used in Catholic countries. The Turks make use of it as an aphrodisiac.' (Beale, ibid., quoting Brande's *Manual of Chemistry*, p. 594)

519. *Brandreth's pills* To blast 'a blasted whale'. One of the first makers of patent medicines in the United States, Benjamin Brandreth emigrated from England in 1834. cf. 'A peck of Morrison's or Brandreth's pills, or his homeopathic dose of a pound of calomel and jalap, would probably remove obstructions in the creature's abdominal viscera...' (Cheever, *The Whale and his Captors*, pp. 115–16)

520. *Bethink thee of that saying of St Paul in Corinthians* 'So also is the resurrection of the dead. It is sown in corruption; it is raised in incorruption; it is sown in dishonour; it is raised in glory: it is sown in weakness; it is raised in power.' (*1 Corinthians* xv, 42–3)

520. *that saying of Paracelsus* 'As Paracelsus encourageth, Ordure makes the best Musk, and from the most foetid substances may be drawn the most odoriferous Essences...' (Sir Thomas Browne, *Pseudodoxia Epidemica*, Bk. III, ch. 26)

Browne drew directly on the *Hermetic and Alchemical Writings* of Paracelsus ('Concerning the Odoriferous Specific'); Melville, however, drew both this reference and the heading for ch. 91, and the initial extract it seems, direct from Beale. (p. 131)

520. *whale cemeteries, in the Greenland dock* From his Green Mountains the greenhorn reaches only this yet more illusory Greenland. From the 'coffin warehouses' of Manhattan Ishmael reaches merely 'these whale cemeteries'. Perfume and plague – life and death – are everywhere mingled: graveyards excavated 'for the foundations of a Lying-in Hospital'.

The old Pittsfield cemetery was transferred in 1850–51. Baptist,

Methodist and Catholic churches had long been built on the oldest parts of the burial ground; but a grammar school – not hospital – was now in the course of construction. 'The new site was dedicated on 9 September 1850, with odes by John C. Hoadley and Mrs J. R. Morewood, both close friends of Melville at this time, and the dedicatory poem by Oliver Wendell Holmes.' (Mansfield and Vincent, p. 795)

520. *the learned Fogo Von Slack* Yet another *alias* to score off Scoresby. See 'Description of Whale-Oil, and Remarks on the Cause of its Offensive Smell' (*An Account of the Arctic Regions*, vol. II, pp. 408–15) and his bogus etymology (vol. II, p. 52).

The Dutch seasonal settlement of Smeerenburg (Blubber-town) dates from the early seventeenth century when whales, harpooned in Spitzbergen bays, had their blubber flensed and boiled out in coppers on the beach. After 1635 Bay Whaling declined and ships, foraging along the ice from Spitzbergen to Greenland into the Davis Strait, flensed and casked their blubber at sea. cf. Friedrich Martens, *The Voyage to Spitzbergen and Greenland*, 1671: 'The next is call'd Schmerenburgh, where formerly the Dutch used to boil their Train-oyl; some of them were left there once for all the Winter, but all perish'd. There were yet remaining several Houses like a small Village...' (Harris Coll. vol. I, ch. 40)

521. *to detect a Jew ... by the nose* See *Pseudodoxia Epidemica* Bk IV 'Of many popular and received Tenents concerning Man', ch. 10: 'That Jews stinke'.

93 THE CASTAWAY

THE CASTAWAY cf.

> No voice divine the storm allay'd,
> No light propitious shone;
> When, snatch'd from all effectual aid,
> We perish'd, each alone:
> But I beneath a rougher sea,
> And whelm'd in deeper gulphs than he.
>
> (Cowper, *The Castaway*, 61–6)

522. *the little negro Pippin by nick-name* The logic of this chapter, evolving by a series of antitheses, is almost Kantian in

its self-defeating dialectic: 'a most significant event' befalling 'the most insignificant of the *Pequod*'s crew'; a 'timorous wight', who is a 'negro'. 'Hoist in Locke's head, you go over that way; but now, on the other side, hoist in Kant's...'

In a craft so 'madly merry', after a midnight 'so gloomy-jolly', reappears little Pippin, evanescent (at a rap) as an apple of Sodom – in explicit contrast to that gigantic 'negro-savage' Daggoo. All is self-contradiction, incapable of resolution: his 'natural lustre' lit by 'unnatural gases'; 'the pure-watered diamond' turned a jewel from Hell.

522. *three hundred and sixty-five Fourth of Julys and New Year's Days* Beyond the good-humoured reference to Negro merry-making lies the dark shadow of impending Civil War. As Frederick Douglass would soon declare: 'What to the American slave is your Fourth of July? I answer: a day that reveals to him, more than all other days in the year, the gross injustice and cruelty to which he is the constant victim. To him your celebration is a sham; your boasted liberty, an unholy licence...' (Rochester, 4 July 1852)

''Tis July's immortal Fourth; all fountains must run wine today!' Stubb had cried; but to the little Negro he adds: 'a whale would sell for thirty times what you would, Pip, in Alabama. Bear that in mind...' A Negroes' Independence Day was not to be pronounced until Lincoln's Emancipation Proclamation of 22 September 1862; not confirmed until the Fourteenth Constitutional Amendment (1868).

522. *his native Tolland County in Connecticut* A northern, or free state – in the Pequot homeland. For this Alabama 'bell-boy' is born in a 'land that tolls' (literally, that lures his kind to capture, that bars their rights and registers them like beasts for sale at market), as the rap (or 'con') of the whale first strikes him with panic.

Like his namesake Father M/*apple*, this *Pippin* too will offer 'a prayer so deeply devout' as to seem 'kneeling and praying at the bottom of the sea'. He too will conclude with a 'continual tolling'. (THE SERMON) His jingle of bells, from birth, sounded a death-knell.

522. *many a fiddler's frolic on the green* cf. Billy Loon, 'royal drummer and pounder of the tamborine' at the Hawaiian court: 'a jolly little negro, tricked out in a soiled blue jacket, studded

all over with rusty bell-buttons, and garnished with shabby gold lace'. (*Omoo*, ch. 65)

523. *several turns around his chest and neck* 'All men live enveloped in whale-lines' – with 'a flash' and a 'blue, choked face' (at 'the chocks') to echo their 'ringed lightnings' and 'hempen blue smoke'.

523. *hated Pip for a poltroon Poltrone*, or lazy coward – another *Scaramuccia*, flinching from the whale. 'What *art* thou afraid of? Wherefore, like a coward, dost thou forever pip and whimper, and go cowering and trembling?' (*Sartor Resartus*, II, vii)

524. *Stick to the boat, Pip* The Fugitive Slave Act became law in September 1850. In April 1851 Thomas Simms, a slave from Georgia, was tried before the Massachusetts Supreme Court. Melville's father-in-law, Lemuel Shaw, was Chief Justice of that court and his friend, Richard Henry Dana Jr, an attorney for the defence. Nine years earlier Shaw had riled abolitionists by returning a fugitive to Virginia. This time he had the court building protected by an iron chain and an armed police guard. Simms too was returned – and publicly whipped in Savannah. (See THE SERMON, p. 143, note.)

524. *like gold-beater's skin hammered out* As the 'great white mass' of the squid rose from under a 'long burnished sun-glade', so from this gold-spangled calm rises Pip's 'big white God'; or rather ('with one half-throttled shriek') Pip himself feels 'carried down alive' to 'the joyous, heartless, ever-juvenile eternities'.

It is this awakening to the heartless horror of his condition which stuns Pip; stuns him not to the cool pose or 'genial, desperado philosophy' of an Ishmael, but shocked idiocy. Deserted in his agony, 'Pip saw the multitudinous, God-omnipresent, coral insects...' 'Heed it well, ye Pantheists!' He had 'trusted in God' (*Matthew* xxvii, 43), yet amid 'such a heartless immensity, my God!' my God! discovered nothing – either 'aloft' or in the 'ringed horizon' of his soul – but blank indifference.

After the crucifixion: descent and resurrection. 'The thing is common in that fishery'; and a 'like abandonment' is soon to befall Ishmael. But Pip returns not as divine saviour ('the divinest symbol of the crystal skies'), nor with gifts of holy wisdom (the prerogative of the mad), but numbed with a sense of confrontation with the void, a meaningless burgeoning chaos, a moral purposelessness at the heart of the infinite. Without belief, without truth, without a refuge in self-deception, neurotic sublimation or moral sanctions, Pip becomes (in Nietzsche's phrase) not a 'superman', but an idiot. His eyes – unlike the monomaniac Ahab's, active even in sleep – are 'passive'.

524. *Bobbing up and down ... Pip's ebon head* As if bobbing for apples, the pippin (Hey presto!) is turned to a 'bobbin' (or spool in the shuttle) which sees 'God's foot upon the treadle of the loom' and speaks it.

525. *The intense concentration of self* cf. 'Delight is to him – a far, far upward, and inward delight – who against the proud gods and commodores of this earth, ever stands forth his own inexorable self.' (THE SERMON)

525. *in the middle of such a heartless immensity* cf. 'Is it that by its indefiniteness it shadows forth the heartless voids and immensities of the universe, and thus stabs us from behind with the thoughts of annihilation ...?' (THE WHITENESS OF THE WHALE)

525. *my God! who can tell? Mark* xv 34: 'And at the ninth hour Jesus cried with a loud voice, saying, Eloi, Eloi, lama sabachthani? which is, being interpreted, My God, my God, why hast thou forsaken me?'

525. *but drowned the infinite of his soul* That at last he lost his identity; took 'the mystic ocean at his feet for the visible image of that deep, blue, bottomless soul, pervading mankind and nature ...' (THE MAST-HEAD, p. 257, note)

525. *the miser-merman Wisdom* Davy Jones, Stubb's 'badger-haired old merman', in his locker.

525. *multitudinous ... coral insects*

> The multitudinous seas incarnadine,
> Making the green one red.
>
> (*Macbeth* II, ii, 62–3)

mingling with memories from *The Tempest*:

> Of his bones are coral made;
> Those are pearls that were his eyes;
> Nothing of him that doth fade
> But doth suffer a sea-change
> Into something rich and strange.

Sea-nymphs hourly ring his knell:
Ding-dong.
Hark! now I hear them – Ding-dong bell.
(I, ii, 397ff.)

525. *He saw God's foot upon the treadle of the loom, and spoke it* But 'woe to him who ... while preaching to others is himself a castaway!' (THE SERMON)

cf. Ishmael's dream-steeped illusions at 'the Loom of Time'. (THE MAT-MAKER, p. 316, note)

cf. 'The weaver-god, he weaves; and by that weaving is he deafened, that he hears no mortal voice; and by that humming, we, too, who look on the loom are deafened; and only when we escape it shall we hear the thousand voices that speak through it.' (A BOWER IN THE ARSACIDES)

526. *So man's insanity is heaven's sense* 'For it is written, I will destroy the wisdom of the wise, and will bring to nothing the understanding of the prudent. Where is the wise? where is the scribe? where is the disputer of this world? hath not God made foolish the wisdom of this world?' (*1 Corinthians* i, 19–20)

The dialectic of the opening paragraphs concludes in the self-defeating metaphysics of the last, where all turns to paradox, 'to reason' (in existentialist jargon) 'absurd': the 'jolly' (with that brightness peculiar to his 'joyous' and 'ever-juvenile' tribe) turned (by these 'joyous' and 'ever-juvenile eternities') to gloom; a youth, who was merry, become truly mad.

Only Ishmael, whom 'nothing dispirits', who can take all 'sly, good-natured hits, and jolly punches in the side', survives. For Pip (with the pip) there is no saving synthesis. To the end 'crazy-witty', he remains a contradiction in terms: an evil-blazing diamond, a Sodom apple, a 'gloomy jolly', a Negro wight.

94 A SQUEEZE OF THE HAND

526. *before a large Constantine's bath* This bath, filled with sperm-like wine, profanes the deathbed baptism of the first Christian Emperor.

526. *my fingers felt like eels ... to serpentine and spiralize* As the whale-line had spiralized the whale, so the sperm-oil, in its turn, now spiralizes the whaleman. The service rendered is mutual.

Such eels and serpents (amid these lumps of sperm, so carefully squeezed into fluid, till they discharge all their opulence) are, of course, blatantly phallic: what should be mollifying (the females) now turning the males themselves into molls; 'after the bitter exertion' (at the windlass), 'a sweet and unctuous duty'.

This homosexual pastoral – as in a musky meadow filled with pansies in *heart's ease* or *love-in-idleness* – is the ultimate illusion. The 'smell of spring violets' mocks scenes of such immodesty: this 'bunch of posies' too masks an unsavoury 'nosegay'; this fraternal eucharist of bursting grapes marks the fellowship of Sodom.

After a love frolic, then, the return to blood frolic: 'the planks stream with freshets of blood and oil.' 'Over Descartian vortices you hover' – of sperm-tub, rope and sea – in spiralizing shapes of universal ruin.

526. *infiltrated tissues, woven almost within the hour* As if *this* were 'the Loom of Time': 'The Sperm of the Whale before it cools, is white and viscid, so that you may draw it like Sealing-wax or Glew, and smells like Wheat boil'd in Water...' (Friedrich Martens, *The Voyage to Spitzbergen and Greenland*, Harris Coll. vol. 1, ch. 42)

527. *I washed my hands and my heart of it* cf:

> And telling me the sovreignest thing on earth
> Was parmaceti for an inward bruise.
>
> (*Henry IV, Part I*, iii, 57–8; Extract 15)

527. *the old Paracelsan superstition* Again from the *Hermetic and Alchemical Writings*.

527. *divinely free from all ill-will* Like Adam and Eve, after eating of the forbidden fruit:

> As with new Wine intoxicated both
> They swim in mirth, and fansie that they feel
> Divinitie within them breeding wings...
>
> (*Paradise Lost* IX, 1008–10)

527. *till I myself almost melted into it* cf. 'I felt a melting in me. No more my splintered heart and maddened hand were turned against the wolfish world.' (A BOSOM FRIEND)

527. *nay, let us all squeeze ourselves into each other* Such longings, while repulsive to one part of the normal personality, are also seductive to another; for they sever sex from its human

context, reducing the world to orifices and organs, action to their combinations. Ishmael's version of sea-pastoral, for all its religious overtones, is peculiarly prone to such day-dreams. Ever after they haunt him; and are never repudiated. Heartfelt bliss *on land* proves a poor second-best to caressing such seamen – in squeezing such semen.

It needed a pre-Freudian self-confidence so unequivocally to reveal so much of Melville's own adolescent obsessions which, leviathan-like in 'his native profundities, sliding along beneath the surface', underlie the myth of Narcissus – the key to *Moby-Dick* in all its metaphysical variations.

527. *let us squeeze ourselves universally* cf. The *Calamus* section of Whitman's *Leaves of Grass* (1860, edn), celebrating this same 'adhesive' love or friendship – a 'beautiful and sane affection of man for man', to 'make the continent indissoluble' and weld the States into a 'Living Union'. cf. Shelley's vision of a future, regenerate world where 'all things are recreated, and the flame of consentaneous love inspires all life.' (*Queen Mab*)

528. *like blocks of Berkshire marble* Grey-veined marble from the very country to which Melville himself had just shifted his 'conceit' of felicity.

528. *from the thigh of Louis le Gros* Louis VI (1081–1137), the French king who was almost continually at war with the Anglo-Norman king, Henry I. As the *ambre gris* had a touch of royal Windsor, this 'plum-pudding' – to complete the paradox – is grossly French. The contradiction is as militant as French Louis and English Henry.

95 THE CASSOCK

530. *for an abomination at the brook Kedron* It is Ishmael, not the priest-chronicler, who is being dark:

> And Asa did that which was right in the eyes of the Lord, as did David his father.
> And he took away the sodomites out of the land, and removed all the idols that his fathers had made.
> And also Maachah his mother, even her he removed from being queen, because she made an idol in a grove; and Asa destroyed her idol, and burnt it by the brook Kidron.
> (*1 Kings* xv, 11–13)

530. *longer than a Kentuckian is tall* 'The Yard of the Whale is a strong Sinew, of six, seven, or eight Foot long, according to the bigness of the Animal: where it is fixed, it has a double Skin, lying just like a Knife in a Sheath ... Where the Yard begins, it is foursquare, consisting of many strong Sinews, which if dry'd, are as transparent as Fishglew, and serve the Sea-men to twist Whips of.' (Friedrich Martens, op. cit. vol. 1, ch. 42)

530. *as an African hunter the pelt of a boa* The true boa (South American, not African) can reach a length of up to twelve feet.

530. *Immemorial to all his order, this investiture* With further hints of masonic rites inverted – presenting this 'candidate' not in white (*candidatus*), but 'arrayed in decent black'.

531. *what a candidate for an archbishoprick* 'I will not conceal his parts, nor his power, nor his comely proportion' (*Job* xli, 12) – with an archaism at last candidly naming the 'cone', 'idol', 'grandissimus', at the rear.

So 'the Archbishop of Savesoul' stands displayed in a black phallic pelt; so this peculiar 'mincer', in full canonical rig, proves but a mincing queer; so this 'cassock', turned inside out, spells 'ass/cock' in the rigging.

531. *Bible leaves! Bible leaves!* Tumbling perverted from his pulpit: 'When Jesus had spoken these words, he went forth with his disciples over the brook Cedron, where was a garden ...' (*John* xviii, 1)

96 THE TRY-WORKS

531. *till they shine within like silver punch-bowls* 'Yea, verily, hearts alive, we'd brew choice punch ... there, and from that live punch-bowl quaff the living stuff.' (PITCHPOLING) These pots – with knees, flanks, lips, mouths – too are now 'hearts alive'; their brew, 'oil, like hot punch'.

531. *profound mathematical meditation* For a nautical Descartes, brooding on those three-dimensional statistics. Ishmael is 'in the left hand try-pot' no doubt as a goatish infidel on 'the left wing of the day of judgment'. This, too, is part of 'the capricious emblazonings of the works'.

532. *the whale supplies his own fuel* For the whale, like *The Whale*, is symbolically self-contained: it supplies its own fuel,

its own squilgee (for clearing the decks), and sperm oil (for cleansing them) – as well as book-marks, magnifying-glasses, folders etc.

533. *the famed Greek fire ... of the bold Hydriote, Canaris* Constantine Canaris (1790–1877) of Psara distinguished himself in the Greek War of Independence by destroying Turkish vessels – notably the flagship of the Turkish admiral in 1822 – by means of small fireships. Revolutionary Hydra, base of the insurgent fleet, was the headquarters of Admiral Miaoulis.

533. *the Tartarean shapes* Confounding, by a single pun, that Tartar helmsman in a Tartarus (for Jack Tars).

533. *laughter forked upwards ... like the flames from the furnace* Turning those 'red men', or 'Red-Men', wholly to fiends in this 'red hell'.

534. *plunging into that blackness of darkness* cf. 'and the preacher's text was about the blackness of darkness'. (THE CARPET-BAG, p. 101, note)

534. *in some enchanted way, inverted* As Ahab was inverted; and Ishmael is inverted by this vision of his 'monomaniac commander's soul'.

535. *Virginia's Dismal Swamp* Stretching south of Norfolk, Virginia.

535. *the truest of all men was the Man of Sorrows* (*Isaiah* liii, 3) cf. 'Knowest thou that "*Worship of Sorrow*"? The temple thereof, founded some eighteen centuries ago, now lies in ruins, overgrown with jungle, the habitation of doleful centuries... To the "*Worship of Sorrow*" ascribe what origin and genesis thou pleasest, *has* not that Worship been originated, and been generated; is it not *here*? Feel it in thy heart, and then say whether it is of God!' (*Sartor Resartus*, II, ix, 'The Everlasting Yea')

535. *unchristian Solomon's wisdom* 'I read Solomon more and more, and every time see deeper and deeper and unspeakable meanings in him... It seems to me now that Solomon was the truest man who ever spoke, and yet that he a little *managed* the truth with a view to popular conservatism; or else there have been many corruptions and interpolations of the text.' (To Hawthorne, June 1851)

In his Bible, inscribed 23 March 1850, thirty-seven verses from *Wisdom* are marked, though Melville knew very well they were not by Solomon. Across the title-page he wrote: 'About a century before Christ this Book was writ by some Alexandrian Jews, who combined Platonism with their Judaism.'

535. *calls Cowper, Young ... poor devils* Like Ishmael, William Cowper too suffered from fits of depression and on several occasions tried to commit suicide. Like Cowper, Ishmael too had just been expounding on 'a sea-sofa'. Edward Young was author of a once popular blank verse poem, *The Complaint, or Night Thoughts on Life, Death and Immortality* (1742–5).

535. *and break the green damp mould* The wisdom is that of *Ecclesiastes*: 'I said of laughter, It is mad: and of mirth, What doeth it?' (ii, 2)

535. *'the man that wandereth out of the way of understanding...'* (*Proverbs* xxi, 16) Which applies as devastatingly to Pip, abandoned by his God, as to Ahab, as to Ishmael squeezing that sperm. ' "I tell ye what it is, men" – cried Stubb to his crew – "It's against my religion to get mad ..." '

535. *There is a wisdom that is woe* cf. *Ecclesiastes*: 'And I gave my heart to know wisdom, and to know madness and folly: I perceived that this also is vexation of spirit. For in much wisdom is much grief: and he that increaseth knowledge increaseth sorrow.' (i, 17–18)

535. *a Catskill eagle* from the Appalachian range in south-east New York State. The highest summits rise to above four thousand feet. This bird, swooping into 'blackest gorges', is in pointed contrast to Ahab's locomotive rush 'over unsounded gorges' on his 'iron way'. (p. 206)

97 THE LAMP

536. *some illuminated shrine of canonized kings and counsellors* This is the whaler's own 'secret inner chamber and *sanctum sanctorum*', where each seaman lies 'coffined, hearsed, and tombed' – the whaler's own forecastle, hidden behind vast outworks like the citadel of Quebec. Yes, we are 'now in that enchanted calm which they say lurks at the heart of every commotion' – the whalemen, like whales, suspended in those vaults.

98 STOWING DOWN AND CLEARING UP

537. *like Shadrach, Meshach, and Abednego* (*Daniel* iii, 19–27)

538. *a potent ley* Lye, or alkaline solution.

538. *as bridegrooms new-leaped from out the daintiest Holland* Meaning linen, of course, but recalling the magnetic world of Leyden jars and Leeuwenhoek's microscopes – De Witt's Holland of Descartes' *Le Discours de la Méthode* (1637), Spinoza's *Ethics* (1665), Locke's *Essay concerning Human Understanding* (1690), and 'the only formal whaling code authorized by legislative enactment' (1695).

Yet this world of Dutch clarity clears nothing up. The mariners' glow is that of bridegrooms, but their chatter that of brides discussing parlours and sea-sofas, fine cambrics and 'tea by moonlight'. Their presence 'dispenses a perfume' as ambiguous 'as when a musk-scented lady rustles her dress in a warm parlor'. Their sexuality is ambivalent as the Sperm Whale's mouth: 'from floor to ceiling, lined, or rather papered with a glistening white membrane, glossy as bridal satins'. (p. 439)

539. *Oh! the metempsychosis! Oh! Pythagoras* 'Ah, Pythagoras' metempsychosis. . .' These shifts and transfigurations culminate in an echo of Faustus' final agony.

Yet the echo is cool as the earlier parody had been lighthearted. That ancient was 'green', and can now be patronized as 'boy', precisely because 'deep down and deep inland' he still bathed 'in eternal mildness of joy'. Even Ishmael can teach him a thing or two.

539. *along the Peruvian coast last voyage* Ishmael was possibly bound for Guayaquil, on the coast of Equador – in transition to. . .

99 THE DOUBLOON

THE DOUBLOON cf. Joseph Addison: 'For this too is an advantage medals have over books, that they tell their story much quicker, and sum up a whole volume in twenty or thirty reverses. They are indeed the best epitomes in the world, and let you see with one cast of an eye the substance of above a hundred pages.' (*Dialogues upon the Usefulness of Ancient Medals*, 1765, p. 14)

540. *hills about Boston ... some morass in the Milky Way* By 1824 Boston's Beacon Hill had been systematically demolished and trundled down to the Mill Pond in tip carts.

540. *many a Pactolus flow* The river in which King Midas bathed to be rid of his fatal touch.

541. *REPUBLICA DEL ECUADOR: QUITO* The coin was recent, dating from after the separation of Ecuador from Columbia (1830) and the inauguration of a national mint (1836). The zodiac with a meridian sun – flanked by Virgo and Libra on the celestial equator – became Ecuador's distinctive device. But what is here called 'a flame' was in fact a vulture; the 'crowing cock', a condor; with a second, across a chasm, perched pensive on a tower. (Plate 6)

Quito lies at the foot of Pichincha, a volcano rising to almost 16,000 feet. Her 'three Andes' summits' then (Ahab is right) may well be volcanic, though coins of Ecuador, unlike those of Peru and Chile, never showed eruptions in action. The value of a Quito doubloon in 1851 was precisely $15.60.

541. *entering the equinoctial point at Libra* viz. the autumnal equinox. For its significance in the Ahab (and Osiris) myth, see p. 575, note.

541. *Ahab, not unobserved by others* cf.

> Thus far these beyond
> Compare of mortal prowess, yet observ'd
> Thir dread Commander: he above the rest
> In shape and gesture proudly eminent
> Stood like a Towr ...
>
> (*Paradise Lost* I, 587–91)

541. *The firm tower, that is Ahab* Such sexual vaunts through the looking-glass are the ultimate illusion: 'dismembered' Ahab (*Ah*, M/*ab*!) – with skirted jacket and 'Tic-Dolly-row' – is neither tower, nor crowing cock, nor ram, nor horn-of-plenty. 'Proud as Lucifer' he parades before his mirror in borrowed plumes. For 'the Lord is my rock,' sang the psalmist, 'and my fortress, and my deliverer; my God, my strength, in whom I will trust; my buckler, and the horn of my salvation, and my high tower.' (*Psalm* xviii, 2)

542. *this coined sun wears a ruddy face* Reflecting his own bronze form, 'tawny scorched face and neck'.

542. *Belshazzar's awful writing* 'ME-NE: God hath numbered thy kingdom, and finished it' (to 'the smallest chip of the *Pequod*').

'TE-KEL: Thou art weighed in the balances, and art found wanting' ('the keystone sun entering the equinoctial point at Libra').

'PE-RES: Thy kingdom is divided...' (between Captains Peleg and Bildad).

(*Daniel* v, 26–8)

542. *the sun of Righteousness still shines* As in the Whaleman's Chapel: 'lo! the sun is breaking through; the clouds are rolling off – serenest azure is at hand'. (THE PULPIT, p. 133, note)

542. *This coin speaks wisely, mildly, truly* Yet how dark is his valley, drained of pastoral joy. Its 'mouldy soil' is of the devil's moulding. *Psalm* xxiii runs so faint through his head that he quits the QUITO coin, lest Truth shake him.

542. *on Negro Hill or in Corlaer's Hook* In a slave market, or on Manhattan's East River.

542. *your doubloons of Popayan* In south-west Columbia, bearing on the reverse two cornucopias, or 'horns-of-plenty'.

542. *gold moidores and pistoles, and joes* Moidores (*moeda d'ouro*, money of gold) and joes (abbreviation of *Joannes*) were both Portuguese gold coins; the pistole, more specifically a Spanish gold coin. The doubloon (*doblon*, or double) was originally worth two pistoles.

542. *By Golconda!* The old name for Hyderabad, long a diamond-cutting centre, celebrated for its wealth.

543. *old Bowditch in his Epitome* Still the sub-title of Nathaniel Bowditch's *The New American Practical Navigator*. (See p. 256, note.)

543. *devils can be raised with Daboll's arithmetic* Nathan Daboll (1750–1818), who also taught navigation, published the first of his New England almanacs in 1773. *Daboll's Complete Schoolmaster's Assistant* (1779) became a widely used arithmetic textbook. But Stubb, 'skylarking' as usual, as well as Melville (himself an ex-schoolmaster's devil), savours the pun.

543. *the Massachusetts calendar* In Melville's day a number of almanacs still contained the 'Man of the Signs' or 'Moon's Man'

– a figure surrounded by the twelve signs of the Zodiac, each referred to some part of his body by a pointed dagger or line. 'Each sign of the zodiac "governed" an organ or part of the body, and, in selecting a day to treat any ailment, or to let blood, it was necessary to know whether the moon was or was not in that sign.' (G. L. Kittredge, *The Old Farmer and his Almanack*, 1904, quoted by Willard Thorp)

Since the most famous of New England almanacs, *The Farmer's Almanac*, never published the 'Man of Signs', Melville may have had Isaiah Thomas's *Massachusetts, Connecticut, Rhode-Island, New-Hampshire and Vermont Almanack* in mind.

543. *Jimini! here's Gemini* The reading of the first English edition.

543. *but we ... supply the thoughts* Promptly breaking his own eleventh commandment: 'Think not.'

543. *Leo, a roaring Lion ... Virgo, the Virgin! that's our first love* But what of Melville's own life? Escaped from the 'roaring' sea and 'fierce bites' of the cannibal Typees, had he not also hailed a virgin – Elizabeth Shaw, daughter of the Chief Justice of Massachusetts – and, in 1847, married? Stubb's guided jaunt seems full of uneasy hints.

543. *here's the battering-ram, Capricornus, or the Goat* Another BATTERING-RAM – like Tashtego ramming his long pole harder and harder till he 'dropped head-foremost ...!' (p. 449)

544. *and so, alow here, does jolly Stubb* And so does the whale. Had not Moby Dick, too, 'been periodically descried ... as the sun, in its annual round, loiters for a predicted interval in any one sign of the Zodiac'? (THE CHART)

544. *at two cents the cigar, that's nine hundred and sixty-cigars* Which, of course, it is not. The materialist, the simple and single-minded pragmatist, alone proves an eternal optimist.

544. *why, there's a horse-shoe nailed on that side* cf. *Omoo*: the old Finn 'laid his hand on the old horse-shoe nailed as a charm to the fore-mast, and solemnly told us that ... not one quarter of our number would remain aboard the ship'. (ch. 12)

544. *The lion is the horse-shoe* To resemble the sign Leo (♌), this horse-shoe must be nailed upside down – perverting its charm!

The sun is in Leo from 23 July to 22 August. H. Bruce Franklin comments: 'The voiceless White Whale is not raised until after Christmas. But the roaring and devouring Typhoon strikes the *Pequod* while she sails the Sea of Japan in summer, on the day she turns to meet her Typhoon in the Season-on-the-Line.' (op. cit. p. 80) See THE CANDLES, p. 611, note.

545. *as the old women talk Surgeon's Astronomy* Meaning 'astrology'.

545. *in the vicinity of his thigh – I guess it's Sagittarius* viz. The great 'Archer' of *Mardi*, 'the god Upi'. Now Stubb, not Sagittarius (♐), 'is amusing himself'.

545. *'I look, you look, he looks...'* Pip's vindication of Kant, or rather of Berkeley. *Esse* is *percipi*: not the doubloon counts, but the eye of the beholder.

545. *Murray's Grammar* Lindley Murray's *English Grammar* (1795, revised 1818), *Reader* (1799) and *Spelling Book* (1804), were still in exclusive use at this time in both English and American schools. A Pennsylvania Quaker, he wrote his *Grammar*, after settling in England in 1784, for a Friends' School.

545. *all bats; and I'm a crow* Pip sees himself in the magic glass not as a fiery crested and 'crowing cock', but merely its initial, black and monosyllabic 'crow' ('Caw! caw! caw!'), not perched on an Andes' peak, but in the *Pequod*'s 'crow's-nest'.

As crow to the house of Cawdor ('in the whirled woods, the last day of the year!') Pip prophesies doom: all turned to bats at dusk; all screwy whirled, all mad.

545. *And where's the scare-crow?* Who 'cursed Pip officially...: "Stick to the boat, Pip, or by the Lord, I wont pick you up if you jump; mind that."' (THE CASTAWAY)

545. *two bones ... poked into the sleeves of an old jacket* Turning 'jolly Stubb' himself into a 'Jim Crow' show. 'There he stands': a blackface minstrel, for Mr Tambo a Mr Bones.

For jollily the sun 'aloft there, wheels through toil and trouble; and so, alow here, does jolly Stubb':

> Weel a-bout and turn a-bout
> And do just so
> Every time I weel a-bout
> I jump Jim Crow.

'Lord! how we suddenly jump..'

545. *I could go hang myself* As Pip's 'unearthly idiot face' is that of another Christ crucified, abandoned by his God, so Stubb, like another Judas, 'saying, I have sinned in that I have betrayed the innocent blood ... departed; and went and hanged himself.' (*Matthew* xxvii, 4–5)

Only Stubb ('Oh, jolly's the word for aye!') quits with a final quip on the QUITO coin.

546. *Here's the ship's navel* For 'this bright coin came from a country planted in the middle of the world'.

But the navel of an ark (symbol of all mankind) suggests older world-centres with holier claims: Jerusalem, by medieval cartographers called 'the navel of the world'; or the Kaaba at Mecca, enclosing its 'jet-black' stone; or the *omphalos* itself, 'that unaccountable cone' in the temple of Apollo at Delphi. All speak in mysteries. Doubloon and Torah and oracle, all need 'interpreters'. And their interpreters – Pip, like the Cabbala, like the Pythian priestess of the sun-god – yet further interpreters.

546. *But, unscrew your navel, and what's the consequence?* With a 'gay ha-ha!' – Ahab! – your bottom drops off. cf. *The Ingenious Boy, or The Bad Effect of Ill-directed Mechanical Genius* (1855), by the Californian wit 'John Phoenix'. The joke, at the expense of Hindu mystics, is in true Western style.

See John D. Seelye, 'The Golden Navel: The Cabalism of Ahab's Doubloon' (*Nineteenth Century Fiction* 14, No. 4, 1960)

546. *for when aught's nailed to the mast* Like colours nailed to the mast: 'a sign that things grow desperate'.

546. *in the resurrection . . . with bedded oysters* 'For now we are too much like oysters observing the sun through the water ...' (THE CHAPEL) Now 'we are imprisoned in the body, like an oyster in his shell'. (Plato, *Phaedrus* 250)

546. *a doubloon lodged . . . the green miser'll hoard ye* For what is the *Pequod* but the 'lodge' of the doubloon? Where is this 'hoard' but in Davy Jones's locker? And 'the miser-merman, Wisdom, revealed his hoarded heaps ...' (THE CASTAWAY)

546. *God goes 'mong the worlds blackberrying* Mansfield and Vincent quote from the prologue to the *Pardoner's Tale*:

> I rekke nevere, whan that they been beryed,
> Though that hir soules goon a-blakeberyed!
> (Chaucer, *Canterbury Tales* VI, 405–6)

– meaning 'wandering at large'. But this alone cannot account for Pip's choice, unless 'blackling' is simply attracted to 'blackberrying'. Most likely two phrases, both Falstaff's from *King Henry IV, Part I*, had stuck in his mind:

> Give you a reason on compulsion! If reasons were as plentiful as blackberries, I would give no man a reason upon compulsion, I. (II, iv, 230ff.)

And neither will Pip:

> Shall the blessed sun of heaven prove a micher [*pilferer*] and eat blackberries? A question not to be ask'd. (ibid., 400ff.)

But wittily enough answered by this crazy darkey.

546. *Jenny! . . . get your hoe-cake done!* Himself a simple crow ('Caw! caw! caw!'), Pip ends his Cassandra prophecy over royal Ahab by humming a snatch of the minstrel song *Old King Crow*:

> 'Jenny git yer hoe-cake.'
> 'Oh! don't bother me.'
> 'Fetch along de hoe-cake.'
> 'I tell you taint done.'
> 'Will you bring de hoe-cake?'
> 'G'long, don't bother me:
> I'll fotch along de hoe-cake
> Soon it am done.'

100 LEG AND ARM

548. *his solitary thigh . . . the crotch of an apple tree* Compared to burly John Bull – fed on 'bull-beef' and dumplings – behind the bulwarks, the Yankee below is all ambiguity: lifted by 'great swells', foiled by 'man-ropes', sliding into a 'crotch' as if to wind himself, like Milton's serpent, up the Forbidden Tree to taste of 'those fair Apples'. (*Paradise Lost* IX, 585)

548. *let us shake bones together! – an arm and a leg!* There they stand; a bone stuck into a pair of old trowsers and another poked into the sleeve of an old jacket. Caw! caw! caw! Mr Tambo and Mr Bones!

552. *what you take for the White Whale's malice is only his awkwardness* Which might well be the truth: of English common sense versus American bravado. But the hallmark of the

Samuel Enderby, after all, is a facetious, teasing relationship where truth and falsehood are not easily disentangled. In a peculiarly English 'roundabout' way, it is a performance put on as much at the stranger's expense, as for his benefit, consisting as it does mostly of private jokes beyond any stranger's comprehension.

Captain Boomer may or may not, for all we know, be spinning a yarn about his surgeon's 'hydrophobia'; Dr Bunger is certainly spinning a yarn about his captain's 'diabolical passions'; and this tall tale of the Ceylonese jack-knife caps their turn. For the truth is that the *Samuel Enderby* neither knows, nor cares, about theories – whether it be of whales' feints or foresight, malice or awkwardness. Nor is it for theories that we look to common sense; but practice. It is Captain Boomer's decision – his pragmatic 'once is enough' – that makes him a tower of good-humoured strength: 'No more White Whales for me.'

Melville's view of the British is kindly. But the implied critique is scalpel-sharp. Both surgeon and captain are dressed in blue. They, too, are Men of Signs; and their facetious good-humour is but one more sign of tranced self-reflection – a form of social, rather than solitary, narcissism no doubt, but 'roundabout' nevertheless, an evasion of ultimate truth, hung 'in festoons of blue'. Yankee compulsion may be neurotic. British common sense may seem reassuring. But can 'one limb' (that is the question) be ever 'enough'? The relaxed narcissism, the mutual self-admiration society of the British, may be charming, but it is correspondingly unaspiring. For the highest accomplishments a dash of 'wild longing' and 'diabolical passions' may be necessary ingredients.

553. *like a dog, strangely snuffing* Another 'godly-looking' prophet in 'patched trowsers': 'In the place where dogs licked the blood of Naboth ...' (*1 Kings* xxi, 19) But who is this Bunger 'late of the reverend clergy'? What is a 'bung' (in naval parlance) but a master's assistant who superintends the grog?

101 THE DECANTER

554. *the famous whaling house of Enderby & Sons* Both Poe (in *The Narrative of Arthur Gordon Pym*) and Bennett pay their respects to 'the late Samuel Enderby'; Melville's paragraphs, however, seem rather to echo Beale. It was Beale who traced the enterprise of Enderby & Sons from the epoch-making voyage of the

Amelia (September 1788–March 1790), via the scouting mission of the *Rattler*, to the experimental cruise of the *Syren*.

555. *the sloop-of-war Rattler ... commanded by a naval Post-Captain* Captain James Colnett, mocked earlier for his diagram outline of the whale. His *Voyage to the South Atlantic and round Cape Horn into the Pacific Ocean, for the Purpose of Extending the Spermaceti Whale Fisheries* (London, 1798) makes quite apparent what service he performed.

555. *a very fast sailor and a noble craft every way* The *Samuel Enderby* was built in 1834 by Thomas White of Cowes. Her dimensions were: length, 107 ft; beam, 29 ft 11 in.; tonnage, 422. Inside a scale replica (1/24), now at the National Maritime Museum, Greenwich, the following note was recently found: 'This model built by Sam White West Cowes Isle of Wight. Completed Christmas 1835 and presented to Messrs Charles, Henry and George Enderby being the model of a ship called the Samuel Enderby (their father) built by my father for the South Sea Whale Fishery in 1834. Sailed 1st voyage to South Seas October 1834.'

During subsequent cruises in the South Seas (1840–46) the *Samuel Enderby* of London may well have gammed the *Acushnet* of Fairhaven (length, 104 ft 8 in.; beam, 27 ft 10 in.; depth, 13 ft 11 in.; tonnage, 358).

555. *good flip* For a flippant ship – a mixture of beer and spirits, sweetened with sugar and heated with a hot iron.

556. *it was an anti-scorbutic* With its 'fresh fare' of weevils! The consumption of lime juice in the British Navy was not enforced till 1884.

556. *an ancient Dutch volume ... "Dan Coopman"* Den Koopman (The Merchant), one of Scoresby's sources for *An Account of the Arctic Regions*. Scoresby, Ishmael's favourite *bête noir*, is here traduced as Dr Snodhead.

557. *2,800 firkins of butter* viz. small tubs holding about 55 lb., or a quarter of a barrel.

557. *550 ankers of Geneva* viz. ten gallon casks of *genever*, juniper or gin.

102 A BOWER IN THE ARSACIDES

A BOWER With a glance at Spenser's 'Bowre of Blisse', also set in the wide ocean, amid 'sea-shouldring Whales':

> With boughes and braunches, which did broad dilate
> Their clasping armes, in wanton wreathings intricate...
> Archt over head with an embracing vine.
> (*The Faerie Queene*, Bk II, canto xii, stanzas 53–4)

IN THE ARSACIDES A group of Pacific atolls near the southern tip of the Solomon Islands. Surville, who visited them soon after their discovery by Bougainville in 1768, gave them their Parthian name – synonymous, to his mind, with 'assassins'. For he found the natives stubbornly fierce and treacherous. (The Arsacidae were a Parthian dynasty ruling Persia from around 250 B.C. to A.D. 226, chief rivals of Rome.)

Yet why did Melville choose this particular remote group for his ecclesiastical bower? The Solomon Islands of course evoke the wisdom of, unfathomably wondrous Solomon'. 'Salomon's House', centuries earlier, had been Lord Bacon's name for a Pacific Institute 'dedicated to the study of the works and creatures of God'. (*The New Atlantis*, 1627) But Ishmael, with a few bleached bones, confounds that master-mason and his vast Temple complex with its Levites, incense, shekels and sacrifices.

559. *for his poke or bag* Or stomach of the whale.

560. *Tranquo, king of Tranque, one of the Arsacides* Tranquil enough names for a Pacific kingdom, though not of assassins. Tranque is not 'one of the Arsacides', in fact, but a tiny island off the south coast of Chile.

560. *his retired palm villa at Pupella* With a hint of *puella* – a 'Bowre of Blisse' for this 'pious Solomon' of the Solomon Isles.

560. *carved woods of wonderful devices ... tribute-rendering waves* 'And Hiram sent to Solomon, saying, I have considered the things which thou sentest to me for: and I will do all thy desire concerning timber of cedar, and concerning timber of fir. My servants shall bring them down from Lebanon unto the sea: and I will convey them by sea in floats unto the place that thou shalt appoint me...' (*1 Kings* v, 8–9)

560. *dead and stranded ... his head against a cocoa-nut tree* This palm tree idyll, with 'verdant jet', is the ultimate mockery: shorn of his 'lordly palms', stripped of his hieroglyphic coat, drained of his aromatic sperm, 'the mighty, misty monster' is transformed (by priests, at last) into a 'mystic head'.

560. *the hair-hung sword that so affrighted Damocles* Whether king Tranquo of Tranque is as inoffensive as his name, or like Sicilian Dionysius (flattered by Damocles) a tyrant, is not made clear. The presence of the trading-ship *Dey* of Algiers, with its suggestion of slave trade, is suspicious. Certainly Ishmael himself lays on the flattery of his 'royal friend'. Yet confronted by the grotesque chapel, the king merely laughs: whether out of shrewdness or blithe good humour is left in the air.

All in all, the rule of this Arsacidean, like that of the Hebrew, Solomon remains ambiguous: peaceful certainly, probably despotic.

560. *green as mosses of the Icy Glen* A private token for Nathaniel Hawthorne – to mark the scramble up Monument Mountain, followed by the lunch in Stockbridge, where he and Melville first met. After a three-hour meal the guests were taken for a tour of the Icy Glen: 'a break in one of the hills of tumbled huge, damp, mossy rocks in whose recesses ice is said to be found all the year round'. (Evert Duyckinck, the following day, 6 August 1850)

Even before meeting Hawthorne, Melville had exalted 'this most excellent Man of Mosses'. (*Hawthorne and his Mosses*) Even before meeting Melville, Hawthorne had already presented just such a youthful, fiery-eyed stranger at just such 'A Select Party': 'And who was he – who but the Master Genius for whom our country is looking anxiously into the mist of Time, as destined to fulfil the great mission of creating an American literature, hewing it, as it were, out of the unwrought granite of our intellectual quarries? From him, whether moulded in the form of an epic poem or assuming a guise altogether new as the spirit itself may determine, we are to receive our first great original work, which shall do all that remains to be achieved for our glory among the nations.' (*Mosses from an Old Manse*)

561. *the great sun seemed a flying shuttle* at 'the Loom of Time' where once, long ago, Ishmael himself had sat, 'a shuttle mechanically weaving and weaving away at the Fates'. (THE MAT-MAKER)

561. *The weaver-god, he weaves; and by that weaving is he deafened* Like Pip, Ishmael sees 'God's foot upon the treadle', and speaks it. But no one calls him mad.

561. *bursting from the opened casements* The subtlest thinking may be overheard, as Stubb, from behind the try-works, overheard Flask, the old Manxman, Queequeg and Fedallah; as Pip, from afar, had 'been watching all of these interpreters'. The whole world, like the spinal column of the whale, proves a 'whispering gallery'.

561. *the great, white, worshipped skeleton* Though themselves South Sea Islanders, their 'worshipped skeleton' is 'white' – white as that great 'white mass floating in the sun, and the white spray heaving high against it'. (THE FUNERAL)

561. *a gigantic idler!* Suggesting the author of *The Idler* – unbuttoned, unfrocked, unbuckled: the investigator of Cock Lane metamorphosed to a god. 'I have invariably used a huge quarto edition of Johnson ... because that famous lexicographer's uncommon personal bulk more fitted him to compile a lexicon to be used by a whale author like me.' (THE FOSSIL WHALE)

561. *seemed the cunning weaver ... all woven over with the vines* For Tranque's (like Martha's) Vineyard teems with tendrils to mask this stranded skeleton with the sacramental grapes of Holy Communion.

561. *Life folded Death; Death trellised Life* Like the whale cemetery in the Greenland dock. Raging gales and palm tree idylls – life and death – are everywhere mixed: graveyards excavated 'for the foundation of a Lying-in Hospital'. cf. *Omoo*, ch. 44.

561. *the skull an altar, and the artificial smoke ascending* 'Behold, I build an house to the name of the Lord my God, to dedicate it to him, and to burn before him sweet incense.' (2 *Chronicles* ii, 4.) – in 'the place Golgotha, which is, being interpreted, The place of a skull' (*Mark* xv, 22).

561. *a chapel as an object of vertù* Confounding royal connoisseurship (of carvings or figured carpets) with virtue. So Solomon had 'carved all the walls of the house round about with carved figures of cherubims and palm trees and open flowers, within and without.' (*1 Kings* vi, 29)

561. *with a ball of Arsacidean twine* Suggesting a clew: for an anagram supplies 'Ariadne'. So these labyrinthine paths retrace a whole Minoan mythology: of the 'interminable Cretan labyrinth' tattooed on Queequeg's arm; of the 'remarkable involved Cretan labyrinth of vermicelli-like vessels' in the whale; of Europa, Minos and Minotaur. So the King Solomon Isles, too, in the end prove another Cyclades, to 'lead us on in barren mazes'.

561. *its many winding, shaded colonnades and arbors* 'For he cast two pillars of brass... And he made two chapiters of molten brass, to set upon the tops of the pillars... And nets of checker work and wreathes of chain work, for the chapiters...' crowned with a profusion of pomegranates and 'lily work'. (*1 Kings* vii, 15–19)

'Boaz' and 'Jachin' survive – as passwords of first and second degree masons. Amid skulls and cross-bones, the 'Entered Apprentice' is taught the assassin-sign: of cutting the throat across with outstretched thumb.

562. *I saw no living thing within; naught was there but bones* 'But will God indeed dwell on the earth? behold, the heaven and heaven of heavens cannot contain thee; how much less this house that I have builded?' (*1 Kings* viii, 27)

562. *From their arrow-slit in the skull ... the altitude of the final rib* 'And the house which king Solomon built for the LORD, the length thereof was three-score cubits, and the breadth thereof twenty cubits, and the height thereof thirty cubits... And for the house he made windows of narrow lights.' (*1 Kings* vi, 2 and 4)

562. *hereupon a fierce contest rose* But these assassin priests, eyeing Ishmael, merely end by cracking 'each other's sconces with their yard-sticks'.

By mid-century theological controversy was, of course, in full spate. David Strauss' *Das Leben Jesu* (1835), the epigraphical work of Georg Grotefend and Henry Rawlinson, Layard's astonishing finds at Babylon and Nineveh (1842–51), all helped to fire the contestants. (cf. JONAH HISTORICALLY REGARDED) In fact, it was Rawlinson's *Persian Cuneiform Inscription at Behistun*, like *Moby-Dick* completed in 1851, which might be said to have finally deciphered these 'Arsacidean annals' carved 'in strange hieroglyphics'.

562. *There is a Leviathanic Museum, they tell me, in Hull ... a certain Sir Clifford Constable*: 'I cannot close these few observations without embracing the opportunity, now presenting itself, of thanking Sir Clifford and Lady Constable for the kind assistance which they rendered me, in procuring the information I required; indeed a pleasant rivalry was manifested among the scientific gentlemen of Hull, in showing and explaining to me all that they knew respecting the leviathans of the deep, of which the Museum of Natural History at Hull can boast of several fine skeletons.' (Beale, p. 76.)

The Burton–Constable skeleton was stranded on the Yorkshire coast in 1825.

563. *a bunch of keys at his side ... the whispering gallery* In Sir Clifford's hands the whole whale becomes a toy. Through Sir Clifford's eyes the vast skull is turned – from a Pantheon or St Peter's – to the dome of St Paul's.

Melville must be recalling his own tour of the cathedral and incessant groping for more pennies; to this day each part of the ascent, from gallery to dome to lantern, is charged separately.

103 MEASUREMENT OF THE WHALE'S SKELETON

563. *a Sperm Whale of the largest magnitude* 'A stout whale of sixty feet in length is of the enormous weight of seventy tons; the blubber weighs about thirty tons; the bones of the head, whalebone, fins and tail, eight or ten; carcass, thirty or thirty-two.' (Scoresby, vol. I, p. 462)

The vital statistics of a blue whale are even more imposing, attaining a length of over 100 feet and, at 170 tons, outweighing 30 elephants, 120 fat oxen, or 1,600 men. Its heart is the size of a bull.

565. *like Pompey's Pillar* Near Alexandria, standing some eighty-eight feet high on its pedestal.

565. *looks something like a white billiard-ball* So that even those 'small, but substantial, symmetrically globular, and indestructible dumplings' on the *Samuel Enderby* are given their due reflection through the looking-glass of *The Whale.*

104 THE FOSSIL WHALE

567. *a condor's quill! ... Vesuvius' crater* 'Oh for a quill plucked from a Seraph's wing!' (Edward Young): Southey opened *The Doctor* with a fantasia on quills, later inserting a twenty-three page digression on the flea in history and literature. (vol. 3, ch. 89)

567. *also a great digger of ditches, canals* A joke at his own expense: as a nineteen-year-old Melville had really taken up engineering and surveying for a time, in the hopes of finding employment on the Erie Canal. Foiled, he shipped on the *St Lawrence* for Liverpool instead (June 1839).

568. *the almost complete vast skeleton of an extinct monster, found ... in Alabama* In 1832 Judge H. Bry of Louisiana sent several fossil vertebrae, found in Arkansas, to the American Philosophical Society; that same year Judge Creagh sent a similar box from his Alabama plantation. Dr Richard Harlan of Philadelphia identified the bones as reptilian. But in 1839 he took some over to London for examination by Sir Richard Owen, who showed them to be the teeth of a sea-going mammal. His 'Observations on the *Basilosaurus* of Dr Harlan (*Zeuglodon cetoides*, Owen)' was read before the London Geological society, 9 January 1839, and concludes: 'We cannot hesitate in pronouncing the colossal *Zeuglodon* to have been one of the most extraordinary of the Mammalia which the revolutions of the globe have blotted out of the number of existing beings.'

569. *the great temple of Denderah* At Tentyra in Upper Egypt, dating from the first century B.C. See Vivant Denon, *Travels in Upper and Lower Egypt*, vol. 2, plates XIX (facing p. 70) and LVIII (facing p. 316). Denon, who had served with Napoleon in Egypt, visited the site to make elaborate drawings of 'the zodiac which is on the ceiling of the portico' and of 'the celestial planisphere, which occupies part of the ceiling of a little apartment built over the nave of the great temple'. Whether or not these whale-like fish on the planisphere are whales, Melville's *Whale* is omnivorous and digests them – stereotype plates and all.

569. *centuries before Solomon was cradled* In 1823 the *North American Review* had ascribed 'the love of the marvelous or worse reasons' to those who urged 'the extreme antiquity' of the

Denderah zodiac and even referred it 'back to an epoch anterior by far to the Mosaic chronology'. (VIII, p. 237) But Ishmael remains a sceptic: 'I take it, that the earliest standers of mast-heads were the old Egyptians ...' Egyptian mythology underlies Hebrew mythology: not Hebrew, Egyptian. cf. pp. 225, 284, notes.

569. *John Leo, the old Barbary traveller* Leo Africanus (Al-Hassan ibn Mohammed), an early sixteenth-century Arab who made extensive journeys throughout North Africa and the Middle East. Captured by pirates, he was sent as a slave to Pope Leo X, and eventually baptized as Johannes Leo. He continued to live in Rome where he taught Arabic and completed an account of his travels (in Arabic, 1526), issued in Italian by G. B. Ramusio as *Descrittione dell' Africa* (vol. I of *Navigazioni e viaggi*, 1550).

It is from the English translation by John Pory (1600) – of the Latin version by J. Florianus (*J. Leonis Africani de totius Africae descriptione*, 1556) – that Melville is paraphrasing.

105 DOES THE WHALE'S MAGNITUDE DIMINISH? – WILL HE PERISH?

570. *Sperm Whales ... near a hundred feet long* cf. Scoresby: 'Yet I believe that whales now occur of as large dimensions, as at any former period since the commencement of the whale fishery.' (vol. 1, p. 452) cf. Charles Wilkes: 'An opinion has indeed gained ground within a few years that the whales are diminishing in numbers; but this surmise, as far as I have learned from the numerous inquiries, does not appear to be well founded.' (*Narrative of the United States Exploring Expedition*, vol. 5, p. 493)

570. *For Pliny tells us* Of 'Whales and Whirlpooles' in the Indian Ocean, that 'take up as much in length as four acres or arpens of land'. (*Historia Naturalis*, Bk IX; Extract 7)

570. *Aldrovandus* The Bolognese naturalist, Ulisse Aldrovandi in *De piscibus et de cetis* (1613).

570. *Rope Walks* A stretch of ground reserved for the manufacture of rope.

570. *Thames Tunnels* i.e. Sir Marc Isambard Brunel's tunnel from Wapping to Rotherhithe. Begun in 1825, it had been open

to the public for six years when Melville visited it in November 1849. Even then its approaches were not finished and it remained principally a tourist attraction.

570. *Banks and Solander* Sir Joseph Banks and Dr Daniel Carl Solander, who accompanied Captain Cook on his circumnavigation of the world (1768–71).

571. *Lacépède* See pp. 228 and 369. Melville's source, once again, is Scoresby: 'One can hardly doubt, says he (p. 3), but that the Mysticetus may have been seen, at certain times, and in certain seas, 100 metres, that is 328 feet, long.' (vol. 1, p. 449 n.)

571. *prize cattle of Smithfield* The London cattle market. 640 pounds was the average weight of cattle sold in 1849.

572. *an irresistible argument ... that the hunted whale cannot now escape speedy extinction.* Today only three whaling nations remain: Japan, Norway and Russia (the Dutch and British both withdrew in 1965). Their activities are controlled by the sixteen nation International Whaling Commission, set up in 1946 to fix catch limits. Figures issued by the Committee of Whaling Statistics show that since 1948 the number of fin whales caught in the Antarctic has fallen from 21,141 to 2,893. The blue whale catch dwindled from 6,908 in 1948 to one in 1964, the last year they were allowed to be taken. By 1965 the catch limit had been reduced from a 1953 quota of 16,000 to 4,500 blue whale units (1 blue whale unit = 2 finbacks, or 2½ humpbacks, or 6 sei whales).

Yet scientists and zoologists failed to persuade the International Whaling Commission, at their 1967 conference in London, to ban the taking of fin whales in the Antarctic – though the total catch of whales permitted was again marginally reduced. Humpback and blue whales, since 1963/4, are completely protected; and there are signs that the blue whale (largest of all known living or extinct creatures) may survive. However Norwegian marine biologists believe that unless a general armistice is declared at once – effective for at least ten years – whale-hunting itself is doomed and the whole species will come rapidly close to extinction.

572. *the census of men now in London* More than two millions in 1850.

572. *Forty men in one ship hunting the Sperm Whale for forty-eight months.* But Melville could not envisage a modern

expedition, with its factory ship (of about 16,000 gross tons) alone carrying over 500 men, plus a dozen attendant 'catchers' (of up to 900 tons), tankers, refrigeration ships and odd auxiliaries amounting to an armada of more than 1,000 men in all. Nor could he foresee steam ousting sail; the diesel engine, steam. Nor the Norwegian sealing captain, Svend Foyn, firing his heavy grenade harpoons from a cannon mounted in the bow; nor slipways for winching carcasses on deck; nor electronic devices, like echo whale-finders, whale-scarers (panicking whales by ultrasonic vibrations), radio buoys and radar screens; nor circling helicopters and other reconnaissance aircraft. In the 1930–1 season forty-one factory ships operated to produce 3,500,000 barrels of oil.

On the factory ship the carcass is flensed of its blubber and the meat stripped from the bone. Blubber, meat and bone are stuffed in separate steam pressure-cookers or rotating drums. Less than forty-five minutes is needed to dispose of a blue whale, weighing more than a hundred tons; thirty minutes is enough to bottle and can a finback. In 1964 annual world whale-oil production was about 370,000 tons – rather less in weight than one third of the butter produced. This oil production, together with some 300,000 tons of by-products for food and fertilizers, came from a world catch of about 63,000 whales, taken by about 360 whale catchers, operating from more than twenty factory ships and about forty shore stations.

573. *two firm fortresses ... their Polar citadels* The North Pacific and the Antarctic are today's main reservoirs, accounting for 60 per cent of world production. But, alas, it is Melville's conceits which are all 'equally fallacious'. The Greenland whale, almost eliminated by over-fishing during the nineteenth century – and left alone for fifty years – is still extremely rare. Now the Antarctic grounds, first exploited in 1904, are almost exhausted. Oil production has fallen from over 2,000,000 barrels in 1948 to 644,263 in 1966. In their heyday, twenty-one factory ships, with attendant flotillas, were busy from December to April and several shore stations in South Georgia and the South Shetlands were also in use. Now the land stations are closing. Nine factory ships went out in 1967; perhaps no more than three or four will in future. The 'charmed circle' is broken.

573. *Harto, the historian of Goa* 'In the two other parts of the world they are in great abundance, as appears by the relation of

Garcias ab Horto, physician to the Viceroy at Goa, who relates that at one venation the King of Siam took four thousand, and is of opinion they are in other parts in greater number than herds of beeves in Europe.' (Sir Thomas Browne, *Pseudodoxia Epidemica*, Bk VI, ch. 6)

573. *by Semiramis, by Porus* viz. the legendary Assyrian queen, who founded Babylon and Nineveh; and the Indian prince, routed by Alexander the Great at the Hydaspes. (p. 493) For his gallantry in battle Porus was later confirmed as Macedonian satrap of the West Punjab.

574. *probably attaining the age of a century or more* (See p. 467, note) The age span of whales, in fact, is very similar to that of man.

574. *upon the topmost crest ... defiance to the skies* The firm tower, that is Leviathan; the volcano, that is Leviathan; the courageous, the undaunted, and victorious fowl, that, too, is Leviathan.

106 AHAB'S LEG

574. *to all appearances lusty* Yet when he wheels about and twists about and jumps (Jim Crow!) 'upon a thwart', his ivory leg is ominously splintered. For the 'bone', far from 'lusty', is 'dead'. 'And there's a mighty difference between a living thump and a dead thump ...'

575. *not ... very long prior to the* Pequod*'s sailing from Nantucket* H. Bruce Franklin comments: 'The Season-on-the-Line forms the chronological and geographical centre of *Moby-Dick*. At that time and place the whale for the first and last times dismembers Ahab. One Season-on-the-Line passes between these two; precisely at this time, Christmas Day, the twice-maimed Ahab begins his fiery hunt. Although Ahab's second injury comes shortly before the Season-on-the-Line, all three injuries coincide with the various dates given for the dismemberment of Osiris, sometime between the autumnal equinox and the winter solstice. Although *Moby-Dick* defines its dates with no more precision than do the accounts of the Osiris myth, this much is explicitly clear: not only is each of Ahab's three injuries related to the position of the sun in the zodiac, but also the annual catastrophe and revival of Ahab, like those of Osiris,

suggest and are suggested by the annual catastrophe and revival of the sun.' (*The Wake of the Gods*, pp. 83–4)

cf. 'As the sky grew less gloomy; indeed, began to grow a little genial, he became still less and less a recluse ...' (AHAB, p. 220)

575. *stake-wise smitten, and all but pierced his groin* The mark, however, is no longer that of castration, but hermaphroditic, 'prone upon the ground', as androgynous as the whales – flukes 'tossed erect' and tails 'flirted high into the air'. (pp. 485–6)

575. *issue of a former woe ... beget their like* After Ahab's strange wound follow his even stranger theories. Fertility, issue, genealogies prey upon his mind, in 'seemingly inexplicable' confusion.

575. *an inference from certain canonic teachings* 'Some natural enjoyments' may well be sexual; but to call sexual enjoyments, incapable of procreation, 'natural' is of course wholly opposed to all the canonical 'Rabbins'. Lusty Ahab lies 'upon a thwart', as his own limb had lain twisted 'upon a thwart'. So too this whole chapter lies thwartwise twisted, in diametrical self-contradictions, *un*canonical in every sense – but that of the mincer 'in the full canonicals of his calling'. (p. 530)

575. *all heart-woes ... an archangelic grandeur* Which is Ahab's delusion, standing 'before them with a crucifixion in his face; in all the nameless regal overbearing dignity of some mighty woe.' As Ishmael well knows: 'in gazing at such scenes, it is all in all what mood you are in; if in the Dantean, the devils will occur to you; if in that of Isaiah, the archangels'. (p. 486)

575. *To trail the genealogies ... among the sourceless primogenitures* In a Gnostic spiritual universe 'of a Supreme Being and a series of "Aeons" emanating from him. One of the outermost of these, called Sophia or Wisdom, "falls" through an excessive aspiration to approach the Supreme God. Out of her grief and passion the Demiurge, Creator of the world, is born.' (Thomas Vargish, 'Gnostic *Mythos* in *Moby-Dick*', *P.M.L.A.* 81, p. 274)

For Ahab's further commitment to Gnostic heresy, see pp. 262, 283, 616–17, notes.

575. *the gods themselves are not for ever glad* On this, at least, Ishmael and Ahab agree: 'The truest of all men was the Man of Sorrows, and the truest of all books is Solomon's, and Ecclesiastes is the fine hammered steel of woe.' (p. 535)

575. *is but the stamp of sorrow in the signers* As that great golden seal affixed by the German emperors to their decrees. It signifies – "God: done this day by my hand".' (THE PRAIRE)

576. *such Grand-Lama-like exclusiveness* Of the Dalai Lama, ruling from Llasa, but here with a hint of Freemasonry, whose God too is called 'Grand'; whose highest office is that of 'Grand Master'.

576. *every revelation ... more of significant darkness than of explanatory light* Like that of the Worshipful Master to initiates of the third degree: 'The light of the master mason is darkness visible.' Their pledge is to keep the secrets of masonry and preserve the confidences of every other master mason: a pledge – 'unwittingly', he claims – just broken by Ishmael.

The whole ritual, and sequence of rituals, is worth restating. Having learnt the words 'Boaz' and 'Jachin' (passwords of the first and second degree) the initiate is ready to be 'raised' to master mason. This is a complex ordeal based on the legend of Hiram Abiff, architect of King Solomon's temple who died rather than reveal the secrets of masonry. It involves the candidate being 'murdered' then 'raised from the dead'. Some masonic temples have a hollow, which is used as a 'grave'. Elsewhere the candidate may be placed in a coffin.

Thus the whole cycle of masonic ceremonies (with their signs and codes) will prove, in the end, a paradigm of *Moby-Dick*. Having stepped in Cycladic circles, as if ascending a spiral staircase (the ritual of the second degree) we are ready at last for the consummate secret – Ishmael's final ordeal of the COFFIN and the LIFE-BUOY.

576. *studs and joists of jaw-ivory (Sperm Whale)* To be transliterated as well as transformed: to a stout stud, for joy, of the clearest-grained 'stuff'.

107 THE CARPENTER

577. *Seat thyself ... among the moons of Saturn* viz. under the astrological influence of the planet: sluggish, cold, gloomy, saturnine.

577. *the Pequod's carpenter was no duplicate* 'Was not God the first shipwright? and all vessels on the water descended from the loyns (or ribs rather) of Noahs ark ...?' (Thomas Fuller, 'The

Good Sea-Captain', *The Holy State and the Profane State*, Bk II, ch. 20)

Who else but a carpenter created the *Pequod* – this 'Noah's ark' – 'this frigate earth'? Like a grizzle-bearded Father Almighty, this antediluvian 'unaccountable old joker' can supply a pagoda as readily as a constellation of vermilion stars. Like the beloved Son – another carpenter – he is both uniquely an individual and 'a stript abstract', both universal craftsman and quack-doctor. Like the Holy Ghost, drowned in the infinite of Pip's soul, he shades off 'into the surrounding infinite of things', 'shoreless, indefinite as God'. (THE LEE SHORE) Like all deity, he is a mass of contradictions – 'lashed athwartships' – 'both useful and capricious', part ewe, part goat, Christ and the Devil. Stolid, heartless, 'the one grand stage where he enacted all his various parts' is 'his *vice*-bench'.

If Ishmael's conception of godhead is capable of projection, this carpenter is its incarnation. That 'unaccountable, cunning life-principle' (*L'évolution créatrice* or *l'élan vital*, as Bergson was to call it) is here embodied in man – a Matse Avatar, wholly anthropomorphized. cf. 'We mortals are all on board a fast-sailing, never-sinking world frigate, of which God was the shipwright; and she is but one craft in a Milky-Way fleet, of which God is the Lord High Admiral.' (*White-Jacket*, 'The End')

578. *the carpenter makes a pagoda-looking cage* Like 'the famous cavern-pagoda of Elephanta' where, the Brahmins maintain, 'all the trades and pursuits, every conceivable avocation of man, were prefigured ages before any of them actually came into being'. (p. 367) For the carpenter is not only a wood-worker, but mechanically gifted; not only mechanically gifted, but 'unhesitatingly expert in all manner of conflicting aptitudes' – including that of dentist. 'Rattle thy teeth, then . . . make a pagoda of thyself.' (MIDNIGHT, FORECASTLE)

578. *Stubb longs for vermillion stars* To wheel, like the sun, through the zodiac? 'Symmetrically' this Grand Geometrician 'supplies the constellation'.

578. *heads he deemed but top-blocks* Literally, the large block suspended below the cap of a smaller mast to hoist, or lower, top-masts.

578. *men themselves . . . for capstans* Because they wheel about and turn about? Or, with 'wheezing humorousness', meaning 'cap-stands'?

578. *while pauselessly active . . . still eternally holds its peace* cf. THE BOWER IN THE ARSACIDES: 'All the trees . . .; all the shrubs; and ferns, and grasses; the message-carrying air; all these unceasingly were active . . .'

579. *this half-horrible stolidity in him* cf. Stubb: 'This way comes Pip – poor boy! would he had died, or I; he's half horrible to me.' (p. 545)

579. *the bearded forecastle* Of Noah's ark, or the *Pequod* for that matter: 'a ship of the old school . . . Her venerable bows looked bearded.'

579. *whose much rolling, to and fro . . . had gathered no moss* For though ancient as those solitary Leviathans – 'those wondrous grey-headed, grizzled whales' – he had gathered no pastoral illusions, no moss; and 'what is more, had rubbed off whatever small outward clingings might have originally pertained to him'.

579. *uncompromised as a new-born babe* viz. 'As newborn babes, desire the sincere milk of the word.' (*1 Peter* ii, 2): to evoke not only 'the unborn whale' but Pip reborn 'uncompromised, indifferent as his God'.

579. multum in parvo, *Sheffield contrivances* So the Christian God is both three-in-one and 'an unfractioned integral': 'As also there are not three incomprehensibles, nor three uncreated: but one uncreated, and one incomprehensible . . . Not three Gods: but one God.' (*Athanasian Creed*)

579. *to use the carpenter for a screw-driver* On the ship's navel? They 'are all on fire to unscrew it'. (THE DOUBLOON)

579. *whether essence of quicksilver, or a few drops of hartshorn* Mercury or ammonia.

580. *like an unreasoning wheel . . . hummingly soliloquizes* cf. Ahab 'without using any words . . . lowly humming to himself, producing a sound so strangely muffled and inarticulate that it seemed the mechanical humming of the wheels of his vitality in him'. (THE QUARTER-DECK)

580. *his body was a sentry-box* For 'man may, in effect, be said to look out on the world from a sentry-box with two joined sashes for his window'. (THE SPERM WHALE'S HEAD)

108 AHAB AND THE CARPENTER

580. *firmly fixed in the vice . . . various tools of all sorts* With its 'straps, pads, screws', this vice-bench seems more like a torturer's rack – or perhaps some retreat, 'lashed athwartships', for scenes of flagellation and other aberrant joys. The red flame from the forge casts a glow of hell.

580. *That is hard which should be soft, and that is soft which should be hard* cf.

Fair is foul, and foul is fair:
Hover through the fog and filthy air.
(*Macbeth* I, i, 10–11)

'Come, come you old Smut . . .'

581. *Well, manmaker!* It is the FIRST NIGHT WATCH. Ahab is in a dourly jesting mood. The carpenter, sneezing amid the bone dust, reminds him of God creating Adam with a sneeze: 'And the Lord God formed man of the dust of the ground, and breathed into his nostrils the breath of life; and man became a living soul.' (*Genesis* ii, 7)

581. *there's a pedlar aboard with a crushing pack* In 'a world full of grave peddlers', another *Hump Back* – or loaded hunchback – on his *Pilgrim's Progress*. cf. *Richard III*, I, iii, 148.

581. *a complete man after a desirable pattern* This heartless, brain-bound, introverted Colossus – with overhead fixtures – is, of course, Melville's own peculiar bogy: 'superior natural force, with a globular brain', beating 'against the solid metal'.

'I stand for the heart,' he wrote to Hawthorne at the time. 'To the dogs with the head! I had rather be a fool with a heart, than Jupiter Olympus with his head.' (June 1851, on reading *Ethan Brand*) *The Modern Prometheus*, sub-title of Mary Shelley's *Frankenstein*, perhaps suggested the figure. Richard Bentley, Melville's English publisher, had presented him with a copy in December 1849.

581. *Imprimis, fifty feet high in his socks* The height of the Phidian Zeus at Olympia (forty feet) on its pedestal (twelve feet).

582. *chest modelled after the Thames Tunnel* See p. 570, note. The great ribbed arches extended over 1,200 feet.

582. *no heart at all* cf. 'But where was the heart? That, indeed, had withered – had contracted – had hardened – had perished! It had ceased to partake of the universal throb.' (Hawthorne, *Ethan Brand*, 1851)

582. *brass forehead* Which inevitably suggests 'the idol Bell' or Baal – or the statue of Helios himself in the harbour of Rhodes. (p. 252)

But as fitting, in this labyrinth of Minoan references, is Talus, a man of brass, who appears in the story of the 'Argo-Navis'. Made by Hephaestos, he was given to King Minos for Crete's coastal defences; like Ahab ('at the boiling point!'), he radiated heat. Another Talus, nephew of Daedalus, was credited with the invention of the saw and compasses – thus, all in all, a peculiarly suitable figure for a captain to order from a carpenter. (See Extract 20.)

582. *a sky-light . . . to illuminate inwards* 'Dominus illuminatio mea' (*Psalm* xxvii, 1, in the Vulgate) – revealing Ahab himself ('made of solid bronze') under his cabin sky-light.

582. *but indifferent architecture to make a blind dome* cf. Sir Clifford's whale with its 'whispering gallery' and 'unrivalled view' from the forehead.

582. *here's one* (touching his own forehead) '. . . And suddenly there shined round about him a light from heaven: And he fell to the earth . . .' (*Acts* ix, 3–4) From the dome of St Paul's Ahab's thoughts turn to the balding, high-domed brow of the saint, illuminated inwards and literally blinded on the road to Damascus – or off Cape Horn, was it? – 'long ago, when he lay like dead for three days and nights'. (THE PROPHET)

582. *or would'st thou rather work in clay? . . . The fellow's impious!* 'Remember, I beseech thee, that thou hast made me as the clay; and wilt thou bring me into dust again?' (*Job* x, 9)

582. *Take the hint, then* That 'Adām' derives from 'Adāmāh', 'made of earth': 'for out of it wast thou taken: for dust thou art, and unto dust shalt thou return'. (*Genesis* iii, 19) Take another from dead Polonius: 'if you find him not within this month, you shall nose him as you go up the stairs into the lobby'. (*Hamlet* IV, iii, 36–7)

582. *Canst thou not drive that old Adam away?* 'Would now St Paul would come along . . .' The text, as if to underline Ishmael's mocking allusion (p. 520), is again from *1 Corinthians* xv: 'For as

in Adam all die, even so in Christ shall all be made alive . . . And so it is written, the first man Adam was made a living soul; the last Adam was made a quickening spirit . . . The first man is of the earth, earthy: the second man is the Lord from heaven.' (verses 22, 45 and 47)

582. *but it will be still pricking him at times* 'Was not Saul of Tarsus converted from unbelief by a similar fright?' (THE AFFIDAVIT): 'And he fell to the earth, and heard a voice saying unto him, Saul, Saul, why persecutest thou me? And he said, Who art thou, Lord? And the Lord said, I am Jesus whom thou persecutest: it is hard for thee to kick against the pricks.' (*Acts* ix, 4–5)

583. *I should humbly call it a poser, sir* Or 'a poseur', maybe, cf. *Ethan Brand*: 'Yet, though the corporeal hand was gone, a spiritual member remained ... an invisible thumb and fingers with as vivid a sensation as before the real ones were amputated.'

583. *some entire, living, thinking thing* '... some unknown but still reasoning thing' putting forth 'the mouldings of its features ...' (THE QUARTER-DECK)

583. *dost thou not fear eavesdroppers?* From 'the land of spirits' and of *whales*? (AHAB'S LEG) For Ahab knows nothing of Ishmael's 'opened casements' – cares less for 'the whispering gallery' of the world.

583. *Hah!* Sign of Ahab. *Good Lord!* And god-like carpenter.

583. *proud as Greek god* Whose 'intense thinking thus makes him a Prometheus'. (THE CHART)

583. *Cursed be that mortal inter-indebtedness* Ishmael's 'Siamese connexion with a plurality of other mortals' (THE MONKEY-ROPE); Queequeg's 'mutual, joint-stock world'. (WHEELBARROW)

583. *dissolve myself down* As his crushed leg is already long dissolved, Ahab's cry (By heavens!) recalls Faustus's last despairing cry.

583. *to one small, compendious vertebra* Which (crucible and all) suggests not so much *The Tragical History of Doctor Faustus* as *The Honorable History of Friar Bacon and Friar Bungay* – who too made a head of brass and conjured up the devil to give it speech.

583. *here's his bed-fellow! ... for a wife!* and a 'queer, very queer' wife 'to mount' with the old one 'still pricking him'.

584. *one leg standing in three places, and all three places standing in one hell* The Three in One, the One in Three. 'Is't a riddle?' 'Not three Gods, but one God' (Athanasian Creed): a poser for this 'unfractioned integral', himself a '*multum in parvo*'.

584. *before the resurrection fellow comes a-calling with his horn* Now the carpenter picks up Paul: 'Behold, I shew you a mystery . . . for the trumpet shall sound, and the dead shall be raised incorruptible, and we shall be changed.' (*1 Corinthians* xv, 51–2)

584. *he'll be taking altitudes on it* A final dig at Ahab's metaphysical wit: cf. 'I love to lose my selfe in a mystery, to pursue my Reason to an *oh altitudo*. 'Tis my solitary recreation to pose my apprehension with those involved aenigma's and riddles of the Trinity, with Incarnation, and Resurrection.' (Sir Thomas Browne, *Religio Medici* Pt I, sec. 9)

But from this carpenter in the bone dust – a mocking boomerang.

109 AHAB AND STARBUCK IN THE CABIN

585. *nigh to Formosa and the Bashee Isles* Or Batan Islands. The *Pequod*, that is, was sailing into the Bashi Channel between Taiwan and the Philippines.

585. *the Japanese islands – Niphon, Matsmai, and Sikoke* The nomenclature is odd: the Japanese call the whole of Japan 'Nippon' (or 'Niphon'), though Ishmael appears to mean only the large central island, the seat of government; 'Matsmai' (or Matsumai, the old name for the city of Fukuyama on the straits) is Hokkaido, the large northern island; 'Sikoke', now Shikoku, is the smaller of the two southern islands. Japan at this time, of course, was still a 'double-bolted land'. (p. 206, note)

585. *new ivory leg . . . against the screwed leg* Snow-white and wrinkled (emblematic signs of Moby Dick), at 'his screwed-down table' (THE CHART), with jack-knife in hand (mark of Peleg, Queequeg and all ruminating tars).

585. *We must up Burtons* viz. rig the tackle and hoist up casks.

586. *those miserly owners* cf. 'Cursed be that mortal inter-indebtedness . . . I would be free as air; and I'm down in the whole world's books.' (p. 583)

586. *Ahab seized a loaded musket from the rack* Himself a loaded musket, racked by unhappiness: for 'thrusted light is worse than presented pistols'. (p. 582)

586. *There is one God that is Lord over the earth* i.e. There is one law for subordinates, but another for Ahab 'proud as Greek god': 'Talk not to me of blasphemy, man; I'd strike the sun if it insulted me . . .' (THE QUARTER-DECK)

Thus Starbuck's reply: 'Thou hast outraged, not insulted me, sir.'

586. *let Ahab beware of Ahab; beware of thyself, old man* cf.

> Macbeth! Macbeth! Macbeth! Beware [Macbeth!]
> (*Macbeth* IV, i, 71)

> Be Kent unmannerly
> When Lear is mad. What wouldst thou do, old man?
> (*King Lear* I, i, 144–6)

586. *unconsciously using the musket* With an iron brow, below those 'iron-grey locks', leaning on a philosophy of iron. cf. John C. Calhoun, in Harriet Martineau's phrase: 'the cast-iron man, who looks as if he had never been born, and could never be extinguished.' (*Retrospect of Western Travel* vol. 1, p. 243; London, 1838) See p. 508, note.

587. *vain to surmise . . . or mere prudential policy* Seeing that 'Starbuck would ever be apt to fall into open relapses of rebellion against his captain's leadership, unless some ordinary, prudential, circumstantial influences were brought to bear upon him.' (SURMISES)

110 QUEEQUEG IN HIS COFFIN

QUEEQUEG IN HIS COFFIN cf. 'And what, Mr President, do you suppose it is? It is a fragment of the coffin of Washington – a fragment of that coffin in which now repose in silence, in sleep, and speechless, all the earthly remains of the venerated Father of his Country. Was it portentous that it should have been thus presented to me? . . . No, sir, no. It was a warning voice, coming from the grave . . .' (Henry Clay's peroration to his 'Compromise Resolutions', 29 January 1850: quoted by Alan Heimert, '*Moby-Dick* and American Political Symbolism')

587. *coins of Captain Noah* cf. The carpenter on 'the bearded forecastle', like the 'Worshipful Master Noah' himself presiding over a gathering of Royal Ark Mariners. (p. 472, note) cf. The 'zig-zag' word-circle of this etymological cruise, whose Ark of Testimony is *An American Dictionary*, whose captain, Noah Webster. (p. 343)

588. *the very sill of the door of death* As 'disembowelled', half disembowelled, leaves a 'well', so 'well', by a series of waning half-rhymes – 'chill', 'sill' – turns to ill, 'till there seemed but little left of him but his frame and tattooing'.

588. *like the rings of Eternity* In ever-widening circles of:

pure and endless light . . .
(Henry Vaughan, *The World*)

588. *when Zoroaster died* According to Greek and Latin tradition Zoroaster 'wished to be struck with thunder and consumed by fire from Heaven.' (Pierre Bayle, *An Historical and Critical Dictionary*, 5, 632)

589. *the rolling sea seemed gently rocking him* Thus a mortal threat 'in a rolling sea' is transformed to a 'rolling sea' gently rocking Queequeg to his mortal rest.

Once again all is antithesis without resolution: 'calm weather' disclosing 'black midnight'; a 'bosom friend' manhandling the casks, bitter sweatings turned to a chill; sharper cheek-bones displaying eyes grown softer. 'Without Contraries,' wrote Blake, 'is no progression.' (*The Marriage of Heaven and Hell*)

589. *mild, uncontinented seas . . . the white breakers of the milky way* Turning to 'serenest azure' all 'thoughts of annihilation, when beholding the white depths of the milky way'. (THE WHITENESS OF THE WHALE)

589. *old lumber . . . of the Lackaday islands* For a coffin (alack-a-day!) – possibly from the Laccadives, a starry archipelago off the Malabar Coast.

591. *sweet Antilles . . . beat with water-lilies* Rig-a-dig, dig, dig! for a chiming lost pastoral world of innocence. Not lilies, but Pip s/lily, will 'beat ye your dying march'.

591. *in violent fevers, men . . . have talked in ancient tongues* Ascribing to *men* a German case study of hysteria (disturbance of

the uterus) discussed by Coleridge: 'A young woman of four or five and twenty, who could neither read, nor write, was seized with a nervous fever; during which . . . she continued incessantly talking Latin, Greek, and Hebrew, in very pompous tones and with most distinct enunciation.' The girl, it turned out, had been brought up by an old pastor, who used to walk up and down reading aloud to himself out of 'a collection of Rabbinical writings, together with several of the Greek and Latin fathers . . .' (*Biographia Literaria* I, Part ii, pp. 117–19)

Melville acquired Coleridge's two volumes in 1848.

591. *Hark! he speaks again* 'Hark! now I hear them, – Ding-dong, bell.'

591. *Form two and two!* For a procession, with military honours: '. . . and in the wild conceits that swayed me to my purpose, two and two there floated into my inmost soul, endless processions of the whale'. (LOOMINGS)

591. *Let's make a General of him!* Another Washington (fellow mason of the Blue Lodge).

591. *Oh for a game cock now to sit upon his head and crow!* 'Caw! caw! caw! . . . Ain't I a crow?' But not a gamecock; not the 'crowing cock' on the doubloon. 'Poor Queequeg!' Poor Pip! No 'cock and bull stories' now at THE SPOUTER-INN, but cock and crow – with a jingle of 'game! game! game!' 'Shame! shame!'

592. *shame upon all cowards* Once again Falstaff's words weigh on Pip's mind: 'A plague of all cowards, I say, and a vengeance too! Marry and amen! . . .' (*Henry IV, Part 1*, II, iv, 109ff.)

But confused, it seems, with memories of Macbeth upbraiding his servant:

> Go, prick thy face, and over-red thy fear,
> Thou lily-liver'd boy. What soldiers, patch?
> Death of thy soul! (*Macbeth* V, iii, 14–16)

592. *a matter of his own sovereign will and pleasure* Though Ishmael, on the monkey-rope, perceived 'a sort of interregnum in Providence', Queequeg, at the other end, retains his faith in 'his own sovereign will' (but for acts of God) undiminished.

Thus 'George Washington', from the grave, recalls Henry Clay's 'little duty ashore': 'a warning voice ... to beware, to pause, to reflect; before they lend themselves to any purposes which shall destroy' the Union. 'Mere sickness' cannot kill states; nothing but some 'violent, ungovernable, unintelligent destroyer'.

593. *those hieroglyphic marks . . . a riddle to unfold* – as the whale's whole 'visible surface', marked with hieroglyphics. (THE BLANKET) This 'mystical treatise on the art of attaining truth' (or *Book of the Dead*) then, like Ishmael's own 'little treatise on Eternity', remains impenetrable. But the transfer of that masonic chequerboard, however clumsy, may yet prove a life-buoy.

III THE PACIFIC

593. *gliding by the Bashee isles* To the north of the Batan Islands, in 'one of the tropical outlets from the China waters . . .' (ch. 109)

593. *the long supplication of my youth was answered* Ishmael greets the Pacific with almost religious adoration. But those 'leagues of blue' – those sea-pastures rolling eastwards – are as always deceptive. The fields are Potters' Fields. Tiger-lilies lurk in those prairies. Below their 'gently awful stirrings' stir the millions drowned of this infatuated world.

593. *those fabled undulations of the Ephesian sod over the buried Evangelist St John* St Augustine relates that some Ephesians 'had assured him, that St John was not dead; that indeed he was buried at Ephesus, but that he was in his grave as a man that sleeps in his bed; and that as we see the bed clothes move up and down, according as a man in his sleep breathes, so the earth of the grave wherein St John was buried, was seen to rise and fall in such like intervals'. (Pierre Bayle, *An Historical and Critical Dictionary*). The passage, as Millicent Bell first noted, faces the opening of the long article on 'Jonas' which Melville had already utilized for chs. 82 and 83.

As Queequeg is Ishmael's poor 'companion and fast bosom-friend', so Jesus, apparently, was John's.

594. *Asiatic lands, older than Abraham* cf. 'centuries before Solomon was cradled'. (THE FOSSIL WHALE, p. 569)

594. *this mysterious, divine Pacific zones . . . the tide-beating heart of earth* Like Queequeg, 'a riddle to unfold . . . whose

mysteries not even himself could read, though his own live heart beat against them'.

594. *Lifted by those eternal swells ... bowing your head to Pan* Not only the Arcadian deity of Ishmael's tossing dreams (capricious goat-god); nor Christ (seductive scapegoat of the Evangelists); but God of 'the world's whole bulk' (*πάν*, all-in-all), and universal Panic.

594. *like an iron statue* On its 'iron brow' wearing the 'Iron Crown of Lombardy', its fixed purpose 'laid with iron rails'.

594. *snuffed the sugary musk* Delusive as the 'fresh cinnamon' snuffed off Java Head; those lovers 'green' as Cockatoo Point!

594. *the vaulted hull ... the White Whale spouts thick blood!* Linking 'the lowermost puncheons' with THE FOUNTAIN; 'empty catacombs' with the Eucharist; the vaulted *Pequod* with the whale.

112 THE BLACKSMITH

594. *Perth* If the carpenter's stolidity shades off 'into the surrounding infinite of things', the blacksmith's grime, like his hammer's beat, is solidly of earth.

595. *at the age of nearly sixty* The 'goodly age' at which Bildad 'had concluded his adventurous career by wholly retiring from active life ... and dedicating his remaining days to the quiet receiving of his well-earned income'. (THE SHIP)

595. *a cheerful-looking church* And, like Queen Maachah's idol, 'planted in a grove'. (*1 Kings* xv, 13) cf.

> Under a spreading chestnut tree
> The village smithy stands ...

The whole chapter plays an ironic counterpoint to Longfellow's:

> Week in, week out, from morn till night,
> You can hear his bellow blow;
> You can hear him swing his heavy sledge,
> With measured beat and slow,
> Like a sexton ringing the village-bell,
> When the evening sun is low ...

He goes on Sunday to the church,
And sits among his boys;
He hears the parson pray and preach,
He hears his daughter's voice
Singing in the village choir;
And it makes his heart rejoice.
(*The Village Blacksmith*, 13–18, 25–30)

596. *It was the Bottle Conjuror!* A djin, or gin:
'For he is cast into a net by his own feet, and he walketh upon a snare.
The gin shall take him by the heel, and the robber shall prevail against him.'
(*Job* xviii, 8–9)

596. *But death plucked down some virtuous elder brother* Like Melville's own elder brother, Gansevoort, who had died five years earlier in London, at the age of thirty (May 1846). For almost half his short life he had been the moral and financial prop of the family. Herman owed him a special debt for arranging the publication of his first novel, *Typee*, with John Murray in London only shortly before his death.

597. *to the death-longing eyes of such men* 'That unsounded ocean you gasp in, is Life.' cf. Ishmael: 'This is my substitute for pistol and ball.' How I 'turned me to admire the magnanimity of the sea which will permit no records'. (WHEELBARROW) cf. *Omoo*, ch. 14.

597. *here are wonders supernatural, without dying* Like the albatross, supernatural bird: 'Through its inexpressible, strange eyes, methought I peeped to secrets which took hold of God. As Abraham before the angels, I bowed myself; the white thing was so white, its wings so wide, and in those for ever exiled waters, I had lost the miserable warping memories of traditions and of towns.' (p. 289)

'It is not an accident,' W. H. Auden has remarked, 'that many homosexuals should show a special preference for sailors, for the sailor on shore is symbolically the innocent god from the sea who is not bound by the law of the land and can therefore do anything without guilt.' (*The Enchaféd Flood*, p. 122, footnote)

597. *Aye, I come! And so Perth went a-whaling* cf.

> Thanks, thanks to thee, my worthy friend,
> For the lesson thou hast taught!
> Thus at the flaming forge of life
> Our fortunes must be wrought;
> Thus on its sounding anvil shaped
> Each burning deed and thought!
> (Longfellow, *The Village Blacksmith*, final stanza)

113 THE FORGE

597. *thy Mother Carey's chickens* For 'man is born unto trouble, as the sparks fly upward'. (*Job* v, 7) Petrels or stormy petrels are, of course, 'birds of ill omen'.

598. *Can'st thou smoothe this seam?* cf.

> Canst thou not minister to a mind diseas'd,
> Pluck from the memory a rooted sorrow,
> Raze out the written troubles of the brain ...?
> (*Macbeth* V, iii, 40–42)

598. *away with child's play; no more gaffs* Jingling his word-hoard, to suggest both a fishing-hook (or ship's spar) and literally child's play – a place of public amusement, stuff and nonsense.

598. *gathered nail-stubbs of ... racing horses* Details of welding the harpoon derive from Scoresby (vol. 2, pp. 225–6). But *his* horse-shoe nails are spelt correctly 'stubs'; and only 'two or three' rods, not this apostolic dozen, are joined together.

599. *the Parsee passed silently* As fire draws the Parsee, these stubborn nail-stubbs inevitably rouse the mulish Stubb.

599. *like a fusee* A kind of match with a large head, also known at this time as a 'lucifer' or 'vesuvian'.

599. *Here are my razors – the best of steel* Steel shoes, steel razors – for 'that accursed white whale that razeed me'. Sleet (steel's anagram) evokes Dante's icy Inferno or Ishmael's own oxymoron: 'the flame Baltic of Hell'.

600. *'Ego non baptizo te in nomine patris, sed in nomine diaboli!'*

'Ego non baptizo te in nominee Patris et
Filii et Spiritus Sancti – sed in nomine
Diaboli. Madness is undefinable –
It & right reasons extremes of one.
Not the (black art) Goetic but Theurgic magic –
seeks converse with the Intelligence, Power, the
Angel.'

(Jottings on the back fly-leaves of vol. 7 of Melville's Shakespeare: 'Devil as Quaker'.)

But Ahab, like his Zoroastrian headman, or the Albigensians of Languedoc, is truly diabolic. 'In no Paradise' himself, he professes a dualism of good and evil, God and the Devil. This latin howl, in fact, proves him the very heir of the Inquisition, above all of the Dominicans who first converted peasant magic into demonology: 'They saw themselves as worshippers of God, their enemies as worshippers of the Devil; and as the Devil is *simia Dei*, the ape of God, they built their diabolical system as the necessary counterpart of their divine system. The new "Aristotelean" cosmology stood firmly behind them, and St Thomas Aquinas, the guarantor of the one, was the guarantor of the other. The two were interdependent ...' (H. R. Trevor-Roper, *The Witch Craze in the Sixteenth and Seventeenth Centuries*)

Which recalls the landlord of the Spouter-Inn 'looking a sort of diabolically funny ... the while grinning like an ape'. Which recalls Queequeg 'wrapped up in his great pilot monkey jacket', or held like 'a dancing-ape' upon the whale – and that matrimonial cord binding him to Ishmael, called 'in the fishery a monkey-rope'. Which recalls Stubb jabbering like 'a St Jago monkey' and 'a baboon'. Which evokes the whole company of Ahab's crew in their monkey-jackets. 'Why, thou monkey'!: the *Pequod* is top-heavy 'as a dinnerless student with all Aristotle in his head'. (For earlier references to the Black Mass, see notes on pp. 104, 293, 334, 354, and 575.)

'The tail is not yet cooked', Melville informed Hawthorne in June 1851, '– though the hell-fire in which the whole book is broiled might not unreasonably have cooked it all ere this. This is the book's motto (the secret one), – Ego non baptiso te in nomine – but make out the rest yourself.'

600. *selecting one of hickory, with the bark still investing it* With a wink at 'Young Hickory', thundered 'higher than a

throne!' For a 'hickory pole', in its bark, served as Democrat standard to display the true line of descent from 'Old Hickory' Jackson to 'Young Hickory' Polk. (It was Gansevoort Melville, in the election of 1844, who had first christened Polk.)

So the diabolist, it seems, is also a militant Democrat! 'Oh! Pip, ... all thy strange mummeries not unmeaningly blended with the black tragedy of the melancholy ship' (of state).

600. *A coil of new tow-line* First twelve rods were spiralized; then a coil stretched and strummed. This *harp*/oon is hallowed to a diabolic hum.

600. *the pole was then driven hard up* 'There's the stuff' (from the pouch): after the blood-rite, a phallic thrust. As the carpenter's limb had rebounded on Ahab's groin, so the blacksmith's harpoon will catch him round the neck.

601. *Oh! Pip, thy wretched laugh, thy ... unresting eye* Aye, 'and standing there in thy spite? In thy most solitary hours, then, dost thou not fear eavesdroppers?' (p. 583)

Castaway mocks castaway in this 'black tragedy': the little negro, a scorched blacksmith – a black wight, a white black – in the '*melan*/choly' chase of a 'white fiend', in the Manichaean forgery of this chequered FORGE.

114 THE GILDER

THE GILDER cf. 'the gilded velvets of butterflies, and the butterfly cheeks of young girls; all these are but subtile deceits ...' (THE WHITENESS OF THE WHALE) cf. 'the long burnished sun-glade on the waters seemed a golden finger laid across them, enjoining some secresy'. (SQUID) cf. 'the spangled sea calm and cool, and flatly stretching away, all round, to the horizon, like gold-beater's skin hammered out to the extremest'. (THE CASTAWAY)

As beaten gold forms a skin, this 'tranquil beauty and brilliance' too is but skin-deep; these 'wonders supernatural' (gilt without guilt), mere siren songs. What seem 'golden keys' to 'golden treasuries' prove, like the gold doubloon, mere mirrors for wish-fulfilment.

601. *a certain filial, confident, land-like feeling towards the sea* And once again a calm and dreamy quietude evokes a pastoral of 'flowery earth' and rolling prairies – wading through Tiger-

lilies: 'consider them both, the sea and the land; and do you not find a strange analogy to something in yourself?' (BRIT)

602. *in ye, men yet may roll* As the live whale 'rolled his island bulk', the vast mass of the dead whale revolved 'like a tread-mill' beneath Queequeg. The waves roll; the *Pequod* rolls in the sea 'like an air-freighted demijohn'. The whalemen themselves, in 'the whole roll' of their order, are rolled in their hammocks. A 'rolling sea' both mocks, and rocks, the harpooneer to heaven.

602. *manhood's pondering repose of If* In Greek, 'Ei', name for the letter 'E'. cf. Plotinus Plinlimmon's lecture, in *Pierre; or, The Ambiguities,* entitled *Ei* (1852). cf. Plutarch, 'The E at Delphi' (which follows 'Of Isis and Osiris' in the *Moralia*).

Circling through scepticism to atheism, Ishmael eventually resorts to something like Coleridge's 'suspension of disbelief' – much as earlier he had settled for something akin to Huxley's 'agnosticism': 'Doubts of all things earthly, and intuitions of some things heavenly; this combination makes neither believer nor infidel, but makes a man who regards them both with equal eye'. (THE FOUNTAIN)

602. *Where is the foundling's father ... the secret of our paternity* Like Jesus, like Ishmael possibly, like Ahab whose 'crazy, widowed mother ... died when he was only a twelve-month old.' (THE SHIP) All are fatherless, wanderers, outcasts.

Add quotation marks – hey, presto! – and Ahab becomes the speaker of the whole paragraph. This is a most inviting emendation (Hayford/Parker, p. 494). For if Ahab is followed by Starbuck who is followed by Stubb, then THE GILDER plays a gilded echo to THE DOUBLOON. In fact, the whole meditation on 'ever vernal endless landscapes in the soul' becomes a much needed transition to Ahab's final Andean pastoral, so shocking to Starbuck: 'Sleep? Aye, and rust amid greenness ...' (THE SYMPHONY)

602. *Let faith oust fact* 'lest Truth shake me falsely'. (THE DOUBLOON) 'I look deep down' into gold (skin-deep) 'and do believe'!

602. *Stubb, fish-like, with sparkling scales* A 'Cape-Cod-man' in the same golden light – and 'happy-go-lucky' who thinks 'to be happy for aye, when pop comes Libra, or the Scales ... to wind up with Pisces' in sleep. (THE DOUBLOON)

115 THE PEQUOD MEETS THE BACHELOR

603. *It was a Nantucket ship, the* Bachelor 'Bachelor' became for Melville a half jocular, private epithet for those who see only half truths, or surface truths, like those gentlemen of London's Temple, to whose bachelor imaginations 'the thing called pain, the bugbear styled trouble – those two legends seemed preposterous ... How could men of liberal sense, ripe scholarship in the world, and capacious philosophical and convivial understandings – how could they suffer themselves to be imposed upon by such monkish fables? Pain! Trouble! As well talk of Catholic miracles. No such thing. – Pass the sherry, sir. – Pooh, pooh! Can't be!' (*The Paradise of Bachelors*, 1855)

603. *The three men at her mast-head* The picture alters – to what Melville may well have intended – if one reads with Hayford/Parker: 'The three men at her mast-heads ...'

603. *slender breakers* Corruption from Spanish *bareca*, a small keg.

603. *nailed to her main truck was a brazen lamp* In contrast to the *Virgin*'s empty oil-can and lamp-feeder. For it is no longer so much a quest of wise or foolish virgins, as of the *Virgin* seeking what the *Bachelor* so abundantly, and so brazenly, displays – casks and barrels and breakers and chests of sperm: '... indeed everything was filled with sperm, except the captain's pantaloons pockets ...'

605. *'No; only heard of him; but don't believe in him at all'* THE GILDER was fitting prelude to such light-hearted insouciance, universal scepticism and self-satisfaction.

605. *'Thou art too damned jolly'* Ahab's oxymoron compounding 'the whole striking contrast of the scene'.

605. *a small vial of sand* A final touch to link the Shaker from Neskyeuna to the Nantucket Quaker.

116 THE DYING WHALE

606. *sun and whale both stilly died together* cf. 'The red tide now poured from all sides of the monster ... The slanting sun playing upon this crimson pond in the sea ...' (STUBB KILLS A WHALE)

606. *inwreathing ... in that rosy air* 'such plaintiveness' to plainsong (as of women's voices in the ecstatic drawn-out 'eee' of the sweet breeze inwreathing over the sea) till rosy horizons blend into their orisons. But 'no roses, no violets, no Cologne-water in the sea'. Nor Manilla convents either, with wanton air: only 'Manilla rope'. (p. 384, note)

606. *sat intently watching his final wanings* cf. 'An awe that cannot be named would steal over you as you sat by the side of this waning savage, and saw strange things in his face, as any beheld who were bystanders when Zoroaster died.' (QUEEQUEG IN HIS COFFIN)

606. *the turning sunwards of the head, and so expiring* A whaling myth recorded by Beale, who adds: 'but of this I have never been convinced'. (pp. 160–61)

606. *He turns and turns him to it ... He too worships fire* In his death-flurry, too, turning and wheeling about his 'mystic brow'.

cf. 'I once saw a large herd of whales in the east, all heading towards the sun ... As it seemed to me at the time, such a grand embodiment of adoration of the gods was never beheld, even in Persia, the home of the fire worshippers.' (THE TAIL)

606. *beyond all hum* Whether pastoral (of weal, 'in some glad May-time') or mechanical (of woe). 'Far water-locked', he is beyond humanity.

606. *in these most candid and impartial seas; where to traditions no rocks furnish tablets* For the ocean is magnanimous. From the ocean sound siren voices to a life free of guilt, exempt from the Mosaic code, beyond good and evil. Itself without rocks, it rocks tradition, razing the Bastille of sensual – and all Judaic – orthodoxy.

So far Ishmael and Ahab are at one. Yet 'O Nature, and O soul of man!' Whereas Ahab is thereby rocked to 'a prouder, if a darker faith', Ishmael had long ago scuttled *all* faith in rocks – whether Mosaic, Christian, or Hindu – to a meaningless 'vacuum'. (THE FUNERAL) What to Ishmael appears cruel farce, becomes for Ahab a cult of darkness and cruelty.

606. *upon the Niger's unknown source* Mungo Park penetrated three hundred miles upstream to Bamako (*Travels in the Interior Districts of Africa*, 1799). Sent out again by the British government in 1805, to trace the Niger to its mouth, he was attacked at Bussa and drowned (1806). Despite two subsequent

expeditions, in 1822–5 and 1825–7, by Hugh Clapperton (who died at Sokoto) and Richard Lander (who returned with his brother John in 1830–31), the source of the Niger was still unknown – though its delta on the Bight of Benin had been established.

Africa seems to weigh on Ahab's mind; and the Niger's very name evokes what Ishmael had called 'the negro heart of Africa': 'serpents, savages, tigers, poisonous miasmas, with all the other common perils incident to wandering in the heart of unknown regions.' (THE AFFIDAVIT)

606. *thou art an infidel, thou queen* Meaning Kali, Siva's consort, black goddess of death, with her necklace of human heads and protruding blood-stained tongue.

But 'Ahab's invocation cannot be understood precisely without a knowledge of the Gnostic myth of the fallen Mother – she who fell from overweening love of the Supreme Being, whose passion produced the Demiurge of whom she is both the mother and "infidel" adversary. Norton associated her with the "female energy" worshipped by the Hindus (*Evidences*, II, 204–5) ...' (Thomas Vargish, op. cit., p. 275)

606. *Oh, trebly hooped* Like a sperm-oil cask, or the carpenter's beer barrels.

607. *I am buoyed by breaths of once living things* Though they will prove no life-buoy: 'for every one knows that this earthly air ... is terribly infected with the nameless miseries of the numberless mortals who have died exhaling it.' (KNIGHTS AND SQUIRES)

607. *though hill and valley mothered me* Foster-child of the Old Testament and the New; of 'thy holy hill' and 'green pasture'; of 'the valley of the shadow' and Sermon on the Mount.

607. *ye billows are my foster-brothers!* Himself a 'landless gull ... rocked to sleep between billows'. (NANTUCKET)

117 THE WHALE WATCH

607. *over Asphaltites* Milton's 'Asphaltick Pool' (*Paradise Lost* I, 411) – or Dead Sea for Jack Tars (p. 106, note).

And 'what too many seamen are when ashore is very well known,' Melville had noted in *White-Jacket*, 'but what some of them become when completely cut off from shore indulgences can hardly be imagined by landsmen. The sins for which the cities of the plain were overthrown still linger in some of these wooden-walled Gomorrahs of the deep.' (ch. 90)

608. *the first not made by mortal hands; and the visible wood of the last* The Parsee speaks darkly as the Apparitions to Macbeth:

SECOND APPARITION Be bloody, bold, and resolute; laugh
to scorn
The pow'r of man, for none of woman born
Shall harm Macbeth.
THIRD APPARITION Macbeth shall never vanquish'd be until
Great Birnam wood to high Dunsinane Hill
Shall come against him.
MACBETH That will never be.
(*Macbeth* IV, i, 79ff.)

(Both Birnam and Dunsinane, incidentally, lie near Perth, which may help account for the fatal blacksmith's name.)

608. *a hearse and its plumes* cf. Stubb: 'here comes our old Manxman – the old hearse-driver ...' (THE DOUBLOON)

608. *I shall still go before thee thy pilot* But not a 'pilot-prophet, or speaker of true things' necessarily (like Jonah); more like a sea-gudgeon perhaps, 'the Whale's guide, for she doth ever follow him, suffering her selfe, as easily to be led and turned by him, as a ship is directed and turned by a sterne.' (Montaigne, *Apology for Raimond Sebond*; cf. Extract 10)

608. *His eyes lighted up like fire-flies* Ahab's *ignis fatuus* – like the blacksmith's 'sparks in thick hovering flights'; like Pip's 'fiery effulgences'.

608. *'Hemp only can kill thee'* And 'hemp is a dusky, dark fellow, a sort of Indian'. (THE LINE)

Indan hemp – *cannibis sativa*, 'grass' or 'hashish' – is, of course, a narcotic. But, then, somnambulist Ahab, like the Shaker Gabriel, looks and moves like an addict. He drugs himself on the Indian's continual presence; he feeds himself his own pastoral illusions; and, in the end, despatches his own 'assassin' (hash-shāshīn).

608. *'The gallows, ye mean'* Playing another prophetic card from the Tarot pack: the Hanged Man 'suspended by asses' ears' – sign of 'The Trap!' (CHOWDER)

118 THE QUADRANT

608. *the vigilant helmsman ... handle his spokes* A further odd discrepancy: see p. 389, note. (STUBB KILLS A WHALE) cf. Ishmael's hallucination of THE TRY-WORKS.

608. *on the nailed doubloon ... upon high noon* A rhyme to signal 'the keystone sun'; and the White Whale too 'seen gliding at high noon ... all spangled with golden gleamings'. (MOBY DICK)

609. *with his astrological-looking instrument* Now Ahab is the Chaldean – between the heavenly Pilot high above and his earthly pilot ('one grand hooded phantom') kneeling below.

610. *yet with thy impotence thou insultest the sun! Science!* Again every word rebounds: 'Talk not to me of blasphemy, man; I'd strike the sun if it insulted me!' (THE QUARTER-DECK) But it is Ahab who is impotent – Ahab/Prometheus with machine-like hum, propelled along the grooves of his 'iron way'.

610. *these old eyes ... scorched with thy light* For Ahab is not 'past scorching'. Scarred though he be, he is not yet, like Perth, a 'burnt-out' case.

610. *not shot from the crown of his head* cf. 'No, but put a sky-light on top of his head to illuminate inwards ... No, no, no; I must have a lantern.' (AHAB AND THE CARPENTER)

610. *Curse thee, thou quadrant!* This cabbalistical toy, 'furnished with colored glasses', yet again carries an echo of Paul:

> When I was a child, I spake as a child, I understood as a child, I thought as a child: but when I became a man, I put away childish things.
> For now we see through a glass, darkly; but then face to face: now I know in part; but then shall I know even as also I am known.
>
> (*1 Corinthians* xiii, 11–12)

But what was once an invocation is now turned to a curse. This crushing of the quadrant is Ahab's final rejection of 'the great Pilot' and his theological virtues of faith, hope and charity. It is this – the supreme peripeteia – which is greeted by the Parsee with sneering triumph.

But also 'a fatalistic despair', at such a heady succession of puns. For now – like Oedipus, like Lear, like every tragic hero – Ahab ('old man of oceans!') is blinded, self-mutilated, moving in darkness by 'level dead-reckoning' to his doom: 'Aye ... thus I split and destroy thee!' Dismissing the light, he lights upon the deck. 'His live and dead feet', trampling the quadrant, become the visible embodiment of his divided manhood – of the diabolism at the Manichaean root of his being.

And 'like wilful travellers in Lapland, who refuse to wear colored and coloring glasses upon their eyes, so the wretched infidel gazes himself blind at the monumental white shroud that wraps all the prospect around him.' (THE WHITENESS OF THE WHALE)

610. *Up helm! – square in!* cf. 'Quitting the common Fleet of herring-busses and whalers ... he desperately steers off, on a course of his own, by sextant and compass of his own.' (*Sartor Resartus*, Bk 2, ch. 5)

610. *as the ship half-wheeled upon her heel* As Ahab 'vehemently wheeled' upon his ivory joist 'with an urgent command to the steersman'. (AHAB'S LEG) For the *Pequod is* Ahab, and responds to Ahab and Ahab's doom.

The Horatii, according to legend, were triplets who, in single combat with a trio of Latin brothers, decided the war between Alba and Rome. They are occasionally shown seated astride a single horse. (See p. 264, note.)

610. *between the knight-heads* Timbers on either side of the bowsprit, at one time carved into figures of knights. Thus, doubtless, the dual chapter-heads, KNIGHTS AND SQUIRES.

610. *wane at last ... down, to dumbest dust* Like Queequeg, like the whale, like all mortality to Adam-dust. But what is numb is not necessarily dumb. Thus the carpenter's little joke: 'Halloa, this bone dust is (*sneezes*) – why it's (*sneezes*) – yes it's (*sneezes*) – bless my soul, it won't let me speak!'

610. *but see coal ashes ... not your common charcoal* Not 'begrimed with charcoal' (like Hawthorne's lime-burner), to be consumed at last by his 'Unpardonable Sin'. cf. *Ethan Brand*, 1851.

611. *some one thrusts these cards* 'The gallows, ye mean'? But first three further cards must be played: Libra (the Scales); the Dark Tower in a lightning flash; the Cleft, or Splintered, Heart.

611. *live in the game, and die in it!* Thus the gay *Bachelor's* commander: 'merry's the play'. Thus Ishmael in the *Samuel Enderby*: 'a short life to them, and a jolly death'.

119 THE CANDLES

611. *the direst of all storms, the Typhoon.*

'... or Typhon, whom the Den
By ancient Tarsus held, or that Sea-beast
Leviathan, which God of all his works
Created hugest that swim th' Ocean stream:'
(*Paradise Lost* I, 199–202)

'Melville used the uncapitalized word "typhoon" frequently in his earliest works and several times early in *Moby-Dick*. Late in *Moby-Dick* the word begins to appear capitalized, and shortly thereafter the "Typhoon" strikes the *Pequod*. This Typhoon is not only capitalized by Melville, but is also addressed as a god by Ahab.' (H. Bruce Franklin, *The Wake of the Gods*, p. 79)

Let 'the pale Usher' dust 'his old lexicons and grammars' (ETYMOLOGY):

'TY-PHOON Ar. tufān, a violent storm; probably fr. Gr. *τυφῶν, τυφώς*, a violent whirlwind.

'TYPHON 1. According to Hesiod, the son of Typhoeus, and father of the winds, but later identified with him. By modern writers *Typhon* is identified with Egyptian Set, who represents physical evil. 2. A violent whirlwind; a typhoon [*Obs.*]'
(Noah Webster, *An American Dictionary of the English Language*)

It is the Typhoon, or Typhon, which singles out Ahab's post in his whale boat and reverses his compasses. It is the Typhon-Typhoon which violently stays the *Pequod*, turns it aside, and whirls it in the direction diametrically opposed to Ahab's course. cf. Plutarch: 'And *Typhon*, as we have already said, is named *Seth, Baebon* and *Smy*, which words betoke all, a violent stay and impeachment, a contrariety and a diversion or turning aside another way.' ('Of Isis and Osiris')

Typhon, according to Plutarch, is 'neither drought alone, nor winde, nor sea ne yet darknesse; but all that is noisome and hurtful whatsoever, and which hath a special part to hurt and destroy, is called *Typhon*'. The Egyptians attribute 'all dangerous wicked beasts . . . unto *Typhon*, as if they were his workes, his parts or motions'. (Philemon Holland's translation, pp. 1305–8.)

611. *bare-poled was left to fight* Like Ahab, 'erectly poised' but 'disabled' – that is to say, impotent.

612. *so the old song says* Melvillean hocus-pocus.

612. *I am a coward; and I sing to keep up my spirits* Like one of Shakespeare's 'jesty, joky, hoky-poky' lads, professional word-riggers or fools. As the Typhoon strikes 'his harp here in our rigging', so Stubb's 'wind-up', he claims, will be a *Gloria in Excelsis*.

613. *the gale comes from the eastward* Like 'that tempestuous wind Euroclydon . . . about poor Paul's tossed craft'. (THE CARPET-BAG)

613. *In the stern-sheets, man; where he is wont to stand* His quadrant smashed, Ahab's boat's bottom too is smashed 'at the stern'. His 'stand-point', that is, as well as his point of view, 'is stove'.

613. *Yes, yes, round the Cape of Good Hope* 'So in this vale of Death . . . the sun of Righteousness still shines a beacon and a hope.' (THE DOUBLOON)

613. *'Who's there?'* cf. 'Oh! how that harmless question mangles Jonah! For the instant he almost turns to flee again. But he rallies.' (THE SERMON)

613. *'Old Thunder!' said Ahab* – Old Thor, son of Odin: 'Aye, among some of us old sailor chaps, he goes by that name.' (THE PROPHET)

614. *to raise rods on the Himmalehs and Andes* In the early 1850s the Pittsfield neighbourhood was subjected to a vigorous advertising campaign, accompanied by door to door salesmen pressing copper rods on eager households. Lightning-rods sprang up as ubiquitously as TV aerials a century later. But 'out on privileges!' Ahab again insists on 'fair play' between man and God.

But does he not himself carry a 'slender rod-like mark' from crown to sole? Such hyperboles, such sermons on 'mountain-tops', are as ever 'egotistical'. (THE DOUBLOON)

614. *'The corpusants! the corpusants!'* Correctly 'corposants' (*corpo santo*), balls of light sometimes seen about the masts or yard-arms of a ship during a storm. Though called St Elmo's fire, the *corpus sancti* is not, it seems, that of the fourth century

martyr, but of yet another Peter – the Dominican Peter Gonzalez of Astorga (c. 1190–1246), who worked among the mariners of Galicia.

But an earlier name, *Hermes' fire*, suggests that something occult is to be divulged, a magical ceremony celebrated: a Witches' Sabbat, in fact, to be Ahab's *Walpurgisnacht* of leaping, and fawning kisses, and burning orgasm.

614. *tipped with a pallid fire . . . three gigantic wax tapers* As the whole ship wheeled to Ahab's purpose, so in thunder and lightning the whole ship celebrates Black Mass ('non . . . in nomine patris, sed in nomine diaboli!') before this 'lofty tri-pointed trinity' of 'tapering upright cones'. The saints 'have mercy on us all!'

614. *in the teeth of the tempest* The typhoon's force caught in that high-pitched 'eeee' of 'the reeling ship's high tetering side' as the topsail yards 'teter over to a seething sea'. (And thus, while the *Bachelor* 'went cheerily before the breeze, the other stubbornly fought against it'.)

614. *when God's burning finger has been laid* 'In the same hour came forth fingers of a man's hand, and wrote over against the candlestick upon the plaister of the wall of the king's palace . . .'

The immediate allusion again is to *Daniel* v. (p. 542, note)

614. *the enchanted crew . . . like a far away constellation of stars* Again a 'trance of the calm' in the midst of a storm. (THE GRAND ARMADA) cf. 'The Captain . . . directed my attention "to those fellows" as he called them, – meaning several "Corposant balls" on the yardarms & mastheads. They were the first I had ever seen, & resembled large, dim stars in the sky.' (*Journal*, 13 October 1849)

615. *The tableau all waned at last* Flambeaux light a tableau: pallidness turns to a pall. Contraries yet again meet in a pun, 'floating over the ocean with the waves for the pall-bearers'. (THE WHALE WATCH)

615. *skeletons in Herculaneum* Caught by the Vesuvius eruption of 79 A.D. – to be buried in the Roman sub-strata of *The Whale*. There is a hint of Arbaces (from Bulwer-Lytton's *The Last Days of Pompeii*) in Ahab: 'half prophet and half fiend' induced, by his superior intellect, to practise 'goetic, or dark and evil necromancy' instead of 'theurgic, or benevolent magic'.

616. *blood against fire!* With a foot on the fusee/Parsee, that match for Lucifer: 'Bless my soul, and curse the foul fiend's... his pulse makes these planks beat!' (LEG AND ARM)

616. *with fixed upward eye* Having dismissed the light, Ahab is greeted by lightning. Scorched by that 'solar fire', Ahab now greets this 'pallid fire' with fixed gaze. But 'it is held a fatal sign to have the pale light of the corposant thrown upon one's face.' (Richard Henry Dana, *Two Years before the Mast*)

cf. Nulli, *alias* John C. Calhoun: 'a cadaverous, ghost-like man; with a low ridge of forehead; hair, steel-gray; and wondrous eyes: – bright, nimble, as the twin corposant balls, playing about the ends of ships' royal-yards in gales.' (*Mardi*, ch. 162)

616. *and high-flung right arm* cf.

> The Lord is thy keeper: the Lord is thy shade upon thy
> right hand.
> The sun shall not smite thee by day, nor the moon by night.
> (*Psalm* cxxi, 5–7)

So Hawthorne's 'Ethan Brand stood erect, and raised his arms on high. The blue flames played upon his face, and imparted the wild and ghastly light which alone could have suited its expression...'

616. *Oh! thou clear spirit of clear fire* 'Then hail, for ever hail': after the baptism of blood, after the 'dark Hindoo' salutation, after the dashing of his quadrant, Ahab is now wholly resolved in his heretic role. All his twisted energies are tensed and gathered for the final kill, whose prologue is this invocation to Lucifer (the light-bringer), Satan (the opposer).

'From storm to storm! So be it, then': 'not Fear or whining Sorrow was it, but Indignation and grim fire-eyed Defiance.' (*Sartor Resartus*, II, vii, 'The Everlasting No')

616. *I as Persian once* For Ahab is no practising Zoroastrian. *Once* he had worshipped 'as Persian': by 'the Persian fire worshippers, the white forked flame being held the holiest on the altar'. (THE WHITENESS OF THE WHALE) But burnt in the sacramental act, Ahab had turned to the eternal adversary of this 'mechanical', 'fiery' Creator (or Gnostic Demiurge), 'foundling' son of Sophia (or Wisdom). His allegiance – his whole personality – is now wholly at the command of the 'fallen Mother'. cf. pp. 262, 267, 283, 575, 606, notes.

616. *to this hour I bear the scar* An 'old Gay-Head Indian ... superstitiously asserted that not till he was full forty years old did Ahab become that way branded ...' (p. 219)

cf. 'For the fire-baptized soul, long so scathed and thunder-riven, here feels its own Freedom, which feeling is its Baphometic Baptism; the citadel of its whole kingdom it has thus gained by assault, and will keep inexpugnable ...' (*Sartor Resartus*, II, viii, 'Centre of Indifference')

616. *No fearless fool now fronts thee* cf. 'By visable truth, we mean the apprehension of the absolute condition of present things as they strike the eye of the man who fears them not, though they do their worst to him, – the man who, like Russia or the British Empire, declares himself a sovereign nature (in himself) amid the powers of heaven, hell, and earth. He may perish; but so long as he exists he insists upon treating with all Powers upon an equal basis. If any of those other Powers choose to withhold certain secrets, let them; that does not impair my sovereignty in myself; that does not make me tributary.' (To Hawthorne, April 1851)

616. *In the midst of the personified impersonal* A 'personality', unlike his impersonally stolid old carpenter; yet rather like the carpenter, 'a point at best'; and very like him, it seems, 'prepared at all points, and alike indifferent and without respect in all'.

Between the carpenter and the blacksmith (both sixty-year-olds) Ahab wavers, sharing something of the impersonality of the one and personality (if extinct) of the other; of the carpenter's 'cunning life-principle' and the blacksmith's 'death-longing eyes'. Both literally and metaphorically he passes to and fro between them, from the vice-bench to the forge. (chs. 107–113)

616. *the queenly personality lives in me* Which is Kali's, not Siva's (of the lingam) 'who creates the elements'. Ahab claims the black goddess as his own; and on his own lips at last (not Stubb's) is dubbed 'a queen'.

For 'into the rational soul which proceeded from the Creator, Achamoth [the Mother or Sophia], unknown to him, infused a portion of the spiritual substance which she had produced, a leaven of immortality, a spirit.' (Andrews Norton, *Evidences* III, 159–60)

616. *the nine flames leap lengthwise to thrice their previous height*

Thrice to thine, and thrice to mine,
And thrice again, to make up nine.
Peace! The charm's wound up.
(*Macbeth* I, iii, 35–7)

616. *Light . . . thou leapest out of darkness* As 'the light of the master mason is darkness visible'.

Hail! mystic holy light,
Heaven born and ever bright
Spread more and more; –
Light of the bold and free,
Honour and loyalty,
Light of freemasonry,
Ne'er leave our shore

sing freemasons at their gatherings (to the tune of 'God Save the Queen').

But what does Ahab here? 'When were you made a Mason?' asks the Worshipful Master. 'When the Sun was at its Meridian,' did you not smash the quadrant? Though 'blindfold', with an initiate's noose about your neck, were you not blinded? And even if the whole *Pequod* – the whole visible world, that is, like a masonic temple floor – is now chequered in black and white, was it not said, old man, 'that neither hearse nor coffin can be thine?'

617. *now I do glory in my genealogy* For to 'trail the genealogies of these high mortal miseries, carries us at last among the sourceless primogenitures of the gods . . .' (AHAB'S LEG)

617. *my sweet mother, I know not* In diabolical contrast to Ishmael's predicament: 'Our souls are like those orphans whose unwedded mothers die in bearing them: the secret of our paternity lies in their grave . . .' (THE GILDER)

For it was Sophia, as well as Kali, Ahab had claimed as 'queen'. It was Sophia who had breathed into Adam at his creation – in defiance of her son, the Demiurge. It was she who had employed the Serpent 'for the purpose of seducing our first parents'. Over the years she had sent a long line of her own prophets – Jesus among them – to impart her spiritual essence, or *gnosis*, to man. It is as last of this line that Ahab here invokes her.

617. *hence callest thyself unbegotten* 'The Father is made of none: neither created, nor begotten.' (*Athanasian Creed*)

617. *all thy creativeness mechanical* Like the carpenter's, like Ahab's inmost wheels 'lowly humming'.

617. *my scorched eyes do dimly see* And 'the thunders that rolled away from off his swarthy brow, and the light leaping from his eye, made all his simple hearers look on him with a quick fear...' (THE SERMON)

617. *thou too hast thy incommunicable riddle* cf. 'We incline to think that God cannot explain His own secrets, and that He would like a little information upon certain points Himself. We mortals astonish Him as much as He us.' (To Nathaniel Hawthorne, April? 1851) See p. 472, note.

617. *Leap! leap up . . . I leap with thee* Up from the spray – straight up, leaps my 'apotheosis!' (THE LEE SHORE)

617. *harpoon burned there like a serpent's tongue* With 'bottom' stove and harpoon projecting, phallus-like, from 'its conspicuous crotch' (the sheath dropped off), Ahab stands stripped at last – burning with passion – nakedly exposed: 'Come in thy lowest form of love, and I will kneel and kiss thee.'

But his pole (fitted with phallic thrust), far from being flush with sap or regenerative sperm, is forked with fire. The flame, far from leaping upward, shoots horizontally by a 'level dead-reckoning'. Not Siva's lingam is revealed but his 'queen' (worshipped as a snake): 'I burn with thee; would fain be welded with thee.' Waving his 'fiery dart' like a torch, this Knight of the Burning Pestle is neither Lucifer (the light-bringer), nor Milton's Satan (*Paradise Lost* XII, 492), but Kali, black goddess of death.

'Wherefore take unto you the whole armour of God, that ye may be able to withstand in the evil day . . . Above all, taking the shield of faith, wherewith ye shall be able to quench all the fiery darts of the wicked.' (*Ephesians* vi, 13–16)

618. *thus I blow out the last fear!* 'The Lord is my light and my salvation; whom shall I fear?' (*Psalm* xxvii, 1) This Quaker is a fighting Quaker: 'Oh, thou'lt like him well enough; no fear, no fear.' (THE SHIP)

'Hang those that talk of fear. Give me mine armour.' (*Macbeth* V, iii, 36)

618. *some lone, gigantic elm* Some 'straight, lofty trunk' of a wych-elm – or *witch* elm: no longer 'Cellini's cast Perseus', but the Medusa.

120 THE DECK TOWARDS THE END OF THE FIRST NIGHT WATCH

618. *he takes me for the hunch-backed skipper* Ahab dismisses hunchbacks as lubbers, oblivious in his frenzy of 'this august hump . . . this high hump the organ of firmness or indomitableness in the Sperm Whale'. (THE NUT)

618. *Ho, gluepots!* Slang term for 'clergymen'.

618. *Oh, none but cowards send down their brain-trucks in tempest time* Thus Father Mapple's dramatic entrance out of the storm: 'he carried no umbrella, and certainly had not come in his carriage'. (THE PULPIT)

619. *What a hooroosh . . . the colic is a noisy malady* cf.

> Blow, winds, and crack your cheeks! rage! blow! . . .
> Rumble thy bellyful! Spit, fire! Spout, rain!
> (*King Lear* III, ii, 1ff.)

121 MIDNIGHT – THE FORECASTLE BULWARKS

619. *you're Aquarius* – the water-flask, or pitcher. But 'Lord! how we suddenly jump . . . when Aquarius, or the Water-bearer, pours out his whole deluge and drowns us.' (THE DOUBLOON)

620. *these two anchors . . . are your iron fists* But 'first take your leg off from the crown': this cast Iron Duke or Czar, it seems, has been deposed. Blinded, lashed, pinioned, 'knotted all over with ropes and hawsers', his hands tied behind his back, he too must face the end, like a condemned man facing the firing squad. (THE MUSKET)

620. *whew! there goes my tarpaulin* Which, rebus-fashion, might be interpreted as 'Pilot Paul overboard'. cf. Father Mapple's storm-pelted apparition in 'his tarpaulin hat . . . and his great pilot cloth jacket'. (THE PULPIT)

122 MIDNIGHT ALOFT – THUNDER AND LIGHTNING

621. *Um, um, um, . . . we want rum* To oil that 'unreasoning wheel' which – like captain's, like carpenter's – 'also hummingly soliloquizes'.

123 THE MUSKET

621. *the whirling velocity with which they revolved* First sign of the impending vortex now 'upon the cards'.

621. *the shivered remnants of the jib* Like Ahab's ivory joist (white truss, or *alba*/tross) after its 'half-splintering shock'.

622. *coming round astern* 'Fair is foul' – and 'aye, the foul breeze became fair!'

622. *burning fitfully, and casting fitful* shadows Of Jonah, 'praying God for annihilation until the fit be passed'; of Ahab's paroxysms; and again Macbeth:

> Then comes my fit again. I had else been perfect,
> Whole as the marble, founded as the rock,
> As broad and general as the casing air,
> But now I am cabin'd, cribb'd, confin'd, bound in
> To saucy doubts and fears.
>
> (*Macbeth* III, iv, 21–25)

622. *the old man's bolted door ... with fixed blinds inserted* Ahab is his own deluded prisoner locked inside his cell. Permanently blinded, isolated within the unceasing mechanic hum of his intellect, hooped round by gloom, he lies behind this door – bolted within – 'more hideous than a caged tiger'; more sluggish than any monster sporting its 'Venetian blind'; more obdurate than Jonah, bolted by the whale.

For 'certain it is, that with the mad secret of his unabated rage bolted up and keyed in him, Ahab had purposely sailed . . . with the one only and all-engrossing object of hunting the White Whale'. (MOBY DICK)

622. *The loaded muskets in the rack* Like Stubb, he too keeps 'a whole row of pipes there ready loaded, stuck in a rack, within easy reach . . .' (KNIGHTS AND SQUIRES)

622. *stood upright* Erect on a heretic's rack, their load is death. But Starbuck, like David 'servant of the Lord', is an 'upright man':

> I was also upright before him, and I kept myself from mine iniquity.
>
> Therefore hath the Lord recompensed me according to my righteousness, according to the cleanness of my hands in his eyesight. (*Psalm* xviii, 23–24)

623. *locked Japan* 'double-bolted' from within – and, likewise, its own deluded prisoner. (p. 206, note)

624. *And would I be a murderer, then, if* – cf. Hamlet:

> Now might I do it pat, now 'a is a-praying;
> And now I'll do't . . . (III, iii, 73–74)

– with sword poised over Claudius.

624. *On this level* lies 'the level dead-reckoning' – not through sight-tube (of the quadrant), but 'death-tube'.

624. *Stern all! Oh Moby Dick* Self-condemned, like Jonah, Ahab lies drowned in tormented sleep. But, unlike Jonah 'in that contracted hole', he 'feels the heralding presentiment' of that exultant hour when *he* shall hold the *whale* 'in the smallest of his bowel's wards' – and clutch his heart.

624. *seemed wrestling with an angel* For 'as a prince hast thou power with God and with men, and hast prevailed'. (*Genesis* xxxii, 28)

124 THE NEEDLE

624. *the whole world boomed* The advance, which is a retreat, being hinted in the very advance and retreat of the letters: the forward roll of the sea, sucked back in 'billows'; 'muffled' reversed to 'full'.

625. *as of crowned Babylonian kings and queens* Again a pointer to Belshazzar in his pride, with his princes, wives and concubines: thou 'hast not humbled thine heart . . . But hast lifted up thyself against the Lord of heaven . . .' (*Daniel* v. 22–3)

625. *to eye the bright sun's rays* Itself now 'invisible':

> . . . and th' excess
> Of Glory obscur'd. (*Paradise Lost* I, 593–4)

625. *how the same yellow rays were blending* No doubt with his purple wake, so that all nature 'absolutely paints like the harlot' (p. 160, note; p. 296):

'Come hither; I will shew unto thee the judgment of the great whore that sitteth upon many waters: . . . And upon her forehead was a name written, MYSTERY, BABYLON THE GREAT, THE MOTHER OF HARLOTS AND ABOMINATIONS OF THE EARTH.' (*Revelation* xvii, 1–5)

625. *Ha, ha, my ship! . . . the sea-chariot of the sun* With a 'ha, ha' and a 'ho, ho', 'this brain-truck of mine . . . sails amid the cloud-scud'. Now Ahab (Lord H/*a-ha*) is playacting Phaeton, or Osiris, or a sea-Viking mounting the Trundholm chariot in all his pride.

cf. The Egyptians 'affirme also, that the Sunne and Moone are not mounted upon chariots, but within bardges or boates continually do moove and saile as it were round about the world.' (Plutarch, 'Of Isis and Osiris', Holland's translation, pp. 1300–1301)

625. *its very blinding palpableness* But Ahab, of course, is already blinded; in an 'unstaggering breeze', almost staggered.

625. *last night's thunder turned our compasses* Inverted 'in some enchanted way', like Ishmael in *his* 'unnatural hallucination of the night.' (p. 534, note)

626. *the supposed fair one had only been juggling her* cf.

> And be these juggling fiends no more believ'd,
> That palter with us in a double sense . . .
> (*Macbeth* V, viii, 19–20)

626. *a certain magnetism shot into their congenial hearts* From 'the Leyden jar of his own magnetic life' (p. 264, note). As the electric storm is to the needles, so Ahab's infidel soul is to the pagan hearts of his harpooneers.

627. *revive the spirits of his crew* For like one-eyed Odin – Nordic god of wisdom and magic – Ahab is host of dead heroes. cf. 'The Hero as Divinity' (first of Carlyle's *Lectures on Heroes*, 1840).

627. *the magnetizing of the steel . . . the awe of the crew* 'By heavens! I'll get a crucible . . .' (p. 583) Now that Ahab too has made his pact, 'heart, soul, and body, lungs and life' bound like Faust, he too can turn alchemist – if not reviving spirits exactly, playact the subtile conjuror over his 'crucible of molten gold': final presage of doom.

628. *lord of the level loadstone!* 'Science! . . . thou vain toy'! The Iron Man is lord of the iron, but all the details of his act are borrowed from Scoresby (*Journal of a Voyage to the Northern Whale-Fishery*, Edinburgh 1823).

cf. also Sir Thomas Browne, 'Concerning the Loadstone' (*Pseudodoxia Epidemica* Bk II, ch. 2).

628. *The sun is East* – *Orientis princeps*, 'O Lucifer, son of the morning!' (*Isaiah* xiv, 12)

628. *In his fiery eyes of scorn* Mark of the beast, 'and with him the false prophet that wrought miracles before him, with which he deceived them ...' (*Revelation* xix, 20)

628. *Ahab in all his fatal pride* A new leviathan:

He maketh the deep to boil like a pot: he maketh the sea like a pot of ointment.
He maketh a path to shine after him; one would think the deep to be hoary.
Upon the earth there is not his like, who is made without fear.
He beholdeth all high things: he is a king over all the children of pride. (*Job* xli, 31–4)

125 THE LOG AND LINE

628. *the billows rolled in riots* In lieu of the crew, who had merely 'raised a half mutinous cry'. (THE CANDLES)

629. *the spindle, round which the spool* Second sign of the impending vortex, revolving in coils.

629. *a patched professor Alias* Professor Diogenes Teufelsdröckh (to wit, Carlyle's 'Sartor Resartus'); *alias* that patched and professorial printer's devil, the captain himself.

629. *granite-founded College* 'Yet dost thou ... rock me with a prouder, if a darker faith.' (THE DYING WHALE) For like Christ's seminary, Kali's too, Ahab claims, is founded on rock: '... and the gates of hell shall not prevail against it. And I will give unto thee the keys of the kingdom ...' (*Matthew* xvi, 18–19)

629. *Thou'st hit the world by that* Ahab's emblematic mind at once seizes on this 'little rocky Isle of Man' to allegorize and conjure with double meanings.

Though the Tynwald is the world's most ancient parliament, the Isle of Man was long a dependency of Viking Norway until sold in 1266, for cash, to become first the appanage of Scotland (under Alexander III), then of England (under Edward I), then again of Scotland (under Robert the Bruce), and finally again of England (under Edward III) – 'unmanned of Man'.

But religious implications seem to underlie the political. For what of Christendom, 'once independent' as Rousseau's savages, now unmanned by the Son of Man to sheep-like subservience? And what of Ahab himself, born free, now 'soul and body' bound? What of his limb 'dismembered', 'unmanned', 'sucked in – by what?' Whose is that 'tripod' spinning on the island's crest (*Gules, three legs armed, conjoined in fesse at the upper part of the thighs . . . or*) but Ahab's: one of flesh, one of bone, one tingling solely to the soul? And what is his whole story, too, but a house of emblems, or keys?

It is the old Manxman – from the parliament of Man, or House of Keys – who has the last word. For he alone holds the key.

629. *The dead, blind wall butts all inquiring heads* And 'how can the prisoner reach outside except by thrusting through the wall?' (THE QUARTER-DECK) But Ahab himself has long been walled up, deadened, blindly 'brain-battering' at all inquiring heads: Starbuck, the carpenter, the Manxman.

629. *the old reelman* The wooden 'reel' beneath the 'railing', lowered into 'rolling' billows, at last causes the Manxman (the pun was irresistible) to 'stagger'.

630. *the skewer seems loosening out of the middle of the world* 'But unscrew your navel, and what's the consequence?': Pip's echo – and cue.

630. *fisherman . . . Jerk him off* 'The thing is common in that fishery . . .' (THE CASTAWAY)

630. *Peace, thou crazy loon* viz.

'The devil damn thee black, thou cream-faced loon!'

(*Macbeth* V, iii, 11)

630. *Hands off from that holiness!* For every fool with an 'unearthly idiot face' was once accounted holy. (cf. Job Pray in James Fenimore Cooper's *Lionel Lincoln*, another half-wit indebted to *King Lear*.)

But Ahab is drawn to Pip with a peculiar attraction. For he too, in his madness, has come to a 'celestial thought'. He, too, 'while preaching to others is himself a castaway'. He too, in the end, will catch it in the neck.

630. *I see not my reflection in the vacant pupils* For Ahab's monomania is frenzied, sleep-walking, active: Pip's vacant, passive.

630. *a thing for immortal souls to sieve through* Itself a rebus – for 'holiness'.

630. *Pip! Pip! Pip! One hundred pounds of clay reward* Parodying the handbills for a runaway slave: 'Five feet high ...' etc. 'Remember, I beseech thee, that thou hast made me as the clay ...' (*Job* x, 9) But there is a babel of politics in Pip's 'clay': for Henry Clay, of Kentucky, that very year had agreed vigorously to enforce fugitive slave law (the 'Compromise of 1850'); while his fellow Kentuckian, the abolitionist Cassius Clay, had made an unsuccessful bid for the governorship in 1849 on an anti-slavery ticket.

630. *Here, boy; Ahab's cabin shall be Pip's home* Not by thrusting pride ('in the living act, the undoubted deed') but pity does Ahab break out from his prison wall:

Come, your hovel.
Poor fool and knave, I have one part in my heart
That's sorry yet for thee ...
In, boy; go first. – You houseless poverty –
Nay, get thee in.

(*King Lear* III, ii and iv)

631. *This seems to me, sir, as a man-rope* What was once 'shirr! shirr! ... that anaconda of an old man' has now turned (sir, sir,) to 'a man-rope ... that weak souls may hold by'. Captain Ahab, striding the blast, is become Pip's 'big white God aloft there somewhere in yon darkness ...'

Shew thy marvellous lovingkindness, O thou that savest by thy right hand them which put their trust in thee from those that rise up against them.
Keep me as the apple of the eye, hide me under the shadow of thy wings,
From the wicked that oppress me, from my deadly enemies, who compass me about.

(*Psalm* xvii, 7–9)

But how can a hand, unmanned by 'man-ropes', itself be 'a man-rope'? Another monkey-rope, rather, wedding the captain (in the crotch of his tree) to Pip (now the apple of his eye).

631. *let old Perth now ... rivet these two hands together* 'I burn with thee; would fain be welded with thee'. (THE CANDLES)

631. *though I grasped an Emperor's!* Exit one Holy Emperor with another, a crowned Charlemagne with his 'little Pip', Pippin, or Pepin the Short. ('But here's the end of the rotten line ...')

126 THE LIFE-BUOY

631. *Ahab's levelled steel* This 'yet levelled' steel discharges images of doom: 'of newly drowned men', seals sobbing, a phantom falling, hemlock, ghosts. If THE MUSKET in the end acquiesced in life, THE LIFE-BUOY paradoxically inclines to death.

632. *stood ... or leaned all transfixedly listening, like the carved Roman slave* Perhaps the 'Dying Gaul', often called the 'Dying Gladiator', is meant. Originally from Pergamon, the statue had long been in Rome. cf. 'motionless as the marble Gladiator, that for centuries had been dying' (*Mardi*, ch. 135). cf. 'only bowed ... and stood as the Dying Gladiator lies' (*White-Jacket*, ch. 87).

632. *sobbing with their human sort of wail* cf. Captain James Colnett: 'These cries continued for upwards of three hours, and seemed to encrease as the ship sailed from it: I conjectured it to be a female seal that had lost its cub, or a cub that had lost its dam; but I never heard any noise whatever that approached so near those sounds which proceed from the organs of utterance in the human species. The crew considered this as another evil omen...' (*A Voyage to the South Atlantic*, p. 169)

632. *when a cry was heard* In 'the fairest weather, with one half-throttled shriek you drop through that transparent air into the summer sea, no more to rise for ever'. (THE MAST-HEAD)

633. *white bubbles in the blue* As of the great white squid disentangling itself from the azure. For phantoms both rise and fall about the *Pequod*.

633. *'A life-buoy of a coffin!'* By 'certain strange signs and innuendoes' hinting a masonic 'hint': Bang it, carpenter! Rig it!

634. *I don't like this cobbling sort of business* 'No man also seweth a piece of new cloth on an old garment: else the new piece that filled it up taketh away from the old, and the rent is made worse.' (*Mark* ii, 21)

634. *Let tinkers' brats do tinkerings* Like John Bunyan in his *Grace Abounding to the Chief of Sinners*? or *Pilgrim's Progress*?

634. *clean, virgin, fair-and-square mathematical jobs* For this god-like carpenter is also the Grand Geometrician, preferring a new start – a clean break or virgin birth, call it. Like all fellow masons and Masters of Grand Lodge too, he is a 'fair-and-square' man, who is 'on the level'.

634. *Lord! what an affection all old women have* Tender-hearted as an 'old lady' with her roly-poly coach-horses, tender as Ahab's infatuation for tender-hearted Pip. 'And in this same last or shoe, that old woman of the nursery tale with the swarming brood' might very well be 'lodged'. (THE RIGHT WHALE'S HEAD)

634. *when I kept my job-shop in the Vineyard* cf. 'My well-beloved hath a vineyard in a very fruitful hill ...' (*Isaiah* v, 1ff., *Luke* xx, 9ff.)

634. *Were ever such things done before* On the *Argo*, yes, with the coffin of Osiris; after the winter solstice, with 'the snap-spring', awaiting rebirth.

634. *knotty Aroostook hemlock* A river to the north of the Saco, rising in Maine and winding east into New Brunswick. In 1838 a clash between Yankee farmers and Canadian lumbermen was narrowly averted – each claiming the valley with an 'I don't budge'.

634. *Cruppered with a coffin!* Turning the ship's stern to a horse's rump: i.e. no longer with a buoy on the buttocks, but a coffin rigged for death.

The carpenter hummingly soliloquizes with his rhymes, half-rhymes and puns: 'off in a huff', he 'baulks' as he caulks; 'hemlock ... Hem!'; 'job shop' and 'grave-yard tray!'

635. *Turk's-headed life-lines* With a turban-ended knot for each infidel *ex officio* professor of Sabbath breaking.

127 THE DECK

635. *The coffin laid upon two line-tubs* Almost as if to say 'the coffin laid upon two prodigious great wedding-cakes' (THE LINE) – to form yet another diptych of life and death. For as the wedding is Ahab's, so is the doom. And this carpenter, unwinding a clue from his bosom, who supplies both legs and coffins and life-buoys in impartial metamorphoses, is no more than a

chip of that 'omnitooled', bisexual, unprincipled, 'cunning life-principle' itself.

635. *Middle aisle of a church!* Lord Ha-ha to Pip's 'gay ha-ha': 'And it came to pass ... that he took to wife Jeze/*bel* the daughter of Ethbaal king of the Zidonians' (*1 Kings* xvi, 31).

But it is a catafalque Ahab means: set out, as at a funeral.

636. *the grave-digger in the play sings*

'In youth, when I did love, did love ...'

(*Hamlet* V, i, 61ff.)

636. *Hark to it* 'Hark! more knocking.' (*Macbeth* II, ii, 69) For the carpenter is now also devil-porter of hell-gate: 'Knock, knock, knock! Who's there, i' th' name of Belzebub? ... Knock knock! Who's there, i' th' other devil's name? Faith ...'

'Will ye never have done, Carpenter, with that accursed sound?'

636. *Dost thou spin thy own shroud* cf. First Clown:

A pick-axe, and a spade, a spade,
For and a shrouding sheet:
O, a pit of clay for to be made
For such a guest is meet.

(*Hamlet* V, i, 91–4)

636. *the Isle of Albemarle, one of the Gallipagos* Or Galapagos Islands, 600 miles west of Ecuador: a whaler's port of call for fresh water and tortoises. On 30 October 1841, in 'pleasant weather', the north head of Albemarle Island was sighted (log-book of the *Acushnet*).

636. *some sort of Equator cuts yon old man ... under the Line – fiery hot* cf:

But to the girdle do the gods inherit,
Beneath is all the fiends';
There's hell, there's darkness, there is the sulphurous pit –
Burning, scalding, stench, consumption.

(*King Lear* IV, vi, 126–9)

637. *I'm the professor of musical glasses – tap, tap!* Not 'a patched professor in Queen Nature's granite-founded College'; not a *sartor resartus* at all ('I don't like this cobbling'), but a professional musician.

For the carpenter is himself a 'harmonica': 'an unfractioned integral' in whom all is resolved, all harmonized, shading off 'into the surrounding infinite of things'. For 'here ye strike but splintered hearts together – there, ye shall strike unsplinterable glasses'. (EXTRACTS)

Musical glasses, introduced in Dublin in 1743, and shown off by Gluck in London three years later, had been skilfully improved by Benjamin Franklin (c. 1761). Franklin's instrument consisted of a series of glass bowls fitted inside one another, supported by a spindle. As the spindle revolved, the edges of the bowls passed through a trough filled with water. A player's fingertips, touching the moistened revolving edges, produced the sound. Both Mozart and Beethoven wrote pieces for the instrument. Even a keyboard was added later.

Thus the carpenter, in his virtuoso guise, has mastery over yet another vortex: now a watery vortex, even a Yankee vortex – third sign of impending doom.

637. *the greyheaded wood-pecker tapping the hollow tree!* There stands his 'deaf and dumb' carpenter at work. There stands the blind, greyheaded captain over 'a sounding-board': with his one live leg making 'lively echoes along the deck', while 'every stroke of his dead limb sounded like a coffin-tap'. (THE SPIRIT-SPOUT)

637. *So man's seconds tick! Oh! how immaterial are all materials!*

> To-morrow, and to-morrow, and to-morrow,
> Creeps in this petty pace from day to day
> To the last syllable of recorded time,
> And all our yesterdays have lighted fools
> The way to dusty death. Out, out, brief candle!
> Life's but a walking shadow...
>
> (*Macbeth* V, v, 19ff.)

For Ahab's condition is now Macbeth's condition; and all Macbeth's imagery – of dust and death, candles and fools – is also Ahab's. He too is a man of fits, rapt in hysterical fantasies of sight and sound. He too is the passionate hypocrite, 'a poor player that struts and frets his hour upon the stage'. He too is the 'idiot, full of sound and fury' – 'full of Leviathanism even, but 'signifying nothing'. (CETOLOGY)

637. *What things real ... but imponderable thoughts?* For, like the Sperm Whale, Ahab 'is both ponderous and profound'.

A 'Platonian' too, he now dismisses the whole world ('O Nature, and O soul of man!') for a universe of ideas.

637. *I'll think of that* Ahab's role wavers: now Macbeth, now Hamlet; and then again King Lear, or perhaps King Richard II in his dungeon. The whole monologue is a cento of Shakespearean allusions. In the hell-porter's phrase: 'he should have old turning the key'.

But one thing irrevocably eludes this Grand Lama, or Master: the masonic aspect of that dread 'symbol', made 'the expressive sign' of help and hope.

637. *I do suck most wondrous philosophies from thee!* Now Ahab, once more, is Lear: 'First let me talk with this philosopher ... I will keep still with my philosopher.' (III, iv, 15ff.) Or Faustus, or Jaques, is it, seeking his 'motley fool', sucking 'melancholy out of a song, as a weasel sucks eggs'? (*As You Like It* II, v, 12)

128 THE PEQUOD MEETS THE RACHEL

638. *a swift gleam of bubbling white water* With a hint of witchcraft:

> The earth hath bubbles, as the water has,
> And these are of them. Whither are they vanish'd?
>
> (*Macbeth* I, iii, 79–80)

639. *For God's sake – ... I conjure* Now a fellow captain tries conjuring; but he too cannot revive spirits. Ahab is icy: 'There can be no hearts above the snow-line. Oh, ye frozen heavens! look down here...' (p. 630)

640. *to pick up the majority first ... for some unknown constitutional reason* The 'three tall cherry trees' at the close seem to link the *Rachel* with another gardener, legendary 'Father of His Country' and mourning patriarch. 'One cannot fail to note' writes Alan Heimert, 'that the most instinctive of majoritarians, Thomas Jefferson, had once served as mate to a Washington whose Constitution did not embody a majority principle.' ('*Moby-Dick* and American Political Symbolism', op. cit.)

640. *his one yet missing boy ... but twelve years old* The most famous twelve-year-old ever missing was doubtless Jesus, on the way home from Jerusalem: 'And it came to pass, that after

three days they found him in the temple, sitting in the midst of the doctors ...' (*Luke* ii, 46). His very age, then, should have aroused Christian sympathies.

640. *For you too have a boy ... though but a child, and nestling* But Ahab is wholly iron-bound – his heart shrunk, beyond the point of no return. This is Herod's murder of the Innocents (*Matthew* ii, 16–18). This is Macbeth's assassination of young Macduff (*Macbeth* IV, ii).

Confined, even in harbour, to his cabin, Ahab had long ago withdrawn from an 'ever-contracting, dropping circle' of Nantucket acquaintanceship: 'Weep so, I will murder thee! have a care ...' (THE CABIN)

641. *clustered with men, as three tall cherry trees* For Captain Gardiner's *Rachel*, as much as Queequeg's coffin, is necessary to Ishmael's salvation: by 1850 'without comfort' no doubt; patriarchal, however, *and* democratic – an emblem of the same undying faith that 'Melville glorified in the apotheoses of Jackson, of Steelkilt and of Bulkington'. (Alan Heimert, op. cit.)

641. *She was Rachel, weeping for her children* 'Thus saith the Lord; A voice was heard in Ramah, lamentation, and bitter weeping; Rahel weeping for her children refused to be comforted for her children, because they were not.' (*Jeremiah* xxxi, 15; *Matthew* ii, 17–18)

129 THE CABIN

641. *thou must not follow Ahab now. The hour is coming* Parodying both Jesus's call to his disciples, 'Follow me', and their final desertion at Gethsemane: 'Sleep on now ... the hour is come; behold the Son of man is betrayed into the hands of sinners.' (*Mark* xiv, 41)

641. *Like cures like* *Similia similibus curantur*, or homeopathy, the medical treatment developed in about 1796 by Samuel Hahnemann of Leipzig.

642. *'Oh good master, master, master!'* As if echoing Judas's appeal: 'Is it I?' But it is Ahab who deserts poor Pip. His 'God for ever bless thee' is as void as his 'God bless ye, man' to Captain Gardiner; his 'God for ever save thee', meaningless for Pip, long deserted by God.

642. *True ... as the circumference to its centre* He speaks like a Grand Master from Grand Lodge, or the Grand Geometrician himself. But all is fraud. Like Stubb, Ahab quits this black who is so 'crazy-witty'. As Starbuck, the Quito coin 'lest Truth shake me falsely'.

642. *Here he this instant stood; I stand in his air* cf.

BANQUO: Wither are they vanish'd?
MACBETH: Into the air; and what seem'd corporal melted
As breath into the wind. Would they had stay'd!
(*Macbeth* I, iii, 80–82)

642. *Ding, dong, ding!*

Nothing of him that doth fade
But doth suffer a sea-change
Into something rich and strange.
(*The Tempest* I, ii, 399–401)

642. *in their black seventy-fours* Mounting seventy-four guns (see p. 286).

642. *epaulets! epaulets! the epaulets all come crowding!* Where once Ahab had sat brooding on St Paul, now only epaulets, epaulets come crowding. And yet they too, in this final vision, seem almost saint-like; or like priests, rather, 'with gold lace upon their coats'. Decantors, in a choir, pace round singing; and 'in the ship's full middle', with 'her three masts before' him (in lieu of the Trinity), a black boy is offered as '[t]*ransom*' (or 'host'), at a white man's mess (or mass), first naval 'lord' on this 'screwed' navel (or altar of the whole world).

'But, unscrew your navel, and what's the consequence?' (THE DOUBLOON)

643. *I hear ivory ... I am indeed down-hearted* For the tap of the ivory is as the 'customary rap' of the whale.

643. *and oysters come to join me* 'And so they'll say in the resurrection, when they come to fish up this old mast ...' (THE DOUBLOON)

130 THE HAT

643. *into an ocean-fold* As if these leviathans had been 'but a flock of simple sheep, pursued over the pasture'. (THE GRAND ARMADA) Here endeth the parable of the 'lost sheep'. (THE CHART)

643. *the very latitude and longitude where his tormenting wound* Which is Ahab's cross – the 'crucifixion in his face' – the omphalos of his entire being.

643. *the demoniac indifference* But so is Pip 'indifferent'. The carpenter, too, is 'indifferent enough'; Stubb, too, taking perils 'with an indifferent air'; and Daggoo sustaining himself with an 'indifferent' majesty; and Queequeg, 'his very indifference speaking a nature in which there lurked no civilized hypocrisies'. Even Ahab, in his most grovelling homage, 'still remains indifferent'. Why then is the White Whale's 'indifference' alone, in Ahab's eyes, 'demoniac'?

643. *whether sinning or sinned against* Because he insists on viewing the world as an Armageddon of good and evil, with himself, of course, in the role of Lear:

> Tremble, thou wretch,
> That hast within thee undivulged crimes
> Unwhipp'd of justice...
>
> (III, ii, 51ff.)

But is it not Ahab ('I'm demoniac, I am madness maddened!') who should tremble? Is it not the White Whale, perhaps, who is 'more sinn'd against than sinning'?

643. *As the unsetting polar star* cf:

> Incenc't with indignation *Satan* stood
> Unterrifi'd, and like a Comet burn'd,
> That fires the length of *Ophiucus* huge
> In th' Artick Sky...
>
> (*Paradise Lost* II 707–10)

643. *a single spear or leaf* of mutiny, or illusion.

644. *Ahab's purpose ... Ahab's iron soul* No longer sharks or sea-dogs but mere machines, the crew is hurled in the wake of Ahab's locomotive force. 'The path to my fixed purpose is laid with iron rails, whereon my soul is grooved to run.' (SUNSET)

644. *the old man's despot eye* 'Such large virtue lurks in these small things ... that in some royal instances even to idiot imbecility they have imparted potency.' (THE SPECKSYNDER)

644. *a tremulous shadow cast upon the deck* 'In this foreshadowing interval', a 'forethrown shadow':

Why, I, in this weak piping time of peace,
Have no delight to pass away the time,
Unless to spy my shadow in the sun
And descant on mine own deformity.
(*Richard III*, I, i, 24–27)

644. *his living foot advanced upon the deck* His dead foot in the scuttle: to scuttle the ship.

644. *his hat slouched heavily over his eyes* 'Oh! most contemptible and worthy of all scorn; with slouched hat and guilty eye, skulking from his God.' (THE SERMON)

645. *nor reaped his beard ... all gnarled, as unearthed roots* Had not Moby Dick 'reaped away Ahab's leg, as a mower a blade of grass'? Now 'reaped', by an anagram, reverts to 'beard': 'where far beneath ... his root of grandeur, his whole awful essence sits in bearded state'. (pp. 284–5)

For pastoral dream and infernal torment, at root, are one; and all hell is laid bare, with green illusion withered.

645. *still fixedly gazing ... his abandoned substance* Still a 'gamboge ghost', a Siamese twin. But their relation is purely Platonic: Ahab turned wholly to his one supreme purpose, an unchanging Platonic 'Idea' which alone is 'form' or 'substance'; the Parsee reduced to a tremulous shadow, which is its flickering appearance in the cave.

As in all Socratic discourse, such knowledge (of the supreme 'good') implies the supreme effort to realize it. As in all Platonic theory, substance is independent of phenomena, the 'Idea' of its shadow. And Ahab – aloof in imponderable thought – at last shines as the sun, in the Platonic myth, over the shadowy world of the senses.

645. *his iron voice ... 'sharp! sharp!'* Sharp as a rib, sharp as a keel, sharp as the edge of his Iron Crown – while 'the old man, with the sharp of his extended hand, now took the precise bearing of the sun'. (THE NEEDLE)

646. *a nest of basketed bowlines* Himself a 'nestling safely at home now' – as if to parody Saul's exit from Damascus: 'And after that many days were fulfilled, the Jews took counsel to kill him: But their laying await was known of Saul. And they watched the gates day and night to kill him. Then the disciples took him by night, and let him down by the wall in a basket.' (*Acts* ix, 23–5)

646. *with one hand clinging round the royal mast* King of infinite space, grand master of the *Pequod*, 'true ... as the circumference to its centre'!

Now Ahab plays look-out, Pip lord of his cabin. That it might be fulfilled which was written by the evangelist: 'But he that is greatest among you shall be your servant. And whosoever shall exalt himself shall be abased; and he that shall humble himself shall be exalted.' (*Matthew* xxiii, 11–12)

647. *one of those red-billed savage sea-hawks* 'Throws his steep flight in many an Aerie wheele ...' (*Paradise Lost* III, 741) – fourth sign of the impending vortex.

cf. Bennett on *Pelicanus Aquila* (the frigate bird): 'sometimes it wheels rapidly, or darts to the surface of the water in pursuit of prey; and at others, soars to so great a height that it is lost to vision, or becomes a mere speck in the sky ...' (vol. 2, pp. 243–4)

647. *'Your hat, your hat, sir!'* Like 'the Manhattoes', doomed. First Queequeg; then Stubb; now Ahab has literally lost his 'head', and:

> ... thus with his stealthy pace,
> With Tarquin's ravishing strides, towards his design
> Moves like a ghost.
>
> (*Macbeth* II, i, 54–6)

647. *cried the Sicilian seaman* Were not giants hurled under volcanic Etna? Are not Sicilians witness to Typhon's doom? Is not the eagle herald of Zeus? In a single swoop this sea-hawk snatches Ahab's Promethean crown.

647. *a minute black spot* 'For a dervish to lose his cap is identical with losing divine grace, since the headgear is held to be of divine origin, an emblem of "the vase of light" which contains the immortal soul of Mohammed' (Dorothée M. Finkelstein, *Melville's Orienda*, p. 202). 'But heigh-ho! there are no caps at sea but snow caps ...'

cf. 'Always there is a black spot in our sunshine; it is even, as I said, the *Shadow of Ourselves*.' (Carlyle, *Sartor Resartus* II, ix).

131 THE PEQUOD MEETS THE DELIGHT

648. *misnamed the Delight* Instead of lightness, light or delight – a weighted hammock, hollow cheeks, a ghostly gloom. In

the name (Oh! God) of 'the resurrection and the life': a religion of the corpse, the skeleton, the tomb.

648. *her broad beams, called shears* Or 'gallows':

> But the fair guerdon when we hope to find,
> And think to burst out into sudden blaze,
> Comes the blind Fury with th' abhorred shears
> And slits the thin-spun life.
>
> (Milton, *Lycidas* 73–6)

648. *the shattered, white ribs ... and bleaching skeleton of a horse* cf. 'the great, white worshipped skeleton'. (A BOWER IN THE ARSACIDES) cf. The *Albatross* 'bleached like the skeleton of a stranded walrus'. 'And I looked, and behold a pale horse: and the name that sat on him was Death ...' (*Revelation* vi, 8)

648. *Perth's levelled iron* Brandishing his phallus, as it were, from the crotch, in defiance of Christian asceticism. But the 'hot place behind the fin' is not only the whale's. It is hell that awaits Ahab in the end.

649. *Oh! God ... may the resurrection and the life* – Invoking Jesus' words to Martha, 'I am the resurrection, and the life: he that believeth in me ...' (*John* xi, 25): part of the Anglican order for burial of the dead.

649. *As Ahab now glided* Which is the *Pequod* gliding, but with the Parsee's 'gliding strangeness'.

649. *from the dejected Delight* An ironic coda to THE SERMON: 'But oh! shipmates! on the starboard hand of every woe, there is a sure delight; and higher the top of that delight, than the bottom of the woe is deep ... Delight, – top-gallant delight is to him, who acknowledges no law or lord, but the Lord his God ...'

132 THE SYMPHONY

THE SYMPHONY All keys and shifts of key, all contrapuntal strains and harmonies of this 131-part prelude, are to be fused at last. Polyphony is turned to 'symphony' – in its prime sense of an instrumental interlude in oratorio, or operatic prelude to the final three part fugue (or three days' flight):

'Sing out for every spout ...' 'Why sing ye not out for him ... ?'

For what is *Moby-Dick*, after all, but an 'incantation'? A mystery play of all that 'has been promiscuously said, thought, fancied and sung of Leviathan'? An oratorio in the fullest sense: semi-dramatic in character, based on biblical themes, for solo voices and 'wild chorus'? Mendelssohn's *St Paul* (1836) and *Elijah* (1846) are its almost exact contemporaries; and it too was composed by 'rehearsing – singing, if I may' for vast stretches – without the aid of either scenery or action:

SOLO	'The ribs and terrors in the whale ...'
CHORUS	*The Girls in Booble Alley.*
SOLO	'Sweet fields beyond the swelling flood ...'
SOLO	'We'll drink tonight with hearts as light ...'
CHORUS	'Farewell and adieu to you, Spanish ladies!'
SOLO AND CHORUS	'Our captain stood upon the deck ...'
SOLO	*Old King Crow.*

etc. etc.

Handel's *Messiah*, of course, was the implicit model. For this, too, is a Pastoral Symphony with 'a mild, mild wind, and a mild looking sky' in 'that all pervading azure': a symphony of blue and white, of transparent innocence and snow-white wings; of male and female longings between sea and sky; and green, green thoughts of land, and a hill, and 'a far away meadow'.

649. *It was a clear steel-blue day* With a touch of the razor – treacherous as Delilah. (*Judges* xvi, 19)

649. *unspeckled birds ... the gentle thoughts* But gliding like serpents, snow-white as the Whale, 'soft and tremulous' as the Parsee's shadow.

650. *Tied up and twisted ... untottering Ahab* is Samson (Hebrew, 'the sun') among the Philistines, blindly tearing his own roof to ruin over his head; 'gnarled and knotted' he seems a witch-like hag, 'close-coiled', with 'eyes glowing like coals'. But, compounded of both, he turns volcanic Titan thrusting 'steel skull' and 'steel shoulder-blades' into the steel-blue sky to claim for himself the title 'royal czar and king'.

650. *so have I seen little Miriam and Martha, laughing-eyed elves* 'But what thinks Lazarus?' (p. 102) The sole survivor of the wreck recalls all womankind in his sisters Mary (Hebrew, *Miriam*) and Martha. (Is this a private allusion, perhaps, meant solely for Hawthorne, whose daughter Una, aged seven now, had herself

been the model for that mischievous American child-sprite, 'that wild and flighty little elf', Pearl of *The Scarlet Letter*?)

650. *the circle of singed locks* 'Locks so grey' suggest Mt Greylock, only recently climbed by Melville (12 August 1851) and long viewed from the 'Melville House' in Pittsfield. Its cleft twin-humped peak, *alias* Saddleback, the highest in Massachusetts, evokes a final *alter ego* for this self-styled hunchback.

Pierre; or, The Ambiguities (1852) was to be dedicated 'To Greylock's Most Excellent Majesty'.

650. *that burnt-out crater of his brain* Like that of Ethan Brand 'in the ashes of ruin'? Like the shape of his heart in its circle of 'snow-white lime'? Like his fiery kiln at the foot of 'Old Graylock . . . glorified with a golden cloud upon his head'? (Hawthorne, *Ethan Brand*, 1851)

650. *a tear into the sea . . . that one wee drop* cf. Milton's Satan:

> Thrice he assayd, and thrice in spite of scorn,
> Tears such as Angels weep, burst forth: at last
> Words interwove with sighs found out their way.
> (*Paradise Lost* I, 619–21)

Unlike Faustus in his agony, then, Ahab can still drop a tear. Unlike the Ancient Mariner, however, he cannot return the blessing. But without 'a spring of love', his remorse is itself delusion: a last chance to wallow in self-pity, to lacerate himself with self-accusations, to castigate himself as 'a demon' and mock himself as a blind, humped fool.

651. *forty years ago! – ago!* 'Forty years of continual' wandering, like Moses, in the wilderness.

651. *the masoned, walled-town of a Captain's exclusiveness* Looking back to the masonic exclusiveness of the Master. But had not whales too, from the start, been 'walled towns'? Wherein we saw 'the rare virtue of thick walls, and the rare virtue of interior spaciousness . . .' (THE BLANKET)

651. *Behold . . . Adam, staggering* But this *Ecce Homo* is still of the old Adam, staggering beneath 'the piled entablatures of ages', not of the new, beneath his cross: 'And when they had mocked him, they took off the purple from him, and put his own clothes on him, and led him out to crucify him.' (*Mark* xv, 20)

652. *God! God! God! – crack my heart! – stave my brain!* cf.

O Lear, Lear, Lear!
Beat at this gate that let thy folly in ...
(I, iv, 270–71)
Crack Nature's moulds ... (III, ii, 8)

652. *this is the magic glass, man* Which, like the doubloon, 'but mirrors back his own mysterious self'. His quadrant gone, Ahab's whole world is reduced to a hall of mirrors – a place of shadows, doppelgängers and reflections. 'Fixedly gazing' at the Parsee, he but sees his own 'forethrown shadow'; now gazing into Starbuck's eye, Narcissus but recognizes himself; finally, gazing down into the water, his eyes but meet the gaze of 'two reflected, fixed eyes'.

652. *'Oh, my Captain! my Captain! ... grand old heart'* 'But Ahab, my Captain ... what shall be grand in thee, it must needs be plucked at from the skies, and dived for in the deep, and featured in the unbodied air!' (THE SPECKSYNDER)

652. *his last cindered apple* Dissolving, according to Josephus, at a touch into smoke and ashes:

... greedily they pluck'd
The Frutage fair to sight, like that which grew
Neer that bituminous Lake where *Sodom* flam'd ...
(*Paradise Lost* X, 560–62)

As Pip's first appearance was on 'the windlass-bitt', so Ahab's last is to be 'turned round and round ... like yonder windlass'. Thus apple is united with apple: the forbidden fruit and apple of Sodom are one.

653. *Is Ahab, Ahab?* Not even a Platonic 'Idea' now ('great sun' of the Platonic system), but an *idée fixe*, an automaton rushing to its doom.

So Ahab in the end, like Ishmael, rejects free will. His God too is no longer the God of the Aristotelian–Thomistic tradition, God the prime mover, but is himself the *perpetuum mobile*, a pantheistic force at all times and everywhere inherent in the world.

The English reading, echoing both the preceding and subsequent clause, reinforces the meaning: 'Is it Ahab, Ahab? Is it I, God, or who ... ?'

653. *Look! see yon Albicore!* Another seeming Albino. But 'albacore' or 'albicore' – a large species of tunny – derives from the arabic (*al bukr*, a young camel).

653. *making hay . . . under the slopes of the Andes* So Ahab's heaven-aspiring thoughts, too, come to pastoral rest – not in 'the far away home', but 'a far-away meadow'. For pastoral dream and infernal torment, at root, are one – to sprout as 'grass' (or witch-grass).

653. *blanched to a corpse's hue* But the Mate, soul-mate of the *Delight*, 'paled, and turned, and shivered'. (THE QUARTER-DECK)

133 THE CHASE – FIRST DAY

654. *as a sagacious ship's dog will ... the dog-vane* Or wind-sock. Thus 'the invisible police officer of the Fates . . . secretly dogs me'. (LOOMINGS)

654. *pleated watery wrinkles . . . metallic-like marks* Sign of the whale, and mark of metallic Ahab with plaited brow: 'He maketh a path to shine after him; one would think the deep to be hoary.' (*Job* xli, 32; Extract 2)

654. *Thundering with the butts* To rouse those 'ground-tier butts': 'Tell 'em it's the resurrection; they must kiss their last, and come to judgment'. (MIDNIGHT, FORECASTLE) From 'their triangular oaken vaults', they seem to exhale like 'breaths of once living things', to face their Doomsday.

654. *he raised a gull-like cry* For this politic hypocrite, this Man in the Iron Mask ('our old Mo/*gul*'), is now himself to be gulled. The *Gull* might well have been a name for his ship, 'as some craft are nowadays christened the "Shark' 'or the "Eagle".' (JONAH HISTORICALLY REGARDED)

655. *in long-drawn, lingering . . . tones* With an almost sensuous response to 'the whale's visible jets'. cf. the 'long, strong, lingering swells' of Samson's chest; or the sea-fowls longingly lingering over Moby Dick.

656. *Like noiseless nautilus shells* Or 'argonauts' – cephalopod molluscs believed to sail on the surface of the sea. The image, picking up Ahab 'heading the onset', is at once projected on the whale which appears, equipped with fleece, as a painted 'argosy'.

656. *a revolving ring of finest, fleecy, greenish foam* The fifth vortex commingling echoes of threat and illusion: of a Golden Fleece, a Christian lamb, and green noon-meadows. At last the

'lost sheep' reappears, but not as a Lamb of God. As a Lamb and Flag, rather – or John the Baptist, under his cloud-like canopy.

656. *Not the white bull Jupiter . . . with ravished Europa clinging* As seen by Rubens in a celebrated painting (now in the Gardner Museum, Boston). But who is who in this Cretan labyrinth? For Ahab, too, plays Jove: not 'leering' sideways, maybe, but 'peering ahead'; his paddles 'plying with rippling swiftness' in the wake of that 'tide-rip'. As 'he slid through the air', the whale now slides 'along the sea'; what was a 'gliding strangeness' in him, a gliding repose in the whale.

657. *his whole marbleized body*, like 'the tied tendons . . . bursting from the marble in the carved Hercules', is rapturously enticing – a theme for erotic contemplation. 'Hundreds of gay fowl' perch and rock on that 'tall but shattered pole'.

657. *a high arch, like Virginia's Natural Bridge* 215 ft high, 90 ft long, in 'Virginia's Blue Ridge' Mountains: 'It is impossible for the emotions, arising from the sublime, to be felt beyond what they are here: so beautiful an arch, so elevated, so light, and springing, as it were, up to heaven, the rapture of the Spectator is really indescribable!' (Jefferson, *Notes on Virginia*, 1784)

657. *the grand god revealed himself* One 'grand hooded phantom', 'grand argosy' of THE GRAND ARMADA, Ahab's true Grand Master at last, who with 'mystic gestures . . . akin to Free-Mason signs and symbols' rules the world. 'Straight as a surveyor's parallel' is this Grand Geometrician's wake.

657. *his eyes seemed whirling* In a sixth vortex 'as he swept the watery circle'.

657. *In long Indian file, as when herons take wing* Or a 'heron-built captain' with his Pequot warriors – 'wheeling round and round' in a seventh vortex.

657. *two long crooked rows* Of 'leviathan the piercing serpent, even leviathan that crooked serpent' (*Isaiah* xxvii, 1), whose jaw, like his tail, is 'scroll-wise coiled'. (p. 484)

658. *The glittering mouth* flashed 'like a marble sepulchre' (THE FUNERAL):

> why the sepulchre
> Wherein we saw thee quietly enurn'd
> Hath op'd his ponderous and marble jaws . . .
> (*Hamlet* I, iv, 48–51)

658. *giving one sidelong sweep* Itself a reflex of the first, sudden 'sweeping' of his lower jaw. (MOBY DICK)

658. *the bluish pearl-white* Of that *vagina dentata*: 'What a really beautiful and chaste-looking mouth! . . . glossy as bridal satins'. (THE SPERM WHALE'S HEAD)

658. *while both elastic gunwales were springing* In a double sense: 'owing to the light buoyancy of the whale-boat, and the elasticity of its materials' (p. 485); owing to 'the unobstructed elasticity' of the Sperm Whale's head. (p. 445)

659. *like an enormous shears* Of another *Delight*, 'serving to carry . . . disabled boats'. (p. 648, note)

659. *by the crafty upraising* Outwitting Ahab's 'craft'. He flattens his face to the sea, as he had flattened it to the sky; while the crew cling to the 'gunwales', as 'ravished Europa' to her bull. Now all is 'wide wooing' vacancy, 'horizontal vacancy', a 'level dead-reckoning'.

For this is the fable of the weasel and the gull.

659. *vertically thrusting . . . up and down* As Ahab lies 'prone'. Each breaching, amid foam, is described in orgastic terms. With this 'up-and-down' toss of the sperm whale, or 'pitchpoling'.

659. *slowly revolving his whole spindled body* Uncoiling the eighth Cartesian vortex.

659. *as if lashing himself up*, while the crew strive to lash their oars. In this hall of mirrors the spray is 'shivered' as the boat is 'splintered'; and the eddies 'eddy' round 'the Eddystone' lighthouse. (p. 157)

John Smeaton's design, using iron braces between the stones, stood from 1759 to 1882. Re-erected on Plymouth Hoe, it still 'triumphantly' stands.

660. *as the blood of grapes and mulberries cast before Antiochus's elephants* That 'they might prepare them for battle'. (*1 Maccabees* vi, 34)

660. *so planetarily swift the ever-contracting circles* True 'as the circumference to its centre', whose sun is Ahab. (THE CABIN)

660. *chancing to rise on a towering crest* For 'the firm tower, that is Ahab; . . . the courageous, the undaunted, and victorious fowl, that, too, is Ahab' – rearing to spout 'his frothed defiance to the skies'. (p. 574, note)

But in all this 'rippling' is concealed 'a cripple'; in that 'appalling' aspect, a 'pall'; in this 'whelmed', a 'helm'.

660. *Ahab's bodily strength did crack* 'God! God! God! – crack my heart!' (p. 652) 'Blood-shot, blinded' Ahab has outfaced his executioner.

661. *Far inland, nameless wails* '*Sail* on the *whale!*' he *hailed.* And the jingle resounds from the 'unsounded gorges' of his rifled heart: no longer 'great lord of Leviathans', but a prince of wails.

661. *In an instant's compass* For the circling of the whale is also a circle of time; and within those circles lies the measureless compass of Ahab's heart. Such is the Cartesian metaphysic that allows Ahab, through sheer intensity, the role of hero.

661. *what a leaping spout! . . . The eternal sap* Again with that melting response to the whale's jet.

662. *like the double-jointed wings of an albatross* cf. the ominous '*Goney* (Albatross) by name': 'bleached like the skeleton of a stranded walrus'. (p. 338)

662. *The thistle the ass refused; it pricked his mouth* A touch of bawdry whose *double-entendres* should not have escaped Ahab (ha! ha!).

662. *as fearless fire (and as mechanical)* cf. 'There is some unsuffusing thing beyond . . .' (THE CANDLES) That was the lesson of THE DYING WHALE: to turn away from the sun, creative fire of the Demiurge, to Kali/Sophia – champions of the spiritual in man against the 'mechanical'.

662. *Omen? omen? – the dictionary!* Not 'sight' but *sound,* corrects the 'patched professor', or Sub-Sub-Librarian, indicating the root, *audire* (to hear). 'If the gods think to speak outright . . .' they speak through a *πρό-φητης* – or PROPHET (in 'patched trowsers'). And their 'sentence' (*fatum,* or *θέσφατον*) is fate: 'Fate is the handspike . . .' (p. 653)

663. *an old wives' darkling hint* But should Pip be the 'darkling', then who is his 'old wife' (ha! ha!)? cf. the carpenter: 'Lord! what an affection all old women have . . .' (p. 634)

663. *Starbuck is Stubb reversed* More literally 'Stubb reversed' prompts 'butts' – the very 'butts' that first roused the sleepers from the 'scuttle'. And 'butt', with its suggestion of turbot ('fish-like, with sparkling scales'), of wine and beer casks, buttocks and butt-heads, thick skin and a goat-like thrust, is every bit Stubb –

the habitual butt of Ahab's ridicule: 'What soulless thing is this . . . ?'

So if 'Starbuck is Stubb reversed', he must be a 'halibut' (or 'holy butt'); if 'Stubb is Starbuck', a *buck*skin *tar*; while Ahab 'alone among the millions of the peopled earth' is clearly a 'sole' (or soul), or common 'perch': 'and to wind up with Pisces, or the Fishes, we sleep'.

663. *till the White Whale is dead; and then, whosoever of ye first raises him* A curious inversion implying that the whale's Doomsday, too, will be a kind of resurrection to match those 'judgment claps', and that exhalation, of the opening.

134 THE CHASE – SECOND DAY

665. *the proverbial evanescence* Of John Keats's own epitaph: 'Here lies one whose name was writ in water.' (Lord Houghton, *Life of Keats*, ii, 91)

665. *as the mighty iron Leviathan of the modern railway* For the whale's path, too, 'is laid with iron rails'; his, too, is a 'wake through the darkness'. (SUNSET)

665. *as when a cannon-ball . . . becomes a plough-share* The pastoral is the infernal reversed; the infernal, the pastoral. Like her captain (a fiend by the mill-stream), or crew (timid hares on the rack), the *Pequod* is compounded of both.

'Fixed, unfearing, blind, reckless' – at the sound of the last 'trump' – all contraries are resolved at last, on a single keel, 'shot' to a single doom.

665. *Ha, ha! we go the gait* 'Enter ye in at the strait gate: for wide is the gate, and broad is the way, that leadeth to destruction . . .' (*Matthew* vii, 13–14)

665. *Ahab will dam off your blood*

> This word 'damnation' terrifies not him,
> For he confounds hell in Elysium.
>
> (*Doctor Faustus*, I, iii, 58–9)

666. *guilt and guiltiness* Mansfield/Vincent's suggested reading, 'guilt and guiltlessness' (p. 827), was adopted by Hayford/Parker. This certainly makes for a decided contrast. But who, after THE QUARTER-DECK, was guiltless? My 'shouts had gone up with the rest; my oath had been welded with theirs . . .'

(MOBY DICK) Possibly Melville intended to pair the fact and the feeling of guilt.

667. *the key-note to an orchestra* For a second 'Pastoral Symphony' – or simultaneous discharge from thirty buckskins – to announce the 'breaching' of the whale.

But 'buckskin' (revolutionary nickname for a native American) itself sounds oddly discordant aboard the cosmopolitan *Pequod*.

667. *in his immeasurable bravadoes the White Whale tossed himself* Himself a 'brave', and 'an Indian juggler', and a 'salmon' too, leaping 'to Heaven' (for a touch of *sal*/vation).

667. *thy hour and thy harpoon are at hand!* Aye, preach your last: 'behold the hour is at hand . . .' (*Matthew* xxvi, 45)

668. *incessantly wheeling like trained chargers*

Wheel a-bout
And turn a-bout . . .

in the 'untraceable evolutions' of the ninth vortex, which is the labyrinth of the whale-fight.

668. *Caught and twisted – corkscrewed* '"Corkscrew!" cried Ahab, "aye, Queequeg, the harpoons lie all twisted and wrenched in him".' (THE QUARTER-DECK) cf. Extract 20.

669. *little Flask . . . twitching his legs* No longer a 'water-bearer' or pitcher, but 'bobbing up and down' like Pip; twitching like an 'old rigger'; like Gabriel's vial, an empty threat.

669. *Stubb was lustily singing . . . to ladle him up* No longer a pitchpoler, pitching; for now the whale has pitchpoled Stubb:

The scud all a flyin',
That's his flip only foamin';
When he stirs in the spicin', –
(p. 612)

669. *drawn up towards Heaven by invisible wires* 'Conducting upwards . . . as by magnetic wires, the life and death throbs of' whalers. (THE PEQUOD MEETS THE VIRGIN)

670. *one short sharp splinter . . . 'tis sweet to lean* 'Sharp, shooting pains' – 'sharp! sharp!' – 'shiver her! – shiver her!': voice, hand, crown, leg, keel, from top to toe all splintered to a 'jagged edge'. Not Starbuck, but Ahab now, is 'the leaner'; not the Parsee, but Ahab, 'the lean shade siding the solid rib'. (p. 645)

670. *even with a broken bone, old Ahab is untouched* cf. 'Then came the soldiers, and brake the legs of the first, and of the other which was crucified with him. But when they came to Jesus, and saw that he was dead already, they brake not his legs . . . For these things were done, that the scripture should be fulfilled. A bone of him shall not be broken.' (*John* xix, 32–3, 36)

671. *What death-knell rings . . . as if he were the belfry* But his cabin is the belfry, where:

> Sea-nymphs hourly ring his knell:
> Ding-dong.
> Hark! now I hear them – Ding-dong bell.

671. *Aloft there! Keep him nailed* Recalling the bell-boy: 'Ha, ha! old Ahab! the White Whale; he'll nail ye!' (THE DOUBLOON)

671. *I'll ten times girdle the unmeasured globe* Like Shakespeare's Puck ('Ere the leviathan can swim a league'):

> I'll put a girdle round about the earth
> In forty minutes.
> (*A Midsummer Night's Dream* II, i, 174–6)

671. *In Jesus' name . . . all good angels mobbing thee with warnings* cf. Faustus' Good Angel, or the Old Man, pleading before the catastrophe.

672. *the palm of this hand – a lipless, unfeatured blank* Thus transforming even Starbuck, at last, to his own 'unreasoning mask'; obliterating the features of brotherhood to a whale's 'blank forehead'. (p. 682)

672. *Fool! I am the Fates' lieutenant* cf. Faustus' Evil Angel:

> Be thou on earth as Jove is in the sky,
> Lord and commander of these elements . . .
> (I, i, 75–6)

672. *but Ahab's soul's a centipede* Wingless, that it, a worm. cf. 'Art thou a silkworm? Dost thou spin thy own shroud out of thyself?' (THE DECK)

673. *his hid, heliotrope glance* Turned sunward, like the dying whale. For the sun-dial, that is Ahab; the reflecting mirror, or heliograph, that is Ahab; the blood-stone and royal purple, that, too, is Ahab; all are Ahab.

135 THE CHASE – THIRD DAY

673. *a fairer day could not dawn* But this is *Genesis* and *Revelation*, alpha and omega. 'So foul and fair a day I have not seen.' (*Macbeth* I, iii, 38)

673. *but Ahab never thinks* Now even the *idée fixe* is dismissed for a Stubb-like tingling 'at the heart'. But with his pipe gone, all 'sereneness' is gone too. Where Stubb was cool, Ahab's calm is 'frozen'. In place of that mystic jet (of 'mild white vapors'), only a cracked glass, shivered with ice, remains.

674. *Greenland ice or in Vesuvius' lava* A final symbiosis of the two landscapes of mind: pastoral illusion and volcanic inferno.

674. *mightiest Mississippies . . . shift and swerve* The first English edition corrected the spoonerism of the American 'swift and swerve'.

675. *once more Ahab swung on high* The Hanged Man – to prefigure that third and final pledge: 'The gallows, ye mean.' (THE WHALE WATCH)

675. *some three points off . . . from the three mast-heads three shrieks* With 'one half-throttled shriek':

> Thrice to thine, and thrice to mine,
> And thrice again, to make up nine.

675. *as if the tongues of fire had voiced it* 'And suddenly there came a sound from heaven as of a rushing mighty wind, and it filled all the house where they were sitting. And there appeared unto them cloven tongues like as of fire, and it sat upon each of them. And they were all filled with the Holy Ghost ...' (*Acts* ii, 2–3)

675. *Forehead to forehead I meet thee* Like Queequeg greeting Ishmael – 'in the most brain-battering fight!' (SUNSET)

675. *good bye, old mast-head! ... aye, tiny mosses in these warped cracks* For 'this pine-tree' too, like Ahab, is green, is warped, is cracked; and grasped by dismasted Ahab with a peculiar affection for its 'most vital stuff'.

675. *But aye, old mast ... Aye, minus a leg* For this perch, this eyrie, this dead wood, aye, is his one solitary eye: 'good bye, good bye ... Will' I 'have eyes at the bottom of the sea ... ?' 'Good bye ... keep a good eye upon the whale, the while I'm gone.'

676. *Aye, aye ... as touching thyself* *O Part/see!* With a parting, blind 'shot' – to close with a distich:

Nay, tonight, when the white whale
Lies down there, tied by head and tail.

676. *in his shallop's stern* French *chaloupe*; Dutch *sloep* or sloop.

678. *drive off that hawk! see! he pecks – he tears* '... my brain'. (THE CHASE – SECOND DAY)

678. *the head-beat waves hammered and hammered* On 'this the critical third day'. 'Aloft there! Keep him nailed' (to the main-royal cross-trees)! Crucify him! Strike 'moody stricken Ahab ... with a crucifixion in his face'. (p. 220)

678. *slowly swelled in broad circles* A swell of ice, which is the tenth vortex spinning with 'the sound of hammers, and the hum of the grindstone'.

678. *shot lengthwise, but obliquely* For, to the last, *The Whale* is a veil, is a wail, 'shrouded' in mist.

678. *the waters flashed ... like heaps of fountains* Or rainbowed 'intuitions' (THE FOUNTAIN) – till 'flashed', at a second shot, resolves to 'lashed'.

679. *churning his tail ... flailed them apart* To 'rolling husks' yet again, in the Sperm Whale's cream.

679. *pinioned in ... the involutions of the lines* The eleventh vortex of death-in-life.

679. *Aay, Parsee! I see ... this then is the hearse* Gulled! Gulled! For 'Parsee', half torn, *is* 'see'. Two 'Ayes' yet again meet the 'eyes' of a 'lean shade' siding 'the solid rib'.

'But I hold thee to the last letter of thy word': in that 'Parsee', as in that 'hearse', there lurks an 'arse'.

679. *Ye are ... but my arms and my legs* And 'Ahab's soul's a centipede, that moves upon a hundred legs'. (p. 672)

680. *so nail it to the mast* That 'is ugly, too ... it's a sign that things grow desperate'. (THE DOUBLOON)

681. *his great, Monadnock hump* Emerson's 'barren cone' – an isolated, bald-topped mountain in southern New Hampshire. Thus the wheel comes full circle: that dream in 'the valley of the Saco' is linked, in the end, to a neighbouring mountain. Pastoral and inferno, 'hill and valley' – both are New England's.

681. *to the socket, as if sucked into a morass* cf. 'the pole was then driven hard up into the socket . . .' (p. 600) cf. 'The thistle the ass refused . . .' (p. 662) cf. the hump-backed merman 'his stern . . . stuck full of marlinspikes . . .' (p. 226) 'Such a sog! such a sogger!' As the iron is sucked up to its lance-head (or socket), so the 'curse' sinks to the 'he*arse*' (or 'mor/*ass*') – another socket 'in that hot place behind the fin'.

681. *the third man helplessly dropping astern* 'Now, in general, *Stick to the boat,* is your true motto in whaling; but cases will sometimes happen when *Leap from the boat,* is still better.' (THE CASTAWAY)

682. *Some sinew cracks! – 'tis whole again* Striking 'the key-note': 'Crack, crack, old ship! so long as thou crackest, thou holdest!' (p. 273)

682. *nobler foe . . . amid fiery showers of foam* 'Out of his mouth go burning lamps, and sparks of fire leap out . . . His breath kindles coals, and a flame goeth out of his mouth . . . His heart is as firm as a stone; yea, as hard as a piece of the nether millstone.' (*Job* xli, 19ff.)

682. *I grow blind; hands! stretch out* Like Oedipus Tyrannos physically blinded at last. Or, still in the brooding presence of Emerson's *Monadnock*:

> Plunges eyeless on forever . . .
> Cooped in a ship he cannot steer, –

682. *half-wrapping him as with a plaid* Like Highlanders above 'the smoky mountain mist', like Queequeg in his 'Highland costume'.

683. *to bed upon a mattrass . . . would it were stuffed* Not a 'mattress', but 'mattr/*ass*' (Italian, *materasso*). Would it were brushwood, that is, piled in layers, to construct a pier or dike.

Stubb lingers to the end, with a grin, on that fateful syllable. For active he remains to the last 'in his drawers', not passively 'drawn' like Flask. But the only glasses yet to be rung are those of 'the professor of musical glasses – tap, tap!' – that 'unsplinter-able' harmonica, harmonizing all.

683. *I grin at thee, thou grinning whale!* Like Ishmael confronting his 'grinning landlord': 'Whether that mattress was stuffed with corn-cobs or broken crockery, there is no telling'. (THE SPOUTER-INN)

683. *Oh, Flask, for one red cherry* Or virgin hymen: with a last defiant echo of 'chéries! chéries! chéries!' (girls! girls! girls!) from those 'three tall cherry trees'. (p. 641) 'Wherefore by their fruits ye shall know them.' (*Matthew* vii, 20)

683. *overspreading semicircular foam* From 'that horizontal, semi-crescentic depression in the forehead's middle' – mark of the Turk.

683. *smote the ship's starboard bow* To recapitulate the fate of the *Essex* (p. 307, note, *passim*).

684. *the whale ran quivering* With a final quiver below to echo the Quaker's 'quiver of 'em' above – and rest 'quiescent': 'Behold the hope of him is in vain: shall not one be cast down even at the sight of him?' (*Job* xli, 9)

684. *I turn my body from the sun* As 'the whale wheeled round', now Ahab turns 'his dying head' (THE DYING WHALE): from his 'fiery father' to the billows; from the light to Kali/Sophia, his dark queen.

684. *my topmost greatness lies in my topmost grief* Condensed 'to one deep pang'. (THE CHASE – FIRST DAY)

cf. 'Man's Unhappiness, as I construe, comes of his Greatness; it is because there is an Infinite in him, which with all his cunning he cannot quite bury under the Finite ... Try him with half of a Universe, of an Omnipotence, he sets to quarrelling with the proprietor of the other half, and declares himself the most maltreated of men.' (*Sartor Resartus*, Bk 2, ch. 9)

684. *Ho, ho! ... this one piled comber* With a final cock-crow, to greet death. *'Towards thee I roll'* (Dut. and Ger. *Wallen*; A. S. *Walw-ian*) – 'a great lord of Leviathans' greeting the whale. *'I grapple with thee'* – to the 'last, cindered apple'. *'From hell's heart'*, 'I clutch thy heart at last!' – *'Thus'*!

> Rodmond unerring o'er his head suspends
> The barbed steel, and every turn attends.
>
> (Extract 45)

684. *the stricken whale flew forward* He 'laugheth at the shaking of a spear' (*Job* xli, 29).

684. *the line ... ran foul*

> ... and foul is fair:
> Hover through the fog ...

as, shrouded in mist, the whale 'hovered for a moment in the rain-bowed air'; as the sea-fowls 'hoveringly . . . lingered over the agitated pool that he left'; as Ahab 'hovered upon the point of the descent'.

684. *the flying turn caught him round the neck* cf. 'The whale was sounding very swiftly when the line became entangled. The boat-steerer, who was at his post in the stern of the boat, tending the line, instantly threw the turn off the loggerhead, and the tangled part ran forward and caught in the bow. The captain was seen to stoop to clear it, and then at once disappeared . . .' (Cheever, pp. 138–9)

'All men live enveloped in whale-lines. All are born with halters round their necks . . .' (THE LINE) Now Ahab (another Pippin) too is 'caught' – choked in the hangman's noose,

'and jump
Jim Crow'

– with a fatal ignition 'shot' out of the boat. 'The lightning flashes through my skull; mine eye-balls ache and ache; my whole beaten brain seems as beheaded, and rolling on some stunning ground.' (THE CANDLES)

'Oh, lonely death on lonely life!' – and both self-inflicted. 'See! Moby Dick seeks thee not.' A fraudulent Freemason in that roll of honour and loyalty, Ahab's end is that of a heretic who has renegued his masonic oath: with 'throat cut across . . . and buried in the sand of the sea'.

684. *voicelessly as Turkish mutes* With swift and oriental treachery, infidels eliminate the infidel,

> . . . took by th' throat the circumcised dog,
> And smote him – thus.
>
> (*Othello* V, ii, 358–9)

'No turbaned Turk . . . could have smote him with more seeming malice.' (MOBY DICK)

684. *the heavy eye-splice* Which is the inexorable, blinding darkness of Ahab's 'final end'. 'Aye, aye, like many more thou told'st direful truth as touching thyself . . .' (p. 676)

684. *the tranced boat's crew stood still* 'But though the picture lies thus tranced . . .' (LOOMINGS), 'Ah, God! what trances of torments . . .' (THE CHART)

684. *her sidelong fading phantom* 'It is the image of the un-

graspable phantom of life ...' Even the *Pequod,* at last, turned to a spectre, a spirit-spout, a Cock-Lane ghost.

684. *as in the gaseous Fata Morgana* A mirage occasionally seen off Calabria and in the straits of Messina. Morgan le Fay (Italian *fata,* a fairy) was a sister of King Arthur. The peculiar feature of this mirage is the dual image – with one side inverted – seen suspended over the masts, say, or on the water. Such reflex inversions, of course, were the key all along to Melville's imagery. As sea mirrors sky, so the *Pequod* mirrored the whale; and both are fairy-like. Queen Mab visions guided the one; a tail, like a 'fairy's arm', the other. But their common root – in *fatum* – is only now revealed.

684. *concentric circles . . . round and round in one vortex* Which is the twelfth and final vortex of life-in-death. 'Round with it, round! Short draughts – long swallows, men ...' (THE QUARTER-DECK)

685. *with long streaming yards of the flag* To the last 'erect', the *Pequod* sounds, like Moby Dick, with 'bannered flukes' and pennons streaming.

685. *hovered backwardly uplifted* With one posthumous spasm, as it were, from that 'one concrete hull': still hovering like Ahab 'upon the point of the descent'; still backwardly uplifted, like Ahab to the poise of the harpoon; for ever frozen to that one iron will.

685. *A sky-hawk that tauntingly had followed* cf. 'They apparently take a delight in soaring over the masthead of a ship, from which they usually tear away the pieces of coloured cloth fixed in the vane. One individual, thus occupied over the *Tuscan,* was taken by hand by the man at the masthead. The lookout at the time was kept by a landsman, remarkably tall and slender, and his mess-mates would never believe but that the poor bird, accustomed to the figure of a sailor, had mistaken him for a spare spar, and thus fallen a victim to a want of discernment.' (Bennett, vol. 2, pp. 243–4)

685. *in his death-gasp* 'death-grasp', in the first English edition.

685. *with archangelic shrieks . . . to hell* Like Satan 'thrusting forth his tormented colossal claw'. (p. 486) What had begun with 'long pampered Gabriel' coming to a close with 'archangelic shrieks'; what had been opened by 'a poor devil of a Sub-Sub' ending submerged in the Nether-lands.

685. *and helmeted herself with it* Picking up Milton's pun:

> O're Shields and Helmes, and helmed heads he rode
> Of Thrones and mighty Seraphim prostrate
> (*Paradise Lost* VI, 840–41)

– of Messiah routing Satan.

685. *over the yet yawning gulf*

> Hell at last
> Yawning receavd them whole, and on them clos'd,
> Hell thir fit habitation . . .
> (*Paradise Lost* VI, 874–6)

cf. The fate of 'Korah and his company'. (BRIT) cf. Moby Dick's mouth yawning 'beneath the boat like an open-doored marble tomb'. (p. 658) cf. The end of Ulysses' expedition off the Mount of Purgatory (Dante, *Inferno* xxvi).

685. *the great shroud of the sea rolled on* So the first verb used of the whale is also the last repeated verb – with a final echo of white horror and 'royal shrouds'. But in that 'roll' there lingers also the roll of ships and the roll of thunder and the whole masonic 'roll of our order', whose calendar too counts 'sixty round centuries'.

685. *as it rolled five thousand years ago* 'The same! . . . the same to Noah as to me' (p. 675): the precise date indicating (by whatever chronology) not the creation, but the flood. As 'the great flood-gates of the wonder-world swung open' to reveal 'two and two . . . endless processions of the whale' (LOOMINGS) – so their vista closes on an Ark Royal drowned.

EPILOGUE

687. *'AND I ONLY AM ESCAPED ALONE TO TELL THEE'* 'And, behold, there came a great wind from the wilderness, and smote the four corners of the house, and it fell upon the young men, and they are dead . . .' (*Job* i, 19)

687. *Because one did survive the wreck* 'Who suffered for our salvation: descended into hell, rose again the third day from the dead . . .' (*Athanasian Creed*)

For what means 'Ishmael' in Hebrew but 'God hears'? Cato, the suicide, was acclaimed at Utica, as 'the only free and only undefeated man'; Ishmael, in a coffin, alone escapes his captain's suicidal catastrophe, to be restored at last to life and liberty.

687. *the place of Ahab's bowsman* Once Starbuck's: 'And God was with the lad; and he grew, and dwelt in the wilderness, and became an archer.' (*Genesis* xxi, 20)

687. *the half-spent suction* Heard in the repeated sibilance of 'the ensuing scene', 'sight', 'sunk', and at last 'subsided' – which is the ultimate doom of the *Pequod*'s 'Pole-pointed prow'; the final solution to Ahab's conundrum: 'and now unmanned of Man; which is sucked in – by what?' (p. 629)

It was the weasel that sucked the gull.

687. *to a creamy pool* The whole 'spotless dairy room' itself now churned. (p. 539)

687. *Round and round* 'He turns and turns him to it' (THE DYING WHALE), 'as one who in that miserable plight still turns and turns in giddy anguish' (THE SERMON) 'beholding the white depths of the milky way'. (THE WHITENESS OF THE WHALE)

A tale launched in circumambulating New York, and set adrift in 'circulating' New Bedford, now closes 'the devious zig-zag world-circle of the *Pequod*'s circumnavigating wake' in this 'slowly wheeling circle' – or 'WHEEL/*BARROW*'.

687. *towards the . . . black bubble at the axis* In final expiation of that levelled 'cross' at the axis of another circle – or ring of stout mariners. (THE QUARTER-DECK)

687. *like another Ixion* Still echoing Ahab, in echoing Lear:

> You do me wrong to take me out o' th' grave.
> Thou art a soul in bliss; but I am bound
> Upon a wheel of fire, that mine own tears
> Do scald like molten lead.
>
> (IV, vii, 45–8)

Ixion murdered his father-in-law, by contriving his fall into a 'fiery pit'.

687. *I did revolve* In a maelstrom, Ish/*mael*, for a last solo turn still wheeling about and turning about, till

'... jump, Jim Crow'

687. *gaining that vital centre* of the circumference, 'the coffin life-buoy shot' – like the Sperm Whale – 'lengthwise from the

sea'. And with that parting 'shot', death is literally restored to life, the coffin to a cradle, holding a buoy.

'Take heart ... Up from the spray of thy ocean-perishing – straight up, leaps thy apotheosis!' Now Ishmael, like Queequeg, is passed to 'the third degree'. Now he alone – once so mocking of 'antique Adam' – is reborn. He alone is 'raised' to master mason.

687. *Buoyed up by that coffin* 'Coffin! Angels! save me!' (THE SPOUTER-INN) Like Arion on his dolphin, he has mounted the whale at last – tossed 'salmon-like to Heaven' to 'leap the topmost skies ...'

'Verily, verily, I say unto thee, Except a man be born of water and of the Spirit, he cannot enter into the kingdom of God.' (*John* iii, 5)

687. *The unharming sharks, they glided by* In a child-like vision of the 'Peaceable Kingdom', of a Golden Age returned, of 'Paradise Regain'd'.

687. *as if with padlocks on their mouths* Like Papageno (that child of nature) in Mozart's opera of masonic ritual transformed to mysteries of Isis, *The Magic Flute*:

> So shall the Truth all untruth banish,
> And Evil yield before the Good,
> And denigrating Envy vanish
> Within the light of Brotherhood.

(in the W. H. Auden/Chester Kallman version of the libretto by Schikaneder and Giesecke, Act I, sc.i)

687. *the devious-cruising Rachel ... after her missing children* What Captain Gardiner finds, however, is not his 'missing boy' but a 'coffin life-buoy'; not a twelve-year-old lad, but Ishmael happily free of both Rahab, 'that crooked serpent', and Ahab, that uncanonical Rabbin, and all Cartesian vortices.

Thus a tale that opened at Christmas closes with a 'cunning spring'. Peter Coffin is translated in the end to a 'coffin life-buoy'; 'that tempestuous wind Euroclydon', to Easter and resurrection.

687. *only found another orphan* For Ishmael and Ahab throughout were matched – two sides of one coin, twin aspects of one author. As Captain Gardiner, then, had lost a son, in Captain Ahab Ishmael has lost a father: 'my sweet mother, I know not'.

Appendix

THE EARLIEST SOURCES

OWEN CHASE

The Wreck of the Whaleship Essex[1]

I HAVE not been able to recur to the scenes which are now to become the subject of description, although a considerable time has elapsed, without feeling a mingled emotion of horror and astonishment at the almost incredible destiny that has preserved me and my surviving companions from a terrible death. Frequently, in my reflections on the subject, even after this lapse of time, I find myself shedding tears of gratitude for our deliverance, and blessing God, by whose divine aid and protection we were conducted through a series of unparalleled suffering and distress, and restored to the bosoms of our families and friends. There is no knowing what a stretch of pain and misery the human mind is capable of contemplating, when it is wrought upon by the anxieties of preservation; nor what pangs and weaknesses the body is able to endure, until they are visited upon it; and when at last deliverance comes, when the dream of hope is realized, unspeakable gratitude takes possession of the soul, and tears of joy choke the utterance. We require to be taught in the school of some signal suffering, privation, and despair, the great lessons of constant dependence upon an almighty forbearance and mercy. In the midst of the wide ocean, at night, when the sight of the heavens was shut out, and the dark tempest came upon us; then it was, that we felt ourselves ready to exclaim, 'Heaven have mercy upon us, for nought but that can save us now.' But I proceed to the recital. – On the 20th November, (cruising in latitude 0° 40′ S. longitude 119° 0′ W.) a shoal of whales was discovered off the lee bow. The weather at this time was extremely fine and clear, and it was about 8 o'clock in the morning, that the man at the mast-head gave the usual cry of,

1. From Owen Chase, *Narrative of the Most Extraordinary and Distressing Shipwreck of the Whale-Ship Essex, of Nantucket; Which Was Attacked and Finally Destroyed by a Large Spermaceti-Whale in the Pacific Ocean,* (New York, 1821), pp. 23–41.

'there she blows'. The ship was immediately put away, and we ran down in the direction for them. When we had got within half a mile of the place where they were observed, all our boats were lowered down, manned, and we started in pursuit of them. The ship, in the mean time, was brought to the wind, and the main-top-sail hove aback, to wait for us. I had the harpoon in the second boat; the captain preceded me in the first. When I arrived at the spot where we calculated they were, nothing was at first to be seen. We lay on our oars in anxious expectation of discovering them come up somewhere near us. Presently one rose, and spouted a short distance ahead of my boat; I made all speed towards it, came up with, and struck it; feeling the harpoon in him, he threw himself, in an agony, over towards the boat, (which at that time was up alongside of him,) and, giving a severe blow with his tail, struck the boat near the edge of the water, amidships, and stove a hole in her. I immediately took up the boat hatchet, and cut the line, to disengage the boat from the whale, which by this time was running off with great velocity. I succeeded in getting clear of him, with the loss of the harpoon and line; and finding the water to pour fast in the boat, I hastily stuffed three or four of our jackets in the hole, ordered one man to keep constantly bailing, and the rest to pull immediately for the ship; we succeeded in keeping the boat free, and shortly gained the ship. The captain and the second mate, in the other two boats, kept up the pursuit, and soon struck another whale. They being at this time a considerable distance to leeward, I went forward, braced around the mainyard, and put the ship off in a direction for them; the boat which had been stove was immediately hoisted in, and after examining the hole, I found that I could, by nailing a piece of canvass over it, get her ready to join in a fresh pursuit, sooner than by lowering down the other remaining boat which belonged to the ship. I accordingly turned her over upon the quarter, and was in the act of nailing on the canvass, when I observed a very large spermaceti whale, as well as I could judge, about eighty-five feet in length; he broke water about twenty rods off our weather-bow, and was lying quietly, with his head in a direction for the ship. He spouted two or three times, and then disappeared. In less than two or three seconds he came up again, about the length of the ship off, and made directly for us, at the rate of about three knots. The ship was then going with about the same velocity. His appearance and attitude gave us at first no alarm; but while I stood watching his movements, and observing him but a ship's length off, coming down for us with great celerity, I involuntarily ordered the boy at the helm to put it hard up; intending to sheer off and avoid him. The words were scarcely out of my mouth, before he came down upon us with full speed, and struck the ship with his head, just forward of the fore-chains; he gave us such an appalling and tremendous jar, as nearly threw us all on our faces. The ship brought up as suddenly and violently as if she had struck a rock, and trembled for a few seconds like a leaf. We looked at each other with perfect amazement, deprived almost of the power of speech. Many minutes elapsed before we were able to realize the dreadful accident; during which time he passed under the ship, grazing her keel as he went along, came up alongside of her to leeward, and lay on the top of the water, (apparently stunned with the violence of the blow,) for the space of a minute; he then suddenly started off, in a direction to leeward. After a few moments' reflection, and recovering, in some measure, from the sudden consternation that had seized us, I of course concluded that he had stove a hole in the ship, and that it would be necessary to set the pumps going. Accordingly they were rigged, but had not been in operation more than one minute, before I perceived the head of the ship to be gradually settling down in the water; I then ordered the signal to be set for the other boats, which, scarcely had I despatched, before I again discovered the whale, apparently in convulsions, on the top of the water, about one hundred rods to leeward. He was enveloped in the foam of the sea, that his continual and violent thrashing about in the water had created around him, and I could distinctly see him smite his jaws together, as if distracted with rage and fury. He remained a short time in this situation, and then started off with great velocity, across the bows of the ship, to windward. By this time the ship had settled down a considerable distance in the water, and I gave her up as lost. I, however, ordered the pumps to be kept constantly going, and endeavoured to collect my thoughts for the occasion. I turned to the boats, two of which we then had with the ship, with an intention of clearing them away, and getting all things ready to embark in them, if there should be no other resource left; and while my attention was thus engaged for a moment, I was aroused with the cry of a man at the hatchway, 'here he is – he is making for us again'. I turned around, and saw him about one hundred rods directly ahead of us, coming down apparently with twice his ordinary speed, and to me at that moment, it appeared with tenfold fury and vengeance in his aspect. The surf flew in all directions about him, and his course towards us was marked by a white foam of a rod in width, which he made with the continual violent thrashing of his tail; his head was about half out of water, and in that way he came upon, and again struck the ship. I was in hopes when I descried him making for us, that by a dexterous movement of putting the ship away immediately, I should be able to cross the line of his approach, before he could get up to us, and thus avoid, what I knew, if he should strike us again, would prove our inevitable destruction. I bawled out to the helmsman, 'hard up!' but she had not fallen off more than a point, before we took the second shock. I should judge the speed of the ship to have been at this time about three knots, and that of the whale about six. He struck her to windward, directly under the cathead, and completely stove in her bows. He passed under the ship again, went off to leeward, and we saw no more of him. Our situation at this juncture can be more readily imagined than described. The shock to our feelings was such, as I am sure none can have an adequate conception of, that were not there: the misfortune befel us at a moment when we least dreamt of any accident; and from the pleasing anticipations we had formed, of realizing the certain profits of our labour, we were dejected by a sudden, most mysterious, and overwhelming calamity. Not a moment, however, was to be lost in endeavouring to provide for the extremity to which it was now certain we were reduced. We were more than a thousand miles from the nearest land, and with nothing but a light open boat, as the resource of safety for myself and companions. I ordered the men to cease pumping, and every one to provide for himself; seizing a hatchet at the same time, I cut away the lashings of the spare boat, which lay bottom up across two spars directly over the quarter deck, and cried out to those near me, to take her as she came down. They did so accordingly, and bore her on their shoulders as far as the waist of the ship. The steward had in the mean time gone down into the cabin twice, and saved two quadrants, two practical navigators, and the captain's trunk and mine; all which were hastily thrown into the boat, as she lay on the deck, with the two compasses which I snatched from the binnacle. He attempted to descend again; but the water by this time had rushed in, and he returned without being able to effect his purpose. By the time we had got the boat to the waist, the ship had filled with water, and was going down on her beam-ends: we shoved our boat as quickly as possible from the plank-shear into the water, all hands jumping in her at the same time, and launched off clear of the ship. We were scarcely two boats' lengths distant from her, when she fell over to windward, and settled down in the water.

Amazement and despair now wholly took possession of us. We contemplated the frightful situation the ship lay in, and thought with horror upon the sudden and dreadful calamity that had overtaken us. We looked upon each other, as if to gather some consolatory sensation from an interchange of sentiments, but every countenance was marked with the paleness of despair. Not a word was spoken for several minutes by any of us; all appeared to be bound in a spell of stupid consternation; and from the time we were first attacked by the whale, to the period of the fall of the ship, and of our leaving her in the boat, more than ten minutes could not certainly have elapsed! God only knows in what way, or by what means, we were enabled to accomplish in that short time what we did; the cutting away and transporting the boat from where she was deposited would of itself, in ordinary circumstances, have consumed as much time as that, if the whole ship's crew had been employed in it. My companions had not saved a single article but what they had on their backs; but to me it was a source of infinite satisfaction, if any such could be gathered from the horrors of our gloomy situation, that we had been fortunate enough to have preserved our compasses, navigators, and quadrants. After the first shock of my feelings was over, I enthusiastically contemplated them as the probable instruments of our salvation; without them all would have been dark and hopeless. Gracious God! what a picture of distress and suffering now presented itself to my imagination. The crew of the ship were saved, consisting of twenty human souls. All that remained to conduct these twenty beings through the stormy terrors of the ocean, perhaps many thousand miles, were three open light boats. The prospect of obtaining any provisions or water from the ship, to subsist upon during the time, was at least now doubtful. How many long and watchful nights, thought I, are to be passed? How many tedious days of partial starvation are to be endured, before the least relief or mitigation of our sufferings can be reasonably anticipated. We lay at this time in our boat, about two ships' lengths off from the wreck, in perfect silence, calmly contemplating her situation, and absorbed in our own melancholy reflections, when the other boats were discovered rowing up to us. They had but shortly before discovered that some accident had befallen us, but of the nature of which they were entirely ignorant. The sudden and mysterious disappearance of the ship was first discovered by the boat-steerer in the captain's boat, and with a horror-struck countenance and voice, he suddenly exclaimed, 'Oh, my God! where is the ship?' Their operations upon this were instantly suspended, and a general cry of horror and despair burst from the lips of every man, as their looks were directed for her, in vain, over every part of the ocean. They immediately made all haste towards us. The captain's boat was the first that reached us. He stopped about a boat's length off, but had no power to utter a single syllable: he was so completely overpowered with the spectacle before him, that he sat down in his boat, pale and speechless. I could scarcely recognize his countenance, he appeared to be so much altered, awed, and overcome, with the oppression of his feelings, and the dreadful reality that lay before him. He was in a short time however enabled to address the inquiry to me, 'My God, Mr Chase, what is the matter?' I answered, 'We have been stove by a whale.' I then briefly told him the story. After a few moments' reflection he observed, that we must cut away her masts, and endeavour to get something out of her to eat. Our thoughts were now all accordingly bent on endeavours to save from the wreck whatever we might possibly want, and for this purpose we rowed up and got on to her. Search was made for every means of gaining access to her hold; and for this purpose the lanyards were cut loose, and with our hatchets we commenced to cut away the masts, that she might right up again, and enable us to scuttle her decks. In doing which we were occupied about three quarters of an hour, owing to our having no axes, nor indeed any other instruments, but the small hatchets belonging to the boats. After her masts were gone she came up about two-thirds of the way upon an even keel. While we were employed about the masts the captain took his quadrant, shoved off from the ship, and got an observation. We found ourselves in latitude 0° 40′ S. longitude 119° W. We now commenced to cut a hole through the planks, directly above two large casks of bread, which most fortunately were between decks, in the waist of the ship, and which being in the upper side, when she upset, we had strong hopes was not wet. It turned out according to our wishes, and from these casks we obtained six hundred pounds of hard bread. Other parts of the deck were then scuttled, and we got without difficulty as much fresh water as we dared to take in the boats, so that each was supplied with about sixty-five gallons; we got also from one of the lockers a musket, a small canister of powder, a couple of files, two rasps, about two pounds of boat nails, and a few turtle. In the afternoon the wind came on to blow a strong breeze; and having obtained every thing that occurred to us could then be got out, we began to make arrangements for our safety during the night. A boat's line was made fast to the ship, and to the other end of it one of the boats was moored, at about fifty fathoms to leeward; another boat was then attached to the first one, about eight fathoms astern; and the third boat, the like distance astern of her. Night came on just as we had finished our operations; and such a night as it was to us! so full of feverish and distracting inquietude, that we were deprived entirely of rest. The wreck was constantly before my eyes. I could not, by any effort, chase away the horrors of the preceding day from my mind: they haunted me the live-long night. My companions – some of them were like sick women; they had no idea of the extent of their deplorable situation. One or two slept unconcernedly, while others wasted the night in unavailing murmurs, I now had full leisure to examine, with some degree of coolness, the dreadful circumstances of our disaster. The scenes of yesterday passed in such quick succession in my mind that it was not until after many hours of severe reflection that I was able to discard the idea of the catastrophe as a dream. Alas! it was one from which there was no awaking; it was too certainly true, that but yesterday we had existed as it were, and in one short moment had been cut off from all the hopes and prospects of the living! I have no language to paint out the horrors of our situation. To shed tears was indeed altogether unavailing, and withal unmanly; yet I was not able to deny myself the relief they served to afford me. After several hours of idle sorrow and repining I began to reflect upon the accident, and endeavoured to realize by what unaccountable destiny or design, (which I could not at first determine,) this sudden and most deadly attack had been made upon us: by an animal, too, never before suspected of premeditated violence, and proverbial for its insensibility and inoffensiveness. Every fact seemed to warrant me in concluding that it was any thing but chance which directed his operations; he made two several attacks upon the ship, at a short interval between them, both of which, according to their direction, were calculated to do us the most injury, by being made ahead, and thereby combining the speed of the two objects for the shock; to effect which, the exact manoeuvres which he made were necessary. His aspect was most horrible, and such as indicated resentment and fury. He came directly from the shoal which we had just before entered, and in which we had struck three of his companions, as if fired with revenge for their sufferings. But to this it may be observed, that the mode of fighting which they always adopt is either with repeated strokes of their tails, or snapping of their jaws together; and that a case, precisely similar to this one, has never been heard of amongst the oldest and most experienced whalers. To this I would answer, that the structure and strength of the whale's head is admirably designed for this mode of attack; the most prominent part of which is almost as hard and as tough as iron; indeed, I can compare it to nothing else but the inside of a horse's hoof, upon which a lance or harpoon would not make the slightest impression. The eyes and ears are removed nearly one-third the length of the whole fish, from the front part of the head, and are not in the least degree endangered in this mode of attack. At all events, the whole circumstances taken together, all happening before my own eyes, and producing, at the time, impressions in my mind of decided, calculating mischief, on the part of the whale, (many of which impressions I cannot now recall,) induce me to be satisfied that I am correct in my opinion. It is certainly, in all its bearings, a hitherto unheard of circumstance, and constitutes, perhaps, the most extraordinary one in the annals of the fishery.

November 21st. The morning dawned upon our wretched company. The weather was fine, but the wind blew a strong breeze from the SE. and the sea was very rugged. Watches had been kept up during the night, in our respective boats, to see that none of the spars or other articles (which continued to float out of the wreck,) should be thrown by the surf against, and injure the boats. At sunrise, we began to think of doing something; what, we did not know: we cast loose our boats, and visited the wreck, to see if any thing more of consequence could be preserved, but every thing looked cheerless and desolate, and we made a long and vain search for any useful article; nothing could be found but a few turtle; of these we had enough already; or at least, as many as could be safely stowed in the boats, and we wandered around in every part of the ship in a sort of vacant idleness for the greater part of the morning. We were presently aroused to a perfect sense of our destitute and forlorn condition, by thoughts of the means which we had for our subsistence, the necessity of not wasting our time, and of endeavouring to seek some relief wherever God might direct us.

RALPH WALDO EMERSON

(*Journal Entry, 1834*)[2]

Boston, Feb. 19 A seaman in the coach told the story of an old sperm whale which he called a white whale which was known for many years by the whalemen as Old Tom & who rushed upon the boats which attacked him & crushed the boats to small chips in his jaws, the men generally escaping by jumping overboard & being picked up. A vessel was fitted out at New Bedford, he said, to take him. And he was finally taken somewhere off Payta head by the Winslow or the Essex.

JULES LECOMTE

Le Cachalot Blanc[3]

Dans les journaux modernes, les récits d'événements causés par la rencontre des grands monstres marins sont assez communs. Une feuille espagnole qui s'imprime à la Havane contenait en 1830 le rapport d'un capitaine qui signalait la rencontre d'un animal d'espèce inconnue. Voici à peu près la traduction de ce rapport:

« Partis de Matanzas le 3 janvier, dit le voyageur, nous faisions

2. From *The Journals and Miscellaneous Notebooks of Ralph Waldo Emerson,* vol. IV, edited by Alfred R. Ferguson (Cambridge, Massachusetts; Belknap Press of Harvard University Press, 1964), p. 256.

3. From 'Études maritimes, de quelques animaux apocryphes et fabuleux de la mer', *Musée des familles, 4,* pp. 97–104 (January, 1837). First reprinted by Janez Stanonik, *Moby-Dick; The Myth and the Symbol* (Ljubljana: Ljubljana University Press, 1962), pp. 189–95.

route vers notre destination, lorsque vers midi nous aperçûmes, à quatre milles de la côte que nous longions, un objet fort élevé au-dessus de la surface de la mer. Mes matelots et les passagers crurent d'abord comme moi que c'était un bâtiment chaviré. Je fis aussitôt gouverner de manière à m'en approacher le plus possible: mais, parvenus à une petite distance de lui, l'objet sur lequel nous avions les yeux parut changer d'aspect, et nous crûmes que c'était une grande embarcation en détresse. Croyant pouvoir être utile à quelques malheureux, je l'accostai à portée de fusil; nos doutes furent alors éclaircis. Cette apparence d'embarcation nous présenta la mâchoire supérieure d'un monstre d'une effroyable dimension. Il s'élevait de l'eau dans une position presque horizontale, à quinze ou vingt pieds, et il était entouré d'une innombrable quantité de poissons de diverses grandeurs, qui nageaient dans toutes les directions, en occupant un espace de près d'un mille autour de lui. En nous rapprochant encore de cet immense cétacé, nous le vîmes mouvoir ses mâchoires, et un bruit terrible et semblable à celui que produit un éboulement de terre se fit entendre. Une nageoire de couleur noire et de près de 9 pieds d'élévation placée à 60 pieds environ de sa gueule, apparut lentement. Nous n'avons pu estimer la longueur totale de ce monstre, dont la queue ne s'est pas montrée au-dessus de la surface de la mer. Sans les instances réitérées de mes passagers dont l'effroi était visible, je m'en serais approché de manière à pouvoir donner sur cette rencontre extraordinaire des détails plus précis.

< A l'instant où nous revirâmes de bord, le monstre disparut dans le nord-ouest, mais il se montra bientôt après dans le nord, à une grande distance, et il nous sembla avoir repris la position qu'il avait lorsque nous l'aperçûmes pour la première fois. Ses dimensions sont infiniment plus grandes que celles que pourrait offrir la plus colossale de toutes les baleines, et sa conformation, qui ne ressemble nullement à celle de ce dernier genre de cétacé, me porte à croire qu'il doit appartenir à une espèce tout-à-fait inconnue jusqu'à présent.

<Certifié véritable et sincère, à la Havane, le 5 janvier 1830. Suivent les signatures des passagers et matelots du *Neptune*, avec celle du capitaine José-Maria Lopez.>

On trouve dans Olaüs Magnus, et dans la cosmographie, quelques mots sur un monstre marin dont la description présente d'assez directes analogies avec l'analyse qui précède. Olaüs surtout parle d'un cétacé énorme qui se tenait à peu près debout dans l'eau et ne montrait conséquemment que sa tête, surmontée d'un évent dont l'eau fortement comprimée et lancée en l'air lui faisait un large panache. La gravure où sont figurés les phoques-sirènes en offre, dans notre premier article, la reproduction d'après le naïf dessin de Belleforest. Les anciens navigateurs redoutaient beaucoup ce monstre, qui du reste avait peur du bruit, et qu'on parvenait souvent à faire fuir à son de trompe. Parfois il attaquait les navires, et leur donnait de violentes secousses; pour s'en débarrasser, on jetait à la mer de vieilles futailles sur lesquelles le géant marin se lançait joyeusement tandis que le bâtiment fuyait à force de rames. Il y a dans la marine américaine, sous le titre de cachalot blanc, une tradition que cette dernière circonstance nous rappelle, parce que ce fut par un semblable moyen de futailles que l'aventure fut menée à fin; la voici:

Les pêcheurs baleiniers de Nantukett, qui à chaque saison se rencontrent aux îles Malouïnes, ne manquaient jamais de retrouver dans les parages où tous les ans ils avaient coutume d'exercer leur pêche, un énorme cachalot qui maintes fois poursuivi par les plus hardis harponneurs, n'avait jamais paru d'humeur à prêter son lard à l'ébullition des vastes chaudières des bords. Une circonstance assez remarquable avait surtout signalé le cétacé à l'attention de tous les navigateurs, de sorte qu'il était impossible qu'ils se trompassent sur la réalité de la présence continuelle du même monstre dans les eaux des Malouïnes; cette circonstance, c'est que ce cachalot, remarquable d'abord par ses proportions anormales, était encore surtout extraordinaire par sa couleur, qui était du blanc le plus pur et le plus éclatant. La plupart des cétacés connus sous le nom de baleines et de cachalots ont bien parfois sous le ventre quelques larges taches laiteuses qui se découpent bizarrement sur le ton foncé de l'enveloppe générale. Mais un cachalot entièrement blanc pouvait à raison passer dans l'imagination des pêcheurs pour le phénomène le plus étonnant que leur montrât l'Ocean; aussi y avait-il, surtout parmi les matelots, une sorte de superstition craintive qui rendait l'approche du monstre une circonstance, à leurs yeux, défavorable au succès de leur navigation. Quand le grand cachalot blanc s'était montré, il était rare que les rameurs trouvassent quelque vigueur pour remuer les avirons de leurs agiles pirogues, et d'ailleurs, convenons-en, mille accidents avaient démontré que le dos brillant du cétacé, mêlé aux flots bleus de certains parages, était un signe fatal. Quelquefois de hardis pêcheurs s'étaient aventurés à sa poursuite, mais tous les efforts des rames et les dispositions les plus heureuses de la mer: surface unie, brise favorable, rien n'avait réussi aux marins découragés. Enfin, bien que la présence du grand cachalot dans les mers du Sud remontât à des temps fort reculés, pas un harponneur n'avait réussi à planter sur son dos l'arme si redoutable aux baleines et aux cachalots vulgaires; la tradition du gaillard-d'avant était absolument muette à cet égard.

Il est inutile, pensons-nous, d'ajouter que chaque nouveau navire qui arrivait du continent sur le théâtre général de la pêche ne manquait jamais de s'informer avec inquiétude de tout ce que ses devanciers pouvaient avoir à lui dire sur le fantastique animal. C'était le récit de ses ruses infinies pour échapper aux pêcheurs, ses apparitions inattendues, ses méfaits envers les pirogues imprudentes dont un nonchalant coup de queue lui faisait justice; c'était l'histoire vraie ou fausse, avec additions et commentaires, la biographie fleurie et aventureuse du cétacé qui formait le peloton d'où se dévidaient toutes les conversations de bord. Les marins les plus haut placés dans l'opinion des baleiniers étaient ceux qui avaient osé poursuivre l'ennemi général, et le comble de l'honneur consistait à avoir eu sa pirogue brisée par un de ses attouchements. Il s'écoula de longues années pendant lesquelles les choses furent perpétuellement ainsi.

En 1828, un beau trois-mâts américain, nommé *l'Océanie*, rentrait à Nantukett avec un copieux chargement de fanons et d'huile de baleine. L'équipage, comme toujours, rapportait les plus curieuses histoires sur les nouveaux méfaits de l'impunissable cachalot blanc. Dix pirogues armées des meilleurs marins du pays, venaient d'être, pendant la dernière saison, victimes de leur chaleureux dévouement à l'extinction du monstre. Des coups de queue pleins de mépris avaient adroitement brisé chaque embarcation et blessé les hommes qui les montaient. Le capitaine de *l'Océanie* avait perdu un de ses proches dans cette formidable joûte. Une exaspération impuissante agitait toute la population maritime de Nantukett.

Le vieux capitaine avait une admirable fille, une de ces créoles américaines dont l'ensemble est le texte vivant d'une fusion de la beauté des filles du Nord es des filles Caraïbes. La jeune personne était donc fort belle, sa dot considérable; il y avait peu de partis dans la ville qu'on pût lui offrir en enjeu. Eh bien! son père, le vieux baleinier, promit sa fille en mariage, son beau trois-mâts *l'Océanie* en commandement, au vaillant pêcheur qui, par quelque ruse que ce soit tuerait le monstre et en apporterait au port la graisse productive, – toison pharmaceutique du nouveau Jason.

Les concurrents ne manquèrent pas; il y eut émeute sur tous les navires en départ. La jeune Américaine, élevée au milieu des merveilleux récits dont le *grand cachalot blanc* offrait le thème inépuisable, était entrée pour quelque chose dans l'enthousiasme de son père. L'idée de devenir l'épouse du vainqueur s'offrait à son esprit à travers de nuageuses visions de gloire et de triomphe qui devaient au besoin rester sur ses yeux pour lui dissimuler les imperfections de l'homme que cette hasardeuse loterie devait lui adjoindre pour la vie. On ne saurait dire les gens de toute sorte qui s'armèrent pour le grand tournoi, et combien d'impatientes expéditions se préparèrent pour aller jeter des combattants dans l'arène. Franchissons les espaces du temps et du lieu, et rejoignons les parages encombrés des îles Malouïnes.

Un splendide soleil faisait de la mer une éblouissante mare de lumière; la brise faisait à peine palpiter les voiles sous les folles et rares bouffées de son haleine endormie. Vingt navires tournés dans des allures différentes pointaient dans l'air immobile leurs blanches voiles, comme de gigantesques albatros au repos. Les vigies attentives planaient des points les plus élevés des mâtures, sur l'horizon immense, qu'un ciel limpide déroulait à leurs yeux. Toutes les pirogues étaient prêtes et les rameurs impatients. Un petit pavillion de couleur tranchante devait se développer à la poupe de chaque canot, dans la colonne d'air formée par la vitesse que donneraient les rames. C'était le panache des combattants, qui devait signaler au loin leur défaite ou leur victoire. Les harpons, les lances, les flèches tranchantes reluisaient au soleil en échangeant avec lui de brillants éclairs. Tout était prêt pour la joûte formidable. Le monstre de son côté, ne se fit point attendre.

Au moment où l'impatience des pêcheurs était surtout extrême, la surface unie de la mer s'entrouvrit tout à coup au milieu de plusieurs navires. Le souffle volumineux du cétacé lança dans l'air brillianté de soleil une immense gerbe d'eau, semblable à une irruption de diamants; puis l'armure blanche du géant des mers se montra, éclatante comme un acier poli. Son chant de guerre, son cri de combat, fut un grognement formidable, semblable à un éboulement de terrain. Il battit l'eau de sa large queue en accolade, et les flots soulevés par lui s'y brisèrent ourlés d'une frange étincelante. C'était un spectacle étourdissant à voir et qui jetait mille éblouissements dans le regard étourdi. Ce ne fut qu'un seul cri de *rescousse* sur la flotte baleinière, quand cette apparition se fût offerte aux yeux de tous les combattants. Les pirogues quittèrent les bords et se dirigèrent sur le champ de bataille. Les couleurs variées des patrons se dessinèrent comme des panaches chevaleresques; le roi de la mer agitait, comme un défi, la mousse blanche qui s'élançait de son évent, semblable aux plumes neigeuses qui ombrageaient le cimier des rois de France. La pensée du gage précieux que promettait la victoire était si ardente, que l'appareil hostile du monstre n'intimida guère les combattants. C'était d'ailleurs un défi jeté à de nombreux amours-propres de marins, – une légende traditionnelle dont un couplet restait à faire, et dans lequel un nom glorieux devait être enchâssé. Les pirogues volaient en contournant les molles ondulations de la surface; on eût dit des feuilles rafflées par un tourbillon. Emportées vers un but inconnu comme ces dernières dont elles avaient la verte couleur, les pauvres barques dévoraient la surface, qui se rayait sous leur faible pression, sans prendre le loisir de regarder leur forme capricieusement réfléchie dans l'inconstant miroir des eaux. Les rameurs trouvaient des forces inépuisables dans l'espérance de la victoire ... Elle fut inconstante à beaucoup.

Les premiers pêcheurs qui abordèrent le monstre n'eurent point le temps de lui jeter leurs vigoureux harpons. Montrant à peine sa tête et une partie de son corps à la surface tourmentée de la mer, il plongeait sa queue redoutable et ne la soulevait que pour briser une pirogue. L'arène se couvrit de débris; les armes, les fers patiemment aiguisés, au lieu de se réfugier dans l'épaisse enveloppe du cétacé, lancés au hasard par le choc, plongeaient en ricochant leurs lames tranchantes dans les membres des malheureux matelots. Ce fut un horrible carnage duquel pas une pirogue, pas un homme n'échappa sans blessures. Une seule embarcation, commandée par un pêcheur qu'une infériorité hiérarchique de position avait, malgré lui, retenu dans certaines limites, flottait encore autour de tant de ruines et de débris; un instant alarmé sur le sort que lui promettaient de semblables préludes, le pêcheur intimidé songea à regagner son navire. Mais soudain son courage se retrempa dans une idée nouvelle. Il courut à bord; une futaille de la plus large dimension fut placée à l'avant de sa pirogue. Il interrogea le zèle de ses rameurs, et désormais confiant dans leur résolution, il se dirigea vers le cachalot qui, peut-être décidé à rester maître du tournoi, venait au-devant de lui comme pour lui présenter la bataille. Le baleinier observa tous ses mouvements et se raffermit dans son espérance.

Quand la distance qui séparait encore le cétacé de la barque fut suffisamment étroite, l'ordre fut donné de lancer sur l'eau la grosse futaille, et au même moment la pirogue dévia de sa route. Le cachalot se précipita sur la barrique en ouvrant sa longue mâchoire, dont les claquements semblaient de nouvelles menaces ou quelque sinistre avertissement. Il y avait là de la peur pour mille Autrichiens; personne dans la barque n'en ressentit les atteintes. Tandis que l'animal, excité par les précédentes escarmouches, s'épluchait les dents avec la futaille abandonée à ses jeux ou à son courroux, le hardi baleinier, qu'un circuit avait rapproché d'un des flancs du monstre, lui jeta avec une adresse et une vigueur merveilleuses sa lance agüe prês d'une certaine cavité que dans ses mouvements protégeait et découvrait tour à tour le nageoire du cachalot.* Le mouvement qu'il fit souleva d'énormes lames à la surface de la mer, et le plus prodigieux hasard put seul sauver la pirogue du contact destructeur d'un de ses mouvements. Son instinct étourdi dans la souffrance, laissa le monstre livré aux soubresauts les plus fougueux; puis, comme pour essayer de se soustraire à la douleur de cette mortelle blessure, il partit avec impétuosité dans une direction sans but; bien que la coutume, ou mieux, les règles de la pêche de la baleine placent un cordage sur toutes les armes qui sont dirigées sur ces monstres, afin que la pirogue reste attachée à leurs courses, cette fois cette mesure avait été jugée trop dangereuse. Aussi le cachalot s'enfuit-il sans entrave, mais avec la mort dans son gigantesque corps. Quand les marins virent le sang épais sortir en bouillonnant du souffle de leur adversaire, ils ressentirent une joie inexprimable. Le reste se devine. La pirogue ensanglantée rejoignit triomphalement son navire. Le cachalot s'en fût mourir dans d'autres eaux où il fut retrouvé et mis en pièces; – le vainqueur revint à Nantukett.

Tout le peuple attendait sur le rivage la descente du pêcheur qui venait de remporter une aussi éclatante victoire, Son navire

*Les baleines et les cachalots ont sur les côtes les plus prochaines de leur nageoire ou aileron un petit espace ou la peau est ridée, et qui livre passage jusqu' aux poumons du monstre, à travers son osseuse et solide charpente. Dirigé sur cette partie, le coup que reçoit le cétacé est mortel; alors, au lieu de jeter par ses évents l'eau que recèlent certaines bourses comprimées dans son arrière-mâchoire, il projette des flots de sang qu'un épanchement abondant livre à ses canaux mystérieux. Sa mort est certaine dès que le sang jaillit de ses évents. Toute l'habilité des pêcheurs de baleines consiste donc à atteindre adroitement cette place.

pavoisé de brillantes flammes avait annoncé le succès par l'explosion de ses carronades. *L'Océanie* hissa ses pavillons pour recevoir son nouveau capitaine; la jeune Américaine, dont les charmes admirables formaient la couronne du vainqueur, attendait sur la plage ... C'était partout mille cris de joie, mille clameurs d'enthousiasme; une mer de peuple roulait ses vagues curieuses jusqu'au point où allait aborder la barque qui approchait couverte de drapeaux flottants ... Une musique militaire jouait dans la foule ses marches les plus retentissantes ... La pirogue accosta et s'avança vers la belle Américaine descendue pour le recevoir d'un splendide palanquin ... Les cris redoublèrent, le nom du vainqueur vola de bouche en bouche ... c'était un gros nègre.

Ceci se passait, nous l'avons dit, en 1828; aujourd'hui le nouvel armateur de *l'Océanie* est colossalement riche; il a de charmants enfants mulâtres.

Après l'histoire du grand cachalot blanc, laquelle est chose croyable et authentique, nous avons grande envie de parler au lecteur d'un certain animal plus apocryphe et plus fabuleux cent fois que telle autre bête que ce soit ...

Translation

In contemporary newspapers tales of encounters with great sea-monsters are fairly common. A Spanish newspaper, printed at Havana, in 1830 published a description by a captain of an encounter with an animal of an unknown species. Here is a rough translation of that report:

'After leaving Matanzas on the 3rd of January, said the captain, we proceeded towards our destination; at midday we noticed, four miles or so from the coast along which we were sailing, a strange object looming out of the water. Passengers, sailors, all took it to be a capsized ship; and so did I, immediately ordering a change of course to bring us up closer. But on approaching, the object seemed to change shape and we decided it was a large boat in distress. Hoping to be of some help, we sailed within a musket-shot; at that moment all our doubts vanished. What had appeared to be a boat, turned out to be the upper jaw of a monster of enormous dimensions. This monster rose from fifteen to twenty feet above the water in an almost horizontal position, surrounded by innumerable quantity of fish swimming in all directions for almost a mile around. Drawing nearer to this immense cetacean we saw it move its jaws and a terrifying roar, loud as a landslide, resounded. A black fin slowly appeared, nearly nine feet high, and some sixty feet removed from its mouth. We could not guess the total length of the monster since it did not reveal its tail. But for the repeated entreaties of the passengers, who were in great distress, I would have approached even closer to give more precise details about this extraordinary encounter.

'At the moment of tacking about, the monster disappeared to the north-west, but reappeared soon after some way to the north. It seemed to be back in the spot where we had first sighted it. Its dimensions are infinitely greater than those observed even in the largest whales (baleines), nor does its shape in any way resemble them. This leads me to conclude that it must belong to a species hitherto wholly unknown.

'Certified as true and genuine, at Havana, on the 3rd of January, 1830. Here follow the signatures of the passengers and crew of the *Neptune*, with the signature of the captain, Jose-Maria Lopez.'

In the work of Olaus Magnus and various, descriptive geographies, there are references to a sea-monster resembling this report. Olaus speaks of an enormous cetacean standing almost upright in the water so that only its head showed, from which a spout shot into the air like a vast plume. The engraving, with the sea-sirens in our first article, reproduces an ingenious drawing by Belleforest. Early navigators stood in great awe of this monster; but the monster was so afraid of noise that they frequently managed to frighten it away with a trumpet blast. Now and then it attacked ships and tossed them violently about. To get rid of it, they threw old tubs into the sea; while the giant hurled itself gleefully upon the tubs, the ship took to the oars. A tradition lingers in the American navy about the *white sperm whale* that this anecdote brings to mind. It runs as follows:

Whalers from Nantucket, whose rendezvous lay near the Falkland Islands, invariably met a huge sperm whale in their seasonal hunting grounds. Though chased often enough, it held coolly aloof from the try-works. One feature alone was conspicuous: this whale, already notable for sheer bulk, was of the purest, most brilliant white. Right Whales and Sperm Whales may well sport a milky patch or two under their belly contrasting with uniform black. But a totally white whale was a living mystery. Sailors are peculiarly prone to superstitious fear; the mere approach of the albino sperm whale was considered an evil portent. Oarsmen could hardly summon the strength to pull their oars. The very brilliance of the white whale mingling with the blue waves proved a fatal sign. Even in giving chase on a calm day with a favouring breeze they never succeeded. Not a single harpooneer ever pierced his back or held him fast; on that point forecastle tradition was unanimous.

Each ship, on arrival from the mainland, made uneasy inquiries. There were accounts of the endless guile with which the monster escaped the whalers, his unexpected appearances, his passes at imprudent boats destroyed with a nonchalant swipe of his flukes. This one whale dominated all tongues. To pursue this whale was to court honour; to lose one's boat in the encounter, a prized distinction. Such was the situation for many years.

In 1828 a fine American three-master, the *Oceania*, returned to Nantucket with a large cargo of whalebone and oil. The crew, as usual, told the strangest stories about the latest misdeeds of the indomitable white sperm whale. Their bravest sailors had fallen prey to his wiles during the season. The contemptuous strokes of his flukes broke every boat to pieces and wounded the men. In one such joust the captain of the *Oceania* had lost a close relation. Impotent rage stirred the whole population of Nantucket.

This old captain had a daughter, a beautiful Creole uniting all the graces of the North and the Caribbean Sea. Her dowry was considerable; few young Nantucketers could hope to be her match. But her father promised the hand of his daughter and the command of the *Oceania* to whoever should slay the monster and – Jason-like – bring the gold fleece of its blubber to port.

There were hordes of competitors; in fact, there was almost a riot on every ship that departed. And the girl, brought up on tales of the great *white sperm whale*, echoed the enthusiasm of her father. Visions of glory shrouded the possible imperfections of the bridegroom to be granted her by this lottery. Suitors of all kinds prepared for the tournament; impatient expeditions set sail. Let us leap space and time to rejoin the busy waters around the Falkland Islands.

A glorious sun bedazzled the sea; sails drooped and fluttered in an occasional breeze. Twenty ships moved in different directions, pointing their white sails in the motionless air like huge albatrosses in repose. Attentive watches clung to their top-masts and swept the immense horizon. The whale-boats were ready; the oarsmen, impatient. On each stern fluttered a small banner – the pennant to signal victory or defeat. Harpoons, lances, spear-heads reflected the brilliant rays of the sun. Everything was prepared for battle.

Suddenly – their patience almost exhausted – the smooth expanse burst open. An enormous spout of water jetted into the gleaming air like an eruption of diamonds. Next a glimpse of white, dazzling as polished steel. His battle-cry was a growl, a rumbling landslide. He thrashed the surface with his huge flukes, starting a ripple of sparkling waves. It was an awesome sight. A shout arose from the whole whaling fleet. The boats left their ships and threaded their way to the field of battle. Their pennants seemed knightly plumes; the monster, dashing foam from his spout, seemed a King of France shaded by his snow white crest. But the prize urged them on. His war-cry, far from scaring them off, only quickened their pride. Here was the very stuff of heroic ballad with only the final couplet still to be sung and a name to be celebrated. The boats flew along, rebounding on the slight undulations like leaves swept into a whirlpool. They were as green as leaves, and as doomed, merely creasing the surface without time to examine their mirror images in the waves.

Nor did the leaders have time even to dart their harpoons. Merely poking head and shoulders out from the tossed waves, the whale thrashed his formidable flukes; with every blow he crushed a boat. The sea was littered with wreckage. Instead of piercing the thick blubber, harpoons haphazardly rebounded, cutting the sailors. It was a massacre; no one escaped unwounded. Only one boat – kept distant by rank rather than resolution – now bobbed among the wrecks and splinters. Momentarily its headman felt alarmed; he considered retreat. Then – struck by an idea – he leapt on deck. A huge tub was lowered into the stern; and rousing his oarsmen, he steered towards the whale. The monster swam to meet him.

Intently watching the whale's movements, and the distance between, the whaleman ordered the tub to be jettisoned and at once changed course. The sperm whale pounced on the barrel, growling and thundering with open jaws – enough to scare a thousand Austrians witless. But in the boat all was calm. While the whale gritted his teeth on the tub, the whaleman stole round his flanks and darted his lance behind a fin. It was a vulnerable spot, now concealed, now revealed, as he swam.* Frantically the monster stirred huge waves; convulsed with pain, made furious, sudden leaps, rushing impetuously this way and that. Only a miracle saved the whaleboat from his mad rushes. But, as a precaution, the harpoon had been left unattached; the whale ran free. Yet death lurked in his enormous body. The sailors felt an inexpressible joy when they saw thick blood jetting in short spurts from the blow-holes. The rest can be imagined. The triumphant boat, stained with blood, returned to the ship. The sperm whale died in another stretch of water where he was later found and cut up; the victor returned to Nantucket.

The whole island awaited the champion's arrival. His ship, with pennants fluttering, boomed out victory salvoes from her carronades. The *Oceania* hoisted her ensigns to receive her new captain; the young American bride, whose charms were the crowning reward for the victor, waited upon the shore ... Shouts of joy sounded everywhere; the people rolled in waves down to the harbour; a military band played the most stirring marches ... The boat drew up alongside; the hero approached his bride who greeted him from a splendid litter ... The cries redoubled; the name of the victor passed from mouth to mouth ... He was a tall Negro.

All this happened, as was noted, in the year 1828. Today the new captain of the *Oceania* is extremely rich; and he has charming mulatto children.

After this story of the great white sperm whale, which is an authentic record, we wish to speak of an animal a hundred times more fabulous than any other ...

*In right whales (baleines) and sperm whales (cachalots) there is a small spot, close to the fin, covered with wrinkled skin, where piercing through the bony frame one can wound the lungs. Hit point blank upon this spot, the wound proves fatal. Instead of spouting up water from the compressed cavities behind his throat, the whale discharges blood; and death is assured.

J. N. REYNOLDS

Mocha Dick:

OR THE WHITE WHALE OF THE PACIFIC: A LEAF FROM A MANUSCRIPT JOURNAL.[4]

We expected to find the island of Santa Maria still more remarkable for the luxuriance of its vegetation, than even the fertile soil of Mocha; and the disappointment arising from the unexpected shortness of our stay at the latter place, was in some degree relieved, by the prospect of our remaining for several days in safe anchorage at the former. Mocha lies upon the coast of Chili, in lat. 38° 28′ south, twenty leagues north of Mono del Bonifacio, and opposite the Imperial river, from which it bears W. S. W. During the last century, this island was inhabited by the Spaniards, but it is at present, and has been for some years, entirely deserted. Its climate is mild, with little perceptible difference of temperature between the summer and winter seasons. Frost is unknown on the lowlands, and snow is rarely seen, even on the summits of the loftiest mountains.

It was late in the afternoon, when we left the schooner; and while we bore up for the north, she stood away for the southern extremity of the island. As evening was gathering around us, we fell in with a vessel, which proved to be the same whose boats, a day or two before, we had seen in the act of taking a whale. Aside from the romantic and stirring associations it awakened, there are few objects in themselves more picturesque or beautiful, than a whaleship, seen from a distance of three or four miles, on a pleasant evening, in the midst of the great Pacific. As she moves gracefully over the water, rising and falling on the gentle undulations peculiar to this sea, her sails glowing in the quivering light of the fires that flash from below, and a thick volume of smoke ascending from the midst, and curling away in dark masses upon the wind; it requires little effort of the fancy, to imagine one's self gazing upon a floating volcano.

As we were both standing to the north, under easy sail, at nine o'clock at night we had joined company with the stranger. Soon

4. From *The Knickerbocker, New York Monthly Magazine*, XIII (May, 1839), pp. 377–92.

after, we were boarded by his whale-boat, the officer in command of which bore us the compliments of the captain, together with a friendly invitation to partake the hospitalities of his cabin. Accepting, without hesitation, a courtesy so frankly tendered, we proceeded, in company with Captain Palmer, on board, attended by the mate of the *Penguin*, who was on his way to St Mary's to repair his boat, which had some weeks before been materially injured in a storm.

We found the whaler a large, well-appointed ship, owned in New-York, and commanded by such a man as one might expect to find in charge of a vessel of this character; plain, unassuming, intelligent, and well-informed upon all the subjects relating to his peculiar calling. But what shall we say of his first mate, or how describe him? To attempt his portrait by a comparison, would be vain, for we have never looked upon his like; and a detailed description, however accurate, would but faintly shadow forth the *tout ensemble* of his extraordinary figure. He had probably numbered about thirty-five years. We arrived at this conclusion, however, rather from the untamed brightness of his flashing eye, than the general appearance of his features, on which torrid sun and polar storm had left at once the furrows of more advanced age, and a tint swarthy as that of the Indian. His height, which was a little beneath the common standard, appeared almost dwarfish, from the immense breadth of his overhanging shoulders; while the unnatural length of the loose, dangling arms which hung from them, and which, when at rest, had least the appearance of ease, imparted to his uncouth and muscular frame an air of grotesque awkwardness, which defies description. He made few pretensions as a sailor, and had never aspired to the command of a ship. But he would not have exchanged the sensations which stirred his blood, when steering down upon a school of whales, for the privilege of treading, as master, the deck of the noblest liner that ever traversed the Atlantic. According to the admeasurement of his philosophy, whaling was the most dignified and manly of all sublunary pursuits. Of this he felt perfectly satisfied, having been engaged in the noble vocation for upward of twenty years, during which period, if his own assertions were to be received as evidence, no man in the American spermaceti fleet had made so many captures, or met with such wild adventures, in the exercise of his perilous profession. Indeed, so completely were all his propensities, thoughts, and feelings, identified with his occupation; so intimately did he seem acquainted with the habits and instincts of the objects of his pursuit, and so little conversant with the ordinary affairs of life; that one felt less inclined to class him in the genus *homo*, than as a sort of intermediate something between man and the cetaceous tribe.

Soon after the commencement of his nautical career, in order to prove that he was not afraid of a whale, a point which it is essential for the young whaleman to establish beyond question, he offered, upon a wager, to run his boat 'bows on' against the side of an 'old bull', leap from the 'cuddy' to the back of the fish, sheet his lance home, and return on board in safety. This feat, daring as it may be considered, he undertook and accomplished; at least so it was chronicled in his log, and he was ready to bear witness, on oath, to the veracity of the record. But his conquest of the redoubtable MOCHA DICK, unquestionably formed the climax of his exploits.

Before we enter into the particulars of this triumph, which, through their valorous representative, conferred so much honor on the lancers of Nantucket, it may be proper to inform the reader who and what Mocha Dick was; and thus give him a posthumous introduction to one who was, in his day and generation, so emphatically among fish the 'Stout Gentleman' of his latitudes. The introductory portion of his history we shall give, in a condensed form, from the relation of the mate. Substantially, however, it will be even as he rendered it; and as his subsequent narrative, though not deficient in rude eloquence, was coarse in style and language, as well as unnecessarily diffuse, we shall assume the liberty of altering the expression; of adapting the phraseology to the occasion; and of presenting the whole matter in a shape more succinct and connected. In this arrangement, however, we shall leave our adventurer to tell his *own story*, although not always in his own words, and shall preserve the person of the original.

But to return to Mocha Dick – which, it may be observed, few were solicitous to do, who had once escaped from him. This renowned monster, who had come off victorious in a hundred fights with his pursuers, was an old bull whale, of prodigious size and strength. From the effect of age, or more probably from a freak of nature, as exhibited in the case of the Ethiopian Albino, a singular consequence had resulted – *he was white as wool*! Instead of projecting his spout obliquely forward, and puffing with a short, convulsive effort, accompanied by a snorting noise, as usual with his species, he flung the water from his nose in a lofty, perpendicular, expanded volume, at regular and somewhat distant intervals; its expulsion producing a continuous roar, like that of vapor struggling from the safety-valve of a powerful steam engine. Viewed from a distance, the practised eye of the sailor only could decide, that the moving mass, which constituted this enormous animal, was not a white cloud sailing along the horizon. On the spermaceti whale, barnacles are rarely discovered; but upon the head of this *lusus naturæ*, they had clustered, until it became absolutely rugged with the shells. In short, regard him as you would, he was a most extraordinary fish; or, in the vernacular of Nantucket, 'a genuine old sog', of the first water.

Opinions differ as to the time of his discovery. It is settled, however, that previous to the year 1810, he had been seen and attacked near the island of Mocha. Numerous boats are known to have been shattered by his immense flukes, or ground to pieces in the crush of his powerful jaws; and, on one occasion, it is said that he came off victorious from a conflict with the crews of three English whalers, striking fiercely at the last of the retreating boats, at the moment it was rising from the water, in its hoist up to the ship's davits. It must not be supposed, howbeit, that through all this desperate warfare, our leviathan passed scathless. A back serried with irons, and from fifty to a hundred yards of line trailing in his wake, sufficiently attested, that though unconquered, he had not proved invulnerable. From the period of Dick's first appearance, his celebrity continued to increase, until his name seemed naturally to mingle with the salutations which whalemen were in the habit of exchanging, in their encounters upon the broad Pacific; the customary interrogatories almost always closing with, 'Any news from Mocha Dick?' Indeed, nearly every whaling captain who rounded Cape Horn, if he possessed any professional ambition, or valued himself on his skill in subduing the monarch of the seas, would lay his vessel along the coast, in the hope of having an opportunity to try the muscle of this doughty champion, who was never known to shun his assailants. It was remarked, nevertheless, that the old fellow seemed particularly careful as to the portion of his body which he exposed to the approach of the boat-steerer; generally presenting, by some well-timed manœuvre, his back to the harpooneer; and dexterously evading every attempt to plant an iron under his fin, or a spade on his 'small'.

Though naturally fierce, it was not customary with Dick, while unmolested, to betray a malicious disposition. On the contrary, he would sometimes pass quietly round a vessel, and occasionally swim lazily and harmlessly among the boats, when armed with full craft, for the destruction of his race. But this forbearance gained him little credit, for if no other cause of accusation remained to them, his foes would swear they saw a lurking deviltry in the long, careless sweep of his flukes. Be this as it may, nothing is more certain, than that all indifference vanished with the first prick of the harpoon; while cutting the line, and a hasty retreat to their vessel, were frequently the only means of escape from destruction, left to his discomfited assaulters.

Thus far the whaleman had proceeded in his story, and was about commencing the relation of his own individual encounters with its subject, when he was cut short by the mate of the *Penguin*, to whom allusion has already been made, and who had remained, up to this point, an excited and attentive listener. Thus he would have continued, doubtless, to the end of the chapter, notwithstanding his avowed contempt for every other occupation than sealing, had not an observation escaped the narrator, which tended to arouse his professional jealousy. The obnoxious expression we have forgotten. Probably it involved something of boasting or egotism; for no sooner was it uttered, than our sealer sprang from his seat, and planting himself in front of the unconscious author of the insult, exclaimed:

'*You*! – you whale-killing, blubber-hunting, light-gathering varmint! – *you* pretend to manage a boat better than a Stonington sealer! A Nantucket whaleman,' he continued, curling his lip with a smile of supreme disdain, 'presume to teach a Stonington sealer how to manage a boat! Let all the small craft of your South Sea fleet range among the rocks and breakers where I have been, and if the whales would not have a peaceful time of it, for the next few years, may I never strip another jacket, or book another skin! What's taking a whale? Why, I could reeve a line through one's blow-hole, make it fast to a thwart, and then beat his brains out with my seal-club!'

Having thus given play to the first ebullition of his choler, he proceeded with more calmness to institute a comparison between whaling and sealing. 'A whaler,' said he, 'never approaches land, save when he enters a port to seek fresh grub. Not so the sealer. *He* thinks that his best fortune, which leads him where the form of man has never before startled the game he's after; where a quick eye, steady nerve, and stout heart, are his only guide and defence, in difficulty and danger. Where the sea is roughest, the whirlpool wildest, and the surf roars and dashes madly among the jagged cliffs, there – I was going to say there *only* – are the peak-nosed, black-eyed rogues we hunt for, to be found, gambolling in the white foam, and there must the sealer follow them. Were I to give you an account of my adventures about the Falkland Isles; off the East Keys of Staten Land; through the South Shetlands; off the Cape, where we lived on salt pork and seal's flippers; and finally, the story of a season spent with a single boat's crew on Diego Ramirez,* you would not make such a fuss about your Mocha Dick. As to the straits of Magellen, Sir, they are as familiar to me, as Broadway to a New-York dandy; though *it* should strut along that fashionable promenade twelve dozen times a day.'

Our son of the sea would have gone on to particularize his 'hair-breadth 'scapes and moving accidents', had we not interposed, and insisted that the remainder of the night should be devoted to the conclusion of Dick's history; at the same time assuring the 'knight of the club' that so soon as we met at Santa Maria, he should have an entire evening expressly set apart, on which he might glorify himself and his calling. To this he assented, with the qualification, that his compliance with the general wish, in thus yielding precedence to his rival, should not be construed into an admission, that Nantucket whalemen were the best boatmen in the world, or that sealing was not as honorable and as pretty a business for coining a penny, as the profession of 'blubber-hunting' ever was.

The whaler now resumed. 'I will not weary you,' said he, 'with the uninteresting particulars of a voyage to Cape Horn. Our vessel, as capital a ship as ever left the little island of Nantucket, was finely manned and commanded, as well as thoroughly provided with every requisite for the peculiar service in which she was engaged. I may here observe, for the information of such among you as are not familiar with these things, that soon after a whale-ship from the United States is fairly at sea, the men are summoned aft; then boats' crews are selected by the captain and first mate, and a ship-keeper, at the same time, is usually chosen. The place to be filled by this individual is an important one; and the person designated should be a careful and sagacious man. His duty is, more particularly, to superintend the vessel while

* Diego Ramirez is a small island, lying s.w. from Cape Horn.

the boats are away, in chase of fish; and at these times, the cook and steward are perhaps his only crew. His station, on these occasions, is at the mast-head, except when he is wanted below, to assist in working the ship. While aloft, he is to look out for whales, and also to keep a strict and tireless eye upon the absentees, in order to render them immediate assistance, should emergency require it. Should the game rise to windward of their pursuers, and they be too distant to observe personal signs, he must run down the jib. If they rise to leeward, he should haul up the spanker; continuing the little black signal-flag at the mast, so long as they remain on the surface. When the 'school' turn flukes, and go down, the flag is to be struck, and again displayed when they are seen to ascend. When circumstances occur which require the return of the captain on board, the colors are to be hoisted at the mizzen peak. A ship-keeper must farther be sure that provisions are ready for the men, on their return from the chase, and that drink be amply furnished, in the form of a bucket of 'switchel'. 'No whale, no switchel', is frequently the rule; but *I* am inclined to think that, whale or no whale, a little rum is not amiss, after a lusty pull.

'I have already said, that little of interest occurred, until after we had doubled Cape Horn. We were now standing in upon the coast of Chili, before a gentle breeze from the south, that bore us along almost imperceptibly. It was a quiet and beautiful evening, and the sea glanced and glistened in the level rays of the descending sun, with a surface of waving gold. The western sky was flooded with amber light, in the midst of which, like so many islands, floated immense clouds, of every conceivable brilliant dye; while far to the northeast, looming darkly against a paler heaven, rose the conical peak of Mocha. The men were busily employed in sharpening their harpoons, spades, and lances, for the expected fight. The look-out at the mast-head, with cheek on his shoulder, was dreaming of the 'dangers he had passed', instead of keeping watch for those which were to come; while the captain paced the quarter-deck with long and hasty stride, scanning the ocean in every direction, with a keen, expectant eye. All at once, he stopped, fixed his gaze intently for an instant on some object to leeward, that seemed to attract it, and then, in no very conciliating tone, hailed the mast-head:

' "Both ports shut?" he exclaimed, looking aloft, and pointing backward, where a long white bushy spout was rising, about a mile off the larboard bow, against the glowing horizon. "Both ports shut? I say, you leaden-eyed lubber! Nice lazy son of a sea-cook *you* are, for a look-out! Come down, Sir!"

'"There she blows! – sperm whale – old sog, sir;" said the man, in a deprecatory tone, as he descended from his nest in the air. It was at once seen that the creature was companionless; but as a lone whale is generally an old bull, and of unusual size and ferocity, more than ordinary sport was anticipated, while unquestionably more than ordinary honor was to be won from its successful issue.

'The second mate and I were ordered to make ready for pursuit; and now commenced a scene of emulation and excitement, of which the most vivid description would convey but an imperfect outline, unless you have been a spectator or an actor on a similar occasion. Line-tubs, water-kegs, and waif-poles, were thrown hurriedly into the boats; the irons were placed in the racks, and the necessary evolutions of the ship gone through, with a quickness almost magical; and this too, amidst what to a landsman would have seemed inextricable confusion, with perfect regularity and precision; the commands of the officers being all but forestalled by the enthusiastic eagerness of the men. In a short time, we were as near the object of our chase, as it was considered prudent to approach.

'"Back the main-top-s'l!" shouted the captain. "There she blows! there she blows! – there she blows!" – cried the look-out, who had taken the place of his sleepy shipmate, raising the pitch of his voice with each announcement, until it amounted to a downright yell: "Right ahead, Sir! – spout as long an 's thick as the mainyard!"

'"Stand by to lower!" exclaimed the captain; "all hands; cook, steward, cooper – every d—d one of ye, stand by to lower!"

'An instantaneous rush from all quarters of the vessel answered this appeal, and every man was at his station, almost before the last word had passed the lips of the skipper.

'"Lower away!" – and in a moment the keels splashed in the water. "Follow down the crews; jump in my boys; ship the crotch; line your oars; now pull, as if the d—l was in your wake!" were the successive orders, as the men slipped down the ship's side, took their places in the boats, and began to give way.

'The second mate had a little the advantage of me in starting. The stern of his boat grated against the bows of mine, at the instant I grasped my steering-oar, and gave the word to shove off.

One sweep of my arm, and we sprang foaming in his track. Now came the tug of war. To become a first-rate oarsman, you must understand, requires a natural gift. My crew were not wanting in the proper qualification; every mother's son of them pulled as if he had been born with an oar in his hand; and as they stretched every sinew for the glory of darting the first iron it did my heart good to see the boys spring. At every stroke, the tough blades bent like willow wands, and quivered like tempered steel in the warm sunlight, as they sprang forward from the tension of the retreating wave. At the distance of half a mile, and directly before us, lay the object of our emulation and ambition, heaving his huge bulk in unwieldy gambols, as though totally unconscious of our approach.

'"There he blows! An old bull, by Jupiter! Eighty barrels, boys, waiting to be towed alongside! Long and quick – shoot ahead! Now she feels it; waist-boat never could beat us; now she feels the touch! – now she walks through it! Again – *now*!" Such were the broken exclamations and adjurations with which I cheered my rowers to their toil, as, with renewed vigor, I plied my long steering-oar. In another moment, we were alongside our competitor. The shivering blades flashed forward and backward, like sparks of light. The waters boiled under our prow, and the trenched waves closed, hissing and whirling, in our wake, as we swept, I might almost say were *lifted*, onward in our arrowy course.

'We were coming down upon our fish, and could hear the roar of his spouting above the rush of the sea, when my boat began to take the lead.

'"Now, my fine fellows," I exclaimed, in triumph, "now we'll show them our stern – only spring! Stand ready, harpooner, but don't dart, till I give the word."

'"Carry me on, and his name's *Dennis*!"* cried the boat-steerer, in a confident tone. We were perhaps a hundred feet in advance of the waist-boat, and within fifty of the whale, about an inch of whose hump only was to be seen above the water, when, heaving slowly into view a pair of flukes some eighteen feet in width, he went down. The men lay on their oars. "There he blows, again!" cried the tub-oarsman, as a lofty, perpendicular spout sprang into the air, a few furlongs away on the starboard side. Presuming from his previous movement, that the old fellow had been "gallied" by other boats, and might prob-

* A whale's name is 'Dennis', when he spouts blood.

ably be jealous of our purpose, I was about ordering the men to pull away as softly and silently as possible, when we received fearful intimation that he had no intention of balking our inclination, or even yielding us the honor of the first attack. Lashing the sea with his enormous tail, until he threw about him a cloud of surf and spray, he came down, at full speed, "jaws on", with the determination, apparently, of doing battle in earnest. As he drew near, with his long curved back looming occasionally above the surface of the billows, we perceived that it was *white as the surf around him*; and the men stared aghast at each other, as they uttered, in a suppressed tone, the terrible name of MOCHA DICK!

' "Mocha Dick or the d—l," said I, "this boat never sheers off from any thing that wears the shape of a whale. Pull easy; just give her way enough to steer." As the creature approached, he somewhat abated his frenzied speed, and, at the distance of a cable's length, changed his course to a sharp angle with our own.

' "Here he comes!" I exclaimed. "Stand up, harpooner! Don't be hasty – don't be flurried. Hold your iron higher – firmer. Now!" I shouted, as I brought our bows within a boat's length of the immense mass which was wallowing heavily by. *"Now! – give it to him solid!"*

'But the leviathan plunged on, unharmed. The young harpooner, though ordinarily as fearless as a lion, had imbibed a sort of superstitious dread of Mocha Dick, from the exaggerated stories of that prodigy, which he had heard from his comrades. He regarded him, as he had heard him described in many a tough yarn during the middle watch, rather as some ferocious fiend of the deep, than a regular-built, legitimate whale! Judge then of his trepidation, on beholding a creature, answering the wildest dreams of his fancy, and sufficiently formidable, without any superadded terrors, bearing down upon him with thrashing flukes and distended jaws! He stood erect, it cannot be denied. He planted his foot – he grasped the coil – he poised his weapon. But his knee shook, and his sinewy arm wavered. The shaft was hurled, but with unsteady aim. It just grazed the back of the monster, glanced off, and darted into the sea beyond. A second, still more abortive, fell short of the mark. The giant animal swept on for a few rods, and then, as if in contempt of our fruitless and childish attempts to injure him, flapped a storm of spray in our faces with his broad tail, and dashed far down into the depths of the ocean, leaving our little skiff among the waters where he sank, to spin and duck in the whirlpool.

'Never shall I forget the choking sensation of disappointment which came over me at that moment. My glance fell on the harpooner. "Clumsy lubber!" I vociferated, in a voice hoarse with passion; "*you* a whaleman! You are only fit to spear eels! Cowardly spawn! Curse me, if you are not *afraid* of a whale!"

'The poor fellow, mortified at his failure, was slowly and thoughtfully hauling in his irons. No sooner had he heard me stigmatize him as "afraid of a whale", than he bounded upon his thwart, as if bitten by a serpent. He stood before me for a moment, with a glowing cheek and flashing eye, then, dropping the iron he had just drawn in, without uttering a word, he turned half round, and sprang head-foremost into the sea. The tub-oarsman, who was re-coiling the line in the after part of the boat, saw his design just in season to grasp him by the heel, as he made his spring. But he was not to be dragged on board again without a struggle. Having now become more calm, I endeavored to soothe his wounded pride with kind and flattering words; for I knew him to be a noble-hearted fellow, and was truly sorry that my hasty reproaches should have touched so fine a spirit so deeply.

'Night being now at hand, the captain's signal was set for our return to the vessel; and we were soon assembled on her deck, discussing the mischances of the day, and speculating on the prospect of better luck on the morrow.

'We were at breakfast next morning, when the watch at the fore-top-gallant head sung out merrily, "There she breaches!" In an instant every one was on his feet. "Where away?" cried the skipper, rushing from the cabin, and upsetting in his course the steward, who was returning from the caboose with a replenished biggin of hot coffee. "Not loud but deep" were the grumblings and groans of that functionary, as he rubbed his scalded shins, and danced about in agony; but had they been far louder, they would have been drowned in the tumult of vociferation which answered the announcement from the mast-head.

' "Where away?" repeated the captain, as he gained the deck.

' "Three points off the leeward bow."

' "How far?"

'About a league, Sir; heads same as we do. There she blows!" added the man, as he came slowly down the shrouds, with his eyes fixed intently upon the spouting herd.

'"Keep her off two points! Steady! – steady, as she goes!"

'"Steady it is, Sir," answered the helmsman.

'"Weather braces, a small pull. Loose to'-gallant-s'ls! Bear a hand, my boys! Who knows but we may tickle their ribs at this rising?"

'The captain had gone aloft, and was giving these orders from the main-to'-gallant-cross-trees. "There she top-tails! there she blows!" added he, as, after taking a long look at the sporting shoal, he glided down the back stay. "Sperm whale, and a thundering big school of 'em!" was his reply to the rapid and eager inquiries of the men. "See the lines in the boats," he continued; "get in the craft; swing the cranes!"

'By this time the fish had gone down, and every eye was strained to catch the first intimation of their reappearance.

'"There she *spouts*!" screamed a young greenhorn in the main chains, "close by; a mighty big whale, Sir!"

'"We'll know that better at the trying out, my son," said the third mate, drily.

'"Back the main-top-s'l!" was now the command. The ship had little headway at the time, and in a few minutes we were as motionless as if lying at anchor.

'"Lower away, all hands!" And in a twinkling, and together, the starboard, larboard, and waist-boats struck the water. Each officer leaped into his own; the crews arranged themselves at their respective stations; the boat-steerers began to adjust their "craft"; and we left the ship's side in company; the captain, in laconic phrase, bidding us to "get up and get fast", as quickly as possible.

'Away we dashed, in the direction of our prey, who were frolicking, if such a term can be applied to their unwieldy motions, on the surface of the waves. Occasionally, a huge, shapeless body would flounce out of its proper element, and fall back with a heavy splash; the effort forming about as ludicrous a caricature of agility, as would the attempt of some over-fed alderman to execute the Highland fling.

'We were within a hundred rods of the herd, when, as if from a common impulse, or upon some preconcerted signal, they all suddenly disappeared. "Follow me!" I shouted, waving my hand to the men in the other boats; "I see their track under water;

they swim fast, but we'll be among them when they rise. Lay back," I continued, addressing myself to my own crew, "back to the thwarts! Spring *hard*! We'll be in the thick of 'em when they come up; only *pull*!"

'And they did pull, manfully. After towing for about a mile, I ordered them to "lie". The oars were peaked, and we rose to look out for the first "noddle-head" that should break water. It was at this time a dead calm. Not a single cloud was passing over the deep blue of the heavens, to vary their boundless transparency, or shadow for a moment the gleaming ocean which they spanned. Within a short distance lay our noble ship, with her idle canvass hanging in drooping festoons from her yards; while she seemed resting on her inverted image, which, distinct and beautiful as its original, was glassed in the smooth expanse beneath. No sound disturbed the general silence, save our own heavy breathings, the low gurgle of the water against the side of the boat, or the noise of flapping wings, as the albatross wheeled sleepily along through the stagnant atmosphere. We had remained quiet for about five minutes, when some dark object was descried ahead, moving on the surface of the sea. It proved to be a small "calf", playing in the sunshine.

'"Pull up and strike it," said I to the third mate; "it may bring up the old one – perhaps the whole school."

'And so it did, with a vengeance! The sucker was transpierced, after a short pursuit; but hardly had it made its first agonized plunge, when an enormous cow-whale rose close beside her wounded offspring. Her first endeavor was to take it under her fin, in order to bear it away; and nothing could be more striking than the maternal tenderness she manifested in her exertions to accomplish this object. But the poor thing was dying, and while she vainly tried to induce it to accompany her, it rolled over, and floated dead at her side. Perceiving it to be beyond the reach of her caresses, she turned to wreak her vengeance on its slayers, and made directly for the boat, crashing her vast jaws the while, in a paroxysm of rage. Ordering his boat-steerer aft, the mate sprang forward, cut the line loose from the calf, and then snatched from the crotch the remaining iron, which he plunged with his gathered strength into the body of the mother, as the boat sheered off to avoid her onset. I saw that the work was well done, but had no time to mark the issue; for at that instant, a whale "breached" at the distance of about a mile from us, on the starboard quarter. The glimpse I caught of the animal in his descent, convinced me that I once more beheld my old acquaintance, Mocha Dick. That falling mass was white as a snow-drift!

'One might have supposed the recognition mutual, for no sooner was his vast square head lifted from the sea, than he charged down upon us, scattering the billows into spray as he advanced, and leaving a wake of foam a rod in width, from the violent lashing of his flukes.

' "He's making for the bloody water!" cried the men, as he cleft his way toward the very spot where the calf had been killed. "Here, harpooner, steer the boat, and let me dart!" I exclaimed, as I leaped into the bows. "May the '*Goneys*' eat me, if he dodge us *this* time, though he were Beelzebub himself! Pull for the red water!"

'As I spoke, the fury of the animal seemed suddenly to die away. He paused in his career, and lay passive on the waves, with his arching back thrown up like the ridge of a mountain. "The old sog's lying to!" I cried, exultingly. "Spring, boys! spring *now*, and we have him! All my clothes, tobacco, every thing I've got, shall be yours, only lay me 'longside that whale before another boat comes up! My *grimky*! what a hump! Only look at the irons in his back! No, don't *look* – PULL! Now, boys, if you care about seeing your sweethearts and wives in old Nantuck! – if you love Yankee-land – if you love *me* – pull ahead, *wont* ye? Now then, to the thwarts! Lay back, my boys! I feel ye, my hearties! Give her the touch. Only five seas off! *Not* five seas off! One minute – *half* a minute more! Softly – no noise. Softly with your oars! That will do –"

'And as the words were uttered, I raised the harpoon above my head, took a rapid but no less certain aim, and sent it, hissing, deep into his thick white side!

' "Stern all! for your lives!" I shouted; for at that instant the steel quivered in his body, the wounded leviathan plunged his head beneath the surface, and whirling around with great velocity, smote the sea violently, with fin and fluke, in a convulsion of rage and pain.

'Our little boat flew dancing back from the seething vortex around him, just in season to escape being overwhelmed or crushed. He now started to run. For a short time, the line rasped, smoking, through the chocks. A few turns round the loggerhead then secured it; and with oars a-peak, and bows tilted to the sea, we went leaping onward in the wake of the tethered monster.

Vain were all his struggles to break from our hold. The strands were too strong, the barbed iron too deeply fleshed, to give way. So that whether he essayed to dive or breach, or dash madly forward, the frantic creature still felt that he was held in check. At one moment, in impotent rage, he reared his immense blunt head, covered with barnacles, high above the surge; while his jaws fell together with a crash that almost made me shiver; then the upper outline of his vast form was dimly seen, gliding amidst showers of sparkling spray; while streaks of crimson on the white surf that boiled in his track, told that the shaft had been driven home.

'By this time, the whole "school" was about us; and spouts from a hundred spiracles, with a roar that almost deafened us, were raining on every side; while in the midst of a vast surface of chafing sea, might be seen the black shapes of the rampant herd, tossing and plunging, like a legion of maddened demons. The second and third mates were in the very centre of this appalling commotion.

'At length, Dick began to lessen his impetuous speed. "Now, my boys," cried I, "haul me on; wet the line, you second oarsman, as it comes in. Haul away, ship-mates! – why the devil don't you haul? Leeward side – *leeward*! I tell you! Don't you know how to approach a whale?"

'The boat brought fairly up upon his broadside as I spoke, and I gave him the lance just under the shoulder blade. At this moment, just as the boat's head was laid off; and I was straitening for a second lunge, my lance, which I had "boned" in the first, a piercing cry from the boat-steerer drew my attention quickly aft, and I saw the waist-boat, or more properly a fragment of it, falling through the air, and underneath, the dusky forms of the struggling crew, grasping at the oars, or clinging to portions of the wreck; while a pair of flukes, descending in the midst of the confusion, fully accounted for the catastrophe. The boat had been struck and shattered by a whale!

'"Good heaven!" I exclaimed, with impatience, and in a tone which I fear showed me rather mortified at the interruption, than touched with proper feeling for the sufferers; "good heavens! – hadn't they sense enough to keep out of the red water! And I must lose this glorious prize, through their infernal stupidity!" This was the first outbreak of my selfishness.

'"But we must not see them drown, boys," I added, upon the instant; "cut the line!" The order had barely passed my lips, when I caught sight of the captain, who had seen the accident from the quarter deck, bearing down with oar and sail to the rescue.

'"Hold on!" I thundered, just as the knife's edge touched the line; "for the glory of old Nantuck, hold on! The captain will pick them up, and Mocha Dick will be ours, after all!"

'This affair occurred in half the interval I have occupied in the relation. In the mean time, with the exception of a slight shudder, which once or twice shook his ponderous frame, Dick lay perfectly quiet upon the water. But suddenly, as though goaded into exertion by some fiercer pang, he started from his lethargy with apparently augmented power. Making a leap toward the boat, he darted perpendicularly downward, hurling the after oarsman, who was helmsman at the time, ten feet over the quarter, as he struck the long steering-oar in his descent. The unfortunate seaman fell, with his head forward, just upon the flukes of the whale, as he vanished, and was drawn down by suction of the closing waters, as if he had been a feather. After being carried to a great depth, as we inferred from the time he remained below the surface, he came up, panting and exhausted, and was dragged on board, amidst the hearty congratulations of his comrades.

'By this time two hundred fathoms of line had been carried spinning through the chocks, with an impetus that gave back in steam the water cast upon it. Still the gigantic creature bored his way downward, with undiminished speed. Coil after coil went over, and was swallowed up. There remained but three flakes in the tub!

'"Cut!" I shouted; "cut quick, or he'll take us down!" But as I spoke, the hissing line flew with trebled velocity through the smoking wood, jerking the knife he was in the act of applying to the heated strands out of the hand of the boat-steerer. The boat rose on end, and her bows were buried in an instant; a hurried ejaculation, at once shriek and prayer, rose to the lips of the bravest, when, unexpected mercy! the whizzing cord lost its tension, and our light bark, half filled with water, fell heavily back on her keel. A tear was in every eye, and I believe every heart bounded with gratitude, at this unlooked-for deliverance.

'Overpowered by his wounds, and exhausted by his exertions and the enormous pressure of the water above him, the immense creature was compelled to turn once more upward, for a fresh supply of air. And upward he came, indeed; shooting twenty feet of his gigantic length above the waves, by the impulse of his ascent. He was not disposed to be idle. Hardly had we succeeded in bailing out our swamping boat, when he again darted away, as it seemed to me with renewed energy. For a quarter of a mile, we parted the opposing waters as though they had offered no more resistance than air. Our game then abruptly brought to, and lay as if paralyzed, his massy frame quivering and twitching, as if under the influence of galvanism. I gave the word to haul on; and seizing a boat-spade, as we came near him, drove it twice into his small; no doubt partially disabling him by the vigor and certainty of the blows. Wheeling furiously around, he answered this salutation, by making a desperate dash at the boat's quarter. We were so near him, that to escape the shock of his onset, by any practicable manoeuvre, was out of the question. But at the critical moment, when we expected to be crushed by the collision, his powers seemed to give way. The fatal lance had reached the seat of life. His strength failed him in mid career, and sinking quietly beneath our keel, grazing it as he wallowed along, he rose again a few rods from us, on the side opposite that where he went down.

'"Lay around, my boys, and let us set on him!" I cried, for I saw his spirit was broken at last. But the lance and spade were needless now. The work was done. The dying animal was struggling in a whirlpool of bloody foam, and the ocean far around was tinted with crimson. "Stern all!" I shouted, as he commenced running impetuously in a circle, beating the water alternately with his head and flukes, and smiting his teeth ferociously into their sockets, with a crashing sound, in the strong spasms of dissolution. "Stern all! or we shall be stove!"

'As I gave the command, a stream of black, clotted gore rose in a thick spout above the expiring brute, and fell in a shower around, bedewing, or rather drenching us, with a spray of blood.

'"*There's the flag!*" I exclaimed; "there! thick as tar! Stern! every soul of ye! He 's going in his flurry!" And the monster, under the convulsive influence of his final paroxysm, flung his huge tail into the air, and then, for the space of a minute, thrashed the waters on either side of him with quick and powerful blows; the sound of the concussions resembling that of the rapid discharge of artillery. He then turned slowly and heavily on his side, and lay a dead mass upon the sea through which he had so long ranged a conqueror.

'"He's fin-up at last!" I screamed, at the very top of my voice. "Hurrah! hurrah! hurrah!" And snatching off my cap, I sent it spinning aloft, jumping at the same time from thwart to thwart, like a madman.

'We now drew alongside our floating spoil; and I seriously question if the brave commodore who first, and so nobly, broke the charm of British invincibility, by the capture of the Guerriere, felt a warmer rush of delight, as he beheld our national flag waving over the British ensign, in assurance of his victory, than I did, as I leaped upon the quarter deck of Dick's back, planted my waif-pole in the midst, and saw the little canvass flag, that tells so important and satisfactory a tale to the whaleman, fluttering above my hard-earned prize.

'The captain and second mate, each of whom had been fortunate enough to kill his fish, soon after pulled up, and congratulated me on my capture. From them I learned the particulars of the third mate's disaster. He had fastened, and his fish was sounding, when another whale suddenly rose, almost directly beneath the boat, and with a single blow of his small, absolutely cut it in twain, flinging the bows, and those who occupied that portion of the frail fabric, far into the air. Rendered insensible, or immediately killed by the shock, two of the crew sank without a struggle, while a third, unable in his confusion to disengage himself from the flakes of the tow-line, with which he had become entangled, was, together with the fragment to which the warp was attached, borne down by the harpooned whale, and was seen no more! The rest, some of them severely bruised, were saved from drowning by the timely assistance of the captain.

'To get the harness on Dick, was the work of an instant; and as the ship, taking every advantage of a light breeze which had sprung up within the last hour, had stood after us, and was now but a few rods distant, we were soon under her stern. The other fish, both of which were heavy fellows, lay floating near; and the tackle being affixed to one of them without delay, all hands were soon busily engaged in cutting in. Mocha Dick was the longest whale I ever looked upon. He measured more than seventy feet from his noddle to the tips of his flukes, and yielded one hundred barrels of clear oil, with a proportionate quantity of "head-matter". It may emphatically be said that "the scars of his old wounds were near his new", for not less than twenty harpoons did we draw from his back; the rusted mementos of many a desperate rencounter.'

The mate was silent. His yarn was reeled off. His story was told; and with far better tact than is exhibited by many a modern orator, he had the modesty and discretion to stop with its termination. In response, a glass of 'o-be-joyful' went merrily round; and this tribute having been paid to courtesy, the vanquisher of Mocha Dick was unanimously called upon for a song. Too sensible and too good-natured to wait for a second solicitation, when he had the power to oblige, he took a 'long pull' and a strong, at the grog as an appropriate overture to the occasion, and then, in a deep, sonorous tone, gave us the following professional ballad, accompanied by a superannuated hand-organ, which constituted the musical portion of the cabin furniture:

I.

'Don't bother my head about catching of seals!
To me there's more glory in catching of eels;
Give me a tight ship, and under snug sail,
And I ask for no more, 'long side the sperm whale,
In the Indian Ocean,
Or Pacific Ocean,
No matter *what* ocean;
Pull ahead, yo heave O!

II.

'When our anchor's a-peak, sweethearts and wives
Yield a warm drop at parting, breathe a prayer for our lives;
With hearts full of promise, they kiss off the tear
From the eye that grows rarely dim – never with fear!
Then for the ocean, boys,
The billow's commotion, boys,
That's our devotion, boys,
Pull ahead, yo heave O!

III.

'Soon we hear the glad cry of "Town O! – there she blows!"
Slow as night, my brave fellows, to leeward she goes:
Hard up! square the yards! then steady, lads, so!
Cries the captain, "My maiden lance soon shall she know!"
Now we get near, boys,
In with the gear, boys,
Swing the cranes clear, boys;
Pull ahead, yo heave O!

IV.

'Our boat's in the water, each man at his oar
Bends strong to the sea, while his bark bounds before,
As the fish of all sizes, still flouncing and blowing,
With fluke and broad fin, scorn the best of hard rowing:
Hang to the oar, boys,
Another stroke more, boys;
Now line the oar, boys;
Pull ahead, yo heave O!

V.

'Then rises long Tom, who never knew fear;
Cries the captain, "Now nail her, my bold harpooner!"
He speeds home his lance, then exclaims, "I am fast!"
While blood, in a torrent, leaps high as the mast:
Starn! starn! hurry, hurry, boys!
She's gone in her flurry, boys,
She'll soon be in "gurry", boys!
Pull ahead, yo heave O!

VI.

'Then give me a whaleman, wherever he be,
Who fears not a fish that can swim the salt sea;
Then give me a tight ship, and under snug sail,
And last lay me 'side of the noble sperm whale;
In the Indian ocean,
Or Pacific ocean,
Not matter *what* ocean;
Pull ahead, yo heave O!'

The song 'died away into an echo', and we all confessed ourselves delighted with it – save and except the gallant knight of the seal-club. He indeed allowed the lay and the music to be well enough, considering the subject; but added: 'If you want to hear genuine, heart-stirring harmony, you must listen to a rookery of fur seal. For many an hour, on the rocks round Cape Horn, have I sat thus, listening to these gentry, as they clustered on the shelving cliffs above me; the surf beating at my feet, while –'

'Come, come, my old fellow!' exclaimed the captain, interrupting the loquacious sealer; 'you forget the evening you are to have at Santa Maria. It is three o'clock in the morning, and more.'

Bidding farewell to our social and generous entertainers, we were soon safely on board our ship, when we immediately made all sail to the north.

To me, the evening had been one of singular enjoyment. Doubtless the particulars of the tale were in some degree highly colored, from the desire of the narrator to present his calling in a prominent light, and especially one that should eclipse the occupation of sealing. But making every allowance for what, after all, may be considered a natural embellishment, the facts presented may be regarded as a fair specimen of the adventures which constitute so great a portion of the romance of a whaler's life; a life which, viewing all the incidents that seem inevitably to grow out of the enterprise peculiar to it, can be said to have no parallel. Yet vast as the field is, occupied by this class of our resolute seamen, how little can we claim to know of the particulars of a whaleman's existence! That our whale ships leave port, and usually return, in the course of three years, with full cargoes, to swell the fund of national wealth, is nearly the sum of our knowledge concerning them. Could we comprehend, at a glance, the mighty surface of the Indian or Pacific seas, what a picture would open upon us of unparalleled industry and daring enterprise! What scenes of toil along the coast of Japan, up the straits of Mozambique, where the dangers of the storm, impending as they may be, are less regarded than the privations and sufferings attendant upon exclusion from all intercourse with the shore! Sail onward, and extend your view around New-Holland, to the coast of Guinea; to the eastern and western shores of Africa; to the Cape of Good Hope; and south, to the waters that lash the cliffs of Kergulan's Land, and you are ever upon the whaling-ground of the American seaman. Yet onward, to the vast expanse of the two Pacifics, with their countless summer isles, and your course is still over the common arena and highway of our whalers. The varied records of the commercial world can furnish no precedent, can present no comparison, to the intrepidity, skill, and fortitude, which seem the peculiar prerogatives of this branch of our marine. These characteristics are not the growth of forced exertion; they are incompatible with it. They are the natural result of the ardor of a free people; of a spirit of fearless independence, generated by free institutions. Under such institutions alone, can the human mind attain its fullest expansion, in the various departments of science, and the multiform pursuits of busy life.

1 Forecastle 2 Forehold 3 Casks for oil 4 Lower Main Hold 5 Blubber Room 6 Steerage 7 Afterhold 8 Galley 9 Captain's Cabin 10 Captain's Store 11 Cabin Skylight 12 Windlass 13 Bowsprit 14 Try-Works 15 Quarter-Deck 16 Taffrail 17 Whaleboats 18 Flying Jib 19 Jib 20 Lower Studding Sail 21 Foresail 22 Forespencer 23 Main Studding Sail 24 Lower Shrouds 25 Main Spencer 26 Spanker 27 Yardarm 28 Mainsail 29 Fore-Topmast Studding Sail 30 Foretop 31 Fore-Topsail 32 Topmast Shrouds 33 Main-Topmast Studding Sail 34 Maintop 35 Main Topsail 36 Mizzen Topsail 37 Fore-Topgallant Studding Sail 38 Fore Topgallant 39 Main-Topgallant Studding Sail 40 Main Topgallant 41 Topgallant Crosstrees 42 Mizzen Topgallant 43 Masthead (look-out) 44 Mizzen Royal 45 Fore-Royal Studding Sail 46 Fore Royal 47 Main Royal Studding Sail 48 Main Royal 49 Dogvane 50 Fore-Truck 51 Main-Truck 52 Mizzen-Truck

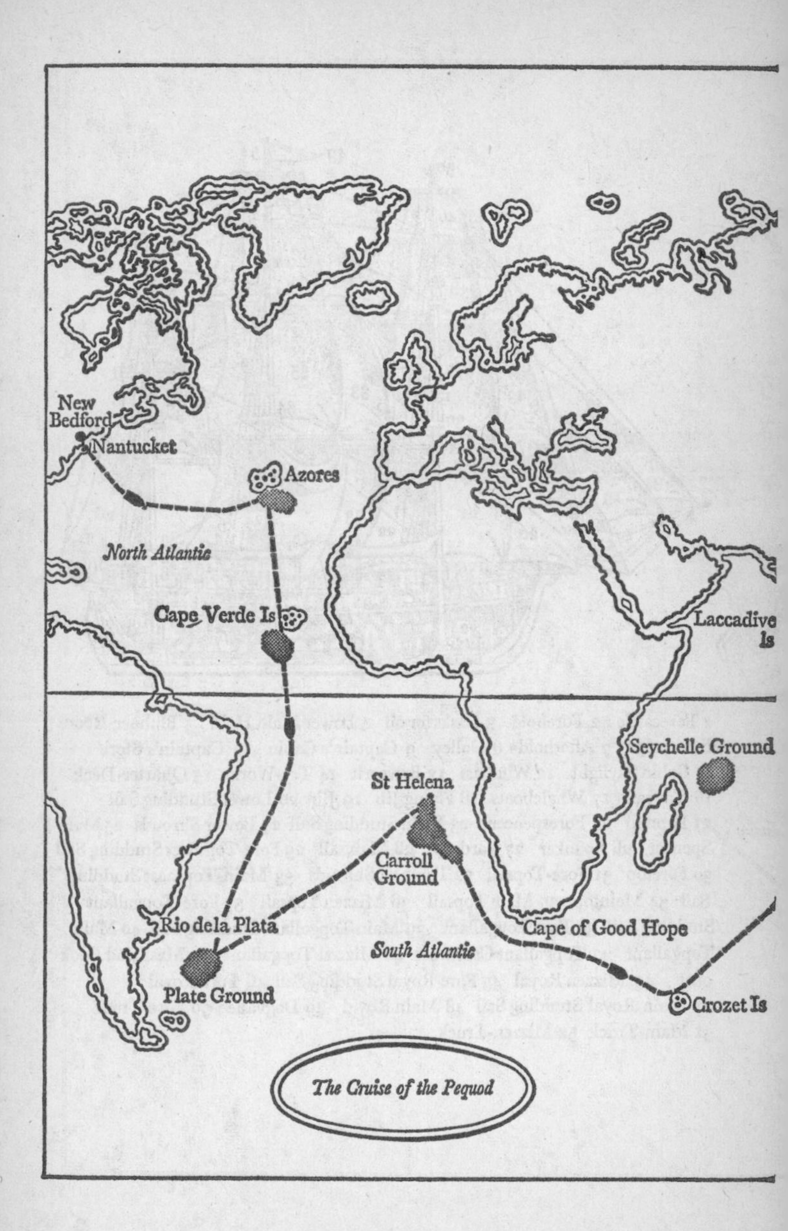
New Bedford
Nantucket
Azores
North Atlantic
Cape Verde Is
Laccadive Is
Seychelle Ground
St Helena
Carroll Ground
Rio de la Plata
Cape of Good Hope
South Atlantic
Plate Ground
Crozet Is
The Cruise of the Pequod

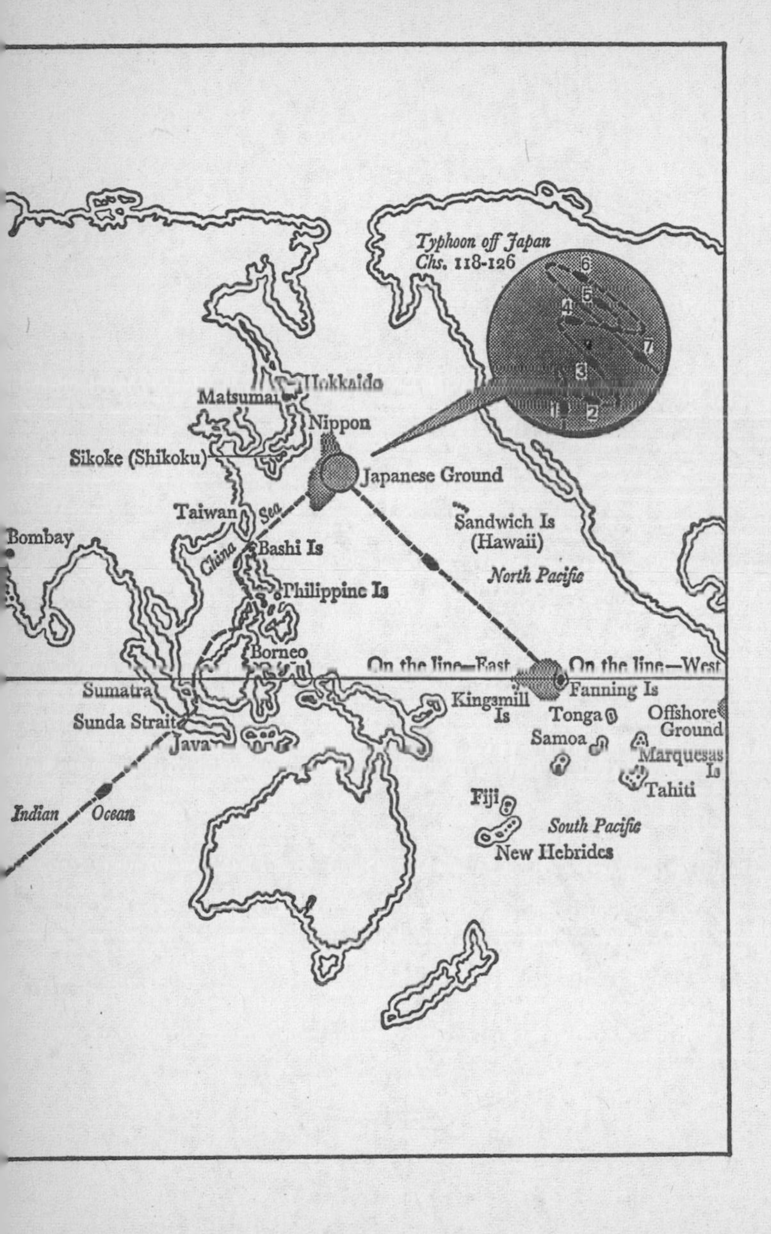

Typhoon off Japan
Chs. 118-126
6
5
4
7
3
1
2
Hokkaido
Matsumai
Nippon
Sikoke (Shikoku)
Japanese Ground
Taiwan
Sea
China
Bombay
Bashi Is
Sandwich Is
(Hawaii)
North Pacific
Philippine Is
Borneo
On the line—East
On the line—West
Sumatra
Fanning Is
Kingsmill
Is
Tonga
Offshore
Ground
Sunda Strait
Java
Samoa
Marquesas
Is
Tahiti
Indian
Ocean
Fiji
South Pacific
New Hebrides

MORE ABOUT PENGUINS, PELICANS, PEREGRINES AND PUFFINS

For further information about books available from Penguins please write to Dept EP, Penguin Books Ltd, Harmondsworth, Middlesex UB7 0DA.

In the U.S.A.: For a complete list of books available from Penguins in the United States write to Dept DG, Penguin Books, 299 Murray Hill Parkway, East Rutherford, New Jersey 07073.

In Canada: For a complete list of books available from Penguins in Canada write to Penguin Books Canada Ltd, 2801 John Street, Markham, Ontario L3R 1B4.

In Australia: For a complete list of books available from Penguins in Australia write to the Marketing Department, Penguin Books Australia Ltd, P.O. Box 257, Ringwood, Victoria 3134.

In New Zealand: For a complete list of books available from Penguins in New Zealand write to the Marketing Department, Penguin Books (N.Z.) Ltd, Private Bag, Takapuna, Auckland 9.

In India: For a complete list of books available from Penguins in India write to Penguin Overseas Ltd, 706 Eros Apartments, 56 Nehru Place, New Delhi 110019.

The Penguin English Library

Nathaniel Hawthorne

THE SCARLET LETTER AND SELECTED TALES

EDITED BY THOMAS E. CONNOLLY

'He has the purest style, the finest taste, the most available scholarship, the most delicate humour, the most touching pathos, the most radiant imagination, the most consummate ingenuity,' wrote Poe of Hawthorne, whose novel, *The Scarlet Letter* (1850), is generally regarded as the first great work of American fiction. It is the story of a 'fallen woman' – fallen, that is, in the eyes of the Calvinist-Puritan society of Boston – and of her daughter and the unacknowledged father.

Charles Maturin

MELMOTH THE WANDERER

EDITED BY ALETHEA HAYTER

Melmoth the Wanderer, first published in 1820, is one of the masterpieces of the school of Terror Romance. The name 'Melmoth' itself has come to stand for that typically Romantic hero, the outsider who has voluntarily exchanged his salvation for the knowledge and power that come with prolonged life and who then desperately tries to lay his fearful burden on another victim.

The Penguin English Library

THREE GOTHIC NOVELS

WALPOLE The Castle of Otranto

BECKFORD Vathek

MARY SHELLEY Frankenstein

With an introduction by Mario Praz

The Gothic novel, that curious literary genre which flourished from about 1765 until 1825, revels in the horrible and supernatural, in suspense and exotic settings. This volume presents three of the most celebrated Gothic novels: *The Castle of Otranto*, published pseudonymously in 1765, is one of the first of the genre and the most truly Gothic of the three. *Vathek* (1786), an oriental tale by an eccentric millionaire, exotically combines Gothic romanticism with the vivacity of *The Arabian Nights*. The story of *Frankenstein* (1818) and the monster he created is as spine-chilling today as it ever was; as in all Gothic novels, horror is the keynote.

Thomas Love Peacock

NIGHTMARE ABBEY
and
CROTCHET CASTLE

EDITED BY RAYMOND WRIGHT

A romantic in his youth and a friend of Shelley, Thomas Love Peacock happily made hay of the romantic movement in *Nightmare Abbey*, clamping Coleridge, Byron, and Shelley himself in a kind of painless pillory. And in *Crotchet Castle* he did no less for the political economists, pitting his gifts of exaggeration and ridicule against scientific progress and the March of Mind.

The Penguin English Library

Mark Twain

THE ADVENTURES OF HUCKLEBERRY FINN

EDITED BY PETER COVENEY

This idyll, intended at first as 'a kind of companion to *Tom Sawyer*', grew and matured under Mark Twain's hand into a work of immeasurable richness and complexity. Critics have argued over the symbolic significance of Huck's and Jim's voyage down the Mississippi: none has disputed the greatness of the book itself.

A CONNECTICUT YANKEE AT THE COURT OF KING ARTHUR

EDITED BY JUSTIN KAPLAN

A Connecticut Yankee, like others among Mark Twain's works, started out as an amusing idea – the Yankee who wakes up to find himself in sixth-century England – and, while never quite losing its comic character, turned into something deeper and darker.

PUDD'NHEAD WILSON

EDITED BY MALCOLM BRADBURY

Mark Twain returns to the idyllic river community of his childhood. The flashes of farce and general comic exuberance which enlivened *Huckleberry Finn* are sustained in this later work; but the mood is altogether more restless and critical. Twain uses certain stock characters and devices to build up a complex, ironical and morally disturbing account of human nature under slavery.

The Penguin English Library

Edgar Allan Poe

THE NARRATIVE OF ARTHUR GORDON PYM OF NANTUCKET

EDITED BY HAROLD BEAVER

'Comprising The Details of a Mutiny and Atrocious Butchery on Board the American Brig *Grampus*, on her way to the South Seas, in the month of June, 1827 ... together with the Incredible Adventures and Discoveries to which that Distressing Calamity gave Rise.'

Edgar Allan Poe's masterly blending of science with romance, the real with the supernatural, is followed in this edition by Jules Verne's ingenious sequel *Le Sphinx des Glaces.*

SELECTED WRITINGS

EDITED BY DAVID GALLOWAY

Poe, unquestioned master of 'the Grotesque and Arabesque', is fully represented here, but the volume also includes generous selections from his poetry and critical writings. Together they amount to a portrait of a complex personality, that of a conscious aesthete, the most exotic of American writers.

THE SCIENCE FICTION OF EDGAR ALLAN POE

EDITED BY HAROLD BEAVER

Presented together for the first time, and including the celebrated *Eureka,* the sixteen stories in this volume reveal Poe as both apocalyptic prophet and pioneer of science fiction. Together with a general introduction and a select chronology of post-Newtonian science in the century preceding *Eureka,* each of the tales in this edition carries an individual critique and full annotation.

The Penguin English Library

Herman Melville

REDBURN

EDITED BY HAROLD BEAVER

From his own experiences as a 'boy' on a packet ship sailing between New York and Liverpool, Melville wove the story of Wellingborough Redburn: a tale of pastoral innocence transformed to disenchantment and disillusionment.

BILLY BUDD, SAILOR AND OTHER STORIES

EDITED BY HAROLD BEAVER

The tales in this selection of Melville's shorter fiction are products of the strange and complex imagination that produced *Moby-Dick*. They include *Bartleby*, *The Encantadas*, *Benito Cereno* (recently dramatized by Robert Lowell) and one of Melville's supreme masterpieces, *Billy Budd, Sailor*.

TYPEE

EDITED BY GEORGE WOODCOCK

Long thought to be an authentic narrative of travel in the South Seas, *Typee* is now recognized as a mixture of fact and fiction, in which the life of the islanders is distorted to emphasize the contrast between the idyllic paradise of the 'Noble Savage' and the nineteenth-century industrial civilization which Melville had left behind.